C. S. FORESTER

C.S. FORESTER

C. S. FORESTER

The Ship
Mr Midshipman Hornblower
The Earthly Paradise
The General
The Captain from Connecticut
The African Queen

Heinemann/Octopus

The Ship first published in Great Britain by Michael Joseph Ltd in 1943
Mr Midshipman Hornblower first published in Great Britain
by Michael Joseph Ltd in 1950
The Earthly Paradise first published in Great Britain
by Michael Joseph Ltd in 1940
The General first published in Great Britain by Michael Joseph Ltd in 1936
The Captain from Connecticut first published in Great Britain
by Michael Joseph Ltd in 1941
The African Queen first published in Great Britain
by William Heinemann Ltd in 1935

This edition first published jointly by

William Heinemann Limited
15–16 Queen Street, London W.1

Martin Secker & Warburg Limited,
14 Carlisle Street, London W.1

and

Octopus Books Limited
59 Grosvenor Street, London W.1

ISBN 0 905712 02 1

Printed in Great Britain by
Jarrold & Sons Ltd, Norwich

CONTENTS

Introduction

Cecil Scott Forester became immensely popular with readers of fiction in the early years of the Second World War and has remained so ever since. He was born in 1899 in Cairo, where his father was a government official in the Egyptian service; educated in England at Alleyn's School and Dulwich College, he went on to study medicine at Guy's Hospital. Like Somerset Maugham, he never completed his medical training and left Guy's without a degree to take up writing as a career.

His first novel, a crime story entitled *Payment Deferred*, was published in 1926 and was subsequently both dramatised and turned into a film. Novels and short stories appeared regularly from that date. With his first wife he went inland voyaging in England, France and Germany, and accounts of their cruises appeared in book form; he also wrote books on historical subjects and did a regular script-writing stint in Hollywood.

The first of his 'Hornblower' novels *The Happy Return*–appeared in 1937. Two sequels–*A Ship of the Line* and *Flying Colours*–quickly followed. These three books were issued in 1939 in one volume with the title *Captain Hornblower, R.N.* It was the publication of this trilogy which greatly widened Forester's readership, putting him into the best-seller class. The robust and challenging adventures of the Napoleonic war hero were magnificent reading for the beleaguered British of the early 1940s. More than this, Horatio Hornblower was not at all a typical hero; he was a splendid leader and a superb seaman, but he was full of introspection and self-doubts, and would often have relapsed into cowardice were it not for his sense of duty and his fear of being thought foolish. He was a very human hero, and someone with whom everyone could identify.

Hornblower provided his creator with material for six more novels, short stories and the unfinished *Hornblower and the Crisis*. In *The Hornblower Companion* Forester described at length and with all his accustomed clarity, the manner in which this fictional character was created and developed; it is an unusual and fascinating account of the novel-writing process, from a born story-teller.

Forester continued to write on other subjects about other historical periods and unfailingly produced work of the highest quality: his technical knowledge of the sea, ships and of warfare was faultless as was his background research into any country about which he wrote. Forester himself explained how a snatch of conversation or a piece of casual reading can float to the surface of the creative artist's mind from the sub-conscious, to provide an idea, or a sequence of ideas which will carry a novel forward, or can in fact be developed into a complete novel. Forester's wide reading and his enquiring and analytical mind were the background to his careful craftsmanship.

This collection of six novels is designed to show the range of his fiction in its widest aspect. Although Forester served briefly as an army cadet towards the end of the First World War, it was not his own experience which provided the background to *The General*, often considered his best novel. It is a savage attack on the military mind of that age, and ironic and harsh in its judgement, although not entirely unsympathetic in its portrayal of the lonely Corps-Commander.

The same theme occurs too in an early sea-faring novel, *The Captain from Connecticut*, a study of the tough New England Captain Peabody in the little-known war of 1812 between Britain and the United States. Forester's historical knowledge is matched by his understanding of seamen and the sea and his humorous portrayal of his characters.

The Earthly Paradise has little of the sea in it, but has as its background the struggles of early Spanish explorers in Central America; disease and disillusion, religious intolerance, greed for gold, the clash of cultures–these are the themes developed with clarity and precision.

Mr Midshipman Hornblower is not so much a novel as a series of linked stories, each episode illustrating the training and development of the raw-boned and gawky Horatio Hornblower from a brand new Midshipman into a skilled and resourceful fighting man. Humour again plays a big part in these tales, as Hornblower learns his seamanship the hard way and absorbs the concept of duty–to the Royal Navy, to the state, to one's comrades.

These themes re-occur in *The Ship*–a brilliant short novel of the Second World War. Forester wrote this after some time at sea in H.M.S. *Penelope*. Not a word is wasted in this vivid account of five or six hours of battle in a light cruiser, described through the eyes of a handful of the crew, as she fights her way through towards Malta escorting, with the rest of the squadron, a vital convoy. Forester's perception and humanity vividly illuminate the minds of these men, from the portly Paymaster-Commander, the solemn Able-Seaman Whipple in the crows-nest and the stolid lollipop-chewing Dawkins steering the ship, to the nervous but articulate Jerningham on the bridge, waiting beside the absorbing figure of the Captain–a sensitive, brilliant and brave man.

Several of Forester's novels have been made into films: by far the most successful of these was *The African Queen*, from the highly characteristic novel included in this volume. Seamanship is here, but seamanship of a peculiar sort as the resourceful cockney engineer and the strait-laced missionary pursue their crazy and adventurous course down an African river at the start of the First World War in an effort to 'do their bit'–a hilarious and breathtaking tale, moving and unforgettable.

Forester's style reflects the man himself–straightforward, honest and wise. The reader's factual knowledge is often increased as some skill or process is lucidly explained; equally his knowledge of people is widened, as a character takes shape and as his, or her, motives are clarified.

Winston Churchill, on one of his many wartime journeys, had been given a copy of *Captain Hornblower, R.N.* for some rare leisure reading. Staff officers were confused by his signal of thanks for the book, thinking he was referring to the code-name of an operation. Many thousands of readers have endorsed his verdict: 'Hornblower is admirable', he telegraphed, 'vastly entertaining'. The same can equally be said of all the work of C. S. Forester.

THE SHIP

C. S. FORESTER

THE SHIP

Dedicated with the deepest respect to the Officers and Ship's Company of H.M.S. *Penelope*

With half a million men in the Royal Navy at the time this story was written, it is inevitable that there should be some coincidence of names and ranks between characters in this book and officers and ratings now serving. This is so inevitable that the author has made no attempt to avoid any such coincidence; all he can do is to assure the reader that he has attempted neither portrait nor caricature of any living person.

I

FROM THE CAPTAIN'S REPORT

. . . and at 11.30 the attacks ceased, although enemy aircraft were still occasionally visible . . .

Paymaster Commander George Brown put his fountain pen back into his pocket, put on his cap and got up from the table where he had been ciphering.

'I'm going for a prowl,' he told the petty officer beside him.

He slid his rather rotund bulk out through the narrow door and down three successive ladders, turning each corner and making each steep descent with the careless facility of long practice, even in the darkness that prevailed with the doors all shut. Emerging on the deck he stood and blinked for a moment in the sunshine, clear, sparkling sunshine which gave less warmth than might be expected in the Mediterranean in March. The sky was blue and the tossing sea was grey, the two colours blending exquisitely, the white caps and the white stretch of the wake completing the colour scheme to an artist's satisfaction.

The Paymaster Commander took a step or two farther into the waist, and stood and blinked again. He was not wasting time, nor idly taking the air; he was, as he might have expressed it himself, engaged in out-thinking Mussolini. The guns' crews at the four-inch guns, at the pompoms and at the .50 calibre machine guns were standing at their stations; as *Artemis* rolled in the heavy sea the brass cases of the ammunition expended in beating off the last attack jangled on the iron decks on which they lay heaped like autumn leaves.

The men at the guns were vigilant and yet relaxed, they would lose no time, not one-tenth of a second, in opening fire should another attack be launched, but they were not wasting their strength in staying keyed up unnecessarily. These men were veterans of nearly three years of war, three years during which at any moment death might swoop at them from the skies, and every movement they made showed it. The weapons they handled were part of their lives by now; not toys for formal parade, nor wearisome nuisances to be kept cleaned and polished in accordance with a meaningless convention; those cannons were of the very essence of life, as was the long rifle to the frontier pioneer, the brush to the artist, the bow to the violinist. In a world where the law was 'kill or be killed' they were determined to be the killers and not the killed–the tiger stalking his prey lived under the same law.

The Paymaster Commander had finished out-guessing Mussolini; his experience of aerial attacks told him that another was unlikely in the immediate future. And at the same time what he knew from the signals he had been deciphering made him certain that the respite was only a respite, and that more desperate work lay ahead even than beating off Italian dive bombers. He turned into the galley, where the Chief Petty Officer Cook, burly and competent, stood waiting for orders–the only man in the ship (until the

Paymaster Commander decided to take his stroll), apparently, not engaged in the business of making the ship the complete fighting machine; and yet he, too, had his part to play.

'Half an hour to send food round,' said the Paymaster Commander. He picked up the telephone. 'Wardroom.'

In the wardroom the telephone squealed plaintively and the Surgeon Lieutenant Commander answered it.

'Wardroom.'

'Hullo, P.M.O. Purser here. Let's have some of my boys back. You can spare 'em.'

The Surgeon Lieutenant Commander looked round him. When H.M.S. *Artemis* was at action stations the wardroom ceased to be the officers' mess and became the Medical Distributing Station. Here the wounded were brought for treatment–the sick bay, forward under the bridge, was both too small and too exposed to be used as anything other than a dressing station. The two casualties were quiet now, and the stretcher-bearer force was squatting on the deck. The Surgeon Lieutenant Commander carried grave responsibility in yielding to the Paymaster Commander's request. A sudden attack might leave twenty–fifty–wounded on the decks; a score of lives might depend on prompt collection and treatment. Wounded left lying were bad for discipline, bad for morale, apart from the guilty conscience which would torment the Surgeon Lieutenant Commander if his job were not properly done. But he had been shipmates for two years with the Paymaster Commander, and could appreciate his cool judgement and sober common sense. Pay was not the kind of man who would make a frivolous or unnecessary or ill-timed request. He could trust him.

'Right-o, Pay. I'll send 'em along.'

He looked along the row of squatting forms.

'You eight. You're all galley party? Report to the Paymaster Commander at the galley.'

The eight queerly dressed men–between them all they hardly bore a single trace of uniform clothing–scrambled to their feet, and doubled forward into the sunshine which illuminated the waist and halted at the galley. The Surgeon Lieutenant Commander watched them go. Perhaps it was the sight of the ragged group running which started a train of subconscious memory, starting with the recollection of an inter-hospital cross-country race; the Surgeon Lieutenant Commander suddenly found before his mind's eye a picture of the interior courtyard at Guy's–the green grass, the dribbling fountain where pigeons tried to wash off London grime, the nurses, white aproned, in blue or lilac uniforms, first year students carrying microscopes, third year men lounging, pipe in mouth and comically manly, out from the gloomy entrance to the dissecting-room, the youthfulness and eager anticipation of the best in life. All bombed to hell now, he had heard. The Surgeon Lieutenant Commander shook the vision from him as though it were water out of his eyes when he was swimming; he turned back to take a fresh look at the rating with the head wound. There was a chance that the wounded man might live and be none the worse for his experience.

In the galley the Paymaster Commander was ready with the scheme he had long mapped out, and tested in a dozen engagements. He had six hundred men to feed, and none of them had eaten for six hours. The Paymaster Commander thought of the hungry six hundred with a queer tenderness. He was a man born for parenthood, for self-sacrifice, to think for others. If Fate had made him a millionaire, he might have been a notable philanthropist; if Fate had given him children, he might have been the much loved father of a family, but Fate had ruled that he should be a childless man and a poor one. And as the senior officer of the paymaster branch in a light cruiser his inborn instincts had play in other directions. At present his thoughts were queerly paralleling those of the housewife planning what would be best for her menfolk getting in the harvest or working at the mill–it was only common sense that they should be given the best available, and it was pleasant that that should be what he liked doing anyway.

There was no flame in the range by which cooking could be done–the oil fuel for the range had all been safely drained away below where it was less likely to start a fire–but there was a steam jet, and superheated steam, not the flabby vapour that issues from a kettle's spout, but steam at four hundred degrees, live, active steam, can do remarkable things in the quickest time. The cook was already putting the ingredients into the cauldron. No economy soup this, but the best the ship could provide, the best the limited imagination of the Admiralty could encompass for the men who fought the battles. To make the forty gallons of soup necessary the cook was ripping open four dozen vast tins of tomatoes; stacked round him were the sixteen tins of corned beef which would go in next. The Paymaster Commander, without wasting time, took the fourteen pounds of corn-flour and began to mix it into a paste with water so as to make it smooth for admixture with the soup. While he was doing so he issued his instructions to the men who came panting up to the galley at the Surgeon Lieutenant Commander's orders.

'Get going on those sandwiches,' he said. 'Hopkins, open the tins. Clarke and Stanton, cut the meat. The rest of you see to the spreading.'

The men fell naturally into the parts they had to play, like actors in a well-rehearsed performance. The long loaves which the cook's crew had made and baked during the night were run through the slicer, the slabs of corned beef were slapped on the buttered slices, and the completed sandwiches were stacked aside; the knives flickered with the speed at which they worked, and they had no time for speech except for brief sentences–'Let's have another tin here, Nobby'; 'More butter here!'

Corn-flour, meat, vegetables, all had gone into the soup cauldron, and now the Chief Petty Officer Cook dropped in the three pounds of sugar and the handfuls of herbs which were his own contribution to the formula for producing appetizing soup. He stirred with his vast ladle, and then moved the lever of the steam valve round its pipe. Only a slight crackling and tremor indicated that steam from the ship's boilers–steam as hot as red-hot iron–was heating up the cauldron.

The Canteen Manager and his assistant came to attention before the Paymaster Commander.

'We've been sent to report to you from the wardroom, sir,' said the Canteen Manager.

'Very good. Start on the cocoa. Murchie, get those pickles opened.'

The Paymaster Commander swept his gaze round the galley. The soup was nearly hot, the forty gallons of cocoa were preparing, the mass of sandwiches nearly completed. He checked the other tubs–they were full of fresh water, in accordance with his standing orders. The Paymaster Commander had fought in another battle, once, in a cruiser which had filled with water nearly to the level of her maindeck. Desperate determination and brilliant seamanship had brought her in tow back to harbour after forty-eight hours of struggle against wind and sea, submarines and aircraft; but those forty-eight hours had been spent without drinking water, thanks to the holing of some tanks and the submersion of the others. The Paymaster Commander remembered the insanity of thirst and fatigue, and never again would he allow his men to suffer that agony as far as it was in his power to mitigate it. These tubs held half a gallon for each man of the ship's company–men could go for days on two pints of water if necessary.

His final inspection completed, the Paymaster Commander stepped out again on deck, balancing against the roll and heave of the sea. The horizon was still clear; there were no planes in the sky. On the port quarter the convoy still rolled along over the grey surface. Mussolini, the Paymaster Commander decided, was not going to cause any more trouble immediately; so he took up the telephone again and said 'Commander'. The Commander answered from his Damage Control Station on the boat deck.

'Pay here, Commander. Dinner's ready to serve. May I pipe to that effect?'

'Yes, carry on,' said the Commander.

The Paymaster Commander made his way forward and heaved himself up over the prodigiously high coaming to the foot of the ladder leading to the bridge.

'Bosun's mate,' he ordered, 'pipe "cooks to the galley".'

The Bosun's mate switched on the loudspeaker, and the eerie squeal of his pipe went echoing through every corner of the ship.

He was a north-country man, and his years in the Navy had not eliminated the north-country tang of his speech. He drew out the double O of the word 'cooks' until it was a treble or quadruple O, and he made no attempt to pronounce the 'the' sound in the 'the'.

'Cooks to t'galley,' he said into the loudspeaker. 'Cooks to t'galley.'

The Paymaster Commander went back to the galley. In the hundreds of years of the history of the British Navy this meaning of the word 'cooks' had suffered a change. They were no longer the men who actually cooked the food of their respective messes; they were merely the men who, each on his appointed day, carried the food from the galley to the mess. Already they were assembling there; men from the six-inch turrets and men from the four-inch H.A. guns; men from the magazines and men from the engine-room–in every quarter of the ship one man knew that it was his duty, as soon as he heard 'cooks to the galley' piped, to come and fetch food for his mates who could not leave their stations. The Paymaster Commander watched the food being served out, from A mess right through the alphabet to Z mess; from AA to ZZ, and then from AAA to EEE–food for five men, food for seven men, food for nine men, according to the number in each quarter; for each mess the food was ready stacked, and the Paymaster Commander nodded in faint self-approval as he saw how smoothly the arrangements were working over which he had sat up late on so many evenings. This was his own special plan, and he thought it improved on the system prevailing in other ships. It called for forethought and organization to feed six hundred men in half an hour, men who could not leave their guns, their gauges, or their instruments even for a moment while death lay only just beyond the horizon.

'I want those mess-traps brought back,' said the Paymaster Commander sharply, 'don't leave them sculling about on the decks.'

It was his duty to fill the bellies of his men, but at the same time it was his duty to safeguard Navy property. Just because a battle was being fought was no excuse for exposing crockery–even crockery of enamelled iron–to needless damage. The cooks had all left, and the Paymaster Commander picked up a sandwich and stood eating it, looking down at the galley party squatting on the decks spooning up soup into their mouths. Five minutes more of this let-up in the battle and everyone in the ship would have food inside him, and be fit and ready to go on fighting until nightfall or later.

He finished his sandwich and pulled out his cigarette case, and then stood with it unopened as a further thought struck him. He looked down fixedly at the Canteen Manager and his assistant.

'The boys'll want cigarettes,' he said. 'I expect half of 'em are short already.'

The Paymaster Commander was of the type that could use the word 'boys' instead of 'men' without being suspected of sentimentality.

'I expect so, sir,' said the Canteen Manager.

'Better take some round,' said the Paymaster Commander. 'You and Murchie see to it.'

'Aye aye, sir,' said the Canteen Manager, and then he hesitated. 'Shall I issue them, sir?'

'Issue them? Good God, no.'

The Paymaster Commander had visions of the endless reports and explanations he would have to make if he gave cigarettes away free to the Navy on the mere excuse that they were in action. And he had been in the service long enough to see nothing incongruous in the idea of sailors having to pay for their cigarettes in a ship which might during the next ten minutes be battered into a shapeless wreck.

'Half of 'em'll have no money, not after Alex., sir,' said the Canteen Manager.

'Well,' said the Paymaster Commander, the struggle between regulations and expediency evident in his face, 'let 'em have credit. See that every man has what he wants. And some of the boys'll like chocolate, I expect–take some round as well.'

The Paymaster Commander really meant 'boys' and not 'men' when he said 'boys' this time–there were plenty of boys on board, boys under eighteen, each with a sweet tooth and a growing frame which would clamour for sweetmeats, especially after the nervous strain of beating off aerial attack for four hours.

The 'mess-traps' about which he had worried–the 'fannies' of soup, the mugs and the plates–were already being returned to the galley. Things were going well. The Canteen Manager and his assistant filled mess-cans with packets of cigarettes and packets of chocolate, and began to make their way from action station to action station, selling their wares as though at a football match. Like the Paymaster Commander, neither the Canteen Manager nor the men saw anything incongruous in their having to put their hands into their pockets to find the pennies for their cigarettes and their bars of chocolate. It was a right and proper thing that they should do so, in fact.

'You men return to your action stations,' said the Paymaster Commander to the galley party.

He looked round the galley once more, and then turned away. He walked forward, stepped over the coaming, took one last glance backward at the blue sky and the grey sea, and then set himself to climb the dark ladders again back to the coding room. Even if he did nothing else in the battle he had supplied the food and the strength to keep the men going during a moment in the future when history would balance on a knife-edge–his forethought and his training and his rapid decision had played their part.

2

FROM THE CAPTAIN'S REPORT

. . . At 1205 smoke was sighted . . .

Ordinary Seaman Harold Quimsby sucked a hollow tooth in which a shred of corned beef had stuck apparently inextricably. He ought to have reported that hollow tooth at least a month ago, but Quimsby was of the type of man who crosses no bridges until he comes to them. He did not let anything worry him very much, for he was of a philosophical nature, filled with the steady fatalism to be expected of a veteran of so much service, even though Quimsby was merely an enlistment for hostilities only. Some men would be uncomfortable up here in the crow's nest–not so Quimsby, whose ideal existence was one something like this, with a full belly and nothing particular to do. As H.M.S. *Artemis* rolled and corkscrewed over the quartering sea the crow's nest swung round and round in prodigious circles against the sky, but Quimsby's seasoned stomach positively enjoyed the motion and untroubled went on with the process of digestion.

Cold meat and pickles; that made a meal fit for a king. Quimsby liked nothing better than that. His portion of pickles had included no fewer than four onions, and Quimsby breathed out reminiscently, conscious of, and delighting in, his flavoured breath. He had swallowed down his soup and his cocoa, but they were only slop, unworthy of the name of food. Cold meat and pickles were the food for a man. He sucked at his tooth again, and breathed out again, sublimely contented with the world.

Everything seemed to be designed for his comfort. The chair in which he sat certainly was–the padded seat and back held him in exactly the right position for keeping the horizon under continuous observation through the binoculars laid upon the direction finder before his eyes. As Quimsby rolled and circled round in the crow's nest he automatically kept the horizon swept by the binoculars; long practice had accustomed him to do so. A thrust of his feet one way or the other kept his stool rotating from port to starboard and back again, while his right hand on the lever kept the elevation in constant adjustment to correspond with the roll of the ship. Thanks to many hours of practice Quimsby was able to watch the whole horizon forward of the beam without allowing any of his automatic movements to break into his internal chain of thought, from the shred of beef in his tooth to the comfortable state of his inside and from that to unholy memories of that little bint at Alex. who had made his last shore leave so lively.

And from there his memories went back to his first arrival at Alex., his first glimpse of the East, and from there to his first voyage to sea back in the almost unbelievably distant days of 1939. He had been up in the crow's nest then, too, he remembered and his forehead wrinkled in faint bewilderment at the certainty that the scared, seasick, self-conscious youth at the direction finder in those days was, unbelievably but beyond all doubt, the same man who sat there so self-assured and competent now. That first report he had to make, when his binoculars picked up the dot on the distant surface and he had rung down to the bridge, his stomach heaving with excitement and sea-sickness.

'Something over on the left,' he had spluttered, all his previous instruction forgotten.

The unhurried voice of the First Lieutenant had steadied him.

'Where are you speaking from?'

'Headmast–I mean masthead, sir.'

'Then that's what you say first, so that we know down here. And you don't say "over on the left", do you? What do you say?'

'On–on the port bow, sir.'

'That's right. But it's better to give a bearing. What does your bearing indicator read?'

'Twenty-one, sir.'

'And how do you say it?'

'I–I've forgotten, sir.'

'Port is red, and starboard is green,' said the First Lieutenant patiently. 'Remember that port wine is red, and then you won't forget. And twenty-one isn't plain enough, is it?'

'No, sir–yes, sir.'

'Now let's have your report. Remember to say where you're speaking from first.'

'M–masthead, sir. Object in sight. Red two-one.'

'Very good, Quimsby. But you must say it twice over. You remember being told that? If the guns are firing we might not hear you the first time.'

'Yes, sir. I mean aye aye, sir.'

He had been a very green hand at that time, decided Quimsby. He felt self-conscious all over again at the thought of how Number One had coaxed him into making his report in the proper form so that it could be instantly understood. The subject was almost unsavoury to him, and his thoughts began to drift farther back still, to the time when he was selling newspapers in

Holborn–the evening rush, the coppers thrust into the one hand as with the other he whipped the copies out from under his arm.

Then he looked more attentively at the horizon, blinked, and looked again with his hand on the buzzer of the voice tube. Then he rang.

'Forebridge,' came the reply up the voice tube.

'Masthead. Smoke on the starboard bow. Green one-nine. Masthead. Smoke on the starboard bow. Green one-nine,' said Quimsby ungratefully, all memory of that early training passing from his mind as he said the words.

3

FROM THE CAPTAIN'S REPORT

. . . and a signal to this effect was immediately made . . .

In H.M.S. *Artemis* a high proportion of the brains of the ship was massed together on the bridge, Captain and Torpedo Officer, Navigating Lieutenant and Officer of the Watch, Asdic cabinet and signalmen. They stood there unprotected even from the weather, nothing over their heads, and, less than shoulder-high round them, the thin plating which served only to keep out the seas when the ship was taking green water in over her bows. Death could strike unhindered anywhere on that bridge; but then death could strike anywhere in the whole ship, for the plating of which she was constructed was hardly thicker than paper. Even a machine gun bullet could penetrate if it struck square. The brains might as well be exposed on the bridge as anywhere else–even the imposing looking turrets which housed the six-inch guns served no better purpose than to keep out the rain. The ship was an egg-shell armed with sledge-hammers, and her mission in life was to give without receiving.

Was it Voltaire who said that first? No, it was Molière, of course. Paymaster Sub-Lieutenant James Jerningham, the Captain's secretary, was sometimes able to project himself out of the ship and look down on the whole organization objectively. It was he who was thinking about Voltaire and Molière as he squatted on the deck of the bridge eating his sandwich. Even after three years in the Navy he still had not learned to spend several hours consecutively on his feet the way these others did–they had learned the trick young (for that matter, save for the Captain, he was at twenty-seven the oldest officer on the bridge) and could stand all day long without fatigue. In the delirious days before the war he had written advertising copy, spending most of his time with his heels on his desk, and to this day he only felt really comfortable with his feet higher than his head.

One way of thinking of the ship was as of some huge marine animal. Here on the bridge was the animal's brain, and radiating from it ran the nerves–the telephones and voice tubes–which carried the brain's decisions to the parts which were to execute them. The engine-room was the muscles which actuated the tail–the propellers–and the guns were the teeth and claws of the animal. Up in the crow's nest above, and all round the bridge where the lookouts sat raking sea and sky with their binoculars, were the animal's eyes, seeking everywhere for enemies or prey, while the signal flags and the wireless transmitter were the animal's voice, with which it could cry a warning to its fellows or scream for help.

It was a nice conceit, all this; Jerningham summoned up all his knowledge of anatomy and physiology (he had spent hours with a medical dictionary when he wrote advertising copy for patent medicines) to continue it in greater detail. The ratings detailed as telephone numbers on the bridge and scattered through the ship, with their instruments over their ears, were the ganglia which acted as relay stations in the animal's nervous system. The rating who had just brought him his sandwich was like the blood vessel which carried food material from the galley–stomach and liver in one–to the unimportant part of the brain which he represented, to enable it to recuperate from fatigue and continue its functions.

The lower animals had important parts of their nervous systems dotted along their spinal cords–large expansions in the dorsal and lumbar regions to control the limbs. The Chief Engineer down in the engine-room would represent the lumbar expansion; the Gunnery Lieutenant in the Director Control Tower would be the dorsal expansion–the one managing the hind-limbs with which the animal swam, and the other the forelimbs with which it fought. Even if the brain were to be destroyed the animal would still move and fight for a time, just as a headless chicken runs round the yard; and, like the very lowest animals, like the earthworm or the hydra, if the head were cut off it could painfully grow itself a new one if given time–the Commander could come forward from his station aft and take command, the Torpedo Gunner take the place of the Torpedo Lieutenant. And, presumably, young Clare would come forward to take his place if he, Jerningham, were killed.

Jerningham shuddered suddenly, and, hoping that no one had noticed it, he pulled out a cigarette and lit it so as to disguise his feelings. For Jerningham was afraid. He knew himself to be a coward, and the knowledge was bitter. He could think of himself as lazy, he could think of himself as an unscrupulous seducer of women, he could tell himself that only because of the absence of need he had never robbed the blind or the helpless, and it did not disturb his equanimity. That was how he was made, and he could even smile at it. But it was far otherwise with cowardice. He was ashamed of that.

He attributed to his brother officers a kindly contemptuous tolerance for the fear that turned his face the colour of clay and set his lips trembling. He could not understand their stolid courage which ignored the dangers around them. He could see things only too clearly, imagine them too vividly. A bomb could scream down from the sky–he had heard plenty that morning. Or from a shadowy ship on the horizon could be seen the bright orange flare that heralded a salvo, and then, racing ahead of the sound they made would come the shells. Bomb or shell, one would burst on the bridge, smashing and rending. Officers and ratings would fall dead like dolls, and he, the Jerningham he knew so well, the handsome smiling Jerningham whose good looks were only faintly marred by having a nose too big for the distance between his eyes, would be dead, too, that body of his torn into fragments of red warm flesh hanging in streamers on the battered steel of the bridge.

Closing his eyes only made the vision more clear to Jerningham. He drew desperately on his cigarette although it was hard to close his lips round the end. He felt a spasm of bitter envy for the other officers so stolid and impassive on the bridge–the Captain perched on his stool (he was a man of sense, and had had the stool made and clamped to the deck to save himself from standing through the days and nights at sea when he never left the bridge). Torps and Lightfoot, the Officers of the Watch, chatting together and actually smiling. They had been unmoved even during the hell of this morning, when planes had come shrieking down to the attack from every point of the compass, and the ship had rocked to the explosion of near-misses and the eardrums had been battered into fatigue by the unremitting din of the guns.

Part of the explanation–but only part, as Jerningham told himself with bitter self-contempt–was that they were so wrapped up in their professional interests that their personal interests became merely secondary. They had spent their lives, from the age of thirteen, preparing to be naval officers, preparing for action, tackling all the problems of naval warfare–it was only natural that they should be interested in seeing whether their solutions were correct. And Jerningham had spent his years rioting round town, drinking and gossiping and making love with a gang of men and women whose every reaction he had come to be able to anticipate infallibly, spending first a handsome allowance from his father and then a handsome salary for writing nonsense about patent medicines. He had always felt pleasantly superior to those men and women; he had felt his abilities to be superior to those of any of the men, and he had taken to his bed any of the women he had felt a fancy for, and they, poor creatures, had been flattered by his attentions and mostly fallen inconveniently in love with him. It was humiliating to feel now so utterly inferior to these officers round him, even though war was their trade while he was merely a temporary officer, drifted into the rank of Paymaster Sub-Lieutenant and the position of Captain's secretary because for his own convenience he had once studied shorthand and typewriting. Those were happy years in which he had never felt this abasement and fear.

Jerningham remembered that in his pocket was a letter, unopened as yet, which he had picked up the day before when they left Alex., and which he had thrust away in the flurry of departure without bothering to open. It was a letter from that other world–it might as well be a letter from Mars, from that point of view–which ought to do something to restore his self-respect. It was in Dora Darby's writing, and Dora was nearly the prettiest, certainly the cleverest, and probably the woman who had been most in love with him of all that gang. She had written him heartbroken letters when he had first joined the Navy, telling how much she missed him and how she longed for his return–clever though she was, she had no idea that Dorothy Clough and Cicely French were receiving from him the same attentions as he was paying her. It would help to bolster up his ego to read what she had written this time, and to think that there were plenty of other women as well who would as eagerly take him into their arms. Only a partial compensation for this fear that rotted him, but compensation and distraction nevertheless. He opened the letter and read it–nearly six months old, of course, now that all mail save that by air was being routed via the Cape.

Dearest J. J.,

I expect you will laugh at what I have to tell you. In fact, I can just picture you doing so, but someone has to break the horrid news to you and I think I am the right person. The fact is that I am *married*!! To Bill Hunt!!! I suppose it will seem odd to you, especially after what I've always said, but marriage is in the air here in England, and Bill (he is a First Lieutenant now) had a spot of leave coming to him, and we didn't see why we shouldn't. What will make you laugh even more is that Bill has been doing his best to get me with child, and I have been aiding and abetting him all I can. That is in the air too. And honestly, it means something to me after all these years of doing the other thing. And another thing is I shouldn't be surprised if Bill's efforts have been successful, although I can't be sure yet—

Dora's letter trailed off after that into inconsequential gossip which Jerningham made no effort to read. That opening paragraph was quite enough for him; was far too much in fact. He felt a wave of hot anger that he should have lost his hold over Dora, even though that hold was of no practical use to him at the moment. It touched his pride most bitterly that Dora should have even thought of marrying a brainless lout like Bill Hunt, and that she should never have expressed a moment's regret at having to accept Bill as a poor sort of substitute for himself.

But this sort of jealousy was very mild compared with the other kind that he felt at the thought of Dora becoming pregnant. This simply infuriated him. He could not, he felt, bear the thought of it. And the brutal phrase Dora used–'to get me with child'–why in hell couldn't she have worded it more gently? He knew that he had always coached Dora to call a spade a spade–not that she needed much coaching–but she might have had a little regard for his feelings, all the same. Those pointed words conjured up in Jerningham's mind mental pictures as vivid as those of bombs dropping on the bridge. Dora and he and the others of his set–Bill among them, for that matter–had always assumed an attitude of lofty superiority towards people who were foolish enough to burden themselves with children and slack-fibred enough to lapse into domesticity; and in moments of high altruism they had always thought it selfish and unkind to bring a child into the sort of world they had to live in. And yet if anyone were going to 'get Dora with child', he wanted to do the job himself, and not have Bill Hunt do it. Up to this minute he had hardly even thought of marrying, far less of becoming the father of a family, and yet now he found himself bitterly regretting that he had not married Dora before *Artemis* left for the Mediterranean, and not merely married her but made her pregnant so that there would be a young Jerningham in England today.

He had never been jealous in his life before, and it hardly occurred to him that he had had almost no cause to be. He had always thought that he would smile a tolerant smile if one of his women before he had quite done with her should transfer her affections to someone else. But this was not the case, very much not the case. He was hot with anger about it, and yet the anger about this was merely nothing compared with his anger at the thought of Dora being made pregnant by Bill Hunt. His jealousy about this was something extraordinary. Jerningham found time even in the heat of his rage to note with surprise the intensity of his feelings on the subject; he had never thought for a moment, during the blasé twenties of his, that he would ever feel the emotions of uncultured humanity. For a harrowing moment he even began to wonder whether all his early cynicism had been quite natural to him. This was certainly the third instance of primitive emotion overcoming him–the first was way back in 1939, when he suddenly realized that Hitler was aiming at the enslavement of the world and he had found himself suddenly determined to fight, willing to risk even death and discomfort sooner than be enslaved; the second was when he had known physical fear, and this was the third time, this frightfully painful jealousy, this mad rage at being helpless here at sea while Bill Hunt enjoyed all the privileges of domesticity with Dora Darby. Self-analysis ceased abruptly as a fresh wave of bitter feeling swamped his reason.

He got on to his feet–he, who never stood when he could sit–because he simply could not remain physically quiescent while emotion banked up inside him. A buzz from the voice tube behind him made him swing round, and he took the message.

'Masthead reports smoke, green one-nine,' he sang out, his voice harsh and unwavering, as it would have been if it had been Dora Darby he had been addressing.

'Very good,' said the Captain, 'Chief Yeoman, make that to the flagship.'

4

FROM THE CAPTAIN'S REPORT

. . . Action was taken in accordance with the orders previously issued . . .

'So that's that,' said Captain the Honourable Miles Ernest Troughton-Harrington-Yorke to himself.

The signal flags were already racing up the halliards–the Chief Yeoman had begun to bellow the names of the flags before the last words of the order had left his lips. It would be the first warning to the Admiral that the possible danger which they had discussed previously was actually materializing. The Italian fleet was out, as the reconnaissance submarines had hinted; and if it was out it could be trusted to be out in full force. How many battleships they had managed to make seaworthy after Taranto and Matapan no British officer knew quite for sure, but now he would know. He would see them with his own eyes, for the Italians would never venture out except in the fullest possible force.

He twisted on his stool and looked round him over the heaving sea. Ahead of the *Artemis* stretched an attenuated line of destroyers, the destroyer screen to keep down possible submarines. Away to port lay the rest of the squadron of light cruisers; the light cruiser silhouette had altered less than that of any type of ship since Jutland, and the ships looked strangely old-fashioned and fragile–mid-Victorian, to exaggerate–in their parti-coloured paint. The White Ensigns with the gay block of colour in the corner, and the red crosses, seemed somehow to accentuate this effect of fragility. Flown by a battleship the White Ensign conveyed a message of menace, of irresistible force; but in a light cruiser it gave an impression of jauntiness, of reckless daring, of proudly flaunting itself in the face of peril.

In the centre flew the Rear-Admiral's flag, beside the signal acknowledging that of the *Artemis*. The Captain wondered faintly what the Rear-Admiral was thinking about at this moment. Away over the port quarter wallowed the convoy, the fat helpless merchant ships, with a frail destroyer screen round them and the anti-aircraft cruiser in the centre. Helpless enough they looked, and yet they bore within them cargoes of most desperate urgency. Malta was threatened with every danger the imagination could conceive–the danger of attack from the air, of attack from the sea, of pestilence and of famine. A civilian population of a quarter of a million, and a garrison of God-only-knew how many were on short rations until the food these ships carried should be delivered to them. The anti-aircraft guns which took such toll of raiding aircraft were wearing their rifling smooth–here came new inner tubes to line them; and the barrages which they threw up consumed a ton of high explosive in five minutes–here were more shells to maintain those barrages. Here were heavy guns of position, with mountings and ammunition, in case the Italians should venture their fleet within range to cover a landing. Here were bandages and dressing and splints for the wounded, and medicines for the sick–the sick must be numerous, huddled below ground on meagre rations.

If the convoy did not get through Malta might fall, and the fall of Malta would mean the healing of a running ulcer which was eating into the strength of Mussolini and Hitler. And to escort the convoy through there were only these five light cruisers and a dozen destroyers–the convoy *had* to get through, and if it were reckless to risk it with such an escort, then recklessness had to be tolerated. The man over there whose Rear-Admiral's flag fluttered so bravely could be relied upon to be reckless when necessary; the Captain knew of half a dozen incidents in which the Rear-Admiral had displayed a cold-blooded calculation of risks and an unwavering acceptance of them. Wars could only be waged by taking chances; no Admiral since history began had ever been able to congratulate himself upon a prospective certainty. The Captain knew how the Admiral proposed to neutralize the chances against him, to counter overwhelming strength with overwhelming skill. The next few minutes would show whether his calculations would be justified.

'You can see the smoke now, sir,' said the Chief Yeoman of Signals.

There it was, heavy and black, on the horizon.

'Green one-o, sir,' said the forward lookout on the starboard side.

The big difference in the bearing proved that whatever it was which was making the smoke was moving sharply across the path of the squadron so as to head it off. The Captain turned and looked up at the vane on the mast, and at the smoke from the funnels of *Artemis*. It was only the slightest breath of smoke, he was glad to see–not the dense mass which the Italians were making, revealing their course and position half an hour before it was necessary.

He doubted if his smoke were visible even yet to the enemy, but it sufficed for his own purpose, which was to show him in what direction the wind was blowing. It was only a moderate breeze–last night's gale which had kicked up the present rough sea had died down considerably–and it was blowing from nearly aft. It was a strange turn of the wheel of fortune that the captain of a modern light cruiser on his way into action should have to bear the direction of the wind in mind and manoeuvre for the weather gauge as if he were the captain of one of Nelson's frigates. But the weather gauge would be of vital importance in this battle, and the squadron held it. The Italians had lost the opening trick, even though they held all the cards in their hands. And this moderate breeze was ideal for the laying of a smoke screen–not strong enough to disperse it, and yet strong enough to roll it down slowly towards the enemy. It was a stroke of good fortune; but the squadron needed all the good fortune there was available if it had to face the whole Italian navy. If the wind had been in any other direction–but yet the Admiral's orders had envisaged that possibility. There might have been some interesting manoeuvring in that case.

The Chief Yeoman of Signals was standing with his binoculars to his eyes, sweeping back and forth from the destroyers ahead to the flagship to port, but his gaze dwelt twice as long upon the flagship as upon all the other ships put together. For the Chief Yeoman, during the twenty-eight years of his service, had been in battles before, from the Dogger Bank to the present day, and he felt in his bones that the next signal would come from the flagship. The discipline and training of twenty-eight years, in gunboats on Chinese rivers, in battle cruisers in the North Sea, were at work upon him to catch that signal the moment it was hoisted, so that it did not matter to him that in addition his life might depend on the prompt obedience of the *Artemis*. He had stood so often, in peace and in war, ready to read a signal, that it was natural to him to ready himself in this fashion, as natural to him as breathing.

The wife he loved, back in England–the service had kept him apart from her during twenty of the twenty-five years of their married life–had been twice bombed out of her home, and all the furniture they had collected and of which he had been so modestly proud was now nothing but charred fragments and distorted springs; he had a son who was a Leading Seaman in one of the new battleships, and a daughter who was causing her mother a good deal of worry because she was seeing too much of a married man whom she had met in the factory. He was a living, sentient human being, a man who could love and who could hate, a man with a heart and bowels like any of his fellows, the grey-haired head of a household, an individual as distinct as any in the world, but at this moment he was merely the eye of H.M.S. *Artemis*–less than that, a mere cell in the body of the marine creature which Jerningham had been visualizing, a cell in the retina of the creature's eyeball specialized to receive visual impressions.

'Signal from the Flag, sir,' said the Chief Yeoman of Signals, 'K for King.'

'Acknowledge,' said the Captain.

The cell in the retina had done its job, had received its visual impression and passed it on to the brain.

The Captain had open on his knee, already, the typewritten orders which laid down what each ship should do in certain specified circumstances, and he had foreseen that the present circumstances were those which would be covered by scheme K–moderate wind abaft, enemy to leeward. A pity in some ways, from the artistic point of view; there would have been some pretty work if it had been necessary to manoeuvre the Italians into the leegauge.

'Signal's down, sir,' said the Chief Yeoman.

'Port ten,' said the Captain. 'Two-one-o revolutions.'

'Port ten,' said the Navigating Lieutenant into the voice pipe, 'two-one-o revolutions.'

The moment when a signal is to be obeyed is the moment when it is hauled down; the squadron was moving out to defend the convoy from the Italian navy in the way that had been planned. The Captain swung his glasses round him; the convoy was executing a wheel to port under full helm, the cruisers were turning more gently and increasing speed so as to remain interposed between it and the enemy, and the destroyers in the advanced screen were doubling round, some to reinforce the immediate escort of the convoy in case of simultaneous aerial attack, some to clear the range for the light cruisers. It was a beautiful geometrical movement, like a figure in some complicated quadrille.

'Midships,' said the Captain.

'Midships,' repeated the Navigating Lieutenant into the voice pipe.

He broke the word into two, distinctly, for Able Seaman Dawkins was at the helm, perhaps the most reliable quartermaster in the ship's company, but once–during that night action–Dawkins had misheard the word and the Navigating Lieutenant was taking no chances in the future. The ship was steady on her course now.

Deep down in the ship, below the water line, where there was the least chance of an enemy's shell reaching him, Able Seaman Dawkins stood with his hands on the wheel and his eyes on the compass before him. With his legs spread wide he balanced himself with the ease of long practice against the roll of the ship; that had to be done automatically down here with no stable thing against which the movement could be contrasted, and with his eyes never straying from the compass. It was only a few minutes back–at noon–that he had come down here and taken over the wheel. He was comfortably full of food, and at the moment his cheek was distended and he was sucking rhythmically. A few years back one would have guessed at once that he was chewing tobacco, but with the new Navy one could not be sure–and in the present case one would have been wrong, for Dawkins was sucking a lollipop, a huge lump like yellow glass which he had slipped into his cheek before going below. He had a two-pound bottle of them in his locker, bought in Alexandria, for as Dawkins would have explained, he was 'partial to a bit of sweet'. One of those vast things would last him during nearly the whole of his trick at the wheel if he did not crunch down upon it when it began to get small.

At the time when he left the deck full of soup, cocoa, and sandwich, and with his lollipop in his cheek to top up with, the aerial attacks had ceased, and convoy and escort had been rolling along at peace with the world. While he had been eating his sandwich Brand had told him that there was a buzz that the Eyety navy was out, but Dawkins was of too stable a temperament to pay much attention. He was a man of immense placidity and immense muscle; in fact, as he stood there sucking on his lollipop one could hardly help being reminded of a cow chewing the cud. It was hard, studying his expressionless face and his huge hairy arms and hands, to credit him with the sensitive reactions necessary to keep a light cruiser steady on her course in a heavy sea. He stood there at the wheel, the two telegraph men seated one on each side of him; he towered over them, the three of them, in that small grey compartment, constituting a group which in its balance and dramatic force seemed to cry out to be reproduced in sculpture.

Above his head the voice pipe curved down at the end of its long course through the ship from the bridge; it, too, had a functional beauty of its own.

'Port ten, two-one-o revolutions,' said the voice pipe unexpectedly in the Navigating Lieutenant's voice; the sound came without warning, dropping into the silence of the compartment suddenly, as on a still day an apple may fall from a tree.

'Port ten, two-one-o revs, sir,' echoed Dawkins instantly, turning the wheel. At the same moment the telegraphman beside him spun the handle of the revolution indicator to two-one-o, and he was at once conscious of the faster beat of the ship's propellers.

A sudden change of course; a sudden increase of speed; that meant action was imminent, but Dawkins had no means of knowing what sort of action. It might be dive bombers again. It might be torpedo bombers. A submarine might have been sighted and *Artemis* might be wheeling to the attack, or the track of a torpedo might have been sighted and *Artemis* might be turning in self-defence. It might be the Eyety navy, or it might be trouble in the convoy.

'Midships,' said the voice pipe.

A man of less placid temperament than Dawkins might be irritated at that pedantic enunciation; the Navigating Lieutenant always pronounced the word that way, but Dawkins was philosophic about it, because it was his fault in the first place; once when he had had to repeat the word he had been caught transferring his lollipop from one cheek to the other and had spluttered in consequence, so that the Navigating Lieutenant believed his order had not been correctly heard.

'Midships,' repeated Dawkins; the ship was lying now much more in the trough of the waves, and he had to bring into play a new series of trained reactions to keep *Artemis* steady on her course. Those minute adjustments of the wheel which he was continually making nipped in the bud each attempt of wind and sea to divert the ship from the straight line; a raw helmsman would do nothing of the sort, but would have to wait for each digression to develop before recognizing it so that the ship would steer a zigzag course infuriating the men controlling the guns.

The guns were not firing yet, perhaps would not fire in this new action, but it would not be Dawkins' fault if they were incorrectly aimed, just as it would not be his fault if there were any time wasted at all between a decision to change course forming itself in the brain of the Captain and its being executed by the ship. He stood there by the wheel, huge and yet sensitive, immobile and yet alert, eyes on the compass, sucking blissfully on his lollipop, satisfied to be doing best the work which he could best do without further thought for the turmoil of the world outside.

5

FROM THE CAPTAIN'S REPORT

. . . an Italian force of two heavy cruisers of the 'Bolzano' type and four cruisers of the 'Regolo' type and 'Bande Nere' type.

Another signal ran to the masthead of the flagship, fluttered to await acknowledgement, and then descended.

'Starboard ten,' said the Captain, with the Navigating Lieutenant repeating the order, 'Midships'.

The squadron now was far ahead of the convoy, and lying a little way distant from a straight line drawn from the convoy astern to the tell-tale smoke ahead, ready at a moment's notice, that was to say, to interpose as might be necessary either with a smoke screen or with gunfire. Italians and British were heading directly for each other now at a combined speed of more than fifty miles an hour. It could not be long before they would sight each other–already the smoke was as thick and dense as ever it would be.

The masthead voice pipe buzzed.

'Forebridge,' said Jerningham, answering it, and then he turned to yell the message to the Captain. 'Ships in sight!'

As Ordinary Seaman Quimsby's binoculars picked out more details he elaborated his reports with Jerningham relaying them.

'Six big ships!' yelled Jerningham. 'Six destroyers. Two leading ships look like battleships. Might be heavy cruisers.'

The crow's nest where Quimsby swayed and circled above the bridge was twenty feet higher than the bridge itself. It was an easy calculation that Quimsby's horizon lay one and a half miles beyond the captain's, and that in two minutes or a little less the Italians would be in sight from the bridge. In two minutes they shot up suddenly over the curve of the world, climbing over it with astonishing rapidity. Visibility was at its maximum; they made hard, sharp silhouettes against the blue and grey background, not quite bows on to the British squadron, the ships ahead not quite masking the ships astern. Jerningham heard the voice of the rangetaker begin its chant, like a priest of some strange religion reciting a strange liturgy.

'Range three-one-o. Range three-o-five. Range three-double-o.'

There were other voices, other sounds, simultaneously. The ship was rushing towards a great moment; every cell in her was functioning at full capacity.

'Port fifteen,' said the Captain, and *Artemis* heeled over as she executed the sudden turn. 'Revolutions for twenty-seven knots.'

The squadron had turned into line ahead, and was working up to full speed to head off the Italians should it become necessary. As Jerningham watched the Italian ships he saw the leader turn sharply to starboard, revealing her profile;

some seconds later the next ship turned to follow her, and then the next, and the next. Jerningham was reminded of some advertising display or other in a shop window. The vicious bad temper which Dora Darby's letter had aroused still endured within him, keying him up. The gap between imaginative fear and sublime courage, in a highly strung person, is only a small one; the residuum of bad temper sufficed to push Jerningham into boldness. He saw those six sharp profiles; the wind, blowing from the British to the Italians, kept them clear of smoke, unsoftened and undisguised. Jerningham went back through his memory, to those hours spent in his cabin of careful study of the pictured profiles of hostile ships, study carried out in a mood of desperate despair, when he knew himself to be a coward but was determined to be a coward deficient in nothing. He had the splendid memory which goes with a vivid pictorial imagination, and he could recall the very pages on which he had seen those profiles, the very print beneath them. He stepped forward to the Captain's side.

'The two leading ships are *Bolzanos*, sir,' he said. 'Nine thousand tons, eight eight-inch, thirty-two knots.'

'You're sure?' asked the Captain mildly. 'Aren't they *Zaras*?'

'No, sir,' said Jerningham with unselfconscious certainty. 'And the last three light cruisers look like *Bande Neres*. I don't know about the first one, though, sir. She's like nothing we've been told about. I suppose she's one of the new ones, *Regolos*, and the Intelligence people didn't get her profile right.'

'I expect you're right,' said the Captain. He had turned a little on his stool to look at Jerningham; he was surprised to see his secretary thus self-assured and well poised, for the Captain had seen his secretary in action before and had struggled against the suspicion that Jerningham had not all the control over his emotions which was desirable in the British Navy. But the Captain had learned to control his own emotions, and not the slightest hint of his surprise appeared in his expression or his voice.

'I think I am, sir,' said Jerningham, dropping back again.

In the Long Acre office he had had the ideal secretary, Miss Horniman, always at hand, always acquainted with the latest development, ready to remind him of the appointment he had forgotten or the copy he had to deliver, sympathetic when his head ached in the morning, and wooden faced and unassuming when she put forward to him an idea which he had not been able to produce, content that her boss should receive the credit that was rightfully hers. Jerningham always modelled his behaviour towards the Captain on Miss Horniman's behaviour towards him. The Captain might possibly have been wrong in his report of what he had seen if his secretary had not put him right, and the Captain would have the credit and the secretary would not, but that was the destiny, the proper fate of Captain's secretaries. He could grin to himself about that; the irony and incongruity of it all appealed to his particular sense of humour.

The Captain was a Captain R.N., thought Jerningham, only a few grades lower than God; out of a hundred who started as naval cadets only very few ever reached that lofty rank–he was a picked man, with Staff College training behind him, but here was something his secretary could do better than he. It was a very considerable help to think about that; it saved Jerningham from some of the feeling of intense inferiority which plagued him.

But he respected the Captain none the less, admired him none the less. Jerningham looked at him in profile, with his glasses trained out to starboard on the Italian squadron. Those black eyebrows were turned up the tiniest trifle at the corners, giving him a faintly Mephistophelian appearance. It was a slightly fleshy face; the big mouth with its thick lips might well have been coarse if it had not been firmly compressed and helped out by the fine big chin. There was something of the artist about the long fingers which held the glasses, and the wrists were slender although muscular. Jerningham suddenly realized that the Captain was a slender man–he had always thought of him as big, powerful, and muscular. It was a surprise to him; the explanation must be that the Captain must have so much personality and force of character that anyone talking to him automatically credited him with physical strength.

It made more piquant still the sensation of discovering that the Captain had been in doubt of the identification of those Italian cruisers. Otherwise it would have been almost insufferable to see the steady matter of fact way in which the Captain looked across at the heavy odds opposed to him, the inhuman coolness with which he treated the situation, as if he were a spectator and not a participant, as if–what was certainly the case, for that matter–as if his professional interest in the tactics of the forthcoming battle, and his curiosity regarding what was going to happen, left him without a thought regarding his own personal danger.

Jerningham felt intense envy of the Captain's natural gifts. It was an envy which blended with, and fed, the fires of the jealousy which Dora Darby's letter had aroused in him.

6

FROM THE CAPTAIN'S REPORT

. . . At 1310 the enemy opened fire . . .

Captain Miles Ernest Troughton-Harrington-Yorke kept his glasses trained on the Italians. Jerningham was undoubtedly right about the identification of them. The six best cruisers the Italians had left; and that was a Vice-Admiral's flag which the leading ship was flying. They could not be more than a few hundred yards out of range, either, with those big eight-inch guns of theirs. The Captain looked to see them open fire at any moment, while the British six-inch still could not drop a shell within three thousand yards of them. With the very detailed reports which must have reached them from the air they could be in no doubt of the situation; they could fear no trap, have no doubt of their superiority of strength. It was possible–likely, in fact, in view of the other intelligence–that this Italian force was only a screen for a still stronger one, of battleships and more heavy cruisers, but there was no need to wait for reinforcements. They were strong enough to do the business themselves, two heavy cruisers and four light against five light cruisers.

Only two months ago the situation had been reversed, when *Artemis* and

Hera had come upon that Italian convoy escorted by the two Italian destroyers. The disproportion of strength had not been very different. If the Italian destroyer captains had been realists they would have simply run away, and by their superior speed they could have saved their own ships while abandoning the convoy to destruction. But they had stayed to fight, like a couple of fools, advancing boldly towards the British cruisers, and endeavouring to lay a smoke screen. The first broadside of six-inch from *Artemis* had hit one of the destroyers–the Captain still felt intense professional pleasure at the recollection–and the third from *Hera* had hit the other. The two destroyers had been blown into flaming, sinking wrecks before even their feeble 120 mm. guns had had a chance to fire; the British cruisers rushing down on them destroyed them in the few seconds which it took to cover the distance representing the difference in range. So the destroyers expended themselves uselessly, not having delayed for a moment the destruction of the transports they were escorting. Very foolish of them indeed.

If the Italian admiral over there–I wonder who he is? Nocentini, perhaps, or is it Pogetti?–knows his business he will turn two points to port and close with us and finish us off. And if we knew our business we would run like hares and save ourselves, and let the convoy go, and let Malta go.

The Captain's tightly shut mouth stretched into a dry grin. That was logic, but logic was not war. If it were, Hitler would be dining in Buckingham Palace this evening, and Napoleon would have dined there a hundred and forty years ago. No, that was a slipshod way of putting it. War was perfectly logical, but to grasp all the premises of war was very difficult and it was as fatally easy to draw incorrect conclusions from incomplete premises in war as in everything else. A mere count of the tonnage and the guns of the opposing sides was insufficient; it was even insufficient to include an estimate of the relative excellence of the training and discipline of the personnel on the two sides. There were other factors–the memory of Matapan, of Taranto, of the River Plate; the memory even of the defeat of the Spaniards of the Armada or of the defeat of the Italians at Lissa eighty years back.

The Captain had read somewhere of an unpleasant child who used to find amusement in chasing the slaves round the compound with a hot poker. The child found out quite early that it was unnecessary to have the poker actually red hot; it would serve just as well if it were painted so that the slaves thought it was hot. The slaves might even suspect that it was only painted, but they would not take the chance involved in finding out. So it was at the present moment; the British Navy had a record of victory over odds, and the Italians one of defeat by inferior numbers. This time the Italians might suspect that the odds were too heavy, the numbers too inferior, for history to repeat itself. But it might call for more resolution than they possessed to put the matter to the proof. It was going to be interesting to see.

Something beautiful showed itself at that moment in the field of the Captain's binoculars, a tall, lovely column of water, rising gracefully out of the sea like the arm clothed in white samite, mystic, wonderful, which rose from the mere to catch Excalibur. The Captain had vague theories of beauty; he had often wondered why one curve should be more beautiful than another, one motion more graceful than another. But he had never tried to crystallize his theories, to give definition to what he felt might be indefinable. Hogarth had once attempted it, with his 'Line of Beauty' on the palette depicted in the corner of his self-portrait, and he had tried again, and failed disastrously, when he wrote his 'Analysis of Beauty'.

But for all that, it might be worth someone's while to try to analyse why the column of water thrown up by an eight-inch shell should be so beautiful. The rate of its rise (and the mathematics of the relative velocities of its constituent particles had their own charm as well), the proportion of height to girth, the very duration of its existence, were all so perfectly related to each other as to give pleasure to the eye. The faint yellow tinge that it possessed (that meant high explosive shell) was an added charm against that sky and sea. And farther away, to left and to right, rose its fellows at the same moment, each as beautiful as the other; they were widespread, and even allowing for the fact that those eight-inch were firing at extreme range that meant that the gunnery control instruments in the Italian ship were not lined up as carefully nor as accurately as they should be.

The leading ship was altering round towards the enemy. That was the way to deal with them; if they won't come and fight, go in and fight them.

'Starboard ten,' said the Navigating Officer into the voice tube, as *Artemis* reached the position where each of her four predecessors had made their two-point turns, and the cruiser heeled again as the rudder brought her round.

7

FROM THE CAPTAIN'S REPORT

. . . the enemy withdrew . . .

All down the line of Italian cruisers ran a sparkle of light, bright yellow flashes competing with faint success against the sunlight. Leading Seaman Alfred Lightfoot saw the flashes in the cruiser upon which he was training his rangefinder; he saw them double, because the rangefinder presented two images of the cruiser, just overlapping. That double image was something like what he had seen once or twice half-way through a binge, after the seventh drink or so. For a few minutes, then, the lights behind the bar, and the barmaid's face, duplicated themselves in just the same fashion, just as substantially, so that one could swear that the girl had two faces, one overlapping the other by half, and that each electric bulb had another hung beside it.

Lightfoot twirled the controlling screws of the rangefinder, and the two images moved into each other; in the same way, when Lightfoot was getting drunk, he could by an effort make the two images of the barmaid's face run together again, so that they would click into sharp unity instead of being hazy and oreoled with light. He read off the scale of the rangefinder.

'Range two-seven-ho,' he announced, his Cockney twang flavouring the dry tone in which he had been trained to make his statements; the vowel sound of the word 'range' was exactly the same as he would have used in the word 'rind'.

The sharp image at which he was peering was obscure again at once; two shadowy cruisers were replacing the single one–there were two red, white and green flags flying aft, a muddled double mass of funnels. With his Cockney quickness of thought Lightfoot could, if he had wanted to, have drawn the obvious conclusion, that the two squadrons were approaching each other rapidly, and he could from there have gone on to the next deduction, which was that in a very few seconds they would be pounding each other to pieces. But Lightfoot did not trouble to think in that fashion. Long ago he had told himself fatalistically that if a shell had his name on it he would cop it, and from no other shell. His job was to take ranges quickly and exactly; that was to be his contribution to the perfect whole which was the fighting ship, and he was set upon doing that without distraction. Just once or twice when he had strayed into self-analysis Lightfoot had felt a little pleased with himself at having attained this fatalistic Nirvana, but it is hard to apportion the credit for it–some of it was undoubtedly due to Lightfoot himself, but some also to the system under which he had been trained, some to the captain for his particular application of that system; and possibly some to Mussolini himself, who had given Lightfoot a cause in which to fight whose justice was so clearly apparent.

Lightfoot twisted the regulating screws again to bring the images together. It was twenty-one seconds since he had seen the flashes of the guns of the cruiser at which he was pointing, and Lightfoot had already forgotten them, so little impression had they made upon him. And during those twenty-one seconds the eight-inch shells had been hurtling towards *Artemis* at a speed through the air of more than a mile in two seconds because their path was curved, reaching far up into the upper atmosphere, higher than the highest Alps into the freezing stratosphere before plunging down again towards their target. Lightfoot heard a sudden noise as of rushing water and of tearing of sheets, and then the field of his rangefinder was blotted out in an immense upheaval of water as the nearest shell of the broadside pitched close beside starboard bow of *Artemis*. Twenty tons of water, yellowed slightly by the high explosive, came tumbling on board, deluging the upper works, flooding over Lightfoot's rangefinder.

'Ringe hobscured,' said Lightfoot.

He reached to sweep the lenses clear, and darkness gave way to light again as he stared into the instrument. For a moment he was still nonplussed, so different was the picture he saw in it from what he had seen just before. The images were double, but the silhouettes were entirely changed, narrow instead of broad, and the two flecks of colour, the double images of the Italian flag, were right in the middle of each silhouette instead of aft of them. Lightfoot's trained reactions were as quick as his mind; his fingers were spinning the screws round in the opposite direction at the same moment as he realized that the Eyeties had turned their sterns towards the British and were heading for the horizon as fast as they could go.

The spectacle astonished him; the surprise of it broke through his professional calm in a way in which the prospect of danger quite failed to do.

'Coo!' said Lightfoot; the exclamation (although Lightfoot did not know it) was a shortening of 'Coo blimey', itself a corruption of 'God blind me'.

'Coo!' and then instantly training and professional pride mastered him again, and he brought the images together with a deft twirl of the screws 'Range two-nine-ho'.

Paymaster Sub-Lieutenant James Jerningham saw the Italian ships turn away, and he gravely noted the time upon his pad. One of his duties was to keep a record of any action in which the ship was engaged, because experience had proved that after an action, even with the help of the ship's plot which was kept up to date in the chart-room, and with the help of the various logs kept in different parts of the ship–signal logs, engine-room logs, and so on–it was difficult for anyone to remember the exact order of events as they had occurred. And reports had to be written, and the lessons of the action digested, if only for the benefit of the vast fleet in all the oceans of the world anxious to improve its professional knowledge.

The Captain slid down from his stool and stretched himself; Jerningham could tell just from his actions that he was relieved at not having to sit for a while–the lucky devil did not know that he was well off. Jerningham's feet ached with standing and he would have given something substantial in exchange for the chance to sit down. The Captain walked briskly up and down for a while, five paces aft and five paces forward; the bridge was too small and too crowded with officers and instruments to allow of a longer walk. And even during that five-pace walk the Captain kept shooting glances round him, at signalmen and flagship and lookouts so as to maintain himself in instant readiness for action.

It might be said that while the ship was at sea the Captain never went more than five paces from his stool; at night he lay on an air mattress laid on the steel deck with a blanket over him, or a tarpaulin when it rained. Jerningham had known him to sleep for as much as four hours at a stretch like that, with the rain rattling down upon him, a fold of the stiff tarpaulin keeping the rain from actually falling on his face. It was marvellous that any man could sleep in those conditions; it was marvellous that any man bearing that load of responsibility could sleep at all; but, that being granted, it was also marvellous that a man once asleep could rouse himself so instantly to action. At a touch on his shoulder the Captain would raise his head to hear a report and would issue his orders without a moment in which to recover himself.

The Captain was tough both mentally and physically, hard like steel–a picked man, Jerningham reminded himself. And no man could last long in command of a light cruiser in the Mediterranean if he were not tough. Yet toughness was only one essential requisite in the make-up of a cruiser captain. He had to be a man of the most sensitive and delicate reflexes, too, ready to react instantly to any stimulus. Mere vulgar physical courage was common enough, thought Jerningham, regretfully, even if he did not possess it himself, but in the Captain's case it had to be combined with everything else, with moral courage, with the widest technical knowledge, with flexibility of mind and rapidity of thought and physical endurance–all this merely to command the ship in action, and that was only part of it. Before the ship could be brought into action it had to be made into an efficient fighting unit. Six hundred officers and men had to be trained to their work, and fitted into the intricate scheme of organization as complex as any jigsaw puzzle, and, once trained and organized, had to be maintained at fighting pitch. There were plenty of men who made reputations by successfully managing a big department store; managing a big ship of war was as great an achievement, even if not greater.

Jerningham, with nearly three years of experience, knew a great deal about the Navy now, and yet his temperament and his early life and his duties in the ship still enabled him to look on the service dispassionately as a disinterested observer. He knew better than anyone else in the ship's company how little work the Captain seemed to do when it came to routine business, how freely he delegated his power, and having delegated it, how cheerfully he trusted his subordinates, with none of those after-thoughts and fussinesses which Jerningham had seen in city offices. That was partly moral courage, of course, again, the ability to abide by a decision once having made it. But partly it was the result of the man's own ability. His judgement was so sound, his sense of justice so exact, his foresight so keen, that everyone could rely on him. Jerningham suspected that there might be ships whose captains had not these advantages and who yet were not plagued with detail because officers and men united in keeping detail from them knowing that the decisions uttered would not be of help. Those would be unhappy ships. But the kind of captain under which he served was also not plagued with detail, because officers and men knew that when they should appeal to him the decisions that would be handed down to them would be correct, human, intelligent. In that case officers and men went on cheerfully working out their own destiny, secure in the knowledge that there was an ability greater than their own ready to help them should it become necessary. That would mean a happy, efficient ship like *Artemis*.

Jerningham's envy of the Captain's capacity flared out anew as he thought about all this. It was a most remarkable sensation for Jerningham to feel that someone was a better man than he–Jerningham's sublime egotism of pre-war days had survived uncounted setbacks. Lost games of tennis or golf, failure to convince an advertising manager that the copy laid before him was ideal for its purpose, could be discounted on the grounds of their relative unimportance, or because of bad luck, or the mental blindness of the advertising manager. In this case there was no excuse of that sort to be found. Jerningham had never yet met an advertising manager whose work he did not think he could do better himself; the same applied to office heads–and to husbands. But Jerningham had to admit to himself that the Captain was better fitted than he was to command a light cruiser, and it was no mitigation that he did not want to command a light cruiser.

To recover his self-respect he called back into his mind again the fact that he had been quicker than the Captain in the identification of the Italian cruisers, and he went on to tell himself that the Captain would not stand a chance in competition with him for the affections of the young women of his set, with–not Dora Darby (Jerningham's mind shied away from that subject hastily)–but with Dorothy Clough or Cicely French, say. That was a comforting line of thought. The Captain might be the finest light cruiser captain, actual or potential, on the Seven Seas–Jerningham thought he was–but he was not to compare with Jerningham in anything else, in the social graces, or in appreciation of art or literature. The man had probably never seen beauty in anything. And it was quite laughable to think of him trying to woo

Cicely French the way Jerningham had, finding her in a tantrum of temper, and subtly coaxing her out of it with womanish sympathy, and playing deftly on her reaction to win her regard, and telepathically noting the play of her mood so as to seize the right moment for the final advance. The very thought of the Captain trying to do anything like that made Jerningham smile through all his misery as he met the Captain's eye.

The Captain smiled back, and stopped in his walk at Jerningham's side.

'Was it a surprise to you, their running away like that?' asked the Captain.

Jerningham had to think swiftly to get himself back on board *Artemis* today from a Paddington flat three years ago.

'No, sir,' he said. 'Not very much.'

That was the truth, inasmuch as he had had no preconceived tactical theories so as to be surprised at all.

'It may be just a trick to get us away from the convoy,' said the Captain. 'Then their planes would have a chance. But I don't think so.'

'No, sir?' said Jerningham.

'There's something bigger than cruisers out today, I fancy. They may be trying to head us into a trap.'

The Captain's eye was still everywhere. He saw at that moment, and Jerningham's glance following him saw too, the flagship leading around in a sixteen-point turn.

'Starboard fifteen,' said the Navigating Lieutenant, and the deck canted hugely as *Artemis* followed her next ahead round. She plunged deeply half a dozen times as she crashed across the stern waves thrown up first by her predecessors and then by herself, and white water foamed across her forecastle.

'Flagship's signalling to convoy, sir,' said the Chief Yeoman of Signals, '"Resume previous course".'

'We're staying between the Eyeties and the convoy,' remarked the Captain, 'and every minute brings us nearer to Malta.'

'Yes, sir,' said Jerningham. He cast frantically about in his mind for some contribution to make to this conversation other than 'Yes, sir,' and 'No, sir.' He wanted to appear bright.

'And night is coming,' said Jerningham, grasping desperately at inspiration.

'Yes,' said the Captain. 'The Eyeties are losing time. The most valuable asset they have, and they're squandering it.'

Jerningham looked at the Satanic eyebrows drawing together over the curved nose, the full lips compressed into a gash, and his telepathic sympathies told him how the Captain was thinking to himself what he would do if he commanded the Italian squadron, the resolution with which he would come plunging down into battle. And then the eyebrows separated again, and the lips softened into a smile.

'The commonest mistake to make in war,' said the Captain, 'is to think that because a certain course seems to you to be the best for the enemy, that is the course he will take. He may not think it the best, or there may be some reason against it which you don't know about.'

'That's true, sir,' said Jerningham. It was not an aspect of war he had ever thought about before; most of his thoughts in action were usually taken up by wondering what his own personal fate would be.

Ordinary Seaman Whipple was climbing the difficult ladder to the crow's nest to relieve the lookout there. The Captain allowed himself to watch the changeover being effected, and Jerningham saw him put back his head and inflate his chest to hail the masthead, and then he relaxed again with the words unspoken.

'And the next commonest mistake,' grinned the Captain, 'is to give unnecessary orders. Whipple up there will keep a sharp lookout without my telling him. He knows that's what he's there for.'

Jerningham gaped at him, wordless now, despite his efforts to appear bright. This was an aspect of the Captain's character which he had never seen before, this courteous gentleman with his smiling common sense and insight into character. It crossed Jerningham's mind, insanely at that moment, that perhaps the Captain after all might be able to make some progress with Cicely French if he wanted to.

8

FROM THE CAPTAIN'S REPORT

... the enemy's cruisers were then joined by a fresh force consisting of two battleships of the 'Littorio' class and another cruiser of the 'Bolzano' class ...

Ordinary Seaman Albert Whipple was a crusader. Like most crusaders he was inclined to take himself a little too seriously, and that made him something of a butt to his friends. When he took over from Quimsby the latter grinned tolerantly and poked him in the ribs while pointing out to him the things in sight–the smoke of the Italian cruiser squadron, and their funnels just visible over the horizon, the distant shapes of the convoy wallowing doggedly along towards Malta.

'An' that thing in the front of the line is the flagship,' concluded Quimsby with heavy-handed humour. 'Give my regards to the Admiral when you get your commission.'

For one of the theories that the lower deck maintained about Whipple's seriousness was that he wanted promotion, aspiring to the quarter deck, for Whipple had a secondary school education. The lower deck was wrong about this. All that Whipple wanted to do was to fight the enemy as efficiently as was in his power, in accordance with the precepts of his mother.

Albert was the youngest of a large family, and his elder brothers and sisters were quite unlike him, big and burly, given to the drinking of beer and to riotous Saturday nights; they had all gone out to work at fourteen, and it was partly because of the consequent relief to the family finances that Albert had been able to set his foot on the lower rungs of the higher education. The brothers and sisters had not objected, had shown no jealousy that the youngest should have had better treatment than they; in fact, they had been mildly proud of him when he came home and reported proudly that he had won the scholarship which might be the beginning of a career. Albert was white-faced and skinny, like his mother, and desperately serious. The brothers and sisters had never paid any attention to their mother's queer behaviour; their work in the tannery and the toy factory had made them good union members, but they had no sympathy with her further aspirations, with her desperate interest in the League of Nations, in the Japanese invasion of China and Franco's rebellion in Spain. They had laughed, as their father had learned to do before they were born. Their father could remember as far back as 1914, when the eldest child–George–was on the way, finding her standing on the kerb watching the soldiers of the new army marching down the street, bands playing and people cheering, and yet she had tears running down her cheeks at the sight of it. Mr Whipple had clapped her on the back and told her to cheer up, and as soon as George was born had gone off and joined the army and had done his bit in Mespot. And when he had come back, long after the war was over, he had found her all worked up about the Treaty of Versailles, and when it was not the Treaty of Versailles it was some new worry about the Balkans or the militarization of the Rhine or something.

She had tried to capture the interest of each of her children in turn regarding the problems of the world, and she had failed with each until Albert began to grow up. He listened to her; it was a help that during his formative years he came home to dinner while the rest ate sandwiches at the factory. Those *tête-à-têtes* across the kitchen table, the skinny little son listening rapt to the burning words of his skinny little mother, had had their effect. Albert had it in mind when he was still quite young that when he grew up it would be his mission to reform the world; he was a little priggish about it, feeling marked out from the rest of humanity, and this conception of himself had been accentuated by the fact that unlike his brothers and sisters he had started a secondary education, and that he passed, the summer in which war began, his school examination a year younger than the average of his fellows and with distinctions innumerable.

The brothers had joined the Air Force or the Army, but with pitiably small sense of its being a sacred duty; they did not hold with Hitler's goings on, and it was time something was done about it, but they did not think of themselves as crusaders and would have laughed at anyone who called them that. And Albert had stayed with his mother, while his father worked double shifts at the tannery, until after a few months Albert and his mother talked over the fact that now he was old enough to join one of the Services at least–a poster had told them how boys could join the Royal Navy. Mrs Whipple kept back her tears as they talked about it; in fact, she jealously hugged her pain to her breast, womanlike. At the back of her mind there was the thought of atonement, of a bloody sacrifice of what she held dearest in the world, to make amends for her country's earlier lethargy and indifference. She was giving up her best loved son, but to him she talked only of his duty, of how his call had come to him when he was hardly old enough for the glory of it. And Albert had answered the call, and his confident certainty in the rightness of his mission had carried him through homesickness and seasickness, had left him unspotted by his messmates' spoken filth and casual blasphemies. He had endured serenely their amused tolerance of his queer ways and priggish demeanour, and he devoted himself to the work in hand with a fanaticism which had raised the eyebrows of the petty officers of H.M.S. *Collingwood* so that now he was Ordinary Seaman in *Artemis* and noted down in the Commander's mental books–and in those of the Captain, too–as certain to make a good Leading Seaman in time.

Sea service weathered his complexion to a healthy tan, but neither good food nor exercise had filled him out at all. Perhaps the thought of his mission kept him thin. He was still hollow-cheeked, and his comparatively wide forehead above his hollow cheeks and his little pointed chin made his face strangely wedge-shaped, which intensified the gleam in his eyes sunk deep under their brows. All his movements were quick and eager; he grabbed feverishly at the binoculars resting in their frame before his face, so anxious was he to take up his duties again, to resume his task of avenging Abyssinia and hastening the coming of the millennium. Lying in a hospital at that moment, her legs shattered by the ruins that a bomb from a German aeroplane had brought down, his mother was thinking of him, two thousand miles away; either through space or through time it was her spirit which was animating him.

Whipple searched the horizon carefully, section by section, from the starboard beam to right ahead and then round to the port beam and back again; there was nothing to report, nothing in sight beyond what Quimsby had pointed out to him. He swivelled back again to the Italian squadron; his hatred might have been focused through lenses and prisms like some death-dealing ray, so intense was it. There were only the funnels of the cruisers to see, and the pall of smoke above them stretching back behind them in a dwindling plume. He swivelled slowly forward again, and checked his motion abruptly. There was a hint of smoke on the horizon at a point forward of the Italians, almost nothing to speak of, and yet a definite trace of smoke, all the same, and clearly it was no residual fragment of the smoke of any of the ships which Whipple had in sight. For five seconds Whipple watched it grow before he pressed the buzzer.

The Captain's secretary answered it–a man Whipple had never cared for. He suspected him of he knew not what, but he had also seen him drunk, only just able to stagger along the brow back into the ship, and Whipple had no use for a man who let himself get drunk when there was work to be done, while there was a mission still unfulfilled. But Whipple did not allow his dislike to interfere with his duty. If anything, it made him more careful than ever with his enunciation, more painstaking to make an exact report of what he could see.

'Forebridge,' said Jerningham.

'Masthead. More smoke visible on the port bow,' said Whipple pedantically. 'Beyond the enemy cruisers. Green three-eight.'

He repeated himself just as pedantically. Back through the voice pipe, before Jerningham closed it, he could hear his report being relayed to the Captain, and that gave him the comforting assurance that Jerningham had got it right. He swept the horizon, rapidly and thoroughly, before looking at the new smoke again; it was always as well to take every possible precaution. But there was nothing further to report except as regards the new smoke. He pressed the buzzer again.

'Masthead,' he said. 'The new lot of smoke is closing us. The same bearing.

No, green three-nine.'

A bigger wave than usual, or a combination of waves, lifted *Artemis* ten feet vertically at the same moment as beyond the horizon another combination of waves lifted the Italian battleship *Legnano* ten feet also. In that crystal clear air against the blue sky, Whipple caught a glimpse of solid grey–funnel tops and upperworks, the latter apparently the top storey of a massive gunnery control tower. It came and went almost instantaneously, but Whipple knew what it was, and felt a wave of fierce excitement pass over him like a flame. Yet excitement could not shake the cold fixity of his purpose to do his duty with exactitude.

'Masthead,' he said down the tube, dryly and unemotionally. 'Battleship in sight. Green four-o.'

The blood was pulsing faster in his veins. A bibliophile finding in the twopenny box a long-sought first edition would know nearly the same thrill as Whipple felt, or a knight of the Round Table at a vision of the Grail. There were thousands of Italians there to be killed, ships which were the pride of the Italian navy were there to be destroyed. 'The thicker the hay,' said Alaric once, when the odds against his army were being pointed out to him, 'the easier it is mown.' 'The bigger they come,' said Bob Fitzsimmons, 'the harder they fall.' Whipple thought along the same lines. The appalling strength of the hostile force meant nothing to him, literally nothing, from the point of view of frightening him. He was merely glad that the enemy were presenting themselves in such numbers to be killed. If at that moment some impossible chance had put Whipple without time for reflexion in command of the English squadron, the light cruisers would have dashed headlong into action and destruction. But Whipple was not in command. He was perfectly conscious that he was merely the masthead lookout in H.M.S. *Artemis*, and as such a man with a definite duty to perform to the best of his ability.

'Two battleships and a heavy cruiser,' he reported down the voice pipe, 'heading a little abaft our beam. On the same bearing now as the other ships. The other ships are turning now astern of them.'

Whipple was reporting the development of the Italian fleet into line of battle, and in exactly the same tone as he would have used if he had been reporting sighting a buoy. That was the contribution he was privileged to make to the cause his mother had talked about to him over the midday dinner table in Bermondsey. Ordinary Seaman Albert Whipple, aged eighteen, was a prig and a self-righteous one. A cynic might well define *esprit de corps* as self-righteous priggishness–the spirit which inspired Sir Richard Grenville or Cromwell's Ironsides. From the yardarm close beside Whipple fluttered the signal flags which he had set a-flying.

9

FROM THE CAPTAIN'S REPORT

. . . the behaviour of the ship's company was most satisfactory . . .

The Italian fleet was up over the horizon now, their upperworks visible under the smoke, and the British squadron had wheeled about once more. The Italians were heading to interpose between the convoy and Malta; if it were not for that slow, lumbering convoy, crawling along at its miserable eleven knots, the light cruisers could have circled round the Italian battleships like a hawk round a heron. As it was the British squadron was like a man with a cannon ball chained to his leg, crippled and slow, forced to keep its position between the convoy and the Italian warships–those battleships were designed for twenty-nine knots and even when mishandled were quite capable of twenty-five. They could work steadily ahead, until they barred the route, forcing the British to attack to clear the path–as if a man with a penknife could clear a path out of a steel safe–and if the British sensibly declined the attempts and turned back, they would be pursued by the Italians, whose superior speed would then compel the light cruisers either to stay and be shot at or move out of the Italian path and leave the convoy to destruction.

It was all perfectly logical, positive, and inevitable when the data were considered–the eleven-knot convoy, the thirty-knot battleships, the Italian fifteen-inch guns, the British six-inch; the four hours remaining of daylight and the extraordinary clearness of the air. Fog might save the English, but there was no chance of fog in that sparkling air. Nightfall might save the English, too, for it would be most imprudent for battleships to engage in a night action with cruisers–that would be like staking guineas against shillings in a game of pitch-and-toss. But it was still early afternoon, and no more than half an hour would be needed for the Italians to reach their most advantageous position. Then five minutes of steady shelling would be sufficient to sink every cruiser in the British line; less than that to destroy the helpless convoy. Then Malta would fall; the running ulcer in Italy's side would be healed; Rommel in Africa, the submarines in the Atlantic would feel an instant lessening of the strain upon them; the Vichy government would be informed of one more step towards the German conquest of the world; the very Japanese in seas ten thousand miles away would be aware of a lightening of their task.

So obvious and logical was all this that the inferences must be clear to the rawest hand anywhere in the ship. It was not necessary to have studied Mahan, or to have graduated from the Staff College, to understand the situation. The ship's company of *Artemis* might not stop to think about Vichy or Rommel or the Japanese; but they knew the speed of the convoy, and the merest whisper of the word 'battleships' would tell them that their situation was a perilous one. And a mere whisper–with implied doubt–would be far more unsettling than any certainty. Not one man in ten in *Artemis* could see what was going on, and in a ship at action stations it was hard for information to filter through by word of mouth.

In the Captain's opinion distorted news was dangerous. He knew his men, and he believed that his men knew him; if they heard the truth he could rely upon them whatever the truth might be. A crisis in the battle was close at hand, and he could spare not one moment from the bridge to tell them himself. He turned a little on his stool, caught Jerningham's eye, and beckoned to him. Jerningham had to wait a second or two while the Captain brought himself up to date again regarding the situation, looking at flagship and convoy and enemy, before he took the glasses from his eyes and turned a searching glance at his secretary. Jerningham was acutely conscious of that glance. He was not being sized up for any trifle; it was not as if he was a mere applicant for a job in a City office. The business he was to do was something touching the whole efficiency of the ship–the safety of Malta–the life or death of England. The Captain would not have trusted him with it if he were not absolutely sure of him. In fact, the Captain was faintly surprised at finding that he *was* sure of him; he wondered a little whether he had previously misjudged his secretary or whether the latter was one of those people who had moods, and was sometimes reliable and sometimes not. But whether he had misjudged him or not, and whether he had moods or not, this was the right time to impose responsibility upon him and to make amends if he had misjudged him, or to give him confidence in the future if this was merely an exalted mood.

'Go down,' said the Captain, 'and tell the ship about the situation.'

Jerningham stood a little startled, but the Captain already had his binoculars to his eyes again. He had given his order, and an order given by a Captain in a ship of war is carried out.

'Aye aye, sir,' said Jerningham, saluting as he jerked himself out of his surprise.

He turned away and started down the ladder. He was an intelligent man, accustomed in his private life to think for himself, accustomed to selling ideas to advertising managers, accustomed to conveying ideas to commercial artists, accustomed to telling the public truths or fictions in the fewest and clearest words. The Captain might easily have expanded the brief order he gave his secretary, telling him what to say and how to say it, but the Captain knew that it was not necessary; and also that to leave the responsibility to his secretary would be good for him.

Jerningham's mind was feverishly turning over words and phrases as he descended the ladder; he did not have time to assemble any, but, on the other hand, he did not have time in those few seconds to become self-conscious, nor had his weakness time to reassert itself.

'I've a message for the ship from the Captain,' he said to the bosun's mate beside the loudspeaker bolted to the bulkhead.

The petty officer switched on and piped shrilly, the sound of his call audible in every part of the ship.

'The Captain has sent me to tell you,' said Jerningham to the mouthpiece, 'we've got the Eyety navy in front of us. Battleships, heavy cruisers, and all. They've run away from us once, the heavy cruisers have. Now we're going to see if the battleships'll run too. Three hours of daylight left, and the convoy's *got* to reach Malta. Good luck to us all. There's none like us.'

Jerningham opened his mouth to say more, but his good judgement came to his rescue and he closed it again. He had said all there was to say, and in an illuminated moment he knew that anything he were to add would be not only superfluous but possibly harmful. Men of the temper of the crew of *Artemis* did not need rhetoric; a plain statement of the facts for the benefit of those men below decks who had no idea what was happening was all that was needed.

He turned away from the unresponsive instrument, not knowing whether he had done well or badly; in the days of wooden ships, before public address systems had even been heard of, his words might have been received with cheers–or boos–which would have been informative. The ludicrous thought crossed his active mind that it was just like an advertising problem. How often had he devised ingenious methods by which to 'key' advertisements to discover which had the greatest pulling power?

His eyes met those of the bosun's mate, and then travelled on to exchange glances with the other ratings–messengers and resting lookouts–stationed here. One or two of the men still wore the expression of philosophic indifference which so often characterized the lower deck, but there was a gleam in the eyes of the others, a smile at the corners of their mouths, which told him that they were excited, and pleasurably excited. That telepathic sympathy of his, which had assisted him to the downfall of so many young women, made him aware that the men were feeling the same inconsequent exhilaration as he felt–inconsequent to him, and novel and strange, but something they had known before and recognized. A climax was at hand, the climax to months and years of training and forethought, to the unobtrusive mental conditioning for which the Mephistophelian Captain on the bridge was responsible, to the life's mission to which men like Ordinary Seaman Albert Whipple had devoted themselves, or to the long line of fighting ancestors, which had generated them–like A.B. Dawkins down at the wheel, whose great-great-grandfather had run with powder charges over the bloody decks of the *Temeraire* at Trafalgar. It was the prospect of such a climax which exhilarated them, just as, ridiculously, it exhilarated him, and left them all careless of any possible consequences to themselves. He ran up the steep ladder again to the bridge, disregarding the way in which it swayed and swung to the send of the sea.

10

FROM THE CAPTAIN'S REPORT

. . . increasing speed and at the same time making smoke . . .

Back on the bridge, Jerningham looked round him to see that there had been no radical change in the situation during the short time of his absence. There were the minutest possible dots on the horizon below the Italian funnel smoke which showed that the Italian fleet was now actually in sight. A new string of flags was breaking out on the halliards of the flagship.

The Captain knew this was the moment. The Admiral had led them round until they were properly stationed with regard to the wind which now blew in a line from them to a point ahead of the Italians–that blessed wind, of such a convenient strength and from such a convenient quarter–and he had timed his arrival in this situation at the very moment when the Italians would be almost within range with their fourteen-inch guns. And so far the Admiral had shown none of his hand, except to display a determination to yield nothing without fighting for it, and the Italians must have been expecting that at least, as was proved by their caution in bringing up their battleships only behind a heavy force of cruisers.

The Chief Yeoman of Signals interpreted the flagship's signal, and the Captain was ready for it–the plan which he held on his knee laid it down as the next step.

'Revolutions for thirty-one knots,' he ordered. 'Make smoke.'

The Navigating Lieutenant repeated the order, and the Officer of the Watch pressed the plunger which ordered smoke.

Down in the engine-room the Commander (E) stood on the iron grating; being a tall man the top of his head was no more than a few inches below the level of the sea. He stood there with the immeasurable patience of his breed, acquired during countless hours of standing on countless gratings, and with his feet apart and his hands clasped behind him in the attitude he had first been taught as a cadet eighteen years before. He was the supreme lord of this underworld of his, like Lucifer, and he seemed marked out as such by the loneliness of his position, without a soul within yards of him, and by the light-coloured boiler suit which he wore, and by the untroubled loftiness of his expression. The very lighting of the engine-room by some strange chance accentuated the fact, glaring down upon his face and figure with a particular brightness, specially illuminating him like a character on the stage. He was a young man to have the rank of Commander and to carry the responsibilities of his position, to have hundreds of men obedient to him, to have sixty-four thousand horse-power under his control, to be master of the pulsating life of a light cruiser, but it would be a hard task to guess his age, so deliberate were his movements and so unlined and yet so mature was his face.

All the Commander (E) had to do was to stand there on the grating and do nothing else. A crisis might be at hand, but it could not affect the Commander (E) unless some catastrophe occurred. His work was done for the moment; it had been accomplished already during the years *Artemis* had been in commission. He had trained the engine-room complement into complete efficiency–the Engine-room Artificers and the Mechanicians and the Stokers; the Lieutenants and Sub-Lieutenants (E) who were his heads of department and his subordinates–not so many years younger than he–loved him as if he were their father, and would have found it hard to explain why if called upon to do so. None could appreciate the magic serenity, that endless patience, who had not served under him. Because of the love they bore him they knew his will without his expressing it, and they laboured constantly to anticipate it, to perfect themselves in their duty because he wished it, so that the organization and routine of the engine-room ran as smoothly and as efficiently as did the turbines at that moment.

And the turbines ran smoothly because of the previous labours of the Commander (E)–the sleepless vigilance which had watched over material and supplies, had read every engine-room log, had studied the temperatures of every bearing, the idiosyncrasies of every oil jet. There had been the endless desk-work, the reports written to the Admiralty (the strange gods of Whitehall whose motives had to be guessed, and who had to be propitiated by exact and complicated paper ceremonial, but who, once propitiated, were lavish like the savage rain gods of Africa), the statistics to be gathered and studied, the plans that had to be made against future contingencies. In time of war a light cruiser repairs and reconditions when she can and not when she should; and the Commander (E) had had to use forethought, and had had to display prompt decision, deciding what should be done, what opportunities snatched at, what might safely be postponed, anticipating future needs, doing today what would have to be done anyway during the next two weeks, leaving until some uncovenanted future doing the things which were not immediately essential.

As a result of all this the Commander (E) had nothing to do now; everything was being done by itself. Even the Senior Engineer, Lieutenant (E) Charles Norton Bastwick, felt a lack of anything to do, and came lounging up to take his stand beside the Commander (E), hands behind him, feet apart, in the 'at ease' position; it would be some minutes before he would once more feel the urge to walk round again, reading gauges and thermometers, and thereby debarring the Commander (E) from doing the same. It would only be if an emergency arose–if some near-miss shook up a condenser so that it leaked, or if a torpedo hit flooded a compartment, or some similar damage was inflicted–that they would have their hands full, improvising and extemporizing, toiling along with their men to keep the ship afloat and the propellers turning. And if the ship were to meet her death, if the sea were to come flooding in and the scalding steam–steam as hot as red-hot iron, steam that could roast meat to a frizzled brown–should pour into boiler-room and engine-room, and the order 'abandon ship' should be given, they would be the last of all to leave, the last to climb the treacherous iron ladders up to sea level and possible safety.

The engine-room was hot, because the ship had been going twenty-seven knots for some time now. The thermometer on the forward bulkhead registered 105 degrees, but for an engine-room, and according to the ideas of men accustomed to working in one, that was not really hot. And the place was full of noise, the high-pitched note of the turbines dominating everything–a curious noise, in its way an unobtrusive noise, which sounded as if it did not want to call attention to itself, the loudest whisper one could possibly imagine. The ears of a newcomer to the engine-room would be filled with it, all the same, so that he could hear nothing else. Only after long experience would he grow so accustomed to the noise that he could distinguish other noises through it, and hear human voices speaking at their normal pitch. Until that should come about he would see lips move and not be able to understand a word.

Bastwick and the Commander (E) were aware that above them, on the surface of the sea some sort of action was taking place. All through the forenoon they had heard the four-inch and the Oerlikons and the pompoms firing in savage bursts, and they had known that the convoy and escort were under aerial attack; but then the guns fell silent over their heads, and food had been brought to them, and there had been a brief moment of tranquillity. But then the bridge had rung down for twenty-seven knots, and they had had to switch over from the cruising turbines to the main engines (that blessed fluid flywheel which made the changeover so rapid and easy!) and the ship had begun rapid manoeuvring. Since then course had been altered so often that it was hard to reconstruct the situation in the mind. And once the ship had rolled and quivered to an explosion close alongside–God only knew what that was, for not a gun had been fired in the ship since the morning.

The squeal of the bosun's pipe suddenly made itself heard through the loudspeaker in the engine-room, attracting everyone's attention to Jerningham's voice which followed it. 'We've got the Eyety navy in front of us . . . now we're going to see if the battleships'll run too . . .' Jerningham's voice came to an end, but the Commander (E) and Bastwick still stood at ease on the iron grating, unmoved and unmoving. At any moment a fifteen-inch shell might come crashing through the deck above them, to burst in the engine-room and rend the ship apart while dashing them to atoms. Around them and beneath them a thousand-odd tons of fuel oil awaited the chance to burst into flame and burn them like ants in a furnace. A hundred tons of high explosive, forward and aft, needed only to be touched off.

But it was of the essence of life down here below the protective deck that destruction might come at any second, without any warning at all, and–more important from the point of view of mental attitude–without any possibility of raising a hand to ward it off. There was nothing to do but one's duty, just as the comic poet once declared that he had nothing to eat save food. Down there Jerningham's announcement on the loudspeaker had the effect of making everyone feel a little superior to the world above them, as the white settlers in Africa in time of drought might watch the natives sacrificing chickens or dancing wild dances to bring rain; the whites could feel contemptuous or compassionate–but they could not make it rain any more than the natives could. Above decks, Jerningham's announcement was like a stone dropped into a pool, sending a ripple of excitement over the surface; below them it was like a stone dropped into treacle, absorbed without any apparent reaction. The Commander (E) and Bastwick were watching Engine-room Artificer Henrose making the routine test of the boiler water, making sure that under the stress of continuous high speed the sea water pumped through the condenser to cool the used steam and to make it available for re-use was not leaking through any one of the thousand joints. Henrose, balancing against the roll of the ship, held the test-tube of boiler water in his left hand and poised the bottle of silver nitrate over it, letting the reagent fall into it drop by drop. Jerningham's announcement made itself heard, but Henrose might just as well not have heard it as far as any apparent reaction was concerned. He levelled the bottle of silver nitrate, squinted at the test-tube, and shook it, and squinted again. There was not the slightest trace of the white precipitate of silver chloride which would indicate that there was salt in the boiler water–salt which would eat through joints and tubes and cripple the ship in a few hours. Henrose went swaying back along the heaving grating to spill out the test-tube of water and replace the silver nitrate bottle. Italian dreadnoughts might be within range; that was interesting, just as was the fact that Henry VIII had six wives, but there was no salt in the boiler water, and it was that which mattered.

To starboard and port the needles of the revolution indicators moved sharply round the dial; the Commander (E) from where he stood–he stood there because although he had ostensibly nothing to do he could see from there everything of importance–could see that the number of revolutions ordered would give the ship thirty-one knots, full speed save for a knot or two in hand for emergencies. The Commander (E) was serenely aware that there was ample pressure available to satisfy this demand; it was because he could foresee such demands and plan economically for them ahead of time that he held the rank of Commander.

The four ratings who stood at the valves admitting steam to the four turbines began to spin the valves open, turning the horizontal wheels while watching the restless needles–two black and one red–of the dials. The note of the turbines began unbelievably to rise, unbelievably because the ear would not have believed that there could be a note higher than the previous one. More and more steam poured into the turbines, a tremendous torrent of steam, steam with a strength of sixty thousand horse-power. The beat of the propellers quickened, the needles crept farther round the dials until they caught up with and rested upon the others. The orders from the bridge were obeyed; the ship was making thirty-one knots, and in the engine-room it felt as if she were leaping like a stag from wave to wave over the lively sea.

A fresh noise broke through the whine of the turbines; this time it was a loud imperious clatter that none could mistake. A red light glowed high up on the bulkhead, and an indicator hand moved across from 'Stop making smoke' to 'Make smoke'. Bastwick moved forward leisurely towards the boiler-room. He knew that the signal was being repeated there–during the night before he had personally tested every communication–and he knew that Stoker Petty Officer Harmsworth was perfectly reliable, but he knew, too, that nothing is certain in war. As he went through the double door his ears clicked with the rise in pressure; at thirty-one knots the furnaces burnt in a few minutes enough oil fuel to warm the average house for a whole winter, and the air to consume that oil was a rushing mighty tempest dragged into the boiler-room by the partial vacuum set up by the combustion.

Harmsworth was completing the adjustment of the valves admitting just too much oil and shutting off just too much air to allow of complete combustion in this furnace. Bastwick stooped and peered through the glazed peephole. Normally it gave a view of a white-hot whirl of flame, but now it showed a hideous gloomy blackness; some of the oil was being burnt, but only just enough to break down the remainder into thick black greasy hydrocarbons whose sooty smoke was being caught up in the draught and poured through the after-funnel.

'Very good,' said Bastwick, straightening up.

The heat in here was oppressive, and the temperature would rise still higher with this increase in speed; there were trickles of sweat down Harmsworth's bull neck and among the hairs of his bare chest. Bastwick looked round the boiler-room, nodded to Sub-Lieutenant (E) Pilkington, and got a grin back in return. Pilkington was a brilliant youngster; one of these days he would be an Admiral. Bastwick completed a brief inspection and found everything satisfactory as it would be with Pilkington there. Then Bastwick made his way back to the engine-room, where the Commander (E) still stood on the iron grating, his handsome ageless face lit up by the harsh electric bulbs like that of a marble saint. But Bastwick knew that the Commander (E) had taken note that he, Bastwick, had recently inspected the boiler-room. The rudder indicator on the bulkhead, below the smoke telegraph, showed that the ship was changing course, and the two red lights beside it confirmed it by showing that the steering engines were at work. Bastwick knew, too, that the Commander (E) had noted this fact as well, and was making deductions from it regarding the battle. The saint might appear lost in contemplation, but when, or if, an emergency should arise he would be as prepared to deal with it as he could be, as any man could be.

II

FROM THE CAPTAIN'S REPORT

. . . I found the smoke screen to be extremely effective . . .

Artemis was flying through the water now; at that speed with the wind abeam and the sea nearly so she lurched savagely and with unremitting regularity, hitting each wave as if it were something solid, her forecastle awash with the white water which came leaping over her port bow. Last of the line, she tore along over a surface already whipped creamy white by the four ships ahead of her; the mountainous waves thrown up by five hulls each of nearly six thousand tons travelling at that speed diverged on either side of her and broke into white water where they crossed the waves thrown up by the destroyers racing in a parallel line. The five cruisers went tearing along in their rigid line. Smoke began to pour from the after-funnel of the flagship in the van, a wisp or two at first, and then a thick greasy never-ending cloud; within two seconds of the first wisps there was smoke pouring from the after-funnels of all five of them–five thick cylinders of smoke, each so dense as to appear liquid rather than gaseous. They drooped down to the surface of the sea, and rolled over it, pushed gently by that convenient wind towards the enemy, and hardly dissipating at all, spreading just enough to blend with each other in a wide bank of smoke diagonal to the squadron's course so that even the second ship in the line, to say nothing of *Artemis* at the rear, was completely obscured from the sight of the Italians. And the thirty-one knots at which the squadron was moving was far faster than anything the dreadnoughts could do, so that although the Italian fleet was faster than the convoy the smoke screen was being laid between the two; to attack the convoy the battleships would still have to come through the screen–they could not work round the end of it.

But to lay a smoke screen and to hide behind it was mere defensive warfare of the most pusillanimous kind. The enemy must be smitten, and smitten again, even though the smiting was with mere six-inch guns against twelve inches of armour-plate. Even though the enemy could not be hurt, his resolution must be broken down, his nerve shattered; he must be taught the lesson that he could not venture out to sea without submitting to vicious attack. And *Artemis* was last of the line of cruisers; abeam of her the smoke lay thickest, and it would be her movements that would be the most unpredictable to the enemy. It was her duty to smite, even though to smite she must expose those eggshell sides of hers to the sledgehammer blows of the enemy, and run the gauntlet of one-ton shells hurled with the velocity of a meteor, with an accuracy which could hit a tennis court from ten miles distance.

The Captain sat on the stool which bucked beneath him like a playful horse; the motion was unnoticed by him even though the reflexes developed during years at sea were continually at work keeping him steady in his seat. He was thinking deeply, but on subjects so logical, and with such a comforting ingredient of mathematics, that his expression gave no sign of it. The Mephistophelian eyebrows were their normal distance apart; and although the plan he was to carry out called for the highest degree of resolution, the firm mouth was no more firmly compressed than usual, for the plan was a part of the Captain's life, something he was going to do, not something he wished to do or did not wish to do; something the advisability of which was not in doubt even though the details of execution had had to be left to this last moment for consideration because of possible freaks of weather or possible unexpected moves on the part of the enemy.

Three minutes of smoke meant a smoke bank a mile and a half long, far too wide for the enemy to watch with care all along its length. And with the smoke being continually added to at one end, the other end would probably not be under observation at all. And the smoke bank, allowing for spread, would be a quarter of a mile thick, but *Artemis* would be going through it diagonally, and it would take her (the Captain solved a Pythagorean problem in his head) fifty-five seconds to emerge on the other side, without allowing for the drift of the bank before the wind. This fifteen-knot breeze added a refreshing complication to the mathematics of it. It would take over two minutes to traverse the smoke bank; two minutes and ten seconds. The Captain turned to the voice pipe beside him.

'Captain–Gunnery Officer,' he said. The Gunnery Lieutenant answered him.

'I am turning to starboard now, Guns. It will take us two minutes and ten seconds approximately to go through the smoke. You'll find the Eyeties about red five when we come out, but I shall turn to port parallel to their course immediately. Open fire when you are ready. All right? Good-bye.'

Artemis was the last ship in the line, and consequently the first to take action independently of the rest of the squadron.

'Turn eight points to starboard, Pilot,' he said to the Navigating Lieutenant.

'Starboard fifteen,' said the Navigating Lieutenant down the voice pipe; *Artemis* leaned far over outwards as she made the right-angle turn–full speed and plenty of helm. 'Midships. Steady!'

'Stop making smoke,' ordered the Captain; he wanted the range clear for the guns when he emerged, and the signal went down through five decks to Stoker Petty Officer Harmsworth in the boiler-room.

So far the wind had been carrying the smoke solidly away to starboard, but now *Artemis* was heading squarely into it. One moment they were out in the clear sunshine with its infinite visibility. The next moment they were in reeking darkness. The stink of unburnt fuel oil was in their nostrils and their lungs. It made them cough. And in the smoke it was dark, far darker than the darkest coloured spectacles would make it; the Captain looked round, and he could only just see the white uniform of the Navigating Lieutenant two yards away. It was most satisfactory smoke as far as he could tell–he looked aft towards the masthead and could see nothing. But there was just the chance that the mast was protruding through the smoke and betraying the movements of the ship to the Italians.

'Call the masthead and see if the lookout is in the smoke,' ordered the Captain, and Jerningham obeyed him.

'Masthead lookout reports he is in the smoke and can't see anything,' he called into the darkness when he had received Ordinary Seaman Whipple's reassurance.

The duty had been useful to him. When they had plunged into the smoke his heart had seemed to rise in his throat, and it was only with an effort that he had seemed to swallow it down. It was beating fast, and the beating seemed to find an echo in his finger tips so that they shook. But the distraction of having to speak to Whipple had saved him, and he was able to recapture his new found sang-froid.

'Thirty seconds,' said the Torpedo Lieutenant. He had switched on the light at the hooded desk and, stooping with his face close down, he was reading the movement of the second-hand of the deck-watch.

'Forty-five seconds.'

It was strange how silent the ship seemed to be, here in the smoke. The sound of the sea overside was much more obvious than out in the sunshine. Within the ship as she pitched over the waves, vibrating gently to the thrust of the propellers, there was a silence in seeming accord with the gloomy darkness that engulfed them. The Captain knew that darkness did not necessitate absence of noise; it was a curious psychic phenomenon this assumption that it was quieter. No, it was not. In the smoke or out of it the wind was still blowing, and the turn which *Artemis* had just made had brought the wind abaft when before it was squarely abeam. That accounted for it; the ship really was quieter.

'One minute,' said the Torpedo Lieutenant.

That was interesting, to discover that it had taken him fifteen seconds to make that deduction about the wind. The opportunity of honestly timing mental processes came quite rarely. And the study of the speed of thought was an important one, with its bearing on the reaction times of officers and men.

'Seventy-five seconds,' said the Torpedo Lieutenant.

He must remember, when he thought about this later, that at the moment he was keyed up and as mentally active as he well could be. Perhaps the brain really did work more quickly in those circumstances, although it was hard to imagine the physiological and anatomical adjustments which such a theory could postulate.

'Ninety seconds,' said the Torpedo Lieutenant.

Presumably the R.A.F. doctors had been on a similar track for years. He must remember at some time or other to find out how much they had discovered; but they would of course be more interested in split seconds than in reactions lasting a quarter of a minute.

'One-o-five seconds,' said the Torpedo Lieutenant.

Not long to go now. But the smoke was just as thick as ever–extremely good. He must remember to put that in his report. The Captain shifted in his position on the stool, poising himself ready for instant action. It seemed to him as if the smoke were thinning. Just possibly the Italians could see by now the shadowy grey form of the *Artemis* emerging.

'Two minutes,' said the Torpedo Lieutenant.

Yes, he could see the Navigating Lieutenant plainly now. There was a second of sunshine, and then darkness again, and then they were out of the smoke, blinded a little by the sun, but not so blind as to be unable to see, full and clear, within six-inch gun range, the massive silhouettes of the Italian battle line almost right ahead of them, every detail plain, the complex gunnery control towers, the tripod masts, the huge guns, the reeking funnels.

'Port fifteen,' said the Captain, and *Artemis*, beautiful in the sunshine, swung round to turn her broadside upon that colossal force, like Ariel coming out to combat a horde of Calibans.

12

FROM THE CAPTAIN'S REPORT

. . . fire was opened . . .

The Gunnery Lieutenant wore the ribbon of the D.S.C. on the breast of his coat. *Artemis* had won victories before, and, under the Captain, it was to the Gunnery Lieutenant's credit that those victories had been so overwhelming. There was the daylight action against the Italian convoy, when the first broadside which he had fired had struck home upon the wretched Italian destroyer which was trying to lay a smoke screen, had blown the destroyer into a wreck, and had enormously simplified the problem of the destruction of the convoy. The night action against another convoy had in certain respects been simpler, thanks to the Italians. They had not been so well trained, and because of their long confinement in harbour they had not had nearly as much experience at sea as the British. They had failed to spot *Artemis* in the darkness, and the Captain had been able to circle, to silhouette the Italians against the declining moon, and to creep up to them with guns trained and ready until they were within point-blank range at which no one could have missed. Two broadsides for one destroyer–the sheets of flame which engulfed her must have killed the men running to their guns, for she never fired a shot in return–and then a quick training-round and another broadside into the other destroyer. The latter actually fired in return, but the shells went into the sky; apparently her guns were trained ready for anti-aircraft action and some startled person just fired them off. Then nothing more from that destroyer after the second broadside crashed into her; only the roaring orange flames and the explosion of shells and torpedoes as the fire reached them and her crew roasted.

But at least *Artemis* had hit, with every broadside she had fired, and the loftiest gunnery officer in the British Navy could not have done better than that. It was proof at least that her gunnery was efficient, her gun crews fully trained, her infinite instruments properly adjusted, her gunnery officer steady of nerve and hand. In itself that was in no way enough to merit a decoration–it was no more than was expected of him–but the Admiralty must have decided that there was something more of credit to be given him, so that now he wore that blue-and-white ribbon.

Today the Gunnery Lieutenant's heart was singing. He was big and burly and fair. Perhaps in his veins there coursed some of the blood of a berserker ancestor; always at the prospect of action he felt this elation, this anticipation of pleasure. He felt it, but he was not conscious of it, for he was not given at all to self-analysis and introspection. Perhaps if someone whom he respected called his attention to it he would recognize it, this rapture of the strife, although years of schooling in the concealment of emotion would make the discovery a source of irritation. He was clear-headed and fierce, a dangerous kind of animal, employing his brain only along certain lines of thought. The men who swung the double axes beside Harold at Hastings and the reckless buccaneers who plundered the Spanish Main in defiance of odds must have been of the same type. With a Morgan or a Nelson or a Wellington or a Marlborough to direct their tireless energy and their frantic bravery, there was nothing that could stand against them.

It was tireless energy which had brought the Gunnery Lieutenant his present appointment. Not for him was the profound study of ballistics, or patient research into the nature of the stresses inside a gun; more clerkly brains than his could correlate experimental results and theoretical data; more cunning minds than his could devise fantastically complicated pieces of apparatus to facilitate the employment of the latent energy of high explosive. For the Gunnery Lieutenant it was sufficient that the results and the data had been correlated, that guns had been built to resist the stresses, that the apparatus for directing them had been invented. Dogged hard work–like that of an explorer unrelentingly making his way across a desert–had carried him through the mathematics of his gunnery courses and had given him a thorough grounding in the weapons he was to use. He knew how they worked–let others bother their heads about why they did. He had personality and patience enough to train his men in their use; the fiddling tiny details of maintenance and repair could be entrusted to highly skilled ratings who knew that their work was to stand the supreme test of action and that in the event of any failure they would have to face the Gunnery Lieutenant's wrath. Endless drills and battle practice had trained both the Gunnery Lieutenant and his men until he and they and the guns worked as a single whole, the berserker now instead of with the double axe was armed with weapons which could strike at twelve miles, could pull down an aeroplane six miles up.

He sat in the Gunnery Control Tower which he had not left since dawn, one knee crossed over the other and his foot swinging impatiently. His big white teeth champed upon the chocolate with which he stuffed his mouth; he was still hungry despite the vast sandwich which the Paymaster Commander had sent up to him, and the soup, and the cocoa. Indeed, it was fortunate that the Canteen Manager had made his way up to him and had sold him that chocolate, for the exertions of the morning had given the Gunnery Lieutenant a keen appetite, partly on account of the irritation he experienced at being on the defensive. Beating off aeroplane attacks, controlling the four-inch A.A. fire, was strictly defensive work and left him irritable–and hungry.

The opening moves of the battle on the surface mollified him to some extent. He admired the neat way in which the Admiral had parried the first feeble thrust of the Italians, and reluctantly he agreed that it was all to the good when the Italian cruiser screen withdrew after having done nothing more than pitch a few salvoes into the sea alongside the British ships. His ancestors had been lured out from the palisade wall at Hastings in a mad charge which had left them exposed to William the Conqueror's mailed horsemen; but the Gunnery Lieutenant, as one of the Captain's heads of department, had been for some time under a sobering influence and had been kept informed as to the possibility of Italian battleships being out. And he was aware of the importance of the convoy; and he was a veteran of nearly three years of life and death warfare. He had learned to wait cheerfully now, and not to allow inaction or defensive war to chafe him too much. But all the same the laying of the smoke screen, which (after all those careful conferences) he knew to be the first move in a greater game brought him a great upsurge of spirits. He listened carefully to what the Captain told him on the telephone.

'Aye aye, sir.'

Then *Artemis* leaned over outwards as she turned abruptly and plunged into the smoke screen.

In the Director Control Tower it remained bright; the smoke found it difficult to penetrate into the steel box, and the electric bulbs were continuously alight. The Gunnery Lieutenant's steel and leather chair was in the centre of the upper tier; on his right sat the spotting officer, young Sub-Lieutenant Raikes, binoculars poised before him, and on his left Petty Officer Saddler to observe the rate of change of range. In front of him sat Chief Petty Officer O'Flaherty, the Irishman from Connaught, at the director, and below him and before him sat a whole group of trained men, the pick of the gunnery ratings–picked by the Gunnery Lieutenant and tried and tested in battle and in practice. One of them was Alfred Lightfoot, his brows against the rubber eyepiece of his rangefinder; in the other corner was John Oldroyd, who had spent his boyhood in a Yorkshire mine and was now a rangetaker as good as Lightfoot. Behind them were the inclinometer operator and the range-to-elevation-and-deflection operator; the latter was a pop-eyed little man with neither chin nor dignity, his appearance oddly at variance with his pompous title, but the Gunnery Lieutenant knew him to be a man who did not allow himself to be flurried by danger or excitement. He was of the prim old-maidish type who could be trusted to keep his complex instrument in operation whatever happened, just as the Gunnery Lieutenant's maiden aunts kept their skirts down come what might. Even the telephone rating, his instrument over his head, had been hand-picked; in the ship's records he was noted as having been a 'domestic servant', and he found his present task of keeping track of telephone calls a little like his pre-war job when as a bachelor's valet he had had to converse over the telephone with creditors and relations and women friends and be polite to all of them. He had acquired then a rather pompous manner which stood him in good stead now in action–he had learned to recall it and employ it at times of greatest stress.

'We shall be opening fire on the enemy,' said the Gunnery Lieutenant into the telephone which connected him with the turrets, 'on a bearing about green eight-five.'

Long ago the Transmitting Station had passed the order 'all guns load', and before that the guns' crew had been in the 'first degree of readiness'. The team in the Director Control Tower, the marines stationed in the Transmitting Station, the men at the guns, were like men down on their marks waiting for the pistol before a sprint race. They would have to be off to a quick start–it would be on the start that everything would depend, because they must hit the enemy and get away again before the enemy could hit them back. Everybody in the ship knew that. Everybody in the ship had contributed something to the effort of making the thing possible, and now it was up to the gunnery men to carry the plan to completion.

Sunshine flicked into the Director Control Tower, flicked off again, and then shone strongly.

'Green five,' said the Spotting Officer as he caught sight of the Italian fleet, but the bearing changed instantly as *Artemis* swung round on a course parallel to the Italians.

'Fire at the leading ship,' said the Gunnery Officer, coldly brave. That was a battleship, least vulnerable of all to *Artemis*'s fire, but she flew the flag of the Italian Admiral. The three rangefinders in the ship were at work on the instant: Lightfoot and Oldroyd and their colleague Maxwell at the after-rangefinder spinning the screws and, as the double image that each saw resolved itself into one, thrusting with their feet at the pedals before them. Down in the Transmitting Station a machine of more than human speed and reliability read off all three recordings and averaged them. Each of the other observers in the Director Control Tower was making his particular estimate and passing it down to the Transmitting Station, and down there, by the aid of these new readings, the calculation having been made of how distant the Italian flagship was at that moment, other machines proceeded to calculate where the Italian flagship would be in fifteen seconds' time. Still other machines had already made other calculations; one of them had been informed of the force and direction of the wind, and would go on making allowance for that, automatically varying itself according to the twists and turns of the ship. Because every gun in the ship had its own little peculiarities, each gun had been given its individual setting to adjust it to its fellows. Variations in temperature would minutely affect the behaviour of the propellant in the guns, which would in turn affect the muzzle velocities of the shells, so that one machine stood by to make the corresponding corrections; and barometric pressure would affect both the propellant and the subsequent flight of the shells–barometric pressure, like temperature, varied from hour to hour and the Transmitting Station had to allow for it. And the ship was rolling in a beam sea–the Transmitting Station dealt with that problem as well.

'Table tuned for deflection, sir,' said the telephone to the Gunnery Lieutenant.

'Broadsides,' said the Gunnery Lieutenant coldly again. That was the way fighting madness affected him, so that he would take the wildest risks with the calmest manner.

All the repeaters before him had stopped moving now, and at this moment the last 'gun ready' lamp came on. There was no need to report to the Captain and ask permission to open fire; that had already been given. In those infinitesimal seconds the observations and calculations had been completed which were necessary to the solution of the problem of how, from a ship moving at thirty-one knots, to throw a quarter of a ton of steel and high explosive at another ship moving at twenty knots nine miles away.

'Shoot!' said the Gunnery Lieutenant loudly and still calmly, and then, as O'Flaherty pressed the trigger, he gave his next order, 'Up ladder, shoot!'

13

FROM THE CAPTAIN'S REPORT

. . . and hits were observed . . .

Chief Petty Officer Patrick O'Flaherty had been born a subject of the United Kingdom of Great Britain and Ireland, and for a short time he had been a subject of the Irish Free State before he enlisted in the British Navy and took the oath of allegiance to His Majesty the King of Great Britain and Northern Ireland. In the early days a few ill-mannered and stupid individuals among his shipmates had questioned him teasingly or casually as to the reason for his enlistment, but not one of them had asked him twice; even the stupidest could learn the lesson which O'Flaherty dealt out to them.

There had been wild times and black doings in Ireland in those days, and O'Flaherty as a child in his early teens had been through scenes of horror and blood; he may possibly have made enemies at that early age, although it is hard to imagine O'Flaherty even at fifteen being frightened of human enemies. One turn or another of Irish politics and of Irish guerrilla warfare may have resulted in O'Flaherty being deemed a traitor by his friends. In that fashion the boy may have found himself alone; or it may have been mere chance, some coincidence of raid and counter-raid that threw suspicion on him. There may have been no suspicion at all; the blood on O'Flaherty's hands may have called for the vengeance of someone too powerful or too cunning for the boy to oppose.

Perhaps, on the other hand, when peace descended upon Ireland, O'Flaherty may have joined the Navy out of mere desire for adventure, out of mere yearning for the sea that he knew in Clew Bay and Blacksod, possibly with the thought at the back of his mind that if he were ready to desert he would find in the British Navy endless opportunities of making a start in a fresh country without having to pay his fare thither.

But whatever was his motive, the British Navy had absorbed him. Its placid routine and its paternal discipline had been able to take a hold even on the wild Irish boy with the nerves of an unbroken colt. The kindly tolerance of the lower deck, where tolerance is the breath of life because there men have to live elbow to elbow for months together, won him over in the end–it cloyed him at first, sickened him at first, before he grew to understand it, and then to rely upon it. He came to love the breath of the sea, under equatorial stars in the Indian Ocean or freezing spray in the North Atlantic, as he had loved the soft air of Joyce's country. There had been black periods when the exile went through the uncontrollable misery of homesickness, but they had grown rarer with the years, as the boy of fifteen grew into the man of thirty-five, and providence, or good luck–or conceivably good management–had saved him during those times from breaches of discipline serious enough to ruin him.

Twenty years of service is a long time. Once he had been a pink-cheeked boy, in the days when, ragged and hungry, he had been a thirteen-year-old soldier of Ireland, sleeping in the hills, hiding in the bogs, crouching behind a bank with half a dozen of his fellows waiting to pitch a bomb into a lorryload of Black-and-Tans at the point where a bend in the road hid the felled tree. Now his cheeks were blue-black, and he was lantern-jawed; there were a few grey hairs among his wavy black ones, although the blue eyes under the black brows were as bright as ever, and the smile of the soft lips was as winning as ever. All the contradictions of Ireland were embodied in his person as in his career, just as obviously as they had been in the old days when the 'fighting blackguards' of Wellington's Connaught Rangers had stormed the castle of Badajoz in the teeth of the flailing musketry of Napoleon's garrison.

Today Chief Petty Officer O'Flaherty faced odds equally dreadful with his fighting blood as much aflame. His Irish sensitiveness and quickness of thought would not desert him, even when the Irish lust for battle consumed him–so that he reached by a different path the same exalted mental condition as the Gunnery Lieutenant who had entrusted him with his present duty. He kept the director sight upon the Italian flagship, holding it steady while the ship rolled, deeply to starboard, deeply to port, sighting for the base of the foremast and easing the director round millimetre by millimetre as *Artemis* head-reached upon the target ship. And with every microscopic variation of the director sight the six guns moved, too, along with their three turrets, five hundred tons of steel and machinery swaying to each featherweight touch upon the director, as miraculous as any wonder an Irish bard had ever sung about over his harp.

'Shoot!' said the Gunnery Lieutenant, loudly, and O'Flaherty pressed the trigger, completing the circuits in the six guns.

They bellowed aloud with their hideous voices, their deafening outcry tapering abruptly into the harsh murmur of the shells tearing through the air. And the shells were still on their way across the grey sea when the 'gun ready' lamps lit before the Gunnery Lieutenant's eyes.

'Shoot!' said the Gunnery Lieutenant.

O'Flaherty pressed the trigger again; the sights were still aligned upon the base of the Italian flagship's foremast.

'Shoot!' said the Gunnery Lieutenant, and again, 'Shoot!'

Twelve shells were in the air at once while the fountains raised by the six preceding ones still hung poised above the surface. This was the moment when heads must be utterly clear and hands utterly steady. Gunnery Lieutenant and Spotting Officer and Sub-Lieutenant Home forward in 'B' turret were watching those fountains, and pressing on the buttons before them to signal 'short' or 'straddle' or 'over'. Down in the Transmitting Station the signals from the three officers arrived together; if they were in agreement, or, if not, in accordance with the majority, the elevation of the guns was adjusted up or down the scale–the 'ladder' which the Gunnery Lieutenant had ordered–and to every round fired there were also added the innumerable other corrections: with an additional one now, because the guns were heating up. Yet every ten seconds the guns were ready and loaded, and every ten seconds the shells were hurled out of them, and the point where they fell, every ten seconds, had to be carefully noted–any confusion between one broadside and its predecessor or successor would ruin the subsequent shooting. The Gunnery Lieutenant could, when he wanted to, cut out completely the signals of the Spotting Officer and of 'B' turret officer, and rely entirely upon his own observations. But Raikes and Home were old and tried companions in arms. He could trust them–he stole a glance at Raikes' profile, composed and steady, and was confirmed in his decision. The Gunnery Lieutenant looked back quickly at the target. The next broadside raised a single splash this side of the target, and along the grey profile of the battleship a sparkling yellow flash, minute in the sunshine–another hit. Four hits with six broadsides was good shooting. That yellow flash was the consummation of a gunnery officer's career. It was for the sake of that that he endured the toil and drudgery of Whale Island, the endless drills, the constant inspection of apparatus; years of unremitting labour in order at the end of them to glimpse that yellow flash which told that the shells were hitting. The Gunnery Lieutenant stirred uneasily in his seat as within him surged the fighting spirit clamouring to hit and hit and go on hitting.

Now those bright flashes from the Italian flagship's sides were not hits. It was three seconds before the fall of another broadside was due. The Gunnery Lieutenant knew what they were. He spotted the fall of the next broadside and signalled it as 'short', and the fall of the next as 'straddle'. His finger was still on the button as the surface of the sea between him and the target rose in mountains, the incredible masses of water flung up by fifteen-inch shells.

'Shoot!' said the Gunnery Lieutenant.

With the bellow of the broadside sounded another tremendous noise, like that of a tube train hurtling through a tunnel–the sound of big shells passing close overhead. The Italian navy was firing back now. There were bright flashes all down the line; sea and air were flung into convulsions.

'Shoot!' said the Gunnery Lieutenant, and he marked up the next fall of shot.

And O'Flaherty at the director still kept the sights steady on the base of the Italian flagship's foremast, pressing the trigger as he was ordered, while the shells roared over him or burst in front of him and the guns thundered below him. That sensitive mouth of his–there was a girl in Southsea who still dreamed about that mouth occasionally–was smiling.

14

FROM THE CAPTAIN'S REPORT

. . . until I turned back again into the smoke screen . . .

On the bridge the sudden crash of the guns made Jerningham jump, the way it always did. He told himself that if he had any means of knowing just when that crash was coming he would not jump, but up here on the bridge there was no warning. He felt the hot blast of the explosion, and looked towards the enemy to see if he could spot the fall of the shot; so the crash of the next broadside caught him off his guard again and made him jump and miss it. He hoped none of the ratings on duty up here had seen him jump–that second time he was sure his feet had left the deck. The third crash came at that moment and he jumped again. The din was appalling, and with every broadside he was shaken by the blast of the guns.

He straightened his cap, which had fallen perilously lopsided: and tried to stiffen himself against the next broadside. It was hard to think in these conditions; those explosions jumbled a man's thoughts like shaking up a jigsaw puzzle. He felt envy, almost hatred, for the Officer of the Watch and the Torpedo Lieutenant and the Navigating Lieutenant standing together like a group of statuary. By the time he pulled himself together half a dozen broadsides had been fired; *Artemis* had been out of the smoke bank a full minute, Jerningham looked again to starboard in time to see the first Italian salvo fling up the sea before his eyes; then he heard another rumble terrifyingly close over his head. He saw the whole Italian line a-sparkle with gunfire. Every one of those ships was firing at him.

He gulped, and then with one last effort regained his self-control, panic fading out miraculously the way neuralgia sometimes did, and he was left savouring, almost doubtingly, his new-won calm, as, when the neuralgia had gone, he savoured doubtingly his freedom from pain. Remembering the notes he had to take regarding the course of the battle he took out pad and pencil again, referring to his wrist watch and making a hasty average of the time which had elapsed since his last entries and now. When he looked up again he saw the sea boiling with shell-splashes. It seemed incredible that *Artemis* could go through such a fire without being hit.

But the Captain was turning and giving an order to the Navigating Lieutenant, and then speaking into the voice pipe; the din was so terrific that Jerningham at his distance could hear nothing that he said. *Artemis* heeled and turned abruptly away from the enemy, and the gunfire ended with equal abruptness. Only a second or two elapsed before they were back again in the comforting smoke and darkness and silence; the smoke bank took the ship into its protection like a mother enfolding her child.

'God!' said Jerningham aloud, 'we're well out of that.'

He heard, but could not see, another salvo strike the water close alongside; some of the spray which it threw up spattered on to the bridge. He wondered if the Italians were purposefully firing, blind, into the smoke, or if this was a salvo fired off by a shaken and untrained ship unable to check its guns' crews; as it became apparent that this was the only salvo fired it seemed that the second theory was the correct one.

The smoke was beginning to thin.

'Hard-a-starboard!' said the Captain, suddenly and a trifle more loudly than was his wont.

Artemis leaned steeply over, so steeply that the empty ammunition cases went cascading over the decks with a clatter that rang through the ship. The Navigating Lieutenant was saying the name of God as loudly as Jerningham had done, and was grabbing nervously at the compass before him. Jerningham looked forward. Dimly visible on the port bow were the upperworks of a light cruiser, and right ahead was another, old *Hera*, the companion of *Artemis* in so many Mediterranean sallies. The ships were approaching each other at seventy miles an hour.

'Je-sus!' said the Navigating Lieutenant, his face contorted with strain.

Jerningham saw *Hera* swing, felt *Artemis* swing. The two ships flashed past each other on opposite courses not twenty yards apart; Jerningham could see the officers on *Hera*'s bridge staring across at them, and the set faces of the ratings posted at *Hera*'s portside Oerlikon gun.

'Midships,' said the Captain. 'Steady!'

Artemis went back to a level keel, dashing along the windward edge of the smoke bank away from the rest of the squadron. The Navigating Lieutenant put two fingers into his collar and pulled against its constriction.

'That was a near thing, sir,' he said to the Captain; the calmness in his voice was artificial.

'Yes, pretty close,' replied the Captain simply.

It must have been very shortly after *Artemis* had turned into the smoke to attack the enemy that the Admiral had led the rest of the squadron back again on an opposite course, so that *Artemis* turning back through the smoke had only just missed collision with the last two ships in the line. But because of good seamanship and quick thinking no collision had taken place; that was the justification of the risk taken.

The Captain smiled, grimly and secretly, as he reconstructed the encounter in his mind. When ships dash about at thirty knots in a fogbank surprising things are likely to happen. A twenty-yard margin and a combined speed of sixty-two knots meant that he had given the order to starboard the helm with just half a second to spare. As a boy he had been trained, and as a man he had been training himself for twenty years, to make quick decisions in anticipation of moments just like that.

Back in 1918 the Captain had been a midshipman in the Grand Fleet, and he had been sent in his picket-boat with a message to the Fleet Flagship one day when they were lying at Rosyth. He had swung his boat neatly under *Queen Elizabeth*'s stern, turning at full speed, then, going astern with his engines, had come to a perfect stop at the foot of *Queen Elizabeth*'s gangway. He had delivered his message and was about to leave again when a messenger stopped him.

'The Admiral would like to see you on the quarter-deck, sir.'

He went aft to where Acting-Admiral Sir David Beatty, G.C.B., commanding the Grand Fleet, was pacing the deck.

'Are you the wart who brought that picket-boat alongside?'

'Yes, sir.'

'Did you see my notice?'

'No, sir.'

'You've flooded my damned cabin with your damned wash. The first time the scuttles have been open for weeks. I go to the trouble of putting out a notice to say "slow" and the first damned little wart in his damned little picket-boat that comes alongside sends half the damned Firth of Forth over my damned furniture. My compliments to your Lieutenant, and you're to have six of the best. Of the *best*, remember.'

The midshipman displayed quickness of thought and firmness of decision to save himself from the pain and indignity of a beating. He stood his ground stubbornly.

'Well?' snapped the Admiral.

'That notice isn't hung so that anyone can see it coming under the ship's stern, sir. It's quite invisible from there.'

'Are you arguing with *me*?'

'Yes, sir. If the notice had been visible I should have seen it.'

That was a downright statement of fact, addressed boldly by a sixteen-year-old midshipman to the Commander-in-Chief. Beatty looked the boy up and down keenly, realizing that in this particular case a midshipman was sure of what he was saying. If his statement were to be put to the test it would probably prove to be correct; and to make the test would be a most undignified proceeding for an Admiral.

'Very good, then. I'll cancel my order. Instead you will report to your Lieutenant that you have been arguing with the Commander-in-Chief. I'll leave the verdict to him. Carry on.'

That was Beatty's quickness of decision. He could not be guilty of an act of injustice, but discipline might suffer if some unfledged midshipman would be able to boast of having bested him in an argument. He could rely on the Lieutenant to see to it that discipline did not suffer, to administer a beating for the purpose of making sure that the midshipman did not get too big for his boots. And in the end, the midshipman had escaped the beating by simply disobeying the Admiral's order. He had made no report to the Lieutenant, thereby imperilling his whole professional career and running the risk of dire punishment in addition; a big stake. But the odds were so heavy against the Commander-in-Chief inquiring as to whether a midshipman had made an obviously trivial report to his Lieutenant that it was a safe gamble which had succeeded.

In the mind of a boy of sixteen to argue with an Admiral and to disobey an order was as great a risk as it was for a captain to face the fire of the Italian navy and to charge through a smoke screen at thirty knots. There was risk in exposing a light cruiser to the fire of battleships. But, carefully calculated, the odds were not so great. *Artemis* emerged from the smoke screen ready to open fire. The Italians had to see her first, and then train their guns around, ascertain the range, open fire. Their instruments would not be as carefully looked after, nor as skilfully handled. It would take them much longer to get on to the target. And the more ships which fired upon *Artemis* the better; the numerous splashes would only serve to confuse the spotters and gunnery officers–a ship that tried to correct its guns' elevations by observing the fall of another ship's shells was lost indeed. The greatest risk to be run was that of pure chance, of a fluke salvo hitting the target, and against that risk must be balanced the utter necessity of hitting the Italians. The Captain had calculated the odds to a close approximation.

15

FROM THE CAPTAIN'S REPORT

. . . I then returned to continue the action . . .

'That was a near one,' said Leading Seaman Harris. He sat in the gunner's seat at the portside pompom and swung his legs as *Hera* tore past them. He grinned hugely, for Harris was of the graceless type that refuses to be impressed.

'Wonder 'ow old Corky's feeling,' said Able Seaman Ryder. 'D'you remember old Corky, Nibs? You know, the crusher. I 'eard 'e was in '*Era* now.'

A crusher is a member of the ship's police, and Ryder was a seaman familiar with those officials, like the majority of the pompom's crew. The ship's bad characters seemed to have gravitated naturally to the pompom. Leading Seaman Harris had been disrated more than once, and only held his responsible position because of a special endowment by nature, for Harris was a natural marksman with a pompom. To handle the gun accurately called for peculiar abilities–one hand controlling elevation and the other hand traversing the gun round, like playing the treble and the bass on a piano. And it had to be done instinctively, for there was no time to think when firing at an aeroplane moving at three hundred miles an hour. The complex four-barrelled gun, a couple of tons of elaborate machinery, had to be swung forward and back, up and down, not to keep on the target but to lead it by fifty yards or more so as to send its two-pound shells to rendezvous with the flying enemy. Even with a gun that fired four shells in a second, each with a muzzle velocity of unimaginable magnitude, and even with the help of tracer shells, it was a difficult task–the gunner had to be a natural shot and at the same time flexible enough of mind to submit to the necessary artificial restrictions of the training gear, lightning quick of hand and eye and mind–with the more vulgar attribute of plain courage so as to face unflurried the appalling attack of the dive bombers.

In *Artemis*, as in every ship, there was courage in plenty, but the ship had been combed unavailingly to find another pompom gunner as good as Leading Seaman Harris. He handled that gun of his as though it were a part of himself, looking along the sights with both eyes open, his unique mind leaping to conclusions where another would calculate. And experience had improved even Harris, because now he could out-think the bomber pilots and anticipate with equal intuition just what manoeuvres they would employ to throw off his aim. He was a virtuoso of the two-pounder pompom; this very morning he had increased his score by five–five shattered aeroplanes lay a hundred miles back at the bottom of the Mediterranean torn open by the shells Harris had fired into them.

So his crew were in higher spirits even than usual, like a successful football team after a match–it was a matter of teamwork, for the crew had to work in close co-ordination, supplying ammunition and clearing jams, like the half-backs making the openings for Harris the gifted centre-forward who shot the goals. Exultation rose high in their breasts, especially as the starboard side pompom could only claim one victim, and that doubtful. If the opportunity were to present itself before the exultation had a chance to die down the success would be celebrated in the way the gang celebrated every success, in indiscipline and lack of respect for superior officers–along with drunkenness and leave-breaking, these offences kept the port-side pompom crew under punishment with monotonous consistency.

'Convoy's copping it,' remarked Able Seaman Nye; a sudden burst of gunfire indicated that the convoy and its depleted escort were firing at the aeroplanes which had renewed the attack now that the cruisers' and destroyers' screen was out of the way.

'They won't come to no 'arm,' said Ryder. 'We got the cream of the Eyeties 'smorning.'

'Remember that one wiv the red stripes on 'is wings?' said Nibs. 'You got 'im properly, Leader.'

Harris nodded in happy reminiscence.

'How're you getting on, Curly?' he asked, suddenly.

Able Seaman Presteign smiled.

'All right,' he said.

Presteign was the right-handed loader of the pompom, his duty being to replace regularly the short heavy belts of shells on that side, a job he carried out accurately and unfailingly; that goes without saying, for if he had not he would never have remained entrusted with it, Harris's friendship notwithstanding. It was odd that he and Harris were such devoted friends. It was odd that Presteign was so quick and efficient at his work. For Presteign was a poet.

Not many people knew that. Jerningham did–one evening in the wardroom the Gunnery Lieutenant had tossed over to him one of the letters he was censoring, with a brief introduction.

'Here, Jerningham, you're a literary man. This ought to be in your line.'

Jerningham glanced over the sheet. It was a piece of verse, written in the typical uneducated scrawl of the lower deck, and Jerningham smiled pityingly as he first observed the shortness of the lines which revealed it to be lower-deck poetry. He nearly tossed it back again unread, for it went against the grain a little to laugh at someone's ineffective soul-stirrings. It was a little like laughing at a cripple; there are strange things to be read occasionally in the correspondence of six hundred men. But to oblige the Gunnery Lieutenant, Jerningham looked through the thing, reluctantly–he did not want to have to smile at crude rhymes and weak scansion. The rhymes were correct, he noted with surprise, and something in the sequence of them caught his notice so that he looked again. The verse was a sonnet in the Shakespearian form, perfectly correct, and for the first time he read it through with attention. It was a thing of beauty, of loveliness, exquisitely sweet, with a honeyed rhythm; as he read it the rhymes rang in his mental ear like the chiming of a distant church bell across a beautiful landscape. He looked up at the Gunnery Lieutenant.

'This is all right,' he said, with the misleading understatement of all the wardrooms of the British Navy. 'It's the real thing.'

The Gunnery Lieutenant smiled sceptically.

'Yes it is,' persisted Jerningham. He looked at the signature. 'Who's this A.B. Presteign?'

'Nobody special. Nice-looking kid. Curly, they call him. Came to us from *Excellent*.'

'Hostilities only?'

'No. Joined the Navy as a boy in 1938. Orphanage boy.'

'So that he's twenty now?'

'About that.'

Jerningham looked through the poem again, with the same intense pleasure. There was genius, not talent, here–genius at twenty. Unless–Jerningham went back through his mind in search of any earlier recollection of that sonnet. The man might easily have borrowed another man's work for his own. But Jerningham could not place it; he was sure that if ever it had been published it would be known to him.

'Who's it addressed to?'

'Oh, some girl or other.' The Gunnery Lieutenant picked out the envelope from the letters before him. 'Barmaid, I fancy.'

The envelope was addressed to Miss Jean Wardell, The Somerset Arms, Page Street, Gravesend; most likely a barmaid, as the Gunnery Lieutenant said.

'Well, let's have it back,' said the Gunnery Lieutenant. 'I can't spend all night over these dam' letters.'

There had been three other sonnets after that, each as lovely as the first, and each addressed to the same public house. Jerningham had wondered often about the unknown Keats on board *Artemis* and made a point of identifying him, but it was some time before he encountered him in person; it was not until much later that this happened, when they found themselves together on the pier waiting for the ship's boat with no one else present. Jerningham was a little drunk.

'I've seen some of your poetry, Presteign,' he said, 'it's pretty good.'

Presteign flushed slightly.

'Thank you, sir,' he said.

'What started you writing sonnets?' asked Jerningham.

'Well, sir—'

Presteign talked with a restrained fluency, handicapped by the fact that he was addressing an officer; also it was a subject he had never discussed before with anyone, never with anyone. He had read Shakespeare, borrowing the copy of the complete works from the ship's library; he gave Jerningham the impression of having revelled in Shakespeare during some weeks of debauch, like some other sailor on a drinking bout.

'And at the end of the book, sir—'

'There were the sonnets, of course.'

'Yes, sir. I never read anything like them before. They showed me something new.'

'"Then felt I like some watcher of the skies,"' quoted Jerningham, '"When a new planet swims into his ken."'

'Yes, sir,' said Presteign respectfully, but with no other reaction that Jerningham's sharp glance could observe.

'That's Keats. Do you know Keats?'

'No, sir.'

'Come to my cabin and I'll lend you a copy.'

There was something strangely dramatic about introducing Presteign to Keats. If ever there were two poets with everything in common, it was those two. In one way Jerningham regretted having made the introduction; he would have been interested to discover if Presteign would evolve for himself the classical sonnet form of octet and sextet. Presteign had undoubtedly been moving towards it already. But on the other hand there had been Presteign's enchanted enthusiasm over the 'Odes', his appreciation of the rich colour of 'The Eve of St Agnes'. There was something fantastically odd about the boy's beauty (there was no other word for it) in the strange setting of a sailor's uniform; his enthusiasm brought more colour to his cheeks and far more sparkle to his eyes. From the way his cropped fair hair curled over his head it was obvious how he came by his nickname.

And it was basically odd, too, to be talking about the 'Ode to a Nightingale' to a man whose duty it was to feed shells into a pompom, when England was fighting for her life and the world was in flames; and when Jerningham himself was in danger. Yet it was charming to listen to Presteign's intuitive yet subtle criticism of the Spenserian stanza as used by Keats in 'St Agnes'.

It was all intuitive, of course. The boy had never been educated; Jerningham ascertained the bald facts of his life partly from his own lips, partly from the ship's papers. He was a foundling (Jerningham guessed that his name of Presteign was given him after that of the Herefordshire village), a mere orphanage child. Institution life might have killed talent, but it could not kill genius; nothing could do that, not even the bleak routine, the ordered time-table, the wearisome drill, the uninspired food, the colourless life, the drab clothing, the poor teaching, the not-unkind guardianship. Sixteen years in an institution, and then the Navy, and then the war. The boy could not write an 'Ode to a Grecian Urn', he had never read an ode nor seen a Grecian urn. He had never heard a nightingale, and the stained glass in the institution chapel could never have suggested to him nor to Keats the rose-bloom falling on Madeline's hands.

He wrote about the beauties he knew of–the following gull; the blue and silver stern wave which curved so exquisitely above the stern of a fast-moving cruiser, as lovely as any Grecian urn; the ensign whipping stiffly from the staff; and he wrote about them in the vocabularies of the institution and the Navy, gaunt, exact words, transmuted by him into glowing jewels. Keats would have done the same, thought Jerningham, save that Milton and Byron had given him a freer choice.

And it is humanly possible that Navy discipline–Whale Island discipline–played its part in forming that disciplined poetic style. Jerningham formed the opinion that it had done so. That interested Jerningham enormously. Outwardly Presteign–save for his handsome face–was as typical a *matelot* as ever Jerningham had seen; if the institution had not taught him how to live in a crowded community the Navy certainly had done so. There was nothing of the rebel against society about Presteign; he had never come into conflict with rules and regulations–he wandered unharmed through them like a sleepwalker through bodily perils, carrying his supreme lyrical gift with him.

Yet in addition Jerningham came to realize that much of Presteign's immunity from trouble was due to his friendship with Harris–a strange friendship between the poet and the hard-headed sailor, but very real and intense for all that. Harris watched over and guarded Presteign like a big brother, and had done so ever since they first came into touch with each other at Whale Island–it was a fortunate chance that had transferred the pair of them simultaneously to *Artemis*. It was Harris who fought the battles for him that Presteign disdained to fight, and Harris who planned the breaches of the regulations that smoothed Presteign's path, and who did the necessary lying to save him from the consequences; Harris saw to it that Presteign's kit was complete and his hammock lashed up and stowed, reminded him of duties for which he had to report, and shielded him from the harsher contacts with his fellow men. Presteign's poetic gifts were something for Harris to wonder at, to admire without understanding; something which played no part in their friendship, something that Harris accepted unquestioning as part of his friend's make-up, on a par with the fact that his hair curled. And it may have been Presteign's exquisite sense of timing and rhythm which made him an efficient loader at the portside pompom, and that was the only return Harris wanted.

Up to the present moment Jerningham had only had three interviews with Presteign–not very long in which to gather all these facts about him, especially considering that he had spoilt the last interview rather badly.

'And who is Miss Jean Wardell?' asked Jerningham, as casually as he could–casually, but a sullen frown closed down over Presteign's sunny face when he heard the words.

'A girl I know,' he said, and then, as Jerningham looked further questions, 'a barmaid. In Gravesend.'

That sullenness told Jerningham much of what he wanted to know. He could picture the type, shopworn and a little overblown, uneducated and insensitive. Jerningham could picture the way a girl like that would receive Presteign's poems–the raised eyebrows, the puzzlement, the pretended interest for fear lest she should be suspected of a lack of culture. Now that they came by post they would be laid aside pettishly with no more than a glance–thrown away, probably. And Presteign knew all this about her, as that sullen glance of his disclosed; he was aware of her blowsiness and yet remained in thrall to her, the flesh warring with the spirit. The boy was probably doomed for the rest of his life to hopeless love for women older and more experienced than him–Jerningham saw that with crystal clearness at that very moment, at the same time as he realized that his rash question had, at least temporarily, upset the delicate relationship existing between officer and seaman, poet and patron. He had to postpone indefinitely the request he was going to put forward for a complete collection of Presteign's poetical works; and he had to terminate the interview as speedily as he decently could. After Presteign had left him he told himself again that poetry was something that did not matter, that a torpedo into a German submarine's side was worth more than all the sonnets in the world; and more bitterly he told himself that he would give all Presteign's poetry, written and to come, in exchange for a promise of personal immunity for himself during this war.

'How're you getting on, Curly?' asked Leading Seaman Harris, swinging his legs in the gunlayer's seat.

'All right,' said Presteign.

Something was forming in his mind; it was like the elaborate gold framework of a carefully designed and beautiful piece of jewellery, before the enamels and the gems are worked into it. It was the formula of a sonnet; the rhymes were grouping themselves together, with an overflow at the fifth line that would carry the sense on more vividly. That falling bomber, with the smoke pouring from it and the pilot dead at the controls, was the inspiration of that sonnet; Presteign could feel the poem forming itself, and knew it to be lovely. And farther back still in his mind there were other frameworks, other settings, constituting themselves, more shadowy as yet, and yet of a promise equally lovely. Presteign knew himself to be on the verge of a great outburst of poetry; a sequence of sonnets; the falling bomber, the Italian Navy ranged along the horizon, the Italian destroyer bursting into flames to split the night, the German submarine rising tortured to the surface; these were what he was going to write about. Presteign did not know whether ever before naval warfare had been made the subject of a sonnet-cycle, neither did he care. He was sure of himself with the perfect certainty of the artist as the words aligned themselves in his mind. The happiness of creation was upon him as he stood there beside the pompom with the wind flapping his clothes, and the stern wave curling gracefully behind the ship; grey water and white wake and blue sky; and the black smoke screen behind him. The chatter of his friends was faint in his ears as the first of the sonnet-cycle grew ever more and more definite in his mind.

''Ere we go again,' said Nibs.

Artemis was heeling over on the turn as she plunged back into the smoke screen to seek out her enemies once more.

16

FROM THE CAPTAIN'S REPORT

. . . further hits were observed until . . .

The smoke screen was only a little less dense this time; it was holding together marvellously well as that beautiful wind rolled it down upon the Italian line. The ventilating shafts took hold of the smoke and pumped it down into the interior of the ship, driving it along with the air into every compartment where men breathed. Acrid and oily at the same time, it dimmed the lights and it set men coughing and cursing. In 'B' turret, forward of the bridge and only just lower than it, the guns' crews stood by with the smoke eddying round them;

their situation was better than that of most, because the ventilation here was speedier and more effective than in any other enclosed part of the ship. The guns were already loaded and they could feel the turret training round. Every man of the guns' crews had a skilled job to do, at some precise moment of the operation of loading and firing, and to keep a six-inch gun firing every ten seconds meant that each man must so concentrate on doing his work that he had no time to think of anything else; after a few minutes of action they would find it hard to say offhand on which side the turret was trained, and unless the loudspeaker or Sub-Lieutenant Home told them they would know nothing about the damage their shots were doing. Their business was to get the guns loaded every ten seconds; the transmitting station would do their calculation for them, the director would point the guns and fire them. But they knew what the return into the smoke screen implied. It was hardly necessary for Sub-Lieutenant Home to tell them quietly.

'We shall be opening fire again in two minutes' time.'

Most of the men in 'B' turret were at least five years older than Home, and most of them, too, were still devotees of the beard-growing fashion which had swept the Royal Navy during the opening months of the war. There were black beards and fair beards and red beards in 'B' turret; the men could well have passed for a pirate crew instead of seamen of the Royal Navy. Most of them were dressed in soiled and ragged clothes, for, very sensibly, none of them saw any purpose in exposing their smart uniforms to damage in battle, especially as the majority of them spent a proportion of their pay in making their clothes smarter and better fitting than when issued by the Government.

A devotee of discipline of the old school would have been just as shocked to see the easy way in which they attended to their duties; a man did not spring to stiff attention when he had completed the operation for which he was responsible. He took himself out of the way of the others and stood poised to spring forward again. There was no need for the outward show of discipline, of the Prussian Guard type, with these men. They understood their business; they had worked those guns in half a dozen victories; they knew what they were fighting for; they were men of independent habit of thought working together with a common aim. They did not have to be broken into unthinking obedience to ensure that they would do what they were told; thanks to their victories and to the age-long victorious tradition of their service they could be sure that their efforts would be directly aimed towards victory.

It was true as well that every man knew that the better he did his work the better would be his chance of life, that for every Italian he helped to kill in this battle there was one less Italian who might kill him, but that was only a minor, a very minor reason for his doing his best. Love of life did not have nearly as much strength as did the love for the service which actuated these men, the love for the ship, and especially the artistic desire to do perfectly the task before them. They were in that way like the instrumentalists in an orchestra, playing their best and obedient to the conductor not through fear of dismissal but solely to produce a good performance. This state of mind of the men–this discipline and *esprit de corps* in other words, which would excite the hopeless envy of admirals not fortunate enough to command such men–made anything possible in the ship save cowardice and wilful inefficiency. The martyr at the stake refusing to recant to save his life, the artist unthinkingly putting his whole best into his work, were actuated by motives similar to those actuating these gunners–although anyone who rashly told those gunners that they were martyrs or artists would at best be answered only with the tolerance extended by the Navy towards an eccentric. They were masters of their craft, balancing easily on the heaving deck, ready for instant action although relaxed, the jokes which were passing among them having nothing to do with the situation in which they found themselves.

The ship passed out of the smoke screen; sunlight came in through the slits, and the smoke within began to dissipate under the forced ventilation. The deck under their feet took up a steep slant as *Artemis* turned; the pointer moved on the dial, and the turret rotated its heavy weight smoothly as Gunlayer Wayne kept his pointer following it. As the pointers coincided, with the guns loaded, the circuit was closed which illuminated the 'gun ready' lamp before the eyes of the Gunnery Lieutenant in the Gunnery Control Tower. And when Chief Petty Officer O'Flaherty pressed the trigger of the director, the little 'bridges' in the ignition tubes heated up, the tubes took fire, the detonators at their ends exploded into the cordite charges, the cordite exploded, and the guns went off in a smashing madness of sound, like a clap of thunder confined in a small room. The solid charges of cordite changed themselves into vast masses of heated gas, so much gas that if expanded at that temperature it would form a volume more than equal to that of the five-thousand-ton ship itself, but confined at the moment of firing into a bulk no bigger than a large loaf of bread under a pressure a hundred times as great as the heaviest pressure in any ship's boiler. The pressure thrust itself against the bases of the shells, forcing them up the twenty-five-feet guns, faster and faster and faster. The lands of the rifling took hold of the driving bands of the shells–that rifling was of the finest steel, for the pressure against the sides of the lands, as the shells inertly resisted rotation, was as powerful as that of a hydraulic press. Up the guns went the shells, faster and faster forward, and spinning faster and faster on their axes, until when they reached the muzzles twenty-five feet from the breech, they were rushing through the air at four times the speed of sound, having each acquired during that brief twenty-five feet an energy equal to that of a locomotive engine travelling at thirty miles an hour. And the recoil was exactly of the same amount of energy, as if each turret had been struck simultaneously by two locomotives moving at thirty miles an hour; but these two enormous blows fell merely on the recoiling systems of the guns–those recoiling systems over which so many ingenious brains had laboured, which represented the labour of so many skilled workmen, and which 'B' turret crew had kept in high condition through years of warfare. Unseen and unfelt, the hydraulic tubes of the recoil systems absorbed those two tremendous shocks; all that could be seen of their activity was the guns sliding slowly back and forward again. The two locomotives had been stopped in two seconds, as quietly as a woman might lean back against a cushion.

Number two at the right-hand gun was Leading Seaman Harley–the bearded seaman with the appearance of a benevolent Old Testament prophet; as the recoil ceased he opened the breech, and by that action sent a huge gust of compressed air tearing up the bore of the gun to sweep away the hot gases and any possible smouldering residue. He flicked out the old firing tube and pushed in a new one, closing the venthole. Numbers four and five were Seamen Cunliffe and Holt; they already had hold of the new shell, taken from the hoist, and they thrust it into the hot chamber of the gun. Cunliffe pushed with the rammer until the shell rested solidly against the rifling.

'Home!' shouted Cunliffe.

Able Seaman James was ready with the charge, and as Cunliffe withdrew the rammer James slid the charge into the breech and sprang back. Harley swung the breech shut, and the forward swing of the screw plug converted itself into a rotatory motion which interlocked the screw threads on breech and plug. As its motion stopped, Harley flicked over the interceptor which had up to that moment been guarding against accidents.

'Ready!' shouted Harley.

Wayne's pointer was exactly above the director pointer, and Harley had scarcely spoken when the guns crashed out anew, and the shells left the muzzles of the guns exactly ten seconds after their predecessors. Sub-Lieutenant Home looked through the glasses that were trained through the narrow slit under the roof of the turret. His gaze was fixed on the Italian flagship, but he was conscious, in the vague outer field of his vision, in the blue sky above the battleship, of a mysterious black line that rose and fell there, erasing itself at one end at the same time as it prolonged itself at the other. What he could see was the actual track of the shells winging their way through the air at two thousand feet a second; his position directly behind the guns gave him the advantage of following them with his glance as they rose three miles high and then descended again. The guns crashed out again below him, but he did not allow that to distract him, for he was looking for splashes. Just after this new explosion of the guns he saw the tiniest white chalk marks against the blue sky, appearing here and there behind the upperworks of the battleship–hard to tell whether before or behind, but these had no visible roots, he was certain. Home snicked the 'over' button decisively, but this was no time to relax, for the next broadside was already on its way, writing its black line against the sky.

A single splash whose root he could see, white against the dark grey of the battleship; two more tiny white tips beyond, and a reddish-yellow gleam, at the base of the foremost funnel.

'Straddle,' muttered Home, marking it up.

He had to keep his head clear despite the din and the excitement. *Artemis* might have the most perfect instruments, the finest guns, the best ammunition ever made, but they were useless without clear heads and steady hands and keen eyes. It took a keen eye to see an 'over', so that it usually called for a bold decision to mark it up, and the three buttons were temptingly close to each other; a nervous man or a clumsy man or a shaken man could easily signal 'over' when he meant to signal 'short'. Home was only twenty years old; a mature man would smile at the idea of buying a house on Home's recommendation, or investing his money on Home's advice, or even backing a horse that Home might fancy. The women who might meet him in drawing-rooms or at cocktail parties would think of him–if they thought of him at all–as a 'nice boy'; even the girls younger than him would hardly bother their heads about a penniless sub-lieutenant–someone they could dance with, a convenient escort on an otherwise empty evening, perhaps, but not someone to be taken seriously. Moreover, Sub-Lieutenant Home was not a young man with social graces, and he had an inborn tendency to mild stupidity; hostesses found him heavy in the hand.

He was not a man of active and ingenious mind, and people who knew him well would predict for him only the most undistinguished future–retirement from the Navy in twenty years or so with the rank of Lieutenant-Commander, presumably. It might in consequence be considered strange to find him in such a responsible position as captain of 'B' turret, but there was really nothing strange about it. Home was a man with all the dogged courage of the society whence he came. He could be relied upon to die where he stood–where he sat, rather–sooner than desert his post. His quiet unimaginative mind was unmoved by fear or by fear of responsibility; as he pressed those buttons he did not dwell mentally on the consequences of pressing the wrong one–the broadside that might miss, the defeat that might ensue from that, the fall of Malta as a consequence of the defeat, the loss of Egypt as a result of the fall of Malta, the victory of Germany, the enslavement of the world. Home may have been worried a little at the thought of a 'ticking-off' from the Gunnery Lieutenant, but beyond that his imagination did not stray. He merely made sure that he pressed the right button and observed the fall of the successive broadsides in their proper sequence. He would go on doing that until the end of time; and if evil fortune should wipe out the Gunnery Control Tower and the Gunnery Lieutenant he was perfectly prepared to take over the direction of the three turrets from where he sat and carry the responsibility of the whole ship's armament.

The bearded ruffians who manned 'B' turret accorded him the respect due to his rank and the devotion they were ready to give anyone who could be relied upon come what might to direct their endeavours to destroy the Eyeties. They knew him well after all these months of service, could predict with complete certainty what would be his attitude towards any of the usual crimes or requests. Even though he still only had to shave alternate days while their beards had grey hairs in them, he wore a gold stripe on his sleeve and he could (with discreet aid from tables) work out problems in ballistics or navigation which they never had any hope of solving–the two attributes were very much on a par with each other in their estimation; in other words they knew him to be a major cog in the complex machine in which they were minor cogs, but they also knew that the major cog would never break under the strain or jam through some unpredictable flaw.

17

FROM THE CAPTAIN'S REPORT

. . . a hit started a small fire . . .

Artemis was shooting superbly. The Captain could see that, with his own eyes, as he turned his binoculars upon the Italian flagship. With the shortened range it was possible to see not merely whether the splashes fell this side or the other of the target, but how close they fell, and they were raining so densely round the battleship that there must be many more hits being scored than were revealed by the fleeting gleams of the bursting shells which he could see; others were being obscured by the splashes or were bursting inside plating. It was impossible that they could do any serious damage to the big battleship with her vitals encased in twelve-inch steel, but they must be discommoding, all the same. The Captain experienced a feeling of elation which was extraordinarily pleasant. He was a man who was profoundly interested in the art of living. Rembrandt gave him pleasure, and so did the Fifth Symphony; so did bouillabaisse at Marseilles or southern cooking at New Orleans or a properly served Yorkshire pudding in the north of England; so did a pretty girl or an elegant woman; so did a successful winning hazard from a difficult position at billiards, or a Vienna coup at bridge; and so did success in battle. These were the things that gilded the bitter pill of life which everyone had to swallow. They were as important as life and death; not because they were very important, but because life and death were not very important. So the Captain allowed himself to enjoy both the spectacle of shells raining down upon the Italian flagship, and the knowledge that it was his own achievement that they should rain down like that.

The enemy's salvoes were creeping closer; it was nearly time to retire again. A mile away *Hera* had emerged from the smoke screen, spitting fire from all her turrets. It seemed for a moment as if she were on fire herself, for during her passage through the smoke screen she had breathed the smoke in through her ventilators, and now her forced ventilation system was blowing it out again in wreathes that curled round her superstructure so that she looked like a ghost ship. *Artemis* must have presented the same appearance when she came through the screen; the Captain was a little annoyed with himself for not having thought of it and borne it in mind–it would be of some importance in hampering the Italian rangefinders and gunlayers.

But with *Hera* out of the screen, and the other cruisers beginning to show beyond her, it was for *Artemis* to withdraw and leave the Italians to their weary task of getting the range of these new elusive targets. It would be ideal if the English ships were only to show themselves for so long that the Italians had no chance of firing on them at all, but that was a council of perfection, and impractical; what was to be aimed at was to strike an exact balance between rashness and timidity, to stay out as long as possible so as to do the most damage and yet not to run undue risks from the enemy's fire.

'Port ten,' said the Captain, waiting until a broadside did not drown his voice, and *Artemis* plunged back into the protecting smoke.

'Gawd!' said Leading Seaman Harris down at the portside pompom, 'back in the smoke again! Slow, I call it.'

Not many of the ship's company of *Artemis* would have called her proceedings slow, but Harris had something of the spoilt prima-donna about him. He wanted to be in action with his gun against dive bombers, and he faintly resented the main battery of the ship having a turn at all.

'It's this blasted smoke I can't stand,' grumbled Nibs. 'It makes me feel filthy under my clothes.'

An Italian salvo rumbled overhead and plunged unseen into the sea beyond.

'Wouldn't call it slow meself,' said Ryder.

'Where's Curly?' asked Harris. 'You all right, Curly?'

'Yes,' said Presteign. He was all right. The sonnet on the falling bomber, plummetting in flames into the sea, was nearly fully shaped in his mind, and he knew it to be good. 'I'm all right, Leader.'

Then it happened. No one can explain it. Fifty salvoes had been fired at *Artemis* without scoring a hit, and now, when she was invisible in the fog, a chance shell hit her. It struck full on the portside pompom, smashing it into jagged splinters of steel as swift as rifle bullets, plunged on and down, through the deck, and there it burst. On the edge of the huge crater it opened in the deck lay what was left of Presteign and Harris, and their blood mingled in the scuppers, so that in their deaths they were joined together.

Artemis staggered under the blow. In the engine-room, in the turrets, on the bridge, men grabbed for handhold to preserve their footing. That shell had struck *Artemis* with the force of an express train travelling at sixty miles an hour, with nothing to cushion the shock, nothing to resist it save the frail plating. But a trifle had saved her from utter destruction; the fact that in its plunging course the shell had struck the heavy pompom, five feet above the deck. The gun had been smashed into unrecognizable fragments by the blow, all its tons of steel torn into splinters, but on the other hand the fuse of the shell had been started into action. The ingenuity of man has progressed so far that as well as being able to throw a shell weighing a ton at a speed of two thousand feet a second, he can divide that second into thousandths, and arrange for the shell to explode either on impact or one two-hundredth of a second later, when it might be expected to be inside any armour plate it might strike. Having struck the pompom, the shell burst only just beneath the upper deck; had it not done so, it would have burst below the main deck, and it would have torn *Artemis* in two.

What it did was bad enough. It tore open a huge crater in the deck–a vast hole ringed round with a rough edge–long jagged blades of steel, blown vertical by the explosion. It tore huge holes in the ship's side, and drove red-hot fragments here, there and everywhere, forward through the frail bulkheads, down through the main deck, aft through the plating into the handling-room of 'X' turret. The mere force of its impact, the conversion of its energy of motion into heat, was sufficient to make steel white hot, and within the shell were hundreds of pounds of high explosive which turned the middle of the ship into a raging furnace. Below the upper deck, at the point where the shell burst, was the wardroom, where were the Surgeon Lieutenant-Commander and his men, and two casualties hit by bomb splinters earlier in the morning. One moment they were alive, and the next they were dead, one moment they were men, and then the shell burst right in their midst, and they were nothing–nothing.

The heat of the explosion was like the heat of an oxy-acetylene flame, like the heat of an electric furnace. The paint on the bulkheads of the wardroom was only the thinnest possible layer–kept thin with this particular emergency in view–but it burst into raging flames, as if the very plating had caught fire. The scant covering of linoleum on the deck burst into flames. The padding of the chairs caught fire. The bulkhead forward, dividing the wardroom from its stores, had been torn open, and the stores caught fire, all the sparse pitiful little things which brought some amenity into the lives of the officers: tablecloths and table-napkins, newspapers and spirits, the very bread and sugar, all blazed together. On the starboard side of the ship beside the wardroom were the senior officers' cabins. They blazed as well–bedding and desks and clothing, paint and woodwork, and photographs of their wives and children, hockey sticks and tennis rackets. From side to side of the ship, from 'X' turret aft beyond the warrant officers' mess forward, the ship was a raging furnace, with flames and smoke pouring out of her riddled hull. Cascading into the flames fell the ammunition of the shattered pompom–deadly little shells, bursting in a devil's tattoo of explosions and feeding the flames which blazed luridly in the gloom of the smoke screen.

The Commander–Commander James Hipkin Rhodes, D.S.O., D.S.C.–had been squatting on the boat deck aft, complaining bitterly to himself. When he had been a young lieutenant it had appeared such an unattainable apotheosis to become a Commander even when he attained the unattainable and won the vital promotion–the most difficult and most significant in a naval officer's career–from lieutenant-commander to commander it had been delightful and gratifying. But to be Commander in a light cruiser in action was to be a fifth wheel to a coach: it meant squatting here on the boat deck doing nothing at all, waiting merely for unpleasantness–waiting in case the Captain should be killed (and the Commander would rather be killed himself, with no sort of pose about that option) and waiting for the ship to be hit (and the Commander loved *Artemis* more dearly than most men love their wives).

On active service it was hard enough to keep the ship at all clean and presentable, the way any self-respecting commander would have his ship appear. He groaned each time *Artemis* dashed into the smoke screen–he knew too well the effect that oily vapour would have on paint and bedding and clothing. A commander's duty in a big ship is largely one of routine, and after two years of that duty it can be understood that Rhodes had become too deeply involved in it, was liable to think too much about details and not about the broad outline of the fact that England was fighting for her life. As *Artemis* went into action he had been wondering what damage would be done to his precious paint, just as a woman's first reaction when she and her husband receive an invitation to some important function might be to wonder what she should wear. Rhodes, in fact, was in grave danger of becoming an old woman.

The shell burst, and the blast of the explosion flung him from his seat sprawling on the deck. His chin was lacerated, and when he got to his feet blood poured down his chest, but he paid no attention to it. He staggered to the rail, sick and shaken, and gazed down at the ruin six feet below him. The heat of the flames scorched his face. Then he rallied.

'Hoses, there!' he bellowed; the crew of the starboard side pompom–those who had not been mown down by the splinters–were picking themselves up out of the fantastic attitudes into which they had been flung, and the light of the flames lit them vaguely in the artificial darkness of the smoke. The voice of an officer pulled them together. Without knowing what they did they got out the hoses, going like automatons through the drill that had been grained into them. *Artemis* came out of the smoke screen, and the flames paled almost into invisibility against the sunshine, masked by the thick grey smoke pouring up through the deck–foul, stinking smoke, for many things were burning there.

Rhodes half fell, half ran down the ladder to the upper deck, calling together the fire-fighting parties in the waist. The pumps began to sing; the prescience of the Commander (E) had provided ample steam for them. Rhodes plunged down to the mess flat below; it was full of smoke both from the screen and from the fire, and pitchy-black with the failure of the electric circuits–so dark that he could see, as he looked aft, the afterbulkhead glowing lurid red with the heat beyond it.

Rhodes was an old woman no longer. The explosion of a fifteen-inch shell had been sufficient to shake him at least temporarily out of his old-womanishness. He organized the fire-fighting arrangements here, and then dashed up again to the boat deck where he could have the clearest view of the damage. There was no way of getting aft from here direct–the ship was ablaze from side to side–and the only way left would be to go down into the boiler-room and aft from there, under the fire. That would take a long time. He caught sight of Richards on the quarterdeck; he was in charge of damage control in the after part of the ship, and as Richards was alive and had a working party with him there was no urgent need for Rhodes' presence. He turned to the telephone.

'Forebridge,' he said, and then when Jerningham answered, 'Commander to Captain.'

The two brief waits, of a second or two each time, gave him time to get his breath and steady himself. For Rhodes there was some advantage about being old-maidish and fussy about detail. Being deeply immersed in his job shut out other considerations from his mind. He had to make a formal report, and it had to be done exactly right.

'Yes, Commander?' said the Captain's voice.

Rhodes reported what he had seen and done.

'Is it a bad fire?' asked the Captain.

The Commander let his eyes roam back aft, to the smoke and flame. From a commander's point of view it was a very bad fire indeed, but Rhodes still had some common sense left to save him from exaggeration. He made himself look at the flames with a dispassionate eye, the eye of a fighting man and not that of the ship's head housemaid.

'No, sir,' he said. 'Not a bad fire. It'll be under control directly.'

He put back the receiver and the instrument squealed at once so that he took it up again. The damage reports were coming in from the different compartments–a small leak here, a shattered bulkhead there. Nothing to call for a serious transference of his damage-control strength. Jerningham showed up beside him, a little white about the gills, but his manner was quite composed. Jerningham and the Commander disliked each other for a variety of reasons, and there was no pretence of cordiality as they spoke to each other. The Commander hastily recapitulated the reports which had come in to him, and Jerningham made notes on his pad, before they turned back to look at the fire.

A score of hoses were pouring water into the flaming crater; one or two pompom shells were still exploding down below, each explosion sending up a torrent of sparks like some vast firework. Another hose party came running down the waist on the portside; the man who held the nozzle dragged Presteign's dead body viciously out of the way. The jets would have mastered the fire soon enough, but a more powerful agency came into play. *Artemis* put her helm over, and as she heeled the hole torn in her side was brought below the surface, and the sea rushed in. Even on the upper deck they could hear the crackling as the water quenched the red-hot surfaces, and steam poured in a huge cloud up through the crater, enwreathing the whole stern of the ship. Then she righted herself as she took up her new course, then leaned a little the other way as the rudder steadied her, sending fifty tons of water washing through the compartment into every corner and cranny before it poured down in sooty warm shower-baths through the few holes torn in the main deck by the shell fragments. Only a little steam and smoke came up through the deck now; Richards stood on the jagged edge of the crater and looked down, while a petty officer beside him jumped down into the wrecked wardroom amid the unspeakable mess inside. Richards with his hands to his mouth bellowed the result of his inspection to the Commander–the holes in both sides of the ship above the water line, the minor holes in the deck.

'I'll get those holes patched in a jiffy,' said the Commander to Jerningham. 'Report that to the Captain.'

'Aye aye, sir,' said Jerningham, remembering the need to salute only in the nick of time as he turned away.

The Commander promptly forgot Jerningham in the happier business of organizing. He was calling up in his mind where he had stored the rubber slabs, the battens and timbers that he would need for patching the holes, the ratings whom he would detail for the work. He had in his mind a clear picture of the things he had to do and the order in which he would do them as he ran down to the upper deck and set about the work, while Jerningham made his way back from the boat deck to the bridge and delivered his message to the Captain.

It had been rank bad luck that *Artemis* had been hit at all, but on the other hand the bad luck was balanced by the good luck that dictated how little damage had been done. A shell in the wardroom, with only the most minor damage below the main deck, would do the ship less harm practically than if it had burst in any other spot. No damage had been done to the ship's main armament, and the casualty list was small. The wardroom flat would flood and flood again as *Artemis* manoeuvred, before the Commander could get his patches into place, but (the Captain worked out the problem roughly in his head) her stability would not be greatly endangered by the weight of that mass of water above the water-line. She had plenty of reserve to deal with that, despite the shifting of weights as a result of firing off thirty tons of shells. A pity about the Surgeon Lieutenant-Commander and his men.

'The port-side pompom's crew's wiped out, you say?' said the Captain.

'Yes, sir.'

'Then Harris has gone.'

'Yes, sir.'

So *Artemis* had lost her phenomenal pompom gunner. Probably he was irreplaceable–the ship would never see his like again.

Jerningham thought of Presteign. He knew–he felt in his bones–that the Gravesend barmaid had crumpled up and thrown away each of those sonnets as they had reached her. And he had never got from Presteign that complete copy of his work. Something had been lost to civilization. Jerningham had been shaken by the explosion into a numbed state of mind; that part of him which had been trained into a naval officer was functioning only dully and semi-automatically, and it was strange that the other part of him should have this piercing insight and feel this bitter sense of loss. He would tell the Captain about Presteign some day if they ever came out of this battle alive.

Four destroyers were racing alongside of *Artemis*, overhauling her as they dashed to head off the Italian line. Signal flags went fluttering to the masthead of the leader, and the Chief Yeoman of Signals began to bellow his interpretation of them.

18

FROM THE CAPTAIN'S REPORT

. . . without serious damage . . .

The ship's company of *Artemis* knew the Torpedo Gunner's Mate to be a misanthrope–they had suffered for long under his misanthropy–and it may have been that which led the lower deck to believe him to be a bigamist. Certainly the most circumstantial stories were told about the Torpedo Gunner's Mate's matrimonial affairs, of the grim wife he had in Pompey, a wife apparently as repellent as himself, and of the charming young girl he was reputed to be bigamously married to in Winchester. Some went as far as to say that this new wife was his first wife's niece, or some blood relation at least, and there was always much speculation about the occult power by which he had contrived to win her affection and induce her to be an accessory in that particular crime of all crimes. He was an old man, too, as sailors count age, called back into service after retiring on pension, and the wags would raise a laugh sometimes by wondering what Nelson had said to the Torpedo Gunner's Mate when they last met.

Whatever might be the Torpedo Gunner's Mate's matrimonial vagaries on shore, at sea he was a single-minded man, a man with only one interest, which probably accounted for the ship's company's jests–a single-minded man is a natural butt. He was engrossed, to the exclusion of all other interests, in the ship's electricity supply and distribution. All his waking thoughts and most of his dreams dealt with electricity, as a miser can only think of his hoard. According to the Torpedo Gunner's Mate, no one else in the ship knew anything worth knowing about electricity; the Torpedo Lieutenant might be able to work out the text-book problems about inductance and hysteresis, but that sort of theoretical nonsense was of no use to a man confronted with the necessity of supplying electricity to every nook and cranny of a ship in every condition. The Torpedo Lieutenant certainly could not shut his eyes and count slowly along the main port-side distributing main, ticking off one by one every branch, every fuse-box, and every switch, but the Torpedo Gunner's Mate could do that, and he could do the same for the accessory port-side distributing main, and then pass over to the starboard side and do it all over again.

The Torpedo Gunner's Mate had the loftiest contempt for anyone who could not do that, which meant that he had the loftiest contempt for everyone in the ship. And because nothing in the ship could operate properly without electricity everybody on board, the Captain, the Commander, whose word was law, the Commander (E), the Torpedo Lieutenant, the Gunnery Lieutenant whose guns' crews considered themselves the most important people in the ship, every man Jack of them, in the Torpedo Gunner's Mate's mind, was a mere puppet dependent upon him for everything beyond the mere breath of life–and, considering the number of electrically-operated fans, they were dependent on him for that as well. He knew, even although no one else knew it, that he was lord and master of H.M.S. *Artemis*; that by opening or closing a few switches he could cut the thread of her life just as the Greek Fates cut the thread of the lives of mankind. He hugged that knowledge to himself secretly, as passionately as he hugged to his bosom the fair-haired charmer of Winchester. It was a constant source of secret gratification to him, not realizing in his blindness that at the same time the power was quite useless to him in consequence of his fixed determination to keep the electricity supply of *Artemis* functioning perfectly–he could no more have flouted that determination than he could have cut off his own nose.

The Torpedo Gunner's Mate's action station was beside the great switchboard, deep down in the bowels of the ship, and that was the place where he would rather be than anywhere else in the world–with the occasional exception of Winchester. He could feast his eyes on the dials and the indicator lights, run them once more over the huge wiring diagram, enjoying every moment of it–like a miser with his hoard again, fingering the coins and adding up the totals for the thousandth time with as much pleasure as the first. He took a glance at the specific gravity of the acid in the storage batteries; there was enough electricity there to fill the demands of the whole ship for three hours if necessary should the generators be damaged, and in three hours either the poor fools could get the generators working again or the damage must be such that the ship was lost. He was checking over the switchboard again when the shell struck and burst, and the deck beneath his feet heaved and flung him crashing down. He was on his feet again directly, disentangling himself from the rating who was stationed there with him to take his place if he became a casualty–as if the miserable ignoramus could possibly take his place!–and turned his eyes at once to the switchboard, to the dials and the indicator lamps. His assistant got to his feet beside him, but the Torpedo Gunner's Mate jealously elbowed him back; no man while he was on duty would touch that switchboard except himself.

Some of the lamps were out; some of the needles on the dials were back to zero. The Torpedo Gunner's Mate ran his hands over the switches like a pianist trying out a piano. He played a scale on them, switched over to the alternative main, and played the scale again, never having to take his eyes from the indicators as he did so–he could lay his hands blindfolded on any switch he chose. The lighting circuit to the after-mess flat was broken, and the Torpedo Gunner's Mate restored it; he did the same for other parts of the ship, for all except the wardroom flat. The indicator here remained obstinate. Nothing he could do could restore the flow of electricity in the wardroom flat. As far as the Torpedo Gunner's Mate was concerned, the wardroom flat had ceased to exist. He grunted as he reached this conclusion; not even his assistant, who was looking now at him instead of at the board, and who had borne with his moods for two and a half years, could tell what that grunt meant, or could interpret the stony expression in his face.

The Torpedo Gunner's Mate grunted again, and let his hand fall from the switchboard. He walked forward, rolling a trifle stiffly with the motion of the ship–he was a little troubled with rheumatism in the knees–and passed through the door into the telephone exchange. Here he surveyed the scene with a jealous eye, for only very partially was the telephone exchange under his charge. He supplied it with electricity, but Seamen Howlett and Grant who manned the telephone switchboard were not under the orders of his department, and the Torpedo Gunner's Mate strongly believed that they would be more efficient if they were. He did not like the fact that men who dispensed electricity–even in the minute quantities necessary to actuate a telephone receiver–should not be under his supervision, and the work they were doing now, of testing the circuits and ascertaining which ones were still functioning, was so like the duty he had just completed as to rouse his jealousy still further.

He watched their deft motions for a brief space–he knew as much about their duty as they did themselves–and ran his eye over the telephone switchboard to check what they were doing. Here and there the board was spanned criss-cross by wires plugged in for the duration of the action, completing circuits which enabled the Gunnery Lieutenant to speak at will with his turrets and magazines, the boiler-room with the engine-room, and so on. The Torpedo Gunner's Mate was a little disappointed to see that the permanent circuits were correct; he could tell by the set of their shoulders that Howlett and Grant, despite the earphones on their ears and their preoccupation with their duty, were aware of his entrance and of the fact that he was brooding over them.

A light glowed on the switchboard and Howlett plugged in.

'Exchange,' he said.

The Torpedo Gunner's Mate could not hear the murmur in Howlett's earphone, but he saw where he plugged in the connexion. Forebridge wanted to speak with sick bay–nothing very remarkable about that.

'One of you lads get me the Damage Control Officer,' said the Torpedo Gunner's Mate, picking up the telephone receiver beside him. 'This is a priority call.'

That was a gratifying thing to be able to say; during his brief watch over the switchboard he had been able to see how much in demand was the Damage Control Officer's telephone, and the fact that he could claim priority and insist on his own call being put through next, was a most satisfactory tribute to the importance of electricity. He heard the Commander's voice, and proceeded to report the result of his tests at the main switchboard.

'Very good,' said the Commander. 'Yes. Yes, the wardroom flat's been burnt out.'

The Torpedo Gunner's Mate put back the receiver and eyed again for a moment the unresponsive backs of Howlett and Grant. He was jealous of these two. They could listen to the telephone conversations, and even if they were too busy to do that they could still guess, from the origins and destinations of the calls coming through, what was going on in the ship. They shared his knowledge about the wardroom flat, and it was not fair–it was actually indecent–that it should be so. What he knew and ought to know by virtue of his position as dispenser of electricity they knew because they could take advantage of the duty to which they happened to be assigned. It was not consistent with the dignity of the Torpedo Gunner's Mate, in charge of the main switchboard–no, much more than that, it was not consistent with the dignity of electricity itself–that he should not be solitary on a pinnacle of exclusive knowledge. He saw Howlett dart a glance at Grant, and he read amusement in it, something almost approaching insolence; what mollified the Torpedo Gunner's Mate and distracted him from taking instant action in defence of his dignity was the sight of the left side of Grant's face–so far he had seen only the back of Grant's head. Grant's left eye was blackened and puffy, the lid swollen and gorged. There was a contusion on his cheekbone which would probably turn black as well, and the cheek itself showed a faint bruise which reappeared lower down over the jawbone in more marked fashion.

'That's a rare shiner you've got there, Grant,' said the Torpedo Gunner's Mate.

'It is an' all,' said Grant, who despite his name, was born and bred in Manchester. Another light glowed on the switchboard, and Grant plugged in. 'Exchange.'

The explosion of the shell must have lifted Grant up from his chair and dashed him, face foremost, against the switchboard.

'Exchange,' said Grant and Howlett simultaneously, plugging in.

It was a trifle of a pill for the Torpedo Gunner's Mate to swallow for him to acknowledge to himself that the telephone switchboard was being properly looked after without his supervision, that these children of twenty or so would do their duty whether he kept his eye on them or not. The Torpedo Gunner's Mate had little faith in the young. He sighed and turned away, walking out of the telephone room back to his own treasured switchboard; his rheumatism gave him an old man's gait. He ran his eye over the dials and indicator lights; all was still well here; even his fool of an assistant rating had not managed to do anything wrong. The Torpedo Gunner's Mate continued to walk aft, through another door and into the most secret part of the ship.

He closed the door behind him and looked round. This was the Transmitting Station; the Torpedo Gunner's Mate knew that any foreign power, even in time of peace, would pay a King's ransom for the chance of having one of their experts stand for half an hour where he stood now. All about him were the superhuman machines upon which the best brains of the Navy had laboured for years in search of perfection, the machines which solved instantaneously the differential equations which would occupy a skilled mathematician for a couple of days or more, the machines which correlated half a dozen different sets of data at once, the machines which allowed for barometric pressure and for gun temperatures, machines that looked into the future and yet never forgot the past.

It was comforting to the Torpedo Gunner's Mate to know that these superhuman things were dependent on him for the supply of electricity which alone allowed them to function; the only crony he had in the ship, Chief

Electrical Artificer Sands (another man with proper ideas regarding the importance of electricity), spent most of his waking hours adjusting them and tuning them, pandering to their weaknesses and being patient with them when they turned obstinate.

In the centre of the room, ranged round a table large enough for a Lord Mayor's banquet to be served on it, sat the Marine band. In the old days travelling theatrical companies expected their players to do a double job, and take their places nightly in the orchestra preliminary to appearing on the stage; there would be advertisements in the theatrical papers for a 'heavy' who could 'double in brass'. Similarly, in *Artemis*, the musicians had a double duty, and the provision of music was the less important. The time they spent rehearsing 'Colonel Bogey' and 'A Life on the Ocean Wave' was only the time that could be spared from rehearsals of a more exacting piece of teamwork. The machines all round them, the superhuman machines, even when the Torpedo Gunner's Mate had supplied them with electricity and Chief Electrical Artificer Sands had tuned them to perfection, were still dependent upon human agency to interpret and implement their findings. Under the glass top of the table there were needles which moved steadily and needles which moved erratically, needles which crept and needles which jumped, and each needle was watched by a bandsman who had his own individual pointer under his control which had to keep pace with it, creep when it crept, jump when it jumped, utterly unpredictably. At the Transmitting Station table every item the Marine band played was unrehearsed and without score; the instrumentalists could never look ahead and find that some individuals among them had been allotted twenty bars' rest by the composer. There was no looking ahead, and each bandsman was obeying a different baton which might at any moment leap into activity and summon him to action.

At the head of the table, sitting on a higher chair which gave him a view over the whole expanse, sat the Commissioned Gunner, Mr Kaile, his telephone instrument clasped over his head, the other telephones within reach. In one sense, Mr Kaile was conductor of this mad hatter's orchestra. He had no control over what air should be played, nor when it should begin or end. He was rather in the position of a band leader who may find his instrumentalists suddenly striking up together at any moment without agreeing on the tune. He had to see that at least every instrument was in the same key and kept the same time, and, in accordance with the orders that came down from the bridge and from the Gunnery Lieutenant, and guided by the triple reports of the spotting officers, he was also expected–to continue the analogy–to swell or diminish the volume of sound as might be considered necessary; in other words, to send the range up or down the ladder, deflect to right or to left, as the direct observation of the fall of the shells might dictate.

However perfect the machines, war in the last analysis is fought by men whose nerves must remain steady to direct the machines, whose courage must remain high when they, as well as their machines, are in danger; whose discipline and training must be such that they work together. Every improvement in the machines does not dispose of this problem, but only pushes it one remove farther along. The Palaeolithic man who first thought of setting his flint axe in a haft instead of holding it clumsily in his hand still had to face and fight his enemy. Nelson's gunners had their ammunition brought to them by powder monkeys instead of by an automatic hydraulic hoist like the gunners in *Artemis*, but in either case the gunners had to stand by their guns to achieve anything.

So similarly round the table of the Transmitting Station it was necessary that there should be discipline and courage. Trembling hands could not keep those pointers steady, nor could minds distracted by fear be alert to follow the aimless wanderings of the guiding needles so that the guns above could continue to hurl forth their broadsides every ten seconds. Down here, far below the level of the sea, the men were comparatively protected from shell fire, but not far below their feet was the outer skin of the ship, and around them were the bunkers of oil fuel. Mine or torpedo might strike there, engulfing them in flame or water. Other compartments of the ship might be holed, and the sea pour in as the ship sank slowly; in that case it would be their duty to remain at their posts to keep the guns firing to the last, while above them there were only the difficult iron ladders up which they might eventually climb to precarious life.

The Marine bandsmen were perfectly aware of all this–they were far too intelligent not to be. It was discipline which kept them at the table; it was even discipline which kept their hands steady and their heads clear. Intangible and indefinable, discipline might perhaps be more clearly understood by consideration of one of its opposites. Panic can seize a crowd or an individual, making men run for no known reason in search of no known objective; in panic men shake with fear, act without aim or purpose, hear nothing, see nothing. Disciplined men stay calm and steady, do their duty purposefully, and are attentive to orders and instructions. The one is a state of mind just as is the other, and every state of mind grows out of the past. A myriad factors contribute to discipline–old habit, confidence in one's fellows, belief in the importance of one's duty. Roman discipline came to be based on fear of consequences; it was axiomatic in the Roman army that the soldier should fear his officers more than the enemy, and Frederick the Great used the same method with the Prussian Guard. An enthusiast will charge into danger, but, once stopped, he is likely to run away, and, running away, he is as hard to stop as when he is charging. Fear and enthusiasm are narrow and precarious bases for discipline. Perhaps the principal element in the Marines' discipline was pride–pride in themselves, pride in the duty entrusted them, pride in the cause in which they fought, and pride in the Navy in which they served.

The Torpedo Gunner's Mate indulged in none of these highly theoretical speculations. His glance round the Transmitting Station told him that the men were doing their duty, and gratified his curiosity; and a glance at Mr Kaile told him that all the apparatus was functioning correctly, thanks to the electricity which he was supplying to them. In reply to the Torpedo Gunner's Mate's lifted eyebrows, Mr Kaile gave a nod, and, having no more excuse to linger, the Torpedo Gunner's Mate withdrew to his action station.

'Nosey old bastard,' said Mr Kaile; he said it half to himself, but the other half into the telephone, and he had to add hastily to the Gunnery Lieutenant who heard it, 'Sorry, sir, I wasn't speaking to you.'

The telephone gurgled back at him with the information that *Artemis* was turning again to the attack.

'Yes, sir,' said Mr Kaile.

Mr Kaile's war experience went back twenty-eight years. At the Battle of the Falkland Islands as a very young Ordinary Seaman he had played an undistinguished part, being merely one of the hands in H.M.S. *Kent* who had been used as living ballast, sent aft with every man who could be spared from his station to stand on the quarter-deck so as to help lift the bows a trifle and add to the speed of the ship in her desperate pursuit of *Nürnberg*. Mr Kaile had stood there patiently while *Kent* plunged through the drizzling rain of that dramatic evening, and he had cheered with the others when *Nürnberg*, shot to pieces, had sunk into the freezing South Atlantic.

He had married a girl when at last *Kent* reached England again, Bessie–Bessie had been no oil-painting even then, as Mr Kaile politely described her looks to himself, but it was largely owing to Bessie that Mr Kaile now held his present exalted rank, with a 'Mr' before his name and a gold stripe on his sleeve. Oil-painting or not, Mr Kaile had loved Bessie from the first, and had never ceased to love her, with her gentleness and sympathy and her unbounded faith in her husband. Nothing was too good for Bessie. On Bessie's account Mr Kaile had become a man of towering ambition, with dreams that he hardly dared admit even to himself; even he had never ventured so far into the realms of the wildly improbable as to imagine his holding commissioned rank, but some of his dreams had been almost equally fantastic–he had dreamed of Bessie living in a house of their own, a house bought and paid for with the money he earned, and filled with furniture, *good* furniture, on which all the instalments were paid. It was too lofty a dream that Bessie should have a maid in the house, wearing cap and apron, but Mr Kaile certainly had aspired in those old days to Bessie's having a charwoman to do the rough work of the dream house–a respectable old body who would call Mrs Kaile 'Mum'. Mr Kaile as a young Leading Seaman had thrilled to the idea of someone doing that, but when he spoke of it to his wife she had only smiled tolerantly and stroked his hair as if he were a child telling about fairies.

And Leading Seaman Kaile had gone back to sea with the ambition rooted more deeply still, to earn his first medal by the way he handled a machine gun on the deck of the old *Vindictive* when she lay against Zeebrugge Mole with her upperworks being torn to splinters by the German artillery. The ambition had stayed with him when the war ended, and sustained him through the years of the peace, while he slaved to supplement an elementary education and master the complexities (complexities which grew ever more complex) of the technical side of gunnery. Mr Kaile was not a brilliant man, but he was a man willing to go to endless effort, and under the stimulus of his ambition his mind grew more and more retentive in its memory for elaborate detail, and more and more orderly in its processes. He fell naturally into the discipline of H.M.S. *Excellent*, and when the text-books that he read went beyond his comprehension he turned patiently back again to page one and started afresh analysing each sentence until he had cleared up the difficulty. He acquired the most complex assortment of rule of thumb knowledge, from the temperature at which cordite should be stored in a magazine to the breaking strain of chain cable. There was no gun in use in the British Navy which he could not repair or serve. He made orderly thinking an efficient substitute for the higher mathematics which he could never hope to learn, so that he could deal with muzzle velocities and trajectories in a workmanlike fashion. And he had risen from Leading Seaman to Petty Officer, and from Petty Officer to warrant rank, until at last he was what he had never hoped to be, a Commissioned Gunner, Mr Kaile; and Bessie lived in her own house–Mr Kaile deeded it over to her the day he paid the last instalment–full of her own furniture, and two days a week, before the war began in 1939, she had a charwoman in who called her 'Mum' to do the washing and the rough work. Mr Kaile did not know whether after the war there would be any servants again who would wear cap and apron, but so many unbelievable things had happened to him in his career that he had even thought this might be possible some day, and that he might have the last, ultimate pleasure of sitting in Bessie's own sitting-room hearing Bessie give instructions to her own servant.

Even without that prospect, merely to keep Bessie in her own house and surrounded by her own furniture, Mr Kaile would fight every Wop in the Eyety navy. He had realized so many of his ambitions, with Bessie undisputably leader of society in the circle in which she moved as wife of a Commissioned Gunner she could queen it, if she willed, over the wives of Chief Petty Officers and Sergeants of Marines. In point of fact, Bessie did not queen it very obviously, as Mr Kaile had noticed just as he noticed everything nice about Bessie. The pleasure for Mr Kaile lay in knowing that she could if she wanted to. Mr Kaile's present position, sitting at the head of the table in the Transmitting Station, was closely enough related in Mr Kaile's mind with the continuance of that pleasure.

Mr Kaile was fully aware that the Eyeties had good machinery of their own. He had read with the utmost care the confidential notes which had been circulated to gunnery officers in the Royal Navy regarding the discoveries made in captured Italian ships. Captured submarines had contributed a little–the submersible six-inch gun mounting was a most ingenious adaptation of an idea which the Navy had been (in Mr Kaile's mind) a little premature in discarding–and the destroyer captured in the Red Sea had told much more. Reconstructing in theory the Italian system of gunnery control in big ships from what could be seen in a destroyer was a sort of Sherlock Holmes job, like guessing a man's height from the length of his stride between footprints, and it was just the sort of thing Mr Kaile was good at. In his pocket at that moment there was a nice letter from the Lords Commissioners of the Admiralty thanking Mr Kaile for some suggestions he had made on the subject. One of these days the English would lay their hands on an intact Italian cruiser, or even a battleship–Mr Kaile hoped when that happened he would be there to see. It would be pretty good material, Mr Kaile was sure, but Mr Kaile was not so wrapped up in materials as to be unaware that the best of material is still dependent on men to be handled properly. He looked down the double row of serious faces along the Transmitting Station table and was satisfied. These kids were sometimes inclined to a frivolity which needed restraint. They were well enough behaved; when the big explosion had come, and the ship had jerked as if she had struck a rock, the lights had gone out instantly. But when they had come on again (Mr Kaile gave grudging credit to the Torpedo

Gunner's Mate for the promptitude with which the circuits had been restored) they were still all sitting in their places, and each had reported quietly that the pointer each was observing was still functioning. They were quite steady, and Mr Kaile was human enough to realize that they might not be so in that atmosphere, for some freak of the ship's ventilation was dragging into the Transmitting Station a horrible stench–of burning paint, perhaps, but with other elements added; possibly burning meat. Mr Kaile could be single-minded and ignore that stench, and he could control his thoughts so as not to speculate about what might be happening elsewhere in the ship to cause that stench, but he knew that might not be the case with these lads. He was glad to see that it was.

'Enemy in sight. Green four-o,' said the telephones to Mr Kaile.

'All guns load,' said Mr Kaile to the turrets. That was an automatic reaction. The Transmitting Station was as quiet as a church, save for the curt sentences passing back and forth. Band Corporal Jones at his telephone was receiving, and repeating aloud, the enemy's course and deflection, as the Rate Officer announced it. The marvellous machines were making their calculations. Mr Kaile swept his eye over the table.

'Table tuned for deflection, sir,' he reported.

'Broadsides,' said the telephone back to him.

'Broadsides,' repeated Mr Kaile to the turrets.

A gong pealed sharply, and then *Artemis* heaved beneath their feet to her own broadside, and the rigid steel of her structure transported the din and the shock of the explosion into the Transmitting Station, astoundingly. And the new data began to pour into the Transmitting Station, and the pointers moved, tracked steadily by the Marine band, while every ten seconds came the crash of the broadside, and the stench from the burning wardroom flat seeped down into the Transmitting Station, polluting their nostrils.

19

FROM THE CAPTAIN'S REPORT

. . . so that the ship was ready to attack again . . .

The battle was approaching a climax. The wind had steadily rolled the smoke screen down upon the Italian battle line, and the British ships had advanced with it, nearer and nearer to the Italian ships. The Captain on the bridge of *Artemis* was considering the possibilities and potentialities of an attack by the destroyers with torpedoes. A destroyer is even more fragile than a light cruiser, and her attack must be launched only after careful preparation of it to be successful. At more than five thousand yards her torpedoes are running too slowly to have much chance of hitting a well-handled target, and the longer the range the more difficult it is to send the torpedo near the target. Fired at a line of ships, a salvo of torpedoes nominally stands a chance of hitting with one torpedo in three, because between each pair of ships there is an empty space twice as long as any ship, but slow torpedoes and alert handling makes this chance far slighter.

A forty-knot torpedo fired at a range of three miles at a ship advancing at twenty knots reaches its target in three minutes having only travelled two miles; but if the ship is retreating instead of advancing the torpedo must run for nine minutes, travelling six miles, before it overtakes its target. So a torpedo attack must always be delivered from ahead of the enemy's line, and it must be pressed home to the farthest limit in the teeth of the enemy's fire. That Italian battle line mounted over a hundred guns, which each fired a shell big enough to cripple a destroyer, over ranges at least three times as long as the maximum efficient torpedo range; if the destroyers were to launch a simple attack they would have a long and perilous gauntlet to run before they could fire their torpedoes with any hope of success. In fact, if even one of the six available destroyers got within torpedo range it would be surprising. And if, more surprisingly, that one destroyer had the opportunity to send off six torpedoes the chances would be against scoring two hits, and even two hits would probably not sink one of those big fellows over there. So the net result would be the loss of six destroyers in exchange for a temporary crippling of one or two major Italian units–a very bad bargain in the beggar-your-neighbour game of war.

The Captain had no need to recapitulate all this in his mind; his reasoning processes started at this point, up to which the facts were as much part of his mental equipment as a musician's knowledge of the number of flats in a scale. For the destroyers to stand any chance of success in the attack which the leader's flag signals were proposing to him the Italians must be distracted, their attention diverted and their aim divided. That meant launching another attack with the cruisers through the smoke screen so that they could attract the Italian fire to themselves, and then the destroyers could slip round the end of the screen ahead of the Italians and charge in. The Italian reply to this would be to keep their big guns firing at the cruisers and turn their secondary armament against the destroyers; but the Captain doubted whether in the stress of action the Italian fire control would be effective enough to master this added complication. And when the Italians attempted it they would be under the rapid fire of the British cruisers, shaken by hits and blinded by splashes. Some of their secondary armament, behind thin armour, might be put out of action–by some good fortune perhaps even the secondary gunnery control in some of the ships might be knocked out by lucky shells. That would make all the difference in the world. Another attack of the cruisers would increase the stake thrown on the board–exposing them again to the Italian fire at ever-lessening range–but it increased the chances of success to a far greater proportion. It made a good gamble of it.

The Captain pulled himself up sharply; his thoughts were running away with themselves. He was allowing himself to be carried away by his emotions. The realization was thrust upon him by the discovery that he was pleased with the prospect of plunging once more through the smoke screen, of being deafened again by the guns of *Artemis*, of seeing the shells he fired striking the Italian line. There was pleasure in the thought, and that meant danger. The Captain was a man of violent passions, although no mere acquaintance would ever have guessed it. People said that 'Methy'–Captain the Hon. Miles Ernest

Troughton-Harrington-Yorke–had ice water in his veins instead of the blue blood one would expect of the son of the tenth Viscount Severne, but the people who said so did not know him, however close their acquaintance with him. The fact that he had a nickname should have warned them of the contrary, for even when their initials run together so conveniently, nicknames are not given to men who are as cold and hard and unemotional as they thought the Captain to be. As a boy and a youth Methy had indulged and indulged again in the rich dark pleasure of insane evil temper. He had revelled in the joy of having no bounds to his passion, of every restraint cast aside–the sort of joy whose intensity not even the drunkard or the drug-addict can know. One of Methy's brothers carried to his grave the scar across his scalp which resulted from a blow Methy dealt him–a blow not dealt to kill, for in his rage Methy never stopped to think of the possibility of killing, but a blow that might have killed. Methy's brother carried that scar to his grave, the unmarked grave amidst the shattered ruins of Boulogne where he fought to the last with the Guards.

Methy's wife knew about the frightful passions that could shake the man, for she had seen something of them. She could remember the young Lieutenant about to sail for the East Indian Station, frantic with jealousy that duty was taking him to the other side of the world while his rival stayed in England. He had been brutal, violent, demanding that she swear to be faithful to him, and she had been cold, aloof–concealing her fright–reminding him that they were not married or betrothed and that she had no intention of being either as long as he behaved like a madman.

That had been a very late manifestation of passion, called forth by his love for a woman; long before that he had come to realize the insidious danger of a lack of self-control, and the insidious habit that could be formed by self-indulgence, more binding even than a drunkard's. He had mastered his passions, slowly and determinedly. Luckily he had matured early; luckily the discipline of the life of a naval cadet had been reinforced by the discipline of the life of a poor man's son–the tenth Viscount Severne had no money to speak of, and his three elder sons were in the army. When Gieves' agent came on board at Gibraltar and displayed shocked disapproval of jacket or cap, Methy had to smile and refuse to take the easy step of ordering new ones; when his rivals thought nothing of dinner at the Savoy or the Berkeley he had to suggest Soho. And he had come through without becoming either embittered or inhuman. Only a very few people knew that the Captain, good humoured, easy going in everything unconnected with the Service, witty and reliable and even tempered, had been compelled to learn to be each of these things; and most people who were in that secret thought the change was absolutely permanent. They looked upon Methy as an extinct volcano; but he himself knew, only too well, that he was only a dormant volcano, that mad rage could still master him–like some half-tamed animal it would still rise against him the moment he took his eye off it.

So the Captain regarded with suspicion his decision in favour of attacking the Italians again; warned by the surge of fighting madness in his brain he waited to cool off before reconsidering. He turned on his stool and looked about him at the homely and familiar surroundings, at the Torpedo

Lieutenant and the Navigating Lieutenant and at Jerningham, at the compass and the voice pipes and the hasty after-thought of the Asdic cabinet. That had been hurriedly knocked together of three-ply; the Captain clairvoyantly foresaw a day when peace-time warships would have Asdic cabinets beautifully constructed of teak, elaborately polished and varnished. Three-ply was good enough for a light cruiser which might not be afloat by evening.

The fighting madness passed, his emotions under control again, the Captain reconsidered the idea of covering the destroyers' attack with the cruiser's fire. It was sound enough; the balance sheet of possible losses weighed against the chances of possible gains showed a profit. It was worth doing. Yet before deciding on a plan, it was as well to think about the enemy's possible plans; the Italians the other side of the smoke screen might be making some movement which could entirely nullify the destroyer attack, and they might also have up their sleeves some counter-move which could bring disaster on the cruiser squadron. The Captain thought seriously about it; if the Italian Admiral had any tactical sense he would have turned towards the smoke screen so that when the British ship emerged again they would find him not ten thousand yards, but only five thousand yards away; at that range the Italian salvoes could hardly miss. In a five-minute advance the Italians could reach the smoke screen, and in another minute they could be through it, with the convoy in sight and in range of their heavy guns. There might be a mêlée in the smoke screen at close quarters, where chance could play a decisive part, and where a light cruiser would be as valuable as a battleship. But chance was always inclined to favour the bigger squadrons and the bigger ships. The Italians could afford to lose heavily if in exchange they could destroy the British squadron first and the convoy, inevitably, later. Malta was worth a heavy cruiser or two or even a battleship. Far more than that; Malta was worth every ship the Italians had at sea, whether the island fortress were considered as the bastion of defence of the Eastern Mediterranean–as it was today–or as the advanced work from which an attack could be launched upon Italy–as it would be tomorrow.

It was only logical that the Italians should plunge forward into the attack–even if there were no other motive than the maintenance of the morale and the self-respect of the Italian crews, shaken by Matapan and Taranto and doomed to utter ruin if once more the Italian high command refused action with a greatly inferior force. That was all logical; the Captain reminded himself, smiling bleakly, that in war logic can be refuted by new arguments, and courage and dash on the part of the light cruisers could supply those. Time was passing, and the sun was sinking lower towards the horizon. The Italians had frittered time away. Even if now they made up their minds to attack there was a bare chance that a well-fought rearguard action might save the convoy–the British ships that survived the smoke screen action might lay another screen, and, when that was pierced, another yet, and so on, until sunset. A bare chance, but it was a chance.

The flagship astern, re-emerging from the smoke screen, was flashing a searchlight signal to *Artemis*, and the Captain heard the Chief Yeoman read off the letters one by one. By the time the message was one-third completed the Captain could guess what the end of it was going to be. The Admiral had reached the same decision regarding the destroyer attack as had the Captain, and this was the order putting into effect the plans discussed so long ago in contemplation of this very state of affairs.

'Acknowledge,' said the Captain to the Chief Yeoman of Signals, and then, to the Navigating Lieutenant, 'We'll attack again, Pilot. Starboard ten.'

20

FROM THE CAPTAIN'S REPORT

. . . and the attack was made . . .

'X' turret was not under the command of a commissioned officer. The Gunnery Lieutenant had found a kindred spirit in his chief gunner's mate; Allonby was one of those inspired fighting men–the Gunnery Lieutenant was another good example–that England produces in such numbers. At twenty-four, with his profound gunnery experience and his powers of leadership, Allonby had a career before him. Chief Petty Officer now, he was obviously destined to be commissioned Sub-Lieutenant shortly and Lieutenant immediately after, as soon as he should fill in the gaps in his technical education. The Captain had his eye on Allonby as a future Admiral. 'Aft through the hawse hole' the expression went, for describing the promotion of a man from the lower deck. Allonby would start with a handicap of six years in age, but prompt promotion would soon remedy that. No one could ever be quite sure how a man would react to promotion and added responsibility; Allonby might be a disappointment, but the Captain did not think it probable. On the contrary, he confidently expected that Allonby would clear all the hurdles before him and that one of these days Rear-Admiral Allonby would hoist his flag in command of a squadron. But that was part of the problematical future. In the pressing, concrete present, Allonby was in command of 'X' turret. He was a hard man and a good-tempered man simultaneously, with no mercy for any lazy or careless individual who came under his orders; a martinet despite his ease of manner and his unconstrained good humour. The energetic men of 'X' turret's crew liked him and admired him; the lazy ones admired him equally and liked him nearly as much despite themselves. It had not been easy for Allonby; the man promoted from the lower deck to a post of great power and responsibility has to face a certain amount of inevitable friction with his subordinates. His good temper was only partly responsible for his success with his men; the most potent factor was his consistency. The man who smarted under Allonby's reprimands or who went under punishment as a result of his charges could see clearly enough that Allonby was not gratifying his own ego, or asserting himself in beggar-on-horseback fashion. There was nothing moody about Allonby. He worked steadily for the efficiency of 'X' turret, and he worked for it in the same way every day. He might rule 'X' turret with a rod of iron, but it was always a rod of iron, not a rod of iron one day and a rod of clay the next.

Even Ordinary Seaman Triggs could appreciate that fact, dimly and without understanding. Triggs was the ship's bad character, careless, lazy, drunken, stupid, dirty–possessed, in other words, of all the qualities likely to get him into trouble. Most likely Triggs was of an intelligence well below standard, having slipped through the Navy's tests by misfortune or oversight. In civil life he would have sunk to the lowest levels of society, or rather have stayed there, among the shiftless drunken dregs which gave him birth. As it was, the Navy could feed him and clothe him, build up his physique and keep him at work which was not too exacting, but even the Navy could not give him the intelligence to profit by all this. His limited brain was almost incapable of grasping an order–the sharpest punishment could not impress upon him the necessity for listening to what he was told to do and then doing it. 'In at one ear and out at the other' as his exasperated shipmates said, and some would add that this was because there was nothing between his ears to act as an impediment. Five minutes after the six-inch guns' crews had been told to fall in for exercise the ship's loudspeaker would always say 'Ordinary Seaman Triggs, close up,' and it might even be two or three times that Ordinary Seaman Triggs was ordered to close up before he came tumbling aft to 'X' turret, his usual inane grin on his face, while Chief Petty Officer Allonby fumed and seethed. Time and place meant nothing to him. As a confirmed leave-breaker he rarely could be trusted ashore; when, after months on board perforce, he had at last purged himself of the sin of leave-breaking and was allowed on shore, it was only to be brought back by the naval police, hideously drunk and long overdue, to begin the weary cycle over again. There was always something of Triggs's in the ship's scranbag–lost property office–it was always Triggs who had to be told to get his hair cut or his nails cleaned. Captain and Commander had learned to sigh when they saw his name among the ship's defaulters and had him brought up before them, the silly smile on his face and his fingers twining aimlessly as he held his cap. The Captain had set in motion the official mechanism which would bring about Triggs's discharge from the Navy as unlikely to become an efficient seaman, but in time of war, with every man needed, and a personnel of a million men to be administered, the mechanism moved slowly, and Triggs was still on board *Artemis* when the battle was fought which decided the fate of the Mediterranean.

Allonby had stationed Triggs down in the magazine of 'X' turret, along with the officers' steward and the other untrained men, where he could do no harm. It was odd to think of Triggs put among tons of high explosive deliberately, but it was perfectly correct that he was harmless there, for cordite is a stubborn material. It will burn readily enough, but nothing save high pressure or another explosive will induce it to explode. As long as there was no chance of their catching fire the big cylinders of high explosive which Triggs handled were as harmless as so many pounds of butter. In the magazine with Triggs was Supply Assistant Burney, with more brains and reliability, and what Triggs and Burney had to do when the guns were in action was to take the tin boxes one by one from the racks in the magazine, extract the cordite charges from the boxes, and pass the charges through the flash-tight shutter in the bulkhead into the handling-room. Every ten seconds the two guns fifty feet above their heads each fired a round; every ten seconds two cordite charges in the magazine had to be stripped of their tin cases and passed through the shutter. That was all that had to be done; possibly in the whole ship when she was in action there was no duty calling for less practice or intelligence. Supply Assistant Burney may have felt himself wasted in the after magazine, but his routine duties in the ship made it hard to train him for a more exacting task, and his friends told him cheerfully that he could devote any attention he had to spare to seeing that Triggs did not strike matches down there. How Burney actually spent his time during the long and dreary waits while the guns were not firing was in squatting on the steel deck, with a couple of tons of high explosive round him and the sea just outside, reading *Economics in Theory and Practice*, for Burney's hobby was economics and he had vague ideas about some sort of career when he should leave the Navy. And Triggs would whistle tunelessly, and fidget about the steel cell that enclosed them, and, possibly, think vaguely whatever thoughts may come by chance into such a mind as Triggs possessed. He would finger the telephone, and peer at the thermometer, and drum with his fingers on the bulkhead. It was always a relief to Burney when the gong jangled and the guns bellowed atrociously overhead and he and Triggs had to resume their task of passing cordite through the shutters.

Down here in the magazine the forced ventilation was always hard at work, for cordite is peculiarly susceptible to changes in temperature, and if the after magazine was ever warmer or colder than the forward magazine the six guns would not shoot identically, the broadsides would 'spread', and all the skill of the spotters, all the uncanny intelligence of the machines, all the training of the guns' crews, would be wasted. So the ventilators hummed their monotonous note as air from the outside was forced down, and with it came the greasy smoke of the smoke screen, and the sickening stench from the burnt-out wardroom flat. For the fifth time now the oil smoke was being drawn into the magazine, as *Artemis* made her third attack, but Burney and Triggs had not troubled to count, and could not have guessed at the number of times; they were probably vaguer about the course of the battle than anyone else in the ship. Petty Officer Hannay, in the handling-room, had not much chance of telling them, during the brief seconds the flash-tight shutter was open, the news he heard over the loudspeaker. Burney had learned to be fatalistic about his ignorance, and Triggs did not care.

21

FROM THE CAPTAIN'S REPORT

. . . in support of the attack made by the destroyers . . .

The Captain made himself ready to meet any emergency as *Artemis* shot out of the smoke screen. Anything might be awaiting him on the other side. He might find himself right under the guns of the Italian battleships and heavy cruisers if they had moved forward to anticipate the attack. The Italian destroyers might be lurking in ambush beyond the smoke screen, ready to send in a salvo of torpedoes. It was hard to believe that the Italian battle line would remain on the defensive under the repeated goading of these attacks.

The smoke wreaths thinned, the blue sky overhead became visible, and there ahead was the Italian line, nine thousand yards away, still fumbling to find an unopposed path round the smoke screen that lay between them and their prey. The Captain kept his glasses on them as he gave his orders. It was the same line of battle–the two elephantine battleships in the van, massive and menacing, their silhouetted upperworks showing no sign of damage at that distance, and the heavy cruisers in their wake, smoke coiling greasily from their funnels. The second cruiser in the line had other smoke leaking from her upperworks–clear proof that a shell had got home somewhere in her.

Artemis came round on a parallel course, and her guns crashed out, the hot blast from them eddying over the bridge, the unbelievable noise of them beating against the eardrums of officers and men, and the faint smoke from the muzzles whirling by alongside. Through his glasses the Captain saw the long stout silhouettes of the leading battleship's big guns against the horizon. Slowly they shortened as the turrets trained round. They disappeared behind a screen of splashes as *Artemis*'s broadside struck–through the splashes the Captain saw the gleam of a hit–and then when the splashes were gone the guns were still no longer visible, and the Captain knew that they were pointed straight at him. *Artemis* had fired two more broadsides, and at this range the shells reached the target a second before the next was fired. Splashes and flashes, smoke and spray made the battleship's outline uncertain, as the Captain held her in the field of his glasses, countering the roll and vibration of his own ship. But then the Captain saw, through all the vagueness, the sudden intense flames of the battleship's salvo. She had fired, and in that second the Captain was aware of four momentary black dots against the blue above her silhouette, come and gone so quickly that he could hardly be quite sure of what he had seen. It might be a subjective illusion, like the black spots that dance before the eyes in a bilious attack. This was no bilious attack; the Captain knew that what he had seen were the four big shells of the Italian's salvo on their way towards him, travelling faster than the speed of sound and charged with destruction and death. The Captain faced their coming unabashed and impersonal. A hundred yards from *Artemis*'s starboard side rose the massive yellow columns of water; surprisingly, one big shell ricocheted from the surface, bouncing up without exploding, turning end-over-end and travelling slowly enough for the eye to follow it as it passed fifty feet above *Artemis*'s stern. Everything was happening at once; a broadside from *Artemis* reached its target while the flash of the Italian salvo still lingered on the Captain's retina, and another was fired at the very moment that shell was passing overhead.

'Turn two points to starboard, Pilot,' said the Captain to the Navigating Lieutenant.

In response *Artemis* sheered towards the enemy's line, shortening the range. The Italian salvo had fallen short; they would lengthen the range for the next. The Captain saw the gleam of it, saw the black spots dance again before his eyes, and then he heard the rumble of the shells overhead, high-pitched for a moment and then dropping two tones in the musical scale as they passed to fling up their vast fountains a hundred and fifty yards to port; *Artemis* had ducked under the arc of their trajectory like a boxer under a punch.

'Four points to port, Pilot,' said the Captain.

The Italians would shorten their range this time, and *Artemis* must withdraw from the blow like a boxer stepping back. All this time her guns were bellowing in reply; the erratic course she was steering would make the Gunnery Lieutenant's task harder, because the range would be opening and closing for her just as much as for the Italians; but the Gunnery Lieutenant, and the machines in the Transmitting Station would be kept informed of the alterations of course, and would not have to guess at them–over in the Italian ships the Captain could imagine the inclinometer operators at work, peering at their smoke-wreathed, splash-surrounded target and trying to guess whether the vague image they saw was growing fatter or thinner. If *Artemis* zigzagged while the Italians maintained a steady course it would be to *Artemis*'s advantage, therefore, and she would have more chance of hitting than the Italians had; while if the Italians should decide to zigzag, too, it would merely make it harder for everyone so as to give the British superiority in training and discipline more opportunity still.

The Captain was handling his ship, watching the Italian gunnery and observing the effect of his own. He turned and looked aft; the other cruisers had broken through the smoke screen and were blazing away at the Italian line, a chain of Davids attacking Goliaths. He turned his attention forward again; that was where the destroyers would launch their attack as soon as the Italians were fully distracted by the light cruisers. It was a matter for the nicest judgement on the part of the destroyer leader, for the cruisers could not be subjected for too long to the fire of the Italian battle line. In the very nature of things, by pure laws of chance, one or other of those innumerable salvoes must strike home at last; he ordered a new change of course, and a sudden flash of thought set him smiling grimly again as it crossed his mind momentarily that perhaps, if the Italian spotters were rattled and the Italian gunnery officers unskilful, the 'short' might be corrected as if it were an 'over' and he might be steering right into the salvo instead of away from it. There was no predicting what unnerved men might do. But still it certainly could not be worse than pure chance, and the sea was wide and the spread even of an Italian salvo was small; the Captain's sane and sanguine temperament reasserted itself. Despite that tremendous din, with *Artemis* rolling in a beam sea, and with a dozen factors demanding his attention and his calculation, and in face of appalling odds it was necessary that he should remain both clear-headed and cheerful.

Jerningham behind the Captain felt physically exhausted. The noise and the nervous strain were wearing him down. This was the third time *Artemis* had emerged from the shelter of the smoke screen to run the gauntlet of the Italian salvoes. How many more times would they have to do this–how many more times would they be able to? He was tired, for many emotions had shaken him that day, from terror under the morning's bombing attack to exasperation at reading Dora Darby's letter, and thence to exultation after the first successful attack. Exultation was gone now, and he only knew lassitude and weariness. He felt he would give anything in the world if only this frightful din would stop and the terrible danger would cease. The hand which held the rail beside him was cramped with gripping tight, and his throat was so dry that although he tried to swallow he could not do so. His eyes were dry too, or so they felt–his lids wanted to droop down over them and seemed to be unable to do so because of the friction with the dry surface. He was caught between the upper millstone of the Captain's inflexible will and the nether millstone of the Italian invulnerability.

It was a six-inch shell that hit the cruiser eventually, fired perhaps from the Italian flagship's secondary armament, or maybe a chance shot from one of the cruisers. The chances of dynamics dictated that it did not deal the *Artemis* nearly as severe a shock as the previous hit had done, although it caused far more damage. It struck the ship's side a yard above the water-line abreast of 'X' turret, and it penetrated the main deck as it burst, flinging red-hot fragments of steel all round it. Beneath the main deck there was No. 7 fuel tank containing fifty tons of oil fuel, and the shell ripped it open as it set everything ablaze. Oil welled up into the blaze and blazed itself, and the heat generated by the fire set more and more of the expanding oil welling up to feed the fire. The roll of the ship sent the burning oil running over the decks, turning the after-part of the ship into one mass of flames.

It was not merely the oil which burnt; it was not merely No. 7 fuel tank which was ripped open by the flying red-hot steel. Inboard of where the shell struck was 'X' turret, and from 'X' turret downwards to the bottom of the ship extended the ammunition supply arrangements for the turret–the lobby below the gunhouse and the magazine below the lobby. Fragments of the shell came flying through that thin steel of the bulkhead of 'X' turret lobby, and with the fragments came the flame of the explosion. The rating at the shell ring, the rating at the ammunition hoist, fell dead at their posts, killed by the jagged steel, and the petty officer in charge of the lobby, and the other ratings survived them only by a second. They died by fire, but it was a quick death. One moment they were alive and hard at work; the next, and the cordite charge in the hoist had caught alight and was spouting flames which filled full the whole interior of the lobby. One quick breath, and the men who took that breath fell dead. It was their dead bodies upon which the flame then played, so hot that the bodies were burned away in smoke and gas during the few seconds that the ammunition blaze lasted. Lobby and crew were wiped out; of the crew nothing remained–nothing–and of the lobby only the red-hot steel box, its sides warped and buckled with the heat.

On the bridge the shock of the blow passed nearly unfelt; the crash of the explosion nearly unheard. Jerningham saw the Chief Yeoman of Signals, on the wing of the bridge, looking anxiously aft. Where Jerningham stood the funnels and super-structure blocked the view astern, and he walked to the side and leaned over, craning his neck to look aft. Dense black smoke was pouring out of the side of the ship and was being rolled by the wind towards the enemy, and as Jerningham looked he saw massive flames sprouting at the root of the smoke, paling as a trick of the wind blew the smoke away, reddening as the smoke screened the sunshine from them. It was a frightening sight.

'Turn two points to starboard, pilot,' said the Captain to the Navigating Lieutenant; he was still handling his ship to avoid the shells raining round her, unconscious of what had happened. Jerningham saluted to catch his attention, and the Captain turned to him.

'Ship's on fire aft, sir,' said Jerningham. His voice quavered, and was drowned as he spoke by the roar of the guns. He repeated himself, more loudly this time, and the need to speak more loudly kept his voice steady. It was two full seconds before the Captain spoke, and then it was only one word, which meant nothing.

'Yes?' said the Captain.

'Pretty badly, apparently, sir,' said Jerningham. Exasperation at the Captain's dullness put an edge to his voice.

'Very good, Jerningham, thank you,' said the Captain.

The guns bellowed again, their hot blast whirling round the bridge.

'The reports will come in soon,' said the Captain. 'Pilot, turn four points to port.'

On the instant he was immersed again in the business of handling the ship. The destroyers were at this very moment dashing out of their ambush round the end of the smoke screen, and this was the time for them to be given all possible support. As long as the guns would fire, as long as the ship would answer her helm, she must be kept in the fighting line–for that matter she must be kept in the fighting line anyway, if for no other reason than to attract to herself as much of the Italian fire as possible. The fact that she was a mass of flames aft did not affect the argument. Whether she was doomed to blow up, or whether eventually she was going to sink, had no bearing on the present. She would or she would not. Meanwhile, there went the destroyers.

The Captain fixed his glasses on them. The attack had been well judged, and the destroyers were racing down to meet the Italians on a course converging at an acute angle. They were going at their highest speed–even at this distance the Captain could see their huge bow-waves, brilliant white against the grey; and their sterns had settled down so deep in the troughs they ploughed in the surface as to be almost concealed. The White Ensigns streamed behind them, and the thin smoke from their funnels lay above the surface of the sea in rigid parallel bars.

The Captain swung his glasses back to the Italian fleet, and from there to the other cruisers steaming briskly along with their guns blazing; for the first time he saw the dense smoke which was pouring out of *Artemis*'s quarter. He saw it, but his mind did not register the sight–the decision to take no action about the ship being on fire had already been made. He changed the ship's course again to dodge the salvoes and looked once more at the destroyers. His glasses had hardly begun to bear on them when he saw the sea all about them leap up into fountains–the Italians had at last opened fire on them. For a full minute of the necessary five that they must survive they had been unopposed. The destroyers began to zigzag; the Captain could see their profiles foreshortening first in one sense and then in the other as they turned from side to side like snipe under gunfire. Evasive action of that sort was a stern test of the gunners firing on them. Not merely was the range decreasing but the bearing was constantly altering–traversing a big gun back and forth to keep the sights on a little ship as handy as a destroyer, zigzagging under the unpredictable whim of her captain, was a chancy business at best.

It was important to note whether the Italian fire was accurate or not. The whole surface of the sea between the destroyers and the Italians was pock-marked with splashes, and far beyond the destroyers too. There were wild shots which threw up the sea hardly a mile from the Italians' bows, and there were wild shots falling three miles astern of the destroyers; over the whole of that length and making a zone a mile and a half wide, a hundred guns were scattering five hundred shells every minute, but the splashes were clustered more thickly about the destroyers than anywhere else–that much at least could be said for the Italian gunnery.

There were flashes darting from the destroyers, too. They were banging away with their 4.7-inch popguns–peashooters would not be much less effective against the massive steel sides of the Italian battleships, but there was always the chance of a lucky hit. The leading destroyer vanished utterly in a huge pyramid of splashes, and the Captain gulped, but two seconds later she emerged unharmed, her guns still firing, jinking from side to side so sharply that her freeboard disappeared as she lay over.

Jerningham was at the Captain's side again, with a report received by telephone.

' "X" turret reports they have flooded the magazine, sir,' said Jerningham to the Captain's profile.

'Thank you,' said the Captain without looking round.

If the after magazine was flooded it would mean that the two guns in 'X' turret would be silent, that was all. There were still the four guns of 'A' and 'B' turrets in action, and four guns fired a large enough salvo for efficiency. *Artemis* would not blow up yet awhile, either; but as the Captain would not have varied his course of action even if he had been utterly certain that she was going to blow up in the next minute that did not matter.

The leading destroyer disappeared again in the splashes, and reappeared again miraculously unhurt. The second destroyer in the line swung round suddenly at right angles, her bows pointed almost straight for *Artemis*. A cloud of white steam enveloped her, and then a moment or two later her black bows crept out of it and she began to crawl slowly away, steam and smoke still pouring from her as she headed for the shelter of the smoke screen. It was the first casualty; some shell had hit her in the boiler-room presumably. The other five were still tearing towards their objective; the Captain swung his glasses back at the Italian line in time to see a bright flash on the side of the Italian flagship–indisputably a hit and not gunfire, for it was a single flash–but he did now know enough about the broadsides *Artemis* had been firing to be able to credit it either to his own ship or to the destroyers. 'A' and 'B' turrets were still firing away, but, amazingly, the ears were so wearied by the tremendous sound that they took no special note of it unless attention was specially directed upon the guns.

By now the destroyers must be nearly close enough to discharge their torpedoes. The Captain tried to estimate the distance between them and their objective. Six thousand yards, maybe. Five thousand, perhaps–it was difficult to tell at that angle. The officers in command had displayed all the necessary courage and devotion. And the Italian destroyers were creeping out ahead of the Italian battle line to meet them now–they had been left behind when the Italian fleet turned about to try and work round the smoke screen, and had been compelled to sheer away widely to get on the disengaged side, and had then had to waste all those precious minutes working their way up to the head of the line where they should have been stationed all along. At the first hint of a British destroyer attack they should have been ready to move forward to fend it off, engaging with their own class beyond torpedo range of the battle line. The Captain fancied that there was a bad quarter-hour awaiting the senior Italian destroyer officer if ever he made port; he would probably be unjustly treated, but a naval officer who expected justice was expecting too much.

The leading British destroyer was wheeling round now, and the others were following her example, turning like swallows. Presumably at that moment the torpedoes were being launched, hurled from the triple tubes at the Italian line. Thirty torpedoes, the Captain hoped, were now dashing through the water, twenty feet below the surface against the Italians–sixty thousand pounds' worth of machinery thrown into the sea on the chance that five pounds' worth of T.N.T. might strike home; that was as typical of war as anything he knew; the dive bombers he had beaten off that morning were a hundred times more expensive still.

He kept his glasses on the Italian line so as to make sure of the effect of the torpedo attack, even while, in the midst of the deafening din, he continued to handle his ship so as to evade the enemy's salvoes. He was wet through from the splash of a shell close overside, and his skin kept reporting to his inattentive mind the fact that it was clammy and cold, just as in the same way he had been listening to reports on the progress of the struggle to extinguish the fire aft. This was the crisis of the battle, the moment which would decide the fate of Malta and of the world. Whatever happened to that fire aft, he must keep his ship in action a little longer, keep his four remaining six-inch guns in action, not merely to cover the retirement of the destroyers but to out-face and out-brave that line of Italian capital ships.

22

FROM THE CAPTAIN'S REPORT

. . . the ship sustained another hit . . .

When that six-inch shell struck *Artemis*'s side they were hardly aware of it forward on the bridge, but aft in 'X' turret there could be no misunderstanding of what had happened–they heard the crash and felt the jar of the explosion, smelt the suffocating stench of high explosive and burning fuel, and saw the red flames that raged round them. Beneath their feet in the gunhouse they felt the whole structure stir uneasily, like the first tremor of an earthquake, but the guns' crews could not allow that to break the smooth rhythm of loading and firing–sliding shells and charges from the hoist to the breeches, inserting the tubes and masking the vents, closing the breeches and then swinging them open again. Yet something else broke that rhythm.

'Hoist's stopped working, Chief,' reported Number Two at the right-hand gun.

'Use the ready-use charges,' said Allonby.

Three rounds for each gun were kept in 'X' turret in contemplation of such an emergency–enough for half a minute's firing. There is no point in keeping ammunition below the surface of the sea in the magazine and yet maintaining large quantities of high explosive above decks behind a trivial inch of steel. And when dealing with high explosive–with cylinders of cordite that can spout flames a hundred feet long a second after ignition–thirty seconds is a long time.

Allonby bent to the steel voice pipe beside him which led down to the lobby beneath his feet. A blast of hot air greeted him, and he hastily re-stoppered the pipe, for actual flame might come through there. The turret walls were hot to the touch–almost too hot to touch; the gunhouse must be seated at that moment in a sea of flame. It was just as well they were firing off those ready-use rounds and getting rid of them the best possible way. The turret was filling with smoke so that they could hardly see or breathe. They could be suffocated or baked alive in this steel box; the party in the lobby below must have been killed instantly. The instinct of self-preservation would have driven Allonby and the guns' crews out of 'X' turret the moment those red flames showed through the slits. It would be hard to believe that flight was actually the last thought that occurred to them, except that our minds are dulled by tales of heroism and discipline. We hear so many stories of men doing their duty that our minds are biased in that direction. The miracle of men staying in the face of the most frightful death imaginable ceases to be a miracle unless attention is directly called to it. Undisciplined men, untrained men, would have seen those flames and felt that heat; they might have halted for one paralysed second, but the moment realization broke in upon them they would have fled in the wildest panic that nothing would have stopped–possibly not even the threat of a worse fate (if one could be imagined) than being baked to death in a steel box. In 'X' turret under Allonby's leadership the thought of flight occurred to no one; they went on loading and reloading. Allonby had to take the decision that would make his turret utterly useless, even if the lobby and the hoist could be repaired; he had to relegate himself from being the proud captain of 'X' turret into the position of being a mere passenger at the same time as he put one-third of the main armament of *Artemis* out of action for good. He had to bear all the responsibility himself; with that fire blazing there was not even time to ask permission from the Gunnery Lieutenant.

Allonby seized the voice pipe to the magazine, and to his intense relief it was answered; Allonby knew Burney's voice as he knew the voice of every man under his command.

'Flood the magazine,' said Allonby.

'Flood the magazine?'

There was a question mark at the end of the sentence–it was not the usual Navy repetition of an order. The crash of the firing of the next round made Allonby pause for a second before he repeated himself, slowly and distinctly, making quite sure that he was understood. The last round was fired from the guns as he plugged the voice pipe.

'Clear the turret,' said Allonby to his men, and they began to scramble out, leaping through the flames to safety as if it were some ceremonial worship of Moloch.

Allonby applied himself to the telephone. The Gunnery Lieutenant and the

Transmitting Station must know at once that 'X' turret had ceased to fire; otherwise both the control and the spotting of the other guns would suffer. When he had finished that it was too late to escape from the turret, which was ringed with fire now and whose steel plates were red hot.

And down below the main deck, below the water-line, Ordinary Seaman Triggs and Supply Assistant Burney came out from the magazine into the handling-room crew. The elaborate mechanisms which had been specially designed for this emergency had played their part in saving the ship from instant destruction. All the way along the chain of ammunition supply, from magazine and shell-room to handling-room, from handling-room to lobby, from lobby to turret, there were flash-proof doors and shutters. At Jutland twenty-six years ago, similar hits had resulted in the destruction of three big battle cruisers; the roaring flames of one ignited charge had flashed from one end to the other, from turret to magazine, setting off the tons of high explosive in a blast which had blown the huge ships to fragments. In *Artemis* only the lobby had been wiped out, and only two charges had added their hundred-foot flames to those of the burning fuel. The flash-proof doors had allowed time, had stretched the period during which safety action could be taken from one-tenth of one second to fifteen seconds–time for Allonby to give his orders; possibly time for Burney or Triggs to carry them out. The alleyway in which the group found themselves was a place of unimaginable horror. It was filled with dense smoke, but no smoke could be thick enough to hide the scene entirely. Through holes in the torn deck above long tongues of red flame were darting intermittently down from the blazing lobby. At the end of the alleyway the bursting shell had blown bulkheads and doors into a porcupine-tangle of steel blades which protruded from a burning sea of oil; and with every movement of the ship the surface lapped over them and the flames ran farther down the alleyway. The heat was terrific, and although the flames were distinct enough the smoke was so thick that only objects directly illuminated by them were visible–the men groped about blinded, their lungs bursting and their eyes streaming.

'Flood the magazine!' shouted Burney in the fog. He ran round to where the twin wheels were which operated the inlet valves, with Triggs behind him; they ran through thin fire. Burney laid his hands on the wheels.

He had been drilled as far as this. Among the innumerable gunnery drills, R.I. exercises and sub-calibre work, sometimes the order had come through 'Clear "X" turret. Flood the magazine,' and Burney had run to the valves, even as he had now, and laid his hands on the wheels, as he did now, with Triggs beside him. Mechanical arrangements for flooding magazines might as well not exist if a man were not detailed to operate them, and practised in what he had to do; and not one man, but two, for men may die in the Navy.

But in this case action was different from practice, for the wheels were too hot to touch. Involuntarily Burney snatched his hands back from them with a cry of pain. They were seared and burnt. A sluggish river of burning oil trickled towards them and stopped five feet from them. Burney put his hands to the wheels again, but when he put his weight on his hands to force the wheels round it was more than his will would endure. He cried out with pain, agonized. Blind reflexes made him put his charred hands under his armpits as he stamped with agony and the burning oil edged nearer to him.

Cordite is a touchy substance, impatient of bonds. Free from confinement it will submit to rough treatment; it can be dropped, or thrown or tossed about without resenting the indignity. It will even burn, two out of three times, without exploding–a block consuming itself in a second, which is its approximate rate of combustion, instead of in a hundredth of a second, which is its rate of explosion. But if it is compressed or confined it will resent it vigorously. A pinch of fulminate then will make it explode, the wave of explosion jumping from molecule to molecule through the whole mass with the speed of light. And cordite is touchy about the temperature at which it is kept, too–let that rise a few degrees, and it begins to decompose. Nitrous fumes begin to rise from it; strange, complex, unstable nitrous acids begin to form within it. It begins to heat itself up spontaneously, accelerating the process in a vicious circle. So that if its temperature is allowed to rise while at the same time it is kept confined a pressure is developed which increases by leaps and bounds, and the decomposing cordite, compressed beyond all bounds, will explode without waiting for a primer to set it off.

Within 'X' turret magazine temperature and pressure were rising rapidly as the magazine's bulkheads passed on their heat to the cordite within. Thick yellow fumes (although there was no human eye within to see them) were flooding into the magazine as the unstable molecules stirred restlessly. A blast was approaching which would tear the ship in two, which might wipe out every human life within her. Pressure was piling up. Ordinary Seaman Triggs heard Burney's cries; the flames from the burning oil dimly illuminated Burney's shadowy figure bowed over his charred hands. Drill and discipline had left a mark even on Trigg's vague mental make-up. He knew orders were meant to be obeyed, although it was so easy to forget them and so easy to be distracted from their execution. When he went on shore he never meant to overstay his leave; it was only that he forgot; only that drink confused and muddled him. When the order came over the loudspeaker '"X" turret crew close up,' he would always obey it promptly except that he was so often thinking about something else. Here amid the smoke and flame of the alleyway, Triggs, oddly enough, was thinking about nothing except the business in hand. He saw Burney try to turn the wheels and fail, and without hesitation he took up the task. The pain in his hands was frightful, but Triggs was able to ignore it. He flung his weight on the wheels and they moved; again and again they moved, turning steadily.

Temperature in the magazine was high; there was a red danger mark on the thermometer hung within and the mercury was far, far above it. Pressure was high, too. Triggs turned the wheels, the steel rods rotated, the worm-gear turned, and the inlet valves in the magazine slowly opened to admit the sea. Momentarily there was a strange reluctance on the part of the sea to enter; the pressure within was so high that the twelve feet below water-line of the valves did not give enough counter-pressure to force the water in. Then *Artemis* rolled, rolling the valves three feet further below the surface, and that added pressure just sufficed. Two jets of water sprang up into the magazine, greedily absorbing the yellow nitrous fumes and cooling the heated gas so that the pressure within the magazine dropped abruptly; even when *Artemis* went back to an even keel the sea still welled up into the magazine, and when she heeled over the next time the jets spouted far higher, cooling and absorbing so that now the sea rushed in like a flood, filling the whole magazine.

Triggs knew now that his hands hurt him; the charred bones were visible where the flesh of his palms had been burned away. He was sobbing with pain, the sobs rising to a higher and higher pitch as the pain grew more intense and the realization of it more and more acute; wounds in the hand seem to be especially unnerving and painful, presumably because of the ample nerve supply to their surfaces. Burney mastered his own agony for a space, sufficient to lead Triggs forward to the sick-bay where Sick Berth Petty Officer Webster was doing his best to attend to the wounded who were being brought in here now that the wardroom and the Surgeon Lieutenant-Commander had been wiped out. Webster could at least bandage those frightful hands, and at least could give morphia to check those high-pitched sobs of Triggs's.

And meanwhile the Commander and his men, with 'X' turret's crew to help, and Sub-Lieutenant Richards with such of his men as the shell had left alive, battled with hoses and chemical extinguishers against the sea of flames that had engulfed the after half of the ship, reducing it bit by bit from a sea to a lake, from a lake to isolated pools, until at last the tons of sea water which the pumps brought on board had extinguished every spark.

23

FROM THE CAPTAIN'S REPORT

. . . with moderate damage . . .

When the crew of *Artemis* was at action stations one of the loneliest men in the ship was Henry Hobbs, Stoker First Class. His station was in the shaft tunnel, aft, a watertight door behind him and a watertight door in front of him, cutting him off from the rest of the world, and his duty was to watch over the eight shaft-bearings and to see that they did not run hot. The shaft tunnel was an inch less than five feet in height, so that Hobbs walked about in it bent double; and it was lighted eerily by a few sparse electric bulbs, and when *Artemis* was under full power, as she had been during this battle, the tunnel was full of the incessant high-pitched note of the shaft, which in that confined space made a continuous noise of a tone such as to make the unaccustomed listener feel he could not bear to listen to it any longer. Stoker Hobbs was used to it; in fact, it might as well be said he liked the noise and that it was no hardship for him to be stationed in the shaft tunnel; it must be further admitted that when action stations were being allotted Hobbs had looked so earnestly at Stoker Petty Officer Harmsworth so as to attract his attention and gain his influence in his favour in the matter. Harmsworth had cheerfully put forward Hobbs's name for duty in the tunnel because Hobbs was essentially reliable. It was unlikely that more than once in a watch an officer would come into the tunnel to inspect, so the stoker on duty there must be someone who could be trusted to do his duty without supervision.

The duty was not a very exacting one, because the main duty that Hobbs had to perform was to watch his eight bearings. He could tell by touch when one was running hot instead of warm, and he had exactly to anticipate this by opening the oil valve regulating the flow of lubricating oil to the bearing. The only other thing he had to do was to watch the bilge below the shaft–the ultimate lowest portion of the ship–and report if it began to deepen. The rest of the time Hobbs could spend in communion with God.

In Hobbs's opinion the shaft tunnel was the ideal place in which to address himself to God, and this opinion was the result of a large variety of factors. It was odd that the least potent of these factors was that he could be alone in the tunnel–solitude is something hard to find in a light cruiser crammed with a full wartime crew. The art of staying sane in a crowd, and of retaining one's individuality when living night and day shoulder to shoulder with one's fellows, has been perfected through generations of seamen since Drake in the give-and-take life of the lower deck, and a man has freedom enough to speak to God if he wishes to. The man who says his prayers is just another individual, as is the man who indulges in the almost forgotten habit of chewing tobacco, or the man who amazingly sleeps face downward in his hammock.

So solitude was to Hobbs's mind only the least attractive aspect of duty in the shaft tunnel–it was of some importance, but not of much. That continuous high-pitched hum was more important. Hobbs found that it led his mind towards the higher things of life. The finest organ playing in the world, the most impassioned sermons were less effective in this way than the note of the shaft as far as Hobbs was concerned. The vibration played its part, too; nowhere in the length and breadth and depth of H.M.S. *Artemis* was the vibration as noticeable as in the shaft tunnel. That vibration, intense and rapid, always set Stoker Hobbs thinking about the wrath of God–the connexion could hardly be apparent to anyone else, but to Hobbs it was clear enough. It was important, for in Hobbs's mind God was a Being who was filled with implacable wrath–implacable towards Hobbs alone, as far as Hobbs knew or cared. It was none of Hobbs's concern how God felt towards all the other men who swarmed through the ship. The naked steel that surrounded Hobbs in the tunnel, and the dreary lighting–harsh patches of light and darkness–reminded Hobbs of God, too, and so did the cramped confinement, and the blind leaps and surges of the tunnel when the ship was in a sea-way. And when the guns were firing the sound of them, by some trick of acoustics, was carried through the steel framework of the ship to a focus in the tunnel, so that it resounded like a steel drainpipe pounded with sledgehammers.

From this picture of the shaft tunnel can be drawn a picture, then, of the aspect of God which Stoker Hobbs thought was turned towards him, seeing that it was here, amid the din and vibration, among these repulsive surroundings, that he thought he was nearest to Him. Hobbs would have been the first to agree, on the other hand, that this was definitely only one aspect of God; just as only one face of the moon is visible to us on earth, however the earth rotates and the moon revolves, so God steadily kept only one side of Him towards Hobbs; there was another, beneficent side which other and more fortunate people could see–just as from another planet the back of the moon is visible–but they were not such frightful sinners, such utterly lost souls as was Henry Hobbs.

Close questioning of him, by someone whom Hobbs could not suspect of flippancy or irreligion, would have elicited from him the fact–not the admission–that all these dreadful sins of Hobbs's were at most venial, and the greater part of them were at least a dozen years old. At twenty Hobbs had kissed a girl or two and drunk a glass of beer or two too many. Possibly he had even gone a shade further in both directions, but only a shade. As a boy he had stolen from his hardworking mother's purse, and once he had stolen a doughnut in a baker's shop. But Hobbs was utterly convinced that his childhood and youth had been one long orgy of sin, meriting eternal damnation a dozen times over; at thirty-two he was still paying for them in penance and submission to a God who might some day forgive and who meanwhile only deigned to acknowledge the sinner's existence in such places as the shaft tunnel.

When he had gone the rounds of his eight bearings and seen that they were all properly lubricated, and after he had tried the bilge and made certain water was not rising in the ship, Hobbs took off the little black skull-cap he wore on duty to cushion the blows his head was always sustaining in the tunnel when the ship rolled. He clasped his hands before him–his head was already bowed, thanks to the lowness of the tunnel–and he prayed once more to God for forgiveness for what had passed between him and Mary Walsh that evening in the darkened cinema.

The second hit on *Artemis* did not extinguish the lights in the shaft tunnel immediately. Hobbs felt it and heard it, but it was fifteen seconds later before the flames burned through the insulation of the wiring somewhere along its course and plunged the tunnel into complete darkness. Hobbs stood quite still, hunched over in the tunnel, with no glimmer of light at all. The shaft went on singing its vast song, and all about him was God. He was not afraid. 'X' turret guns above his head fell silent–he could distinguish between a full broadside and the fire merely of 'A' and 'B' turrets–but the framework of the ship transmitted a great many new noises to him, crashes and thumps and bangs, as the flames roared through the stern and the damage control party fought them down. He waited a while for the lights to come on again, but the fire was so far aft that the emergency circuit to the shaft tunnel was involved as well; there would be no more light in the shaft tunnel until–if *Artemis* ever came out of this battle–the wiremen could, under the instructions of the Torpedo Gunner's Mate, restore the circuit. Hobbs took his electric torch out of the pocket of his dungarees and made the round of the bearings again, turning the valves on and off, and when he finished he switched the torch off again. If there was no light there was no light, and that was an end to the business. He certainly was not going to waste the electricity in his torch, for no one–except God who shared the darkness with him–knew how long this action was going to last and how long it would be before he was relieved. God was all about him in the shaft tunnel. He could stand there, bent half double, and wait.

One moment he was alone with God in the darkness of the tunnel; the next, it seemed to him, and he was knee deep in water, so suddenly it poured in. The surprising thing about that water was that it was *hot*. It had not come in direct from the sea–it was sea-water which had been pumped on the flames, had quenched areas of red-hot steel plating, and had thence found its way by devious routes–a fragile light cruiser after two heavy hits and two fires was likely to have many passages open in it–down into the shaft tunnel. As the ship rolled and pitched the water surged up and down the tunnel, almost carrying Hobbs off his feet and splashing up into his face when it broke against the obstacle of his body.

He groped his way through the darkness to the telephone and lifted the receiver. It was some seconds before Howlett or Grant at the telephone switchboard were able to attend to the red light which glowed at the foot of the board to show that the hardly-used telephone in the shaft tunnel was off its hook. During that interval the water rose suddenly again to Hobbs's waist–not hot this time but icy cold, for the red-hot plating was all quenched by now. When the ship rolled the water surged clear over Hobbs's head, throwing him down still holding the receiver. Howlett plugged in–Hobbs heard the welcome click–and said 'Exchange'.

'Engine-room,' said Hobbs, and when he heard the answer, 'Hobbs–shaft tunnel here. I want the officer of the watch.'

The water dashed him against the tunnel walls as he waited again until Lieutenant Bastwick answered him and he made his report.

'We'll pump you out,' said Bastwick. 'Open up the discharge valves.'

Hobbs put back the telephone–under water–and felt his way to the valves. The motion of the ship sent the water up and down the tunnel; not merely did it wash over Hobbs's head, but when his head was clear it also compressed or rarefied the air at the end of the tunnel where Hobbs was so that his eardrums crackled and his breath laboured on those occasions when he had the chance to breathe. The water still flooded into the tunnel–overhead where the damage control party fought the flames it naturally occurred to no one that down in the shaft tunnel their efforts were fast drowning one of their shipmates–and there were twenty tons of it now, hurtling from end to end and from side to side. It picked Hobbs up and dashed him against the watertight door; the point of his shoulder took the shock, and he felt his collar-bone break. It was painful to raise his right arm after that, but he stuck his hand into the front of his dungarees as a substitute sling. The discharge valves were open now, and he hoped the pumps were at work.

The next rush of water up the tunnel was less violent, although it jarred him against the watertight door and hurt his collar-bone again, and the next one was weaker still, hardly over his waist. There were pumps at work all over the ship–some pumping water in as fast as possible to quench the fire, and others pumping it out again as fast as possible from those compartments down into which it drained in torrents, for watertight doors and watertight hatchways work only moderately well after a ship has been struck by heavy shells and has had a bad fire rage through a quarter of her length. Hundreds of horse-power were being consumed in this effort, and for hours now the engine-room had been called upon to supply the sixty-five thousand horse-power needed for full speed. The Commander (E) had had the responsibility of seeing to it that engines and boilers would produce more power than they had been designed to produce, and for a longer time than it was fair that they should be asked to do so: the fact that First Class Stoker Hobbs was not drowned miserably in the shaft tunnel was some measure of the Commander (E)'s success in his task.

Hobbs was still alive. His right hand was thrust into the breast of his dungarees, and his shoulder pained him. He was utterly in the dark, for his saturated electric torch refused to function. But he was alive, and he knew his way about the shaft tunnel, from one bearing to another, to the oil valves and back again, and his work which could be carried out one-handed. These were not circumstances in which he felt himself to be justified in asking for relief, and he made no such request; indeed, it did not occur to himself to do so. God was with him in the darkness, and as it happened Hobbs had never been in the shaft tunnel in darkness before. It seemed to him as if in the darkness God was not as implacable, as remorseless, as he was when the tunnel was lit up–that may easily be explained by the harsh black-and-white lighting of the tunnel, for there were no soft tones about it when the bulbs functioned. Very deep down within him, very faintly, Hobbs may have felt that this experience, this being flung about by tons of water in a confined space, his broken collar-bone and his near-drowning, was an expiation of his goings-on with Mary Walsh, but Hobbs was a man of slow mental reactions and of morbidly sensitive conscience, and if this feeling was there at all it was very slight, even if later, after mature consideration, it grew stronger. It was just the solid darkness which was comforting to Hobbs, and his reaction to it was to feel as if God were not quite so angry with him. He felt his way round the eight bearings with his left hand, and as he did so he whistled between his teeth, which he had not done since first the conviction of sin had come upon him. It was a very faint little whistle, not audible at all through the high-pitched song of the shaft, and when Hobbs realized what he was doing he cut himself off, but not very abruptly.

24

FROM THE CAPTAIN'S REPORT

. . . but firing was maintained . . .

At some time during the few minutes–during the interval measured perhaps in seconds–following immediately after the launching of their torpedoes by the destroyers, a shell was fired from H.M.S. *Artemis* which changed the face of the war, altered the whole history of the world. Men and women in Nigeria or Czechoslovakia would feel the impact of that shell upon their lives. Head-hunting cannibals in Papua, Siberian nomads seeking a scant living among the frozen tundra of Asia, toddling babies in the cornfields of Iowa, and their children's children, would all, in the years to come, owe something to that shell.

For the correct apportionment of the credit the history of that shell and the charge which sent it on its way should be traced back to their origins. There were, somewhere in England, women whose skin was stained yellow by the picric acid which entered into the composition of the bursting charge, who sacrificed strength and beauty in the munitions factory that filled that shell; their hair was bound under caps and their feet encased in felt slippers lest the treacherous material they handled should explode prematurely. There were women at the precision lathes who turned that shell until it fitted exactly, to the thousandth of an inch, into the rifling of the gun that fired it. There were the men that mined the iron and the coal, and the slaving foundry-workers who helped to cast the shell. There were the devoted sailors of the Mercantile Marine, who manned the ship that bore the nickel that hardened the steel from Canada to England, in the teeth of the fiercest blockade Germany could maintain. There were the metallurgists who devised the formula for the steel, and there were the chemists who worked upon the explosive. There were the railwaymen and the dockyard workers who handled the deadly thing under the attack of the whole strength of the Nazi air power. The origins of that shell spread too far back and too widely to be traced–forty millions of people made their contribution and their sacrifice that that shell might be fired, forty millions of people whose dead lay in their streets and whose houses blazed round them, working together in the greatest resurgence of patriotism and national spirit that the world has known, a united effort and a united sacrifice which some day may find an historian. Perhaps he will be able to tell of the women and the children and the men who fought for freedom, who gave life and limb, eyesight and health and sanity, for freedom in a long-drawn and unregretted sacrifice.

The miners and the sailors, the munition workers and the railwaymen, had played their part, and now the shell stood in its place in 'A' turret shell-room, and the charge that was to dispatch it lay in its rack in the forward turret magazine. There were only humble workers down there, men like Triggs and Burney who worked in the after turret magazine. Harbord, the Captain's steward, was stationed in the forward magazine–a thin, dried-up little man, who was aware of the importance of serving bacon and eggs in the most correct manner possible when his Captain called for them. Harbord had come into the Navy from the Reserve, and had passed the earlier years of his life as a steward in the Cunard White Star. He had found promotion there, rising from steward in the second-class to steward in a one-class ship, and from there to steward in the first-class in a slow ship, and eventually supreme promotion, to steward in the first-class in a five-day ship, where the tips were pound notes and five-dollar bills, and where he waited upon film stars and industrial magnates, millionaires and politicians.

He gave them good service; perhaps the best service the world has ever known was that given in the trans-Atlantic luxury liners in the twenties and thirties. He devoted his ingenuity to anticipating the wants of his passengers so that they would be spared even the trouble of asking for what they wanted–he learned to read their characters, sizing them up the first day so that during the next four they would perhaps not have to ask for anything. He could put a basin at the bedside of a seasick millionaire as tactfully as he could serve a midnight supper for two–pork chops and champagne!–in the cabin of a nymphomaniac film star. He was unobtrusive and yet always available. When passengers tried to pump him about their fellow passengers he could supply what appeared to be inside information without disclosing anything at all. He knew the great, the wealthy, and the notorious, in their weakest moments, and to him they were not in the least heroic figures. Yet of his feelings he gave no sign; he was deferential without being subservient, helpful without being fulsome.

The trade agreement between the shipping lines regulated the fares charged so that the only way in which they could compete with each other was in the services they could offer–menus ten pages long, food from every quarter of the globe, masterpieces of art hanging on the bulkheads, orchestras and gymnasiums and swimming baths; the concerted efforts of ingenious minds were at work devising fresh ways of pampering the first-class passengers so that a thousand miles from land they were surrounded by luxuries of which Nero or Lucullus never dreamed, by comforts such as Queen Victoria never enjoyed. And the service which the stewards could give was an important part of this system. If by a particular manner and bearing Harbord could make his charges more comfortable, he was ready to display that manner and bearing–it was his job for the moment. The social system which permitted–encouraged–such luxury and waste, and which made him the servant of drunken ne'er-do-wells and shifty politicians was obviously in need of reform, but the reformation must start with the system, not with the symptoms. Meanwhile he had work to do, and Harbord took pride in doing to the best of his ability the work which was to be done.

And when war came and the Navy claimed his services it was far easier to reconcile his prejudices with the type of work to which he was allotted. He was a steward, still, but the Captain's steward–trust the Captain to select the best available. The arts he had acquired in the Cunard White Star were of real use now, to serve a breakfast without breaking in on the Captain's train of thought, to attend to the trivial and mechanical details of the Captain's day so that it was only the war which made demands upon the Captain's reserves of mental energy. At sea when the Captain was day and night on the bridge, it was Harbord's duty to keep him well fed and well clad, and in port Harbord had to shield him from nervous irritation so as to allow him a chance to recuperate. His discretion and his trustworthiness were of real value nowadays; the desk in the Captain's cabin held papers which the German staff would gladly pay a million pounds to see–Harbord never allowed his mind to record the writing which his eyes rested upon. Visitors came to the Captain's cabin, officers of the ship, officers of other ships, Intelligence officers of the Army and Air Force Staffs, Admirals and Generals.

They talked freely with the Captain, and Harbord in his pantry or offering sherry and pink gin from a tray could hear all they said. Sometimes it would be things that would make the spiciest shipboard gossip–news as to where the ship was going, or alterations in routine, or promotions, or transfers, or arrangements for shore leave. Sometimes it would be matters of high policy, the course of the naval war, the tactics to be employed in the next battle, or the observed effects of new weapons or new methods. Sometimes it would merely be reminiscence, tales of battle with submarine or aeroplane or armed raider. Whatever it was bound to be of the most engrossing interest. An advance word to the lower deck on the subject of leave would make his confidants his grateful clients; when talking to his friends on shore Harbord could have been most gratifyingly pontifical about the progress of the war; and in every port there lurked men and women who would pay anything in money and kind for news of how such-and-such a submarine was sunk or what happened to such-and-such a raider. But Harbord was deaf and dumb and blind, just as he had been in peacetime when the newspaper reporters had tried to find out from him who it was who shared the politician's cabin at night.

When the hands went to action stations his was a position of no such responsibility. He was like Triggs, merely a man who stripped the tin cover from the cordite charges and thrust the cardboard-cased cylinders of explosive through the flashtight shutter of the magazine into the handling-room–his duties about the Captain allowed neither the time nor the opportunity to train him to do more responsible work. He was hardly aware of his unimportance; that much effect, at least, his previous experience had had on him. He handed the cordite with as much solemnity as when he offered sherry to a Vice-Admiral, although with a greater rapidity of movement. A lifetime of self-control had left him with little surface light-heartedness, just as the habitual guard he maintained over his tongue made the men who worked beside him think him surly and unfriendly. At his action station he was in close contact with half a dozen men, because 'A' and 'B' magazines were combined into one, with a flash-tight shutter both forward and aft, the one opening into 'A' turret handling-room and the other into 'B'. During the periods of idleness when the guns were not firing the men could stand about and gossip, all except Harbord, who would not. His fellow workers–the queerest mixture, from Clay, the ship's painter, to Sutton of the canteen staff–had, as a result of their different employments, the most varied gossip to exchange, and Harbord's could have been a valued contribution. But he kept his mouth shut, and was repaid by his shipmates saying he put on all the airs of an admiral. Of all these it was Harbord who was privileged to be the man who handled the propellant charge that sent to its target the shell that changed history.

Forward in the shell-room it was Able Seaman Colquhoun who handled the shell–a big curly-haired young giant from Birkenhead, whose worst cross in life was the tendency of the uninitiated to mispronounce his name and give the 'l' and 'q' their full value. It was always a ticklish job telling petty officers that he called himself 'Ca-hoon'; self-important petty officers were inclined to look on that as an impertinence. The six-inch shell that Colquhoun handled weighed one hundred pounds, which was why his youthful thews and sinews were employed here in the shell-room. In a rolling ship it called for a powerful man to heave as big a weight as that with certainty into the hoist.

Colquhoun was proud of his strength, and to put it to good use gratified some instinct within him. He smiled reminiscently as he bent and heaved. In the early days of the black-out in England, when his ship was under orders to sail, he had spent his last night's leave ashore with Lily Ford, the big blonde friend of his boyhood, who had repelled every advance made to her by every man she had met. She had kept her virginity as though it were a prize in a competition, not selfishly, not prudishly, but as if she looked on herself as if she were as good as any man and would not yield until she should meet one whom she could admit to be her better. But that night on the canal bank, under the bright moon of the first September of the war, Colquhoun had put out all his strength. It had been careless of Lily to let herself be lured by Colquhoun's tact to such a deserted spot as the canal bank, but it would really have been the same if there had been help within call–Lily would not have called for help to deal with a situation she could not deal with single-handed. She fought with him, silently, desperately, at first, and even when he was pressing her hard she would not do more than whisper hoarsely, 'Get away, you beast.' She writhed and struggled, putting out all the strength of her tough body, trained by the factory labours which had given her her glorious independence. Then she yielded to his overpowering force, breaking down suddenly and completely, her savage words trailing off into something between a sigh and a sob, her stiff body relaxing into submission, the mouth she had kept averted seeking out his in the darkness.

It was a succulent memory for the graceless Colquhoun something to be rolled over the tongue of reminiscence, every detail just as it should have been, even to the walk back from the canal bank with Lily clinging to him, her boasted self-sufficiency all evaporated, and the fact that Colquhoun's ship was under orders to sail terrifying in its imminence and inevitability. She had clung and she had even wept, although the day before she would have laughed at any suggestion that she would waste a tear on any man. Well, that was two and a half years ago, and it was to be presumed that she had got over it by now.

'Come up, you bastard!' said Colquhoun without ill temper, for he was still grinning to himself; the arms that had clasped Lily Ford clasped the shell that was to change history, and slid it forward into the hoist.

At the same moment in the handling-room Able Seaman Day, the man who lost his left forefinger as a result of a premature explosion at the Battle of the River Plate, took the charge that Harbord had thrust through the flash-tight shutter and pushed it into a pocket on the endless chain that ran up above his head through another flash-tight hatchway. The hoist rose, the endless chain revolved, the shell and charge arrived simultaneously in 'A' turret lobby.

The designer of a ship of war encounters difficulties at every turn. One school of naval thought clamours for guns, the largest possible guns in the greatest possible number, with which an enemy may be overwhelmed without the opportunity of hitting back. Another school demands speed, and points out that the best guns in the world are useless unless they can be carried fast enough to catch the enemy. A third school prudently calls for armour because, as Nelson once pointed out, a battle at sea is the most uncertain of all conflicts, and speed and guns may vanish in a fiery holocaust as a result of a single hit. And armour means weight, and guns mean weight, the one at the expense of the other and both at the expense of the weight that can be allotted to engines.

The designer reaches a compromise with these conflicting demands only to come against new incompatibles. Men must be able to live in a ship; the mere processes of living demand that they should be able to go from one part of the ship to another, and when she is in action it may well be that they have to do so with the greatest possible speed. But, once again, she may be struck by shells or bombs or torpedoes, and to minimize the damage of the hit she must be divided up into the greatest possible number of compartments bulkheaded off from each other, and those bulkheads must be free of all openings–except that there is the most urgent need for wires and voice pipes and ventilating shafts to pass through them.

In the same way the gunnery expert insists that his guns should be placed as high as possible, so as to give the greatest possible command, and his insistence is met with the reply that guns and gun-mountings are the heaviest things in a ship and putting them high up means imperilling the ship's stability like standing up in a rowing boat. Not merely that, but the gunnery expert, wise to the danger of high explosives, demands that although his guns should be as high above the level of the sea as possible the shells and the charges for the guns should be out of harm's way and as far below that level as possible; then, unreasonable as a spoilt child, he goes on to clamour for guns that will fire with the greatest rapidity and in consequence needing to be supplied every minute with a great weight of ammunition regardless of the distance it must be raised from shell-room and magazine. Even that is not all. The moment his wishes appear to be granted he baulks at the thought of a long chain of high explosive extending unbroken from top to bottom of the ship, and he insists that the chain be broken up and interrupted with flash-tight hatchways and shutters that must on no account delay the passage of the ammunition from the magazine to the precious guns.

Ingenious mechanisms solve this problem–so that when 'X' turret lobby in *Artemis* was set on fire the flames did not flash up into the turret nor down into the magazine–and then the designer is faced with a new difficulty, because the turret must, of course, be able to revolve, to turn from side to side, so that the belts and hoists are attached at one end to the stationary lobby, and at the other to the revolving turret; and this is the difficulty which designers for eighty years have struggled against. When Ericsson built *Monitor* he had a hole cut in the floor of the turret and another in the roof of the magazine below, and in order for ammunition to be passed up the turret had to be revolved until the two holes corresponded and the turret had to remain stationary until it was re-ammunitioned–a state of affairs no gunnery officer, intent on annihilating the enemy, would tolerate for a moment.

Even the apparently insoluble problem of the revolving turret and the stationary lobby has been solved now, so that whichever way the turret may be turning two shells of a hundred pounds each and two charges of cordite arrive in it every ten seconds to feed the guns, but the complication has forced another compromise upon the unfortunate designer. He is faced by the choice between employing men or machines–elaborate, complicated machines which may be disabled by a hit, or men who have to be fed, and given water to drink, and somewhere to sling a hammock, and who, in a nation exerting the last ounce of its strength, could be employed on some other urgent duty if not engaged in manhandling ammunition. Faced by this choice, the designer compromises, as he has compromised in his designs all through the ship. He makes the mechanisms as simple as he can without necessitating too great use of manpower, and he cuts down his manpower as far as he can without complicating the mechanisms too much. He ends, of course, by satisfying neither the Commander who is responsible for the men's living conditions nor the Gunnery Officer who is responsible for the guns, but that is the natural fate of designers of ships–the speed enthusiasts and the gunnery experts and the advocates of armour protection, the men who have to keep the ships at sea and the men who have to handle them in action all combine to curse the designer. Then comes the day of battle, and the mass of compromises which is a ship of war encounters another ship of war which is a mass of different compromises, and then, ten to one, the fighting men on the winning side will take all the credit to themselves and the losers–such of them as survive–will blame the designer all over again.

So the thews and sinews of Able Seaman Colquhoun and the fussy diligence of Harbord were necessary to start the shell and its propelling charge on the way up from shell-room and magazine to 'A' turret lobby. Then Able Seaman Mobbs tipped the shell out of the hoist into the shell ring; to him it was just one more shell, and not the shell on which the destinies of the world depended. With one shell arriving up the hoist every five seconds he had no time for profound thought. He had to be as diligent as a beaver, and he was a man of full body, oddly enough. The stooping and the heaving which he had to do in the warm atmosphere of the lobby had no apparent effect on the waistline which week by week grew a little more salient as Mobbs left youth further behind and advanced further into maturity. He swept the sweat from his forehead with the back of his right forearm, avoiding the use of his hands, which were filthy from contact with the shells. But by now his forearm was nearly as dirty as his hands, and the sweat and the dirt combined into fantastic streaks diagonally across his pink face. On his cheeks and chin there was a fuzz of fair beard like a chicken's down, for Mobbs had been carried away early in the war by the revived Naval craze for beards, and the poverty of the result had not yet induced him to reapply for permission to shave. The fuzz was dirty in patches, too, and there were little rivers of sweat running through it. Anyone in the lobby with leisure for thought would have smiled at the sight of him, his plethoric pink face and his ridiculous beard, his blue pop-eyes as innocent as a child's, and the streaked dirt over all. He moved the shell ring round for a quarter of a revolution to where Ordinary Seaman Fiddler awaited it, and then he brushed his face with his left forearm and managed to streak it again in the diagonally opposite direction, thereby giving the finishing touch to his ludicrous appearance. No one had time to notice it, however. Another shell had come up the hoist, dispatched by Able Seaman Colquhoun, and he had to deal with it–just another shell, no different in its appearance from its important predecessor now under the charge of Ordinary Seaman Fiddler, no different from the scores that had gone before, or from the scores which, for all Mobbs knew, would follow after. It seemed to him as if he had been at work for hours tipping shells from hoist to ring and would go on doing so to the end of time. The thunder of the guns just above his head, the motion of the ship, made no impression on him; for that matter he was not even actively conscious of the stuffy heat of the lobby. Word had come through over the telephone system that 'X' turret lobby had been wiped out, and after magazine flooded, 'X' turret guns silenced. Mobbs heard the news as he toiled and sweated; some of his messmates were gone, and it must have been only by a miracle that he and *Artemis* together had escaped being blown into microscopic fragments. None of that was as important as this business of keeping the shell ring full and the hoist empty, not as important at the moment, at least.

Meanwhile Ordinary Seaman Filmore took from the endless chain the cordite charge that Harbord below him had put into it, and transferred it to the cordite hoist of the revolving structure–three neat movements did it all, in far less than the five seconds allowed him. It was an easy job for Filmore. He had time to think and talk. The empty pocket in the endless chain flicked out of sight through the flash-tight hatchway.

'Coo!' said Filmore. 'That means old Nobby's gone. *You* know. Not Nobby the Leading Cook. The other one wiv the red 'air. 'E owes me a couple o' pints, too. Last time—'

'Shut up,' snapped Petty Officer Ransome.

He should not have snapped; he should have given the order naturally and easily, as orders which must be obeyed under pain of death should be given, and he was conscious of his error the moment the words were out of his mouth. But he was newly promoted and not quite sure of himself, and the responsibility of 'A' turret lobby weighed heavily on him.

'Keep yer 'air on!' said Filmore to himself, very careful that he should not be overheard. By diligent testing he knew just how far he could go with every Petty Officer and Leading Seaman in the ship. He had the Cockney quick wit, and the Cockney interest in disaster and death. He felt about the death of the red-haired Nobby Clark in the same way as his mother in her Woolwich slum felt about the death of a neighbour. It was a most interesting event; although the daily miracles of sunrise and sunset quite failed to impress him, he was always struck by the miracle that someone he knew, had talked to and talked about, should now be something quite different, a mere lump of flesh destined to immediate mouldering and decay. It was not intrinsically a morbid interest, and certainly the death of Nobby Clark was something to be talked about, like a birth in the Royal family. Petty Officer Ransome thought otherwise. If he had been a mere seaman he would gladly have entered into the discussion, recalling old memories of Nobby, and wondering how his widow would get along on her pension. But as a Petty Officer, responsible for 'A' turret lobby, and with an unjustified fear that it was bad for the morale of the men to dwell on the death of a shipmate, he cut the discussion short. As a distraction he gave another order.

'Keep it moving, Fiddler.'

'Aye, aye,' said Fiddler.

The shell vanished into the hoist in the revolving structure as a fresh broadside blared overhead. Ransome, in this his first action as a Petty Officer, was worried. From the time of going to action stations he had felt a nagging fear lest his lobby should not be as efficient as the other two, lest a broadside should be delayed because ammunition was supplied more slowly to 'A' turret than to 'B' and 'X'. If that should happen there would be a sharp reprimand from Sub-Lieutenant Coxe over his head; even worse, the Gunnery Lieutenant, watching the 'gun ready' lamps, might–certainly would–be moved to inquire into the cause of the delay. It was not fear of actual reprimand, or of punishment or disrating, which Ransome felt, any more than the crew of a racing eight fears defeat as it waits at the starting point. It was mere nervousness, which sharpened his voice and led him into giving unnecessary orders, and it remained to be seen if time and experience would enable him to overcome this weakness. No man's capacity for command can be known until it has been tried in actual battle.

In point of fact, 'A' turret was easier to keep supplied than 'B' turret just aft of it. 'B' turret was superimposed, raised higher above the deck than 'A', so as to enable its guns, when pointed directly forward, to fire over it. Yet 'A' and 'B' turrets drew their ammunition from the same magazine, and from shell-rooms at the same level below the sea, with the result that 'B's' shells and charges had to be sent up on a journey a full seven feet longer that 'A's', enough to make an appreciable difference in the time of transmission and to demand a proportionate increase in efficiency on the part of 'B's' turret crew. Since his promotion Ransome had not begun to reason this out and comfort himself with the knowledge, which was a pity, for when nervousness begins to reason it ceases to be nervousness. Instead, he snapped, 'Keep it moving, Fiddler,' quite unnecessarily.

'Aye, aye,' grumbled Fiddler, a little resentfully, for he knew that there was nothing slow about his supervision of the shell ring. He was an old, old sailor who had seen Petty Officers come and Petty Officers go, who had been through battle and shipwreck and hardship and pestilence, sturdily refusing promotion despite the recommendations of Lieutenants and the suggestions of Commanders. The life of an Able Seaman was a comfortable one, a satisfactory one, and he did not want the even tenor of his existence broken by the responsibilities of promotion. He did not look upon his experiences when the destroyer *Apache* was lost in a snowstorm in the Hebrides, and he had clung to a ledge of a cliff for a night and half a day with the waves beating just below him, as an interruption of his placid existence, nor the fighting at Narvik, nor the week he spent in an open boat when his sloop was torpedoed. Those were mere incidents, but to be even a Leading Seaman meant disturbing all the comfortable habits and daily routine acquired during twenty years of service. All he wanted to do was to go steadily along performing the duties allotted him, gaining neither credit nor discredit, neither promotion nor punishment, but reserving to himself the right to feel that he knew much more about seamanship and gunnery than did these whipper-snapper young Petty Officers whom they promoted nowadays. Ransome's order to him called forth the mechanical response to his lips, but did not quicken his movements in the least, for he knew he was doing his job perfectly, and probably a great deal better than Ransome could. The shell slid under his guidance from the shell ring to the revolving hoist, and soared up to the turret and out of his life, keeping pace as before with the cordite charge in the cordite hoist.

Sub-Lieutenant Coxe allowed his eyes to rest idly on the shell as it lay in its trough on its arrival, with its ugly distinctive paint on it, and ugly in its harsh cylindro-conical outline. There was not even a functional beauty about it, unlike most of the weapons of war, nor was it large enough to be impressive in its bulk. A six-inch shell, even one which is destined to free humanity, is unredeemingly ugly. Coxe never stopped to think for a moment whether it was ugly or beautiful. He was keeping a sharp eye on his guns' crews, watching each of their intricate movements. Coxe knew all about this turret and the principles that it embodied. He knew all the details of its mechanism, all the bolts and all the levers. If every six-inch turret in the Royal Navy, and every blueprint and every working drawing were to be destroyed in some unheard-of cataclysm, they could be replaced by reference to Sub-Lieutenant Coxe. When he was seasick (which was often) Coxe could forget his troubles by closing his eyes and calling up before him the obturator on the vent axial bolt or the tapered grooves in the recoil cylinder, but there was no need for sea-sickness to set him free thinking about gunnery. It occupied most of his thoughts; and in the same way that a man at dinner turns satisfied from a joint to complete the meal with cheese, so Coxe could turn from the comparatively simple mechanics of the gun-mountings to the mathematics of ballistics, and Henderson and Hasse's differential form of Resal's fundamental equation.

Coxe was an example of the mathematical prodigy, as his first-class certificates showed; at twenty his facility in the subject was striking. The fact that England was at war was at least postponing his specializing; a prolonged period of peace would almost inevitably have resulted in his being confined to desk work in a state of voluntary servitude, hugging his chains, respected, perhaps, in his own speciality, but unknown beyond a limited circle. In those conditions he would have been likely to forget that war is not a clash of mathematical formulae, but a contest waged by men of flesh and blood and brain. If anything would help to keep him human, to develop him into a wise leader of men instead of into a learned computer, it was his present command, where under his own eye he could see formulae and machinery and men in action together. The proving ground and the testing station could confirm or destroy theories about internal pressures and the toughness of armour plate, but only the proving ground of war could test men. The most beautiful machines, the most elaborate devices, were useless if the men who handled them were badly trained or shaken by fear, and there was the interesting point that the more complex the machinery, and the more human effort it saved, and the more exactly it performed its functions, the greater need there was for heroes to handle it. Not mere individual heroes either, but a whole team of heroes. Disaster would be the result of a weak link anywhere along the long chain of the ship's organization. A frightened rangetaker, a jumpy Marine bandsman at the Transmitting Station table, a shaken steward in the magazine, and all the elaborate mechanism, the marvellous optical instruments, the cannons that cost a king's ransom, and the machine which embodied the ingenuity of generations, were all of them useless. It would be better then if there had never been any development in gunnery, and they were still in the days when the gunnery handbook made use of the elastic expression, 'take about a shovelful of powder'. Euclid had pointed out that the whole is equal to the sum of all its parts, and it was dawning upon Coxe that there was not merely a mathematical application of that axiom.

With a new eye he saw Numbers Four and Five ram home the shell into the left-hand gun; he was familiar with the very abstruse mathematics involved in calculations regarding compensation for wear at the breech of the gun, and those calculations always assumed that the projectile would be firmly seated against the rifling. Some dry-as-dust individual at Woolwich made those calculations, some withered officer with rings on his sleeve and gold oak-leaves on his cap brim, but unless Number Five, there, the hairy individual with the crossed flags of England and France tattooed on his forearms, kept his head and wielded the rammer efficiently, those calculations might as well never have been put on paper.

Number Six was pushing in the charge. It had never occurred to Coxe before that the instructions which ordered this were no guarantee that it would be done. Number Six might drop the charge, or if his hands were shaking or he was not seaman enough to keep his footing, he might break it open against the sharp edge. Number Six might even become frightened enough to dash out of the turret and run below to take shelter under the main deck–that was a possibility that had never crossed Coxe's mind before, he realized, and yet it was a possibility. Number Six had a tendency to boils on the back of his neck; Coxe had never noticed that before either, but a man who could suffer from boils was a man and not a piece of machinery that shoved the propellant up the breech. Number Six–what the devil was his name? Stokes? Something like that. No, it was Merivale, of course–Number Six was a fallible human being. Coxe became guiltily conscious that it was even conceivable that Number Six would be less likely to run away when he should be pushing in charges if the officer of the quarters did not call him Stokes when his name was Merivale. That was not something that could be reduced to a mathematical formula. It was courage, morale, *esprit de corps*, discipline–of a sudden these were pregnant words for Coxe now.

He turned with a fresh interest to Number Two, who was closing the breech. Coxe was nearly sure that Number Two's name was Hammond. He really must make an effort to remember. Hammond–if that was his name–was having trouble with his wife. The matter had come up when the Commander was interviewing request-men. Some neighbour, officious or well-intentioned or spiteful or over-moral, had written to Hammond telling him about nocturnal visitors to Hammond's home. White-faced and sick with despair, on the sunny quarter-deck, Hammond had admitted to the Commander that he would not be surprised if the accusation were true. 'She was like that,' said Hammond. Once she had promised that it would never occur again, and Hammond had believed her, but standing before the Commander, Hammond had reluctantly admitted that he had been an optimistic fool; yet clearly that had not made it easier for Hammond, his life in ruins, and only half-hearted even now in his desire to cut off his allotment of pay to the wife he was still, obviously, besotted about.

A man whose wife was being unfaithful to him was liable to neglect his business. Coxe was academically aware of that even though he could not conceive of anything, certainly not domestic unhappiness, coming between him and gunnery. He darted a glance to see that Hammond had inserted the tube and masked the vent. Hammond swung the breech shut and closed the interruptor.

'Ready!' he said quietly–Number Two at the other gun shouted the word excitedly. Hammond was cool; cold might be a better word for it. It might be merely the deadly coldness of an embittered man; but, on the other hand, it might be the effect of discipline and training. Coxe actually found himself wondering which it was.

Shell and charge were in the gun now. Magazine and shell-room and handing-room, lobby and turret, had all made their contribution. So had every man in the ship, from Hobbs down in the shaft tunnel to the Captain on the bridge and Whipple at the masthead. The fact that the shell now lying in the breech of the left-hand gun 'A' turret was going assuredly to alter the history of the world was something to the credit of every one of them. The whole is equal to the sum of all its parts.

'Shoot!' said the Gunnery Lieutenant for the hundredth time that day. His fighting blood was still roused; the long battle had not brought weariness or lassitude. He controlled and directed this broadside as thoroughly as he had controlled the first.

The elevation and deflection of the guns was fixed by the Transmitting Station; this broadside meant no more and no less to the men there than any other in the long fight. The Marine bandsmen followed their pointers and Mr Kaile handled his complex orchestra as always, and the fire gong rang for the hundredth time in the Transmitting Station as Chief Petty Officer O'Flaherty in the Director Control Tower obeyed the Gunnery Lieutenant's order and pressed the trigger, to fire the broadside that would decide the future of neutral Ireland just as much as that of the rest of the belligerent world. The tubes heated, the charges exploded, and the four shells went shrieking over nine thousand yards of sea to their destined ends. Three of them missed, and the fourth one–the shell from the left-hand gun in 'A' turret–hit. The spotters in *Artemis* recorded 'straddle' and set themselves in ignorance of what that straddle meant to observe the next fall of shot.

25

FROM THE CAPTAIN'S REPORT

. . . until the enemy turned away . . .

Kapitän-sur-See Helmuth von Bödicke stood on the signal bridge of His Italian Majesty's battleship *Legnano* with Vice-Ammiráglio Gasparo Gaetano Nocentini. They were out of earshot of their staffs, who stood decently back so as not to overhear the conversation of the two great men, who were talking French to each other; only when French failed them did they turn and summon Korvetten Kápitan Klein and Luogotenènte Lorenzetti to translate for them from German into Italian and from Italian into German. At the time when von Bödicke was young enough to learn languages it never occurred to any German naval officer that it might some day be specially useful to speak Italian, and Nocentini had learned French in the nursery and had never had either the desire or the intention to acquire the language of the barbarians of the north.

The signal bridge in *Legnano* was windy and exposed, but it was the most convenient place in the ship for the commanding admiral; the conning tower was too crowded and its view too limited, while the signal bridge afforded the most rapid means of communication with the rest of the fleet. On the port side where Bödicke and Nocentini stood they had the best view of whatever was visible. Abeam of them was the immensely long black smudge of the smoke screen which the English had laid down, and against that background, vague and shadowy, were the English light cruisers, screened from view during much of the time by the splashes thrown up by the Italian salvoes. Fine on the port bow were the English destroyers, just wheeling round like swallows on the wing, after presumably launching their torpedoes against the Italian line. Astern of *Legnano* came the other Italian ships, the battleship *San Martino*, the heavy cruisers and the light cruisers. What Bödicke and Nocentini could not see from the port side of the signal bridge were the Italian destroyers advancing too late against the English destroyers, but as they undoubtedly were too late it did not matter so much that they could not be seen.

The din that assailed the ears of the men on the signal bridge was enormous, frightful. Every twenty-five seconds the fifteen-inch guns let loose a salvo louder than the loudest thunderclap, whose tremendous detonation shook them like a violent blow, and, deep-toned behind them, *San Martino*'s big guns echoed those salvoes. These were intermittent noises; the din of the secondary armament went on without cessation, six-inch and four-inch and twelve-pounder all banging away as fast as they could be loaded and fired in the endeavour to beat back the destroyer attack. It was ear-splitting and made it hard to think clearly. And all round the ship were raining the broadsides from the English light cruiser, deluging the decks with splashes, or bursting against the armour with a piercing crash, straddling the ship so closely that the shells that passed overhead were audible through the detonations of the secondary armament.

Von Bödicke trained his glasses on the leading English cruiser. She was badly on fire aft, with thick smoke pouring out of her, and yet she was still firing superbly and fast. The rest of the line appeared to have suffered little damage, which was quite absurd seeing how much they had been under fire. These excitable Italians could never steady themselves quickly enough to hit an elusive target. Brave enough men, perhaps (presumably because of the infiltration of Nordic blood into their Mediterranean veins), but unsteady. He experienced a momentary feeling of helplessness when he thought of his mission; he had been sent here to crush the British fleet by the aid of the Italian, and now he was conscious of the weakness of the tool he had to employ. He was like a man setting out to move a heavy rock and finding his crowbar buckling in his hand.

He let his glasses hang by their cord from his neck, and he plucked at the torpedo beard he wore as a tribute to the memory of von Hipper. Naval warfare, a naval battle, was like a game of poker. A good hand was of no avail if it met a better; confronted with four of a kind a full house was as unprofitable as a pair of deuces; the winner scooped the pool and the loser had nothing. In land warfare, or in air warfare, the loser might hope for a profitable defeat, to gain so much time or to inflict so much loss as to nullify the other's victory, but at sea it was all or nothing.

It was all or nothing for him, von Bödicke, as well. Von Bödicke remembered receiving supplementary verbal orders at the Marineamt, and the thin lips and the almost colourless eyes of Admiral Fricke, the Chief of the Naval Staff. He could expect no mercy from Fricke if he were to fail, and it was no comfort to think that Fricke could expect no mercy either. Fricke was primarily a Nazi and only secondarily a naval officer, who had won his position through all the clashes and fierce jealousies of the Party. If the command of the Mediterranean were not achieved other ambitious young men would pull Fricke down. And Fricke would die, of heart disease or a motoring accident, for a man who tried for power by way of the Party staked his life on the result; successful rivals would never run the risk of his regaining power and avenging himself, nor would the Führer. The blackguards of the Party acted on the principle that dead men knife no one in the back. Fricke would die, and old von Bödicke would merely be ruined, put on beggarly retired pay under police supervision. He would not even have enough to eat, for he would be a useless mouth, on the lowest scale of rations, and doomed to slow starvation because no one would help a man with no return favours in his gift to supplement his diet illegally. He turned to Nocentini beside him.

'We must turn towards the enemy, your excellency,' he said.

Nocentini looked down at von Bödicke, Nocentini tall and gangling and clean-shaven, von Bödicke short and stocky with a little bristling beard. Nocentini had received verbal instructions as well, and his came direct from the lips of Il Duce. Il Duce had been most explicit on the point that nothing was to be risked. An easy victory was to be grasped at eagerly, but only as long as there was no prospect of loss. The battleships with which Nocentini was entrusted were the only ones left serviceable in the Italian navy, and very precious in consequence. Il Duce had far-reaching theories about war; one was that it was most necessary to husband one's strength against the possible demands of an always dangerous future, and the other was that by biding one's time one always found opportunities to pick up highly profitable gains for almost nothing as long as one had not dissipated one's strength prematurely. Il Duce had been most eloquent about this, making his points one after the other with much slapping of his fat white hands on the table while the sweat made his flabby jowls shine in the lamplight. He preached caution in the privacy of his office with just as much fervour as he preached recklessness from his balcony. But the fervour had an unhappy ring, and the arguments were those of a beaten man, of a tired man. Il Duce was growing old.

That was one of the considerations Nocentini had to bear in mind. One of these days Il Duce would die, and no one could tell what régime would find itself in power; there might be prolonged chaos. A powerful fleet would be a potent factor in the struggle, and Nocentini had ideas about how to use it. So he was in complete agreement with the Chief of the State about the desirability of easy victories and the necessity to avoid crippling losses. He knew that it was only with the utmost reluctance that Il Duce had consented to risking the fleet three hundred miles from its base, even when the Germans, in their usual cocksure fashion, had assured him that the English had no capital ships whatever available in the Eastern Mediterranean. Nocentini fancied that the Germans had been using a great deal of pressure, threatening in the event of a refusal to cut down still further the tiny shipments of coal that just enabled Italian civilization to exist.

If he could wipe out this British squadron and its convoy it would add to his own prestige and that of the fleet, but it would restore something to the prestige of Il Duce as well. The wiping out would not be easy, for the English had already shown their readiness to fight to the last. Those early moves of his, cautious feelers to determine the British attitude, had proved this. To turn towards the enemy, to plunge into the smoke screen, would mean a muddled battle, an undignified scuffle, and possibly heavy losses in a close-range action. Nocentini simply did not believe the optimistic reports with which the Naval Intelligence kept bombarding him regarding the extremities to which Malta was reduced. He was not a natural optimist; and with regard to Malta, he had the unhappy suspicion that its fall would be just another chestnut pulled out of the fire for the benefit of the Germans.

Italy? Nocentini was not sure now what Italy was. Not Mussolini, assuredly. The vulgarian who had built up the Italian fleet, who had given it more men and more money than Nocentini had ever dreamed of, had something once to recommend him. But the frightened worn-out man, prematurely old, cowering in the Quirinal, pathetically pleading with Nocentini to be cautious, and with the haunting fear of the Nazis to be read in his face, was not a leader to be followed with devotion, and certainly not the embodiment of the Italy which Nocentini vaguely dreamed about.

The continuous crash of the guns, the constant arrival of reports, the very wind that whipped round their ears, confused Nocentini's mind and made thinking difficult. He stood and gazed down at von Bödicke, wasting precious seconds while the torpedoes were actually on their way towards them.

'Your Excellency,' said von Bödicke, 'it is absolutely necessary that you should give the order.'

Von Bödicke was in a desperate mood. He was disillusioned on every side. He suspected a policy of deliberate obstruction. In the opening moves of the battle heavy smoke had poured from the funnels first of this ship and then of that one prematurely revealing the position of the fleet. Any engineer ought to be ashamed of himself for permitting such a thing to happen; the lowest *maschinist-maat* in the German navy would know better. He had goaded Nocentini into signalling reprimands, and the replies that came back had been decidedly unsettling. One captain had blamed the oil fuel, and in the wording of his message had insolently suggested that the fuel's defects were due to the culpable carelessness of the German authorities who had supplied it. The worst of that suggestion was that it was possibly true; von Bödicke knew a little about Albert Speer, who made use of his position as Oil Fuel Controller to make profits for the dummy company which was really Albert Speer. With boiler-room crews as excitable as the Italians, it was too much to expect that they should keep their heads clear enough to deal instantly and accurately with crises like fluctuations in the quality of the oil in the pipes.

These damned Italians were all alike. They were jumpy and excitable. Most of them had had too little training at sea either to be able to master seasickness or to be able to carry out their duties in a crisis with a seaway running. They had been firing away at the cruisers all this time and hardly scored a hit–when the action began he had visited turrets and gunnery control towers, to find officers and men chattering like apes and getting in each other's way. Von Bödicke suspected that half the salvoes they fired off had been unaimed as a result of inefficiency on the part of the guns' crews or the gunnery control crews; it was too much to expect that somewhere along the complicated chain there would not be at least one weak link–especially as the veteran seamen were being drained away from the ships to make good the steady losses in submarine crews.

Von Bödicke's desperation was being eaten away by a growing weariness. He hated Fricke for sending him on this thankless duty. Victory would confirm Fricke in his position; and Bödicke suddenly realized that bloody defeat might do the same. If he, Bödicke, were able to persuade Nocentini to make an attack, and this *Legnano* were to be sunk, and Bödicke along with her, Bödicke having done his best and the Italian navy proved to be obviously not up to its work, then no one could possibly blame Fricke. He would continue to lord it at the Marineamt. Self-pity came to soften von Bödicke's desperations as well. It was a frightful dilemma in which he found himself. This was no simple marine problem which he faced. It was a complex of political and personal factors intricately entangled. With a German fleet under his command, in German waters, he would not hesitate for a moment about what to do, but out here in the Mediterranean with these Italians it was quite different. The very name of the ship in which he found himself was an insult to Germany. Legnano was the name of the battlefield where der Alte Barbarossa had by chance met with defeat at the hands of the Lombard League. Mussolini had no business to recall to memory that unfortunate accident of seven hundred years ago. But it was just like the Italians; when they decided to call their battleships after Italian victories they soon found themselves running out of names. *San Martino* astern was named after a battle which was really an Austrian victory, terminated by an Austrian retreat merely because of the success of the French on the other battlefield of Solferino. At Vittorio Veneto the decisive blow was struck by an English army, and then only after Austria had been stabbed in the back by the Jews and separatists. Von Bödicke remembered the sneer in which German naval officers so often indulged when they asked the rhetorical question why the Italians had named no battleship of theirs after Caporetto. The question was on the tip of his tongue as he looked at Nocentini, so bitter was his mood.

He had asked to have the Italian fleet turned towards the enemy, but he had no sooner said the words when he experienced a revulsion of spirit. He could not recall them, but he was in two minds about it. He simply did not know what he wanted. He was balanced on a knife edge of indecision, and Nocentini, looking down at him, knew it telepathically. He was just as undetermined, just as unsettled in his mind as was Bödicke. The minutest influence would decide him, like Bödicke, one way or the other.

'We must turn either towards or away,' said Nocentini slowly, groping with difficulty, in his dazed preoccupation, for the French words.

He would have liked more time to discuss it, so as to postpone the moment of decision, but he knew that was vain. It was twenty seconds at least since the British destroyers had launched their torpedoes. Nocentini looked over at the British squadron, at the smoke-wreathed silhouettes aflame with gun flashes. He knew much about the British Navy, and in that clairvoyant moment he visualized the disciplined sailors bending to their work, the shells quietly passed up from the magazine, the rapid loading and the accurate firing. And at that moment there was flung into the scale that factor that tipped it down and swayed the balance of von Bödicke's and Nocentini's hesitating minds. A six-inch shell struck full upon 'B' turret, below them and forward of them, and burst against the twelve-inch steel.

To the ship itself it did no particular damage. It did not slow the working of the turret; in fact, it left hardly a mark on the diamond-hard steel. Its fragment sang viciously through the air, ripping up planking here and cutting through a stanchion there, but they found no one in an exposed position, and they took no lives. The force of its explosion shook the group on the signal bridge, they felt the hot breath of its flame, and their nostrils were filled with the penetrating stink of its fumes, but they were unhurt. Perhaps of all the hits scored by *Artemis*'s guns this one did the least physical damage, but for all that it was the one which turned the scale. All the other shells fired by *Artemis* had played their part, had leaded the scale so far, had worked upon the minds of Nocentini and von Bödicke, convincing them that here were no easy victims, no weak-minded enemies to be driven off by a mere show of force; but it was this last shell, which Colquhoun had lifted so casually, and which Mobbs and Filmore had sent up to 'A' turret with their minds occupied by Ransome's peevishness, and upon which Sub-Lieutenant Coxe had cast an unseeing eye while Merivale rammed it home, it was this shell bursting vainly against the turret that actually decided the history of the world.

Nocentini and von Bödicke looked at each other again as they steadied themselves after the explosion. Each was unhurt, each of them hoped breathlessly in his heart of hearts that the other was not. For one second more they hesitated, each hoping that the other would assume the responsibility for the next move, and during that second each of them read the added weakness in the other's face, and they both of them realized that there was no need to state formally what was in their minds. It would be better not to do so, they both decided; it gave each of them more chance to shuffle off the blame–if there was to be blame–upon the other. They did not meet each other's eyes after that; von Bödicke looked at Klein while Nocentini turned to Lorenzetti.

'Signal all ships turn together eight points to starboard,' said Nocentini. He was shoulder to shoulder with von Bödicke, and he did his best to convey by his bearing the impression that the two of them were in agreement on the decision, while von Bödicke, the moment he heard the decisive words tried to put himself in an attitude of ineffective protest without attracting Nocentini's attention to it.

The flags ran up to the yardarm, flapped there in the smoke, were answered and were hauled down. Slowly *Legnano* turned her ponderous bulk about, her bows towards Italy, her stern to the British squadron.

'We had to do it,' said Nocentini. 'Otherwise we would have crossed the course of the torpedoes.'

Von Bödicke kept his mouth shut; he only just grasped the meaning of the Italian words, and he was not going to commit himself to anything that might later be construed as approval. He felt much happier in the probability that Nocentini could be saddled with the blame. He walked stiffly to the other end of the bridge, meeting no one's eye as the staffs made way for him, and for Nocentini at his elbow.

From the starboard wing of the bridge he could look down the long line abreast of the Italian fleet. The heavy cruiser on the far side of *San Martino* was still badly on fire. That would be part of his defence, if he should need defence. The guns had fallen silent, for the sudden change of course had disconcerted the trainers, and only half of *Legnano*'s armament could bear on a target right astern. And yet at that very moment another broadside from the British came crashing home as though the ship were suddenly struck by a Titanic sledgehammer. Some fragment hurled by the explosion rang loudly against the stanchion at his side. It was the last straw to von Bödicke that the British should persist in continuing the fight when he had allowed it to be broken off on the Italian side. He wanted to relax, to allow the tension to lessen, and yet the British were set upon continuing the action to the last possible moment.

Legnano's upperworks aft were riven into picturesque ruin, he saw. No vital damage done, but enough to make a deep impression on any civilian who might see it. That was all to the good. But Klein knew better. Klein, who had crossed the bridge and was standing at his elbow again, and whom he suspected strongly of being a spy on behalf of Fricke. Von Bödicke hated Klein.

'They are holding their course,' said Nocentini from behind his binoculars, which were trained on the British cruisers. He was speaking careful French, and von Bödicke realized that although the words were apparently addressed to him, Nocentini meant them to be recorded by Klein. 'They will not leave their smoke screen.'

'That is clear,' said von Bödicke, agreeing speedily. He hoped as he spoke them Klein would not perceive the stilted artificiality of his tone; it was ingenious of Nocentini to suggest that the turn-away was really planned to lure the British cruisers away from their smoke screen.

'We will re-form line ahead when the torpedoes have passed,' said Nocentini.

'Of course,' said von Bödicke. He had himself under control now. He kept his eyes steadily on the Italian and did now allow them to waver towards Klein for a moment. It was undignified and sordid, but defeat is always undignified and sordid. They were beaten men.

They were already out of range of the British cruisers, and the distance was increasing every minute. When they should form line ahead again and circle round to reopen the engagement it would be nearly dark, and no sane officer would court a night action with an inferior force. Someone was yelling madly from the masthead, his high-pitched voice clearly audible from the signal bridge, although von Bödicke could not understand the excited Italian. *Legnano* swung ponderously round again, under full helm, first to port and then to starboard–it was that, combined with the rush of the Italian officers to the side, and the way they peered down at the water, which told von Bödicke that the track of a torpedo had been sighted, and that *Legnano* was manoeuvring to avoid it. He caught his breath quickly. The gestures of the Italians showed that the torpedo had passed, and then directly afterwards there came the roar of an explosion to split the eardrums. The torpedo which *Legnano* had avoided had struck *San Martino* full in the side. An enormous column of water, higher than the funnel top, obscured the battleship momentarily before it cascaded back into the sea and revealed her with smoke pouring out of her side and listing perceptibly.

He caught Nocentini's eye again as the Admiral stood rapping out orders. The anxiety and strain had gone from the man's face. He was dealing with a familiar emergency, one with which he was competent to deal. Salving and protecting an injured ship was not like carrying the burden of the responsibility of battle. And not only that, but the problems of battle were solved for him. No one could expect him to leave an injured Dreadnought to shift for herself while he turned and re-engaged the enemy. No one could expect him to. A Nelson or a Beatty might take the risk, but no man could be condemned for not being a Nelson or Beatty. Nocentini actually smiled a little as he met von Bödicke's eye, and von Bödicke smiled back. Whatever happened now, they had at least an explanation and an excuse.

26

FROM THE CAPTAIN'S REPORT

. . . and the action terminated.

The Captain had known temptation. With *Artemis* all ablaze aft, and one turret out of action, it was a strain to keep her in action, dodging the continual salvoes of the enemy. The very din of the continual broadsides was exhausting. Close at hand, on the port side, was the shelter of the smoke screen. He had only to utter two words and *Artemis* could dive into it just as she had done before. There would be a relief from strain and danger and responsibility, and the thought even of relief that might be only momentary was alluring. And the whole principle of the tactics of the British cruisers was to make use of the smoke screen as it rolled down on the Italian line; now that the destroyers had delivered their attack and turned back would be a fitting moment, ostensibly, for a temporary withdrawal. That was the temptation on the one hand, while on the other was the doubt of his own judgement that it was desirable to continue in action. That might be just fighting madness. He knew that his judgement might be clouded, that this decision of his to keep his guns firing might be the result of mere berserk rage. Yet his instinct told him that it was not so.

His instinct; something developed in him by years of study of his profession, of deep reading and of mental digestion of innumerable lessons, supplemented by his inborn qualities. That instinct told him that this was the crisis of the battle, the moment when one side or the other must give way. He knew that he had only to hold on a little longer–after that a little longer still, perhaps–for the battle to be decided. The whole series of thoughts, from the decision to cover the retreat of the destroyers to the momentary doubt, and then back again to the decision to maintain the action took only the briefest possible time, two or three seconds at most.

It was not to the discredit of the Captain that he should have experienced that two or three seconds of doubt, but to his credit. Had he not been tried so far as that it would have been no trial at all. War is something to try the very strongest, and it is then that those crack who are almost the strongest, the Nocentinis and the von Bödickes, oppressed by a complexity of motives.

The Captain was aware that his pipe was empty, and that he wanted to refill and relight it, but he did not want to take his binoculars from his eyes. The guns of 'A' and 'B' turrets roared out below him; the Captain did not know that from the left-hand gun of 'A' turret had flown the decisive shell. He saw the flight of the broadside, and he saw the yellow flash of the hit. Then, as another broadside roared out disregarded, he saw the long silhouette of the leading Italian battleship foreshorten and alter, the two funnels blend into one, the stern swinging towards him and the bow away. The Captain gulped excitedly. He traversed his binoculars round. Every Italian ship had her stern to him; it was a withdrawal, a retreat; the Italian flagship was not merely trying to disconnect the English gunners. This was victory.

He turned his gaze back to the Italian flagship in time to see the flash of another hit upon her. Good gunnery, that, to hit at that extreme range and with the range altering so fast. He dropped his glasses on his chest and took out pipe and pouch, feeding tobacco into the bowl with his long sensitive fingers, but his eyes still strained after the distant shapes on the horizon. They had turned away. They were refusing battle. The Captain knew in his bones that they would never turn back again to reopen the fight. A motive strong enough to induce them to break off the fight would be amply strong enough to keep them from renewing it; one way or the other they would find excuses for themselves.

His pipe was filled, and he was just reaching for his matches when the voice pipe buzzer sounded:

'Director Control,' said the pipe. 'The enemy is out of range.'

'Thank you, Guns,' said the Captain. 'I have no orders for you at present.'

The Chief Yeoman of Signals saluted.

'I think I saw a torpedo 'it on the second ship from the left,' he said, 'while you was speaking.'

'Thank you,' said the Captain again.

He was about to take up his binoculars to look, but he changed his mind and felt for his matches instead. He could afford to be prodigal of his time and his attention now. Even a torpedo hit on a Dreadnought was nothing in the scale compared with the fact of the Italian turn-away. The tobacco tasted good as he drew the flame of the match down upon it, stoppered it down with the finger that long use had rendered comparatively fireproof, and drew on the flame again. He breathed out a lungful of smoke and carefully dropped the stump of the match into the spit-kid. The silence and the cessation of the enemy's fire were ceasing to be oppressive; the normal sounds of the ship's progress, the noise of the sea under the bows and of the wind about his ears, were asserting themselves.

So this was victory. The proof that the history of the world had reached a turning-point was that he was conscious again of the wind about his ears. History books would never write about today. Even sober, scientific historians needed some more solid fact on which to hang a theme; a few ships sunk and a few thousand men killed, not a mere successful skirmish round half a dozen transports. Even in a month's time the memory of today would be faded and forgotten by the world. Two lines in a communiqué, a few remarks by appreciative commentators, and then oblivion.

Somewhere out in the Russian plain Ivan Ivanovich, crouching in a hole in the dusty earth, and looking along the sights of his anti-tank gun, would never know about *Artemis* and her sisters. Ivan Ivanovich might comment on the slightness of the aerial attack, on the scarcity of hostile dive bombers; it might even occur to him as a realist that a few well-placed bombs, wiping out him and his fellows, could clear the way into Moscow for Hitler, but even as a realist Ivan Ivanovich had never heard of *Artemis*, and never would hear.

To Hitler, Malta was a prize still more desirable than Moscow, and more vital to his existence. With the failure of the Italian navy to get it for him he would have to use his own air force; a thousand planes, and a ground staff scores of thousands strong would have to be transferred from the Russian front to Italy in the desperate need to conquer every bastion that could buttress his top-heavy empire. A thousand planes; planes that could blind the Russian command, planes that could blast a path through the Russian lines, planes that could succour isolated detachments and supply advance guards, planes that could hunt Russian guerilla forces far in the rear of the Germans or menace Russian communications far in advance. The Captain had no doubt whatever that as a result of today's work those thousand planes would be brought south.

Whether they would achieve their object or not was more doubtful. The Captain had the feeling that the advocates of air power talked about today as if it were tomorrow. Tomorrow command of the air might take the place of command of the sea, but this was today. Today those half-dozen fat transports wallowing along on the far side of the smoke screen were on their way to Malta, and it was today they had to be stopped, if at all. Today the convoys were still pouring in to English harbours, while across a tiny strip of water lay an enemy whose greatest ambition was to prevent them from doing so. It was sea power that brought them safely in. Tomorrow it might be air power; tomorrow the Captain might be an antiquated old fogey, as useless as a pikeman on a modern battlefield, but the war was being fought today, today, today. Rommel in Libya clamouring for reinforcement could have everything his heart desired if the British Navy did not interfere. The crippling of the American Navy at Pearl Harbor had put an eighth of the world's population and a quarter of the world's surface temporarily at the mercy of Japan and her twelve Dreadnoughts. Ships–ships and the men in them–were still deciding the fate of the world. The Arab fertilizing date palms at Basra, the Negro trading cattle for a new wife in Central Africa, the gaucho riding the Argentine pampas, did so under the protection of the British Navy, of which the Captain and his ship were a minor fraction, one of many parts whose sum was equal to the whole.

'Signal from the flagship, sir,' said the Chief Yeoman of Signals, reading if off through his glass: 'Resume–convoy–formation.'

'Acknowledge,' said the Captain.

He gave the order to turn *Artemis* back towards the transports, back through the smoke screen which had served them so well. The revolution indicator rang down a reduction of speed, and peace seemed to settle closer about the ship as the vibration caused by full speed died away. Only a tiny bit of the sun was left, a segment of gold on the clear horizon–ten seconds more and it would be gone and night would close in. The Italians were already invisible from the bridge, and the Captain strode abruptly over to the masthead voice pipe.

'Masthead,' said the tube to him in answer to his buzz. It was Ordinary Seaman Whipple's voice.

'Can you see anything of the enemy?' asked the Captain.

'Only just in sight, sir. They're still heading away from us. They'll be gone in a minute.'

They were close clipped, incisive sentences which Whipple used. Whipple was conscious of victory, too. He was fighting for an ideal, and he was fanatical about that ideal, and this afternoon's work had brought that ideal a great deal closer. Yet Whipple did not indulge in idle exhilaration. The fact that he had to fight for his ideal, that the generation preceding his had once had the same ideal in their grasp and allowed it to slip through their fingers, had left him without illusions. Whipple was ready to go on fighting. He knew there was still a long bitter struggle ahead before final victory, and he guessed that after victory it would be another bitter struggle to put it to the best use, to forward the ideal, and he was ready for both struggles.

The Captain in his present clairvoyant mood could sense all this in the tone of Whipple's voice, and he drew once, meditatively, on his pipe before he turned away. One part of his mind was concerned in practical fashion with the future promotion of Whipple to Leading Seaman; the other was thinking how Whipple's generation, twenty years younger than his own, must take up the task of building the good of the new world as unfalteringly as they were applying themselves to the task of tearing down the evil of the old world, in each case facing random defeat, and unexpected disappointment, and peril and self-sacrifice, with selfless self-discipline.

As he looked up from the voice pipe his eyes met those of his secretary.

'Congratulations, sir,' said Jerningham.

So Jerningham was aware of the importance of today, too. The rest of the ship's company, going quietly about their duties, had not yet attained to that realization. But it was to be expected of Jerningham. His civilian background, the breadth of his experience and the liveliness of his imagination, made him able–when he was not too closely concerned personally–to take a wide view of the war, and to realize how proper attention to his own duties would help Ivan Ivanovich in his hole in the ground, of Lai Chao tearing up a railway line in Shantung. There was a moment of sympathy between Jerningham and the Captain, during which brief space of time they were *en rapport*, each appreciative of the other.

'Thank you, Jerningham,' said the Captain.

This was no time to relax, to indulge either in futile congratulations or in idle speculation. The smoke screen suddenly engulfed the ship; it was not nearly as dense as when it had first been laid, but with the rapid approach of night now that the sun was below the horizon the darkness inside the smoke screen was intense. The Captain took three strides in the darkness to the end of the bridge and craned his neck to look aft. There was only the faintest glow to be seen of the fire which had raged there, and a few more minutes with the hoses would extinguish even that.

They emerged into the evening light again; the scant minute during which they had been in the smoke screen seemed to have brought night far closer. There was just light enough to see how the fires and the enemy's hits had left the whole after third of the ship above water-line a tangle of burnt-out steel, a nightmare of buckled plates and twisted girders, desolate and dead.

Artemis under the orders of the Navigating Lieutenant was wheeling round to take the station allotted her by the standing orders for convoy escort at night. It was as well that the fires had been subdued, for otherwise the flames would be a welcoming beacon inviting a torpedo. The aeroplanes had attacked in the morning; in the afternoon they had beaten off the surface ships; tonight they would have to be on their guard against submarines, for the enemy, like the devil, was capable of taking many forms. One battle completed, one victory achieved, merely meant that *Artemis* and her men must plunge headlong into the next, into the long struggle of sea power against tyranny; the struggle that the Greeks had waged at Salamis, that the Captain's ancestors had waged against the Armada of Spain, against the fleets of Louis XIV and Napoleon and Wilhelm II, the long struggle which some day would have an end, but not now, and not for months and years to come. And even when it should end the freedom which the struggle would win could only be secured by eternal vigilance, eternal probity, eternal good will, and eternal honesty of purpose. That would be the hardest lesson of it; peace would be a severer test of mankind even than war. Perhaps mankind would pass that test when the time came; and when that time came (the Captain said to himself) he would fight to the last, he would die in the last ditch, before he would compromise in the slightest with the blind or secret enemies of freedom and justice. He must remember this mood; when he became an old man he must remember it. He must remember in time to come how nothing now was further from his thoughts than the least yielding to the open enemies of mankind, and that would help to keep him from the least indolent or careless or cynical yielding in that future.

The Captain suddenly tensed himself as his roving eyes caught sight of a twinkle of light ahead, and then he was able to relax again and even smile a little to himself in the twilight. For that was the evening star shining out over the Mediterranean.

Mr Midshipman Hornblower

C. S. Forester

I

THE EVEN CHANCE

A January gale was roaring up the Channel, blustering loudly, and bearing in its bosom rain squalls whose big drops rattled loudly on the tarpaulin clothing of those among the officers and men whose duties kept them on deck. So hard and so long had the gale blown that even in the sheltered waters of Spithead the battleship moved uneasily at her anchors, pitching a little in the choppy seas, and snubbing herself against the tautened cables with unexpected jerks. A shore boat was on its way out to her, propelled by oars in the hands of two sturdy women; it danced madly on the steep little waves, now and then putting its nose into one and sending a sheet of spray flying aft. The oarswoman in the bow knew her business, and with rapid glances over her shoulder not only kept the boat on its course but turned the bows into the worst of the waves to keep from capsizing. It slowly drew up along the starboard side of the *Justinian*, and as it approached the mainchains the midshipman of the watch hailed it.

'Aye aye' came back the answering hail from the lusty lungs of the woman at the stroke oar; by the curious and ages-old convention of the Navy the reply meant that the boat had an officer on board–presumably the huddled figure in the sternsheets looking more like a heap of trash with a boat-cloak thrown over it.

That was as much as Mr Masters, the lieutenant of the watch, could see; he was sheltering as best he could in the lee of the mizzen-mast bitts, and in obedience to the order of the midshipman of the watch the boat drew up towards the mainchains and passed out of his sight. There was a long delay; apparently the officer had some difficulty in getting up the ship's side. At last the boat reappeared in Masters's field of vision; the women had shoved off and were setting a scrap of lugsail, under which the boat, now without its passenger, went swooping back towards Portsmouth, leaping on the waves like a steeplechaser. As it departed Mr Masters became aware of the near approach of someone along the quarterdeck; it was the new arrival under the escort of the midshipman of the watch, who, after pointing Masters out, retired to the mainchains again. Mr Masters had served in the Navy until his hair was white; he was lucky to have received his commission as lieutenant, and he had long known that he would never receive one as captain, but the knowledge had not greatly embittered him, and he diverted his mind by the study of his fellow men.

So he looked with attention at the approaching figure. It was that of a skinny young man only just leaving boyhood behind, something above middle height, with feet whose adolescent proportions to his size were accentuated by the thinness of his legs and his big half-boots. His gawkiness called attention to his hands and elbows. The newcomer was dressed in a badly fitting uniform which was soaked right through by the spray; a skinny neck stuck out of the high stock, and above the neck was a white bony face. A white face was a rarity on the deck of a ship of war, whose crew soon tanned to a deep mahogany, but this face was not merely white; in the hollow cheeks there was a faint shade of green–clearly the newcomer had experienced seasickness in his passage out in the shore boat. Set in the white face were a pair of dark eyes which by contrast looked like holes cut in a sheet of paper; Masters noted with a slight stirring of interest that the eyes, despite their owner's seasickness, were looking about keenly, taking in what were obviously new sights; there was a curiosity and interest there which could not be repressed and which continued to function notwithstanding either seasickness or shyness, and Mr Masters surmised in his far-fetched fashion that this boy had a vein of caution or foresight in his temperament and was already studying his new surroundings with a view to being prepared for his next experiences. So might Daniel have looked about him at the lions when he first entered their den.

The dark eyes met Masters's, and the gawky figure came to a halt, raising a hand selfconsciously to the brim of his dripping hat. His mouth opened and tried to say something, but closed again without achieving its object as shyness overcame him, but then the newcomer nerved himself afresh and forced himself to say the formal words he had been coached to utter.

'Come aboard, sir.'

'Your name?' asked Masters, after waiting for it for a moment.

'H-Horatio Hornblower, sir. Midshipman,' stuttered the boy.

'Very good, Mr Hornblower,' said Masters, with the equally formal response. 'Did you bring your dunnage aboard with you?'

Hornblower had never heard that word before, but he still had enough of his wits about him to deduce what it meant.

'My sea chest, sir. It's–it's forrard, at the entry port.'

Hornblower said these things with the barest hesitation; he knew that at sea they said them, that they pronounced the word 'forward' like that, and that he had come on board through the 'entry port', but it called for a slight effort to utter them himself.

'I'll see that it's sent below,' said Masters. 'And that's where you'd better go, too. The captain's ashore, and the first lieutenant's orders were that he's not to be called on any account before eight bells, so I advise you, Mr Hornblower, to get out of those wet clothes while you can.'

'Yes, sir,' said Hornblower; his senses told him, the moment he said it, that he had used an improper expression–the look on Masters's face told him, and he corrected himself (hardly believing that men really said these things off the boards of the stage) before Masters had time to correct him.

'Aye aye, sir,' said Hornblower, and as a second afterthought he put his hand to the brim of his hat again.

Masters returned the compliment and turned to one of the shivering messengers cowering in the inadequate shelter of the bulwark. 'Boy! Take Mr Hornblower down to the midshipmen's berth.'

'Aye aye, sir.'

Hornblower accompanied the boy forward to the main hatchway. Seasickness alone would have made him unsteady on his feet, but twice on the short journey he stumbled like a man tripping over a rope as a sharp gust brought the *Justinian* up against her cables with a jerk. At the hatchway the boy slid down the ladder like an eel over a rock; Hornblower had to brace himself and descend far more gingerly and uncertainly into the dim light of the lower gundeck and then into the twilight of the 'tweendecks. The smells that entered his nostrils were as strange and as assorted as the noises that assailed his ears. At the foot of each ladder the boy waited for him with a patience whose tolerance was just obvious. After the last descent, a few steps–Hornblower had already lost his sense of direction and did not know whether it was aft or forward–took them to a gloomy recess whose shadows were accentuated rather than lightened by a tallow dip spiked on to a bit of copper plate on a table round which were seated half a dozen shirt-sleeved men. The boy vanished and left Hornblower standing there, and it was a second or two before the whiskered man at the head of the table looked up at him.

'Speak, thou apparition,' said he.

Hornblower felt a wave of nausea overcoming him–the after effects of his trip in the shore boat were being accentuated by the incredible stuffiness and smelliness of the 'tweendecks. It was very hard to speak, and the fact that he did not know how to phrase what he wanted to say made it harder still.

'My name is Hornblower,' he quavered at length.

'What an infernal piece of bad luck for you,' said a second man at the table, with a complete absence of sympathy.

At that moment in the roaring world outside the ship the wind veered sharply, heeling the *Justinian* a trifle and swinging her round to snub at her cables again. To Hornblower it seemed more as if the world had come loose from its fastenings. He reeled where he stood, and although he was shuddering with cold he felt sweat on his face.

'I suppose you have come,' said the whiskered man at the head of the table, 'to thrust yourself among your betters. Another soft-headed ignoramus come to be a nuisance to those who have to try to teach you your duties. Look at him'–the speaker with a gesture demanded the attention of everyone at the table–'look at him, I say! The King's latest bad bargain. How old are you?'

'S-seventeen, sir,' stuttered Hornblower.

'Seventeen!' the disgust in the speaker's voice was only too evident. 'You must start at twelve if you ever wish to be a seaman. Seventeen! Do you know the difference between a head and a halliard?'

That drew a laugh from the group, and the quality of the laugh was just noticeable to Hornblower's whirling brain, so that he guessed that whether he said 'yes' or 'no' he would be equally exposed to ridicule. He groped for a neutral reply.

'That's the first thing I'll look up in Norie's *Seamanship*,' he said.

The ship lurched again at that moment, and he clung on to the table.

'Gentlemen,' he began pathetically, wondering how to say what he had in mind.

'My God!' exclaimed somebody at the table. 'He's seasick!'

'Seasick in Spithead!' said somebody else, in a tone in which amazement had as much place as disgust.

But Hornblower ceased to care; he was not really conscious of what was going on round him for some time after that. The nervous excitement of the last few days was as much to blame, perhaps, as the journey in the shore boat and the erratic behaviour of the *Justinian* at her anchors, but it meant for him that he was labelled at once as the midshipman who was seasick in Spithead, and it was only natural that the label added to the natural misery of the loneliness and homesickness which oppressed him during those days when that part of the Channel Fleet which had not succeeded in completing its crews lay at anchor in the lee of the Isle of Wight. An hour in the hammock into which the messman hoisted him enabled him to recover sufficiently to be able to report himself to the first lieutenant; after a few days on board he was able to find his way round the ship without (as happened at first) losing his sense of direction below decks, so that he did not know whether he was facing forward or aft. During that period his brother officers ceased to have faces which were mere blurs and came to take on personalities; he came painfully to learn the stations allotted him when the ship was at quarters, when he was on watch, and when hands were summoned for setting or taking in sail. He even came to have an acute enough understanding of his new life to realize that it could have been worse–that destiny might have put him on board a ship ordered immediately to sea instead of one lying at anchor. But it was a poor enough compensation; he was a lonely and unhappy boy. Shyness alone would long have delayed his making friends, but as it happened the midshipmen's berth in the *Justinian* was occupied by men all a good deal older than he; elderly master's mates recruited from the merchant service, and midshipmen in their twenties who through lack of patronage or inability to pass the necessary examination had never succeeded in gaining for themselves commissions as lieutenants. They were inclined, after the first moments of amused interest, to ignore him, and he was glad of it, delighted to shrink into his shell and attract no notice to himself.

For the *Justinian* was not a happy ship during those gloomy January days. Captain Keene–it was when he came aboard that Hornblower first saw the pomp and ceremony that surrounds the captain of a ship of the line–was a sick man, of a melancholy disposition. He had not the fame which enabled some captains to fill their ships with enthusiastic volunteers, and he was devoid of the personality which might have made enthusiasts out of the sullen pressed men whom the press gangs were bringing in from day to day to complete the ship's complement. His officers saw little of him, and did not love what they saw. Hornblower, summoned to his cabin for his first interview, was not impressed–a middle-aged man at a table covered with papers, with the hollow and yellow cheeks of prolonged illness.

'Mr Hornblower,' he said formally, 'I am glad to have this opportunity of welcoming you on board my ship.'

'Yes, sir,' said Hornblower–that seemed more appropriate to the occasion than 'Aye aye, sir', and a junior midshipman seemed to be expected to say one or the other on all occasions.

'You are–let me see–seventeen?' Captain Keene picked up the paper which apparently covered Hornblower's brief official career.

'Yes, sir.'

'July 4th, 1776,' mused Keene, reading Hornblower's date of birth to himself. 'Five years to the day before I was posted as captain. I had been six years as lieutenant before you were born.'

'Yes, sir,' agreed Hornblower–it did not seem the occasion for any further comment.

'A doctor's son–you should have chosen a lord for your father if you wanted to make a career for yourself.'

'Yes, sir.'

'How far did your education go?'

'I was a Grecian at school, sir.'

'So you can construe Xenophon as well as Cicero?'

'Yes, sir. But not very well, sir.'

'Better if you knew something about sines and cosines. Better if you could foresee a squall in time to get t'gallants in. We have no use for ablative absolutes in the Navy.'

'Yes, sir,' said Hornblower.

He had only just learned what a topgallant was, but he could have told his captain that his mathematical studies were far advanced. He refrained nevertheless; his instincts combined with his recent experiences urged him not to volunteer unsolicited information.

'Well, obey orders, learn your duties, and no harm can come to you. That will do.'

'Thank you, sir,' said Hornblower, retiring.

But the captain's last words to him seemed to be contradicted immediately. Harm began to come to Hornblower from that day forth, despite his obedience to orders and diligent study of his duties, and it stemmed from the arrival in the midshipmen's berth of John Simpson as senior warrant officer. Hornblower was sitting at mess with his colleagues when he first saw him–a brawny good-looking man in his thirties, who came in and stood looking at them just as Hornblower had stood a few days before.

'Hullo!' said somebody, not very cordially.

'Cleveland, my bold friend,' said the newcomer, 'come out from that seat. I am going to resume my place at the head of the table.'

'But—'

'Come out, I said,' snapped Simpson.

Cleveland moved along with some show of reluctance, and Simpson took his place, and glowered round the table in reply to the curious glances with which everyone regarded him.

'Yes, my sweet brother officers,' he said, 'I am back in the bosom of the family. And I am not surprised that nobody is pleased. You will all be less pleased by the time I am done with you, I may add.'

'But your commission—?' asked somebody, greatly daring.

'My commission?' Simpson leaned forward and tapped the table, staring down the inquisitive people on either side of it. 'I'll answer that question this once, and the man who asks it again will wish he had never been born. A board of turnip-headed captains has refused me my commission. It decided that my mathematical knowledge was insufficient to make me a reliable navigator. And so Acting-Lieutenant Simpson is once again Mr Midshipman Simpson, at your service. At your service. And may the Lord have mercy on your souls.'

It did not seem, as the days went by, that the Lord had any mercy at all, for with Simpson's return life in the midshipmen's berth ceased to be one of passive unhappiness and became one of active misery. Simpson had apparently always been an ingenious tyrant, but now, embittered and humiliated by his failure to pass his examination for his commission, he was a worse tyrant, and his ingenuity had multiplied itself. He may have been weak in mathematics, but he was diabolically clever at making other people's lives a burden to them. As senior officer in the mess he had wide official powers; as a man with a blistering tongue and a morbid sense of mischief he would have been powerful anyway, even if the *Justinian* had possessed an alert and masterful first lieutenant to keep him in check, while Mr Clay was neither. Twice midshipmen rebelled against Simpson's arbitrary authority, and each time Simpson thrashed the rebel, pounding him into insensibility with his huge fists, for Simpson would have made a successful prize-fighter. Each time Simpson was left unmarked; each time his opponent's blackened eyes and swollen lips called down the penalty of mast heading and extra duty from the indignant first lieutenant. The mess seethed with impotent rage. Even the toadies and lickspittles among the midshipmen–and naturally there were several–hated the tyrant.

Significantly, it was not his ordinary exactions which roused the greatest resentment–his levying toll upon their sea chests for clean shirts for himself, his appropriation of the best cuts of the meat served, nor even his taking their coveted issues of spirits. These things could be excused as understandable, the sort of thing they would do themselves if they had the power. But he displayed a whimsical arbitrariness which reminded Hornblower, with his classical education, of the freaks of the Roman emperors. He forced Cleveland to shave the whiskers which were his inordinate pride; he imposed upon Hether the duty of waking up Mackenzie every half hour, day and night, so that neither of them was able to sleep–and there were toadies ready to tell him if Hether ever failed in his task. Early enough he had discovered Hornblower's most vulnerable points, as he had with everyone else. He knew of Hornblower's shyness; at first it was amusing to compel Hornblower to recite verses from Gray's 'Elegy in a Country Churchyard' to the assembled mess. The toadies could compel Hornblower to do it; Simpson would lay his dirk-scabbard on the table in front of him with a significant glance, and the toadies would close round Hornblower, who knew that any hesitation on his part would mean that he would be stretched across the table and the dirk-scabbard applied; the flat of the scabbard was painful, the edge of it was agonizing, but the pain was nothing to the utter humiliation of it all. And the torment grew worse when Simpson instituted what he aptly called 'The Proceedings of the Inquisition' when Hornblower was submitted to a slow and methodical questioning regarding his homelife and his boyhood. Every question had to be answered, on pain of the dirk-scabbard; Hornblower could fence and prevaricate, but he had to answer and sooner or later the relentless questioning would draw from him some simple admission which would rouse a peal of laughter from his audience. Heaven knows that in Hornblower's lonely childhood there was nothing to be ashamed of, but boys are odd creatures, especially reticent ones like Hornblower, and are ashamed of things no one else would think twice about. The ordeal would leave him weak and sick; someone less solemn might have clowned his way out of his difficulties and even into popular favour, but Hornblower at seventeen was too ponderous a person to clown. He had to endure the persecution experiencing all the black misery which only a seventeen-year-old can experience; he never wept in public, but at night more than once he shed the bitter tears of seventeen. He often thought about death; he often even thought about desertion, but he realized that desertion would lead to something worse than death, and then his mind would revert to death, savouring the thought of suicide. He came to long for death, friendless as he was, and brutally ill-treated, and lonely as only a boy among men–and a very reserved boy–can be. More and more he thought about ending it all the easiest way, hugging the secret thought of it to his friendless bosom.

If the ship had only been at sea everyone would have been kept busy enough to be out of mischief; even at anchor an energetic captain and first lieutenant would have kept all hands hard enough at work to obviate abuses, but it was Hornblower's hard luck that the *Justinian* lay at anchor all through that fatal January of 1794 under a sick captain and an inefficient first lieutenant. Even the activities which were at times enforced often worked to Hornblower's disadvantage. There was an occasion when Mr Bowles, the master, was holding a class in navigation for his mates and for the midshipmen, and the captain by bad luck happened by and glanced through the results of the problem the class had individually been set to solve. His illness made Keene a man of bitter tongue, and he cherished no liking for Simpson. He took a single glance at Simpson's paper, and chuckled sarcastically.

'Now let us all rejoice,' he said, 'the sources of the Nile have been discovered at last.'

'Pardon, sir?' said Simpson.

'Your ship,' said Keene, 'as far as I can make out from your illiterate scrawl, Mr Simpson, is in Central Africa. Let us now see what other *terrae incognitae* have been opened up by the remaining intrepid explorers of this class.'

It must have been Fate–it was dramatic enough to be art and not an occurrence in real life; Hornblower knew what was going to happen even as Keene picked up the other papers, including his. The result he had obtained was the only one which was correct; everybody else had added the correction for refraction instead of subtracting it, or had worked out the multiplication wrongly, or had, like Simpson, botched the whole problem.

'Congratulations, Mr Hornblower,' said Keene. 'You must be proud to be alone successful among this crowd of intellectual giants. You are half Mr Simpson's age, I fancy. If you double your attainments while you double your years, you will leave the rest of us far behind. Mr Bowles, you will be so good as to see that Mr Simpson pays even further attention to his mathematical studies.'

With that he went off along the 'tweendecks with the halting step resulting from his mortal disease, and Hornblower sat with his eyes cast down, unable to meet the glances he knew were being darted at him, and knowing full well what they portended. He longed for death at that moment; he even prayed for it that night.

Within two days Hornblower found himself on shore, and under Simpson's command. The two midshipmen were in charge of a party of seamen, landed to act along with parties from the other ships of the squadron as a press gang. The West India convoy was due to arrive soon; most of the hands would be pressed as soon as the convoy reached the Channel, and the remainder, left to work the ships to an anchorage, would sneak ashore, using every device to conceal themselves and find a safe hiding-place. It was the business of the landing parties to cut off this retreat, to lay a cordon along the waterfront which would sweep them all up. But the convoy was not yet signalled, and all arrangements were completed.

'All is well with the world,' said Simpson.

It was an unusual speech for him, but he was in unusual circumstances. He was sitting in the back room of the Lamb Inn, comfortable in one armchair with his legs on another, in front of a roaring fire and with a pot of beer with gin in it at his elbow.

'Here's to the West India convoy,' said Simpson, taking a pull at his beer. 'Long may it be delayed.'

Simpson was actually genial, activity and beer and a warm fire thawing him into a good humour; it was not time yet for the liquor to make him quarrelsome; Hornblower sat on the other side of the fire and sipped beer without gin in it and studied him, marvelling that for the first time since he had boarded the *Justinian* his unhappiness should have ceased to be active but should have subsided into a dull misery like the dying away of the pain of a throbbing tooth.

'Give us a toast, boy,' said Simpson.

'Confusion to Robespierre,' said Hornblower lamely.

The door opened and two more officers came in, one a midshipman while the other wore the single epaulette of a lieutenant–it was Chalk of the *Goliath*, the officer in general charge of the press gangs sent ashore. Even Simpson made room for his superior rank before the fire.

'The convoy is still not signalled,' announced Chalk. And then he eyed Hornblower keenly. 'I don't think I have the pleasure of your acquaintance.'

'Mr Hornblower–Lieutenant Chalk,' introduced Simpson. 'Mr Hornblower is distinguished as the midshipman who was seasick in Spithead.'

Hornblower tried not to writhe as Simpson tied that label on him. He imagined that Chalk was merely being polite when he changed the subject.

'Hey, potman! Will you gentlemen join me in a glass? We have a long wait before us, I fear. Your men are all properly posted, Mr Simpson?'

'Yes, sir.'

Chalk was an active man. He paced about the room, stared out of the window at the rain, presented his midshipman–Caldwell–to the other two when the drinks arrived, and obviously fretted at his enforced inactivity.

'A game of cards to pass the time?' he suggested. 'Excellent! Hey, potman! Cards and a table and another light.'

The table was set before the fire, the chairs arranged, the cards brought in.

'What game shall it be?' asked Chalk, looking round.

He was a lieutenant among three midshipmen, and any suggestion of his was likely to carry a good deal of weight; the other three naturally waited to hear what he had to say.

'Vingt-et-un? That is a game for the half-witted. Loo? That is a game for the wealthier half-witted. But whist, now? That would give us all scope for the exercise of our poor talents. Caldwell, there, is acquainted with the rudiments of the game, I know. Mr Simpson?'

A man like Simpson, with a blind mathematical spot, was not likely to be a good whist player, but he was not likely to know he was a bad one.

'As you wish, sir,' said Simpson. He enjoyed gambling, and one game was as good as another for that purpose to his mind.

'Mr Hornblower?'

'With pleasure, sir.'

That was more nearly true than most conventional replies. Hornblower had learned his whist in a good school; ever since the death of his mother he had made a fourth with his father and the parson and the parson's wife. The game was already something of a passion with him. He revelled in the nice calculation of chances, in the varying demands it made upon his boldness or caution. There was even enough warmth in his acceptance to attract a second glance from Chalk, who–a good card player himself–at once detected a fellow spirit.

'Excellent!' he said again. 'Then we may as well cut at once for places and partners. What shall be the stakes, gentlemen? A shilling a trick and a guinea on the rub, or is that too great? No? Then we are agreed.'

For some time the game proceeded quietly. Hornblower cut first Simpson and then Caldwell as his partner. Only a couple of hands were necessary to show up Simpson as a hopeless whist player, the kind who would always lead an ace when he had one, or a singleton when he had four trumps, but he and Hornblower won the first rubber thanks to overwhelming card strength. But Simpson lost the next in partnership with Chalk, cut Chalk again as partner, and lost again. He gloated over good hands and sighed over poor ones; clearly he was one of those unenlightened people who looked upon whist as a social function, or as a mere crude means, like throwing dice, of arbitrarily transferring money. He never thought of the game either as a sacred rite or as an intellectual exercise. Moreover, as his losses grew, and as the potman came and went with liquor, he grew restless, and his face was flushed with more than the heat of the fire. He was both a bad loser and a bad drinker, and even Chalk's punctilious good manners were sufficiently strained so that he displayed a hint of relief when the next cut gave him Hornblower as a partner. They won the rubber easily, and another guinea and several shillings were transferred to Hornblower's lean purse; he was now the only winner, and Simpson was the heaviest loser. Hornblower was lost in the pleasure of playing the game again; the only attention he paid to Simpson's writhings and muttered objurgations was to regard them as a distracting nuisance; he even forgot to think of them as danger signals. Momentarily he was oblivious to the fact that he might pay for his present success by future torment.

Once more they cut, and he found himself Chalk's partner again. Two good hands gave them the first game. Then twice, to Simpson's unconcealed triumph, Simpson and Caldwell made a small score, approaching game, and in the next hand an overbold finesse by Hornblower left him and Chalk with the odd trick when their score should have been two tricks greater–Simpson laid his knave on Hornblower's ten with a grin of delight which turned to dismay when he found that he and Caldwell had still only made six tricks; he counted them a second time with annoyance. Hornblower dealt and turned the trump, and Simpson led–an ace as usual, assuring Hornblower of his re-entry. He had a string of trumps and a good suit of clubs which a single lead might establish. Simpson glanced muttering at his hand; it was extraordinary that he still had not realized the simple truth that the lead of an ace involved leading a second time with the problem no clearer. He made up his mind at last and led again; Hornblower's king took the trick and he instantly led his knave of trumps. To his delight it took the trick; he led again and Chalk's queen gave them another trick. Chalk laid down the ace of trumps and Simpson with a curse played the king. Chalk led clubs of which Hornblower had five to the king queen–it was significant that Chalk should lead them, as it could not be a singleton lead when Hornblower held the remaining trumps. Hornblower's queen took the trick; Caldwell must hold the ace, unless Chalk did. Hornblower led a small one; everyone followed suit, Chalk playing the knave, and Caldwell played the ace. Eight clubs had been played, and Hornblower had three more headed by the king and ten–three certain tricks, with the last trumps as re-entries. Caldwell played the queen of diamonds, Hornblower played his singleton, and Chalk produced the ace.

'The rest are mine,' said Hornblower, laying down his cards.

'What do you mean?' said Simpson, with the king of diamonds in his hand.

'Five tricks,' said Chalk briskly. 'Game and rubber.'

'But don't I take another?' persisted Simpson.

'I trump a lead of diamonds or hearts and make three more clubs,' explained Hornblower. To him the situation was as simple as two and two, a most ordinary finish to a hand; it was hard for him to realize that foggy-minded players like Simpson could find difficulty in keeping tally of fifty-two cards. Simpson flung down his hand.

'You know too much about the game,' he said. 'You know the backs of the cards as well as the fronts.'

Hornblower gulped. He recognized that this could be a decisive moment if he chose. A second before he had merely been playing cards, and enjoying himself. Now he was faced with an issue of life or death. A torrent of thought streamed through his mind. Despite the comfort of his present surroundings he remembered acutely the hideous misery of the life in the *Justinian* to which he must return. This was an opportunity to end that misery one way or the other. He remembered how he had contemplated killing himself, and into the back of his mind stole the germ of the plan upon which he was going to act. His decision crystallized.

'That is an insulting remark, Mr Simpson,' he said. He looked round and met the eyes of Chalk and Caldwell, who were suddenly grave; Simpson was still merely stupid. 'For that I shall have to ask satisfaction.'

'Satisfaction?' said Chalk hastily. 'Come, come. Mr Simpson had a momentary loss of temper. I am sure he will explain.'

'I have been accused of cheating at cards,' said Hornblower. 'That is a hard thing to explain away.'

He was trying to behave like a grown man; more than that, he was trying to act like a man consumed with indignation, while actually there was no indignation within him over the point in dispute, for he understood too well the muddled state of mind which had led Simpson to say what he did. But the opportunity had presented itself, he had determined to avail himself of it, and now what he had to do was to play the part convincingly of the man who has received a mortal insult.

'The wine was in and the wit was out,' said Chalk, still determined on keeping the peace. 'Mr Simpson was speaking in jest, I am sure. Let's call for another bottle and drink it in friendship.'

'With pleasure,' said Hornblower, fumbling for the words which would set the dispute beyond reconciliation. 'If Mr Simpson will beg my pardon at once before you two gentlemen, and admit that he spoke without justification and in a manner no gentleman would employ.'

He turned and met Simpson's eye with defiance as he spoke, metaphorically waving a red rag before the bull, who charged with gratifying fury.

'Apologize to *you*, you little whippersnapper!' exploded Simpson, alcohol and outraged dignity speaking simultaneously. 'Never this side of Hell.'

'You hear that, gentlemen?' said Hornblower. 'I have been insulted and Mr Simpson refuses to apologize while insulting me further. There is only one way now in which satisfaction can be given.'

For the next two days, until the West India convoy came in, Hornblower and Simpson, under Chalk's orders, lived the curious life of two duellists forced into each other's society before the affair of honour. Hornblower was careful–as he would have been in any case–to obey every order given him, and Simpson gave them with a certain amount of self-consciousness and awkwardness. It was during those two days that Hornblower elaborated on his original idea. Pacing through the dockyards with his patrol of seamen at his heels he had plenty of time to think the matter over. Viewed coldly–and a boy of seventeen in a mood of black despair can be objective enough on occasions–it was as simple as the calculations of the chances in a problem at whist. Nothing could be worse than his life in the *Justinian*, not even (as he had thought already) death itself. Here was an easy death open to him, with the additional attraction that there was a chance of Simpson dying instead. It was at that moment that Hornblower advanced his idea one step further–a new development, startling even to him, bringing him to a halt so that the patrol behind him bumped into him before they could stop.

'Beg your pardon, sir,' said the petty officer.

'No matter,' said Hornblower, deep in his thoughts.

He first brought forward his suggestion in conversation with Preston and Danvers, the two master's mates whom he asked to be his seconds as soon as he returned to the *Justinian*.

'We'll act for you, of course,' said Preston, looking dubiously at the weedy youth when he made his request. 'How do you want to fight him? As the aggrieved party you have the choice of weapons.'

'I've been thinking about it ever since he insulted me,' said Hornblower temporizing. It was not easy to come out with his idea in bald words, after all.

'Have you any skill with the small-sword?' asked Danvers.

'No,' said Hornblower. Truth to tell, he had never even handled one.

'Then it had better be pistols,' said Preston.

'Simpson is probably a good shot,' said Danvers. 'I wouldn't care to stand up before him myself.'

'Easy now,' said Preston hastily. 'Don't dishearten the man.'

'I'm not disheartened,' said Hornblower, 'I was thinking the same thing myself.'

'You're cool enough about it, then,' marvelled Danvers.

Hornblower shrugged.

'Maybe I am. I hardly care. But I've thought that we might make the chances more even.'

'How?'

'We could make them exactly even,' said Hornblower, taking the plunge. 'Have two pistols, one loaded and the other empty. Simpson and I would take our choice without knowing which was which. Then we stand within a yard of each other, and at the word we fire.'

'My God!' said Danvers.

'I don't think that would be legal,' said Preston. 'It would mean one of you would be killed for certain.'

'Killing is the object of duelling,' said Hornblower. 'If the conditions aren't unfair I don't think any objection can be raised.'

'But would you carry it out to the end?' marvelled Danvers.

'Mr Danvers—' began Hornblower; but Preston interfered.

'We don't want another duel on our hands,' he said. 'Danvers only meant he wouldn't care to do it himself. We'll discuss it with Cleveland and Hether, and see what they say.'

Within an hour the proposed conditions of the duel were known to everyone in the ship. Perhaps it was to Simpson's disadvantage that he had no real friend in the ship, for Cleveland and Hether, his seconds, were not disposed to take too firm a stand regarding the conditions of the duel, and agreed to the terms with only a show of reluctance. The tyrant of the midshipmen's berth was paying the penalty for his tyranny. There was some cynical amusement shown by some of the officers; some of both officers and men eyed Hornblower and Simpson with the curiosity that the prospect of death excites in some minds, as if the two destined opponents were men condemned to the gallows. At noon Lieutenant Masters sent for Hornblower.

'The captain has ordered me to make inquiry into this duel, Mr Hornblower,' he said. 'I am instructed to use my best endeavours to compose the quarrel.'

'Yes, sir.'

'Why insist on this satisfaction, Mr Hornblower? I understand there were a few hasty words over wine and cards.'

'Mr Simpson accused me of cheating, sir, before witnesses who were not officers of this ship.'

That was the point. The witnesses were not members of the ship's company. If Hornblower had chosen to disregard Simpson's words as the ramblings of a drunken ill-tempered man, they might have passed unnoticed. But as he had taken the stand he did, there could be no hushing it up now, and Hornblower knew it.

'Even so, there can be satisfaction without a duel, Mr Hornblower.'

'If Mr Simpson will make me a full apology before the same gentlemen, I would be satisfied, sir.'

Simpson was no coward. He would die rather than submit to such a formal humiliation.

'I see. Now I understand you are insisting on rather unusual conditions for the duel?'

'There are precedents for it, sir. As the insulted party I can choose any conditions which are not unfair.'

'You sound like a sea lawyer to me, Mr Hornblower.'

The hint was sufficient to tell Hornblower that he had verged upon being too glib, and he resolved in future to bridle his tongue. He stood silent and waited for Masters to resume the conversation.

'You are determined, then, Mr Hornblower, to continue with this murderous business?'

'Yes, sir.'

'The captain has given me further orders to attend the duel in person, because of the strange conditions on which you insist. I must inform you that I shall request the seconds to arrange for that.'

'Yes, sir.'

'Very good, then, Mr Hornblower.'

Masters looked at Hornblower as he dismissed him even more keenly than he had done when Hornblower first came on board. He was looking for signs of weakness or wavering–indeed, he was looking for any signs of human feeling at all–but he could detect none. Hornblower had reached a decision, he had weighed all the pros and cons, and his logical mind told him that having decided in cold blood upon a course of action it would be folly to allow himself to be influenced subsequently by untrustworthy emotions. The conditions of the duel on which he was insisting were mathematically advantageous. If he had once considered with favour escaping from Simpson's persecution by a voluntary death it was surely a gain to take an even chance of escaping from it without dying. Similarly, if Simpson were (as he almost certainly was) a better swordsman and a better pistol shot than him, the even chance was again mathematically advantageous. There was nothing to regret about his recent actions.

All very well; mathematically the conclusions were irrefutable, but Hornblower was surprised to find that mathematics were not everything. Repeatedly during that dreary afternoon and evening Hornblower found himself suddenly gulping with anxiety as the realization came to him afresh that tomorrow morning he would be risking his life on the spin of a coin. One chance out of two and he would be dead, his consciousness at an end, his flesh cold, and the world, almost unbelievably, would be going on without him. The thought sent a shiver through him despite himself. And he had plenty of time for these reflections, for the convention that forbade him from encountering his destined opponent before the moment of the duel kept him necessarily in isolation, as far as isolation could be found on the crowded decks of the *Justinian*. He slung his hammock that night in a depressed mood, feeling unnaturally tired; and he undressed in the clammy, stuffy dampness of the 'tweendecks feeling more than usually cold. He hugged the blankets round himself, yearning to relax in their warmth, but relaxation would not come.

Time after time as he began to drift off to sleep he woke again tense and anxious, full of thoughts of the morrow. He turned over wearily a dozen times, hearing the ship's bell ring out each half hour, feeling a growing contempt at his cowardice. He told himself in the end that it was as well that his fate tomorrow depended upon pure chance, for if he had to rely upon steadiness of hand and eye he would be dead for certain after a night like this.

That conclusion presumably helped him to go to sleep for the last hour or two of the night, for he awoke with a start to find Danvers shaking him.

'Five bells,' said Danvers. 'Dawn in an hour. Rise and shine!'

Hornblower slid out of his hammock and stood in his shirt; the 'tweendecks was nearly dark and Danvers was almost invisible.

'Number One's letting us have the second cutter,' said Danvers. 'Masters and Simpson and that lot are going first in the launch. Here's Preston.'

Another shadowy figure loomed up in the darkness.

'Hellish cold,' said Preston. 'The devil of a morning to turn out. Nelson, where's that tea?'

The mess attendant came with it as Hornblower was hauling on his trousers. It maddened Hornblower that he shivered enough in the cold for the cup to clatter in the saucer as he took it. But the tea was grateful, and Hornblower drank it eagerly.

'Give me another cup,' he said, and was proud of himself that he could think about tea at that moment.

It was still dark as they went down into the cutter.

'Shove off,' said the coxswain, and the boat pushed off from the ship's side. There was a keen cold wind blowing which filled the dipping lug as the cutter headed for the twin lights that marked the jetty.

'I ordered a hackney coach at the George to be waiting for us,' said Danvers. 'Let's hope it is.'

It was there, with the driver sufficiently sober to control his horse moderately well despite his overnight potations. Danvers produced a pocket flask as they settled themselves in with their feet in the straw.

'Take a sip, Hornblower?' he asked, proffering it. 'There's no special need for a steady hand this morning.'

'No thank you,' said Hornblower. His empty stomach revolted at the idea of pouring spirits into it.

'The others will be there before us,' commented Preston. 'I saw the quarter boat heading back just before we reached the jetty.'

The etiquette of the duel demanded that the two opponents should reach the ground separately; but only one boat would be necessary for the return.

'The sawbones is with them,' said Danvers. 'Though God knows what use he thinks he'll be today.'

He sniggered, and with overlate politeness tried to cut his snigger off short.

'How are you feeling, Hornblower?' asked Preston.

'Well enough,' said Hornblower, forbearing to add that he only felt well enough while this kind of conversation was not being carried on.

The hackney coach levelled itself off as it came over the crest of the hill, and stopped beside the common. Another coach stood there waiting, its single candle-lamp burning yellow in the growing dawn.

'There they are,' said Preston; the faint light revealed a shadowy group standing on frosty turf among the gorse bushes.

Hornblower, as they approached, caught a glimpse of Simpson's face as he stood a little detached from the others. It was pale, and Hornblower noticed that at that moment he swallowed nervously, just as he himself was doing. Masters came towards them, shooting his usual keen inquisitive look at Hornblower as they came together.

'This is the moment,' he said, 'for this quarrel to be composed. This country is at war. I hope, Mr Hornblower, that you can be persuaded to save a life for the King's service by not pressing this matter.'

Hornblower looked across at Simpson, while Danvers answered for him.

'Has Mr Simpson offered the proper redress?' asked Danvers.

'Mr Simpson is willing to acknowledge that he wishes the incident had never taken place.'

'That is an unsatisfactory form,' said Danvers. 'It does not include an apology, and you must agree that an apology is necessary, sir.'

'What does your principal say?' persisted Masters.

'It is not for any principal to speak in these circumstances,' said Danvers, with a glance at Hornblower, who nodded. All this was as inevitable as the ride in the hangman's cart, and as hideous. There could be no going back now; Hornblower had never thought for one moment that Simpson would apologize, and without an apology the affair must be carried to a bloody conclusion. An even chance that he did not have five minutes longer to live.

'You are determined, then, gentlemen,' said Masters. 'I shall have to state that fact in my report.'

'We are determined,' said Preston.

'Then there is nothing for it but to allow this deplorable affair to proceed. I left the pistols in the charge of Doctor Hepplewhite.'

He turned and led them towards the other group–Simpson with Hether and Cleveland, and Doctor Hepplewhite standing with a pistol held by the muzzle in each hand. He was a bulky man with the red face of a persistent drinker; he was actually grinning a spirituous grin at that moment, rocking a little on his feet.

'Are the young fools set in their folly?' he asked; but everyone very properly ignored him as having no business to ask such a question at such a moment.

'Now,' said Masters. 'Here are the pistols, both primed, as you see, but one loaded and the other unloaded, in accordance with the conditions. I have here a guinea which I propose to spin to decide the allocation of the weapons. Now, gentlemen, shall the spin give your principals one pistol each irrevocably–for instance, if the coin shows heads shall Mr Simpson have this one–or shall the winner of the spin have choice of weapons? It is my design to eliminate all possibility of collusion as far as possible.'

Hether and Cleveland and Danvers and Preston exchanged dubious glances.

'Let the winner of the spin choose,' said Preston at length.

'Very well, gentlemen. Please call, Mr Hornblower.'

'Tails!' said Hornblower as the gold piece spun in the air.

Masters caught it and clapped a hand over it.

'Tails it is,' said Masters, lifting his hand and revealing the coin to the grouped seconds. 'Please make your choice.'

Hepplewhite held out the two pistols to him, death in one hand and life in the other. It was a grim moment. There was only pure chance to direct him; it called for a little effort to force his hand out.

'I'll have this one,' he said; as he touched it the weapon seemed icy cold.

'Then now I have done what was required of me,' said Masters. 'The rest is for you gentlemen to carry out.'

'Take this one, Simpson,' said Hepplewhite. 'And be careful how you handle yours, Mr Hornblower. You're a public danger.'

The man was still grinning, gloating over the fact that someone else was in mortal danger while he himself was in none. Simpson took the pistol Hepplewhite offered him and settled it into his hand; once more his eyes met Hornblower's, but there was neither recognition nor expression in them.

'There are no distances to step out,' Danvers was saying. 'One spot's as good as another. It's level enough here.'

'Very good,' said Hether. 'Will you stand here, Mr Simpson?'

Preston beckoned to Hornblower, who walked over. It was not easy to appear brisk and unconcerned. Preston took him by the arm and stood him up in front of Simpson, almost breast to breast–close enough to smell the alcohol on his breath.

'For the last time, gentlemen,' said Masters loudly. 'Cannot you be reconciled?'

There was no answer from anybody, only deep silence, during which it seemed to Hornblower that the frantic beating of his heart must be clearly audible. The silence was broken by an exclamation from Hether.

'We haven't settled who's to give the word!' he said. 'Who's going to?'

'Let's ask Mr Masters to give it,' said Danvers.

Hornblower did not look round. He was looking steadfastly at the grey sky past Simpson's right ear–somehow he could not look him in the face, and he had no idea where Simpson was looking. The end of the world as he knew it was close to him–soon there might be a bullet through his heart.

'I will do it if you are agreed, gentlemen,' he heard Masters say.

The grey sky was featureless; for this last look on the world he might as well have been blindfolded. Masters raised his voice again.

'I will say "one, two, three, fire",' he announced, 'with those intervals. At the last word, gentlemen, you can fire as you will. Are you ready?'

'Yes,' came Simpson's voice, almost in Hornblower's ear, it seemed.

'Yes,' said Hornblower. He could hear the strain in his own voice.

'One,' said Masters, and Hornblower felt at that moment the muzzle of Simpson's pistol against his left ribs, and he raised his own.

It was in that second that he decided he could not kill Simpson even if it were in his power, and he went on lifting his pistol, forcing himself to look to see that it was pressed against the point of Simpson's shoulder. A slight wound would suffice.

'Two,' said Masters. 'Three. Fire!'

Hornblower pulled his trigger. There was a click and a spurt of smoke from the lock of his pistol. The priming had gone off but no more–his was the unloaded weapon, and he knew what it was to die. A tenth of a second later there was a click and spurt of smoke from Simpson's pistol against his heart. Stiff and still they both stood, slow to realize what had happened.

'A miss-fire, by God!' said Danvers.

The seconds crowded round them.

'Give me those pistols!' said Masters, taking them from the weak hands that held them. 'The loaded one might be hanging fire, and we don't want it to go off now.'

'Which was the loaded one?' asked Hether, consumed with curiosity.

'That is something it is better not to know,' answered Masters, changing the two pistols rapidly from hand to hand so as to confuse everyone.

'What about a second shot?' asked Danvers, and Masters looked up straight and inflexibly at him.

'There will be no second shot,' he said. 'Honour is completely satisfied. These two gentlemen have come through this ordeal extremely well. No one can now think little of Mr Simpson if he expresses his regret for the occurrence, and no one can think little of Mr Hornblower if he accepts that statement in reparation.'

Hepplewhite burst into a roar of laughter.

'Your faces!' he boomed, slapping his thigh. 'You ought to see how you all look! Solemn as cows!'

'Mr Hepplewhite,' said Masters, 'your behaviour is indecorous. Gentlemen, our coaches are waiting on the road, the cutter is at the jetty. And I think all of us would be the better for some breakfast; including Mr Hepplewhite.'

That should have been the end of the incident. The excited talk which had gone round the anchored squadron about the unusual duel died away in time, although everyone knew Hornblower's name now, and not as the midshipman who was seasick in Spithead but as the man who was willing to take an even chance in cold blood. But in the *Justinian* herself there was other talk; whispers which were circulated forward and aft.

'Mr Hornblower has requested permission to speak to you, sir,' said Mr Clay, the first lieutenant, one morning while making his report to the captain.

'Oh, send him in when you go out,' said Keene, and sighed.

Ten minutes later a knock on his cabin door ushered in a very angry young man.

'Sir!' began Hornblower.

'I can guess what you're going to say,' said Keene.

'Those pistols in the duel I fought with Simpson were not loaded!'

'Hepplewhite blabbed, I suppose,' said Keene.

'And it was by your orders, I understand, sir.'

'You are quite correct. I gave those orders to Mr Masters.'

'It was an unwarrantable liberty, sir!'

That was what Hornblower meant to say, but he stumbled without dignity over the polysyllables.

'Possibly it was,' said Keene patiently, rearranging, as always, the papers on his desk.

The calmness of the admission disconcerted Hornblower, who could only splutter for the next few moments.

'I saved a life for the King's service,' went on Keene, when the spluttering died away. 'A young life. No one has suffered any harm. On the other hand, both you and Simpson have had your courage amply proved. You both know you can stand fire now, and so does every one else.'

'You have touched my personal honour, sir,' said Hornblower, bringing out one of his rehearsed speeches, 'for that there can only be one remedy.'

'Restrain yourself, please, Mr Hornblower.' Keene shifted himself in his chair with a wince of pain as he prepared to make a speech. 'I must remind you of one salutary regulation of the Navy, to the effect that no junior officer can challenge his superior to a duel. The reasons for it are obvious–otherwise promotion would be too easy. The mere issuing of a challenge by a junior to a senior is a court-martial offence, Mr Hornblower.'

'Oh!' said Hornblower feebly.

'Now here is some gratuitous advice,' went on Keene. 'You have fought one duel and emerged with honour. That is good. Never fight another–that is better. Some people, oddly enough, acquire a taste for duelling, as a tiger acquires a taste for blood. They are never good officers, and never popular ones either.'

It was then that Hornblower realized that a great part of the keen excitement with which he had entered the captain's cabin was due to anticipation of the giving of the challenge. There could be a morbid desire for danger–and a morbid desire to occupy momentarily the centre of the stage. Keene was waiting for him to speak, and it was hard to say anything.

'I understand, sir,' he said at last.

Keene shifted in his chair again.

'There is another matter I wanted to take up with you, Mr Hornblower. Captain Pellew of the *Indefatigable* has room for another midshipman. Captain Pellew is partial to a game of whist, and has no good fourth on board. He and I have agreed to consider favourably your application for a transfer should you care to make one. I don't have to point out that any ambitious young officer would jump at the chance of serving in a frigate.'

'A frigate!' said Hornblower.

Everybody knew of Pellew's reputation and success. Distinction, promotion, prize money–an officer under Pellew's command could hope for all these. Competition for nomination to the *Indefatigable* must be intense, and this was the chance of a lifetime. Hornblower was on the point of making a glad acceptance, when further considerations restrained him.

'That is very good of you, sir,' he said 'I do not know how to thank you. But you accepted me as a midshipman here, and of course I must stay with you.'

The drawn, apprehensive face relaxed into a smile.

'Not many men would have said that,' said Keene. 'But I am going to insist on your accepting the offer. I shall not live very much longer to appreciate your loyalty. And this ship is not the place for you–this ship with her useless captain–don't interrupt me–and her worn-out first lieutenant and her old midshipmen. You should be where there may be speedy opportunities of advancement. I have the good of the service in mind, Mr Hornblower, when I suggest you accept Captain Pellew's invitation–and it might be less disturbing for me if you did,'

'Aye aye, sir,' said Hornblower.

2

THE CARGO OF RICE

The wolf was in among the sheep. The tossing grey water of the Bay of Biscay was dotted with white sails as far as the eye could see, and although a strong breeze was blowing every vessel was under perilously heavy canvas. Every ship but one was trying to escape; the exception was His Majesty's frigate *Indefatigable*, Captain Sir Edward Pellew. Farther out in the Atlantic, hundreds of miles away, a great battle was being fought, where the ships of the line were thrashing out the question as to whether England or France should wield the weapon of sea power; here in the Bay the convoy which the French ships were intended to escort was exposed to the attack of a ship of prey at liberty to capture any ship she could overhaul. She had come surging up from leeward, cutting off all chance of escape in that direction, and the clumsy merchant ships were forced to beat to windward; they were all filled with the food which revolutionary France (her economy disordered by the convulsion through which she was passing) was awaiting so anxiously, and their crews were all anxious to escape confinement in an English prison. Ship after ship was overhauled; a shot or two, and the newfangled tricolour came fluttering down from the gaff, and a prize-crew was hurriedly sent on board to conduct the captive to an English port while the frigate dashed after fresh prey.

On the quarterdeck of the *Indefatigable* Pellew fumed over each necessary delay. The convoy, each ship as close to the wind as she would lie, and under all the sail she could carry, was slowly scattering, spreading farther and farther with the passing minutes, and some of these would find safety in mere dispersion if any time was wasted. Pellew did not wait to pick up his boat; at each surrender he merely ordered away an officer and an armed guard, and the moment the prize-crew was on its way he filled his main-topsail again and hurried off after the next victim. The brig they were pursuing at the moment was slow to surrender. The long nine-pounders in the *Indefatigable*'s bows bellowed out more than once; on that heaving sea it was not so easy to aim accurately and the brig continued on her course hoping for some miracle to save her.

'Very well,' snapped Pellew. 'He has asked for it. Let him have it.'

The gunlayers at the bow chasers changed their point of aim, firing at the ship instead of across her bows.

'Not into the hull, damn it,' shouted Pellew–one shot had struck the brig perilously close to her waterline. 'Cripple her.'

The next shot by luck or by judgement was given better elevation. The slings of the foretopsail yard were shot away, the reefed sail came down, the yard hanging lopsidedly, and the brig came up into the wind for the *Indefatigable* to heave to close beside her, her broadside ready to fire into her.

Under that threat her flag came down.

'What brig's that?' shouted Pellew through his megaphone.

'*Marie Galante* of Bordeaux,' translated the officer beside Pellew as the French captain made reply. 'Twenty-four days out from New Orleans with rice.'

'Rice!' said Pellew. 'That'll sell for a pretty penny when we get her home. Two hundred tons, I should say. Twelve of a crew at most. She'll need a prize-crew of four, a midshipman's command.'

He looked round him as though for inspiration before giving his next order.

'Mr Hornblower!'

'Sir!'

'Take four men of the cutter's crew and board that brig. Mr Soames will give you our position. Take her into any English port you can make, and report there for orders.'

'Aye aye, sir.'

Hornblower was at his station at the starboard quarterdeck carronades –which was perhaps how he had caught Pellew's eye–his dirk at his side and a pistol in his belt. It was a moment for fast thinking, for anyone could see Pellew's impatience. With the *Indefatigable* cleared for action, his sea chest would be part of the surgeon's operating table down below, so that there was no chance of getting anything out of it. He would have to leave just as he was. The cutter was even now clawing up to a position on the *Indefatigable*'s quarter, so he ran to the ship's side and hailed her, trying to make his voice sound as big and as manly as he could, and at the word of the lieutenant in command she turned her bows in towards the frigate.

'Here's our latitude and longitude, Mr Hornblower,' said Soames, the master, handing a scrap of paper to him.

'Thank you,' said Hornblower, shoving it into his pocket.

He scrambled awkwardly into the mizzen-chains and looked down into the cutter. Ship and boat were pitching together, almost bows on to the sea, and the distance between them looked appallingly great; the bearded seaman standing in the bows could only just reach up to the chains with his long boat-hook. Hornblower hesitated for a long second; he knew he was ungainly and awkward–book learning was of no use when it came to jumping into a boat–but he had to make the leap, for Pellew was fuming behind him and the eyes of the boat's crew and of the whole ship's company were on him. Better to jump and hurt himself, better to jump and make an exhibition of himself, than to delay the ship. Waiting was certain failure, while he still had a choice if he jumped. Perhaps at a word from Pellew the *Indefatigable*'s helmsman allowed the ship's head to fall off from the sea a little. A somewhat diagonal wave lifted the *Indefatigable*'s stern and then passed on, so that the cutter's bows rose as the ship's stern sank a trifle. Hornblower braced himself and leaped. His feet reached the gunwale and he tottered there for one indescribable second. A seaman grabbed the breast of his jacket and he fell forward rather than backward. Not even the stout arm of the seaman, fully extended, could hold him up, and he pitched headforemost, legs in the air, upon the hands on the second thwart. He cannoned onto their bodies, knocking the breath out of his own against their muscular shoulders, and finally struggled into an upright position.

'I'm sorry,' he gasped to the men who had broken his fall.

'Never you mind, sir,' said the nearest one, a real tarry sailor, tattooed and pigtailed. 'You're only a featherweight.'

The lieutenant in command was looking at him from the sternsheets.

'Would you go to the brig, please, sir?' he asked, and the lieutenant bawled an order and the cutter swung round as Hornblower made his way aft.

It was a pleasant surprise not to be received with the broad grins of tolerantly concealed amusement. Boarding a small boat from a big frigate in even a moderate sea was no easy matter; probably every man on board had arrived headfirst at some time or other, and it was not in the tradition of the service, as understood in the *Indefatigable*, to laugh at a man who did his best without shirking.

'Are you taking charge of the brig?' asked the lieutenant.

'Yes, sir. The captain told me to take four of your men.'

'They had better be topmen, then,' said the lieutenant, casting his eyes aloft at the rigging of the brig. The foretopsail yard was hanging precariously, and the jib halliard had slacked off so that the sail was flapping thunderously in the wind. 'Do you know these men, or shall I pick 'em for you?'

'I'd be obliged if you would, sir.'

The lieutenant shouted four names, and four men replied.

'Keep 'em away from drink and they'll be all right,' said the lieutenant. 'Watch the French crew. They'll recapture the ship and have you in a French gaol before you can say "Jack Robinson" if you don't.'

'Aye aye, sir,' said Hornblower.

The cutter surged alongside the brig, white water creaming between the two vessels. The tattooed sailor hastily concluded a bargain with another man on his thwart and pocketed a lump of tobacco–the men were leaving their possessions behind just like Hornblower–and sprang for the mainchains. Another man followed him, and they stood and waited while Hornblower with difficulty made his way forward along the plunging boat. He stood, balancing precariously, on the forward thwart. The mainchains of the brig were far lower than the mizzen-chains of the *Indefatigable*, but this time he had to jump upwards. One of the seamen steadied him with an arm on his shoulder.

'Wait for it, sir,' he said. 'Get ready. Now jump, sir.'

Hornblower hurled himself, all arms and legs, like a leaping frog, at the mainchains. His hands reached the shrouds, but his knee slipped off, and the brig, rolling, lowered him thigh deep into the sea as the shrouds slipped through his hands. But the waiting seamen grabbed his wrists and hauled him on board, and two more seamen followed him. He led the way onto the deck.

The first sight to meet his eyes was a man seated on the hatch cover, his head thrown back, holding to his mouth a bottle, the bottom pointing straight up to the sky. He was one of a large group all sitting round the hatch cover; there were more bottles in evidence; one was passed by one man to another as he looked, and as he approached a roll of the ship brought an empty bottle rolling past his toes to clatter into the scuppers. Another of the group, with white hair blowing in the wind, rose to welcome him, and stood for a moment with waving arms and rolling eyes, bracing himself as though to say something of immense importance and seeking earnestly for the right words to use.

'Goddam English,' was what he finally said, and, having said it, he sat down with a bump on the hatch cover and from a seated position proceeded to lie down and compose himself to sleep with his head on his arms.

'They've made the best of their time, sir, by the Holy,' said the seaman at Hornblower's elbow.

'Wish we were as happy,' said another.

A case still a quarter full of bottles, each elaborately sealed, stood on the deck beside the hatch cover, and the seaman picked out a bottle to look at it curiously. Hornblower did not need to remember the lieutenant's warning; on his shore excursions with press gangs he had already had experience of the British seaman's tendency to drink. His boarding party would be as drunk as the Frenchmen in half an hour if he allowed it. A frightful mental picture of himself drifting in the Bay of Biscay with a disabled ship and a drunken crew rose in his mind and filled him with anxiety.

'Put that down,' he ordered.

The urgency of the situation made his seventeen-year-old voice crack like a fourteen-year old's, and the seaman hesitated, holding the bottle in his hand.

'Put it down, d'ye hear?' said Hornblower, desperate with worry. This was his first independent command; conditions were absolutely novel, and excitement brought out all the passion of his mercurial temperament, while at the same time the more calculating part of his mind told him that if he were not obeyed now he never would be. His pistol was in his belt, and he put his hand on the butt, and it is conceivable that he would have drawn it and used it (if the priming had not got wet, he said to himself bitterly when he thought about the incident later on), but the seaman with one more glance at him put the bottle back into the case. The incident was closed, and it was time for the next step.

'Take these men forrard,' he said, giving the obvious order. 'Throw 'em into the forecastle.'

'Aye aye, sir.'

Most of the Frenchmen could still walk, but three were dragged by their collars, while the British herded the others before them.

'Come alongee,' said one of the seamen. 'Thisa waya.'

He evidently believed a Frenchman would understand him better if he spoke like that. The Frenchman who had greeted their arrival now awakened, and, suddenly realizing he was being dragged forward, broke away and turned back to Hornblower.

'I officer,' he said, pointing to himself. 'I not go wit' zem.'

'Take him away!' said Hornblower. In his tense condition he could not stop to debate trifles.

He dragged the case of bottles down to the ship's side and pitched them overboard two at a time–obviously it was wine of some special vintage which the Frenchmen had decided to drink before the English could get their hands on it, but that weighed not at all with Hornblower, for a British seaman could get drunk on vintage claret as easily as upon service rum. The task was finished before the last of the Frenchmen disappeared into the forecastle, and Hornblower had time to look about him. The strong breeze blew confusingly round his ears, and the ceaseless thunder of the flapping jib made it hard to think as he looked at the ruin aloft. Every sail was flat aback, the brig was moving jerkily, gathering sternway for a space before her untended rudder threw her round to spill the wind and bring her up again like a jibbing horse. His mathematical mind had already had plenty of experience with a well-handled ship, with the delicate adjustment between after sails and headsails. Here the balance had been disturbed, and Hornblower was at work on the problem of forces acting on plane surfaces when his men came trooping back to him. One thing at least was certain, and that was that the precariously hanging foretopsail yard would tear itself free to do all sorts of unforeseeable damage if it were tossed about much more. This ship must be properly hove to, and Hornblower could guess how to set about it, and he formulated the order in his mind just in time to avoid any appearance of hesitation.

'Brace the after yards to larboard,' he said. 'Man the braces, men.'

They obeyed him, while he himself went gingerly to the wheel; he had served a few tricks as helmsman, learning his professional duties under Pellew's orders, but he did not feel happy about it. The spokes felt foreign to his fingers as he took hold; he spun the wheel experimentally but timidly. But it was easy. With the after yards braced round the brig rode more comfortably at once, and the spokes told their own story to his sensitive fingers as the ship became a thing of logical construction again. Hornblower's mind completed the solution of the problem of the effect of the rudder at the same time as his senses solved it empirically. The wheel could be safely lashed, he knew, in these conditions, and he slipped the becket over the spoke and stepped away from the wheel, with the *Marie Galante* riding comfortably and taking the seas on her starboard bow.

The seamen took his competence gratifyingly for granted, but Hornblower, looking at the tangle on the foremast, had not the remotest idea of how to deal with the next problem. He was not even sure about what was wrong. But the hands under his orders were seamen of vast experience, who must have dealt with similar emergencies a score of times. The first–indeed the only–thing to do was to delegate his responsibility.

'Who's the oldest seaman among you?' he demanded–his determination not to quaver made him curt.

'Matthews, sir,' said someone at length, indicating with his thumb the pigtailed and tattooed seaman upon whom he had fallen in the cutter.

'Very well, then. I'll rate you petty officer, Matthews. Get to work at once and clear that raffle away forrard. I'll be busy here aft.'

It was a nervous moment for Hornblower, but Matthews put his knuckles to his forehead.

'Aye aye, sir,' he said, quite as a matter of course.

'Get that jib in first, before it flogs itself to pieces,' said Hornblower, greatly emboldened.

'Aye aye, sir.'

'Carry on, then.'

The seaman turned to go forward, and Hornblower walked aft. He took the telescope from its becket on the poop, and swept the horizon. There were a few sails in sight; the nearest ones he could recognize as prizes, which, with all sail set that they could carry, were heading for England as fast as they could go. Far away to windward he could see the *Indefatigable*'s topsails as she clawed after the rest of the convoy–she had already overhauled and captured all the slower and less weatherly vessels, so that each succeeding chase would be longer. Soon he would be alone on this wide sea, three hundred miles from England. Three hundred miles–two days with a fair wind; but how long if the wind turned foul?

He replaced the telescope; the men were already hard at work forward, so he went below and looked round the neat cabins of the officers; two single ones for the captain and the mate, presumably, and a double one for the bos'un and the cook or the carpenter. He found the lazarette, identifying it by the miscellaneous stores within it; the door was swinging to and fro with a bunch of keys dangling. The French captain, faced with the loss of all he possessed, had not even troubled to lock the door again after taking out the case of wine. Hornblower locked the door and put the keys in his pocket and felt suddenly lonely–his first experience of the loneliness of the man in command at sea. He went on deck again, and at sight of him Matthews hurried aft and knuckled his forehead.

'Beg pardon, sir, but we'll have to use the jeers to sling that yard again.'

'Very good.'

'We'll need more hands than we have, sir. Can I put some o' they Frenchies to work?'

'If you think you can. If any of them are sober enough.'

'I think I can, sir. Drunk or sober.'

'Very good.'

It was at this moment that Hornblower remembered with bitter self-reproach that the priming of his pistol was probably wet, and he had not scorn enough for himself at having put his trust in a pistol without re-priming after evolutions in a small boat. While Matthews went forward he dashed below again. There was a case of pistols which he remembered having seen in the captain's cabin, with a powder flask and bullet bag hanging beside it. He loaded both weapons and reprimed his own, and came on deck again with three pistols in his belt just as his men appeared from the forecastle herding half a dozen Frenchmen. He posed himself in the poop, straddling with his hands behind his back, trying to adopt an air of magnificent indifference and understanding. With the jeers taking the weight of yard and sail, an hour's hard work resulted in the yard being slung again and the sail reset.

When the work was advancing towards completion, Hornblower came to himself again to remember that in a few minutes he would have to set a course, and he dashed below again to set out the chart and the dividers and parallel rulers. From his pocket he extracted the crumpled scrap of paper with his position on it–he had thrust it in there so carelessly a little while back, at a time when the immediate problem before him was to transfer himself from the *Indefatigable* to the cutter. It made him unhappy to think how cavalierly he had treated that scrap of paper then; he began to feel that life in the Navy, although it seemed to move from one crisis to another, was really one continuous crisis, that even while dealing with one emergency it was necessary to be making plans to deal with the next. He bent over the chart, plotted his position, and laid off his course. It was a queer uncomfortable feeling to think that what had up to this moment been an academic exercise conducted under the reassuring supervision of Mr Soames was now something on which hinged his life and his reputation. He checked his working, decided on his course, and wrote it down on a scrap of paper for fear he should forget it.

So when the foretopsail yard was re-slung, and the prisoners herded back into the forecastle, and Matthews looked to him for further orders, he was ready.

'We'll square away,' he said. 'Matthews, send a man to the wheel.'

He himself gave a hand at the braces; the wind had moderated and he felt his men could handle the brig under her present sail.

'What course, sir?' asked the man at the wheel, and Hornblower dived into his pocket for his scrap of paper.

'Nor'-east by north,' he said, reading it out.

'Nor'-east by north, sir,' said the helmsman; and the *Marie Galante*, running free, set her course for England.

Night was closing in by now, and all round the circle of the horizon there was not a sail in sight. There must be plenty of ships just over the horizon, he knew, but that did not do much to ease his feeling of loneliness as darkness came on. There was so much to do, so much to bear in mind, and all the responsibility lay on his unaccustomed shoulders. The prisoners had to be battened down in the forecastle, a watch had to be set–there was even the trivial matter of hunting up flint and steel to light the binnacle lamp. A hand forward as a lookout, who could also keep an eye on the prisoners below; a hand aft at the wheel. Two hands snatching some sleep–knowing that to get in any sail would be an all-hands job–a hasty meal of water from the scuttle-butt and of biscuit from the cabin stores in the lazarette–a constant eye to be kept on the weather. Hornblower paced the deck in the darkness.

'Why don't you get some sleep, sir?' asked the man at the wheel.

'I will, later on, Hunter,' said Hornblower, trying not to allow his tone to reveal the fact that such a thing had never occurred to him.

He knew it was sensible advice, and he actually tried to follow it, retiring below to fling himself down on the captain's cot; but of course he could not sleep. When he heard the lookout bawling down the companionway to rouse the other two hands to relieve the watch (they were asleep in the next cabin to him) he could not prevent himself from getting up again and coming on deck to see that all was well. With Matthews in charge he felt he should not be anxious, and he drove himself below again, but he had hardly fallen on to the cot again when a new thought brought him to his feet again, his skin cold with anxiety, and a prodigious self-contempt vying with anxiety for first glance in his emotions. He rushed on deck and walked forward to where Matthews was squatting by the knightheads.

'Nothing has been done to see if the brig is taking in any water,' he said–he had hurriedly worked out the wording of that sentence during his walk forward, so as to cast no aspersion on Matthews and yet at the same time, for the sake of discipline, attributing no blame to himself.

'That's so, sir,' said Matthews.

'One of those shots fired by the *Indefatigable* hulled her,' went on Hornblower. 'What damage did it do?'

'I don't rightly know, sir,' said Matthews. 'I was in the cutter at the time.'

'We must look as soon as it's light,' said Hornblower. 'And we'd better sound the well now.'

Those were brave words; during his rapid course in seamanship aboard the *Indefatigable* Hornblower had had a little instruction everywhere, working under the orders of every head of department in rotation. Once he had been with the carpenter when he sounded the well–whether he could find the well in this ship and sound it he did not know.

'Aye aye, sir,' said Matthews, without hesitation, and strolled aft to the pump. 'You'll need a light, sir. I'll get one.'

When he came back with the lantern he shone it on the coiled sounding line hanging beside the pump, so that Hornblower recognized it at once. He lifted it down, inserted the three-foot weighted rod into the aperture of the well, and then remembered in time to take it out again and make sure it was dry. Then he let it drop, paying out the line until he felt the rod strike the ship's bottom with a satisfactory thud. He hauled out the line again, and Matthews held the lantern as Hornblower with some trepidation brought out the timber to examine it.

'Not a drop, sir!' said Matthews. 'Dry as yesterday's pannikin.'

Hornblower was agreeably surprised. Any ship he had ever heard of leaked to a certain extent; even in the well-found *Indefatigable* pumping had been necessary every day. He did not know whether this dryness was a remarkable phenomenon or a very remarkable one. He wanted to be both noncommittal and imperturbable.

'H'm,' was the comment he eventually produced. 'Very good, Matthews. Coil that line again.'

The knowledge that the *Marie Galante* was making no water at all might have encouraged him to sleep, if the wind had not chosen to veer steadily and strengthen itself somewhat soon after he retired again. It was Matthews who came down and pounded on his door with the unwelcome news.

'We can't keep the course you set much longer, sir,' concluded Matthews. 'And the wind's coming gusty-like.'

'Very good, I'll be up. Call all hands,' said Hornblower, with a testiness that might have been the result of a sudden awakening if it had not really disguised his inner quaverings.

With such a small crew he dared not run the slightest risk of being taken by surprise by the weather. Nothing could be done in a hurry, as he soon found. He had to take the wheel while his four hands laboured at reefing topsails and snugging the brig down; the task took half the night, and by the time it was finished it was quite plain that with the wind veering northerly the *Marie Galante* could not steer north-east by north any longer. Hornblower gave up the wheel and went below to the chart, but what he saw there only confirmed the pessimistic decision he had already reached by mental calculation. As close to the wind as they could lie on this tack they could not weather Ushant. Shorthanded as he was he did not dare continue in the hope that the wind might back; all his reading and all his instruction had warned him of the terrors of a lee shore. There was nothing for it but to go about; he returned to the deck with a heavy heart.

'All hands wear ship,' he said, trying to bellow the order in the manner of Mr Bolton, the third lieutenant of the *Indefatigable*.

They brought the brig safely round, and she took up her new course, close hauled on the starboard tack. Now she was heading away from the dangerous shores of France, without a doubt, but she was heading nearly as directly away from the friendly shores of England–gone was all hope of an easy two days' run to England; gone was any hope of sleep that night for Hornblower.

During the year before he joined the Navy Hornblower had attended classes given by a penniless French émigré in French, music, and dancing. Early enough the wretched émigré had found that Hornblower had no ear for music whatever, which made it almost impossible to teach him to dance, and so he had endeavoured to earn his fee by concentrating on French. A good deal of what he had taught Hornblower had found a permanent resting place in Hornblower's tenacious memory. He had never thought it would be of much use to him, but he discovered the contrary when the French captain at dawn insisted on an interview with him. The Frenchman had a little English, but it was a pleasant surprise to Hornblower to find that they actually could get along better in French, as soon as he could fight down his shyness sufficiently to produce the halting words.

The captain drank thirstily from the scuttlebut; his cheeks were of course unshaven and he wore a bleary look after twelve hours in a crowded forecastle, where he had been battened down three parts drunk.

'My men are hungry,' said the captain; he did not look hungry himself.

'Mine also,' said Hornblower. 'I also.'

It was natural when one spoke French to gesticulate, to indicate his men with a wave of the hand and himself with a tap on the chest.

'I have a cook,' said the captain.

It took some time to arrange the terms of a truce. The Frenchmen were to be allowed on deck, the cook was to provide food for everyone on board, and while these amenities were permitted, until noon, the French would make no attempt to take the ship.

'Good,' said the captain at length; and when Hornblower had given the necessary orders permitting the release of the crew he shouted for the cook and entered into an urgent discussion regarding dinner. Soon smoke was issuing satisfactorily from the galley chimney.

Then the captain looked up at the grey sky, at the close reefed topsails, and glanced into the binnacle at the compass.

'A foul wind for England,' he remarked.

'Yes,' said Hornblower shortly. He did not want this Frenchman to guess at his trepidation and bitterness.

The captain seemed to be feeling the motion of the brig under his feet with attention.

'She rides a little heavily, does she not?' he said.

'Perhaps,' said Hornblower. He was not familiar with the *Marie Galante*, nor with ships at all, and he had no opinion on the subject, but he was not going to reveal his ignorance.

'Does she leak?' asked the captain.

'There is no water in her,' said Hornblower.

'Ah!' said the captain. 'But you would find none in the well. We are carrying a cargo of rice, you must remember.'

'Yes,' said Hornblower.

He found it very hard at that moment to remain outwardly unperturbed, as his mind grasped the implications of what was being said to him. Rice would absorb every drop of water taken in by the ship, so that no leak would be apparent on sounding the well–and yet every drop of water taken in would deprive her of that much buoyancy, all the same.

'One shot from your cursed frigate struck us in the hull,' said the captain. 'Of course you have investigated the damage?'

'Of course,' said Hornblower, lying bravely.

But as soon as he could he had a private conversation with Matthews on the point, and Matthews instantly looked grave.

'Where did the shot hit her, sir?' he asked.

'Somewhere on the port side, forrard, I should judge.'

He and Matthews craned their necks over the ship's side.

'Can't see nothin', sir,' said Matthews. 'Lower me over the side in a bowline and I'll see what I can find, sir.'

Hornblower was about to agree and then changed his mind.

'I'll go over the side myself,' he said.

He could not analyse the motives which impelled him to say that. Partly he wanted to see things with his own eyes; partly he was influenced by the doctrine that he should never give an order he was not prepared to carry out himself–but mostly it must have been the desire to impose a penance on himself for his negligence.

Matthews and Carson put a bowline round him and lowered him over. He found himself dangling against the ship's side, with the sea bubbling just below him; as the ship pitched the sea came up to meet him, and he was wet to the waist in the first five seconds; and as the ship rolled he was alternately swung away from the side and bumped against it. The men with the line walked steadily aft, giving him the chance to examine the whole side of the brig above water, and there was not a shot hole to be seen. He said as much to Matthews when they hauled him on deck.

'Then it's below the waterline, sir,' said Matthews, saying just what was in Hornblower's mind. 'You're sure the shot hit her, sir?'

'Yes, I'm sure,' snapped Hornblower.

Lack of sleep and worry and a sense of guilt were all shortening his temper, and he had to speak sharply or break down in tears. But he had already decided on the next move–he had made up his mind about that while they were hauling him up.

'We'll heave her to on the other tack and try again,' he said.

On the other tack the ship would incline over to the other side, and the shot-hole, if there was one, would not be so deeply submerged. Hornblower stood with the water dripping from his clothes as they wore the brig round; the wind was keen and cold, but he was shivering with expectancy rather than cold. The heeling of the brig laid him much more definitely against the side, and they lowered him until his legs were scraping over the marine growths which she carried there between wind and water. They then walked aft with him, dragging him along the side of the ship, and just abaft the foremast he found what he was seeking.

'Avast, there!' he yelled up to the deck, mastering the sick despair that he felt. The motion of the bowline along the ship ceased. 'Lower away! Another two feet!'

Now he was waist-deep in the water, and when the brig swayed the water closed briefly over his head, like a momentary death. Here it was, two feet below the waterline even with the brig hove to on this tack–a splintered, jagged hole, square rather than round, and a foot across. As the sea boiled round him Hornblower even fancied he could hear it bubbling into the ship, but that might be pure fancy.

He hailed the deck for them to haul him up again, and they stood eagerly listening for what he had to say.

'Two feet below the waterline, sir?' said Matthews. 'She was close hauled and heeling right over, of course, when we hit her. But her bows must have lifted just as we fired. And of course she's lower in the water now.'

That was the point. Whatever they did now, however much they heeled her, that hole would be under water. And on the other tack it would be far under water, with much additional pressure; yet on the present tack they were headed for France. And the more water they took in, the lower the brig would settle, and the greater would be the pressure forcing water in through the hole. Something must be done to plug the leak, and Hornblower's reading of the manuals of seamanship told him what it was.

'We must fother a sail and get it over that hole,' he announced. 'Call those Frenchmen over.'

To fother a sail was to make something like a vast hairy doormat out of it, by threading innumerable lengths of half-unravelled line through it. When this was done the sail would be lowered below the ship's bottom and placed against the hole. The inward pressure would then force the hairy mass so tightly against the hole that the entrance of water would be made at least much more difficult.

The Frenchmen were not quick to help in the task; it was no longer their ship, and they were heading for an English prison, so that even with their lives at stake they were somewhat apathetic. It took time to get out a new topgallant sail–Hornblower felt that the stouter the canvas the better–and to set a party to work cutting lengths of line, threading them through, and unravelling them. The French captain looked at them squatting on the deck all at work.

'Five years I spent in a prison hulk in Portsmouth during the last war,' he said. 'Five years.'

'Yes,' said Hornblower.

He might have felt sympathy, but he was not only preoccupied with his own problems but he was numb with cold. He not only had every intention if possible of escorting the French captain to England and to prison again but he also at that very moment intended to go below and appropriate some of his spare clothing.

Down below it seemed to Hornblower as if the noises all about him–the creaks and groans of a wooden ship at sea–were more pronounced than usual. The brig was riding easily enough hove-to, and yet the bulkheads down below were cracking and creaking as if the brig were racking herself to pieces in a storm. He dismissed the notion as a product of his over-stimulated imagination but by the time he had towelled himself into something like warmth and put on the captain's best suit it recurred to him; the brig was groaning as if in stress.

He came on deck again to see how the working party was progressing. He had hardly been on deck two minutes when one of the Frenchmen, reaching back for another length of line, stopped in his movement to stare at the deck. He picked at a deck seam, looked up and caught Hornblower's eye, and called to him. Hornblower made no pretence of understanding the words; the gestures explained themselves. The deck seam was opening a little; the pitch was bulging out of it. Hornblower looked at the phenomenon without understanding it–only a foot or two of the seam was open, and the rest of the deck seemed solid enough. No! Now that his attention was called to it, and he looked further, there were one or two other places in the deck where the pitch had risen in ridges from out of the seams. It was something beyond his limited experience, even beyond his extensive reading. But the French captain was at his side staring at the deck too.

'My God!' he said. 'The rice! The rice!'

The French word 'riz' that he used was unknown to Hornblower, but he stamped his foot on the deck and pointed down through it.

'The cargo!' he said in explanation. 'It–it grows bigger.'

Matthews was with them now, and without knowing a word of French he understood.

'Didn't I hear this brig was full of rice, sir?' he asked.

'Yes.'

'That's it, then. The water's got into it and it's swelling.'

So it would. Dry rice soaked in water would double or treble its volume. The cargo was swelling and bursting the seams of the ship open. Hornblower remembered the unnatural creaks and groans below. It was a black moment; he looked round at the unfriendly sea for inspiration and support, and found neither. Several seconds passed before he was ready to speak, and ready to maintain the dignity of a naval officer in face of difficulties.

'The sooner we get that sail over that hole the better, then,' he said. It was too much to be expected that his voice should sound quite natural. 'Hurry those Frenchmen up.'

He turned to pace the deck, so as to allow his feelings to subside and to set his thoughts running in an orderly fashion again, but the French captain was at his elbow, voluble as a Job's comforter.

'I said I thought the ship was riding heavily,' he said. 'She is lower in the water.'

'Go to the devil,' said Hornblower, in English–he could not think up the French for that phrase.

Even as he stood he felt a sudden sharp shock beneath his feet, as if someone had hit the deck underneath them with a mallet. The ship was springing apart bit by bit.

'Hurry with that sail!' he yelled, turning back to the working party, and then was angry with himself because the tone of his voice must have betrayed undignified agitation.

At last an area five feet square of the sail was fothered, lines were rove through the grommets, and the working party hurried forward to work the sail under the brig and drag it aft to the hole. Hornblower was taking off his clothes, not out of regard for the captain's property but so as to keep them dry for himself.

'I'll go over and see that it's in place,' he said. 'Matthews, get a bowline ready for me.'

Naked and wet, it seemed to him as if the wind blew clear through him; rubbing against the ship's side as she rolled he lost a good deal of skin, and the waves passing down the ship smacked at him with a boisterous lack of consideration. But he saw the fothered sail placed against the hole, and with intense satisfaction he saw the hairy mass suck into position, dimpling over the hole to form a deep hollow so that he could be sure that the hole was plugged solid. They hauled him up again when he hailed, and awaited his orders; he stood naked, stupid with cold and fatigue and lack of sleep, struggling to form his next decision.

'Lay her on the starboard tack,' he said at length.

If the brig were going to sink, it hardly mattered if it were one hundred or two hundred miles from the French coast; if she were to stay afloat he wanted to be well clear of that lee shore and the chance of recapture. The shot hole with its fothered sail would be deeper under water to increase the risk, but it seemed to be the best chance. The French captain saw them making preparations to wear the brig round, and turned upon Hornblower with voluble protests. With this wind they could make Bordeaux easily on the other tack. Hornblower was risking all their lives, he said. Into Hornblower's numb mind crept, uninvited, the translation of something he had previously wanted to say. He could use it now.

'Allez au diable,' he snapped, as he put the Frenchman's stout woollen shirt on over his head.

When his head emerged the Frenchman was still protesting volubly, so violently indeed that a new doubt came into Hornblower's mind. A word to Matthews sent him round the French prisoners to search for weapons. There was nothing to be found except the sailors' knives, but as a matter of precaution Hornblower had them all impounded, and when he had dressed he went to special trouble with his three pistols, drawing the charges from them and reloading and repriming afresh. Three pistols in his belt looked piratical, as though he were still young enough to be playing imaginative games, but Hornblower felt in his bones that there might be a time when the Frenchmen might try to rise against their captors, and three pistols would not be too many against twelve desperate men who had makeshift weapons ready to hand, belaying pins and the like.

Matthews was awaiting him with a long face.

'Sir,' he said, 'begging your pardon, but I don't like the looks of it. Straight, I don't. I don't like the feel of her. She's settlin' down and she's opening up, I'm certain sure. Beg your pardon, sir, for saying so.'

Down below Hornblower had heard the fabric of the ship continuing to crack and complain; up here the deck seams were gaping more widely. There was a very likely explanation; the swelling of the rice must have forced open the ship's seams below water, so that plugging the shot-hole would have only eliminated what would be by now only a minor leak. Water must still be pouring in, the cargo still swelling, opening up the ship like an overblown flower. Ships were built to withstand blows from without, and there was nothing about their construction to resist an outward pressure. Wider and wider would gape the seams, and faster and faster the sea would gain access to the cargo.

'Look'e there, sir!' said Matthews suddenly.

In the broad light of day a small grey shape was hurrying along the weather scuppers; another one followed it and another after that. Rats! Something convulsive must be going on down below to bring them on deck in daytime, from out of their comfortable nests among the unlimited food of the cargo. The pressure must be enormous. Hornblower felt another small shock beneath his feet at that moment, as something further parted beneath them. But there was one more card to play, one last line of defence that he could think of.

'I'll jettison the cargo,' said Hornblower. He had never uttered that word in his life, but he had read it. 'Get the prisoners and we'll start.'

The battened-down hatch cover was domed upwards curiously and significantly; as the wedges were knocked out one plank tore loose at one end with a crash, pointing diagonally upwards, and as the working party lifted off the cover a brown form followed it upwards–a bag of rice, forced out by the underlying pressure until it jammed in the hatchway.

'Tail on to those tackles and sway it up,' said Hornblower.

Bag by bag the rice was hauled up from the hold; sometimes the bags split, allowing a torrent of rice to pour on to the deck, but that did not matter. Another section of the working party swept rice and bags to the lee side and into the ever-hungry sea. After the first three bags the difficulties increased, for the cargo was so tightly jammed below that it called for enormous force to tear each bag out of its position. Two men had to go down the hatchway to pry the bags loose and adjust the slings. There was a momentary hesitation on the part of the two Frenchmen to whom Hornblower pointed–the bags might not all be jammed and the hold of a tossing ship was a dangerous place wherein a roll might bury them alive–but Hornblower had no thought at that moment for other people's human fears. He scowled at the brief check and they hastened to lower themselves down the hatchway. The labour was enormous as it went on hour after hour; the men at the tackles were dripping with sweat and drooping with fatigue, but they had to relieve periodically the men below, for the bags had jammed themselves in tiers, pressed hard against the ship's bottom below and the deck beams above, and when the bags immediately below the hatchway had been swayed up the surrounding ones had to be pried loose, out of each tier. Then when a small clearance had been made in the neighbourhood of the hatchway, and they were getting deeper down into the hold, they made the inevitable discovery. The lower tiers of bags had been wetted, their contents had swelled, and the bags had burst. The lower half of the hold was packed solid with damp rice which could only be got out with shovels and a hoist. The still intact bags of the upper tiers, farther away from the hatchway, were still jammed tight, calling for much labour to free them and to manhandle them under the hatchway to be hoisted out.

Hornblower, facing the problem, was distracted by a touch on his elbow when Matthews came up to speak to him.

'It ain't no go, sir,' said Matthews. 'She's lower in the water an' settlin' fast.'

Hornblower walked to the ship's side with him and looked over. There could be no doubt about it. He had been over the side himself and could remember the height of the waterline, and he had for a more exact guide the level of the fothered sail under the ship's bottom. The brig was a full six inches lower in the water–and this after fifty tons of rice at least had been hoisted out and flung over the side. The brig must be leaking like a basket, with water pouring in through the gaping seams to be sucked up immediately by the thirsty rice.

Hornblower's left hand was hurting him, and he looked down to discover that he was gripping the rail with it so tightly as to cause him pain, without knowing he was doing so. He released his grip and looked about him, at the afternoon sun, at the tossing sea. He did not want to give in and admit defeat. The French captain came up to him.

'This is folly,' he said. 'Madness, sir. My men are overcome by fatigue.'

Over by the hatchway, Hornblower saw, Hunter was driving the French seamen to their work with a rope's end, which he was using furiously. There was not much more work to be got out of the Frenchmen; and at that moment the *Marie Galante* rose heavily to a wave and wallowed down the further side. Even his inexperience could detect the sluggishness and ominous deadness of her movements. The brig had not much longer to float, and there was a good deal to do.

'I shall make preparations for abandoning the ship, Matthews,' he said.

He poked his chin upwards as he spoke; he would not allow either a Frenchman or a seaman to guess at his despair.

'Aye aye, sir,' said Matthews.

The *Marie Galante* carried a boat on chocks abaft the mainmast; at Matthews's summons the men abandoned their work on the cargo and hurried to the business of putting food and water in her.

'Beggin' your pardon, sir,' said Hunter aside to Hornblower, 'but you ought to see you have warm clothes, sir. I been in an open boat ten days once, sir.'

'Thank you, Hunter,' said Hornblower.

There was much to think of. Navigating instruments, charts, compass –would he be able to get a good observation with his sextant in a tossing little boat? Common prudence dictated that they should have all the food and water with them that the boat could carry; but–Hornblower eyed the wretched craft dubiously–seventeen men would fill it to overflowing anyway. He would have to leave much to the judgement of the French captain and of Matthews.

The tackles were manned and the boat was swayed up from the chocks and lowered into the water in the tiny lee afforded on the lee quarter. The *Marie Galante* put her nose into a wave, refusing to rise to it; green water came over the starboard bow and poured aft along the deck before a sullen wallow on the part of the brig sent it into the scuppers. There was not much time to spare–a rending crash from below told that the cargo was still swelling and forcing the bulkheads. There was a panic among the Frenchmen, who began to tumble down into the boat with loud cries. The French captain took one look at

Hornblower and then followed them; two of the British seamen were already over the side fending off the boat.

'Go along,' said Hornblower to Matthews and Carson, who still lingered. He was the captain; it was his place to leave the ship last.

So waterlogged was the brig now that it was not at all difficult to step down into the boat from the deck; the British seamen were in the sternsheets and made room for him.

'Take the tiller, Matthews,' said Hornblower; he did not feel he was competent to handle that over-loaded boat. 'Shove off, there!'

The boat and the brig parted company; the *Marie Galante*, with her helm lashed, poked her nose into the wind and hung there. She had acquired a sudden list, with the starboard side scuppers nearly under water. Another wave broke over her deck, pouring up to the open hatchway. Now she righted herself, her deck nearly level with the sea, and then she sank, on an even keel, the water closing over her, her masts slowly disappearing. For an instant her sails even gleamed under the green water.

'She's gone,' said Matthews.

Hornblower watched the disappearance of his first command. The *Marie Galante* had been entrusted to him to bring into port, and he had failed, failed on his first independent mission. He looked very hard at the setting sun, hoping no one would notice the tears that were filling his eyes.

3

THE PENALTY OF FAILURE

Daylight crept over the tossing waters of the Bay of Biscay to reveal a small boat riding on its wide expanses. It was a very crowded boat; in the bows huddled the French crew of the sunken brig *Marie Galante*, amidships sat the captain and his mate, and in the sternsheets sat Midshipman Horatio Hornblower and the four English seamen who had once constituted the prize-crew of the brig. Hornblower was seasick, for his delicate stomach, having painfully accustomed itself to the motion of the *Indefatigable*, rebelled at the antics of the small boat as she pitched jerkily to her sea-anchor. He was cold and weary as well as seasick after his second night without sleep–he had been vomiting spasmodically all through the hours of darkness, and in the depression which seasickness brings he had thought gloomily about the loss of the *Marie Galante*. If he had only remembered earlier to plug that shot hole! Excuses came to his mind only to be discarded. There had been so much to do, and so few men to do it with–the French crew to guard, the damage aloft to repair, the course to set. The absorbent qualities of the cargo of rice which the *Marie Galante* carried had deceived him when he had remembered to sound the well. All this might be true, but the fact remained that he had lost his ship, his first command. In his own eyes there was no excuse for his failure.

The French crew had wakened with the dawn and were chattering like a nest of magpies; Matthews and Carson beside him were moving stiffly to ease their aching joints.

'Breakfast, sir?' said Matthews.

It was like the games Hornblower had played as a lonely little boy, when he had sat in the empty pig-trough and pretended he was cast away in an open boat. Then he had parcelled out the bit of bread or whatever it was which he had obtained from the kitchen into a dozen rations, counting them carefully, each one to last a day. But a small boy's eager appetite had made those days very short, not more than five minutes long; after standing up in the pig-trough and shading his eyes and looking round the horizon for the succour that he could not discover, he would sit down again, tell himself that the life of a castaway was hard, and then decide that another night had passed and that it was time to eat another ration from his dwindling supply. So here under Hornblower's eye the French captain and mate served out a biscuit of hard bread to each person in the boat, and filled the pannikin for each man in turn from the water breakers under the thwarts. But Hornblower when he sat in the pig-trough, despite his vivid imagination, never thought of this hideous seasickness, of the cold and the cramps, nor of how his skinny posterior would ache with its constant pressure against the hard timbers of the sternsheets; nor, in the sublime self-confidence of childhood, had he ever thought how heavy could be the burden of responsibility on the shoulders of a senior naval officer aged seventeen.

He dragged himself back from the memories of that recent childhood to face the present situation. The grey sky, as far as his inexperienced eye could tell, bore no presage of deterioration in the weather. He wetted his finger and held it up, looking in the boat's compass to gauge the direction of the wind.

'Backing westerly a little, sir,' said Matthews, who had been copying his movements.

'That's so,' agreed Hornblower, hurriedly going through in his mind his recent lessons in boxing the compass. His course to weather Ushant was nor'-east by north, he knew, and the boat close hauled would not lie closer than eight points off the wind–he had lain-to to the sea-anchor all night because the wind had been coming from too far north to enable him to steer for England. But now the wind had backed. Eight points from nor'-east by north was nor'-west by west, and the wind was even more westerly than that. Close hauled he could weather Ushant and even have a margin for contingencies, to keep him clear of the lee shore, which the seamanship books and his own common sense told him was so dangerous.

'We'll make sail, Matthews,' he said; his hand was still grasping the biscuit which his rebellious stomach refused to accept.

'Aye aye, sir.'

A shout to the Frenchmen crowded in the bows drew their attention; in the circumstances it hardly needed Hornblower's halting French to direct them to carry out the obvious task of getting in the sea-anchor. But it was not too easy, with the boat so crowded and hardly a foot of freeboard. The mast was already stepped, and the lug sail bent ready to hoist. Two Frenchmen, balancing precariously, tailed on to the halliard and the sail rose up the mast.

'Hunter, take the sheet,' said Hornblower. 'Matthews, take the tiller. Keep her close hauled on the port tack.'

'Close hauled on the port tack, sir.'

The French captain had watched the proceedings with intense interest from his seat amidships. He had not understood the last, decisive order, but he grasped its meaning quickly enough when the boat came round and steadied on the port tack, heading for England. He stood up, spluttering angry protests.

'The wind is fair for Bordeaux,' he said, gesticulating with clenched fists. 'We could be there by tomorrow. Why do we go north?'

'We go to England,' said Hornblower.

'But–but–it will take us a week! A week even if the wind stays fair. This boat–it is too crowded. We cannot endure a storm. It is madness.'

Hornblower had guessed at the moment the captain stood up what he was going to say, and he hardly bothered to translate the expostulations to himself. He was too tired and too seasick to enter into an argument in a foreign language. He ignored the captain. Not for anything on earth would he turn the boat's head towards France. His naval career had only just begun, and even if it were to be blighted on account of the loss of the *Marie Galante* he had no intention of rotting for years in a French prison.

'Sir!' said the French captain.

The mate who shared the captain's thwart was protesting too, and now they turned to their crew behind them and told them what was going on. An angry movement stirred the crowd.

'Sir!' said the captain again. 'I insist that you head towards Bordeaux.'

He showed signs of advancing upon them; one of the crew behind him began to pull the boat-hook clear, and it would be a dangerous weapon. Hornblower pulled one of the pistols from his belt and pointed it at the captain, who, with the muzzle four feet from his breast, fell back before the gesture. Without taking his eyes off him Hornblower took a second pistol with his left hand.

'Take this, Matthews,' he said.

'Aye aye, sir,' said Matthews, obeying; and then, after a respectful pause, 'Beggin' your pardon, sir, but hadn't you better cock your pistol, sir?'

'Yes,' said Hornblower, exasperated at his own forgetfulness.

He drew the hammer back with a click, and the menacing sound made more acute still the French captain's sense of his own danger, with a cocked and loaded pistol pointed at his stomach in a heaving boat. He waved his hands desperately.

'Please,' he said, 'point it some other way, sir.'

He drew farther back, huddling against the men behind him.

'Hey, avast there, you,' shouted Matthews loudly–a French sailor was trying to let go the halliard unobserved.

'Shoot any man who looks dangerous, Matthews,' said Hornblower.

He was so intent on enforcing his will upon these men, so desperately anxious to retain his liberty, that his face was contracted into a beast-like scowl. No one looking at him could doubt his determination for a moment. He would allow no human life to come between him and his decisions. There was still a third pistol in his belt, and the Frenchmen could guess that if they tried a rush a quarter of them at least would meet their deaths before they overpowered the Englishmen, and the French captain knew he would be the first to die. His expressive hands, waving out from his sides–he could not take his eyes from the pistol–told his men to make no further resistance. Their murmurings died away, and the captain began to plead.

'Five years I was in an English prison during the last war,' he said. 'Let us reach an agreement. Let us go to France. When we reach the shore–anywhere you choose, sir–we will land and you can continue on your journey. Or we can all land, and I will use all my influence to have you and your men sent back to England under cartel, without exchange or ransom. I swear I will.'

'No,' said Hornblower.

England was far easier to reach from here than from the French Biscay coast; as for the other suggestion, Hornblower knew enough about the new government washed up by the revolution in France to be sure that they would never part with prisoners on the representation of a merchant captain. And trained seamen were scarce in France; it was his duty to keep these dozen from returning.

'No,' he said again, in reply to the captain's fresh protests.

'Shall I clout 'im on the jaw, sir?' asked Hunter, at Hornblower's side.

'No,' said Hornblower again; but the Frenchman saw the gesture and guessed at the meaning of the words, and subsided into sullen silence.

But he was roused again at the sight of Hornblower's pistol on his knee, still pointed at him. A sleepy finger might press that trigger.

'Sir,' he said, 'put that pistol away, I beg of you. It is dangerous.'

Hornblower's eye was cold and unsympathetic.

'Put it away, please. I will do nothing to interfere with your command of this boat. I promise you that.'

'Do you swear it?'

'I swear it.'

'And these others?'

The captain looked round at his crew with voluble explanations, and grudgingly they agreed.

'They swear it too.'

'Very well, then.'

Hornblower started to replace the pistol in his belt, and remembered to put it on half-cock in time to save himself from shooting himself in the stomach. Everyone in the boat relaxed into apathy. The boat was rising and swooping rhythmically now, a far more comfortable motion than when it had jerked to a sea-anchor, and Hornblower's stomach lost some of its resentment. He had been two nights without sleep. His head lowered on his chest, and then he leaned sideways against Hunter, and slept peacefully, while the boat, with the wind nearly abeam, headed steadily for England. What woke him late in the day was when Matthews, cramped and weary, was compelled to surrender the tiller to Carson, and after that they kept watch and watch, a hand at the sheet and a hand at the tiller and the others trying to rest. Hornblower took his turn at the sheet, but he would not trust himself with the tiller, especially when night fell; he knew he had not the knack of keeping the boat on her course by the feel of the wind on his cheek and the tiller in his hand.

It was not until long after breakfast the next day–almost noon in fact–that they sighted the sail. It was a Frenchman who saw it first, and his excited cry roused them all. There were three square topsails coming up over the horizon on their weather bow, nearing them so rapidly on a converging course that each time the boat rose on a wave a considerably greater area of canvas was visible.

'What do you think she is, Matthews?' asked Hornblower, while the boat buzzed with the Frenchmen's excitement.

'I can't tell, sir, but I don't like the looks of her,' said Matthews doubtfully. 'She ought to have her t'gallants set in this breeze–and her courses too, an' she hasn't. An' I don't like the cut of her jib, sir. She–she might be a Frenchie to me, sir.'

Any ship travelling for peaceful purposes would naturally have all possible sail set. This ship had not. Hence she was engaged in some belligerent design, but there were more chances that she was British than that she was French, even in here in the Bay. Hornblower took a long look at her; a smallish vessel, although ship-rigged. Flush-decked, with a look of speed about her–her hull was visible at intervals now, with a line of gunports.

'She looks French all over to me, sir,' said Hunter. 'Privateer, seemly.'

'Stand by to jibe,' said Hornblower.

They brought the boat round before the wind, heading directly away from the ship. But in war as in the jungle, to fly is to invite pursuit and attack. The ship set courses and topgallants and came tearing down upon them, passed them at half a cable's length and then hove-to, having cut off their escape. The ship's rail was lined with a curious crowd–a large crew for a vessel that size. A hail came across the water to the boat, and the words were French. The English seamen subsided into curses, while the French captain cheerfully stood up and replied, and the French crew brought the boat alongside the ship.

A handsome young man in a plum-coloured coat with a lace stock greeted Hornblower when he stepped on the deck.

'Welcome, sir, to the *Pique*,' he said in French. 'I am Captain Neuville, of this privateer. And you are—?'

'Midshipman Hornblower, of His Britannic Majesty's ship *Indefatigable*,' growled Hornblower.

'You seem to be in evil humour,' said Neuville. 'Please do not be so distressed at the fortunes of war. You will be accommodated in this ship, until we return to port, with every comfort possible at sea. I beg of you to consider yourself quite at home. For instance, those pistols in your belt must discommode you more than a little. Permit me to relieve you of their weight.'

He took the pistols neatly from Hornblower's belt as he spoke, looked Hornblower keenly over, and then went on.

'That dirk that you wear at your side, sir. Would you oblige me by the loan of it? I assure you that I will return it to you when we part company. But while you are on board here I fear that your impetuous youth might lead you into some rash act while you are wearing a weapon which a credulous mind might believe to be lethal. A thousand thanks. And now might I show you the berth that is being prepared for you?'

With a courteous bow he led the way below. Two decks down, presumably at the level of a foot or two below the water line, was a wide bare 'tweendecks, dimly lighted and scantily ventilated by the hatchways.

'Our slave deck,' explained Neuville carelessly.

'Slave deck?' asked Hornblower.

'Yes. It is here that the slaves were confined during the middle passage.'

Much was clear to Hornblower at once. A slave ship could be readily converted into a privateer. She would already be armed with plenty of guns to defend herself against treacherous attacks while making her purchases in the African rivers; she was faster than the average merchant ship both because of the lack of need of hold space and because with a highly perishable cargo such as slaves speed was a desirable quality, and she was constructed to carry large numbers of men and the great quantities of food and water necessary to keep them supplied while at sea in search of prizes.

'Our market in San Domingo has been closed to us by recent events, of which you must have heard, sir,' went on Neuville, 'and so that the *Pique* could continue to return dividends to me I have converted her into a privateer. Moreover, seeing that the activities of the Committee of Public Safety at present make Paris a more unhealthy spot even than the West Coast of Africa, I decided to take command of my vessel myself. To say nothing of the fact that a certain resolution and hardihood are necessary to make a privateer a profitable investment.'

Neuville's face hardened for a moment into an expression of the grimmest determination, and then softened at once into its previous meaningless politeness.

'This door in this bulkhead,' he continued, 'leads to the quarters I have set aside for captured officers. Here, as you see, is your cot. Please make yourself at home here. Should this ship go into action–as I trust she will frequently do–the hatches above will be battened down. But except on those occasions you will of course be at liberty to move about the ship at your will. Yet I suppose I had better add that any harebrained attempt on the part of prisoners to interfere with the working or wellbeing of this ship would be deeply resented by the crew. They serve on shares, you understand, and are risking their lives and their liberty. I would not be surprised if any rash person who endangered their dividends and freedom were dropped over the side into the sea.'

Hornblower forced himself to reply; he would not reveal that he was almost struck dumb by the calculating callousness of this last speech.

'I understand,' he said.

'Excellent! Now is there anything further you may need, sir?'

Hornblower looked round the bare quarters in which he was to suffer lonely confinement, lit by a dim glimmer of light from a swaying slush lamp.

'Could I have something to read?' he asked.

Neuville thought for a moment.

'I fear there are only professional books,' he said. 'But I can let you have Grandjean's *Principles of Navigation*, and Lebrun's *Handbook on Seamanship* and some similar volumes, if you think you can understand the French in which they are written.'

'I'll try,' said Hornblower.

Probably it was as well that Hornblower was provided with the materials for such strenuous mental exercise. The effort of reading French and of studying his profession at one and the same time kept his mind busy during the dreary days while the *Pique* cruised in search of prizes. Most of the time the Frenchmen ignored him–he had to force himself upon Neuville once to protest against the employment of his four British seamen on the menial work of pumping out the ship, but he had to retire worsted from the argument, if argument it could be called, when Neuville icily refused to discuss the question. Hornblower went back to his quarters with burning cheeks and red ears, and, as ever, when he was mentally disturbed, the thought of his guilt returned to him with new force.

If only he had plugged that shot hole sooner! A clearer-headed officer, he told himself, would have done so. He had lost his ship, the *Indefatigable*'s precious prize, and there was no health in him. Sometimes he made himself review the situation calmly. Professionally, he might not–probably would not–suffer for his negligence. A midshipman with only four for a prize-crew, put on board a two-hundred-ton brig that had been subjected to considerable firing from a frigate's guns, would not be seriously blamed when she sank under him. But Hornblower knew at the same time that he was at least partly at fault. If it was ignorance–there was no excuse for ignorance. If he had allowed his multiple cares to distract him from the business of plugging the shot hole immediately, that was incompetence, and there was no excuse for incompetence. When he thought along those lines he was overwhelmed by waves of despair and of self-contempt, and there was no one to comfort him. The day of his birthday, when he looked at himself at the vast age of eighteen, was the worst of all. Eighteen and a discredited prisoner in the hands of a French privateersman! His self-respect was at its lowest ebb.

The *Pique* was seeking her prey in the most frequented waters in the world, the approaches to the Channel, and there could be no more vivid demonstration of the vastness of the ocean than the fact that she cruised day after day without glimpsing a sail. She maintained a triangular course, reaching to the north-west, tacking to the south, running under easy sail north-easterly again, with lookouts at every masthead, with nothing to see but the tossing waste of water. Until the morning when a high-pitched yell from the foretopgallant masthead attracted the attention of everybody on deck, including Hornblower, standing lonely in the waist. Neuville, by the wheel, bellowed a question to the lookout, and Hornblower, thanks to his recent studies, could translate the answer. There was a sail visible to windward, and next moment the lookout reported that it had altered course and was running down towards them.

That meant a great deal. In wartime any merchant ship would be suspicious of strangers and would give them as wide a berth as possible; and especially when she was to windward and therefore far safer. Only someone prepared to fight or possessed of a perfectly morbid curiosity would abandon a windward position. A wild and unreasonable hope filled Hornblower's breast; a ship of war at sea–thanks to England's maritime mastery–would be far more probably English than French. And this was the cruising ground of the *Indefatigable*, his own ship, stationed there specially to fulfil the double function of looking out for French commerce-destroyers and intercepting French blockade-runners. A hundred miles from here she had put him and his prize crew on board the *Marie Galante*. It was a thousand to one, he exaggerated despairingly to himself, against any ship sighted being the *Indefatigable*. But–hope reasserted itself–the fact that she was coming down to investigate reduced the odds to ten to one at most. Less than ten to one.

He looked over at Neuville, trying to think his thoughts. The *Pique* was fast and handy, and there was a clear avenue of escape to leeward. The fact that the stranger had altered course towards them was a suspicious circumstance, but it was known that Indiamen, the richest prizes of all, had sometimes traded on the similarity of their appearance to that of ships of the line, and by showing a bold front had scared dangerous enemies away. That would be a temptation to a man eager to make a prize. At Neuville's orders all sail was set, ready for instant flight or pursuit, and, close-hauled, the *Pique* stood towards the stranger. It was not long before Hornblower, on the deck, caught a glimpse of a gleam of white, like a tiny grain of rice, far away on the horizon as the *Pique* lifted on a swell. Here came Matthews, red-faced and excited, running aft to Hornblower's side.

'That's the old *Indefatigable*, sir,' he said. 'I swear it!' He sprang on to the rail, holding on by the shrouds, and stared under his hand.

'Yes! There she is, sir! She's loosing her royals now, sir. We'll be back on board of her in time for grog!'

A French petty officer reached up and dragged Matthews by the seat of his trousers from his perch, and with a blow and a kick drove him forward again, while a moment later Neuville was shouting the orders that wore the ship round to head away directly from the *Indefatigable*. Neuville beckoned Hornblower over to his side.

'Your late ship, I understand, Mr Hornblower?'

'Yes.'

'What is her best point of sailing?'

Hornblower's eyes met Neuville's.

'Do not look so noble,' said Neuville, smiling with thin lips. 'I could undoubtedly induce you to give me the information. I know of ways. But it is unnecessary, fortunately for you. There is no ship on earth–especially none of His Britannic Majesty's clumsy frigates–that can outsail the *Pique* running before the wind. You will soon see that.'

He strolled to the taffrail and looked aft long and earnestly through his glass, but no more earnestly than did Hornblower with his naked eye.

'You see?' said Neuville, proffering the glass.

Hornblower took it, but more to catch a closer glimpse of his ship than to confirm his observations. He was homesick, desperately homesick, at that moment, for the *Indefatigable*. But there could be no denying that she was being left fast behind. Her topgallants were out of sight again now, and only her royals were visible.

'Two hours and we shall have run her mastheads under,' said Neuville, taking back the telescope and shutting it with a snap.

He left Hornblower standing sorrowful at the taffrail while he turned to berate the helmsman for not steering a steadier course; Hornblower heard the explosive words without listening to them, the wind blowing into his face and ruffling his hair over his ears, and the wake of the ship's passage boiling below him. So might Adam have looked back at Eden; Hornblower remembered the stuffy dark midshipmen's berth, the smells and the creakings, the bitter cold nights, turning out in response to the call for all hands, the weevilly bread and the wooden beef, and he yearned for them all, with the sick feeling of hopeless longing. Liberty was vanishing over the horizon. Yet it was not these personal feelings that drove him below in search of action. They may have quickened his wits, but it was a sense of duty which inspired him.

The slave-deck was deserted, as usual, with all hands at quarters. Beyond the bulkhead stood his cot with the books upon it and the slush lamp swaying above it. There was nothing there to give him any inspiration. There was another locked door in the after bulkhead. That opened into some kind of boatswain's store; twice he had seen it unlocked and paint and similar supplies brought out from it. Paint! That gave him an idea; he looked from the door up to the slush lamp and back again, and as he stepped forward he took his claspknife out of his pocket. But before very long he recoiled again, sneering at himself. The door was not panelled, but was made of two solid slabs of wood, with the cross-beams on the inside. There was the keyhole of the lock, but it presented no point of attack. It would take him hours and hours to cut through that door with his knife, at a time when minutes were precious.

His heart was beating feverishly–but no more feverishly than his mind was working–as he looked round again. He reached up to the lamp and shook it; nearly full. There was a moment when he stood hesitating, nerving himself, and then he threw himself into action. With a ruthless hand he tore the pages out of Grandjean's *Principes de la Navigation*, crumpling them up in small quantities into little loose balls which he laid at the foot of the door. He threw off his uniform coat and dragged his blue woollen jersey over his head; his long powerful fingers tore it across and plucked eagerly at it to unravel it. After starting some loose threads he would not waste more time on it, and dropped the garment on to the paper and looked round again. The mattress of the cot! It was stuffed with straw, by God! A slash of his knife tore open the ticking, and he scooped the stuff out by the armful; constant pressure had almost solidified it, but he shook it and handled it so that it bulked out far larger in a mass on the deck nearly up to his waist. That would give him the intense blaze he wanted. He stood still, compelling himself to think clearly and logically–it was impetuosity and lack of thought which had occasioned the loss of the *Marie Galante*, and now he had wasted time on his jersey. He worked out the successive steps to take. He made a long spill out of a page of the *Manuel de Matelotage*, and lighted it at the lamp. Then he poured out the grease–the lamp was hot and the grease liquid–over his balls of paper, over the deck, over the base of the door. A touch from his taper lighted one ball, the flame travelled quickly. He was committed now. He piled the straw upon the flames, and in a sudden access of insane strength he tore the cot from its fastenings, smashing it as he did so, and piled the fragments on the straw. Already the flames were racing through the straw. He dropped the lamp upon the pile grabbed his coat and walked out. He thought of closing the door, but decided against it–the more air the better. He wriggled into his coat and ran up the ladder.

On deck he forced himself to lounge nonchalantly against the rail, putting his shaking hands into his pockets. His excitement made him weak, nor was it lessened as he waited. Every minute before the fire could be discovered was important. A French officer said something to him with a triumphant laugh and pointed aft over the taffrail, presumably speaking about leaving the *Indefatigable* behind. Hornblower smiled bleakly at him; that was the first gesture that occurred to him, and then he thought that a smile was out of place, and he tried to assume a sullen scowl. The wind was blowing briskly, so that the *Pique* could only just carry all plain sail; Hornblower felt it on his cheeks, which were burning. Everyone on deck seemed unnaturally busy and preoccupied; Neuville was watching the helmsman with occasional glances aloft to see that every sail was doing its work; the men were at the guns, two hands and a petty officer heaving the log. God, how much longer would he have?

Look there! The coaming of the after hatchway appeared distorted, wavering in the shimmering air. Hot air must be coming up through it. And was that, or was it not, the ghost of a wreath of smoke? It was! In that moment the alarm was given. A loud cry, a rush of feet, an instant bustle, the loud beating of a drum, high-pitched shouts–'Au feu! Au feu!'

The four elements of Aristotle, thought Hornblower insanely–earth, air, water, and fire–were the constant enemies of the seaman, but the lee shore, the gale, and the wave, were none of them as feared in wooden ships as fire.

Timbers many years old and coated thick with paint burnt fiercely and readily. Sails and tarry rigging would burn like fireworks. And within the ship were tons and tons of gunpowder waiting its chance to blast the seamen into fragments. Hornblower watched the fire parties flinging themselves into their work, the pumps being dragged over the decks, the hoses rigged. Someone came racing aft with a message for Neuville, presumably to report the site of the fire. Neuville heard him, and darted a glance at Hornblower against the rail before he hurled orders back at the messenger. The smoke coming up through the after hatchway was dense now; at Neuville's orders the after guard flung themselves down the opening through the smoke. And there was more smoke, and more smoke; smoke caught up by the following wind and blown forward in wisps–smoke must be pouring out of the sides of the ship at the waterline.

Neuville took a stride towards Hornblower, his face working with rage, but a cry from the helmsman checked him. The helmsman, unable to take his hands from the wheel, pointed with his foot to the cabin skylight. There was a flickering of flame below it. A side pane fell in as they watched, and a rush of flame came through the opening. That store of paint, Hornblower calculated–he was calmer now, with a calm that would astonish him later, when he came to look back on it–must be immediately under the cabin, and blazing fiercely. Neuville looked round him, at the sea and the sky, and put his hands to his head in a furious gesture. For the first time in his life Hornblower saw a man literally tearing his hair. But his nerve held. A shout brought up another portable pump; four men set to work on the handles, and the clank-clank, clank-clank made an accompaniment that blended with the roar of the fire. A thin jet of water was squirted down the gaping skylight. More men formed a bucket chain, drawing water from the sea and passing it from hand to hand to pour in the skylight, but those buckets of water were less effective even than the stream from the pumps. From below came the dull thud of an explosion, and Hornblower caught his breath as he expected the ship to be blown to pieces. But no further explosion followed; either a gun had been set off by the flames or a cask had burst violently in the heat. And then the bucket line suddenly disintegrated; beneath the feet of one of the men a seam had gaped in a broad red smile from which came a rush of flame. Some officer had seized Neuville by the arm and was arguing with him vehemently, and Hornblower could see Neuville yield in despair. Hands went scurrying aloft to get in the foretopsail and forecourse, and other hands went to the main braces. Over went the wheel, and the *Pique* came up into the wind.

The change was dramatic, although at first more apparent than real; with the wind blowing in the opposite direction the roar of the fire did not come so clearly to the ears of those forward of it. But it was an immense gain, all the same; the flames, which had started in the steerage in the farthest afterpart of the ship, no longer were blown forward, but were turned back upon timber already half consumed. Yet the after-part of the deck was fully alight; the helmsman was driven from the wheel, and in a flash the flames took hold of the driver and consumed it utterly–one moment the sail was there, and the next there were only charred fragments hanging from the gaff. But, head to wind, the other sails did not catch, and a mizzen-trysail hurriedly set kept the ship bows on.

It was then that Hornblower, looking forward, saw the *Indefatigable* again. She was tearing down towards them with all sail set; as the *Pique* lifted he could see the white bow wave foaming under her bowsprit. There was no question about surrender, for under the menace of that row of guns no ship of the *Pique*'s force, even if uninjured, could resist. A cable's length to windward the *Indefatigable* rounded-to, and she was hoisting out her boats before even she was fully round. Pellew had seen the smoke, and had deduced the reason for the *Pique*'s heaving to, and had made his preparations as he came up. Longboat and launch had each a pump in their bows where sometimes they carried a carronade; they dropped down to the stern of the *Pique* to cast their jets of water up into the flaming stern without more ado. Two gigs full of men ran straight aft to join in the battle with the flames, but Bolton, the third lieutenant, lingered for a moment as he caught Hornblower's eye.

'Good God, it's you!' he exclaimed. 'What are you doing here?'

Yet he did not stay for an answer. He picked out Neuville as the captain of the *Pique*, strode aft to receive his surrender, cast his eyes aloft to see that all was well there, and then took up the task of combating the fire. The flames were overcome in time, more because they had consumed everything within reach of them than for any other reason; the *Pique* was burnt from the taffrail forward for some feet of her length right to the water's edge, so that she presented a strange spectacle when viewed from the deck of the *Indefatigable*. Nevertheless, she was in no immediate danger; given even moderate good fortune and a little hard work she could be sailed to England to be repaired and sent to sea again.

But it was not her salvage that was important, but rather the fact that she was no longer in French hands, would no longer be available to prey on English commerce. That was the point that Sir Edward Pellew made in conversation with Hornblower, when the latter came on board to report himself. Hornblower had begun, at Pellew's order, by recounting what had happened to him from the time he had been sent as prize master on board the *Marie Galante*. As Hornblower had expected–perhaps as he had even feared–Pellew had passed lightly over the loss of the brig. She had been damaged by gunfire before surrendering, and no one now could establish whether the damage was small or great. Pellew did not give the matter a second thought. Hornblower had tried to save her and had been unsuccessful with his tiny crew–and at that moment the *Indefatigable* could not spare him a larger crew. He did not hold Hornblower culpable. Once again, it was more important that France should be deprived of the *Marie Galante*'s cargo than that England should benefit by it. The situation was exactly parallel to that of the salvaging of the *Pique*.

'It was lucky she caught fire like that,' commented Pellew, looking across to where the *Pique* lay, still hove-to with the boats clustering about her but with only the thinnest trail of smoke drifting from her stern. 'She was running clean away from us, and would have been out of sight in an hour. Have you any idea how it happened, Mr Hornblower?'

Hornblower was naturally expecting that question and was ready for it. Now was the time to answer truthfully and modestly, to receive the praise he deserved, a mention in the *Gazette*, perhaps even appointment as acting-lieutenant. But Pellew did not know the full details of the loss of the brig, and might make a false estimate of them even if he did.

'No, sir,' said Hornblower. 'I think it must have been spontaneous combustion in the paint-locker. I can't account for it otherwise.'

He alone knew of his remissness in plugging that shot hole, he alone could decide on his punishment, and this was what he had chosen. This alone could re-establish him in his own eyes, and when the words were spoken he felt enormous relief, and not one single twinge of regret.

'It was fortunate, all the same,' mused Pellew.

4

THE MAN WHO FELT QUEER

This time the wolf was prowling round outside the sheep-fold. H.M. frigate *Indefatigable* had chased the French corvette *Papillon* into the mouth of the Gironde, and was seeking a way of attacking her where she lay at anchor in the stream under the protection of the batteries at the mouth. Captain Pellew took his ship into shoal water as far as he dared, until in fact the batteries fired warning shots to make him keep his distance, and he stared long and keenly through his glass at the corvette. Then he shut his telescope and turned on his heel to give the order that worked the *Indefatigable* away from the dangerous lee shore–out of sight of land, in fact. His departure might lull the French into a sense of security which, he hoped, would prove unjustified. For he had no intention of leaving them undisturbed. If the corvette could be captured or sunk not only would she be unavailable for raids on British commerce, but also the French would be forced to increase their coastal defences at this point and lessen the effort that could be put out elsewhere. War is a matter of savage blow and counter blow, and even a forty-gun frigate could strike shrewd blows if shrewdly handled.

Midshipman Hornblower was walking the lee side of the quarterdeck, as became his lowly station as the junior officer of the watch, in the afternoon, when Midshipman Kennedy approached him. Kennedy took off his hat with a flourish and bowed low as his dancing master had once taught him, left foot advanced, hat down by the right knee. Hornblower entered into the spirit of the game, laid his hat against his stomach, and bent himself in the middle three times in quick succession. Thanks to his physical awkwardness he could parody ceremonial solemnity almost without trying.

'Most grave and reverend signor,' said Kennedy, 'I bear the compliments of Captain Sir Ed'ard Pellew, who humbly solicits Your Gravity's attendance at dinner at eight bells in the afternoon watch.'

'My respects to Sir Edward,' replied Hornblower, bowing to his knees at the mention of the name, 'and I shall condescend to make a brief appearance.'

'I am sure the captain will be both relieved and delighted,' said Kennedy. 'I will convey him my felicitations along with your most flattering acceptance.'

Both hats flourished with even greater elaboration than before, but at that moment both young men noticed Mr Bolton, the officer of the watch, looking at them from the windward side, and they hurriedly put their hats on and assumed attitudes more consonant with the dignity of officers holding their warrants from King George.

'What's in the captain's mind?' asked Hornblower.

Kennedy laid one finger alongside his nose.

'If I knew that I should rate a couple of epaulettes,' he said. 'Something's brewing, and I suppose one of these days we shall know what it is. Until then all that we little victims can do is to play unconscious of our doom. Meanwhile, be careful not to let the ship fall overboard.'

There was no sign of anything brewing while dinner was being eaten in the great cabin of the *Indefatigable.* Pellew was a courtly host at the head of the table. Conversation flowed freely and along indifferent channels among the senior officers present–the two lieutenants, Eccles and Chadd, and the sailing master, Soames. Hornblower and the other junior officer–Mallory, a midshipman of over two years' seniority–kept silent, as midshipmen should, thereby being able to devote their undivided attention to the food, so vastly superior to what was served in the midshipmen's berth.

'A glass of wine with you, Mr Hornblower,' said Pellew, raising his glass.

Hornblower tried to bow gracefully in his seat while raising his glass. He sipped cautiously, for he had early found that he had a weak head, and he disliked feeling drunk.

The table was cleared and there was a brief moment of expectancy as the company awaited Pellew's next move.

'Now, Mr Soames,' said Pellew, 'let us have that chart.'

It was a map of the mouth of the Gironde with the soundings; somebody had pencilled in the positions of the shore batteries.

'The *Papillon*,' said Sir Edward (he did not condescend to pronounce it French-fashion), 'lies just here. Mr Soames took the bearings.'

He indicated a pencilled cross on the chart, far up the channel.

'You gentlemen,' went on Pellew, 'are going in with the boats to fetch her out.'

So that was it. A cutting-out expedition.

'Mr Eccles will be in general command. I will ask him to tell you his plan.'

The grey-haired first lieutenant with the surprisingly young blue eyes looked round at the others.

'I shall have the launch,' he said, 'and Mr Soames the cutter. Mr Chadd and Mr Mallory will command the first and second gigs. And Mr Hornblower will command the jolly boat. Each of the boats except Mr Hornblower's will have a junior officer second in command.'

That would not be necessary for the jolly boat with its crew of seven. The launch and cutter would carry from thirty to forty men each, and the gigs twenty each; it was a large force that was being despatched–nearly half the ship's company.

'She's a ship of war,' explained Eccles, reading their thoughts. 'No merchantman. Ten guns a side, and full of men.'

Nearer two hundred men than a hundred, certainly–plentiful opposition for a hundred and twenty British seamen.

'But we will be attacking her by night and taking her by surprise,' said Eccles, reading their thoughts again.

'Surprise,' put in Pellew, 'is more than half the battle, as you know, gentlemen–please pardon the interruption, Mr Eccles.'

'At the moment,' went on Eccles, 'we are out of sight of land. We are about to stand in again. We have never hung about this part of the coast, and the Frogs'll think we've gone for good. We'll make the land after nightfall, stand in as far as possible, and then the boats will go in. High water tomorrow morning is at four-fifty; dawn is at five-thirty. The attack will be delivered at four-thirty so that the watch below will have had time to get to sleep. The launch will attack on the starboard quarter, and the cutter on the larboard quarter. Mr Mallory's gig will attack on the larboard bow, and Mr Chadd's on the starboard bow. Mr Chadd will be responsible for cutting the corvette's cable as soon as he has mastered the forecastle, and the other boats' crews have at least reached the quarterdeck.'

Eccles looked round at the other three commanders of the large boats, and they nodded understanding. Then he went on.

'Mr Hornblower with the jolly boat will wait until the attack has gained a foothold on the deck. He will then board at the main chains, either to starboard or larboard as he sees fit, and he will at once ascend the main rigging, paying no attention to whatever fighting is going on on deck. He will see to it that the maintopsail is loosed and he will sheet it home on receipt of further orders. I myself, or Mr Soames in the event of my being killed or wounded, will send two hands to the wheel and will attend to steering the corvette as soon as she is under way. The tide will take us out, and the *Indefatigable* will be awaiting us just out of gunshot from the shore batteries.'

'Any comments, gentlemen?' asked Pellew.

That was the moment when Hornblower should have spoken up–the only moment when he could. Eccles's orders had set in motion sick feelings of apprehension in his stomach. Hornblower was no maintopman, and Hornblower knew it. He hated heights, and he hated going aloft. He knew he had none of the monkey-like agility and self-confidence of the good seaman. He was unsure of himself aloft in the dark even in the *Indefatigable*, and he was utterly appalled at the thought of going aloft in an entirely strange ship and finding his way among strange rigging. He felt himself quite unfitted for the duty assigned to him, and he should have raised a protest at once on account of his unfitness. But he let the opportunity pass, for he was overcome by the matter-of-fact way in which the other officers accepted the plan. He looked round at the unmoved faces; nobody was paying any attention to him, and he jibbed at making himself conspicuous. He swallowed; he even got as far as opening his mouth, but still no one looked at him, and his protest died stillborn.

'Very well, then, gentlemen,' said Pellew. 'I think you had better go into the details, Mr Eccles.'

Then it was too late. Eccles, with the chart before him, was pointing out the course to be taken through the shoals and mudbanks of the Gironde, and expatiating on the position of the shore batteries and on the influence of the lighthouse of Cordouan upon the distance to which the *Indefatigable* could approach in daylight. Hornblower listened, trying to concentrate despite his apprehensions. Eccles finished his remarks and Pellew closed the meeting.

'Since you all know your duties, gentlemen, I think you should start your preparations. The sun is about to set and you will find you have plenty to do.'

The boats crews had to be told off; it was necessary to see that the men were armed, and that the boats were provisioned in case of emergency. Every man had to be instructed in the duties expected of him. And Hornblower had to rehearse himself in ascending the main shrouds and laying out along the main-topsail yard. He did it twice, forcing himself to make the difficult climb up the futtock shrouds, which, projecting outwards from the mainmast, made it necessary to climb several feet while hanging back downwards, locking fingers and toes into the ratlines. He could just manage it, moving slowly and carefully, although clumsily. He stood on the footrope and worked his way out to the yardarm–the footrope was attached along the yard so as to hang nearly four feet below it. The principle was to set his feet on the rope with his arms over the yard, then, holding the yard in his armpits, to shuffle sideways along the footrope to cast off the gaskets and loose the sail. Twice Hornblower made the whole journey, battling with the disquiet of his stomach at the thought of the hundred-foot drop below him. Finally, gulping with nervousness, he transferred his grip to the brace and forced himself to slide down it to the deck–that would be his best route when the time came to sheet the topsail home. It was a long perilous descent; Hornblower told himself–as indeed he had said to himself when he had first seen men go aloft–that similar feats in a circus at home would be received with 'ohs' and 'ahs' of appreciation. He was by no means satisfied with himself even when he reached the deck, and at the back of his mind was a vivid mental picture of his missing his hold when the time came for him to repeat the performance in the *Papillon*, and falling headlong to the deck–a second or two of frightful fear while rushing through the air, and then a shattering crash. And the success of the attack hinged on him, as much as on anyone–if the topsail were not promptly set to give the corvette steerage way she would run aground on one of the innumerable shoals in the river mouth to be ignominiously recaptured, and half the crew of the *Indefatigable* would be dead or prisoners.

In the waist the jolly boat's crew was formed up for his inspection. He saw to it that the oars were properly muffled, that each man had pistol and cutlass, and made sure that every pistol was at half cock so that there was no fear of a premature shot giving warning of the attack. He allocated duties to each man in the loosening of the topsail, laying stress on the possibility that casualties might necessitate unrehearsed changes in the scheme.

'I will mount the rigging first,' said Hornblower.

That had to be the case. He had to lead–it was expected of him. More than that; if he had given any other order it would have excited comment–and contempt.

'Jackson,' went on Hornblower, addressing the coxswain, 'you will quit the boat last and take command if I fall.'

'Aye aye, sir.'

It was usual to use the poetic expression 'fall' for 'die', and it was only after Hornblower had uttered the word that he thought about its horribly real meaning in the present circumstances.

'Is that all understood?' asked Hornblower harshly; it was his mental stress that made his voice grate so.

Everyone nodded except one man.

'Begging your pardon, sir,' said Hales, the young man who pulled stroke oar, 'I'm feeling a bit queer-like.'

Hales was a lightly built young fellow of swarthy countenance. He put his hand to his forehead with a vague gesture as he spoke.

'You're not the only one to feel queer,' snapped Hornblower.

The other men chuckled. The thought of running the gauntlet of the shore batteries, of boarding an armed corvette in the teeth of opposition, might well raise apprehension in the breast of a coward. Most of the men detailed for the expedition must have felt qualms to some extent.

'I don't mean that, sir,' said Hales indignantly. ''Course I don't.'

But Hornblower and the others paid him no attention.

'You just keep your mouth shut,' growled Jackson. There could be nothing but contempt for a man who announced himself sick after being told off on a dangerous duty. Hornblower felt sympathy as well as contempt. He himself had been too much of a coward even to give voice to his apprehensions–too much afraid of what people would say about him.

'Dismiss,' said Hornblower. 'I'll pass the word for all of you when you are wanted.'

There were some hours yet to wait while the *Indefatigable* crept inshore, with the lead going steadily and Pellew himself attending to the course of the frigate. Hornblower, despite his nervousness and his miserable apprehensions, yet found time to appreciate the superb seamanship displayed as Pellew brought the big frigate in through these tricky waters on that dark night. His interest was so caught by the procedure that the little tremblings which had been assailing him ceased to manifest themselves; Hornblower was of the type that would continue to observe and to learn on his deathbed. By the time the *Indefatigable* had reached the point off the mouth of the river where it was desirable to launch the boats, Hornblower had learned a good deal about the practical application of the principles of coastwise navigation and a good deal about the organization of a cutting-out expedition–and by self-analysis he had learned even more about the psychology of a raiding party before a raid.

He had mastered himself to all outward appearance by the time he went down into the jolly boat as she heaved on the inky-black water, and he gave the command to shove off in a quiet steady voice. Hornblower took the tiller–the feel of that solid bar of wood was reassuring, and it was old habit now to sit in the sternsheets with hand and elbow upon it, and the men began to pull slowly after the dark shapes of the four big boats; there was plenty of time, and the flowing tide would take them up the estuary. That was just as well, for on one side of them lay the batteries of St Dye, and inside the estuary on the other side was the fortress of Blaye; forty big guns trained to sweep the channel, and none of the five boats–certainly not the jolly boat–could withstand a single shot from one of them.

He kept his eyes attentively on the cutter ahead of him. Soames had the dreadful responsibility of taking the boats up the channel, while all he had to do was to follow in her wake–all, except to loose that maintopsail. Hornblower found himself shivering again.

Hales, the man who had said he felt queer, was pulling stroke oar; Hornblower could just see his dark form moving rhythmically back and forward at each slow stroke. After a single glance Hornblower paid him no more attention, and was staring after the cutter when a sudden commotion brought his mind back into the boat. Someone had missed his stroke; someone had thrown all six oars into confusion as a result. There was even a slight clatter.

'Mind what you're doing, blast you, Hales,' whispered Jackson, the coxswain, with desperate urgency.

For answer there was a sudden cry from Hales, loud but fortunately not too loud, and Hales pitched forward against Hornblower's and Jackson's legs, kicking and writhing.

'The bastard's having a fit,' growled Jackson.

The kicking and writhing went on. Across the water through the darkness came a sharp scornful whisper.

'Mr Hornblower,' said the voice–it was Eccles putting a world of exasperation into his *sotto voce* question–'cannot you keep your men quiet?'

Eccles had brought the launch round almost alongside the jolly boat to say this to him, and the desperate need for silence was dramatically demonstrated by the absence of any of the usual blasphemy; Hornblower could picture the cutting reprimand that would be administered to him tomorrow publicly on the quarterdeck. He opened his mouth to make an explanation, but he fortunately realized that raiders in open boats did not make explanations when under the guns of the fortress of Blaye.

'Aye aye, sir,' was all he whispered back, and the launch continued on its mission of shepherding the flotilla in the tracks of the cutter.

'Take his oar, Jackson,' he whispered furiously to the coxswain, and he stooped and with his own hands dragged the writhing figure towards him and out of Jackson's way.

'You might try pouring water on 'im, sir,' suggested Jackson hoarsely, as he moved to the afterthwart. 'There's the baler 'andy.'

Seawater was the seaman's cure for every ill, his panacea; seeing how often sailors had not merely wet jackets but wet bedding as well they should never have a day's illness. But Hornblower let the sick man lie. His struggles were coming to an end, and Hornblower wished to make no noise with the baler. The lives of more than a hundred men depended on silence. Now that they were well into the actual estuary they were within easy reach of cannon shot from the shore–and a single cannon shot would rouse the crew of the *Papillon*, ready to man the bulwarks to beat off the attack, ready to drop cannon balls into the boats alongside, ready to shatter approaching boats with a tempest of grape.

Silently the boats glided up the estuary; Soames in the cutter was setting a slow pace, with only an occasional stroke at the oars to maintain steerage way. Presumably he knew very well what he was doing; the channel he had selected was an obscure one between mudbanks, impracticable for anything except small boats, and he had a twenty-foot pole with him with which to take the soundings–quicker and much more silent than using the lead. Minutes were passing fast, and yet the night was still utterly dark, with no hint of approaching dawn. Strain his eyes as he would Hornblower could not be sure that he could see the flat shores on either side of him. It would call for sharp eyes on the land to detect the little boats being carried up by the tide.

Hales at his feet stirred and then stirred again. His hand, feeling round in the darkness, found Hornblower's ankle and apparently examined it with curiosity. He muttered something, the words dragging out into a moan.

'Shut up!' whispered Hornblower, trying, like the saint of old, to make a tongue of his whole body, that he might express the urgency of the occasion without making a sound audible at any distance. Hales set his elbow on Hornblower's knee and levered himself up into a sitting position, and then levered himself further until he was standing, swaying with bent knees and supporting himself against Hornblower.

'Sit down, damn you!' whispered Hornblower, shaking with fury and anxiety.

'Where's Mary?' asked Hales in a conversational tone.

'Shut up!'

'Mary!' said Hales, lurching against him. 'Mary!'

Each successive word was louder. Hornblower felt instinctively that Hales would soon be speaking in a loud voice, that he might even soon be shouting. Old recollections of conversations with his doctor father stirred at the back of his mind; he remembered that persons emerging from epileptic fits were not responsible for their actions, and might be, and often were, dangerous.

'Mary!' said Hales again.

Victory and the lives of a hundred men depended on silencing Hales, and silencing him instantly. Hornblower thought of the pistol in his belt, and of using the butt, but there was another weapon more conveniently to his hand. He unshipped the tiller, a three-foot bar of solid oak, and he swung it with all the venom and fury of despair. The tiller crashed down on Hales's head, and Hales, an unuttered word cut short in his throat, fell silent in the bottom of the boat. There was no sound from the boat's crew, save for something like a sigh from Jackson, whether approving or disapproving Hornblower neither knew nor cared. He had done his duty, and he was certain of it. He had struck down a helpless idiot; most probably he had killed him, but the surprise upon which the success of the expedition depended had not been imperilled. He reshipped the tiller and resumed the silent task of keeping in the wake of the gigs.

Far away ahead–in the darkness it was impossible to estimate the distance–there was a nucleus of greater darkness, close on the surface of the black water. It might be the corvette. A dozen more silent strokes, and Hornblower was sure of it. Soames had done a magnificent job of pilotage, leading the boats straight to that objective. The cutter and launch were diverging now from the two gigs. The four boats were separating in readiness to launch their simultaneous converging attack.

'Easy!' whispered Hornblower, and the jolly boat's crew ceased to pull.

Hornblower had his orders. He had to wait until the attack had gained a foothold on the deck. His hand clenched convulsively on the tiller; the excitement of dealing with Hales had driven the thought of having to ascend strange rigging in the darkness clear out of his head, and now it recurred with redoubled urgency. Hornblower was afraid.

Although he could see the corvette, the boats had vanished from his sight, had passed out of his field of vision. The corvette rode to her anchor, her spars just visible against the night sky–that was where he had to climb! She seemed to tower up hugely. Close by the corvette he saw a splash in the dark water–the boats were closing in fast and someone's stroke had been a little careless. At the same moment came a shout from the corvette's deck, and when the shout was repeated it was echoed a hundredfold from the boats rushing alongside. The yelling was lusty and prolonged, of set purpose. A sleeping enemy would be bewildered by the din, and the progress of the shouting would tell each boat's crew of the extent of the success of the others. The British seamen were yelling like madmen. A flash and a bang from the corvette's deck told of the firing of the first shot; soon pistols were popping and muskets banging from several points of the deck.

'Give way!' said Hornblower. He uttered the order as if it had been torn from him by the rack.

The jolly boat moved forward, while Hornblower fought down his feelings and tried to make out what was going on on board. He could see no reason for choosing either side of the corvette in preference to the other, and the larboard side was the nearer, and so he steered the boat to the larboard mainchains. So interested was he in what he was doing that he only remembered in the nick of time to give the order, 'In oars.' He put the tiller over and the boat swirled round and the bowman hooked on. From the deck just above came a noise exactly like a tinker hammering on a cooking-pot–Hornblower noted the curious noise as he stood up in the sternsheets. He felt the cutlass at his side and the pistol in his belt, and then he sprang for the chains. With a mad leap he reached them and hauled himself up. The shrouds came into his hands, his feet found the ratlines beneath them, and he began to climb. As his head cleared the bulwark and he could see the deck the flash of a pistol shot illuminated the scene momentarily, fixing the struggle on the deck in a static moment, like a picture. Before and below him a British seaman was fighting a furious cutlass duel with a French officer, and he realized with vague astonishment that the kettle-mending noise he had heard was the sound of cutlass against cutlass–that clash of steel against steel that poets wrote about. So much for romance.

The realization carried him far up the shrouds. At his elbow he felt the futtock shrouds and he transferred himself to them, hanging back downward with his toes hooked into the ratlines and his hands clinging like death. That only lasted for two or three desperate seconds, and then he hauled himself on to the topmast shrouds and began the final ascent, his lungs bursting with the effort. Here was the topsail yard, and Hornblower flung himself across it and felt with his feet for the footrope. Merciful God! There was no footrope–his feet searching in the darkness met only unresisting air. A hundred feet above the deck he hung, squirming and kicking like a baby held up at arm's length in its father's hands. There was no footrope; it may have been with this very situation in mind that the Frenchmen had removed it. There was no footrope, so that he could not make his way out to the yardarm. Yet the gaskets must be cast off and the sail loosed–everything depended on that. Hornblower had seen daredevil seamen run out along the yards standing upright, as though walking a tightrope. That was the only way to reach the yardarm now.

For a moment he could not breathe as his weak flesh revolted against the thought of walking along that yard above the black abyss. This was fear, the fear that stripped a man of his manhood, turning his bowels to water and his limbs to paper. Yet his furiously active mind continued to work. He had been resolute enough in dealing with Hales. Where he personally was not involved he had been brave enough; he had not hesitated to strike down the wretched epileptic with all the strength of his arm. That was the poor sort of courage he was capable of displaying. In the simple vulgar matter of physical bravery he was utterly wanting. This was cowardice, the sort of thing that men spoke about behind their hands to other men. He could not bear the thought of that in himself–it was worse (awful though the alternative might be) than the thought of falling through the night to the deck. With a gasp he brought his knee up on to the yard, heaving himself up until he stood upright. He felt the rounded, canvas-covered timber under his feet, and his instincts told him not to dally there for a moment.

'Come on, men!' he yelled, and he dashed out along the yard.

It was twenty feet to the yardarm, and he covered the distance in a few frantic strides. Utterly reckless by now, he put his hands down on the yard, clasped it, and laid his body across it again, his hands seeking the gaskets. A thump on the yard told him that Oldroyd, who had been detailed to come after him, had followed him out along the yard–he had six feet less to go. There could be no doubt that the other members of the jolly boat's crew were on the yard, and that Clough had led the way to the starboard yardarm. It was obvious from the rapidity with which the sail came loose. Here was the brace beside him. Without any thought of danger now, for he was delirious with excitement and triumph, he grasped it with both hands and jerked himself off the yard. His waving legs found the rope and twined about it, and he let himself slide down it.

Fool that he was! Would he never learn sense and prudence? Would he never remember that vigilance and precaution must never be relaxed? He had allowed himself to slide so fast that the rope seared his hands, and when he tried to tighten his grip so as to slow down his progress it caused him such agony that he had to relax it again and slide on down with the rope stripping the skin from his hands as though peeling off a glove. His feet reached the deck and he momentarily forgot the pain as he looked round him.

There was the faintest grey light beginning to show now, and there were no sounds of battle. It had been a well-worked surprise–a hundred men flung suddenly on the deck of the corvette had swept away the anchor watch and mastered the vessel in a single rush before the watch below could come up to offer any resistance. Chadd's stentorian voice came pealing from the forecastle.

'Cable's cut, sir!'

Then Eccles bellowed from aft.

'Mr Hornblower!'

'Sir!' yelled Hornblower.

'Man the halliards!'

A rush of men came to help–not only his own boat's crew but every man of initiative and spirit. Halliards, sheets and braces; the sail was trimmed round and was drawing full in the light southerly air, and the *Papillon* swung round to go down with the first of the ebb. Dawn was coming up fast, with a trifle of mist on the surface of the water.

Over the starboard quarter came a sullen bellowing roar, and then the misty air was torn by a series of infernal screams, supernaturally loud. The first cannon balls Hornblower ever heard were passing him by.

'Mr Chadd! Set the headsails! Loose the foretops'l. Get aloft, some of you, and set the mizzen tops'l.'

From the port bow came another salvo–Blaye was firing at them from one side, St Dye from the other, now they could guess what had happened on board the *Papillon.* But the corvette was moving fast with wind and tide, and it would be no easy matter to cripple her in the half light. It had been a very near-run thing; a few seconds' delay could have been fatal. Only one shot from the next salvo passed within hearing, and its passage was marked by a loud snap overhead.

'Mr Mallory, get that forestay spliced!'

'Aye aye, sir!'

It was light enough to look round the deck now; he could see Eccles at the break of the poop, directing the handling of the corvette, and Soames beside the wheel conning her down the channel. Two groups of red-coated marines, with bayonets fixed, stood guard over the hatchways. There were four or five men lying on the deck in curiously abandoned attitudes. Dead men; Hornblower could look at them with the callousness of youth. But there was a wounded man, too, crouched groaning over his shattered thigh–Hornblower could not look at him as disinterestedly, and he was glad, maybe only for his own sake, when at that moment a seaman asked for and received permission from Mallory to leave his duties and attend to him.

'Stand by to go about!' shouted Eccles from the poop; the corvette had reached the tip of the middle ground shoal and was about to make the turn that would carry her into the open sea.

The men came running to the braces, and Hornblower tailed on along with them. But the first contact with the harsh rope gave him such pain that he almost cried out. His hands were like raw meat, and fresh-killed at that, for blood was running from them. Now that his attention was called to them they smarted unbearably.

The headsail sheets came over, and the corvette went handily about.

'There's the old *Indy*!' shouted somebody.

The *Indefatigable* was plainly visible now, lying-to just out of shot from the shore batteries, ready to rendezvous with her prize. Somebody cheered, and the cheering was taken up by everyone, even while the last shots from St Dye, fired at extreme range, pitched sullenly into the water alongside. Hornblower had gingerly extracted his handkerchief from his pocket and was trying to wrap it round his hand.

'Can I help you with that, sir?' asked Jackson.

Jackson shook his head as he looked at the raw surface.

'You was careless, sir. You ought to 'a gone down 'and over 'and,' he said, when Hornblower explained to him how the injury had been caused. 'Very careless, you was, beggin' your pardon for saying so, sir. But you young gennelmen often is. You don't 'ave no thought for your necks, nor your 'ides, sir.'

Hornblower looked up at the maintopsail yard high above his head, and remembered how he had walked along that slender stick of timber out to the yardarm in the dark. At the recollection of it, even here with the solid deck under his feet, he shuddered a little.

'Sorry, sir. Didn't mean to 'urt you,' said Jackson, tying the knot. 'There, that's done, as good as I can do it, sir.'

'Thank you, Jackson,' said Hornblower.

'We got to report the jolly boat as lost, sir,' went on Jackson.

'Lost?'

'She ain't towing alongside, sir. You see, we didn't leave no boatkeeper in 'er. Wells, 'e was to be boatkeeper, you remember, sir. But I sent 'im up the rigging a'head o' me, seeing that 'Ales couldn't go. We wasn't too many for the job. So the jolly boat must 'a come adrift, sir, when the ship went about.'

'What about Hales, then?' asked Hornblower.

''E was still in the boat, sir.'

Hornblower looked back up the estuary of the Gironde. Somewhere up there the jolly boat was drifting about, and lying in it was Hales, probably dead, possibly alive. In either case the French would find him, surely enough, but a cold wave of regret extinguished the warm feeling of triumph in Hornblower's bosom when he thought about Hales back there. If it had not been for Hales he would never have nerved himself (so at least he thought) to run out to the maintopsail yardarm; he would at this moment be ruined and branded as a coward instead of basking in the satisfaction of having capably done his duty.

Jackson saw the bleak look in his face.

'Don't you take on so, sir,' he said. 'They won't 'old the loss of the jolly boat agin you, not the captain and Mr Eccles, they won't.'

'I wasn't thinking about the jolly boat,' said Hornblower. 'I was thinking about Hales.'

'Oh, 'im?' said Jackson. 'Don't you fret about 'im, sir. 'E wouldn't never 'ave made no seaman, not no 'ow.'

5

THE MAN WHO SAW GOD

Winter had come to the Bay of Biscay. With the passing of the Equinox the gales began to increase in violence, adding infinitely to the labours and dangers of the British Navy watching over the coast of France; easterly gales, bitter cold, which the storm-tossed ships had to endure as best they could, when the spray froze on the rigging and the labouring hulls leaked like baskets; westerly gales, when the ships had to claw their way to safety from a lee shore and make a risky compromise between gaining sufficient sea-room and maintaining a position from which they could pounce on any French vessel venturing out of harbour. The storm-tossed ships, we speak about. But those ships were full of storm-tossed men, who week by week and month by month had to endure the continual cold and the continual wet, the salt provisions, the endless toil, the boredom and misery of life in the blockading fleet. Even in the frigates, the eyes and claws of the blockaders, boredom had to be endured, the boredom of long periods with the hatches battened down, with the deck seams above dripping water on the men below, long nights and short days, broken sleep and yet not enough to do.

Even in the *Indefatigable* there was a feeling of restlessness in the air, and even a mere midshipman like Hornblower could be aware of it as he was looking over the men of his division before the captain's regular weekly inspection.

'What's the matter with your face, Styles?' he asked.

'Boils, sir. Awful bad.'

On Styles's cheeks and lips there were half a dozen dabs of sticking plaster.

'Have you done anything about them?'

'Surgeon's mate, sir, 'e give me plaister for 'em, an' 'e says they'll soon come right, sir.'

'Very well.'

Now was there, or was there not, something strained about the expressions on the faces of the men on either side of Styles? Did they look like men smiling secretly to themselves? Laughing up their sleeves? Hornblower did not want to be an object of derision; it was bad for discipline–and it was worse for discipline if the men shared some secret unknown to their officers. He glanced sharply along the line again. Styles was standing like a block of wood, with no expression at all on his swarthy face; the black ringlets over his ears were properly combed, and no fault could be found with him. But Hornblower sensed that the recent conversation was a source of amusement to the rest of his division, and he did not like it.

After divisions he tackled Mr Low the surgeon, in the gunroom.

'Boils?' said Low. 'Of course the men have boils. Salt pork and split peas for nine weeks on end–what d'you expect but boils? Boils–gurry sores–blains–all the plagues of Egypt.'

'On their faces?'

'That's one locality for boils. You'll find out others from your own personal experience.'

'Does your mate attend to them?' persisted Hornblower.

'Of course.'

'What's he like?'

'Muggridge?'

'Is that his name?'

'He's a good surgeon's mate. Get him to compound a black draught for you and you'll see. In fact, I'd prescribe one for you–you seem in a mighty bad temper, young man.'

Mr Low finished his glass of rum and pounded on the table for the steward. Hornblower realized that he was lucky to have found Low sober enough to give him even this much information, and turned away to go aloft so as to brood over the question in the solitude of the mizzen-top. This was his new station in action; when the men were not at their quarters a man might find a little blessed solitude there–something hard to find in the crowded *Indefatigable*. Bundled up in his peajacket, Hornblower sat in the mizzen-top; over his head the mizzen-topmast drew erratic circles against the grey sky; beside him the topmast shrouds sang their high-pitched note in the blustering gale, and below him the life of the ship went on as she rolled and pitched, standing to the northward under close reefed topsails. At eight bells she would wear to the southward again on her incessant patrol. Until that time Hornblower was free to meditate on the boils on Styles's face and the covert grins on the faces of the other men of the division.

Two hands appeared on the stout wooden barricade surrounding the top, and as Hornblower looked up with annoyance at having his meditations interrupted a head appeared above them. It was Finch, another man in Hornblower's division, who also had his station in action here in the mizzen-top. He was a frail little man with wispy hair and pale blue eyes and a foolish smile, which lit up his face when, after betraying some disappointment at finding the mizzen-top already occupied, he recognized Hornblower.

'Beg pardon, sir,' he said. 'I didn't know as how you was up here.'

Finch was hanging on uncomfortably, back downwards, in the act of transferring himself from the futtock shrouds to the top, and each roll threatened to shake him loose.

'Oh come here if you want to,' said Hornblower, cursing himself for his soft-heartedness. A taut officer, he felt, would have told Finch to go back whence he came and not bother him.

'Thank 'ee, sir. Thank 'ee,' said Finch, bringing his leg over the barricade and allowing the ship's roll to drop him into the top.

He crouched down to peer under the foot of the mizzen-topsail forward to the mainmast head, and then turned back to smile disarmingly at Hornblower like a child caught in moderate mischief. Hornblower knew that Finch was a little weak in the head–the all-embracing press swept up idiots and landsmen to help man the fleet–although he was a trained seaman who could hand, reef and steer. That smile betrayed him.

'It's better up here than down below, sir,' said Finch, apologetically.

'You're right,' said Hornblower, with a disinterested intonation which would discourage conversation.

He turned away to ignore Finch, settled his back again comfortably, and allowed the steady swing of the top to mesmerize him into dreamy thought that might deal with his problem. Yet it was not easy, for Finch was as restless almost as a squirrel in a cage, peering forward, changing his position, and so continually breaking in on Hornblower's train of thought, wasting the minutes of his precious half-hour of freedom.

'What the devil's the matter with you, Finch?' he rasped at last, patience quite exhausted.

'The Devil, sir?' said Finch. 'It isn't the Devil. He's not up here, begging your pardon, sir.'

That weak mysterious grin again, like a mischievous child. A great depth of secrets lay in those strange blue eyes. Finch peered under the topsail again; it was a gesture like a baby's playing peep-bo.

'There!' said Finch. 'I saw him that time, sir. God's come back to the maintop, sir.'

'God?'

'Aye indeed, sir. Sometimes He's in the maintop. More often than not, sir. I saw Him that time, with His beard all a-blowing in the wind. 'Tis only from here that you can see Him, sir.'

What could be said to a man with that sort of delusion? Hornblower racked his brains for an answer, and found none. Finch seemed to have forgotten his presence, and was playing peep-bo again under the foot of the mizzen-topsail.

'There He is!' said Finch to himself. 'There He is again! God's in the maintop, and the Devil's in the cable tier.'

'Very appropriate,' said Hornblower cynically, but to himself. He had no thought of laughing at Finch's delusions.

'The Devil's in the cable tier during the dog watches,' said Finch again to no one at all. 'God stays in the maintop for ever.'

'A curious timetable,' was Hornblower's *sotto voce* comment.

From down on the deck below came the first strokes of eight bells, and at the same moment the pipes of the bosun's mates began to twitter, and the bellow of Waldron the bos'un made itself heard.

'Turn out the watch below! All hands wear ship! All hands! All hands! You, master-at-arms, take the name of the last man up the hatchway. All hands!'

The interval of peace, short as it was, and broken by Finch's disturbing presence, was at an end. Hornblower dived over the barricade and gripped the futtock shrouds; not for him was the easy descent through the lubber's hole, not when the first lieutenant might see him and reprimand him for unseamanlike behaviour. Finch waited for him to quit the top, but even with this length start Hornblower was easily outpaced in the descent to the deck, for Finch, like the skilled seaman he was, ran down the shrouds as lightly as a monkey. Then the thought of Finch's curious illusions was temporarily submerged in the business of laying the ship on her new course.

But later in the day Hornblower's mind reverted inevitably to the odd things

Finch had been saying. There could be no doubt that Finch firmly believed he saw what he said he saw. Both his words and his expression made that certain. He had spoken about God's beard–it was a pity that he had not spared a few words to describe the Devil in the cable tier. Horns, cloven hoof, and pitchfork? Hornblower wondered. And why was the Devil only loose in the cable tier during the dog watches? Strange that he should keep to a timetable. Hornblower caught his breath as the sudden thought came to him that perhaps there might be some worldly explanation. The Devil might well be loose in the cable tier in a metaphorical fashion during the dog watches. Devil's work might be going on there. Hornblower had to decide on what was his duty; and he had to decide further on what was expedient. He could report his suspicions to Eccles, the first lieutenant; but after a year of service Hornblower was under no illusions about what might happen to a junior midshipman who worried a first lieutenant with unfounded suspicions. It would be better to see for himself first, as far as that went. But he did not know what he would find–if he should find anything at all–and he did not know how he should deal with it if he found anything. Much worse than that, he did not know if he would be able to deal with it in officer-like fashion. He could make a fool of himself. He might mishandle whatever situation he found, and bring down obloquy and derision upon his head, and he might imperil the discipline of the ship–weaken the slender thread of allegiance that bound officers and men together, the discipline which kept three hundred men at the bidding of their captain suffering untold hardship without demur; which made them ready to face death at the word of command. When eight bells told the end of the afternoon watch and the beginning of the first dog watch it was with trepidation that Hornblower went below to put a candle in a lantern and make his way forward to the cable tier.

It was dark down here, stuffy, odorous; and as the ship heaved and rolled he found himself stumbling over the various obstacles that impeded his progress. Yet forward there was a faint light, a murmur of voices. Hornblower choked down his fear that perhaps mutiny was being planned. He put his hand over the horn window of the lantern, so as to obscure its light, and crept forward. Two lanterns swung from the low deck-beams, and crouching under them were a score or more of men–more than that, even–and the buzz of their talk came loudly but indistinguishably to Hornblower's ears. Then the buzz increased to a roar, and someone in the centre of the circle rose suddenly to as near his full height as the deck-beams allowed. He was shaking himself violently from side to side for no apparent reason; his face was away from Hornblower, who saw with a gasp that his hands were tied behind him. The men roared again, like spectators at a prize-fight, and the man with his hands tied swung round so that Hornblower could see his face. It was Styles, the man who suffered from boils; Hornblower knew him at once. But that was not what made the most impression on Hornblower. Clinging to the man's face, weird in the shifting meagre light, was a grey writhing shape, and it was to shake this off that Styles was flinging himself about so violently. It was a rat; Hornblower's stomach turned over with horror.

With a wild jerk of his head Styles broke the grip of the rat's teeth and flung the creature down, and then instantly plunged down on his knees, with his hands still bound behind him, to pursue it with his own teeth.

'Time!' roared a voice at that moment–the voice of Partridge, bosun's mate. Hornblower had been roused by it often enough to recognize it at once.

'Five dead,' said another voice. 'Pay all bets of evens or better.'

Hornblower plunged forward. Part of the cable had been coiled down to make a rat pit ten feet across in which knelt Styles with dead and living rats about his knees. Partridge squatted beside the ring with a sandglass–used for timing the casting of the log–in front of him.

'Six dead,' protested someone. 'That 'un's dead.'

'No, he ain't.'

''Is back's broken. 'E's a dead 'un.'

''E ain't a dead 'un,' said Partridge.

The man who had protested looked up at that moment and caught sight of Hornblower, and his words died away unspoken; at his silence the others followed his glance and stiffened into rigidity, and Hornblower stepped forward. He was still wondering what he should do; he was still fighting down the nausea excited by the horrible things he had seen. Desperately he mastered his horror, and, thinking fast, took his stand on discipline.

'Who's in charge here?' he demanded.

He ran his eye round the circle. Petty officers and second-class warrant officers, mainly; bosun's mates, carpenter's mates. Muggridge, the surgeon's mate–his presence explained much. But his own position was not easy. A midshipman of scant service depended for his authority on board largely on the force of his own personality. He was only a warrant officer himself; when all was said and done a midshipman was not nearly as important to the ship's economy–and was far more easily replaced–than, say, Washburn, the cooper's mate over there, who knew all about the making and storage of the ship's water barrels.

'Who's in charge here?' he demanded again, and once more received no direct reply.

'We ain't on watch,' said a voice in the background.

Hornblower by now had mastered his horror; his indignation still flared within him, but he could appear outwardly calm.

'No, you're not on watch,' he said coldly. 'You're gambling.'

Muggridge took up the defence at that.

'Gambling, Mr Hornblower?' he said. 'That's a very serious charge. Just a gentlemanly competition. You'll find it hard to sub–substantiate any charges of gambling.'

Muggridge had been drinking, quite obviously, following perhaps the example of the head of his department. There was always brandy to be got in the medical stores. A surge of wrath made Hornblower tremble; the effort necessary to keep himself standing stock still was almost too much for him. But the rise in internal pressure brought him inspiration.

'Mr Muggridge,' he said icily, 'I advise you not to say too much. There are other charges possible, Mr Muggridge. A member of His Majesty's forces can be charged with rendering himself unfit for service, Mr Muggridge. And similarly there might be charges of aiding and abetting which might include *you*. I should consult the Articles of War if I were you, Mr Muggridge. The punishment for such an offence is flogging round the fleet I believe.'

Hornblower pointed to Styles, with the blood streaming from his bitten face, and gave more force to his argument by the gesture. He had met the men's arguments with a more effective one along the same lines; they had taken up a legalistic defence and he had legalistically beaten it down. He had the upper hand now and could give vent to his moral indignation.

'I could bring charges against every one of you,' he roared. 'You could be court-martialled–disrated–flogged–every man Jack of you. By God, one more look like that from you, Partridge, and I'll do it. You'd all be in irons five minutes after I spoke to Mr Eccles. I'll have no more of these filthy games. Let those rats loose, there you, Oldroyd, and you, Lewis. Styles, get your face plastered up again. You, Partridge, take these men and coil this cable down properly again before Mr Waldron sees it. I'll keep my eye on all of you in future. The next hint I have of misbehaviour and you'll all be at the gratings. I've said it, and by God I mean it!'

Hornblower was surprised both at his own volubility and at his self-possession. He had not known himself capable of carrying off matters with such a high hand. He sought about in his mind for a final salvo with which to make his retirement dignified, and it came to him as he turned away so that he turned back to deliver it.

'After this I want to see you in the dog watches skylarking on deck, not skulking in the cable tiers like a lot of Frenchmen.'

That was the sort of speech to be expected of a pompous old captain, not a junior midshipman, but it served to give dignity to his retirement. There was a feverish buzz of voices as he left the group. Hornblower went up on deck, under the cheerless grey sky dark with premature night, to walk the deck to keep himself warm while the *Indefatigable* slashed her way to windward in the teeth of a roaring westerly, the spray flying in sheets over her bows, the straining seams leaking and her fabric groaning; the end of a day like all the preceding ones and the predecessor probably of innumerable more.

Yet the days passed, and with them came at last a break in the monotony. In the sombre dawn a hoarse bellow from the lookout turned every eye to windward, to where a dull blotch on the horizon marked the presence of a ship. The watch came running to the braces as the *Indefatigable* was laid as close to the wind as she would lie. Captain Pellew came on deck with a peajacket over his nightshirt, his wigless head comical in a pink nightcap; he trained his glass on the strange sail–a dozen glasses were pointing in that direction. Hornblower, looking through the glass reserved for the junior officer of the watch saw the grey rectangle split into three, saw the three grow narrow, and then broaden again to coalesce into a single rectangle again.

'She's gone about,' said Pellew. 'Hands 'bout ship!'

Round came the *Indefatigable* on the other tack; the watch raced aloft to shake out a reef from the topsails while from the deck the officers looked up at the straining canvas to calculate the chances of the gale which howled round their ears splitting the sails or carrying away a spar. The *Indefatigable* lay over until it was hard to keep one's footing on the streaming deck; everyone without immediate duties clung to the weather rail and peered at the other ship.

'Fore- and maintopmasts exactly equal,' said Lieutenant Bolton to

Hornblower, his telescope to his eye. 'Topsails white as milady's fingers. She's a Frenchie all right.'

The sails of British ships were darkened with long service in all weathers; when a French ship escaped from harbour to run the blockade her spotless unweathered canvas disclosed her nationality without real need to take into consideration less obvious technical characteristics.

'We're weathering on her,' said Hornblower; his eye was aching with staring through the glass, and his arms even were weary with holding the telescope to his eye, but in the excitement of the chase he could not relax.

'Not as much as I'd like,' growled Bolton.

'Hands to the mainbrace!' roared Pellew at that moment.

It was a matter of the most vital concern to trim the sails so as to lie as close as possible to the wind; a hundred yards gained to windward would count as much as a mile gained in a stern chase. Pellew was looking up at the sails, back at the fleeting wake, across at the French ship, gauging the strength of the wind, estimating the strain on the rigging, doing everything that a lifetime of experience could suggest to close the gap between the two ships. Pellew's next order sent all hands to run out the guns on the weather side; that would in part counteract the heel and give the *Indefatigable* more grip upon the water.

'Now we're walking up to her,' said Bolton with grudging optimism.

'Beat to quarters!' shouted Pellew.

The ship had been expecting that order. The roar of the marine bandsmen's drums echoed through the ship; the pipes twittered as the bosun's mates repeated the order, and the men ran in disciplined fashion to their duties. Hornblower, jumping for the weather mizzen shrouds, saw the eager grins on half a dozen faces–battle and the imminent possibility of death were a welcome change from the eternal monotony of the blockade. Up in the mizzen-top he looked over his men. They were uncovering the locks of their muskets and looking to the priming; satisfied with their readiness for action Hornblower turned his attention to the swivel gun. He took the tarpaulin from the breech and the tompion from the muzzle, cast off the lashings which secured it, and saw that the swivel moved freely in the socket and the trunnions freely in the crotch. A jerk of the lanyard showed him that the lock was sparking well and there was no need for a new flint. Finch came climbing into the top with the canvas belt over his shoulder containing the charges for the gun; the bags of musket balls lay handy in a garland fixed to the barricade. Finch rammed home a cartridge down the short muzzle; Hornblower had ready a bag of balls to ram down on to it. Then he took a priming-quill and forced it down the touch-hole, feeling sensitively to make sure the sharp point pierced the thin serge bag of the cartridge. Priming-quill and flintlock were necessary up here in the top, where no slow match or port-fire could be used with the danger of fire so great and where fire would be so difficult to control in the sails and the rigging. Yet musketry and swivel-gun fire from the tops were an important tactical consideration. With the ships laid yardarm to yardarm Hornblower's men could clear the hostile quarterdeck where centred the brains and control of the enemy.

'Stop that, Finch!' said Hornblower irritably; turning, he had caught sight of him peering up at the maintop and at this moment of tension Finch's delusions annoyed him.

'Beg your pardon, sir,' said Finch, resuming his duties.

But a moment later Hornblower heard Finch whispering to himself.

'Mr Bracegirdle's there,' whispered Finch, 'an' Oldroyd's there, an' all those others. But *He's* there too, so He is.'

'Hands wear ship!' came the shouted order from the deck below.

The old *Indefatigable* was spinning round on her heel, the yards groaning as the braces swung them round. The French ship had made a bold attempt to rake her enemy as she clawed up to her, but Pellew's prompt handling defeated the plan. Now the ships were broadside to broadside, running free before the wind at long cannon shot.

'Just look at 'im!' roared Douglas, one of the musket men in the top. 'Twenty guns a side. Looks brave enough, doesn't he?'

Standing beside Douglas Hornblower could look down on the Frenchman's deck, her guns run out with the guns' crews clustering round them, officers in white breeches and blue coats walking up and down, the spray flying from her bows as she drove headlong before the wind.

'She'll look braver still when we take her into Plymouth Sound,' said the seaman on the far side of Hornblower.

The *Indefatigable* was slightly the faster ship; an occasional touch of starboard helm was working her in closer to the enemy, into decisive range, without allowing the Frenchman to headreach upon her. Hornblower was impressed by the silence on both sides; he had always understood that the French were likely to open fire at long range and to squander ineffectively the first carefully loaded broadside.

'When's he goin' to fire?' asked Douglas, echoing Hornblower's thoughts.

'In his own good time,' piped Finch.

The gap of tossing water between the two ships was growing narrower. Hornblower swung the swivel gun round and looked along the sights. He could aim well enough at the Frenchman's quarterdeck, but it was much too long a range for a bag of musket balls–in any case he dared not open fire until Pellew gave permission.

'Them's the men for us!' said Douglas, pointing to the Frenchman's mizzen-top.

It looked as if there were soldiers up there, judging by the blue uniforms and the crossbelts; the French often eked out their scanty crews of trained seamen by shipping soldiers; in the British Navy the marines were never employed aloft. The French soldiers saw the gesture and shook their fists, and a young officer among them drew his sword and brandished it over his head. With the ships parallel to each other like this the French mizzen-top would be Hornblower's particular objective should he decide on trying to silence the firing there instead of sweeping the quarterdeck. He gazed curiously at the men it was his duty to kill. So interested was he that the bang of a cannon took him by surprise; before he could look down the rest of the Frenchman's broadside had gone off in straggling fashion, and a moment later the *Indefatigable* lurched as all her guns went off together. The wind blew the smoke forward, so that in the mizzen-top they were not troubled by it at all. Hornblower's glance showed him dead men flung about on the *Indefatigable*'s deck, dead men falling on the Frenchman's deck. Still the range was too great–very long musket shot, his eye told him.

'They're shootin' at us, sir,' said Herbert.

'Let 'em,' said Hornblower.

No musket fired from a heaving masthead at that range could possibly score a hit; that was obvious–so obvious that even Hornblower, madly excited as he was, could not help but be aware of it, and his certainty was apparent in his tone. It was interesting to see how the two calm words steadied the men. Down below the guns were roaring away continuously, and the ships were nearing each other fast.

'Open fire now, men!' said Hornblower. 'Finch!'

He stared down the short length of the swivel gun. In the coarse V of the notch on the muzzle he could see the Frenchman's wheel, the two quartermasters standing behind it, the two officers beside it. He jerked the lanyard. A tenth of a second's delay, and then the gun roared out. He was conscious, before the smoke whirled round him, of the firing quill, blown from the touch-hole, flying past his temple. Finch was already sponging out the gun. The musket balls must have spread badly; only one of the helmsmen was down and someone else was already running to take his place. At that moment the whole top lurched frightfully; Hornblower felt it but he could not explain it. There was too much happening at once. The solid timbers under his feet jarred him as he stood–perhaps a shot had hit the mizzen-mast. Finch was ramming in the cartridge; something struck the breech of the gun a heavy blow and left a bright splash of metal there–a musket bullet from the Frenchman's mizzen-top. Hornblower tried to keep his head; he took out another sharpened quill and coaxed it down into the touch-hole. It had to be done purposefully and yet gently; a quill broken off in the touch-hole was likely to be a maddening nuisance. He felt the point of the quill pierce the cartridge; Finch rammed home the wad on top of the musket balls. A bullet struck the barricade beside him as Hornblower trained the gun down, but he gave it no thought. Surely the top was swaying more even than the heavy sea justified? No matter. He had a clear shot at the enemy's quarterdeck. He tugged at the lanyard. He saw men fall. He actually saw the spokes of the wheel spin round as it was left untended. Then the two ships came together with a shattering crash and his world dissolved into chaos compared with which what had gone before was orderly.

The mast was falling. The top swung round in a dizzy arc so that only his fortunate grip on the swivel saved him from being flung out like a stone from a sling. It wheeled round. With the shrouds on one side shot away and two cannon balls in its heart the mast tottered and rolled. Then the tug of the mizzen-stays inclined it forward, the tug of the other shrouds inclined it to starboard, and the wind in the mizzen-topsail took charge when the back stays parted. The mast crashed forward; the topmast caught against the mainyard and the whole structure hung there before it could dissolve into its constituent parts. The severed butt-end of the mast must be resting on the deck for the moment; mast and topmast were still united at the cap and the trestle-trees into one continuous length, although why the topmast had not snapped at the cap was hard to say. With the lower end of the mast resting precariously on the deck and the topmast resting against the mainyard, Hornblower and Finch still had a chance of life, but the ship's motion, another shot from the Frenchman, or the parting of the over-strained material could all end that chance. The mast could slip outwards, the topmast could break, the butt-end of the mast could slip along the deck–they had to save themselves if they could before any one of these imminent events occurred. The maintopmast and everything above it was involved in the general ruin. It too had fallen and was dangling, sails spars and ropes in one frightful tangle. The mizzen-topsail had torn itself free. Hornblower's eyes met Finch's; Finch and he were clinging to the swivel gun, and there was no one else in the steeply inclined top.

The starboard side mizzen-topmast shrouds still survived; they, as well as the topmast, were resting across the mainyard, strained taut as fiddle strings, the mainyard tightening them just as the bridge tightens the strings of a fiddle. But along those shrouds lay the only way to safety–a sloping path from the peril of the top to the comparative safety of the mainyard.

The mast began to slip, to roll, out towards the end of the yard. Even if the mainyard held, the mizzen-mast would soon fall into the sea alongside. All about them were thunderous noises–spars smashing, ropes parting; the guns were still bellowing and everyone below seemed to be yelling and screaming.

The top lurched again, frightfully. Two of the shrouds parted with the strain, with a noise clearly audible through the other din, and as they parted the mast twisted with a jerk, swinging farther round the mizzen-top, the swivel gun, and the two wretched beings who clung to it. Finch's staring blue eyes rolled with the movement of the top. Later Hornblower knew that the whole period of the fall of the mast was no longer than a few seconds, but at this time it seemed as if he had at least long minutes in which to think. Like Finch's, his eyes stared round him, saw the chance of safety.

'The mainyard!' he screamed.

Finch's face bore its foolish smile. Although instinct or training kept him gripping the swivel gun he seemingly had no fear, no desire to gain the safety of the mainyard.

'Finch, you fool!' yelled Hornblower.

He locked a desperate knee round the swivel so as to free a hand with which to gesticulate, but still Finch made no move.

'Jump, damn you!' raved Hornblower. 'The shrouds–the yard. Jump!'

Finch only smiled.

'Jump and get to the maintop! Oh, Christ–!' Inspiration came in that frightful moment. 'The maintop! God's there, Finch! Go along to God, quick!'

Those words penetrated into Finch's addled brain. He nodded with sublime unworldliness. Then he let go of the swivel and seemed to launch himself into the air like a frog. His body fell across the mizzen-topmast shrouds and he began to scramble along them. The mast rolled again, so that when Hornblower launched himself at the shrouds it was a longer jump. Only his shoulders reached the outermost shroud. He swung off, clung, nearly lost his grip, but regained it as a counter-lurch of the leaning mast came to his assistance. Then he was scrambling along the shrouds, mad with panic. Here was the precious mainyard, and he threw himself across it, grappling its welcome solidity with his body, his feet feeling for the footrope. He was safe and steady on the yard just as the outward roll of the *Indefatigable* gave the balancing spars their final impetus, and the mizzen-topmast parted company from the broken mizzen-mast and the whole wreck fell down into the sea alongside. Hornblower shuffled along the yard, whither Finch had preceded him, to be received with rapture in the maintop by Midshipman Bracegirdle. Bracegirdle was not God, but as Hornblower leaned across the breastwork of the maintop he thought to himself that if he had not spoken about God being in the maintop Finch would never have made that leap.

'Thought we'd lost you,' said Bracegirdle, helping him in and thumping him on the back. 'Midshipman Hornblower, our flying angel.'

Finch was in the top, too, smiling his fool's smile and surrounded by the crew of the top. Everything seemed mad and exhilarating. It was a shock to remember that they were in the midst of a battle, and yet the firing had ceased, and even the yelling had almost died away. He staggered to the side of the top–strange how difficult it was to walk–and looked over. Bracegirdle came with him. Foreshortened by the height he could make out a crowd of figures on the Frenchman's deck. Those check shirts must surely be worn by British sailors. Surely that was Eccles, the *Indefatigable*'s first lieutenant on the quarterdeck with a speaking trumpet.

'What has happened?' he asked Bracegirdle, bewildered.

'What has happened?' Bracegirdle stared for a moment before he understood. 'We carried her by boarding. Eccles and the boarders were over the ship's side the moment we touched. Why, man, didn't you see?'

'No, I didn't see it,' said Hornblower. He forced himself to joke. 'Other matters demanded my attention at that moment.'

He remembered how the mizzen-top had lurched and swung, and he felt suddenly sick. But he did not want Bracegirdle to see it.

'I must go on deck and report,' he said.

The descent of the main shrouds was a slow, ticklish business, for neither his hands nor his feet seemed to wish to go where he tried to place them. Even when he reached the deck he still felt insecure. Bolton was on the quarterdeck supervising the clearing away of the wreck of the mizzen-mast. He gave a start of surprise as Hornblower approached.

'I thought you were overside with Davy Jones,' he said. He glanced aloft. 'You reached the mainyard in time?'

'Yes, sir.'

'Excellent. I think you're born to be hanged, Hornblower.' Bolton turned away to bellow at the men. ''Vast heaving, there! Clynes, get down into the chains with that tackle! Steady, now, or you'll lose it.'

He watched the labours of the men for some moments before he turned back to Hornblower.

'No more trouble with the men for a couple of months,' he said. 'We'll work 'em 'til they drop, refitting. Prize-crew will leave us shorthanded, to say nothing of our butcher's bill. It'll be a long time before they want something new. It'll be a long time for you, too, I fancy, Hornblower.'

'Yes, sir,' said Hornblower.

6

THE FROGS AND THE LOBSTERS

'They're coming,' said Midshipman Kennedy.

Midshipman Hornblower's unmusical ear caught the raucous sounds of a military band, and soon, with a gleam of scarlet and white and gold, the head of the column came round the corner. The hot sunshine was reflected from the brass instruments; behind them the regimental colour flapped from its staff, borne proudly by an ensign with the colour guard round him. Two mounted officers rode behind the colour, and after them came the long red serpent of the half battalion, the fixed bayonets flashing in the sun, while all the children of Plymouth, still not sated with military pomp, ran along with them.

The sailors standing ready on the quay looked at the soldiers marching up curiously, with something of pity and something of contempt mingled with their curiosity. The rigid drill, the heavy clothing, the iron discipline, the dull routine of the soldier were in sharp contrast with the far more flexible conditions in which the sailor lived. The sailors watched as the band ended with a flourish, and one of the mounted officers wheeled his horse to face the column. A shouted order turned every man to face the quayside, the movements being made so exactly together that five hundred boot-heels made a single sound. A huge sergeant-major, his sash gleaming on his chest, and the silver mounting of his cane winking in the sun, dressed the already perfect line. A third order brought down every musket-butt to earth.

'Unfix–bayonets!' roared the mounted officer, uttering the first words Hornblower had understood.

Hornblower positively goggled at the ensuing formalities, as the fuglemen strode their three paces forward, all exactly to time like marionettes worked by the same strings, turned their heads to look down the line, and gave the time for detaching the bayonets, for sheathing them, and for returning the muskets to the men's sides. The fuglemen fell back into their places, exactly to time again as far as Hornblower could see, but not exactly enough apparently, as the sergeant-major bellowed his discontent and brought the fuglemen out and sent them back again.

'I'd like to see him laying aloft on a stormy night,' muttered Kennedy. 'D'ye think he could take the maintops'l earring?'

'These lobsters!' said Midshipman Bracegirdle.

The scarlet lines stood rigid, all five companies, the sergeants with their halberds indicating the intervals–from halberd to halberd the line of faces dipped down and then up again, with the men exactly sized off, the tallest men at the flanks and the shortest men in the centre of each company. Not a finger moved, not an eyebrow twitched. Down every back hung rigidly a powdered pigtail.

The mounted officer trotted down the line to where the naval party waited, and Lieutenant Bolton, in command, stepped forward with his hand to his hat rim.

'My men are ready to embark, sir,' said the army officer. 'The baggage will be here immediately.'

'Aye aye, major,' said Bolton–the army title and the navy reply in strange contrast.

'It would be better to address me as "My lord",' said the major.

'Aye aye, sir–my lord,' replied Bolton, caught quite off his balance.

His Lordship, the Earl of Edrington, major commanding this wing of the 43rd Foot, was a heavily built young man in his early twenties. He was a fine soldierly figure in his well-fitting uniform, and mounted on a magnificent charger, but he seemed a little young for his present responsible command. But the practice of the purchase of commissions was liable to put very young men in high command, and the Army seemed satisfied with the system.

'The French auxiliaries have their orders to report here,' went on Lord Edrington. 'I suppose arrangements have been made for their transport as well?'

'Yes, my lord.'

'Not one of the beggars can speak English, as far as I can make out. Have you got an officer to interpret?'

'Yes, sir. Mr Hornblower!'

'Sir!'

'You will attend to the embarkation of the French troops.'

'Aye aye, sir.'

More military music–Hornblower's tone-deaf ear distinguished it as making a thinner noise than the British infantry band–heralded the arrival of the Frenchmen farther down the quay by a side road, and Hornblower hastened there. This was the Royal, Christian, and Catholic French Army, or a detachment of it at least–a battalion of the force raised by the émigré French nobles to fight against the Revolution. There was the white flag with the golden lilies at the head of the column, and a group of mounted officers to whom Hornblower touched his hat. One of them acknowledged his salute.

'The Marquis of Pouzauges, Brigadier General in the service of His Most Christian Majesty Louis XVII' said this individual in French by way of introduction. He wore a glittering white uniform with a blue ribbon across it.

Stumbling over the French words, Hornblower introduced himself as an aspirant of his Britannic Majesty's Marine, deputed to arrange the embarkation of the French troops.

'Very good,' said Pouzauges. 'We are ready.'

Hornblower looked down the French column. The men were standing in all attitudes, gazing about them. They were all well enough dressed, in blue uniforms which Hornblower guessed had been supplied by the British government, but the white crossbelts were already dirty, the metalwork tarnished, the arms dull. Yet doubtless they could fight.

'Those are the transports allotted to your men, sir,' said Hornblower, pointing. 'The *Sophia* will take three hundred, and the *Dumbarton*–that one over there–will take two hundred and fifty. Here at the quay are the lighters to ferry the men out.'

'Give the orders, M. de Moncoutant,' said Pouzauges to one of the officers beside him.

The hired baggage carts had now come creaking up along the column, piled high with the men's kits, and the column broke into chattering swarms as the men hunted up their possessions. It was some time before the men were reassembled, each with his own kit-bag; and then there arose the question of detailing a fatigue party to deal with the regimental baggage, and the men who were given the task yielded up their bags with obvious reluctance to their comrades, clearly in despair of ever seeing any of the contents again. Hornblower was still giving out information.

'All horses must go to the *Sophia*,' he said. 'She has accommodation for six chargers. The regimental baggage—'

He broke off short, for his eye had been caught by a singular jumble of apparatus lying in one of the carts.

'What is that, if you please?' he asked, curiosity overpowering him.

'That, sir,' said Pouzauges, 'is a guillotine.'

'A guillotine?'

Hornblower had read much lately about this instrument. The Red Revolutionaries had set one up in Paris and kept it hard at work. The King of France, Louis XVI himself, had died under it. He did not expect to find one in the train of a counter-revolutionary army.

'Yes,' said Pouzauges, 'we take it with us to France. It is in my mind to give those anarchists a taste of their own medicine.'

Hornblower did not have to make reply, fortunately, as a bellow from Bolton interrupted the conversation.

'What the hell's all this delay for, Mr Hornblower? D'you want us to miss the tide?'

It was of course typical of life in any service that Hornblower should be reprimanded for the time wasted by the inefficiency of the French arrangements–that was the sort of thing he had already come to expect, and he had already learned that it was better to submit silently to reprimand than to offer excuses. He addressed himself again to the task of getting the French aboard their transports. It was a weary midshipman who at last reported himself to Bolton with his tally sheets and the news that the last Frenchman and horse and pieces of baggage were safely aboard, and he was greeted with the order to get his things together quickly and transfer them and himself to the *Sophia*, where his services as interpreter were still needed.

The convoy dropped quickly down Plymouth Sound, rounded the Eddystone, and headed down channel, with H.M.S. *Indefatigable* flying her distinguishing pennant, the two gun-brigs which had been ordered to assist in convoying the expedition, and the four transports–a small enough force, it seemed to Hornblower, with which to attempt the overthrow of the French republic. There were only eleven hundred infantry; the half battalion of the 43rd and the weak battalion of Frenchmen (if they could be called that, seeing that many of them were soldiers of fortune of all nations) and although Hornblower had enough sense not to try to judge the Frenchmen as they lay in rows in the dark and stinking 'tweendecks in the agonies of seasickness he was puzzled that anyone could expect results from such a small force. His historical reading had told him of many small raids, in many wars, launched against the shores of France, and although he knew that they had once been described by an opposition statesman as 'breaking windows with guineas' he had been inclined to approve of them in principle, as bringing about a dissipation of the French strength–until now, when he found himself part of such an expedition.

So it was with relief that he heard from Pouzauges that the troops he had seen did not constitute the whole of the force to be employed–were indeed only a minor fraction of it. A little pale with seasickness, but manfully combating it, Pouzauges laid out a map on the cabin table and explained the plan.

'The Christian Army,' explained Pouzauges, 'will land here, at Quiberon. They sailed from Portsmouth–these English names are hard to pronounce–the day before we left Plymouth. There are five thousand men under the Baron de Charette. They will march on Vannes and Rennes.'

'And what is your regiment to do?' asked Hornblower.

Pouzauges pointed to the map again.

'Here is the town of Muzillac,' he said. 'Twenty leagues from Quiberon. Here the main road from the south crosses the River Marais, where the tide ceases to flow. It is only a little river, as you see, but its banks are marshy, and the road passes it not only by a bridge but by a long causeway. The rebel armies are to the south, and on their northward march must come by Muzillac. We shall be there. We shall destroy the bridge and defend the crossing, delaying the rebels long enough to enable M. de Charette to raise all Brittany. He will soon have twenty thousand men in arms, the rebels will come back to their allegiance, and we shall march on Paris to restore His Most Christian Majesty to the throne.'

So that was the plan. Hornblower was infected with the Frenchmen's enthusiasm. Certainly the road passed within ten miles of the coast, and there, in the broad estuary of the Vilaine, it should be possible to land a small force and seize Muzillac. There should be no difficulty about defending a causeway such as Pouzauges described for a day or two against even a large force. That would afford Charette every chance.

'My friend M. de Moncoutant here,' went on Pouzauges, 'is Lord of Muzillac. The people there will welcome him.'

'Most of them will,' said Moncoutant, his grey eyes narrowing. 'Some will be sorry to see me. But I shall be glad of the encounter.'

Western France, the Vendée and Brittany, had long been in a turmoil, and the population there, under the leadership of the nobility, had risen in arms more than once against the Paris government. But every rebellion had ended in defeat; the Royalist force now being convoyed to France was composed of the fragments of the defeated armies–a final cast of the dice, and a desperate one. Regarded in that light, the plan did not seem so sound.

It was a grey morning–a morning of grey sky and grey rocks–when the convoy rounded Belle Ile and stood in towards the estuary of the Vilaine River. Far to the northward were to be seen white topsails in Quiberon Bay–Hornblower, from the deck of the *Sophia*, saw signals pass back and forth from the *Indefatigable* as she reported her arrival to the senior officer of the main expedition there. It was a proof of the mobility and ubiquity of naval power that it could take advantage of the configuration of the land so that two blows could be struck almost in sight of each other from the sea yet separated by forty miles of roads on land. Hornblower raked the forbidding shore with his glass, reread the orders for the captain of the *Sophia*, and stared again at the shore. He could distinguish the narrow mouth of the Marais River and the strip of mud where the troops were to land. The lead was going in the chains as the *Sophia* crept towards her allotted anchorage, and the ship was rolling uneasily; these waters, sheltered though they were, were a Bedlam of conflicting currents that could make a choppy sea even in a calm. Then the anchor cable rumbled out through the hawsehole and the *Sophia* swung to the current, while the crew set to work hoisting out the boats.

'France, dear beautiful France,' said Pouzauges at Hornblower's side.

A hail came over the water from the *Indefatigable*.

'Mr Hornblower!'

'Sir!' yelled Hornblower back through the captain's megaphone.

'You will go on shore with the French troops and stay with them until you receive further orders.'

'Aye aye, sir.'

So that was the way in which he was to set foot on foreign soil for the first time in his life.

Pouzauges's men were now pouring up from below; it was a slow and exasperating business getting them down the ship's side into the waiting boats. Hornblower wondered idly regarding what was happening on shore at this moment–without doubt mounted messengers were galloping north and south with the news of the arrival of the expedition, and soon the French Revolutionary generals would be parading their men and marching them hurriedly towards this place; it was well that the important strategic point that had to be seized was less than ten miles inland. He turned back to his duties; as soon as the men were ashore he would have to see that the baggage and reserve ammunition were landed, as well as the horses, now standing miserably in improvised stalls forward of the mainmast.

The first boats had left the ship's side; Hornblower watched the men stagger up the shore through mud and water, the French on the left and the red-coated British infantry on the right. There were some fishermen's cottages in sight up the beach, and Hornblower saw advance parties go forward to seize them; at least the landing had been effected without a single shot being fired. He came on shore with the ammunition, to find Bolton in charge of the beach.

'Get those ammunition boxes well above high-water mark,' said Bolton. 'We can't send 'em forward until the Lobsters have found us some carts for 'em. And we'll need horses for those guns too.'

At that moment Bolton's working party was engaged in manhandling two six-pounder guns in field carriages up the beach; they were to be manned by seamen and drawn by horses commandeered by the landing party, for it was in the old tradition that a British expeditionary force should always be thrown on shore dependent for military necessities on the countryside. Pouzauges and his staff were waiting impatiently for their chargers, and mounted them the moment they had been coaxed out of the boats on to the beach.

'Forward for France!' shouted Pouzauges, drawing his sword and raising the hilt to his lips.

Moncoutant and the others clattered forward to head the advancing infantry, while Pouzauges lingered to exchange a few words with Lord Edrington. The British infantry was drawn up in a rigid scarlet line; farther inland occasional red dots marked where the light company had been thrown forward as pickets. Hornblower could not hear the conversation, but he noticed that Bolton was drawn into it, and finally Bolton called him over.

'You must go forward with the Frogs, Hornblower,' he said.

'I'll give you a horse,' added Edrington. 'Take that one–the roan. I've got to have someone I can trust along with them. Keep your eye on them and let me know the moment they get up to any monkey tricks–God knows what they'll do next.'

'Here's the rest of your stores coming ashore,' said Bolton. 'I'll send 'em up as soon as you send some carts back to me. What the hell's *that*?'

'That's a portable guillotine, sir,' said Hornblower. 'Part of the French baggage.'

All three turned and looked at Pouzauges, sitting his horse impatiently during this conversation, which he did not understand. He knew what they were referring to, all the same.

'That's the first thing to be sent to Muzillac,' he said to Hornblower. 'Will you have the goodness to tell these gentlemen so?'

Hornblower translated.

'I'll send the guns and a load of ammunition first,' said Bolton. 'But I'll see he gets it soon. Now off you go.'

Hornblower dubiously approached the roan horse. All he knew about riding he had learned in farmyards, but he got his foot up into the stirrup and climbed in the saddle, grabbing nervously at the reins as the animal started to move off. It seemed as far down to the ground from there as it did from the maintopgallant yard. Pouzauges wheeled his horse about and started up the beach, and the roan followed its example, with Hornblower hanging on desperately, spattered by the mud thrown up by the French horse's heels.

From the fishing hamlet a muddy lane, bordered by green turf banks, led inland, and Pouzauges trotted smartly along it, Hornblower jolting behind him. They covered three or four miles before they overtook the rear of the French infantry, marching rapidly through the mud, and Pouzauges pulled his horse to a walk. When the column climbed a slight undulation they could see the white banner far ahead. Over the banks Hornblower could see rocky fields; out on the left there was a small farmhouse of grey stone. A blue-uniformed soldier was leading away a white horse pulling a cart, while two or three more soldiers were holding back the farmer's frantic wife. So the expeditionary force had secured some of its necessary transport. In another field a soldier was prodding a cow along with his bayonet–Hornblower could not imagine with what motive. Twice he heard distant musket shots to which no one seemed to pay any attention. Then, coming down the road, they encountered two soldiers leading bony horses towards the beach; the jests hurled at them by the marching column had set the men's faces in broad grins. But a little way farther on Hornblower saw a plough standing lonely in a little field, and a grey bundle lying near it. The bundle was a dead man.

Over on their right was the marshy river valley, and it was not long before Hornblower could see, far ahead, the bridge and the causeway which they had been sent to seize. The lane they were following came down a slight incline into the town, passing between a few grey cottages before emerging into the high-road along which there lay the town. There was a grey stone church, there was a building that could easily be identified as an inn and postinghouse with soldiers swarming round it, a slight broadening of the high-road, with an avenue of trees, which Hornblower assumed must be the central square of the town. A few faces peered from upper windows, but otherwise the houses were shut and there were no civilians to be seen except two women hastily shuttering their shops. Pouzauges reined up his horse in the square and began issuing orders. Already the horses were being led out of the posthouse, and groups of men were bustling to and fro on seemingly urgent errands. In obedience to Pouzauges one officer called his men together–he had to expostulate and gesticulate before he succeeded–and started towards the bridge. Another party started along the highway in the opposite direction to guard against the possible surprise attack from there. A crowd of men squatted in the square devouring the bread that was brought out from one of the shops after its door had been beaten in, and two or three times civilians were dragged up to Pouzauges and at his orders were hurried away again to the town gaol. The seizure of the town of Muzillac was complete.

Pouzauges seemed to think so, too, after an interval, for with a glance at Hornblower he turned his horse and trotted towards the causeway. The town ended before the road entered the marshes, and in a bit of waste ground beside the road the party sent out in this direction had already lighted a fire, and the men were gathered round it, toasting on their bayonets chunks of meat cut from a cow whose half-flayed corpse lay beside the fire. Farther on, where the causeway became the bridge over the river, a sentry sat sunning himself, with his musket leaning against the parapet of the bridge at his back. Everything was peaceful enough. Pouzauges trotted as far as the crown of the bridge, with Hornblower beside him, and looked over the country on the farther side. There was no sign of any enemy, and when they returned there was a mounted red-coated soldier waiting for them–Lord Edrington.

'I've come to see for myself,' he said. 'The position looks strong enough in all conscience here. Once you have the guns posted you should be able to hold this bridge until you can blow up the arch. But there's a ford, passable at low water, half a mile lower down. That is where I shall station myself–if we lose the ford they can turn the whole position and cut us off from the shore. Tell this gentleman–what's his name?–what I said.'

Hornblower translated as well as he could, and stood by as interpreter while the two commanders pointed here and there and settled their respective duties.

'That's settled, then,' said Edrington at length. 'Don't forget, Mr Hornblower, that I must be kept informed of every development.'

He nodded to them and wheeled his horse and trotted off. As he left a cart approached from the direction of Muzillac, while behind it a loud clanking heralded the arrival of the two six-pounders, each drawn painfully by a couple of horses led by seamen. Sitting upon the front of the cart was Midshipman Bracegirdle, who saluted Hornblower with a broad grin.

'From quarterdeck to dung cart is no more than a step,' he announced, swinging himself down. 'From midshipman to captain of artillery.'

He looked along the causeway and then around him.

'Put the guns over there and they'll sweep the whole length,' suggested Hornblower.

'Exactly,' said Bracegirdle.

Under his orders the guns were wheeled off the road and pointed along the causeway, and the dung cart was unloaded of its contents, a tarpaulin spread on the ground, the gunpowder cartridges laid on it and covered with another tarpaulin. The shot and the bags of grape were piled beside the guns, the seamen working with a will under the stimulus of their novel surroundings.

'Poverty brings strange bedfellows,' said Bracegirdle. 'And wars strange duties. Have you ever blown up a bridge?'

'Never,' said Hornblower.

'Neither have I. Come, and let us do it. May I offer you a place in my carriage?'

Hornblower climbed up into the cart with Bracegirdle, and two seamen led the plodding horse along the causeway to the bridge. There they halted and looked down at the muddy water–running swiftly with the ebb–craning their heads over the parapet to look at the solid stone construction.

'It is the keystone of the arch which we should blow out,' said Bracegirdle.

That was the proverbial recipe for the destruction of a bridge, but as Hornblower looked from the bridge to Bracegirdle and back again the idea did not seem easy to execute. Gunpowder exploded upwards and had to be held in on all sides–how was that to be done under the arch of the bridge?

'What about the pier?' he asked tentatively.

'We can but look and see,' said Bracegirdle, and turned to the seaman by the cart. 'Hannay, bring a rope.'

They fastened the rope to the parapet and slid down it to a precarious foothold on the slippery ledge round the base of the pier, the river gurgling at their feet.

'That seems to be the solution,' said Bracegirdle, crouching almost double under the arch.

Time slipped by fast as they made their preparations; a working party had to be brought from the guard of the bridge, picks and crowbars had to be found or extemporized, and some of the huge blocks with which the pier was built had to be picked out at the shoulder of the arch. Two kegs of gunpowder, lowered gingerly from above, had to be thrust into the holes so formed, a length of slow match put in at each bunghole and led to the exterior, while the kegs were tamped into their caves with all the stones and earth that could be crammed into them. It was almost twilight under the arch when the work was finished, the working party made laboriously to climb the rope up to the bridge and Bracegirdle and Hornblower left to look at each other again.

'I'll fire the fuses,' said Bracegirdle. 'You go next, sir.'

It was not a matter for much argument. Bracegirdle was under orders to destroy the bridge, and Hornblower addressed himself to climbing up the rope while Bracegirdle took his tinderbox from his pocket. Once on the roadway of the bridge Hornblower sent away the cart and waited. It was only two or three minutes before Bracegirdle appeared, frantically climbing the rope and hurling himself over the parapet.

'Run!' was all that was said.

Together they scurried down the bridge and halted breathless to crouch by the abutment of the causeway. Then came a dull explosion, a tremor of the earth under their feet, and a cloud of smoke.

'Let's come and see,' said Bracegirdle.

They retraced their steps towards where the bridge was still shrouded in smoke and dust.

'Only partly—' began Bracegirdle as they neared the scene and the dust cleared away.

And at that moment there was a second explosion which made them stagger as they stood. A lump of the roadbed hit the parapet beside them and burst like a shell, spattering them with fragments. There was a rumble and a clatter as the arch subsided into the river.

'That must have been the second keg going off,' said Bracegirdle, wiping his face. 'We should have remembered the fuses were likely to be of different lengths. Two promising careers might have ended suddenly if we had been any nearer.'

'At any rate, the bridge is gone,' said Hornblower.

'All's well that ends well,' said Bracegirdle.

Seventy pounds of gunpowder had done their work. The bridge was cut clear across, leaving a ragged gap several feet wide, beyond which the roadway reached out towards the gap from the farther pier as a witness to the toughness of the mortar. Beneath their feet as they peered over they could see the river bed almost choked with lumps of stone.

'We'll need no more than an anchor watch tonight,' said Bracegirdle.

Hornblower looked round to where the roan horse was tethered; he was tempted to return to Muzillac on foot, leading the animal, but shame forbade. He climbed with an effort into the saddle and headed the animal back up the road; ahead of him the sky was beginning to turn red with the approach of sunset.

He entered the main street of the town and rounded the slight bend to the central square, to see something that made him, without his own volition, tug at his reins and halt his horse. The square was full of people, townsfolk and soldiers, and in the centre of the square a tall narrow rectangle reached upwards towards the sky with a glittering blade at its upper end. The blade fell with a reverberating thump, and the little group of men round the base of the rectangle dragged something to one side and added it to the heap already there. The portable guillotine was at work.

Hornblower sat sick and horrified–this was worse than any flogging at the gratings. He was about to urge his horse forward when a strange sound caught his ear. A man was singing, loud and clear, and out from a building at the side of the square emerged a little procession. In front walked a big man with dark curly hair, wearing a white shirt and dark breeches. At either side and behind him walked soldiers. It was this man who was singing; the tune meant nothing to Hornblower, but he could hear the words distinctly–it was one of the verses of the French revolutionary song, echoes of which had penetrated even across the Channel.

'Oh, sacred love of the Fatherland . . .' sang the man in the white shirt; and when the civilians in the square heard what he was singing, there was a rustle among them and they dropped to the knees, their heads bowed and their hands crossed upon their breasts.

The executioners were winding the blade up again, and the man in the white shirt followed its rise with his eyes while he still sang without a tremor in his voice. The blade reached the top, and the singing ceased at last as the executioners fell on the man with the white shirt and led him to the guillotine. Then the blade fell with another echoing crash.

It seemed that this was to be the last execution, for the soldiers began to push the civilians back towards their homes, and Hornblower urged his horse forward through the dissolving crowd. He was nearly thrown from his saddle when the animal plunged sideways, snorting furiously–it had scented the horrid heap that lay beside the guillotine. At the side of the square was a house with a balcony, and Hornblower looked up at it in time to see Pouzauges still standing there, wearing his white uniform and blue ribbon, his staff about him and his hands on the rail. There were sentries at the door, and to one of them Hornblower handed over his horse as he entered; Pouzauges was just descending the stairs.

'Good evening, sir,' said Pouzauges with perfect courtesy. 'I am glad you have found your way to headquarters. I trust it was without trouble? We are about to dine and will enjoy your company. You have your horse, I suppose? M. de Villers here will give orders for it to be looked after, I am sure.'

It was all hard to believe. It was hard to believe that this polished gentleman had ordered the butchery that had just ended; it was hard to believe that the elegant young men with whom he sat at dinner were staking their lives on the overthrow of a barbarous but lusty young republic. But it was equally hard to believe, when he climbed into a four-poster bed that night, that he, Midshipman Horatio Hornblower, was in imminent deadly peril himself.

Outside in the street women wailed as the headless corpses, the harvest of the executions, were carried away, and he thought he would never sleep, but youth and fatigue had their way, and he slept for most of the night, although he awoke with the feeling that he had just been fighting off a nightmare. Everything was strange to him in the darkness, and it was several moments before he could account for the strangeness. He was in a bed and not–as he had spent the preceding three hundred nights–in a hammock; and the bed was steady as a rock instead of swaying about with the lively motion of a frigate. The stuffiness about him was the stuffiness of bed curtains, and not the stuffiness of the midshipmen's berth with its compound smell of stale humanity and stale bilgewater. He was on shore, in a house, in a bed, and everything about him was dead quiet, unnaturally so to a man accustomed to the noises of a wooden ship at sea.

Of course; he was in a house in the town of Muzillac in Brittany. He was sleeping in the headquarters of Brigadier General the Marquis de Pouzauges, commanding the French troops who constituted part of this expedition, which was itself part of a larger force invading Revolutionary France in the Royalist cause. Hornblower felt a quickening of the pulse, a faint sick feeling of insecurity, as he realized afresh that he was now in France, ten miles from the sea and the *Indefatigable* with only a rabble of Frenchmen–half of them mercenaries only nominally Frenchmen at that–around him to preserve him from death or captivity. He regretted his knowledge of French–if he had had none he would not be here, and good fortune might even have put him among the British half battalion of the 43rd guarding the ford a mile away.

It was partly the thought of the British troops which roused him out of bed. It was his duty to see that liaison was kept up with them, and the situation might have changed while he slept. He drew aside the bed curtains and stepped down to the floor; as his legs took the weight of his body they protested furiously–all the riding he had done yesterday had left every muscle and joint aching so that he could hardly walk. But he hobbled in the darkness over to the window, found the latch of the shutters, and pushed them open. A three-quarter moon was shining down into the empty street of the town, and looking down he could see the three-cornered hat of the sentry posted outside, and the bayonet reflecting the moonlight. Returning from the window, he found his coat and his shoes and put them on, belted his cutlass about him, and then he crept downstairs as quietly as he could. In the room off the entrance hall a tallow dip guttered on the table, and beside it a French sergeant slept with his head on his arms, lightly, for he raised his head as Hornblower paused in the doorway. On the floor of the room the rest of the guard off duty were snoring stertorously, huddled together like pigs in a sty, their muskets stacked against the wall.

Hornblower nodded to the sergeant, opened the front door and stepped out into the street. His lungs expanded gratefully as he breathed in the clean night air–morning air, rather, for there to the east the sky was assuming a lighter tinge–and the sentry, catching sight of the British naval officer, came clumsily to attention. In the square there still stood the gaunt harsh framework of the guillotine reaching up to the moonlit sky, and round it the black patch of the blood of its victims. Hornblower wondered who they were, who it could have been that the Royalists should seize and kill at such short notice, and he decided that they must have been petty officials of the Revolutionary government–the mayor and the customs officer and so on–if they were not merely men against whom the émigrés had cherished grudges since the days of the Revolution itself. It was a savage, merciless world, and at the moment he was very much alone in it, lonely, depressed, and unhappy.

He was distracted from these thoughts by the sergeant of the guard emerging from the door with a file of men; the sentry in the street was relieved, and the party went on round the house to relieve the others. Then across the street he saw four drummers appear from another house, with a sergeant commanding them. They formed into a line, their drumsticks poised high before their faces, and then at a word from the sergeant, the eight drumsticks fell together with a crash, and the drummers proceeded to march slowly along the street beating out a jerky exhilarating rhythm. At the first corner they stopped, and the drums rolled long and menacingly, and then they marched on again, beating out the previous rhythm. They were beating to arms, calling the men to their duties from their billets, and Hornblower, tone-deaf but highly sensitive to rhythm, thought it was fine music, real music. He turned back to headquarters with his depression fallen away from him. The sergeant of the guard came marching back with the relieved sentries; the first of the awakened soldiers were beginning to appear sleepily in the streets, and then, with a clatter of hoofs, a mounted messenger came riding up to headquarters, and the day was begun.

A pale young French officer read the note which the messenger brought, and politely handed it to Hornblower to read; he had to puzzle over it for a space–he was not accustomed to hand-written French–but its meaning became clear to him at length. It implied no new development; the main expeditionary force, landed yesterday at Quiberon, would move forward this morning on Vannes and Rennes while the subsidiary force to which Hornblower was attached must maintain its position at Muzillac, guarding its flank. The Marquis de Pouzauges, immaculate in his white uniform and blue ribbon, appeared at that moment, read the note without comment, and turned to Hornblower with a polite invitation to breakfast.

They went back to the big kitchen with its copper cooking pans glittering on the walls, and a silent woman brought them coffee and bread. She might be a patriotic Frenchwoman and an enthusiastic counter-revolutionary, but she showed no signs of it. Her feelings, of course, might easily have been influenced by the fact that this horde of men had taken over her house and were eating her food and sleeping in her rooms without payment. Maybe some of the horses and wagons seized for the use of the army were hers too–and maybe some of the people who had died under the guillotine last night were her friends. But she brought coffee, and the staff, standing about in the big kitchen with their spurs clinking, began to breakfast. Hornblower took his cup and a piece of bread–for four months before this his only bread had been ship's biscuit–and sipped at the stuff. He was not sure if he liked it; he had only tasted coffee three or four times before. But the second time he raised his cup to his lips he did not sip; before he could do so, the distant boom of a cannon made him lower his cup and stand stock still. The cannon shot was repeated, and again, and then it was echoed by a sharper, nearer note–Midshipman Bracegirdle's six-pounders on the causeway.

In the kitchen there was instant stir and bustle. Somebody knocked a cup over and sent a river of black liquid swirling across the table. Somebody else managed to catch his spurs together so that he stumbled into somebody else's arms. Everyone seemed to be speaking at once. Hornblower was as excited as the rest of them; he wanted to rush out and see what was happening, but he thought at that moment of the disciplined calm which he had seen in H.M.S. *Indefatigable* as she went into action. He was not of this breed of Frenchmen, and to prove it he made himself put his cup to his lips again and drink calmly. Already most of the staff had dashed out of the kitchen shouting for their horses. It would take time to saddle up; he met Pouzauges's eye as the latter strode up and down the kitchen, and drained his cup–a trifle too hot for comfort, but he felt it was a good gesture. There was bread to eat, and he made himself bite and chew and swallow, although he had no appetite; if he was to be in the field all day, he could not tell when he would get his next meal, and so he crammed a half loaf into his pocket.

The horses were being brought into the yard and saddled; the excitement had infected them, and they plunged and sidled about amid the curses of the officers. Pouzauges leapt up into his saddle and clattered away with the rest of the staff behind him, leaving behind only a single soldier holding Hornblower's roan. That was as it had better be–Hornblower knew that he would not keep his seat for half a minute if the horse took it into his head to plunge or rear. He walked slowly out to the animal, which was calmer now when the groom petted him, and climbed with infinite slowness and precaution into the saddle. With a pull at the bit he checked the brute's exuberance and walked it sedately into the street and towards the bridge in the wake of the galloping staff. It was better to make sure of arriving by keeping his horse down to a walk than to gallop and be thrown. The guns were still booming and he could see the puffs of smoke from Bracegirdle's six-pounders. On his left, the sun was rising in a clear sky.

At the bridge the situation seemed obvious enough. Where the arch had been blown up a few skirmishers on either side were firing at each other across the gap, and at the far end of the causeway, across the Marais, a cloud of smoke revealed the presence of a hostile battery firing slowly and at extreme range. Beside the causeway on this side were Bracegirdle's two six-pounders, almost perfectly covered by a dip in the ground. Bracegirdle, with his cutlass belted round him, was standing between the guns which his party of seamen were working, and he waved his hand lightheartedly at Hornblower when he caught sight of him. A dark column of infantry appeared on the distant causeway. Bang–bang went Bracegirdle's guns. Hornblower's horse plunged at the noise, distracting him, but when he had time to look again, the column had disappeared. Then suddenly the causeway parapet near him flew into splinters; something hit the roadbed beside his horse's feet a tremendous blow and passed on with a roar–that was the closest so far in his life that a cannon shot had missed him. He lost a stirrup during the resultant struggle with his horse, and deemed it wiser, as soon as he regained moderate control, to dismount and lead the animal off the causeway towards the guns. Bracegirdle met him with a grin.

'No chance of their crossing here,' he said. 'At least, not if the Frogs stick to their work, and it looks as if they're willing to. The gap's within grapeshot range, they'll never bridge it. Can't think what they're burning powder for.'

'Testing our strength, I suppose,' said Hornblower, with an air of infinite military wisdom.

He would have been shaking with excitement if he had allowed his body to take charge. He did not know if he were being stiltedly unnatural, but even if he were that was better than to display excitement. There was something strangely pleasant, in a nightmare fashion, in standing here posing as a hardened veteran with cannon balls howling overhead; Bracegirdle seemed happy and smiling and quite master of himself, and Hornblower looked sharply at him, wondering if this were as much a pose as his own. He could not tell.

'Here they come again,' said Bracegirdle. 'Oh, only skirmishers.'

A few scattered men were running out along the causeway to the bridge. At long musket range they fell to the ground and began spasmodic firing; already there were some dead men lying over there and the skirmishers took cover behind the corpses. On this side of the gap the skirmishers, better sheltered, fired back at them.

'They haven't a chance, here at any rate,' said Bracegirdle. 'And look there.'

The main body of the Royalist force, summoned from the town, was marching up along the road. While they watched it, a cannon shot from the other side struck the head of the column and ploughed into it–Hornblower saw dead men flung this way and that, and the column wavered. Pouzauges came riding up and yelled orders, and the column, leaving its dead and wounded on the road, changed direction and took shelter in the marshy fields beside the causeway.

With nearly all the Royalist force assembled, it seemed indeed as if it would be utterly impossible for the Revolutionaries to force a crossing here.

'I'd better report on this to the Lobsters,' said Hornblower.

'There was firing down that way at dawn,' agreed Bracegirdle.

Skirting the wide marsh here ran a narrow path through the lush grass, leading to the ford which the 43rd were guarding. Hornblower led his horse on to the path before he mounted; he felt he would be more sure in that way of persuading the horse to take that direction. It was not long before he saw a dab of scarlet on the river bank–pickets thrown out from the main body to watch against any unlikely attempt to cross the marshes and stream round the British flank. Then he saw the cottage that indicated the site of the ford; in the field beside it was a wide patch of scarlet indicating where the main body was waiting for developments. At this point the marsh narrowed where a ridge of slightly higher ground approached the water; a company of redcoats was drawn up here with Lord Edrington on horseback beside them. Hornblower rode up and made his report, somewhat jerkily as his horse moved restlessly under him.

'No serious attack, you say?' asked Edrington.

'No sign of one when I left, sir.'

'Indeed?' Edrington stared across the river. 'And here it's the same story. No attempt to cross the ford in force. Why should they show their hand and then not attack?'

'I thought they were burning powder unnecessarily, sir,' said Hornblower.

'They're not fools,' snapped Edrington, with another penetrating look across the river. 'At any rate, there's no harm in assuming they are not.'

He turned his horse and cantered back to the main body and gave an order to a captain, who scrambled to his feet to receive it. The captain bellowed an order, and his company stood up and fell into line, rigid and motionless. Two further orders turned them to the right and marched them off in file, every man in step, every musket sloped at the same angle. Edrington watched them go.

'No harm in having a flank guard,' he said.

The sound of a cannon across the water recalled them to the river; on the other side of the marsh a column of troops could be seen marching rapidly along the bank.

'That's the same column coming back, sir,' said the company commander. 'That or another just like it.'

'Marching about and firing random shots,' said Edrington. 'Mr Hornblower, have the émigré troops any flank guard out towards Quiberon?'

'Towards Quiberon, sir?' said Hornblower, taken aback.

'Damn it, can't you hear a plain question? Is there, or is there not?'

'I don't know, sir,' confessed Hornblower miserably.

There were five thousand émigré troops at Quiberon, and it seemed quite unnecessary to keep a guard out in that direction.

'Then present my compliments to the French émigré general, and suggest he posts a strong detachment up the road, if he has not done so.'

'Aye aye, sir.'

Hornblower turned his horse's head back up the path towards the bridge. The sun was shining strongly now over the deserted fields. He could still hear the occasional thud of a cannon shot, but overhead a lark was singing in the blue sky. Then as he headed up the last low ridge towards Muzillac and the bridge he heard a sudden irregular outburst of firing; he fancied he heard screams and shouts, and what he saw as he topped the rise, made him snatch at his reins and drag his horse to a halt. The fields before him were covered with fugitives in blue uniforms with white crossbelts, all running madly towards him. In among the fugitives were galloping horsemen, whirling sabres that flashed in the sunshine. Farther out to the left a whole column of horsemen were trotting fast across the fields, and farther back the sun glittered on lines of bayonets moving rapidly from the high road towards the sea.

There could be no doubt of what had happened; during those sick seconds when he sat and stared, Hornblower realized the truth; the Revolutionaries had pushed in a force between Quiberon and Muzillac, and, keeping the émigrés occupied by demonstrations from across the river, had rushed down and brought off a complete surprise by this attack from an unexpected quarter. Heaven only knew what had happened at Quiberon–but this was no time to think about that. Hornblower dragged his horse's head round and kicked his heels into the brute's sides, urging him frantically back up the path towards the British. He bounced and rolled in his saddle, clinging on madly, consumed with fear lest he lose his seat and be captured by the pursuing French.

At the clatter of hoofs every eye turned towards him when he reached the British post. Edrington was there, standing with his horse's bridle over his arm.

'The French!' yelled Hornblower hoarsely, pointing back. 'They're coming!'

'I expected nothing else,' said Edrington.

He shouted an order before he put his foot in the stirrup to mount. The main body of the 43rd was standing in line by the time he was in the saddle. His adjutant went galloping off to recall the company from the water's edge.

'The French are in force, horse, foot, and guns, I suppose?' asked Edrington.

'Horse and foot at least, sir,' gasped Hornblower, trying to keep his head clear. 'I saw no guns.'

'And the émigrés are running like rabbits?'

'Yes, sir.'

'Here come the first of them.'

Over the nearest ridge a few blue uniforms made their appearance, their wearers still running while stumbling with fatigue.

'I suppose we must cover their retreat, although they're not worth saving,' said Edrington. 'Look there!'

The company he had sent out as a flank guard was in sight on the crest of a slight slope: it was formed into a tiny square, red against the green, and as they watched they saw a mob of horsemen flood up the hill towards it and break into an eddy around it.

'Just as well I had them posted there,' remarked Edrington calmly. 'Ah, here comes Mayne's company.'

The force from the ford came marching up. Harsh orders were shouted. Two companies wheeled round while the sergeant-major with his sabre and his silver-headed cane regulated the pace and the alignment as if the men were on the barrack square.

'I would suggest you stay by me, Mr Hornblower,' said Edrington.

He moved his horse up into the interval between the two columns, and Hornblower followed him dumbly. Another order, and the force began to march steadily across the valley, the sergeants calling the step and the sergeant-major watching the intervals. All round them now were fleeing émigré soldiers, most of them in the last stages of exhaustion–Hornblower noticed more than one of them fall down on the ground gasping and incapable of further movement. And then over the low slope to the right appeared a line of plumes, a line of sabres–a regiment of cavalry trotting rapidly forward. Hornblower saw the sabres lifted, saw the horses break into a gallop, heard the yells of the charging men. The redcoats around him halted; another shouted order, another slow, deliberate movement, and the half battalion was in a square with the mounted officers in the centre and the colours waving over their heads. The charging horsemen were less than a hundred yards away. Some officer with a deep voice began giving orders, intoning them as if at some solemn ceremony. The first order brought the muskets from the men's shoulders, and the second was answered by a simultaneous click of opened priming pans. The third order brought the muskets to the present along one face of the square.

'Too high!' said the sergeant-major. 'Lower, there, number seven.'

The charging horsemen were only thirty yards away; Hornblower saw the leading men, their cloaks flying from their shoulders, leaning along their horses' necks with their sabres pointed forward at the full stretch of their arms.

'Fire!' said the deep voice.

In reply came a single sharp explosion as every musket went off at once. The smoke swirled round the square and disappeared. Where Hornblower had been looking, there were now a score of horses and men on the ground, some struggling in agony, some lying still. The cavalry regiment split like a torrent encountering a rock and hurtled harmlessly past the other faces of the square.

'Well enough,' said Edrington.

The deep voice was intoning again; like marionettes all on the same string the company that had fired now reloaded, every man biting out his bullet at the same instant, every man ramming home his charge, every man spitting his bullet into his musket barrel with the same instantaneous inclination of the head. Edrington looked keenly at the cavalry collecting together in a disorderly mob down the valley.

'The 43rd will advance!' he ordered.

With solemn ritual the square opened up again into two columns and continued its interrupted march. The detached company came marching up to join them from out of a ring of dead men and horses. Someone raised a cheer.

'Silence in the ranks!' bellowed the sergeant-major. 'Sergeant, take that man's name.'

But Hornblower noticed how the sergeant-major was eyeing keenly the distance between the columns; it had to be maintained exactly so that a company wheeling back filled it to make the square.

'Here they come again,' said Edrington.

The cavalry were forming for a new charge, but the square was ready for them. Now the horses were blown and the men were less enthusiastic. It was not a solid wall of horses that came down on them, but isolated groups, rushing first at one face and then at another, and pulling up or swerving aside as they reached the line of bayonets. The attacks were too feeble to meet with company volleys; at the word of command sections here and there gave fire to the more determined groups. Hornblower saw one man–an officer, judging by his gold lace–rein up before the bayonets and pull out a pistol. Before he could discharge it, half a dozen muskets went off together; the officer's face became a horrible bloody mask, and he and his horse fell together to the ground. Then all at once the cavalry wheeled off, like starlings over a field, and the march could be resumed.

'No discipline about these Frogs, not on either side,' said Edrington.

The march was headed for the sea, for the blessed shelter of the *Indefatigable*, but it seemed to Hornblower as if the pace was intolerably slow. The men were marching at the parade step, with agonizing deliberation, while all round them and far ahead of them the fugitive émigrés poured in a broad stream towards safety. Looking back, Hornblower saw the fields full of marching columns–hurrying swarms, rather–of Revolutionary infantry in hot pursuit of them.

'Once let men run, and you can't do anything else with them,' commented Edrington, following Hornblower's gaze.

Shouts and shots over to the flank caught their attention. Trotting over the fields, leaping wildly at the bumps, came a cart drawn by a lean horse. Someone in a seaman's frock and trousers was holding the reins; other seamen were visible over the sides firing muskets at the horsemen hovering about them. It was Bracegirdle with his dung cart; he might have lost his guns but he had saved his men. The pursuers dropped away as the cart neared the columns; Bracegirdle, standing up in the cart, caught sight of Hornblower on his horse and waved to him excitedly.

'Boadicea and her chariot!' he yelled.

'I'll thank you, sir!' shouted Edrington with lungs of brass, 'to go on and prepare for our embarkation.'

'Aye aye, sir!'

The lean horse trotted on with the cart lurching after it and the grinning seamen clinging on to the sides. At the flank appeared a swarm of infantry, a mad, gesticulating crowd, half running to cut off the 43rd's retreat. Edrington swept his glance round the fields.

'The 43rd will form line!' he shouted.

Like some ponderous machine, well oiled, the half battalion fronted towards the swarm; the columns became lines, each man moving into his position like bricks laid on a wall.

'The 43rd will advance!'

The scarlet line swept forward, slowly, inexorably. The swarm hastened to meet it, officers to the front waving their swords and calling on their men to follow.

'Make ready!'

Every musket came down together; the priming pans clicked.

'Present!'

Up came the muskets, and the swarm hesitated before that fearful menace. Individuals tried to get back into the crowd to cover themselves from the volley with the bodies of their comrades.

'Fire!'

A crashing volley; Hornblower, looking over the heads of the British infantry from his point of vantage on horseback, saw the whole face of the swarm go down in swathes. Still the red line moved forward, at each deliberate step a shouted order brought a machine-like response as the men reloaded; five hundred mouths spat in five hundred bullets, five hundred right arms raised five hundred ramrods at once. When the muskets came to the present the red line was at the swathe of dead and wounded, for the swarm had withdrawn before the advance, and shrank back still further at the threat of the volley. The volley was fired; the advance went on. Another volley; another advance. Now the swarm was shredding away. Now men were running from it. Now every man had turned tail and fled from that frightful musketry. The hillside was as black with fugitives as it had been when the émigrés were fleeing.

'Halt!'

The advance ceased; the line became a double column, and the retreat began again.

'Very creditable,' remarked Edrington.

Hornblower's horse was trying jerkily to pick its way over a carpet of dead and wounded, and he was so busy keeping his seat, and his brain was in such a whirl, that he did not immediately realize that they had topped the last rise, so that before them lay the glittering waters of the estuary. The strip of muddy beach was packed solid with émigrés. There were the ships riding at anchor, and there, blessed sight, were the boats swarming towards the shore. It was high time, for already the boldest of the Revolutionary infantry were hovering round the columns, taking long shots into them. Here and there a man fell.

'Close up!' snapped the sergeants, and the files marched on stolidly, leaving the wounded and dead behind them.

The adjutant's horse suddenly snorted and plunged, and then fell first to its knees, and, kicking, to its side, while the freckle-faced adjutant freed his feet from the stirrups and flung himself out of the saddle just in time to escape being pinned underneath.

'Are you hit, Stanley?' asked Edrington.

'No, my lord. All safe and sound,' said the adjutant, brushing at his scarlet coat.

'You won't have to foot it far,' said Edrington. 'No need to throw out skirmishers to drive those fellows off. This is where we must make our stand.'

He looked about him, at the fishermen's cottages above the beach, the panic-stricken émigrés at the water's edge, and the masses of Revolutionary infantry coming up in pursuit, leaving small enough time for preparation. Some of the redcoats poured into the cottages, appearing a moment later at the windows; it was fortunate that the fishing hamlet guarded one flank of the gap down to the beach while the other was guarded by a steep and inaccessible headland on whose summit a small block of redcoats established themselves. In the gap between the two points the remaining four companies formed a long line just sheltered by the crest of the beach.

The boats of the squadron were already loading with émigrés among the small breakers below. Hornblower heard the crack of a single pistol-shot; he could guess that some officer down there was enforcing his orders in the only possible way to prevent the fear-driven men from pouring into the boats and swamping them. As if in answer came the roar of cannon on the other side. A battery of artillery had unlimbered just out of musket range and was firing at the British position, while all about it gathered the massed battalions of the Revolutionary infantry. The cannon balls howled close overhead.

'Let them fire away,' said Edrington. 'The longer the better.'

The artillery could do little harm to the British in the fold of ground that protected them, and the Revolutionary commander must have realized that as well as the necessity for wasting no time. Over there the drums began to roll–a noise of indescribable menace–and then the columns surged forward. So close were they already that Hornblower could see the features of the officers in the lead, waving their hats and swords.

'43rd, make ready!' said Edrington, and the priming pans clicked as one. 'Seven paces forward–march!'

One–two–three–seven paces, painstakingly taken, took the line to the little crest.

'Present! Fire!'

A volley nothing could withstand. The columns halted, swayed, received another smashing volley, and another, and fell back in ruin.

'Excellent!' said Edrington.

The battery boomed again; a file of two redcoat soldiers was tossed back like dolls, to lie in a horrible bloody mass close beside Hornblower's horse's feet.

'Close up!' said a sergeant, and the men on either side had filled the gap.

'43rd, seven paces back–march!'

The line was below the crest again, as the redcoated marionettes withdrew in steady time. Hornblower could not remember later whether it was twice or three times more that the Revolutionary masses came on again, each time to be dashed back by that disciplined musketry. But the sun was nearly setting in the ocean behind him when he looked back to see the beach almost cleared and Bracegirdle plodding up to them to report.

'I can spare one company now,' said Edrington in reply but not taking his eyes off the French masses. 'After they are on board, have every boat ready and waiting.'

One company filed off; another attack was beaten back–after the preceding failures it was not pressed home with anything like the dash and fire of the earlier ones. Now the battery was turning its attention to the headland on the flank, and sending its balls among the redcoats there, while a battalion of French moved over to the attack at that point.

'That gives us time,' said Edrington. 'Captain Griffin, you can march the men off. Colour party, remain here.'

Down the beach went the centre companies to the waiting boats, while the colours still waved to mark their old position, visible over the crest to the French. The company in the cottages came out, formed up, and marched down as well. Edrington trotted across to the foot of the little headland; he watched the French forming for the attack and the infantry wading out to the boats.

'Now, grenadiers!' he yelled suddenly. 'Run for it! Colour party!'

Down the steep seaward face of the headland came the last company, running, sliding, and stumbling. A musket, clumsily handled, went off unexpectedly. The last man came down the slope as the colour party reached the water's edge and began to climb into a boat with its precious burden. A wild yell went up from the French, and their whole mass came rushing towards the evacuated position.

'Now, sir,' said Edrington, turning his horse seawards.

Hornblower fell from his saddle as his horse splashed into the shallows. He let go of the reins and plunged out, waist deep, shoulder deep, to where the longboat lay on its oars with its four-pounder gun in its bows and Bracegirdle beside it to haul him in. He looked up in time to see a curious incident; Edrington had reached the *Indefatigable*'s gig, still holding his horse's reins. With the French pouring down the beach towards them, he turned and took a musket from the nearest soldier, pressed the muzzle to the horse's head, and fired. The horse fell in its death agony in the shallows; only Hornblower's roan remained as prize to the Revolutionaries.

'Back water!' said Bracegirdle, and the longboat backed away from the beach; Hornblower lay in the eyes of the boat feeling as if he had not the strength to move a limb, and the beach was covered with shouting, gesticulating Frenchmen, lit redly by the sunset.

'One moment,' said Bracegirdle, reaching for the lanyard of the four-pounder, and tugging at it smartly.

The gun roared out in Hornblower's ear, and the charge cut a swathe of destruction on the beach.

'That was canister,' said Bracegirdle. 'Eighty-four balls. Easy, port! Give way, starboard!'

The longboat turned, away from the beach and towards the welcoming ships. Hornblower looked back at the darkening coast of France. This was the end of an incident; his country's attempt to overturn the Revolution had met with a bloody repulse. Newspapers in Paris would exult; the *Gazette* in London would give the incident five cold lines. Clairvoyant, Hornblower could foresee that in a year's time the world would hardly remember the incident. In twenty years it would be entirely forgotten. Yet those headless corpses up there in Muzillac; those shattered redcoats; those Frenchmen caught in the four-pounder's blast of canister–they were all as dead as if it had been a day in which history had been changed. And he was just as weary. And in his pocket there was still the bread he had put there that morning and forgotten all about.

7

THE SPANISH GALLEYS

The old *Indefatigable* was lying at anchor in the Bay of Cadiz at the time when Spain made peace with France. Hornblower happened to be midshipman of the watch, and it was he who called the attention of Lieutenant Chadd to the approach of the eight-oared pinnace, with the red and yellow of Spain dropping at the stern. Chadd's glass made out the gleam of gold on epaulette and cocked hat, and bellowed the order for sideboys and marine guard to give the traditional honours to a captain in an allied service. Pellew, hurriedly warned, was at the gangway to meet his visitor, and it was at the gangway that the entire interview took place. The Spaniard, making a low bow with his hat across his stomach, offered a sealed envelope to the Englishman.

'Here, Mr Hornblower,' said Pellew, holding the letter unopened, 'speak French to this fellow. Ask him to come below for a glass of wine.'

But the Spaniard, with a further bow, declined the refreshment, and, with another bow, requested that Pellew open the letter immediately. Pellew broke the seal and read the contents, struggling with the French which he could read to a small extent although he could not speak it at all. He handed it to Hornblower.

'This means the Dagoes have made peace, doesn't it?'

Hornblower struggled through twelve lines of compliments addressed by His Excellency the Duke of Belchite (Grandee of the First Class, with eighteen other titles ending with Captain-General of Andalusia) to the Most Gallant Ship-Captain Sir Edward Pellew, Knight of the Bath. The second paragraph was short and contained only a brief intimation of peace. The third paragraph was as long as the first, and repeated its phraseology almost word for word in a ponderous farewell.

'That's all, sir,' said Hornblower.

But the Spanish captain had a verbal message with which to supplement the written one.

'Please tell your captain,' he said, in his lisping Spanish-French, 'that now as a neutral power, Spain must enforce her rights. You have already been at anchor here for twenty-four hours. Six hours from now'–the Spaniard took a gold watch from his pocket and glanced at it–'if you are within range of the batteries at Puntales there they will be given orders to fire on you.'

Hornblower could only translate the brutal message without any attempt at softening it, and Pellew listened, white with anger despite his tan.

'Tell him—' he began, and then mastered his rage. 'Damme if I'll let him see he has made me angry.'

He put his hat across his stomach and bowed in as faithful an imitation of the Spaniard's courtliness as he could manage, before he turned to Hornblower.

'Tell him I have received his message with pleasure. Tell him I much regret that circumstances are separating him from me, and that I hope I shall always enjoy his personal friendship whatever the relations between our countries. Tell him–oh, you can tell him the sort of thing I want said, can't you, Hornblower? Let's see him over the side with dignity. Sideboys! Bosun's mates! Drummers!'

Hornblower poured out compliments to the best of his ability, and at every phrase the two captains exchanged bows, the Spaniard withdrawing a pace at each bow and Pellew following him up, not to be outdone in courtesy. The drums beat a ruffle, the marines presented arms, the pipes shrilled and twittered until the Spaniard's head had descended to the level of the maindeck, when Pellew stiffened up, clapped his hat on his head, and swung round on his first lieutenant.

'Mr Eccles, I want to be under way within the hour, if you please.'

Then he stamped down below to regain his equanimity in private.

Hands were aloft loosing sail ready to sheet home, while the clank of the capstan told how other men were heaving the cable short, and Hornblower was standing on the portside gangway with Mr Wales the carpenter, looking over at the white houses of one of the most beautiful cities in Europe.

'I've been ashore there twice,' said Wales. 'The wine's good–vino, they calls it–if you happens to like that kind o' muck. But don't you ever try that brandy, Mr Hornblower. Poison, it is, rank poison. Hello! We're going to have an escort, I see.'

Two long sharp prows had emerged from the inner bay, and were pointing towards the *Indefatigable*. Hornblower could not restrain himself from giving a cry of surprise as he followed Wales's gaze. The vessels approaching were galleys; along each side of them the oars were lifting and falling rhythmically, catching the sunlight as they feathered. The effect, as a hundred oars swung like one, was perfectly beautiful. Hornblower remembered a line in a Latin poet which he had translated as a schoolboy, and recalled his surprise when he discovered that to a Roman the 'white wings' of a ship of war were her oars. Now the simile was plain; even a gull in flight, which Hornblower had always looked upon until now as displaying the perfection of motion, was not more beautiful than those galleys. They lay low in the water, immensely long for their beam. Neither the sails nor the lateen yards were set on the low raking masts. The bows blazed with gilding, while the waters of the bay foamed round them as they headed into the teeth of the gentle breeze with the Spanish red and gold streaming aft from the masthead. Up–forward–down–went the oars with unchanging rhythm, the blades not varying an inch in their distance apart during the whole of the stroke. From the bows of each two long guns looked straight forward in the direction the galleys pointed.

'Twenty-four pounders,' said Wales. 'If they catch you in a calm, they'll knock you to pieces. Lie off on your quarter where you can't bring a gun to bear and rake you till you strike. An' then God help you–better a Turkish prison than a Spanish one.'

In a line-ahead that might have been drawn with a ruler and measured with a chain the galleys passed close along the port side of the *Indefatigable* and went ahead of her. As they passed the roll of the drum and the call of the pipes summoned the crew of the *Indefatigable* to attention out of compliment to the flag and the commission pendant going by, while the galleys' officers returned the salute.

'It don't seem right, somehow,' muttered Wales under his breath, 'to salute 'em like they was a frigate.'

Level with the *Indefatigable*'s bowsprit the leader backed her starboard side oars, and spun like a top, despite her length and narrow beam, across the frigate's bows. The gentle wind blew straight to the frigate from the galley, and then from her consort as the latter followed; and a foul stench came back on the air and assailed Hornblower's nostrils, and not Hornblower's alone, clearly, for it brought forth cries of disgust from all the men on deck.

'They all stink like that,' explained Wales. 'Four men to the oar an' fifty oars. Two hundred galley slaves, that is. All chained to their benches. When you goes aboard one of them as a slave you're chained to your bench, an' you're never unchained until they drop you overside. Sometimes when the hands aren't busy they'll hose out the bilge, but that doesn't happen often, bein' Dagoes an' not many of 'em.'

Hornblower as always sought exact information.

'How many, Mr Wales?'

'Thirty, mebbe. Enough to hand the sails if they're making a passage. Or to man the guns–they strike the yards and sails, like now, before they goes into action, Mr Hornblower,' said Wales, pontifical as usual, and with that slight emphasis on the 'Mister' inevitable when a warrant officer of sixty with no hope of further promotion addresses a warrant officer of eighteen (his nominal equal in rank) who might some day be an admiral. 'So you see how it is. With no more than thirty of a crew an' two hundred slaves they daren't let 'em loose, not ever.'

The galleys had turned again, and were now passing down the *Indefatigable*'s starboard side. The beat of the oars had slowed very noticeably, and Hornblower had ample time to observe the vessels closely, the low forecastle and high poop with the gangway connecting them along the whole length of the galley; upon that gangway walked a man with a whip. The rowers were invisible below the bulwarks, the oars being worked through holes in the sides closed, as far as Hornblower could see, with sheets of leather round the oar-looms to keep out the sea. On the poop stood two men at the tiller and a small group of officers, their gold lace flashing in the sunshine. Save for the gold lace and the twenty-four-pounder bow chasers Hornblower was looking at exactly the same sort of vessel as the ancients used to fight their battles. Polybius and Thucydides wrote about galleys almost identical with these–for that matter it was not much more than two hundred years since the galleys had fought their last great battle at Lepanto against the Turks. But those battles had been fought with hundreds of galleys a side.

'How many do they have in commission now?' asked Hornblower.

'A dozen, mebbe–not that I knows for sure, o' course. Carthagena's their usual station, beyond the Gut.'

Wales, as Hornblower understood, meant by this through the Strait of Gibraltar in the Mediterranean.

'Too frail for the Atlantic,' Hornblower commented.

It was easy to deduce the reasons for the survival of this small number–the innate conservatism of the Spaniards would account for it to a large extent. Then there was the point that condemnation to the galleys was one way of disposing of criminals. And when all was said and done a galley might still be useful in a calm–merchant ships becalmed while trying to pass the Strait of Gibraltar might be snapped up by galleys pushing out from Cadiz or Carthagena. And at the very lowest estimate there might be some employment for galleys to tow vessels in and out of harbour with the wind unfavourable.

'Mr Hornblower!' said Eccles. 'My respects to the captain, and we're ready to get under way.'

Hornblower dived below with his message.

'My compliments to Mr Eccles,' said Pellew, looking up from his desk, 'and I'll be on deck immediately.'

There was just enough of a southerly breeze to enable the *Indefatigable* to weather the point in safety. With her anchor catted she braced round her yards and began to steal seaward; in the disciplined stillness which prevailed the sound of the ripple of water under her cutwater was clearly to be heard–a musical note which told nothing, in its innocence, of the savagery and danger of the world of the sea into which she was entering. Creeping along under her topsails the *Indefatigable* made no more than three knots, and the galleys came surging past her again, oars beating their fastest rhythm, as if the galleys were boasting of their independence of the elements. Their gilt flashed in the sun as they overtook to windward, and once again their foul stench offended the nostrils of the men of the *Indefatigable*.

'I'd be obliged if they'd keep to leeward of us,' muttered Pellew, watching them through his glass. 'But I suppose that's not Spanish courtesy. Mr Cutler!'

'Sir!' said the gunner.

'You may commence the salute.'

'Aye aye, sir.'

The forward carronade on the lee side roared out the first of its compliments, and the fort of Puntales began its reply. The sound of the salute rolled round the beautiful bay; nation was speaking to nation in all courtesy.

'The next time we hear those guns they'll be shotted, I fancy,' said Pellew, gazing across at Puntales and the flag of Spain flying above it.

Indeed, the tide of war was turning against England. Nation after nation had retired from the contest against France, some worsted by arms, and some by the diplomacy of the vigorous young republic. To any thinking mind it was obvious that once the step from war to neutrality had been taken, the next step would be easy, from neutrality to war on the other side. Hornblower could foresee, close at hand, a time when all Europe would be arrayed in hostility to England, when she would be battling for her life against the rejuvenescent power of France and the malignity of the whole world.

'Set sail, please, Mr Eccles,' said Pellew.

Two hundred trained pairs of legs raced aloft; two hundred trained pairs of arms let loose the canvas, and the *Indefatigable* doubled her speed, heeling slightly to the gentle breeze. Now she was meeting the long Atlantic swell. So were the galleys; as the *Indefatigable* overtook them, Hornblower could see the leader put her nose into a long roller so that a cloud of spray broke over her forecastle. That was asking too much of such frail craft. Back went one bank of oars; forward went the other. The galleys rolled hideously for a moment in the trough of the sea before they completed their turn and headed back for the safe waters of Cadiz Bay. Someone forward in the *Indefatigable* began to boo, and the cry was instantly taken up through the ship. A storm of boos and whistles and catcalls pursued the galleys, the men momentarily quite out of hand while Pellew spluttered with rage on the quarterdeck and the petty officers strove in vain to take the names of the offenders. It was an ominous farewell to Spain.

Ominous indeed. It was not long before Captain Pellew gave the news to the ship that Spain had completed her change-over; with the treasure convoy safely in she had declared war against England; the revolutionary republic had won the alliance of the most decayed monarchy in Europe. British resources were now stretched to the utmost; there was another thousand miles of coast to watch, another fleet to blockade, another horde of privateers to guard against, and far fewer harbours in which to take refuge and from which to draw the fresh water and the meagre stores which enabled the hard-worked crews to remain at sea. It was then that friendship had to be cultivated with the half savage Barbary States, and the insolence of the Deys and the Sultans had to be tolerated so that North Africa could provide the skinny bullocks and the barley grain to feed the British garrisons in the Mediterranean–all of them beleagured on land–and the ships which kept open the way to them. Oran, Tetuan, Algiers wallowed in unwontedly honest prosperity with the influx of British gold.

It was a day of glassy calm in the Strait of Gibraltar. The sea was like a silver shield, the sky like a bowl of sapphire, with the mountains of Africa on the one hand, the mountains of Spain on the other as dark serrations on the horizon. It was not a comfortable situation for the *Indefatigable*, but that was not because of the blazing sun which softened the pitch in the deck seams. There is almost always a slight current setting inwards into the Mediterranean from the Atlantic, and the prevailing winds blow in the same direction. In a calm like this it was not unusual for a ship to be carried far through the Strait, past the Rock of Gibraltar, and then to have to beat for days and even weeks to make Gibraltar Bay. So that Pellew was not unnaturally anxious about his convoy of grain ships from Oran. Gibraltar had to be revictualled–Spain had already marched an army up for the siege–and he dared not risk being carried past his destination. His orders to his reluctant convoy had been enforced by flag and gun signals, for no short-handed merchant ship relished the prospect of the labour Pellew wished to be executed. The *Indefatigable* no less than her convoy had lowered boats, and the helpless ships were now all in tow. That was backbreaking, exhausting labour, the men at the oars tugging and straining, dragging the oar blades through the water, while the towlines tightened and bucked with superhuman perversity and the ships sheered freakishly from side to side. It was less than a mile an hour, that the ships made in this fashion, at the cost of the complete exhaustion of the boats' crews, but at least it postponed the time when the Gibraltar current would carry them to leeward, and similarly gave more chance for the longed-for southerly wind–two hours of a southerly wind was all they wished for–to waft them up to the Mole.

Down in the *Indefatigable*'s longboat and cutter the men tugging at their oars were so stupefied with their toil that they did not hear the commotion in the ship. They were just tugging and straining, under the pitiless sky, living through their two hours' spell of misery, but they were roused by the voice of the captain himself, hailing them from the forecastle.

'Mr Bolton! Mr Chadd! Cast off there, if you please. You'd better come and arm your men at once. Here come our friends from Cadiz.'

Back on the quarterdeck, Pellew looked through his glass at the hazy horizon; he could make out from here by now what had first been reported from the masthead.

'They're heading straight for us,' he said.

The two galleys were on their way from Cadiz; presumably a fast horseman from the lookout point at Tarifa had brought them the news of this golden opportunity, of the flat calm and the scattered and helpless convoy. This was the moment for galleys to justify their continued existence. They could capture and at least burn, although they could not hope to carry off, the unfortunate merchant ships, while the *Indefatigable* lay helpless hardly out of cannon's range. Pellew looked round at the two merchant ships and the three brigs; one of them was within half a mile of him and might be covered by his gunfire, but the others–a mile and a half, two miles away–had no such protection.

'Pistols and cutlasses, my lads!' he said to the men pouring up from overside. 'Clap on to that stay tackle now. Smartly with that carronade, Mr Cutler!'

The *Indefatigable* had been in too many expeditions where minutes counted to waste any time over these preparations. The boats' crews seized their arms, the six-pounder carronades were lowered into the bows of the cutter and longboat, and soon the boats, crowded with armed men, and provisioned against sudden emergency, were pulling away to meet the galleys.

'What the devil d'you think you're doing, Mr Hornblower?'

Pellew had just caught sight of Hornblower in the act of swinging out of the jolly boat which was his special charge. He wondered what his midshipman thought he could achieve against a war-galley with a twelve-foot boat and a crew of six.

'We can pull to one of the convoy and reinforce the crew, sir,' said Hornblower.

'Oh, very well then, carry on. I'll trust to your good sense, even though that's a broken reed.'

'Good on you, sir!' said Jackson ecstatically, as the jolly boat shoved off from the frigate. 'Good on you! No one else wouldn't never have thought of that.'

Jackson, the coxswain of the jolly boat, obviously thought that Hornblower had no intention of carrying out his suggestion to reinforce the crew of one of the merchant ships.

'Those stinking Dagoes,' said stroke oar, between his teeth.

Hornblower was conscious of the presence in his crew of the same feeling of violent hostility toward the Spanish galleys as he felt within himself. In a fleeting moment of analysis, he attributed it to the circumstances in which they had first made the galleys' acquaintance, as well as to the stench which the galleys trailed after them. He had never known this feeling of personal hatred before; when previously he had fought it had been as a servant of the King, not out of personal animosity. Yet here he was gripping the tiller under the scorching sky and leaning forward in his eagerness to be at actual grips with his enemy.

The longboat and cutter had a long start of them, and even though they were manned by crews who had already served a spell at the oars they were skimming over the water at such a speed that the jolly boat with all the advantage of the glassy-smooth water only slowly caught up to them. Overside the sea was of the bluest, deepest blue until the oar blades churned it white. Ahead of them the vessels of the convoy lay scattered where the sudden calm had caught them, and just beyond them Hornblower caught sight of the flash of oar blades as the galleys came sweeping down on their prey. Longboat and cutter were diverging in an endeavour to cover as many vessels as possible, and the gig was still far astern. There would hardly be time to board a ship even if Hornblower should wish to. He put the tiller over to incline his course after the cutter; one of the galleys at that moment abruptly made its appearance in the gap between two of the merchant ships. Hornblower saw the cutter swing round to point her six-pounder carronade at the advancing bows.

'Pull, you men! Pull!' he shrieked mad with excitement.

He could not imagine what was going to happen, but he wanted to be in the fray. That six-pounder popgun was grossly inaccurate at any range longer than musket shot. It would serve to hurl a mass of grape into a crowd of men, but its ball would have small effect on the strengthened bows of a war galley.

'Pull!' shrieked Hornblower again. He was nearly up to them, wide on the cutter's quarter.

The carronade boomed out. Hornblower thought he saw the splinters fly from the galley's bow, but the shot had no more effect on deterring her than a peashooter could stop a charging bull. The galley turned a little, getting exactly into line, and then her oars' beat quickened. She was coming down to ram, like the Greeks at Salamis.

'Pull!' shrieked Hornblower.

Instinctively, he gave the tiller a touch to take the jolly boat out into a flanking position.

'Easy!'

The jolly boat's oars stilled, as their way carried them past the cutter. Hornblower could see Soames standing up in the sternsheets looking at the death which was cleaving the blue water towards him. Bow to bow the cutter might have stood a chance, but too late the cutter tried to evade the blow altogether. Hornblower saw her turn, presenting her vulnerable side to the galley's stem. That was all he could see, for the next moment the galley herself hid from him the final act of the tragedy. The jolly boat's starboard side oars only just cleared the galley's starboard oars as she swept by. Hornblower heard a shriek and a crash, saw the galley's forward motion almost cease at the collision. He was mad with the lust of fighting, quite insane, and his mind was working with the rapidity of insanity.

'Give way, port!' he yelled, and the jolly boat swung round under the galley's stern. 'Give way all!'

The jolly boat leaped after the galley like a terrier after a bull.

'Grapple them, damn you, Jackson!'

Jackson shouted an oath in reply, as he leaped forward, seemingly hurdling the men at the oars without breaking their stroke. In the bows Jackson seized the boat's grapnel on its long line and flung it hard and true. It caught somewhere in the elaborate gilt rail on the galley's quarter. Jackson hauled on the line, the oars tugged madly in the effort to carry the jolly boat up to the galley's stern. At that moment Hornblower saw it, the sight which would long haunt his dreams–up from under the galley's stern came the shattered forepart of the cutter, still with men clinging to it who had survived the long passage under the whole length of the galley which had overrun them. There were straining faces, empurpled faces, faces already relaxing in death. But in a moment it was past and gone, and Hornblower felt the jerk transmitted through the line to the jolly boat as the galley leaped forward.

'I can't hold her!' shouted Jackson.

'Take a turn round the cleat, you fool!'

The galley was towing the jolly boat now, dragging her along at the end of a twenty-foot line close on her quarter, just clear of the arc of her rudder. The white water bubbled all around her, her bows were cocked up with the strain. It was a mad moment, as though they had harpooned a whale. Some one came running aft on the Spaniard's poop, knife in hand to cut the line.

'Shoot him, Jackson!' shrieked Hornblower again.

Jackson's pistol cracked, and the Spaniard fell to the deck out of sight–a good shot. Despite his fighting madness, despite the turmoil of rushing water and glaring sun, Hornblower tried to think out his next move. Inclination and common sense alike told him that the best plan was to close with the enemy despite the odds.

'Pull up to them, there!' he shouted–everyone in the boat was shouting and yelling. The men in the bows of the jolly boat faced forward and took the grapnel line and began to haul in on it, but the speed of the boat through the water made any progress difficult, and after a yard or so had been gained the difficulty became insurmountable, for the grapnel was caught in the poop rail ten or eleven feet above water, and the angle of pull became progressively steeper as the jolly boat neared the stern of the galley. The boat's bow cocked higher out of the water than ever.

'Belay!' said Hornblower, and then, his voice rising again, 'Out pistols, lads!'

A row of four or five swarthy faces had appeared at the stern of the galley. Muskets were pointing into the jolly boat, and there was a brief but furious exchange of shots. One man fell groaning into the bottom of the jolly boat, but the row of faces disappeared. Standing up precariously in the swaying sternsheets, Hornblower could still see nothing of the galley's poop deck save for the tops of two heads, belonging, it was clear, to the men at the tiller.

'Reload,' he said to his men, remembering by a miracle to give the order. The ramrods went down the pistol barrels.

'Do that carefully if you ever want to see Pompey again,' said Hornblower.

He was shaking with excitement and mad with the fury of fighting, and it was the automatic, drilled part of him which was giving these level-headed orders. His higher faculties were quite negatived by his lust for blood. He was seeing things through a pink mist–that was how he remembered it when he looked back upon it later. There was a sudden crash of glass. Someone had thrust a musket barrel through the big stern window of the galley's after cabin. Luckily having thrust it through he had to recover himself to take aim. An irregular volley of pistols almost coincided with the report of the musket. Where the Spaniard's bullet went no one knew; but the Spaniard fell back from the window.

'By God! That's our way!' screamed Hornblower, and then, steadying himself, 'Reload.'

As the bullets were being spat into the barrels he stood up. His unused pistols were still in his belt; his cutlass was at his side.

'Come aft, here,' he said to stroke oar; the jolly boat would stand no more weight in the bows than she had already. 'And you, too.'

Hornblower poised himself on the thwarts, eyeing the grapnel line and the cabin window.

'Bring 'em after me one at a time, Jackson,' he said.

Then he braced himself and flung himself at the grapnel line. His feet grazed the water as the line sagged, but using all his clumsy strength his arms carried him upwards. Here was the shattered window at his side; he swung up his feet, kicked out a big remaining piece of the pane, and then shot his feet through and then the rest of himself. He came down on the deck of the cabin with a thud; it was dark in here compared with the blinding sun outside. As he got to his feet, he trod on something which gave out a cry of pain–the wounded Spaniard, evidently–and the hand with which he drew his cutlass was sticky with blood. Spanish blood. Rising, he hit his head a thunderous crash on the deck-beams above, for the little cabin was very low, hardly more than five feet, and so severe was the blow that his senses almost left him. But before him was the cabin door and he reeled out through it, cutlass in hand. Over his head he heard a stamping of feet, and shots were fired behind him and above him–a further exchange, he presumed, between the jolly boat and the galley's stern rail. The cabin door opened into a low half-deck, and Hornblower reeled along it out into the sunshine again. He was on the tiny strip of maindeck at the break of the poop. Before him stretched the narrow gangway between the two sets of rowers; he could look down at these latter–two seas of bearded faces, mops of hair and lean sunburned bodies, swinging rhythmically back and forward to the beat of the oars.

That was all the impression he could form of them at the moment. At the far end of the gangway at the break of the forecastle stood the overseer with his whip; he was shouting words in rhythmic succession to the slaves–Spanish numbers, perhaps, to give them the time. There were three or four men on the forecastle; below them the half-doors through the forecastle bulkhead were hooked open, through which Hornblower could see the two big guns illuminated by the light through the port holes out of which they were run almost at the water level. The guns' crews were standing by the guns, but numerically they were far fewer than two twenty-four pounders would demand. Hornblower remembered Wales's estimate of no more than thirty for a galley's crew. The men of one gun at least had been called aft to defend the poop against the jolly boat's attack.

A step behind him made him leap with anxiety and he swung round with his cutlass ready to meet Jackson stumbling out of the half deck, cutlass in hand.

'Nigh on cracked my nut,' said Jackson.

He was speaking thickly like a drunken man, and his words were chorused by further shots fired from the poop at the level of the top of their heads.

'Oldroyd's comin' next,' said Jackson. 'Franklin's dead.'

On either side of them a companion ladder mounted to the poop deck. It seemed logical, mathematical, that they should each go up one but Hornblower thought better of it.

'Come along,' he said, and headed for the starboard ladder, and, with Oldroyd putting in an appearance at that moment, he yelled to him to follow.

The handropes of the ladder were of twisted red and yellow cord–he even could notice that as he rushed up the ladder, pistol in hand and cutlass in the other. After the first step, his eye was above deck level. There were more than a dozen men crowded on the tiny poop, but two were lying dead, and one was groaning with his back to the rail, and two stood by the tiller. The others were looking over the rail at the jolly boat. Hornblower was still insane with fighting madness. He must have leaped up the final two or three steps with a bound like a stag's, and he was screaming like a maniac as he flung himself at the Spaniards. His pistol went off apparently without his willing it, but the face of the man a yard away dissolved into bloody ruin, and Hornblower dropped the weapon and snatched the second, his thumb going to the hammer as he whirled his cutlass down with a crash on the sword which the next Spaniard raised as a feeble guard. He struck and struck and struck with a lunatic's strength. Here was Jackson beside him shouting hoarsely and striking out right and left.

'Kill 'em! Kill 'em!' shouted Jackson.

Hornblower saw Jackson's cutlass flash down on the head of the defenceless man at the tiller. Then out of the tail of his eye he saw another sword threaten him as he battered with his cutlass at the man before him, but his pistol saved him as he fired automatically again. Another pistol went off beside him–Oldroyd's, he supposed–and then the fight on the poop was over. By what miracle of ineptitude the Spaniards had allowed the attack to take them by surprise Hornblower never could discover. Perhaps they were ignorant of the wounding of the man in the cabin, and had relied on him to defend that route; perhaps it had never occurred to them that three men could be so utterly desperate as to attack a dozen; perhaps they never realized that three men had made the perilous passage of the grapnel line; perhaps–most probably–in the mad excitement of it all, they simply lost their heads, for five minutes could hardly have elapsed altogether from the time the jolly boat hooked on until the poop was cleared. Two or three Spaniards ran down the companion to the maindeck, and forward along the gangway between the rows of slaves. One was caught against the rail and made a gesture of surrender, but Jackson's hand was already at his throat. Jackson was a man of immense physical strength; he bent the Spaniard back over the rail, farther and farther, and then caught him by the thigh with his other hand and heaved him over. He fell with a shriek before Hornblower could interpose. The poop deck was covered with writhing men, like the bottom of a boat filled with flapping fish. One man was getting to his knees when Jackson and Oldroyd seized him. They swung him up to toss him over the rail.

'Stop that!' said Hornblower, and quite callously they dropped him again with a crash on the bloody planks.

Jackson and Oldroyd were like drunken men, unsteady on their feet, glazed of eye and stertorous of breath; Hornblower was just coming out of his insane fit. He stepped forward to the break of the poop, wiping the sweat out of his eyes while trying to wipe away the red mist that tinged his vision. Forward by the forecastle were gathered the rest of the Spaniards, a large group of them; as Hornblower came forward, one of them fired a musket at him but the ball went wide. Down below him the rowers were still swinging rhythmically, forward and back, forward and back, the hairy heads and the naked bodies moving in time to the oars; in time to the voice of the overseer, too, for the latter was still standing on the gangway (the rest of the Spaniards were clustered behind him) calling the time–'Seis, siete, ocho.'

'Stop!' bellowed Hornblower.

He walked to the starboard side to be in full view of the starboard side rowers. He held up his hand and bellowed again. A hairy face or two was raised, but the oars still swung.

'Uno, doce, tres,' said the overseer.

Jackson appeared at Hornblower's elbow, and levelled a pistol to shoot the nearest rower.

'Oh, belay that!' said Hornblower testily. He knew he was sick of killings now. 'Find my pistols and reload them.'

He stood at the top of the companion like a man in a dream–in a nightmare. The galley slaves went on swinging and pulling; his dozen enemies were still clustered at the break of the forecastle thirty yards away; behind him the wounded Spaniards groaned away their lives. Another appeal to the rowers was as much ignored as the preceding ones. Oldroyd must have had the clearest head or have recovered himself quickest.

'I'll haul down his colours, sir, shall I?' he said.

Hornblower woke from his dream. On a staff above the taffrail fluttered the yellow and red.

'Yes, haul 'em down at once,' he said.

Now his mind was clear, and now his horizon was no longer bounded by the narrow limits of the galley. He looked about him, over the blue, blue sea. There were the merchant ships; over there lay the *Indefatigable*. Behind him boiled the white wake of the galley–a curved wake. Not until that moment did he realize that he was in control of the tiller, and that for the last three minutes, the galley had been cutting over the blue seas unsteered.

'Take the tiller, Oldroyd,' he ordered.

Was that a galley disappearing into the hazy distance? It must be, and far in its wake was the longboat. And there, on the port bow, was the gig, resting on her oars–Hornblower could see little figures standing waving in bow and stern, and it dawned upon him that this was in acknowledgement of the hauling down of the Spanish colours. Another musket banged off forward, and the rail close at his hip was struck a tremendous blow which sent gilded splinters flying in the sunlight. But he had all his wits about him again, and he ran back over the dying men; at the after end of the poop he was out of sight of the gangway and safe from shot. He could still see the gig on the port bow.

'Starboard your helm, Oldroyd.'

The galley turned slowly–her narrow length made her unhandy if the rudder were not assisted by the oars–but soon the bow was about to obscure the gig.

'Midships!'

Amazing that there, leaping in the white water that boiled under the galley's stern, was the jolly boat with one live man and two dead men still aboard.

'Where are the others, Bromley?' yelled Jackson.

Bromley pointed overside. They had been shot from the taffrail at the moment that Hornblower and the others were preparing to attack the poop.

'Why in hell don't you come aboard?'

Bromley took hold of his left arm with his right; the limb was clearly useless. There was no reinforcement to be obtained here, and yet full possession must be taken of the galley. Otherwise it was even conceivable that they would be carried off to Algeciras; even if they were masters of the rudder the man who controlled the oars dictated the course of the ship if he willed. There was only one course left to try.

Now that his fighting madness had ebbed away, Hornblower was in a sombre mood. He did not care what happened to him; hope and fear had alike deserted him, along with his previous exalted condition. It might be resignation that possessed him now. His mind, still calculating, told him that with only one thing left to do to achieve victory he must attempt it, and the flat, dead condition of his spirits enabled him to carry the attempt through like an automaton, unwavering and emotionless. He walked forward to the poop rail again; the Spaniards were still clustered at the far end of the gangway, with the overseer still giving the time to the oars. They looked up at him as he stood there. With the utmost care and attention he sheathed his cutlass, which he had held in his hand up to that moment. He noticed the blood on his coat and on his hands as he did so. Slowly he settled the sheathed weapon at his side.

'My pistols, Jackson,' he said.

Jackson handed him the pistols and with the same callous care he thrust them into his belt. He turned back to Oldroyd, the Spaniards watching every movement fascinated.

'Stay by the tiller, Oldroyd. Jackson, follow me. Do nothing without my orders.'

With the sun pouring down on his face, he strode down the companion ladder, walked to the gangway, and approached the Spaniards along it. On either side of him the hairy heads and naked bodies of the galley slaves still swung with the oars. He neared the Spaniards; swords and muskets and pistols were handled nervously, but every eye was on his face. Behind him Jackson coughed. Two yards only from the group, Hornblower halted and swept them with his glance. Then, with a gesture, he indicated the whole of the group except the overseer; and then pointed to the forecastle.

'Get forrard, all of you,' he said.

They stood staring at him, although they must have understood the gesture.

'Get forrard,' said Hornblower with a wave of his hand and a tap of his foot on the gangway.

There was only one man who seemed likely to demur actively, and Hornblower had it in mind to snatch a pistol from his belt and shoot him on the spot. But the pistol might misfire, the shot might arouse the Spaniards out of their fascinated dream. He stared the man down.

'Get forrard, I say.'

They began to move, they began to shamble off. Hornblower watched them go. Now his emotions were returning to him, and his heart was thumping madly in his chest so that it was hard to control himself. Yet he must not be precipitate. He had to wait until the others were well clear before he could address himself to the overseer.

'Stop those men,' he said.

He glared into the overseer's eyes while pointing to the oarsmen; the overseer's lips moved, but he made no sound.

'Stop them,' said Hornblower, and this time he put his hand to the butt of his pistol.

That sufficed. The overseer raised his voice in a high-pitched order, and the oars instantly ceased. Strange what sudden stillness possessed the ship with the cessation of the grinding of the oars in the tholes. Now it was easy to hear the bubbling of the water round the galley as her way carried her forward. Hornblower turned back to hail Oldroyd.

'Oldroyd! Where away's the gig?'

'Close on the starboard bow, sir!'

'How close?'

'Two cable's lengths, sir. She's pulling for us now.'

'Steer for her while you've steerage way.'

'Aye aye, sir.'

How long would it take the gig under oars to cover a quarter of a mile? Hornblower feared anti-climax, feared a sudden revulsion of feeling among the Spaniards at this late moment. Mere waiting might occasion it, and he must not stand merely idle. He could still hear the motion of the galley through the water, and he turned to Jackson.

'This ship carries her way well, Jackson, doesn't she?' he said, and he made himself laugh as he spoke, as if everything in the world was a matter of sublime certainty.

'Aye, sir, I suppose she does, sir,' said the startled Jackson; he was fidgeting nervously with his pistols.

'And look at the man there,' went on Hornblower, pointing to a galley slave. 'Did you ever see such a beard in your life?'

'N-no, sir.'

'Speak to me, you fool. Talk naturally.'

'I–I dunno what to say, sir.'

'You've no sense, damn you, Jackson. See the welt on that fellow's shoulder? He must have caught it from the overseer's whip not so long ago.'

'Mebbe you're right, sir.'

Hornblower was repressing his impatience and was about to make another speech when he heard a rasping thump alongside and a moment later the gig's crew was pouring over the bulwarks. The relief was inexpressible. Hornblower was about to relax completely when he remembered appearances. He stiffened himself up.

'Glad to see you aboard, sir,' he said, as Lieutenant Chadd swung his legs over and dropped to the maindeck at the break of the forecastle.

'Glad to see *you*,' said Chadd, looking about him curiously.

'These men forrard are prisoners, sir,' said Hornblower. 'It might be well to secure them. I think that is all that remains to be done.'

Now he could not relax; it seemed to him as if he must remain strained and tense for ever. Strained and yet stupid, even when he heard the cheers of the hands in the *Indefatigable* as the galley came alongside her. Stupid and dull, making a stumbling report to Captain Pellew, forcing himself to remember to commend the bravery of Jackson and Oldroyd in the highest terms.

'The Admiral will be pleased,' said Pellew, looking at Hornblower keenly.

'I'm glad, sir,' Hornblower heard himself say.

'Now that we've lost poor Soames,' went on Pellew, 'we shall need another watch-keeping officer. I have it in mind to give you an order as acting-lieutenant.'

'Thank you, sir,' said Hornblower, still stupid.

Soames had been a grey-haired officer of vast experience. He had sailed the seven seas, he had fought in a score of actions. But, faced with a new situation, he had not had the quickness of thought to keep his boat from under the ram of the galley. Soames was dead, and acting-lieutenant Hornblower would take his place. Fighting madness, sheer insanity, had won him this promise of promotion. Hornblower had never realized the black depths of lunacy into which he could sink. Like Soames, like all the rest of the crew of the *Indefatigable*, he had allowed himself to be carried away by his blind hatred for the galleys, and only good fortune had allowed him to live through it. That was something worth remembering.

8

THE EXAMINATION FOR LIEUTENANT

H.M.S. *Indefatigable* was gliding into Gibraltar Bay, with Acting-Lieutenant Horatio Hornblower stiff and self-conscious on the quarterdeck beside Captain Pellew. He kept his telescope trained over toward Algeciras; it was a strange situation, this, that major naval bases of two hostile powers should be no more than six miles apart, and while approaching the harbour it was as well to keep close watch on Algeciras, for there was always the possibility that a squadron of Spaniards might push out suddenly to pounce on an unwary frigate coming in.

'Eight ships–nine ships with their yards crossed, sir,' reported Hornblower.

'Thank you,' answered Pellew. 'Hands 'bout ship.'

The *Indefatigable* tacked and headed in toward the Mole. Gibraltar harbour was, as usual, crowded with shipping, for the whole naval effort of England in the Mediterranean was perforce based here. Pellew clewed up his topsails and put his helm over. Then the cable roared out and the *Indefatigable* swung at anchor.

'Call away my gig,' ordered Pellew.

Pellew favoured dark blue and white as the colour scheme for his boat and its crew–dark blue shirts and white trousers for the men, with white hats with blue ribbons. The boat was of dark blue picked out with white, the oars had white looms and blue blades. The general effect was very smart indeed as the drive of the oars sent the gig skimming over the water to carry Pellew to pay his respects to the port admiral. It was not long after his return that a messenger came scurrying up to Hornblower.

'Captain's compliments, sir, and he'd like to see you in his cabin.'

'Examine your conscience well,' grinned Midshipman Bracegirdle. 'What crimes have you committed?'

'I wish I knew,' said Hornblower, quite genuinely.

It is always a nervous moment going in to see the captain in reply to his summons. Hornblower swallowed as he approached the cabin door, and he had to brace himself a little to knock and enter. But there was nothing to be alarmed about; Pellew looked up with a smile from his desk.

'Ah, Mr Hornblower, I hope you will consider this good news. There will be an examination for lieutenant tomorrow, in the *Santa Barbara* there. You are ready to take it, I hope?'

Hornblower was about to say 'I suppose so, sir,' but checked himself.

'Yes, sir,' he said–Pellew hated slipshod answers.

'Very well, then. You report there at three p.m. with your certificates and journals.'

'Aye aye, sir.'

That was a very brief conversation for such an important subject. Hornblower had Pellew's order as acting-lieutenant for two months now. To-morrow he would take his examination. If he should pass the admiral would confirm the order next day, and Hornblower would be a lieutenant with two months' seniority already. But if he should fail! That would mean he had been found unfit for lieutenant's rank. He would revert to midshipman, the two months' seniority would be lost, and it would be six months at least before he could try again. Eight months' seniority was a matter of enormous importance. It would affect all his subsequent career.

'Tell Mr Bolton you have my permission to leave the ship tomorrow, and you may use one of the ship's boats.'

'Thank you, sir.'

'Good luck, Hornblower.'

During the next twenty-four hours Hornblower had not merely to try to read all through Norie's *Epitome of Navigation* again, and Clarke's *Complete Handbook of Seamanship*, but he had to see that his number one uniform was spick and span. It cost his spirit ration to prevail on the warrant cook to allow the gunroom attendant to heat a flatiron in the galley and iron out his neck handkerchief. Bracegirdle lent him a clean shirt, but there was a feverish moment when it was discovered that the gunroom's supply of shoe blacking had dried to a chip. Two midshipmen had to work it soft with lard, and the resultant compound, when applied to Hornblower's buckled shoes, was stubbornly resistant to taking a polish; only much labour with the gunroom's moulting shoebrush and then with a soft cloth brought those shoes up to a condition of brightness worthy of an examination for lieutenant. And as for the cocked hat–the life of a cocked hat in the midshipman's berth is hard, and some of the dents could not be entirely eliminated.

'Take it off as soon as you can and keep it under your arm,' advised Bracegirdle. 'Maybe they won't see you come up the ship's side.'

Everybody turned out to see Hornblower leave the ship, with his sword and his white breeches and his buckled shoes, his bundle of journals under his arm and his certificates of sobriety and good conduct in his pocket. The winter afternoon was already far advanced as he was rowed over to the *Santa Barbara* and went up the ship's side to report himself to the officer of the watch.

The *Santa Barbara* was a prison hulk, one of the prizes captured in Rodney's action off Cadiz in 1780 and kept rotting at her moorings, mastless, ever since, a storeship in time of peace and a prison in time of war. Redcoated soldiers, muskets loaded and bayonets fixed, guarded the gangways; on forecastle and quarterdeck were carronades, trained inboard and depressed to sweep the waist, wherein a few prisoners took the air, ragged and unhappy. As Hornblower came up the side he caught a whiff of the stench within, where two thousand prisoners were confined. Hornblower reported himself to the officer of the watch as come on board, and for what purpose.

'Whoever would have guessed it?' said the officer of the watch–an elderly lieutenant with white hair hanging down to his shoulders–running his eye over Hornblower's immaculate uniform and the portfolio under his arm. 'Fifteen of your kind have already come on board, and–Holy Gemini, see there!'

Quite a flotilla of small craft was closing in on the *Santa Barbara*. Each boat held at least one cocked-hatted and white-breeched midshipman, and some held four or five.

'Every courtesy young gentleman in the Mediterranean Fleet is ambitious for an epaulet,' said the lieutenant. 'Just wait until the examining board sees how many there are of you! I wouldn't be in your shoes, young shaver, for something. Go aft, there, and wait in the portside cabin.'

It was already uncomfortably full; when Hornblower entered, fifteen pairs of eyes measured him up. There were officers of all ages from eighteen to forty, all in their number one's, all nervous–one or two of them had Norie's *Epitome* open on their laps and were anxiously reading passages about which they were doubtful. One little group was passing a bottle from hand to hand, presumably in an effort to keep up their courage. But no sooner had Hornblower entered than a stream of newcomers followed him. The cabin began to fill, and soon it was tightly packed. Half the forty men present found seats on the deck, and the others were forced to stand.

'Forty years back,' said a loud voice somewhere, 'my grandad marched with Clive to revenge the Black Hole of Calcutta. If he could but have witnessed the fate of his posterity!'

'Have a drink,' said another voice, 'and to hell with care.'

'Forty of us,' commented a tall, thin, clerkly officer, counting heads. 'How many of us will they pass, do you think? Five?'

'To hell with care,' repeated the bibulous voice in the corner, and lifted itself in song. 'Begone, dull care; I prithee be gone from me—'

'Cheese it, you fool!' rasped another voice. 'Hark to that!'

The air was filled with the long-drawn twittering of the pipes of the bos'n's mates, and someone on deck was shouting an order.

'A captain coming on board,' remarked someone.

An officer had his eye at the crack of the door. 'It's Dreadnought Foster,' he reported.

'He's a tail twister if ever there was one,' said a fat young officer, seated comfortably with his back to the bulkhead.

Again the pipes twittered.

'Harvey, of the dockyard,' reported the lookout.

The third captain followed immediately. 'It's Black Charlie Hammond,' said the lookout. 'Looking as if he'd lost a guinea and found sixpence.'

'Black Charlie?' exclaimed someone, scrambling to his feet in haste and pushing to the door. 'Let's see! So it is! Then here is one young gentleman who will not stay for an answer. I know too well what that answer would be. "Six months more at sea, sir, and damn your eyes for your impertinence in presenting yourself for examination in your present state of ignorance." Black Charlie won't ever forget that I lost his pet poodle overside from the cutter in Port-o'-Spain when he was first of the *Pegasus*. Good-bye, gentlemen. Give my regards to the examining board.'

With that he was gone, and they saw him explaining himself to the officer of the watch and hailing a shore boat to take him back to his ship. 'One fewer of us, at least,' said the clerkly officer. 'What is it, my man?'

'The board's compliments, sir,' said the marine messenger, 'an' will the first young gentleman please to come along?'

There was a momentary hesitation; no one was anxious to be the first victim.

'The one nearest the door,' said an elderly master's mate. 'Will you volunteer, sir?'

'I'll be the Daniel,' said the erstwhile lookout desperately. 'Remember me in your prayers.'

He pulled his coat smooth, twitched at his neckcloth, and was gone, the remainder waiting in gloomy silence, relieved only by the glug-glug of the bottle as the bibulous midshipman took another swig. A full ten minutes passed before the candidate for promotion returned, making a brave effort to smile.

'Six months more at sea?' asked someone.

'No,' was the unexpected answer. 'Three! . . . I was told to send the next man. It had better be you.'

'But what did they ask you?'

'They began by asking me to define a rhumb line. . . . But don't keep them waiting, I advise you.' Some thirty officers had their textbooks open on the instant to reread about rhumb lines.

'You were there ten minutes,' said the clerkly officer, looking at his watch. 'Forty of us, ten minutes each–why, it'll be midnight before they reach the last of us. They'll never do it.'

'They'll be hungry,' said someone.

'Hungry for our blood,' said another.

'Perhaps they'll try us in batches,' suggested a third, 'like the French tribunals.'

Listening to them, Hornblower was reminded of French aristocrats jesting at the foot of the scaffold. Candidates departed and candidates returned, some gloomy, some smiling. The cabin was already far less crowded; Hornblower was able to secure sufficient deck space to seat himself, and he stretched out his legs with a nonchalant sigh of relief, and he no sooner emitted the sigh than he realized that it was a stage effect which he had put on for his own benefit. He was as nervous as he could be. The winter night was falling, and some good Samaritan on board sent in a couple of purser's dips to give a feeble illumination to the darkening cabin.

'They are passing one in three,' said the clerkly officer, making ready for his turn. 'May I be the third.'

Hornblower got to his feet again when he left; it would be his turn next. He stepped out under the halfdeck into the dark night and breathed the chill fresh air. A gentle breeze was blowing from the southward, cooled, presumably, by the snow-clad Atlas Mountains of Africa across the Strait. There was neither moon nor stars. Here came the clerkly officer back again.

'Hurry,' he said. 'They're impatient.'

Hornblower made his way past the sentry to the after cabin; it was brightly lit, so that he blinked as he entered, and stumbled over some obstruction. And it was only then that he remembered that he had not straightened his neckcloth and seen to it that his sword hung correctly at his side. He went on blinking in his nervousness at the three grim faces across the table.

'Well, sir?' said a stern voice. 'Report yourself. We have no time to waste.'

'H-Hornblower, sir. H-Horatio H-Hornblower. M-Midshipman–I mean

Acting-Lieutenant, H.M.S. *Indefatigable.*'

'Your certificates, please,' said the right-hand face.

Hornblower handed them over, and as he waited for them to be examined, the left-hand face suddenly spoke. 'You are close-hauled on the port tack, Mr Hornblower, beating up Channel with a nor-easterly wind blowing hard, with Dover bearing north two miles. Is that clear?'

'Yes, sir.'

'Now the wind veers four points and takes you flat aback. What do you do, sir? What do you do?'

Hornblower's mind, if it was thinking about anything at all at that moment, was thinking about rhumb lines; this question took him as much aback as the situation it envisaged. His mouth opened and shut, but there was no word he could say.

'By now you're dismasted,' said the middle face–a swarthy face; Hornblower was making the deduction that it must belong to Black Charlie Hammond. He could think about that even if he could not force his mind to think at all about his examination.

'Dismasted,' said the left-hand face, with a smile like Nero enjoying a Christian's death agony. 'With Dover cliffs under your lee. You are in serious trouble, Mr–ah–Hornblower.'

Serious indeed. Hornblower's mouth opened and shut again. His dulled mind heard, without paying special attention to it, the thud of a cannon shot somewhere not too far off. The board passed no remark on it either, but a moment later there came a series of further cannon shots which brought the three captains to their feet. Unceremoniously they rushed out of the cabin, sweeping out of the way the sentry at the door. Hornblower followed them; they arrived in the waist just in time to see a rocket soar up into the night sky and burst in a shower of red stars. It was the general alarm; over the water of the anchorage they could hear the drums rolling as all the ships present beat to quarters. On the portside gangway the remainder of the candidates were clustered, speaking excitedly.

'See there!' said a voice.

Across half a mile of dark water a yellow light grew until the ship there was wrapped in flame. She had every sail set and was heading straight into the crowded anchorage.

'Fire ships!'

'Officer of the watch! Call my gig!' bellowed Foster.

A line of fire ships was running before the wind, straight at the crowd of anchored ships. The *Santa Barbara* was full of the wildest bustle as the seamen and marines came pouring on deck, and as captains and candidates shouted for boats to take them back to their ships. A line of orange flame lit up the water, followed at once by the roar of a broadside; some ship was firing her guns in the endeavour to sink a fire ship. Let one of those blazing hulls make contact with one of the anchored ships, even for a few seconds, and the fire would be transmitted to the dry, painted timber, to the tarred cordage, to the inflammable sails, so that nothing would put it out. To men in highly combustible ships filled with explosives fire was the deadliest and most dreaded peril of the sea.

'You shore boat, there!' bellowed Hammond suddenly. 'You shore boat! Come alongside! Come alongside, blast you!'

His eye had been quick to sight the pair-oar rowing by.

'Come alongside or I'll fire into you!' supplemented Foster. 'Sentry, there, make ready to give them a shot!'

At the threat the wherry turned and glided towards the mizzen-chains.

'Here you are, gentlemen,' said Hammond.

The three captains rushed to the mizzen-chains and flung themselves down into the boat. Hornblower was at their heels. He knew there was small enough chance of a junior officer getting a boat to take him back to his ship, to which it was his bounden duty to go as soon as possible. After the captains had reached their destinations he could use this boat to reach the *Indefatigable*. He threw himself off into the sternsheets as she pushed off, knocking the breath out of Captain Harvey, his sword scabbard clattering on the gunwale. But the three captains accepted his uninvited presence there without comment.

'Pull for the *Dreadnought*,' said Foster.

'Dammit, I'm the senior!' said Hammond. 'Pull for *Calypso*.'

'*Calypso* it is,' said Harvey. He had his hand on the tiller, heading the boat across the dark water.

'Pull! Oh, pull!' said Foster, in agony. There can be no mental torture like that of a captain whose ship is in peril and he not on board.

'There's one of them,' said Harvey.

Just ahead, a small brig was bearing down on them under topsails; they could see the glow of the fire, and as they watched the fire suddenly burst into roaring fury, wrapping the whole vessel in flames in a moment, like a set piece in a fireworks display. Flames spouted out of the holes in her sides and roared up through her hatchways. The very water around her glowed vivid red. They saw her halt in her career and begin to swing slowly around.

'She's across *Santa Barbara*'s cable,' said Foster.

'She's nearly clear,' added Hammond. 'God help 'em on board there. She'll be alongside her in a minute.'

Hornblower thought of two thousand Spanish and French prisoners battened down below decks in the hulk.

'With a man at her wheel she could be steered clear,' said Foster. 'We ought to do it!'

Then things happened rapidly. Harvey put the tiller over. 'Pull away!' he roared at the boatmen.

The latter displayed an easily understood reluctance to row up to that fiery hull.

'Pull!' said Harvey.

He whipped out his sword from its scabbard, and the blade reflected the red fire as he thrust it menacingly at the stroke oar's throat. With a kind of sob, stroke tugged at his oar and the boat leaped forward.

'Lay us under her counter,' said Foster. 'I'll jump for it.'

At last Hornblower found his tongue. 'Let me go, sir. I'll handle her.'

'Come with me, if you like,' replied Foster. 'It may need two of us.'

His nickname of Dreadnought Foster may have had its origin in the name of his ship, but it was appropriate enough in all circumstances. Harvey swung the boat under the fire ship's stern; she was before the wind again now, and just gathering way, just heading down upon the *Santa Barbara*.

For a moment Hornblower was the nearest man in the boat to the brig and there was no time to be lost. He stood up on the thwart and jumped; his hands gripped something, and with a kick and a struggle he dragged his ungainly body up on to the deck. With the brig before the wind, the flames were blown forward; right aft here it was merely frightfully hot, but Hornblower's ears were filled with the roar of the flames and the crackling and banging of the burning wood. He stepped forward to the wheel and seized the spokes, the wheel was lashed with a loop of line, and as he cast this off and took hold of the wheel again he could feel the rudder below him bite into the water. He flung his weight on the spoke and spun the wheel over. The brig was about to collide with the *Santa Barbara*, starboard bow to starboard bow, and the flames lit an anxious gesticulating crowd on the *Santa Barbara*'s forecastle.

'Hard over!' roared Foster's voice in Hornblower's ear.

'Hard over it is!' said Hornblower, and the brig answered her wheel at that moment, and her bow turned away, avoiding the collision.

An immense fountain of flame poured out from the hatchway abaft the mainmast, setting mast and rigging ablaze, and at the same time a flaw of wind blew a wave of flame aft. Some instinct made Hornblower while holding the wheel with one hand snatch out his neckcloth with the other and bury his face in it. The flame whirled round him and was gone again. But the distractions had been dangerous; the brig had continued to turn under full helm, and now her stern was swinging in to bump against the *Santa Barbara*'s bow. Hornblower desperately spun the wheel over the other way. The flames had driven Foster aft to the taffrail, but now he returned.

'Hard-a-lee!'

The brig was already responding. Her starboard quarter bumped the *Santa Barbara* in the waist, and then bumped clear.

'Midships!' shouted Foster.

At a distance of only two or three yards the fire ship passed on down the *Santa Barbara*'s side; an anxious group ran along her gangways keeping up with her as she did so. On the quarterdeck another group stood by with a spar to boom the fire ship off; Hornblower saw them out of the tail of his eye as they went by. Now they were clear.

'There's the *Dauntless* on the port bow,' said Foster. 'Keep her clear.'

'Aye, aye, sir.'

The din of the fire was tremendous; it could hardly be believed that on this little area of deck it was still possible to breathe and live. Hornblower felt the appalling heat on his hands and face. Both masts were immense pyramids of flame.

'Starboard a point,' said Foster. 'We'll lay her aground on the shoal by the Neutral Ground.'

'Starboard a point,' responded Hornblower.

He was being borne along on a wave of the highest exaltation; the roar of the fire was intoxicating, and he knew not a moment's fear. Then the whole deck only a yard or two forward of the wheel opened up in flame. Fire spouted out of the gaping seams and the heat was utterly unbearable, and the fire moved rapidly aft as the seams gaped progressively backward.

Hornblower felt for the loopline to lash the wheel, but before he could do so the wheel spun idly under his hand, presumably as the tiller ropes below him were burned away, and at the same time the deck under his feet heaved and warped in the fire. He staggered back to the taffrail. Foster was there.

'Tiller ropes burned away, sir,' reported Hornblower.

Flames roared up beside them. His coat sleeve was smouldering.

'Jump!' said Foster.

Hornblower felt Foster shoving him–everything was insane. He heaved himself over, gasped with fright as he hung in the air, and then felt the breath knocked out of his body as he hit the water. The water closed over him, and he knew panic as he struggled back to the surface. It was cold–the Mediterranean in December is cold. For the moment the air in his clothes supported him, despite the weight of the sword at his side, but he could see nothing in the darkness, with his eyes still dazzled by the roaring flames. Somebody splashed beside him.

'They were following us in the boat to take us off,' said Foster's voice. 'Can you swim?'

'Yes, sir. Not very well.'

'That might describe me,' said Foster; and then he lifted his voice to hail, 'Ahoy! Ahoy! Hammond! Harvey! Ahoy!'

He tried to raise himself as well as his voice, fell back with a splash, and splashed and splashed again, the water flowing into his mouth cutting short something he tried to say. Hornblower, beating the water with increasing feebleness, could still spare a thought–such were the vagaries of his wayward mind–for the interesting fact that even captains of much seniority were only mortal men after all. He tried to unbuckle his sword belt, failed, and sank deep with the effort, only just succeeding in struggling back to the surface. He gasped for breath, but in another attempt he managed to draw his sword half out of its scabbard, and as he struggled it slid out the rest of the way by its own weight; yet he was not conscious of any noticeable relief.

It was then that he heard the splashing and grinding of oars and loud voices, and he saw the dark shape of the approaching boat, and he uttered a spluttering cry. In a second or two the boat was up to them, and he was clutching the gunwale in panic.

They were lifting Foster in over the stern, and Hornblower knew he must keep still and make no effort to climb in, but it called for all his resolution to make himself hang quietly on to the side of the boat and wait his turn. He was interested in this overmastering fear, while he despised himself for it. It called for a conscious and serious effort of willpower to make his hands alternately release their death-like grip on the gunwale, so that the men in the boat could pass him round to the stern. Then they dragged him in and he fell face downward in the bottom of the boat, on the verge of fainting. Then somebody spoke in the boat, and Hornblower felt a cold shiver pass over his skin, and his feeble muscles tensed themselves, for the words spoken were Spanish–at any rate an unknown tongue, and Spanish presumably.

Somebody else answered in the same language. Hornblower tried to struggle up, and a restraining hand was laid on his shoulder. He rolled over, and with his eyes now accustomed to the darkness, he could see the three swarthy faces with the long black moustaches. These men were not Gibraltarians. On the instant he could guess who they were–the crew of one of the fire ships who had steered their craft in past the Mole, set fire to it, and made their escape in the boat. Foster was sitting doubled up, in the bottom of the boat, and now he lifted his face from his knees and stared round him.

'Who are these fellows?' he asked feebly–his struggle in the water had left him as weak as Hornblower.

'Spanish fire ship's crew, I fancy, sir,' said Hornblower. 'We're prisoners.'

'Are we indeed!'

The knowledge galvanized him into activity just as it had Hornblower. He tried to get to his feet, and the Spaniard at the tiller thrust him down with a hand on his shoulder. Foster tried to put his hand away, and raised his voice in a feeble cry, but the man at the tiller was standing no nonsense. He brought out, in a lightning gesture, a knife from his belt. The light from the fire ship, burning itself harmlessly out on the shoal in the distance, ran redly along the blade, and Foster ceased to struggle. Men might call him Dreadnought Foster, but he could recognize the need for discretion.

'How are we heading?' he asked Hornblower, sufficiently quietly not to irritate their captors.

'North, sir. Maybe they're going to land on the Neutral Ground and make for the Line.'

'That's their best chance,' agreed Foster.

He turned his neck uncomfortably to look back up the harbour.

'Two other ships burning themselves out up there,' he said. 'There were three fire ships came in, I fancy.'

'I saw three, sir.'

'Then there's no damage done. But a bold endeavour. Whoever would have credited the Dons with making such an attempt?'

'They have learned about fire ships from us, perhaps, sir,' suggested Hornblower.

'We may have "nursed the pinion that impelled the steel," you think?'

'It is possible, sir.'

Foster was a cool enough customer, quoting poetry and discussing the naval situation while being carried off into captivity by a Spaniard who guarded him with a drawn knife. Cool might be a too accurate adjective; Hornblower was shivering in his wet clothes as the chill night air blew over him, and he felt weak and feeble after all the excitement and exertions of the day.

'Boat ahoy!' came a hail across the water; there was a dark nucleus in the night over there. The Spaniard in the sternsheets instantly dragged the tiller over, heading the boat directly away from it, while the two at the oars redoubled their exertions.

'Guard boat–' said Foster, but cut his explanation short at a further threat from the knife.

Of course there would be a boat rowing guard at this northern end of the anchorage; they might have thought of it.

'Boat ahoy!' came the hail again. 'Lay on your oars or I'll fire into you!'

The Spaniard made no reply, and a second later came the flash and report of a musket shot. They heard nothing of the bullet, but the shot would put the fleet–towards which they were heading again–on the alert. But the Spaniards were going to play the game out to the end. They rowed doggedly on.

'Boat ahoy!'

This was another hail, from a boat right ahead of them. The Spaniards at the oars ceased their efforts in dismay, but a roar from the steersman set them instantly to work again. Hornblower could see the new boat almost directly ahead of them, and heard another hail from it as it rested on its oars. The Spaniard at the tiller shouted an order, and the stroke oar backed water and the boat turned sharply; another order, and both rowers tugged ahead again and the boat surged forward to ram. Should they succeed in overturning the intercepting boat they might make their escape even now, while the pursuing boat stopped to pick up their friends.

Everything happened at once, with everyone shouting at the full pitch of his lungs, seemingly. There was the crash of the collision, both boats heeling wildly as the bow of the Spanish boat rode up over the British boat but failed to overturn it. Someone fired a pistol, and the next moment the pursuing guard boat came dashing alongside, its crew leaping madly aboard them. Somebody flung himself on top of Hornblower, crushing the breath out of him and threatening to keep it out permanently with a hand on his throat. Hornblower heard Foster bellowing in protest, and a moment later his assailant released him, so that he could hear the midshipman of the guard boat apologizing for this rough treatment of a post captain of the Royal Navy. Someone unmasked the guard boat's lantern, and by its light Foster revealed himself, bedraggled and battered. The light shone on their sullen prisoners.

'Boats ahoy!' came another hail, and yet another boat emerged from the darkness and pulled towards them.

'Cap'n Hammond, I believe!' hailed Foster, with an ominous rasp in his voice.

'Thank God!' they heard Hammond say, and the boat pulled into the faint circle of light.

'But no thanks to you,' said Foster bitterly.

'After your fire ship cleared the *Santa Barbara* a puff of wind took you on faster than we could keep up with you,' explained Harvey.

'We followed as fast as we could get these rock scorpions to row,' added Hammond.

'And yet it called for Spaniards to save us from drowning,' sneered Foster. The memory of his struggle in the water rankled, apparently. 'I thought I could rely on two brother captains.'

'What are you implying, sir?' snapped Hammond.

'I make no implications, but others may read implications into a simple statement of fact.'

'I consider that an offensive remark, sir,' said Harvey, 'addressed to me equally with Captain Hammond.'

'I congratulate you on your perspicacity, sir,' replied Foster.

'I understand,' said Harvey. 'This is not a discussion we can pursue with these men present. I shall send a friend to wait on you.'

'He will be welcome.'

'Then I wish you a very good night, sir.'

'And I, too, sir,' said Hammond. 'Give way there.'

The boat pulled out of the circle of light, leaving an audience open-mouthed at this strange freak of human behaviour, that a man saved first from death and then from captivity should wantonly thrust himself into peril again. Foster looked after the boat for some seconds before speaking; perhaps he was already regretting his rather hysterical outburst.

'I shall have much to do before morning,' he said, more to himself than to anyone near him, and then addressed himself to the midshipman of the guard boat, 'You, sir, will take charge of these prisoners and convey me to my ship.'

'Aye aye, sir.'

'Is there anyone here who can speak their lingo? I would have it explained to them that I shall send them back to Cartagena under cartel, free without exchange. They saved our lives, and that is the least we can do in return.' The final explanatory sentence was addressed to Hornblower.

'I think that is just, sir.'

'And you, my fire-breathing friend. May I offer you my thanks? You did well. Should I live beyond tomorrow, I shall see that authority is informed of your actions.'

'Thank you, sir.' A question trembled on Hornblower's lips. It called for a little resolution to thrust it out, 'And my examination, sir? My certificate?'

Foster shook his head. 'That particular examining board will never reassemble, I fancy. You must wait your opportunity to go before another one.'

'Aye aye, sir,' said Hornblower, with despondency apparent in his tone.

'Now lookee here, Mr Hornblower,' said Foster, turning upon him. 'to the best of my recollection, you were flat aback, about to lose your spars and with Dover cliffs under your lee. In one more minute you would have failed–it was the warning gun that saved you. Is not that so?'

'I suppose it is, sir.'

'Then be thankful for small mercies. And even more thankful for big ones.'

9

NOAH'S ARK

Acting-Lieutenant Hornblower sat in the sternsheets of the longboat beside Mr Tapling of the diplomatic service, with his feet among bags of gold. About him rose the steep shores of the Gulf of Oran, and ahead of him lay the city, white in the sunshine, like a mass of blocks of marble dumped by a careless hand upon the hillsides where they rose from the water. The oar blades, as the boat's crew pulled away rhythmically over the gentle swell, were biting into the clearest emerald green, and it was only a moment since they had left behind the bluest the Mediterranean could show.

'A pretty sight from here,' said Tapling, gazing at the town they were approaching, 'but closer inspection will show that the eye is deceived. And as for the nose! The stinks of the true believers have to be smelt to be believed. Lay her alongside the jetty there, Mr Hornblower, beyond those xebecs.'

'Aye aye, sir,' said the coxswain, when Hornblower gave the order.

'There's a sentry on the waterfront battery here,' commented Tapling, looking about him keenly, 'not more than half asleep, either. And notice the two guns in the two castles. Thirty-two pounders, without a doubt. Stone shot piled in readiness. A stone shot flying into fragments on impact effects damage out of proportion to its size. And the walls seem sound enough. To seize Oran by a *coup de main* would not be easy, I am afraid. If His Nibs the Bey should choose to cut our throats and keep our gold it would be long before we were avenged, Mr Hornblower.'

'I don't think I should find any satisfaction in being avenged in any case, sir,' said Hornblower.

'There's some truth in that. But doubtless His Nibs will spare us this time. The goose lays golden eggs–a boatload of gold every month must make a dazzling prospect for a pirate Bey in these days of convoys.'

'Way 'nough,' called the coxswain. 'Oars!'

The longboat came gliding alongside the jetty and hooked on neatly. A few seated figures in the shade turned eyes at least, and in some cases even their heads as well, to look at the British boat's crew. A number of swarthy Moors appeared on the decks of the xebecs and gazed down at them, and one or two shouted remarks to them.

'No doubt they are describing the ancestry of the infidels,' said Tapling. 'Sticks and stones may break my bones, but names can never hurt me, especially when I do not understand them. Where's our man?'

He shaded his eyes to look alongside the waterfront.

'No one in sight, sir, that looks like a Christian,' said Hornblower.

'Our man's no Christian,' said Tapling. 'White, but no Christian. White by courtesy at that–French-Arab-Levantine mixture. His Britannic Majesty's

Consul at Oran *pro tem.*, and a Mussulman from expediency. Though there are very serious disadvantages about being a true believer. Who would want four wives at any time, especially when he pays for the doubtful privilege by abstaining from wine?'

Tapling stepped up on to the jetty and Hornblower followed him. The gentle swell that rolled up the Gulf broke soothingly below them, and the blinding heat of the noonday sun was reflected up into their faces from the stone blocks on which they stood. Far down the Gulf lay the two anchored ships–the storeship and H.M.S. *Indefatigable*–lovely on the blue and silver surface.

'And yet I would rather see Drury Lane on a Saturday night,' said Tapling.

He turned back to look at the city wall, which guarded the place from sea-borne attack. A narrow gate, flanked by bastions, opened on to the waterfront. Sentries in red caftans were visible on the summit. In the deep shadow of the gate something was moving, but it was hard with eyes dazzled by the sun to see what it was. Then it emerged from the shadow as a little group coming towards them–a half-naked Negro leading a donkey, and on the back of the donkey, seated sideways far back towards the root of the tail, a vast figure in a blue robe.

'Shall we meet His Britannic Majesty's Consul halfway?' asked Tapling. 'No. Let him come to us.'

The Negro halted the donkey, and the man on the donkey's back slid to the ground and came towards them–a mountainous man, waddling straddle-legged in his robe, his huge clay-coloured face topped by a white turban. A scanty black moustache and beard sprouted from his lip and chin.

'Your servant, Mr Duras,' said Tapling. 'And may I present Acting-Lieutenant Horatio Hornblower, of the frigate *Indefatigable*?'

Mr Duras nodded his perspiring head.

'Have you brought the money?' he asked, in guttural French; it took Hornblower a moment or two to adjust his mind to the language and his ear to Duras's intonation.

'Seven thousand golden guineas,' replied Tapling, in reasonably good French.

'Good,' said Duras, with a trace of relief. 'Is it in the boat?'

'It is in the boat, and it stays in the boat at present,' answered Tapling. 'Do you remember the conditions agreed upon? Four hundred fat cattle, fifteen hundred fanegas of barley grain. When I see those in the lighters, and the lighters alongside the ships down the bay, then I hand over the money. Have you the stores ready?'

'Soon.'

'As I expected. How long?'

'Soon–very soon.'

Tapling made a grimace of resignation.

'Then we shall return to the ships. Tomorrow, perhaps, or the day after, we shall come back with the gold.'

Alarm appeared on Duras's sweating face.

'No, do not do that,' he said, hastily. 'You do not know His Highness the Bey. He is changeable. If he knows the gold is here he will give orders for the cattle to be brought. Take the gold away, and he will not stir. And–and–he will be angry with me.'

'Ira principis mors est,' said Tapling, and in response to Duras's blank look obliged by a translation. 'The wrath of the prince means death. Is not that so?'

'Yes,' said Duras, and he in turn said something in an unknown language, and stabbed at the air with his fingers in a peculiar gesture; and then translated, 'May it not happen.'

'Certainly we hope it may not happen,' agreed Tapling with disarming cordiality. 'The bowstring, the hook, even the bastinado are all unpleasant. It might be better if you went to the Bey and prevailed upon him to give the necessary orders for the grain and the cattle. Or we shall leave at nightfall.'

Tapling glanced up at the sun to lay stress on the time limit.

'I shall go,' said Duras, spreading his hands in a deprecatory gesture. 'I shall go. But I beg of you, do not depart. Perhaps His Highness is busy in his harem. Then no one may disturb him. But I shall try. The grain is here ready–it lies in the Kasbah there. It is only the cattle that have to be brought in. Please be patient. I implore you. His Highness is not accustomed to commerce, as you know, sir. Still less is he accustomed to commerce after the fashion of the Franks.'

Duras wiped his streaming face with a corner of his robe.

'Pardon me,' he said, 'I do not feel well. But I shall go to His Highness. I shall go. Please wait for me.'

'Until sunset,' said Tapling implacably.

Duras called to his Negro attendant, who had been crouching huddled up under the donkey's belly to take advantage of the shade it cast. With an effort Duras hoisted his ponderous weight on to the donkey's hind quarters. He wiped his face again and looked at them with a trace of bewilderment.

'Wait for me,' were the last words he said as the donkey was led away back into the city gate.

'He is afraid of the Bey,' said Tapling watching him go. 'I would rather face twenty Beys than Admiral Sir John Jervis in a tantrum. What will he do when he hears about this further delay, with the Fleet on short rations already? He'll have my guts for a necktie.'

'One cannot expect punctuality of these people,' said Hornblower with the easy philosophy of the man who does not bear the responsibilty. But he thought of the British Navy, without friends, without allies, maintaining desperately the blockade of a hostile Europe, in face of superior numbers, storms, disease, and now famine.

'Look at that!' said Tapling pointing suddenly.

It was a big grey rat which had made its appearance in the dry storm gutter that crossed the waterfront here. Regardless of the bright sunshine it sat up and looked round at the world; even when Tapling stamped his foot it showed no great signs of alarm. When he stamped a second time it slowly turned to hide itself again in the drain, missed its footing so that it lay writhing for a moment at the mouth of the drain, and then regained its feet and disappeared into the darkness.

'An old rat, I suppose,' said Tapling meditatively. 'Senile, possibly. Even blind, it may be.'

Hornblower cared nothing about rats, senile or otherwise. He took a step or two back in the direction of the longboat and the civilian officer conformed to his movements.

'Rig that mains'l so that it gives us some shade, Maxwell,' said Hornblower. 'We're here for the rest of the day.'

'A great comfort,' said Tapling, seating himself on a stone bollard beside the boat, 'to be here in a heathen port. No need to worry in case any men run off. No need to worry about liquor. Only about bullocks and barley. And how to get a spark on this tinder.'

He blew through the pipe that he took from his pocket, preparatory to filling it. The boat was shaded by the mainsail now, and the hands sat in the bows yarning in low tones, while the others made themselves as comfortable as possible in the sternsheets; the boat rolled peacefully in the tiny swell, the rhythmic sound as the fendoffs creaked between her gunwale and the jetty having a soothing effect while city and port dozed in the blazing afternoon heat. Yet it was not easy for a young man of Hornblower's active temperament to endure prolonged inaction. He climbed up on the jetty to stretch his legs, and paced up and down; a Moor in a white gown and turban came staggering in the sunshine along the waterfront. His gait was unsteady, and he walked with his legs well apart to provide a firmer base for his swaying body.

'What was it you said, sir, about liquor being abhorred by the Moslems?' said Hornblower to Tapling down in the sternsheets.

'Not necessarily abhorred,' replied Tapling, guardedly. 'But anathematized, illegal, unlawful, and hard to obtain.'

'Someone here has contrived to obtain some, sir,' said Hornblower.

'Let me see,' said Tapling, scrambling up; the hands, bored with waiting and interested as ever in liquor, landed from the bows to stare as well.

'That looks like a man who has taken drink,' agreed Tapling.

'Three sheets in the wind, sir,' said Maxwell, as the Moor staggered.

'And taken all aback,' supplemented Tapling, as the Moor swerved wildly to one side in a semicircle.

At the end of the semicircle he fell with a crash on his face; his brown legs emerged from the robe a couple of times and were drawn in again, and he lay passive, his head on his arms, his turban fallen on the ground to reveal his shaven skull with a tassel of hair on the crown.

'Totally dismasted,' said Hornblower.

'And hard aground,' said Tapling.

But the Moor now lay oblivious of everything.

'And here's Duras,' said Hornblower.

Out through the gate came the massive figure on the little donkey; another donkey bearing another portly figure followed, each donkey being led by a Negro slave, and after them came a dozen swarthy individuals whose muskets, and whose pretence at uniform, indicated that they were soldiers.

'The Treasurer of His Highness,' said Duras, by way of introduction when he and the other had dismounted. 'Come to fetch the gold.'

The portly Moor looked loftily upon them; Duras was still streaming with sweat in the hot sun.

'The gold is there,' said Tapling, pointing. 'In the sternsheets of the longboat. You will have a closer view of it when we have a closer view of the stores we are to buy.'

Duras translated this speech into Arabic. There was a rapid interchange of sentences, before the Treasurer apparently yielded. He turned and waved his arms back to the gate in what was evidently a prearranged signal. A dreary procession immediately emerged–a long line of men, all of them almost naked, white, black, and mulatto, each man staggering along under the burden of a sack of grain. Overseers with sticks walked with them.

'The money,' said Duras, as a result of something said by the Treasurer.

A word from Tapling set the hands to work lifting the heavy bags of gold on to the quay.

'With the corn on the jetty I will put the gold there too,' said Tapling to Hornblower. 'Keep your eye on it while I look at some of those sacks.'

Tapling walked over to the slave gang. Here and there he opened a sack, looked into it, and inspected handfuls of the golden barley grain; other sacks he felt from the outside.

'No hope of looking over every sack in a hundred ton of barley,' he remarked, strolling back again to Hornblower. 'Much of it is sand, I expect. But that is the way of the heathen. The price is adjusted accordingly. Very well, Effendi.'

At a sign from Duras, and under the urgings of the overseers, the slaves burst into activity, trotting up to the quayside and dropping their sacks into the lighter which lay there. The first dozen men were organized into a working party to distribute the cargo evenly into the bottom of the lighter, while the others trotted off, their bodies gleaming with sweat, to fetch fresh loads. At the same time a couple of swarthy herdsmen came out through the gate driving a small herd of cattle.

'Scrubby little creatures,' said Tapling, looking them over critically, 'but that was allowed for in the price, too.'

'The gold,' said Duras.

In reply Tapling opened one of the bags at his feet, filled his hand with golden guineas, and let them cascade through his fingers into the bag again.

'Five hundred guineas there,' he said. 'Fourteen bags, as you see. They will be yours when the lighters are loaded and unmoored.'

Duras wiped his face with a weary gesture. His knees seemed to be weak, and he leaned upon the patient donkey that stood behind him.

The cattle were being driven down a gangway into another lighter, and a second herd had now appeared and was waiting.

'Things move faster than you feared,' said Hornblower.

'See how they drive the poor wretches,' replied Tapling sententiously. 'See! Things move fast when you have no concern for human flesh and blood.'

A coloured slave had fallen to the ground under his burden. He lay there disregarding the blows rained on him by the sticks of the overseers. There was a small movement of his legs. Someone dragged him out of the way at last and the sacks continued to be carried to the lighter. The other lighter was filling fast with cattle, packed into a tight, bellowing mass in which no movement was possible.

'His Nibs is actually keeping his word,' marvelled Tapling. 'I'd 'a settled for the half, if I had been asked beforehand.'

One of the herdsmen on the quay had sat down with his face in his hands; now he fell over limply on his side.

'Sir–' began Hornblower to Tapling, and the two men looked at each other with the same awful thought occurring to them at the same moment.

Duras began to say something; with one hand on the withers of the donkey and the other gesticulating in the air it seemed that he was making something of a speech, but there was no sense in the words he was roaring out in a hoarse voice. His face was swollen beyond its customary fatness and his expression was widely distorted, while his cheeks were so suffused with blood as to look dark under his tan. Duras quitted his hold of the donkey and began to reel about in half circles, under the eyes of Moors and Englishmen. His voice died away to a whisper, his legs gave way under him, and he fell to his hands and knees and then to his face.

'That's the plague!' said Tapling. 'The Black Death! I saw it in Smyrna in '96.'

He and the other Englishmen had shrunk back on the one side, the soldiers and the Treasurer on the other, leaving the palpitating body lying in the clear space between them.

'The plague, by St Peter!' squealed one of the young sailors. He would have headed a rush to the longboat.

'Stand still, there!' roared Hornblower, scared of the plague but with the habits of discipline so deeply engrained in him by now that he checked the panic automatically.

'I was a fool not to have thought of it before,' said Tapling. 'That dying rat–that fellow over there who we thought was drunk. I should have known!'

The soldier who appeared to be the sergeant in command of the Treasurer's escort was in explosive conversation with the chief of the overseers of the slaves, both of them staring and pointing at the dying Duras; the Treasurer himself was clutching his robe about him and looking down at the wretched man at his feet in fascinated horror.

'Well, sir,' said Hornblower to Tapling, 'what do we do?'

Hornblower was of the temperament that demands immediate action in face of a crisis.

'Do?' replied Tapling with a bitter smile. 'We stay here and rot.'

'Stay *here*?'

'The fleet will never have us back. Not until we have served three weeks of quarantine. Three weeks after the last case has occurred. Here in Oran.'

'Nonsense!' said Hornblower, with all the respect due to his senior startled out of him. 'No one would order that.'

'Would they not? Have you ever seen an epidemic in a fleet?'

Hornblower had not, but he had heard enough about them–fleets where nine out of ten had died of putrid fevers. Crowded ships with twenty-two inches of hammock space per man were ideal breeding places for epidemics. He realized that no captain, no admiral, would run that risk for the sake of a longboat's crew of twenty men.

The two xebecs against the jetty had suddenly cast off, and were working their way out of the harbour under sweeps.

'The plague can only have struck today,' mused Hornblower, the habit of deduction strong in him despite his sick fear.

The cattle herders were abandoning their work, giving a wide berth to that one of their number who was lying on the quay. Up at the town gate it appeared that the guard was employed in driving people back into the town–apparently the rumour of plague had spread sufficiently therein to cause a panic, while the guard had just received orders not to allow the population to stream out into the surrounding country. There would be frightful things happening in the town soon. The Treasurer was climbing on his donkey; the crowd of grain-carrying slaves was melting away as the overseers fled.

'I must report this to the ship,' said Hornblower; Tapling, as a civilian diplomatic officer, held no authority over him. The whole responsibility was Hornblower's. The longboat and the longboat's crew were Hornblower's command, entrusted to him by Captain Pellew whose authority derived from the King.

Amazing how the panic was spreading. The Treasurer was gone; Duras's Negro slave had ridden off on his late master's donkey; the soldiers had hastened off in a single group. The waterfront was deserted now except for the dead and dying; along the waterfront, presumably, at the foot of the wall, lay the way to the open country which all desired to seek. The Englishmen were standing alone, with the bags of gold at their feet.

'Plague spreads through the air,' said Tapling. 'Even the rats die of it. We have been here for hours. We were near enough to–that–' he nodded at the dying Duras–'to speak to him, to catch his breath. Which of us will be the first?'

'We'll see when the time comes,' said Hornblower. It was his contrary nature to be sanguine in the face of depression; besides, he did not want the men to hear what Tapling was saying.

'And there's the fleet!' said Tapling bitterly. 'This lot'–he nodded at the deserted lighters, one almost full of cattle, the other almost full of grain sacks–'this lot would be a God-send. The men are on two-thirds rations.'

'Damn it, we can do something about it,' said Hornblower. 'Maxwell, put the gold back in the boat, and get that awning in.'

The officer of the watch in H.M.S. *Indefatigable* saw the ship's longboat returning from the town. A slight breeze had swung the frigate and the *Caroline* (the transport brig) to their anchors, and the longboat, instead of running alongside, came up under the *Indefatigable*'s stern to leeward.

'Mr Christie!' hailed Hornblower, standing up in the bows of the longboat.

The officer of the watch came aft to the taffrail.

'What is it?' he demanded, puzzled.

'I must speak to the Captain.'

'Then come on board and speak to him. What the devil—?'

'Please ask the Captain if I may speak to him.'

Pellew appeared at the after-cabin window; he could hardly have helped hearing the bellowed conversation.

'Yes, Mr Hornblower?'

Hornblower told him the news.

'Keep to loo'ard, Mr Hornblower.'

'Yes, sir. But the stores—'

'What about them?'

Hornblower outlined the situation and made his request.

'It's not very regular,' mused Pellew. 'Besides—'

He did not want to shout aloud his thoughts that perhaps everyone in the longboat would soon be dead of plague.

'We'll be all right, sir. It's a week's rations for the squadron.'

That was the point, the vital matter. Pellew had to balance the possible loss of a transport brig against the possible gain of supplies, immeasurably more important, which would enable the squadron to maintain its watch over the outlet to the Mediterranean. Looked at in that light Hornblower's suggestion had added force.

'Oh, very well, Mr Hornblower. By the time you bring the stores out I'll have the crew transferred. I appoint you to the command of the *Caroline*.'

'Thank you, sir.'

'Mr Tapling will continue as passenger with you.'

'Very good, sir.'

So when the crew of the longboat, toiling and sweating at the sweeps, brought the two lighters down the bay, they found the *Caroline* swinging deserted at her anchors, while a dozen curious telescopes from the *Indefatigable* watched the proceedings. Hornblower went up the brig's side with half a dozen hands.

'She's like a blooming Noah's Ark, sir,' said Maxwell.

The comparison was apt; the *Caroline* was flush-decked, and the whole available deck area was divided by partitions into stalls for the cattle, while to enable the ship to be worked light gangways had been laid over the stalls into a practically continuous upper deck.

'An' all the animiles, sir,' said another seaman.

'But Noah's animals walked in two by two,' said Hornblower. 'We're not so lucky. And we've got to get the grain on board first. Get those hatches unbattened.'

In ordinary conditions a working party of two or three hundred men from the *Indefatigable* would have made short work of getting in the cargo from the lighters, but now it had to be done by the longboat's complement of eighteen. Luckily Pellew had had the forethought and kindness to have the ballast struck out of the holds, or they would have had to do that weary job first.

'Tail on to those tackles, men,' said Hornblower.

Pellew saw the first bundle of grain sacks rise slowly into the air from the lighter, and swung over and down the *Caroline*'s hatchway.

'He'll be all right,' he decided. 'Man the capstan and get under way, if you please, Mr Bolton.'

Hornblower, directing the work on the tackles, heard Pellew's voice come to him through the speaking trumpet.

'Good luck, Mr Hornblower. Report in three weeks at Gibraltar.'

'Very good, sir. Thank you, sir.'

Hornblower turned back to find a seaman at his elbow knuckling his forehead.

'Beg pardon, sir. But can you hear those cattle bellerin', sir? 'Tis mortal hot, an' 'tis water they want, sir.'

'Hell,' said Hornblower.

He would never get the cattle on board before nightfall. He left a small party at work transferring cargo, and with the rest of the men he began to extemporize a method of watering the unfortunate cattle in the lighter. Half *Caroline*'s hold space was filled with water barrels and fodder, but it was an awkward business getting water down to the lighter with pump and hose, and the poor brutes down there surged about uncontrollably at the prospect of water. Hornblower saw the lighter heel and almost capsize; one of his men–luckily one who could swim–went hastily overboard from the lighter to avoid being crushed to death.

'Hell,' said Hornblower again, and that was by no means the last time.

Without any skilled advice he was having to learn the business of managing livestock at sea; each moment brought its lessons. A naval officer on active service indeed found himself engaged on strange duties. It was well after dark before Hornblower called a halt to the labours of his men, and it was before dawn that he roused them up to work again. It was still early in the morning that the last of the grain sacks was stowed away and Hornblower had to face the operation of swaying up the cattle from the lighter. After their night down there, with little water and less food, they were in no mood to be trifled with, but it was easier at first while they were crowded together. A bellyband was slipped round the nearest, the tackle hooked on, and the animal was swayed up, lowered to the deck through an opening in the gangways, and herded into one of the stalls with ease. The seamen, shouting and waving their shirts, thought it was great fun, but they were not sure when the next one, released from its bellyband, went on the rampage and chased them about the deck, threatening death with its horns, until it wandered into its stall where the bar could be promptly dropped to shut it in. Hornblower, looking at the sun rising rapidly in the east, did not think it fun at all.

And the emptier the lighter became, the more room the cattle had to rush about in it; to capture each one so as to put a bellyband on it was a desperate adventure. Nor were those half-wild bullocks soothed by the sight of their companions being successively hauled bellowing into the air over their heads. Before the day was half done Hornblower's men were as weary as if they had fought a battle, and there was not one of them who would not gladly have quitted this novel employment in exchange for some normal seaman's duty like going aloft to reef topsails on a stormy night. As soon as Hornblower had the notion of dividing the interior of the lighter up into sections with barricades of stout spars the work became easier, but it took time, and before it was done the cattle had already suffered a couple of casualties–weaker members of the herd crushed underfoot in the course of the wild rushes about the lighter.

And there was a distraction when a boat came out from the shore, with swarthy Moors at the oars and the Treasurer in the stern. Hornblower left Tapling to negotiate–apparently the Bey at least had not been so frightened of the plague as to forget to ask for his money. All Hornblower insisted upon was that the boat should keep well to leeward, and the money was floated off to it headed up in an empty rum-puncheon. Night found not more than half the cattle in the stalls on board, with Hornblower worrying about feeding and watering them, and snatching at hints diplomatically won from those members of his crew who had had bucolic experience. But the earliest dawn saw him driving his men to work again, and deriving a momentary satisfaction from the sight of Tapling having to leap for his life to the gangway out of reach of a maddened bullock which was charging about the deck and refusing to enter a stall. And by the time the last animal was safely packed in Hornblower was faced with another problem–that of dealing with what one of the men elegantly termed 'mucking out'. Fodder–water–mucking out; that deck-load of cattle seemed to promise enough work in itself to keep his eighteen men busy, without any thought of the needs of handling the ship.

But there were advantages about the men being kept busy, as Hornblower grimly decided; there had not been a single mention of plague since the work began. The anchorage where the *Caroline* lay was exposed to north-easterly winds, and it was necessary that he should take her out to sea before such a wind should blow. He mustered his men to divide them into watches; he was the only navigator, so that he had to appoint the coxswain and the under-coxswain, Jordan, as officers of the watch. Someone volunteered as cook, and Hornblower, running his eye over his assembled company, appointed Tapling as cook's mate. Tapling opened his mouth to protest, but there was that in Hornblower's expression which cut the protest short. There was no bos'n, no carpenter–no surgeon either, as Hornblower pointed out to himself gloomily. But on the other hand if the need for a doctor should arise it would, be hoped, be mercifully brief.

'Port watch, loose the jibs and main tops'l,' ordered Hornblower. 'Starboard watch, man the capstan.'

So began that voyage of H.M. transport brig *Caroline* which became legendary (thanks to the highly coloured accounts retailed by the crew during innumerable dog-watches in later commissions) throughout the King's navy. The *Caroline* spent her three weeks of quarantine in homeless wanderings about the western Mediterranean. It was necessary that she should keep close up to the Strait, for fear lest the westerlies and the prevailing inward set of the current should take her out of reach of Gibraltar when the time came, so she beat about between the coasts of Spain and Africa trailing behind her a growing farmyard stench. The *Caroline* was a worn-out ship; with any sort of sea running she leaked like a sieve; and there were always hands at work on the pumps, either pumping her out or pumping sea water on to her deck to clean it or pumping up fresh water for the cattle.

Her top hamper made her almost unmanageable in a fresh breeze; her deck seams leaked, of course, when she worked, allowing a constant drip of unspeakable filth down below. The one consolation was in the supply of fresh meat–a commodity some of Hornblower's men had not tasted for three months. Hornblower recklessly sacrificed a bullock a day, for in that Mediterranean climate meat could not be kept sweet. So his men feasted on steaks and fresh tongues; there were plenty of men on board who had never in their whole lives before eaten a beef steak.

But fresh water was the trouble–it was a greater anxiety to Hornblower than even it was to the average ship's captain, for the cattle were always thirsty; twice Hornblower had to land a raiding party at dawn on the coast of Spain, seize a fishing village, and fill his water casks in the local stream.

It was a dangerous adventure, and the second landing revealed the danger, for while the *Caroline* was trying to claw off the land again a Spanish guarda-costa lugger came gliding round the point with all sail set. Maxwell saw her first, but Hornblower saw her before he could report her presence.

'Very well, Maxwell,' said Hornblower, trying to sound composed.

He turned his glass upon her. She was no more than three miles off, a trifle to windward, and the *Caroline* was embayed, cut off by the land from all chance to escape. The lugger could go three feet to her two, while the *Caroline*'s clumsy superstructure prevented her from lying nearer than eight points to the wind. As Hornblower gazed, the accumulated irritation of the past seventeen days boiled over. He was furious with fate for having thrust this ridiculous mission on him. He hated the *Caroline* and her clumsiness and her stinks and her cargo. He raged against the destiny which had caught him in this hopeless position.

'Hell!' said Hornblower, actually stamping his feet on the upper gangway in his anger. 'Hell *and* damnation!'

He was dancing with rage, he observed with some curiosity. But with his fighting madness at the boil there was no chance of his yielding without a struggle, and his mental convulsions resulted in his producing a scheme for action. How many men of a crew did a Spanish guarda-costa carry? Twenty? That would be an outside figure–those luggers were only intended to act against petty smugglers. And with surprise on his side there was still a chance, despite the four eight-pounders that the lugger carried.

'Pistols and cutlasses, men,' he said. 'Jordan, choose two men and show yourselves up here. But the rest of you keep under cover. Hide yourselves. Yes, Mr Tapling, you may serve with us. See that you are armed.'

No one would expect resistance from a laden cattle transport; the Spaniards would expect to find on board a crew of a dozen at most, and not a disciplined force of twenty. The problem lay in luring the lugger within reach.

'Full and by,' called Hornblower down to the helmsman below. 'Be ready to jump, men. Maxwell, if a man shows himself before my order shoot him with your own hand. You hear me? That's an order, and you disobey me at your peril.'

'Aye aye, sir,' said Maxwell.

The lugger was romping up towards them; even in that light air there was a white wave under her sharp bows. Hornblower glanced up to make sure that the *Caroline* was displaying no colours. That made his plan legal under the laws of war. The report of a gun and a puff of smoke came from the lugger as she fired across the *Caroline*'s bows.

'I'm going to heave to, Jordan,' said Hornblower. 'Main tops'l braces. Helm-a-lee.'

The *Caroline* came to the wind and lay there wallowing, a surrendered and helpless ship apparently, if ever there was one.

'Not a sound, men,' said Hornblower.

The cattle bellowed mournfully. Here came the lugger, her crew plainly visible now. Hornblower could see an officer clinging to the main shrouds ready to board, but no one else seemed to have a care in the world. Everyone seemed to be looking up at the clumsy superstructure and laughing at the farmyard noises issuing from it.

'Wait, men, wait,' said Hornblower.

The lugger was coming alongside when Hornblower suddenly realized, with a hot flood of blood under his skin, that he himself was unarmed. He had told his men to take pistols and cutlasses; he had advised Tapling to arm himself, and yet he had clean forgotten about his own need for weapons. But it was too late now to try to remedy that. Someone in the lugger hailed in Spanish, and Hornblower spread his hands in a show of incomprehension. Now they were alongside.

'Come on, men!' shouted Hornblower.

He ran across the superstructure and with a gulp he flung himself across the gap at the officer in the shrouds. He gulped again as he went through the air; he fell with all his weight on the unfortunate man, clasped him round the shoulders, and fell with him to the deck. There were shouts and yells behind him as the *Caroline* spewed up her crew into the lugger. A rush of feet, a clatter and a clash. Hornblower got to his feet empty-handed. Maxwell was just striking down a man with his cutlass. Tapling was heading a rush forward into the bows, waving a cutlass and yelling like a madman. Then it was all over; the astonished Spaniards were unable to lift a hand in their own defence.

So it came about that on the twenty-second day of her quarantine the *Caroline* came into Gibraltar Bay with a captured guarda-costa lugger under her lee. A thick barn-yard stench trailed with her, too, but at least, when Hornblower went on board the *Indefatigable* to make his report, he had a suitable reply ready for Mr Midshipman Bracegirdle.

'Hullo, Noah, how are Shem and Ham?' asked Mr Bracegirdle.

'Shem and Ham have taken a prize,' said Hornblower. 'I regret that Mr Bracegirdle can't say the same.'

But the Chief Commissary of the squadron, when Hornblower reported to him, had a comment to which even Hornblower was unable to make a reply.

'Do you mean to tell me, Mr Hornblower,' said the Chief Commissary, 'that you allowed your men to eat fresh beef? A bullock a day for your eighteen men. There must have been plenty of ship's provisions on board. That was wanton extravagance, Mr Hornblower, I'm surprised at you.'

10

THE DUCHESS AND THE DEVIL

Acting-Lieutenant Hornblower was bringing the sloop *Le Rêve*, prize of H.M.S. *Indefatigable*, to anchor in Gibraltar Bay. He was nervous; if anyone had asked him if he thought that all the telescopes in the Mediterranean Fleet were trained upon him he would have laughed at the fantastic suggestion, but he felt as if they were. Nobody ever gauged more cautiously the strength of the gentle following breeze, or estimated more anxiously the distances between the big anchored ships of the line, or calculated more carefully the space *Le Rêve* would need to swing at her anchor. Jackson, his petty officer, was standing forward awaiting the order to take in the jib, and he acted quickly at Hornblower's hail.

'Helm-a-lee,' said Hornblower next, and *Le Rêve* rounded into the wind. 'Brail up!'

Le Rêve crept forward, her momentum diminishing as the wind took her way off her.

'Let go!'

The cable growled a protest as the anchor took it out through the hawsehole–that welcome splash of the anchor, telling of the journey's end. Hornblower watched carefully while *Le Rêve* took up on her cable, and then relaxed a little. He had brought the prize safely in. The commodore–Captain Sir Edward Pellew of H.M.S. *Indefatigable*–had clearly not yet returned, so that it was Hornblower's duty to report to the port admiral.

'Get the boat hoisted out,' he ordered, and then, remembering his humanitarian duty, 'and you can let the prisoners up on deck.'

They had been battened down below for the last forty-eight hours, because the fear of a recapture was the nightmare of every prizemaster. But here in the Bay with the Mediterranean Fleet all round that danger was at an end. Two hands at the oars of the gig sent her skimming over the water, and in ten minutes Hornblower was reporting his arrival to the admiral.

'You say she shows a fair turn of speed?' said the latter, looking over at the prize.

'Yes, sir. And she's handy enough,' said Hornblower.

'I'll purchase her into the service. Never enough despatch vessels,' mused the Admiral.

Even with that hint it was a pleasant surprise to Hornblower when he received heavily sealed official orders and, opening them, read that 'you are hereby requested and required' to take H.M. sloop *Le Rêve* under his command and to proceed 'with the utmost expedition' to Plymouth as soon as the despatches destined for England should be put in his charge. It was an independent command; it was a chance of seeing England again (it was three years since Hornblower had last set foot on the English shore) and it was a high professional compliment. But there was another letter, delivered at the same moment, which Hornblower read with less elation.

'Their Excellencies, Major-General Sir Hew and Lady Dalrymple, request the pleasure of Acting-Lieutenant Horatio Hornblower's company at dinner today, at three o'clock, at Government House.'

It might be a pleasure to dine with the Governor of Gibraltar and his lady, but it was only a mixed pleasure at best for an acting-lieutenant with a single sea chest, faced with the need to dress himself suitably for such a function. Yet it was hardly possible for a young man to walk up to Government House from the landing ship without a thrill of excitement, especially as his friend Mr Midshipman Bracegirdle, who came from a wealthy family and had a handsome allowance, had lent him a pair of the finest white stockings of China silk–Bracegirdle's calves were plump, and Hornblower's were skinny, but that difficulty had been artistically circumvented. Two small pads of oakum, some strips of sticking plaster from the surgeon's stores, and Hornblower now had a couple of legs of which no one need be ashamed. He could put his left leg forward to make his bow without any fear of wrinkles in his stockings, and sublimely conscious, as Bracegirdle said, of a leg of which any gentleman would be proud.

At Government House the usual polished and languid aide-de-camp took charge of Hornblower and led him forward. He made his bow to Sir Hew, a red-faced and fussy old gentleman, and to Lady Dalrymple, a red-faced and fussy old lady.

'Mr Hornblower,' said the latter, 'I must present you–Your Grace, this is Mr Hornblower, the new captain of *Le Rêve*. Her Grace the Duchess of Wharfdale.'

A duchess, no less! Hornblower poked forward his padded leg, pointed his toe, laid his hand on his heart and bowed with all the depth the tightness of his breeches allowed–he had still been growing when he bought them on joining the *Indefatigable*. Bold blue eyes, and a once beautiful middle-aged face.

'So this 'ere's the feller in question?' said the duchess. 'Matilda, my dear, are you going to hentrust me to a hinfant in harms?'

The startling vulgarity of the accent took Hornblower's breath away. He had been ready for almost anything except that a superbly dressed duchess should speak in the accent of Seven Dials. He raised his eyes to stare, while forgetting to straighten himself up, standing with his chin poked forward and his hand still on his heart.

'You look like a gander on a green,' said the duchess. 'I hexpects you to 'iss hany moment.'

She struck her own chin out and swung from side to side with her hands on her knees in a perfect imitation of a belligerent goose, apparently with so close a resemblance to Hornblower as well as to excite a roar of laughter from the other guests. Hornblower stood in blushing confusion.

'Don't be 'ard on the young feller,' said the duchess, coming to his defence and patting him on the shoulder. ''E's on'y young, an' thet's nothink to be ashamed of. Somethink to be prard of, for thet matter, to be trusted with a ship at thet hage.'

It was lucky that the announcement of dinner came to save Hornblower from the further confusion into which this kindly remark had thrown him. Hornblower naturally found himself with the riff-raff, that ragtag and bobtail of the middle of the table along with the other junior officers – Sir Hew sat at one end with the duchess, while Lady Dalrymple sat with a commodore at the other. Moreover, there were not nearly as many women as men; that was only to be expected, as Gibraltar was, technically at least, a beleaguered fortress. So Hornblower had no woman on either side of him; at his right sat the young aide-de-camp who had first taken him in charge.

'Your health, Your Grace,' said the commodore, looking down the length of the table and raising his glass.

'Thank'ee,' replied the duchess. 'Just in time to save my life. I was wonderin' 'oo'd come to my rescue.'

She raised her brimming glass to her lips and when she put it down again it was empty.

'A jolly boon companion you are going to have,' said the aide-de-camp to Hornblower.

'How is she going to be my companion?' asked Hornblower, quite bewildered.

The aide-de-camp looked at him pityingly.

'So you have not been informed?' he asked. 'As always, the man most concerned is the last to know. When you sail with your despatches tomorrow you will have the honour of bearing Her Grace with you to England.'

'God bless my soul,' said Hornblower.

'Let's hope He does,' said the aide-de-camp piously, nosing his wine. 'Poor stuff this sweet Malaga is. Old Hare bought a job lot in '95, and every governor since then seems to think it's his duty to use it up.'

'But who *is* she?' asked Hornblower.

'Her Grace the Duchess of Wharfdale,' replied the aide-de-camp. 'Did you not hear Lady Dalrymple's introduction?'

'But she doesn't talk like a duchess,' protested Hornblower.

'No. The old duke was in his dotage when he married her. She was an innkeeper's widow, so her friends say. You can imagine, if you like, what her enemies say.'

'But what is she doing here?' went on Hornblower.

'She is on her way back to England. She was at Florence when the French marched in, I understand. She reached Leghorn, and bribed a coaster to bring her here. She asked Sir Hew to find her a passage, and Sir Hew asked the Admiral – Sir Hew would ask anyone for anything on behalf of a duchess, even one said by her friends to be an innkeeper's widow.'

'I see,' said Hornblower.

There was a burst of merriment from the head of the table, and the duchess was prodding the governor's scarlet-coated ribs with the handle of her knife, as if to make sure he saw the joke.

'Maybe you will not lack for mirth on your homeward voyage,' said the aide-de-camp.

Just then a smoking sirloin of beef was put down in front of Hornblower, and all his other worries vanished before the necessity of carving it and remembering his manners. He took the carving knife and fork gingerly in his hands and glanced round at the company.

'May I help you to some of this beef, Your Grace? Madam? Sir? Well done or underdone, sir? A little of the brown fat?'

In the hot room the sweat ran down his face as he wrestled with the joint; he was fortunate that most of the guests desired helpings from the other removes so that he had little carving to do. He put a couple of haggled slices on his own plate as the simplest way of concealing the worst results of his own handiwork.

'Beef from Tetuan,' sniffed the aide-de-camp. 'Tough and stringy.'

That was all very well for a governor's aide-de-camp–he could not guess how delicious was this food to a young naval officer fresh from beating about at sea in an over-crowded frigate. Even the thought of having to act as host to a duchess could not entirely spoil Hornblower's appetite. And the final dishes, the meringues and macaroons, the custards and the fruits, were ecstasy for a young man whose last pudding had been currant duff last Sunday.

'Those sweet things spoil a man's palate,' said the aide-de-camp–much Hornblower cared.

They were drinking formal toasts now. Hornblower stood for the King and the royal family, and raised his glass for the duchess.

'And now for the enemy,' said Sir Hew, 'may their treasure galleons try to cross the Atlantic.'

'A supplement to that, Sir Hew,' said the commodore at the other end, 'may the Dons make up their minds to leave Cadiz.'

There was a growl almost like wild animals from round the table. Most of the naval officers present were from Jervis's Mediterranean squadron which had beaten about in the Atlantic for the past several months hoping to catch the Spaniards should they come out. Jervis had to detach his ships to Gibraltar two at a time to replenish their stores, and these officers were from the two ships of the line present at the moment in Gibraltar.

'Johnny Jervis would say amen to that,' said Sir Hew. 'A bumper to the Dons then, gentlemen, and may they come out from Cadiz.'

The ladies left them then, gathered together by Lady Dalrymple, and as soon as it was decently possible Hornblower made his excuses and slipped away, determined not to be heavy with wine the night before he sailed in independent command.

Maybe the prospect of the coming on board of the duchess was a useful counter-irritant, and saved Hornblower from worrying too much about his first command. He was up before dawn–before even the brief Mediterranean twilight had begun–to see that his precious ship was in condition to face the sea, and the enemies who swarmed upon the sea. He had four popgun four-pounders to deal with those enemies, which meant that he was safe from no one; his was the weakest vessel at sea, for the smallest trading brig carried a more powerful armament. So that like all weak creatures his only safety lay in flight–Hornblower looked aloft in the half-light, where the sails would be set on which so much might depend. He went over the watch bill with his two watch-keeping officers, Midshipman Hunter and Master's Mate Winyatt, to make sure that every man of his crew of eleven knew his duty. Then all that remained was to put on his smartest seagoing uniform, try to eat breakfast, and wait for the duchess.

She came early, fortunately; Their Excellencies had had to rise at a most unpleasant hour to see her off. Mr Hunter reported the approach of the governor's launch with suppressed excitement.

'Thank you, Mr Hunter,' said Hornblower coldly–that was what the service demanded, even though not so many weeks before they had been playing follow-my-leader through the *Indefatigable*'s rigging together.

The launch swirled alongside, and two neatly dressed seamen hooked on the ladder. *Le Rêve* had such a small freeboard that boarding her presented no problems even for ladies. The governor stepped on board to the twittering of the only two pipes *Le Rêve* could muster, and Lady Dalrymple followed him. Then came the duchess, and the duchess's companion; the latter was a younger woman, as beautiful as the duchess must once have been. A couple of aides-de-camp followed, and by that time the minute deck of *Le Rêve* was positively crowded, so that there was no room left to bring up the duchess's baggage.

'Let us show you your quarters, Your Grace,' said the governor.

Lady Dalrymple squawked her sympathy at sight of the minute cabin, which the two cots almost filled, and everyone's head, inevitably, bumped against the deck-beam above.

'We shall live through it,' said the duchess stoically, 'an' that's more than many a man makin' a little trip to Tyburn could say.'

One of these aides-de-camp produced a last minute packet of despatches and demanded Hornblower's signature on the receipt; the last farewells were said, and Sir Hew and Lady Dalrymple went down the side again to the twittering of the pipes.

'Man the windlass!' bellowed Hornblower the moment the launch's crew bent to their oars.

A few seconds' lusty work brought *Le Rêve* up to her anchor.

'Anchor's aweigh, sir,' reported Winyatt.

'Jib halliards!' shouted Hornblower. 'Mains'l halliards!'

Le Rêve came round before the wind as her sails were set and her rudder took grip on the water. Everyone was so busy catting the anchor and setting sail that it was Hornblower himself who dipped his colours in salute as *Le Rêve* crept out beyond the mole before the gentle south-easter, and dipped her nose to the first of the big Atlantic rollers coming in through the Gut. Through the skylight beside him he heard a clatter and a wail, as something fell in the cabin with that first roll, but he could spare no attention for the women below. He had the glass to his eye now, training it first on Algeciras and then upon Tarifa–some well-manned privateer or ship of war might easily dash out to snap up such a defenceless prey as *Le Rêve*. He could not relax while the forenoon watch wore on. They rounded Cape Marroqui and he set a course for St Vincent, and then the mountains of Southern Spain began to sink below the horizon. Cape Trafalgar was just visible on the starboard bow when at last he shut the telescope and began to wonder about dinner; it was pleasant to be captain of his own ship and to be able to order dinner when he chose. His aching legs told him he had been on his feet too long–eleven continuous hours; if the future brought him many independent commands he would wear himself out by this sort of behaviour.

Down below he relaxed gratefully on the locker, and sent the cook to knock at the duchess's cabin door to ask with his compliments if all was well; he heard the duchess's sharp voice saying that they needed nothing, not even dinner. Hornblower philosophically shrugged his shoulders and ate his dinner with a young man's appetite. He went on deck again as night closed in upon them; Winyatt had the watch.

'It's coming up thick, sir,' he said.

So it was. The sun was invisible on the horizon, engulfed in watery mist. It was the price he had to pay for a fair wind, he knew; in the winter months in these latitudes there was always likely to be fog where the cool land breeze reached the Atlantic.

'It'll be thicker still by morning,' he said gloomily, and revised his night orders, setting a course due west instead of west by north as he originally intended. He wanted to make certain of keeping clear of Cape St Vincent in the event of fog.

That was one of those minute trifles which may affect a man's whole after life–Hornblower had plenty of time later to reflect on what might have happened had he not ordered that alteration of course. During the night he was often on deck, peering through the increasing mist, but at the time when the crisis came he was down below snatching a little sleep. What woke him was a seaman shaking his shoulder violently.

'Please, sir. Please, sir. Mr Hunter sent me. Please, sir, won't you come on deck, he says, sir.'

'I'll come,' said Hornblower, blinking himself awake and rolling out of his cot.

The faintest beginnings of dawn were imparting some slight luminosity to the mist which was close about them. *Le Rêve* was lurching over an ugly sea with barely enough wind behind her to give her steerage way. Hunter was standing with his back to the wheel in an attitude of tense anxiety.

'Listen!' he said, as Hornblower appeared.

He half-whispered the word, and in his excitement he omitted the 'sir' which was due to his captain–and in his excitement Hornblower did not notice the omission. Hornblower listened. He heard the shipboard noises he could expect–the clattering of the blocks as *Le Rêve* lurched, the sound of the sea at her bows. Then he heard other shipboard noises. There were other blocks clattering; the sea was breaking beneath other bows.

'There's a ship close alongside,' said Hornblower.

'Yes, sir,' said Hunter. 'And after I sent below for you I heard an order given. And it was in Spanish–some foreign tongue, anyway.'

The tenseness of fear was all about the little ship like the fog.

'Call all hands. Quietly,' said Hornblower.

But as he gave the order he wondered if it would be any use. He could send his men to their stations, he could man and load his four-pounders, but if that ship out there in the fog was of any force greater than a merchant ship he was in deadly peril. Then he tried to comfort himself–perhaps the ship was some fat Spanish galleon bulging with treasure, and were he to board her boldly she would become his prize and make him rich for life.

'A 'appy Valentine's day to you,' said a voice beside him, and he nearly jumped out of his skin with surprise. He had actually forgotten the presence of the duchess on board.

'Stop that row!' he whispered furiously at her, and she pulled up abruptly in astonishment. She was bundled up in a cloak and hood against the damp air, and no further detail could be seen of her in the darkness and fog.

'May I hask—' she began.

'Shut up!' whispered Hornblower.

A harsh voice could be heard through the fog, other voices repeating the order, whistles being blown, much noise and bustle.

'That's Spanish, sir, isn't it?' whispered Hunter.

'Spanish for certain. Calling the watch. Listen!'

The two double-strokes of a ship's bell came to them across the water. Four bells in the morning watch. And instantly from all round them a dozen other bells could be heard, as if echoing the first.

'We're in the middle of a fleet, by God!' whispered Hunter.

'Big ships, too, sir,' supplemented Winyatt who had joined them with the calling of all hands. 'I could hear half a dozen different pipes when they called watch.'

'The Dons are out, then,' said Hunter.

And the course I set has taken us into the midst of them, thought Hornblower bitterly. The coincidence was maddening, heartbreaking. But he forebore to waste breath over it. He even suppressed the frantic gibe that rose to his lips at the memory of Sir Hew's toast about the Spaniards coming out from Cadiz.

'They're setting more sail,' was what he said. 'Dagos snug down at night, just like some fat Indiaman. They only set their t'gallants at daybreak.'

All round them through the fog could be heard the whine of sheaves in blocks, the stamp-and-go of the men at the halliards, the sound of ropes thrown on decks, the chatter of a myriad voices.

'They make enough noise about it, blast 'em,' said Hunter.

The tension under which he laboured was apparent as he stood straining to peer through the mist.

'Please God they're on a different course to us,' said Winyatt, more sensibly. 'Then we'll soon be through 'em.'

'Not likely,' said Hornblower.

Le Rêve was running almost directly before what little wind there was; if the Spaniards were beating against it or had it on their beam they would be crossing her course at a considerable angle, so that the volume of sound from the nearest ship would have diminished or increased considerably in this time, and there was no indication of that whatever. It was far more likely that *Le Rêve* had overhauled the Spanish fleet under its nightly short canvas and had sailed forward into the middle of it. It was a problem what to do next in that case, to shorten sail, or to heave to, and let the Spaniards get ahead of them again, or to clap on sail to pass through. But the passage of the minutes brought clear proof that fleet and sloop were on practically the same course, as otherwise they could hardly fail to pass some ship close. As long as the mist held they were safest as they were.

But that was hardly to be expected with the coming of day.

'Can't we alter course, sir?' asked Winyatt.

'Wait,' said Hornblower.

In the faint growing light he had seen shreds of denser mist blowing past them–a clear indication that they could not hope for continuous fog. At that moment they ran out of a fog bank into a clear patch of water.

'There she is, by God!' said Hunter.

Both officers and seamen began to move about in sudden panic.

'Stand still, damn you!' rasped Hornblower, his nervous tension releasing itself in the fierce monosyllables.

Less than a cable's length away a three-decked ship of the line was standing along parallel to them on their starboard side. Ahead and on the port side could be seen the outlines, still shadowy, of other battleships. Nothing could save them if they drew attention to themselves; all that could be done was to keep going as if they had as much right there as the ships of the line. It was possible that in the happy-go-lucky Spanish navy the officer of the watch over there did not know that no sloop like *Le Rêve* was attached to the fleet–or even possibly by a miracle there *might* be one. *Le Rêve* was French built and French rigged, after all. Side by side *Le Rêve* and the battleship sailed over the lumpy sea. They were within point-blank range of fifty big guns, when one well-aimed shot would sink them. Hunter was uttering filthy curses under his breath, but discipline had asserted itself; a telescope over there on the Spaniard's deck would not discover any suspicious bustle on board the sloop. Another shred of fog drifted past them, and then they were deep in a fresh fog bank.

'Thank God!' said Hunter, indifferent to the contrast between this present piety and his preceding blasphemy.

'Hands wear ship,' said Hornblower. 'Lay her on the port tack.'

There was no need to tell the hands to do it quietly; they were as well aware of their danger as anyone. *Le Rêve* silently rounded-to, the sheets were hauled in and coiled down without a sound; and the sloop, as close to the wind as she would lie, heeled to the small wind, meeting the lumpy waves with her port bow.

'We'll be crossing their course now,' said Hornblower.

'Please God it'll be under their stern and not their bows,' said Winyatt.

There was the duchess still in her cloak and hood, standing right aft as much out of the way as possible.

'Don't you think Your Grace had better go below?' asked Hornblower, making use by a great effort of the formal form of address.

'Oh, no, *please*,' said the duchess. 'I couldn't bear it.' Hornblower shrugged his shoulders, and promptly forgot the duchess's presence again as a new anxiety struck him. He dived below and came up again with the two big sealed envelopes of despatches. He took a belaying pin from the rail and began very carefully to tie the envelopes to the pin with a bit of line.

'Please,' said the duchess, 'please, Mr Hornblower, tell me what you are doing?'

'I want to make sure these will sink when I throw them overboard if we're captured,' said Hornblower grimly.

'Then they'll be lost for good?'

'Better that than that the Spaniards should read 'em,' said Hornblower with all the patience he could muster.

'I could look after them for you,' said the duchess. 'Indeed I could.'

Hornblower looked keenly at her.

'No,' he said, 'they might search your baggage. Probably they would.'

'Baggage!' said the duchess. 'As if I'd put them in my baggage! I'll put them next my skin–they won't search *me* in any case. They'll never find 'em, not if I put 'em up my petticoats.'

There was a brutal realism about those words that staggered Hornblower a little, but which also brought him to admit to himself that there was something in what the duchess was saying.

'If they capture us,' said the duchess,'—I pray they won't, but if they do–they'll never keep me prisoner. You know that. They'll send me to Lisbon or put me aboard a King's ship as soon as they can. Then the despatches will be delivered eventually. Late, but better late than never.'

'That's so,' mused Hornblower.

'I'll guard them like my life,' said the duchess. 'I swear I'll never part from them. I'll tell no one I have them, not until I hand them to a King's officer.'

She met Hornblower's eyes with transparent honesty in her expression.

'Fog's thinning, sir,' said Winyatt.

'Quick!' said the duchess.

There was no time for further debate. Hornblower slipped the envelopes from their binding of rope and handed them over to her, and replaced the belaying pin in the rail.

'These damned French fashions,' said the duchess. 'I was right when I said I'd put these letters up my petticoats. There's no room in my bosom.'

Certainly the upper part of her gown was not at all capacious; the waist was close up under the armpits and the rest of the dress hung down from there quite straight in utter defiance of anatomy.

'Give me a yard of that rope, quick!' said the duchess.

Winyatt cut her a length of the line with his knife and handed it to her. Already she was hauling at her petticoats; the appalled Hornblower saw a gleam of white thigh above her stocking tops before he tore his glance away. The fog was certainly thinning.

'You can look at me now,' said the duchess; but her petticoats only just fell in time as Hornblower looked round again. 'They're inside my shift, next to my skin as I promised. With these Directory fashions no one wears stays any more. So I tied the rope round my waist outside my shift. One envelope is flat against my chest and the other against my back. Would you suspect anything?'

She turned round for Hornblower's inspection.

'No, nothing shows,' he said. 'I must thank Your Grace.'

'There is a certain thickening,' said the duchess, 'but it does not matter what the Spaniards suspect as long as they do not suspect the truth.'

Momentary cessation of the need for action brought some embarrassment to Hornblower. To discuss with a woman her shift and stays–or the absence of them–was a strange thing to do.

A watery sun, still nearly level, was breaking through the mist and shining in his eyes. The mainsail cast a watery shadow on the deck. With every second the sun was growing brighter.

'Here it comes,' said Hunter.

The horizon ahead expanded rapidly, from a few yards to a hundred, from a hundred yards to half a mile. The sea was covered with ships. No less than six were in plain sight, four ships of the line and two big frigates, with the red-and-gold of Spain at their mastheads, and, what marked them even more obviously as Spaniards, huge wooden crosses hanging at their peaks.

'Wear ship again, Mr Hunter,' said Hornblower. 'Back into the fog.'

That was the once chance of safety. Those ships running down towards them were bound to ask questions, and they could not hope to avoid them all. *Le Rêve* spun round on her heel, but the fog-bank from which she had emerged was already attentuated, sucked up by the thirsty sun. They could see a drifting stretch of it ahead, but it was lazily rolling away from them at the same time as it was dwindling. The heavy sound of a cannon shot reached their ears, and close on their starboard quarter a ball threw up a fountain of water before plunging into the side of a wave just ahead. Hornblower looked round just in time to see the last of the puff of smoke from the bows of the frigate astern pursuing them.

'Starboard two points,' he said to the helmsman, trying to gauge at one and the same moment the frigate's course, the direction of the wind, the bearing of the other ships, and that of the thin last nucleus of that wisp of fog.

'Starboard two points,' said the helmsman.

'Fore and main sheets!' said Hunter.

Another shot, far astern this time but laid true for line; Hornblower suddenly remembered the duchess.

'You must go below, Your Grace,' he said curtly.

'Oh, no, no, no!' burst out the duchess with angry vehemence. 'Please let me stay here. I can't go below to where that seasick maid of mine lies hoping to die. Not in that stinking box of a cabin.'

There would be no safety in that cabin, Hornblower reflected–*Le Rêve*'s scantlings were too fragile to keep out any shot at all. Down below the water line in the hold the women might be safe, but they would have to lie flat on top of beef barrels.

'Sail ahead!' screamed the lookout.

The mist there was parting and the outline of a ship of the line was emerging from it, less than a mile away and on almost the same course as *Le Rêve*'s. Thud–thud from the frigate astern. Those gunshots by now would have warned the whole Spanish fleet that something unusual was happening. The battleship ahead would know that the little sloop was being pursued. A ball tore through the air close by, with its usual terrifying noise. The ship ahead was awaiting their coming; Hornblower saw her topsails slowly turning.

'Hands to the sheets!' said Hornblower. 'Mr Hunter, jibe her over.'

Le Rêve came round again, heading for the lessening gap on the port side. The frigate astern turned to intercept. More jets of smoke from her bows. With an appalling noise a shot passed within a few feet of Hornblower, so that the wind of it made him stagger. There was a hole in the mainsail.

'Your Grace,' said Hornblower, 'those aren't warning shots—'

It was the ship of the line which fired them, having succeeded in clearing away and manning some of her upper-deck guns. It was as if the end of the world had come. One shot hit *Le Rêve*'s hull, and they felt the deck heave under their feet as a result as if the little ship were disintegrating. But the mast was hit at the same moment, stays and shrouds parting, splinters raining all round. Mast, sails, boom, gaff and all went from above them over the side to windward. The wreckage dragged in the sea and turned the helpless wreck round with the last of her way. The little group aft stood momentarily dazed.

'Anybody hurt?' asked Hornblower, recovering himself.

'On'y a scratch, sir,' said one voice.

It seemed a miracle that no one was killed.

'Carpenter's mate, sound the well,' said Hornblower and then, recollecting himself, 'No, damn it. Belay that order. If the Dons can save the ship, let 'em try.'

Already the ship of the line whose salvo had done the damage was filling her topsails again and bearing away from them, while the frigate which had pursued them was running down on them fast. A wailing figure came scrambling out of the afterhatch way. It was the duchess's maid, so mad with terror that her seasickness was forgotten. The duchess put a protective arm round her and tried to comfort her.

'Your Grace had better look to your baggage,' said Hornblower. 'No doubt you'll be leaving us shortly for other quarters with the Dons. I hope you will be more comfortable.'

He was trying desperately hard to speak in a matter-of-fact way, as if nothing out of the ordinary were happening, as if he were not soon to be a prisoner of the Spaniards; but the duchess saw the working of the usually firm mouth, and marked how the hands were tight clenched.

'How can I tell you how sorry I am about this?' asked the duchess, her voice soft with pity.

'That makes it the harder for me to bear,' said Hornblower, and he even forced a smile.

The Spanish frigate was just rounding-to, a cable's length to windward.

'Please, sir,' said Hunter.

'Well?'

'We can fight, sir. You give the word. Cold shot to drop in the boats when they try to board. We could beat 'em off once, perhaps.'

Hornblower's tortured misery nearly made him snap out 'Don't be a fool', but he checked himself. He contented himself with pointing to the frigate. Twenty guns were glaring at them at far less than point-blank range. The very boat the frigate was hoisting out would be manned by at least twice as many men as *Le Rêve* carried–she was no bigger than many a pleasure yacht. It was not odds of ten to one, or a hundred to one, but odds of ten thousand to one.

'I understand, sir,' said Hunter.

Now the Spanish frigate's boat was in the water, about to shove off.

'A private word with you please, Mr Hornblower,' said the duchess suddenly.

Hunter and Winyatt heard what she said, and withdrew out of earshot.

'Yes, Your Grace?' said Hornblower.

The duchess stood there, still with her arm round her weeping maid, looking straight at him.

'I'm no more of a duchess than you are,' she said.

'Good God!' said Hornblower. 'Who–who are you, then?'

'Kitty Cobham.'

The name meant a little to Hornblower, but only a little.

'You're too young for that name to have any memories for you, Mr Hornblower, I see. It's five years since I last trod the boards.'

That was it. Kitty Cobham the actress.

'I can't tell it all now,' said the duchess–the Spanish boat was dancing over the waves towards them. 'But when the French marched into Florence that was only the last of my misfortunes. I was penniless when I escaped from them. Who would lift a finger for a onetime actress–one who had been betrayed and deserted? What was I to do? But a duchess–that was another story. Old Dalrymple at Gibraltar could not do enough for the Duchess of Wharfedale.'

'Why did you choose that title?' asked Hornblower in spite of himself.

'I knew of her,' said the duchess with a shrug of the shoulders. 'I knew her to be what I played her as. That was why I chose her–I always played character parts better than straight comedy. And not nearly so tedious in a long role.'

'But my despatches!' said Hornblower in a sudden panic of realization. 'Give them back, quick.'

'If you wish me to,' said the duchess. 'But I can still be the duchess when the Spaniards come. They will still set me free as speedily as they can. I'll guard those despatches better than my life–I swear it, I swear it! In less than a month, I'll deliver them, if you trust me.'

Hornblower looked at the pleading eyes. She might be a spy, ingeniously trying to preserve the despatches from being thrown overboard before the Spaniards took possession. But no spy could have hoped that *Le Rêve* would run into the midst of the Spanish fleet.

'I made use of the bottle, I know,' said the Duchess. 'I drank. Yes, I did. But I stayed sober in Gibraltar, didn't I? And I won't touch a drop, not a drop, until I'm in England. I'll swear that, too. Please, sir–please. I beg of you. Let me do what I can for my country.'

It was a strange decision for a man of nineteen to have to make–one who had never exchanged a word with an actress in his life before. A harsh voice overside told him that the Spanish boat was about to hook on,

'Keep them, then,' said Hornblower. 'Deliver them when you can.'

He had not taken his eyes from her face. He was looking for a gleam of triumph in her expression. Had he seen anything of the sort he would have torn the despatches from her body at that moment. But all he saw was the natural look of pleasure, and it was then that he made up his mind to trust her–not before.

'Oh, thank you, sir,' said the duchess.

The Spanish boat had hooked on now, and a Spanish lieutenant was awkwardly trying to climb aboard. He arrived on the deck on his hands and knees, and Hornblower stepped over to receive him as he got to his feet. Captor and captive exchange bows. Hornblower could not understand what the

Spaniard said, but obviously they were formal sentences that he was using. The Spaniard caught sight of the two women aft and halted in surprise; Hornblower hastily made the presentation in what he hoped was Spanish.

'Señor el tenente Espanol,' he said. 'Señora la Duquesa de Wharfedale.'

The title clearly had its effect; the lieutenant bowed profoundly, and his bow was received with the most lofty aloofness by the duchess. Hornblower could be sure the despatches were safe. That was some alleviation of the misery of standing here on the deck of his water-logged little ship, a prisoner of the Spaniards. As he waited he heard, from far to leeward, roll upon roll of thunder coming up against the wind. No thunder could endure that long. What he could hear must be the broadsides of ships in action–of fleets in action. Somewhere over there by Cape St Vincent the British fleet must have caught the Spaniards at last. Fiercer and fiercer sounded the roll of the artillery. There was excitement among the Spaniards who had scrambled on to the deck of *Le Rêve*, while Hornblower stood bareheaded waiting to be taken into captivity.

Captivity was a dreadful thing. Once the numbness had worn off Hornblower came to realize what a dreadful thing it was. Not even the news of the dreadful battering which the Spanish navy had received at St Vincent could relieve the misery and despair of being a prisoner. It was not the physical conditions–ten square feet of floor space per man in an empty sail loft at Ferrol along with other captive warrant officers–for they were no worse than what a junior officer often had to put up with at sea. It was the loss of freedom, the fact of being a captive, that was so dreadful.

There were four months of it before the first letter came through to Hornblower; the Spanish government, inefficient in all ways, had the worst postal system in Europe. But here was the letter, addressed and re-addressed, now safely in his hands after he had practically snatched it from a stupid Spanish non-commissioned officer who had been puzzling over the strange name. Hornblower did not know the handwriting, and when he broke the seal and opened the letter the salutation made him think for a moment that he had opened someone else's letter.

'Darling Boy,' it began. Now who on earth would call him that? He read on in a dream.

> 'Darling Boy,
>
> I hope it will give you happiness to hear that what you gave me has reached its destination. They told me, when I delivered it, that you are a prisoner, and my heart bleeds for you. And they told me too that they were pleased with you for what you had done. And one of those admirals is a shareholder in Drury Lane. Whoever would have thought of such a thing? But he smiled at me, and I smiled at him. I did not know he was a shareholder then, and I only smiled out of the kindness of my heart. And all that I told him about my dangers and perils with my precious burden were only histrionic exercises, I am afraid. Yet he believed me, and so struck was he by my smile and my adventures, that he demanded a part for me from Sherry, and behold, now I am playing second lead, usually a tragic mother, and receiving the acclaim of the groundlings. There are compensations in growing old, which I am discovering too. And I have not tasted wine since I saw you last, nor shall I ever again. As one more reward, my admiral promised me that he would forward this letter to you in the next cartel–an expression which no

doubt means more to you than to me. I only hope that it reaches you in good time and brings you comfort in your affliction.

I pray nightly for you.

Ever your devoted friend,
Katharine Cobham.'

Comfort in his affliction? A little, perhaps. There was some comfort in knowing that the despatches had been delivered; there was some comfort in a second-hand report that Their Lordships were pleased with him. There was comfort even in knowing that the duchess was re-established on the stage. But the sum total was nothing compared with his misery.

Here was a guard come to bring him to the commandant, and beside the commandant was the Irish renegade who served as interpreter. There were further papers on the commandant's desk–it looked as if the same cartel which had brought in Kitty Cobham's note had brought in letters for the commandant.

'Good afternoon, sir,' said the commandant, always polite, offering a chair.

'Good afternoon, sir, and many thanks,' said Hornblower. He was learning Spanish slowly and painfully.

'You have been promoted,' said the Irishman in English.

'W-what?' said Hornblower.

'Promoted,' said the Irishman. 'Here is the letter–"The Spanish authorities are informed that on account of his meritorious service the acting-commission of Mr Horatio Hornblower, midshipman and acting-lieutenant, has been confirmed. Their Lordships of the Admiralty express their confidence that Mr Horatio Hornblower will be admitted immediately to the privileges of commissioned rank." There you are, young man.'

'My felicitations, sir,' said the commandant.

'Many thanks, sir,' said Hornblower.

The commandant was a kindly old gentleman with a pleasant smile for the awkward young man. He went on to say more, but Hornblower's Spanish was not equal to the technicalities he used, and Hornblower in despair looked at the interpreter.

'Now that you are a commissioned officer,' said the latter, 'you will be transferred to the quarters for captured officers.'

'Thank you,' said Hornblower.

'You will receive the half pay of your rank.'

'Thank you.'

'And your parole will be accepted. You will be at liberty to visit in the town and the neighbourhood for two hours each day on giving your parole.'

'Thank you,' said Hornblower.

Perhaps, during the long months which followed, it was some mitigation of his unhappiness that for two hours each day his parole gave him freedom; freedom to wander in the streets of the little town, to have a cup of chocolate or a glass of wine–providing he had any money–making polite and laborious conversation with Spanish soldiers or sailors or civilians. But it was better to spend his two hours wandering over the goat paths of the headland in the wind and the sun, in the companionship of the sea, which might alleviate the sick misery of captivity. There was slightly better food, slightly better quarters.

And there was the knowledge that now he was a lieutenant, that he held the King's commission, that if ever, ever, the war should end and he should be set free he could starve on half pay–for with the end of the war there would be no employment for junior lieutenants. But he had earned his promotion. He had gained the approval of authority, that was something to think about on his solitary walks.

There came a day of south-westerly gales, with the wind shrieking in from across the Atlantic. Across three thousand miles of water it came, building up its strength unimpeded on its way, and heaping up the sea into racing mountain ridges which came crashing in upon the Spanish coast in thunder and spray. Hornblower stood on the headland above Ferroll harbour, holding his worn greatcoat about him as he leaned forward into the wind to keep his footing. So powerful was the wind that it was difficult to breathe while facing it. If he turned his back he could breathe more easily, but then the wind blew his wild hair forward over his eyes, almost inverted his greatcoat over his head, and furthermore forced him into little tottering steps down the slope towards Ferrol, whither he had no wish to return at present. For two hours he was alone and free, and those two hours were precious. He could breathe the Atlantic air, he could walk, he could do as he liked during that time. He could stare out to sea; it was not unusual to catch sight, from the headland, of some British ship of war which might be working slowly along the coast in the hope of snapping up a coasting vessel while keeping a watchful eye upon the Spanish naval activity. When such a ship went by during Hornblower's two hours of freedom, he would stand and gaze at it, as a man dying of thirst might gaze at a bucket of water held beyond his reach; he would note all the little details, the cut of the topsails and the style of the paint, while misery wrung his bowels. For this was the end of his second year as a prisoner of war. For twenty-two months, for twenty-two hours every day, he had been under lock and key, herded with five other junior lieutenants in a single room in the fortress of Ferrol. And today the wind roared by him, shouting in its outrageous freedom. He was facing into the wind; before him lay Corunna, its white houses resembling pieces of sugar scattered over the slopes. Between him and Corunna was all the open space of Corunna Bay, flogged white by the wind, and on his left hand was the narrow entrance to Ferrol Bay. On his right was the open Atlantic; from the foot of the low cliffs there the long wicked reef of the Dientes del Diablo–the Devil's Teeth–ran out to the northward, square across the path of the racing rollers driven by the wind. At half-minute intervals the rollers would crash against the reef with an impact that shook even the solid headland on which Hornblower stood, and each roller dissolved into spray which was instantly whirled away by the wind to reveal again the long black tusks of the rocks.

Hornblower was not alone on the headland; a few yards away from him a Spanish militia artilleryman on lookout duty gazed with watery eyes through a telescope with which he continually swept the seaward horizon. When at war with England it was necessary to be vigilant; a fleet might suddenly appear over the horizon, to land a little army to capture Ferrol, and burn the dockyard installations and the ships. No hope of that today, thought Hornblower–there could be no landing of troops on that raging lee shore.

But all the same the sentry was undoubtedly staring very fixedly through his telescope right to windward; the sentry wiped his streaming eyes with his coat sleeve and stared again. Hornblower peered in the same direction, unable to see what it was that had attracted the sentry's attention. The sentry muttered something to himself, and then turned and ran clumsily down to the little stone guardhouse where sheltered the rest of the militia detachment stationed there to man the guns of the battery on the headland. He returned with the sergeant of the guard, who took the telescope and peered out to windward in the direction pointed out by the sentry. The two of them jabbered in their barbarous Gallego dialect; in two years of steady application Hornblower had mastered Galician as well as Castilian, but in that howling gale he could not intercept a word. Then finally, just as the sergeant nodded in agreement, Hornblower saw with his naked eyes what they were discussing. A pale grey square on the horizon above the grey sea–a ship's topsail. She must be running before the gale making for the shelter of Corunna or Ferrol.

It was a rash thing for a ship to do, because it would be no easy matter for her to round-to into Corunna Bay and anchor, and it would be even harder for her to hit off the narrow entrance to the Ferrol inlet. A cautious captain would claw out to sea and heave-to with a generous amount of sea room until the wind moderated. These Spanish captains, said Hornblower to himself, with a shrug of his shoulders; but naturally they would always wish to make harbour as quickly as possible when the Royal Navy was sweeping the seas. But the sergeant and the sentry were more excited than the appearance of a single ship would seem to justify. Hornblower could contain himself no longer, and edged up to the chattering pair, mentally framing his sentences in the unfamiliar tongue.

'Please, gentlemen,' he said, and then started again, shouting against the wind. 'Please, gentlemen, what is it that you see?'

The sergeant gave him a glance, and then, reaching some undiscoverable decision, handed over the telescope–Hornblower could hardly restrain himself from snatching it from his hands. With the telescope to his eye he could see far better; he could see a ship-rigged vessel, under close-reefed topsails (and that was much more sail than it was wise to carry) hurtling wildly towards them. And then a moment later he saw the other square of grey. Another topsail. Another ship. The foretopmast was noticeably shorter than the maintopmast, and not only that, but the whole effect was familiar–she was a British ship of war, a British frigate, plunging along in hot pursuit of the other, which seemed most likely to be a Spanish privateer. It was a close chase; it would be a very near thing, whether the Spaniard would reach the protection of the shore batteries before the frigate overhauled her. He lowered the telescope to rest his eye, and instantly the sergeant snatched it from him. He had been watching the Englishman's face, and Hornblower's expression had told him what he wanted to know. Those two ships out there were behaving in such a way as to justify his rousing his officer and giving the alarm. Sergeant and sentry went running back to the guardhouse, and in a few moments the artillerymen were pouring out to man the batteries on the verge of the cliff. Soon enough came a mounted officer urging his horse up the path; a single glance through the telescope sufficed for him. He went clattering down to the battery and the next moment the boom of a gun from there alerted the rest of the defences. The flag of Spain rose up the flagstaff beside the battery, and Hornblower saw an answering flag rise up the flagstaff on San Anton where another battery guarded Corunna Bay. All the guns of the harbour defences were now manned, and there would be no mercy shown to any English ship that came in range.

Pursuer and pursued had covered quite half the distance already towards Corunna. They were hull-up over the horizon now to Hornblower on the headland, who could see them plunging madly over the grey sea–Hornblower momentarily expected to see them carry away their topmasts or their sails blow from the bolt-ropes. The frigate was half a mile astern still, and she would have to be much closer than that to have any hope of hitting with her guns in that sea. Here came the commandant and his staff, clattering on horseback up the path to see the climax of the drama; the commandant caught sight of Hornblower and doffed his hat with Spanish courtesy, while Hornblower, hatless, tried to bow with equal courtesy. Hornblower walked over to him with an urgent request–he had to lay his hand on the Spaniard's saddlebow and shout up into his face to be understood.

'My parole expires in ten minutes, sir,' he yelled. 'May I please extend it? May I please stay?'

'Yes, stay, señor,' said the commandant generously.

Hornblower watched the chase, and at the same time observed closely the preparations for defence. He had given his parole, but no part of the gentlemanly code prevented him from taking note of all he could see. One day he might be free, and one day it might be useful to know all about the defences of Ferrol. Everyone else of the large group on the headland was watching the chase, and excitement rose higher as the ships came racing nearer. The English captain was keeping a hundred yards or more to seaward of the Spaniard, but he was quite unable to overhaul her–in fact it seemed to Hornblower as if the Spaniard was actually increasing his lead. But the English frigate being to seaward meant that escape in that direction was cut off. Any turn away from the land would reduce the Spaniard's lead to a negligible distance. If he did not get into Corunna Bay or Ferrol Inlet he was doomed.

Now he was level with the Corunna headland, and it was time to put his helm hard over and turn into the bay and hope that his anchors would hold in the lee of the headland. But with a wind of that violence hurtling against cliffs and headlands strange things can happen. A flaw of wind coming out of the bay must have caught her aback as she tried to round-to. Hornblower saw her stagger, saw her reel as the backlash died away and the gale caught her again. She was laid over almost on her beam-ends and as she righted herself Hornblower saw a momentary gap open up in her maintopsail. It was momentary because from the time the gap appeared the life of the topsail was momentary; the gap appeared and at once the sail vanished, blown into ribbons as soon as its continuity was impaired. With the loss of its balancing pressure the ship became unmanageable; the gale pressing against the foretopsail swung her round again before the wind like a weathervane. If there had been time to spare to set a fragment of sail farther aft she would have been saved, but in those enclosed waters there was no time to spare. At one moment she was about to round the Corunna headland; at the next she had lost the opportunity for ever.

There was still the chance that she might fetch the opening to the Ferrol inlet; the wind was nearly fair for her to do that–nearly. Hornblower on the Ferrol headland was thinking along with the Spanish captain down there on the heaving deck. He saw him try to steady the ship so as to head for the narrow entrance, notorious among seamen for its difficulty. He saw him get her on her course, and for a few seconds as she flew across the mouth of the bay it seemed as if the Spaniard would succeed, against all probability, in exactly hitting off the entrance to the inlet. Then the backlash hit her again. Had she been quick on the helm she might still have been safe, but with her sail pressure so outbalanced she was bound to be slow in her response to her rudder. The shrieking wind blew her bows round, and it was instantly obvious too, that she was doomed, but the Spanish captain played the game out to the last. He would not pile his ship up against the foot of the low cliffs. He put his helm hard over; with the aid of the wind rebounding from the cliffs he made a gallant attempt to clear the Ferrol headland altogether and give himself a chance to claw out to sea.

A gallant attempt, but doomed to failure as soon as begun; he actually cleared the headland, but the wind blew his bows round again, and, bows first, the ship plunged right at the long jagged line of the Devil's Teeth. Hornblower, the commandant, and everyone, hurried across the headland to look down at the final act of the tragedy. With tremendous speed, driving straight before the wind, she raced at the reef. A roller picked her up as she neared it and seemed to increase her speed. Then she struck, and vanished from sight for a second as the roller burst into spray all about her. When the spray cleared she lay there transformed. Her three masts had all gone with the shock, and it was only a black hulk which emerged from the white foam. Her speed and the roller behind her had carried her almost over the reef–doubtless tearing her bottom out–and she hung by her stern, which stood out clear of the water, while her bows were just submerged in the comparatively still water in the lee of the reef.

There were men still alive on her. Hornblower could see them crouching for shelter under the break of her poop. Another Atlantic roller came surging up, and exploded on the Devil's Teeth, wrapping the wreck round with spray. But yet she emerged again, black against the creaming foam. She had cleared the reef sufficiently far to find shelter for most of her length in the lee of the thing that had destroyed her. Hornblower could see those living creatures crouching on her deck. They had a little longer to live–they might live five minutes, perhaps, if they were lucky. Five hours if they were not.

All round him the Spaniards were shouting maledictions. Women were weeping; some of the men were shaking their fists with rage at the British frigate, which, well satisfied with the destruction of her victim, had rounded-to in time and was now clawing out to sea again under storm canvas. It was horrible to see those poor devils down there die. If some larger wave than usual, bursting on the reef, did not lift the stern of the wreck clear so that she sank, she would still break up for the survivors to be whirled away with the fragments. And, if it took a long time for her to break up, the wretched men sheltering there would not be able to endure the constant beating of the cold spray upon them. Something should be done to save them, but no boat could round the headland and weather the Devil's Teeth to reach the wreck. That was so obvious as not to call for a second thought. But . . . Hornblower's thoughts began to race as he started to work on the alternatives. The commandant on his horse was speaking vehemently to a Spanish naval officer, clearly on the same subject, and the naval officer was spreading his hands and saying that any attempt would be hopeless. And yet . . . For two years Hornblower had been a prisoner; all his pent-up restlessness was seeking an outlet, and after two years of the misery of confinement he did not care whether he lived or died. He went up to the commandant and broke into the argument.

'Sir,' he said, 'let me try to save them. Perhaps from the little bay there. . . . Perhaps some of the fishermen would come with me.'

The commandant looked at the officer and the officer shrugged his shoulders.

'What do you suggest, sir?' asked the commandant of Hornblower.

'We might carry a boat across the headland from the dockyard,' said Hornblower, struggling to word his ideas in Spanish, 'but we must be quick–quick!'

He pointed to the wreck, and force was added to his words by the sight of a roller bursting over the Devil's Teeth.

'How would you carry a boat?' asked the commandant.

To shout his plan in English against that wind would have been a strain; to do so in Spanish was beyond him.

'I can show you at the dockyard, sir,' he yelled. 'I cannot explain. But we must hurry!'

'You want to go to the dockyard, then?'

'Yes–oh, yes.'

'Mount behind me, sir,' said the commandant.

Awkwardly Hornblower scrambled up to a seat astride the horse's haunches and clutched at the commandant's belt. He bumped frightfully as the animal wheeled round and trotted down the slope. All the idlers of the town and garrison ran beside them.

The dockyard at Ferrol was almost a phantom organization, withered away like a tree deprived of its roots, thanks to the British blockade. Situated as it was at the most distant corner of Spain, connected with the interior by only the roughest of roads, it relied on receiving its supplies by sea, and any such reliance was likely with British cruisers off the coast to be disappointed. The last visit of Spanish ships of war had stripped the place of almost all its stores, and many of the dockyard hands had been pressed as seamen at the same time. But all that Hornblower needed was there, as he knew, thanks to his careful observation. He slid off the horse's hindquarters–miraculously avoiding an instinctive kick from the irritated animal–and collected his thoughts. He pointed to a low dray–a mere platform on wheels–which was used for carrying beef barrels and brandy kegs to the pier.

'Horses,' he said, and a dozen willing hands set to work harnessing a team.

Beside the jetty floated half a dozen boats. There was tackle and shears, all the apparatus necessary for swinging heavy weights about. To put slings under a boat and swing her up was the work of only a minute or two. These Spaniards might be dilatory and lazy as a rule, but inspire them with the need for instant action, catch their enthusiasm, present them with a novel plan, and they would work like madmen–and some of them were skilled workmen, too. Oars, mast and sail (not that they would need the sail), rudder, tiller and balers were all present. A group came running from a store shed with chocks for the boat, and the moment these were set up on the dray the dray was backed under the tackle and the boat lowered on to them.

'Empty barrels,' said Hornblower. 'Little ones–so.'

A swarthy Galician fisherman grasped his intention at once, and amplified Hornblower's halting sentences with voluble explanation. A dozen empty water breakers, with their bungs driven well home, were brought, and the swarthy fisherman climbed on the dray and began to lash them under the thwarts. Properly secured, they would keep the boat afloat even were she filled to the gunwale with water.

'I want six men,' shouted Hornblower, standing on the dray and looking round at the crowd. 'Six fishermen who know little boats.'

The swarthy fisherman lashing the breakers in the boat looked up from his task.

'I know whom we need, sir,' he said.

He shouted a string of names, and half a dozen men came forward; burly, weather-beaten fellows, with the self-reliant look in their faces of men used to meeting difficulties. It was apparent that the swarthy Galician was their captain.

'Let us go, then,' said Hornblower, but the Galician checked him.

Hornblower did not hear what he said, but some of the crowd nodded, turned away, and came hastening back staggering under a breaker of fresh water and a box that must contain biscuit. Hornblower was cross with himself for forgetting the possibility of their being blown out to sea. And the commandant, still sitting his horse and watching these preparations with a keen eye, took note of these stores too.

'Remember, sir, that I have your parole,' he said.

'You have my parole, sir,' said Hornblower–for a few blessed moments he had actually forgotten that he was a prisoner.

The stores were safely put away into the sternsheets and the fishing-boat captain caught Hornblower's eye and got a nod from him.

'Let us go,' he roared to the crowd.

The iron-shod hoofs clashed on the cobbles and the dray lurched forward, with men leading the horses, men swarming alongside, and Hornblower and the captain riding on the dray like triumphing generals in a procession. They went through the dockyard gate, along the level main street of the little town, and turned up a steep lane which climbed the ridge constituting the backbone of the headland. The enthusiasm of the crowd was still lively; when the horses slowed as they breasted the slope a hundred men pushed at the back, strained at the sides, tugged at the traces to run the dray up the hillside. At the crest the lane became a track, but the dray still lurched and rumbled along. From the track diverted an even worse track, winding its way sideways down the slope through arbutus and myrtle towards the sandy cove which Hornblower had first had in mind–on fine days he had seen fishermen working a seine net on that beach, and he himself had taken note of it as a suitable place for a landing party should the Royal Navy ever plan a descent against Ferrol.

The wind was blowing as wildly as ever; it shrieked round Hornblower's ears. The sea as it came in view was chaotic with wave-crests, and then as they turned a shoulder of the slope they could see the line of the Devil's Teeth running out from the shore up there to windward, and still hanging precariously from their jagged fangs was the wreck, black against the seething foam. Somebody raised a shout at the sight, everybody heaved at the dray, so that the horses actually broke into a trot and the dray leaped and bounced over the obstructions in its way.

'Slowly,' roared Hornblower. 'Slowly!'

If they were to break an axle or smash a wheel at this moment the attempt would end in ludicrous failure. The commandant on his horse enforced Hornblower's cries with loud orders of his own, and restrained the reckless enthusiasm of his people. More sedately the dray went on down the trail to the edge of the sandy beach. The wind picked up even the damp sand and flung it stinging into the faces, but only small waves broke here, for the beach was in a recess in the shoreline, the south-westerly wind was blowing a trifle off shore here, and up to windward the Devil's Teeth broke the force of the rollers as they raced along in a direction nearly parallel to the shoreline. The wheels plunged into the sand and the horses stopped at the water's edge. A score of willing hands unharnessed them and a hundred willing arms thrust the dray out into the water–all these things were easy with such vast manpower available. As the first wave broke over the floor of the dray the crew scrambled up and stood ready. There were rocks here, but mighty heaves by the militiamen and the dockyard workers waist-deep in water forced the dray over them. The boat almost floated off its chocks, and the crew forced it clear and scrambled aboard, the wind beginning to swing her immediately. They grabbed for their oars and put their backs into half a dozen fierce strokes which brought her under command; the Galician captain had already laid a steering oar in the notch in the stern, with no attempt at shipping rudder and tiller. As he braced himself to steer he glanced at Hornblower, who tacitly left the job to him.

Hornblower, bent against the wind, was standing in the sternsheets planning a route through the rocks which would lead them to the wreck. The shore and the friendly beach were gone now, incredibly far away, and the boat was struggling out through a welter of water with the wind howling round her. In those jumbled waves her motion was senseless and she lurched in every direction successively. It was well that the boatmen were used to rowing in broken water so that their oars kept the boat under way, giving the captain the means by which, tugging fiercely at the steering oar, he could guide her through that maniacal confusion. Hornblower, planning his course, was able to guide the captain by his gestures, so that the captain could devote all the necessary attention to keeping the boat from being suddenly capsized by an unexpected wave. The wind howled, and the boat heaved and pitched as she met each lumpy wave, but yard by yard they were struggling up to the wreck.

If there was any order in the waves at all, they were swinging round the outer end of the Devil's Teeth, so that the boat had to be carefully steered, turning to meet the waves with her bows and then turning back to gain precarious yards against the wind. Hornblower spared a glance for the men at the oars; at every second they were exerting their utmost strength. There could never be a moment's respite–tug and strain, tug and strain, until Hornblower wondered how human hearts and sinews could endure it.

But they were edging up towards the wreck. Hornblower, when the wind and spray allowed, could see the whole extent of her canted deck now. He could see human figures cowering under the break of the poop. He saw somebody there wave an arm to him. Next moment his attention was called away when a jagged monster suddenly leaped out of the sea twenty yards ahead. For a second he could not imagine what it was, and then it leaped clear again and he recognized it–the butt end of a broken mast. The mast was still anchored to the ship by a single surviving shroud attached to the upper end of the mast and to the ship, and the mast, drifting down to leeward, was jerking and leaping on the waves as though some sea god below the surface was threatening them with his wrath. Hornblower called the steersman's attention to the menace and received a nod in return; the steersman's shouted 'Nombre de Dios' was whirled away in the wind. They kept clear of the mast, and as they pulled up along it Hornblower could form a clearer notion of the speed of their progress now that he had a stationary object to help his judgement. He could see the painful inches gained at each frantic tug on the oars, and could see how the boat stopped dead or even went astern when the wilder gusts hit her, the oar blades pulling ineffectively through the water. Every inch of gain was only won at the cost of an infinity of labour.

Now they were past the mast, close to the submerged bows of the ship, and close enough to the Devil's Teeth to be deluged with spray as each wave burst on the farther side of the reef. There were inches of water washing back and forth in the bottom of the boat, but there was neither time nor opportunity to bale it out. This was the trickiest part of the whole effort, to get close enough alongside the wreck to be able to take off the survivors without stoving in the boat; there were wicked fangs of rock all about the after end of the wreck, while forward, although the forecastle was above the surface at times the forward part of the waist was submerged. But the ship was canted a little over to port, towards them, which made the approach easier. When the water was at its lowest level, immediately before the next roller broke on the reef, Hornblower, standing up and craning his neck, could see no rocks beside the wreck in the middle part of the waist where the deck came down to water level. It was easy to direct the steersman towards that particular point, and then, as the boat moved in, to wave his arms and demand the attention of the little group under the break of the poop, and to point to the spot to which they were approaching. A wave burst upon the reef, broke over the stern of the wreck, and filled the boat almost full. She swung back and forth in the eddies, but the kegs kept her afloat and quick handling of the steering oar and lusty rowing kept her from being dashed against either the wreck or the rocks.

'Now!' shouted Hornblower–it did not matter that he spoke English at this decisive moment. The boat surged forward, while the survivors, releasing themselves from the lashings which had held them in their shelter, came slithering down the deck towards them.

It was a little of a shock to see there were but four of them–twenty or thirty men must have been swept overboard when the ship hit the reef. The bows of the boat moved towards the wreck. At a shouted order from the steersman the oars fell still. One survivor braced himself and flung himself into the bows. A stroke of the oars, a tug at the steering oar, and the boat nosed forward again, and another survivor plunged into the boat. Then Hornblower, who had been watching the sea, saw the next breaker rear up over the reef. At his warning shout the boat backed away to safety–comparative safety–while the remaining survivors went scrambling back up the deck to the shelter of the poop. The wave burst and roared, the foam hissed and the spray rattled, and then they crept up to the wreck again. The third survivor poised himself for his leap, mistimed it, and fell into the sea, and no one ever saw him again. He was gone, sunk like a stone, crippled as he was with cold and exhaustion, but there was no time to spare for lamentation. The fourth survivor was waiting his chance and jumped at once, landing safely in the bows.

'Any more?' shouted Hornblower, and receiving a shake of the head in reply; they had saved three lives at the risk of eight.

'Let us go,' said Hornblower, but the steersman needed no telling.

Already he had allowed the wind to drift the boat away from the wreck, away from the rocks–away from the shore. An occasional strong pull at the oars sufficed to keep her bows to wind and wave. Hornblower looked down at the fainting survivors lying in the bottom of the boat with the water washing over them. He bent down and shook them into consciousness; he picked up the balers and forced them into their numb hands. They must keep active or die. It was astounding to find darkness closing about them, and it was urgent that they should decide on their next move immediately. The men at the oars were in no shape for any prolonged further rowing; if they tried to return to the sandy cove whence they had started they might be overtaken both by night and by exhaustion while still among the treacherous rocks off the shore there. Hornblower sat down beside the Galician captain, who laconically gave his views while vigilantly observing the waves racing down upon them.

'It's growing dark,' said the captain, glancing round the sky. 'Rocks. The men are tired.'

'We had better not go back,' said Hornblower.

'No.'

'Then we must get out to sea.'

Years of duty on blockade, of beating about off a lee shore, had ingrained into Hornblower the necessity for seeking searoom.

'Yes,' said the captain, and he added something which Hornblower, thanks to the wind and his unfamiliarity with the language, was unable to catch. The captain roared the expression again, and accompanied his words with a vivid bit of pantomime with the one hand he could spare from the steering oar.

'A sea anchor,' decided Hornblower to himself. 'Quite right.'

He looked back at the vanishing shore, and gauged the direction of the wind. It seemed to be backing a little southerly; the coast here trended away from them. They could ride to a sea anchor through the hours of darkness and run no risk of being cast ashore as long as these conditions persisted.

'Good,' said Hornblower aloud.

He imitated the other's bit of pantomime and the captain gave him a glance of approval. At a bellow from him the two men forward took in their oars and set to work at constructing a sea anchor–merely a pair of oars attached to a long painter paid out over the bows. With this gale blowing the pressure of the wind on the boat set up enough drag on the float to keep their bows to the sea. Hornblower watched as the sea anchor began to take hold of the water.

'Good,' he said again.

'Good,' said the captain, taking in his steering oar.

Hornblower realized only now that he had been long exposed to a winter gale while wet to the skin. He was numb with cold, and he was shivering uncontrollably. At his feet one of the three survivors of the wreck was lying helpless; the other two had succeeded in baling out most of the water and as a result of their exertions were conscious and alert. The men who had been rowing sat drooping with weariness on their thwarts. The Galician captain was already down in the bottom of the boat lifting the helpless man in his arms. It was a common impulse of them all to huddle down into the bottom of the boat, beneath the thwarts, away from that shrieking wind.

So the night came down on them. Hornblower found himself welcoming the contact of other human bodies; he felt an arm round him and he put his arm round someone else. Around them a little water still surged about on the floorboards; above them the wind still shrieked and howled. The boat stood first on her head and then on her tail as the waves passed under them, and at the moment of climbing each crest she gave a shuddering jerk as she snubbed herself to the sea anchor. Every few seconds a new spat of spray whirled into the boat upon their shrinking bodies; it did not seem long before the accumulation of spray in the bottom of the boat made it necessary for them to disentangle themselves, and set about, groping in the darkness, the task of baling the water out again. Then they could huddle down again under the thwarts.

It was when they pulled themselves together for the third baling that in the middle of his nightmare of cold and exhaustion Hornblower was conscious that the body across which his arm lay was unnaturally stiff; the man the captain had been trying to revive had died as he lay there between the captain and Hornblower. The captain dragged the body away into the sternsheets in the darkness, and the night went on, cold wind and cold spray, jerk, pitch, and roll, sit up and bale and cower down and shudder. It was hideous torment; Hornblower could not trust himself to believe his eyes when he saw the first signs that the darkness was lessening. And then the grey dawn came gradually over the grey sea, and they were free to wonder what to do next. But as the light increased the problem was solved for them, for one of the fishermen, raising himself up in the boat, gave a hoarse cry, and pointed to the northern horizon, and there, almost hull-up, was a ship, hove-to under storm canvas. The captain took one glance at her–his eyesight must have been marvellous–and identified her.

'The English frigate,' he said.

She must have made nearly the same amount of leeway hove-to as the boat did riding to her sea anchor.

'Signal to her,' said Hornblower, and no one raised any objections.

The only white object available was Hornblower's shirt, and he took it off, shuddering in the cold, and they tied it to an oar and raised the oar in the maststep. The captain saw Hornblower putting on his dripping coat over his bare ribs and in a single moment peeled off his thick blue jersey and offered it to him.

'Thank you, no,' protested Hornblower, but the captain insisted; with a wide grin he pointed to the stiffened corpse lying in the sternsheets and announced he would replace the jersey with the dead man's clothing.

The argument was interrupted by a further cry from one of the fishermen. The frigate was coming to the wind; with treble-reefed fore and maintopsails she was heading for them under the impulse of the lessening gale. Hornblower saw her running down on them; a glance in the other direction showed him the Galician mountains, faint on the southern horizon– warmth, freedom and friendship on the one hand; solitude and captivity on the other. Under the lee of the frigate the boat bobbed and heaved fantastically; many inquisitive faces looked down on them. They were cold and cramped; the frigate dropped a boat and a couple of nimble seamen scrambled on board. A line was flung from the frigate, a whip lowered a breeches ring into the boat, and the English seamen helped the Spaniards one by one into the breeches and held them steady as they were swung up to the frigate's deck.

'I go last,' said Hornblower when they turned to him. 'I am a King's officer.'

'Good Lor' lumme,' said the seamen.

'Send the body up, too,' said Hornblower. 'It can be given decent burial.'

The stiff corpse was grotesque as it swayed through the air. The Galician captain tried to dispute with Hornblower the honour of going last, but Hornblower would not be argued with. Then finally the seamen helped him put his legs into the breeches, and secured him with a line round his waist. Up he soared, swaying dizzily with the roll of the ship; then they drew him in to the deck, lowering and shortening, until half a dozen strong arms took his weight and laid him gently on the deck.

'There you are, my hearty, safe and sound,' said a bearded seaman.

'I am a King's officer,' said Hornblower. 'Where's the officer of watch?'

Wearing marvellous dry clothing, Hornblower found himself soon drinking hot rum-and-water in the cabin of Captain George Crome, of His Majesty's frigate *Syrtis*. Crome was a thin pale man with a depressed expression, but Hornblower knew of him as a first-rate officer.

'These Galicians make good seamen,' said Crome. 'I can't press them. But perhaps a few will volunteer sooner than go to a prison hulk.'

'Sir,' said Hornblower, and hesitated. It is ill for a junior lieutenant to argue with a post captain.

'Well?'

'Those men came to sea to save life. They are not liable to capture.'

Crome's cold grey eyes became actively frosty–Hornblower was right about it being ill for a junior lieutenant to argue with a post captain.

'Are you telling me my duty, sir?' he asked.

'Good heavens no, sir,' said Hornblower hastily. 'It's a long time since I read the Admiralty Instructions and I expect my memory's at fault.'

'Admiralty Instructions, eh?' said Crome, in a slightly different tone of voice.

'I expect I'm wrong, sir,' said Hornblower, 'but I seem to remember the same instruction applied to the other two–the survivors.'

Even a post captain could only contravene Admiralty Instructions at his peril.

'I'll consider it,' said Crome.

'I had the dead man sent on board, sir,' went on Hornblower, 'in the hope that perhaps you might give him proper burial. Those Galicians risked their lives to save him, sir, and I expect they'd be gratified.'

'A Popish burial? I'll give orders to give 'em a free hand.'

'Thank you, sir,' said Hornblower.

'And now as regards yourself. You say you hold a commission as lieutenant. You can do duty in this ship until we meet the admiral again. Then he can decide. I haven't heard of the *Indefatigable* paying off, and legally you may still be borne on her books.'

And that was when the devil came to tempt Hornblower, as he took another sip of hot rum-and-water. The joy of being in a King's ship again was so keen as to be almost painful. To taste salf beef and biscuit again, and never again to taste beans and garbanzos. To have a ship's deck under his feet, to talk English. To be free–to be free! There was precious little chance of ever falling again into Spanish hands. Hornblower remembered with agonizing clarity the flat depression of captivity. All he had to do was not to say a word. He had only to keep silence for a day or two. But the devil did not tempt him long, only until he had taken his next sip of rum-and-water. Then he thrust the devil behind him and met Crome's eyes again.

'I'm sorry, sir,' he said.

'What for?'

'I am here on parole. I gave my word before I left the beach.'

'You did? That alters the case. You were within your rights, of course.'

The giving of parole by captive British officers was so usual as to excite no comment.

'It was in thc usual form, I suppose?' went on Crome. 'That you would make no attempt to escape?'

'Yes, sir.'

'Then what do you decide as a result?'

Of course Crome could not attempt to influence a gentleman's decision on a matter as personal as a parole.

'I must go back, sir,' said Hornblower, 'at the first opportunity.'

He felt the sway of the ship, he looked round the homely cabin, and his heart was breaking.

'You can at least dine and sleep on board tonight,' said Crome. 'I'll not venture inshore again until the wind moderates. I'll send you to Corunna under a flag of truce when I can. And I'll see what the Instructions say about those prisoners.'

It was a sunny morning when the sentry at Fort San Anton, in the harbour of Corunna, called his officer's attention to the fact that the British cruiser off the headland had hove-to out of gunshot and was lowering a boat. The sentry's responsibility ended there, and he could watch idly as his officer observed that the cutter, running smartly in under sail, was flying a white flag. She hove-to within musket shot, and it was a mild surprise to the sentry when in reply to the officer's hail someone rose up in the boat and replied in unmistakable Gallego dialect. Summoned alongside the landing slip, the cutter put ashore ten men and then headed out again to the frigate. Nine men were laughing and shouting; the tenth, the youngest, walked with a fixed expression on his face with never a sign of emotion–his expression did not change even when the others, with obvious affection, put their arms round his shoulders. No one ever troubled to explain to the sentry who the imperturbable young man was, and he was not very interested. After he had seen the group shipped off across Corunna Bay towards Ferrol he quite forgot the incident.

It was almost spring when a Spanish militia officer came into the barracks which served as a prison for officers in Ferrol.

'Señor Hornblower?' he asked–at least Hornblower, in the corner, knew that was what he was trying to say. He was used to the way Spaniards mutilated his name.

'Yes?' he said, rising.

'Would you please come with me? The commandant has sent me for you, sir.'

The commandant was all smiles. He held a despatch in his hands.

'This, sir,' he said, waving it at Hornblower, 'is a personal order. It is countersigned by the Duke of Fuentesauco, Minister of Marine, but it is signed by the First Minister, Prince of the Peace and Duke of Alcudia.'

'Yes, sir,' said Hornblower.

He should have begun to hope that moment, but there comes a time in a prisoner's life when he ceases to hope. He was more interested, even, in that strange title of Prince of the Peace which was now beginning to be heard in Spain.

'It says: "We, Carlos Leonardo Luis Manuel de Godoy y Boegas, First Minister of His Most Catholic Majesty, Prince of the Peace, Duke of Alcudia and Grandee of the First Class, Count of Alcudia, Knight of the Most Sacred Order of the Golden Fleece, Knight of the Holy Order of Santiago, Knight of the Most Distinguished Order of Calatrava, Captain General of his Most Catholic Majesty's forces by Land and Sea, Colonel General of the Guardia de Corps, Admiral of the Two Oceans, General of the cavalry, of the infantry, and of the artillery"–in any event, sir, it is an order to me to take immediate steps to set you at liberty. I am to restore you under flag of truce to your fellow countrymen, in recognition of "your courage and self-sacrifice in saving life at the peril of your own".'

'Thank you, sir,' said Hornblower.

THE EARTHLY PARADISE

C. S. FORESTER

I

The learned Narciso Rich was washing his shirt. He had dropped a wooden bucket over the side on the end of a rope, and, having filled it–with difficulty because of its tendency to float and the lack of motion of the ship–he had swung it up to the fore-deck. Although it was late afternoon, it was still stifling hot, and Rich endeavoured to stay as much as possible in the shadow cast by the mast and sail, but that was not easy, because the ship was swinging about slowly and aimlessly in the flat calm. The sun stung his bare skin, brown though the latter was, when it reached it. Yet Rich could not postpone what he was doing until nightfall, because the work in hand necessitated a good light–he was freeing his shirt of the insect pests which swarmed in it.

There were grim thoughts running through his mind as he bent over his revolting task. Firstly, he knew by experience that his shirt was far easier to clean than the leather breeches which he wore, and on which he would have to start work next. Next, he would not stay clean very long, not in this ship, where every man was alive with lice, and where the very planking swarmed with loathsome creatures which hastened out at nightfall to suck human blood. At this very moment, when he stopped to think about it, he thought he could distinguish their hideous stench among the other stinks which reached his nostrils. It was a strange piece of work for him to be doing. Not since his student days had he had to abase himself in this fashion, and for the last five years he had had servants to wait on him in his own house, after he had attained eminence in his profession. Without immodesty he could look on himself as in the first rank of jurisconsults in the triple kingdom of Arragon, and as certainly the second, and possibly the first, authority on the universal maritime code of Catalonia. Merchant princes from Pisa and Florence and Marseille–the very Doge of Venice, for that matter–had sent deputations, almost embassies, to request his judgment upon points in dispute, and had listened attentively to his explanations of the law, and had paid in gold for them. Now he was washing his own shirt under an equinoctial sun.

And–he admitted it to himself with all a lawyer's realism–it was his own fault. He need not have joined this expedition. The King had summoned him to consultation; a pretty tangle they had got their affairs into, His Highness and the Admiral, as a result of not consulting expert legal opinion when drawing up their first agreement, which was exactly what always happened when two laymen tried to save lawyer's fees. Rich remembered His Highness's inquiring glance; the subject under discussion was as to which able-bodied young lawyer would be best suited to send out to the Indies to watch over the royal interests and to try to straighten out the legal muddles there. A hot wave of recklessness had swept Rich away.

'I could go myself, Highness,' he said, with an appearance of jesting.

At that moment he had felt weary of the dull round of a lawyer's life, of the dignified robes, of the solemn pretence to infallibility, of the eternal weariness of explaining to muddled minds the petty points–often the same points over and over again–which to him were clarity itself. He had suddenly realized that he was forty, and ageing, and that the twenty years which had elapsed since his journey back to Barcelona from Padua had brought him nothing except the worldly success which seemed to him, momentarily, of small account. With pitiless self-analysis Rich, sousing his shirt in the bucket, reminded himself that at that time the prospect of wearing a sword at his side had made a definite appeal to him, as though he had been a hare-brained boy to be attracted by toys.

His Highness's lantern jaw had dropped a little in surprise.

'There is nothing we would like better,' he had said.

There had still been a chance of escape. Instant retraction would have left him at peace in his quiet house in Barcelona, and yet he had thrown away the opportunity.

'There is no reason why I should not go, Highness,' he had said, like a fool, and after that there was no chance of withdrawal save at the risk of royal displeasure, and the displeasure of King Ferdinand was more perilous even than a voyage to the Indies.

So here he was, eaten alive by vermin, and roasting under a tropical sun in a ship which seemed as though she would never again feel a breath of wind, so long had she drifted in these equatorial calms. He was indeed the only person on board, of all the hundred and thirty who crowded her, who was displaying any sign of activity. The Admiral and his servants were invisible in the great after-cabin, and the rest of the horde were lying idly in the shade of the bulwarks and of the break of the fore-deck. They were more accustomed to filth and vermin than he was; his fastidious nostrils could distinguish the reek of their dirty bodies and unwashed clothing as one strand of the tangled skein of stinks–salted cod, not too well preserved, and rotting cheese, and fermenting beans. The least unpleasing and most prevalent odour was the vinegary smell of spilt wine drying in the heat–the wine barrels in the waist had been badly coopered, and wine was continually sweating out between the staves, the supply dwindling daily, although to them it was more value now than the gold they were seeking. The tremendous rainstorms, accompanied, alas, by hardly a breath of wind, of the last few days, had brought them drinking water, but it was having to be caught in sails before being run into the casks. It was vastly unattractive water, especially to Spaniards with their discriminating taste in drinking water; Rich suspected the water of being the cause of the bowel complaint which was beginning to plague them all.

His shirt was finished now, and he put it on, revelling in the coolness of the wet material against his skin while he stripped off his breeches–it was repulsive and unpleasing to be naked. It was strange that among all the dangers and discomforts he had expected–the fevers, the poisoned arrows, the fire-breathing dragons, the tempests and rocks, he had never anticipated the vermin which now held so important a place in his thoughts. St Francis of Assisi, of blessed memory, had spoken of lice as the pearls of poverty. Rich, bending over his disgusting task, shuddered at the unorthodoxy of disapproving of anything St Francis had said, until he reassured himself with the thought that divine Providence had not blessed him with the Saint's humility. There was a whiff of heresy about that, too, now he came to think about it. But he pulled himself together sturdily; his immortal soul could not really be endangered by his cleansing the seam of his breeches. De minimis non curat lex. He could argue a good case with St Peter on that point.

These breeches were fiendishly difficult to clean; cold sea-water was not the most helpful medium in which to attempt it. Boiling water, if he could be sure of not hardening the leather, would be far more efficacious. Or a hot knife-blade, run along the seams. But there was no chance of heating a knife-blade or of boiling water; the cooking fire on the stone hearth in the waist was out, and had not been lighted for–how many days? Five? Six?–the days had been so much alike that he could not remember. The heat had been too great for the cooks to do their work, so the cooks had said, and the Admiral had believed them. The Admiral did not care whether his food was hot or cold, sweet or rotten; probably he did not even notice. Presumably he was now in his great cabin, dreaming over his charts, revolving fresh theories. Rich pointed out to himself that the Admiral, even if he were too gentle with the men, was hard enough on himself, and even though he was grasping in his efforts to adhere to the letter of that absurd agreement with the Crown, he was at least prepared to devote every thought in his head and every breath in his body to the furtherance of the objects of that agreement.

This southerly course which they were following now–or would be following, if there was only a wind–would take them into a region of burning sun and brilliant moon; it had done so, for that matter, already. That would greatly increase their chances of obtaining precious metals. The golden glory of the sun and the silver brightness of the moon must obviously engender and stimulate the growth of gold and silver. The soil should be thick with them in this climate, when they reached land. The Portuguese had discovered more and more gold the farther south they pushed their exploration of Africa, which was a clear confirmation of the theory. Shiploads of gold and silver would make Spain rich and powerful. There would be content and plenty in the land. There would be bread on the table of every peasant, and the court of Their Highnesses would be the most brilliant in Christendom.

The Admiral saw this plainly enough. It would be a much shorter cut than the tedious methods of trade. The other Indian islands he had discovered had obviously been pretty close to the dominions of the Grand Khan. That wealthy region of Cibao that the natives of Española talked about must most probably be the island of Japan, often referred to as Cipangu, which was known to lie adjacent to the coast of China. For that matter the Admiral had reached the confines of the Grand Khan's dominions in his previous voyage. The great land of Cuba at which he had touched–the name obviously recalled that of Kubla Khan, whom Marco Polo had encountered in his travels to the East. Rich was aware that more than one wild theorist had put forward the suggestion that Cuba was just another island, vaster than any yet known, larger even than Sicily, but the Admiral did not agree. The Admiral was much the more likely to be right. He had proved himself right over the tremendous question of the practicability of reaching the Indies by sailing westward, so that he was hardly likely to be wrong over the simple question as to whether Cuba was part of the mainland or not. Kubla Khan's court was wealthy, and his empire wide; trade with him might produce benefits, but nothing nearly as great as winning great shiploads of gold without the tiresome necessity of trading.

So Rich had thoroughly approved of this southerly course, which would carry them to the gold-bearing, barbaric countries and keep them clear of Cuba and Japan and the other Chinese territories. He was only a tiny bit doubtful now, and that merely on account of practical details. To the north of them lay a region where the wind blew eternally from the eastward; he had sailed through it, he had observed the phenomenon with his own senses. Always from the eastern quarter, sometimes from the north of east, very occasionally from the south of east, that wind blew. If there was a region where there was always a wind blowing, was it not likely that there was another where the wind never blew? They had had days and days of calm. If they were to push farther south still they might reach an area where the calm would be eternal, where they would drift helpless until they died.

Rich looked about him. Westward the sky was beginning to display the marvellous reds and golds of another sunset. Over-side was the deep clear blue of the sea, in which lay a long wreath of golden weed–a pleasing colour contrast. A little flock of flying fish rose from the sea as he looked, and skimmed along, and vanished again; the dark furrows they left behind them on the glassy surface vanished as quickly. In the bows, black against the colouring sky, stood the look-out, his hand resting on the forestay. Aft stood the helmsman, the tiller idle at his side. Far astern, almost on the horizon, he could see the brown sail and the red sail of their consorts, wallowing, like them, helpless in the calm. Lovely, and yet sinister, was how the scene appeared to Rich. Standing barelegged on the fore-deck of the *Holy Name*, his breeches in his hand, and with the sunset lowering round him, he felt a twinge of lonely fear.

At that very moment a little wind began to blow. He felt it first on his bare legs, damp with the water that had dripped from his shirt–a tiny coolness, the merest ghost of a breath. At first the coolness was all he noticed, never thinking of the cause. Then the big sail above him flapped a trifle, and then louder. Alonso Sanchez de Carvajal, the sailing master, was on his feet now on the poop, looking round at the sea and the sky, and up at the long red-cross pennant which was stirring itself at the masthead. He bellowed orders, and at the sound of his voice the sailors bestirred themselves, rousing themselves up from where they lounged on the decks, moving to halliards and braces with more cheerfulness than they had been accustomed to show during the last few days. The yards were braced round and the sails bellied a little to the wind. Already the motion of the *Holy Name* had changed, from the indolent indifferent lurching to a more purposeful swoop. Rich heard a sound he had forgotten–the musical bubbling of water under the bows. In itself that was enough to rouse him from his depression. He could feel his spirits rise as he hopped on one leg trying to pull on his breeches and not impede the sailors in their duties.

There was the Admiral on the poop now, in his blue satin doublet with the gold chain glittering round his neck, his white hair hanging to his shoulders. He, too, was looking round the horizon. Now he was speaking to Carvajal, and Carvajal was bellowing more orders to the crew. The yards were being braced farther round. They were altering course; Rich looked forward as the ship steadied herself. Right ahead the sun hovered close above the horizon in a glory of red and gold. The *Holy Name* was heading due west–the Admiral must have changed his mind at last about holding to the south-westward. To the westward probably lay the nearest land; Rich felt a little thrill of anticipation.

Alonso Perez came shambling past him–the Admiral's servant, major-domo and general factotum, stoop-shouldered and with arms disproportionately long. He stepped to the rail and cleared his throat noisily, standing waiting.

'Go!' came the Admiral's high clear voice from the poop, and Perez spat into the indigo sea.

The Admiral was by the rail on the poop, the fingers of his right hand clasping his left wrist. He was counting the number of times his pulse beat while the white fleck of mucus drifted back to him, which would enable him to estimate the speed of the ship through the water. Rich had helped in the initial tedious calculations by which the table of speeds had been constructed–for example, if the ship travels XCI feet while the pulse beats XLIII times, and the number of times the pulse beats in a minute is LXX, how many leagues does the ship travel in an hour? But there was no need to make those calculations now, because the table was constructed once for all, and a mere knowledge of the number of pulse beats enabled anyone to read off the speed of the ship; and Carvajal's pulse, and the pulse of Diego Osorio the boatswain, had been compared with the Admiral's so that any one of the three could take an observation.

It was highly ingenious–one of the many highly ingenious devices which Rich had admired since he had come to sea and interested himself in navigation. The astrolabe, which enabled one to guess which point one had reached of the earth's rotundity from north to south, was another ingenious device. By its aid a ship's captain could always return to a place he had previously visited, if only he sailed long enough along the line which ran through it parallel to the equinoctial line. If only–Rich was beginning again, as he had often done before to try and work out a similar method of ascertaining longitude, but he was interrupted by his noticing that the ship's company was assembling aft.

He hastened after them, and took his place among the group of gentlemen and priests at the starboard side. The Admiral stood by the tiller, Carvajal at his side, the seamen in line athwartships, and the landsmen to port. Only the look-out and the helmsman took no part in the prayer. Heads were bowed. Horny hands made the sign of the cross. They prayed to the Queen of Heaven, the unlettered among them stumbling through the Latin words following the others. Rich glanced up under his eyelids at the Admiral, who was standing with clasped hands gazing up at the darkening sky. There was a happy exaltation in his face, a fixed and fanatical enthusiasm–everyone was aware of the Admiral's special devotion to the Blessed Virgin. His blue eyes were still bright in the growing darkness, his white beard ghost-like.

The prayer ended, and the massed ship's company began to break up again into groups. Overhead the stars were coming into sight–strange stars, with the Great Bear almost lost on the northern horizon, and new constellations showing in the south, glowing vividly against the velvet of the sky. Like another star appeared the taper borne by a ship's boy to light the shaded lamp that hung above the compass before the steersman.

2

The blessed new coolness of the night gave sweet sleep to Narciso Rich, despite the foulness of his sleeping quarters with twenty gentlemen of coat-armour on the berth-deck below the great cabin aft, despite the snores of his companions, despite the lumpiness of his chaff mattress and the activity of its inhabitants. He told himself, as he stepped into the fresh air in the waist, just before dawn, that they must be nearing the fountain of youth, for he felt none of the weight of his forty years on his shoulders, and his bones had ceased to protest about that chaff mattress. Carvajal had told him of the curious type of bed used by the natives of the Indian islands–a network of interlaced creepers, secured to posts at either end, and called a 'hammock' in their pagan tongue–and Rich had once suggested that they would be ideal for use on board ship, where space was limited and motion violent, but Carvajal had pursed his lips and shaken his head at such a preposterous notion. Chaff mattresses had always been used at sea, and always would; and Christian sailors could do better than to adopt ideas from naked unbelievers.

Rich dipped his bucket and rinsed his face and hands, ran his comb through his hair and beard, and looked about him. The sky was lavender-hued now with the approaching dawn, in such lovely contrast with the blue of the sea as to rouse an ache in his breast, and that blessed breeze was still blowing from the east, driving the *Holy Name* steadily westward over the rhythmic rise and fall of the sea. He walked over and glanced at the slate hanging beside the helmsman. There was bunch after bunch of little strokes recorded there–they must have made at least twenty leagues during the night. Quite soon they much reach land, and they were a hundred leagues or more farther south than Española–one of the southern islands which Polo had heard about, Sumatra, perhaps, with its sandalwood and spices.

A ship's boy came pattering up, barefooted; the last grains were running out of the hour-glass and he turned it and lifted his voice in a loud cry to Diego Osorio. The ship's day was begun, and by coincidence just as the first rays of the sun were gleaming over the sea, touching the crests of the waves into gold. Carvajal came up on to the poop, crossed himself before the painted Virgin by the taffrail, and looked keenly at the slate. He nodded curtly to Rich, but he had no words to spare for him at this time in the morning, for it was during this cool hour that the work of the ship must be done. Soon he was bellowing orders at the sleepy men who came crawling out of the forecastle to join those already on deck. Twelve of them were set to work at bailing out the ship–seven of them as a living chain passing up buckets from the bilge to the rail, and five returning the empty buckets again. It was a slow and weary process, which Rich had watched daily for five weeks, and every day the work was harder, because in these seas there lived creatures who bored holes in the bottoms of ships, as clean as an auger.

Rich had dallied with several ideas bearing on the subject, both to reduce the labour of bailing and to evade the necessity for it. There was the Archimedean screw, about which he had read in an Arabic mathematical treatise. A single man turning a handle might do more with such an apparatus–if it could be set up in a ship–than twelve men with buckets. Or there were pumps about which he had vaguely heard–the Netherlanders and Frisians were using them to drain their drowned fields. Here, too, they might be worked by the force of the wind and keep the ship dry without any labour at all. And if the marine creatures bored through wood, why not protect the wood from them? A thin coating of lead, say, or of copper. Perhaps the weight would be too great for the ship to bear, and certainly the cost would be enormous, but it might be worth while thinking about.

It would be no use discussing such innovations with Carvajal, as he was painfully aware. Nor–Rich decided reluctantly–with the Admiral. The latter regarded him with suspicion, as a royal agent sent to try and devise methods of entrenching upon his cherished privileges as Viceroy of the Ocean, and in that he was not far wrong. Where he was wrong was in seeing traps laid for him in the most innocent suggestions, such as for copper-bottoming ships. The Admiral was in such a state of mind as to believe every man's hand against him.

The ship was fully awake now. Here came the friars in their robes, and after them Rich's recent cabin mates, the hidalgos, lounging out on deck, their swords at their hips; the two Acevedo brothers, Cristobal Garcia and his followers, Bernardo de Tarpia, still a little unsure of himself from seasickness, and the others. Their lisping Castilian contrasted oddly with the rougher, aspirated Andalusian of the crews and with the sweet Catalan which was music to Rich's ears. João de Setubal spoke the barbarous Portuguese, which put him on better terms with the Admiral, who spoke Portuguese well, but who, when he spoke Castilian, was liable to lapse with startling unintelligibility into his native Italian. When that happened it was not unusual for him to go on talking, for several minutes without realizing what had happened, and for him only to be recalled to Spanish by the look of blank incomprehension on the face of the person addressed.

Here he came on deck now, wearing scarlet velvet–the fact that he could wear velvet in that heat was a clear enough proof of the way in which personal discomfort meant nothing to him–his gold chain and his jewelled sword and dagger. His four pages followed him–it was as if they were carrying a five-yard ermine train–and Perez with his white staff of office and Antonio Spallanzani his Italian squire. The hidalgos, Rich among them, fell into line and bowed deeply as he approached, with all the deference due to the Regent of the Indies. He bowed stiffly in return–it was rheumatism which made him so unbending–and then turned, with head bowed and uncovered, to murmur a prayer to the Virgin by the taffrail. Carvajal awaited his attention at his elbow, and the Admiral, when he had finished his devotions, turned to him with a slow dignity. Carvajal made his report on the night's run, the Admiral's keen blue eyes running over the slate to confirm it. They had run twenty-one leagues. Two great shooting stars had been seen during the middle watch. At dawn the look-out had seen a flight of pelicans.

'Then land is near,' said the Admiral. 'Pelicans never fly far to sea.'

'Yes, Excellency,' said Carvajal, bowing again. 'But the western horizon was clear at daybreak.'

'No matter. We shall see land today. We are close upon it.'

The Admiral directed his glance forward, to where the look-out stood gazing ahead. There was a little petulance in the Admiral's manner, a little impatience, as though he suspected the look-out of not doing his duty. Rich felt a little puzzled, because the Admiral could have no certain knowledge that land was within five hundred miles of them in that direction; the Indies already discovered were far to the northward, and no one could tell exactly where were Java and Sumatra and the islands of the roc and the island of pearls where Sinbad had traded.

'It may even be in sight now,' said the Admiral. 'Here, Perez, go aloft and see for me.'

Perez handed his white staff in silence to one of the pages and shambled forward. He leaped with ungraceful agility up into the shrouds of the mainmast, and climbed like a cat or an ape up the unstable rope ladder. Every eye watched him as he reached the mast-head and steadied himself with one arm linked round a rope and shaded his eyes with his other hand. For a long time he stared to the westward over the indigo sea, looked away to relieve his aching eyes, and then stared again. Suddenly he waved his hand.

'Land!' he shouted 'Land!'

The ship broke into a bustle of excitement. Everyone began to scramble for a better point of view. Two or three sailors sprang for the shrouds, and were instantly checked by a high-pitched cry from the Admiral. No one except the faithful Perez should set eyes on this new domain of his before its legitimate ruler should. He walked to the shrouds with the dignity that concealed his rheumatic gait, and slowly began the climb. His bulky clothes and his sword impeded him, but he never hesitated until the mast-head was reached. They saw Perez make place for him and point forward, and then, clearly dismissed, slide down the halliard to the deck. The Admiral stayed at the mast-head, the sun gleaming on his jewellery and his scarlet and gold. It was long before he began the descent again, longer still before he reached the deck.

'Gentlemen,' he said gravely to the group of hidalgos–gravely, but with a sparkle of happiness in his eyes. 'Yet one more miracle has been vouchsafed to us by the mercy of God.'

He crossed himself, and they waited for him to say more, patiently.

'This voyage, as you know, gentlemen, the third expedition to the Indies which I have commanded, was undertaken in the name of the Most Holy Trinity. The third voyage, gentlemen, and in the name of the Trinity. And now the first land we sight is a triple peak, three mountain-tops conjoined at their base, the emblem of the Trinity, Three in One and One in Three. I have named the land in sight Trinidad, in perpetual memory of this stupendous event. Let us give thanks to God the Father, and to the Blessed Saviour, and to the Holy Spirit.'

The harsh voice of the Dominican friar began at once to recite the prayer; heads were bared and bowed as they followed the words. And when the prayer was finished the Admiral turned to the ship's boys behind him.

'Sing, boys,' he commanded. 'Sing the Salve Regina.'

They sang like angels, their clear high treble soaring up to the cloudless blue sky, the deep bass of the crew blending in harmony with it. It was only after the hymn was finished that the Admiral, with a gesture, dismissed the excited ship's company so that they could climb the rigging and view the land in sight, but at the same time his eyes met Rich's and detained him.

'You see, Don Narciso,' said the Admiral, gravely, 'how clearly the hand of God is visible in this enterprise.'

'Yes, Your Excellency,' said Rich. He felt the same. The sighting of the triple mountain-top as the first incident of a voyage undertaken in the name of the Trinity might–so Rich's legal mind insisted–have been only a coincidence. But that land should be sighted on the very day the Admiral had predicted it, at a moment when Rich was acutely aware how insignificant were the data on which to base any calculations–that was also proof of God's providence. The two facts together made the deduction indisputable.

'We are no more than ten degrees north of the equinoctial line,' went on the Admiral. 'It will be the gold-bearing land whose existence was postulated by my friend Ferrer, the jeweller, as well as by the ancients. Pliny and Aristotle both have passages bearing on the subject. It seems likely enough to me that this will prove to be the land of Ophir of which the Bible tells us.'

'Yes, sir,' said Rich.

The possibility of the new land being Ophir seemed to him not too great. It was only a possibility, not a probability. If it were so they must have progressed at least two-thirds of the way round the globe, and their moontime must differ by sixteen hours from that of Cadiz. If only by some fresh miracle they could know what was the time at that moment in Spain! Or if only their hour-glasses could be relied upon to give accurate time over a period of weeks, without a cumulative and unknown error of hours! So much that was doubtful would be settled by that.

'My hope is,' said the Admiral, 'that we shall obtain such quantities of gold that there will be no need for dispute between me and the other servants of Their Highnesses.'

'We must hope so, sir,' said Rich. He tried to imagine how much gold would have to be imported before King Ferdinand considered it too much trouble to go into the accounts. He felt there was not that much gold in the whole world, even though Queen Isabella would be more easily satisfied.

'With Ophir found, and with shiploads of gold returning to Spain,' went on the Admiral, 'it will not be long before the Holy Places are free and the unbeliever ceases to defile Jerusalem.'

'I beg your pardon, sir?' said Rich, a little bewildered. This was something new to him.

'Did not Their Highnesses tell you?' asked the Admiral, surprised. 'The dearest wish of my heart, in achieving which I will die happy, is to set free the Holy Places. It is to that end that I intend to employ the gold of Ophir. I have visited the ports of the Levant, and I have studied the problem on the spot. With four thousand horse and fifty thousand foot three campaigns would reconquer the Holy Land for Christendom. I vowed my wealth to that end when I first reached the Indies, and I have no doubt of the assistance of Their Highnesses when the money becomes available.'

'Yes, sir,' said Rich, feebly. His mind struggled with the details of the plan–with the expense of maintaining an army of fifty thousand men for three years, with the question as to whether such a force would attain any success against the most powerful military state in Europe, and, lastly, whether Their Highnesses were likely to set the whole Mediterranean into a turmoil and wage a bloody war at the instigation of a vassal whose power they suspected even on the other side of the ocean. The whole scheme seemed utterly wild; and yet–six years ago the Admiral had discovered the Indies, in face of the hostile criticism of all the world. Today his prediction of the presence of land in a place where no one could be certain land existed had been dramatically confirmed. Nothing he said could be dismissed casually as an old man's maunderings.

'Nazareth!' said the Admiral in a kind of ecstasy. His mind was evidently still running on the same subject, but presumably in a very different way from Rich's. Yet his enthusiasm was infectious.

'It is a glorious project,' said Rich, in spite of himself.

'Yes,' replied the Admiral. 'And we are approaching the country which will provide the means to realize it. The land of the Trinity!'

There was dismissal in the gesture he made. His mind was wrapped now in lofty schemes like a mountain among the clouds. Rich bowed and withdrew. He was glad enough, too, to do so, for he was excited and impatient for his first sight of the Indies. He hoisted himself up on the bulwark, but the approaching land was still below the horizon from there, and he set himself to make the unaccustomed climb up the main shrouds–the whole rigging of the ship was still thick with clusters of men, like fruit in a tree. At the mast-head there were a dozen of the soldiers whom Bernardo de Tarpia commanded, and they grudgingly made room for him. Rich clung wildly to the yard, breathless and giddy. He was unaccustomed both to exercise and to heights, and up here the motion of the ship was greatly exaggerated. The horizon swooped round him for a few wild seconds until he regained his breath and his self-control. He wiped off the sweat which was streaming into his eyes and looked forward. There was the land; bright green slopes illuminated by the morning sun. The Indies! The most westerly and the most easterly limit of man's knowledge of the world he lived in. It was raining there to the northward–the sun behind him was lighting up a dazzling rainbow at that extremity of the island. From there southward there stretched luxuriant green hills; when the *Holy Name* rose on a wave he could see a line of white foam as the waves broke against the beach at their feet.

The sun was beating on his back like a flail; he wiped the sweat from his face again and continued his observations. It looked a rich enough country–that vivid green spoke well for its fertility–but it seemed virgin. No axe had ever plied among those forests. His straining eyes could see no sign of human habitation. Trying to compel himself to think clearly, he came to admit that at that distance he could not expect to see individual houses. But a town would be visible enough, for all that, and there was not the slightest hint of the existence of a town. A busy and prosperous coast would be thick with shipping, and there was no shipping in sight at all, not even–what was the word the Indian islanders used?–not even a canoe to make a speck on the flawless blue. Depression settled on him for a moment, which he told himself was unreasonable.

But God had vouchsafed a sign–the Admiral had announced to them the sight of the triple peak from which he had already named this new island. Rich swept his gaze along the skyline to identify the mountain. It was odd that he did not see it at once. He had looked from north to south; now he looked from south to north, more carefully. There was still no triple peak to be seen, and yet it ought to be obvious. The Admiral had been very positive about it indeed. It occurred to Rich that the explanation probably lay in the long interval which had elapsed since the Admiral had first seen the land. During that time the three peaks must have moved round into line relative to the new position of the ship.

With this in mind, he looked again. It was puzzling, for the ship had been heading straight for the land ever since it had first come in sight, and the relative movement could not have been great. Nowhere was there any outstanding peak which might be resolved into three summits from another point of view. With a little sinking at heart he began to realize another possibility–that the Admiral had not seen any triple peak at all, and had merely imagined it, the wish being father to the thought. That at least was humanly possible, and as far as he could see was the only hypothesis which fitted the facts; in that case, his study of logic assured him, he should work on that hypothesis until either it was disproved or a better one presented itself.

Nevertheless, it was disquieting, not merely to be at sea under an admiral who saw mountains which did not exist, but because–this was quite as disturbing–it tended to shake his faith in miracles. He had just disproved one for himself, and it was tempting to imagine that all miracles had a similar foundation in wishful thinking. That cut at the base of all religion, and led to doubt and heresy, and from that to polygamy and unsound theories on the distribution of property, to the fines of the Inquisition and the flames of Hell. He shuddered at the thought of the damnation of his soul, and clung to the yard in front of him, a little sick. The soldiers beside him were joking coarsely–their words came faintly to his ears as if from another room–about the naked women who were, they hoped, looking out at the ship from the island and awaiting their arrival. He tried to shake off his depression as he set himself to descend the shrouds.

As his feet touched the deck he found himself face to face with Rodrigo Acevedo, the elder of the two brothers.

'Well, doctor?' said Rodrigo. He was a tall, wiry man, of a bitter humour; his high arched nose and his flashing black eyes hinted at his Moorish blood, and he bore himself with an easy athleticism which made Rich conscious of his own ungainly plumpness, and this despite the fact that Rich had been at some pains to acquire that plumpness as increasing the dignity of a young doctor of law.

'Well?' said Rich, defensively.

'What do you think of the promised land?'

'It looks green and fertile enough,' answered Rich, still defensive.

'Did you see the great city of Cambaluc?'

'No. That must lie more to the north and west.'

'Yes. More to the north and west. How far? A hundred leagues? A thousand?'

Rich was silent.

'Five thousand, then?' sneered Acevedo.

'Not as far,' said Rich, hotly.

'And did you see the Grand Khan putting off to welcome us in his gilded galleon?'

'No,' said Rich. 'We have come this far south so as to avoid the Grand Khan's dominions.'

'We have avoided them in all conscience,' said Acevedo. 'Did you see any mountains of gold?'

'No,' replied Rich.

'None? You are quite sure? Did you see any mountain with a triple peak?'

'I went up the mast a long time after land was sighted,' said Rich, uneasily. 'The appearances had changed by then.'

'Yes,' sneered Acevedo again. 'Doubtless they had.'

'What do you think then?' asked Rich, his dignity reasserting itself. He was tired of being teased.

'I? I think nothing.'

Acevedo's mouth was distorted in a lopsided smile. Rich remembered what he had heard about Acevedo's past–of the Inquisition's descent upon the family of his betrothed; his prospective father-in-law had been burned at the stake in Toledo, and his prospective bride had been paraded in a fool's coat to make a solemn act of contrition before disappearing for life into a dungeon where the bread and water of affliction awaited her. The Holy Office must have questioned Acevedo closely enough. He was wise not to think; he was wise to come here to the Indies where the Holy Office would not have its attention called to him again so easily.

'That is sensible of you,' said Rich.

Their eyes met, with a gleam of understanding, before Acevedo was called away by a group clustered forward.

The backgammon boards were out, and the dice were already rattling there. Half the ship's company had already recovered from the excitement of sighting land and had plunged again into the diversions which had become habitual during the long voyage. The people were indifferent to their fates, careless as to where they were going, and that was only to be expected, seeing that three-quarters of them at least were on board either against their will or, like Acevedo, because Spain had grown too hot to hold them.

It was like the first voyage over again, when the ships had to be manned by criminals and ne'er-do-wells. For the second voyage there had been no lack of money nor of volunteers. Seventeen tall ships had sailed, with full complements, and a score of stowaways had been found on board, after sailing, so great had been the eagerness to join, as a result of the marvellous stories the Admiral had brought back of the wealth and the marvels of the newly discovered lands. But during the years that followed bad news had drifted back across the ocean. The original garrison left in Española were all dead by the time the second expedition arrived, and death had followed death in terrifying succession. Death by disease, death by poisonous serpents, death even from the pointed canes which were all the weapons the Indians possessed. Then death by famine, death by the gallows after mutiny. The stories told by the broken men who were lucky enough to make their way back to Spain had discouraged the nation. The adventurous spirits now followed Gonsalvo de Cordoba to the conquest of Italy. King Ferdinand, struggling in the whirlpool of European affairs, had naturally been dubious about expending further strength on chimerical conquests. Twenty ships from the Basque ports had been necessary to convey the Princess Katherine and a suitable train to her wedding with the Prince of Wales. It was not surprising that compulsion was necessary to man the ships for this present third expedition.

Rich remembered the sullen evidence given by the wretched survivors whom he had examined. Every man had cherished a grievance, mainly against the Admiral. It was his digest of the evidence which had influenced His Highness to despatch a lawyer to the Indies to investigate. Rich told himself that, like the eagle in the fable, it was he himself who had winged the arrow of his fate.

3

'By order of the Admiral!' announced the harsh voice of Alonso Perez in the stifling 'tweendecks. 'All gentlemen on board the *Holy Name* will wear half-armour and swords today. By order of the Admiral!'

It was nearly dawn, and still comparatively dark. The harsh voice awakened Rich from a tumultuous sleep; the heat and the excitement had kept him awake most of the night. He sat up on his chaff mattress in his shirt and listened to the yawns and groans around him. Someone pulled the deadlight away from the scuttle and let in a little more light and a whiff of fresher air; the sky visible through the hole was a rich dark blue. Twenty tousled men were stretching and rubbing their eyes, their hair and beards in disorder. Some were experimentally running their tongues over their palates, savouring the foul taste in their mouths resulting from a night in the poisonous atmosphere of the 'tweendecks.

He got to his knees–the deck above was too low to admit of standing, with the 'tweendecks floored with chests–rolled up his mattress and struggled to open the chest beneath it. Cristobal Garcia lay next to him, against the bulkhead; he was big and burly and bearded to the eyes and clearly in a bad temper. An unexpected movement of the ship caught Rich off his balance and rolled him against him. Garcia growled like a wounded bear.

'I beg your pardon, sir,' said Rich, hastily.

He tugged the heavy bundle of his armour out of the chest and allowed the lid to fall with a crash. Garcia yelped at the noise in his ear.

'God, what a devilish din!' he said. He got on to his elbow and eyed Rich sardonically. 'So our little fat Doctor of Law becomes a soldier today?'

'The Admiral's orders,' said Rich.

'The Admiral can work miracles by his orders, apparently,' growled Garcia.

Rich kept his mouth shut. It saved trouble, although he could have replied that he was entitled to wear the gentlemanly sword although he was merely a vintner's son; half the artisans of Catalonia could do so–much to the amusement of fine gentlemen–thanks to the peculiar laws of the kingdom. He comforted himself with the thought that although not yet forty he had already accumulated more wealth than was owned by all the segundones–younger sons–in this crowded space put together. He had acquired it honestly, too, and with no advantage over them save a good education. In the whole fleet he was perhaps the only man who had not been driven by necessity to join, the only man save the Admiral who had already made a name for himself in his own walk of life.

Yet it was cold comfort, all the same. He could not meet them in the lists, which was the only kind of argument they understood, he had never seen a battlefield, he could only just manage to sit a horse. More important still, they were completely convinced of their superiority over him in consequence of their ancestry. In their eyes he was hardly more of an equal than, say, an ape or a mule. Without one hundred and twenty-eight quarterings of nobility he could no more reckon himself their equal than he could reckon himself the equal of the archangels of God.

It was quite an athletic feat to wriggle into clothes and armour under the low deck while crouched on his mattress. He was sweating profusely by the time the leather coat and breeches were on, and the back and breastplates buckled about him. He grabbed his sword and his helmet and scrambled out, bent double.

There was the dull gleam of armour to be seen everywhere about the ship. He put on his helmet and felt its unaccustomed weight upon his forehead. He slung his sword by its broad leather belt over his shoulder and saw to it that its hilt was clear. The deck was crowded with crossbowmen in helmet and jerkin, and spearmen with helmet and leather shield. On the forecastle the bombardier and his two mates were cleaning the two swivel cannons ready for use. They had a barrel of gunpowder and a chest full of their enormous bullets, each nearly the size of a man's fist. The six hand-gunmen were aft, by the taffrail, each with his ponderous weapon and his rest. Of a certainty, it was all extremely impressive, and grew more so each minute as the hidalgos came crawling out of the 'tweendecks in helmet and armour. No embassy from the shore but could could fail to be struck by all this display.

Rich could see, as he peered under the peak of his helmet, the gleam of more armour on the decks of the two caravels lying hove-to a short distance away. The fleet was close up to the land, and had been lying-to through the dark hours. Rich gazed across the intervening water; easy green slopes, lush vegetation, dazzling white surf where the ocean swell burst upon the beaches. The steady east wind blew, but it hardly tempered the sweltering heat; Rich in his armour and helmet felt as if he were being roasted alive.

Here came the Admiral, in his usual dignified procession, walking stiffly on account of his rheumatism. Orders were bellowed and stamping men hauled at ropes. Round came the ships, westward before the wind, heading close along shore. Now Rich could understand why the Admiral had so persistently, when the expedition was being got together, demanded only little ships–nothing more than a hundred tons. The two small caravels sailed far nearer the beach and had the land under far closer observation than could the *Holy Name*. A sailor in the bows of each vessel was heaving the lead and chanting the depths, but apart from the men engaged in the actual work of the ship, everyone's attention was fixed upon the land.

It was a silent shore. There were birds wheeling overhead, but save for the birds there was no sound, no sign of life. Only the expressionless green slopes and the monotonous surf; a dead landscape, changing and yet in no way different as they cruised along beside it. They had hoped for the teeming millions of Asia, opulent cities and luxurious princes–to impress whom they were wearing the armour that burdened them. Even at the worst they had hoped at least to see the laughing naked peoples whom they had discovered in the other islands, but here there was nothing. Nothing at all.

The Admiral was giving an order now, and the bombardier fussed over his swivel cannon. He ladled powder into the muzzle, and stuffed it down with a mop. He clicked his flint and steel over his tinder, blew at the spark, tried again, got his match alight, whirled it round to make it glow, and pressed it on the touch-hole. There was a loud bang and a puff of smoke. The birds screamed and a little cloud of them appeared above the trees on the island. The echo of the report ran flatly along the shore, and that was all. No welcoming human appeared; the armoured men stood stupid and silent on the decks.

'A lovely land, Don Narciso,' said the Admiral's voice in Rich's ear–he started with surprise. 'Green and fertile, like Andalusia in spring time.'

'Yes, Your Excellency,' said Rich, unhappily.

The Admiral was breathing great lungfuls of air. There was a fresh colour to his cheeks and a fresh light in his eyes. He wore his armour and his cloak over it as if they were gossamer.

'There is something rejuvenating about the air here,' said the Admiral. 'Do you not notice how fresh and sweet it is?'

'The sun is hot,' protested Rich, feebly.

'Naturally, seeing that at noon it is directly overhead at this time of year. But that calls forth the treasures of the soil, the fruits, the minerals. This will prove to be the richest quarter of the earth, Don Narciso.'

'We must hope so.'

'Hope? We know it to be so already. The ancients proved it, and the Scriptures tell us so. Last night, Don Narciso, instead of sleeping, I pondered over our new discoveries. I thought about this new balminess of the air, as compared with the windless and torrid regions of the ocean which we have crossed. I compared this blessed land with the stifling unhealthiness of those regions of Africa which the Portuguese have discovered and which lie as close to the equinoctial line as does this. There must be an explanation of the difference. Is it not likely to be that the earth is not a perfect sphere, as one might deduce from what one knows of the northern half, but drawn out and prolonged towards this point, like, say, the thinner end of a pear? Or perhaps on a smaller scale–one can naturally not be certain yet of exact proportions–like the nipple of a woman's breast?'

'The possibility had not occurred to me, Your Excellency,' said Rich, bewildered.

'But now you must appreciate it. Here we must be farther from the earth's centre, closer to heaven, remote from evil. I think we must be close beside the Garden of Eden, the Earthly Paradise, where the Tree of Knowledge grows, and where man is near to God.'

Rich stared up, under his helmet's peak, at the tall, gaunt Admiral and the ecstasy in his face. Yesterday they had reached Ophir, today it was the Garden of Eden. He could think of no passages either in the ancients or in the Scriptures to justify either theory. He was at a loss for words with which to make any pretence at a reply. But he was preserved from the necessity, for the Admiral's keen eyes had detected an indentation in the shore line. He turned to give orders in his clear, penetrating tenor, and the seamen leaped to obey him. The steersman dragged the tiller over; the sails were clewed up; the anchor was let go and the cable roared through the hawse-hole. Even Rich, with his mere theoretical knowledge of the sea, was impressed by the neatness of the manoeuvre–as impressed as he was by the Admiral's sudden change from a dreamer of lunatic dreams to a sailor of profound practical ability. As the *Holy Name* swung to her anchor the Admiral turned to Rich.

'A stream comes down to the sea at that beach, Don Narciso. I shall send ashore for fresh water. Would you care to go with the landing party and take possession of the island in the name of Their Highnesses?'

'Indeed yes. I must thank Your Excellency.'

There was no denying the thrill of excitement which ran through him at the suggestion. Rich forgot the weight of his armour and the heat of the sun; he fidgeted with his sword hilt while the sailors rigged the yardarm tackles with which to swing out the longboat from the waist. The cooper supervised the lowering of the empty barrels into the boat; six seamen scrambled down and took their places at the oars; Osorio the boatswain took the tiller. At a sharp command from the Admiral four of Bernardo de Tarpia's crossbowmen followed him. Them came Antonio Spallanzani, the Admiral's Italian squire, with the Admiral's standard, bearing the lions and castles of Leon and Castile, recently granted him, quartered with the barry wavy, argent and azure, charged with green islands, to represent his discoveries. Those lions and castles in the flag might be of use if ever a legal argument arose regarding the sovereignty over this new land. They would help to make out Their Highnesses' case–but although the Admiral might be suspected of much, no one had yet openly accused him of dreaming of an independent sovereignty.

They were awaiting for him. Rich clambered down into the boat, ungracefully, conscious of many eyes upon him, and only realizing after he had settled himself at Spallanzani's side that if he had slipped into the sea his armour would have carried him straight to the bottom. The sailors tugged at the oars, and they went dancing over the sea towards the shore.

The Italian sat silent–he had a reputation for taciturnity–while they rowed past the anchored caravels, busy hoisting out their boats, and crept in closer to the shore. There was still only the golden beach and the white surf and the tangled greenery to be seen. The sailors rested on their oars for a space while Osorio stood up and studied the surf. He gave a hoarse cry; the sailors tugged sharply at the oars, and the boat leaped forward on the shoulder of a wave, hurrying on until its motion died away and the sand scraped under the keel and the white foam eddied back past them. The sailors leaped out, thigh deep, in the water, and hauled the boat up as far as it would go, until by a wave of his hand Osorio indicated to the two gentlemen that it was time for them to step ashore. Rich scrambled up into the bows and from there over the side; a dying wave swirled past his knees as he stepped into the water and his feet sank in the sand. He struggled up the beach, oppressed by the weight of his armour, until he was beyond the water's edge. The Italian was close behind him, and the crossbowmen followed, their crossbows on their shoulders. Spallanzani struck the shaft of the flag into the sand and took a paper from his breast.

'We,' he read, a barbarous Tuscan accent colouring his Castilian, 'Don Cristopher Columbus, Admiral of the Ocean, Viceroy and Governor of the Islands of the Indies, Captain-General and Grandee of Spain—' it was a solemn formula of possession.

When he had finished Rich took off his helmet.

'This is done,' he proclaimed, bareheaded, to the four solemn crossbowmen, 'in the names of Their Highnesses Don Ferdinand and Donna Isabella, by the grace of God King and Queen of Castile, Leon, Arragon, Sicily, Granada, Toledo, Valencia, Galicia, Mallorca, and Seville, Count and Countess of Barcelona, Roussillon and Cerdagne, Duke and Duchess of Athens and Neopatra, Marquis and Marchioness of Oristano and Goziano, Lord and Lady of Biscay and Molina.'

He had left out quite a number of the titles, but he had done enough to ensure the legality of the Royal possession, especially as the only witnesses were crossbowmen, standing with ox-like stupidity in the sunshine. Osorio and his men had put out the boat's anchor, and were carrying empty water breakers up the beach. At a roar from the boatswain two of the crossbowmen joined in the work; the other two wound up their bows, laid bolts in the grooves, and walked forward to where the stream came bubbling down out of the greenery, to stand as sentries on guard against surprise. It was an elementary precaution to take, so elementary that Rich experienced a feeling of annoyance that he had not thought of it and ordered it himself.

He cleared the hilt of his sword and walked curiously up the beach, conscious now of a particular thrill at making these, his first steps in the New World. The little stream bubbled and gurgled, and he stooped and filled his hands and drank, over and over again, rejoicing in the water's cool freshness and having enough to drink after six weeks of a ration of only three leathern cups of water a day. He walked on beside the stream, to be engulfed in the delicious shade of the vegetation, so dense and tangled that it was only by walking ankle deep in the pebbles that he was able to make any progress. He turned a corner and the forest behind him cut him off from the sea more effectively than the closing of a door. The sounds of the beach–the surf, and the voices of the watering party–ended abruptly.

Here he could only hear the sound of the brook and the clatter of birds' wings above him. Looking upward, he could see the birds flitting through the tangle of the branches, birds of gay colours, crying harshly to each other. Some brilliant red flowers grew just out of his reach to his left; there were some strange greenish-yellow blooms growing on a decaying stump on the other side of the stream. The noise of his passage disturbed half a dozen more birds–like starlings, he thought at first, and then he saw that they were all of a sombre black, beak and claw and all, funereal birds, with something repellent about their metallic chirping.

There was a breathless heat here in the forest. The shade had been grateful enough at first, but out in the open there was at least a wind, and here the air was stagnant and warm. The sweat streamed down from under his helmet, and his skin began to itch furiously inside his armour where he could not scratch. A mosquito sang into his ear and then bit his neck. He brushed it off, and soon he was busy brushing off flies from neck and face and hands and wrists. He burst through into a little clear space, where the stream expanded into a small pool and marshy banks. There was a startled croaking of frogs, and a dozen splashes told how they had dived back into the pool on his approach. On the surface of the water lay two fallen trees, their exposed parts green with moss; so wide was the pool that the interlaced branches hardly met overhead, and, looking upward, he could see the blue sky again. Tall canes grew here, each twice the height of a man and thicker than his wrist. The gay birds with hooked beaks flew thick–parrots, they were. He remembered that in the Admiral's triumphal procession through Barcelona, when he was received by Their Highnesses on his return from his first voyage of discovery, there had been a great many parrots displayed. Probably there was nothing to be found at this landing place which was not to be seen in Guanahani or Española.

He turned back and made his way down the stream again. Were those bees, beating the air above the scarlet flowers? Rich looked at them more closely. They were tiny birds, brilliant in their colouring. He thought they were the most lovely things he had ever seen in his life. He plunged into the thorns in order to view them more closely, but they flew away, erratically, at his slow approach, and would not return. With a twinge of real regret he continued his way. A loud challenge greeted him at the edge of the wood, and he replied, a little self-consciously, 'Friend.' It was the first time in his life a sentinel had ever challenged him.

The crossbowman lowered his weapon and allowed him to pass, blinking in the sunshine. Someone was kneeling at the water's edge, above the point where the men were filling their barrels. He had a flat pan in his hand, which, with a gentle rocking motion, he was holding at the surface of the water. There was gravel in the bottom of the pan, and under the influence of the current and of the man's raking fingers it was gradually being swept away. Rich recognized the man and guessed what he was doing–it was Diego Alamo the assayer, who had sailed in the caravel *Santa Anna* along with them. Alamo had dealt in gold and precious stones; he was learned in the languages of the East and with his knowledge of Hebrew and Chaldean might be useful when they made contact with Asiatic civilization. Under suspicion of being a crypto-Jew he had thought it well to accept the appointment of Royal Assayer to escape the attention of the Holy Office.

Alamo with a skilful jerk flirted the remaining water from the pan and studied the layer of sediment closely, inclining the pan to this side and to that so as to catch the faintest gleam of colour. Then he shrugged his shoulders and washed the pan clean, looking up to meet Rich's eyes upon him.

'Ha, good day, Don Narciso,' he said, white teeth showing in a smile.

'Good day,' said Rich. 'Are there signs of gold?'

'Not so far. The country looks as if it might bear gold, but I'll certify that this stream has none.'

Rich forgot any disappointment he might feel at that statement in the pleasure of this re-encounter with a friend–Alamo and he were old acquaintances. He made the conventional enquiries as to whether Alamo had enjoyed his passage across the ocean–conventional and yet sincere. It was odd to ask those questions here, on the shores of the Indies.

'Well enough, thank you,' answered Alamo. There was a wry smile on his dark intelligent face; Rich guessed that Alamo was as much out of place among the seamen and gentlemen-adventurers of the *Santa Anna* as he himself was in the *Holy Name*.

Alamo rose to his feet, brushing his hands clean. The beach was a scene of animation now, with three boats lying in the shallows and a score of men carrying water casks. The two caravels lay beyond, black upon the blue, and farther out the *Holy Name* rode to her anchor.

'Have you been into the forest?' asked Alamo.

'Yes.'

'Did you see any animals? Any rocks?'

'Only the pebbles and boulders of the stream bed. The forest is too thick to see more.'

Alamo was looking around the beach.

'Over there,' he said, pointing. 'The rock comes down to the sea there.'

They walked over the sand to the place he had indicated, and Alamo ran his hands over the rocky ledges.

'Gold is unlikely here,' he announced. 'These rocks are dead. They are smooth and lifeless–feel them for yourself, Don Narciso. It is the spirited, lively rocks which bear the noble metals.'

He climbed over the ridge and dropped on to the sand the other side. There were more rocks beyond, running out to the water.

'Now this is strange,' announced Alamo.

He went down on to his knees to examine his find more closely. Among the brown rocks there were patches and dabs and seams of black, and he pawed at them, clearly puzzled.

'This appears to be pitch,' he said. 'Bitumen. I have seen specimens brought from the Holy Land, but never before have I seen it *in situ*. Now how comes it here?'

He looked up at the forest and out at the sea.

'It is found on the shores of the Dead Sea,' he explained, 'at the foot of arid cliffs. It was with fiery pitch that God overwhelmed Sodom and Gomorrah, but the Moslems believe it to be formed by the great excess of salt in the water, under the influence of a burning sun. Now, is the ocean here more salt than usual?'

'It is not dead, at least,' said Rich. 'There is weed growing. And the gulls prove that there must be fish.'

'Quite right. I should have thought of that. Yet it is hard to think of any other explanation of this pitch. The Dead Sea lies in the midst of deserts. There is no life, no plants, no birds, although I am assured by credible authority that the story is incorrect that birds drop dead who fly over its mephitic surface. Two places more unlike than that and this it is hard to imagine.'

'Very hard,' agreed Rich, thinking of the lush vegetation and the teeming bird life around them.

'Has a Sodom been overwhelmed here, too?' asked Alamo.

'Not unless the name of God has penetrated here,' answered Rich, fairly sure of his theology on this point.

'Exactly. That is why I sought for a naturalistic explanation.'

Alamo walked on among the rocks of the beach, Rich straying a little apart from him along the water's edge. It was he who made the final discovery, and his sharp cry brought Alamo hurrying back to him. There was a little stretch of smooth sand here, at which Rich was staring; in the sand was a wide, shallow groove, and around it were the half-obliterated prints of bare feet. Rich had already made the deductions from the appearances.

'No ship's boat made that mark,' he said. 'There is no sign of a keel.'

Alamo nodded agreement, stooping to peer at the footprints.

'There is little enough left to see,' he said. 'But I should think that the feet that made those marks were longer and narrower than any Spaniard's.'

'Yes.'

'And how long ago were they made? An hour? Two hours?'

They looked at each other, a little helpless. Neither of them had the faintest idea.

'We can be sure of one thing at least,' said Rich. 'The people here are not as eager to meet us as were those of Cuba and Española.'

A bellowing behind them made them turn; the watering party was waving arms to them in recall. They picked their way back over the rocks.

4

The squadron was still sailing westward along the south coast of Trinidad, while the Admiral listened to Rich's report. His face fell a little when he heard that Alamo had found no sign of gold, but he grew cheerful again over the undoubted evidence that the island was inhabited, and over the other details which Rich conveyed.

'Pitch?' he said. 'Bitumen?'

He ran his fingers through his beard as he pondered the phenomenon.

'What did Alamo say about it?'

'He said that it was found beside the Dead Sea,' said Rich. He was a little shocked to notice an inward quaver as he said it; he was actually dreading some new theory as to the fleet's whereabouts.

'That is so. It is found in Egypt, too, in the deserts that border the Nile.'

'There is no desert here, Your Excellency,' said Rich, stoutly.

'No.' The Admiral looked over at the luxurious green coast. 'Yet it makes me more sure of the Earthly Paradise being at hand–I shall write to Their Highnesses to that effect–but perhaps I shall have more evidence still by the time I can spare a ship to return to Spain.'

'I have no doubt you will, sir,' said Rich, strangely sick at heart.

The armoured men were lounging about the deck. Spallanzani had his lute, and was singing Italian love-songs to the accompaniment of soft chords from it, to an audience of hidalgos. They had eaten their meal of weevilly biscuits and rancid cheese with its flavour of cockroach. Rich remembered with regret the roast sucking pig on which he had dined his last day on shore, and was quite startled to note that all the same he did not wish himself home. This crushing heat, this wearisome armour, the foul food, the wild talk of Ophir and the Earthly Paradise–notwithstanding all these things he was happier where he was, here in the New World, than sitting in his furred robe in the admiralty hall in Barcelona listening to the crooked pleadings of crooked lawyers paid by crooked merchants. Seventeen years of it–the Consulate of the Sea, the Laws of Oleron, and the Code of Wisby, Justinian and the fueros of Barcelona; it was better to be able to raise his head and sniff the scented air of Trinidad.

A loud cry from a look-out brought everybody to their feet again. There was a canoe, a black speck under the glaring sun, full in sight as they rounded a headland. It was well out to sea, on passage between cape and cape; they could see the flash of the paddles as the men bent to their work. With the wind right aft the squadron overhauled it fast; it turned frantically to make for the shore, but the *Santa Anna* was there, cutting it off, and it headed back. Fifty yards from the *Holy Name* the paddles ceased work, and the canoe drifted idly on the blue.

Brown and naked, with streaming black hair, the Indians stared with frightened eyes at the huge hull drifting down upon them. One of them stood up, overcome with curiosity, in the desire to see better, revealing herself as a woman, quite naked save for her necklace. A loud roar of laughter burst from the ship–a naked woman was so rare a sight as naturally to excite laughter. She sat down abruptly, with hands over her face, and in her place a man rose to his feet, balancing precariously in the rocking canoe. He set an arrow to the string of the bow he held, raised the weapon and drew it to his breast, and loosed off the shaft.

Rich saw the arrow in the air; it struck his breastplate with a slight tap, and dropped on the deck with a faint clatter. It was effort as feeble as a child's–the shaft was already spent in its fifty yards' flight by the time it reached him. His furred judicial robe would have been as effective protection as his steel breastplate. The arrow was merely a thin cane, crudely sharpened at one end, and with a single parrot's feather at the other. But the gesture had excited the Spaniards. A crossbowman lifted his lumbering weapon to reply, and lowered it again at a hasty order from the Admiral.

'Put that crossbow down!' he called in his high tenor. 'We are at peace with them. Hey, Diego, there, beat your tambourine, and you boys dance to it. Show them that we mean no harm.'

It was a ludicrous scene, the ship's boys capering on the forecastle, and the sullen Indians gazing up at them uncomprehending. The canoe was in the lee of the *Holy Name* now, and the wind was gradually drifting the big ship down upon it. The Admiral himself was up on the bulwark, jingling hawk's bells–hawk's bells had been found to be an unfailing attraction in the other Indian islands–and Alonso Perez was beside him, a red woollen cap in either hand held temptingly towards them

'Jorge,' muttered the Admiral out of the corner of his mouth to a seaman close at hand. 'Strip off your coat and make ready to upset the canoe.'

The canoe was close alongside as Jorge swung himself over the bulwark and dropped amid a wild scream from the Indians. The canoe overturned, and the occupants were flung into the sea. They were glad to clutch the ropes thrown to them and to be pulled on deck, where they stood, dripping water, with the Spaniards clustered round them. Four of them were men and two women, the women quite naked, but three of the men were wearing cloths of coarse cotton about their shoulders–Rich examined the material. It was of poorer weave than any he had ever seen.

'Make fast the canoe!' called the Admiral over the bulwark. 'Put those paddles back in her!'

The Indians made a frightening group, their arms about each other and their teeth chattering in fright, while the Spaniards pushed and elbowed to see more closely these strange humans, who felt no shame at nudity, who had never heard the name of God, who knew nothing of steel or gunpowder. Someone stretched out a hand and stroked a woman's shoulder; she shrank from the touch at first, but when it was renewed she gradually recovered from her shyness and smiled a little over her shoulder at the man who caressed her, like a child, but a new bellow of laughter made her seek safety again beside her fellows.

The Admiral pushed through the mob, resplendent in his scarlet velvet with his glittering helmet and armour; the Spaniards falling back to make room for him revealed him and his position of authority to the Indians. He was uttering strange words learned in Cuba and Española, and they responded to his soothing tone of voice even though they clearly could not understand what he said.

'Guanahani,' said the Admiral. 'Cibao. Cuba. Hayti.'

The names of these places meant nothing to them.

'Canoa,' said the Admiral, pointing overside.

That they understood; they nodded and smiled.

'Canoa,' they said, in chorus, and one of them went on to say more, in a sing-song tune.

It was the Admiral's turn to shake his head.

'Their speech is not unlike that of Española,' he said to Rich. 'But it is not the same, save for a few words, like canoa.'

'Canoa,' repeated one of the Indians, parrot fashion.

The Admiral jingled one of his hawk's bells enticingly, and they eyed it with wonder. He offered it, and they shrank back a little. He took the hand of one of the men and put the bell into it, shutting his fingers over it, and then setting the bell a-rattle again by shaking the man's fist. An awed expression crept over the man's face as he realized that this bell was actually to be his. He could hardly credit his good fortune, cautiously opening his hand and finally jingling the bell delightedly. All the Indians were smiling broadly now.

Rich's eyes were on the necklace worn by the woman in the background. He stretched out his hand to examine it; she shrank away for a moment, and he tried to make soothing noises. But immediately she understood what he wanted, and stepped forward, proffering a loop of the necklace to him. He examined it closely. It was a string of pearls–two yards of pearls. The other Spaniards noticed what he was doing, and surged towards them, frightening her; a score of hands were stretched out for the necklace, when the Admiral turned fiercely upon them and they dropped back again.

'They are pearls,' said the Admiral after examination. He took one of the red woollen caps from Alonso Perez and offered it to her with a gesture of exchanging it for the necklace. She did not understand. He jingled a hawk's bell, and reached for the necklace again. Suddenly her expression changed to one of comprehension, and with two swift movements she uncoiled the necklace from her neck and thrust it, a great double handful, into his hands. Her puzzled look as he proffered the cap in exchange revealed that she had intended the necklace as a gift.

'It is the same as in Española,' said the Admiral. 'The heathen have no notion of barter. They think that because a stranger wants a thing that is sufficient reason for giving it.'

The surging Spaniards round laughed at such folly.

'She does not know what that cap is for, either, Your Excellency,' remarked someone in the background.

'True,' said the Admiral.

At his order Perez took of his helmet and the Admiral perched the cap on top of his mass of hair, stood back with a gesture of admiration, took the cap again and put it on the head of the trembling woman. The other Indians chattered at the sight, teeth flashing in smiles.

'And look at this, Your Excellency. Look!' said a Spaniard, loudly.

One of the Indian men had something hanging on a string round his neck, a little fleck of something with a yellow glint. It was a tiny fragment of gold, smaller than half a castellano but gold all the same. Rich heard the quick intake of breath all round the ring. Gold! The Admiral strode up, his expression so hard and fierce that the Indian raised his arm to ward off a blow.

'Where did you get this?' demanded the Admiral.

The Indian still cowered away, and the Admiral, with an obvious effort at self-control, changed his tone.

'Send for Alamo from the *Santa Anna*,' he said, aside, and then, turning back to the Indian, he smiled winningly. He raised his eyebrows in an obvious question, pointed to the bit of gold, and then away to the island. The Indian thought for a moment and pointed westward. There was a general murmur from the crowd–there was gold in the west.

'Much?' asked the Admiral, making a gesture with widespread arms. 'Much?'

The Indian after a moment of puzzlement extended his arms in agreement, to the sound of a renewed murmur from the crowd. There was much gold to be found; but Rich, watching the by-play, was not quite sure. The Indian was clearly doubtful of the significance of the question asked him. He might be meaning that the gold was far away, or even, conceivably, that it was hard to come by. Years of sifting evidence had given Rich an insight into the extraordinary ways in which misunderstandings can arise.

The Admiral was jingling another hawk's bell and offering to barter it for the gold, and the Indian made the exchange gladly as soon as he grasped what the Admiral wanted.

'This piece of gold would buy five hundred hawk's bells,' commented the Admiral; he reached for another scarlet cap and set it on the Indian's head, to the accompaniment of a renewed chorus of admiration from the others.

'They like caps equally as much as hawk's bells,' said the Admiral to Rich. 'In that they are more like the cannibal Indians of Dominica than those of Española. That is what one would expect.'

The longboat, rowed as fast as a dozen stout arms could drive her, had returned now from the *Santa Anna*, and Alamo reported himself to the Admiral. He looked at the string of pearls which the Admiral gave him for inspection.

'They are pearls undoubtedly,' he said, feeling their texture with his lips. He shaded them from the sun with his body to see their lustre. 'Yet they are different from the pearls of the Orient. Their tinge and lustre are not the same.'

'Are they valuable?' demanded the Admiral.

'Oh, yes. Half their value has disappeared because of the clumsy way in which they have been bored, but I would give you a good price for them in the Calle del Paradis. As rarities, even if for no other reason, they would stand high. And there are some good specimens here, too. These two match well and are of superb lustre. A queen could have no better ear-drops.'

'And what of this gold?'

Alamo took the fragment of metal, poised it on a finger-tip, tested it against his teeth, turned it to obtain a flash of the sun from it.

'That is gold,' he said. 'Without my acids and scales I cannot assay it, but I am certain it is pure and virgin. It contains no base metal, in other words, and it is in a state of nature, as it was found.'

'And where would that be?'

Alamo shrugged.

'In the bed of a stream, most likely. Or in sand or loam close to a stream. Gold found in the heart of a rock is never in pieces as large as this.'

'Thank you. Now speak to these men in the tongues of the East.'

Alamo addressed the Indians in a language of which Rich understood no word. Nor did the Indians, to judge by the blankness of their expressions. Alamo tried again, this time in Arabic with which Rich was faintly familiar, but without result. He spoke to them in Greek, of which Rich had a working knowledge, and then again in a language faintly reminiscent of Arabic to Rich. The Indians' faces remained impassive.

'That is Hebrew, Greek, the Arabic of the East and the Arabic of the West, Your Excellency,' said Alamo.

'Thank you. We can let them go now,' said the Admiral.

He took more caps, and set one on the head of each Indian. He pressed a hawk's bell into each of their hands, and then he waved them over the side to where their canoe, gunwale deep, floated at the end of a line.

'Go in peace,' he said, as they still stood awestruck at the magnificence of the presents pressed upon them. He drew one by the wrist to the ship's side to make his meaning plain. They slid down the line into the water-logged canoe; one of the women took hold of a big shell tied to the gunwale and with it began to scoop the water swiftly out–it was obvious that they were perfectly accustomed to having their cranky craft capsized. The line was cast off, and the men took the paddles. Slowly the canoe stood away from the ship, heading in for the land. The scarlet caps danced over the water, bright in the light of the setting sun. The Indians never looked back; Rich, watching their course, saw the canoe turn abruptly aside in fright, like a shying horse, from the caravels as the big sails were trimmed to the wind again.

'With kind treatment and presents,' said the Admiral, coming to stand beside Rich, 'we can hope that they will tell their fellows and send them to us. We need pearls and we need gold.'

Not merely for any mad scheme for reconquering the Holy Land either, thought Rich. He knew how precarious was the Admiral's hold on the Royal favour, despite the presence of his two sons–one of them a bastard, too–as pages at court.

'We have made a start,' he said, cheerfully.

'So we have,' said the Admiral; in his two fists was the long string of pearls, luminous in the failing light.

5

In the lavender dawn next morning, when the ships had hardly gathered way after lying-to all night, the look-out cried that he saw more land. It was a low peak on their port bow; to starboard the southern coast of the island of Trinidad terminated in a similar peak, with a narrow strait between, towards which the easterly breeze was briskly pushing them. The Admiral came with his limping step to see for himself. He gave two hurried orders, hailing the caravels himself, in his high voice, as they converged upon the *Holy Name* towards the strait. Rich did not understand at the time all that happened next. He saw the anchors let go and the sails got in, and the longboat manned to go up the strait and take soundings, but before the boat could cast off the sailors in the ships were running and shouting with excitement. The anchors were not holding on the rocky bottom, there was a fierce current running here of which they could have no knowledge until they tried to stop, and the wind was still pushing briskly against hulls and rigging. Stern first, and with anchors dragging helplessly, the ships were moving fast towards the unknown passage–a fact which Rich found it hard to realize at the time, and of the danger of it all he was quite unconscious.

He saw the *Santa Anna* lurch as her anchor caught, saw her cable part, and saw her swing round and race them on their course towards the strait. The rocks to the right, all a-boil with surf, seemed to be coming nearer, dangerously near. The Admiral was shouting orders; Osorio was running forward with an axe, and the Admiral himself was hounding the panicky sailors up the shrouds. The cable was cut, the mainsail dropped. High and clear the Admiral's voice called to the steersman. Over went the tiller. For a few more harrowing seconds the ship, nearly aback, hesitated; they could hear the surf on the rocks. Then slowly she turned and gathered way. She lurched in a sudden boil of current, and a moment after she was running free, as if nothing had happened at all, on a sea mirror-smooth, with the rocks far astern and the land already far distant on either hand.

The Admiral was smiling as he returned from setting the men to work at preparing the spare anchor and cable.

'Sailors are ignorant and superstitious,' he said, limping up to Rich. 'On seas where no Christian has ever sailed before I suppose it is excusable. When they found that anchors did not hold and that we were in the grip of a current they imagined all sorts of things. They thought we were near Sinbad's loadstone mountain, being dragged by the attraction of our iron. Or they thought we had reached the edge of the world and were about to slide off. They thought of everything, in fact, except the need for getting the ship under control again.'

'*You* thought of that, Your Excellency,' said Rich. The incident confirmed what he knew well enough already, that the Admiral was a first-rate seaman with a clear head for any emergency.

'That is thanks to the Blessed Virgin,' said the Admiral, simply and devoutly. 'She has never deserted me. Not even in worse perils than that. But that was a strange current between those islands.'

He shaded his eyes from the sun and looked back at the perilous passage.

'So it appears,' said Rich.

'The caravels are safe. They were nearer the centre of the strait. It was well that we hove-to last night,' commented the Admiral, half to himself. 'I shall call the new land the Isle of Grace. And the strait must have a name, too, for my chart. The Serpent's Mouth!'

'Your Excellency is ingenious at devising names. But of course you have had much practice.'

The Admiral flushed a little at the compliment. He smiled confidently, and made a deprecating gesture with his hand; the smile almost became a grin.

'Even of the devising of names one can grow tired,' he said. 'And the places must have names. To me they are each distinct enough, but in my letters to Their Highnesses I must have something by which to call them.'

At that human moment Rich felt himself to be more in sympathy with, and fonder of, the Admiral than he had ever been before. He must have been in this mood at the time when he made his famous demonstration with the egg. The

Admiral showed in a far better light as a practical seaman and as a man of the world than as a highfalutin theorist. But one at least of his theories–that there was a route to the Indies across the ocean–had most certainly been proved correct.

'I could wish,' said the Admiral, ' that we should see more Indians. We need to trade. And we shall need labour for the mines.'

He called a request to Carvajal, and the *Holy Name* headed once more towards the coast of Trinidad, a seaman at the lead to ascertain the safe limit of their approach. The land was tantalizingly just too far away for close observation.

'Might I—' began Rich, and then he hesitated, surprised at himself, before he took the plunge. 'Might I take the longboat closer in to shore?'

'I would be glad if you did,' said the Admiral. 'You must take every possible opportunity to be able to report favourably to Their Highnesses on the wealth of these islands.'

Rich had no time to repent. It was a surprisingly short interval before he found himself in the sternsheets of the longboat, indubitably invested with his first command at sea, and experiencing a tremor of fearful excitement in consequence. The old sailor Jorge sat at the tiller beside him, two more sailors were at the sheet, and forward there sat five gentlemen of coat-armour, glad of the opportunity of escaping for a while from the confinement of the ship and ready in consequence to acquiesce in the command with which the Admiral had tacitly invested him. Rodrigo Acevedo was one of them, however–there was a hint of a smile in his handsome swarthy face as he met Rich's eye, which told Rich that Acevedo was aware of the inner doubts which were troubling him.

The wind was off the land, blowing briskly enough, and the boat lay over gaily on her side as they headed parallel to the shore, the sailors handling sheet and tiller deftly as they translated Rich's vague directions into action. The coast curved here in a wide bay, shelving so gradually that even the longboat had to keep two hundred yards from the beach, and everywhere the monotonous green vegetation came down to the very water's edge–green, eternally green. There were irregularly shaped hills in the background, but never a sign of a clearing, no hint of smoke to betray the habitation of man. The wind blew more briskly yet, and the sky was overcast, yet it was stifling hot. As Rich stirred uncomfortably in his seat he felt the sweat trickling in the folds of his clothes. A rainstorm changed the colour of the hills from green to grey; it came drifting towards them over the grey sea. Soon it was upon them–they heard the hiss of the drops upon the water as it approached. The first drops rang sharply on the helmet which Rich wore–he had discarded his armour–but immediately the distinctive sound was blurred in his ears by the roar of the rain beating everywhere about them. Entirely exposed as they were, they could neither think nor see. The rain fell in cataracts, blotting out both ships and shore from view, soaking them and dazing them as it drove into their faces.

Rich was still unconscious of Jorge moving beside him. He was still attending to his duties, presumably by touch and instinct, and his example diverted Rich from his first instinct to order the longboat to run back for shelter to the ship. Rich set his teeth; he would not be the first to give in. As captain, even though it was only of a longboat, it was his duty to make no complaint about the conditions, and the thought of Rodrigo Acevedo's earlier amused tolerance acted as a new stimulant. It was worth suffering discomfort if the hidalgos–hijos de alguna, sons of somebody–had to share it. They might be better swordsmen than he, better horsemen; they might think of him as a pot-bellied little lawyer, but sitting in the rain was a thing anyone could do without either practice or grandfathers. He wiped the rain out of his eyes to peer at the five gentlemen huddled in mute discomfort in the bows, and grinned to himself and settled down to endure.

For an hour they crept along through the downpour, and then, when the rain had almost killed the wind, it stopped as suddenly as it began. Within a few seconds the sun was shining in all its majesty, and the wind, hot and sticky, had almost died away. Rich stood up to wring the water from his clothes; the thwarts steamed in the glaring sunlight. There was no change in the appearance of the shore–the hills may have grown a little loftier, but they were still clothed in their eternal green. He scanned the coast carefully, and looked to seaward, where the *Holy Name*, in all the glory of her coloured sails and ensigns, preceded the two caravels on her slow northerly course. Only then did he pay any attention to the group in the bows, and, even so, he waited for them to speak first.

'God, what rain!' said Bernardo de Tarpia. His hair hung lank over his cheeks, his trim beard was a mere ludicrous wisp. The water trickled out of the skirts of his coat as he stood up.

'What of the food?' asked Cristobal Garcia. 'I suppose the bread is no better than a pudding.'

'No, gentlemen,' explained Jorge. 'It is a tarred sack in which it is kept.'

'It is hard to decide,' said Garcia, 'whether a flavour of tar is preferable to rain water.'

'Tar or no tar,' interrupted Rich, fumbling in his pocket, 'I mean to dine today on fresh fish, newly broiled.'

'Fresh fish!' exclaimed Garcia.

'That is what I said,' said Rich, demurely. 'It will be odd if we cannot catch enough for our dinners here.'

The little bundle he produced from his pocket contained lines and hooks; he felt a gratified glow as he heard the delighted exclamations of his crew. He thought of the other contents of his chest in the 'tweendecks in the *Holy Name*–his anxiety during the three weeks between his deciding to join the expedition and its sailing had at least stimulated him into wondering what might be of most use in the New World, and he had stocked his chest accordingly. These penniless younger sons, their heads full of battles and gold mines, had done nothing of the sort.

He doled out lines and hooks; a biscuit from the bag was crumbled into a paste for bait.

'Please God,' said Garcia, piously, 'that the fish here like the flavour of weevils.'

With shortened sail, before the faint air, the longboat crept slowly over the glassy sea. The gentlemen fished as enthusiastically as the seamen; it was amusing to note how they cheered up at the thought of fish for dinner, and how earnestly they plunged into the business. Two months of weevilly biscuits, of stinking dried cod and of boiled barley porridge and stale olives made the prospect of fresh fish ineffably attractive. But Rich could guess how they would round on him, their tempers sharpened by disappointment, if no fish were caught. He bent his head secretly and prayed earnestly to Saint Peter–he had prayed to Saint Peter for good fortune in fishing often before, on pleasant outings in the roadstead of Barcelona, but this time there was an edge to his prayer. He wanted desperately to catch fish.

Saint Peter was kind. They caught fish in plenty while the wind died away to nothing. They landed and built a fire and toasted their fish on sticks before it–not very efficiently. Rich wondered secretly to himself what comment these young men would have made if in their father's houses they had been served with fish half charred and half raw, but here, stretching their legs on land for the first time for months, and in the blessed shade at the edge of the sand, they ate with gusto, and with only moderate curses for the mosquitoes which bit them. Rich could see a new light in their eyes when, full fed and comfortable, they regarded him now. There was a faint respect for him as a giver of good things; he sat with his back against a tree and his helmet on the ground beside him and felt happier than he had done for months.

The ships still lay becalmed on the blue, blue seas under the glaring sun.

'We can explore for a little while,' he announced. 'Who'll come with me?'

They all wanted to, seamen and gentlemen both, looking eagerly to him for orders.

'Two men must guard the boat,' decided Rich. 'Will anyone volunteer? Then you must stay, Jorge. And you, Don Diego. Come on, you others.'

As they plunged into the forest Rich decided to himself, remembering the disappointment in the eyes of those left behind, that the hardest task of a man in command was the arbitrary allotting of distasteful duty. He was glad he had not hesitated, but had given his orders instantly without allowing time for argument. He was conscious that he was learning fast.

The forest was dense and nearly impenetrable; in places they had to hack a path through it with their heavy swords, for the gurgling watercourse they followed was too small to allow easy passage along it. They sweltered in the stagnant air, plunging knee deep into slime and rotting vegetation. Gaudy birds clattered among the branches over their heads. Bernardo de Tarpia uttered a sudden sharp cry, slashing with his sword–a red and black snake coiled and writhed at his feet. It was a lucky blow which had taken off its head before it could strike; they had all of them heard stories, of those red and black snakes of the Indies and the death they could inflict. A huge goggling lizard ran frantically among the branches away from them. Then they saw monkeys, scurrying among the tree-tops for all the world like mice on the floor of a barn. They laughed at their antics and the monkeys chattered down at them in reply.

'There is everything here save the Grand Khan and the mines of Ophir,' said Rodrigo de Acevedo in an undertone to Rich, but Rich would not allow himself to be drawn; he could not enter into a discussion of that sort while in a position of responsibility.

And at this place where they had stopped for a moment there seemed, for the first time, to be a possibility of humans near them. There might almost be a path through the undergrowth here, nearly imperceptible, probably only a wild beast run. Rich looked up at the sky; there was a wisp of cloud there which was quite stationary–in the absence of wind they could continue the exploration without fear of being parted from the *Holy Name*.

'Follow me quietly,' he said to the others, and he turned his steps up the path, his sword in his hand.

But they could not hope to move quietly in the forest. Dead wood crackled under their feet, low twigs rang on their helmets, their scabbards rattled and their accoutrements creaked. There was precious little hope, Rich realized, of ever surprising a party of Indians in this fashion, especially after he stumbled and fell full length. As he picked himself up someone came running down the path and stopped and looked at them–it was a little Indian boy, naked and pot-bellied. He put his fingers in his mouth and stared, the sunlight through the branches making strange markings on his brown skin. His features began to work, and it was clearly only a matter of seconds before he started to cry.

'Seize hold of him!' hissed Garcia into Rich's ear.

'Quiet!' muttered Rich in reply over his shoulder.

He held out his hand, peacefully.

'Hullo, little one,' he said.

The little boy took his finger from his mouth and stared all the harder, postponing his tears.

'Come to me,' said Rich. 'Come along, little one. Come and talk to me.'

Clearly while he spoke gently the child would not be frightened. He racked his brains for things to say, chattering ludicrously, and the little boy slowly began to sidle towards him, with many hesitations.

'There!' said Rich, squatting down on his heels to bring their two faces on a level.

The little boy piped out something incomprehensible; his eyes were fixed on Rich's helmet, and he stretched out a small hand and touched it.

'Pretty!' said Rich. 'Pretty!'

The little boy replied in his own strange language, still engrossed in the helmet. When at last his interest died away Rich cautiously straightened himself.

'There!' he said again, and pointed slowly up the path. 'Mother? Father?'

He began gently to walk forward, and the little boy put his hand in his and trotted with him.

They came out into a little clearing. There was a tiny wisp of smoke rising in the centre, marking the position of a small fire. On one side there were five strange houses of dead leaves, but no human stirred; as they stood grouped at the edge of the clearing they could hear no sound save that of the birds and the insects. The little boy tugged at Rich's hand to draw him forward, and then raised his voice, calling. An Indian woman broke from the forest beyond the clearing and came running heavily towards them. She, too, was naked, and far gone in pregnancy; she caught up the little boy in her arms and stared at them, asking urgent questions of the child meanwhile.

Rich spread his left hand again in the instinctive gesture of peace, even though his right still held his drawn sword.

'We come in peace,' he said. He tried to make soothing noises; the little boy pointed at the glittering helmets and chattered shrilly to his mother.

Now there was a bustle and stir in the forest; a score of Indians came forth into the clearing, old and young, men and women and children. Rich, looking to see if any of them were armed, saw that one man carried a little cane bow–as feeble as a ten-year-old child's–and two small cane arrows, and two others carried headless cane spears, against which ordinary clothes–leaving leather coats out of account–would be adequate protection. He took off his helmet.

'We are here,' he announced, forcing his voice down into quiet conversational tones, 'in the name of Their Highnesses the King and Queen of Castile and Leon.'

The Indians smiled, with flashing white teeth, chattering to each other in their high-pitched voices.

'The woman there has pearls!' said Garcia at Rich's shoulder.

Round each arm above the elbow she wore a rope of pearls, each pearl larger than any they had obtained before.

'Look at them, by God!' said Tarpia.

The Indians noticed their gestures and turned to see what it was which was attracting so much attention; it was obvious enough to them that it was the pearls. They chattered and laughed to each other, the wearer of the pearls–a fine, handsome woman of early middle age–laughing as much as any of them, a little bashfully. The wrinkled old man beside her–husband or father, it was not apparent which–laughed and clapped her on the shoulder, urging her forward. She approached them modestly, eyes cast down. She stripped the pearls from her arms, stood hesitating for a moment, and then thrust one rope into Garcia's hand and the other into Tarpia's, scuttling back to her companions with a laugh. The Spaniards eyed their treasures.

'We must give them something in exchange,' said Rich. The Admiral's orders had been very strict on the point that all treasure should be bartered for and never taken.

'I know what I should give her,' said Garcia, eyeing her nudity.

Rich tried to ignore him; he sheathed his sword–a simple act which yet caused a new outburst of piping comment from the Indians–and fumbled through his pockets. He had two silver coins and a handful of copper ones, and he walked towards the Indians and dropped a coin into each hand as long as the supply lasted. The Indians looked curiously at the money. One of them suddenly spied the Queen's head on the coin and pointed it out to the others. Instantly they were all laughing again. To them it appeared to be the greatest joke in the world that someone should represent human features on an inanimate object–such an idea had never occurred to them. The wrinkled man presented Rich with his spear–a mere cane with the point charred with fire–and made a gesture embracing all his fellows and the encampment. There was an inquiring look in his face; clearly he was anxious to know if there was anything else the Spaniards would like. It dawned upon Rich, remembering also the interview with the other Indians in the canoe, that the first instinct of these people on meeting strangers was to give them presents. He smiled and nodded pacifically, a little embarrassed.

A fresh idea suddenly struck the wrinkled man, and he turned and cried out to the others. His suggestion was greeted with obvious acclamation. The Indians laughed again and clapped their hands. Some ran towards the huts, some came and took the Spaniards' hands and led them towards the space between the huts and the fire, skipping like children at the new prospect. There was a fallen log near the fire. From the huts the Indians dragged out a few more blocks of wood, and most of the Spaniards found seats in this way. To tempt the others to sit down the Indians patted the earth invitingly. The women ran in and out of the huts, all a-bustle, while the men took sticks and began to open the earth near the fire.

A girl put a big leaf on Rich's lap; another girl brought him a flimsy basket filled with lumps of strange bread and offered it to him.

'Cassava,' she said; Rich remembered the word as occurring in the depositions of survivors returned from the Indies.

The men had by now completed their task. They had laid open a hole beside the fire, and from it arose a savoury steam which smelt deliciously, even to the Spaniards who had eaten only an hour ago; obviously the Spaniards had reached the clearing at a moment when the Indians were about to dine. With sticks the Indians hoisted from the hole what looked at first to be a bundle of dead leaves, and when they peeled the leaves off the smell grew more delicious than ever. The operation was not completed with ease–two of the men contrived to burn their fingers, to the accompaniment of fresh peals of laughter–but at last the unrecognizable roast was laid bare. The wrinkled man took a leaf in each hand and began to break up the meat; the women scurried back and forth with more leaves. Rich found a savoury bit on his lap; he bit cautiously into it. It was a delicious tender meat. Another woman brought him a little gourd; it was only fresh water, for, as Rich knew already, the Indians of these islands knew no other beverage.

'What the devil is this we're eating?' asked Bernardo de Tarpia. 'It's good.'

'What is this?' asked Rich of one of the women. He pointed to the meat and raised his eyebrows inquiringly.

'Iguana,' said the woman. 'Iguana.'

The name meant nothing to any of the Spaniards, as their expression showed. One of the Indian men came to the rescue. He pointed up into the trees, and, going down on his hands and knees, made a pretence of scurrying along a branch.

'Monkey, by God!' said Tarpia.

'Monkey?' asked Acevedo.

He made a series of gestures like a monkey, much to the amusement of everybody. The Indians clung to each other and laughed and laughed. Then one of them wiped the tears from his eyes and began a new pantomime. He went down on all fours. He turned his head this way and that. He put the edge of his hand on the base of his spine and waved it from side to side. He projected two fingers from his face beside his eyes and moved them in different directions.

'Iguana,' he said, rising.

It was a graphic piece of work. There could be no doubt what he meant–he had imitated the lashing of the iguana's tail and the goggling of its strange eyes to perfection.

'He means a lizard,' said Rich, trying to keep a little of the consternation out of his voice.

'Does he?' said Tarpia. 'Well, lizard is good enough for me.'

'My God, yes,' said Garcia. 'Look at this.'

He had drawn one of the girls to his knee, and was caressing her naked body. She stood stock-still, with eyes downcast, trembling a little. Rich looked anxiously round the ring. He saw the smile die away from the face of one of the Indian men. The merriment ceased, it was as if a shadow had come over the sun.

'Remember the Admiral's orders, Don Cristobal,' said Rich, anxiously.

'Oh, to Hell with orders,' expostulated Garcia.

'Don Cristobal's talking treason,' interjected Acevedo. He grinned as he said it, but that did not blunt the point of what he said.

'Oh, very well then,' grumbled Garcia. He clapped the girl on the flank and pushed her from him, and the tension died away from the attitudes of the Indians. The women hastened round, offering more bread; the wrinkled man broke off more meat. There were fruits being offered, too, like pale yellow eggs, faintly aromatic when Rich smelled one, vaguely acid and pleasant when he bit into the pulp.

'Guava,' said the lad who gave it to him, explanatorily.

The shadow had passed from over the sun now; there was giggling and talking again. It dawned upon Rich that these people had given away the meal they had been about to eat themselves; he wondered if they had anything left over, and he realized that he need not let his conscience trouble him too much on the point. Their pleasure in giving was so obvious and unassumed. It was the Spaniards who were conferring the favour by accepting. He felt a sudden wave of melancholy come over him. These laughing, generous people, naked from the day of their birth, with sticks for weapons and houses of leaves, and destined to the damnation awaiting the unenlightened, had no need or desire for gold or jewels. They had no more knowledge of labour than they had of property or of civilized warfare. To try to make an empire out of them, as the Admiral dreamed of doing, meant either suffering for them or weakness in the empire. They would be happier left alone–he caught himself up on the verge of heresy as well as of treason. It was the Christian man's duty to see that their feet were set in the way of God, and it was the sensible Spaniard's duty to seek out the treasures of this land to the increase of the wealth of Spain. Yet he still revolted from all the implications. Weakly, he tried to brush the problem from him as he brushed his hands together and rose. The shadow of the forest stretched from side to side of the clearing; it was late afternoon. Only this morning they had dragged their anchors in the Serpent's Mouth, and it seemed like a month ago.

'Back to the ship!' he called to the others. He was conscious of the invidiousness of his condition of uncertainty as to whether he had to request or could command; more, he knew with a qualm that he was not of the stuff to whom command came naturally. But they rose to obey him. Tarpia and Garcia were arm in arm, muttering to each other with their eyes on the women–he could guess the sort of filth they were saying to each other.

The wrinkled man came with a new question, pointing up to the sky, repeating his question and tapping Rich on the breast and pointing upwards again. He was asking if they were going to return to their habitation in the sky.

'Oh, no, no, no,' laughed Rich.

He thought for a moment of trying to explain all the complexities of ships and sea passages and the kingdom of Spain in sign language, and gave up the notion as soon as he thought of it. Others who might follow him could tackle that task. He shook the old man's hand, and he waved good-bye to the women. As he set his feet on the homeward path with his own flock, he looked back at them, standing grouped in the clearing, each with his arm on another's shoulder. The melancholy he had felt before flooded back within him, and he plunged without a word along the narrow path, the others trailing after him.

The journey back to the boat was not as toilsome as the upward climb. At one corner, by the brook, they caught a glimpse of the sea–the ships had drifted a league or more along the coast, but were still within easy reach; from the way their bows were turned to all points of the compass it was obvious that they were quite becalmed. The brook gurgled sleepily, the parrots overhead squawked and fluttered, and all the noises of the forest engulfed them again as they went on down the hill. Far away, Rich heard the faint cry of a strange bird, high and shrill, repeated more than once.

They came out at last into the bright evening sunshine of the beach, where Don Diego Moret dozed on his back and Jorge whittled at a stick with his knife. They looked up as the party approached.

'Is all well?' asked Rich, and then, in the same moment, he knew that all was not well. Gonzalo Acevedo was close behind him. One of the seamen was a little farther back. Rodrigo Acevedo emerged from the forest as he stood and waited, and after him there came–nobody.

'Where's Don Cristobal? Where's Don Bernardo?' he demanded.

'I thought they were in front with you,' said Acevedo, a little surprised.

'Where's Diego?' asked Jorge of the seaman.

'I thought he was following me.'

'Perhaps they are coming,' said Acevedo. But his eyes met Rich's, and they both knew they were thinking the same thoughts.

'Shall I give them a call?' suggested Jorge.

He lifted up his voice in a loud seaman's bellow. Startled birds rose from the trees; an echo came faintly from above, but no answering cry. He bellowed again, and there was still no answer.

'I shall go back for them,' announced Rich. The unaccustomed exercise in the sweltering heat had tired him out; his legs were stiff and weary already. It had been an effort to cover the last few hundred yards to the beach, and it was only the prospect of resting there which had brought him down to the sea without a halt. His heart sank as he thought of the stiff climb back through the forest.

'It's an hour's march to the village,' said Rodrigo Acevedo warningly, 'and not more than an hour of daylight.'

The sun was dipping towards the horizon.

'They may be coming down another way,' suggested Gonzalo Acevedo. 'You could miss them easily. Wait a few minutes.'

Rich wavered. There was a great deal in both arguments; and if what he suspected was the case, if the missing men had made their way back to the village, they must have already had an hour or more to work their will there, and would have another hour before he got back again. And what was he to do when he got there? And how was he to find his way back to the boat in darkness?

'I'll wait,' he said, bitterly, turning his back on them to hide his feelings.

He had been flattering himself he was learning to command men, and this was the first of his achievements. He sat down on a fallen tree and gnawed at his fists.

'What's all this about a village?' asked Moret, curiously, of the Acevedos.

They began to tell him of their experiences and discoveries; the eager babble went on unheeded by Rich, who sat with his back to them, his joints aching and his heart sick. Suddenly a new recollection came to him, one that set his heart beating fast and increased his feeling of nausea. That wild, high-pitched cry which he had heard repeated, far back in the forest, and which he had thought to be the cry of a strange bird–he knew what it was now. He could guess what bloody work it told of, back in the village. He got to his feet, and paced the sand stiffly, boiling with helpless fury. He found himself gripping his sword hilt, he who had never crossed blades with an enemy in his life, and he snatched his hand away in self-contempt. He started for the forest, and turned back. The sun was setting in a wild glory of scarlet; the lower edge of its disk was almost touching the sea, and the level light strangely illuminated the beach and the boat with the little waves lapping round it.

A dull report reached his ears, and, looking towards the ships, he saw a little puff of smoke at the bows of the *Holy Name*. The great standard at her mainmast-head came slowly down, rose again, descended and rose.

'That's a signal to us, sir,' called Jorge. 'We'll have to go back.'

'Very well,' said Rich, his mind made up. 'The others will be left in the forest.'

They began to put their gear back into the boat, and they made preparations for pushing her out. Rich climbed in and sat in the sternsheets. A shout from the forest made them pause and look round.

'That's Garcia,' said Rodrigo Acevedo.

The three of them came in sight now at the edge of the trees, running over the sand towards the boat. Rich saw their faces in the light of the last of the sun, like a trio of schoolboys caught in a piece of mischief, guilty and yet impudent, meeting his eyes and looking away again.

'Where have you been?' asked Moret as they came up, panting.

'Oh, we missed our way,' said Tarpia, looking sidelong at Rich in the sternsheets.

They followed the example of the others, throwing their weight against the boat and splashing out with her in the shallows. There was no opportunity of talking for a moment, and then they all came tumbling in over the sides. Garcia was on the aftermost thwart beside Jorge and face to face with Rich. He reached for an oar along with the others.

'Shall we have to use these things?' he asked, loudly, dropping the oar clumsily into the rowlock.

Rich was staring at Garcia's hand and Garcia caught sight of his expression and followed his gaze. The hand was stained with dried blood, hand and wrist, black in the light of the fast-dying sunset. Very coolly, Garcia leaned over the side and washed clean his hands in the sea.

'It will be a long pull back to the ships,' he said, and took hold of his oar again. His teeth showed white in his swarthy face as he smiled.

6

In the Admiral's cabin, vaguely lit with its two horn lanterns, accusation and denial were hotly exchanged.

'I say we missed our way,' said Garcia. 'You know what the forests in these Indian islands are like, Your Excellency. It is easy enough.'

'And you, Don Narciso?' asked the Admiral. 'You say—'

'I say they went back to the village,' said Rich, unhappily. He was beginning to be sorry that the argument had started; if he had worded his report to the Admiral more tactfully it might not have began at all, and now Garcia and Tarpia had been called in and he had fears as to what the end would be.

'You have no right to say that at all!' burst out Tarpia.

'Gentlemen, moderation, please,' expostulated the Admiral. 'What makes you think so, Don Narciso?'

Rich thought of the way in which they had looked at the women, of the furtive conversation they had held as they started their homeward march, of what he thought was a human cry of fear and agony, and he knew all this was not evidence. He remembered the contempt he had in his own court for people who had no better sort of case than this to present.

'You see, Your Excellency,' sneered Garcia. 'He finds it hard to think of something to say.'

'And what right has he to accuse us?' demanded Tarpia. 'Is he in authority over us?'

'I represent Their Highnesses' interests,' said Rich.

'I have represented Their Highnesses' interests in a dozen battles,' said Tarpia. 'There are twenty soldiers on board this very ship who follow me.'

There was a threat behind that last statement, as anyone could see who caught the glance at the Admiral which accompanied it. Rich looked at the Admiral, hoping against hope that he would take up this challenge to his authority.

'Gentlemen,' said the Admiral. 'We are on a holy mission–a crusade. Must you wrangle like this?'

'The wrangling,' said Garcia, haughtily, 'is not the fault of Don Bernardo and me. The blue blood of Spain does not wrangle willingly with the base-born.'

Rich checked himself as he was about to counter hotly with the statement that he was a caballero de fuero of Catalonia. It would be of no avail. No hidalgo would dream of admitting, even inwardly, any equality between himself and a caballero de fuero–legally a gentleman–and, what was worse (and it was this which sent a little shudder of fear through Rich's plump body) Garcia might take advantage of the statement to challenge him to a duel. In that event Garcia would kill him for certain, and Rich shrank from the imminent prospect of death, as presented harshly to him by his imagination. He had not mentioned to the Admiral the bloodstains he had seen on Garcia's hands because he knew that Garcia would give a flat denial that they had ever existed; now he realized that he had been doubly wise, because if he were given the lie direct the incident could not end until more blood–his own–had been shed.

'Very well, gentlemen,' said the Admiral, when the struggle of emotion in Rich's face had died away and there was clearly no reply to be expected of him. 'I have heard your explanation and of course I accept it. But with regard to the pearls which I understand you received from the Indians?'

Garcia and Tarpia exchanged glances, and then Garcia looked across at Rich with no friendly expression.

'All gold and all treasure,' said the Admiral, sharply, 'must be handed to me–to me, the Viceroy. That is the Royal order, as you are aware, gentlemen.'

There was no weakness in his attitude now, that was obvious enough. He was prepared to enforce his will in the matter of money, just as he was not prepared to enforce it in the matter of discipline. Sulkily the two gentlemen produced the pearl armlets and handed them over.

'Thank you, gentlemen. I need take up no more of your time.'

They swaggered out of the cabin with all the dignity the low deck beams over their heads would allow, leaving the Admiral fondling the glistening treasure and Rich staring malignantly after them.

'These hot-blooded gentlemen,' said the Admiral, 'are a little unruly. Even unreasonably so, occasionally.'

'Without a doubt,' agreed Rich, bitterly.

What was he to do or say? he wondered bitterly. The moment had clamoured for a sharp example, and had been allowed to pass. In the essential matter of discipline the Admiral had allowed his authority to be challenged successfully. The dissensions and squabbles and final anarchy in the colony of the Española were explained by that one incident. He thought of that ludicrous agreement between Their Highnesses and the Admiral, which made the latter Viceroy of all the lands he might discover. The fact that a man was a capable navigator, or even that he had ideas and was tenacious of them, did not imply that he would be an effective governor. The agreement handed over unlimited territory to a man who could not control his subordinates–there was no blinking the fact. Rich wondered to himself how Caesar Borgia, conquering Central Italy, would have treated those two.

'The pearls we have already obtained on this voyage,' remarked the Admiral, 'are nearly sufficient to repay the cost of the expedition. There will be much profit.'

'Let us hope so,' said Rich.

He felt himself to be friendless and desolate; he had incurred the hatred of Garcia and Tarpia, which meant that his very life was in danger. He did not dare to risk antagonizing the Admiral as well with untimely criticism. No one would trouble much about the fate of a wretched lawyer, not even Their Highnesses across two thousand miles of sea. He was very sorry he had come.

'And I expect,' went on the Admiral, 'that when we reach Española we shall find a shipload of gold awaiting us there. I made arrangements for its collection. The Royal fifth should be a large sum. So should my eighth and tenth!'

That absurd agreement gave Their Highnesses a fifth of all treasure. But to the Admiral it gave a tenth of everything shipped home, not merely of treasure, but of merchandise or spices. And besides that he could claim an eighth share of the gross profit, and an additional one-tenth share of the net profit, of each individual expedition that sailed from Spain. And the agreement itself made the Admiral the judge as to what was or was not merchandise, and what was or was not profit, it made hîm Admiral and Viceroy with the right to nominate all his officers; and, lastly, it empowered him to leave by will all these varied privileges and powers in perpetuity to whomsoever he should think proper. It occurred to Rich that perhaps it was as well for Spain that the Admiral was not the ruthless leader of men he would have liked him to be five minutes back. Such a man could make himself greater than Their Highnesses themselves. If the choice lay between anarchy and independence he would have to choose anarchy for the Admiral's empire.

The consideration had made him forget his own misery for the moment. Outside the cabin awaited him the hatred of the men he feared; he felt like a tale-telling schoolboy, safe for an instant with his teacher, but doomed sooner or later to have to face the resentment of his fellows. He yearned to stay a little longer here in the light and safety. Why, oh why had he ever allowed his restless curiosity to carry him off on that infernal expedition in the longboat?

Antonio Spallanzani came into the cabin and broke the chain of his thoughts.

'Ah, you are in time to lock these away,' said the Admiral in his native Italian, handing over the armlets, and then in Castilian, 'Thank you, Don Narciso.'

There was nothing for it now but to leave. Rich took a deep breath as he set his hand to the door, for he was by nature a timorous man. Then he passed out into the darkness of the after-deck, under the break of the poop. The inky blackness here, even after the dim light of the cabin, left him blind for a second or two. Somebody brushed against him, and he jumped with nervousness, and then breathed with relief as he heard Rodrigo Acevedo's voice.

'Who is that?' asked Acevedo.

'It is I,' said Rich, trying to keep the quaver out of his voice.

'Don Narciso? Our two companions of today have been here breathing fire and murder against you.'

Acevedo's voice was pitched low, and Rich whispered when he replied.

'Where–where are they now?'

'Over on that side, talking with Moret and the others.'

The night was warm, but to Rich the sweat that beaded his face was cold.

'I don't know what to do,' whispered Rich, pathetically, and was promptly startled by hearing Acevedo suddenly start speaking in a normal tone, loud enough to be heard by the dark mass of figures on the far side of the ship.

'Oh, no, Don Narciso,' said Acevedo, speaking with a distinctness which was agony at first to Rich. 'You can hardly do that. I feel for you, and sympathize with you. But you ought to know the rules of shipboard life if anyone on board does.'

'What do you mean?' whispered Rich.

'Brawling on board is terribly punished. The hand that draws a weapon is nailed by it to the mast, and remains nailed there until the owner tears himself free. If you were to kill him you would be tied to his dead body and thrown overboard.'

'Oh, not so loud, not so loud,' whispered Rich, wringing his hands, but Acevedo continued quite calmly.

'So all I can advise is that you swallow your resentment, at least for a time–althought I quite appreciate how unpleasant it is for you. Diego de Arana of Cordoba is alguazil mayor–master-at-arms–on board here, and you know his reputation. He holds his commission direct from the crown.'

'But why–?' began Rich, still too stupid with fright to see the trend of what Acevedo was saying.

'He'd stick at nothing,' continued Acevedo. 'Gentle or simple, seaman or hidalgo, it's all one to him. At the first sound of steel he'd be upon you with his chains and his fetters. Twenty stinking seamen would throw you into the hold, and next morning we'd see you nailed up. You'd never hold a sword again, and I for one would be sorry for that.'

'So would I,' said Rich, taking his cue at last.

'By God!' said Acevedo, striking one fist into the other. 'Do you remember disarming that swashbuckling lout that night outside the Santo Spirito in Florence? If I'd been in your place I should have killed him–he deserved it. With his French sword-play and all, behaving like a boor because he thought he was the best fencer in Florence. Holy Mary, the look on his face as his sword fell on the ground!'

Acevedo laughed, lightly and reminiscently.

'That was 'ninety-two, wasn't it? Or was it 'ninety-three?' said Rich, desperately trying to heap on the local colour, and feeling a fearful joy in doing so.

'It was my second visit, anyway. But as I was saying, we can have nothing like that on board here, Don Narciso. No point of honour can be satisfied if the successful combatant is liable to execution. All courts of heralds are agreed upon that. Any offence given must be passed over in those circumstances–dishonour is confined to the man who offers the offence.'

'Yes,' said Rich, remembering the frequent teasing he had undergone at the hands of his bedmates of the 'tweendecks. 'Yes. I knew that. It was only because I was so angry this evening that I had forgotten it.'

Don Rodrigo yawned elaborately.

'Well,' he said, 'I for one am sleepy. There is little enough to do–shall we go to bed? Or are you still too wrought up to sleep?'

'Oh,' said Rich. 'I think we might as well.'

Perhaps Acevedo sensed the intoxication which Rich felt at that moment, and appreciated the danger of his saying a word too many which might spoil the whole effect so elaborately built up. He slipped his hand under Rich's elbow and guided him firmly to the companion way. As they fumbled their way in the darkness the silence which had overlain the shadowy group against the opposite bulwark was broken by a thin nervous cough.

Rich stripped to his shirt in the cramped 'tweendecks in a wild exultation, hardly knowing what he was doing. The reaction from his earlier terror was profound. He began a jocular remark to Acevedo at the farther end of the tier of chests, but the almost invisible figure there made no reply and offered no encouragement to conversation, so that Rich realized that in a ship anything he said might be overheard, if he did not desire it as much as if he did. One of the philosophers had said: 'I have often regretted having spoken, but I have never regretted holding my tongue.' Rich remembered the saying, and got himself into bed with no more speech.

Of course he was not yet asleep when the rest of the party came into the 'tweendecks and prepared for bed, groping about in the puzzling light of the single evil-smelling tallow dip. Don Cristobal Garcia came to his bed beside him, and Rich would not even feign sleep, only sleepiness, opening his eyes and then closing them again as if the sight of Garcia was not enough to discompose him. And Garcia, crouching under the deck beams as he undressed, was much more careful than usual not to discommode his neighbour.

That may have been, decided Rich, thinking tumultuously, because of his new reputation as a swordsman. Or it may have been because Garcia now realized that any squabble might end in disaster for both of them. Or just conceivably he might have taken to heart Acevedo's remark that it was ungentlemanly to offer provocation without the chance of satisfaction. Or it might be because Garcia was in a sober mood. Or it might be just coincidence. In any case, it seemed a lifetime since, some fifteen hours ago, they had first sighted the Serpent's Mouth. Rich's agitated mind began to turn over afresh all the numerous occurrences since then, from the moment of sighting the Island of Grace to that of Garcia's retirement to bed.

7

There was a very marked northerly current along this eastern shore of Trinidad. Hove-to during the night, the squadron was carried steadily northwards, until at last the late-rising moon had revealed such looming masses of land ahead that the Admiral had been roused, and the sleeping men on board had been awakened by the bustle and noise of letting go the anchors. Now, at dawn, everyone could see more clearly what lay ahead. There were several small steep-sided islands in a chain across their course, with narrow passages between, over which soared and wheeled innumerable sea birds. The Admiral beside the taffrail was studying the sea on their quarter towards these passages–Rich was still landsman enough to feel a slight shock at the realization that in an anchored ship one does not necessarily look ahead to examine the course one intends to pursue.

'More dangerous passages, Don Narciso,' announced the Admiral. 'There are current and eddies there as bad as the Serpent's Mouth yesterday. These channels are narrower, and more dangerous. The Mouths of the Dragon, do you think?'

They both smiled as they remembered their conversation of yesterday.

'A very appropriate name, Your Excellency,' said Rich.

'I am not justified in risking the passage,' announced the Admiral. 'I intend heading eastward along this chain of islands until we find an easier one.'

'It is not for me to discuss questions of navigation with Your Excellency,' said Rich in perfect sincerity; the Admiral was the best practical seaman the world could show.

Orders were bellowed back and forth from the ship to the caravels; men set to work at the capstan while others loosened the sails

'It is better if we head eastward in any case,' went on the Admiral, turning back to Rich from the business of getting the squadron under way. 'It cannot be far to the east of here that the Earthly Paradise is to be found. I am convinced of it–the air blows fresher and purer with every league.'

'I had not noticed it, Your Excellency,' said Rich, boldly.

'You are insensitive, and you have not had my experience of this climate. And besides, you were present when Alamo discovered bitumen in the island, weren't you? He told me that there was obviously some undiscovered central source of bitumen in Trinidad. The analogy with the Dead Sea is very close. The Euphrates–only across the desert from the Dead Sea–was one of the four rivers of Eden, and not even the most learned fathers of the Church have been able to identify the other three. They have remained unknown for as long as all our knowledge was derived from the westward. Now we are approaching from the east and shall solve the mystery.'

'But between us and the Euphrates must lie all India, and the Spice Islands, and the empire of the Great Khan, Your Excellency,' protested Rich, bewildered.

'Undoubtedly they must lie to the northward,' admitted the Admiral. 'It would be hard to reconcile the theory with that of a perfectly spherical earth. But remember what I suggested to you before, and assume that in this quarter of the world the sphere is prolonged into a pear-shaped extension. That would then allow room enough to the northward for Asia, and at the same time account for the balminess of this air, and for the fierce ocean currents here–probably, when our knowledge is more advanced, for the existence of sources of bitumen on either side of Eden, and for the steep-sided shape of those islands there.'

'I see, Your Excellency,' said Rich.

The theory was a difficult one, but no more difficult than that of an earth which was not flat, nor than the postulate of the existence of antipodes, and the Admiral and the Portuguese had between them established these firmly enough. Rich began to feel a new excitement at the thought of fresh discoveries and began restlessly to pace the deck, exchanging a courteous formal bow with Garcia as he did so. After Garcia's deeds of yesterday Rich wondered what men of that stamp would be guilty of in the Earthly Paradise, and at the same moment he found himself wondering heretically whether perhaps the Earthly Paradise had not already been discovered, and whether those laughing hospitable folk who entertained them were not dwellers in it, pagans though they were. The thought struck him with sadness, and he turned again to look at the land.

They left the islands of the Dragon's Mouths to starboard and crept slowly before the wind on an easterly course. The north-eastern corner of Trinidad, which they were leaving behind them, had been steeper and loftier than the central part where they had landed yesterday, and this chain of islands appeared to be a continuation of the ridge. The last island of the chain in sight was not quite so bold in outline, but as they drew up to it Rich could see that it was steep enough, all the same, and as wooded and green as the others. Slowly they coasted along it, but it was a good deal bigger than the rest of the chain. Rich could see no end to it as he looked along its green flank.

Throughout the ship there was a bustle and an interest in what they were discovering, oddly at variance with the comparative apathy of yesterday. Rich told himself that the enthusiasms of men in a mass ebbed and flowed like the tides of the ocean. They ate their food today with one eye over the ship's side; they stayed voluntarily exposed to the two tremendous rainstorms which swept down on them from Trinidad. Even the hidalgos were interested, talking freely and imperilling their dignity with their pointings and gesticulations. The look-out at the mast-head announced land right ahead, across their course–low green hills again. With land to the west of them now, as well as land to the north and land to the east, and the water shoaling fast, the Admiral ordered a southerly course in his determination to circle round this large island. He had ordered a chair to be brought up to the poop, and sat there with his white beard fluttering and Perez and Spallanzani at his elbow. He feared lest his squadron might be embayed here, where the wind blew always from the east, and it was well before sunset that, as the sea grew shallower and the land ahead was seen to trend farther and farther to the southward, he ordered the anchors to be let go.

'I shall send the longboat tomorrow, Don Narciso,' he announced, 'to discover if there is a passage ahead or to the southward. Would you care for another jaunt?'

'I am no seaman, Your Excellency,' said Rich, taken a little aback. He had not been ready for this question.

'There will be seamen with you to take the soundings and set the course,' said the Admiral. 'I would go myself, but, as you see—'

With a gesture the Admiral indicated his rheumaticky joints. There was a hurt, pleading look in his eyes. Rich had won his trust, and there were few enough people on earth whom the Admiral trusted. Ever since Pinzon had deserted him on his first historic voyage of discovery, and set out to discover new countries for himself, he had been cautious about despatching expeditions which could make themselves independent. It was dangerous–in his view, at least–to delegate authority either to turbulent and needy hidalgos or to adventurous captains. Rich might be an agent of the King and Queen, but he was an honest one; he could be trusted not to plunder the inhabitants nor–much worse–to conceal treasure, not to go off on expeditions of his own nor (the Admiral's suspicions were unbounded) to bring back false information which might wreck the whole voyage.

'It would please me very much if you would go, Don Narciso,' said the Admiral. Several hidalgos were listening.

'I will come and pull an oar,' said Rodrigo Acevedo.

'I, too,' said his brother.

There was a little ripple of volunteering round the circle. A respite from the cramped conditions of the ship, the chance of fresh food and new sights, the possibility of finding women and pearls and gold–they were all willing to come for the sake of these. They all eyed Rich, with his new reputation as a bold fighting man, and for the sake of that reputation he could not refuse.

'Thank you, Your Excellency,' he said. 'I shall much appreciate the honour.'

Five seconds later Garcia was addressing him as privately as a crowded ship permitted.

'May I be one of the party?' he asked.

Their eyes met–the burly young hidalgo with his bristling beard and his shabby flaunting clothes, and the stout little lawyer with the sharp eye belied by the unobtrusive manner. It was strange for the one to be asking a favour of the other, and yet he undoubtedly was.

'There are others who have not been ashore at all,' Rich temporized.

'Yes,' answered Garcia with a placatory grin, 'but I should like to go again.'

'And you remember what happened?' said Rich. He did not want Garcia in his party; he was afraid.

'I remember. But—'

Rich knew that if he refused him he would offend him. On the other hand there was a chance of loyal service from him now–only a chance, but that was better than making a certain enemy of him.

'Will you stay with me if you come?' he asked.

It was a big effort to screw himself up to talk like a superior to this haughty young man who could wring his neck like a chicken's–who had been on the point of doing so the night before. But it was the only course open to him.

'Yes,' said Garcia.

So Garcia was one of the twenty men who crowded the longboat at dawn next day when they pushed off from the *Holy Name* and headed for the low green shore while the ones left behind waved farewell. The air was hot and sticky; it had rained heavily during the night and the overcast sky bore promise of more rain still. There was only just enough wind to fill the sail and push them slowly forward; it was fluky and variable, too–twice Osorio at the tiller had to shout an order as the sail flapped heavily over to the other side. A flight of pelicans flapped solemnly overhead.

There was no sign of a break in the land to the northward; to the south the hills grew lower and died away into a flat green coast. It was to the south, then, that Rich directed Osorio to steer the boat. The sun broke through the clouds and glared upon them with a terrible eye, illuminating the shore to which they were trending; a seaman standing in the bows cried out that he could see a break in the coast. Rich climbed to his feet and stood precariously balancing in the sternsheets–he had no faith in his own judgment, and yet, as commander of the expedition, he had to make some pretence at employing it. So low and flat was the shore that it was hard to distinguish where the sea ended and the land began, but Rich thought he saw what the seaman indicated–there was at least an arm of the sea running up into the land there.

With the dying wind they were compelled to take in the sail and set to work with the oars, and they took an occasional cast of the lead as they headed in. Three fathoms–two and a half fathoms–three fathoms again.

'Hardly enough for the flagship,' commented Osorio, spitting loudly over the side.

They were close to the shore now; the trees that fringed the sea were a sad grey, not the bright green of Trinidad, and they seemed to have their roots set actually in the water. Osorio put the tiller over until the boat was close in, and the men rested on their oars while she drifted, the gurgle and bubble at the bows dying away along with her motion.

'Look there!' said somebody, pointing to the trees.

On the bare grey stems close to the surface of the water there were oysters clustered thick. Osorio reached out and snapped off a brittle branch–the tip that trailed in the water bore four of them.

'We know now where those pearls come from,' commented Rich.

Osorio eagerly prised an oyster open with his knife, and poked a gnarled forefinger into its interior.

'None there,' he said, hesitated a moment, and then swallowed it noisily.

The boat lurched as everyone tried to grab for oysters; there was an interval as oysters were gathered and knives were borrowed. Food and pearls were sought with equal eagerness, but no pearls were found. Osorio turned over the shell he held in his hand and examined it curiously.

'They are nothing like our oysters at home,' he said, with his mouth full, and then, looking across at the birds wheeling over the sea, 'It is more than pearls that they make. No wonder there are so many sea birds here.'

'So the birds eat oysters, then?' asked Rich.

'No,' said Osorio, 'the oysters grow into birds.'

He opened a fresh specimen for the purpose of his lecture.

'These half-tide shell fish always do that. Many's the goose I've eaten which was a barnacle once. I expect these become pelicans. See here, sir. You can see the wings starting to sprout. And this must be the head–the long beak must grow later, when they are fledglings. Every spring tide brings them out in thousands, the same as butterflies come from chrysalises.'

It was an interesting point in natural history, and an apt comparison. Rich told himself that it was no more marvellous that a pelican should develop from a half-tide oyster than that a butterfly should emerge from a dull chrysalis, and yet somehow it did appear so; the one was a wonder to which he had been accustomed all his life, and the other was new. He supposed that when at last the expedition reached the Asiatic plains he would experience the same sensations on seeing the unicorns that only a virgin could tame, and the upas tree which destroyed all animal life within half a mile.

They took to the oars again, and the boat crept along up the inlet. Monkeys appeared on the shore, chattering loudly at them from the tree-tops; gaudy birds flew over their heads, and the steaming heat closed in upon them. The inlet was no more than half a mile broad when it divided, one portion continuing easterly and the other trending off to the south. Osorio at the tiller looked to Rich for orders.

'Which do you think looks more promising?' asked Rich as casually as he could manage.

Osorio shrugged enormously and spat again.

'Go to the right, then,' said Rich; if one way appeared as good as another to Osorio it was no use for himself to try to judge by appearances. Southward lay the Isle of Grace, opposite to Trinidad across the Serpent's Mouth; that was one solid bit of knowledge. The best chance of finding a passage was to keep to the northward of Gracia.

Now it began to rain, the usual relentless downpour to which they had grown accustomed in these latitudes. The roar of it drowned the noise of the oars in the rowlocks and the squeaking of the stretchers. The near-by land was almost blotted from sight, and the jesting conversation in the longboat came to an untimely end. The men at the oars rowed in dogged silence, and the rest sat patiently suffering. The channel divided again, and Rich again took the northern arm, but this immediately divided once more, and he took the southern arm this time in the hope of preserving as direct an easterly course as possible. And these were only the main channels; peering through the rain Rich fancied that there were plenty of minor waterways, mere threads of water by comparison, diverging from the wide channels. It was bewildering.

Then at last the rain stopped, and the sun shone once more. The forest beside them steamed, and they could hear again the innumerable sounds of the life within it. The men at the oars were relieved by their companions, and the longboat pushed on along the channel. And here they were balked; the channel split into two channels, at right angles to each other, and each was barely wide enough–the oars caught against the vegetation on either side.

'There's no way through here for the flagship,' said Osorio.

'No,' agreed Rich, hoarsely.

At Osorio's orders they backed water again until they could turn the boat, and they retraced their course; there was a resentful murmur at this wasted labour.

'We must try again,' said Rich, loudly. 'The Admiral relies on us to discover a passage.'

But the mention of the Admiral had small effect–he did not command these men's devotion.

The bank where the nose of the boat touched it in turning was soft and oozy; this was an amphibious sort of island, plainly; the distinction between land and water was not a sharp one. Still they rowed along winding channels, turning now south and now north, yet in general holding steadily eastward, rowing interminably.

'We must be three leagues from the sea,' said Osorio.

'That at least,' agreed Rich.

'And no sign of a spring yet.'

Everyone on board would be glad of fresh water to drink, instead of the flat and unpalatable reserve carried in the two casks. In these salt marshes there would be no chance of finding drinking water. Rich wondered what the birds and the monkeys drank–presumably these torrential rains made pools among the greenery. Anything was possible here; yet it was strange to find a marshly island surviving in the midst of the ocean, where one would expect the great waves to wash it away. To the east Trinidad gave it protection, but what of the north, and the west, and the south? It was puzzling.

The channel in which they found themselves now was wider than several they had previously traversed. And here the vegetation did not come quite to the water's edge. There was rock–pebbles–in sight. The same idea seemed to strike Osorio and Rich at the same moment. Osorio moved restlessly in his seat, staring at the bank. Rich cautiously put one hand into the water and tasted the drops which he lifted out. It was palatable water, almost fresh.

'We're in a river, by God!' said Osorio.

'Yes. The water is drinkable,' said Rich.

The rowers rested on their oars at the announcement, mopping their sweat. Two or three men leaned dangerously over the side and sucked up water like horses. There was a babble of talk.

'Under that bank,' mused Osorio, 'there's quite an eddy. Look! There is a current running here. And it's a big river.'

A river a quarter a mile wide, thought Rich. And those innumerable marshy channels through which they had struggled! Rich thought of Padua, of the innumerable arms of the Po, embanked by the labour of centuries. And there were all the mouths of the Ebro, too, in the dreary marshland beyond Tarragona. He had seen the mouths of the Rhône, too, and he had heard of the mouths of the Rhine and of the Nile. This must be a delta, too; and the deductions to be drawn from that simply staggered the imagination. It could be no small island which they were exploring; a river the size of Ebro implied a land the size of Arragon at least. Larger still, most probably. Perhaps–perhaps it was the mainland of Asia at last.

But then again there were difficulties. Rich remembered the description by the Venetian, Marco Polo, of the Asiatic countries and of the court of the Grand Khan, its wealth and its fleets and armies. If this were the mainland those armies must have pushed hither to conquer this productive country, and those fleets must have coasted along these shores. Certainly the land would not be sparsely peopled by naked Indians with no knowledge of metals–and wearing pearls worth a king's ransom. If the Grand Khan's fleets had not come here, it must be because it was not part of the mainland of Asia at all, but a mere island–a large island–and far enough from Asia not to have been discovered from that side. That implied a wide stretch of ocean to the westward of it, as large a stretch, perhaps, as the ocean they had already traversed on their way from Spain. And this in turn implied that the world was far larger than anyone thought, that the Admiral's calculations were vastly at fault, and that they had not reached the Indies at all. That was as nonsensical as the other theory.

It was a dangerous thought, too. There had been doubters before, on the Admiral's second voyage, and the Admiral had not only compelled everyone to swear a solemn oath that they had believed Cuba to be part of the mainland of Asia, but also had publicly threatened to cut out the tongue of any man who affirmed the contrary–very right and proper treatment for dangerous sceptics, thought Rich, involuntarily, until he came back with a shock to the thought that it would take very little more to push him himself over into the abyss of scepticism as well. And he had never yet been a sceptic in his life.

Osorio was addressing him–apparently had been trying to attract his attention for some time.

'Shall we land and eat our food?' asked Osorio.

'No,' said Rich, after a moment's thought. 'Let's push a mile or two more up the river first.'

As far as he was concerned, he would have no appetite for food while consumed by his present doubts. There was just a chance that the theories were all wrong, that this was not a river at all, current and fresh water notwithstanding. A little further effort might resolve all doubts, might carry them to a place where all was clear–might even take them again to the open sea on the farther side of this mysterious island.

The oars groaned in the rowlocks, the blades splashed monotonously alongside, and the boat crawled steadily up the channel round a vast bend. Another bend succeeded to that, the banks here lined with a wide stretch of golden sand. Some vast dull-coloured creatures lay sunning themselves there; at the sound of the oars they bestirred themselves and wallowed down into the water.

'Iguanas,' said Garcia, in reply to a question from a companion. 'Lizards.'

They certainly looked like lizards, like large specimens of the kind of creature they had seen scuttling along the branches in Trinidad, and of which they had eaten at the Indians' invitation.

'Tender and sweet as chicken,' said Tarpia, with a smacking of his lips. All hands stared over at the sandbank, now quite deserted.

Round the next bend the character of the river changed. A long way upstream they could see rocks, and a sparkling of wavelets, and a hint of white water.

'Rapids,' said Osorio.

'I fancy so,' agreed Rich. At that rate they had reached the limit of their expedition in this direction; no sensible purpose could be served by dragging the boat over the rapids, even if it were possible. Yet Rich was conscious of a feeling of disappointment; he did not want to turn back. He wanted to push on and on into the depths of this new and mysterious island. But the men were hungry and tired, and already the current was running faster.

'We'll land,' said Rich, curtly.

A narrow deep channel ran aimlessly up between a sandbank and the sand of the shore, and Osorio guided the longboat into it. The sharp shelving edge made a suitable landing place; while the oarsmen scratched ineffectively at the sand with their blades a seaman in the bow took a grip with the boathook and drew the heavy boat in, so that Rich was able to step ashore almost dry-shod. The heat and glare from the sand came up into his face like a fountain of fire, and he hurried forward to the shade of the trees with the rest of them capering and chattering after him. A little crowd of monkeys overhead peeped through the branches at them and chattered more shrilly back until misgivings overcame them and they fled over the tops of the trees like thistledown over a field before they stopped again to peep.

'That would be meat for our dinner,' roared Tarpia, pointing. 'Better than mouldy olives.'

They all looked eagerly to Rich for permission, and he gave it after a glance at Osorio's expressionless countenance.

'Bring your crossbow this way, Pepe. We can cut them off,' said Tarpia. 'Will you go along the shore, Cristobal? Take Estaban with you. Try round there, Acevedo.'

They clattered and crashed off into the forest, leaving Osorio and Rich standing in the edge of the shade, the food bags at their feet and the river shining in front of them beyond the glaring sand. Shouts and cries came from the hunting party. They heard the sudden clatter of a discharged crossbow, a burst of laughter, and more cries. Birds were fluttering over the tree-tops in panic.

'The gentlemen are full of life,' said Osorio, philosophically. 'Let us hope St Hubert will favour them.'

St Hubert apparently did, for they came back soon along the sand dragging their spoils with them.

'These little men,' said Garcia, exultantly, 'have never seen a crossbow before. That is plain. They squeaked with surprise when a bolt reached them at the top of a tree–that was a good shot of yours, Estaban.'

He turned over with his foot one of the limp bodies on the sand; the greyish brown fur was clotted with blood.

'Pepe got these two with one shot,' said Tarpia. 'It broke this one's leg and hit that one in the belly.'

'Pedro got a parrot,' said someone else, displaying the dead bird.

Garcia drew his dagger and knelt by the dead animals.

'Who'll light a fire?' he asked over his shoulder. 'Holy Mary, the last game I gutted was a seven-point stag in the forest of St Ildefonso.

8

Everyone had eaten; everyone had swallowed at least a mouthful or two of monkey's flesh despite the brutal jokes which were passed; everyone had decided that parrot's meat tasted of tough carrion and was not food for Christians. Two or three of the more phlegmatic were asleep in the shade; most of the men, too excited with their run ashore to wish for a siesta, were lying talking in low tones. Rich was too restless even to lie still; he heaved himself to his feet and asked Osorio to walk with him, and the boatswain obeyed even though he would clearly have preferred to continue to take his ease in the shade.

'I want your opinion on the rapid there,' said Rich.

With notable self-control Osorio refrained from pointing out that whether the rapid were easy or difficult its mere existence made it impossible for the *Holy Name* to pass it, even if, unlike all the other rivers which Osorio knew, this particular one ran from sea to sea. They plodded doggedly side by side over the blazing sand, which scorched their feet through their boots.

'I have the Admiral's order,' said Rich, 'to spend four days if necessary seeking a passage.'

'We will need every minute of four days,' said Osorio in an elaborately neutral tone. 'Four weeks or four months. You do not find rivers this size on a small island.'

'I am afraid so,' said Rich. 'But we can at least report to the Admiral whether it is possible for a force to get up into the interior of the island this way.'

'Yes, sir,' said Osorio, non-committally, and they plodded on in silence.

The rapid when they reached it was clearly a difficult one. Flat grey rocks showed everywhere above the surface of the water, which swirled sullenly round them. Upstream, as far as their vision extended, the rocks were to be seen scattered over the river. Here and there they were so thick that the water came tumbling through the gaps in cataracts.

'M'm,' said Osorio. 'A league of broken water. I can tell you this, sir. It would take the twenty men we have with us now a week at least to drag the longboat up there.'

'Thank you,' said Rich, 'that was what I had to find out. We must go back and look for another passage.'

'We must,' said Osorio.

Yet Rich lingered for a while longer beside the rushing water, reluctant to turn back; he was surprised at himself, both for this unexpected yearning to push on, to explore, to make discoveries, and at his disappointment at having to retrace his steps. Osorio waited patiently until at last he made up his mind to return to the boat. Rich was silent as they walked back, puzzling over this unexpected development in himself, and Osorio's sudden remark roused him with a jerk from his brown study.

'The gentlemen are hunting again,' he said.

Half-way between them and the boat lay three bulky shapes sunning themselves on the sand–iguanas like the ones they had disturbed on their passage up the river in the boat. Half a dozen gentlemen were stealthily approaching them over the sand, Garcia, conspicuous in his glittering helmet, in the lead. Their cautious movements brought them to within a score of yards of the creatures while Rich and Osorio were still a hundred yards away in the opposite direction. Rich watched one of the men kneel down and aim with a crossbow; the faint clatter of the released steel reached Rich's ears over the heated sand.

From them on events moved rapidly. Two of the creatures vanished into the river; Garcia, leaping forward with a rope, noosed the third before it could escape. A whirl of the brute's tail sent him flying, but the others grabbed the end of the rope and hauled manfully, while the one with the crossbow was frantically working his windlass. The iguana, oddly agile for a thing so deformed, made at the prostrate Garcia with open mouth, but the drag of the rope just deflected him and Garcia was barely able to roll out of reach of the snapping jaws.

Rich and Osorio came running up to see the fun, but Rich stopped, appalled at the spectacle of mad ferocity exhibited by the iguana. This was no harmless tree lizard to fall a victim to the sticks and stones of naked savages; it was a ton weight of hideous strength. Its jaws were frightening and its lashing tail a formidable weapon. Coursing through Rich's mind, like a river in spate, came a torrent of recollections of what he had heard and read of the crocodile of the Nile. This was more like a crocodile than anything he had imagined. Its left foreleg was crippled by the crossbow bolt driven deeply into it, to which perhaps Garcia owed his life, but it was still lively enough and fierce enough to face eight men with every chance of success, despite the noose round its neck.

With a whirl of oaths Osorio snatched the knife from his belt and sprang forward into the fray while Rich stood rooted to the sand, his hand clutching the hilt of his undrawn sword. As he slowly pulled out the weapon a sudden swerve on the lizard's part swept off their feet the men at the end of the rope. they tumbled in the sand, and the beast, after a futile snap at the rope, caught sight of Rich and rushed straight at him. Rich stood still fascinated for a second by its little dead eyes which yet were so malignant; the shouts of the others reached his ears so faintly that he hardly heard them. Yet his mind was racing; he knew in that moment that if he ran away, as his every instinct dictated, he would forfeit any regard which the others, thanks to Acevedo, might feel for him. He changed his movement for flight into a clumsy evasion of the rush, and swung his sword frantically at the brute's head; he felt and heard the blade ring loudly on the bone. Three times he slashed; it seemed like a long minute that he was at grips with the thing. A crossbow bolt whizzed harshly past him–apparently the gentleman with the crossbow had taken a hurried and ineffective aim for his second shot.

Then suddenly and unexpectedly the brute, as it swung round, turned over on to its back, revealing its whitish belly; the others had grabbed the rope again, which, passing under its body, had twisted round its right foreleg. The thing squirmed insanely for a second or two while Rich slashed again; Garcia was beside him now, slashing too. Rich saw the pale green-grey belly gape widely in a red wound. As it righted itself, the creature's tail knocked Garcia violently against him, but in an instant of time, as he reeled, he saw a hindleg within the sweep of his sword, and he slashed once more. There was a thrill as the blade bit deep; Rich had the gratifying feeling that the muscles of his back and loins–all his strength–had been behind that blow. Red blood spouted in a dark trail over the sand from beneath the animal. The rush the thing was about to make at Osorio was crippled and disjointed, and a fresh drag upon the rope flung it on its side.

Moret was here now, sword in hand, too. He plunged the weapon deep into the thing's side behind the foreleg, and the other men dropped the rope and came running in, plucking out their swords. The thing died under the sword blades, its huge jaws still snapping together with a ringing sound, and the mad yelling–they had all apparently been shouting at the tops of their voices–died away as they looked at each other across the corpse.

'Holy Mary, Mother of God,' said Osorio, solemnly. He stood dagger in hand and looked round at the sweating gentlemen, at the torn-up sand with its bloodstains, and the dead lizard.

'Did you say the Indians kill these things?' asked João de Setubal of Garcia; the latter was cautiously feeling the bruises on his thigh.

'Smaller ones. I said smaller ones before we attacked it.'

'I should well think so,' said João.

'And you say you have eaten their flesh?' asked another. 'Jesus, how the thing stinks!'

It stank indeed; their nostrils were assailed with the foul musky stench which arose from the corpse.

'This is more like a crocodile of the Nile,' said Rich, and there was a murmur of agreement as they recognized the likeness.

'The brute is armoured with scales,' said Garcia by way of diversion. 'Is the armour proof against a sword blade?'

He thrust with all his strength at the armoured back; the sword point pierced the hide with difficulty and sank into the flesh below. At the prick of the steel the dead thing twitched convulsively, causing a roar of laughter. They all hastened to prick at the brute with their swords, but the life of the thing–the half-life of the dead organism–was ebbing fast and hardly a movement rewarded their efforts. Alfonso de Avila came up with the crossbow and shot it off into the soft underpart of the tail, but the only response was a languid flap.

'That's a better shot than your last one,' said Garcia, rounding on him. 'I'll swear it went within a yard of me–and Don Narciso, here, it must have gone past his ear. It did, Don Narciso, did it not?'

'Maybe so,' said Rich as indifferently as he could manage. He had no wish to be involved in any controversy.

'I hit the brute well enough with my first shot,' retorted Avila, hotly. 'Look, you can see the bolt still in the bone. I was the first of us to wound it.'

There might have been a quarrel if Moret had not intervened.

'It was Don Narciso who first struck it with steel,' he said.

'By God, that is so!' said Osorio. 'I heard the sword ring against the thing's head.'

'It is for Don Narciso to claim the kill, then,' said Moret.

In the tradition of the chase the honour of the kill in the case of dangerous game went to the man who first set steel in the quarry.

'Yes,' said João de Setubal in his half-intelligible Portuguese. 'And look at that hind leg! I saw him strike that blow myself.'

The creature's left hind leg was cut nearly through close to the body, hanging merely by a bit of hide.

'A good blow that,' said Osorio.

They all looked at Rich, he felt himself blushing in the hot sunlight.

'Gentlemen,' he said, feebly, and then experience in court loosened his tongue and found him words to say, despite his embarrassment. 'It was the efforts of all of us that killed this crocodile. There was the skill and courage of Don Cristobal, who dropped the noose over its head. There was our worthy boatswain, who came rushing into battle with no more than a dagger. There were the intelligent men who dragged at the rope at exactly the right moment. Why, gentlemen, there is no need for us to dispute for honour.'

They murmured in pleased agreement at that; they all had a better opinion of themselves now, and there were no hard feelings. It was odd, the influence trifles had over these hot-blooded gentlemen.

9

A fresh distraction came when one of the seamen cried out that a canoe was approaching. Every eye turned down the river; they could see the canoe paddling briskly against the current towards them. The sun flashed on the paddle blades. Rich walked to the water's edge and waved a welcome, and the canoe came steadily on towards them until it grated on the sand and the five Indians in it stepped out and lifted it–it was a tiny, cranky thing–beyond the water. The Indians wore cloaks of white cotton, and aprons of the same material. They were handsome, of the palest copper colour, and with long straight hair hanging to their shoulders.

What Rich noticed specially was their lack of surprise at finding the white men here; he decided immediately that they had been watching them for some time, probably from across the river. The initial shyness displayed by the Indians of Trinidad was wanting; immediately after salutations with raised hands they came forward and examined the Spaniards as curiously as the Spaniards examined them. The Spaniards' clothing and armour and beards came in for specially close study; the two older Indians displayed a curious tendency to smell at the things that excited their curiosity, lifting the sleeve of Rich's coat to their noses in turn. They all fingered Garcia's polished steel helmet–Rich guessed that the sight of it, glittering across the water, had been the cause of considerable argument among them. They stood in a group and admired the longboat, marvelling at its size and its accessories and at the cunning way in which the planks were joined together–their own wretched boat was made of a single piece of wood and had hardly three inches of freeboard.

Three of them wore thin metal collars–half the Spaniards hurriedly called Rich's attention to them–which seemed to be of pale gold, but Rich forbore to offer to barter for them until their curiosity might be satisfied. With inquiring looks and beckoning gestures they walked away from the longboat towards the dead lizard, confirming Rich's theory that they had been studying the Spaniards' actions from across the water, and they stood and stared at the dead body with ejaculations of wonder. Garcia approached them and pointed to it.

'Iguana?' he said inquiringly, and, when they only looked puzzled, he repeated the word, varying the intonation. 'Iguana? Iguana?'

A look of understanding came over their faces and they made emphatic gestures of negation.

'Caiman,' said one, and then, pointing to the trees, 'Iguana.'

He helped his meaning out with more gestures; clearly the iguanas who lived in trees were vastly different creatures from the caimans that lived in rivers.

'Eat caiman?' asked Garcia. He pointed to the body and then to his mouth and then rubbed his belly.

The gestures of dissent were still more emphatic now; they made wry faces and held their noses. One of them, too, made all the gestures of fear, pretending to run away, and holding his hands to represent the snapping jaws of the caiman. That brought them back to their wonder that this ferocious animal had been killed at all. They marvelled loudly at the severed hind leg, and one of them turned to Garcia in an attempt to discover the magic means by which such a blow had been dealt. Politely he put out his hand to Garcia's sword hilt–he must have seen swords drawn already. Garcia pulled the weapon from its sheath.

'Hey! Careful!' said Garcia; the Indian had grasped the blade with his bare hand. Garcia's involuntary gesture and the Indian's withdrawal between them gashed the palm–fortunately not deeply; the Indian looked with amazement at the blood, while Garcia was voluble in apology and prodigal of gesture. But the Indian only smiled and shut his fist upon the cut; from the chattering that went on it was apparent that they were explaining to each other that a weapon which could cut at a touch could sever a caiman's leg at a blow.

Rich judged it to be as well to be conciliatory. He produced some of the trade goods with which the longboat had been supplied, and jingled a hawk's bell enticingly. There was just the same awe and delight displayed at the gifts as Rich had seen on the first occasion. He tapped at one of the collars of gold, and without a moment's hesitation the Indian unsnapped it from his neck and thrust it into his hand. It was harder and tougher than pure gold would have been; it was clearly an alloy, but its weight demonstrated that it must contain a large proportion of gold. Rich tried to display in dumb show great affection for the gold, and pointed inquiringly to the horizon. Instantly the Indian pointed south, with many words and gestures. Rich caught one word–'Guanin.'

'Guanin?' he said.

'Guanin,' said the Indian, tapping the collar.

They knew now the Indian word for gold. The two other collars were put into Rich's hands without his even asking for them. These uncultured folk clearly were possessed of the instinct to present strangers with whatever they desired. One of them began a new pantomine, pointing to his mouth, pointing to the whole group of Spaniards, and then, in a wide gesture, away across the river.

'He's inviting us to dinner,' said Garcia.

'I fancy so,' said Rich. 'He wants to take us to his village.'

He nodded in acceptance, and with little more ado the matter was settled satisfactorily. They pushed the longboat out from its mooring place and pulled after the canoe, which preceded them down the river with the Indian in the stern looking anxiously back at them and calling to see that they understood what they had to do. His gesture towards the setting sun indicated his wish to arrive at their destination before nightfall.

The current bore them down the river, while they quartered steadily across. Down where the delta began the canoe turned abruptly into a side channel which led them into a broader arm again, where trees grew with their feet in the water. It was not very far up here; the forest receded from the river bank leaving a wide clearing. Four more canoes floated moored to the bank, and a little crowd of Indians stood at the landing place to welcome them, men, women, and children, some in cotton aprons, many of them naked, and all of them chattering and laughing with pleasure at the success of their embassy in inducing these strangers to visit them.

Everything was on a much larger scale here than in Trinidad, as Rich saw when he mounted the bank with the others bustling like schoolboys behind him. The clearing was wider, and there were obvious patches of cultivated crops; Rich's attention was caught by the yellow hue of corn–presumably that strange golden Indian corn which he had heard about from Spaniards returned from Española. The Indians were laughing and chattering around them, leading them towards the leaf-built huts grouped to one side. It was a sort of triumphal procession, the naked children scampering in front of them, the adults leading the Spaniards by the hand, the original party which had found them talking loudly to everyone, apparently telling of all the extraordinary things these strangers could do. There was plenty of laughter, shouts of it–the Indians had to stop in the progress more than once while they all clasped midriffs and doubled up with mirth.

'You left no guard on the boat, sir,' muttered Osorio to Rich. He made a strange spectacle when Rich looked at him, his hat pulled awry and a naked girl clasping each arm; they had stuffed a handful of scarlet flowers into the breast of his leather coat. It was with a shock that Rich remembered that he had indeed neglected the precaution suggested by Osorio–nothing of the sort had occurred to him at all.

'No guard is necessary,' he said; he meant it, and yet he would have posted a guard if it had occurred to him.

'They might steal the boat's gear,' suggested Osorio.

'No,' said Rich. 'Oh, no.'

He was absolutely certain that these people would not steal; when the matter was presented to him as bluntly as that he realized that there was certainly no need to leave a guard with the boat.

'Very well, then, sir,' said Osorio, clearly washing his hands of the whole business. Nor could he had continued the conversation, for another girl was distracting him. She was presenting him with a small live parrot–a gorgeous green bird, with touches of yellow and red–which perched on her forefinger and looked at him with its head on one side in the most comical fashion. Laughing, she put the bird on his breast; it clung to his leather coat with beak and claws, pecked for a moment at the red flowers, and then, climbing desperately, reached the summit of his shoulder, from which it squawked into Osorio's ear its own contribution to the din around them.

A dignified Indian, taller than his fellows, met them at the huts, and for the moment chatter ceased. The speech he made was obviously one of welcome.

'Thank you,' said Rich. He said something about Their Highnesses, and about His Excellency the Admiral. He mentioned the Church of Christ, and to all of this they listened with grave attention. The chief tapped his own chest.

'Malalé,' he said.

Rich tried to reproduce the name. The chief listened courteously, and repeated it.

'Malalé,' said Rich.

The chief clapped his hands with pleasure, and all the mob round clapped as well. Yet the chief still waited for a second or two, and then with extreme deference he began again.

'Malalé,' he said, pointed to himself, and then pointed to Rich, who grasped his meaning at last.

'Rich,' he said, touching his breast.

Malalé hesitated.

'Rich,' said Rich again, encouragingly.

'Lish,' said Malalé with an effort.

'Rich,' said Rich.

'Lish,' said Malalé.

It was too much for anybody's gravity, certainly too much for the very precarious gravity of the Indians. Everybody laughed, including the chief. Everybody was saying 'Lish' in a hundred different intonations. The harsh 'r' and 'ch' were clearly beyond their powers of articulation.

'Lish,' said the girls on Osorio's arms.

'Lish,' said a pot-bellied little boy, laughing with his head thrown back and his stomach protruding.

'Lish,' said everyone else; it was like the wind rustling in a grove of willows.

The chief waved his arms to terminate the séance; Rich was irresistibly reminded of the kindly young teaching friar in his first school breaking off the chorused repetition when it grew too riotous. Everyone remembered the real business of the meeting, and the Spaniards were led by their chattering escorts up to the leafy huts. There were hammocks in there, standing on the earthen floors; a few gourds; a headless spear; some fantastic shells–practically nothing. Rich was led into the main hut, and seated on a couch of trellised creeper beside the doorway. It wobbled under his weight; it was as impermanent as the hut in which it stood. Osorio was given a block of wood on which to sit at Rich's side, and Garcia another–apparently these two were singled out to share the place of honour, the one because he had been seen much in Rich's company and the other because of his glittering helmet.

It was almost dark by now. Someone stirred the two fires into a bright blaze, and the rest of the Spaniards were led to seats by them. Then came the food, a prodigal display. There was fish and there was fruit, yellow cornbread, and grey cassava bread. There was roast meat of a nature quite unidentifiable, all served by the women and young men, while the older men stood by anxiously watchful that their guests should want for nothing.

'A cup of wine, now—' said Garcia. 'Hey, Don Malalé.'

He made a gesture of drinking, and in obedience to Malalé's request a girl approached him, carrying under each arm a bulky gourd. Another girl followed her with a couple of small drinking gourds. She put one in each of Garcia's hands. The first girl filled one of them, and stood by while Garcia tasted it.

'Queer,' said Garcia, savouring it on his palate. 'Sickly. I can't say that I like it.'

The expression on his face was sufficient indication for the girl to stoop and fill the other cup from the other gourd.

'Sour,' said Garcia. 'But still—Drinkable, at any rate.'

He drained the cup, and it was refilled for him. When Rich came to taste the drink he found it sour, as Garcia has said. The flavour was indefinable, and he simply could not guess whether it was fermented or not.

Malalé was standing ready to make polite conversation. It called for a good deal of effort to make him understand that he wanted to know the name of this little town.

'Paria,' said Malalé at length. He pointed all about him into the surrounding darkness. 'Paria.'

So this country was called Paria. Rich could remember no geographical name that resembled it, in the way that Cibao resembled Cipangu.

'Guanin?' asked Rich, and the chief evinced a little surprise at Rich's knowing a word of his language. One of the Indians who had been in the canoe interposed with a voluble explanation in which Rich heard the word repeated more than once. Malalé called to his subjects. There was a good deal of bustling about, and people brought Rich ornaments of gold and put them at his feet–two more collars, and several shapeless lumps, the largest the size of a walnut.

'This wench here has pearls on,' said Osorio.

'I was going to ask about them next,' said Rich.

He reached out and touched the armlet, and at his touch the girl stood stock-still, quivering a little like a frightened horse. At a word from Malalé she stripped off the armlet and put it in his hand, still stood for a second, and then, presumably deciding that it was only the pearls that interested Rich, quietly withdrew. More pearls were brought; a little pile of wealth lay at Rich's feet.

Beyond the ring of light round the fires something was happening in the darkness. The circle of Spaniards had grown thin. The din and chatter had died away into a more secretive murmur. Uneasily Rich guessed what was going on, and felt a little sick both with apprehension and disgust. He himself had lived celibate for nearly twenty years, ever since he had said good-bye to Paoletta in Padua after he had received his doctorate, and he had not been conscious of missing anything, thanks to his interest in his work and in the minor pleasures of life. He could feel only small sympathy with the animal grossness of these hot-blooded Castilians; he was a dozen years older than the eldest of the hidalgos, and he felt as if it were more like thirty or forty. Nothing, not even gold, could cause quarrelling and bloodshed so easily as could women, but that was only a practical point. Morally, Rich felt an uneasy sensation of sin at the thought of condonation of promiscuousness. He had his own immortal soul to think about.

But a casuist might argue that there was no sin in promiscuousness with these simple pagans who knew nothing of God, who gave so gladly and who submitted so willingly. Their souls were put in no further peril by it; the devil, although he wished to entrap Christian souls, would not assume the guise of these girls whose simple nakedness stripped the glamour–to Rich's mind–from the act and reduced it to a mere function of brutish nature. Rich found himself lapsing into heresy again; it was perilous to try and distinguish between deliberate sin and instinctive sin. And no thief would ever be hanged and no heretic would ever be burned if it were once admitted that inability to resist temptation constituted an excuse. That way lay chaos and anarchy. Natural instincts were in themselves suspect.

All the same, it was dangerous to interfere, physically dangerous. To take a girl from these men was like taking a kill from a wild cat. They would challenge him, perhaps. Any of these brawny louts could kill him five seconds after crossing swords. Rich vividly pictured to himself a sword blade slicing through his soft flesh, and his red blood flowing; the thought made him sick, and decided him instantly to take no action. After all, he did not know–he was not certain–what was going on. That was sufficient excuse, although he despised himself for his weakness at the same time as he yielded to it.

Somewhere in the darkness a woman screamed sharply, and Rich felt his heart sink. He tried to act as if he had not heard, and the cry came again. Garcia was eyeing him curiously in the firelight, and Osorio was looking at him sidelong, to see what he would do. The Indians were tense; everything seemed to be waiting on his decision. In a few moments there might be a bloody massacre, he realized now. He got slowly to his feet, and as he did so an Indian girl came running into the firelight. She made straight for one of the men and threw herself into his arms; she pointed back into the darkness with tearful explanations as he stood with an arm round her shoulders.

As she pointed, two figures came into sight, blinking a little sheepishly in the firelight, João de Setubal and Diego Moret. They saw everyone on their feet, and they felt the tension, and they were self-conscious with every eye on them.

'What is this?' said Rich. Every word was a torment to utter.

'I found the girl first,' said Moret, sullenly.

'You found her first? *You* found her?' protested Setubal in his slobbering Portuguese. 'She promised me an hour ago.'

'Can you talk this monkey-talk, then?' Moret was a fat and lazy man, but he was thoroughly roused now.

'No. But she knew what I meant, well enough,' said Setubal. 'She promised me.'

'Nonsense. She was willing enough for me, or would have been if you had not interfered and frightened her.'

'You had no right to her.'

'Nor had you.'

'I claimed her first!'

'That's a lie!'

Their hands went to their sword hilts at those words. To give the lie was as much an invitation to bloodshed as to give a blow. Someone was at Setubal's elbow in the half-light, and someone else at Moret's. In a moment there would be a dozen swords drawn. Everyone's life would be in peril, with these Indians uneasily looking on, and Rich had to plunge in, lest worse befall.

'Don Diego! Don João!' he cried, hurrying forward from the hut between the two fires.

His words barely sufficed to check the men as they stood with their swords half drawn. They looked round at him, their bodies turned towards each other, right feet advanced, left shoulders thrown back. In the tenth part of a second those blades could cross.

'Take your hands from your swords!' roared Rich. The desperate urgency of the moment gave power to his voice–it was like shouting at a child who was about to touch unwittingly a brazier of burning charcoal. They hesitated, and then, as Rich strode between them, they dropped their melodramatic poses; their right hands left their sword hilts even if their left still retained their grasp on the scabbards.

'Are you fools enough to want to fight with a hundred Indians looking on?' spluttered Rich. 'They may think us gods now, but how long will they think it if one of you had a yard of steel in his belly?'

A training in rhetoric may have enabled his tongue to move more freely, but he had never before been so desperately anxious to win a cause, and the idiom he used and the tactics he employed were the proof of the inspiration of necessity. The sound of the quarrel had called back to the firelight the other Spaniards who were out in the shadow; they were coming back to the ring one by one, and taking their places in it, while the Indian women were grouping together in the background behind the screen of their menfolk–Rich was conscious out of the tail of his eye of this by-play.

'Will the women be so easy for you if they see you think 'em worth squabbling about?' he asked, wondering, as he said it, whether his tone of self-confident coarse good-fellowship rang true. 'Twenty of you came with me in the longboat, and I've got to take twenty of you back, or there'll be the devil to pay when I make my report to the Admiral.'

He ran his eyes round the ring; every Spaniard was present now. Somebody damned the Admiral in an undertone, but low enough for Rich to be able to pretend he had not heard.

'If it comes to that,' he went on, amplifying his earlier speech, 'what'll these women think of us anyway if you go on as you do? With our clothes on, and our helmets, and our sword belts, and our white skins we're gods to them now. There's gold and there's pearls for the asking. But with our breeches off we're men. Aren't we, now? And you've been taking the surest way of making the men angry and dangerous. Think of your own case. If an archangel visited you in Spain you'd give him dinner, wouldn't you? But if you caught that archangel with your wife? What then?'

He got a laugh at that–a most encouraging sound.

'Let's have no more of this nonsense,' he said, taking the bull by the horns at last, and assuming the attitude of authority which he dreaded. 'It's time for sleep, and we'll sleep close together for safety's sake. I'm not going to take chances with my eyes shut. Seamen can sleep by the fire here. Gentlemen here. Don Diego, you can make yourself obeyed by these hot-headed lads. See that nobody wanders off in the night and gets his throat cut. Boatswain, you can do the same with your seamen.'

To delegate the responsibilty to Garcia was a bold and successful move. Garcia would not like it to be demonstrated that he could not make himself obeyed after Rich had assumed he could, and he certainly could fight if necessary, which was more than Rich could do. And the simple assumption of authority and of Garcia's support worked a miracle, too. The young men were impressed by it–and perhaps Rich did not realize that they were the less ready to resent his authority after he had withstood sword in hand the first mad charge of the wounded caiman. Nor was the hint that their lives might be in peril, here in this unknown land, without its weight.

10

For the four full days which the Admiral had allotted as a maximum Rich explored this new coast in the longboat. Southward they went, and southward again, finding the land continuous. The marshy delta-formation continued for miles–more than one big river contributed to its formation. There was a freshwater lagoon where flocked countless white aigrettes, beautiful in the sunshine. There were cranes and monkeys and parrots, while each sandbank bore its two or three caimans–the sight of them always raised a laugh in the longboat, at the memory of Garcia's temerity in attempting to kill one with a noose and the bare steel. There were Indians in little groups everywhere, each group with a hospitable welcome, and ready to accompany them to the next group even though it was impossible to explain to them by sign language that they were seeking an easterly passage to the open sea–they were never able to make them understand this. The Spaniards' gesticulations were met with a wooden lack of understanding which their utmost efforts could not enlighten. The Indians knew of no sea to the east, but the evidence was not convincing, seeing that it appeared unlikely that any one of them had ever been more than ten miles from his birthplace.

One little piece of useful information they acquired, however. They were eating some of the little half-tide oysters which grew on trees, and Rich, showing pearls, was able to make it clear to one of their guides that he wanted to know if these oysters produced them. The suggestion met with an emphatic negative. By signs the guide was able to indicate that pearls were found in another kind of oyster, one with a much bigger shell, for which one had to dive deep, and which was only found in certain places to the north. It was a useful confirmation of Rich's already well-developed theory that these little oysters would be quite fully occupied in developing into pelicans without wasting further strength on producing pearls, and it agreed with what he knew vaguely of the pearl fisheries of the East. Rich wondered how extensive these new fisheries were. Certainly there were pearls in plenty to be seen in this country, but these Indians had lived here for countless generations undisturbed, and the pearls they wore might be the accumulation of centuries. With no idea of barter or trade, and wearing the things purely for ornament, it might easily be the case that the pearls they owned might represent the annual produce of the fisheries a hundred times over.

Of the Indians' ignorance of barter, or their utter improvidence, the longboat bore ample proof. She was laden deep with gifts; every village had stripped itself bare to supply the strangers with anything they might require–bread and fruit and strange edible roots in addition to gold and pearls. The weary crews of the ships would experience a welcome change of diet on the longboat's return, but Rich wondered a little about how the Indians were going to live until their next crops ripened. Hawk's bells and red caps and steel mirrors would not fill empty bellies, but the Indians seemed to have no qualms on the subject. There might be a word in their limited vocabulary for 'tomorrow'–although he doubted even that–but there certainly was none for 'the future.' He felt a little pang of sympathy for them each time the longboat pushed away from the creek-side landing places.

Southward, through the lagoons and waterways, the longboat sought for the passage to an eastern sea. Then westward as well as southward, as the trend of the land forced them that way. The sun roasted them, and the rain saturated them, insects bit them. There were tiny creatures, some flat and some cylindrical, which found their way under their clothes when they were on land and sank their jaws so deeply into their skin that their heads parted company from their bodies sooner than loose their holds when the Spaniards tried to pull them off. Next day there was an itching sore where the head had been left in the wound, and each day the soreness and irritation grew worse. Wrists and faces swelled with the bites of the mosquitoes.

In the sweltering nights there were things even worse than mosquitoes to be dreaded. On the third night they slept in an abandoned Indian clearing at the water's edge, under the crude shelter of the boat's sails spread to protect them from the rainstorms, and Rich found himself awakened at dawn by Osorio shaking his shoulder. Rich was stupid with sleep–it was not until the early morning that he had been able to lose consciousness in the heavy heat–and it was with bleared eyes that he followed the line of Osorio's pointing forefinger. From under the shelter of the mainsail two yards away projected the naked leg and foot of one of the seamen, thrust out, Rich presumed, in search of coolness during the night. And resting on the foot was a greyish lump, which moved a little as Rich looked. There was hardly light to see, for the faint dawn could as yet barely penetrate the forest around them, and the thing was too vague to be seen clearly, but it was ugly, menacing, obscene.

Bernardo de Tarpia had shared the shelter of the mizzensail with Rich and Osorio, and he, too, was awake and staring at the thing, crossing himself and breathing hard. Then the leg moved and the thing dropped off the foot to the ground with a flutter of wings; it made towards them. There was something vile about it and they all three flinched back. The wings fluttered again in the short undergrowth; it was trying to fly and yet was unable to rise, and its course brought it close to Rich. His hand was on the hilt of his sword, which he had grasped instinctively at the first alarm, and he whirled the sheathed weapon and struck the thing, shuddering. Again and again he struck, but Tarpia had his sword out by now, and with a cry, half prayer and half blasphemy, he slashed at the thing and the flutterings ended abruptly.

It was a bat, a furry thing, brownish above and greyish below, with wide-spread leathery wings, dead with its open mouth revealing a gleam of sharp white teeth. The revolting ugliness of the face made Rich shudder again, and the spreading pool of blood in which the creature lay disclosed the work it had been at, it had gorged itself until it was unable to rise in the air. The occupants of the other tent had awakened, and were on their feet and out now; one of them was bare-legged and pale under his tan. At Rich's order, he showed his foot. A patch of skin the size of a finger nail had been shaved from off it at the root of the great toe, and a broad stream of blood still flowed from the wound, even though the seaman was ignorant of its existence until his attention was called to it. He paled still further when he learned what had happened, and during that day they waited for him to die of the poison they thought the bat had injected into the wound. But he did not die, and the flow from the wound ceased after it had soaked the cloth in which they bound it. On their return to the ships the surgeon bled him from the right elbow, as was of course necessary after a wound in the left foot, and he recovered some days later with the help of purges. But they did not foresee his recovery at the time. During the exploration of that day Rich was thinking of the wretched man with pity, and watching him as he lay in the bottom of the boat with the oars creaking over him.

A shallow exit from a lagoon brought them out into open water again; there lay Trinidad to the westward, well up over the horizon, while to the eastward and the southward was the land they had been exploring. There was only a narrow gap between the two–the Serpent's Mouth. The Admiral's Isle of Grace, as he had named the land across the Serpent's Mouth from Trinidad, was something more than an island, then. It was a part of the big island whose innumerable river mouths they had been examining.

'That settles it, sir, I should think,' said Osorio, peering round under his hand. 'If the Admiral wants to find a passage to the eastward he'll have to come back through here first. And I don't expect he'll want to do that–not with that current running.'

'Perhaps not,' said Rich, looking at the green slopes of Trinidad and of what he had thought of so far as the Isle of Grace. But now they had circumnavigated the whole of this sea of Paria and there were only the two exits–the Serpent's Mouth to the south and the Dragon's Mouths, which they had hardly examined, to the north; if the Admiral would not use the one, he would have to use the other. Yet Rich was reluctant to give up the search for another way round. He had a strange feeling that this land of Paria held the secret of the Indies. He wanted to know how far it extended, and what ocean lay beyond it. He felt a little thrill of pleasure–at which he was inclined to smile–at the thought that his foot had been the first from Europe to be set upon it. Trinidad was a mere small island, but Paria–no one knew the limits of Paria yet.

'Take the boat in again,' he said, hoarsely, and Osorio swung the tiller over and they headed in towards the flat delta once more.

There was a bigger river mouth even than usual here; Osorio tasted the water which he lifted in his hand from over-side.

'Fresh,' he said laconically–it meant that the volume of water coming down the river was considerable, if here at the edge of the sea there was no taste of salt.

But save in the matter of size, this channel was like the others they had explored; mud and jungle, mosquitoes and aigrettes. Rich wondered whether he would be able to persuade the Admiral to bring the squadron back to here and push a strong expedition, equipped for weeks of exploration, up this river. He felt a sudden yearning to lead such an expedition–he felt in his bones, ridiculous though he knew such an idea to be, that this river drained no mere island, but a new unguessed-at continent. A mad theory, contrary to all the ideas held by the Admiral, a dangerous, almost an heretical, theory. If only there was some means of ascertaining how far round this revolving globe they had sailed, whether it was one-third the way round, as the Admiral's theories demanded, or one-eighth the way, as Rich saw would have to be the case if his own mad guesses were correct! If only some miracle would let them know, even just for once, what time of day it was at that moment in Cadiz!

Sand-glasses turned half-hourly for a ten weeks' voyage, could be as much as a week out in their record at the end of that time, he knew. Ingenious mechanics were constructing engines in Germany which could tell the time with an error of not more than an hour a day. If some remarkable man could devise one accurate to a second a day, and able to withstand the shocks of a sea voyage, the problem would be solved, but no such miraculous workmanship could ever be hoped for. Wilder and more chimerical ideas flowed through Rich's brain. Supposing a string were to be laid by a ship on the bottom of the ocean from Cadiz to the Indies, so that a twitch from one end would announce the hour of noon to the other end! Supposing some vast explosion, some flash of light, could be contrived at Cadiz at noon which could be observed in the Indies! That was plain madness, said Rich to himself, terminating his meditations with a jerk. Three thousand miles of ocean sundered Spain from the Indies. It was a gap which no wild theories could bridge and no one–at least no one without the help of the magical powers–would ever be able to tell at one place what was the time at another; neither the Greek philosophers nor the Fathers of the Church held out any hope of the contrary.

'Another Indian boat, sir,' announced a seaman in the bow. 'See! He's gone up that creek over there to starboard.'

They turned the longboat and headed across the river to the creek, and sharp eyes detected the canoe hiding among the trees whose feet stood in the water. The two young Indian men who were in her had no concrete fears for their personal safety, just like all the other Indians they had encountered. They had merely taken flight before the unknown, and their confidence had only to be won for them to begin to smile broadly, with white teeth showing in contrast with their pale copper skins. The technique of handling them so as to reassure them was being acquired rapidly. Jingling hawk's bells, bright red caps–the young men were soon enraptured by the acquisition of treasures whose very possibility had been unguessed at by them an hour ago. But they had no treasures to give in exchange; the canoe contained nothing save a few fibre fishing lines with fish-bone hooks attached.

'Guanin?' said Tarpia to them; as they showed no understanding a dozen voices repeated the word in a dozen different intonations. One of them understood at last, saying the word over again. It was the initial sound which troubled these Castilians and Andalusians, noted Rich. The 'gu-' pronunciation which they used did not exactly reproduce the real sound because the latter had no place in their language. It was more like the beginning of a good many Arabic words–'Wadi,' for instance–which was reminiscent of the way in which he himself, speaking Catalan, or the Provençals speaking their native tongue, pronounced an initial 'v.'

'Guanin?' repeated everybody eagerly.

The Indian spread his hands deprecatingly. He had no gold.

'Where can we find guanin?' asked Acevedo; he went through the motions of someone seeking something, steadily repeating the word meanwhile.

The Indian grinned and pointed south. It was always to some other quarter that these Indians pointed, south or north or west; they knew no mines of gold close to them.

Rich was trying to question the other Indian about the geography of the neighbourhood–a heartbreaking task in dumb show, but the Indian paid courteous attention to his strained gesticulations. He partly understood at last and replied in a long speech, pointing round about him. Twice in the rapid sentences Rich caught the name 'Paria,' and he knew already that was the name of this country. He pointed to the river, and peered along it under his hand, pointed back to the sea, and then inland again, in a desperate effort to inquire about the existence of a westward passage. The Indian grasped some of his meaning. He smiled and nodded his head; he spread his arms wide, striving with his body to convey the impression of something big–big–big. Did that mean there was a big sea beyond, wondered Rich. The other Indian joined in. He, too, pointed to the river and spread his arms.

'Orinoco,' he said, and the other eagerly echoed the word, 'Orinoco.'

'Orinoco?' asked Rich.

The Indians were delighted, and gesticulated more vehemently than ever. This Orinoco, whatever it was, was something very big, and was somehow connected with the river by which they were. One of the Indians hissed and shushed, swinging his arms horizontally with twittering fingers–the Orinoco must be a rushing river, and, judging by the way the other Indian pointed and spread his arms, far wider somewhere in the interior than this arm of it. The Indians chattered together and then one of them turned back to Rich; he was clearly faced with a difficult explanation, but that could not account for the reverent solemnity of their expressions. He was about to try to describe something which they considered very important, perhaps connected with some god of theirs. He held his hands high, the fingers dancing, and moved slowly along–this was the steady course of a wavelet-capped river.

'Whoosh!' he said, and his hands dropped suddenly to the level of his knees. 'Whoosh!'

His hands indicated a turmoil in the water at a lower level.

'A waterfall!' said Osorio,

'Of course,' said Rich. 'How far?'

He made a gesture of walking towards this Orinoco waterfall, and the Indian dissented emphatically. The Indian closed his eyes and inclined his head sideways against his folded hands in a gesture of sleep. Then he held up his finger. He slept again, and held up his finger again, and then again. After that repetition he gave up the effort of trying to convey the exact number, and spread all his fingers, over and over again. A man would have to sleep many nights before he penetrated as far as this waterfall. Two more vivid gestures disclosed the fact that he had himself seen this marvellous phenomenon, while his companion had not.

'Are there people to be found on the way?' asked Rich. 'Many people?'

The Indians presumably grasped the meaning of his signs, and dissented doubtfully. There were some people, a few people, apparently, along the river–but apparently these Indians had no notion of an uneven distribution of population.

'Guanin?' asked Rich.

The Indians were puzzled. There might be gold there, a little, but clearly they were not interested in gold, and could not understand this persistent questioning about the existence of gold. Rich tried to work by analogy in his effort to understand their mentality. Supposing a negro of unknown tongue landed in Catalonia, and was not interested in the service of God or in money, and yet persistently asked about the existence of, say, sandstone–or even birds' nests–something of no special appeal, his questions might be received with the same blank lack of sympathy.

One of the Indians was examining Pedro's crossbow with more interest. Pedro was always glad of the opportunity of demonstrating the effectiveness of his weapon. He wound the thing up, making great play of the amount of strength necessary to turn the windlass, while the Indians looked on, deeply interested but entirely without understanding. When the cord clicked over the catch and the windlass spun free they actually thought the demonstration was complete, and smiled politely.

'No,' said Pedro; he was one of the school which believed that people who did not understand good Spanish might understand bad Spanish. 'Big shooting. Look. See.'

He laid a heavy bolt into the groove against the string and looked round for a target. A few score yards away, out on the broad surface of the river, a sea bird drifted with the current. Pedro called their attention to it, raised his heavy weapon, took careful aim, and shot. The bolt splashed into the water not more than a couple of yards from the bird, which squawked with surprise. Such an amazing result naturally impressed the Indians as much as did the clatter of the released bow. They looked with reverence upon the man who could do such extraordinary things, and these Spaniards who manned the longboat took a childish delight in displaying their powers–the sharpness of their heavy swords, and the impenetrability of their armour, and the way their clothes fastened with brooches and buttons. Rich allowed them plenty of time for it before he suggested a move.

They would have to turn back and seek the ships now, and it was with a curious sinking of heart that he directed the longboat's course away from the mouth of the Orinoco, and northward, with the easterly wind just fair enough to enable them to proceed under sail. As they coasted along, leaving on their left the flat delta which they had explored, Rich looked across at the land with this persistent feeling of unhappiness. He might never return here, to this land of the laughing Indians, he might never explore the vast Orinoco, and he felt that it was this that he wanted to do, despite the heat, and the rain, and the insect pests, and the vampire bats. Whatever might be the wonders awaiting him in Española, he felt as if this vast new land where he had been the first Spaniard to set foot was peculiarly his own. He hardly paid attention when Osorio announced, after cautious experiments, that even out here the water was hardly brackish.

II

The Admiral listened courteously to Rich's report. His eyes brightened at the sight of the gold and the pearls which Rich handed over, and he seemed pleased at the news that the longboat was full of fresh food. The Admiral had no interest in food himself–his bad teeth alone would have limited it–and with him it was an article of faith, not of knowledge, that weaker men found benefit in a varied diet. He laughed at Rich's account of how they had attacked a caiman under the impression that it was an iguana.

'It is a pity you had no men with you with experience of the Indies,' he said, and then his face hardened as he realized what he said. When the squadron sailed from Spain no inducement offered had been great enough to tempt a single one of those survivors of the previous expedition who had returned to Spain to sail again for the Indies.

Rich noticed the Admiral's hurt expression, and went on hastily with his report so as to smooth over the difficulty.

'It is a vast land, Your Excellency,' he said, and the Admiral nodded doubtfully. 'The rivers are huge.'

'You mean the channels between the islands?'

'Rivers, Your Excellency. Vast rivers of fresh water. So vast that they freshen the water far out in this inland sea.'

'That freshness is interesting–we have noticed it here, near the ships, while you have been away. I have decided on the cause.'

'It is caused by these big rivers, Your Excellency.'

'Oh, no. There is no land near which could support a river of that size. It is far more likely that—'

'We found a river the Indians called Orinoco, Your Excellency,' said Rich. He was desperate enough to interrupt in his anxiety not to hear the theory. 'They said one could ascend it for many days' journey, as far as a great waterfall.'

'There is nothing so easy to misunderstand as the signs these Indians make,' said the Admiral, kindly. 'Believe me on that point; I have had sufficient experience to know.'

Rich remembered the Admiral's early reports and their frequent mentions of the consequences of such misunderstandings, and yet he was sure that on this occasion there had been no misunderstanding.

'Their gestures left me in no doubt,' he said.

'That is often enough the case, believe me. Could they have been referring to a fountain, perhaps? The fountain of youth–what did you say this river was called?'

'Orinoco, Your Excellency.'

'There were four rivers in Eden. Euphrates, Hiddekel, Pishon, and Gihon.' The Admiral thought for a while; Rich could see the struggle in his face as he gave up the attempt to reconcile one of the last three names with 'Orinoco.' 'No matter. These Indians often have several different names for their rivers. Let us hear more.'

Rich told of the oysters which grew upon trees.

'Ah, that is the source of these pearls. Pliny has a passage on the subject. Did you notice any clinging with their shells open?'

'No, Your Excellency.'

'Pliny tells that oysters exposed by the tide open their shells to receive drops of dew from the skies, and then solidify these drops into pearls. It is natural to meet with confirmation here.'

Rich kept his mouth tight shut. He was not going to risk a further snub by advancing the further information given him by the Indians about the pearls. And then with a shock he realized that the Admiral was right. He remembered perfectly plainly now the passage in *De Rerum Natura* that dealt with the point. He certainly must have mistaken the Indians' gestures in this case, at least. Pliny could not be wrong; Rich withdrew in horror from the brink of the abyss of free-thinking into which he had been about to plunge.

'What is the matter, Don Narciso?' asked the Admiral, politely. 'You look unwell.'

'Oh, no, Your Excellency, thank you,' said Rich, hastily. Not for words would he confess to a proximity to heretical unbelief. 'I am perfectly well.'

'Then let us hear more.'

Rich told of the endless marshy channels, of the vampire bat, of their eventual recognition of the Isle of Grace as they emerged beside the Dragon's Mouths.

'So that between here and the Isle of Grace you think the channels impracticable for the squadron, then?'

'Yes, Your Excellency.'

That was one way of saying that he thought the Isle of Grace a peninsula jutting out from a vast continent, and it was one which saved argument. Besides, after the incident of Pliny and the pearls Rich was in a bewilderment of doubt again.

'Then we shall have to risk the passage of the Dragon's Mouths. We have no more time to spare at the moment–my presence is probably urgently needed in Española. We shall make the passage tomorrow morning.'

'Yes, Your Excellency.'

Rich had foreseen this development some time back–he was coming to know the Admiral so well and to anticipate his reactions. It was the Admiral's way to touch lightly upon one subject of investigation and then dash on to the next, to formulate a theory and neglect the confirmation of it, to find the distant prospect always more alluring than the present–an extraordinary trait in a man with the obstinacy and firmness of character to pursue, as the Admiral had done, a single aim through eighteen early years of rebuffs and poverty. It was as if that effort had drained him of all his single-purposedness.

'My brother, I hope, will have reduced the colony to order, and will have several shiploads of treasure awaiting us. As Adelantado I left him full powers.'

'Yes, Your Excellency.'

Bartholomew Columbus was one of the few men whom the Admiral trusted–but these clannish Genoese could be, of course, expected to trust their brothers. And Bartholomew had sailed with Diaz to the Cape of Good Hope, and was generally reputed to be a man of parts. With the powers of Adelantado–deputy to the Viceroy–he certainly might by now have effected a change in the colony since the date of the last depressing reports; but Rich was aware that it would call for a man of vast ability and courage to enforce an orderly government on the adventurers and gaolbirds who had accompanied the Admiral to Española on his second voyage. He hoped it had been done.

'If all is well in Española, Your Excellency,' ventured Rich, 'I hope you will consider it advisable to despatch a new expedition to explore these parts.'

'I hope I shall,' said the Admiral. 'But there is so much to explore–there is so much to do.'

The Admiral sighed, and his heavy lids drooped over his blue eyes; the man was weary.

'But here there is so much to discover,' said Rich.

'Yes, indeed,' agreed the Admiral with more animation; his face brightened as he spoke. 'I have written it all in the report I am sending to Their Highnesses. The Earthly Paradise, the mines of Ophir, the Fountain of Youth–I am glad that you are with me, Don Narciso, to confirm me in all these matters.'

Rich had not the least intention of affirming to King Ferdinand the presence of any such phenomena in these parts; he wanted a great deal more evidence before he could do that, even though he knew that the counter theories at the back of his mind were ridiculous and dangerous enough to call for instant repression with nothing to replace them. But he had to swallow twice before his innate theory forced him to hint as much to the Admiral.

'The gold and the pearls which you will send will be better evidence of the wealth of the country, perhaps, Your Excellency,' he said, 'and I am not geographer enough to venture an opinion on the other points.'

The straight deep line reappeared between the Admiral's eyebrows at the suggestion of an opinion contrary to his own.

'The ultimate exploration of this group of islands,' he said finally, 'will reveal many wonders. I should be accustomed by now to having my ideas mocked at by those unqualified to judge.'

'At least, Your Excellency,' pleaded Rich, 'I am aware of my lack of qualification.'

For the first time in his life Rich was feeling sympathy towards heretics faced with a demand for a recantation. Someone, who should know, spoke of a group of islands where he considered lay a mass of land, and in the face of superior experience Rich could not help but cling to his own opinion, despite himself. Whether he would go to the stake for it or not Rich could not decide; certainly he would face a good deal of unpleasantness, and he was decidedly glad that it was a geographical point, and only distantly a theological one, which was at issue.'

'Then you need not continue to weary me with argument,' said the Admiral, dismissing him.

Rich went on deck again depressed and unhappy, to watch the sun descend slowly towards this unknown land–or islands.

A little group of canoes came stealing out to the squadron over the glassy waters of the Gulf of Paria; they were the usual cranky craft of which Rich had seen a good many specimens during the longboat's voyage, mere strips of bark two or three feet wide. The two ends were tied into thin bundles and bent upwards, so as to accentuate the natural trough-like curve of the bark, thus making a boat which a venturesome boy might use on a millpond, but which would roll over at the first incentive and which buckled about, snake-like in its lack of rigidity, under the impulse of the paddles. Two or three such groups had already visited the squadron during the longboat's absence, and the ships' companies watched the approach of this one without excitement; Rich was too deeply sunk in his own thoughts to pay any attention at all.

It was Acevedo who raised him from his depression.

'Don Narciso,' he said, crossing the deck. 'A friend of yours is hailing you.'

A small canoe was creeping alongside the ship, propelled slowly by the paddles of two boys, and in the middle a naked Indian half stood, half crouched on his precarious foothold.

'Lish!' he was calling. 'Lish!'

He saw Rich's head and shoulders appear over the bulwark, and nearly capsized the canoe in the enthusiasm of his arm waving. It was Malalé, the chief of the first village which Rich had visited here; he smiled wildly and stooped to seek something down by his feet as the boys brought the canoe to the ship's side.

'Perhaps it is a royal collar of gold and pearls which he has brought you,' suggested Acevedo–someone was throwing a rope for Malalé to climb into the waist.

The Indian swung himself up over the bulwarks; he blinked for a moment, like a man emerging into strong sunlight, at the proximity of all the massive wonders about him, but he had confidence in Rich and was still smiling with the pleasure of seeing him again.

'No, it's a parrot, by God,' said Acevedo; perched on Malalé's hand was a big blood-red bird, which, as it moved, betrayed bewildering markings of a vivid blue–it was an extraordinary stimulating combination of colours.

Malalé approached, talking volubly but deferentially; it was not hard to guess that he was employing formal phrases which for once had a real meaning. He stopped, and waited for Rich to speak.

'I am delighted to see you again, Malalé,' said Rich. 'I hope you are well.'

He might as well say that as anything else, and it was all true. Malalé lifted the red parrot and offered it to Rich, and at the latter's hesitation burst into voluble pleading; Rich held out his hand and Malalé set the parrot upon it. Rich was about to utter formal thanks, but was checked by a new outburst of speech from Malalé. He was chattering to the parrot, stroking its feathers and rubbing the back of its head, and the parrot contorted its neck and goggled up at Rich with beady eyes. Still Malalé chattered and caressed; the parrot put its head on the other side and said something in reply–but evidently not the right thing, for Malalé continued to address it, coaxingly. Suddenly the parrot seemed to realize what was expected of it.

'Lish,' it said, clearly and unmistakably. 'Lish, Lish, Lish.'

Everybody laughed, and Malalé stood by with modest pride while the parrot looked round the ring with its inhuman eyes and ruffled its blood-red feathers and repeated 'Lish' half a dozen more times before it trailed off again first into Indian speech and then into silence, with its long claws gripping Rich's finger.

'They must have started teaching the bird to say that the moment we left the village,' commented Acevedo.

Rich did not need Acevedo's friendly comment to call his attention to the forethought that contributed to the gift. He was inexpressibly moved by it–foolishly, he told himself–and he was surprised to find such a strong emotion in him, impeding his utterance and blurring his vision for a second or two. Not many people had ever made gifts to the learned Narciso Rich save in payment for his professional services. He found it hard to stammer his thanks, and it moved him still more to see Malalé's obvious delight in the pleasure he had given. The parrot flapped impotent wings and began to sidle along his sleeve with beak and claws.

'Lish,' it said, peering up at him.

Malalé's visit and the gift he bore drew some at least of the sting from out of the necessity of saying farewell to the Gulf of Paria.

12

They sailed next morning by the central channel of the Dragon's Mouths. It was reassuring to see the drastic change which came over the Admiral when he was confronted with a problem in seamanship. He was no longer a touchy old gentleman rather set in his ideas; his very rheumatism seemed to leave him, and he paced the deck like a young man, his high clear voice as he called his orders to the captains of the caravels reaching easily across the intervening sea.

Rich stood beside him and watched the manoeuvre; there was a fascination about seeing the actual practice of an art with which he was theoretically well acquainted. Close-hauled, they reached to the southward–that was obviously to avoid the necessity of having to go about when they were at the point of entering the straits. Rich had to look up at the masthead, where the red-cross pennant flapped, to make sure of the direction of the wind, but the Admiral was under no such necessity. Presumably he based his judgment on a whole host of trivial indications to which Rich was insensitive–the wind upon his cheek, the heel of the deck, the action of the sails and the general behaviour of the ship.

Osorio was out in the longboat at the entrance to the straits; he had to be allowed plenty of time to make the passage, because he had to sound carefully every yard of the way, lest there might be a hidden transverse reef which would allow the passage of the longboat and yet would rip the bottom out of the ships; when the latter came hurtling down with the wind on their quarter and the current behind them there would be no chance of changing their minds–and yet the longboat must be kept in sight for her signals to be seen. The Admiral gauged the force of the wind and measured the distance to the straits with a considering eye. He gave a quiet order to Carvajal and turned to hail the caravels again. Round came the *Holy Name*, her canvas flapping and her rigging rattling while the crew scuttled round in the flurry of going about. She steadied on her new course, the caravels in her wake and her bows pointing to the passage. Far ahead the longboat danced in the turbulent race–they could see the flash of her oars as her crew strove to hold her on a steady course in the eddies.

They ran down towards the islands; a brief order from the Admiral corrected the course a trifle to allow for the leeway the clumsy ship was making and which was carrying her a trifle away from the exact centre of the passage. The lofty green hills of the north-western corner of Trinidad approached them nearer and nearer on their right hand–Rich guessed from the glances the Admiral darted at them that he was wondering what effect they would have on the wind as the ships came under their lee. The longboat was through–Osorio was standing in the sternsheets waving the white flag which indicated an absence of shoals. But the wind was growing fluky, thanks to the hills of Trinidad. Twice the sails flapped angrily; Carvajal was pulling at his beard and watching the man at the tiller. The steep-sided island that rose midway between Trinidad and the land of Paria was close upon them now; that, too, would have its effect on the wind. Rich saw the island swing round in relation to the foremast. Carvajal snapped angrily at the steersman and was answered with excuses–the dying wind was leaving the ship at the mercy of the eddies. But another puff came to steady her on her course, and the island was drawing up beside them.

Now they were through, and the longboat was waiting to come alongside. The wind, the eternal east wind, was blowing again here more freshly after an unimpeded course over three thousand miles of sea, and the long ocean swell was waiting for them–Rich felt the *Holy Name*'s bows lift to it, and heard its music, strangely welcome, under her stern. Behind them now lay Trinidad and Paria, the islands of the Dragon's Mouths ringed with white where the swell burst against their feet. To his right hand, as he looked aft, Rich saw the green coast of Paria stretching until it was lost in the faint haze; whatever the Admiral might think, it was certainly a much larger country than Trinidad.

But curiously enough, that question was not so urgent in Rich's mind now. An hour ago his memories of Paria had been sharp and distinct–Malalé, and the rivers, and the caimans, and the myriad fireflies at night, and the croaking frogs, but now they were already vague. Ahead lay the open sea, and beyond it, Española. The lift and surge of the *Holy Name*, the fresh wind, the prospect of a new voyage–all these things distracted him. The relief from tension after the passage of the Dragon's Mouths helped as well. Rich found himself all a-bubble with pleasurable anticipation, and for the life of him he could not tell why. Bernardo de Tarpia's crossbowmen seemed to have caught the infection; they were strutting a measure on the foredeck to the rhythmical thumping of a tambourine, while Antonio Spallanzani looked on smiling, his lute across his knees.

The Admiral was giving the man at the tiller a new course to steer, and that recalled Rich a little to reality. He wondered by what process the Admiral had reached his conclusions as to the correct course. Española lay at least two hundred leagues away, and he was approaching it from a point as to whose exact whereabouts (Rich knew only too well) the Admiral could be none too certain. Even the compass was no longer the steadfast friend which they knew in the Mediterranean–in these waters it pointed for some unknown reason a little east of north instead of west of north, and allowance would have to be made for its variation, even though that variation were unknown. Vaguely–very vaguely–they knew their distance from Spain, and the distance of Española from Spain. Within ten leagues or so they knew the distance of each point from the equinoctial line, but all that gave only small data for a calculation as to the direction of the one from the other. And in these waters they had already had proof of the existence of currents which might confound all calculations, and even when the calculations were made and the currents allowed for there was still the variation of the compass; all this in addition to the normal mariners' problems of leeway and drift–and in the dark hours, in these unknown seas, they would have to lie-to for fear of shoals, thus doubling the effect of the currents and of their leeway.

'I shall spend the rest of today, Don Narciso,' explained the Admiral, 'in examining the northern coast of this island of Paria, as you say it is called. But it would be inadvisable for us to proceed westward after that–it would carry us too far to leeward of our destination. Tomorrow we shall head for San Domingo; I think that will be the best point in Española to make for.'

'Whatever Your Excellency decides,' said Rich.

He would be quite content if they reached Española at all, without any conditions as to which bay or inlet they should sight first. He could well imagine themselves lost altogether when they left Paria and headed north-westward in search of Española across an uncharted ocean. They might blunder about for days–for weeks–seeking the island; provisions and water might fail; disease might break out among them even if they struck no reef or shoal. He certainly did not share the Admiral's bland confidence regarding what landfall they would make, and he felt a great deal more sober now than half an hour ago when they had passed through the Dragon's Mouths. The antics of the dancers on the forecastle were not at all to his taste.

'There is more land there, right to windward,' said the Admiral, staring with narrowed eyes.

Rich's sight was not as good. Stare as he would, he could see nothing on the horizon resembling land, but Osorio, called into consultation, confirmed the Admiral's opinion.

'Two islands, Your Excellency,' he said. 'One much to the northward.'

'They must be the end of the chain I explored last voyage,' said the Admiral. 'Dominica, Matinino, and the rest. That is the Cannibal region–these islands to windward have a different people from those of Española and Cuba and here in Trinidad. They are anthropophagous–they raid the other islands for prey. Caribs, Canibs, Cannibals, or some such name they bear. We shall root them out, extirpate them. They are magicians as well as eaters of human flesh. And I cannot permit them to put my own people in fear of their lives.'

Rich pondered that expression 'my own people.' It was fit and right that cannibals with magical powers should be rooted out–that was a Christian duty–but it was hardly fit and right that the Admiral should speak of 'my own people.' That was an expression emphatically reserved for royalty; Their Highnesses might see treason in it. Yet on the other hand the Indians, as pagans, might be considered the Admiral's property, after deduction of the Royal percentage. In that case the expression might pass, drawing a nice distinction between slaves and subjects. Legally, as the wielder of the Royal power, the Admiral was entitled to treat as slaves any of his Indians who were not expressly protected by charter–and no charter had yet been, or would ever be, granted to the naked and illiterate. Morally and ethically the position might be different; at the time Rich left Spain the Church there was trying to decide whether the Admiral was justified in sending shiploads of slaves–as he had begun to do in default of other cargo–for sale in Spain. It was a nice point, Rich would have liked to have heard it argued, even though he was no theological expert; but Aristotle and the Institutes would have no authority in an ecclesiastical court, and equity would stand little chance against the law (or the absence of law)–unless indeed Queen Isabella should intervene. Rich wished he knew what decision had been reached, yet with his worldly knowledge of judges he could guess that men who had been encouraged to expect cargoes of gold would not look with favour on the arrival of cargoes of slaves which would have to be paid for. That might give the slaves a chance.

The Admiral had left his side while he had been allowing his thoughts to digress in this fashion; the coast of Paria was still unfolding itself as the *Holy Name* ran along it before the wind. It was a coast of steep green hills, and every hour that the ship progressed demonstrated it to be five or six miles longer; a big island, therefore, if it were not the coast of Asia, or–the continent Rich dared not think about. At nightfall the coast was still close to the south of them, and at dawn next morning, after a dozen miles of drifting while lying-to, it was still there. The first break they saw was at noon, and when they came up to it they found that it was only a channel between the Parian coast and an island lying off it. A nearer approach revealed two islands instead of one, but Paria still continued beyond them.

And in these islands there were Indians–Indians who fled as the vast ships came sailing in, and who soon lost their shyness when they were approached with gifts. And they were Indians who wore pearls, great strings of them, which they were glad to give to the bearded white men who seemed to want them. Rich watched the bartering going on; the squadron, as it lay at anchor in the lagoon, was surrounded by canoes and the decks were thick with Indians while treasures which could have ransomed a prince were being handed over in exchange for broken fragments of painted earthenware.

The Admiral was trying to discover by means of signs whence came all these pearls, and the Indians, when they understood him, pointed over-side, to the lagoon whereon the *Holy Name* floated. The Admiral pressed for details, and two of the Indians swung themselves over-side into their canoe and pushed off to a short distance away. The younger Indian crept forward into the bows and rose cautiously to his feet. He was young and tall and slender–a handsome figure of a man. He poised himself with a foot on either gunwale, the twisted stempiece of the canoe rising to his waist, and then he dived with a sideways wrench of his body which took him clear of the stempiece and yet, miraculously, did not capsize the canoe. He went straight down–for several feet they could watch his progress through the clear water–and it seemed a long time before he rose again, shaking the water from his eyes, and with his hands full of grey objects which he dropped into the bottom of the canoe without troubling to climb in. He swam back to the *Holy Name* as quickly as his companion could paddle, and, running up on deck again, he laid the oysters at the Admiral's feet. An upward gesture showed that he expected to wait until the sun caused them to open, but Osorio's dagger did it at once, to the chattered amazement of the Indians. There were no pearls in the half-dozen oysters he had brought up, but it was clear enough to everybody that they were to be found, and the Indians pointed here and there over most of the lagoon to indicate the presence of oyster beds.

'God!' said Garcia. 'If we could set a thousand men diving here–there must be a thousand men to be caught–we should have pearls by the bushel. Don Narciso, can't you suggest it to the Admiral?'

'We have pearls by the quart, at least,' commented Acevedo. The Admiral was measuring the takings into a leathern cup.

Rich had not heard Garcia's suggestion, for his thoughts were digressing again. Those vast flat oysters were far different from the little ones which grew on the trees above low water in Paria, and they lived always under the sea. They would never have a chance of catching a falling dew drop and converting it into a pearl, and yet they produced pearls–pearls by the quart, as Acevedo said. So Pliny was wrong–was more ignorant than a naked Indian.

It was an appalling discovery, shaking Rich's faith to its foundations. With Pliny proved incorrect, where was the thing to end? Rich stood stock-still, while the pearls poured in a milky cascade from the leathern measure into a canvas bag before his unseeing eyes. The structure of his world was rocking unstably.

There was a loud squawk in his ear as the red parrot launched itself, with a fluttering of almost ineffectual wings, from the rigging beside him and just managed to reach his shoulder, retaining its balance there with a vigorous use of a beak and claws.

'Lish,' it said. 'Lish.'

It nibbled at his ear with a gentle beak, and maundered off, like an old man, into unintelligible Indian speech. Rich smoothed the ruffled feathers and felt in his pocket for a bit of weevilly ship's biscuit which he had already begun to carry there for the parrot's benefit–to the parrot this new kind of food appeared to be a supreme delicacy. Rodrigo Acevedo came along; he carried the jesses and the swivel and leash of the unhappy hawk which had died on the voyage out, and with long, busy fingers he quickly looped the jesses round the parrot's legs and attached the leash.

'There will be no need to cut his wing feathers now,' he remarked; he rubbed the parrot under the beak, and the parrot dug his claws into Rich's shoulder in an ecstasy.

'It is very generous of you, sir,' said Rich.

'Oh, a mere nothing, Don Narciso,' answered Acevedo.

'And I am in your debt for more than that,' went on Rich.

It was to Acevedo that he owed his baseless reputation as a swordsman, perhaps life itself as well, and certainly the satisfactory settlement of an incident which might have caused the gravest possible trouble. There had never yet been an opportunity, in the crowded ship, for Rich to express his gratitude, and Rich had never attempted to make an opportunity, even though he had repeatedly told himself that he ought to. Shyness had held him back–he was blushing now as he spoke.

'That was a mere nothing, sir,' said Acevedo. His handsome face wore a smile, but he was as much embarrassed as Rich was.

'Nothing to you, perhaps,' said Rich.

'I think it is going to rain,' said Acevedo; Garcia had drifted within earshot from the crowd round the pearls. Acevedo petted the parrot, which squawked and flapped and dug its claws with delight. Garcia came and joined in. The fantastic blue and red–a colour combination so bold as to be on the verge of the unpleasing–played under his hands.

13

They had left behind them the Pearl Islands and the coast of Paria, and had turned boldly to the north-west towards Española. The wind blew steadily from the east–sometimes backing towards the north so that the ships could hardly hold their course, sometimes veering southerly so that, with the wind over her quarter, the *Holy Name* put on her best speed, the spray flying from her bluff bows in gorgeous rainbows. Dolphins accompanied them, leaping in the waves of the wake like children playing a game. At the mastheads the look-outs kept keen watch over these seas which no ship had ever sailed before, but they saw no shoals, no land, only the blue, clear water with the white wave crests in dazzling contrast. At noon the sun passed over their heads, so that a man's shadow lay round his feet; at evening it sank into the sea, leaving the eastward sky already dark with night even while the glows of sunset still coloured the west.

Every hour they measured the speed of the ship through the water, chalking the figure on the board; at noontide, the Admiral, balanced stiffly on the heaving deck, took the altitude of the sun as best he could with his astrolabe, and at night that of the Pole Star as it peeped over the horizon, while the ship, hove-to, pitched steadily over the regular swell. In his great cabin the Admiral had a grubby parchment, cracked along its folds, on which some German philosopher had inscribed, with coloured pigments, the signs of the zodiac and the corresponding heights of the sun–the sun was in Leo now, and it should have been easy to calculate their distance from the equator. But Rich, observing the pendulum of the astrolabe, swinging uncontrollably with the heave of the ship, was not so sure; and even in those clear, vivid nights the vagueness of the horizon–as he discovered when he timidly handled the quadrant–made the altitude of the Pole Star an equally vague figure.

He mentioned his doubts in conversation with the Admiral; in his opinion they could not be certain of their latitude within five or six degrees, a hundred leagues or so. As for the other co-ordinate which would help them to fix their position–the longitude about which the Greek philosophers argued so glibly–he already knew the difficulty regarding that. With a compass of unknown variation, and with unknown currents deflecting them from their course, it seemed to Rich quite unlikely that they would ever see Española–they might miss even San Juan Bautista or Cuba, and arrive in China or some new discovered land. But so diplomatically did he express his doubts that the Admiral hardly guessed at them.

'In five days,' he said, 'if the wind holds and no undiscovered land lies on our course, we shall sight Española.'

He looked up from the chart, in the dim light of the lanterns, and Rich could see the calm certainty of his expression. The Admiral had no doubt at all regarding his own ability in the practice of his art. But it was the same certainty which he had displayed regarding the proximity of the Earthly Paradise, or regarding the transmutation of dewdrops into pearls. Rich did not know what to believe; but one thing only was certain, and that was that nothing he could do would make any difference. At sea one was never one's own master unless in command. He tried to compose himself to wait in patience.

And five days later at noon the look-out, hailing from the masthead, announced land. The Admiral was summoned, and came limping on deck; right ahead lay the land like a chalk mark of a different blue on the horizon where the blue of the sky met the blue of the sea.

'You see, we have sighted land within five days, as I foretold, Don Narciso,' said the Admiral.

'And it is Española, Your Excellency?' ventured Rich. The question brought the Admiral's brows together.

'Naturally!' he said, but there was more surprise than anger in his voice. He had not thought Rich such a fool as still to have doubts on that score.

Yet as the squadron drew closer, and the land acquired definition, Rich saw him looking more anxiously towards it under his shaggy white eyebrows. The deep-set blue eyes strained in their effort to make out the details. He consulted with Alonso Perez, his servant and the only other man in the squadron who had sailed these waters before.

'Don Narciso,' said the Admiral at length, 'my navigation has been faulty.'

'It gives me pain to hear Your Excellency say that,' said Rich, and waited to hear whether they had sighted Cuba.

'It must be that the currents are stronger than I have allowed for,' said the Admiral. 'Or perhaps it is the needle–yet I think it must have been the currents. We are not in sight of San Domingo, as I intended to be. That point there is the island of Beata, five full leagues to leeward.'

'Only five leagues!' exclaimed Rich.

He could only marvel; it was miraculous to him.

'Five leagues to leeward!' snapped the Admiral. 'Thirty leagues to windward would have caused less delay.'

He stumped about the deck on his rheumaticky legs in irritation.

'But, Your Excellency,' protested Rich. 'It is seven weeks to the day since we left Cape Verdes, and that was the last known land which we sighted. An error of five leagues in a voyage of seven weeks! It is amazing–extraordinary.'

The enthusiasm and astonishment in his voice were so obviously genuine that the Admiral could not help but be touched by them.

'It is kind of you to say so, Don Narciso,' he said, a little flush of pleasure showing in his cheekbones above his white beard. 'But I am all impatience. I wish to reach San Domingo. There is my brother, the Adelantado–I want to hear an account of his viceroyalty. And the gold mines of Hayna; they should be in full bearing by now. And the three ships we sent on from Ferro–I want to know if they have arrived yet. I am worried, Don Narciso.'

The Admiral had reason to be, as Rich knew, judging by the year-old reports which had reached Spain regarding the conditions in the colony. Rich looked about the crowded deck, at Garcia, fleshy and arrogant, swaggering at Tarpia's side; at the uncouth soldiers, who were plaguing Alonso Perez for information regarding this new land. It would not be many hours now before this fresh horde would be poured into the island. Now that he had had experience of Trinidad and Paria Rich could visualize better the conditions prevailing here on the Admiral's first landing–it had been an Earthly Paradise, too, a pagan paradise of few wants and all of them satisfied, and he could guess what a hell the first settlers had made of it; he had learned much since he had sailed from Spain. It would be his duty to advise the Admiral on how to repair the damage, how to render the island peaceful and productive again, and the instruments for the work would be this undisciplined mob. Rich felt a sinking at heart.

The hidalgos were grouped near him now, all talking together, the fresh wind ruffling their beards, for the squadron was now close-hauled, trying to claw up to windward towards San Domingo. They drew him into their conversation, and he stood among them a little awkwardly, for he never felt at ease among these men of war with their hundred and twenty-eight quarterings of nobility apiece.

'What is the delay?' fumed Bernardo de Tarpia. 'We are coming no nearer to the land.'

'Look, by God!' said Avila. 'We are turning away from the land now!'

'We are going on the other tack,' explained Rich. 'San Domingo lies to windward.'

They looked at him without understanding. Despite the length of the voyage none of them had acquired any knowledge of how a ship is worked. Horses and hawks and hounds, they understood, because they had been taught about them from boyhood, but none of them was possessed with the lively curiosity that urged Rich to learn about everything that came under his notice.

'How far is this San Domingo?' asked Garcia.

'Five leagues.'

'And we shall not reach there tonight?'

'Perhaps not. But after dark there may be a wind off the land which would help us. There usually is.'

'Did the Admiral say so?'

'No.'

Rich could not explain that he had learned about land- and sea-breezes by night and day from simple observations while fishing in Barcelona roadstead.

'But how will a wind off the land help us to reach the land?' asked Avila; his contorted features showed how hard he was trying to think.

'We shall have it on our beam and can get well to windward of San Domingo tonight, so that in the morning we can go straight in with the first of the sea breeze,' said Rich.

'You're as good a pilot as the Admiral, Don Narciso,' said Garcia, looking at him curiously.

'Not a bit of it,' said Rich.

'At least it is not *your* fault that we have arrived the wrong side of San Domingo,' put in Acevedo. Rich rounded on him.

'You don't appreciate what a marvellous navigator the Admiral is,' he said. 'There is no other sailor living who could have brought the squadron so directly here. That is true, believe me. With ordinary piloting we might have been a hundred leagues away instead of five.'

'You must never say a word against the Admiral in Don Narciso's presence,' said Garcia, half bantering and half serious; perhaps he was remembering the occasions when Rich had conscientiously reported the acquisition of treasure.

'Hullo, we're chasing our tails again,' said Tarpia.

The ship was going about again and standing in to the shore, and Rich was for a moment puzzled as to the motive of this manoeuvre. But he guessed it when he saw the Admiral looking keenly shorewards and followed his gaze.

'There's a canoe coming out to us,' he said.

There it was, a dark spot bobbing on the waves; the sinking sun lit up a white speck in motion on it–somebody was waving to the ships from it.

'We'll get news of our friends now!' exclaimed Tarpia, eagerly.

Everybody rushed to the side of the ship and watched the canoe as it danced over the glittering water towards them. It was an Indian who paddled it, but not a naked one. He wore a shirt of coarse towcloth, as everyone could see when he scrambled up the side, but it was not that which specially caught Rich's notice–and the Admiral's notice, too. In his hand he carried a crossbow; it was rusted, and the cord was frayed, and the winding handle was bent lopsided, but it was a crossbow for all that, and in the Indian's belt of creeper was a single bolt. Before the Indian, blinking round at the ring of Spaniards, had time to collect himself the Admiral was demanding where he had obtained the weapon. The seriousness of natives of the island possessing such weapons of precision was apparent to all.

'Loldan gave it me,' said the Indian; he could speak Spanish after a fashion.

'Roldan!' exclaimed the Admiral. 'The Alcalde Mayor?'

'Yes. We friends,' said the Indian, proudly. 'I shoot bad Indians. Christian I am.'

He bent his head and made the sign of the cross, and intoned something in a weird sing-song, which was just recognizable as the Pater Noster. Some of the group round him laughed, as they might at the antics of a performing ape.

'Where is my brother, His Excellency the Adelantado?' asked the Admiral.

'In the town,' said the Indian, pointing down the coast with an appearance of indifference. 'He's not Loldan's friend.'

'Not Roldan's friend?' repeated the Admiral, blankly.

'No. He fight. Loldan fight. Indian fight.'

The Indian grinned a simpleton's grin. A gesture more eloquent than his bad Spanish called up a picture of bloody confusion throughout the island. Someone in the background whistled in amazement at his words.

'But why? *Why*?' groaned the Admiral. The Indian grinned again and tried to explain. There was no sense in his words. Spanish quarrels meant nothing to him. Rich suspected him of being mentally subnormal, even when allowance was made for the difficulties of language.

At least the Admiral was prepared to waste no more time on him.

'Take that crossbow away from him,' he ordered, curtly. 'Put him over the side. Captain, lay the ship on the other tack.'

This was decision, activity. Only a few seconds was necessary to bundle the protesting Indian back into his canoe and to begin to claw seaward again away from the lee shore. Rich admired the Admiral as he stood on the high poop rapping out his orders. Firmness and decision of this sort would soon stamp out any disloyalty when they reached San Domingo.

The wind blew briskly past them as the *Holy Name* ploughed along, lying as close to the wind as she could; it set Rich's clothes flapping and blew the Admiral's white hair out in horizontal streamers as he stood, staring forward. If intensity of desire could carry the *Holy Name* along, the clumsy ship would fly, thought Rich, watching the Admiral's face. The Admiral did not take his eyes from the ship's course as he began to speak.

'It was bad news that Indian bore, Don Narciso,' he said.

'We know nothing of the truth of the matter yet, Your Excellency.'

'No. I find it hard to believe that Roldan would oppose himself to my brother, the Adelantado whom I myself appointed.'

'Who is this Roldan, Your Excellency?'

'The Alcade Mayor–the Chief Magistrate. He owes that position to me.'

'Naturally,' said Rich. There was no appointment in the Indies which was not in the Admiral's direct gift. 'But who is he, Your Excellency? I do not know the name. Is he a gentleman? What rank did he hold before this appointment?'

'He was my servant,' said the Admiral. 'But I thought he was honest. I thought he was loyal. I thought—'

The Admiral checked himself with a sigh.

'Perhaps he is,' said Rich, with cheerful optimism. 'We cannot condemn him without knowing the facts.'

'If he has been fighting my brother he must be disloyal,' said the Admiral, conclusively. Rich was not so sure; it may have been mere professional sympathy, but he felt that a Chief Justice might easily find himself at odds with a Columbus and still have right on his side.

'Is he learned in the law, Your Excellency?' he asked. 'As I said, I am not acquainted with his name.'

'Of course he is not,' said the Admiral, petulantly. 'Did I not say he was my servant? He was my body-servant, my valet.'

After that, Rich felt there was nothing more to be said. A Chief Justice who had been a valet would certainly be as great a source of trouble as any

Columbus. Rich could only gaze forward as anxiously as the Admiral himself, wondering what would be the situation he would find awaiting him when at last he reached San Domingo.

14

They entered the river mouth in the late afternoon, after two weary days of beating against headwinds. The Spaniards on board were pleased and excited at the thought that at last their voyaging was really at an end, and at the prospect of seeing new white faces. The details grew clearer under their eager gaze as the sea breeze pushed them briskly into the inlet; there was the wooden church with its square tower, and beside it the fort–only the simplest arrangement of ditch, palisade, and parapet, but quite impregnable to the simple unarmed folk who were its only possible assailants. At the Admiral's order the *Holy Name* swung round the point of the shoal and headed across to the anchorage, where there was deep water up to the foot of the church. Close on their left hand they opened up a clearing in the wild tangle of trees that came down to the water's edge, and there, starkly visible to all the interior, stood a gallows, from which dangled two corpses.

'Holy Mary!' said Moret, with genuine sincerity. 'It is good to be in a Christian country again!'

He pointed to the gallows.

'Are they Indians or Spaniards?' asked Garcia, shading his eyes with his hands, but no one could answer that question. Rich read a moral lesson in the fact that death and putrefaction made the European indistinguishable from the Indian.

Cannon thundered with wreaths of white smoke from the citadel in salute to the Admiral's flag; the Admiral was standing proudly on the poop looking across at his town; armour winked and glittered in the setting sun over the citadel walls. A small crowd of people were already launching boats and canoes to come out and welcome them.

The leading boat was distinguished by a flag held up in the bows, displaying the Admiral's arms within a white bordure to indicate the presence of the Admiral's deputy, the Adelantado. Bartholomew Columbus, when he came on board, looked round him with piercing blue eyes which at first glance gave him a striking resemblance to his brother, but he was more heavily built–a stoop-shouldered, burly man whose dense beard did not disguise the heavy jaw and the thick lips. An Indian woman mounted next after him; there were pearls in her ears, round her neck, and in her long loose hair. She was cloaked in blue velvet, but she made no effort to keep the cloak about her to conceal the slender naked body beneath. She was smiling and chattering excitedly, white teeth flashing, with her hand laid on the Adelantado's arm. Not even the harsh contrast between the blue velvet and her nudity could mar her beauty.

The brothers kissed, under the gaze of every eye in the ship; the Admiral had a brief word for the woman before he received the bows of the Adelantado's escort. Rich watched the little ceremony keenly from a distance, anxious to form his opinion of the Adelantado–the latter's undoubted influence with the Admiral would count for so much in the future of the New World. He saw Bartholomew pluck at Christopher's sleeve; he pointed ashore and glanced anxiously at the sun–clearly there was work to be done ashore that demanded the Admiral's immediate attention. The Admiral nodded distractedly; Carvajal and Osorio and Tarpia were all asking for his attention, and the decks were crowding with people from the shore, so that there was hardly room to stand. The din and bustle were tremendous. Carvajal wanted instructions regarding the ship and crew, Osorio regarding the stores, Tarpia permission to take his soldiers ashore. Each had a brief unsatisfactory word in reply, and continually Batholomew plucked at the Admiral's sleeve and begged him to come ashore.

'Yes,' said the Admiral, 'I will come. One moment—'

He caught Rich's eye and beckoned to him.

'Bartholomew, I want to present the learned Don Narciso Rich. Their Highnesses have lent me his services to help on the legal side of the administration.'

'A lawyer, eh?' said the Adelantado, turning a coldly belligerent eye upon him.

'Yes, Your Excellency.'

'We need men of action more than men of law.'

'I expect so, Your Excellency. But I am here at Their Highnesses' express command.'

That scored the first point for Rich; he had no intention of being browbeaten, and though his reply was in a humble tone it made a clear statement of the strength of his position. As long as no one knew that his mission was to find a means of curtailing the Admiral's cherished power, he would have all the prestige of a court favourite and there would be no reason for anyone to dislike him. He was a long way from home, and he wished to see Barcelona again.

'It is as a man of law that I welcome Don Narciso here,' interposed the Admiral. 'What you have told me about what you want to do this afternoon—'

'I will have no interference in that,' said Bartholomew, loudly.

The tall Dominican friar at his shoulder broke into the conversation.

'Indeed not. The Crown itself–Queen Isabella in person–could not interfere there. The Holy See long ago decided that matter. The secular arm had only to do its duty after the Church has reached its decision.'

'I beg your pardon, but I do not understand,' said Rich. 'What is the point at issue?'

'It is not at issue,' said Bartholomew, loudly. 'Brother, please come. Soon night will fall and make an excuse for the Indians to steal away. It has been hard enough assembling them.'

'Come with me, Don Narciso,' said the Admiral hastily.

The boat in which they rowed to shore was loaded to the water's edge–it had been full enough on its way to the ship, but now it held the Admiral and his squire and Rich in addition. Rich was crowded in the bow, wedged so tight that he could not even turn his head to see the approaching shore as the boat moved slugglishly over the little waves, so different from the big rollers outside. He could make a guess at the point under consideration–some heretic had been detected and was about to make solemn recantation. He would lose his goods and would vanish into the dungeons of the Inquisition. Certainly it was a matter in which he could not interfere, nor would he if he could.

The boat took the ground with a jerk–it was strange that no pier had as yet been built–and Rich swung himself, with the others, over the side. He might perhaps have stayed and kept his feet dry, as did the Admiral and the Adelantado and the Dominican, but he judged that it might be better if he remained inconspicuous. He splashed ashore, the Indian woman, her cloak held high, beside him. She gabbled something to him, hastily.

'I beg your pardon?' he asked.

The queer Spanish which she spoke suddenly took shape as she repeated herself.

'Save them, sir. Please try and save them.'

There was a frightful anxiety in her face as she spoke–her features were working with the stress of her emotion.

'I will try,' said Rich, cautiously, and puzzled.

'Try. Speak to *him*. Speak to the Admiral.'

Next moment her face had resumed its earlier animated interest, and she was smiling at the Adelantado as he stepped out of the boat.

'This is where the pier will be built,' said the Adelantado to his brother.

'I expected to find it built already,' said the Admiral in a tone of mild expostulation.

'It would have been, if the lazy dogs of Indians would only work. But they would sooner die. I have seen them die under my very eyes, in the quarries, sooner than labour. It was all I could do to get in the quotas of gold and cotton and build the church and the citadel. We put a hundred corpses a week into the sea, even before the present troubles began.'

They were at the summit of the beach now, with the town before them–a hundred or so of brown huts built of timber and leaves.

'Where are all the people?' asked the Admiral.

'They are awaiting Your Excellency.'

Someone in the Adelantado's following had run on ahead up one of the straight narrow lanes between the houses. They could see him wave his arm as he reached the farther corner, and they followed him. Pigs and fowls were rooting among the filth underfoot, but no human creature was to be seen. Now they emerged from the lane into a wide open space. The houses were on three sides, on the fourth was the forest. Two trumpets brayed in the heated air; there was a long roll of drums.

It took the sun-dazzled eye some time to note all the details. The three sides of the square other than the one in the middle of which they stood were lined with naked Indians, packed in dense masses; there must have been thousands of them, five or six thousand. At intervals before and behind the crowd stood Spaniards, conspicuous in their armour, all at the salute while the trumpets blew and while the Admiral returned the compliment.

'There is a pavilion for Your Excellency,' said the Adelantado–close beside where they had emerged was a flat-roofed, open-fronted shed of leaves, in which stood a row of chairs, and beside which the colours of Spain and of the Admiral drooped in the heat. But that was not all which the eye slowly took in. Standing in the square were a whole series of lofty stakes, on which hung chains. And round the foot of every stake was a pile of wood. Rich counted them; there were sixteen stakes, each with its chains and faggots. He felt a little chill, for he had an irrational dislike of burnings–he had witnessed very few. The Indian woman was trembling, he could see. There was appeal in her eyes as they met his.

'The ceremony will begin now,' said the Adelantado, ushering his brother to the central chair with the utmost formality. 'Have I Your Excellency's permission to sit?'

'I don't like this business, Bartholomew,' said the Admiral. 'I used to think them very harmless people. Must it go on?'

'They are relapsed heretics,' said the Dominican. 'It is God's law that they should burn.'

'I've kept five thousand Indians herded here all day,' said the Adelantado, 'expressly to see this. What would be the effect if I let them go?'

'But if it were I who pardoned them,' said the Admiral. 'What have they done? Is their guilt certain?'

'They are blasphemers as well as relapsed heretics,' explained the Dominican. 'After they had accepted baptism they not merely relapsed into idolatry. They burned down a chapel, and they broke the holy vessels and images to pieces.'

'Did they know what they were doing?'

'Having listened once to our teaching they must have known. But even if they did not it makes no difference to their guilt.'

'But why?' asked the Admiral. 'Why did they do it?'

'The devil prompted them,' said the Dominican.

'They were in rebellion over the gold quota,' said Bartholomew behind his hand.

'They are like children,' said the Admiral. 'Trying to do the wickedest thing they can think of.'

'And they succeeded,' said the Dominican. 'Children can be guilty of heresy and relapse.'

That was perfectly true, as Rich knew well. With his training in Roman law he found it hard to hear of condemnation for a crime committed without guilty intent–this was one of the points over which Roman law and the Church law disagreed–but at the same time it was heresy to question the principles of the Church, and he had no intention of being guilty of heresy himself. He simply could not argue on this point, and he resolutely kept his eyes from meeting the pleading glance of the Indian woman's.

'It is a golden opportunity,' said the Adelantado, 'of teaching these people a real lesson. I have given instructions that the heretics are not to be strangled at the stake. Perhaps then those that see them die will learn what it means to incur our wrath.'

'You misunderstand the intentions of the Church, Don Bartholomew,' said the Dominican, sternly. 'This is not intended as a punishment. It is to save these poor people's souls that they must pass through the fire.'

'It coincides all the same with the needs of government,' said the Adelantado, complacently.

'We are saving sixteen souls today,' returned the Dominican. 'We are not trying to make the collection of the gold quota easier.'

A drum was beating in a measured tone up at the citadel. The victims were about to be brought down. Rich realized that any intervention in his power must be made at once.

'There are sixteen souls to be saved,' he said, 'but as a matter of pure expediency in God's cause, Reverend Sir, might it not be better to risk the loss of these sixteen in hope of winning many more?'

'How do you mean?' asked the Dominican; his black brows approached each other, and his eyes narrowed as he turned his gaze on Rich.

'Perhaps if the lives of these sixteen were spared the rejoicing would be so great that many more souls would be won to God.'

'Perhaps–and perhaps there would be many doomed to Hell. These thousands who witness this act of faith will take care in future to keep heretical thoughts out of their minds. They will pay closer attention to the teaching of the Church. They will have a glimpse of what Hell is like. No, sir, there is no substance in your argument. And it is an evil thing to gamble in human salvation.'

'Don't you think there is something in what the learned doctor says?' asked the Admiral.

'No, Your Excellency. A thousand times no. They must burn, so that their souls may be saved and that a thousand other souls may not be imperilled.

The procession was filing into the square. A friar bore a crucifix at the head of it, and following him a dozen Spaniards herded the victims along, pricking them with their swords' points to force them to walk. The resources of the island had been sufficient to provide yellow fools' coats, gaudily daubed with red symbols, for the victims, whose hands were tied behind them. One of them screamed at the sight of the stakes; two of them collapsed into the dust of the square, writhing there until the escort kicked them to their feet again. The Indian woman beside Rich screamed, too. She ran round between the Admiral and his deputy and flung herself on the earth before them, one hand on the knee of each of them, frantically jabbering the while.

'What does she say?' asked the Admiral.

'She wants us to spare these people,' explained his brother. 'Anacaona, don't be a fool.'

Anacaona lifted a face slobbered with tears, her beautiful mouth all distorted. She was trying to talk Spanish, but Indian words tumbled from her lips as well.

'She says some of these men are her brothers,' went on Bartholomew. 'She means cousins by that–it is the same word to them. But every Indian is everyone else's cousin, thanks to their mothers' habits.'

Anacaona bowed her head in the dust before them, her shoulders shaking under the blue velvet, before she lifted face and hands again to beg for mercy. There was a low moaning from all round the square, through which could be heard the rattle of chains as one man after another was fastened to the stakes.

'Can we not commute the punishment, as an act of grace, by virtue of the powers I hold for Their Highnesses?' said the Admiral. 'The dungeons, or the quarries? Would not that be sufficient.'

'Does not your heart tell you it would not, Your Excellency?' retorted the Dominican. 'And I must remind you that not even Their Highnesses can interfere with an act of faith.'

'Stop that noise, Anacaona,' said Bartholomew. 'Here, you two, here. Take this woman to my house and keep her there.'

Two Spaniards of the guard beside the pavilion dragged Anacaona away. To every stake now a victim was chained, fourteen men and two women. Already the torch was being borne from pile to pile; the man who had screamed was still screaming–they could hear his chains rattle as he strove against them.

'Laetabitur justus cum viderit vindicatam,' said the Dominican, solemnly. 'The righteous shall rejoice when he seeth the vengeance.'

That quotation from the Psalms had been given its full weight by St Thomas Aquinas, the greatest of Dominicans. But Rich thought that St Thomas must have given it too much weight–or else he himself was not of the just who could rejoice. Smoke was issuing from the piles of wood now; in one or two of them the sticks were already crackling and banging with the flames. Rich, looking against his will, saw one of the women try to move her feet away from the heat that burned them. He tore his glance away, staring up at the blue evening sky as he stood behind the Admiral's chair. But he could not shut his nostrils to the stench that drifted to them, nor close his ears to the horrible sounds that filled the square. He felt faint and ill and oppressed with guilt. St Bernardino of Siena had pointed out that just as harmonious singing demands deep voices as well as high, so God's harmony demands the bellowings of the damned to complete it. But these bellowings and screams caused him no pleasure, and even did very much the reverse. He feared lest his faith were shaken, lest his Christianity were unsound and this weakness of his should be a proof of it.

He tried to tell himself of St Gregory's comment upon a text of St Ambrose, pointing out that as St Peter cut off a man's ear, which Christ restored, so must the Church smite off the ear of those who will not hear, for Christ to restore them. But his fiercest concentrations upon his authorities did not relieve his senses of the assaults made upon them, did not give strength to his weak legs nor solidity to his watery bowels. He feared for his soul.

15

Next morning Rich was desperately weary. There had been long debate the night before in the Adelantado's house within the citadel walls–and even here they were not quite free from whiffs of stinking smoke from the square–while through the town the newly landed Spaniards rioted as if they had taken it by storm. One of Bernardo de Tarpia's handgunmen had allowed his spirits to rise so high that he had twice let off his weapon to the peril of passers-by, sadly interrupting the anxious argument regarding the treason of Francisco Roldan. Nothing had been settled then; this morning the debate was to continue, and yet in the meanwhile he had not slept a moment, what with the strangeness of his new surroundings, the hideous events of the evening, and the plague of mosquitoes which had hung round him in a cloud all through the night—and Antonio Spallanzani, who had shared a leaf hut with him, had snored fantastically. Rich's head ached and he felt numb and stupid as he made his way past the sentry at the citadel gate up to the governor's house again.

The debate began afresh, with all the Columbus clan present–the Admiral in his best clothes, and Bartholomew the Adelantado, and James, rather weak and foolish, and John Antony, more weak and foolish still. But hardly had the session opened when something happened to terminate it. The man who entered wore spurs which jingled as he strode in over the earthen floor; his face was yellow with fever–like most of the new faces Rich had seen lately–but he wore an expression of unruffled gravity. The Adelantado checked himself to hear what he had to say.

'The Indians are in rebellion again, Your Excellency,' he announced. 'Seriously, this time.'

'Where?'

'In the Llanos. By tonight there'll be twenty thousand of them at Soco.'

'How do you know this?'

'One of my Indian girls told me. I was the only Spaniard with a horse, so I left the others gathering at the fort and rode here through the night. At dawn five hundred or so tried to stop me at the ford, but they were too frightened of my horse, and I broke through. Were those Indians burned yesterday, Your Excellency?'

'Yes.'

'That explains it, then. The rising depended on that, and the news has spread already.'

'You are not speaking with proper deference. Don't you recognize the Admiral here?'

'Your pardon, Admiral,' said the newcomer. 'But I was trying to tell my news in the shortest way possible.'

'What is your name?' asked the Admiral.

'Juan Ruiz, Excellency.'

'I remember you now. Go on with what you have to say.'

'I have said all that is necessary, Excellency. The Indians all have their sticks and stones. Some of those at the ford this morning were painted. They seem more bent on fighting than I have ever known them this last four years.'

'Is this Roldan's doing?' asked James Columbus; the words were no sooner out of his mouth than he received an angry look from Bartholomew.

'No,' replied Ruiz.

'Thank you. You may leave us now,' said Bartholomew, and the moment Ruiz was out of the room he turned on James. 'Will you never learn sense? Do you want the whole island to know we are afraid of Roldan? Over in the Vega Real how can he influence the Indians of the Llanos? You only open your mouth to utter idiocies.'

James shrank abashed before his brother's anger.

'We must send at once,' said the Admiral, 'and pacify these poor wretches. I know they have grievances. I wish I could go myself–they would listen to me.'

'Pacify them?' asked Bartholomew.

'That is what I said.'

'Brother, leave the pacification to me. *I* will pacify them as they ought to be pacified. This is the moment I've been waiting for. A sharp lesson is what they need.'

'I know your sharp lessons, Bartholomew,' said the Admiral, sadly.

'By God,' said Bartholomew, 'I'm glad I have your two hundred men. Without them I would hardly have two hundred men to take out against them. If only the ships with the horses had come! I've barely fifty horses, and in those plains it's horses we need.'

'Bartholomew,' said the Admiral. 'I forbid you to be cruel. You must show them all the mercy possible.'

'That is what I will do,' said Bartholomew, grimly. 'Brother, you are too good for this world. And supposing I did what you think you want? Supposing I encouraged them to think they can rebel against our authority with impunity? What would happen to the gold quota? How much cotton do you think they'd grow for us? What would you say then, brother? Who was it who was complaining at the shortage of gold only five minutes ago? Kind words won't make these people work, as you know. Only the fear of death'll do that–and even then half of 'em prefer to die.'

'I suppose you've been promising them in Spain gold by the ton, as usual,' put in James, taking the side of his younger brother against the elder, who sat shaken and helpless before the double attack.

'I never expected my own brothers to turn against me,' he said, pitifully.

'We haven't turned against you,' snapped Bartholomew. 'We're doing your work for you. And there's no time to lose unless we want the whole island in a blaze. We'll march this afternoon. James, set the drums beating and the church bells ringing.'

The room was in an immediate bustle. Bartholomew flung open the door and began to shout orders through it to the guard at the gate. The three Dominican friars–Brother Bernard who had supervised yesterday's act of faith and the two who had just arrived–were whispering together in one corner.

'Don Narciso,' said the Admiral, and Rich went across to him. 'You must go with my brother. With this cursed gout I can neither walk nor sit a horse. And there are so few I can trust.'

Rich contemplated with some distaste the prospect of marching out with four hundred men to fight ten thousand painted savages.

'I doubt if Don Bartholomew will welcome my presence,' he said.

'You must go. You must. Bartholomew told me last night he had a horse of mine in his stables. Bartholomew, I am giving Don Narciso my horse so that he can ride with you.'

'Come if you like,' said the Adelantado after a momentary grimace. 'I'd rather put a man-at-arms on that horse. Have you armour as well as that long robe?'

'I have,' said Rich.

Bartholomew was a man of action. It took him no more than two hours to assemble every European round, to select his expeditionary force and to detail the fifty men he was leaving behind to their duties as garrison. The few stores which had been brought up out of the ships he divided out among his army.

'There'll be food to be got in the villages,' he explained, 'but with savages to fight, the whole secret lies in being able to march without a halt and give them no time to rally.'

Four hundred men marched out of San Domingo in the blazing heat of the day. Juan Ruiz rode ahead with six horsemen as an advanced guard in case of an ambush. Then came the long column of leather coats and dull armour, Bernardo de Tarpia with his handgunmen, and Moret's crossbowmen, the spearmen and handgunmen led by Juan Antonio Columbus–four years in Española had made these last familiar with the island, even to the extent of calling it by its native name of Hayti–and forty sailors from the ships under Carvajal's command, armed with pikes and swords. Bartholomew Columbus rode with forty horsemen, Cristobal Garcia and Rodrigo and Gonzalo Acevedo among them. Rich had his place with these, a little uneasy even astride the grey horse with which he had been provided, spiritless nag though it was.

The sun roasted him in his half-armour, but he was determined to utter no complaint until his companion should, and they were full of high spirits at being mounted again and faced with the imminent prospect of action. On their right was the blue, blue sea, and on their left the high mountains, vivid green from base to summit, towering to the sky. Ahead of them lay a wide, rolling plain, stretching from the mountains to the sea, green and luxuriant, broken only here and there by thickets and woodland. There were herds of cattle to be seen here–in four years the few beasts brought by the second expedition had multiplied beyond all count–and scattered patches of cultivated land where the Indians grew their roots and their corn. This was the famous plain of the Llanos, which the Admiral had compared, in extent and fertility, with the valley of Guadalquivir.

But at the moment there was not a soul to be seen, save the long column of Spaniards trudging along the faint track. Ruiz and his horsemen turned aside repeatedly to examine the hamlets which lay in sight, but each in turn was found to be deserted, and from each in turn rose the smoke of their burning as the torch was applied to the frail structures.

'Where are these Indians?' grumbled Avila. His visored helmet was at his saddlebow, his painted shield at his back, his long lance at his elbow, as if he was on his way to joust at a king's court.

'Perhaps you may see some,' said the veteran Robion. 'They may perhaps stand to fight here in the plains. They fight like sheep–you will be able to spike six of them at once on that skewer of yours. I doubt if they have learned even yet that they are safer from us in the mountains.'

'They are not worthy enemies, then?'

Robion gave a short harsh laugh.

'Not worthy of a knight errant like you. They know nothing of war, nothing at all. One might as well fight with children.'

'With children?' broke in someone else. 'A Spanish shepherd boy would be more dangerous than ten of their grown men. They had never fought in all their lives until we came among them–they didn't know what fighting was!'

'And I came here to gain honour!' said Avila, drawing a fresh laugh from the old hands.

Rich was pondering over what he had heard. In a land in which there was no tradition of violence at all, how long would it take to develop the art of war afresh? How long would it be before its people learned the axioms which even to a man of peace like himself were as natural as the air he breathed–the value of discipline and of order, the efficacy of surprise, the importance of a position. Why, he himself had read the foremost military treatise in history, Vegetius' *Epitoma rei militaris*, and was conversant with the principles of war, even if he would not be able to put them into practice. The laughing, thoughtless people of the islands, who had never had even to avoid a flung stone or dodge a blow, would not learn them in a generation.

'I expect they are all howling round the fort at Soco,' said Robion. 'Twice I've stood a siege like that. They howl until they are tired, and then you can go out and drive them back to work. But this is the first time I've ever known so many of them unite together, all the same.'

They were filing over a ford now, and everybody eagerly slipped out of their saddles to drink from the dark water; Rich found himself, after two hours' riding, already so stiff that he could hardly swing his leg over, but fortunately no one noticed. The column halted to rest in the shade along the banks, the sweating infantry lying stretched out flat with their weapons beside them until the Adelantado set the trumpet blowing to call them to their feet again. Rich scrambled somehow back into the saddle–he was already sore and his body shrank from contact with the harsh leather. By the end of the day he was in misery. The chatter went on unnoticed round him, blended with the squeaking of leather and the occasional ringing of hoofs or accoutrements. The final order to halt found him quite stupid with fatigue. He tried vainly to make some pretence to attending to the sorry grey horse, and experienced unfathomable relief and gratitude when Rodrigo Acevedo relieved him of the task unobtrusively.

'I can't thank you,' was all Rich was able to say, white-faced.

Ruiz and his companions had driven a small herd of cattle up to the encampment, and fires were lighted for roasting the meat. There was cheerful chatter round the fires, where the meat was roasted upon huge grids of green boughs–'barbecues' or 'boucans,' strange Haytian words which the old-timers used naturally and at which the newcomers made tentative attempts with as realistic an appearance of habit as possible. No more than five sentries were necessary to protect the camp while the others slept.

That had been a day of sunshine; the next was a day of rain, perpetual rain falling in torrents from a grey sky. It soaked everyone to the skin, finding its way remorselessly down inside the necks of leather coats and from there into the leather breeches, so that the horsemen had wet, squelching bags of water round their thighs. The men on foot sank to their ankles in the mud, the horses to their fetlocks. The little streams from the mountains became broad rivers bordered by knee-deep marsh; armour and weapons rusted almost perceptibly under their very eyes, and every man was daubed and streaked with mud. In those conditions not nearly so prolonged a march could be made as the

Adelantado had wished–it had been his plan to camp that night so near to Soco as to make it possible to surprise the besiegers at dawn. With ten miles of slippery ground and three water-courses still between his army and the fort the Adelantado was forced to give up the project.

'But marching at dawn we shall be at Soco by noon,' he said to the disgruntled group of hidalgos round him. 'Time enough then for the lesson I want to teach them.'

It rained until dawn, men and horses suffering miserably under the continued drenching, but with morning came a fiery sun which put new life into them–into all save a score or so of the earlier colonists who lay shuddering and with chattering teeth despite the heat. They were in the grip of malaria–everyone who lived long in the island went down with it in course of time, apparently, and exposure to wet and to night air was certain to bring on an attack. One of the shivering victims begged with blue lips to be left with his companions where they lay.

'So that when we have gone the Indians can beat you to death with their clubs, I suppose,' commented the Adelantado. 'You could not raise a finger to stop them if they did. No. You must come with us. There are horses enough until we reach Soco.'

So Rich completed the march on foot, leading the grey horse and with another man on the other side to help him keep one of the invalids in the saddle. Nor was he specially sorry, for two days of riding, even at foot pace, had rubbed his flesh raw. He trudged along with his sword tapping against his leg, while the sick man on his horse blasphemed wearily about the island and the Indians and the fate which had led him thither. Rich tried to make himself listen, because unguarded speech of this sort would be a valuable source of evidence for the report he would later have to make to His Highness, but it was hard to concentrate on the business with the imminent prospect of a battle before him. The handgunmen had their pieces loaded, and two of them had their matches smouldering whereby a light could quickly be given to their companions; the Adelantado was riding along the column reminding his subordinates of his orders for the line of battle. With every step he took, Rich knew that he was coming nearer to his first battlefield; it was a strange sensation. Once a false alarm ran down the column, and swords were drawn as they halted, but the mounted hidalgos reassured them and they plodded on.

And then they came over a low rise to open up a fresh vista of the plain. Two miles ahead stood a low, grey building with a black speck fluttering over it–the fortress of Soco with its flag; evidently the dozen colonists who had taken refuge there had made good their defence.

'Here they come!' said the Adelantado. 'Form your square, men.'

Rich had no time to see more during the bustle of forming up.

'Invalids here in the centre!' called the Adelantado. 'Gentlemen, mount your horses. Pikemen! Crossbowmen!'

Rich helped his invalid to the ground. There were a dozen helpless men lying there already, but his own invalid was convalescent by now and with one more curse, lurched away to join the ranks of his fellows. Ruiz and the advanced guard came clattering up as Rich climbed on the grey horse. Other horses cannoned into him and he lost a stirrup and nearly lost his helmet before he found himself in the mass of cavalry grouped round the invalids. The foot soldiers had formed a square round the cavalry, facing outwards, the handgunmen with their matches alight, the crossbowmen with their bows wound up.

Pouring up towards them was an enormous crowd of naked Indians. It was like a brown sea rolling upon them, thousands and thousands of them–not merely men, Rich saw as they approached, but women and children as well, all shrieking and yelling, as they waved their arms over their heads, with a noise like surf on the beach.

'Please God they charge,' said the Adelantado, and then, raising his voice: 'Remember, no man is to fire a shot until I give the word. Don Bernardo, see to it.'

Rich, fidgeting with his reins and his sword, marvelled at the Adelantado's sentiments. It seemed to him the most necessary thing in the world that the guns should start firing at once. Through his muddled brain coursed a sudden desire to wheel his horse round and break through the ranks and gallop away; panic was making his heart beat painfully fast and clouding his intellect, and it was only with difficulty that he restrained himself from acting on the impulse.

'If we shoot one now the whole lot'll run away,' explained the Adelantado to the hidalgos round him. 'I want to close with them.'

The huge crowd poured up towards the square. Then it halted a hundred yards from the nearest face, came on again, halted again in the centre, while at the sides it still poured forward until in the end the whole square was surrounded at a discreet distance. A few more daring of the Indians ran closer still and, with frantic gestures, flung stones which fell to earth far in front of the waiting Spaniards.

'No shooting!' said the Adelantado loudly again.

The crowd eddied round the square like mist, forward here and back there. The din was tremendous. Then at last came the rush, as some indetectable impulse carried the whole mob inwards towards the square.

'Fire!' yelled the Adelantado.

The crash of the handguns drowned the noise of the discharge of the crossbows. Rich saw no Indian fall, and next moment the two nations were at grips. The Indians carried heavy sticks for the most part, with which they struck clumsily at the helmets in front of them, clumsily, like clowns in a comedy. Perched up on his horse Rich caught vivid glimpses of brown faces, some of them striped with red paint, distorted with passion. He saw the expression on one turn to mild dismay as a Spaniard drove his sword home. Rich's horse was chafing at the bit as the smell of blood reached his nostrils; close in front of him a crossbowman was winding frantically at his moulinet. There came a loud bang as one of the re-charged handguns went off, and then another and another. The brown masses began to hesitate, and ceased to crowd up against the sword-points.

'They're going to break!' said the Adelantado. 'Gentlemen, are you ready?'

The crossbowmen thrust his loaded weapon forward between the two swordsmen who were protecting him, and released the bolt with a whizz and a clatter.

'Open out when you charge, gentlemen. Ride them down and show no mercy,' said the Adelantado. 'There! They're breaking! Sailors, make way! Open your ranks, sailors! Come on, gentlemen!'

The sailors who formed one face of the square huddled off to either side, making a gap for the horsemen who poured through it in a torrent, the maddened horses jostling each other. Rich kept his seat with difficulty as his horse dashed out along with his fellows; reins and sword seemed to have become mixed in his grip. Avila was riding in front of him, his horse stretched to a gallop and his lance, with its fluttering banderol, in rest before him. The point caught a flying Indian in the back below the ribs, and lifted him forward in a great leap before he dropped spreadeagled on the ground and Avila rode forward to free his point. The swords were wheeling in great arcs of fire under the sun. There was an Indian running madly close by Rich's right knee, his hands crossed over his head to ward off the impending blow. Rich had his sword hand free now, and he swung and struck at the hands, and the Indian fell with a dull shriek.

This was madly exciting, this wild pursuit on a horse galloping at top speed with Indians scurrying in all directions before him. Behind him the handguns were still banging, and faint shouts indicated that the infantry were in pursuit as well. Rich struck again and again. He found himself leaning far out of the saddle, like any accomplished cavalier, to get a fairer sweep, and the discovery delighted him. He was carried away by the violence of his reaction from his previous panic; there were enemies all about him, running like rabbits. He yelled with excitement and slashed again. An Indian, crazed with panic, ran blindly across his course, and fell with a scream under the forelegs of the grey horse. The grey horse came down with a crash, and Rich found himself sailing through the air. The earth which received him was soft, and he was not stunned by the fall, but the breath was driven from his body as if he were a burst bladder. Dazed and winded, sword and helmet gone, he grovelled about on the ground trying to recover himself. And Indian woman saw his plight; she still had her club in her hand, and apparently she was not as affected by panic as most of her companions. She ran up and struck at Rich, screaming the while for assistance. Two more women arrived, one with a pointed cane which she stuck painfully into Rich's left arm, overbalancing him just as he was on the point of regaining his feet. The club clanged on his breastplate, the sharpened cane scraped over it. But then the screams of the women changed from excitement to fright. A horse's head loomed hugely over them; one women fell across Rich, deluging him with blood from her half-severed neck, the others disappeared. Garcia was there riding a maddened chestnut stallion with graceful dexterity; the blood slowly dripped from his reddened sword and his white teeth flashed in a smile.

'Wounded? Hurt?' he asked.

'No,' said Rich, sliding disgustedly from under the woman's corpse.

'I'll catch your horse,' said Garcia, wheeling the chestnut towards where the grey was standing, his reins over his head and his sides heaving.

Rich picked up his sword and helmet and received the reins which Garcia handed him.

'All well?' asked Garcia. 'Right!'

Garcia uttered some inarticulate yell and urged his horse into a gallop again, wheeling his sword in circles; Rich stood with the reins in his hand and watched him catch an Indian and strike him down.

Rich had to sheathe his bloody sword in order to mount. It was an effort to raise his foot in the stirrup, a worse effect to swing himself up into the saddle even though the blown horse stood stock-still for him; he gathered up the reins and wondered what to do next. Behind him the scattered infantry were chasing Indians with small chance of catching them–a few Indians were still running towards him from the direction of the battlefield and swerving frantically away when they caught sight of him. Far ahead the cavalry were still on the fringe of the great mass of flying Indians; the shouts came back to Rich's ears like the distant cry of gulls at sea. He shook his horse into activity and rode forward towards Soco at a ponderous trot–he passed dead and wounded Indians scattered here and there over the plain as witness of the efficacy of the pursuit. The shouting and screaming ahead suddenly redoubled; the distant crowd wavered and hesitated and then broke up into two halves, one flying to the right and one to the left amid the loud reports of gunfire.

The firing enabled Rich to guess what had happened; the garrison of Soco had come charging out across the line of retreat of the Indians, a dozen men against ten thousand and yet sufficient to check their speed enough to give the horsemen's swords a fresh opportunity. There were plenty of Indians even near him, stragglers whom the pursuit had left behind ungleaned–exhausted Indians squatting gasping for breath, crippled Indians limping over the plain and Indians running madly back towards him from the slaughter ahead. Rich put his hand to his sword-hilt and then found himself, rather to his own surprise, leaving the weapon where it was. He did not want to kill any more.

He rode slowly up towards the fort of Soco, where the horsemen were rallying, breathing their horses and tightening their girths. A dozen men on foot–the garrison of Soco, presumably–were standing with them, everyone talking and laughing excitedly. Dead Indians lay in swathes all about them, marking the area wherein their retreat had been cut off by the garrison's sally.

'Mount again, gentlemen,' said the Adelantado, as Rich came within earshot. 'We can beat back over the ground. Plenty of game broke back and the foot are there to head them off for us.'

The Spaniards who had dismounted got back into their saddles. They were like men who had been drinking–some were giggling like schollboys with excitement of slaughter.

'One long line,' said the Adelantado. 'Fifty yards apart. My standard is the centre. Spread yourselves out, gentlemen.'

The Adelantado ran an interested eye over Rich as he trotted up–Rich was conscious of the blood and mud with which he was smeared. He bore clear enough proof that he had played his part in the battle.

'Don Cristobal said you had a fall,' said the Adelantado.

'I had,' said Rich, 'but nothing serious.'

'Are you wounded?'

'Nothing serious again,' answered Rich.

'You can have your revenge now.'

'Do you really mean what you say, Don Bartholomew? Are you going on with this killing?'

'Why, of course. There are four hours more of daylight.'

'Haven't enough been killed?'

'No, by God. I mean this to be a lesson that they will never forget.'

'But they are your brother's subjects–your subjects, Your Excellency. Don't you want them to earn revenue for you?'

'They'll breed again. And we've had no chance of sport like this for months. Don't be mealy-mouthed, Doctor. Trumpeter!'

The trumpet set the long line in motion again in its sweep back across the plain. It was sport for the infantry, too; crossbows and handguns found plenty of targets as the frantic Indians were driven within range. The spearmen and swordsmen, even, hampered though they were with clothes and equipment, were often able to run down on foot the naked Indians who were already exhausted. Some of them showed a pretty wit in their choice of the place in which to plant their weapons when they caught their victims–the same idea had occurred to the horsemen, and shouts of laughter and approval ran along the line as each man vied with the others in displaying his dexterity or strength of arm. Rich followed fascinated.

16

'Torture?' said Don Bartholomew surprisingly that night in reply to a question from Garcia. 'There's no need for torture with these miserable wretches. Just keeping 'em in one place and preventing 'em from wandering about is torture for 'em. I'll guarantee that tomorrow morning every one of the fifty in the corral will blab all we want 'em to. Three days of it, and they die, like fish in a bucket. But if they won't talk tomorrow morning they will in the afternoon, after a morning in the sun without food or water. And if not, even then, the slow match that these handguns use will find tongues for 'em. But mark my words, Don Cristobal, by two hours after dawn we'll know all we want to know and we'll be on our way.'

They were discussing the next move in the suppression of the rebellion. The Adelantado had announced his intention of ascertaining from the prisoners who was the ringleader in the affair and whither he was likely to have fled; he was going to hunt him down, him and every other rebel he could catch, even if he had hidden in the heart of the unexplored mountains.

'Are these people likely to have a ringleader?' asked Rich. 'They don't appear to me to have enough sense.'

The Adelantado turned a cold eye upon him, and Rich was conscious of an uneasy feeling of being in a decided minority. It was by no means the first time since his arrival in the island that he had made suggestions in favour of moderation, and he was aware of the danger of being looked upon as a persistent wet blanket.

'Could ten thousand people rise in rebellion *without* a ringleader?' asked the Adelantado, sarcastically.

'With these people I should say it was more likely in the case of ten thousand than in the case of ten,' said Rich.

It was a sweltering hot night, and all those present were feeling trickles of sweat running down inside their clothes, and were moving uneasily on their wooden benches inside the bare room with its earthen walls.

'I don't believe,' went on Rich, as the others remained silent, 'that there's an Indian alive in this island who could imagine a rebellion of ten thousand people, let alone organize one.'

'Perhaps,' said the Adelantado with elaborate irony, 'the learned doctor will explain to these assembled gentlemen the events of today. I fancied I saw ten thousand Indians armed and in rebellion. Did my imagination deceive me? Were there really only ten?'

'I think they took up arms spontaneously,' said Rich. 'Rebellion grows in misery, like maggots in putrid meat.'

'Misery?' said the Adelantado, genuinely surprised.

'Yes, misery,' said Rich. This was a different argument altogether from the one he had begun, but he was equally ready to debate it now that it had arisen. 'The Indians work now when they never worked before. They see their friends burned alive, and hanged. Their women are raped. They believe that there will be no end to all this unless the Spaniards are all killed–and until the Spaniards came the Indians did not know what it meant to kill people!'

'So!' said the Adelantado. 'They work. How else would we have the gold and the cotton we need? Of course they must work. Men work, relapsed heretics are burned and rebels are hanged, as in any Christian country. Rape? To an Indian woman there is no such thing. And if an Indian intends to kill me, I intend to kill him first. The learned doctor would not, I suppose. He would have us submit to being killed. No, of course, I know what he would advise. We ought all to get on board our ships and sail home again, leaving the gold in the earth and the pagans in their ignorance.'

Most of the men present were smiling now, even Acevedo, to whom Rich looked for sympathy. There was nobody present who could see his point of view, or understand what he was trying to say. Because the Indians were weaker than the Spaniards, because they were pagans, the Spaniards assumed it to be quite natural that they should be forced to work at unaccustomed labour to provide gold and cotton. The Spaniards could see no injustice in that. To them it was a natural law that the weaker should labour for the stronger. And as regards the question of cruelty, these countrymen of his had a tradition of centuries of warfare behind them; the shedding of human blood was a feat that redounded to a man's credit. The man who killed was performing a natural function of a gentleman; justice in the abstract had no meaning for them. Rich remembered the reminiscent grins which had accompanied their comments on the day's work, and was forced to a further conclusion; these were men who found pleasure in cruelty, apart from considering it merely as means to an end. They liked it.

Suetonius had written the lives of the twelve Caesars of Rome, and had shown how each in turn had been maddened by absolute power; their lust and their bloodthirstiness had grown with indulgence, like a wine-bibber's thirst, until no crime was too monstrous for them. These Spaniards in Española found themselves each in the position of a Caesar towards the feeble Indians. They were intoxicated with the power of life and death, and it was as hopeless to argue with them as it would be with drunken men. He could only sigh and remain silent while the discussion of the plans went on.

So Rich remained a witness of the taming of the Llanos, of all the great plain which stretched between the mountains and the sea in the south-east of the island. He saw the hangings and the floggings. He saw the great troops of Indians rounded up and driven back, after a sufficient number of examples had been made, to their labours. In the foothills of the mountains there ran little streams, in the sands of whose beds there were rare specks of gold; a hundred gourdfuls of sand, washed and painfully picked over, might contain one such speck. Every adult Indian had to produce, every three months, a hawk's bell full of gold–the hawk's bells which had once been so coveted in the island were now symbols of servitude.

Up in the mountains there hid little groups of Indians, those rare ones who had sufficient inventiveness to realize that there they had best chance of evading their oppressors. Every day little detachments marched out from Soco in pursuit. They were fierce men, trained in every ruse of war. They climbed the passes in the foothills, they hacked their way through the mountain forests; they moved by night to surprise their quarry at dawn, or spread out to make a wide drive that pinned the hapless refugees against impassable declivities. The hardships of the campaign were great, the exertions enormous. The nights spent in the drenching tropical rains brought on ague; not only the two hundred original colonists who followed the Adelantado's banner, but the two hundred newcomers began to show a high proportion of fever victims in their ranks. Food was short; the little patches of roots and corn which the Indians cultivated soon went wild again with lack of attention. Everything, in fact, was short. There was no leather to repair the shoes which the forced marches wore out–no one could tan the hides of the slaughtered cattle, and the rawhide slippers which the men wore lasted only a few days. Clothing wore out, and there was only the flimsy cotton cloth of native weaving to replace it–and not much of that. Every luxury was missing, and every necessity was scarce.

Discontent began to show itself among the Spaniards. The gentlemen wearied of inglorious hardship in the end; the common soldiers and sailors wearied of their exertions even sooner. There was death as well as disease. One Spaniard only died of his wounds–a deep stab by a sharpened cane in his thigh mortified and turned black–but two died of snake bite, several of fever. The survivors began to murmur a little. They even began to come to Rich with their grievances. The old colonists wanted to be allowed to return to their estates and their harems of Indian girls; the new arrivals wanted to be allowed the chance to set up similar establishments. For these latter three weeks of violent activity on land was quite long enough following their months at sea. They yearned for debauch and for ease. Bartholomew Columbus had led them when they had first arrived; now he had to drive, and he was a tactless taskmaster.

Rich was not present at the quarrel between the Adelantado and Bernardo de Tarpia, but he could picture it easily when it was described to him–the bitter words, the challenge given and insolently declined, the smouldering ill-temper badly hidden. And two days after he was gone, and his handgunmen with him, and Cristobal Garcia and half a dozen more gentlemen, half the sailors and a score of soldiers. It was the Adelantado himself who told Rich about the defection.

'Gone? But where has he gone to?'

'To join Roldan. God blast the souls of both of them!' said the Adelantado. 'And I know whose doing it is. You remember that crop-eared blackguard with a squint? Martinez, he called himself. He lost his ears when someone forebore to hang him in Spain. I ought to have hanged him myself. He came to San Domingo weeks back from Roldan. He said he wanted to resume his allegiance–he was a spy all the time for Roldan.'

'Roldan?' said Rich. 'Always Roldan. Who is this Roldan, Excellency?'

The subject of Roldan had been dexterously side-stepped by everyone from whom Rich had attempted to find out anything; it had been (so he had said to himself) like trying to discuss rope with a man whose father had been hanged. It was only now that he was able to hear the truth, and that thanks to the Adelantado.

'Roldan was once my brother's valet,' said Bartholomew. 'He was given the position of Chief Magistrate. After my brother had left Spain he began to act as if he was not merely Chief Magistrate, but Adelantado as well. You lawyers are infernal nuisances enough, but a valet with a judge's authority—!'

'You could have deprived him.'

'No, I could not, by God,' said Bartholomew. He was lapsing into Italian in the excitement of the moment. 'He held his post from the Admiral. The mere Adelantado could not revoke an appointment by the Viceroy!'

That was obvious enough; Rich ought to have seen it for himself. And with a flash of insight he could guess at more than the obvious. The Admiral returning to Spain would not trust even his own brother with the full powers he himself held. Fearful for his own authority, he had divided the power between his deputy and the chief magistrate.

'And what happened?'

'You can guess,' said the Adelantado with a shrug. 'I did not put him in gaol when I had the chance. All the shiftless men of the colony, all the lazy ones who grew tired of trying to screw gold out of the Indians, all the men who wanted to snore in the sun with fifty women to wait on them, they all joined him.'

All the men with whom the hot-tempered Adelantado happened to quarrel, in other words, thought Rich, but he did not say so. He remained tactfully silent and allowed the Adelantado to run on.

'Most of them were out in the Vera–the open valley to the north of the island. There they have all settled; they have left off seeking gold, and live idly, with a hundred miles of mountains between us and them. Roldan is a little king among them. I was going to march on them, now that I have tamed the Llanos. With four hundred men I would have been too strong for them. Roldan would have hanged. But now Tarpia has joined him with sixty men at least, all able-bodied, and I have fifty sick and another hundred whom I can't trust. Roldan has a new lease of life. But not for long.'

'What are you going to do?'

'There are other ships still to come. Any day they may arrive–the ships under my cousin's command. They sailed from Spain with you, and they ought to have arrived weeks ago, while you were exploring, but I suppose they have lost their way among the islands–my cousin was always a poor fool. But sooner or later they will come. Those ships bear a hundred horses. There will be two hundred men. Tarpia took no more than ten horses–Roldan has no more than five, thank God. In the Vera the horseman reigns supreme, the same as in these plains here. Once I get those horses landed, and the two hundred men, Roldan's little hour is finished. I shall hang him on my gallows at San Domingo, and Tarpia and Garcia and half a dozen others beside him.'

That was the right way to treat rebellion, thought Rich, although it occurred to him that the axe would be more fitting than the gallows for men of such blue blood as Tarpia. He found his dislike for the Adelantado diminishing. Rich was heart and soul on the side of orderly government and decent respect for authority, even though it was a shock to him to find himself approving of the execution of Spaniards when he had spent days in silent protest against the killing of heathen Indians. A man who could speak lightly of hanging a terrible man like Tarpia won his admiration for such daring. Rich was a little ashamed of his pity for the Indians; this bold talk of suppressing rebellion was much more the sort of thing he felt he ought to like. All his life so far he had lived as a spectator, and there was something peculiarly gratifying in being at last behind the scenes, in being at least a potential actor. It was better than splitting legal hairs and wrapping up the result in pages of Latin.

17

In San Domingo, when the Adelantado returned from his chastizing of the Llanos, there was nothing new. The fifty men of the garrison who had remained there with the Admiral had done nothing, heard nothing. Most of them were fever-ridden and asked nothing more than to stay tranquil. Apparently the Admiral had made some attempt to persuade them to heave up the three ships which lay in the harbour and make them ready for the sea again, but they had vehemently refused to do such heavy work, and the Admiral had abandoned his attempt. Those sailors who had not deserted to Roldan took more kindly to the suggestion when it was put to them on their return with the conquering army. The ships would sail for Spain when they were ready, with messages and treasure, and the sailors were sure of a passage home.

'There are two hundredweights of gold,' said Diego Alamo the assayer–Rich had had hardly a word with him since they had left Trinidad, and it was delightful to encounter him again and hear the results of his observations.

'That sounds enormous to me,' said Rich.

'Large enough,' said Alamo with a shrug. 'Their Highnesses do not receive that amount of gold in a year's revenue. And there are pearls beside, of more value still, I should fancy, if the market is not too hurriedly flooded with them.'

'This one island, then, is worth more than all Spain?' said Rich, eagerly. Solid facts of this sort were reassuring especially when retailed by someone as hard-headed and learned as Alamo. But Alamo shrugged again in dampening fashion.

'Perhaps,' he said. 'But part of that gold is what the Indians have saved for generations. And nowhere does the earth breed gold rapidly. A speck here, a grain there, in the sand. One gathers them, and it is years before another speck is formed. During the last few years most of the grains available have been gathered, and in my opinion the annual amount of gold found in the island will diminish rapidly.'

'Oh,' said Rich, disappointed. 'Does everyone think that?'

'No. They know nothing about the subject. Nor have they read the ancients. You, Doctor, you have read your Livy, your Polybius? Don't you remember how our own Spain was conquered by the Romans and Carthaginians? They found gold there, quantities of gold. Spain was to Carthage what these islands are to Spain. But what gold is there now to be found in Spain? A vein or two in the Asturias. A vein or two in the South. No more.'

'And how do you account for that?'

'Spain was a new country. The simple Iberians had little use for the gold which had been breeding there since the creation. From the rivers and valleys all the gold was soon cleared out when the Carthaginians came. Even the seeds of the gold were taken away, so that the country became barren of the metal. I can predict the same of this island.'

'The gold breeds from seeds, you think?'

Alamo shrugged yet once more.

'If I knew how gold breeds I should be as rich as Midas,' he said. 'But every philosopher knows that, however it is, the process is slow.'

'So that the value of this island will diminish, year by year?'

Alamo pulled at his beard and looked at Rich, considering deeply. He hesitated before he spoke, and when at last he allowed the words to come he glanced over his shoulder nervously lest anyone should overhear the appalling heresies he was about to utter.

'Perhaps,' he said, 'gold is not the most important merchandise this island can produce. I have often wondered whether a country is the richer for possessing gold. We may find the other products of this island far more valuable.'

'The spices, you mean? But I thought—'

'The spices are unimportant compared with those which reach Spain via the Levant. The cinnamon which the Admiral thought grew here so freely is poor stuff. There are no real spices here–no cloves, no nutmegs. The pepper is not true pepper, even though one can acquire a taste for it quickly enough.'

Rich found all this a little frightening. If the gold returns were to diminish, as Alamo predicted, and the spice trade were to prove valueless, as Rich had long ago suspected, the colony of Española could not be worth having discovered. The three thousand Spanish lives which had already been expended were quite wasted. But Alamo was ready to reassure him.

'The island has treasures beside gold and spices,' he said. 'It has a soil fifty times more fruitful than Andalusia. The rain and the sun give it a fertility which it is hard to estimate. One man's labour will grow food for ten–see how these wretched Indians have always contrived to live in abundance. Cattle multiply here amazingly. My calculations go to prove that by breeding cattle here a handsome profit would be shown merely by selling the hides in Spain–and I know well enough the cost of sailing a ship from here to there.'

'Cattle? Hides?' said Rich. There was a queer sense of disappointment. A prosaic trade in hides was not nearly as interesting as a deal in hundredweights of gold.

'Oh, there are other possibilites,' said Alamo, hastily. 'Have you ever tasted sugar?'

'Yes. It is a brown powder beneficent in cases of chills and colds. There is a white variety, too, in crystals. I have had packets sent me as presents occasionally. It has a sweet taste, like honey, or even sweeter. Why, is there sugar to be found in this island?'

'Not as yet. But it could grow here–it is expressed from a cane exactly like the canes we see growing everywhere in this country. The sugar cane is grown in Malaga a little, and in Sicily. My friend Patino retails it at five hundred *marvavedis* an ounce. Once start the cultivation here and in a few years we might be exporting sugar not by the ounce, but by the ton.'

That was a more alluring prospect than chaffering in hides. A spark of enthusiasm lit in Rich's breast, and then died away to nothing again as he began to consider details.

'It means husbandry,' he said, despondingly.

'It means hard work,' agreed Alamo, a smile flickering over his lips.

Each knew what the other was thinking about. Knight-errants and adventurers like Garcia, or like Avila, would never reconcile themselves to labouring in the cultivation of sugar, or even in the breeding of cattle. They had come to seek gold and spices, and for those they were willing to risk their lives or undergo hardship. It would be far below the dignity of a hidalgo to settle down to prosaic labour. Nor would the lower-class Spaniards who had reached Hayti–the gaol-birds–the bankrupts–take kindly to arduous work.

'There is no labour to be got out of the Indians,' said Rich, despairingly.

'That is so,' agreed Alamo. 'They die rather than work. And pestilences sweep them away even when they are not killed for sport. There were two millions when the Admiral first landed. Now there is not more than half that number, after six years. Perhaps soon there will not be a single Indian left alive in Española.'

'Impossible!' said Rich.

'Possible enought,' said Alamo, gravely.

'But what then?' asked Rich, wildly. The thought of the blotting out of a population of two million left him a little dizzy. Their Highnesses of Spain had no more than ten million subjects in all their dominions. And he was appalled at the thought both of this green land of Española reduced to an unpeopled desert and of the extinction of a pleasant useless race of mankind. This discovery of the Indies was a Dead Sea fruit–alluring to the sight and yet turning to ashes in the mouth.

'There is another possibility,' said Alamo.

'What?'

'It was João de Setubal who put it in my mind,' said Alamo.

It was a queer world in which a cultured man like Alamo could be indebted for ideas to a clumsy barbarian like the Portuguese knight; Rich must have looked his surprise, because Alamo hastened to explain.

'He was complaining of the uselessness of the Indians, just as everyone else does,' said Alamo. 'And then he went on to say how in Lisbon they have negro slaves nowadays. Stout, dependable labourers, brought from the African coast. I had heard about that before, but it had slipped my memory until Don João reminded me of it. They breed freely, do the negroes. If Their Highnesses could arrange with the King of Portugal for a supply of negroes to be sent here—'

'You are right, by God!' said Rich.

'This hot climate would be native to them,' said Alamo. 'They could do the heavy work and our Spanish gentlemen fresh out of the gaols would not think it beneath them to supervise.'

'And the Indians could be spared,' said Rich, with kindly enthusiasm. 'Perhaps part of the island could be set aside for them to live without interference. Save for Christian teaching, of course.'

This last was a hurried addition.

'The Church would give her blessing,' went on Alamo. 'The negroes would be brought out of heathen darkness in Africa to lead a Christian life here.'

They eyed each other a little flushed and excited.

'Sir,' said Rich, solemnly. 'I think that today you have made a suggestion which may change the history of Spain. In my report to His Highness—'

'I would rather, if possible, that His Highness was not reminded of my existence,' said Alamo. 'Torquemada—'

'I understand,' said Rich, sadly.

But this was the most cheerful thing which had been brought to his notice since his arrival in Española. Rich had been worrying about the report he had to write, and which would go to Spain as soon as the *Holy Name* was ready for sea again. It would have been a cheerless thing without this creative suggestion added to it–merely a sweeping condemnation of the Admiral's administrative system, and of the methods of the colonists, combined with the gloomiest prophecies regarding the future of the island. Rich knew quite well what favour was given to those advisers of the Crown who brought nothing but unpalatable truths to the council board. If he could sketch out a future of plenteous cargoes of sugar at five hundred *maravedis* an ounce, and suggest a profitable trade in negro slaves, his state paper would be a great deal more acceptable and would not prejudice his own future–would not imperil his own life–nearly as much.

'But,' said Rich, half to himself, 'there's a lot to be done before that.'

He was thinking of the disorder in the island–of Roldan's passive rebellion, the vague property laws, the muddled policies.

'That is not my concern, thank God,' said Alamo, guessing–as was not difficult–what was in Rich's mind. 'You will have to settle all that with the

Admiral. I am no more than assayer and naturalist. Politics are not my province.'

Rich thought how lucky Alamo was. There had been a time when he himself had been delighted at the thought of taking part in the administration of a new empire, but there was no pleasure in it now for him. Those endless conferences in the citadel of San Domingo only left him with an exasperated sense of frustration. It was hard for any decicion to be reached–at least, it was hard for the Admiral to reach a decision. There was the pitiful difficulty that Roldan, thanks to his appointment as Alcalde Mayor, could claim a legal justification for his actions.

'Why not revoke the appointment, Your Excellency?' asked Rich. 'Any disobedience then would be treason and could be punished as such.'

'That would drive him to desperate measures,' said the Admiral. 'God knows what he would do then.'

'But what *could* he do?'

'He could march on San Domingo. He could fight us.'

Rich looked at Bartholomew Columbus. This was clearly his cue.

'He *might*,' said Bartholomew. 'But I doubt it.'

'What force has he got?'

'As many men as we have. More perhaps,' interposed the Admiral. 'And–and–perhaps all our men would not fight for us.'

That was perfectly possible, at least in a few cases.

'But would all Roldan's men fight for him?' asked Rich. He was wondering what he himself would do in such a case. Certainly he would think long before he appeared in arms, an obvious rebel.

Bartholomew glanced at him for once with approval. 'Now you're on the right road,' he said. 'Treason is treason either side of the ocean. Some would fear for their necks, and would wait to see what would happen. Proclaim Roldan dismissed. Give him a month to come in and submit. If he does not, march against him. Half his men would not fight.'

'But what would they say in Spain?' said the Admiral, pathetically.

That was the trouble. Once let the Court of Spain know that there was rebellion in her new colony, that the Admiral could not control his subordinates, and Their Highnesses would have every justification for removing their Viceroy from office. There was suspicion in the old man's eyes as he looked round the room. Who would be his successor in that case? Bartholomew, the hero of the Indian rebellion? Rich, who had been sent out for no obvious good purpose? Rich could see the struggle in the Admiral's face. His position, his power–even such as it was–were very dear to him. After a lifetime of unimportance, he now found himself Admiral and Viceroy, and he did not want to lose the splendid position his genius had won for him, even though his genius was not of the kind to make his position supportable. He was bound to regard with suspicion any advice which came from those who might hope to succeed him. He felt alone and friendless, and his first instinct was to temporize.

And Rich, knowing quite well what sort of secret report was awaiting transmission by the *Holy Name* to Their Highnesses, could hardly blame him. But Rich's sense of justice and order, quite apart from his sympathy for the poor old man, urged him to try and make some sort of settlement of this disastrous state of affairs. He wanted to be able to add a postscript to his report, saying he hoped that shortly the situation would be in hand.

'But something ought to be done,' he said.

'What do you suggest?' asked Bartholomew, curiously.

'Proclaiming Roldan's dismissal would deprive him of the support of some of his people,' said Rich. 'Isn't it possible to split his party still further? Can't we make offers which would bring over a large number? Garcia might come back, for instance, or Tarpia, if we bribed heavily enough. Then with Roldan once caught and hanged we could deal with them on a new basis.'

Rich was a little surprised at himself for making such proposals. He had never believed he had it in him to contemplate any such vigorous action. He remembered Tarquin in Rome, cutting off the heads of the tallest poppies; he thought of Caesar Borgia in the Romagna, dividing his enemies and striking them down one by one. All that was very well in theory, to a book-learned man; he was genuinely astonished to find himself advocating the actual practice–prepared even, if need be, to put it into execution himself. He hated the thought of fighting just as much as the Admiral did–although he concealed it better–but he was not nearly so averse to this kind of intrigue.

'But how can we bribe them?' asked James Columbus, his foolish jaw gaping.

'The Admiral has more in his gift than Roldan has. Titles. Offices. Estates.'

Rich was searching in his mind for the sort of thing that would appeal to the Garcia he visualized standing before him. 'Some new expedition to seek for the Grand Khan–Garcia would desert anyone in exchange for the command of that.'

He was proposing treachery of the meanest possible sort, he knew. Yet he was only proposing to meet treachery by treachery, and then only when it seemed impossible to employ any other means.

'No one but me sails from Española on any expedition at all,' said the Admiral, instantly. That showed what was necessary to rouse him.

'It need only be promised him,' said Rich, wearily. 'Your Excellency can reconsider it when Roldan is once hanged.'

The Admiral peered at him with narrowed eyes. It was only too obvious that he suspected Rich of planning something more than he had actually suggested–that he was subtly endeavouring to filch from him a little of his precious power and possessions.

'Never!' said the Admiral. 'I shall never allow such a subject to be discussed!'

This was the sort of exasperating deadlock to which Rich had grown accustomed in these last few days.

'As Your Excellency wishes, of course,' he said. 'I am merely making what suggestions occur to me.'

That meeting, like the preceding ones, broke up without anything having been decided. The next one seemed to call even more urgently for a decision, because now there was a new and disastrous development. The sentinel on the citadel ramparts announced a ship–she was the caravel *Rosa*, one of the three which had parted from the main expedition to sail direct to Española and which should have arrived three months back. Anxiously they watched her, running gaily down before the eternal east wind, the Admiral and the Adelantado and the rest of the Columbus clan, Rich and Alamo and the Acevedo brothers.

'She's the *Rosa*!' said Perez with satisfaction.

'She carried most of the horses,' said the Admiral.

'Did she, by God!' said Bartholomew. 'Then that will end our friend Roldan's career, if enough have survived this infernal long voyage thay have made.'

'A big "if",' whispered Alamo to Rich.

'Why?'

'I know more about those horses than the Admiral does. The horses that came on board are not the same ones as Their Highnesses paid for. The contractors showed the Admiral two hundred horses on land for his approval, and shipped two hundred quite different horses when they had received it. Four months at sea? Half of them would not survive four days!'

They watched the *Rosa* catch the sea breeze and head for the river mouth.

'No sign of the other two,' said Bartholomew, anxiously. He scanned the horizon unavailingly. 'Lost at sea? Parted company? We shall know soon.'

They knew soon enough; there were three captains on board the *Rosa* with reports to make. It was a rambling story, of losing their way, of finding themselves among the unexplored cannibal islands to the south-eastward, and of finally anchoring at Isabella in the north of the island–Roldan's headquarters.

'Holy Mary!' said Bartholomew. 'What next?'

Ballester, the captain of the *Rosa*, spread helpless hands.

'Half our crew's left us,' he said. 'Sixty men–there had been much sickness, as I said. They took the other two caravels. They took the stores out of the *Rosa*. Those of us who would not join them they allowed to sail round to here. That man with no ears–Martinez–would have made us walk across the mountains, sick though we all were. But Roldan let us take the *Rosa*. He said—'

Ballester checked himself.

'What did he say?'

Ballester had no desire to repeat what Roldan had said.

'Really, sir, it was not important. I could not—'

'What did he say?'

'Well, he said we should soon come sailing back to him after a little experience of San Domingo.'

There was an awkward pause, until Bartholomew changed the subject.

'How many men did you leave at Isabella?'

'Sixty-two. Twenty of them were sick.'

'How many horses?'

'Five.'

'Five? Where are the other hundred?'

'Dead, sir. We were short of water for a long time. And on the voyage—'

'That's all right, man. If Roldan has them, I would rather they were all dead. How many men have you brought in the *Rosa*?'

'Forty-seven, sir. That includes five sick who are likely to die, and two friars.'

The council looked at each other.

'The balance is hardly altered, then,' was Bartholomew's comment. 'We can still fight him.'

Despite the heat and the drumming of the rain outside Rich found his brain working fast. The newly landed Spaniards at Isabella would be a source of dissension there, very likely. They would not–gaol-birds though they might be–take kindly to fighting Spaniards the moment they had landed. They might have slipped easily into mutiny after the hardships of the voyage, but they might hesitate at treason. An immediate move on Isabella would cause them to hesitate, and hesitation is infectious. Roldan's men would hesitate as well. The passive rebellion might be borne down by a bold stroke.

'The sooner the better,' he said, without time to wonder at himself for such advocacy of energetic action.

Everyone looked at the Admiral now, and the Admiral shifted in his seat and eyed them uneasily. With the arrival of the squadron there could be no question of further postponement of the decision. And Rich, watching him, noticed how he gazed first at him and then at the Adelantado; he guessed what wild conclusions the Admiral was drawing from the unwonted circumstance of two of them being of one mind. Rich was paralleling the Admiral's thoughts quite closely yet even he was surprised at what the Admiral decided eventually to do. The decision was not reached easily. There was argument–of course there was argument–and a little spurt of old man's rage, but it was agreed to in the end. The Admiral was to sail round in the *Rosa* to Isabella, and there he was to make the last effort to recall Roldan and his supporters to their allegiance, and, in the event of their refusal, he was to denounce them as traitors.

'One more wasted month,' sneered the Adelantado, reluctantly agreeing.

Rich thought the same, but in the face of the old man's unreasoning obstinacy there was only one alternative to agreement, and that was to raise a fresh mutiny in San Domingo.

18

The Admiral had sailed, and Rich had leisure now for his other duties, to make plans for the future government of the colony, to try to estimate its future worth, to put the final touches on the report to Their Highnesses which had already grown to such inordinate length. It called for a good deal of consideration to discover the right wording of the suggestion that in place of shiploads of gold and pearls Their Highnesses would be better advised to expect sugar and hides, and of the advice that negotiations should be opened with the half-hostile Court of Lisbon for the supply of negroes.

Still deeper consideration was necessary to suggest a working system of government. There was one precedent to follow in this case–the constitution of the late Kingdom of Jerusalem. The Holy Land, like Española, was to all intents a new country conquered from the heathen by the Christians, and its constitution had been drawn up in the Assize of Jerusalem in clear-cut legal Latin which embodied the deepest thought of the Middle Ages on the knotty problem of how to erect a stable government on the shaky foundation of the feudal system. But the Kingdom of Jerusalem had fallen through its own rottenness, after all. And there was, as Rich came wearily to realize, time and again, that thrice-accursed agreement between Their Highnesses and the Admiral which would hinder any attempt on the part of the Court of Spain to make any laws for the Indies, as long as the Admiral clung so frantically to every bit of the power which that fantastic document had granted him.

At every turn Rich was reminded of the difficulties around him. The Admiral had borne off to Isabella with him the last horn of ink which the island possessed–before Rich could even set pen to paper (and paper was scarce) he had to consult Alamo regarding this difficulty and wait until, out of burnt bones, Alamo managed to compound a horrid sludge which would just answer the purpose. There were two hundredweights of gold, there was a gallon of pearls, in San Domingo–enough wealth to build a city in Spain–and yet he had to live in a wretched timber hut in a corner of the citadel ramparts, where the rain leaked in through the gaps, and where bugs were already well established, and which had the sole merit of being private now that Antonio Spallanzani had sailed with his master to Isabella.

Food was scarce. The fifty men who constituted the garrison should have been amply fed from the surrounding country, where thousands of Indians cultivated the soil under the direction of the Spaniards. But naturally these supplies for the government had to be paid for with government funds with the gold that came from the fifths and tenths and thirds that were levied on the treasures of the island as collected by the Spaniards outside the town. And when the Spaniards paid it in again, being gold it was subject once more to those fifths and tenths and thirds until it was a most unprofitable business even to sell roots to the garrison, certainly not worth the enormous trouble of bringing them in. In San Domingo the healthy sickened and the sick died and discontent seethed, and the Adelantado dared not use strong measures for fear of further defections to Roldan, and Rich scratched his head unavailingly to try and make some sense out of the tangle of laws and privileges which had already grown up in that part of the island which still remained lukewarm in the government's cause.

There were times when Rich wondered whether he were really awake, or whether he were not deep in some prolonged and fantastic nightmare, from which he would presently awake to find himself safe in bed in Barcelona. All this might well be a dream; in clairvoyant moments he realized how quite unlikely it was that it should be reality–that he should have crossed the ocean, and explored new lands, and ridden in a cavalry charge striking down living men with his sword, and should have taken part in high political debate seriously discussing the hanging of hidalgos. It was a marvellous moment to be invited to the Adelantado's table, there to eat gluttonously of turtle when a fortunate catch had provided several of the creatures. Rich remembered his shuddering disgust at turtles in the Cape Verdes, where lepers congregated to seek a cure by daubing themselves with turtles' blood. Now he was hungry enough to eat them with appetite–that was a nightmare in itself.

The parrot that Malalé had given him in Paria had died long since, while under Diego Alamo's care during his absence at Soco. It had been a disappointing piece of news to receive on his return; in the brief time that he had owned the lovely thing of red and blue he had grown fond of it, with its comic habits and its crowbar of a beak which prised open any buckle which bound it. Rich had an uneasy feeling that this island was fated, that everything Spanish that lived in it was doomed to an early end, whether it should be parrots or codes of law. He was aware of a growing disgust for the place.

And then the *Rosa* came sailing back into the harbour, the Admiral's flag flying at the masthead, and Alonso Perez blowing fanfares on his trumpet, startling the sea birds into flight all round the river mouth. The Adelantado put off hastily from the shore to welcome his brother; everyone else congregated on the beach in anxious expectancy, wondering what had been the outcome of the negotiations with Roldan. They watched for some time before they saw the Admiral descend slowly and painfully into the boat–apparently the brothers had plunged immediately into a long discussion without waiting to return to land.

Apparently, too, the discussion had not been very friendly, to judge by the Adelantado's black brow as he splashed through the shallows to the shore; he stood digging his toes irritably into the sand and meeting no one's eyes while the Admiral was being helped ashore, feeble, almost tottering, by Alonso Perez and a couple of Indians. But the Admiral was no sooner within earshot again than Bartholomew turned upon him to renew the discussion.

'Have you a copy of this precious treaty, brother?' he asked.

'Yes,' said the Admiral. He halted in his slow course up the beach and fumbled in his pocket.

'Oh, it can wait until we reach the citadel,' said Bartholomew. 'Gentlemen, come with us and hear what His Excellency the Admiral has agreed upon.'

The Admiral fluttered a thin hand in protest, only to call forth another bitter comment from his brother.

'Why should they not know?' demanded Bartholomew. 'You say the news is to be proclaimed publicly. That is one of the terms.'

It was only the least of the terms. Bartholomew read the document aloud in the council room, while Rich and the others looked at each other in unbelieving astonishment. It seemed quite incredible that such a treaty could have been made. Item by item Bartholomew read it out, with its unlettered travesty of legal terminology, its 'whereases' and 'aforesaids' which a group of ignorant people had put in in an attempt to imitate lawyer's expressions. By the first clause Roldan and all who followed him were given a pardon for anything they might have done during their stay in the Indies. By the second clause they were, each and severally, to receive from the Admiral a certificate of good conduct. By the third clause a proclamation was to be made throughout the island, to the effect that everything Roldan and his followers had done had met with the Admiral's entire approval. By the fourth clause Roldan was to select who should be allowed to go back to Spain, and those that he should nominate should be allowed to transport whatever property they might desire, either of valuables or of slaves. By the fifth clause the Admiral guaranteed that whoever should remain in Española should receive, free of obligation, as much land as a horse could encircle in a day, with the inhabitants thereof; the recipients to select both the land and the horse. The sixth clause merely confirmed that Roldan was invested with the office and powers of Alcade Mayor, but added that these powers–as the original document had merely implied without express statement–were of course given in perpetuity to Roldan and his heirs for ever, as long as the Admiral's viceregal authority and that of his heirs should endure.

The Adelantado interrupted his reading and tapped the document with a gnarled forefinger.

'You did not tell me about this last one, brother,' he said, and then turning to the rest of the meeting: 'That appears to be all of importance, gentlemen. The rest is merely a résumé of the titles of His Excellency the Admiral of the Ocean and of the Right Honourable the Alcade Mayor of the Indies; I think I can spare myself the trouble of reading them.'

There was only a murmur in reply, and a shuffling of feet. Rich's mind was already deeply engaged upon a legal analysis of the treaty he had just heard read, and the others were too stunned to speak.

'Would any of you gentlemen care to comment?' asked the Adelantado, but the Admiral spoke before anyone else could open his mouth.

'I will not have the matter discussed,' he said. 'This treaty is your Viceroy's decision, and it would be treason to question it.'

The Admiral sat in his chair, with his hands on his thin knees. He had spoken with an old man's querulousness, and yet–and yet–there was a suspicion of triumph in his glance, a self-satisfied gleam in the blue eyes. It was as if he thought he had done something clever, hard though that was to believe. Rich remembered earlier discussions. Perhaps the Admiral had decided that to retain his power he needed to create some new party for himself which he could play off against the Adelantado's brutal bullying, or against Rich's vague powers. Or possibly he wanted to send a despatch to Spain saying that he had arrived to find the island in disorder, and had dissipated the disorder immediately by a few judicious concessions. Or perhaps he knew he had been weak and would not admit it. Or–anything was possible–he might by now have deluded himself into thinking that he had brought off a really creditable coup, just as he believed he had discovered the mines of Ophir and the Earthly Paradise. Meanwhile, Rich saw various loopholes of escape from this treaty.

'Your Excellency signed of your own free will?' he asked. 'You were not coerced into it?'

'Of course not,' said the Admiral, indignantly.

'A promise entered into under compulsion is not binding, Your Excellency,' persisted Rich.

'I know that.'

'And these gifts of land, Your Excellency. Land is a tricky thing to deed away. It is Crown property. I doubt–please pardon me, Your Excellency, but of course we are all anxious to have everything as legal as possible–if Your

Excellency's Viceregal authority entitles you to dispose of the property of the Crown. The recipients would be well advised to have their title confirmed by Their Highnesses, and until Their Highnesses have given that confirmation I myself, for one, would be chary of entering into any dealings regarding those properties.'

'My agreement with Their Highnesses gives me full powers.'

'Powers can only be expressly given, Your Excellency. Any powers not named are by every rule of law retained by Their Highnesses.'

'Oh, why split these hairs?' broke in the Adelantado. 'Their Highnesses are two thousand leagues from here, the treaty is signed, and there's an end of it for a year or so. Roldan and his men will have the land if anything my brother can do can ensure it. There is no profit in continuing this debate, I fancy, gentlemen.'

Rich was of the same opinion. He escaped from the room as soon as he could and went to sit in the tiny apartment which he shared with Antonio Spallanzani. The *Holy Name* and the *Santa Anna* would be sailing soon, and his report must go in one ship while he sailed in the other. He thought longingly of Spain, of his cool stone house and fountain in the courtyard, the while he sat sweating and fighting the flies. It would be a long voyage home reaching far to the northward to avoid the path of the eternal easterly breezes, but in three months at most he would be in Spain. The King would be at Valladolid or Toledo, and he might be kept cooling his heels round the court for weeks. But six months at most, and he would be home again, in his own house, leading a decent and orderly life. He could sit in his big leather chair reading through the pleadings of law-abiding merchants, or, with a hushed band of students behind him, he could issue his judgments, in stately Latin, to the expectant litigants assembled in his hall.

That was the world he knew and loved, not this mad new world of rain and mosquitoes, of slaughter and mutiny, of mad theories and madder politics. And yet mad though it all was, he was conscious of a queer regret that he was leaving it. He would have liked to have stayed a while longer, even though he knew that he would be bitterly disappointed if some unforeseen circumstance compelled him to stay. He told himself that he was as mad as everyone else in Española.

Meanwhile the report had to be written, and he had to make up his mind what to write. As he re-pointed his pen he began to form phrases in his mind. He did not want to word them too strongly–the contents of the report would need no emphasis of phrasing.

19

Roldan and his followers had come to San Domingo under the protection of the free pardon which had been solemnly proclaimed at the foot of the flagstaff. They were swaggering about the place, Roldan and Bernardo de Tarpia and

Cristobal Garcia and of all them. They had brought a long train of Indian slaves with them, well set up and handsome young women, each bearing burdens. Slaves and burdens, in accordance with the recent treaty, were to be sent to Spain in the *Holy Name*; the crop-eared Martinez was to sail with them as agent for all the recent mutineers, and he was to be armed with a long list of the luxuries which he was to buy with the proceeds of this plunder.

Rich's report was completed, signed and sealed. Rich had given it with his own hands to Ballester, who was sailing as captain in the *Santa Anna*. The action had reminded him–if reminding was needed–of the impermanence of life in this world. He was taking the precaution lest the *Holy Name* with him on board should never reach Spain at all. Perhaps the next week would find him with the saints in Paradise, or suffering the pangs of Purgatory, or–he felt a shudder of fear–more likely cast into the eternal flames of Hell as a result of his recent heretical thoughts. He was in a state of profound dejection and agitation of mind which was not relieved in the least by the suspicious glance which Ballester darted at him when he received the letter; Ballester could suspect only too well what the contents were, and Ballester was one of those who loved the Admiral.

Should anyone of the Admiral's party come to know exactly what was written in his report, Rich knew that his life might be in danger. There were subtle poisons in this island–the deadly manchineel was one–even if it would not be a more simple matter of a knife in his back. He had to set himself for these last few days before the ships sailed to play the part of the conscientious supporter, critical but not too much so–certainly not the man who would write to the King that the Admiral was not fit to govern a farmyard, let alone an empire. It was a comfort to him now that Roldan knew of the letter. Certainly neither the Admiral nor Ballester would dare to incur the penalties of high treason by tampering with a sealed document addressed to His Highness himself–at least, not while an enemy knew that such a letter existed. Rich could not trust either the Italians or the Andalusians, and he waited with impatience during the interminable delays in fitting out the *Holy Name*.

He was walking back in the dark after dining with the Adelantado. The *Santa Anna* had actually sailed with his report on board; the *Holy Name* was almost ready; another thirty-six hours and he would have seen the last of this island. Overhead the stars were brilliant; the moon would rise soon in all her splendour. The cicadas were singing wildly all round him, and the lusty croaking of the frogs in the stream supplied a cheerful bass. Fireflies were lighting and relighting their lamps about his path, far more brilliant and mysterious than their duller brothers of Spain. Altogether he was in a cheerful mood–two cups of the Admiral's wine may have had something to do with that.

A denser shadow appeared in the darkness close at his right hand, and then another at his left. There was a man at either elbow walking silently in step with him; Rich felt the skin creep on the back of his neck, while between his shoulder blades he felt the actual spot where the stiletto would enter. Yet even in that moment he found time to wonder why they were troubling to murder him while his report was on its way to the King and beyond recall.

And then the walking shadow on his right spoke to him with the voice of Garcia.

'Don Narciso,' he said, 'I must trouble you to turn back and come with us.'

'And if I do not, Don Cristobal?'

Both men pressed in close upon him, forcing his elbows against his sides.

'I have a dagger here, Don Narciso. I will use it if you cry out.'

'And I have another,' said the voice of Diego Moret on his left. 'And I will use it, too. There will be one in your back and one in your belly.'

'Turn back with us, Don Narciso,' said Garcia, insinuatingly.

Rich turned; he felt there was nothing else he could do.

'Where are you taking me?' he asked; he had to try hard to keep the quaver out of his voice.

'This is not the time for explanations,' said Garcia, grimly. 'I would prefer you to keep quiet.'

They were walking down the slope from the citadel; the little town lay on their right, and there was only one solitary gleam of light from it. Rich decided they were going to lead him into the forest and kill him there. His body might lie for ever in that tangle of vegetation and never be discovered, even within a mile of the place. But he was still puzzled as to the motive, so puzzled that quite involuntarily he broke the silence with another question.

'What do you want to kill me for?' he asked.

'Be quiet. And we are not going to kill you,' said Garcia.

'Probably not going to,' amended Moret in the darkness on his left.

Even with this amendment the statement was reassuring. The wave of relief which surged over Rich astonished him; he realized that he had been far more afraid than he suspected at the time. He trembled a little with the reaction, and then battled with himself to stop it. He did not want these two men at his elbows to know he was trembling. They were coming nearer to the trees and the forest.

'There are four horses here, Don Narciso,' said Garcia. 'One of them is for you. The others are for Don Diego and myself and Don Ramon who is waiting for us. There will be no reins for you to hold–the reins will be in my charge. But I hope you can stay in the saddle by holding on to the saddle bow.'

'I can try,' said Rich–the whinny of a horse told that they were drawing near to them.

'Did you find him?' asked an unknown voice.

'Yes,' said Garcia, and then to Rich: 'Mount.'

Rich felt in the darkness for the stirrup, and with the effort usual to him he hoisted up his foot and got it in. By the time he had swung himself into the saddle Moret was already mounted; Garcia sprang into the saddle of the third horse. They began to move along a path; the unknown Ramon who had been waiting with the horses in front, followed by Rich and Garcia, while Moret brought up the rear. The horses blundered along in the darkness; Rich felt his face whipped painfully occasionally by branches, and his knees received several excruciating knocks. For a space his mind was too much occupied with these troubles, and with the necessity of keeping his seat in the saddle, to have any thoughts to spare for the future, but as soon as the forest began to thin, and the rising moon gave them light to an extent quite remarkable compared with the previous blackness, he inevitably began to wonder once more. Suddenly a new aspect of the situation broke upon him, with a shock which made him sweat and set him moving restlessly in the saddle.

'Mother of God!' he said. 'The *Holy Name* sails tomorrow. You will let me get back in time to sail in her?'

The first reply he had was a light-hearted chuckle from Moret behind; the question seemed to amuse him immensely. Garcia allowed a painful second or two to elapse before answering.

'No, my pretty one,' he said. 'You will not be sailing in the *Holy Name*. Rest assured about that.' Assured was not at all the right adjective to describe Rich's mental condition. There was bitter disappointment at the thought of not returning to Spain, but his other doubts overlaid that at the moment; he was intensely puzzled. It could hardly be ransom that these kidnappers were seeking; they must know that in the island he possessed practically nothing that anyone could desire. Then it occurred to him that perhaps he was being carried off to give legal colour to some plan they had in mind. They might be intending to force him to construct some binding agreement regarding their grants of land.

'I will do nothing,' he announced, stoutly, 'to distort the law for you. I have my professional honour to consider.'

Moret seemed to find this announcement extremely funny, too. He broke into high-pitched laughter again; Rich, who could not see him, could imagine him writhing convulsed with merriment in his saddle.

'Be damned to your professional honour,' said Garcia. 'Do you think a man like me needs a lawyer to chop straws for him in this island?'

'Then why, in the name of God—?'

They wanted neither his wealth nor his legal services, and he could think of nothing else they could want of him. Unless perhaps–it was a most uncomfortable thought–they wanted him as a hostage. If that were the case his doom was certain; nobody of the Admiral's party would lift a finger to save him. The sweat on his face suddenly cold, and he shuddered in the warm light.

'We want you—' began Garcia, slowly.

'It's too good a joke to spoil yet,' interjected Moret, but Garcia ignored him.

'We want you as a navigator,' said Garcia.

'As a navigator?'

'Didn't you hear what I said?' snapped Garcia.

'But I'm no navigator,' protested Rich. 'I know nothing about it.'

'We saw you on the voyage out,' said Garcia. 'The Admiral was giving you lessons. You looked at the sun every day through his astrolabe, and at the stars each night. You were enough of a navigator to lecture us about it. Or have you forgotten?'

Rich certainly had forgotten until he was reminded of it.

'But I could no more take a ship to Spain—' he began.

'Spain? Who said anything about Spain? It's West we sail, not East. And I'll warrant you could find your way to Spain, too.'

'Holy Mary!' said Rich faintly. 'Sainted Narciso of Gerona!'

He was too stunned for a space to say more, but slowly realization came to him.

'I will not go with you,' he burst out. 'I will not. Let me go back. Please. I beg of you.'

He writhed about in his saddle, entertaining some frantic notion of flinging himself to the ground and taking to his heels. The sound of a sharp whirr of steel behind him made him refrain; Moret had drawn his sword and was ready to cut him down. He forced himself to sit still, and from that he proceeded to force himself to appear calm. He was suddenly ashamed of his exhibition of weakness; it was especially shameful that he should have been guilty of an undignified outburst before men like Garcia and Moret, whom he despised. And–such is human nature–there was the faint hope growing in his breast already that he might yet escape.

'What is the plan?' he asked, steadying his voice.

'A week back,' said Garcia, 'we caught an Indian. He is not of this island, although our Indians can understand him. He is taller and stronger, and his lower lip has been cut off in a V, so that we call him el Baboso, the slobberer.'

'But what has he to say?'

'He has told us of a land to the north and west, a vast country full of gold. Gold vases and gold dishes. There are vast palaces, he says, reaching to the sky, and the chiefs have their clothes sewn all over with precious stones so that in the sunshine the eye cannot bear their brightness. That is where we are going. We shall bury our arms elbow deep in gold dust.'

'But in what ship?'

'The caravel *Santa Engracia* lies less than twenty leagues from here. Her captain is dead of fever, and her crew tried to run off, but we have caught four sailors who can work the sails, and now we have you to navigate her.'

'My God!' said Rich. 'I suppose Roldan is captain?'

Moret giggled again behind him.

'Roldan? Good God, no! Who would want to sail under that lout? It is I who am captain, as you will do well to remember in future. We are twenty gentlemen of coat armour, and we shall carve out our own empire in the west.'

The first thought that came up in Rich's mind as he considered all these amazing statements was that the whole expedition was grossly illegal. Only the Admiral or those licensed by him had any right to explore the Indies; anyone else who should do so offended against not merely the Admiral but against the Crown. The gallows and the block awaited such offenders on their return. But a resounding success and a prodigious treasure might avert the penalty.

The immediate reaction to that notion was one of wonder at the incredible hardihood or rashness of those who had conceived the notion. Twenty gentlemen of coat armour, forsooth, with four sailors and a lawyer, were presuming to sail in a ridiculous caravel to 'carve out an empire' in a land wealthy enough to build palaces reaching to the sky. It would be a very different matter from the conquest of the helpless and lovable Indians of Española.

But this story told by the Slobberer with the missing lower lip had a chance of being true. It sounded a more likely tale than any Rich had yet heard; the facts that the Slobberer was of a different breed, and that he was mutilated in a fashion unknown in these islands, constituted valuable evidence that his story was not like the wild tales which the Admiral had first gathered, of Cibao with its golden mountains and of the valley of emeralds. The Slobberer might have some authentic knowledge of a real kingdom which certainly ought to be found in a north-westerly direction; if not the kingdom of the Grand Cham, then at least a dependency of it.

For a moment Rich felt a sensation almost of pleasurable excitement at the thought of such an adventure. He had to catch himself up suddenly and bring down his thoughts to a matter-of-fact level. How could he possibly navigate a ship from Española to China or Cipangu? Perhaps, as Garcia had in mind, the sailors would know how to trim the sails and attend to the other details of the practical handling of the ship. Perhaps he himself was capable of estimating the speed of the ship, and with the needle he would know something of her course. The astrolabe would give him a notion of their position relative to the equinoctial line; he raked back in his memory to see what he knew of the Admiral's table of the sun's height above the horizon–he could at least make a rough allownace for its variation, or perhaps there was a copy of the table on board the *Santa Engracia*. That would be a check on the other calculation, and would help him in the matter of allowing for currents and leeway and the uncertainty of the needle. Vaguely, very vaguely, he would have some sort of notion as to where they were. He could never hope to find his way back to Española if they wanted to return, but he could at least turn the ship's head and sail her eastward–eastward–eastward until he had found Africa or Spain or Portugal or France or even England. The Old World was too big a place even for him to miss.

Then, like a cold douche, common sense returned again. The whole plan was too mad, too insane. How could he be expected to handle a ship, with only his sketchy theoretical knowledge? There would be all kinds of emergencies to deal with–he remembered how the Admiral had brought the *Holy Name* through the Serpent's Mouth and then through the Dragon's Mouths. He could not handle a ship like that. He knew nothing about beating to windward off a lee shore. He did not have the practised seaman's uncanny knack of guessing the trend of a shoal from the successive casts of the lead. These hot-headed Spanish caballeros had no conception at all of the difficulty of the task they proposed to set him–if for no other reason, they were accustomed to the Admiral's phenomenal seamanship.

'I never heard of such a ridiculous plan in all my life,' he burst out.

'So that is what you think?' replied Garcia. There was a polite lack of interest in his manner.

'Yes!' said Rich. 'And what's more—'

Nobody appeared to listen to what more he had to say. The horses broke into a trot, and Rich, joggling about in his saddle, found his flow of eloquence impeded. He knew then that nothing he could say would deter these hotheads from their plan. Nothing would induce them to set him free to return to San Domingo and the *Holy Name*. He relapsed again into miserable silence, while the horses pushed on in the darkness, trotting whenever their fatigue and the conditions would allow, and walking in the intervals. Fatigue soon came to numb his misery. He was sleepy, and an hour or two on horseback was quite sufficient exercise for his soft limbs. The men of iron who rode with him had no idea of fatigue. The loss of a night's rest, the riding of a dozen leagues on horseback were nothing to them. Rich bumped miserably along with them through the night; before dawn he had actually dozed once or twice in the saddle for a few nightmare seconds, only saving himself from falling headlong by a wild clutch at his horse's invisible mane.

20

At dawn Garcia broke his long silence.

'There's the *Santa Engracia*,' he said.

The path had brought them down to the sea's edge here, and the horses were trotting over a beach of firm black sand overhung by the luxuriant green cliffs. A mile ahead a torrential stream notched the steep scarp, and in the shelter of the tiny bay there lay a little ship, a two-masted caravel, her curving lateen yards with their furled sails silhouetted in black against the blue and silver sea. There were huts on the beach, and at their approach people came forth to welcome them. There was Bernardo de Tarpia and Mariano Giraldez, Julio Zerain and Mauricio Galindo–all the hot-headed young gentlemen; Rich could have listed their names without seeing them. There were four or five swaggerers whom he did not know; he presumed they were followers of Roldan whom he had never met before, and the notion was confirmed by the raggedness of their clothing. There were a few depressed Indians, and one with a gap where his lower lip should have been, though which his teeth were visible; this must be el Baboso of whom Garcia had spoken. There were a dozen Indian women whose finery proved that they were the mistresses of Spaniards and not the wives of Indians.

'You found him, then?' commented Tarpia. 'Welcome, learned doctor sailing-master.'

'Good morning,' said Rich.

He was sick with fatigue and fright, but he was determined not to allow the young bloods' gibes to hurt him visibly. If the inevitable really were inevitable, he could cultivate a stoical resignation towards it. His mind went off at a tangent, all the same, refusing to face the present. It groped wildly about trying to recall half-forgotten memories of some learned Schoolman's disquisition on the intrinsically inevitable as compared with the inevitable decreed by God. He slid stiffly off his horse and looked round him, dazed.

'Gold and pearls and emeralds!' said young Alfonso de Avila, clapping him on the shoulder. 'And no grubbing in the earth for them, either.'

It was extraordinary how the lure of easily won gold persisted, despite disillusionments. But young Avila was excited like a child about this new move. He was babbling pleasurably about the kingdoms they were going to assail, and the glory they were going to win; for him the treasure would be merely a measure of their success, just as a lawyer's eminence might be roughly estimated by the size of his fees.

Garcia's voice broke through the chatter.

'Everyone on board,' he said, curtly. 'We may have Roldan or the Admiral on our tracks at any minute. Tarpia, take charge of Rich.'

The longboat lay beside the beach; the Indians pulled at the oars–the hidalgos could not sink their dignity sufficiently to do manual work as long as there was someone else who could be made to do it for them–and within five minutes of Garcia's order Rich was hoisting himself wearily up over the side of the caravel. João de Setubal, the eccentric Portuguese, was there, and three or four others; apparently their duty had been to prevent the escape of the remaining four seamen.

'Here's your crew, sailing-master,' said Tarpia.

The four seamen grinned at him half nervously, half sullenly. It was clear that the new venture was not at all to their taste. Rich looked as sullenly back at them. The sun was already hot, and pained his eyes; he felt the *Santa Engracia* heave under his feet as a big roller lifted her.

'Who are you?' he said. 'What service have you seen?'

They answered him in Catalan, like sweet music after the harsh Castilian. They were fishermen from Villanueva, pressed the year before for service on the Ocean. They could reef and steer, and had spent their lives at sea.

'One of you must be boatswain,' said Rich. 'Which is it to be?'

Fortunately there seemed to be no doubt about that. Three thumbs were pointed at once to the fourth man, the blue-eyed and broad-shouldered Tomas–stoop-shouldered, too, for middle age had begun to curve his spine.

'Tomas, you are boatswain,' said Rich. It was a relief to have found someone on whom he could fob off some of his responsibility.

The second boatload from the shore was already alongside; Garcia had come with it.

'Don Narciso,' he said, 'the horses have to be got on board.'

They were swimming the horses out the short distance from the shore behind the longboat; even at her low waist the *Santa Engracia*'s rail was six good feet above the water's edge. Rich looked at Tomas in a panic.

'Shall I get the slings ready, sir?' asked Tomas.

'Yes,' said Rich.

The sailors pelted up the shrouds; there was tackle already rove on the yards–apparently they had been hoisting in stores and water yesterday. The slings were dropped to the boat, and passed under the belly of one of the horses.

'Here,' said Tomas to a bewildered Indian standing by. 'Tail on.'

The ropes were pushed into the hands of the Indians, and, under Tomas's urging, they walked away with them, and the horse, plunging helplessly, rose into the air. Tomas himself swung the brute inboard, the Indians walking cautiously forward again, and the horse was lowered into the waist. It was amazing how easy it was when one knew exactly how to do it. At a word from Garcia half a dozen young hidalgos took charge of the beasts–there was nothing undignified or unknightly about attending to horses when necessary. To learn how to do so had been part of the education of every hidalgo in his boyhood.

'We are ready to sail now, sailing-master,' said Garcia.

This was all mad, unreal. It must be a nightmare–it could not really be happening to him, the learned Narciso Rich. As though battering with a nightmare he strove to postpone the moment of departure; he felt that if only he could postpone it long enough he might wake up and find himself back in San Domingo, about to sail for Spain in the *Holy Name*.

'But what about stores?' he asked. 'Food? Water?'

'We have spent the last week collecting food,' said Garcia. 'The ship has dried meat, cassava and corn for forty people for two months. There is forage for the horses, and every water-cask is full.'

'And charts? And instruments?'

'Everything the captain had is still in his cabin. He found his way here with them from Spain when he came with Ballester.'

'I had better see them first.'

Garcia's thick brows came together with irritation.

'This is not the moment for wasting time,' he said. 'Hoist sail at once–you can do the rest when we are on our way.'

Garcia's little eyes were like an angry pig's. He glowered at Rich, his hands on his hips and his body inclined forward towards him.

'I know enough about navigation,' he said, menacingly, 'to know we must sail westward along this island before we turn north. I might find I could do without a navigator altogether, and in that case—'

He took his right hand from his hip and pointed significantly, over-side. Rich could not meet his gaze, and was ashamed of himself because of it. He turned away.

'Very well,' he said faintly.

And even then the prayer that he began to breathe was cut short without his realizing it by the way the problem of getting under way captured his interest–if his active mind were employed it was hard for him to remain frightened. He looked up at the mast-head; the pennant there was flapping gently in an easterly wind; the land wind had dropped and the sea breeze had not begun yet to blow. The ship was riding bows on to the wind; he had to turn her about as she got under way. The theory of the manoeuvre was simple, and he had often enough seen it put into practice. It was an interesting experience to have to do it himself.

'Tomas,' he said. 'Set the Indians to up anchor. And I want the foresail ready to set.'

Tomas nodded at him, blinking in the sun.

'Who'll take the tiller, sir? It'll take the four of us to set sail.'

'I will,' said Rich, desperately. He had never held a ship's tiller in his life before, but he knew the theory of it.

He walked aft and set his hand on the big lever, swinging it tentatively. It seemed easy enough. Tomas had collected a band of Indians at the windlass–from the docility with which they obeyed him it was obvious that they were already accustomed to working under him, presumably during the business of provisioning the ship. The windlass began to clack, the Indians straining at the handles as they dragged the ship up to her anchor against the wind. The seamen were ready to set the foresail–two of them had just finished casting off the gaskets.

'Straight up and down, sir!' shouted Tomas, leaning over the bows to look at the cable.

'Hoist away!' shouted Rich; he swallowed hard as soon as the words were out of his mouth.

The anchor came up, and Tomas rushed back to help with the foresail. As the ponderous canvas spread Rich felt the tiller in his hand come to life; the ship was gathering sternway. He knew what he had to do. He put the tiller hard over, for the ship had only to lie in the tiniest fraction across the wind for the big foresail to wing her round like a weathercock. She lurched and hesitated, and Rich in a sudden panic brought the tiller across to the other side. Tomas was watching him, apparently awaiting more orders, but Rich had none to give. Nevertheless, Tomas kept his head–he saw on which side Rich had at last decided to hold the tiller, and ran with his men to brace the yard round. Rich felt the motion of the ship change as she swung across the swell; a glance at the island revealed the shore to be slowly revolving round him. He struggled wildly to keep his head clear; it was the ship that was turning, not the island. The big foresail was doing its work, and he flung his weight against the tiller to catch the ship lest she swung too far. There was some new order he ought to give to Tomas, but he did not know what it was, so he took one hand from the tiller and waved it in the hope that Tomas would understand.

Fortunately Tomas did so; he braced the yard square and the ship steadied on her course before the wind with no more than a lurch or two. Rich looked up at the mast-head pennant–it was streaming ahead. The shore lay on his right hand, and the ship must be pointing west nearly enough. As he centred the tiller he glanced at the compass, but that was still chasing its tail round and round in its basin; it would be several minutes before it settled down. He experimented timidly with the tiller as soon as he saw that the ship was heading a trifle in shore; the ship answered, but with more of a sullen obstinacy than he expected. It was only with a considerable exertion of strength that he was able to hold her on her proper course.

'Set the mainsail, sir?' asked Tomas. He was so obviously expecting an affirmative answer that Rich was constrained to give him one, but it was with an inward qualm–he had as much as he could do to steer as it was, and he doubted his strength to hold her if more canvas were spread. But the mainsail expanded inexorably while the ropes squealed in the blocks; Rich distinctly felt the ship under his feet gather increased speed as the mainsail bellied out in the wind and it seemed to him as if the tiller would soon pull his arms out of their sockets. And then, as Tomas took his men to the braces, Rich suddenly felt the ship become more manageable. The tiller ceased to be a thing to be fought and struggled with. It became a sweet tool of whose every motion–as his tentative experiments soon proved–the ship was immediately conscious.

Of course, he told himself, he should have expected that. Mainsail and foresail were designed to counterpoise each other almost exactly, so that the tiller and rudder held the delicate balance between two nearly equal forces. A touch, now, and she swung to the right. A touch, and she swung to the left–the feeling of mastery was most impressive. Rich came back to his senses with a guilty start; Tomas was looking at him curiously as he swayed the ship about in unseamanlike fashion, and he hurriedly steadied her. The wind blew on the back of his neck, and he was unconscious of the heat of the sun and of his fatigue. In that triumphant moment he felt as if he could steer the ship for ever.

He would rather steer a ship than ride a horse any day–never in the saddle had he felt this superb confidence. But he felt he could not indulge himself at present. He had to make up his mind about what course to steer, and as the numerous factors governing that problem came tumbling into his mind he felt the need for giving it his undivided attention.

'Send a hand to the tiller, Tomas,' he called.

One of the seamen came shambling aft, and took over the steering. He looked at Rich inquiringly for the course; Rich took a stride or two up and down the deck as he made his calculations. He remembered the glimpses he had had of the Admiral's chart–somewhere not far ahead the cape of Alta Vela trended far to the south and would have to be circumnavigated, while soon the wind would shift so as to blow direct upon the shore. It would undoubtedly be as well to get as far to the southward now as he could, so as to have reserve in hand. And the needle in these waters pointed to the east of north–he would have to allow for that, too. On the other hand, if he set too southerly a course it might take him out of sight of land. Rich suddenly realized that he was not nearly as afraid of that as he was of finding himself on a lee shore during the night. He yearned to have plenty of sea all round him, and it was delightful to discover that he was quite confident of finding Española again should he run it out of sight. He bent over the compass and took in his hand the white peg which marked the course to be set, hesitated for a space, and then with decision he put it into the next hole to the east of south.

'So!' he said.

The helmsman brought the tiller over, and the ship began to swing round. Rich knew that the sails must be trimmed to the wind, but he was vague about the exact wording of the orders necessary. He looked over at Tomas, and saw with pleasure that he was making ready to brace the yards round without orders. Rich nodded to him to continue.

The *Santa Engracia* now had the wind almost abeam; she was lying over to it, with plenty of spray coming over the weatherside, making music through the water, and all the rigging harping together, and the green mountains of Española falling fast astern. Rich looked round to find Garcia staring fixedly at him.

'Our course should be west, along the island,' said Garcia, suspiciously. 'Why are we going south?'

'Because it is necessary,' said Rich, crossly, 'because—'

As soon as he had begun upon it he gave up, before the prospect of all the difficulties, the attempt to explain his technique. He had just performed successfully the feat of getting the *Santa Engracia* under way and on her course, and perhaps his feeling of achievement gave him sufficient elation, combined with his annoyance, to answer Garcia with spirit.

'You want me to navigate this ship,' he said. 'Then allow me to navigate her. If you could do it better yourself there was no need to kidnap me to do it for you.'

'Holy Mary!' said Garcia, 'how quick we are to take offence!'

But he himself had taken none, apparently, and Rich actually forgot him, momentarily, as he looked round the ship of which he was in charge. The feeling of elation still persisted, despite his fatigue–or perhaps because of it, for he was a little light-headed through lack of sleep. The beginning of his captaincy had been marked with brilliant success. Perhaps this business was not nearly as difficult as he had thought it to be. Perhaps he would steer the *Santa Engracia* safely to China and home again to Spain. Perhaps—

The cold fit of common sense broke over him again in a wave. He had been thinking nothing but nonsense–he must beware of these fits of misguided enthusiasm. One such, during his conversation with the King, had been responsible for his ever coming to the Indies. He was acting like a hot-headed boy instead of like a man of a mature forty who had already risen to the topmost height of his own profession. He was quite as mad as Garcia, who was setting out with a single caravel with twenty men and four horses to find and conquer the Grand Khan. And–it was extraordinary how muddled his mind was now–he had been on the point of forgetting again that he himself was just as involved as Garcia in this mad attempt. Sick despair closed in upon him again.

Tomas had come aft; he hesitated for a moment between Garcia and Rich, and then finally addressed himself to Rich.

'Shall I start the Indians baling, sir?' he asked. 'She hasn't been baled to-day, and she makes water fast. And there's the stores we put in the forehold, sir. I don't like—'

Apparently Tomas had a great deal on his mind regarding the condition of the ship. He talked volubly, while Rich only half heard him. Rich remembered how the captain ought to make a tour of inspection round his command every morning and settle the day's work. He allowed Tomas to lead him forward, and below. He agreed about the necessity for baling. He looked dubiously at a pile of stores in the forehold, packed in queer containers, half sack, half basket, peculiar to Española, and he left it to Tomas to decide how they should be re-stowed. What with weed and worms and wear and tear the *Santa Engracia* was in poor condition, he was told–Tomas went as far as to say, when they were in solitude of the afterhold, that he would be dubious about sailing her from Palma to Barcelona on a summer's day.

But Rich was growing more and more dizzy with fatigue and lack of sleep. He tried to display an owlish intelligence as Tomas poured out his troubles, answering his remarks with non-committal monosyllables. He escaped from him in the end and found his way to the captain's cabin under the poop. In a drawer of the little table there he came across the late captain's papers and instruments. There was a roll of accounts of one sort and another, all dealing with the outward voyage and apparently of no more importance. There was a paper of sailing instructions in the handwriting of the Admiral himself, dealing with the problem of finding Española from Spain–Rich's swimming eyes could not struggle with that now. There was a rough chart of the Indies, apparently by the same hand; that might be useful. There was astrolabe and cross staff, and, in a leather pouch, a table of the sun's declination at weekly intervals throughout the year. That was all Rich wanted to know. He pushed the other things aside, and laid his head upon his arms on the table as he sat on the stool screwed to the deck. And in that attitude, despite the rolling of the ship, he slept heavily for a couple of hours.

21

The voyage went on, somehow. On the third day they doubled Cape Alta Vela and were able to set a westerly course along the southern coast of Española, the old *Santa Engracia*, leaking like a sieve and encumbered with weeds a yard long on her bottom, lumbering along before the persistent urging of the wind. Far on the horizon to the north rose the green mountains of the island. Each day brought its scorching sunshine and its torrential rain, its blue skies and its rainbows.

Each day brought afresh to Rich the strange feeling of the unreality of it all, despite the harsh realism of the ship's routine, the baling and the constant repairs. He practised diligently each day with astrolabe and cross staff–he told himself that his very life might depend on his skilful use of them, while at the same time he found it impossible to believe. He worked out the little calculation necessary to ascertain the speed of the ship by measuring with his pulse the time taken by an object thrown overboard from the bow to reach the stern. He pored long and diligently over the Admiral's chart of the Indies, at the long sweep of islands at its eastern end where–as the last voyage had ascertained–lay Trinidad and the mysterious country of the Orinoco and the Earthly Paradise. Westmost of the chain lay Española, divided by a narrow strait from the long peninsula of Cuba which jutted out two hundred leagues or so from the unknown mainland of China or India. So the Admiral had drawn it; Rich was aware that there had been whispers that Cuba was merely another island, the vastest of them all. The Admiral had silenced the whispers by decreeing that any such whisperer would lose his tongue.

But whether Cuba were an island or not, the task Garcia had laid upon him was to steer the *Santa Engracia* up through the strait between Cuba and Española, and then north-westerly, on and on until they reached the country el Baboso knew of, the land where the temples reached the sky and where worked gold was to be seen everywhere. Rich fancied it must be the land of the Great Khan which Marco Polo the Venetian had visited, but he occasionally had doubts. It might be some new unvisited empire, if it existed at all. If it existed at all–Rich could picture the *Santa Engracia* sailing on and on over the blue sea until her motley crew died of hunger and thirst and disease, himself among them. Or perhaps in that direction there really was an edge to the earth, despite the Admiral's denials, and the *Santa Engracia* might find herself hurtling over it to plunge into the depths. He tried to hint at his fear to Garcia, but Garcia only shrugged his shoulders and laughed callously. Despite his comfortable plumpness, Garcia was a man of iron will and quite without fear–without heart in his body, Rich came to think.

Certainly without a heart in his body. Three of the sailors–not Tomas–and four Indians were caught the second night by Julio Zerain trying to desert in the longboat; Rich heard the judgment which issued from Garcia's lips the next morning and heard the wild screams of the wretched men as their punishment was dealt out to them. He could not bear to listen–more especially as he would certainly have joined in the attempt if the sailors had taken him into their confidence. He might be screaming there on the deck now, in that case. It was something to thank God for that he had not been allowed the captain's cabin, but had had to sleep in the 'tweendecks with a dozen Spaniards. They had kept him from any such perilous endeavour. He would die–he was sure of it–if ever he were punished in that manner. That morning he knew worse misery of soul than ever since he had left Spain; more could not be said than that.

There was other bloodshed on board. Rich did not know how the quarrel started, but he heard shouts and the clash of steel forward; Fernando Berrocal and Pablo Mourentan had their swords out–the blades flashed fiercely in the sunshine–and were fighting out their quarrel in the manner of hot-blooded youth. Garcia came up from below on the run; he roared like a bull and dashed forward drawing his sword. Tarpia appeared from nowhere, sword drawn, too. Berrocal's blade was beaten out of his hand. Mourentan, thrusting wildly at Garcia in his excitement, received a sword cut on his shoulder which sent him staggering and helpless to the rail.

'Fools!' bellowed Garcia. 'I will have no fighting in this ship. That fool there has less than he deserves. The next man to draw steel will hang. I swear it by the Holy Sacrament.'

He glowered round at the silent crowd and pointed to the yardarm, magnificently animal despite his fat and his rags. Perhaps he remembered the rules on board the *Holy Name* of which Acevedo had once reminded him. He needed every fighting man in the campaign he was planning, and he had come to appreciate not only how easily quarrels may arise in the cramped life aboard ship, but also how easily the whole ship's company might become involved. Rich thought bitterly of the time when he had believed himself to be acquiring the art of managing men–including this same Garcia. He knew now that he could never compare himself with him. He was no man of action; in a great shaking-up like this expedition to the Indies every man found his own level in time.

Seventy leagues to the west of Alta Vela lay Cape San Miguel, the westernmost point of Española; it interested Rich to find that they reached it at the very moment which he predicted. His dead reckoning had been correct, and so was the Admiral's chart–or else they both contained the same error. Rich might at one time have speculated deeply on the philosophy of compensating errors, but nowadays he was too engrossed in hourly problems to waste time. He accepted God's mercy with gratitude and left it at that; as soon as he saw the shore of Española trending away back to the eastward from the bluff green eminence of San Miguel, and knew he had made all the westing necessary, he had to lay a fresh course through the straits, for there was no leeway to spare at all on this next leg of the passage.

No leeway to spare; indeed it became apparent that they would never double Cuba in a single tack. For as they bore northward the wind backed northward as well. Rich and Tomas laid the *Santa Engracia* as close to the wind as they could, striving to make northing while they still had sea room, but she drifted away to leeward spiritlessly, encumbered by her weeds. Rich gazed despairingly at the tell-tale angle which his unaided eye could observe between the trace of her wake and the line of her masts. The cliffs of Cuba loomed in sight, a hard line on the horizon ahead, and still the wind blew from the north. They had to wear the ship round, heading back almost in the direction in which they had come.

Garcia watched the manoeuvre curiously and suspiciously.

'Why back to Española, navigator?' he asked. There was a grim jocularity in his tone. 'I ask you to sail north-west and'–he glanced up at the sun–'even a poor landsman like myself can see you are sailing south-east.'

Rich endeavoured to explain the difficulty he was encountering. Today there was none of the elation which previously had led him to answer with spirit. He was too frightened of Garcia again now.

'I see,' said Garcia, consideringly, but with still a hint of unsatisfied suspicion in his voice. 'But you do not want to go *too* close to Española, do you? We would not like to lose you, learned doctor–not now that you have proved your worth. And I might add that we will see that we do not.'

Hastily Rich disclaimed any thought of attempting to desert from the *Santa Engracia*, but the words died away lamely in face of the cynical smile on Garcia's face.

'I have no need of further assurance of your loyalty, learned Don Narciso,' said Garcia, with a glance forward to where the previous deserters had suffered.

But he grew more human as he stood beside Rich watching the ship's progress on the other tack.

'These zigzag methods call for much explanation to me,' he said. 'I served for a term in His Highness's galleys against the Moors. We never used them there. The slaves took the oars and we went wherever we wished. When the time serves I will have galleys built for use in these waters. There are slaves enought to be found.'

There were two days when the wind failed altogether, and the *Santa Engracia* wallowed helplessly in the calm, with San Miguel still in sight to the eastward, and the porpoises sported round her as if to show their contempt for her sluggishness, and the flying fish furrowed the deep blue of the water. When it blew again, the wind was still hardly east of north, and day by day the *Santa Engracia* beat back and forth across the wide channel, gaining hardly more than a few yards each day, while tempers grew short on board and the murmuring hidalgos, who had actually come to recognize the shores, which encompassed them, asked bitterly how long the blundering incompetence of their navigator was going to keep them confined. Rich began to pray for a southerly wind, which would carry them off towards the mad adventure which he so much dreaded.

22

Long afterwards Rich remembered those prayers; he suspected that it was because of his impiety and incipient heresy that his petition was granted in the fashion which God chose. It was two weeks before the feast of San Narciso of Gerona (who had always stood his friend) to which he had been looking forward as perhaps bringing relief from his troubles. The wind had died away again when they had nearly clawed their way northward to the open sea, and the *Santa Engracia* drifted helplessly with Cuba barely in sight from the masthead and Española invisible over the horizon. It was oppressively hot, although there was a thin veil of cloud over the sky, through which the sun showed only at rare intervals and then a mere ghost of his usual self. The *Santa Engracia* pitched and rolled in a swell which was extraordinarily heavy for the narrow waters in which they lay. Spaniards and Indians sat helpless about the decks, gasping in the heat; Rich felt his clothes wet upon his back.

He prayed for a wind, any wind, and the wind came. Gently it came at first, only a mild puff, steadying the ship in her rolling and making the sails flap loudly. Rich started from the deck in wild excitement. Those puffs of wind were from the south–a few hours of this would see them through the straits, and free. Tomas noticed the puffs of wind, too; he was having the yards braced round in haste. Soon there was quite a breeze blowing from the southward, piping in the rigging, and the *Santa Engracia* was under full sail before it, heading gallantly to the northward over the grey sea.

But the breeze had brought no relief from the heat, curiously enough. It was a hot wind, a fiery wind. Rich felt his skin still drip even while the breeze blew upon him. There was an Indian on the forecastle chattering excitedly to Tomas, and Tomas was trying to puzzle out what he was saying. He led the Indian aft to where Rich stood with Garcia, and the Indian babbled in panic.

'Hurricane,' he was saying, or some word like that. He was frantic with the desire to express his meaning–it was a most vivid example of the curse of Babel with which God had afflicted the world because of its impiety.

'Hurricane,' said the Indian again, wreathing his hands. 'Hurricane–big wind.'

He pointed up to the sky and waved his arms; the clouds to which he was pointing had a baleful yellow gleam now which was echoed in the sea below.

'Big wind,' said the Indian, and now that he had the Spanish words he had sought he amplified them.

'Big–big–big–big wind,' he said, wildly. He was trying to convey to his stolid taskmasters the impression of a wind bigger than their imagination could conceive. Rich and Tomas exchanged glances.

'Wind's freshening,' said Tomas. It was blowing half a gale, certainly, and

Santa Engracia was heaving and plunging before it over the topaze sea.

'You had better shorten sail, Tomas,' said Rich, and then, as bigger gusts came, 'No, heave her to.'

Tomas nodded decided approval and rushed forward; the Indians there were all scurrying to and fro, wringing their hands and wailing, 'Hurricane, hurricane'–there was something about the strange Indian word which filled them with terror. Only two or three were in a fit condition to help Tomas and his men as they battled with the foresail. Rich saw Tomas, clearly frightened now, beckon to some of the Spaniards at hand for assistance, and some of them in the urgency of the moment actually ran to help him. Rich went to the tiller to help the man there heave her to–it was a muddled moment, but the ship came round under the pressure of the mainsail while only the top of one wave came in over the waist amid screams from the Indians. The seamen got the mainsail in, leaving only the lower corner spread; with the yard braced right round and the tiller hard over the ship rode nearly bows on to the wind, meeting the sea with her starboard bow. She was as safe as they could make her, now, and already the wind was blowing a full gale. Garcia came, blown by the wind, aft to Rich, with Manuel Abello, the only one of the old colonists who had joined the expedition, behind him.

'Abello here knows what the Indians are saying,' he shouted in Rich's ear. 'He has seen these hurricanes before.'

Abello was hatless, and his long hair and beard were blown into a wild mop in front of his face.

'Nothing can live in a hurricane,' he shouted. 'Make for land.'

Rich had no words for him. It was not the moment to try to explain that the poor old *Santa Engracia*, hove to before a full gale, could do nothing more now except try to live through it–the Admiral himself would attempt no more. Tomas was clawing his way round the deck with his men, driving the Indians below and making all as secure as might be.

'Why don't you do as he says?' shouted Garcia.

'I can't–' said Rich.

The force of the wind suddenly redoubled itself. It shifted a couple of points and flung itself howling upon the *Santa Engracia*–Rich saw the line of the wind hurtling over the surface of the water. The *Santa Engracia* lay over, took a huge wave over her bows, and then wearily came up to the wind again. The wind was nearly taking them off their feet. They felt as if they were being pushed by something solid, and it was still increasing in force; they had all been dashed against the lee rail, and it was with incredible difficulty that they regained their footing. Rich felt himself being swept away again. He seized a rope's end and began to tie himself to the rail, with great clumsy knots–it seemed mad for a grown man to tie himself to his ship for fear of being blown away, but everything in this world was mad. The deck forward was strangely bare–only Tomas and another man were to be seen there, clutching the rail. The sea they had shipped must have swept the others away. Tomas saw Rich looking at him and pointed up to the mainsail. The small rag of canvas which had been left spread there was blowing out, expanding like a bladder as the gaskets gave way. Next moment the whole sail was loose; a moment later it had flogged itself into fragments which cracked like gigantic whips in the gale with a noise which even the gale could not drown.

The ship must be hurtling to leeward at an astonishing pace, thought Rich, with a mad clarity of mind. He wondered how, when he next worked out the ship's position, he could allow for all this leeway whose pace and direction were quite unknown to him. Then he told himself he would most likely never work out the ship's position again. And he was in mortal sin–he had been intending to confess before sailing in the *Holy Name*. He was frightened now, for the first time since the gale began, and he tried to pray into the shrieking wind.

A huge wave suddenly popped up from nowhere and came tumbling over the poop. Rich felt himself dashed against the rail with terrific force; he choked and strangled and struggled in the water until the *Santa Engracia* shook herself free. Garcia and Abello were gone from beside him, and Rich felt nothing more than a neutral callousness for their fate. The masts went directly after–Rich actually was unaware of the loss of the foremast, but he saw the weather shrouds of the mainmast part and the wind whirl the mast away like a chip. Everything else on deck was going, too–tiller and windlass and boat and all. Only Tomas was still there, bound to the forecastle rail. The *Santa Engracia* was rolling like a spiritless log on the surface of the sea.

A little crowd of people, Spaniards and Italians, came suddenly pouring into the waist, as it rolled awash, from out of the forecastle. The sea took them, too; they must have been driven out of their shelter by the rising of the water within. For the *Santa Engracia* was low in the water by now; the numerous seas she had shipped must have practically filled her, and every sea now was sweeping across her decks and burying Rich in its foam. He realized dully that she would not sink now, for she carried insufficient ballast and cargo for that, and tried to think what would happen to her next as she drifted waterlogged and almost below the surface. Presumably her fastenings would give way under the continual drenching, and she would go to pieces in the end, and that would be the time when he would drown. But while this infernal wind blew and while he was so continually submerged he was incapable of sufficient thought to be afraid any more–it was as if he were standing aside and incuriously watching the body of the learned Narciso Rich battered by the waves.

At nightfall he was still alive, drooping half conscious in his bonds as the seas swept over him, and deaf to the wild roaring of the wind in his ears. He was not aware of the moment when the ship struck land, although he must have come to his senses directly after. Wind and sea were more insensate than ever in the roaring night; there was white foam everywhere, faintly visible in the darkness, and huge waves seemed to be beating upon him with a more direct violence than before. Under his feet and through the mad din of wind and water he was conscious of a thundering noise as the ship pounded and broke. He guessed that the ship had struck land and in panic, like waking from a nightmare, he struggled to free himself from the rope that had bound him fast so far. The deck heaved and canted, smothered under a huge roller. Then the poop broke clear, hurtling over the reef and across the lagoon. Rich felt himself and the deck tossed over and over, and they struck solid land in a welter of crashing fragments. The wind took charge of him as he hit the beach and blew him farther inshore. He clutched feebly and quite ineffectively at the darkness, while the wind flung him through and over, up the slope. He felt vegetation–some kind of cane–under him. Then he fell down another slope; there was water in his face until he struggled clear. A freak of the wind had dropped him into the lee of a nearly vertical bank, so that the giant's fingers of the hurricane could no longer reach under him and hurl him farther. He lay there half-conscious; at rare intervals a shattering sob broke from his lips, while overhead the gale howled and yelled in the pitchy black.

23

It was down into the depths of a ravine that the wind had dropped Rich, perhaps the safest place in a hurricane that chance could have chosen for him. There was a stream flowing in the depths–Rich lay half in and half out of it for most of one day until he roused himself to crawl clear. The fresh water probably saved his life, for he was much too battered and bruised and ill to be able to move far. Overpowering thirst compelled him to bend his tortured neck and drink, the first time and at intervals after that; he felt no hunger, only the dreadful pain of his bruises, and he moaned like a sick child at every slight movement that he made. He had neither thought nor feeling for anything other than his pain and his thirst; late on the second day he raised himself for an instant on his hands and knees and looked around the ravine, but he collapsed again on his face. It was not until the day after that the feeble urge of life within him caused him to pull himself to his feet and stand swaying, while every tiny part of him protested fiercely against the effort. He was like a man flayed alive. He had hardly an atom of skin left upon him–his only clothes were his shoes and his leather breeches–and in addition to his innumerable deep bruises he had several serious cuts, caked now with black blood. He was weak and dizzy, but he made himself stagger along the ravine; he could not hope to attempt its steep sides, but after the first few steps progress became easier as his aching joints loosened, until fatigue caused him to sit down and rest again.

He emerged in the end upon the beach at the point where the ravine cut through the low cliff, round the corner from where the *Santa Engracia* had been blown ashore. The dazzling sunshine, in contrast with the comparative darkness of the ravine, blinded him completely for a space–the silver sand was as dazzling as the cloudless sky above. He sat on a rock again with his hands to his eyes while he recovered, but as he sat he became conscious of hunger, and it was the prodigious urge of hunger which drove him again to wander along the beach, seeking something to devour.

For several days, even in that smiling island, the problem of food occupied his attention to the exclusion of all else. The first solution was supplied by the discovery of a bag of unground Indian corn, cast up on the beach from the wreck of the *Santa Engracia*, all that he ever found of her except a few timbers. The grain was soggy with seawater, but he pounded it between two rocks and made a sort of raw porridge out of it which at least sufficed to fill his belly and give him strength to continue his search. Then he managed to kill a land crab with a rock, and ate the disgusting creature raw–he became accustomed very quickly to a diet of raw land crab. Most of the trees in the little island had been broken off short by the hurricane, and at his second attempt to push through the wild tangle to the low summit of the island he found a plantain tree-top full of fruit, tasteless and tough and not very digestible, but of considerable use in keeping his soul in his body–although the very violent reaction of his interior to this stimulating diet made him wonder more than once if the frail partnership were going to dissolve.

There were queer shell-fish to be discovered in enormous numbers among the rocks; he ate them, too, and survived. But the catch that really turned the scale was that of a turtle on the beach, crawling seaward after laying her eggs. Rich had just enough strength to struggle with her, avoiding the frantic snaps of her bony jaws, and with one wild effort he managed to turn her over by the aid of a bit of driftwood. The rest of the business was horrible, or would have been if he had not been so hungry–he had neither knife nor fire, and he had to make use of rocks and sharp shells. The lepers on the Cape Verdes had bathed in turtles' blood in the hopes of a cure; Rich very nearly did. Nevertheless, it was when he had eaten his fill of the rich food–gorging himself in the knowledge that in that hot sun the meat would be uneatable in a few hours–that he was able to come back to intellectual life again, and cease to be a mere food-hunting animal and become again a man able to think and look about him and to make plans for the future.

He was alone in this little island; of that he was sure by now. He was master of a little hummock of land, a mile long and half a mile wide, rising in the centre to a height of four hundred feet or so, surrounded by a white sandy beach and beyond that by almost continuous coral banks, and covered with the usual dense greenery which was already hastily repairing the ravages of the hurricane. He was unarmed–sword and belt and scabbard had vanished in the storm along with his coat and shirt. He had no tools save sticks and two big nails which he found in a fragment of the *Santa Engracia*. He was not at all sure where he was, but when he climbed as high as he could up the island summit he could see other small islands in the distance, while away to the southward there was a kind of different colouring to the sky and a faint mark on the horizon which he was almost sure must be Española.

He was not very conscious of the curse of loneliness. Indeed, rather on the contrary, he caught himself almost on the point of smiling once or twice at the irony of it that, of all the complement of the *Santa Engracia*, he should be the sole survivor. Garcia with his bull's strength, Tarpia with his skill at arms, Moret, young Avila, Tomas the seaman–the storm had killed them all except him, and he felt no particular regret for any of them save perhaps for Tomas. And even for Tomas he was mainly regretful because with his aid it might have been easier to build a boat.

For he was naturally determined to build a boat. Española lay only just over the horizon, and even if he hated Española he wanted to return there if only as the first stage of his road to Spain. His chances of being rescued if he waited were negligible, he knew–it might be ten years before a ship came even into sight, and with those coral banks littering the sea he knew that any ship would give his little island a wide berth, as unlikely to contain any reward for the danger of approaching it. He had not the least intention of ending his days on a diet of raw shell-fish and plantains; he wanted to return to Spain, to his comfortable house and his dignified position. His mind was running on food. He had eaten roast sucking-pig for his last meal in Spain, and he wanted most unbearably to eat roast sucking-pig again, with plenty of wholesome bread–not ship's biscuit, nor golden cakes of Indian corn, but good honest wheaten bread, although barley bread would serve at a pinch. He could have none of these until as a first step he had built a boat and traversed the fifty miles of sea that lay between him and Española. He set himself again to serious consideration of this question of a boat; his recent experiences had had this profound effect upon him, that he was prepared now to stake his life on the work of his own hands in a fashion he would have shrunk from doing a year ago.

There was driftwood in plenty, and he could supplement it by tearing branches from trees. With creepers he could bind it into faggots, and he could bind the faggots into some kind of raft. It would be a desperately unhandy craft, though, and it might take him as much as a week to paddle it fifty miles to Española. It would not be easy to contrive containers for a week's food and water–and would a craft tied together with creeper sustain for a week the working and straining of the big rollers which beat so steadily on his beaches? He doubted it. The thing might go to pieces in mid-ocean, even without a storm to help. He needed something much more like a boat; and in a boat he could use his corn sack as a sail, for there was plenty of north in the wind in these waters–as he had already painfully learned–and he could make the passage to Española in a single day, then.

Rich was altogether of much too intellectual a turn of mind to have any illusions as to the magnitude of the work before him; it is all the more to his credit that he set himself doggedly at his task, exploring the island for timber that might serve his purpose, and perfectly prepared with shells and stones and his two big nails to dig himself a dug-out canoe from a suitable tree-trunk–his mind was already busy with schemes for tying a keel of rock under the bottom to stabilize the thing and make it not merely less likely to roll over but to save the labour of hollowing it out more than a sketchy amount.

It only took him a single day to discover a suitable tree-trunk, but it took him two weeks to discover stones suitable to work with and to chip them to any sort of edge, for he spoiled nine-tenths of them. He was consumed with a furious energy for the work–his busy mind could not tolerate the empty idleness of the island with only the monotonous beating of the surf to windward and the cries of the birds. He chipped away remorselessly, sparing himself only the minimum of time to hunt for food; he grew lean and hard, and the sun burnt him almost to blackness. He reminded himself that when he was home again at last he would have a delightful time building up once more the corpulence essential to the dignity of a successful professional man. His most exciting discovery was of a thin vein of rock in an exposed scar in the very ravine where he had first fallen. It was of a dark green, nearly black, and when he chipped out a lump and smashed it, it broke like glass into a series of points best adapted for spearheads, perhaps, but with a dull cutting edge which made them possible for use as knives. With infinite patience he quarried out one heavy lump with as perfect an edge as he could hope for. Using that as an axe he quite doubled his rate of progress in the weary business of trimming off the boughs of his tree-trunk.

He went through a period of convulsive labour when he began the process of getting his log down to the beach–even when his canoe were fashioned it would still be too heavy to move with any ease, and it was better to move the log itself where the damage done would be immaterial. He learned much about the use of levers and ramps while he was engaged upon his task; the log lay on the side of a slope so that most of the work was straightforward, but twice he encountered cross ridges which had to be painfully surmounted. He slept each night in the open, hardly troubling to shelter himself under overhanging vegetation, for he was so weary each night that the heavy showers did not wake him. Certainly the winking white fireflies did not, as they danced round him–nor the ceaseless chirpings of the grasshoppers and the bellowing of the frogs.

Rich had made one miscalculation when he was considering his chances of being rescued. He had only had Spanish ships in mind, and he had never given a thought to Indians in canoes, and so it came about that all his labour was quite wasted. It was one noontide that the canoe came, at a moment when his log was poised on the brink of the last slope down to the beach and a few more heaves upon his lever would have sent it careering down to the water's edge. How long the canoe had been in sight he did not know, for he had been engrossed in his work; it was only when he paused that he saw it, with three men at the paddles, threading its way in through the shoals. He threw himself down into hiding the moment he perceived it–instant decision was easy to him now–and waited until it reached the shore and the three Indians had dragged it up the beach, before he seized his heavy lever and rushed down upon them.

They looked up at him in fright as he arrived, and scattered, squeaking with dismay; they may have recognized him as one of the terrible white men of whom they had heard, but just as likely his mere appearance was sufficiently terrifying to strike them with panic. One ran along the beach and the other two dived into the vegetation, and Rich found himself master of a canoe which, crude as it was, was far better than anything he could have hoped to make in three months. But it was a big boat for a single man to handle, and Española was far away. He would prefer to have a crew for the voyage, and he set himself to wonder how he could catch the Indians.

The Admiral had always managed to play upon their curiosity, he knew–he had studied his reports closely enough to remember that–and somehow he must manage to coax them within his reach. He looked into the canoe; it contained only a crude creeper fishing net and gourds of water and a few cakes of cassava bread–the sight even of cassava bread made his mouth water after his recent diet–nothing by which he could get them into his power. He wanted to eat their bread, but he thought that the sight of a man eating bread would be hardly sufficient to excite their curiosity. He took up his big lever, balanced it upright on his open hand, and walked solemnly down the beach with it. Then he raised it to his chin, and he was able to keep it poised there for a few unstable seconds. He picked up three white lumps of stone and tried to juggle with them–as a boy he had been able to keep three balls in the air at once, and he managed to make a clumsy effort to recapture his old skill. Stealing a glance sideways he saw that the Indian who had run along the beach had halted and was looking back, mystified; he was even retracing a few of his steps, hesitant, just like a child. Rich juggled all the harder, tossing the white stones higher and higher. He took his lever again, and spun it in his fingers, and he sat down on the thick gunwale of the canoe with his back to the land, twisting his lever and working his left elbow as if he was doing something mysterious with his left hand out of the Indian's sight. It was while he was so engaged that he heard soft footfalls on the sand behind him, and whisperings; he was careful to turn round as slowly as possible, lest a sudden movement should scare them away like the wild animals they were.

They were standing in a row, half a dozen yards off, and staring at him big-eyed; they jumped when he turned, and were poised for flight again, but they did not flee. Rich put down his lever and extended his hand in the gesture of peace.

'Good day,' he said soothingly.

They looked at each other, and nudged each other, but they said nothing.

'This is a very charming island,' he said. 'Do you come here for fish or turtles?'

They actually were smiling at the strange noise he made–these children of nature were never far from laughter if the white man had not actually laid his hands on them. He racked his brains in an effort to be more conversational. He pointed south-westwards.

'Cuba?' he asked.

They knew that name, and stirred with recognition.

'Cuba,' said one of them, nodding, and another added something unintelligible.

Rich pointed to the south.

'Española?' he asked, and then, correcting himself, 'Hayti? Hayti?'

They shrank back a little at that–to them clearly the name of Hayti was accursed. But the boldest one managed to nod in reply.

'Hayti,' he said.

The assurance was worth having, even if nothing else came from the interview. One of them stepped forward again, asking a question. He pointed to Rich and then to the south; Rich caught the word 'Hayti' repeated several times–he was being asked if he came from there, and he judged it best to disclaim all acquaintance with the place.

'Oh no, no, no,' he said, shaking his head. 'Me Cuba. Me Cuba. Hurricane.'

They knew that word, too, and there was a faint light of understanding in their faces; they chattered to each other as they debated how a hurricane could possibly have blown this queer bearded stranger all the way from Cuba. One of them sidled past him to the canoe, picked out a cassava cake, and gave it to him. He nodded and smiled his thanks, and ate, the cooked food grateful to his stomach although he did his best not to appear too hungry. The more normal his reactions the easier it would be to win their confidence. He rubbed his stomach and pointed down his throat–a plan was forming in his mind.

He picked up the end of the creeper net and pointed to the sea; they knew something of what he meant. He pointed to the sea again with a sweeping gesture of his arm, and rubbed his stomach again. They grasped what he wanted; this simple stranger needed some fish, and they were perfectly willing to oblige, here on this admirable seining beach. They came fearlessly forward now; one of them took up the end of the net while the other two, smiling, prepared to push the canoe into the water. Rich smiled, too, and casually picked up his lever and dropped it into the canoe before he bent to help them shove out. The canoe floated, and one of the two Indians prepared to paddle while the other paid out the net; they were only a little surprised when Rich climbed in behind them.

The canoe danced over the small surf as the single paddle drove it slowly forward; the other Indian, standing precariously, dropped the net over-side armful by armful. Farther and farther out they went, in a curve, until Rich, watching narrowly, decided that half the net was out and they about to curve back to the beach. The decisive moment had come. He scrambled forward and seized the whole remainder of the net, and lifted it in his arms and dumped it overboard amid the Indians' ejaculations of mild protest. He picked up his lever, poised it menacingly.

'Hayti,' he said, and pointed southward.

They protested much more strenuously at that, piping in their shrill voices and gesticulating despairingly.

'Hayti,' said Rich, inexorably. He swung his club back; he was ready to strike one Indian down if by so doing he could terrorise the other into paddling. The one he menaced screamed and cowered under the impending blow.

'Hayti,' said Rich, again, pointing to the paddles.

They gave way before his snarling ferocity–Rich was desperate now that there was this chance of reaching home. They picked up their paddles and began work; one of them was weeping like a girl. They headed out through the shallows to the open sea, while from the distant beach came the wailing of the third Indian, standing there puzzled and deserted. His voice mingled with the weird cry of the seabirds.

The canoe effected its passage to Española in the course of that night, with Rich steering by the sun while daylight lasted and by the North Star–he had to stand up in the unsteady canoe to discover it low down on the horizon–at night. The steady hours of paddling wore out the frail Indians entirely, even before darkness fell they were sobbing with fatigue and Rich had to goad them to work. Then later he allowed one to rest, sitting hunched up with his forehead on his knees, while the other worked; at first it had been hard to make them understand what he wanted, as they shrank and cowered before him, but they understood at last and paddled alternatively while Rich sat in the stern, sleeping in cat naps of a minute or two each, and waking with a jerk to see that his unwilling crew were still at their tasks and to set the canoe on her course again. The canoe rose and fell with dizzy insecurity over the dark invisible waves in whose depths the stars were reflected and the wind sighed overhead.

Just before dawn there was a sudden squall of wind and rain which blotted the world from sight, and for a few minutes Rich felt for the first time a sense of danger. He turned the canoe bows on into the wind and sea, and had to struggle hard to hold her there, but the odd little canoe, with its thick sides of light wood, rode the waves in a fantastically self-confident manner, threading her way through difficulties as though endowed with an intelligence of her own. Then the squall passed, and with the end of the squall dawn was lighting the eastern horizon, and to the southward there were mountains reaching to the sky, wild and jagged.

'Hayti!' said the Indians.

They turned faces yellow with fatigue towards him, dumbly imploring him not to force them to approach nearer to the accursed land, but Rich hardened his heart. With a stroke or two of his paddle he swung the canoe round towards the island, and then used the paddle to prod them into activity. The canoe danced and lurched over a quartering sea in response to a last effort from their weary arms, and the mountains grew steadily nearer until the white ribbon of surf at the base of the rocks was visible, and then the canoe ran alongside a natural pier of rock and Rich stepped out, so stiff and cramped that he could hardly stand straight.

The Indians still looked up at him apprehensively. They had not the spirit–or else the strength–to try to escape, and they could only sit and wonder what awful fate now awaited them in this land which the white devils had come to plague. Rich returned their gaze, looking thoughtfully down on them. He could still find a good use for the canoe, employing it to take him along the coast until he found a Spanish settlement, but the two Indians were so depressed and apprehensive and pitiful in appearance, that he found if difficult to bring himself to detain them further. He tried to debate the pros and cons of it coldly and practically, but he suddenly thought of what might happen to the poor wretches if his fellow Spaniards laid hands on them.

'Go!' he said, suddenly. 'Go home!'

They looked at him without comprehension, and he swept his hand in a wide gesture towards the horizon and pushed the canoe out a little way from the rock. Still they hardly understood until he turned his back on them and walked a little way inland. When he looked round again they were paddling bravely out to sea again, their fatigue forgotten in their new freedom. Rich found time to hope that they would remember to call at his own island to pick up their marooned companion, and then a great wave of elation caught him up to the exclusion of all other thoughts. He was back again in Española, whence ships sometimes sailed to Spain, and he was the sole survivor of a shipload of men all far tougher and stronger than he. He was all a-bubble with excitement as he breasted the cliff and set out to find his fellow men.

Rich walked a hundred and fifty miles through the forests before he found what he sought, and he spent sixteen days doing it. There were tracks through the forest, now almost vanished again as the Indians had ceased to use them. Three times they brought him to ruined villages whose decayed huts and deserted gardens had almost become part of primitive nature again, but there he found a few ears of corn and was able to dig up a few roots which kept him alive. The Indian inhabitants, he supposed, had died in battle or of disease, or were toiling away to the south gathering grains of gold in the mountains of

Cibao. But the fort of Isabella was somewhere to the eastward, and even though Isabella had been Roldan's late headquarters he would be able to obtain assistance to make his way to San Domingo. So Rich walked through the forest to Isabella.

They gave him help when he reached it; they even were anxious to make him welcome when once he had explained who he was and whence he came. They gave him clothing and food–it was good to set his teeth into meat again–and listened sympathetically while he told them of Garcia's wild scheme to discover a land of gold to the north-westward. They had heard of that land themselves–more than one vague account of it had drifted in to Española. In return they told him their news, of the wild disorders which had spread through the island again; how Anacaona, the mistress of Bartholomew Columbus, had been hanged for treason, and sixteen petty chiefs roasted alive at the same time.

They told him of madness and battle and bloodshed, but what they were most interested in was the fact that a new expedition had just reached San Domingo from Spain. It was under the command of one Francisco de Bobadilla, a High Steward of the Royal household in Spain, and the greatest noble who had as yet set foot in Española. He had some mysterious new powers; he had an army with which to enforce them. At the first news of his coming Roldan himself had made his way to San Domingo. How matters stood between the Admiral and Bobadilla they did not know, but–was Don Narciso acquainted with Don Francisco? That was very interesting. Did Don Narciso wish to repair at once to San Domingo? Of course. They would provide him with a horse and a guide immediately. Was there anything else they could do for him? A sword? Armour? He had only to ask. And if Don Francisco were to consult him on the legality of their recent behaviour, and of their grants of lands and slaves, Don Narciso would go to the trouble of assuring him that at Isabella they were all devoted subjects of the Crown, would he not? Rich nodded without committing himself, and took his guide and mounted his horse and rode for San Domingo.

It was five months and a week since Garcia had kidnapped him. The Court of Spain must have acted with unusual promptitude on receipt of his report, and he could guess what sort of orders and what sort of powers had been given to Don Francisco de Bobadilla and at the haste with which he had been sent out. But he hardly cared about that. Soon one at least of the ships which had come out would be sailing back to Spain–perhaps it might already have sailed. That was the rub. Rich urged his horse forward in his panic lest he should arrive too late to be able to sail in her.

24

There had been a hazy dream-like quality about many of his adventures when Rich had been experiencing misfortune; there was the same unreality about his good fortune. Rich could hardly believe that this was really he, sitting in the sternsheets of a boat pulling out to the caravel *Vizcaya* on his way to Spain. The boat's side on which his hand rested, the ladder which he climbed, the deck on which he set his feet, all were quite surprising in their solidarity, considering how he felt that they might at any moment dissolve like wreaths of cloud. The bustle of the ship making ready for departure, the screaming of the seabirds, were like noises heard in a dream. He was free, and he was returning home; perhaps at that very moment the sucking-pig was being engendered which he would eat as soon as he set foot in his own house again–sucking-pig with onions and a big slice of wheaten bread.

He looked over at the island. For him it was a place of only evil memories, and he never wanted to set eyes on it again; as he decided this he was conscious of the faintest incredible twinge of regret that his adventures were over. It was so incredible that he refused to pay any attention to it, even while he was prepared to admit that if time had been of no value he would have liked on his little island to have completed his own boat himself and sailed her back to Española instead of making use of the Indians and their canoe. But if that had been the case he would not have reached San Domingo for months, and he would not be sailing today in the *Vizcaya*, escaping from these pestilential Indies and on his way to Spain.

The Indies would get on without him–he was of no use there. Bobadilla had listened with patience to his account of the legal abuses in the island, and to his rough sketch of a system of government, but Bobadilla had his own ideas and would not act on his advice. Perhaps Bobadilla might be able to tame the headstrong mass of his subjects–he had started firmly enough by putting both the Admiral and Roldan under arrest. Certainly no scheme of reform whatever could be put in hand while those two were free. What would happen next, what would be the future of this empire, no one could foretell. He could guess that its boundaries would expand, that island after island would be steadily overrun and conquered, but whether condemned to ruin or prosperity would depend on Bobadilla and his successors. Conquest was certain, as long as Spain could supply restless and daring spirits like Garcia, prepared to attack any kingdom with a handful of men and horses. Someone in the future would take up Garcia's project again, and discover the land of gold to the north-west, and conquer it, even if it should be the kingdom of the Great Khan itself. That would be a notable commerce, the export merely of stout hearts and the import of rich gold; Spain would be wealthy and prosperous then. Rich found himself smiling when he remembered how he had been almost converted by Diego Alamo's prosaic suggestions about establishing a trade in hides and sugar and Africa negroes. Now that the island was already receding into his mental perspective he could see things clearer and wonder how he could ever have been carried away by such notions.

A boat was coming out to the *Vizcaya*; presumably it had on board Alonso de Villegio the captain, with Bobadilla's final despatches for Spain, and they would be under way directly. Villegio was a man of capacity, who had listened, at Bobadilla's side, with much attention to Rich's account of the island. He would be pleasant, sane company for Rich during the long voyage home, and a word in the King's ear (for Rich could be certain of the King's attention for a space on his arrival) could give him much deserved promotion, But in the stern of the boat, beside Villegio, was a strangely familiar figure. Rich recognized the bent shoulders and the white hair and beard immediately, and only hesitated to be certain because of the unlikeliness of what he saw.

The boat came alongside, and Villegio sprang lightly to the deck, his captain's eye taking in at a flash all the preparations for departure. Then he stood by the rail to help up the man who followed him; another sailor came to help and the head of a third was visible over the side engaged on the same task. And the man who mounted was in need of this help, for he was old and feeble and stiff. Furthermore, as he raised his hands to the rail there was a dull clanking to be heard. The Admiral was coming aboard with chains upon his wrists.

Rich was inexpressibly shocked. He had approved of the temporary confinement of the Admiral, on the grounds that it was necessary to keep him harmless until the reforms should be under way. But that the Admiral of the Ocean, the Viceroy of the Indies, the man who had discovered a new world, should be thus publicly put to shame by being packed off home in chains, without either trial or sentence, was a dreadful thing, and the more dreadful because it showed that Bobadilla was a tactless man who would never manage the Indies.

Rich hurried across to where the Admiral still stood by the ship's side, looking about him blindly and unseeing, the chain dangling from his wrists and the land breeze ruffling his white beard.

'Your Excellency,' he said, and bowed low. His heart was wrung with pity as the Admiral peered at him with rheumy eyes.

'Ah, Don Narciso,' said the Admiral, slowly.

All about them was clamour and bustle, as Villegio was giving orders for sail to be set and the anchor to be got in. Farewells were already being shouted from the boat alongside.

'It is dreadful to see Your Excellency treated in this fashion,' said Rich.

'It is not dreadful for me,' said the Admiral. 'This is the sort of gratitude that benefactors can always expect of the world. And Christ had his cross and crown of thorns, while I have only this chain.'

The ship was under way now, with her sails filled with the last of the land breeze, as she plunged southward to make an offing. Villegio returned to them now that the immediate business of departure was completed. He, too, bowed low.

'Your Excellency,' he said. 'I can remove that chain now, thank God.'

'And why?' asked the Admiral. 'What about the orders given by His genuine Excellency, Don Francisco de Bobadilla?'

Villegio snapped his fingers.

'I am at sea now,' he said. 'I am master of my ship, and no orders here have any weight save mine. I shall call the armourer.'

The Admiral restrained him with a gesture, the chain clattering as he put out his hand.

'No!' said the Admiral. 'Never! I wear this chain by order of the King, through his mouthpiece Bobadilla, and I shall continue to wear it until I am freed by the King's own order again. The world will see the sort of treatment the discoverer of the Indies has received.'

Villegio stood hesitant.

'Your Excellency,' interposed Rich. 'Take the chain off now for the sake of your own comfort. You can put it on again when we sight Spain.'

'No, no, no!' said the Admiral. 'I will not!'

Rich and Villegio exchanged glances. They both of them recognized the sort of fanaticism which brooked no argument.

'As Your Excellency pleases,' said Villegio, bowing again. He was already looking round him at his ship; there must have been scores of matters clamouring for his attention.

'I must ask Your Excellency's kindness to spare me for a few minutes again.'

The Admiral motioned him away with superb dignity.

'I understand,' he said. 'I myself was once a captain of a ship.'

As Villegio departed the Admiral rounded upon Rich.

'I had forgotten until now,' he said. 'But I suppose, Don Narciso, that I have you to thank for this treatment. What did you say in that lying report of yours to Their Highnesses?'

'I said nothing but what I saw to be the truth,' said Rich, taken quite aback and only collecting himself slowly; it was the Admiral himself who gained for him the necessary time to take up the defensive.

'Who bribed you?' asked the Admiral. 'What friend at Court have you to put in my place?'

'No one,' said Rich, hotly, stung by the monstrous imputation. 'I have done my duty, that and no more.'

His genuine indignation may perhaps have been remarked by the Admiral.

'No matter,' he said. 'I care not whether you are my friend or my enemy. I am strong enough to stand alone against all the liars and detractors in Spain or in the Indies. Half an hour with Their Highnesses and these chains will be struck off and I shall be Admiral and Viceroy again. I have only to tell them of the discoveries I have made this voyage, of the mines of Ophir, of the Earthly Paradise, of the westerly passage to Arabia. I have only to remind them of the wealth to be won, the new kingdoms to be discovered.'

The dull blue eyes had a light in them now, and the wrinkled face, until now wooden and impassive, was animated and alive. The Admiral had forgotten Rich's presence, and was staring at the horizon and dreaming dreams, just as he had always dreamed them. Rich, gazing at him, realized quite fully that the Admiral was right, that he had only to talk in that fashion, as he undoubtedly would, to Their Highnesses for a few minutes to have all he wanted again. Within a year, perhaps, he would be at sea again in command of a squadron provided by Their Highnesses, and seeking the Fountain of Youth, or the Tree of Knowledge, or the Golden City of Cambaluk. And he would find–God only knew what he would find, but, being the Admiral, he would find something.

Rich glanced astern to where Española's mountains were fast sinking into the sea. There was a magnificent rainbow across them, adding fresh richness to their superb green summits towering above the blue, blue sea. He caught his breath a little at the sight, and felt a fresh twinge of regret at leaving the Indies behind. He had to think very hard about the solid realities of the island to allay that twinge. He shook off his momentary depression. He was on his way home.

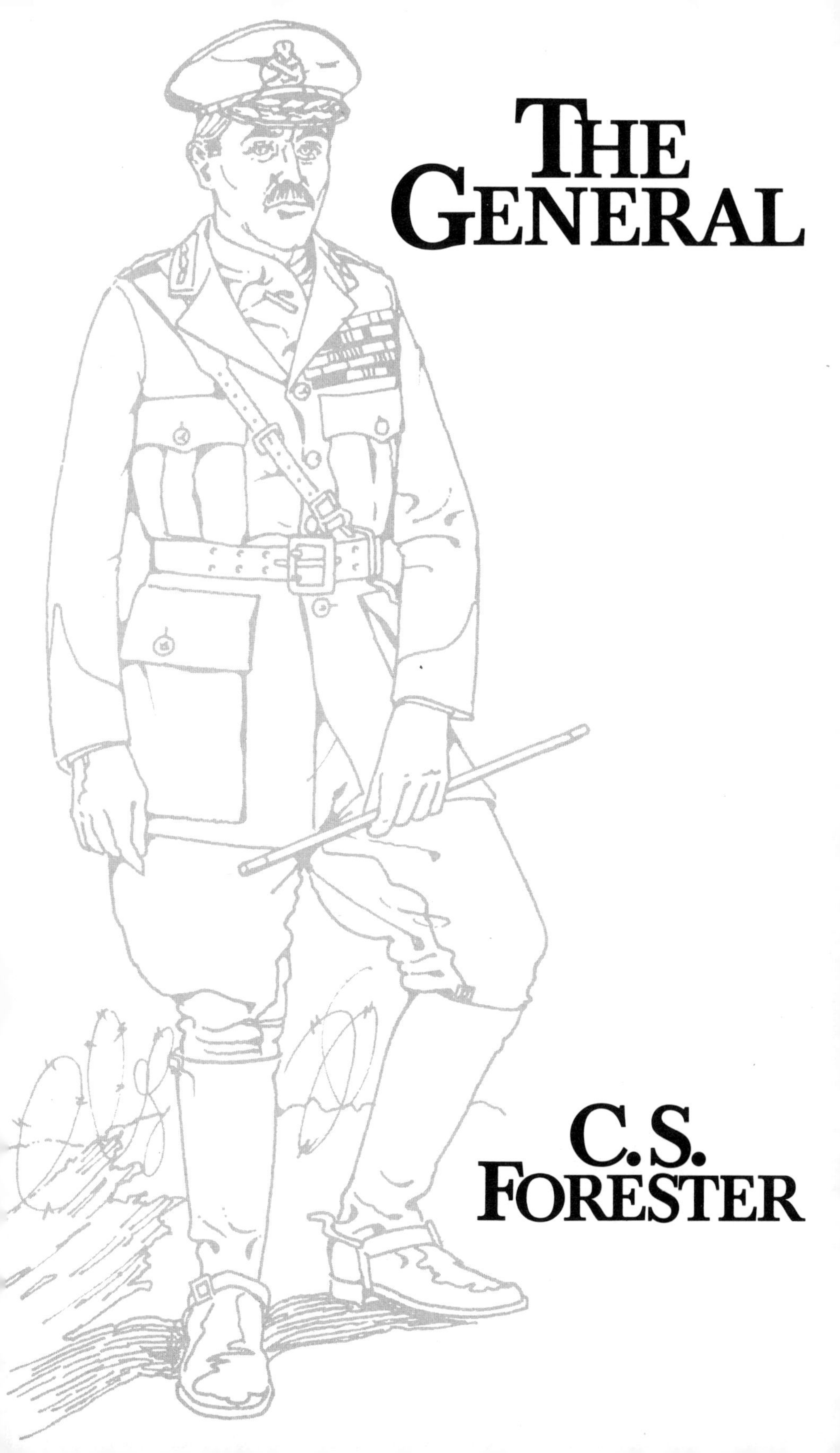
THE GENERAL
C.S. FORESTER

I

Nowadays Lieutenant-General Sir Herbert Curzon, K.C.M.G., C.B., D.S.O., is just one of Bournemouth's seven generals, but with the distinction of his record and his social position as a Duke's son-in-law, he is really far more eminent than those bare words would imply. He is usually to be seen in his bathchair with Lady Emily, tall, raw-boned, tweed-skirted, striding behind. He has a large face, which looks as if it had been rough-carved from a block of wood and his white hair and moustache stuck on afterwards, but there is a kindly gleam in his prominent blue eyes when he greets his acquaintances, and he purses up his lips in the queerest old-maidish smile. He clings to the habit of the old-fashioned bathchair largely for the reason that it is easier from a bathchair to acknowledge one's friends; he has never taught himself to walk with ease with any of the half-dozen artificial limbs he has acquired since the war, and the stump of his amputated thigh still troubles him occasionally. Besides, now that he is growing old he is a tiny bit nervous in a motor car.

Everybody is glad to have him smile to them on Bournemouth promenade, because his smile is a patent of social eminence in Bournemouth. And he wears his position with dignity, and is generous with his smiles, so that his popularity is great although he plays very bad bridge. He goes his way through the town a plaid rug over his knees, the steering-handle in his gloved hands, and on his approach newcomers are hurriedly informed by residents about his brilliant career and his life of achievement. Nowadays, when the memory of the war is fading, these verbal accounts are growing like folk legends, and public opinion in Bournemouth is inclined to give Sir Herbert Curzon more credit than he has really earned, although perhaps not more than he deserves.

The day on which Curzon first stepped over the threshold of history, the day which was to start him towards the command of a hundred thousand men, towards knighthood–and towards the bathchair on Bournemouth promenade–found him as a worried subaltern in an early South African battle. The landscape all about him was of a dull reddish brown; even the scanty grass and the scrubby bushes were brown. The arid plain was seamed with a tangle of ravines and gullies, but its monotony was relieved by the elevation in the distance of half a dozen flat-topped rocky hills, each of them like the others, and all of them like nearly every other kopje in South Africa.

Curzon was in command of his squadron of the Twenty-second Lancers, the Duke of Suffolk's Own, an eminence to which he had been raised by the chances of war. Three officers senior to him were sick, left behind at various points on the lines of communication, and Captain the Honourable Charles

Manningtree-Field, who had been in command when the squadron went into action, was lying dead at Curzon's feet with a Mauser bullet through his head. Curzon was not thinking about Manningtree-Field. His anxiety was such that immediately after the shock of his death, and of the realization that men really can be killed by bullets, his first thought had been that now he could use the captain's Zeiss binoculars and try and find out what was happening. He stood on the lip of the shallow depression wherein lay Manningtree-Field's body, the two squadron trumpeters, and two or three wounded men, and he stared round him across the featureless landscape.

In a long straggling line to his right and left lay the troopers of the squadron, their forage caps fastened under their chins, firing away industriously at nothing at all, as far as Curzon could see. In a gully to the rear, he knew, were the horses and the horseholders, but beyond that Curzon began to realize that he knew extraordinarily little about the battle which was going on. The squadron was supposed to be on the right flank of an advancing British firing line, but when they had come galloping up to this position Curzon had not been in command, and he had been so preoccupied with keeping his troop properly closed up that he had not paid sufficient attention to what Manningtree-Field had been doing.

Probably Manningtree-Field had not been too sure himself, because the battle had begun in a muddle amid a cascade of vague orders from the Staff, and since then no orders had reached them–and certainly no orders had envisaged their coming under heavy fire at this particular point. As an accompaniment to the sharp rattle of musketry about him Curzon could hear the deeper sound of artillery in the distance, echoing over the plain with a peculiar discordant quality, and against the intense blue of the sky he could see the white puffs of the shrapnel bursts far out to the left, but it was impossible to judge the position of their target at that distance, and there was just enough fold in the flat surface of the plain to conceal from him any sight of troops on the ground.

Meanwhile an invisible enemy was scourging them with a vicious and well-directed fire. The air was full of the sound of rifle bullets spitting and crackling past Curzon's ears as he stood staring through the binoculars. Curzon had an uneasy feeling that they were coming from the flank as well as from the front, and in the absence of certain knowledge he was rapidly falling a prey to the fear that the wily Boers were creeping round to encircle him. A fortnight ago a whole squadron of Lancers–not of his regiment, thank God–had been cut off in that way and forced to surrender, with the result that that regiment was now known throughout South Africa as 'Kruger's Own'. Curzon sweated with fear at the thought of such a fate overtaking him. He would die rather than surrender, but–would his men? He looked anxiously along the straggling skirmishing line.

Troop Sergeant-Major Brown came crawling to him on his hands and knees. Brown was a man of full body, and his face was normally brick-red, but this unwonted exertion under a scorching sun coloured his cheeks like a beetroot.

'Ain't no orders come for us, sir?' asked Brown, peering up at him.

'No,' said Curzon sharply. 'And stand up if you want to speak to me.'

Brown stood up reluctantly amid the crackle of the bullets. After twenty years' service, without having had a shot fired at him, and with his pension in sight, it went against his grain to make a target of himself for a lot of farmers whose idea of war was to lay ambushes behind rocks.

'Come down 'ere, sir, please, sir,' pleaded Brown in a fever of distress. 'We don't want to lose *you*, sir, too, sir.'

The loss of the only officer the squadron had left would place Sergeant-Major Brown in command, and Brown was not at all desirous of such a responsibility. It was that consideration which caused Curzon to yield to his solicitations, and to step down into the comparative safety of the depression.

'D'you fink we're cut orf, sir?' asked Brown, dropping his voice so as to be unheard by the trumpeters squatting on the rocks at the bottom of the dip.

'No, of course not,' said Curzon. 'The infantry will be up in line with us soon.'

'Ain't no sign of them, is there, sir?' complained Brown. 'Expect the beggars are 'eld up somewhere, or lorst their way, or something.'

'Nonsense,' said Curzon. All his training, both military and social, had been directed against his showing any loss of composure before his inferiors in rank, even if those inferiors should actually be voicing his own fears. He stepped once more to the side of the hollow and stared out over the rolling plains. There was nothing to be seen except the white shrapnel bursts.

'Our orders was to find their flank,' said Brown, fidgeting with his sword hilt. 'Looks to me more like as if they've found ours.'

'Nonsense,' repeated Curzon. But just exactly where the Boer firing-line was to be found was more than he could say. Those infernal kopjes all looked alike to him. He looked once more along the line of skirmishers crouching among the rocks, and as he looked he saw, here and there, faces turned towards him. That was a bad sign, for men to be looking over their shoulders in the heat of action. The men must be getting anxious. He could hardly blame them, seeing that they had been trained for years to look upon a battle as a series of charges knee to knee and lance in hand against a serried enemy. This lying down to be shot at by hidden enemies a mile off was foreign to their nature. It was his duty to steady them.

'Stay here, sergeant-major,' he said. 'You will take command if I'm hit.'

He stepped out from the hollow, his sword at his side, his uniform spick and span, and walked in leisurely fashion along the firing-line. He spoke to the men by name, steadily and unemotionally, as he reached each in turn. He felt vaguely as he walked that a joke or two, something to raise a laugh, would be the most effective method of address, but he never was able to joke, and as it was his mere presence and unruffled demeanour acted as a tonic on the men. Twice he spoke harshly. Once was when he found Trooper Haynes cowering behind rocks without making any attempt to return the fire, and once was when he found Trooper Maguire drinking from his water-bottle. Water out here in the veld was a most precious possession, to be hoarded like a miser's gold, for when there was no more water there would be no fight left in the men.

He walked down the line to one end; he walked back to the other. Sergeant-Major Brown, peeping out from his hollow, watched his officer's fearless passage, and, with the contrariness of human nature, found himself wishing he was with him. Then, when Curzon was nearly back in safety again, Brown saw him suddenly swing right round. But next instant he was walking steadily down to the hollow, and only when he was out of sight of the men did he sit down sharply.

'Are you hit, sir?' asked Brown, all anxiety.

'Yes. Don't let the men know. I'm still in command.'

Brown hastily called the squadron first-aid corporal with his haversack of dressings. They ripped open Curzon's coat and bound up the entrance and exit wounds. The destiny which directs the course of bullets had sent this one clean through the fleshy part of the shoulder without touching bone or artery or nerve.

'I'm all right,' said Curzon manfully, getting to his feet and pulling his torn coat about him. The arrival of a crawling trooper interrupted Sergeant-Major Brown's protests.

'Message from Sergeant Hancock, sir,' said the trooper. 'Ammunition's running short.'

'Um' said Curzon thoughtfully, and a pause ensued while he digested the information.

'There ain't fifty rounds left in our troop, sir,' supplemented the trooper, with the insistence of his class upon harrowing detail.

'All right,' blazed Curzon irritably. 'All right. Get back to the line.'

''Ave to do somethink now, sir,' said Sergeant-Major Brown as the trooper crawled away.

'Shut up and be quiet,' snapped Curzon.

He was perfectly well aware that he must do something. As long as his men had cartridges to fire they would remain in good heart, but once ammunition failed he might expect any ugly incident to occur. There might be panic, or someone might show a white flag.

'Trumpeter!' called Curzon, and the trumpeter leaped up to attention to receive his orders.

The squadron came trailing back to the gully where the horses were waiting. The wounded were being assisted by their friends, but they were all depressed and ominously quiet. A few were swearing, using words of meaningless filth, under their breath.

'What about the dead, sir?' asked Sergeant Hancock, saluting. 'The captain, sir?'

The regiment was still so unversed in war as to feel anxiety in the heat of action about the disposal of the dead–a reminiscence of the warfare against savage enemies which constituted the British Army's sole recent experience. This new worry on top of all the others nearly broke Curzon down. He was on the point of blazing out with 'Blast the dead,' but he managed to check himself. Such a violation of the Army's recent etiquette would mean trouble with the men.

'I'll see about that later. Get back into your place,' he said. 'Prepare to mount!'

The squadron followed him down the ravine, the useless lances cocked up at each man's elbow, amid a squeaking of leather and a clashing of iron hoofs on the rocks. Curzon's head was beginning to swim, what with the loss of blood, and the pain of his wound, and the strain he had undergone, and the heat of this gully. He had small enough idea of what he wanted to do–or at least he would not admit to himself that what he wanted was to make his way back to some area where the squadron would not be under fire and he might receive orders. The sense of isolation in the presence of an enemy of diabolical cunning and strength was overwhelming. He knew that he must not expose the squadron to fire while in retreat. The men would begin to quicken their horses' pace in that event–the walk would become a trot, the trot a gallop, and his professional reputation would be blasted. The gully they were in constituted at least a shelter from the deadly hail of bullets.

The gully changed direction more than once. Soon Curzon had no idea where he was, nor whither he was going, but he was too tired and in too much pain to think clearly. The distant gun-fire seemed to roll about inside his skull. He drooped in his saddle and with difficulty straightened himself up. The fortunate gully continued a long way instead of coming to a rapid indefinite end as most gullies did in that parched plain, and the men–and Sergeant-Major Brown–were content to follow him without question. The sun was by now well down towards the horizon, and they were in the shade.

It was in fact the sight of the blaze of light which was reflected from the level plain in front which roused Curzon to the realization that the gully was about to end beyond the tangle of rocks just in front. He turned in his saddle and held up his hand to the column of men behind; they came sleepily to a halt, the horses cannoning into the hind-quarters of the horses in front, and then Curzon urged his horse cautiously forward, his trumpeter close behind.

Peering from the shelter of the rocks, Curzon beheld the finest spectacle which could gladden the eyes of a cavalry officer. The gully had led him, all unaware, actually behind the flank of the Boer position. Half a mile in front of him, sited with Boer cunning on the reverse slope of a fold in the ground, was a battery of field guns sunk in shallow pits, the guns' crews clearly visible round them. There were groups of tethered ponies. There was a hint of rifle trenches far in front of the guns, and behind the guns were wagons and mounted staffs. There was all the vulnerable exposed confusion always to be found behind a firing-line, and he and his squadron was within easy charging distance of it all, their presence unsuspected.

Curzon fought down the nightmare feeling of unreality which was stealing over him. He filed the squadron out of the gully and brought it up into line before any Boer had noticed them. Then, forgetting to draw his sword, he set his spurs into his horse and rode steadily, three lengths in front of his charging line, straight at the guns. The trumpeters pealed the charge as the pace quickened.

No undisciplined militia force could withstand the shock of an unexpected attack from the flank, however small the force which delivered it. The Boer defence which had all day held up the English attack collapsed like a pricked balloon. The whole space was black with men running for their ponies. Out on the open plain where the sweltering English infantry had barely been maintaining their firing-lines the officers sensed what was happening. Some noticed the slackening of the Boer fire. Some saw the Boers rise out of their invisible trenches and run. One officer heard the cavalry trumpets faint and sweet through the heated air. He yelled to his bugler to sound the charge. The skirmishing line rose up from flank to flank as bugler after bugler took up the call. Curzon had brought them the last necessary impetus for the attack. They poured over the Boer lines to where Curzon, his sword still in its sheath, was sitting dazed upon his horse amid the captured guns.

The Battle of Volkslaagte–a very great battle in the eyes of the British public of 1899, wherein nearly five thousand men had been engaged a side–was won, and Curzon was marked for his captaincy and the D.S.O. He was not a man of dreams, but even if he had been, his wildest dreams would not have envisaged the future command of a hundred thousand British soldiers–nor the bathchair on Bournemouth promenade.

2

To Curzon the rest of the South African War was a time of tedium and weariness. His wound kept him in hospital during the Black Week, while England mourned three coincident defeats inflicted by an enemy whom she had begun to regard as already at her mercy. He was only convalescent during Robert's triumphant advance to Pretoria. He found himself second-in-command of a detail of recruits and reservists on the long and vulnerable line of communications when the period of great battles had come to an end.

There were months of tedium, of army biscuit and tough beef, of scant water and no tobacco. There were sometimes weeks of desperate marching, when the horses died and the men grumbled and the elusive enemy escaped by some new device from the net which had been drawn round him. There were days of scorching sun and nights of bitter cold. There was water discipline to be enforced so as to prevent the men from drinking from the polluted supplies which crammed the hospitals with cases of enteric fever. There was the continuous nagging difficulty of obtaining fodder so as to keep horses in a condition to satisfy the exacting demands of column commanders. There were six occasions in eighteen months during which Curzon heard once more the sizzle and crack of bullets overhead, but he did not set eyes on an enemy–except prisoners–during that period. Altogether it was a time of inconceivable dreariness and monotony.

But it could not be said that Curzon was actively unhappy. He was not of the type to chafe at monotony. The dreariness of an officers' mess of only two or three members did not react seriously upon him–he was not a man who needed mental diversion. His chill reserve and ingrained frigid good manners kept him out of mess-room squabbles when nerves were fraying and tempers were on edge; besides, a good many of the officers who came out towards the end of the war were not gentlemen and were not worth troubling one's mind about. Yet all the same, it was pleasant when the war ended at last, and Curzon could say good-bye to the mixed rabble of mounted infantry who had made up the column to which he was second-in-command.

He rejoined the Twenty-second Lancers at Cape Town–all the squadrons together again for the first time for two years–and sailed for home. The new king himself reviewed them after their arrival, having granted them time enough to discard their khaki and put on again the glories of blue and gold, schapska and plume, lance pennons and embroidered saddle-cloths. Then they settled down in their barracks with the fixed determination (as the Colonel expressed it, setting his lips firmly) of 'teaching the men to be soldiers again.'

The pleasure of that return to England was intense enough, even to a man as self-contained as Curzon. There were green fields to see, and hedgerows, and there was the imminent prospect of hunting. And there were musical comedies to go to, and good food to eat, and pretty women to be seen in every street, and the Leicester Lounge to visit, with a thrill reminiscent of old Sandhurst days. And there was the homage of society to the returned warriors to be received–although that was not quite as fulsome as it might have been, because public enthusiasm had begun to decline slowly since the relief of Mafeking, and there was actually a fair proportion of people who had forgotten the reported details of the Battle of Volkslaagte.

There was naturally one man who knew all about it–a portly, kindly gentleman with a keen blue eye and a deep guttural voice who had been known as H.R.H. at the time when the Lancers had been ordered to South Africa, but who was now King of England. He said several kindly words to Curzon at the investiture to which Curzon was summoned by the Lord Chamberlain. And Curzon bowed and stammered as he received his D.S.O.–he was not a man made for courts and palaces. In the intimacy of his hotel bedroom he had felt thrilled and pleased with himself in his Lancer full dress, with his plastron and his schapska, his gold lace and glittering boots and sword, and he had even found a sneaking pleasure in the stir among the people on the pavement as he walked out to get into the waiting cab, but his knees knocked and his throat dried up in Buckingham Palace.

On the same leave Curzon had in duty-bound to go and visit Aunt Kate, who lived in Brixton. The late Mr Curzon, Captain Herbert Curzon's father, had married a trifle beneath him, and his wife's sister had married a trifle beneath her, and the Mr Cole whom she had married had not met with much success in life, and after marriage Mr Curzon had met with much, so that the gap between Curzon and his only surviving relatives–between the Captain in the Duke of Suffolk's Own and the hard-up city clerk with his swarm of shrieking children–was wide and far too deep to plumb. Curzon drove to Brixton in a cab, and the appearance of the cab caused as much excitement in that street as did his full-dress uniform in the West End. Aunt Kate opened the door to him–a paint-blistered door at the end of a tile path three yards long, leading from a gate in the iron railings past a few depressed laurels in the tiny 'front garden.' Aunt Kate was momentarily disconcerted at the sight of the well-dressed gentleman who had rat-tat-tatted on her door, but she recovered herself.

'Why, it's Bertie,' she said. 'Come in, dear. Uncle Stanley ought to be home soon. Come in here and sit down. Maud! Dick! Gertie! Here's your cousin Bertie home from South Africa!'

The shabby children came clustering into the shabby parlour; at first they were shy and constrained, and when the constraint wore off they grew riotous, making conversation difficult and hindering Aunt Kate in her effort to extract from her nephew details of his visit to Buckingham Palace.

'What's it like in there?' she asked. 'Is it all gold? I suppose there's cut-glass chandeliers?'

Curzon had not the least idea. And—

'Did the king *really* speak to you? What was he wearing?'

'Field-Marshal's uniform,' said Curzon briefly.

'Of course, you've been presented to him before, when you went into the Army,' said Aunt Kate enviously. 'That was in the dear queen's time.'

'Yes,' said Curzon.

'It must be lovely to know all these people,' said Aunt Kate. 'Are there any lords in your regiment now?'

'Yes,' said Curzon. 'One or two.'

It was irritating, because he himself found secret pleasure in serving in the same regiments as lords, and in addressing them without their titles, but the pleasure was all spoilt now at finding that Aunt Kate was of the same mind.

More irritating still was the arrival of Stanley Cole, Aunt Kate's husband, whom Curzon felt he could not possibly address now as 'Uncle Stanley', although he had done so as a boy. Mr Cole was an uncompromising Radical, and no respecter of persons, as he was ready to inform anyone.

'I didn't 'old with your doings in South Africa,' he announced, almost before he was seated. 'I didn't 'old with them at all, and I said so all along. We didn't ought to 'ave fought with the Boers in the first place. And burning farms, and those concentration camps. Sheer wickedness, that was. You shouldn't have done it, you know, Bertie.'

Curzon, with an effort, maintained an appearance of mild good manners, and pointed out that all he had done was to obey orders.

'Orders! Yes! It's all a system. That's what it is.'

Mr Cole seemed to think that in this case the word 'system' was deeply condemnatory–to Curzon, of course, the word was, if anything, of the opposite implication. He was roused far enough to suggest to his uncle that if he had undergone the discomforts of two years of guerrilla warfare he might not be so particular as to the methods employed to suppress it.

'I wouldn't have gone,' said Mr Cole. 'Not if they had tried to make me. Lord Roberts, now. 'E's trying to introduce conscription. Ought to 'ave more sense. And now there's all this talk about a big Navy. Big fiddlestick!'

There was clearly no ground at all which was common to Mr Cole and his nephew by marriage.

'Look at the rise in the income tax!' said Mr Cole. 'Two shillings in the pound! Peace, retrenchment, and reform. That's what we want. And a sane Government, and no protection.'

Curzon might have replied that Mr Cole had nothing to complain about in the matter of income tax, seeing that his income was clearly below the taxable limit, but his good manners would not permit him to say so while he was conscious of his own seven hundred a year from his private means. Instead, he rose to go, apologizing for the briefness of his visit and pleading further urgent matters demanding his attention. He declined the tea which Aunt Kate belatedly remembered to offer him; he said truthfully enough, that he never had tea, and the children goggled up in surprise at a man who could so lightly decline tea, and Aunt Kate said, 'You'll be going to have late dinner, I suppose.'

She accompanied him to the door.

'Good-bye, then, Bertie,' she said. 'It was nice of you to come. We'll be seeing you again soon, I suppose?'

'Yes, of course,' said Curzon, and he knew it was a lie as he said it, that he would never be able to bring himself again to penetrate into Brixton. He thought the lie had succeeded, if he thought about it at all, but Aunt Kate dabbed furtively at her eyes before she went back into the parlour to talk over the visitor with her family. She knew perfectly well that she would never see 'Lily's boy' again.

Meanwhile Curzon, out in the cabless suburban street, had to make his way on foot to the main road to some means of conveyance to take him back to his hotel. Before he took a cab he was constrained to go into a saloon bar and order himself a large whisky-and-soda, and while he drank it he had to mop his forehead and run his fingers round underneath his collar as recollections of his visit surged up within him. He thanked God fervently that he was an orphan, that he was an only child, and that his father was an only child, and that his mother had had only one sister. He thanked God that his father's speculations in Mincing Lane had been early successful, so that preparatory school and Haileybury and Sandhurst had come naturally to his son.

In a moment of shuddering self-revelation he realized that in other circumstances it might have been just possible that he should have breathed naturally in the air of Brixton. Worse still he felt for a nauseating moment that in that environment he too might have been uncertain with his aitches and spoken about late dinner in a respectful tone of voice. It was bad enough to remember that as a child he had lived in Bayswater–although he could only just remember it, as they had early moved to Lancaster Gate. He had ridden in the Park then, and his father had already decided that he should go into the Army and, if possible, into the cavalry among the real swells.

He could remember his father using that very expression, and he could remember his father's innocent pride in him at Sandhurst and when he had received his commission in the Duke of Suffolk's Own. Curzon struggled for a moment–so black was his mood–with the realization that the Twenty-second Lancers was not really a crack regiment. He could condescend to infantrymen and native Indian army–poor devils–of course, but he knew perfectly well when he came to admit it to himself, as on this black occasion, that the Households and Horse Gunners and people like the Second Dragoons could condescend to him in their turn.

His father, of course, could not appreciate these distinctions and could have no realization that it was impossible for a son of a Mincing Lane merchant to obtain a nomination to one of these exclusive regiments.

Perhaps it was as well that the old man had died when he did, leaving his twenty-year-old son the whole of his fortune–when his partnership had been realized and everything safely invested it brought in seven hundred a year.

Seven hundred a year was rather on the small side, regarded as the private means of a cavalry subaltern, but it sufficed, and as during the South African War he had been unable to spend even his pay, he was clear of debt for once, and could look forward to a good time.

The world was growing rosier again now, with his second whisky-and-soda inside him. He was able to light a cigar and plan his evening. By the time his cab had carried him up to town he was able to change into dress clothes without its crossing his mind even once that in other circumstances to change might not have been so much of a matter of course.

3

There were twelve years of peace between the two wars. It was those twelve years which saw Herbert Curzon undergo transformation from a young man into a middle-aged, from a subaltern into a senior major of cavalry. A complete record in detail of those twelve years would need twelve years in the telling to do it justice, so as to make it perfectly plain that nothing whatever happened during those twelve years; the professional life of an officer in a regiment of cavalry of the line is likely to be uneventful and Curzon was of the type which has no other life to record.

They were twelve years of mess and orderly room; twelve years of inspection of horses' feet and of inquiry why Trooper Jones had been for three days absent without leave. Perhaps the clue to Curzon's development during this time is given by his desire to conform to type, and that desire is perhaps rooted too deep for examination. Presumably preparatory school and Haileybury and Sandhurst had something to do with it. Frequently it is assumed that it is inherent in the English character to wish not to appear different from one's fellows, but that is a bold assumption to make regarding a nation which has produced more original personalities than any other in modern times. It is safer to assume that the boldness and insensitiveness which is found sporadically among the English have developed despite all the influences which are brought to bear to nip them in the bud, and are therefore, should they survive to bear fruits, plants of sturdy growth.

Whether or not Herbert Curzon would have displayed originality, even eccentricity, if he had been brought up in another environment–in that of his cousins, Maudie and Gertie and Dick Cole, for instance–it is impossible to say. It sounds inconceivable to those of us who know him now, but it might be so. There can be no doubt whatever, on the other hand, that during the middle period of his life Curzon was distinguished by nothing more than his desire to be undistinguishable. The things which he did, he did because other people had done before him, and if a tactful person had been able to persuade him to defend himself for so doing he could only have said that to him that appeared an entirely adequate reason for doing them.

When as a senior captain in the regiment he quelled with crushing rudeness the self-assertiveness of some newly arrived subaltern in the mess, he did not do so from any feeling of personal animosity towards the wart in question (although the wart could not help feeling that this was the case), but because senior captains have always quelled self-assertive young subalterns.

He was a firm supporter of the rule that professional subjects should not be discussed in the mess. Whether the subject rashly brought up was 'The Tactical Employment of Cavalry in the Next War' or the new regulations regarding heelropes, Curzon was always on the side of propriety, and saw to it that the discussion was short-lived. It did not matter to him–probably he did not know–that the convention prohibiting the discussion in mess of professional matters and of women dated back to the days of duelling, and that these two subjects about which men are more likely to grow angry had been barred then out of an instinct of self-preservation. It was sufficient to him that the convention was established; it was that fact which justified the convention.

And that his conviction was sincere in this respect was obvious. No one who knew him could possibly doubt that he would far rather receive another wound as bad as the one at Volkslaggte–more, that he would far rather go again through all the mental agony of Volkslaagte–than appear in public wearing a bowler hat and a morning coat. Even if he had thought such a combination beautiful (and he really never stopped to wonder whether anything was beautiful or not) he could not have worn it; indeed, it is difficult to imagine anything which would have induced him to do so. The example of the royal family over a series of years might have contrived it, but even then he would have been filled with misgivings.

The feeling of distaste for everything not done by the majority of those among whom he moved (wherever this feeling originated, in the germ or in the womb or at school, or in the Army) had its effect, too, on his professional career. The majority of his fellows did not apply to go through the Staff College; therefore he did not apply. There was only a small proportion of officers who by their ebullient personalities attracted the attention of their seniors; therefore Curzon made no effort to be ebullient in his personality–quite apart from his dislike of attracting attention.

These pushful, forceful persons had a black mark set against them in Curzon's mind for another reason as well, distinct although closely connected. They disturbed the steady even tenor of life which it was right and proper to expect. If routine made life more comfortable and respectable (just as did the prohibition of shop in mess) the man who disturbed that routine was an enemy of society. More than that, no man had any right whatever to upset the arrangements of his seniors.

There was a very painful occasion when Curzon was commanding a squadron and had just arranged a much-desired shooting leave–it was during the five years that the regiment was stationed in India. Squires, his senior captain, came to him in high spirits, and announced that the War Office had at last seen fit to sanction his application for the Staff College; he would be leaving in a month. Curzon's face fell. A month from now his leave was due; a fortnight from now would arrive the new draft of recruits and remounts–hairy of heel all of them, as years of experience of recruits and remounts had taught him to expect. He had counted on Squires to get them into shape; Squires could be relied upon to keep the squadron up to the mark (as Curzon frankly admitted to himself) better than any of the remaining officers. Curzon had no hesitation when it came to choosing between the squadron and his leave. He must postpone his shooting, and he had been looking forward so much to the thrill and danger of following a gaur through blind cover.

'If the orders come through, of course you must go,' said Curzon. 'But it's devilishly inconsiderate of you, Squires. I'll have to disappoint Marlowe and Colonel Webb.'

'Blame the War Office, don't blame me,' said Squires lightly, but of course it was Squires whom Curzon really blamed. The situation would never have arisen if he had not made his untimely application. It was years before Curzon could meet without instinctive distrust officers with p.s.c. after their name.

That may have been at the root of Curzon's distrust of theorists about war. It was not often that Curzon could be brought to discuss the theory of war although he would argue gladly about its practical details, such as the most suitable ration of fodder or the pros and cons of a bit and snaffle. But apart from this distrust of theorists because of their tendency to be different, there was also the more obvious reason that the majority of theorists were mad as hatters, or even madder. As soon as any man started to talk about the theory of war one could be nearly sure that he would bring forward some idiotic suggestion, to the effect that cavalry had had its day and that dismounted action was all that could be expected of it, or that machine-guns and barbed wire had wrought a fundamental change in tactics, or even–wildest lunacy of all–that these rattletrap aeroplanes were going to be of some military value in the next war.

There was even a feather-brained subaltern in Curzon's regiment who voluntarily, in his misguided enthusiasm, quitted the ranks of the Twenty-second Lancers, the Duke of Suffolk's Own, to serve in the Royal Flying Corps. He actually had the infernal impudence to suggest to the senior major of his regiment, a man with ribbons on his breast, who had seen real fighting, and who had won the Battle of Volkslaagte by a cavalry charge, that the time was at hand when aeroplane reconnaissance would usurp the last useful function which could be performed by cavalry. When Major Curzon, simply boiling with fury at this treachery, fell back on the sole argument which occurred to him at the moment, and accused him of assailing the honour of the regiment with all its glorious traditions, he declared light-heartedly that he would far sooner serve in an arm with only a future than in one with only a past, and that he had no intention whatever of saying anything to the discredit of a regiment which was cut to pieces at Waterloo because they did not know when to stop charging, and that Major Curzon's argument was a *non sequitur* anyway.

With that he took his departure, leaving the major livid with rage; it was agony to the major that the young man's confidential report from the regiment had already gone in to the War Office and could not be recalled for alteration (as the young man had been well aware). Curzon could only fume and mutter, complaining to himself that the Army was not what it was, that the manners of the new generation were infinitely worse than when he was a young man, and that their ideas were dangerously subversive of everything worth preserving.

This picture of Curzon in the years immediately before the war seems to verge closely on the conventional caricature of the Army major, peppery, red-faced, liable under provocation to gobble like a turkey-cock, hide-bound in his ideas and conventional in his way of thought, and it is no more exact than any other caricature. It ignores all the good qualities which were present at the same time. He was the soul of honour; he could be guilty of no meannesses, even boggling at those which convention permits. He would give his life for the ideals he stood for, and would be happy if the opportunity presented itself. His patriotism was a real and living force, even if its symbols were childish. His courage was unflinching. The necessity of assuming responsibility troubled him no more than the necessity of breathing. He could administer the regulations of his service with an impartiality and a practised leniency admirably suited to the needs of the class of man for which those regulations were drawn up. He shirked no duty, however tedious or inconvenient; it did not even occur to him to try to do so. He would never allow the instinctive deference which he felt towards great names and old lineage to influence him in the execution of anything he conceived to be his duty. The man with a claim on his friendship could make any demand upon his generosity. And while the breath was in his body he would not falter in the face of difficulties.

So much for an analysis of Curzon's character at the time when he was about to become one of the instruments of destiny. Yet there is something sinister in the coincidence that when destiny had so much to do she should find tools of such high quality ready to hand. It might have been–though it would be a bold man who would say so–more advantageous for England if the British Army had not been quite so full of men of high rank who were so ready for responsibility, so unflinchingly devoted to their duty, so unmoved in the face of difficulties, of such unfaltering courage.

It might be so. But in recounting the career of Lieutenant-General Sir Herbert Curzon it would be incongruous to dwell on 'mays' or 'mights'. There are more definite matters to record in describing the drama of his rise.

4

The first step came even before the declaration of war, during the tense forty-eight hours which followed mobilization. Curzon was in the stables supervising the arrival of the remounts which were streaming in when a trooper came running up to him and saluted.

'Colonel's compliments, sir, and would you mind coming and speaking to him for a minute.'

Curzon found the Colonel alone–he had passed the adjutant emerging as he entered–and the Colonel was standing erect with an opened letter in his hand. His face was the same colour as the paper he held.

'You're in command of the regiment, Curzon,' said the Colonel.

'I–I beg your pardon, sir?' said Curzon.

'You heard what I said,' snapped the Colonel, and then recovered himself with an effort and went on with pathetic calm. 'These are War Office orders. You are to take command of the regiment with the temporary rank of Lieutenant-Colonel. I suppose it'll be in the *Gazette* tomorrow.'

'And what about you, sir?' asked Curzon.

'I? Oh, I'm being given command of a brigade of yeomanry. Up in the Northern Command somewhere.'

'Good God!' said Curzon, genuinely moved.

'Yes, yeomanry, man,' blazed the Colonel. 'Yokels on plough horses. It'll take a year to do anything with them at all, and the war'll be over in three months. And *you* are to take the regiment overseas.'

'I'm damned sorry, sir,' said Curzon, trying his best to soften the blow, 'but it's promotion for you, after all.'

'Promotion? Who cares a damn about promotion? I wanted to go with the regiment. You'll look after them, won't you, Curzon?'

'Of course I will, sir.'

'You'll be in France in a fortnight.'

'France, sir?' said Curzon, mildly surprised. The destination of the Expeditionary Force had been an object of some speculation. It might possibly have been Belgium or Schleswig.

'Yes,' said the Colonel. 'Of course, you don't know about that. It's in the secret mobilization orders for commanding officers. You had better start reading them now, hadn't you? The British Army comes up on the left of the French. Maubeuge, and thereabouts. Here you are.'

That moment when he was given the printed sheets, marked 'Most Secret. For Commanding Officers of Cavalry Units Only', was to Curzon the most important and vital of his career. It marked the finite change from a junior officer's position to a senior officer's. It was the opening of the door to real promotion. It made it possible that the end of the war would find him a General. Naturally it was not given to Curzon to foresee that before the war should end he would be in command of more men than Wellington or Marlborough ever commanded in the field. And he never knew to what fortunate combination of circumstances he owed this most fortunate bit of promotion, for the secrets of War Office patronage are impenetrable. Of course, the memory of the Battle of Volkslaagte had something to do with it. But presumably someone in the War Office had marked the fact that the Colonel of the Twenty-second Lancers was verging on the age of retirement and had debated whether it would not be better for the regiment to be commanded by a forceful younger man, and at the same time the question of the yeomanry brigade command had arisen, so that Curzon's promotion had solved a double difficulty. It maintained a reputable trainer of peace-time cavalry in a situation where his talents could be usefully employed, and it gave a man of proved ability in war a command in which he would find full scope.

If Curzon had had time to think about it at all, and if his self-conscious modesty had permitted it, he would undoubtedly have attributed these motives to the War Office; and as it was, his subconscious approval of them sent up his opinion of the Higher Command a good many degrees. Moreover, this approval of his was heightened by the marvellous way in which mobilization was carried through. Reservists and remounts poured in with perfect smoothness. His indents for equipment were met instantly by the Command headquarters. In six brief days the Twenty-second Lancers had expanded into a regiment of three full squadrons, complete in men and horses and transport, ammunition and supplies, ready to move on the first word from London–nor was the word long in coming.

Curzon, of course, had worked like a slave. He had interviewed every returning reservist; he had inspected every horse; he had studied his orders until he knew them by heart. Nor was this from personal motives, either. His anxiety about the efficiency of the regiment sprang not at all from the consideration that his professional future depended upon it. The job was there to be done, and done well, and it was his business to do it. Somewhere within his inarticulate depths was the feeling that England's future turned to some small extent upon his efforts, but he could not put that feeling into words even to himself. He could faintly voice his feelings regarding the credit of the Army, and of the cavalry arm in particular. He could speak and think freely about the honour of the regiment, because that was a subject people did speak about. But he could not speak of England; not even of the King–in just the same way the inarticulate regiment which followed its inarticulate colonel sang popular ballads instead of hymns to the Motherland.

Someone in London had done his work extraordinarily well. There never had been a mobilization like this in all British history. In contrast with the methods of the past, which had scraped units together from all parts and flung them pell-mell on to the Continental shore, without guns or transport or cavalry like Wellington in Portugal, or to die of disease and privation like the Army in the Crimea, the present system had built up a real Army ready for anything, and had means and arrangements perfected to put that Army ashore, lacking absolutely nothing which might contribute to its efficiency and its mobility.

One morning at dawn Curzon's servant called him exceptionally early; that same evening Curzon was on the quay at Le Havre supervising the disembarkation of the horses. That day had for Curzon a sort of dream-like quality; certain details stood out with extraordinary clarity although the general effect was blurred and unreal. All his life Curzon could remember the faces of the officers whom he had ordered to remain with the depot squadron, looking on unhappily at the dawn parade, while the band played 'God Save the King', and the men cheered themselves hoarse. He remembered the fussy self-importance of Carruthers, the brigade-major, who came galloping up to the railway sidings at which the regiment was entraining, to be greeted with cool self-confidence by Valentine, the adjutant, who had every detail of the business at his fingers' ends. There was the lunch on board the transport, interrupted by the flight overhead of a non-rigid airship which formed part of the escort. And then, finally, the landing at Le Havre, and the business of getting men and horses into their billets, and someone here had done his work again so efficiently that there was no need for Curzon to recall to himself the cavalry colonel's active service maxim: 'Feed the horses before the men, and the men before the officers, and the officers before yourself.'

The feeling of unreality persisted during the long train journey which followed. The conveyance of the three thousand horses which belonged to the brigade was a business ineffably tedious. Feeding and watering the horses took up much time, and the men needed to have a sharp eye kept on them, because everyone in France seemed to have entered into a conspiracy to make the men drunk–there was free wine for them wherever they came in contact with civilians, and the young soldiers drank in ignorance of its potency and the old soldiers drank with delighted appreciation.

Curzon could not understand the French which the civilians talked with such disconcerting readiness. He had early formed a theory that French could only be spoken by people with a malformed larynx, and in his few visits to Paris he had always managed very well without knowing French; in fact he had been known to declare that 'everyone in France knows English.' That this was not the case was speedily shown in frequent contacts with village *maires* and with French railway officials, but Curzon did not allow the fact to distress him. Valentine spoke good French, and so did half a dozen of the other officers. It was sufficient for Curzon to give orders about what was to be said–in fact an inattentive observer of Curzon's impassive countenance would never have guessed at his ignorance of the language.

Then at last, on a day of sweltering sunshine, the regiment detrained in some gloomy sidings in the heart of a manufacturing and mining district. The brigade formed a column of sections two miles long on a dreary-paved road and began to move along it, with halts and delays as orders came in afresh. The officers were bubbling with excitement, looking keenly at their maps and scanning the countryside eagerly to see if it would be suitable for mounted action; and in that they were disappointed. There were slag heaps and enclosures. There was barbed wire in the hedges, and there were deep, muddy ditches–there could be no hell-for-leather charging, ten squadrons together, on this terrain.

Curzon rode at the head of his regiment. Frequently he turned and looked back along the long column of sections, the khaki-clad men and the winding caterpillar of lance points. Try after self-control as he would, his heart persisted in beating faster. He even noticed a slight trembling of his hands as he held his reins, which was a symptom which roused his self-contempt and made him spurn himself as being as excitable as a woman. The Brigadier, riding along the column, reined in beside him for a moment and dropped a compliment about the condition of the regiment, but the brief conversation was suddenly interrupted by the roar of artillery close ahead. The General galloped forward to be on hand when orders should arrive, and Curzon was left riding wordlessly with Valentine at his elbow, waiting with all his acquired taciturnity for the moment of action.

Unhappily it was not given to the Twenty-second Lancers to distinguish themselves at Mons. To this day, when Curzon can be induced to talk about his experiences in the war, he always slurs over the opening period. Other regiments, more fortunate, fought real cavalry actions–but they were divisional cavalry or part of the brigade out on the left, who were lucky in encountering German cavalry of like mind to themselves, without wanton interference by cyclists or infantry. Curzon's brigade stayed in reserve behind the line while the Battle of Mons was being fought. Twice during that dreary day, they were moved hither and thither as the fortune of the battle in their front swayed back and forth. They heard the wild roar of the firing; they saw the river of wounded flowing back past them, and they saw the British batteries in action, but that was all. Even the Brigadier knew no more than they, until, towards evening, the wounded told them that Mons had been lost to a converging attack by overwhelming numbers. Night fell with the men in bivouac; the general opinion was that next day would see a great counter-attack in which the cavalry would find its opportunity.

Curzon lay down to sleep in the shelter of a hedge; he did not share the opinion of his officers, but neither could be oppose it. That feeling of unreality still held him fast, numbing the action of his mind. It was absurd to feel as he did, if these things were not really happening, as if nothing would ever happen, and yet he could not shake himself free from the feeling. Then he was wakened with a start in the darkness by someone shaking his shoulder.

'Orders, sir,' said Valentine's voice.

He read the scrap of paper by the light of the electric torch which Valentine held. It told him briefly that the brigade was to form on the road preparatory to a fresh march–nothing more.

'Get the regiment ready to move off at once,' he said, forcing himself into wakefulness.

There was a rush and bustle in the darkness, the whinnying of horses and the clattering of hoofs as the troopers, stupid with cold and sleep, prepared for the march. There was an interminable delay as the brigade formed up on the road, and dawn was just breaking as the march began. The march went on for eleven mortal days.

Curzon remembered little enough about those eleven days. At first there was a sense of shame and disappointment, for the British Army was in retreat, and the Twenty-second Lancers were near the head of the column, while far in the rear the boom and volleying of the guns told how the rearguard was still hotly engaged. But as the retreat went on the artillery fire waned, and exhaustion increased. Every day was one of blazing sun and suffocating dust. Sometimes the marches were prolonged far into the night; sometimes they began long before day was come, so that the men fell asleep in their saddles. The horses fell away in condition until even Curzon's fine, black hunter could hardly be forced into a trot by the stab of the sharpened spurs into his thick-coated flanks. The trim khaki uniforms were stained and untidy; beards sprouted on every cheek. Every day saw the number of absentees increase–two or three one day, ten or twelve the next, twenty or thirty the next, as the horses broke down and the regimental bad characters drank themselves into stupor to forget their fatigue. In the rear of the regiment trailed a little band of dismounted men, limping along with blistered feet under the burden of as much of their cavalry equipment as they could carry. Curzon scanned the nightly lists of missing with dumb horror. At the halts he hobbled stiffly among the men, exhorting them to the best of his limited ability to keep moving for the honour of the regiment, but something more than dust dried up his throat, and he was not a good enough actor to conceal entirely the despondency which was overpowering him.

Then there came a blessed day when the orders to continue the retreat were countermanded at the very moment when the brigade was formed up on the road. A moment later the Brigadier himself came up. He could give Curzon no reason for the change, but after half an hour's wait he gave permission for the regiment to fall out. There were pleasant meadows there, marshy presumably in winter, but hardly damp at the moment, by the side of a little stream of black water. They had a whole day of rest in those meadows. They cleaned and polished and shaved. As many as forty stragglers came drifting in during the morning–they had not been permanently lost, but, having fallen out for a moment, they had got jammed in the column farther to the rear and had never been able to rejoin. Everybody's spirits rose amazingly during those sunny hours. The Quartermaster-General's department achieved its daily miracle and heaped rations upon them, so that the men drank quarts of tea, brewed over bivouac fires, and then slept in heaps all over the meadows.

Curzon was able to find time to sit in his portable bath in a screened corner of the field, and to shave himself carefully and to cut his ragged moustache into its trim Lancer shape again–it was that afternoon that he first noticed grey hairs in it (there had been a few in his temples for some time now) and characteristically it never occurred to him to attribute their presence to the fatigues and anxieties of the last month. One servant brushed his clothes, the other groomed his horse, until by late afternoon Curzon, for the first time since he landed in France, began to feel his old efficient clear-thinking self again.

A motor-cyclist with a blue and white brassard came tearing along the road and stopped his machine at the entrance to the field. Valentine tore his dispatch from him and came running across the grass to Curzon.

'Are we going to advance, sir?' he asked eagerly, and Curzon nodded as he read the orders.

'Trumpeter!' yelled Valentine, all on fire with excitement.

The whole regiment seemed to have caught the infection, for as soon as the men saw that the column was headed back the way they had come they began to cheer, and went on cheering madly for several minutes as they got under way. They went back up the white road, over the little bridge with its R.E. demolition party still waiting, and forward towards where the distant low muttering of the guns was beginning to increase in volume and rise in pitch.

And yet the advance soon became as wearisome as the retreat had been. The regiment marched and marched and marched, at first in the familiar choking white dust, and then, when the weather broke, in a chilly and depressing rain. They saw signs of the fighting they had missed–wrecked lorries in the ditches, occasional abandoned guns, and sometimes dead Englishmen, dead Frenchmen, dead Germans. It seemed as if the Twenty-second Lancers were doomed to be always too late. They had not lost a man at Mons; the Marne had been fought while they were twenty miles away; they arrived on the Aisne just as the attempt to push back the German line farther still died away.

The Brigadier saw fit to rage in confidence to Curzon about this one evening in Curzon's billet. He bore it as a personal grudge that his brigade should have had no casualties save stragglers during a month's active service. But before midnight that same evening the situation changed. Curzon hurried round to brigade headquarters, his sword at his side, in response to a brief note summoning commanding officers. The Brigadier greeted his three colonels with a smile of welcome.

'There's work for us now, gentlemen,' he said eagerly, leading them to the map spread on the table. 'There's more marching ahead of us, but—'

He poured out voluble explanations. It appeared that during the retreat the Expeditionary Force's base had been transferred from Havre to Saint-Nazaire, and now would be changed again to the Channel ports. The German right flank was 'in the air' somewhere here, at Armentières. Clearly it would be best if it were the British Army which was dispatched to find that flank and turn the German line so as to roll it back on the Rhine and Berlin. The transfer was to begin next day, infantry and artillery by rail, cavalry by road, and he, the Brigadier, had been given a promise that the brigade would be in the advanced guard this time. It would be *here*, said the General, pointing to Ypres, that the attack would be delivered, up *this* road, he went on, pointing to Menin. The Belgian Army cavalry school was at Ypres, so that was clear proof that the country round about was suitable for mounted action. There were six men bending over that map–the General, three colonels, the brigade-major, and some unknown staff officer, and five of them were to find their graves at the point where the General's gnarled finger was stabbing at the map. Yet with Curzon at the moment his only reaction at this, his first hearing of the dread name of Ypres, was that it should be spelt in such an odd fashion and pronounced in a still odder one.

5

The weary marches were resumed, mostly in the rain. The brigade toiled along by by-roads to the rear of the French line, crossing often only after long delays, one line of communication after the other. They saw unsoldierly French territorial divisions, French coloured divisions, French ammunition and supply columns. After the second day came the order to hasten their march, with the result that they were on the move now from dawn till dark, hurrying through the rain, while the list of absent lengthened with each day.

For the flank of the Allies was as much 'in the air' as was that of the Germans, and Falkenhayn was making a thrust at the weak point just as was Joffre. The units which were gathering about Ypres were being pushed forward hurriedly into action, and every reinforcement which could be scraped together was being called upon to prolong the line. At Hazebrouck the roar of battle round about Armentières was clearly to be heard; it was the sight of British ammunition columns pouring up the road from Poperinghe and the stream of English wounded down it which first told Curzon that this was to be no case of heading an advance upon an unprotected and sensitive German flank.

It had been soon after midnight that fresh orders came to call them out of their muddy bivouac. Dawn found them plodding along the road through the rain. There were motor cars, motor-cycle dispatch riders, mounted orderlies hastening along the straight tree-lined road. An order came back to Curzon to quicken his pace; before very long Carruthers, the brigadier-major, came back at the gallop to reiterate it. But the horses were very weary. It was only a spiritless trot which could be got out of them as the regiment with jingling of accoutrements and squeaking of leather pounded heavily down the road.

The rain fell piteously, numbing the faculties. Suddenly there was a roar like an express train overhead, a shattering explosion, and a column of black smoke at the very edge of the road twenty yards behind Curzon. Somebody yelped with dismay. A horse screamed. Curzon looked back over his shoulder. There was a gap in the long column of dancing lance points.

'Keep them closed up, Browning,' he growled to the major at his side commanding the squadron, and Browning swung his horse out of the column, while Curzon rode on, Valentine at his side, jinglety-bump, jinglety-bump, over the slippery *pavé*.

More shells followed. Curzon found himself riding round the edge of a gaping hole in the road. There was a horrible litter of fragments of men and horses there, but Curzon found he was able to look at it without sensation; he could even note that none of the dead men had lances, and therefore belonged to the dragoon regiment at the head of the brigade, of which two squadrons had sabres only. They were in among houses now–several houses had shell-holes in walls or roof–and a pale staff officer with his left sleeve missing and a bloodstained bandage round his bare arm suddenly appeared and guided Curzon off by a by-road.

'Halt here, please, sir,' he said. 'You will receive orders in a minute.'

And the regiment stood still in the narrow street, the horses steaming in the rain, while the shells burst round them and Curzon tugged at his moustache. To judge by the noise, there was half a dozen batteries in action close at hand; the regiment was in the heart of a battle greater than Mons. The rain began to fall more heavily still, suddenly, just at the moment when the Brigadier came round the corner with his staff and the pale staff officer. Curzon moved to meet them, to be abruptly greeted.

'What in hell are you doing, Curzon?' blazed the General. 'Get your men dismounted and horseholders told off. Quick!'

Generals, of course, had to be allowed their fits of bad temper. It was only natural that a colonel of a cavalry regiment should keep his men ready for mounted action in the absence of express orders to the contrary. Curzon left Valentine to see to the dismounting of the men, while he got off his horse and looked at the map which the brigadier-major held open.

'The brigade is to prolong the line *here*,' said the brigade-major. 'You will come up on the right of the Surreys *here*. The Dragoons will be on your right.'

Curzon stared at the map, on which the raindrops fell with a steady pitter-patter. It was a featureless affair, with featureless names like Saint-Éloi and Kemmel and Messines–he had one like it in his leather map-case.

'Major Durrant, here, will guide you,' went on the brigade-major. 'Site your machine-guns with a good field and get your line entrenched as quick as you can.'

'Very good,' said Curzon. It seemed incredible that Carruthers could be talking to a cavalry colonel about machine-guns and entrenchments like this–Carruthers, who, that very summer in England, had argued so vehemently in favour of lance versus sabre. The words brought back that nightmare feeling of unreality again, but the General dispelled it a moment afterwards.

'Curzon,' he said quietly. 'We're the last troops that can arrive, and we're going straight into the line. There's nothing behind us. Nothing at all. If we give way, the war's lost. So there's nothing for you to do except to hold your position to the last man. At all costs, Curzon.'

'Yes, sir,' said Curzon, and the mist lifted from his brain immediately. That was the kind of order he could understand.

'Right,' said the General, and then, to Carruthers: 'Let's get along to the Dragoons.'

'Bring your regiment this way, sir,' said the wounded staff officer, and then, seeing the regimental officers still mounted, he added: 'They won't want their horses. You won't want your horse, sir, either.'

They marched, already weary with much riding, through the streets. Curzon took notice slightly of a long building which reminded him a little of the Houses of Parliament, and then they were out of the town again in flat green fields rising before them in the faintest of elevations.

'There go the Surreys,' said the staff officer, pointing over to their left front. 'You come up on their right.'

As he said the words, the First Battle of Ypres engulfed the Twenty-second Lancers. For two days now each successive parcel of British troops, as it arrived, had just sufficed to patch or extend the wavering front in face of the masses which the Germans were hurrying to the same point. The arrival of the last cavalry brigade enabled the British command to close the last gap with less than a quarter of an hour to spare, for the German attack here was launched just as the Twenty-second Lancers extended into line. There was no time for Curzon to think about entrenchments or a good field of fire for his machine-guns. A sudden hail of bullets and shells fell all about the regiment, and then even as cavalry tradition evaporated and primeval instinct asserted itself in search for cover, monstrous grey masses came looming through the rain over the slight crest half a mile in front.

There was no time for orders or scientific fire control. It was every man's business to seize his rifle and begin firing as rapidly as he could at the advancing lines. They wavered and hesitated, came on again, and finally shredded away. Immediately afterwards fresh masses came pouring over the crest, gathering up with them the remains of their predecessors. There were mounted officers in the front, waving swords over their heads as if this were Malplaquet or Waterloo. Curzon, standing staring through his glasses, watched them toppling down one by one as the attack died away. He stared mesmerized until he suddenly awoke to the realization that bullets were crackling all round him. The enemy were lying down firing until fresh impetus could be gathered to renew the attack.

He looked along the line of his regiment. There was no trace of order there; half the men had established themselves in a drainage ditch which miraculously ran roughly in the desired direction and afforded cover to anyone who could bring himself to lie down in its thick black mud. That meant the centre was as solidly established as one could hope to be. Young Borthwick–Lieutenant the Honourable George Borthwick–was in an angle of a tributary ditch to the front with his machine-gun section, the men digging frantically with anything that came to hand, so as to burrow into the bank for shelter. Borthwick had been given the machine-guns, not as the most promising machine-gun officer in the regiment (a distinction the whole mess scorned), but because he had the most slovenly seat on a horse that had ever disgraced the ranks of the Twenty-second Lancers. Curzon realized with a twinge of anxiety that the reputation of the regiment suddenly had come to depend to a remarkable extent on how much efficiency young Borthwick had acquired at his job.

He strode over to inspect Borthwick's efforts, Valentine beside him. He leaped the muddy ditch, in which the regiment was crouching, so as not to soil his boots, and stood on the lip of the bank looking down at where Borthwick was sitting in the mud with the lock of a machine-gun on his lap.

'Are you all right, Borthwick?' he asked.

'Yes, sir,' said Borthwick, sparing him just a glance, and then to his sergeant: 'Is that belt ready?'

Curzon left him to his own devices; this much was certain, that however little Borthwick knew about machine-guns it was more than Curzon did. They went back to the ditch.

'Better have a look at the flanks,' said Curzon, and took his leisurely way to the right. The men stared at him. In that pelting hail of bullets they felt as if they could not get close enough to the ground, and yet here was the Colonel standing up and walking about as cool as a cucumber. It was not so much that Curzon was unafraid, but that in the heat of action and under the burden of his responsibility he had not stopped to realize that there was any cause for fear.

The right flank was not nearly as satisfactorily posted as the centre. The little groups of men scattered along here were almost without cover. They were cowering close to the ground behind casual inequalities of level–several men were taking cover behind the dead bodies of their comrades–and only the accident that there were three shell craters close together at this point gave any semblance of solidity to the line. Moreover, there was only a pretence of touch maintained with the Dragoons on the right; there was a full hundred yards bare of defenders between the Lancers' right and the beginning of the ditch wherein was established the Dragoons' left.

'Not so good,' said Curzon over his shoulder to Valentine, and received no reply. He looked round. Ten yards back one of those bullets had killed Valentine, silently, instantly, as Curzon saw when he bent over the dead body.

And as he stooped, he heard all the rifles in the line redouble their fire. Borthwick's two machine-guns began to stammer away on his left. The Germans were renewing their advance; once more there were solid masses of grey-clad figures pouring over the fields towards them. But one man with a rifle can stop two hundred advancing in a crowd–more still if he is helped by machine-guns. Curzon saw the columns reel under the fire, and marvelled at their bravery as they strove to struggle on. They bore terrible losses before they fell back again over the crest.

Curzon did not know–and he did not have either time or inclination at the moment to ponder over the enemy's tactics–that the attacking troops at this point were drawn from the six German divisions of volunteers, men without any military training whatever, who were being sent forwards in these vicious formations because they simply could not manoeuvre in any other. What he did realize was that as soon as the enemy realized the hopelessness of these attacks, and turned his artillery against the regiment, the latter would be blasted into nothingness in an hour of bombardment unless it could contrive shelter. He walked along the line, with the bullets still crackling round him.

'Get your men digging,' he said to Captain Phelps, the first officer he saw.

'Yes, sir,' said Phelps. 'Er–what are they going to dig with, sir?'

Curzon looked Phelps up and down from his cropped fair hair and pop-eyes to his sword-belt and his boots. It was a question which might reasonably have been asked on manoeuvres. Cavalry had no entrenching tools, and the Twenty-second Lancers had, from motives of pride, evaded throughout their corporate existence the annual two hours' instruction in field fortification which the regulations prescribed for cavalry. But this was war now. A battle would be lost, England would be endangered, if the men did not entrench. Curzon boiled with contempt for Phelps at that moment. He felt he could even see trembling on Phelps's lips a protest about the chance of the men soiling their uniforms, and he was angered because he suspected that he himself would have been stupid and obstructive if his brain had not been activated by his urgent, imminent responsibility.

'God damn it, man,' he blazed. 'Get your men digging, and don't ask damn-fool questions.'

The fear of death or dishonour will make even cavalry dig, even without tools–especially when they were urged on by a man like Curzon, and when they were helped by finding themselves in muddy fields whose soil yielded beneath the most primitive makeshift tools. A man could dig in that mud with his bare hands–many men did. The Twenty-second sank into the earth just as will a mole released upon a lawn. The crudest, shallowest grave and parapet quadrupled a man's chance of life.

The fortunate ditch which constituted the greater part of the regiment's frontage, and the shallow holes dug on the rest of it, linked together subsequently by succeeding garrisons, constituted for months afterwards the front line of the British trench system in the Salient–a haphazard line, its convolutions dictated by pure chance, and in it many men were to lose their lives for the barren honour of retaining that worthless ground, overlooked and searched out by observation from the slight crests (each of which, from Hill 60 round to Pilckem, was to acquire a name of ill-omen) which the cavalry brigade had chanced to be too late, by a quarter of an hour, to occupy.

For the moment there could be no question of readjustment of the line. Some time in the late afternoon the bombardment began–a rain of shells compared with which anything Curzon had seen in South Africa was as a park lake to the ocean. It seemed impossible for anything to live through it. The bombardment seemed to reduce men to the significance of ants, but, like ants, they sought and found shelter in cracks in the ground; the very pits the shells dug gave them protection, for this bonbardment, so colossal to their dazed minds, was not to be compared with the later bombardments of the war when mathematical calculations showed that every patch of ground must be hit by three separate shells.

When it was falling dark the bombardment ceased and the German volunteers came forward in a new attack, climbing over their heaped dead, to leave fresh swathes of corpses only a few yards farther on. It was the lifting of the bombardment and the roar of musketry from the Surreys on the left which the dazed men huddled in the mud first noticed, but it was Curzon who repelled that attack. There was no limit to his savage energy in the execution of a clear-cut task. He had no intention in the least of impressing his men with his ability to be everywhere at once, but that was the impression which the weary troopers formed of him. In his anxiety to see that every rifle was in action he hurried about the line rasping out his orders. The wounded and the faint-hearted alike brought their rifles to their shoulders again under the stimulus of his presence. It was this kind of leadership for which all his native talents, all his experience and all his training were best suited. While Curzon was at hand not the most fleeting thought of retreat could cross a man's mind.

The attack withered away, and darkness came, and the pitiless chilling rain continued to fall. Curzon, with every nerve at strain with the responsibility on his shoulders, felt no need for rest. There was much to be done–ammunition to be gathered from the pouches of the dead, patrols to be sent out to the front to guard against a night surprise, wounded to be got out of the way, back to the shell-hole where the medical officer crouched trying to save life by the last glimmerings of a dying electric torch. The earth still shook to the guns, the sky was still lighted by the flame of the explosions. Shells were still coming over, and every little while a tremor of alarm ran down the attenuated line and men grabbed their rifles and fired blindly into the darkness while patrols out in front fell flat on their faces and cursed their own countrymen.

There was an alarm from the rear while Curzon was stumbling along through the dark seeing that the line was evenly occupied. He heard the well-remembered voice of the Brigadier saying: 'Point that rifle the other way, you fool,' and he hastened back to where a trooper was sheepishly allowing the General and a dozen looming forms behind him to approach.

'Ah, Curzon,' said the General when he heard his voice. 'All well here?'

'Yes, sir,' said Curzon.

'I've had to bring up the supply column myself,' said the General.

A brighter flash than usual lit up the forms of the men in his train; the leader was in R.E. uniform and bent under a load of spades.

'Thank God for those,' said Curzon. He would not have believed, three months back, that he would ever have thanked God for a gift of spades, but now he saw no incongruity.

'I thought you'd be glad of 'em,' chuckled the General. 'I've got you fifty spades. The rest's S.A.A. I suppose you can do with that, too?'

'My God, yes,' said Curzon. The supply of small arms ammunition had fallen away to less than a dozen rounds a man. He had not dared to think what would happen when it was finished.

'Take it over, then,' said the General. 'I've got a lot more for these men to do.'

'Can't they stay here, sir?' said Curzon. He longed inexpressibly for a reinforcement of a dozen riflemen.

'No,' snapped the General, and then, to the carrying party: 'Put that stuff down and get back as quick as you can.'

There was a bustle in the darkness as the regiment took charge of the loads. The voice of Lieutenant Borthwick could be heard demanding ammunition for his precious guns. Curzon left Major Browning to supervise the distribution while, obedient to a plucked sleeve, he followed the General away out of earshot of the men.

'I couldn't send you up any food,' said the General. 'But you're all right until tomorrow for that, with your emergency rations. You'll have two a man, I suppose, counting what you'll get off the dead.'

'Pretty nearly, sir,' said Curzon.

'You'll be able to hold on, I suppose?' went on the General, his voice dropping still lower. His face was invisible in the darkness.

'Of course, sir,' said Curzon.

'Speak the truth–lying's no use.'

Curzon ran his mind's eye over the line, visualizing the improvements those fifty spades would bring about, the new life the fresh ammunition would bring to Borthwick's guns, the piled dead on the hill-top above, the exhaustion of his troopers.

'Yes, we ought to get through tomorrow all right,' he said.

'Tomorrow? You'll have to hold on for a fortnight, perhaps. But let's get through tomorrow first. You've got patrols out? You're strengthening your line?'

'Yes, sir.'

'I knew I could trust you all right. I couldn't get over here during the day–had to stay with the Surreys. Browne's dead, you know.'

'Not really, sir?'

'Yes. And so's Harvey of the Dragoons. You succeed to the brigade if I'm hit.'

'Don't say that, sir.'

'Of course I must say it. But I've no orders to give you in case I am. It'll just mean holding on to the last man.'

'Yes, sir.'

'There's two hundred men in the brigade reserve. Horseholders. R.E.s., A.S.C. Don't be lavish with 'em, because that's all there are between here and Havre. And don't trust that major who's commanding the Surreys now. You know who I mean–Carver's his name.'

'Yes, sir.'

'I'm getting a second line dug on the edge of the wood back there. But it won't be any use if they break through. Not enough men to man it. So you've got to hold on. That's all.'

'Yes, sir.'

'Good-night, Curzon.'

'Good-night, sir.'

The darkness engulfed the General as he plodded back alone across the sodden earth, and Curzon went back into the trench, to goad the men into more furious digging, to see that the sentries were alert. Yet even despite Curzon's activity, despite the guns, and the shells, and the pitiless rain, there were men who slept, half-buried in the mire–there never was a time when at least a few British private soldiers in any unit could not contrive an opportunity for sleep.

6

Perhaps it had been a premonition which had caused the Brigadier-General to talk so freely to Curzon about what should be done should the latter succeed to his command. It was no later than next morning, when the German bombardment was searching for the shallow seam in the earth wherein crouched the Twenty-second Lancers, that a mud-daubed runner came crawling up the drainage ditch which had already assumed the function of a communication trench in this section, and gave Curzon a folded scrap of paper. The writing was blurred and shaky, and the signature was indecipherable, but the meaning was clear. The General was dead and Curzon was in command of the brigade. The runner was able to supplement the information–a shell had hit the brigade headquarters and had killed or wounded everyone there and left everything disorganized. It was clearly necessary that Curzon should waste no time in taking over his duties.

He passed the word for Major Browning, and briefly handed over the command of the regiment to him.

'What are the orders, sir?' asked Browning.

A Frenchman would have shrugged his shoulders at that question. Curzon could only eye Browning with a stony expressionless gaze.

'None, except to hold on to the last man,' he said, not taking his eyes off Browning's face. Perhaps this was as well, for he saw a flicker of despair in Browning's eyes. 'You understand, Browning?'

'Yes, sir,' said Browning, but Curzon had already made a mental note that Browning of the Twenty-second Lancers would need stiffening as much as Carver of the Surreys.

'Those are positive orders, Browning,' he said. 'There's no chance of their being modified, and you have no discretion.'

'Yes, sir,' said Browning. Whatever motives had led Browning to join the Twenty-second Lancers as a pink-faced subaltern, twenty years ago, he was being condemned for them now to mutilation or death, and Curzon did not feel sorry for him, only irritated. Men who stopped to think about their chances of being killed were a nuisance to their superior officers.

'Right,' said Curzon. 'I'll come up again and inspect as soon as I can.'

He picked his way along the ditch, the runner crawling behind him. But such was his appreciation of the need for haste that Curzon ignored the danger of exposing himself, and walked upright across the fields pitted with shell-holes while the runner cursed him to himself. The cottage beside the lane to which the runner guided him had been almost completely demolished by a high-explosive shell. As Curzon approached the first sound to strike his ear was a high-pitched, querulous stream of groans and blasphemies. There were some dead bodies and fragments of bodies lying on the edge of the lane, and the red tabs on one obscene fragment showed what had happened to the Brigadier. The groans and blasphemies came from Carruthers the brigadier-major, or what was left of him. There was an orderly bending over him, as he lay on the grass, but the orderly was despairing of inducing this shrieking thing which had graced so many race meetings ever to be silent. Five or six runners were squatting stoically in the ditch near the cottage; there was an R.E. detachment stumbling through the cabbages in the garden with a reel of telephone wire.

Within the shattered walls, down in the cellar now exposed to the light of day, lay Durrant, the staff officer, who yesterday had guided the Twenty-second into action. His left arm was still bare, but the bandage round it was no longer red, but black, and his tunic was torn open at the breast showing white skin. He was putting a field telephone back on its hook as Curzon arrived, and, catching sight of him, he snatched it up again with a hasty:

'Hullo. Hold on. Here he is.'

Then he looked up at Curzon and went on:

'We're through to the First Corps, sir. Just re-established communication.'

Curzon lowered himself into the cellar and took up the instrument. There was a moment of murmurings and grumblings before the earpiece spoke.

'Commanding the Cavalry Brigade?' it asked.

'Yes. This is Colonel Curzon, Twenty-second Lancers, just taken over.'

'Right. You'll go on reporting to us for the present. We've told your division.'

'Very well. Any orders?'

'You are to hold your position at all costs. At–all–costs. Good-bye.'

Curzon put down the receiver and stood silent. The pain-extorted ravings of Carruthers, twenty yards away, came pouring down to him, cutting through the roar of the battle, but he heard neither sound. He was tugging at his moustache; his rather full, rather loose lips were set hard and straight. He was adjusting his mind to the business of commanding a brigade; and he was ready for the responsibility in ten seconds, and turned to the wounded staff officer.

'Any report from the Dragoons?' he demanded.

That was the beginning of eleven days of anxiety and danger and responsibility and desperate hard work. Even if Curzon had the necessary literary ability, he could never write an account of the First Battle of Ypres in which he took so prominent a part, for his later recollections of it could never be sorted out from the tangle into which they lapsed. He could never recover the order in which events occurred. He could never remember which day it was that the commander of the First Corps, beautifully groomed, superbly mounted, came riding up the lane to see for himself what were the chances of the Cavalry Brigade maintaining its precarious hold upon its seemingly untenable position, nor which day it was that he had spent in the trenches of the Surreys, leading the counter-attack which caused the Germans to give back at the moment when there were only a hundred or two exhausted Englishmen to oppose the advance of an army corps.

Curzon's work during these eleven days resembled that of a man trying to keep in repair a dam which is being undermined by an unusual flood. He had to be here, there, and everywhere plastering up weak points–the materials at his disposal being the two hundred men of the brigade reserve whom he had found ready to his hand, and the scrapings of other units, reservists, L. of C. troops, which were sent up to him once or twice from G.H.Q. There was the ammunition supply to be maintained, food to be sent up into the line–for water the troops drank from the stagnant pools in the shell-holes–and bombs to be doled out from the niggardly supply which the R.E. detachments in the field were just beginning to make.

He had to watch over his reserves like a miser, for he was pestered every minute with pathetic appeals from his subordinates for aid–and in this conservation of his resources his natural temperament was of use to him, because he found no difficulty in saying 'no', however urgently the request was drafted, if his judgment decided against it. He put new heart into the men by the way in which he disregarded danger, for to his natural courage was added the mental preoccupation which gave him no chance to think about personal risks. No soldier in the world could have remained unmoved by the nonchalant fashion in which he was always ready to lead into danger. In every crisis his big arrogant nose and heavy black moustache were to be seen as he came thrusting forward to judge for himself. Over and over again during those eleven days it was his arrival which turned the scale.

He was one of the fortunate ones. In the battle where the old British Army found its grave, where more than two-thirds of the fighting men met with wounds or death, he came through unscathed even though there were bullet holes in his clothes. It was as unlikely that he should survive as that a spun penny should come down heads ten times running, and yet he did; it was only men with that amount of good fortune who could come through long enough to make the tale of their lives worth the telling.

He was fortunate, too, in the chance of war which had put his brigade into line separate from the rest of the cavalry corps. There was no divisional general to reap the credit of the work done by his men, and the corps headquarters under whose direction he was placed regarded with approval the officer who carried out his orders with so little protest or complaint or appeal for further assistance, and who was always ready to try and wring another ounce of effort out of his exhausted men.

The old army died so gloriously at Ypres because the battle they had to fight called for those qualities of unflinching courage and dogged self-sacrifice in which they were pre-eminent. They were given the opportunity of dying for their country and they died uncomplaining. It occurred to no one that they had to die in that fashion because the men responsible for their training had never learned any lessons from history, had never realized what resources modern invention had opened to them, with the consequence that men had to do at the cost of their lives the work which could have been done with one-quarter the losses and at one-tenth the risk of defeat if they had been adequately armed and equipped. And of the surviving officers the ones who would be marked out for promotion and high command in the new army to be formed were naturally the ones who had proved themselves in the old-fashioned battle–men like Curzon of the Twenty-second Lancers.

For there could be no doubt at all that the High Command looked with approval on Curzon. When eventually the arrival of new units from distant garrisons and of an army corps from India enabled the exhausted front-line troops to be withdrawn a very great general indeed sent for Curzon at headquarters. The message arrived the very day that Curzon brought the cavalry brigade out of the line. He saw the brigade into billets–not much accommodation was necessary for those few score survivors, filthy, vermin-ridden men who fell asleep every few minutes–and did his best to smarten himself up. Then he got on his horse–it was good to feel a horse again between his knees–and rode slowly over in the dark of the late afternoon.

To Curzon there was something incredibly satisfying in his arrival at that pleasant château. He had seen enough of ruin and desolation, of haggard men in tatters, of deaths and wounds and misery, during the past weeks. Some of his beliefs and convictions had been almost shaken lately. It was a nightmare world from which he had emerged–a world in which cavalry regiments had clamoured for barbed wire, reels and reels of it, and in which horses had been ungroomed and neglected so that their holders could be sent into action with rifles and bayonets, and in which he had almost begun to feel doubts as to England's ultimate victory.

It was like emerging from a bad dream to ride in at the gates of the château, to have a guard turn out to him all spick and span, and to have his horse taken in charge by a groom whose uniform did not detract in the least from his general appearance of an old family retainer. There were beautiful horses looking out from loose-boxes; there were half a dozen motor cars polished to a dazzling glitter.

Then inside the house the atmosphere changed a little. Outside, it was like a country house with a military flavour. Inside it was like a court with a dash of monastery. There were the court functionaries moving about here and there, suave, calm and with an air of unfathomable discretion. There were the established favourites with a bit of swagger. There were anxious hangers-on, wondering what sort of reception would be accorded them today, and the rare visitors of Curzon's type who were not in the court uniform–the red tabs–and who only knew by sight the great ones who went to and fro.

The man who occupied the position corresponding to that of Grand Chamberlain came up to greet Curzon. Anyone better acquainted with courts would have been delighted with the cordiality of his reception, but to Curzon it only appeared as if he were receiving the politeness expected from a gentleman. It was good to drink whisky and soda again–only yesterday he had been drinking army rum out of an enamelled mug–and to exchange a few polite platitudes about the weather with no bearing on the military situation. The nightmare feeling of desperate novelty dropped away from Curzon as he stood and talked. This was life as it should be. His very weariness and the ache in his temples from lack of sleep was no more than he had often felt on his first return to the mess after a night in town. He was inexpressibly glad that he had recovered his kit at his billet and so had been able to change from his muddy tunic with the bullet holes in the skirt. A junior chamberlain came out of a blanket-hung door on the far side of the hall and came up to them with a significant glance at his senior. The time had come for Curzon's admission to the presence.

They went through the blanket-covered door into a long room, with windows extending along the whole of one side giving a fine view over a beautiful park.

There were tables covered with papers; clerks at work with typewriters; maps on the wall; more green baize tables; half a dozen red-tabbed officers with telephones before them at work in a very pleasant smell of cigars; and a door at the far end which gave entrance to a smaller room with the same view, the same green baize tables, and a chair which was politely offered to Curzon.

The actual interview was brief enough. Curzon had the impression that he was being sized up, but he felt no resentment at this–after all, less than four months ago he had been a mere major of cavalry, and his recent tenure of the command of a brigade began to assume an unsubstantial form in his mind in the presence of all this solid evidence of the existence of another world. He conducted himself with the modesty of his humble station. Nevertheless, he must have made a personal impression good enough to support that given by his record, for he came out of that room with a promise of his confirmation in a brigade command.

Not of his present brigade–that would be too much to expect, of course. The command of a regular brigade of cavalry was not the sort of appointment likely to be given to a newly promoted brigadier–and the speaker hastened to point out that additional consolation that the brigade would hardly be fit for action again for months after its recent losses even though by the special dispensation of Providence it had lost very few horses. But in England there were new armies being raised. There seemed to be a growing conviction (and here the speaker was elaborately non-committal) that the war would last long enough for them to be used as new formations and not as drafts. A mere hint to the War Office would ensure Curzon's appointment to a new army brigade. With his regiment out of action as it was at present Curzon might just as well take leave and go to London to see about it.

Curzon hesitated. There was not much attraction for him in the command of four raw battalions of infantry. But he knew the Army well enough; a man who declined a proffered promotion was likely to be left on the shelf from that time onwards unless he had powerful friends; and moreover he was only a temporary lieutenant-colonel. For all he knew, he might at any moment have to revert to his substantive rank of major. Better an infantry brigade than that. If good fortune came his way he might have a chance of commanding the brigade in action during the closing campaign of the war next summer. He left off tugging at his moustache and accepted the offer.

'Good!' said his host. 'And I think it's time for dinner now.'

7

Outwardly the London to which Curzon returned was not very different from the London he had always known. The streets were darker and there were more uniforms to be seen, but that was all. After the first paralysing blow of the declaration of war the city had made haste to recover its balance to the cry of 'Business as Usual.' The theatres were as gay as ever–gayer, if anything; the restaurants more crowded. Most of the people in the streets were so convinced of England's approaching victory in the war that now that the front was stabilized the war had ceased to be a matter of more interest to them than their own personal concerns.

But here and there were cases of interest. The Club, for instance. When Curzon went in there he found the place crowded with men he did not recognize. In addition to many men in the khaki which had scarcely ever been seen in the Club in the old days, all the retired officers who hardly set foot in the Club from year's end to year's end had now crowded up to London to besiege the War Office for employment, and were spending their time of waiting listening all agog for rumours. Curzon had not realized the efficiency of the censorship until he found men crowding round him all intent on acquiring first-hand information. Birtles started it–Birtles had been a major in the regiment when Curzon was only a subaltern.

''Morning, Curzon,' said Birtles when they encountered each other on the stairs, and would have passed him by if he had not suddenly remembered that Curzon must have come back from France on leave from the regiment; he halted abruptly. 'On leave, eh?'

'Yes,' said Curzon.

'What–er,' said Birtles, checking himself in the midst of a question as he suddenly had a spasm of doubt lest Curzon had been 'sent home'. But he reassured himself quickly on that point, because no man who had been sent home would show his face in the Club–at least, not for years. So he was able to continue. 'What's the regiment doing?'

Curzon said what he could about the regiment's achievements.

'Dismounted action, eh?' said Birtles. 'That's bad. Very bad. And what about you? Short leave, or something?'

Curzon was in civilian clothes, so that Birtles had nothing to go on. Yet he was obviously painfully anxious to ask questions. His old eyes were watering with anxiety. Curzon said he was home to take up a fresh command.

'Yeomanry or something?'

'No, an infantry brigade,' said Curzon.

'A brigade? A brigade!' gasped Birtles, who, naturally, having once known Curzon as a subaltern, could not think of him as anything else. 'Here, come and have a drink. I mean–have you time for a drink?'

Curzon was in need of a drink after his busy morning. He had called at the War Office and had had a very satisfactory interview, because a note about him from G.H.Q. in France had already arrived; and he had been told that his promotion to the temporary rank of brigadier-general would appear in the next *Gazette*. Not merely that, either. There would undoubtedly be a brigade for him at the end of his fortnight's leave. More still; besides his inevitable mention in dispatches there would be a decoration for him–most likely a commandership of the Most Honourable Order of the Bath. Three eminent soldiers had cross-examined him in turn about the state of affairs in Flanders–there was a general anxiety to try and supplement the information doled out by telegram from G.H.Q.–and he had answered questions as well as he knew how.

And from the War Office he had gone to his military tailor's. They did not seem to remember him at first, which had annoyed him, and they had expressed doubt about their ability in face of a torrent of orders, to supply his demands in the next week. Their attitude had changed a little when he told them who he was, and still more when he gave his order for a general's uniform with the red tabs and crossed sword and baton of his rank. There had been more excitement than he had expected in giving that order–Curzon was still conscious of a little thrill when he remembered it, and he really badly needed his drink.

Yet by the time the drink had come to him he had precious little opportunity of drinking it, because Birtles hastened to spread the news that he was entertaining a brigadier-general home from the Front, and from every corner of the Club men came crowding to hear his news and to ask him questions, or merely to look at the man newly returned from a European war. They were grey-headed old men, most of them, and they eyed him with envy. With anxiety, too; they had been gathering their information from the all-too-meagre *communiqués* and from the all-too-extensive casualty lists. They feared to know the worst at the same time as they asked, and they raised their voices in quavering questions about this unit and that, and to every question Curzon could only give a painful answer. There was not a unit in the Expeditionary Force which had not poured out its best blood at Mons or at Le Cateau or at Ypres.

For a long time Curzon dealt out death and despair among those old men; it was fortunate that he did not feel the awkwardness which a more sensitive man might have felt. After all, casualties were a perfectly natural subject for a military man to discuss. It was need for his lunch which caused him in the end to break off the conversation, and even at lunch he was not free from interruption. Someone came up and spoke to him as he began on his soup–a tall, heavily built bald old man in the uniform of a captain of a very notable regiment of infantry. He displayed all the embarrassment of an English gentleman addressing a stranger with an unconventional request.

'I beg your pardon for interrupting you,' he began. Curzon tried to be polite, although it was a strain when he had hardly begun his lunch.

'The fact is'–went on the captain–'of course, I must apologize for being unconventional–I was wondering if you had made any arrangements for dinner tonight?'

Curzon stared at him. But his arrangements were of the vague sort an officer home on leave without a relation in the world might be expected to have.

'Well—' began Curzon. It was the fact that this stranger belonged to that very crack regiment which caused him to temporize.

'You see,' went on the captain hastily. 'I was hoping–I know all this sounds most impertinent–I was hoping that I could induce you to dine at my brother's tonight.'

He had fumbled out his card by now, and proffered a card with embarrassed fingers. Curzon read upon it the simple words: 'Lord George Winter-Willoughby'. He only half heard what Lord George, voluble at last, went on to say, while he co-ordinated in his mind what the name meant to him. The Winter-Willoughbys were the Bude family, whose head was the Duke of Bude with a score of other titles, who had held office in the last Conservative

Government. The courtesy title of Lord implied that the present speaker was a son of a duke–more, it meant that he was brother of the present Duke–in fact, it meant that the invitation now being given was to dine with the Duke of Bude. Confirmation trickled through into Curzon's consciousness from the bits of Lord George's speech which Curzon heard–'Bude House'–'Eight o'clock'–'Quite informal–war-time, you know'–'Telephone'–'The Duke and Duchess will be delighted if you can come.'

The self-control which had enabled Curzon for fifteen years to conceal the part which chance had played in the battle of Volkslaagte made it possible for him to accept an invitation to dine at one of the greatest London houses as though he were thoroughly accustomed to such invitations and Lord George displayed immense relief at not being snubbed, apologized once more for the informality of his behaviour, pleaded the present national crisis as his excuse, and withdrew gracefully.

It was fortunate that Curzon was not a man given to analysis of sociological conditions; if he had been he would certainly have wasted the rest of that day in thinking about how extensive must be the present upheaval if it resulted in hasty invitations to Bude House addressed to men of no family at all–he was fully aware that six months ago there would have been no perceptible difference between such an invitation and a Royal Command. As it was, he merely savoured pleasantly of his success and went out and bought a new set of buttons for his white waistcoat.

In December 1914 'war-time informality' at Bude House implies something quite different from what those words meant in, say, Bloomsbury in 1918. There was a footman as well as a butler to open the door to Curzon, but they were both over military age and the footman's livery was inconspicuous. For the first time in his life Curzon described himself as 'General Curzon' for the butler to announce him.

'It's very good of you to come, General,' said a tall woman with dyed hair, offering her hand as he approached her across the deep carpet of the not-too-large drawing-room.

'It's very good of you to ask me,' Curzon managed to say. The bulky figure of Lord George showed itself at the Duchess's side, and beside it a bulkier counterpart of itself, as if the law of primogeniture ensured that the holder of the title should be a size larger than the young son. There were introductions effected. The Duke was as bald as his brother–only a wisp of grey hair remaining round his ears. Lady Constance Winter-Willoughby was apparently Lord George's wife, and was as lovely and as dignified as was to be expected of a daughter of an earldom six generations older than the Dukedom of Bude.

Lady Emily Winter-Willoughby was the Duke's daughter; she was nearly as tall as her father, but she was not conspicuous for beauty of feature or of dress. For a fleeting moment Curzon, as his eyes wandered over her face, was conscious of a likeness between her features and those of Bingo, the best polo pony he ever had, but the thought vanished as quickly as it came when he met her kindly grey eyes. Lady Emily, especially now that she had left thirty behind, had always been a woman who preferred the country to London, and felt more at home with horses and dogs and flowers than with the politicians whom she was likely to encounter at Bude House. A few more years might see her an embittered spinster; but at the moment she only felt slightly the tediousness of this life–just enough to sense the slight awkwardness Curzon was careful not to display. When their eyes met they were both suddenly conscious of a fellow feeling, and they smiled at each other almost as if they were members of some secret society.

It was with an odd reluctance that Curzon left the warm glow of Lady Emily's proximity to meet the other two guests, a Sir Henry Somebody (Curzon did not catch the name) and his wife. They were a sharp-featured pair, both of them. Curzon formed the impression that Sir Henry must be some sort of lawyer, and that his wife had wits just as keen. There was a depressing moment of impersonal conversation with them before dinner was announced.

The advent of the war had accelerated the already noticeable decline from the great days of the Edwardians; dinners were very different now from the huge meals and elaborate service of ten years before; twelve courses had diminished to six; there was some attempt to please by simplicity instead of to impress by elaboration. The dining-room was lit by candles so that it was hard to see the painted arched ceiling; there was not a great deal of silver displayed upon the circular table. But the food was perfection, and the wine marvellous–Bude House had not seen fit to follow the example of Buckingham Palace and eschew all alcoholic liquor for the duration of the war.

As the Vouvray was being served Lady Constance on Curzon's right recounted how, a short time before, at another dinner-party where the hostess had to do like Queen Mary and confine her guests to lemonade and barley water, the guests had one and all produced pocket flasks to make up for the absence of liquor. With eight people at a circular table general conversation was easy, and the Duchess on Curzon's left announced incisively that if she had been the hostess in question she would never receive one of those guests again, but she went on to agree only the dear Queen could expect people to dine without drinking.

'It's bad enough having to do without German wines,' she said. 'We had some Hock that the Duke was very proud of, but of course we can't drink it *now*, can we?'

Curzon agreed with her, and not out of deference, either. He was quite as convinced as she was that there was no virtue left in Hock or in Wagner or in Goethe or in Drüer. From the innate badness of German art to the recent deeds of the German Government was but a step in the conversation–a step easily taken as at least seven of the eight people present were anxious to take it. Before very long Curzon found himself talking about his recent experiences, and he was listened to with rapt attention. It was generally a question either from Sir Henry (on the other side of the Duchess) or from Sir Henry's wife (on the other side of the Duke) which moved him steadily on from one point to the next–at one moment Curzon noted to himself that Sir Henry simply must be a lawyer of some sort as he had already surmised, because the tone of his questions had a ring of the law courts about it.

The conversation had a different trend from that at the Club in the morning. There was not so much anxiety displayed as to the fates of regiments and battalions. The party seemed to be far more interested in the general conduct of the war–Sir Henry, in particular, seemed to know a good deal more already about Mons and Le Cateau than Curzon did. Curzon almost began to form the idea that they would have relished criticism of the Higher Command, but he put the notion away before it crystallized. That was inconceivable; moreover, there was no chance of his disparaging his superiors to anyone–to say nothing of the fact that he had only the haziest ideas about the conduct of a great deal of the war. The British Army had been pitted against superior numbers over and over again, and had emerged each time from the ordeal with honour. Of crisis at headquarters he knew no more than any subaltern, and he denied their existence with all his soldier's pride. Besides, no soldier who had served under Kitchener could lightly give away anything approaching a military secret.

If the company, as it appeared reasonable to suppose, had been expecting any juicy bits of scandal, they were doomed to disappointment. In fact, the disappointment on the faces of the Duchess, Lady Constance, and Sir Henry's wife was almost noticeable even to Curzon, who got as far as feeling that his conversation was not as brilliant as it should have been–a feeling which did not surprise him in the least. It only made him take more notice of Lady Emily, who showed no disappointment at all.

When the conversation moved from the general to the particular, Curzon was still rather at sea. All his life he had been a regimental officer; these people were far more familiar with individuals on the General Staff than he was–to him they were only surnames, while at this table they were spoken of as 'Bertie' and 'Harry' and 'Arthur'. There was only one moment of tense reality, and that was when young Carruthers was mentioned. For a tiny interval Curzon forgot where he was; he forgot the polished table, and the glittering silver, and the exquisite food within him, and the butler brooding over his shoulder like a benevolent diety. It seemed as if he was back at brigade headquarters again, with the tortured screams of Carruthers sounding in his ears. A flood of memories followed–of Major Browning combating the deadly fear which was shaking him like a leaf, of the four headless troopers lying in a huddled heap in one bay of the trench, of the mud and the stench and the sleeplessness.

It was only for a moment. The extraordinary feeling that these men and women here should be forced somehow to realize that these things were part of the same framework as Arthur's appointment to the Adjutant-General's department passed away, killed by its own absurdity, before the others had finished their kind words about Carruther's fate and had passed on to the discussion of someone still alive. After all, it would be as bad taste to force these inevitable details of war upon the notice of these women and civilians as it would be to do the same with the details of digestive processes or any other natural occurrence.

Then the women rose to leave the table and gave Curzon a further opportunity to come back to normal again, as the men closed up round the Duke. The war tended to disappear from the conversation from that moment, while later in the drawing-room where they rejoined the ladies, Lady Constance played the piano very brilliantly indeed so that conversation was not necessary. The music was a little over Curzon's head, but he had a very good dinner inside him and some excellent port, and he was quite content to sit beside Lady Emily and listen vaguely. It was with quite a shock that he found himself nodding in his chair–it was typical of Curzon not to realize what enormous demands those eleven days of furious action and eleven nights of little sleep at Ypres had made upon his strength.

So that it was with relief that he saw Lord George and Lady Constance rise to take their leave, making it possible for him to go immediately afterwards. And Sir Henry's wife said to him as he said good-bye to her: 'Perhaps you'll come and dine with *us* if you can spare another evening of your leave?' so that he felt he had not been quite a failure in society.

8

The same morning that Curzon's promotion to the temporary rank of Brigadier-General appeared in the Press, there arrived the invitation to dinner, which enabled Curzon to confirm his suspicion that Sir Henry was really Sir Henry Cross, the barrister and Conservative Member of Parliament; and the other letter which the waiter brought him was a note from the War Office:

> Dear Curzon,
> Sorry to interrupt your leave, but could you possibly come and see me here in room 231 at your earliest convenience?
> Yours,
> G. Mackenzie, Major-Gen.

Curzon puzzled over this note as he ate his kidneys and bacon solitary in the hotel dining-room–his early-rising habit persisted even in a West End hotel, so that he was bound to be the only one having breakfast at that gloomy hour. It was a surprise to him to be addressed as 'Dear Curzon' by General Mackenzie. Mackenzie had been one of the eminent officers who had discussed the war with him two days before, but half an hour's conversation did not seem sufficient reason for the Director-General of Tactical Services to address him without a prefix and to preface with an apology what might just as well have been a simple order. It was possible that now that he was a General himself he was being admitted into the confraternity of Generals who might have their own conventions of behaviour among themselves, but Curzon did not think that very likely.

He smoked a comfortable cigar while he read *The Times*–he could not help reading the announcement of his promotion three times over–and then he walked across St James's Park and the Horse Guards to the War Office. Relays of commissionaires and Boy Scouts led him through the corridors to Room 231. There was only the briefest of delays before he was brought into the office of the Director-General of Tactical Services, and Mackenzie offered him a chair and a cigar and made three remarks about the weather before he began to say what he meant to say.

'I didn't know you were acquainted with the Budes, Curzon?' he began.

'I know them slightly,' replied Curzon cautiously. 'I dined there a night or two ago.'

'Yes, I know that,' was the surprising rejoinder. Mackenzie drummed with his fingers, and looked across his desk at Curzon with a hint of embarrassment on his large pink face. His ginger hair was horribly out of harmony with the red tabs on his collar. 'That fellow Cross was there, too.'

'Yes,' said Curzon.'

'You've never had anything to do with politicians, Curzon,' went on Mackenzie. 'You've no idea how gossip spreads.'

'I don't gossip, sir,' said Curzon indignantly.

'No,' said Mackenzie. 'Of course not.'

He looked meditatively at his finger-nails before he spoke again.

'Cross has put down a question to ask in the House today–the House of Commons, I mean. It's about Le Cateau.'

'That's nothing to do with me,' said Curzon, more indignantly still, as the implication became obvious to him.

'That was all I wanted to know,' said Mackenzie, simply. His bright eyes, of a pale grey, were scrutinizing Curzon very closely, all the same. Mackenzie could not make up his mind as to whether or not this was yet another example of the plain blunt soldier with secret political affiliations.

'We can put the lid on friend Cross all right,' he went on. 'We can always say that it is opposed to public interest to answer his question, if we want to.'

'I suppose so,' agreed Curzon.

'But the House of Commons is not a very important place just now, thank God,' said Mackenzie. 'It isn't there that things happen.'

Curzon felt bewildered at that. If Mackenzie was not accusing him of betraying military secrets he could not imagine what he was driving at. He had no conception of the power residing in the casual conversation of about fifty or so luncheon and dinner tables in London. He did not realize that high position in the Army–even the post of Director-General of Tactical Services–was, if not exactly at the mercy of, at any rate profoundly influenced by, whispers which might circulate in a particular stratum of society. More especially was this the case when a rigid censorship left public opinion unable to distribute praise or blame except under the influence of gossip or of prejudice. All these circumstances were aggravated by the fact that England had entered upon the war under a government not at all representive of the class accustomed to the dispensing of military patronage; there were already hints and signs that to prolong its existence the government must allow some of the opposition to enter its ranks, and in that case the foolish ones who had staked their careers on its continuance unchanged in power would be called upon to pay forfeit.

Mackenzie felt strongly opposed to explaining all this to Curzon. It might be construed as a confession of weakness. Instead, he harked back to the original subject.

'The Bude House set,' he said, '–the women, I mean, not the men–want a finger in every pie.'

'I didn't know that,' said Curzon perfectly truthfully. Of course, throughout his life, he had heard gossip about petticoat influence. But he had not believed–in fact, he still did not believe–that people played at politics as at a game, in which the amount of patronage dispensed acted as a useful measure of the score, so that to have brought about the appointment of one's own particular nominee to an Under-Secretaryship of State was like bringing off a little slam at bridge.

Now that the war had become such a prominent feature in the news, and friends and relations were taking commissions or returning from retirement, the value of military appointments as counters in the game was higher than ever before. And at the moment the Army was especially entangled in politics, thanks to the Irish business. When certain people returned to power there would be a good many old scores to pay off. There would be distinctions drawn between the men who had declared their unwillingness to obey orders and the men who had not seen fit to make a similar declaration. Besides, in some strange way the fact that there was a war in progress accentuated the intensity of this hidden strife between the Ins and the Outs, and made it more of a cut-and-thrust business than ever before.

'Well, you know now,' said Mackenzie grimly.

'Yes,' said Curzon. He was no fool. He could see that he was in a strong position, even if he could not guess what it was that constituted its strength. 'I'm due to dine with Cross next week, too.'

'Really?' said Mackenzie, contriving to give no hint of meaning at all in his intonation, but drumming with his fingers all the same. He was convinced now that if the man he was talking to was not yet a political soldier, he would be quite soon, and one with very valuable connexions. In fact, he did not feel strong enough to nip the development in the bud by commanding Curzon, on pain of losing his promised brigade, to have nothing to do with the Bude House set.

'Cross gives damned good dinners,' he said. 'I don't know why these lawyer sharks should always be able to get the best chefs. More money, I suppose.'

'I suppose so,' agreed Curzon, and Mackenzie changed the subject.

'By the way, the Foreign Office has just been through to us on the telephone,' he said. 'The Belgian Government wants to present decorations to some English officers, and I have to give my opinion about their distribution. Seeing what you did at Ypres it would be appropriate if one came to you, don't you think? I suppose you wouldn't mind?'

'Of course not,' said Curzon.

'Right,' said Mackenzie, making a note on a memorandum tablet. 'I expect it will be the Order of Leopold–a nice watered red ribbon. It'll look well with your C.M.G. and D.S.O.'

'Thank you very much,' said Curzon.

'Don't thank me,' said Mackenzie, with a certain peculiar emphasis in his tone. 'It's yourself you have to thank.'

Curzon came away from that momentous interview with no very clear idea of what had happened. He was delighted, of course, with the offer of the Belgian decoration. Including his two South African medals he would have five ribbons on his breast now; it would not be long before he could start a second row. Ribbons and promotion were the two signs of success in his profession and now he had both. Success was sweet; he swung his walking stick light-heartedly as he strode across the park. He even laughed when a spiteful old lady said to him as he passed: 'Why aren't you in the army?'

That Curzon could perceive the humour of a situation and laugh at it was a remarkable state of affairs in itself. As he walked, he debated with himself as to whether or no he should telephone Cissie Barnes and see if he could spend the afternoon with her–Cissie Barnes was a lady with whom he had often spent afternoons and week-ends before the war began. If Curzon had been given to self-analysis he might have been seriously alarmed at finding that he was not specially anxious to go and see Cissie.

And then although he was quite sure what he wanted to do he ran through in his mind the other ways open to him of spending the afternoon. He might go round to the Club, and at the Club he might talk or play bridge–the latter, more likely. There would be more than a chance that at the Club he might run across an acquaintance with whom he could share a couple of stalls at a musical comedy or at one of these revues which seemed to have suddenly become fashionable. That might serve very well for the evening. He was not so sure about the afternoon.

There were a few houses at which he might call–he ran over them in his mind and decided against each one in turn. He could go down into Leicestershire so as to hunt next day; presumably Clayton could be relied upon to produce a hireling, and he could stay at the Somerset Arms. The illustrated papers he had read yesterday had informed him that, of course, hunting was still being carried on in the Shires. He could do that tomorrow, though. This afternoon–he admitted it to himself now, having decided that there was a good reason to put forward against all the other courses–he would call at Bude House. It was growing a little old-fashioned to pay a call two days after dinner, but, damn it, he was content to be old-fashioned. Lady Emily might be there. Once he had formed this decision the hours seemed to drag as he ate his lunch and waited for the earliest possible moment at which he could ring the bell at Bude House.

'Her Grace is not at home, sir,' said the butler at the door. By a miracle of elocution he managed to drop just enough of each aitch to prove himself a butler without dropping the rest.

'Is Lady Emily at home?' asked Curzon.

'I will inquire, sir.'

Lady Emily was glad to see the General. She gave him her hand and a smile. She offered him tea, which he declined, and a whisky and soda, which he accepted.

Lady Emily had been brought up very strictly, in the way a child should be during the eighties and nineties, especially when she had had the impertinence to be a girl instead of the boy who would inherit the title. Men, she had been taught, were the lords of the universe, under God. With regard to the subjection of women an important exception was to be made in the case of her mother–the Duchess undoubtedly occupied a place between men and God. What with her parents' ill-concealed disappointment at the accident of her sex, and the prevailing doctrine of the unimportance of women, and her mother's rapacious personality, and the homeliness of her own looks, there was not much self-assertiveness about Lady Emily. To such a pitch had her conviction of innate sin been raised that she even felt vaguely guilty that Lloyd George's pestilent budgets from 1911 onwards had weighed so heavily upon the ducal income.

It was no wonder she had never married. Of course, there were plenty of men who would have been glad of the opportunity of marrying a Duke's only child, but, being a Duke's only child, it had been easy to make sure that she never met that kind of man, and suitable matches had never been attracted. It might be said that Curzon was the first adventurer she had ever met–Curzon would have been furious if anyone had called him an adventurer, but such he was to pay his respects to Lady Emily when he had no more than seven hundred a year of private means, however ample might be his prospects of professional eminence.

Curzon's motives were hardly susceptible to analysis. There could be no denying that for some very obscure reason he liked Lady Emily very much indeed. When her eyes met his as she drank her tea he felt a warm unusual pleasure inside him–but there is nothing that so defies examination as the mutual attraction of two apparently not very attractive people. He was glad to be near her, in a fashion whose like he could not remember regarding any of his light loves or the wives of brother officers with whom he had exchanged glances.

Women had never paid much attention to Curzon; it was gratifying to find one who did, and especially gratifying (there is no shirking this point) in that she was the daughter of a Duke. Success was a stimulating thing. He had risen in four months from Major to Brigadier-General. He had always fully intended to marry at forty, and here he was at forty-one with nothing impossible to him–why should a Duke's daughter be impossible to him? The daring of the thought was part of the attraction; and that business with Mackenzie this morning added to the feeling of daring.

He was so much above himself that he was able to talk more readily than he had ever been able to talk to a woman in his life, and Lady Emily listened and nodded and smiled until they both of them felt very much the better for each other's company. They talked about horses and dogs. Lady Emily had much experience of one kind of sport which Curzon had never sampled–stag-hunting in Somersetshire, where lay the greater part of the Duke's estates. She actually found herself talking about this with animation, and Curzon, fox-hunting man though he was, found himself listening with something more than toleration. They exchanged reminiscences, and Curzon told his two tall fox-hunting stories (the regimental mess had grown tired of them away back in 1912) with complete success. They found, of course, that they had friends in common in the Shires, and they were talking about them when the Duchess came in with a fragile old gentleman trailing behind her.

Her Grace was mildly surprised at finding Curzon in her house, and she endeavoured to freeze him by displaying exactly that mildness of surprise which could not be construed as rudeness but which most definitely could not be called overwhelming hospitality. It was all very well to have a successful general to dinner at a time when successful generals were more fashionable than poets or pianists, but that gave him no excuse for presuming on his position–especially when he promised to be of no use at all in her political manoeuvres. But before

Curzon had time to take note of the drop in temperature and to take his leave Lady Emily had interposed–unconsciously, perhaps.

'Tea, Mr Anstey?' she asked.

'Thank you, yes,' said the frail old gentleman. 'I shall be glad of some tea. My work at the Palace is unusually tiring nowadays in consequence of the war.'

The Duchess made the introductions:

'General Curzon–Mr Anstey.'

'Curzon?' repeated Mr Anstey with mild animation. 'Brigadier-General Herbert Curzon?'

'Yes,' said Curzon.

'Then you are one of the people responsible for my present fatigue.'

'I'm sorry to hear you say that, sir,' said Curzon.

'Oh, there's no need to be sorry, I assure you. I am only too delighted to have the honour of doing the work I do. It is only today that I made out two warrants for you.'

'Indeed, sir?' said Curzon vaguely.

'Yes. There is, of course, no harm in my telling you about them, seeing that they are already in the post and will be delivered to you tomorrow. One of them deals with the Companionship of the Bath and the other with the Belgian Order of Leopold–I must explain that I combine in my humble person official positions both in the department of the Lord Chamberlain and in the registry of the Order of the Bath. You will find you have been commanded to be present at an investiture to be held next week.'

'Thank you,' said Curzon. He remembered vaguely having heard of the Ansteys as one of the 'Court families' who occupied positions at the Palace from one generation to the next.

'The Order of Leopold,' went on Mr Anstey, 'is a very distinguished order indeed. It is the Second Class which is being awarded to you, General–the First Class is generally reserved for reigning monarchs and people in corresponding positions. Or course, it is not an order with a very lengthy history–it can hardly be that, can it?–but I think an order presented by a crowned head far more distinguished than any decoration a republic can award. I hope you agree with me, General?'

'Oh yes, of course,' said Curzon, perfectly sincerely.

The Duchess merely nodded. The orders her husband wore were such as no mere general could ever hope to attain, and possessed the further recommendation (as has frequently been pointed out) that there was no 'damned nonsense about merit' attached to them. The Duke's ribbons and stars were given him, if a reason must be assigned, because his great-great-great-great grandfather had come over in the train of William of Orange–certainly not because ten years ago he had been chivvied by his wife into accepting minor office under a tottering Conservative Government. Her Grace was sublimely confident in her share of the universal opinion that it was far better to receive distinctions for being someone than for doing something.

'You are one of the Derbyshire Curzons, I suppose, General?' said Mr Anstey.

Curzon was ready for that. He had been an officer in India during Lord Curzon's vice-royalty and had grown accustomed to having the relationship suggested–in the course of years even his unimaginative mind had been able to hammer out a suitable answer.

'Yes, but a long way back,' he said. 'My branch has been settled in Staffordshire for some time, and I am the only representative now.'

Curzon always remembered that his father had a vague notion that *his* father had come to London from the Potteries as a boy; moreover, he thought it quite unnecessary to add that these mystic Staffordshire Curzons had progressed from Staffordshire to the Twenty-second Lancers via Mincing Lane.

'That is extremely interesting,' said Mr Anstey. 'Even though the Scarsdale peerage is of comparatively recent creation the Curzons are one of the few English families of undoubtedly Norman descent.'

Mr Anstey checked himself with a jerk. Despite his Court tact, he had allowed himself to mention Norman descent from a follower of William the Conqueror in the presence of a representative of a family of Dutch descent from a follower of William of Orange. To his mind the difference was abysmal and the gaffe he had committed inexcusable. He glanced with apprehension at the Duchess, but he need not have worried. Coronets meant far more to her than did Norman blood.

'How very interesting,' said the Duchess coldly.

'Yes, isn't it?' said Lady Emily eagerly, and attracted every eye by the warmth with which she said it.

The Duchess ran a cold glance over every inch of her thirty-year-old daughter's shrinking form.

'There are a great number of fresh letters arrived,' she said, 'about the Belgian Relief Clothing Association. You will find them in the library, Emily. I think they had better be answered at once.'

Curzon saw Lady Emily's face fall a little, and it was that which made him take the plunge. He cut in with what he had to say just as Lady Emily, with the obedience resulting from years of subjection, was rising from her arm-chair.

'I was wondering, Lady Emily,' he said, 'if I might have the pleasure of your company at the theatre this evening?'

Lady Emily looked at her mother, as ingrained instinct directed. Mr Anstey sensed an awkwardness, and hastened to try and smooth it over with his well-known tact.

'We all of us need a little relaxation in these strenuous days,' he said.

'Thank you, I should very much like to come,' said Lady Emily–perhaps she, too was infected by the surge of revolt against convention and parental control which the newspapers had noted as a concomitant of war-time. The Duchess could hardly countermand a decision publicly reached by a daughter of full age and more.

'What is the play to which you are proposing so kindly to take my daughter?' she asked icily, which was all she could do.

'I was going to leave the choice to Lady Emily,' said Curzon–a reply, made from sheer ignorance, which left the Duchess with no objection to raise, and that emboldened Curzon still further.

'Shall we dine together first?' he asked.

'That would be very nice,' said Lady Emily, her bonnet soaring clean over the windmill in this, her first flourish of emancipation.

'Seven o'clock?' said Curzon. 'It's a pity having to dine so early, but it's hard to avoid it. Shall I call for you?'

'Yes,' said Lady Emily.

9

'Damn it all, Maud,' said the Duke of Bude to the Duchess a week after Curzon had gone to the theatre with Lady Emily. 'Anyone would think you didn't want the girl to get married.'

That was so true that the Duchess had to deny it.

'I don't want Emily to marry a man of no family at all–a mere adventurer,' said she, and the Duke chuckled as he made one of his irritating silly jokes.

'As long as he's got no family it doesn't matter. We won't have to invite his Kensington cousins to the Hall then. The man assured us only yesterday that he hasn't a relation in the world. And as for being an adventurer–well, a man can't help having adventures in time of war, can he?'

'Tcha!' said the Duchess. 'You know perfectly well what I mean.'

'He's a perfectly presentable man. He's Haileybury, after all–everyone can't be an Etonian. Colonel of a good regiment—'

'The Twenty-second Lancers,' sneered the Duchess.

'It might have been black infantry,' said the Duke. 'He's got a C.B. and a D.S.O., and Borthwick at the Lords was telling me that his boy wrote reams about him from the Front. He's a man with a future.'

'But they hardly know each other,' said the Duchess.

'Well, they're old enough to be able to make up their minds. Emily's thirty-two, isn't she, or is it thirty-three? And he's turned forty. I think it's very suitable. I can't imagine why you're objecting so much.'

That, of course, was a lie. The Duke knew perfectly well why the Duchess was objecting, and in his heart of hearts he objected too. But he could bow gracefully to the inevitable, in a way his stiff-necked wife found more difficult.

'Marrying's in the air these war-time days,' went on the Duke. 'There'll be no stopping 'em if they set their minds on it. Much better start getting used to the idea now. Besides, we may as well be in the fashion.'

'Fashion, indeed!' said the Duchess. Her disregard for fashion was one of the things about her which no one who saw her even once could possibily avoid remarking.

'Besides,' said the Duchess, unanswerably, 'he's got no money.'

'M'yes,' said the Duke, undoubtedly shaken. 'That's a point I shall have to go into very carefully when the time comes.'

The time came no later than the day after tomorrow. The courtship had blossomed with extraordinary rapidity in the hot-house air of war-time London. So high above the windmill had Lady Emily's bonnet soared that she had actually accompanied Curzon to a night-club so as to dance. They had shuffled and stumbled through the ultra-modern one-steps and two-steps until the pampered orchestra had at last consented to play a waltz. Curzon certainly could waltz; he had learned the art in the great days of waltzing. And it might have been the extra glass of rather poor champagne which she had drunk at dinner which made Lady Emily's feet so light and her eyes so bright. As the last heart-broken wail of the violins died away and they stopped and looked at each other the thing was as good as settled. No sooner had they sat down than Curzon was able to stumble through a proposal of marriage with less difficulty than he had found in the one-step; and to his delighted surprise he found himself accepted.

Lady Emily's eyes were like stars. They made Curzon's head swim a little. His heart had plunged so madly after his inclinations that never again, not once, did it occur to him that her face was not unlike a horse's. To Curzon Lady Emily's gaunt figure, stiffly corseted–almost an old maid's figure–was a miracle of willowy grace, and her capable ugly hands, when he kissed them in the taxicab on the way home, were more beautiful than the white hands of Lancelot's Yseult.

The interview with the Duke in the morning was not too terrible. It was a relief to the Duke to discover that the General actually had seven hundred pounds a year–especially as under the stimulus of war-time demands some of the dividends which contributed to make up this sum showed an undoubted tendency to expand. It might have been a much smaller income and still not have been incompatible with Curzon's position in life. Besides, the General offered, in the most handsome fashion, to settle every penny of his means upon his future wife. No one could make a fairer offer than that, after all. And when one came to total up his general's pay, and his allowances, under the new scale just published, and his forage allowances and so forth, it did not fall far short of twelve hundred a year, without reckoning on the possibility of promotion or command pay or the less likely sources of income. A general's widow's pension (after all, every contingency must be considered) was only a small amount, of course, but it was as good as any investment in the Funds.

And two thousand a year (for so the Duke, in an expansive moment, generously estimated Curzon's income) really could not be called poverty, not even by a Duke with thirty thousand a year, especially when the Duke belonged to a generation whose young men about town had often contrived to make a passable appearance on eight hundred. The Duke proposed to supplement the newly married couple's income with two thousand a year from his private purse, and they ought to be able to manage very well, especially while the General was on active service.

'I think you've been weak, Gilbert,' said the Duchess later.

'Oh, for goodness' sake, Maud!' said the Duke. 'I don't see that at all. We owe our national existence at present to the Army. And we can spare the money all right. You know that. It'll only go to George and his boys if Emily doesn't get it. That is, if these blasted death duties leave anything over at all.'

'I don't think,' said the Duchess, 'that there is any need for you to use disgusting language to me even though your daughter is marrying beneath her.'

The Duchess grew more reconciled to her daughter's marriage when she came to realize that at least while Curzon was on active service she would still be able to tyrannize over her daughter, and the public interest in the wedding reconciled her still more. The formal announcement was very formal, of course. 'A marriage has been arranged and will shortly take place between Lady Emily Gertrude Maud Winter-Willoughby, only daughter of the Duke and Duchess of Bude, and Brigadier-General Herbert Curzon, C.B., D.S.O., Twenty-second Lancers.'

The newspapers built a marvellous edifice upon this bare foundation. 'Duke's Daughter to Wed War Hero', they said, 'Lightning Wooing'. It was not every day of the week, by any manner of means, that a duke's daughter married; and war news, now that the campaign in Flanders had dwindled away into a stalemate in the mud and rain, was not likely to stimulate sales. There was something piquant about the union of a Winter of the bluest blood with a Curzon whose relationship to Lord Curzon of Kedleston was at best only ill-defined. All the same, the Press played up nobly. The daily Press had a great deal to say about the future bridegroom's military achievements–although the exigencies of the censorship compelled them to say more about Volkslaagte than about Ypres–and the snobbish weekly papers laid stress upon the splendours of Bude Hall in Somersetshire, and the interest the Royal Family was taking in the wedding; there were dozens of photographs taken showing the happy pair walking in the Park or at some party in aid of something. A war-time bride had more popular appeal, undoubtedly, than a war-time widow, or than those other ladies underneath whose photograph the papers could only publish the already hackneyed caption, 'Takes great interest in war work'–Lady Emily and her mother, the Duchess, were always represented as the hardest workers in the Belgian Relief Clothing Association, and perhaps they were. And because a duke's daughter at the time of her betrothal could not possibly be other than young and beautiful, all the Press loyally forbore to mention the fact that Emily was thirty-two years old, and no one dreamed of mentioning that her features were large and irregular, nor that her clothes always had a look of the second-hand about them.

Meanwhile a Field-Marshal and a General and a Major-General were in conference at the War Office.

'The man's on the verge of senile decay,' said the General. 'Over the verge, I should say. He's no more fit to be trusted with a division than to darn the Alhambra chorus's tights.'

'Who are his brigadiers?' asked the Field-Marshal.

'Watson and Webb,' said the Major-General apologetically. 'Yes, sir, I know they're no good, but where am I to get three hundred good brigadiers from?'

'That's your pigeon,' said the Field-Marshal.

'I'm sending Curzon down there tomorrow,' said the Major-General. 'The third brigade of the division has never had a general yet. I think he'll stiffen them up all right.'

'He'll have his work cut out, from what I've seen of that lot,' said the General.

'Curzon?' said the Field-Marshal. 'That's the Volkslaagte fellow, isn't it?'

'Yes, sir,' said the Major-General. 'You read the letter a fortnight ago which G.H.Q. wrote about him.'

'I remember,' said the Field-Marshal. He raised his big heavy face to the window, and stared out contemplatively with squinting blue eyes, while he called up isolated recollections out of a packed memory. Volkslaagte had been fought before he went to South Africa, but he remembered reading the dispatches about it very plainly indeed–it was in this very room in the War Office. There was that race meeting in India, and the mob of horses all coming over the last hurdle together, and a Lancer officer doing a brilliant bit of riding in shouldering off a riderless horse which got in the way and might have caused a nasty accident. That was Curzon. That was not the first time he had been pointed out to him, though. Where was that? Oh yes, at the Aldershot review in the old days before India. That was the chap. A big-nosed fellow with the centre squadron.

'How old is he now?' asked the Field-Marshal.

'Forty-one, sir,' said the Major-General.

At forty-one the Field-Marshal had been Sirdar of the Egyptian Army. He would like to be forty-one again instead of sixty-five with a game leg–but that was nothing to do with the business under discussion. It was this Curzon fellow he was thinking about. He had never put in any time holding a regimental command, apparently, except for a few weeks in France. But that was nothing against him, except that it made it a bit harder to judge him by ordinary standards. The Field-Marshal had done no regimental duty in his life, and it hadn't hurt him.

But there was something else he had heard, or read, about Curzon, somewhere, quite recently. He could not remember what it was, and was vaguely puzzled.

'Is there anything against this Curzon fellow?' he asked tentatively. It was a little pathetic to see him labouring under the burden of all the work he had been doing during these months of war.

'No, sir,' said the Major-General, and because Curzon was obviously allied by now to the Bude House set, and would be a valuable friend in the approaching Government reshuffle, he added, 'He's a man of very decided character.'

That turned the scale. What the Field-Marshal had seen, of course, had been the flaming headlines that very morning announcing Curzon's betrothal. He had put the triviality aside, and yet the memory lingered in his subconscious mind. It was because of that that he had pricked up his ears at the first mention of Curzon's name. Neither the General nor the Major-General saw fit to waste the Field-Marshal's time by a mention of today's newspaper gossip, and the vague memory remained to tease him into action. His mind was not fully made up when he began to speak, but he was positive in his decision by the time the sentence was completed.

'You must unstick Coppinger-Brown,' he said. 'Shunt him off gracefully, though. There's no need to be too hard on him. He's done good work in his time. And Watson'll have to go too. He's no good. I never thought he was. Give Webb another chance. He can still turn out all right if he's properly looked after. You'll have to give the division to Curzon, though. He ought to make a good job of it.'

'Yes, sir,' said the Major-General. He was reluctant to continue, because it was not safe to pester his chief with a request for further instructions once a decision had been reached, but in this case the Service regulations left him no option. 'He's junior to Webb as brigadier, of course.'

'Then you'll have to promote him major-general. Get the orders out today.'

A wave of the Field-Marshal's massive hand told the General and the Major-General that their presence was no longer required, and they left the Field-Marshal to plunge once more into the mass of work piled before him–into the business of constructing a modern army out of the few antiquated remains left over after the departure of the Expeditionary Force.

That was how Curzon obtained his appointment to the command of the Ninety-first Division and his promotion to the temporary rank of Major-General. There were not wanting unkind people who hinted that he owed his new rank to his prospective father-in-law, but the Duke had not raised a finger in the matter. There had been no scheming or bargaining, not even by the little scheming group which centred round the Duke and Lady Constance. He had been selected out of a hundred possible officers who could have filled the vacancy because, while their capacities were all equally unexplored, an adventitious circumstance had singled him out for particular notice. Without that the Major-General would never have had the opportunity of putting in the single sentence which ultimately turned the scale. And it must be specially noticed that the Major-General had not the slightest hint that he might receive favours in return; neither Curzon nor his new relations had been parties to anything underhand of that sort.

10

Curzon was at Bude House when the butler came in to announce–the tone of his voice indicating that he realized the importance of this official business–that the War Office was asking on the telephone if they could speak to General Curzon.

Curzon left his lady's side and went out to the telephone.

'Hullo?' he said.

'Is that General Curzon?' asked a sharp-tongued female voice.

'Speaking.'

'Hold on a minute, please. General Mackenzie would like to speak to you.'

There was a click and a gurgle and then Mackenzie's voice.

'Hullo, Curzon. I thought I'd find you at Bude House when you weren't at your hotel. Hope I'm not disturbing you?'

'Not very much.'

'I think you'll find it's worth being disturbed for. You've been given the Ninety-first Division.'

'I beg your pardon?'

'You've been given the Ninety-first Division–the one you were going to have a brigade in. And you're promoted to Major-General with seniority from today.'

'That's very good news.'

'I said you'd think so, didn't I? When can you take up your command?'

'Whenever you like.'

'Tomorrow?'

'Yes.'

'Very well. Call here in the morning. I want to hear your ideas about a staff. It'll be a pretty makeshift one, anyway, I'm afraid, but that can't be helped.'

'I suppose not.'

'But there's a good house as headquarters, with stabling just as it should be. Trust old Coppinger-Brown for that. You'll have a use for the house, won't you?'

'Yes, I suppose so.'

'That reminds me. I haven't congratulated you on your engagement yet. My very best wishes.'

'Thanks very much.'

'I was wondering when you were going to offer me thanks. You haven't sounded very grateful up to now.'

'Oh, thank you very much.'

'That's better. You remember this, Curzon; the closer you and I stay by each other, the better it will be for both of us. That's a word to the wise.'

'Er–yes.'

'But that can wait a bit. I'll be seeing you tomorrow morning. Nine o'clock?'

'Very well.'

'All right, then. Good-bye.'

'Good-bye.'

Back in Emily's sitting-room he told the glad news, his eyes bright with pleasure and excitement, and, because of that, Emily's eyes shone too. Until a week or two ago Emily had hardly known that such things as brigades and divisions existed, and she had been decidedly vague about the difference between them, but already she was beginning to grasp the essentials of this Army business. The Duke's valet was sent out hurriedly to buy stars at a military tailor's, and then, with a note to the hotel management admitting him to Curzon's room, he was sent on to sew those stars above the crossed swords and batons on the shoulder-straps of Curzon's tunics all ready for the morning, while Curzon and Emily carried on a muddled conversation in which Army promotion and houses and horses and future domesticity were all intermingled.

But next day had its awkward moments. A War Office motor car took Curzon and his kit down into Hampshire, where the division was scattered in billets or under canvas over a five-mile radius, and stopped at the end of the long gravelled drive outside Narling Priory, the headquarters of the Ninety-first Division. A young red-tabbed subaltern led Curzon round the side of the house through french windows into a spacious room wherein stood a group of khaki-clad figures with a tall, thin officer, bent and feeble, the sword of ceremony hanging from his belt, standing in advance of them.

'Good morning,' he said, standing very stiff and still.

Curzon nodded.

'General Coppinger-Brown?' he asked in return.

'Yes.'

It was then that Curzon realized what an embarrassing business it was to relieve a man of his command, because Coppinger-Brown made no effort to put him at ease, but merely stood and waited.

'I have been sent down by the War Office,' began Curzon hesitantly; he waited for help, received none, and had to continue without it. 'I am to take command of the division.'

'So I understood from orders I received this morning,' said Coppinger-Brown. There was the faintest of accents upon the last two words. Curzon realized that it was dashed hard luck on the old chap to be flung out of his command like this at an hour's notice. He wanted for a moment to say 'I'm sorry,' but one man can hardly say that to another, especially in the presence of inferiors. He could only stand and feel awkward while Coppinger-Brown left him to drink the cup of his embarrassment to the full. By the time Coppinger-Brown relented Curzon was decidedly uncomfortable.

'I must introduce,' said Coppinger-Brown at last, 'the officers of my staff–of your staff, I mean; I beg your pardon, General.'

He waved his hand at the group behind him, and each officer in turn came up to attention as his name was spoken.

'General Webb, commanding the Three-hundredth Brigade. General Webb is the only brigadier in the division at present. I made so bold as to give General Watson immediate leave of absence, as I wished to spare him the humiliation of having to leave under orders.'

There was something very acid in Coppinger-Brown's tone as he made this speech, but Curzon did not notice it, as he was too busy sizing-up his second-in-command, a beefy, red-faced infantryman, of whom Mackenzie at the War Office that morning had said that he was being given one more chance.

'Colonel Miller, my G.S.O.1. Captain Frobisher, G.S.O.3. Colonel Hill, C.R.A. Colonel Septimus, A.D.M.S.—'

For a space it simply rained initials in a manner which would have left a civilian gasping, but Curzon was more accustomed to hearing these initials used than to the words they stood for. He nodded formally to each in turn, to the officers of the General Staff, to the Officer commanding Royal Artillery, to Assistant Director of Medical Services, and the Deputy Assistant Quartermaster-General, and the Assistant Provost-Marshal, and the Officer commanding Royal Engineers, and the rag-tag and bobtail of aides-de-camp.

Mackenzie at the War Office had given him thumbnail character portraits of each of these officers; Curzon himself had no knowledge of most of them, and only a hearsay acquaintance with the rest. Hill the Gunner had won a D.S.O. in the Tirah. Webb had commanded a battalion before Curzon had been given a squadron. Runcorn the Sapper had left the Army before the war on account of some scandal about drink and women, which was a very remarkable thing to have occurred to a Sapper, so that Runcorn had better be watched with all attention a freak merited. Miller of the General Staff had been described by Mackenzie as 'a bloke with twice the brains of you and me put together,' and had left it to Curzon to form his own opinion after this somewhat ominous beginning.

'What's been the matter down there,' Mackenzie had said, 'as far as I can make out from what Somerset says–he's just been inspecting them–it's just sheer dam' laziness on someone's part or other. They've had their troubles, of course. We've let 'em down badly from here once or twice, but you couldn't have run the old Army, let alone a new one ten times the size, on the staff I've got left to me here. But old Coppinger-Brown's the real cause of the trouble. He's too old. You can't expect an old boy of seventy-two with bronchial tubes or something to go out in all weathers in the sort of winter we're having, and go charging about on a horse keeping an eye on twelve raw battalions an' two dozen other units. It's not in human nature. Coppinger-Brown swore he was all right when he came here after a job–he produced all sorts of chits from doctors to that effect. And he looked all right too. But you know how it is, Curzon. You've got to work like a blasted nigger to get anything done with new formations. Otherwise everything's held up while everyone's waiting for something else to get done which they think they can't do without. Or else somebody's getting in everybody else's way, and'll go on doing it until you come down on 'em. Doesn't matter how good a staff you've got when you're in that kind of muddle. It's only the boss who can put it straight. Nobody gives a hoot for what a staff officer says when they know the general won't take action. But you'll put ginger into them, Curzon, I know.'

That had been all very well at the War Office, but it was rather different by the time General Coppinger-Brown had finished the introductions and had shuffled out of the room with his aides-de-camp beside him. Curzon stood and faced his staff–nearly all of them ten or twenty years his senior, and most of them until a few weeks back immeasurably his senior in military rank. He felt as awkward and as embarrassed as at the time of General Coppinger-Brown's first greeting of him. It was not in him to be conciliatory. His whole instinct in a time of difficulty was to be unbending and expressionless. It was a natural reaction that there should creep into his voice the tone he employed on parade–he felt as if he were on parade for the first time with some new recalcitrant unit.

'Gentlemen,' he rasped, and paused. He had not anticipated having to make a speech. He tugged at his moustache until he saw the light; he felt at a loss at remembering that there was no regimental *esprit de corps* to which to appeal. But he could, at any rate, appeal to the spirit of the Division. 'Gentlemen, it is my responsibility now to prepare the Ninety-first Division in readiness to go to France. We can never have it said that our Division, one of the earliest to be raised, was the last to be sent overseas. That would be too bad. We must make up our minds that we are not going to be left behind by the other divisions. We must work hard to catch up on them and pass them. I am quite sure we can.'

His expression hardened as he remembered the precariousness of his own temporary rank. It flashed through his mind that the Duchess's elegant friends would sneer delightedly if he were to be unstuck like poor old Coppinger-Brown.

'I am going to see that we do,' he added grimly, looking round the group from one to another. Each pair of eyes dropped as they met his, such was the savage force of his glance as he thought of Emily and the urgency of the need to justify himself to her. And the mention of the corporate existence of the Ninety-first Division had served its purpose in starting him off in what he had to say. He was able to wind up his little speech on the note he wanted.

'This is war-time,' he said. 'A time of great emergency. There will be no mercy at all in this Division for officers who are not up to their work.'

It was a speech which served its purpose as well as any other might have done, and better than some. Some generals might have appealed to their subordinates' loyalty, or might have put new vigour into them by force of personality, but Curzon, if such suggestions had been put forward to him, would have dismissed them as 'claptrap' or 'idealism'. As it was, a subdued and impressed staff crept quietly out of the room, all quite decided to work a great deal harder for the new major-general with the scowl on his face and the barely concealed threat in his speech.

The pink-cheeked aide-de-camp came back into the room. General Coppinger-Brown would be very much obliged if General Curzon could spare him a few minutes for the discussion of private business. Curzon followed the aide-de-camp out of the headquarters office and across the tiled hall to the wing of the house which still remained furnished as a private residence. There was an old, old lady sitting in an arm-chair in the drawing-room with Coppinger-Brown standing beside her.

'Lucy,' said Coppinger-Brown. 'This is my successor, General Curzon. Curzon, may I introduce my wife?'

Curzon bowed, and the old lady nodded icily to him across the room, while the aide-de-camp retired with the tact expected of aides-de-camp.

'The first thing we wanted to say,' said Coppinger-Brown, 'was whether we might expect the pleasure of your company at lunch? It is one o'clock now, and lunch can be served at any time to suit you.'

'Thank you,' said Curzon, 'but I have just arranged to lunch in the staff officers' mess.'

He forebore from adding that he was itching to start work with his chief of staff, and make up for the time lost by Coppinger-Brown, and intended to start as soon as lunch began.

'What a pity,' replied Coppinger-Brown. 'I hope you can spare us a few minutes, all the same, so that we can settle our private arrangements.'

'I am at your service now,' said Curzon.

'That's very good of you,' said Coppinger-Brown. 'Because we are anxious to hear from you how soon we must vacate this house.'

Coppinger-Brown and his wife stared at Curzon with an unvoiced appeal in their eyes. The house was one taken over furnished by the War Office; half of it had been adapted as Staff Offices, and the other half was retained as a residence for the Major-General commanding the division. The last two months had been a wonderful time for the old couple. It had been an end of retirement; they had turned their backs on the Cheltenham boarding-house; there had been a future once more ahead of them; they were back again in the Army in which he had served for forty-five years. Now they were being condemned once more to exile, with all the added bitterness of disappointment and consciousness of failure. Until this morning they had felt secure in the pomp and power of their official position. It was a shock for old people to be flung out like this without warning. They were loth to leave the substantial comfort of the Priory; they shrank from the last open acknowledgement of failure implied by their leaving, as they might shrink from an icy bath. With the tenacity of very old people for the good things of life they wanted to spin out their stay here, even for only a few days.

Curzon, unsympathetic though he was, had a glimpse of these emotions, and stopped for a moment to think. The Coppinger-Browns might be considered harmless old folk, and to allow them to remain for a week or two longer at the Priory might be a kindness which would do no one any harm. But he knew he must not; he felt it in his bones. Coppinger-Brown would never be able to resist the temptation to put his nose into the new organization of the division. Young officers could hardly be expected to order off a Major-General under whom they had only recently been serving, even though he was again retired. There would be hitches, perhaps nasty scenes. And for all he knew Mrs Coppinger-Brown might make trouble among the women–Curzon had all an unmarried man's suspicions of Army women's capacity for making trouble. There must be no chance, not the faintest possibility, of trouble in his division. Moreover, it might weaken his authority a little if people assumed that Coppinger-Brown was staying on to see him firmly in the saddle. He was not going to run the least risk of any of these unpleasant contingencies when a little firmness at the start would obviate them.

'I am afraid,' he said slowly, 'that I need the house myself. It would be convenient if you could see your way to leaving at the earliest possible moment. Perhaps if I put the divisional motor car at your disposal tomorrow morning you would have your kit and luggage ready?'

They looked at each other, all three of them.

'Very well, since you insist,' said Coppinger-Brown–Curzon had made no show of insisting. 'We had better not keep you any longer from your lunch. We shall be ready to leave at ten o'clock tomorrow. Is that all right, Lucy?'

Mrs Coppinger-Brown nodded; from beginning to end of the interview she had said no word, but even a wooden-headed man like Curzon was conscious of the hatred she felt towards him as the supplanter of her husband, the man who was driving her out once more into the lonely, pitiable exile of the Cheltenham boarding-house. Curzon withdrew as quickly as he could, and he comforted himself as he walked back across the hall by telling himself that after all a soldier's wife should be reconciled by now to having to make sudden migrations, while Coppinger-Brown was a doddering old fool who should never have been entrusted with a division. Which was all perfectly true.

II

The Ninety-first Division was composed of troops of a sort Curzon had never even thought of. They were the first flower of England; of a standard of education, enthusiasm and physique far superior to anything the recruits of the old regiments of the line could show. In the old days, for every man who joined the Army because he actively wanted to there were ten who did so because they could find nothing better to do; but in the new units of 1914 every single man had joined because he felt it to be his duty. To Curzon and his like (who in the old days had thoroughly appreciated the value of the occasional 'born soldier' in the ranks) the merit of the new material should have been obvious. These were no unemployable riff-raff, no uneducable boys, but men who had made some part of their way already in the world, men of some experience and education, quicker witted, more accustomed to think for themselves, and filled with the desire to avenge Belgium and to give their best for England–the same stuff as Cromwell (who in an early speech had pointed out its virtues) had employed when he had made of the Ironsides the finest troops in Europe.

But Cromwell had not been a regular soldier, nor–save for the presence of an occasional veteran of the Thirty Years War–was there any framework of a regular army, any procrustean bed of tradition, to which the Ironside army was compelled to adapt itself as in 1914. Kitchener's army was organized by a War Office which had already forgotten the Boer War and clung to the ideals of the Peninsula; but that statement is only correct in a very limited degree, because most of the great body of rules and precedents dealt not with the training of an army for war, but with keeping it inexpensive and out of the way in time of peace. The system was, moreover, adapted to the needs of an army recruited from the very young and the very stupid, officered by men of uniform ideas and training; what the system did for the new armies has been told over and over again.

Besides all this, the War Office was found wanting (perhaps not through its own fault) even in the very elementary duties it might have been expected to perform efficiently. The new armies were left unclothed, unhoused, and unarmed. Units rotted through the winter of 1914–15 under canvas on the bleak exposed hills and plains which had been passed as suitable for a summer camp. They shivered in tents pitched in seas of mud; they ate food prepared by inefficient cooks on inefficient apparatus; they were practised in the evolutions of 1870 by sexagenarian non-commissioned officers, and they used make-believe rifles and make-believe guns under the co-ordination of make-believe staffs.

Of such good stuff, nevertheless, were the new armies that they came through the ordeal successfully, their spirits unimpaired by what had been done to them, and made of themselves, despite the efforts of their commanders, the finest fighting force ever seen, and able to carry that reputation through years of slaughter and mismanagement, despite the constant filling up with drafts whose quality steadily and persistently declined as the war continued.

By a fortunate combination of circumstances Curzon was able to prove himself during these months of training one of the best generals appointed to the new armies. He was full of energy, so that the curse of inertia was not allowed to settle down over the Ninety-first Division. He had no preconceived ideas about the employment of infantry in the field. His barrack traditions were confined to cavalry, and in young Frobisher, his third-grade General Staff Officer, he found an assistant whose desperate laziness had no play under his supervision, and who came of a family in which revolutionary ideas were traditional, so that he did not badger the infantrymen with peace-time regulations nearly as much as occurred in some units.

That very first day at Narling, Curzon showed the stuff he was made of. He had no personal staff at all–no aides-de-camp, no servants, no grooms; until tomorrow he had no home, for that matter. It never occurred to him to attend to the very important business of settling himself in first. He sent his kit to the local hotel, and made Frobisher telephone to the nearest unit to find him a servant. Before this concession to his immediate needs was fulfilled he was calling for the regimental returns, reading the lists of sick and of those found guilty recently of military crime so as to form his first estimate of the quality of the troops under his command, and half-way through the afternoon, finding this office work unsatisfying, he borrowed a horse from Miller and set off, with Frobisher riding beside him in the rain, in his anxiety to see things for himself.

He dropped like a bolt from the blue into the troops he had been given to command, trotting in over the rolling downs into the camps of the Three-hundred-and-first Brigade, the rain streaming from his cap brim and the hem of his cape. There was a moment of hesitation when he confronted his work face to face for the first time–when he realized how extraordinarily little he knew about infantry. But he knew something about men in uniform, at least. There were certain things he could inspect–six months ago he had been inspecting similar arrangements from a regimental aspect. There were the cookhouses; he went stalking into the battalion cooking-huts, to be appalled by their filth and squalor. Frightened cooking staffs stood shivering at attention while he blistered them with his tongue, and startled commanding officers, summoned by flying orderlies, stood scared at his shoulder while he peered into dixies and cauldrons and sampled the contents.

General Coppinger-Brown had not been seen in a cookhouse since the weather broke six weeks ago; here was the new general inspecting them before even the rumour of his appointment had run round the regimental headquarters. Curzon plodded through the mud down the lines of tents with the icy wind blowing through his burberry–it was that walk which first gave him an insight into the quality of his men, for any regular unit before the war compelled to submit to such conditions would have shown its resentment by going sick in hundreds. Startled soldiers, huddled under blankets turned out hastily to stare at him. That morning the bugles had blown 'No parade', for no soldiers' work could have been done in those dreadful conditions, and they had settled down to another day of shivering idleness. The sight of a major-general come to see how they were getting on was a most welcome break in the day, reviving hope in breasts where hope of anything was fast dying altogether.

Far more was this the case with the wretched Special Service battalion of Fusiliers who were farther out still–moved there when cerebrospinal meningitis had appeared in their ranks, to endure the life of outcasts during their period of quarantine. The sense of isolation and guilt had been bad for the Fusiliers, huddled in their tents waiting for the spotted fever. Frobisher had ventured to protest when Curzon announced his intention of visiting the Fusiliers, but Curzon was heedless.

'There's no quarantine for generals,' said Curzon. He had no intention of being epigrammatic either.

He got on his horse again and rode furiously along the slippery chalk track over the summit of the downs to where the Fusiliers languished. A spiritless guard, besodden with misery, turned out to present arms to this extraordinary spectacle of a brass hat in the icy rain, and Curzon, without waiting for the arrival of the commanding officer, began his inspection. Three weeks of quarantine, of isolation, of rain and spotted fever, had taken the heart nearly out of the Fusiliers, but it was the sight of Curzon which put it back. Someone raised a faint cheer, even, when he rode out of the entrance afterwards, in the gathering darkness.

And the word passed round the division, from battalion to battalion, that the new general was crazy on the subject of military cookery. Generals, as the Army had long ago resigned itself to believe, are always crazy on some point or other. Coppinger-Brown's particular weakness (as far as anyone had been able to guess from the little seen of him) had been bootlaces. Under Coppinger-Brown's régime colonels had chivvied captains and captains had chivvied sergeants, into seeing that every man had two pairs at least of spare bootlaces, and had quoted Coppinger-Brown's dictum that 'a division might be held up any day on the march if a man's bootlace broke.' Nowadays it was cookery instead, and no one knew when the General's big nose and moustache might not be seen coming round the cookhouse corner as he demanded to taste whatever indescribable mess was to be found in the dixies. It was a matter which the men in the ranks, after the food they had been enduring for the last two months, could thoroughly appreciate.

There seemed to be no limit to Curzon's abounding energy in those days when he took over the command of the Ninety-first Division. Mason, the soldier-servant whom Miller found for him in the infantry, was under orders always to call him at five–and usually found him awake at that time. Officers, sleepy-eyed and weary, crawling into the divisional headquarters at seven o'clock, found Curzon at his desk running through the pile of returns and 'states' which previously had been seen by no other eye than theirs. Isolated companies on the downs, practising the open-order advance in alternate rushes which none of them was to live to see employed in action, were surprised to find him riding up to watch them at their work.

After ten days of it Curzon had himself whirled up to London in the divisonal motor car and had his presence announced to General Mackenzie with an urgent request for an interview. Mackenzie had him sent up, and blenched a little at the comprehensive sequence of demands which Curzon made on behalf of his division.

'My dear fellow,' said Mackenzie, 'it's not me whom you should ask for all this. It's all the Q.M.G.'s department, most of it, except for this officer question, and I've promised already to see to that for you. Go round and look up the Q.M.G.–I'll give you a chit to the right quarter, if you like.'

Curzon shook his head. He knew a great deal about the Army method of passing on inconvenient requests to the next man.

'No,' he said, 'they don't know me there. I wouldn't be able to get anything done. I'd far rather you saw about it; unofficially, for that matter, if you like. You could get it done in no time, even though it's not your department.'

Mackenzie began to show some signs of irritation at this upstart young general's behaviour. The fellow was certainly growing too big for his boots. He took a breath preparatory to administering a proper 'telling off'.

'You see,' said Curzon, eyeing him attentively as he made his first essay in diplomatic converse. 'I've got a lot to do, and I could only spare one day away from the Division. I've got an appointment to lunch with Lady Cross and one or two other people–newspaper editors or something, I think they are.'

'H'm,' said Mackenzie. The struggle behind the scenes for power was rising to a climax, and he knew it. 'All right, I'll see what I can do.'

When Mackenzie said that, Curzon knew that he could expect immediate attention to be paid to the sweeping indents he had sent in–demands for duckboards and all the other things to make life bearable for the Ninety-first Division in the chalky downland mud, huts and stoves and so on, of which the War Office had such a meagre store. Curzon could leave the War Office now with a clear conscience. He was not lunching with Lady Cross, of course. That had been a blank lie just to apply pressure on Mackenzie. It was his Emily, naturally, with whom he had his next appointment. The big Vauxhall car rolled him smoothly round to Bude House, and the butler showed Curzon into Emily's sitting-room.

Curzon's heart was beating fast, for it was ten days since he had last seen Emily, and she might have changed her mind in that long time. He came into the room stiffly and formally, ready to meet his fate if need be, but all doubts were instantly dispelled on his entrance, and it was as though they had never been separated, as Emily came to him with both hands out and a murmur of 'My dear, my dear.' She came into his arms as if she were no duke's daughter. With her head on his shoulder she fingered his row of medal ribbons, and he caught her hand and raised it to his lips, pressing his cruel black moustache upon her fingers. Even if Curzon had taken care to give his affections to a suitable person, there was no doubt that he had given them thoroughly enough. He was head over ears in love with her, just as she was with him.

When sanity came back to them, Curzon spoke straight to the point, as might be expected of him. To him, love was not a thing to be soiled by roundabout ways of approach, or delicate diplomacy.

'Dear,' he said, 'can we be married on Christmas Eve?'

'Christmas Eve?' Emily's eyes opened a little wider, for Christmas Eve was only five days off.

'Yes,' said Curzon. He made no attempt to mask his reasons. 'I've had to take this morning away from the Division, which I didn't want to. I can't spare another one, except Christmas morning. There won't be a lot to do on that day. I could come up the afternoon before, and we could get married and go down to Narling the same evening. I mustn't be away from the Division.'

'Of course not, dear,' said Emily. She was rather dazed. She had not seen the house she would have to live in; she knew nothing about it in fact, except that Curzon's brief notes had assured her that it was quite a nice one. She had made no preparations for housekeeping there–in fact she had made no preparations for being married at all. But she knew quite well that there was nobody and nothing in the world as important as the General and the Division he commanded.

'We'll do whatever you think we ought to do, dear,' said Emily, and Curzon kissed her hard on the lips in a way he had never kissed her before. Her head swam and her knees went weak so that she leaned against him and clung to him trembling, and they kissed again until the trembling passed and her kind eyes were bright with a passion she had never known before. She found–what she had never expected–that when the world obtruded itself upon them again she was able to meet it boldly face to face, encountering her mother and father across the luncheon table as though a quarter of an hour before she had not been in a man's arms and glad to be there.

At lunch they had to discuss practical details regarding the servants Emily must find for Narling Priory, housekeeper and cook and parlourmaid and kitchenmaid. Curzon's three soldier servants (the regulation number allotted to a Major-General) could be relied upon to do the other work. The Duchess was perturbed when she heard how hurried was the wedding they had decided upon, but she raised no objection. The Duke took on the responsibility of making the arrangements regarding the licence; the Duchess said she would see to it that St Margaret's was available for the ceremony–it had to be St Margaret's, of course. In return, Curzon was able to tell the Duke and Duchess that he had applied for the services of Captain Horatio Winter-Willoughby and Mr Bertram Greven as his aides-de-camp, and that his application had been approved and orders issued for the officers in question to join him. The Duke and Duchess were undoubtedly grateful to him. Horatio Winter-Willoughby was Lord George's son and the ultimate heir to the title, while Greven was a nephew of the Duchess, and somehow no one had as yet made application for his services on the staff. Curzon felt remarkably pleased with himself when he received the thanks of the Duke and the Duchess. Even though they were about to become his parents-in-law it was gratifying to be able to do them favours.

Then when lunch was finished there was only time for one last embrace before Curzon tore himself away to get into the Vauxhall and be driven away through Guildford and Petersfield back to the Division. There was this to be said in favour of war-time conditions, that there was no time for shilly-shallying argument.

12

So that the next two or three days witnessed a whole sequence of arrivals at Narling Priory. There came the grim under-housekeeper from Bude Hall, Somersetshire–the Duchess had made a present of her to her daughter, and with her the trio of servants selected from the staff of the three ducal houses. It had rather frightened the Duchess to hear that her daughter would have to be lady's-maided by the parlourmaid; it was not so easy for her to reconcile herself to that as one of the necessary sacrifices of war-time, but as the Priory was only a medium-sized house and half of it was occupied by the divisional headquarters there had to be a line drawn somewhere, and this was Emily's own suggestion.

Curzon's soldier servants regarded the arrival of the women with unconcealed interest, but they were disappointed in the reception accorded their advances. Not even the kitchen-maid–at any rate, with the cook's eye on her–would allow mere grooms and private soldiers any liberties with one who represented the fifth greatest house in all England. Curzon handed over house and keys to the housekeeper–he was living with the headquarters' mess at the moment–and went on with his work for the Division.

The two brigadiers for whom he had been clamouring turned up next. One was Challis, who as a battalion commander had lost half a hand at Mons and had miraculously escaped capture during the retreat; the other was Daunt, brought home from some South African colony, Nigeria or somewhere. Curzon looked them over and was pleased with them both, although he deferred final judgment. Men had to be good before he could be assured of their suitability for the Ninety-first Division. He was not nearly so satisfied with his two aides-de-camp, who turned up unfeignedly glad at having been released by this miracle from the rigours of service in the Guards' depot at Caterham. Winter-Willoughby was nearly as bald as his father, Lord George, and nearly as fat. Despite the fact that he was indebted to Curzon for this staff appointment he was inclined to be a little resentful and patronizing towards the bounder who was marrying his cousin. And Greven had no forehead and no chin and wore riding breeches whose khaki dye carried the particular admixture of pink which was growing fashionable among the younger officers and for which Curzon had a peculiar dislike. Curzon began to see that there were some special disadvantages about marrying into a ducal family.

He disliked his two aides-de-camp at sight the afternoon on which they reported themselves, and the very next day they deepened his prejudice further still, for they were both of them ten minutes late, on the very first morning on which they were on duty. Curzon had to sit fretting in his office while the horses were being walked up and down outside. Curzon told them off furiously as he got into the saddle, and they sulked as they cantered through the rain over the downs to where there was an artillery brigade to be inspected.

Curzon was a little more at home inspecting artillery than infantry. An infantry battalion's horse-lines were so small and insignificant that one could not in decency spend much time over them, but it was different with artillery. Horses were as important as gunners, and Curzon felt justified in devoting most of his attention to the horses, which he knew something about, rather than to the artillery technicalities, about which he knew nothing at all. The inspection was long and meticulous, and Curzon found fault with everything he saw. The battery commanders wilted under the lash of his tongue, the sergeant-majors flinched, the veterinary surgeons trembled.

When Curzon rode away the rumour was ready to circulate through the division that 'Curzon was just as mad about horse-lines as about cookhouses'. Yet nobody knew the reason of this savage bad temper which he had displayed–those who were in the secret of the General's private life were inclined to attribute it to the fact that he was being married that afternoon, but they were wrong. A letter had come to Curzon that morning, in a cheap shabby envelope, addressed originally to the regimental depot, and readdressed three times before it had reached him. Curzon had read it while he ate his breakfast, and the sight of it had spoiled his day.

117 Shoesmith St
Brixton
16th December, 1914

My Dear Bertie,

I suppose I must call you that still although you are a General now and going to marry a great Lady. We are all of us here very pleased to see how well you are getting on. Your Uncle Stanley reads the papers a great deal and has shown us lots about you in them. He did not approve of the war at first but when he heard about what the Germans did in Belgium he feels differently about it now. Maud has just got married, too, to a gentleman in a very good way of business as a tailor. It seems only like yesterday since she was a little girl like when you saw her last. Gertie is in a government office and doing very well, and our Dick has just made up his mind that he must do his bit and he is going to join the army as soon as Christmas is over. Your Uncle Stanley is very well considering although his chest troubles him a lot, and of course I am all right as usual except for my leg. This is just a line to wish you much joy and happiness in your new life with your bride and to say that if ever you are in Brixton again we shall be glad the same as ever, although you are so grand now, if you would pop in and see us just for a minute.

Your loving
Aunt Kate

P.S.–We saw your photograph in the paper and you look just the same as ever which is why I wrote to you dear.

That was a very disturbing letter for a man about to marry a duke's daughter to receive on his wedding morning. Curzon's flesh had crept as he read it. He had been perfectly sincere when he told Emily and the Duchess that he had not a relation in the world–he had forgotten all about the Coles of Brixton, honestly and sincerely forgotten all about them. It was a shock to be reminded of their existence. If any word about them should reach the Duchess's ears it would make her into his deadly enemy, for she would never forgive him the deception. Even now she was hardly a benevolent neutral. Any revelation would turn the scale. It would lose him Emily's good opinion and regard. Probably it would ruin his life and his career as well, and that was an important although a minor consideration. Curzon felt slightly sick, like a man with no head for heights looking over the edge of a precipice. Why in the world had Aunt Kate married beneath her station instead of above it as his own mother had very sensibly seen fit to do?

He had plenty of time to think about it during the long motor journey up to London. There had been no time for lunch after the artillery inspection, and he and Horatio Winter-Willoughby and Greven ate sandwiches in the stuffy saloon car as they raced along past the Devil's Punchbowl and on to Guildford. They were cumbered with their greatcoats and swords. Curzon actually found himself thankful that he had been compelled to put aside the Duchess's suggestion that he should be married in all the glory of his Lancer full-dress. He simply had not been able to make allowance in the day's timetable for that change of clothing, and he was glad now, swaying about in the motor car, feeling slightly sick, what with the motion, and the sandwiches, and the imminence of marriage, and that letter from Aunt Kate. From Guildford onwards he was looking at his watch. It was going to be a near-run thing. There were only a few minutes left when they ran through Esher, and he called on the driver for yet more speed. Kingston–Putney Bridge–King's Road, crowded with people shopping industriously on this, the first Christmas Eve of the war.

Big Ben showed one minute to two as they swung out of Victoria Street. The paragraphs in the newspapers about the romantic war wedding of a duke's daughter and the sight of the carpet and awning outside St Margaret's had called together a big crowd on the pavement. The Vauxhall stopped at the end of the awning, and Curzon and his two aides got out while the crowd surged under the control of the police. They had hardly sat down up by the chancel rails when the organ changed its tune and up the aisle came Emily in her bridal white, her bridesmaids and her pages behind her, and the Duke in support.

As the Duchess had said, the fact that Emily was marrying a General was a very adequate excuse for so much ceremony at the wedding, when otherwise it might not be quite good taste in war-time. The Bishop (he was a Winter-Willoughby too; by common report the only one with any brains, and he had too many) went through the service, while Curzon rasped out the responses and Emily whispered them . Then the signing of the register, and the march out through the church, while the guests stood up on their seats to catch a better glimpse of the bride and the beribboned bridegroom.

While Curzon was waiting for Emily, encumbered with train and veil, to get into the motor car, the crowd surged more violently than ever. He looked round. Between two policemen, and waving violently, was Aunt Kate–there was no mistaking her; and the two women beside her were presumably Maud and Gertie. It was only for a second that their eyes met. Aunt Kate had the decency and the common sense not to call out 'Bertie!' although for an idiotic second Curzon was filled with fear in case she should say something about her sore leg. He had not time to betray recognition, as he had to climb in at once beside Emily. Next instant they were off, with Curzon sitting shaken beside Emily, who for some woman's reason or other had tears on her face.

So that on the way to Bude House Curzon had time to reflect that there were some relatives of his at his wedding. The church had been crammed with Winter-Willoughbys and Grevens, hordes of them. There had not been more than half a dozen people invited at Curzon's request–three or four members of the Cavalry Club, and Mackenzie, who (perhaps for reasons of his own) had intimated that he might be able to get away from his duties at the War Office for an hour. Curzon had not even been able to find a friend close enough to be asked to be groom's man–the one or two possibles were in France, which was why the egregious Horatio had had to fulfil that duty.

There was an hour's torment in Bude House, where even those colossal rooms were not big enough to shelter all the seething horde without crushing. The sparse khaki amidst the morning coats and the elaborate dresses would have been significant to an attentive observer. Those uniforms were like the secret seeds of decay in the midst of an apparently healthy body. They were significant of the end of a great era. The decline had set in, although those most intimately concerned (despite the fact that they already were talking sorrowfully about the good old days, and lamenting the changes all about them) obstinately refused to recognize it. In ten years' time the world would have no room for Bude House. It would be torn to pieces; the British public would be blackmailed into buying its paintings by the threat of selling them to America; its Adams fireplaces would be sold with less advertisement to the same country; and the people who thronged its rooms would be stockbroking on half-commission or opening little hat shops in the side streets.

But nobody cared to think about all this at the moment, least of all Curzon, the most significant figure present, with his hand nervously resting on his sword hilt and the letter from Aunt Kate in his pocket. He greeted starchily the people who came up to wish him happiness and to look him over covertly; he did not feel in the least complimented when he overheard withered little Mr Anstey whispering to an aged female crony, 'Most romantic. A real cloak and sword wedding just like Napoleon's'; he had not even found any real pleasure in the contemplation of the inkstand which was a present from the King. The longer the reception lasted, the stiffer and more formal be became, and the attempts at boisterousnesss made by the few younger people (among whom should be reckoned his two aides-de-camp) irritated him unbearably.

By the time Emily appeared again in a sober travelling costume, and still in unaccountable tears, his nerves were on edge–although Curzon would have indignantly denied the possession of any nerves at all if anyone had been rash enough to impute them to him. The premature evening had already fallen as he climbed after Emily into the big Vauxhall. They slid through the darkened streets (the A.S.C. driver keeping his eye rigidly in front) and Curzon sat cold and formal in his corner, while Emily drooped from her stiff uprightness in hers. From the darkness that surrounded her there came at intervals something suspiciously like a sniff–unbelievable though it might be that a duke's daughter, and one moreover of her Spartan upbringing, should ever sniff.

Curzon was not given to self-contemplation. He would have seen nothing incongruous in the spectacle of the Major-General, who that morning had reduced an artillery brigade to a condition of gibbering terror, caressing his bride on their bridal journey. When he held aloof from her during that first hour was merely because he did not feel like doing otherwise. The events of the day had left him unfitted for love. Emily was like a stranger to him at present.

Later on, as the headlights tore lanes through the darkness, and the car weaved its way precariously round the curves at Hindhead, he put his hand out and groped for hers. He touched it, and she leaped in panic. Her nerves were in as bad a state as his, and for all this hour she had been expecting and dreading this contact. She was consumed with misgivings regarding the unbelievable thing that men do to women when they are married to them, and to which the woman has to submit–the half-knowledge she had gained of these matters during her cloistered existence made the future absolutely terrifying to her. It was five days since she had last had the comfort and stimulus of Curzon's presence, and during those five days she had lapsed from her mood of reckless passion into one more consonant with an upbringing dating from the eighties. She was brooding darkly over the prospect of 'that kind of thing'; and the new, wordless, reserved, cold, formal Curzon beside her was of no help to her. From the way she jumped at his touch one might have guessed that she feared lest he should begin at once.

There was no fear of that, nor of the least resemblance to it. When Curzon felt the gloved hand snatched away from him he withdrew further into himself than ever. They sat stiffly silent, one in each corner, while the Vauxhall nosed its way through Petersfield, out into the main road beyond, and then swung aside into the by-roads which led to Narling Priory. The servants came out to welcome them–the grim housekeeper, and the prim elderly parlourmaid, and Curzon's groom and soldier servant. The A.S.C. driver was left to unstrap the trunks from the grid at the back, while the housekeeper walked up the stairs to the bridal chamber with the bride, while Curzon trailed behind. They found themselves alone together at last in her bedroom. Emily looked round for comfort, and found none in the unpleasant furniture which the War Office had taken over at a thumping rental along with the house. She saw Curzon standing waiting, with the predatory nose and cruel moustache.

'I–I want to lie down,' she said wildly. 'I–I'm tired.'

The arrival of the parlourmaid and servant with the trunks eased the situation for a moment. As the servant withdrew the parlourmaid addressed herself with decision to the business of unpacking. Curzon was glad that in the circumstances he could be expected to say nothing beyond pure formalities.

'I shall see you at dinner, then,' he said, backing away with his spurs clinking.

Dinner was an ordeal, too, with the elderly parlourmaid breathing discretion at every pore. They looked at each other across the little table and tried to make conversation, but it was not easy. Both of them would have been interested if they had told each other the stories of their lives, for they were still extraordinarily ignorant of each other's past, but it hardly became a husband and wife to tell facts about themselves to the other. In the absence of that resource, and after the inevitable comments about the dreariness of the weather, conversation came to a standstill. Lady Emily looked with bewilderment at the spruce dinner-jacketed man with the red face whom she had married. She told herself that he did not look in the least like the man she had fallen in love with. And Curzon looked at Emily, a little drawn and haggard, and marvelled to himself at the contrariness of women, and felt ill at ease because on other occasions when he had dined with a woman previous to sleeping with her the circumstances had not been in the least like this.

As soon as dinner was over Emily withdrew to the drawing-room, leaving Curzon alone to his port and his brandy, and when Curzon came into the drawing-room she shrank down nervously in her chair and fluttered the weekly newspaper she had been pretending to read. Curzon sat on the edge of his chair and tugged at his moustache; the clock ticked away inexorably on the mantelpiece while he stared into the fire. Emily kept her eyes on the page before her although she could read no word of its print; she was making an effort now at this late hour to rally her self-control as became one of her blue blood and to go stoically through the ordeal before her without a sign of weakness, like a French aristocrat on the way to the guillotine. It was not easy, all the same.

She put down her paper and got to her feet.

'I think I shall go to bed now,' she said; only the acutest ear could have caught the quaver in her voice.

'Yes,' said Curzon. He could not help drawling on occasions like the present of extreme nervous tension. 'You've had a tiring day, m'dear.'

By an effort of rigid self-control Emily kept her upper lip from trembling. Curzon's face was blank and expressionless, like a block of wood, as though he were playing at poker, and when he looked at her he looked right through her–he could not help it; it was only a natural reaction to his shyness. He opened the door for her, and she cast one more glance at that wooden countenance before she fled up the stairs.

Curzon went back beside the fire and drew deeply on a fresh cigar. He stared again into the fire. Somehow this thoughts were jumbled. He tried to think about the Division, that hotchpotch of jarring personalities which he had to straighten out, but he could not think of it for long. For some reason other mental pictures obtruded themselves. For the first time for years he found himself thinking about Manningtree-Field, his captain at Volkslaagte, lying in a mess of blood and brains at his feet. Then his thoughts leaped back a dozen years more, until he was a small boy coming home from preparatory school, being met at Victoria Station by his mother. He thought of Mackenzie with his pink face and sandy hair. He thought of Miss Cissie Barnes, the lady with whom he had spent many joyful evenings. Miss Barnes wore decorative garters whose clasps were miniature five-barred gates with 'trespasser will be prosecuted' engraved upon them. Curzon remembered vividly how they had looked encircling the black-stockinged leg with the luscious white thigh showing above the stocking. Curzon flung the cigar into the fire and strode twice up and down the room. Then he went out, up the stairs, to the upper landing. On the right was the door into his small bedroom and dressing-room. On the left was the door into Emily's room–there was a connecting door between the two, but he did not consider that. He stood still for a moment before he knocked on the door on the left and entered abruptly.

Emily stood by the fire. There were candles alight on the dressing-table, on the mantelpiece, beside the wardrobe, so that the room was brightly illuminated. Emily's clothes, save for the evening frock, lay neatly on the chair where her maid had placed them; the long formidable corset was on the top, with the suspenders hanging down. Emily was wearing a nightdress of the kind considered by orthodox people in 1914 as the most frivolous possible (the kind of nightdress worn by suburban housewives thirty years later was at that time only worn by prostitutes) and she stood there by the fire with a cataract of lace falling over her breast and her long hair in a rope down her back.

She saw him come in, his face a little flushed, the cruel mouth and the big nose much in evidence, and she saw him shut and lock the door.

'Bertie,' she said, and she wanted to add: 'be kind to me,' but she could say no more than the one word, because pride on the one hand and passion on the other dried up in her throat. Curzon came slowly over to her, his face wearing the expression of stony calm which always characterized it at tense moments. He put out his hands to her, and she came towards him, fascinated.

13

Perhaps it was Emily's stoic upbringing which made that marriage a success. Certainly she knew more misery in the opening few weeks of her married life than she had ever known before–the misery of loneliness, and the misery of doubt. But she had long been taught to bear her troubles uncomplaining, along with the doctrine, comforting in its fatalism, that the ways of mankind (as compared with those of womankind) are inscrutable. Thanks to her patience and powers of endurance they learned after a short interval to live together as happy as two people of their limited capacity for happiness could expect to be.

Miss Cissie Barnes had much to answer for. The memory of joyous unrepressed evenings with her influenced Curzon profoundly. He could not dream of treating his wife in the same way as he had once treated Cissie Barnes, with the unfortunate result that he made love to Emily with a stern aloofness that could raise no response in her virginal body. As Emily never expected anything else, however, not so much harm was done as might have been the case. Emily went through that part of the business as her necessary duty, like opening Girl Guides' displays or going to church. It was her duty, something it was incumbent upon her to do, so she did it with the best grace possible short of taking an active interest in it–women were not supposed to do that.

For the rest, she was everything a general's wife should be. On Christmas morning, the very day after her wedding, she breakfasted with him with every appearance of cheerfulness, and saw him off on his tour of inspection with a wave of her hand that told the inquisitive world that they were absolutely happy. There were not many generals of division in England who spent that Christmas Day with the troops, but Curzon was one of them. He managed to visit every one of the twenty units under his command. For nearly all the men it was their first Christmas in the Army; for a great number of them it would also be their last, but no one–certainly not Curzon and not even Emily–stopped to think about that. Curzon had not the time to visit the men in the ranks, but he called in to every officers' mess, and the surprise and delight of the regimental officers at this condescension on the part of high authority filtered in the end down to the men in the ranks and did its part in tuning up the Ninety-first Division to the pitch of excellence which it eventually displayed.

It did Curzon no harm that everyone knew he was newly married, nor that regimental wits were busy producing obscene jokes about him and his wife. It made him known, gave him a personality for the private soldiers, just as did his acquisition of the nickname of 'Bertie'–which reached the troops of the line from the Staff, who had heard Lady Emily address him by that name. Neither Emily nor Curzon saw anything comic or undignified about the name of 'Bertie', and to the Army the irony of the name's suggestion of weak good fellowship as contrasted with his reputation for savage energy and discipline appealed to the wry sense of humour of the sufferers, making a deeper impression still. The catchword 'Bertie's the boy' was current in the Ninety-first Division long before it spread among the troops in France.

Everyone knew that Bertie would tolerate no inefficiency or slackness. The whole Army was aware of the reasons why Lieutenant-Colonel Ringer of the Fusiliers was removed from his command and sent into retirement, and of the energy of Bertie's representations to the War Office which brought this about. Yet not so many people knew that the leakage of gossip regarding this affair was the cause of the return of Lieutenant Horatio Winter-Willoughby to regimental duty. The information regarding the leakage reached Curzon through Emily. Emily had plunged in duty bound into the business of leading Army society locally–most of the senior officers of the division had brought down their wives to be near them, and installed them at exorbitant prices in hotels and cottages round about. Sooner or later someone told her how much they knew about the Ringer scandal, and what was the source of the information.

Emily told Curzon in all innocence–she had not yet learned what a crime gossip was in Curzon's eyes. Curzon struck at once. That same day a report went into the War Office saying that Major-General Curzon much regretted being under the necessity of informing the Director-General of Staff Personnel that Lieutenant Horatio Winter-Willoughby had been found unsuitable for work on the Staff, and of requesting that he be ordered to return to his unit. There was a wail of despair from Horatio when the news reached him–a wail expressed in indignant letters to London, which brought down the Duchess of Bude and Lady Constance Winter-Willoughby, simply seething with indignation.

The Duchess was angry largely because this upstart son-in-law of hers was betraying the family which had condescended to admit him into its circle. What was the good of having a general in the family if he did not find places on the staff for the nephews? And the suggestion that a Winter-Willoughby was not up to his work was perfectly preposterous–more preposterous still, because the Duchess could never imagine that it mattered a rap which man did which work as long as she had a finger in the pie. There was the question of the succession of the title too. If Horatio was sent back into the Guards as a result of this ridiculous notion of Curzon's it was possible that he might be killed–not likely, of course, because Winter-Willoughbys were not killed, but possible–and that would make the continued existence of the title almost precarious.

'So you see,' said the Duchess, putting down her teacup, 'you simply can't go on with this wicked idea. You must write to the War Office *at once*–or it would be better to telephone to them perhaps–and tell them that you have made a mistake and you want Horatio to stay here with you.'

Curzon would have found it difficult to have answered politely if he had cast about for words with which to tell his mother-in-law that he was not going to do what she said. But as it was he did not stop to try to be polite. He was not going to have the efficiency of his Division interfered with by anyone not in authority, least of all a woman.

'I'm not going to do anything of the sort,' he said briefly.

'Bertie!' said the Duchess, scandalized.

'No,' said Curzon. 'This isn't the first time I've had to find fault with Horatio. I'm sorry, he's no good, but I can't have him on my Staff. I hope he will find regimental duty more–more congenial.'

'Do you mean,' said the Duchess, 'that you're not going to do what I ask–what the Family ask you to do?'

'I'm not going to keep him as my A.D.C.,' said Curzon sturdily.

'I think,' said Lady Constance, 'that is perfectly horrible of you.'

Lady Constance happened to be more moved by anxiety for her son that by Curzon's blasphemous denial of the family.

'I'm sorry,' said Curzon, 'but I can't help it. I have the Division to think about.'

'Division fiddlesticks,' said the Duchess, which made Curzon exceedingly angry. Lady Constance saw the look in his eye, and did her best to soothe him.

'Perhaps Horatio was a little indiscreet,' she said, 'but he's only young. I think he will have learned his lesson after this. Don't you think you might give him another chance?'

Lady Constance made play with all her beauty and all her elegance as she spoke. Curzon would certainly have wavered if it had not been the concern of the Division. He was suddenly able to visualize with appalling clarity Horatio, lazy, casual, and unpunctual, confronted suddenly with a crisis like any one of the fifty which had occurred during the eleven days at Ypres. If the existence of the Division should at any time depend on Horatio, which was perfectly possible, the Division would cease to exist. It was unthinkable that Horatio should continue in a position of potential responsibility.

'No,' said Curzon. 'I can't have him.'

Lady Constance and the Duchess looked at each other and with one accord they turned to Emily, who had been sitting mute beside the tea things.

'Emily,' said Lady Constance. 'Can't you persuade him?'

'Horatio is your first cousin,' said the Duchess. 'He's a future Duke of Bude.'

Emily looked in distress, first at her mother and her aunt, and then at her husband in his khaki and his red tabs beside the fire. Anyone–even a woman only three weeks married to him–could see by his stiff attitude that the matter was very near to his heart, that his mind was made up, and that his temper was growing short. In the last two months the family had declined in importance in her eyes; it was her husband who mattered. Yet it was frightening that they should be debating a matter on which Horatio's very life might depend–it was that thought which distressed her more than the need to oppose her mother.

'Don't ask me,' she said. 'I can't interfere with the Division. I don't think you ought to ask me.'

The Duchess snapped her handbag shut with a vicious click and rose to her feet.

'It appears to me,' she said, 'as if we were unwelcome even in my daughter's house.'

She rose superbly to her feet, carrying Lady Constance along with her by sheer force of personality.

'I can see no profit,' she went on, 'in continuing this subject. Perhaps, Bertie, you will be good enough to send and have my car brought round?'

Curzon tugged at the bell-rope and gave the order to the parlourmaid; it is just possible that the Duchess had not expected to be taken quite so readily at her word. At any rate, Lady Constance made a last appeal.

'I don't want to have to part in anger like this,' she said. 'Can't something be arranged, Emily–Bertie?'

'Something will doubtless be arranged,' said the Duchess, with a venomous glance at her daughter and son-in-law. 'Please do not be too distressed, Constance.'

Curzon and Emily walked out to the door with them, but the Duchess so far forgot her good manners as to climb into the car without saying good-bye. Enough had happened that afternoon to make her angry; that a Winter-Willoughby should be denied something apparently desirable, and that a Duchess of Bude should be forced to plead with an upstart little General and then be refused was a state of affairs calculated to make her perfectly furious.

The sequel followed promptly, materializing in the arrival of the Duke the next day, preceded by a telegram. Curzon talked with him alone, at his special request, Emily withdrawing after receiving his fatherly greetings. They sat one each side of the fire and pulled at their cigars in silence for several minutes until the Duke began in the inevitable subject.

'You've made my wife a bit annoyed over this business of young Horatio, Curzon, you know,' said the Duke. 'As a matter of fact I've never seen her so angry before in my life.'

The tone of the Duke's voice suggested that he had frequently seen her fairly angry.

'I'm sorry,' said Curzon.

'Trouble is, with women,' went on the Duke, 'they never know when to stop. And they don't draw any distinctions between a man's private life and his official one–they don't render unto Caesar the things that are Caesar's, you know. My wife's determined to put the screw on you somehow or other–you know what women are like. You can guess what she made me do last night–first shot in the campaign, so to speak?'

'No,' said Curzon.

'She made me sit down there and then, with dinner half an hour late already, and write an order to Coutts'. Dash it all, you can guess what that was about, can't you?'

'I suppose so,' said Curzon.

'It was to countermand my previous order to pay one-seventy a month into your account. Women never know what's good form, and what isn't.'

Curzon said nothing. The prospect of losing the Duke's two thousand a year was disturbing; it would mean altering the whole scale of his domestic arrangements, but it did absolutely nothing towards making him incline again in the direction of retaining Horatio's services.

'I suppose,' said the Duke nervously, 'there isn't any chance of your changing your mind about Horatio?'

'Not the least,' snapped Curzon. 'And I don't think we had better discuss the subject.'

'Quite right,' said the Duke. 'I was sure you would say that. Dam' good thing you didn't kick me out of the house the minute I said what I did. Of course, I wrote another order to Coutts' this morning, saying that they were to continue paying that seventy-one. But I'd rather you didn't let the Duchess know all the same.'

'Thank you,' said Curzon.

'Now,' said the Duke, with enormous relief, 'is there any way out of this mess? Can you think of any job Horatio *could* do?'

'He might make a good regimental officer,' said Curzon. Most of the regimental officers he had known had not been much more distinguished for capacity than Horatio. The Duke nodded.

'I suppose so,' he said. 'There aren't many brains in us Winters, when all is said and done. Fact is, I don't think we'd be very important people if the first Winter hadn't married William of Orange's lady friend. But it's not much good telling the Duchess that. I've got to do something about it.'

The Duke looked quite pathetic.

'There are some staff positions,' said Curzon, 'where he couldn't do much harm.'

Curzon was quite incapable of expressing that awkward truth any less awkwardly.

'M'm,' said the Duke. 'And none of them in your gift, I suppose?'

'No.'

'It's awkward,' said the Duke. 'But I'll have to see what I can do up in town. I suppose you know that I'll be in office again soon?'

'No,' said Curzon. Despite the revelations of the last few weeks he was still abysmally ignorant of the behind-the-scenes moves in politics.

'Yes,' said the Duke. 'I don't think it matters if I tell you. The Radicals won't be able to keep us out much longer. Then I may be able to do a bit more for Horatio and satisfy the Duchess. There's a good many points I want your advice about, too. What's this man Mackenzie like? Any good?'

'First rate,' said Curzon without hesitation. Had not Mackenzie been instrumental in promoting him to Major-General, in giving him the Ninety-first Division, and in supplying that Division with material far beyond its quota? Quite apart from that, it would have needed a very serious deficiency indeed to induce Curzon not to give the simple loyalty which he in turn expected from his subordinates.

'You really mean that?' asked the Duke anxiously.

'Of course,' said Curzon. 'He's one of the best soldiers we've got. Works like a nigger and plenty of brains.'

'M'm,' said the Duke meditatively, pulling at his long fleshy chin. 'You see–well, it doesn't matter. If you think he's satisfactory, and you ought to know, I don't think I ought–anyway, that's all right.'

Having made this cryptic speech the Duke fell silent again, tranferring his attentions from his chin to his cigar, while Curzon smoked opposite to him, silent also, for the adequate enough reason that he had nothing more to say. Finally, the Duke got to his feet.

'Well,' he said. 'There's going to be a hot reception awaiting me when I get back to London again, but it's no use putting if off. I'll start back now, I think. No, thank you very much, I won't stay to dinner. It won't be very late by the time I'm home. Good-bye, Curzon. Don't be too gloomy.'

Captain Horatio Winter-Willoughby did not serve his country at the risk of his life despite Curzon's adverse report upon him. It only needed the War Office's attention to be seriously drawn to the reference to him in the Peerage for him to be found a safe position on the staff of the military attaché to a neutral government–the War Office was quite well aware of the importance of safeguarding the ultimate heir to a dukedom, just as when the threat of air-raids became more than a threat they sent the masterpieces of the National Gallery into safe storage in Wales.

Yet in one respect the Duke's conversation bore fruit. The inevitable spy who tries to serve both sides was able to report a discussion which had been held among the prospective Ins, and his report had come to the knowledge of General Mackenzie. The spy had had a respectable education, and he was able to compare that discussion with the famous debate among the Triumvirate in Julius Caesar, when they prick off the prospective victims.

'No,' the Duke had said. 'I can't say I agree with you about this fellow Mackenzie. My son-in-law, who's in command of a division–I've told you about him before, Haven't I?–well, he says that Mackenzie's all right. Swears by him, in fact. And my son-in-law's got his head screwed on the right way. He wouldn't say a thing like that if he didn't think it was true, either. I don't think Mackenzie ought to go. Hang it, someone's got to do the brainwork.'

That was why–and Mackenzie knew it–that when the Liberal Government at last yielded to the overwhelming pressure and admitted some of the Opposition to the sweets of office, while men in high position fell right and left, General Mackenzie remained Director-General of Tactical Services. Others greater than he–among them the greatest Minister of War that England ever had–were flung out of office, but Mackenzie remained despite his very unsound attitude in the Ulster crisis. Perhaps that is the most important contribution Curzon ever made to the history of England.

In addition, as a born intriguer, Mackenzie could not possibly credit Curzon with ordinary honesty, but considered him as just a fellow intriguer, an ally worth having and especially a potential enemy worth placating.

14

The training of the Ninety-first Division proceeded apace, even though every day added to the total amount to be learned. A good many wounded and convalescent officers rejoined its ranks, and regarded with quiet amusement the parade movements and formal battle tactics which the Division was slowly learning to perform. Their recent experience of Flanders mud, and barbed wire, and German machine-guns had deprived them of their faith in rigid attacking movements.

Besides these informal ambassadors, the War Office began to send instructors with more explicit credentials–trench warfare experts, barbed wire maniacs, bombing officers, machine-gun enthusiasts, and–after the Second Battle of Ypres–gas-warfare specialists. These men were attached to Curzon's staff with orders to teach the Ninety-first Division all they knew, and every one of them was quite convinced that his particular speciality was the vital necessity in the new kind of warfare which was being waged, and clamoured for wider and wider powers to be given.

Curzon had to listen to them patiently and arbitrate among them; sometimes, under the urging of express orders from the War Office, he had to acquiesce in the teaching of doctrines which to him were only a shade less than heretical He had no sooner made arrangements for an intensive instruction in bayonet fighting than he had to coerce his colonels into submitting to an enlargement of the battalion machine-guns establishments which would diminish very seriously the number of bayonets that could be put in line. He had to see to it that the artillery brigades received instruction regarding the new but already highly technical business of spotting from the air. He had to let the sappers have their way and try to make every infantryman an expert in matters which before the war had been strictly left to the engineers.

Curzon himself had small belief still in the theories of a long war to be conducted exclusively in trenches. That would leave such small scope for the kind of soldiering he appreciated that he simply could not believe in it. Even in the spring of 1915, when the line in France reeled under the blow dealt it at Ypres, he was in a fever of apprehension lest the Allied victory should come too quickly, before the Ninety-first Division could arrive to take its share of the glory. In March the first reports of the Battle of Neuve-Chapelle were construed by him as indicating a great victory, the first step in the advance to Berlin, and he was left puzzled, even after the circulation of the War Office confidential memoranda on the battle, by the subsequent inactivity.

He threw himself more ardently than ever into his duty of preparing the Ninety-first Division for active service. His brigadiers–Daunt and Challis and Webb–needed no goading. They were prepared to work until they dropped.

The main part of Curzon's work consisted in co-ordinating the activities of all the officers under him. It would have called for a Solomon to adjudicate between the conflicting claims put before him. Curzon was able to keep the peace not by the ingenuity or justice of his decisions, but solely by the strictness of the discipline maintained. There was no one who dared to dispute or evade his orders. He was the terror of the shirkers and of the wrigglers. His reputation as a relentless disciplinarian stood him in good stead, and after he had made an example of Colonel Ringer he had no more trouble with his subordinates.

The paper work which all this involved was a sore trial to him. Despite the growth of the Headquarters Staff, of the introduction of clerks, of the multiplication of specialist officers, the office work which he personally had to attend to increased inordinately. His anxiety regarding his Division prevented him from delegating more of his authority than he was compelled to, and early morning and late night found him patiently reading courts martial records and confidential reports on junior officers. He signed no indents or statements which he had not read; he set himself painfully to learn all about the idiosyncrasies and strengths and weaknesses of every officer and unit with which he came in contact. He exercised his mind over the Rifles' regrettable tendency to absence without leave, and the proneness of the Seventh (Service) Battalion of the Cumberland Light Infantry to acquire sore feet on route marches.

It was his duty to make the Division efficient; that was why he slaved and toiled over the business. His desire for his own professional advancement, his anxiety to stand well in Emily's eyes and in those of her family, were undoubtedly acute, but they were not the motives which guided him. He had been given a job of work to do, and he did it to the best of his ability, although the desk work made him thin and irritable and spoilt his digestion and his eyesight, and although he could never find time now to have all the exercise for which he craved.

He usually had to leave Lady Emily to hunt by herself, or under the escort of either Greven or Follett, his aides-de-camp–there was a good deal of fox-hunting to be enjoyed, because various patriotic people had decided that hunting must go on, so that when the boys returned from the trenches they would find this essential characteristic of England still flourishing, while officers in England should be provided with sport; nor might foxes be allowed to diminish the food supply of England; nor might the breed of English horses, so essential in war-time, be allowed to decline; nor might the hunt servants be thrown out of employment–there were dozens of reasons put forward for the maintenance of fox-hunting besides the real one that the hunters did not believe a war to be nearly as serious as the suspension of fox-hunting. It was highly convenient for all concerned that their patriotic feelings should run so closely parallel to their own desires.

Yet it is possible that fox-hunting played its part in welding the Ninety-first Division into a living, active whole, for every officer did his best to hunt, and the friendships formed in the hunting field may have influenced subsequent events in no-man's-land. At any rate, the Major-General commanding the Division gave his approval and his blessing to fox-hunting, and when the season came to an end at the approach of summer he condoled with his wife on the subject. Emily looked at him a little queerly–they were dining, at the time, alone for once in the absence of any guests from the Division, but the parlourmaid was in the room and her presence caused Lady Emily not to say immediately what she was going to say. Later on, when they sat in the drawing-room with their coffee beside them, Emily reverted to the subject, nervously.

'You were saying I must be sorry that hunting was coming to an end, Bertie,' said Emily.

'That's right,' said Curzon. 'I always think it's a pity.'

'Well,' said Emily, 'it doesn't matter to me now. I couldn't go on hunting in any case.'

Curzon looked across at Emily with surprise in his face. He had naturally, like any sane newly married man, thought occasionally of the possibility of his wife having a child, but now that she was trying to tell him about it that was the last idea to occur to him.

'Why, m'dear,' he asked, 'is anything the matter?'

'Not really the *matter*,' said Emily. Her eyes were wide and she made herself meet Curzon's glance without flinching.

'But–but—' said Curzon. 'What is it, then?'

Emily went on looking at him without speaking, and yet still he would not jump to the right conclusion. For a moment he was honestly worried lest Emily should have decided that fox-hunting was unpatriotic or cruel. And Emily was not at all deterred at the thought of saying she was pregnant (although that was not the word she would use). What was holding her back was the thought that after the announcement she would have to tell her husband her reasons for thinking herself to be in that condition, and that would involve discussion of matters she had never mentioned to any man at all, not even (as yet) to a doctor. Curzon and she had skated safely (only those of Victorian upbringing can guess how) during three months of married life over the thin ice of female weakness without crashing through into revelations.

'But, my good girl,' protested Curzon, and then the truth dawned upon him.

'God bless my soul,' said Curzon, his coffee cup chattering into its saucer. He grinned with surprised delight; already, in this his early middle-age, there was just noticeable the old-maidish quality about his smile which was later to become so pronounced.

For some unaccountable reason Emily found tears in her eyes; they were soon rolling down her cheeks.

'Oh, my dear, my darling,' said Curzon, hurrying across the room to her. Words of endearment did not come too easily to him; in part that was because of lurking memories of having used them to Cissie Barnes. He patted her on the shoulder, and then, as that did not avail, he knelt in stiff dinner-jacketed awkwardness beside her in her low chair. Emily wiped her eyes and smiled at him, tear-dazzled.

'You're–you're not sorry, m'dear, are you?' said Curzon.

'No,' replied Emily boldly. 'I'm glad. I'm glad.'

'So am I,' endorsed Curzon, and his imagination awoke.

'My son. I shall have a son,' he said. Mental pictures were streaming through his mind like a cinematograph–he thought of the boy at school; later on in

Sandhurst uniform; he could picture all the triumphs which would come the boy's way and which he would enjoy vicariously. As a young man he had envied the representatives of military families, with a long record of service from generation to generation. His son would be one of a military family now, General Curzon's eldest boy, and after him there would be a long unbroken succession of military Curzons. It was as good to be an ancestor as to have ancestors.

'He'll be a fine little chap,' said Curzon, gazing into the future.

Emily was able to smile at the light in his face even though she had no intention of bringing a son into the world–her wish was for a daughter to whom she had already promised a childhood far happier than ever she had enjoyed.

'Darling,' she said to Curzon, taking the lapels of his coat in her hands.

'Darling,' said Curzon to her, his face empurpling as he craned over his stiff collar to kiss her hands. He toppled forward against her, and her arms went around him, and his about her, and they kissed, and Emily's cheek was wet against his, and Curzon's eyes did not remain absolutely dry. Curzon went to bed that night without having read through the Deputy Judge Advocate-General's comments on the conflicting evidence in the court martial on Sergeant-Major Robinson, accused of having been drunk on parade. But he got up early next morning to read them all the same.

The news brought the Duke and Duchess swooping down upon the Priory despite the fact that the crisis in the Cabinet was at its height. Curzon found that his mother-in-law, while almost ignoring him as a mere male in this exclusively feminine business, had practically forgiven him for his obstinacy with regard to Horatio Winter-Willoughby–time, the finding of a new appointment for the young man, and Emily's pregnancy had between them taken the sting out of her enmity. Yet she irritated Curzon inexpressibly by the way in which she took charge of Emily. Emily must leave this old-fashioned house *at once*, and come to London where the finest professional advice was to be obtained. She had already retained the services of Sir Trevor Choape for the event. Bude House would of course be open to Emily all this summer; Sir Trevor had recommended a nurse to whom she had written that very day. The child must have all the care a Winter deserved.

At that even the Duke ventured a mild protest.

'Hang it all, my dear,' he said. 'The child's a Curzon, not a Winter, when all is said and done.'

The Duchess only shot a glance of freezing contempt at him.

'The child will by my grandchild, and yours,' she said–but what she left unspoken about the infant's other grand-parents was far more weighty. The Duchess went on to declare, either expressly or by implication, her distrust of Curzon in a crisis of this sort, her doubts as to the suitability of Hampshire as a pre-natal environment, and her certainty of the undesirability of Narling Priory as a home for a pregnant woman. She made such skilful play with the most obvious points of her argument that it was difficult to pick up the weak ones. Narling Priory was a hideously old-fashioned house; it was lit by oil lamps and candles; it had only two bathrooms, and its hot-water system was a mid-Victorian relic in the last stages of senility. The Duchess did not say that it was indecent for a woman to be pregnant in a house half of which was occupied by a horde of staff officers, but she implied it. The nearest doctor of any reputation was at Petersfield or Southampton, miles away–the Duchess brushed aside Curzon's tentative reminder that there were fifty regimental doctors within five miles.

The Duchess had taken it for granted that they would take Emily back to London with them that very day, leaving Curzon to revert to his primitive bachelorhood; she was quite surprised when both Emily and Curzon protested against this separation. In the end they compromised on a decision that Emily was to return to London with them so as to keep the appointment with Sir Trevor, but was to come back to Narling Priory for as long as Sir Trevor gave permission.

'As a matter of fact,' said the Duke to Curzon, when Lady Emily and the Duchess had left them to themselves while they retired to discuss women's secrets, 'as a matter of fact, I suppose neither of us will be much surprised if Emily has to be put in charge of the Duchess and me quite soon.'

He looked across at Curzon significantly, and Curzon was instantly all attention.

'You haven't heard anything about going to France?' went on the Duke.

'No,' said Curzon. 'Nothing more than rumours.'

'I don't know what's been settled about your Division,' went on the Duke, 'even although I am in office again. I don't hear everything, you know.'

'Have any new formations gone to France already, then?' demanded Curzon, sick at heart.

'Yes,' said the Duke. 'Two divisions went this week. There's no harm in your knowing, after all. There are two more earmarked for the Mediterranean too–I don't know which. The news will be public property in a week.'

Curzon sat tugging at his moustache. He knew how rapidly the Army had expanded. There were fifteen divisions in England which had been created after the Ninety-first. In France the expansion, thanks to the arrival of the Indian Corps and other units, had been such that a new sub-division of a nature never previously contemplated had been devised–the Expeditionary Force was divided into three armies now, each comprising several army corps. After his flying start he was being left behind again in the race for promotion. He was shocked to hear that other new divisions had preceded his to France. He had not the least wish to be ordered to the Mediterranean–and in that he displayed intuition, even though the Dardanelles landing had not yet taken place. The whole opinion of the Army, expressed in all the discussions in which he had taken part, was emphatically that France was the decisive area. It was in France that glory and promotion, therefore, were to be won. It was essential to his career that the Ninety-first Division should be dispatched to France, and quickly.

'There's a good deal of talk,' went on the Duke, 'about a big offensive soon. One that will win the war at a blow. They've got to accumulate a big reserve of munitions, and have all the available troops to hand first, of course, but I don't think it will be long. Everybody's talking about it in London, especially the women, though God knows how these things leak out.'

This final speech made up Curzon's mind for him definitely. The Ninety-first Division must take part in this knock-out blow. Something very decided must be done to ensure that.

'Do you know,' said Curzon meditatively, 'I think I'll come back to town with you tonight, as well? You don't mind, do you?'

'Of course not, my dear fellow,' said the Duke. 'Of course, we shall have to be starting soon.'

'I shall be ready when you are,' said Curzon, getting out of his chair with astonishing rapidity. His mind was already racing through the programme he had planned with his staff for the morrow, and devising means whereby it could be carried through without his presence.

'I'll just go through and give orders to my staff, if you will excuse me,' said Curzon.

'Of course,' said the Duke once more, and, left alone, he gazed into the fire and called up memories of his own prospective fatherhood, and how jumpy he had been, and how unwilling he would have been to allow his wife out of his sight for twenty-four hours. It did not occur to the Duke that Curzon's decision to travel to London was not influenced by his wife's condition, but was simply caused by the gossip he had been retailing about the military situation.

15

A deferential staff-captain came quietly into Major-General Mackenzie's room at the War Office–there was a notice on the door saying, 'Don't knock'.

'It's General Curzon speaking on the telephone, sir,' said the captain. 'He says he would be glad if you could spare the time to see him for a few minutes today.'

'Oh, hell,' said Mackenzie irritably. 'Tell him I'm just off to York on a tour of inspection.'

Two minutes later the captain was back again.

'General Curzon says it is a matter of great importance, and he would be very much obliged if you would see him before you go to York.'

'Blast the man,' said Mackenzie.

'He said that he was only in town for today, and must return to his division tonight, sir. But he asked me to tell you that he was lunching with the Duke of Bude and that it would be more convenient if he could see you first.'

'Damn his eyes,' said Mackenzie. 'Oh, all right. Tell him to come round now. Have him sent straight in.'

Despite the language Mackenzie had used about him, there was cordiality in his reception of Curzon, in his offering of a chair and a cigar. Curzon smoked and waited for Mackenzie to open the conversation.

'Well,' said Mackenzie, 'what do you want this time?'

Curzon pulled at his cigar. He was doing his best to keep himself calm and well in hand while playing this unaccustomed game of diplomacy.

'I want,' he said eventually, 'orders for France.'

'For France?'

'Yes, for me and my division.'

'The hell you do,' said Mackenzie. 'Who's been talking?'

Curzon said nothing in reply to that; he judged that in his case silence would be more effective than speech.

'It's blasted impertinence on your part,' said Mackenzie, 'to come in like this asking for the earth. You're a temporary major-general, but you're only a substantive major. It wouldn't be hard to gazette you back to your substantive rank.'

Curzon had faced this possibility; he was well aware of the risk he was running, but the prize before him was worth the risk. He pulled at his cigar while weighing his words.

'I dare say,' he said, 'but I was hoping you wouldn't do that.'

Curzon's mind was seething with memories, despite his outward calm. He remembered Mackenzie's words on his appointment to his division: 'The closer you and I stay by each other, the better it will be for both of us.' That necessarily implied that Mackenzie credited him with the ability to do him harm if he wanted to. There was that question the Duke had asked only a short time ago, about whether Mackenzie was 'any good'. That had been more than a hint that the Duke could influence Mackenzie's dismissal from office. There had been Mackenzie's pliability with regard to special issues for the Ninety-first Division in the early winter days. That had not been a matter of any great importance, but it constituted good confirmatory evidence.

'You're asking for trouble, you know,' said Mackenzie, with a warning note in his voice.

'What, in asking to go to France?' said Curzon.

'Your division's told off to join Hamilton's command in the Mediterranean, and you know it,' said Mackenzie. Curzon judged it best not to say he did not know it. 'How it's got out I can't imagine. These bloody women, I suppose. Of course you don't want to go there. Of course you want to go to France. So does everybody else. D'you think I'm going to listen to every little poop of a temporary major-general who doesn't want to do what he's told? You'd have had your orders next week, and you'd have been out of England in three shakes of a duck's tail where you couldn't have made this fuss. Somebody's got to go, haven't they. Don't you start thinking I'm in love with this Constantinople idea, because I'm not. It hurts me just as much to have to find troops for it as it does you to go. But I've got my duty to do, the same as the rest of us.'

'There are other divisions besides the Ninety-first,' said Curzon. This was the first he had ever heard about any venture being made against Constantinople, and his opinion was against it from the start. It appeared to him to involve an unmilitary dispersal of force, and now he was more anxious than ever for his division to go to France where the real fighting was to be had.

'Yes,' admitted Mackenzie. 'There *are* other divisions. But yours was the one I had selected as the most suitable.'

'On what grounds?' asked Curzon, and his interest nearly betrayed his ignorance.

There was a struggle on Mackenzie's face as he looked back at the variety of motives which had influenced his choice, some military, some not. Curzon's lack of seniority as a major-general had played its part, as making it easy to fit him into the hierarchy of a small army; so had the fact that Miller, his G.S.O.1, had had experience in Egypt and Cyprus. But also there was the wish to get someone who might be a dangerous enemy and had served most of his purpose as a friend removed well away from London. Incidentally, there were other generals commanding divisions who also had influential connexions in need of propitiation. Mackenzie much regretted the failure of his original plan to order Curzon off without leaving him time to protest. He would have to send someone else now–a decision which would cause him further trouble but which must be adhered to, he was afraid. A man whose father-in-law held office with the certain prospect of a seat in the Cabinet, and who was hand in glove with the Bude House women, must not be offended, the more so because Mackenzie had sure and certain knowledge that Curzon had saved him once from annihilation.

'It's too long a story for me to tell you now,' said Mackenzie. 'Anyway, since you're so damned keen about it, I'll see what I can do about France for you.'

Mackenzie allowed no indication to creep into his tone of his fervent wish that as soon as the Ninety-first Division arrived in France some bomb or shell would relieve him of this Old Man of the Sea who was clinging so tightly to his shoulders.

'Thank you very much,' said Curzon. 'I'm very much obliged to you. And I'd better not take up any more of your time. Good-bye.'

'Good-bye,' said Mackenzie, resignedly.

Curzon ran down the War Office stairs like a schoolboy, without waiting for the lift. The bathchair on Bournemouth promenade had been brought appreciably nearer by that interview, but no thought of bathchairs had ever crossed his mind. He walked briskly back across war-time London; his red tabs and his row of ribbons brought him the salutes of every uniform he passed. At Bude House the butler opened the door for him with all the reverence to be accorded to one who was nearly a son of the house and who had the additional merit of being a General. He sat down and fidgeted as he re-read *The Times* and waited for Emily to return with her mother from her visit to Sir Trevor Choape.

The women came back soon enough, and the moment Curzon heard the subdued noise of their arrival in the hall he hastened down to greet them. Emily put off her furs with a little gesture of weariness; she had vomited badly that morning and still felt slightly upset, and Sir Trevor's brusque treatment of her had not helped to make her more comfortable.

'Well?' said Curzon, smiling at her, but for the moment Emily could only nod to him as a sign that her suspicions had been confirmed–there were too many servants about, relieving her and the Duchess of their coats, for her to say more at present. And later the Duchess was still very much in charge of her daughter. It was she who told Curzon about what Sir Trevor had said.

'Everything's quite all right, Bertie,' said the Duchess. 'Sir Trevor agrees with me that it will be about the end of October. He says we must take care of her, of course.'

'What about this sickness?' asked Curzon, consumed with the anxiety which was only natural to him as an unexperienced prospective father.

'Oh, that's only to be expected,' said the Duchess, echoing Sir Trevor's bluff words–Sir Trevor was one of the old school who took it for granted that a pregnant woman must always vomit her heart out every morning.

'I suppose so,' said Curzon feebly. From the little he had heard about pregnancy he found it easy to believe the same, although some instinct or intuition inspired him with tiny doubts which he naturally put aside.

'At the same time, Bertie,' said the Duchess, clearing for action, 'I think it would be *most unwise* for Emily to make the journey to Narling today, as I believe you were intending.'

The Duchess clearly anticipated violent opposition to this suggestion.

'I certainly must get back,' said Curzon. 'I can't be away from the Division any longer.'

He glanced at Emily, lying back lax in her chair.

'I should like to come to,' said Emily, 'but–but I think I'm going to be sick again.'

There was an immediate bustle and upheaval.

'I'll have that nurse here today or know the reason why,' said the Duchess decisively when the excitement passed. 'You see, it's impossible for Emily to come with you, Bertie.'

Curzon could only agree, weakly.

'At the same time—' he began hesitantly, and paused, looking first at Emily and then at the Duchess, wondering whether he ought to continue.

'Well?' said the Duchess. Now that she had gained her point she had little more attention to spare for this mere man. 'Speak up, and don't dither like that. You'll upset Emily again.'

The fact that a man like Curzon should dither ought to have made her believe that he had something important to say, but it did not.

'I expect I shall be receiving orders for France very shortly,' Curzon managed to blurt out in the end.

'Indeed?' said the Duchess. She did not feel that her son-in-law's prospective re-entry into active service was a tiny bit as important as her daughter's pregnancy.

'Oh, Bertie,' said Emily. She was feeling too limp to say more.

But Emily had known for months that Curzon's greatest wish was to command a division in France; she was glad that his ambition was going to be gratified so soon. And she felt little fear for him. The war had not yet lasted long enough for the fear of death to their best loved to have crept into every heart, and she had so much confidence in him that she felt it to be impossible for him to come to any harm–and, beyond all these considerations there was the fact that he was a general. No one, not even a loving wife, can be quite as afraid for a general as for a subaltern. She would miss him sadly, but not so much now that her mother was reasserting her old dominion over her. There might perhaps even be the slightest suspicion of pique in her attitude, that he should be going off on his own concerns and leave her to bear her troubles alone.

'When do you think you will be going?' asked the Duchess, as a concession to politeness.

Curzon came as near to a shrug of his shoulders as a man of his upbringing can.

'I don't know for certain,' he said. 'Next week, perhaps. Any time.'

'Then,' said the Duchess, 'Emily need not worry any more about this house of yours. I suppose you will have to give it back to the War Office when you go?'

'Yes.'

'That's all right then. You can trust Thompson, my dear, to settle about the inventories and so on, of course. Perhaps you will be good enough, Bertie, when you reach Narling, to instruct Hammett to return to us here and bring Emily's clothes with her?'

For a moment Curzon was on the verge of acquiescence. The domineering woman who was addressing him seemed to exert a spell on all who came into contact with her, by virtue of her calm assumption that no one could deny her. And then Curzon braced himself up. He was nettled that his announcement that he was shortly going to risk his life for King and Country should be received as calmly as if he had said he was going shooting in Scotland. He wanted to have his wife with him for his last few days in England.

'No,' he said. 'I don't think I want to do that.'

'I beg your pardon?' said the Duchess, in a tone which left a doubt as to whether she did anything of the kind.

'I should like Emily to come back to Narling as soon as she's well enough to travel. I think tomorrow she might be, easily.'

The Duchess turned to Emily.

'I think so too,' said Emily. 'That's what we settled yesterday, wasn't it, mother?'

Curzon had only to speak to bring Emily back to his side again, and the Duchess had the perspicacity to see it.

'Just as you like,' she said, washing her hands of them. 'I have already expressed my opinion, and if you two wish to act in a manner contrary to it I cannot say more.'

So that although Curzon dined that night in the headquarters mess, the next afternoon as he sat discussing with Hill the newest instructions from France regarding liaison between infantry and artillery, there was a sound of wheels on the gravel outside, and Curzon just had time to see the ducal motor car come slowly past the window with Emily inside. It was typical of Curzon that after glancing up he was able, despite the throb of excitement in his breast, to go on in an even tone with what he was saying. Curzon had the feeling that it would be harmful to discipline if a Major-General were to admit to his subordinates that he had human attributes–that he was capable of making a woman pregnant, or of being anxious about her afterwards. He prided himself on the way in which he brought the discussion to an end without apparently cutting it short, and on the unhurried and disinterested manner in which he said good-bye to Hill and walked calmly out of the office towards the private half of the house.

He might have been disconcerted if he had seen the quiet wink which Hill exchanged with Runcorn the C.R.E.–in a headquarters which buzzed with rumours like a hive of bees no one could hope to have any private life at all. Headquarters knew of Emily's little secret already–although it would be difficult to discover how. Any private in the Ninety-first Division who might be interested would know of it before a week was out, but, as Curzon would not know he knew, there was no harm in it.

Curzon ran with clinking spurs up the stairs to Emily's bedroom, reaching the door just as Hammett, the parlourmaid and lady's maid, was coming out. Inside, Emily, without her frock, was lying down on the ugly Victorian bed. She smiled with pleasure at sight of him.

'All safe and sound?' asked Curzon bluffly.

'Yes, dear,' said Emily, and then she stretched out her thin arms to him and drew him to her. That brought about the new miracle, whereby Curzon forgot the self-consciousness and the formality acquired during forty years of bachelorhood, and felt surging up within him the wave of hot passion which submerged his cold manner so that he kissed his wife with an ardour which otherwise he would have felt to sit incongruously upon a Major-General.

In this fashion there began a second instalment of their honeymoon, into which in a few days they managed to cram as much happiness as they had succeeded in finding in the previous three months–and this despite the handicaps under which they laboured, of Curzon's increasing work and the wretchedness which Emily experienced each morning when sickness overtook her. It might have been the fault of the long formidable corset which Emily had worn since her childhood, or it may have been the result of a faulty heredity, but Emily's pregnancy was highly uncomfortable to her, and Curzon found himself tortured with apprehension and remorse even while he rejoiced in the coming of that son for whom he was making such lofty plans.

Not very long after the last interview with Mackenzie there came a large official envelope for Major-General H. Curzon, C.B., D.S.O., and Curzon read its contents with a grimly neutral expression. They were his orders for France. Curzon was instructed temporarily to hand over the command of the Ninety-first Division to Brigadier-General J. Webb, D.S.O., and proceed with his personal staff and Colonel Miller to the headquarters of the Forty-second Corps, Lieutenant-General Sir Charles Wayland-Leigh, K.C.M.G., D.S.O. His division was to follow in accordance with the orders enclosed.

Emily felt a sudden pang when Curzon told her the news, and brought her face to face with the reality instead of merely the possibility. In that first spring of the war the passing of every month altered the attitude of the civilians towards it. It was growing usual now for families, who in 1914 had no military connexions whatever, to have relations killed. Even in the last month Emily had developed a fear lest Curzon, although he was her invulnerable husband and a General to boot, might soon be lost to her for more than just a few weeks.

'Now the boy's on his way, m'dear,' said Curzon, 'it almost makes me wish I wasn't going. But there it is. And with any luck the war'll be won and I'll be back with you before he's born.'

Curzon's pathetic faith in the sex of the child to be born raised a wan smile on Emily's face–she had never yet had the courage to break the news to him of her perfect certainty that she was going to bear a daughter.

'I hope you will,' she said bravely, and then, her tone altered, 'I *do* hope you will, dear.'

'Why, are you going to miss me?' said Curzon.

'Yes.'

No one had ever said that to Curzon before in his life. It gave him a sudden thrill; it brought reality to his statement that he almost wished that he had not been ordered to France. He kissed her desperately.

But there was small time for love-making for a General anxious about his professional success, who was shortly due to lose sight of his division completely until he next saw it under conditions of active service. Curzon spent his last days reassuring himself about his division. Time and again the sweating battalions, plodding along the dusty roads on the route marches which were getting them finally into condition, received the order 'March at attention. Eyes left,' and gazed with interest at the stiffly erect figure at the roadside who controlled their destinies. The red and gold on his cap and the ribbons on his breast marked him off as one far different from themselves, and to those amateur soldiers, who never yet had experienced the muddle and slaughter of battle, a general was an object of interest, about whom they felt curiosity but little else.

During those glorious days of 1915, the Hampshire lanes echoed with the music of bands (Curzon had laboured long and hard to see that every battalion had its band) as the finest division in the finest army England had ever raised put a final polish on its training under the anxious eyes of its general. Strangely, he, a cavalryman, had come to love the long-ordered ranks of infantry. He could thrill to the squeal of the fifes and the roar of the sidedrums where once the sweetest music to his ears had been kettledrums and trumpets. He loved this division of his now, with the love the single-minded and the simple-minded can give so readily to what they have laboured over. He could not feel the least doubt but that these big battalions of weatherbeaten men would crash their way almost unimpeded through the German line. He looked forward with confidence now to riding with them across the Rhine to Berlin.

The thought of his wonderful division sustained him when he kissed Emily good-bye, which was as well, for the parting was an even bigger wrench than he had feared. He had no doubt about himself; but there was the coming of the child, and Emily's constant sickness (about which his fears were steadily increasing) and his apprehension lest his mother-in-law should succeed in alienating his wife from him.

'Look after yourself, dear,' he said, his old-time brusqueness concealing his anxiety as he patted her on the shoulder with the gesture which seems universal among departing husbands.

'You must do the same,' said Emily, trying to smile, and he tore himself away and climbed into the waiting Vauxhall where his chief-of-staff and his two aides-de-camp (the latter perched uncomfortably on the stools of repentance with their backs to the driver) sat waiting for him. The tyres tore up the gravel, and they had started, for Southampton and France.

Two days later the party, four officers, eight horses, and eight grooms and servants, reached Saint-Cérisy, the headquarters of the Forty-second Corps, and Curzon reported his arrival to Lieutenant-General Sir Charles Wayland-

Leigh. The Lieutenant-General was a huge man with a face the colour of mahogany and a suspicion of corpulence.

'Glad to see you, Curzon,' he said, although he showed no signs of it at all and made no attempt to shake hands. He ran his eyes up and down Curzon, from his military crop to his glittering field-boots, sizing up with cold, green eyes the new subordinate upon whose capacity depended in part his own reputation.

Curzon felt no inclination to resent his manner, for Wayland-Leigh was a much more eminent general than he was himself–he had been a general in the original expeditionary force of 1914. He stood stiffly to attention and submitted to scrutiny.

'Ha!' said Wayland-Leigh, abruptly and without committing himself–or he might even have been merely clearing his throat. 'Here, Norton. This is Norton, my B.G.G.S. I expect you'll know him better quite soon. General Curzon.'

The Brigadier-General, General Staff–chief staff officer of the Corps–was dark and pale, but his face was stamped with the same truculent and imperious expression as his Chief's, as befitted a man whose word swayed the destinies of forty thousand men. There was the same cold eye, the same slight scowl between the eyebrows, and same thrust-forward jaw and cruel mouth. Yet despite Curzon's more modest attitude as a newcomer, his face had just the same trade-marks, curiously enough. He met the stare of the two generals without flinching. No observer could have witnessed that encounter without thinking of the proverb about the meeting of Greek with Greek.

'What's your division like?' said Wayland-Leigh suddenly.

'All right,' said Curzon, and then, throwing traditional modesty to the winds, 'first rate. As good as anyone could hope for.'

'Let's hope you're right,' said Wayland-Leigh. 'Don't think much of these New Army divisions myself. We've seen a couple of'em, haven't we, Norton?'

'Mine's good stuff,' persisted Curzon, refusing to be brow-beaten.

'We'll see for ourselves soon enough,' said Wayland-Leigh brutally. 'And look here, Curzon, we may as well begin as we mean to go on. There are certain standing orders in this Corps which you'd better hear about now–they're not written orders. In this Corps there are no excuses. A man who's got to find excuses–goes, just like that.'

His thick hand cut the air with an abrupt gesture.

'Yes, sir,' said Curzon.

'This Corps does not retire,' went on Wayland-Leigh. 'It never gives up ground. And in the same way if it is given an objective to reach, it reaches it. You understand?'

'Yes, sir.'

'We don't have any bloody weak-kneed hanky-panky. You've never commanded a division in action, have you, Curzon?'

'No, sir.'

'Well, you'll find that the commanders of units are always looking out for a chance to dodge the dirty work and pass it on to someone else–anxious to spare their own men and all that. Take my advice and don't listen to 'em. It'll be a dam' sight better for you, believe me.'

'Yes, sir.'

'Most of the officers in this army want *driving*, God knows why–the Army's changed since I was a regimental officer. You drive 'em, and you're all right. *I'll* back you up. And if you don't–I'll have to find someone who will.'

'I understand.'

'I hope you do. What about a drink before dinner? Norton, you can look after him. I'll see you at dinner, Curzon.'

Dinner at Corps headquarters was a stiffly military function. It was served at a long table in what had once been the state bedroom of the jewel-like little château. There were silver candlesticks on the table, and a fair show of other silver–somehow Saint-Cérisy had escaped being looted by any of the three armies which had fought in its streets. The Lieutenant-General sat at the head of the table, huge and silent, with Curzon as the newest arrived guest on his right. Looking down the table Curzon saw a long double row of red-tabbed officers whose rank dwindled in accordance with their distance from him as though in perspective–generals and colonels at the head, and aides-de-camp and signal officers at the foot. There was small attempt at conversation at the far end. The brooding immobility of the Lieutenant-General seemed to crush the young men into awed silence. Even their requests to the mess waiters were couched in half-whispers.

On Curzon's right was another major-general commanding a division. Bewly, his name was, and he reminded Curzon of Coppinger-Brown, his predecessor of the Ninety-first Division. Bewly was able to talk despite the presence of his corps commander; he spent dinner-time complaining unnecessarily to Curzon about the lack of social position of the officers of the New Army.

'I should have thought,' said Bewly, 'that they would have drawn the line *somewhere*, but they haven't. There's a battalion of my old regiment in my division. The subalterns come from *anywhere*, literally *anywhere*. I suppose we had to have stock-brokers and schoolmasters. But there are *clerks* in the regiment now, no better than office boys. And that's not all. There's a *linen draper*! It's enough to make one weep. What was your regiment?'

Curzon told him.

'Ah!' said Bewly, and there crept into his voice the slight deference which Curzon was accustomed to hear from infantrymen. 'I don't expect it has happened in your regiment? You can keep that kind of thing out of the cavalry.'

'I suppose so,' said Curzon. He was not very interested in this question of the introduction of the lower orders into the commissioned ranks of the infantry. Partly that may have been because he was a cavalryman, but partly it must have been because he was conscious of his own Mincing Lane parentage. As regards his own division he would have wished for no change in its present constitution, and being without blue blood himself, he failed to see the necessity of blue blood as a qualification for leadership.

At the same time he found himself wondering vaguely how long Bewly would last under Wayland-Leigh's command, and he guessed it would not be long. Bewly's division was a New Army formation which had been in France for three weeks. The other two divisions in the Corps besides the Ninety-first were of an older pedigree, although, as Bewly pessimistically informed Curzon, they had lost so many men and had been filled up so often with drafts that they retained precious little likeness to their originals.

The dinner was admirable and the service more efficient than that of any mess Curzon had ever known. This was due–Bewly was his informant again, speaking with dropped voice, and with nods, and winks at Curzon's left-hand neighbour–to the fact that Wayland-Leigh systematically combed his Corps for ex-waiters and ex-cooks. The mess sergeant was lately a *maître d'hôtel*; the cook had been an assistant chef in a famous restaurant.

'Trust the Buffalo to have the best of everything,' murmured Bewly, and Curzon suddenly remembered that far back in the old Indian Army days Wayland-Leigh had been nicknamed 'the Buffalo'. The original reason for the name had long been forgotten, but the name remained, distinguished by its appropriateness.

As soon as dinner was over the Buffalo rose abruptly from his chair without a glance either to left or to right, and strode away from the table to vanish through an inconspicuous door behind him. A second later Curzon heard another door slam in the farther depths of the house.

'He's settled for the night, thank God,' said Bewly, heaving a sigh of relief. Curzon was reminded (until he put the similarity out of his mind as ludicrous) of the attitude of a small boy at school at the disappearance of a dreaded master.

16

Next morning Curzon formed one of a select party sent round a section of the front line to be initiated into the new developments of trench warfare. Their guide was a tall lean captain named Hodge, who occupied some ill-defined position on the Corps Headquarters' staff, and who wore not merely the blue and red ribbon of the Distinguished Service Order, but the purple and white one of the new-fangled Military Cross. More noticeable than his ribbons was his air of weary lackadaisical tolerance towards his seniors, even major-generals. His uninterested apathy made a bad impression on Curzon, but Bewly took no notice of it, and with Bewly present and senior to him he could not pull him up for it. Life seemed to hold no more secrets and no more attraction for Captain Hodge, who lounged in front of the party along the winding trenches with a weary indifference in striking contrast to the keen interest of the newcomers.

Motor cars had brought them to a cross-roads close behind the line; on the journey up Captain Hodge condescended to point out to them all sorts of things which were new to Curzon, in the way of ammunition dumps (tiny ones, the mere microcosm of their successors, but an innovation as far as Curzon was concerned) and rest billets for troops out of the line, and all the other unheard-of accessories of static warfare.

At the cross-roads Hodge actually was sufficiently awake to say: 'Dangerous place for shelling here,' and to display some sign of haste as he walked across with the staff officers scuttling behind him. But the sky was blue and peace seemed to have settled down upon the tortured landscape. There was hardly a sound of firing to be heard. The armies of both sides seemed to be basking like lizards in the unwonted sunshine. A tiny breath of wind fanned Curzon's face, and brought with it the stink of the front-line trenches, compounded of carrion and mud, and latrines ripened by the present warmth. When Curzon had last quitted the trenches after the First Battle of Ypres that stink had been in its immaturity, only just beginning, but the present whiff called up a torrent of memories of those wild days, of the peril and the fatigue and the excitement. Curzon felt vaguely irritated by the prevailing tranquillity. First Ypres had been real fighting; this was nothing of the sort.

The road they were on had ceased to be a road at the cross-roads, where the red-hatted military policeman had stopped the cars. A vague indication of a trench had grown up around them as they progressed, and soon it was quite definitely a trench, floored with mud in which they sank ankle deep–the warm weather had not dried it–crumbling and slipshod in appearance for lack of revetting. They floundered in single file along the trench. Twice Hodge turned and said: 'Keep low here. They've got a fixed rifle on this point.' Hodge made no bones at all at bending himself double, despite his lackadaisical air, as he made his way round the dangerous bay. Curzon stopped, but could not bring himself to adopt Hodge's cowardly and undignified attitude. He heard a sharp *zzick* and felt the breath of a bullet past the back of his neck.

'Better be careful,' said Hodge.

A little later they had to crowd themselves against the side of the trench to allow a stretcher to go by; the stretcher bearers were breathing deeply, and on the stretcher lay a soldier, deathly pale, his boots protruding beyond the blanket which covered him. That was all the traffic they met in the communication trench.

They reached the support line and went along it. There were soldiers here, lounging about, sleeping in the sun, making tea over little smokeless flames of solid methylated spirit. They came up to attention not very promptly at sight of the string of brass hats making their way along the trench. Battalion headquarters was established in a dug-out burrowed into the front of the trench; not a very good dug-out, a mere rabbit scrape compared with the dug-outs of the future, but the first Curzon had seen. A worn-looking colonel greeted them, and offered them drinks, which all of them except Curzon drank thirstily; Curzon had no desire at all to drink whisky and water at ten in the morning. The battalion runners were waiting on duty in a smaller dug-out still, next door; in the headquarters dug-out was the telephone which linked precariously the battalion to brigade, and thence through Division and Corps and Army to G.H.Q.

They went on by a muddy communication trench to the front line. Here there was the same idleness, the same lack of promptitude in acknowledging the General's presence. There were men asleep squatting on the firestep who had to be wakened for discipline's sake. There were certain concessions made to active-service conditions; the sentries peering into the periscopes were rigidly attentive and stirred not at all at the bustle passing them by; the shell cases hung inverted in every bay to act as gongs for a gas warning should gas come over.

Curzon took a periscope and gazed eagerly over the parapet. He saw a few strands of barbed wire with a tattered dead man–a sort of parody of a corpse–hanging on the farthest one. Then there was a strip of mud pocked with shell craters, more barbed wire beyond, and then the enemy's front line, whose sand-bagged parapet, although neater and more substantial than the British, showed no more sign of life. It was hard to believe that a wave of disciplined men could not sweep across that frail barrier, and as Curzon began to think of that he found himself believing that it would be better even that they should try and fail than moulder here in unsoldierly idleness–it would be the more appropriate, the more correct thing.

The other generals, and Captain Hodge, waited patiently while he peered and stared, twisting the periscope this way and that–it was not easy to form a military estimate of a landscape while using a periscope for the first time–and were clearly relieved when at last his curiosity was satisfied and he handed back the periscope to the platoon officer from whom he had taken it.

'We shall be late for lunch if we don't hurry on our way back, Hodge,' said Bewly.

'Yes, sir,' said Hodge. 'I'll try and get you back in time.'

Bewly's anxiety about lunch irritated Curzon–there was a good deal about Bewly which had begun to irritate him. He almost sympathized with Hodge in his attitude of scarcely concealed contempt for Bewly, even though it was reprehensible in a junior officer. They pushed on along the front-line trench, round bays and traverses innumerable; one bit of trench was very like another, and everywhere the men seemed half asleep, as might have been expected of soldiers who had spent five nights in the trenches–except by Curzon, who could not imagine the physical and still less the moral effects of experiences he had not shared and which were not noticed in the military text-books

The sparseness of the garrison of the trenches made a profound effect on him; it was a continual source of surprise to him to see how few men there were in each sector. He had long known, of course, the length of line allotted on the average to a division, and he had laboriously worked out sums giving the number of rifles per yard of trench from the data issued by the War Office (Most Secret. For the information of Officers Commanding Divisions Only), but he was not gifted with the power of visualizing in actual pictures the results obtained. Now that he could see for himself he marvelled; presumably the German trenches over there were as scantily manned–it seemed to him impossible that such a frail force could withstand a heavy artillery preparation and then a brisk attack with overwhelming numbers.

He already itched with the desire to make the attempt, to head a fierce offensive which would end this slovenly, unmilitary, unnatural kind of warfare once and for all. There must have been mismanagement at Festubert and Neuve-Chapelle, or bad leadership, or bad troops. Nothing else could account for their failure to put an end to a situation against which all Curzon's training caused him to revolt with loathing. His feverish feeling made him reply very shortly indeed to Bewly's droned platitudes on the way back to Corps Headquarters and at lunch, and later, when Miller and he were called in to discuss with Wayland-Leigh and Norton what they had seen, his sincerity lent a touch of eloquence to his unready tongue.

He spoke vehemently against the effect on the troops of life in the trenches, and of this system of petty ambuscades and sniping and dirt and idleness. And, with his experience of improvised attacks and defence to help him, he was able to say how advantageous it must be to be allowed ample time to mount and prepare a careful attack in which nothing could go wrong and overwhelming force could be brought upon the decisive point. Curzon checked himself at last when he suddenly realized how fluently he was talking. It was lawyer-like and un-English to be eloquent, and his little speech ended lamely as he looked in embarrassment from Wayland-Leigh to Norton and back again.

But Wayland-Leigh apparently was too pleased with the sentiments Curzon had expressed to be suspicious of his eloquence. There was a gleam of appreciation in his green eyes. He exchanged glances with Norton.

'That's the stuff, Curzon,' he said. 'That's different from what I've been hearing lately from these can't-be-doners and better-notters and leave-it-to-youers that the Army's crowded with nowadays. What about you, Miller?'

Miller, dark, saturnine, silent, had said nothing so far, and now, after a Lieutenant-General and a Major-General had expressed themselves so enthusiastically, it could not be expected of a mere colonel to go against their opinions–not a colonel, at any rate, who placed the least value on his professional career.

'I think there's a lot in it sir,' said Miller, striving to keep the caution out of his voice and to meet Wayland-Leigh's sharp glance imperturbably.

'Right,' said Wayland-Leigh. 'Norton's got a lot of trench maps and appreciations and skeleton schemes for local offensives. I want you to start going through them with him. We all know that the real big push can't come for a month or two while these bloody politicians are muddling about with munitions and conscription and all the rest of it–why in hell they can't put a soldier in to show them how to run the affair properly I can't imagine. Your division's due to arrive in two days. We'll give 'em a couple of turns in the front line to shake 'em together, and then we'll start in and get something done. Your lot and Hope's Seventy-ninth are the people I'm relying on.'

Curzon ate his dinner with enjoyment that night–it was enough to give any man pleasure in his food to be told that the Buffalo relied upon him. There was a letter from Emily too–full of the shy half-declarations of love which were as far as Emily could be expected to write and as far as Curzon wished. Burning phrases in black and white would have made Curzon uncomfortable; he was well satisfied with Emily's saying that she missed him and hoped he would soon be back again with her, and with the timid 'dears', three in all, interpolated in the halting sentences. Emily was at Bude House, which the Duke had decided to keep open all the summer, but she would soon be going for a few weeks to Bude Manor, in Somerset. She was still being a little sick–Curzon fidgeted with a premonition which he told himself to be unfounded when he read that. The last paragraph but one brought a grin to his lips both because of its contents and its embarrassing phrasing. The grim gaunt housekeeper who had ruled Narling Priory under their nominal control had been found to be with child after forty-one years of frozen virginity, and obstinately refused to name her partner beyond saying he was a soldier. As Emily said, the war was changing a lot of things.

Curzon wrote back the next day, bluffly as usual. The only 'dear' he was able to put in his letter was the one that came in 'my dear wife', and the only sentiment appeared in the bits addressed in reply to Emily's statement that she missed him. He devoted three or four lines to the excellent weather prevailing, and he committed himself to a cautiously optimistic sentence or two regarding the future of the war. He bit the end of his pen in the effort of trying to think of something more to say, but found inspiration slow in coming, and ended the letter with a brief recommendation that Emily should take great care of herself, and a note of amused surprise at the fall of the housekeeper.

He did not think the letter inadequate (nor did Emily when she received it) but it was a relief to turn aside from these barren literary labours and to plunge once more into the living business of the Army. The Division arrived, and Curzon rode over to join it with all the thrill and anticipation of a lover–he had been separated from it for more than a week, and it was with delight that he sat his horse at the side of the road, watching the big bronzed battalions stream past him. He gave a meticulous salute in reply to each salute he received, and his eyes scanned the dusty ranks with penetrating keeness. He heard an ejaculation from the ranks: 'Gawd, there's old Bertie again,' and he looked on with grim approval while a sergeant took the offender's name–not because he objected to being called Bertie, but because the battalion was marching at attention and therefore to call out in that fashion was a grave breach of discipline.

It was an indication, all the same, of the high spirits of the men, who were bubbling over with the excitement of the journey and with the prospect of action. They took a childlike interest in everything–in French farming methods, in the aeroplanes overhead with the white puffs of anti-aircraft shells about them, in the queer French words written over shop windows, in the uncanny ability of even the youngest children to talk French, in the distant nocturnal firework display that indicated the front line.

They showed a decided tendency to let their high spirits grow too much for them, all the same. The arrival of the Division coincided with a large increase in the military crimes in which the British soldier never ceases to indulge. They stole fruit (horrible unripe apples) and poultry and eggs. Their inappeasable yearning for fuel led them to steal every bit of wood, from fence rails and doors to military stores, which they could lay their hands on. They drank far too much of the French wine and beer even while they expressed their contempt for them, and sometimes they conducted themselves familiarly towards Frenchwomen who were not ready to appreciate the compliment.

Curzon read the statistics of regimental crime with growing indignation. All this gross indiscipline must be checked at once. He circulated a scathing divisional order, and strengthened the hands of the military police, and saw to it that a score of offenders received exemplary punishments. The effect was immediate and gratifying, because the amount of crime decreased abruptly–as soon as the men had grown accustomed to the new conditions and to the methods of those in authority, so that they could evade detection; for no disciplinary methods on earth could keep British soldiers from wine, women, and wood.

The Ninety-first Division took its place in the line without any great flourish of trumpets. Norton chose a quiet section for them, and the ten days went by with nothing special to report. There were a hundred casualties–the steady drain of losses to be expected in trench warfare–and a general court martial on a man caught asleep while on sentry duty, from which the culprit was lucky enough to escape with his life.

Curzon fretted a little at the conditions in which he had to command his men. It went against his conscience to a certain extent to spend his time, while his men were in the line, in a comfortable house. He could eat good dinners, he could ride as much as he wanted, he could sleep safely in a good bed; and it was not easy to reconcile all this with his memory of First Ypres. He chafed against the feeling of impotence which he experienced at having to command his Division by telephone. He was still imbued with the regimental ideal of sharing on active service the dangers and discomforts of his men.

During the Division's turns of duty in the trenches his anxiety drove him repeatedly up into the front line to see that all was well. He plodded about along the trenches trying to ignore fatigue–for a journey of a dozen miles through the mud, stooping and scrambling, was the most exhausting way of spending a day he had ever known. His aide-de-camp, Greven, bewailed his fate to unsympathetic audiences; the other one, Follett, was more hardy–but then Curzon had selected him with care and without regard to family connexions, on the recommendation that Follett had once ridden in the Grand National and completed the course. Follett endured the mud and the weariness and the danger without complaint.

There was inconvenience in making these trench tours. Miller had to be left in charge at headquarters, and however capable Miller might be the ultimate responsibility–as Curzon well appreciated–was Curzon's own. During the dozen hours of Curzon's absence orders calling for instant decision might come by telephone or by motor-cycle dispatch rider. While Curzon was in the trenches he found himself to be just as anxious about what was happening at headquarters as he was about the front line when he was at headquarters. It took all the soothing blandishments which Greven could devise with the aid of Curzon's personal servants to keep him from making an unbearable nuisance of himself, and quite a little while elapsed before he was able to reconcile himself to this business of leading by telephone.

On the Division's third turn in the front line Curzon was allowed by Wayland-Leigh to put into practice some of the principles he had been forming. Curzon came to believe, in the event, that it was more harassing to sit by a telephone looking at his watch waiting for news, than to take part in the operations which he had ordered. The first one was the merest trifle, a matter of a raid made by no more than a company, but two o'clock in the morning–the hour fixed–found Curzon and all his staff fully dressed in the office and consumed with anxiety. It was a battalion of a Minden regiment which was making the raid–the colonel had begged the honour for his unit because it was Minden day without realizing that this was a tactless argument to employ to a cavalryman–and Curzon spent an anxious half-hour wondering whether he had been wise in his selection. The buzz of the telephone made them all start when at last it came. Frobisher answered it while Curzon tugged at his moustache.

'Yes,' said Frobisher. 'Yes. Right you are. Yes.'

The studied neutrality of his tone enabled Curzon to guess nothing of the import of the message until Frobisher looked up from the telephone.

'It's all right, sir,' he said. 'They rushed the post quite easily. Seven prisoners. Bombed the other bit of trench and heard a lot of groans. The party's back now, sir. We won't get their casualty return until the morning.'

'All right,' said Curzon. His first independent operation had been crowned with success.

He got up from the table and walked out to the front door, and stood in the porch looking towards the line, his staff following. There was far more commotion there than usually. The sky was lighted by the coloured lights which were being sent up, and the ground shook with the fire of the guns, whose flashes made a dancing line of pin points of lights on the horizon. The raid had put the line on the alert, and expectancy had led to the inevitable 'wind-up' until ten thousand rifles and two hundred guns were all blazing away together–and killing a man or two here and there, while wiring parties and patrols, caught in no-man's-land by the unexpected activity, crouched in shell holes and cursed the unknown fool who had started the trouble.

The glare in the sky which indicated unusual nocturnal activity was to be seen frequently after that over the sector occupied by the Ninety-first Division. There were all sorts of little local operations awaiting their attention–small salients to be pinched out and exposed listening posts to be raided–and the Ninety-first Division engaged in them whole-heartedly.

Moreover, as Curzon had suspected, a certain amount of a live-and-let-live convention had grown up in the line. Each side had inclined to refrain from inflicting casualties on the other side at moments when retaliation would cause casualties to themselves–ration parties were being mutually spared, and certain dangerous localities received reciprocal consideration. Curzon would have none of this. It seemed to him to be a most dangerous and unsoldierly state of affairs; if a soldier whose duty it was to kill the enemy refrained from doing so he was clearly not doing his duty and it might lead to untold damage to discipline. Drastic Divisional orders put a stop to this. The keenness of the new troops and the energy of their commander brought renewed activity into the line; the number of snipers was increased, and places where the enemy had been inclined to be careless were regularly sprayed with machine-gun fire, with, as far as headquarters could tell, a most gratifying increase in German casualties.

Naturally the enemy retaliated. British divisions accustomed to a peaceful turn of duty were annoyed and surprised, when they relieved the Ninety-first, to find that localities hitherto regarded as safe were now highly dangerous, and that sniping had vastly increased, and that the Germans had developed a system of sudden bombing raids which made life in the trenches a continual strain on the nerves. This was especially noticeable because, as the Germans had the advantage of direct observation from the low heights which they occupied, and did not trouble themselves nearly as much as the British about holding on to dangerous salients, and worked far harder at making their trenches safe and habitable, they could make things far more uncomfortable for the British than the British could for them.

Both officers and men of the other divisions complained of the new state of affairs to their fellows of the Ninety-first, but they found small satisfaction in doing so. The Ninety-first Division pleaded the direct orders of their commander. 'Bertie's the boy,' they said, half-proud and half-rueful, and the daily drain of casualties increased–Curzon was already making application for drafts and new officers for his battalions.

The new system met with one protest from an unexpected quarter. Young Captain Frobisher, the General Staff Officer, third grade, found an opportunity while he and Miller and Curzon, sitting at the table littered with trench maps, were drafting the orders for fresh activity. The weak points of the German line in their sector had by now been blotted out, and Curzon casually admitted in conversation that it was not easy now to find suitable objects for attention.

'Perhaps,' said Frobisher, 'it might be wise to quiet down for a bit, sir?'

'No, it's not good for the men,' replied Curzon.

'Casualties are getting a bit high,' said Frobisher.

'You can't make war without casualties,' said Curzon. He had been a casualty himself, once, and he had freely exposed himself to the chance of its occuring again.

'Wellington tried to keep 'em down, sir,' said Frobisher, suddenly bold.

'What on earth do you mean, boy?' asked Curzon.

'Wellington always discouraged sniping and outpost fighting and that sort of thing.'

'Good God!' said Curzon. 'Wellington lived a hundred years ago.'

'Human nature's the same now, though, sir.'

'Human nature? What in hell are you talking about? Anyone would think you were a poet or one of these beastly intellectuals. I don't like this, Frobisher.'

Curzon was definitely angry. There was a frosty gleam in his eyes and a deep line between his brows. It was not so much because a captain was venturing to argue with him, a major-general, as that the captain was putting forward suggestions of a suspicious theoretical nature in direct opposition to the creed of the Army, that the side which does not attack is bound to lose.

'Frobisher's had too much history and not enough practical experience, yet, sir,' said Miller. He put his word in hastily, because he did not want to lose the services of the best G.S.O.3 he could hope to get hold of.

'So I should think,' said Curzon, still staring indignantly at the delinquent, but somewhat appeased. He had grown fond of young Frobisher after six months of work with him, and had been pained as well as shocked at his heresy, just as if his son (supposing he had one) had announced his intention of marrying a tobacconist's daughter. His fondness for Frobisher even led him into defending his own actions by argument.

'We're giving the Germans hell, aren't we?' said Curzon.

'Yes, sir,' said Frobisher, with dropped eyes. A word from Curzon would take him from his staff position, where he could think even though his mouth remained shut, and put him into an infantry battalion where he would not be able to think at all.

'Well, don't let me hear any more of this nonsense. Pass me that map and let's get down to business.'

17

The next time that the Ninety-first Division came out of the line Curzon was summoned to attend a conference at Corps Headquarters. Wayland-Leigh and Norton were jubilant. The Big Push was being planned at last–the great offensive which was to bring with it the decisive victory and the march to Berlin. There were nine divisions available, about three times as many Englishmen–as Curzon jovially pointed out to Frobisher on his return–as Wellington had commanded at Waterloo. There were more field-guns ready for use in the preliminary bombardment than the entire British Army had owned in 1914, and there was a stock of ammunition accumulated for them sufficient for fifty hours of continuous steady firing–a longer bombardment than had ever been known in the field before. Besides all this, they were going to take a leaf out of the Germans' book and employ poison gas, but on a far larger scale than the Germans' timorous attempt at Ypres. There were mountainous dumps already formed of cylinders of chlorine, and every ship that crossed the Channel was bringing further supplies.

But the great cause for rejoicing was that the Forty-second Corps had been selected to take part in the attack–the Buffalo was to be turned loose to crash through the gap made by the leading divisions. The maps were brought out–not the finicking little trench maps on which Curzon had planned his little petty offensives, but big maps, covering all North-eastern France. The French were to attack at Vimy, storm the ridge, and push forward; the British were to strike at Loos, break the German line, and join hands with the French behind Lens, which was to fall as the first ripe fruit of victory into the Allies' hands unassailed. At this stage of the battle the Forty-second Corps would be in the van, with open country before them, and nothing to stop them.

'It's a pity in a way,' said Norton, 'that we've had to wait until autumn for this attack. It makes it just possible that the Huns will be able to hold us up for a winter campaign on the Rhine.'

Before this campaign on the Rhine could be begun, there was more work to be done. The Ninety-first Division had to take another turn of duty in the front-line trenches, working like beavers over the preparations for the great attack. One morning Frobisher brought the Divisional orders for Curzon to sign, and Curzon, as ever, read them carefully through before assuming responsibility for them.

'Here, what's this, boy?' he said suddenly. 'Two men to carry up each gas cylinder? We've only been using one for the empty ones.'

'Yes, sir,' said Frobisher. 'These are full, and they're heavier in consequence.'

'Nonsense,' said Curzon. He was glad to be able to find something he was quite certain he was right about while Frobisher was wrong even though he bore him no ill will. 'Everyone knows that gas makes things lighter. They put it in balloons and things.'

'That's coal gas, sir,' said Frobisher, with deference. 'This is chlorine, and highly compressed.'

'You mean I'm talking nonsense?' demanded Curzon.

'No, sir,' said Frobisher, treading warily as he could over this dangerous ground, 'but we've never had to deal with full cylinders before.'

Curzon glared at this persistent young captain, and decided that his victory would be more crushing still if he gained it without recourse to his hierarchical authority.

'Well, if you don't believe *me*,' he said, with all the dignity he could summon, 'you'd better ring up the gas officer at Corps Headquarters and see what *he* says. You may believe him, if he's had the advantage of an education at Camberley, too, as well as you.'

'Yes, sir,' said Frobisher.

It took Frobisher ten minutes to make his call and get his answer, and he was decidedly nervous on his return.

'Well?' said Curzon.

'The gas officer says that the full cylinders are fifty pounds heavier than the empty ones, sir,' said Frobisher.

Curzon looked very sharply at him, but Frobisher's face was immobile. Without a word Curzon drew the orders to him, dashed off his signature, and handed them back. It must be recorded to Curzon's credit that he never afterwards allowed that incident to prejudice him against Frobisher–and it is significant of his reputation for fairness that Frobisher had no real fear that he would.

By the time the Ninety-first Division came out of the line the preparations for the attack were nearly complete. The ammunition dumps were gorged. There were drafts to fill the ranks of the waiting divisions up to their full establishment, and further drafts ready at the base to make up for the inevitable casualties of the initial fighting. There were hospitals, and prisoners' cages, and three divisions of cavalry ready to pursue the flying enemy.

Curzon's heart went out to these latter when he saw them. For a moment he regretted his infantry command. He felt he would gladly give up his general officer's rank just to hear the roar of the hoofs behind him as he led the Lancers in the charge again. He rode over to their billets, and visited the Twenty-second, to be rapturously received by those men in the ranks who had survived First Ypres. Browning, in command, was not quite so delighted to see him–he had unhappy memories of their previous contacts, when Curzon had been to no trouble to conceal his contempt for his indecision and loss of nerve in the climax of the battle. The officers' mess was full of strange faces, and familiar ones were missing–Borthwick, for instance, when he had recovered from his wounds, had been transferred to the staff and was organizing some piratical new formation of machine-gunners with the rank of Colonel. The fact that Borthwick should ever be a colonel when he had never properly learned to ride a horse was sufficient proof of what a topsy-turvy war this was, as Curzon and his contemporaries agreed over a drink in the mess.

Curzon bade the Twenty-second a sorrowful good-bye at the end of the day. He could not stay to dinner, as he had an invitation to Corps Headquarters. As he stood shaking hands with his friends they heard the roar of the bombardment–in its third day now–which was opening the Battle of Loos.

'They're getting Hell over there,' said a subaltern, and everyone agreed.

'You'll be having your chance in less than a week,' said Curzon, and regret surged up in him again as he mounted his horse. He had gained nothing in forsaking a regiment for a division. He would never know now the rapture of pursuit; all there was for him to do now was to make the way smooth for the cavalry.

There were high spirits at Corps Headquarters, all the same, to counter his sentimental depression. Wayland-Leigh had provided champagne for this great occasion, and in an unwonted expansive moment he turned to Curzon with his lifted glass.

'Well, here's to the Big Push, Curzon,' he said. His green eyes were aflame with excitement.

'Here's to it, sir,' said Curzon fervently.

'It's like a bit of Shakespeare,' said Wayland-Leigh–and the fact that Wayland-Leigh should quote Shakespeare was a sufficient indication of the greatness of the occasion. ' "When shall we three meet again?" Or rather we five, I ought to say.'

He looked round at his four divisional generals.

'On the Rhine, sir,' said Hope of the Seventy-ninth.

'Please God,' said Wayland-Leigh.

The horizon that night was all sparkling with the flashes of the guns as Curzon went back to his headquarters; the bombardment was reaching its culminating point, and the gentle west wind–Curzon wetted his finger and held it up to make sure–was still blowing. It would waft the poison gas beautifully towards the German lines, and those devils would have a chance of finding out what it was like.

At dawn next morning Curzon was waiting in his headquarters for orders and news. The horses of the staff were waiting saddled outside; within half a mile's radius the battalion and batteries of the Division were on parade ready to march. Neither orders nor news came for some time, while Curzon restlessly told himself that he was a fool to expect anything so early. Nothing could come through for seven or eight hours. But Frobisher looked out at the Divisional flag drooping on its staff, and he went outside and held up a wet finger, and came in again gloomily. There was no wind, or almost none. In fact, Frobisher had a suspicion that what little there was came from the east. There could be small hope today for a successful use of gas.

'We can win battles without gas, gentlemen,' said Curzon, looking round at his staff.

As time went on Curzon grew seriously alarmed. They were fifteen miles from the line, and if orders to move did not come soon they might be too late to exploit the initial advantage. Curzon knew that the Forty-second Corps was being held directly under the command of General Headquarters, so that he could try to quiet his fears by telling himself that there was no question of a muddle in the command; G.H.Q. must know more than he did. The orders came in the end some time after noon, brought by a goggled motor cyclist. He and Miller ran through them rapidly; all they said was that the Division was to move up the road at once–it was not more than a quarter of an hour after the motor cyclist's arrival that Curzon had his leading battalion stepping out briskly towards the battle.

By the time the Division was on the march there was news of sorts to be picked up on the road as the debris of the battle drifted back. Ambulance drivers and lorry drivers and wounded contributed their quota, and the tales told brought the deepest depression and revived the wildest hope alternately. A light infantry officer told of disastrous failure, of the ruin of his division amid a tangle of uncut wire. An ambulance load of wounded Scots reported a triumphant advance, the overrunning of miles of German trenches, and desperate fighting still in progress. From a Seventh Division major Curzon learned of the failure of the gas, and how it was released in some sectors and not in others, and how it had drifted over the German lines, or had stayed stagnant in no-man's-land, or had blown sideways over the advancing British troops as if moved by a spirit of murderous mischief. Then on the other hand there came the news that the British had reached Hill 70 and Hulluch, that the German line was definitely broken, and that the enemy was fighting desperately hard to stave off disaster.

A big motor car with the flag of the Forty-second Corps fluttering at the bonnet come bouncing up the road. Inside could be caught glimpses of scarlet and gold–it was Wayland-Leigh and his staff. The car stopped where Curzon's horse pranced over the *pavé*, and Curzon dismounted, gave his reins to Greven, and hurried to the door.

'Keep your men stepping out, Curzon,' said Wayland-Leigh, leaning forward in his seat and speaking in a hoarse whisper.

'Yes, sir,' answered Curzon. 'Can–can you give me any news?'

'I don't know any myself,' said Wayland-Leigh grimly. 'G.H.Q. has hashed it all up, as far as I can see. Your division's ten miles back from where it ought to be. We broke through this morning, and hadn't the reserves to make a clean thing of it. You'll have to break through again tomorrow, Curzon. And I know you'll do it. Good luck.'

The motor car jolted on along the road, while Curzon swung himself back into the saddle. His division might be late, but he would see to it that it made up for some of the lost time. All down the five-mile-long column the pace quickened as his orders reached each unit to lengthen the pace. Then the head of the column came to a halt, and as Curzon was spurring furiously forward to ascertain the cause of the delay word came back that the road was jammed with broken-down transport. So it was, as Curzon saw when he reached there five minutes later, but it did not remain so long. His blazing anger goaded the transport drivers into a final effort to clear the road. An empty lorry was heaved bodily clear into the ditch, where it lay with its wheels in the air. A distracted officer was bullied into organizing a party to empty the lorry with the broken wheel of the ammunition in it so that the same could be done with that, but before the party had even set to work the Ninety-first Division was pouring through the gap Curzon had contrived.

They marched on while darkness fell and the battle flamed and flickered before them. Long ago the men had lost their brisk stride and air of eager anticipation; now they were merely staggering along under the burden of their packs. No one sang, and the weary sergeants snapped at the exhausted men as they blundered on the slippery *pavé*. At midnight they reached what billets were available–half the division slept in wet bivouacs at the roadside, while Curzon slept in his boots and clothes in an arm-chair in the back room of the estaminet which became his temporary headquarters.

The order he had been waiting for came during the night. The division was given an objective and a sector and a time in tomorrow's attack. Miller and Curzon compared the orders with the maps spread on the marble-topped tables. Miller made his measurements, looked involuntarily at his watch, and said: 'It can't be done.'

'It's got to be done,' said Curzon, with a rasp in his voice.

'Dawn's at six-fifteen,' said Miller. 'We'll have two hours of daylight for seven miles on these roads.'

'Can't help that,' snapped Curzon. 'The division'll have to move at five. We'll have to get the orders for the brigades out now. Here, Frobisher—'

A weary staff wrote out the orders, and weary orderlies took them to Brigade Headquarters, where tired brigadiers were roused from sleep to read them and to curse the higher command which forced their men to go into action with no more than four hours' rest–and those, for most of them, passed in muddy bivouacs.

In the half-light the division formed up on the road, trying to loosen its stiff joints. The march began long before dawn, and they toiled forward up the road to the summons of grumbling guns. Dawn had hardly come when there was another hitch ahead. Curzon was almost beside himself with rage as he rode forward, and what he found made him boil over completely. The road was crammed with cavalry, two whole brigades of it, a forest of leaden-hued lance points. Their transport was all over the road, apparently in the process of being moved from one end of the column to the other. What miracles of staff work had brought that cavalry there at that time in that place and in that condition Curzon did not stop to inquire.

He turned his horse off the road and galloped madly along the side of the column over the muddy fields; not even Follett could keep pace with him. Curzon's quick eye caught sight of a cluster of red cap-bands. He leaped his horse over the low bank again, risking a nasty fall on the greasy *pavé*, and addressed himself to the general of the cavalry division.

'Get your men off this road at once, sir!' he blared. 'You're stopping the march of my division. Orders? I don't care a damn what your orders are. Clear the road this minute! No, sir, I will *not* be careful what I say to you. I've got my duty to do.'

The two major-generals glared fiercely at each other for a moment, before the cavalry man turned to his staff and said: 'Better see to it.'

Curzon was tapping with impatience on his saddle-bow with his crop during the slow process of moving the cavalry with their lances and their forage nets and their impedimenta over the bank into the fields, but it was done at last; soon Curzon saw his leading battalion come plodding up the road, a few staunch spirits singing, 'Hullo, hullo, who's your lady friend?' with intervals for jeers and boos for the disgruntled cavalry watching them go by.

A precious quarter of an hour had been wasted; it seemed almost certain that the division would be late at the rendezvous appointed for it. Soon afterwards it became quite certain, for the narrow road, only just wide enough for two vehicles side by side, was utterly jammed with transport. There was a road junction just ahead, and no military police in the world could have combated successfully with the confusion there, where every vehicle in nine divisions seemed to have converged from all four directions.

Frobisher and Follett galloped hither and thither to find someone in authority who could compel the way to be cleared for the Ninety-first Division, but it was Curzon who achieved it in the end, riding his maddened horse into the thick of the turmoil, and using the weight of his authority and the urge of his blazing anger to hold up the traffic.

It was not for Curzon to decide whether the state of the battle made it desirable that the division should have precedence; that was for the General Staff, but as the General Staff was seemingly making no effort to tackle the problem he had to deal with it himself–and as his division was an hour late his decision was a natural one. For Curzon was not to know that German counter-attacks launched in the early morning had completely stultified the orders he had received that night, and that the task before the Ninety-first Division was not now to exploit a success, but to endeavour to hold on to precarious gains.

They were nearing the line now. There were battery positions beside the road, firing away with a desperate rapidity which indicated the severity of the fighting ahead. Curzon rode on through the drifting flotsam of the battle to the house which his orders had laid down should be established as his headquarters. There was a signal section already there, as Curzon saw with satisfaction. Telephonic communication with the new front line had at last been established, and Headquarters would not have to rest content with the news dribbled out an hour too late by scribbled messages borne by runners.

Curzon had no intention of staying in these headquarters of his. He was determined upon going forward with his division. Miller could be trusted with the task of communicating with Corps Headquarters. Curzon knew the value of a commander on the spot in a confused battle; as Curzon saw it, a divisional general among his men even if they were occupying a mile of tangled front was of more use than a divisional general two miles behind.

The division came on up the road–it was hardly a road by now. The artillery branched off, rocking and swaying over the drab shell-torn fields to take up the position assigned them. Webb and Challis rode up for their final orders, and then the division began to plunge forward into action, while Curzon waited, with Daunt's brigade still in hand, in case new orders should come during this period of deployment.

New orders came right enough. Frobisher came running out of the headquarters to where Curzon stood chatting with Daunt and staring forward at the battle he could not see.

'Please, sir,' said Frobisher, breaking into the conversation, and discarding prefixes and circumlocutions with the urgency of the situation. 'Miller wants you. Quickly, sir. Buffalo's on the phone.'

When Curzon arrived indoors Miller was listening at the telephone, writing hard with his free hand. He waved Curzon impatiently into silence at his noisy entrance.

'Yes,' said Miller. 'Yes. All right. Hold on now while I repeat.'

Miller ran slowly through a list of map references and cryptic sentences about units of the division.

'All correct? Then General Curzon is here if General Wayland-Leigh would care to speak to him.'

He handed the instrument to Curzon. A moment later Wayland-Leigh's voice came through.

'Hullo, Curzon. You've got your new orders?'

'Miller has.'

'Right. I've nothing to add, except to remind you of the standing orders of this Corps. But I can trust you, Curzon. There's all hell let loose, but as far as I can see it's just a last effort on the part of the Huns. You've got to hold until I can persuade G.H.Q. to reinforce you. Sorry to break up your division. Good-bye.'

Curzon turned to Miller, appalled at these last words. Miller was already engaged in writing orders in a bold, careful hand.

'What's all this about?' demanded Curzon, and Miller told him, briefly.

There was no intention now of sending the Ninety-first Division in to break through an attenuated line. The German reserves had arrived and were counter-attacking everywhere. So difficult had been communication with troops a mile forward that only now was the higher command able to form an approximately correct picture of the situation of units far forward with their flanks exposed, and other units beating themselves to pieces against strong positions, units in retreat and units holding on desperately in face of superior numbers. The Ninety-first Division was to be used piecemeal to sustain the reeling line. The new orders prescribed that two battalions should be sent in here, and another employed in a counter-attack there, a brigade held in reserve at this point, and support given at that.

'Christ damn and blast it all!' said Curzon as the situation was explained.

He had had enough experience in South Africa as well as elsewhere of the confusion which follows countermanded orders in the heat of action. His artillery were already getting into action, two brigades of infantry were in movement on points quite different from new objectives. He tore at his moustache while Miller went on steadily writing, and then mastered his fury.

'All right,' he said. 'There's nothing for it. Show me these orders of yours.'

So the Ninety-first Division, after a morning of interminable delays on the road, was now subjected to all the heart-breaking checks which were inevitable with the change of scheme. The bewildered rank and file, marched apparently aimlessly first here and then there, cursed the staff which heaped this confusion upon them. They were short of sleep and short of food. They came under fire unexpectedly; they came under the fire of British artillery who had been left in the dark regarding the fluctuations in the line; and then, when that mistake had been set right, they remained under the fire of shells, from British artillery–shells bought in Japan and America, the trajectory and the time of flight of ten per cent of which were quite unpredictable.

Curzon had perforce to fight his battle from headquarters. Wayland-Leigh, besieged by requests for help and by orders to give help, coming from all quarters, was persistent in his demands upon the Ninety-first. Challis with a fraction of his 302nd Brigade reported that he had stormed the redoubt whose enfilade fire had caused such losses in the Guards' Division, but an hour later was appealing for permission to use another of his battalion to consolidate his position. Daunt in another part of the line sent back a warning that a counter-attack was being organized in front of him apparently of such strength that he doubted whether he would be able to stop it. From every hand came appeals for artillery support, at moments when Colonel Miller was warning Curzon that he must persuade Corps Headquarters to send up yet more ammunition.

To reconcile all these conflicting claims, to induce Corps Headquarters to abate something of their exacting demands, and to try and find out from the hasty reports sent in which patch of the line might be left unreinforced, and in which part a renewed attack was absolutely necessary, constituted a task which Curzon could leave to no one else. All through the evening of September 26th, and on through the night, Curzon had to deal with reports and orders brought in by runner, by telephone, and by motor cyclist. There was no possible chance of his being in the line with his men–there was no chance either of guessing in which part of the line his presence would do most good. Miller and Frobisher, Greven and Follett, slept in turns on the floor of the next room, but Curzon stayed awake through the night, dealing with each crisis as it came.

He was red-eyed and weary by the morning, but in the morning there were fresh counter-attacks to be beaten back. All through the night German divisions had been marching to the point of danger, and now they were let loose upon the unstable British line. The nine British divisions had been prodigal of their blood and strength. The mile or half-mile of shell-torn ground behind them impeded communications and supply; the inexperienced artillery seemed to take an interminable time to register upon fresh targets. It was all a nightmare. Units which had lost their sense of direction and position in the wild landscape reported points strongly held by the enemy which other units at the same moment were reporting as being in their possession.

Wayland-Leigh's voice on the telephone carried a hint of anxiety with it. General Headquarters, dealing with the conflicting reports sent it by two Armies and an Army Corps, had changed its mood from one of wild optimism to one of equally wild despair. They had begun to fear that where they had planned a break-through the enemy instead would effect a breach, and they were dealing out threats on all sides in search of a possible scapegoat.

'Somebody's going to be for it,' said Wayland-Leigh. 'You've got to hold on.'

Curzon was not in need of that spur. He would hold on without being told. He held on through that day and the next, while the bloody confusion of the battle gradually sorted itself out. General Headquarters had found one last belated division with which to reinforce the weak line, and its arrival enabled Curzon at last to bring Daunt's brigade into line with Challis's and have his division a little more concentrated–although, as Miller grimly pointed out, the two brigades together did not contain as many men as either of them before the battle. The front was growing stabilized now, as parapets were being built in the new trenches, and carrying parties toiled through the night to bring up the barbed wire which meant security.

Curzon could actually sleep now, and he was not specially perturbed when a new increase in the din of the bombardment presaged a fresh flood of reports from the trenches to the effect that the German attacks were being renewed. But once more the situation grew serious. The German command was throwing away lives now as freely as the British in a last effort to recover important strategic points. Fosse 8 and the quarries were lost again; the British line was bending, even if it would not break. Webb's 300th Brigade, in the very process of transfer to the side of its two fellows, was caught up by imperative orders from Wayland-Leigh and flung back into the battle–Curzon had to disregard a wail of protest from Webb regarding the fatigue of his men. Later in the same day Curzon, coming into the headquarter's office, found Miller speaking urgently on the telephone.

'Here's the General come back,' he said, breaking off the conversation. 'You'd better speak to him personally.'

He handed over the instrument.

'It's Webb,' he explained, *sotto voce*. 'Usual sort of grouse.'

Curzon frowned as he took the receiver. Webb had been making difficulties all through the battle.

'Curzon speaking.'

'Oh, this is Webb here, sir. I want to withdraw my line a bit. P.3–8. It's a nasty bit of salient—'

Webb went on with voluble explanations of the difficulty of his position and the losses the retention of the line would involve. Curzon looked at the map which Miller held out to him while Webb's voice went on droning in the receiver. As far as he could see by the map Webb's brigade was undoubtedly in an awkward salient. But that was no argument in favour of withdrawal. The line as at present constituted had been reported to Corps Headquarters, and the alteration would have to be explained to Wayland-Leigh–not that Curzon would flinch from daring the Buffalo's wrath it he thought it necessary. But he did not think so; it never once crossed his mind to authorize Webb to withdraw from the salient. Retreat was un-English, an admission of failure, something not to be thought of. There had never been any suggestion of retreat at First Ypres, and retreat there would indubitably have spelt disaster. Curzon did not stop to debate the pros and cons in this way–he dismissed the suggestion as impossible the moment he heard it.

'You must hold on where you are,' he said harshly, breaking into Webb's voluble explanations.

'But that's absurd,' said Webb. 'The other line would be far safer. Why should—'

'Did you hear what I said?' asked Curzon.

'Yes, but–but—' Webb had sufficient sense to hesitate before taking the plunge, but not enough to refrain from doing so altogether. 'I'm on the spot, and you're not. I'm within my rights if I make the withdrawal without your permission!'

'You think you are?' said Curzon. He was tired of Webb and his complaints, and he certainly was not going to have his express orders questioned in this way. After that last speech of Webb's he could not trust him, however definitely he laid down his orders. 'Well, you're not going to have the chance. You will terminate your command of your brigade from this moment. You will leave your headquarters and report here on your way down the line at once. No, I'm not going to argue about it. Call your brigade-major and have him speak to me. At once, please. Is that Captain Home? General Webb has ceased to command the brigade. You will be in charge of your headquarters until Colonel Meredith can be informed and arrives to take command. Understand? Right. Send the message to Colonel Meredith immediately, and ask him to report to me on his arrival.'

So Brigadier-General Webb was unstuck and sent home, and lost his chance of ever commanding a division. The last Curzon saw of him was when he left Divisional Headquarters. There was actually a tear–a ridiculous tear–on one cheek just below his blue eye as he went away, but Curzon felt neither pity for him nor dislike. He had been found wanting, as men of that type were bound to be sooner or later. Curzon would have no man in the Ninety-first Division whom he could not trust.

And as Webb left the headquarters the divisional mail arrived. There were letters for each unit in the division, sorted with the efficiency the Army Postal Service always managed to display. They would go up with the rations that night, but the letters for the headquarters personnel could be delivered at once. For the General, besides bills and circulars, and the half-dozen obviously unimportant official ones, there was one letter in a heavy cream envelope addressed to him in a sprawling handwriting which he recognized as the Duke's. He hesitated a moment when Greven gave it to him, but he could not refrain from opening it there and then. He read the letter through, and the big sprawling writing became suddenly vague and ill defined as he did so. The wording of the letter escaped him completely; it was only its import which was borne in upon him.

That vomiting of Emily's, about which he had always felt a premonition, had actually been a serious symptom. There had been a disaster. Young Herbert Winter Greven Curzon (Curzon had determined on those names long ago) would never open his eyes to the wonder of the day. He was dead–he had never lived; and Emily had nearly followed him. She was out of the wood now, the Duke wrote, doing his best to soften the blow, but Sir Trevor Choape had laid it down very definitely that she must never again try to have a child. If she did, Sir Trevor could not answer for the consequences.

Curzon turned a little pale as he stood holding the letter, and he sat down rather heavily in the chair beside his telephone.

'Not bad news, sir, I hope?' said Greven.

'Nothing that matters,' answered Curzon stoically, stuffing the letter into his pocket.

'Colonel Runcorn would like to speak to you, sir,' said Follett, appearing at the door.

'Send him in,' said Curzon. He had no time to weep for Herbert Winter Greven Curzon, just as Napoleon at Marengo had no time to weep for Desaix.

18

The Battle of Loos had come to an end, and at last the Ninety-first Division was relieved and could march out to its billets. It was not the division which had gone into action. Curzon stood by the road to see them march by, as he had so often done in Hampshire and France, and they took far less time to pass him. Each brigade bulked no larger on the road than a battalion had done before the battle; each battalion was no larger than a company. The artillery had suffered as badly; there were woefully few men with the guns, and to many of the guns there were only four horses, and to many of the wagons there were only two mules. Curzon's heart sank a little as he returned the salute of the skeleton units. Even with the drafts which were awaiting them they would not be up to establishment; it would be a long time before the Ninety-first Division would be built up again into the fine fighting unit it had been a fortnight ago.

He did not attempt to conceal from himself that Loos had been a disaster for the British Army; he could only comfort himself with the thought that it had been a disaster for the German Army as well. The next attack to be made would have to be planned very differently. The bombardment had been insufficient. Then they must have a bombardment which would make certain of it–fifty days, instead of fifty hours, if the ammunition supply could be built up to bear the strain. There must be reserves at hand, instead of seventeen miles back, to exploit the success. The Flying Corps must intensify its operations so that maps of the German second line could be ready in the utmost detail, to enable the artillery to register on fresh targets from new positions without delay. Equally important, there must be none of the muddle and confusion behind the line which caused so much harm at Loos.

Curzon, despite his red tabs and oak leaves on his cap-peak, could still feel the fighting man's wrath against the staffs that were responsible for that muddle. It was their business to prevent muddle, and they had failed. Curzon was quite well aware of his own incapacity to do that sort of staff officer's work. He was not too reliable in the matter of addition and multiplication and division; the mathematical problems involved in the arrangement of supply and transport and of march timetables would have certainly been too much for him. But it was not his job to solve them; it was the responsibility of the men at Army Headquarters and G.H.Q., and they had not been equal to it. Curzon felt if he were in chief command he would make a clean sweep of the gilded young men who had made such a hash of the timetables and replace them by efficient mathematicians. Hang it, he would put civilians on the staff for that matter, if they could do the job better–and for Curzon to permit himself even for a moment to be guilty of a heresy of that sort showed how strongly he felt about it.

There were others of the same opinion, as Curzon discovered when he reported himself at Corps Headquarters. Over the whole personnel there lay a brooding sense of disaster both past and to come. Someone would have to bear the responsibility of failure. It would not be long before heads began to fly. Some were gone already–Bewly had been sent home by Wayland-Leigh just as Webb had been sent back by Curzon. Hope of the Seventy-ninth was in hospital, dying of his wounds–rumour said he had gone up to the line to seek death, and death was not so hard to find in the front-line trenches. No one in that gloomy assembly dared to think of the brave words at the last Headquarters dinner, and the brave anticipants of an immediate advance to the Rhine.

Wayland-Leigh, bulky yet restless, sat at the head of the conference table and looked round with his sidelong green eyes. Everyone knew that it would be touch and go with him. He might be selected as the scapegoat, and deprived of his command and packed off at any moment, if G.H.Q. should decide that such a sacrifice would be acceptable to the strange gods of Downing Street. He was conscious of the trembling of his throne even while he presided at this meeting to discuss what suggestions should be put forward regarding future operations.

Curzon was inevitably called upon for his opinion. He spoke hesitatingly, as might be expected of him; as he told himself, he was no hand at these infernal board-meetings, and speech-making was the bane of his life. He was conscious of the eyes upon him, and he kept his own on the table, and fumbled with pen and pencil as he spoke. Yet he had something very definite to say, and no man with that advantage can speak without point. He briefly described what he thought must be considered essentials for the new battle. More men. More guns. More ammunition. More artillery preparation. More energy. He fumbled with his pencil more wildly than ever when he had to pass on from these, to his mind the obvious things, to the other less tangible desiderata. The arrangements behind the lines had been disgraceful. There must be an efficient staff created which would handle them properly. Someone must work out an effective method of bringing fresh troops into the front line at the decisive moments. Someone must see to it that reserves should be ready in the right place at the right time.

Curzon was surprised by the little murmur of applause which went round the table when he had finished. More than one of the subsequent speakers alluded in complimentary terms to General Curzon's suggestions. The whole opinion of the assembly was with him. The attack at Loos had been correct enough in theory. There had only been a failure in practical details and an insufficiency of men and materials. It could all be made good. A staff that could handle half a million men in action could be found. So could the half-million men. So could the guns and ammunition for a really adequate artillery preparation.

Quite noticeably the spirits of the gathering rose; within a very few minutes they were discussing the ideal battle, with forty divisions to draw upon, and elaborate timetables, and a preliminary bombardment which would transcend anything the most vaulting imagination could depict, and a steady methodical advance which nothing could stop–in a word, they were drawing up designs to put forward before higher authority for the Battle of the Somme. With visions like this before them, they could hardly be blamed for ignoring the minor details of machine-guns and barbed wire. Minor details vanished into insignificance when compared with the enormous power they pictured at their disposal.

Wayland-Leigh sat in his chair and writhed his bulk about, grinning like an ogre as the suggestions assumed more and more concrete form, while Norton beside him took industrious notes to form the skeleton of the long reports he would have to send in to Army Headquarters and to G.H.Q. In some ways it was like the debate of a group of savages as to how to extract a screw from a piece of wood. Accustomed only to nails, they had made one effort to pull out the screw by main force, and now that it had failed they were devising methods of applying more force still, of obtaining more efficient pincers, of using levers and fulcrums so that more men could bring their strength to bear. They could hardly be blamed for not guessing that by rotating the screw it would come out after the exertion of far less effort; it would be a notion so different from anything they had ever encountered that they would laugh at the man who suggested it.

The generals round the table were not men who were easily discouraged–men of that sort did not last long in command in France. Now that the first shock of disappointment had been faced they were prepared to make a fresh effort, and to go on making those efforts as long as their strength lasted. Wayland-Leigh was pleased with their attitude; indeed, so apparent was his pleasure that Curzon had no hesitation in asking him, after the conference, for special leave to England for urgent private affairs. Curzon was able to point out (if it had not been the case he would never have dreamed of making the application, despite the urgency of his desire to see Emily) that the division would not be fit to go into the line for some time, and that the knocking into shape of the new drafts could safely be left to the regimental officers.

'Oh, yes, you can go all right,' said Wayland-Leigh. 'You've earned it, anyway. We can spare you for a bit.'

'Thank you, sir,' said Curzon.

'But whether you'll find me here when you come back is quite another matter.'

'I don't understand,' said Curzon. He had heard rumours, of course, but he judged it to be tactless to admit it.

'I've got half an idea I'm going to be unstuck. Sent home because those bloody poops at G.H.Q. have got to find someone to blame besides themselves.'

'I hope not, sir,' said Curzon.

Wayland-Leigh's huge face writhed into an expression of resignation.

'Can't be helped if I am,' he said. 'I've done nothing to be ashamed of, and people will know it some time, even if they don't now. I'm sorry for your sake, though.'

'For me, sir?'

'Yes. I was hoping they'd give you one of the new corps which are being formed. I've written recommending it in the strongest terms. I wanted Hope to have one too, but he'll never be fit enough for active service again if he lives. But what my recommendation's good for is more than I can say. Probably do you more harm than good, as things are.'

'Thank you, sir. But I don't care about myself. It's you that matters.'

Curzon meant what he said.

'Very good of you to say so, Curzon. We'll see what happens. G.H.Q. have got their eye on you anyway, one way or the other. I've had a hell of a lot of bother with 'em about your unsticking that beggar Webb, you know.'

'Sorry about that, sir.'

'Oh, I didn't mind. I backed you up, of course. And I sent your report on him in to G.H.Q. with "concur" written on it as big as I could make it. Push off now. Tell Norton you've got my permission. If you drive like hell to Boulogne you'll catch the leave boat all right.'

In reply to Curzon's telegram the Duke's big motor car was at Victoria Station to meet the train, and in it was Emily, very wan and pale. She was thinner than usual, and in the front of her neck the sterno-mastoid muscles had assumed the prominence they were permanently to retain. She smiled at Curzon and waved through the window to attract his attention although she did not stand up.

'It was splendid to have your telegram, Bertie,' she said as the car slid through the sombre streets of war-time London. 'Mother's been wanting to move me off to Somerset ever since the air raids started to get so bad. But I wouldn't go, not after your letter saying you might be home any minute. We want every hour together we can possibly have, don't we, Bertie?'

They squeezed hands, and went on squeezing them all the short time it took the car to reach Bude House.

The Duke and Duchess welcomed Curzon hospitably, the latter almost effusively. Yet to Curzon's mind there was something incongruous about the Duchess's volubility about the hardships civilians were going through. If it were not for the supplies they could draw from the model farm and dairy in Somerset, the family and servants might almost be going short of food, and if it were not for the Duke's official position petrol and tyres for the motor cars would be nearly unobtainable. That ducal servants should be given margarine instead of butter seemed to the Duchess to be far more unthinkable than it did to Curzon, although he had the wit not to say so; and it gave the Duchess an uneasy sense of outraged convention that aeroplane bombs should slay those in high places as readily as those in low. She described the horrors of air raids to Curzon as though he had never seen a bombardment.

The Duke's sense of proportion was less warped than his wife's, although naturally he was inclined to attribute undue importance to his activities under the new Government. Between Curzon's anxiety for Emily, and the Duchess's desire to tell him and to hear a little from him, it was some time before Curzon and the Duke were able to converse privately and at leisure, but when they did the conversation was a momentous one. The Duke was as anxious as all his other colleagues in the Government to receive an unbiased account of what was really happening on the Western Front, freed from official verbiage and told by someone without a cause to plead. Out of Curzon's brief sentences–for the conversation was of the fashion of small talk, in which the state of military affairs usurped the time-honoured pre-eminence of the weather as a topic of conversation–the Duke was able to form a clearer picture than ever before of the bloody confusion which had been the Battle of Loos. He stroked his chin and said, 'H'm' a great many times, but was able to keep the conversational ball rolling by the aid of a few conjunctive phrases.

'You say it wasn't this chap Wayland-Leigh's fault?' he asked.

'Good God, no. He wouldn't stand anything like that for a moment. It'll be a crime if they unstick him.'

'Why, is there any talk about it?'

'Yes. You see, someone's got to go, after all that was said beforehand.'

'I see. H'm.'

The Duke was aware that anxiety in the Cabinet was reaching a maximum. The decline of Russian power, the alliance of Bulgaria with the Central Powers, the crushing of Serbia, the failure at Gallipoli, Townshend's difficultics in Mesopotamia, and now the fiasco at Loos had been a succession of blows which might well shake anyone's nerve. Yet there were three million Allied troops in France opposed to only two million Germans. That superiority at the decisive point about which the military were so insistent seemed to be attained, and yet nothing was being done. The Duke knew as well as any soldier that a crushing victory in France would make all troubles and difficulties vanish like ghosts, and he yearned and hungered for that victory.

'H'm,' he said again, rousing himself from his reverie. 'Then there's this business about conscription too.'

Curzon's views on the matter of conscription were easily ascertained. When forty divisions began their great attack in France the need for drafts would become insistent. However decisive the victory they won, the volunteer divisions would need to be brought promptly up to strength. Not all the recruiting songs and propaganda–not even the shooting of Nurse Cavell– would ensure an inflow of recruits as reliable as a drastic conscription law like the French. In Curzon's opinion, too, this was a golden opportunity for bringing in a measure which he had always favoured, even before the war.

'It is every man's duty to serve his country,' said Curzon, remembering fragments of what Lord Roberts had said in peace-time.

'It won't be easy to do,' said the Duke, visualizing a harassed Cabinet striving to avoid disruption while being dragged in every direction by conflicting forces.

'Drafts have got to be found, all the same,' said Curzon. He thought of the effect it would have on his own attitude if he were warned that the supply of recruits was uncertain and dwindling. It would mean caution; it would mean an encroachment upon his liberty to attack; it would mean thinking twice about every offensive movement, and an inevitable inclination towards a defensive attitude; it might conceivably come to mean the breaking up of some of the units which had been built up with such care–the Ninety-first Division even.

He was filled with genuine horror at such a prospect–a horror that made him almost voluble. He laid down as stiffly and as definitely as he possibly could the extreme urgency of a lavish supply of recruits. He thumped his knee with his hand to make himself quite clear on the subject. The Duke could not help but be impressed by Curzon's animation and obvious sincerity–they were bound to be impressive to a man who had had experience of Curzon's usual tongue-tied formality of manner.

19

Curzon found his leave as bewilderingly short as any young subaltern home from France. It seemed to him as though he had scarcely reached England before he was back again in the steamer at Folkestone; and when he had rejoined the flood of khaki pouring across the Channel, and heard once more the old military talk, and received the salutes of soldiers stiffened into awed attention by the sight of his brass hat and medal ribbons, he experienced the odd sensation known to every returning soldier–as if his leave had never happened, as if it had been someone else, and not himself, who had revelled in the delights of London and received the embraces of his wife.

Curzon had to think very hard about Emily, about her last brave smile, and her waving handkerchief, before he could make the events of the last week lose their veneer of unreality. He had to make himself remember Emily stroking his hair, and speaking soberly about the amount of grey to be seen in it. Emily had held his hand to her breast, kissing his forehead and his eyes, that time when they had at last brought themselves to mention the brief sojourn in this world of Herbert Winter Greven Curzon. She had offered herself up to him again, a mute voluntary sacrifice, and he had declined like a gentleman; like a gentleman who in the year of grace 1915 had only the vaguest hearsay knowledge of birth-control methods and did not want to extend it. There would never be a Herbert Winter Greven Curzon now. He was the last of his line. He blew his nose, harshly, with a military sort of noise, and made himself forget Emily and England again while he turned back to the problems of his profession and his duty.

Miller had thoughtfully sent a motor car to meet him at Boulogne–not for him the jolting, uncomfortable, endless journey by train. He sat back in the car fingering his moustache as the well-remembered countryside sped by. There were French troops on the roads, and French Territorials guarding bridges. Then the British zone; grooms exercising charges; villages full of British soldiers in shirt-sleeves with their braces hanging down by their thighs; aeroplanes overhead. Divisional Headquarters; Challis ready to hand over the command, Greven and Follett with polite questions about how he had enjoyed his leave, piles of states and returns awaiting his examination.

And there was something new about the atmosphere of headquarters too. Miller and Frobisher bore themselves towards him with a slight difference in their manner. Curzon, none too susceptible to atmosphere, was only aware of the difference and could not account for it. He could only tell that they had heard some rumour about him; whether good news or bad he could not tell.

The General Staff, as he bitterly told himself, were as thick as thieves with one another, and passed rumours from mouth to mouth and telephone to telephone, so that these men, his juniors and assistants, were always aware of things long before they reached his ears, because he was not one of the blood-brotherhood of Camberley.

He asked Miller tentatively about news, and Miller was ready with a vast amount of divisional information, but nothing that would in the least account for the new atmosphere. In the end he ordered out his motor car again, without even waiting to go round the stables and see how his horses had been looked after during his leave, and had himself driven over to Corps Headquarters at Saint-Cérisy. He had to report his return to Wayland-Leigh, and he felt that if he did so in person he might discover what this new unannounced development was.

But at Saint-Cérisy the affair only became more portentous and no less mysterious. Wayland-Leigh and Norton were both of them away. Stanwell, the senior staff officer in charge, told Curzon that they were at G.H.Q. He conveyed this piece of information in a manner which gave full weight to it, and when he went on to suggest that General Curzon should stay to dinner at the headquarters mess, he did so in such a manner likewise as to leave Curzon in no doubt at all that he would be glad later that he had done so. The atmosphere of Corps Headquarters was yet more tensely charged with expectancy even than Divisional Headquarters had been. Fortunately it was the hour before dinner, and Curzon was able to fall back upon gin-and-angostura to help him through the trying wait. He actually had four drinks before dinner, although it was rare for him to exceed two. Then at last the ante-room door opened and Wayland-Leigh came in, followed by Norton, and one glance at their faces told everyone that the news they brought was good.

The news was historic, as well as good. There had been complete upheaval at General Headquarters. The Field-Marshal Commanding-in-Chief had fallen; the new Cabinet at home had decided they would prefer to risk their reputations upon someone different. His exit was to be made as dignified as possible–a Peerage, the Commandership-in-Chief of the Home Forces, Grand Crosses and ribbons and stars were to be given him, but no one present at the headquarters of the Forty-second Corps cared a rap about this aspect of his fate. It was far more important to them to know that his successor was to be a man after their own heart, an Army commander, another cavalry man, a man of the most steadfast determination of purpose. Under his leadership they could look forward to a relentless, methodical, unremitting pressure upon the enemy; nothing fluky, nothing temperamental; something Scottish instead of Irish. Curzon remembered how he had come riding up to his brigade headquarters at First Ypres, and his unmoved calm in the face of the most desperate danger.

But there was a personal aspect as well as a general one. One Army commander had been promoted; one had gone home; the creation of a new Army made a vacancy for a third. Three Army Corps commanders would receive promotion to the full rank of General and the command of an army–and Wayland-Leigh was to be one of them. He was a man cast in the same mould as the new Commander-in-Chief; where the previous one would have cast him down the new one had raised him higher yet. It meant promotion, power, and new opportunities for distinction for all the officers of his staff.

Next there was the question of the lower ranks still. Three Army Corps commanders were being promoted to armies; three divisional commanders would be promoted to take their places. And ten new divisions had now reached France, or were on their way. Three new Army Corps would have to be formed to control these, so that altogether six Major-Generals could expect promotion to Lieutenant-General. Wayland-Leigh did not know yet all their names, but he knew that Curzon had been selected. He clapped Curzon on the shoulder as he told him, with extraordinary *bonhomie*. Curzon flushed with pleasure as he received the congratulations of those present. He was destined for the command of four divisions, for the control of something like a hundred thousand men in battle–as many as Wellington or Marlborough ever commanded. He was destined, too, to the bathchair on Bournemouth promenade, but Bournemouth and bathchairs were far from his thoughts as he sat, a little shy, his cheeks red and his eyes on his plate, contemplating his future.

The personality of the new Commander-in-Chief was already noticeable in his selection of his subordinates, and so through them to the holders of the lesser commands. The men who were wanted were men without fear of responsibility, men of ceaseless energy and of iron will, who could be relied upon to carry out their part in a plan of battle as far as flesh and blood–their own and their men's–would permit. Men without imagination were necessary to execute a military policy devoid of imagination, devised by a man without imagination. Anything resembling freakishness or originality was suspect in view of the plan of campaign. Every General desired as subordinates officers who would meticulously obey orders undaunted by difficulties or losses or fears for the future; every General knew what would be expected of him (and approved of it) and took care to have under him Generals of whom he could expect the same. When brute force was to be systematically applied only men who could fit into the system without allowance having to be made for them were wanted. Curzon had deprived Brigadier-General Webb of his command for this very reason.

In point of fact, Curzon's report on this matter had been the factor which had turned the scale and won him his promotion against the rival influences of seniority and influence. Read with painstaking care by those highest in authority, the sentiments expressed in it had so exactly suited the mood of the moment that Wayland-Leigh had been allowed to have his way in the matter of Curzon's promotion.

Curzon himself did not trouble to analyse the possible reason for his promotion. If some intimate had ventured to ask him what it was likely to be, he would have answered, as convention dictated, that it must have been merely good luck. Right far within himself, in that innermost sanctuary of his soul where convention ceased to rule, would have dwelt the admission that his rise was due to his own merit, and that admission would not have indicated hollow pride. It was his possession of the qualities which he most admired, and which he strove most to ingrain into himself, and which he thought were the necessary characteristics of true greatness, which had won for him the distinction of being almost the youngest Lieutenant-General in the British Army.

The conversation round the mess table was light-hearted. The shadow of calamity had been lifted, for if Wayland-Leigh had been removed from his command the careers of all the staff officers under him would have been gravely checked. As it was, Norton, Brigadier-General, General Staff, would now become Major-General and Chief of Staff of an Army; Commanding Officers of Artillery and Engineers could confidently look forward to a new step in rank, and so on down to the most junior G.S.O.s. Everybody drank champagne and became a littler noisier than was usual at dinner at headquarters' messes, while Wayland-Leigh at the head of the table allowed his big face to wrinkle into an expression of massive good humour. Soldiers had once drunk to 'a bloody war and sickly season'; the bloody war had come, and an expansion of the Army far beyond the calculation of the wildest imagination was bringing with it promotion more rapid than any sickly season could have done.

Curzon drove back to his headquarters with his brain whirling with something more than champagne. He was trying to build up in his mind his conception of the perfect Army Corps, the sort of Army Corps he really wanted. He would have little say in the choice of the divisions under his command, for individual divisions came under and out of Army Corps control according to the needs of the moment. All he could do in that connexion was to see that his major-generals knew what he expected of them–in the darkness of the motor car, Curzon's expression hardened and his lips tightened; he did not anticipate much trouble from major-generals.

It was not in the matter of subordination that his mind chiefly exercised itself. He was preoccupied with the less obvious and more detailed aspect of high command. He had seen something of muddled staff work, and he still retained much of the fighting man's suspicion of the ability of staff officers to handle simple problems of space and time. There was going to be no muddling in *his* Corps. Everything was going to be exact, systematic, perfect–to Curzon the adjective 'systematic' implied a supremely desirable quality. If his officers could not attain to such a standard then he would replace them by others who would.

Curzon made all this abundantly clear to Miller and Frobisher next morning, when he summoned them to hear his news and decisions. He would retain Miller as his chief staff officer, putting him forward, as would be necessary, for promotion to brigadier-general, General Staff. He would advance Frobisher from third to second grade, always provided, of course, that the War Office consented. He would listen to their suggestions in the selection of their assistants–the more readily because he knew very little still about the relative merits of the men of the General Staff.

But Miller and Frobisher in return must pick the best men who could be got, and must remain uninfluenced by fear or favour. They must work for him with a whole-hearted devotion, and the standard of their work would be judged necessarily by results. Curzon could tell as easily as anyone else whether arrangements were working smoothly or not, and if they did not, then Miller and Frobisher would feel the whole weight of his displeasure.

Curzon darted frosty glances at his staff when he said this. Ever since he had passed out from Sandhurst he had been unable to do tricky problems of the type of: 'If A can do a piece or work in four days, and B can do it in five days, how long will they take working together?' and he knew it, and knew that his staff knew it. Curzon now would be responsible for the correct solution of problems of the same order, but far more complicated, dealing with the traffic-capacity of roads, and divisional march timetables, and artillery barrages, and even with railway management–for railways came to a certain extent under Corps control. If things went wrong he would have to bear the blame, and he was not going to trust his military reputation to incompetents.

'You've got to find blokes I can rely on,' said Curzon. 'Some of these University wallahs, or those railway men and engineer fellows who carry slide rules about with them. They make bloody bad soldiers, I know, but I don't care about that. *I*'ll do the soldiering.'

Curzon's experience of his brother officers left him in no doubt at all that in the ranks of what was left of the old professional Army there were not nearly men enough to go round capable of dealing with these semi-military problems, and as the last comer and the junior lieutenant-general he would never have a chance of getting any of them. In these circumstances Curzon had no scruple in making use of the services of civilians in uniform. He could rely upon himself to see that they had no opportunity given them for dangerous theorizing or for interfering in the real management and direction of the Army.

So in this fashion the staff of Curzon's Forty-forth Corps came to include a collection of characters whom a year ago Curzon would not have expected to see as soldiers, far less in the brass hats of field officers and the red tabs of the staff. The Gas Officer was a University of London chemist, Milward, who was blessed with a Cockney accent that would have upset Curzon every time he heard it had he allowed it to. Spiller, who had been a Second Wrangler, was a deputy assistant quartermaster-general, and Colquhoun, whose Lancashire accent was as noticeable as Milward's Cockney, was another–he had had several years' experience in railway management. Runcorn (who had been Curzon's commanding engineer in the Ninety-first Division, and had come on to the Forty-fourth Corps in the same capacity) had as his assistants a major who had built bridges in India and a captain who had built cathedrals in America.

There was no love lost between the Regulars and the others who gaily styled themselves Irregulars. After a short trial it was found impossible for the two sections to mingle without friction in the social life of the headquarters mess, and by an unspoken agreement the staff fell into two separate cliques, only coming together for the purpose of work. It would have been a vicious arrangement had it not been for the authority of Curzon. He wanted the work done, and under his pressure the work was well done–he wanted no theorizing or highfalutin suggestions; all he asked was technical efficiency and that he got.

The Forty-fourth Corps began to make a name for itself, just as the Ninety-first Division had done. The sector of the front line which it held was always an area of great liveliness. Divisional generals were encouraged or coerced–the former usually, as no lieutenant-general had any use for a major-general in need of coercion–to plan and execute local operations of a vigour and enterprise which called forth German retaliation of extreme intensity. Disciplinary measures, carried out with all the severity which Curzon could wring from courts-martial, kept the Corps freer than its neighbours of the plagues of trench feet and trench fever which afflicted the British Army during that miserable winter.

It became noticeable that in the Forty-fourth Corps area there were fewer lorries ditched while taking up supplies to the line at night. A ditched lorry meant that the driver was saved for that night from undergoing personal danger, whatever privations were caused to the men in the line. Curzon knew nothing of lorry driving, but he saw to it that a driver who was ditched suffered so severely that no one else was encouraged to follow his example. Motor-transport drivers remained influenced by the fear of a sentence of imprisonment to an extent far greater than in the infantry (the time was at hand when plenty of infantrymen would have welcomed a sentence of imprisonment which took them out of the line), and the savage sentences which Curzon obtained for delinquents made the chicken-hearted use their headlights at the risk of drawing fire, and to go on across dangerous cross-roads however easily they could have staged a breakdown.

20

Emily was able to eke out of the meagreness of her letters with occasional Press cuttings. The notice in the *Gazette*–'Major (temp. Major-General) Herbert Curzon, C.B., D.S.O.., to be temp. Lieut-General, 4th Dec., 1915', had attracted the attention of the Press. They printed paragraphs about his phenomenal rise, and in the absence of the details which the censorship prohibited, they fell back upon the old information that he was the husband of Lady Emily Winter-Willoughby, only daughter of the Duke of Bude, Minister of Steel, and that he was connected (they did not say how) with the family of Lord Curzon of Kedleston, leader of the House of Lords and member of the War Cabinet.

Not much was known about generals in the present war–a contrast with the Boer War, when people wore in their button-holes portraits of Buller or White or Baden-Powell. Generals in 1914–15 had ignored the value to them of publicity, and were only just beginning to realize how foolish it had been to do so. Few people could list off-hand the names of Haig's Army commanders; and yet the public desire for news about generals was quite definite although unsatisfied. In consequence the newspapers grasped eagerly at the opportunity of saying something about Curzon, and he became better known than, say, Plumer or Horne.

Curzon read the paragraphs about 'this brilliant young general', and 'the satisfaction the public must feel about the promotion of such a young officer' in the privacy of his room with an odd smile on his face. They gave him a feeling of satisfaction without a doubt; he liked publicity, as simple-minded people often do–even though his satisfaction was diminished by the thought that he was indebted for it to 'these newspaper fellows', for whom he had a decided contempt. It did not occur to him that the publicity was of priceless value to him, and established him more firmly in his new rank than any military virtue could have done. It was left for the Army to discover much later that publicity may so strengthen a general's hand that even a Cabinet would risk its own destruction if it should hint at incapacity in the general who was nominally their servant.

Probably it was those paragraphs which brought Curzon the rewards which he was able to write to Emily about. Foreign decorations flowed in to him–G.H.Q. were generous in apportioning his share. He received the Legion of Honour (submitting stoically to the accolade of the French general who invested him with it) and the Italian Order of St Maurice and St Lazarus, and the Russian Order of St George, and the Portuguese Order of St Benedict of Aviz, so that there were three rows of gay ribbons now on his breast. It was not much to write about to Emily, but it was at least something; Curzon could not bring himself to write 'I love you,' and by the time he had said 'I wish I was with you' (which was only partly true, but could be allowed to stand) and remarked on the weather, the page was still only half full. He did not discuss military topics–not so much because of the needs for secrecy but because it was difficult to describe trench raids and local offensives without maps, and he doubted whether Emily could read a trench map.

Emily was fortunate in finding plenty to say. She told how her father had given up the hopeless task of keeping Bude House properly heated and staffed in war-time, and had solved his difficulties by lending the place to the Government as offices. She described her rural life in Somersetshire, and the patriotic efforts she was making to increase the national food supply. She dwelt in happy reminiscence on Curzon's last leave, and told how much she was looking forward to his next, although she appreciated how difficult it was for a man in his position to get away. In fact Emily chattered away in her letters with a spirit and freedom only to be explained by her delight in having a confidant for the first time in her life.

As the winter ended and the summer began a new topic crept into Emily's letter. Her mother (whose work on committees caused her to spend half her time in London) was full of the news that a battle was about to be fought which was to end the war. The Duchess said that July 1st was the date fixed. Emily hoped it was true, because at that rate she would have her husband home with her in time for the beginning of the hunting season.

Curzon boiled with anger as he read the artless words–not anger with his wife, but with the thoughtless civilians who were gossiping about matters of the utmost military importance. He was absolutely certain that no soldier could have made the disclosure. It must be in the fault of the politicians and the women. Curzon knew well enough that the Germans must be aware of the prospect of an offensive on the Somme. The huge ammunition dumps, the accumulation of gun positions, the new roads and the light railways, for much of which his own staff was responsible, must have given that away long ago. But that the very date should be known was an appalling thought. He wrote with fury to the Duke, and the Duke replied more moderately. It was not he who had told the Duchess–he had learned not to entrust her with secrets of state–but the fact was common gossip in politico-social circles in London. He would be more ready to blame the staff in France than the politicians in England.

That was poor comfort to Curzon, who could only set his teeth and urge on his staff to further efforts to ensure certain success on the great day. In the conferences at Army Headquarters statistics were brought forward to show how certain success would be. For every division employed at Loos there would be five on the Somme. For every gun, twenty. For every shell, two hundred. It was inconceivable that an effort on such a scale should fail; there had never been such an accumulation of force in the history of the world. It was doubtful, bearing in mind the heavy losses the Germans had been experiencing at Verdun, whether it was all quite necessary, but as the Chief of Staff of the Sixth Army pointed out, no one ever yet lost a battle by being too strong.

The divisions were slowly moving up into place. The elaborate timetables for the reinforcement and relief of units in the heat of action were settled to the last minute. Then with a crash the bombardment opened. Curzon went up the line to watch the effect. It seemed quite impossible for anything to live a moment under that hell of fire. The German trenches were blotted out by the smoke and the debris. And that bombardment extended for miles back from the front line, and was to endure for a hundred and sixty-eight hours. He had signed orders drawn up by his Commanding Officer of Artillery which had cunningly distributed the fire of the mass of guns at his disposal over every important point in the German defences on his sector–and five other Lieutenant-Generals had signed similar orders.

A week of expectation followed, a week during which the bombardment raved louder than the loudest brief thunderstorm anyone had ever heard; the biggest noise which had shaken the world since it had steeled down into its present shape, louder than avalanches, louder than the crackling of ice-floes or the explosion of volcanoes. The preparations continued without a hitch. Ingenious people solved the problem of finding drinking water for half a million men on that bare chalk plain; ammunition flowed in steadily from railheads to dumps, from dumps to guns; divisions packed themselves neatly into the camps and bivouacs awaiting them. There were no last-minute difficulties, no sudden emergencies. Curzon drove and rode hither and thither through his area and was satisfied. He had done good work for England.

He was stern and unmoved on the morning of July 1st. He shaved himself with a steady hand, long before dawn; he drank his coffee and ate his eggs and bacon (he experienced a momentary distaste for them at first sight, but he fought that down) while the bombardment rose to its maximum pitch. With a calm that was only partly assumed he stalked into the inner headquarters office where Miller and Frobisher, Spiller and Runcorn, Follett and Greven, and a dozen other officers were waiting, drumming on the green-baize tables with their fingers and looking at their watches. Colquhoun was biting his nails. Curzon lit his cigar with care; as he struck the match, under the furtive gaze of his staff, came the moment for the lifting of the barrage. There was a moment's appalling silence, followed by a crash which seemed louder than it was in consequence of the silence which had preceded it. Curzon held the flame to the cigar with steady fingers, drawing slowly until the cigar was lit as well as a good cigar deserved to be lit. As the tobacco flared a hundred and twenty thousand Englishmen were rising up from the shelter of their trenches and exposing their bodies to the lash of the German machine-guns hastily dragged from the dug-outs; but that was no reason for an English general to show un-English emotion.

Even now, despite all the elaborate precautions which had been taken to ensure the prompt passage of messages, despite telephones and buzzers and runners and pigeons and aeroplanes and dispatch riders, there must necessarily be a long wait before the reports came in. Runcorn rose and paced about the cramped space between the tables, to Curzon's unspoken irritation. Greven blew his nose. Colquhoun dealt with a couple of messages whose arrival made everyone stir expectantly, but proved to be no more than railway routine matters.

Then, in a flood, the reports began to pour in. Divisional commanders were reporting progress. The Army Command telephoned, demanding news, describing the result of the attacks on the flanks of the Forty-fourth Corps, issuing hasty orders to meet the new situation. Irascible messages came in form the Corps Headquarters on each side. Miller sat with Curzon, the maps before them, and a tray of coloured pins with which to indicate the situation. Despite the rush and the bustle, there was a strange lack of force about the general tenor of the reports, considered in sum. One unit or other seemed to be always behind the rest with its news, and that gave unreality to the situation. Terry's division had found the wire in their front uncut over wide sectors; it was only in places that they had reached the enemy's front line, and heavy fighting was in progress. Franklin reported that his division was still progressing, but he reported heavy losses–fifty per cent was his estimate, at which Curzon tugged at his moustache with annoyance. The man must be unnerved to say a thing like that. He would have small enough means of knowing yet, and no division could possibly suffer fifty per cent of losses in an hour's attack on an enemy who had just been subjected to seven days' bombardment. Similarly Terry must be exaggerating the amount of uncut wire.

What about Green? Follett brought the message from Green. His men were all back in their trenches again, such as survived. They had made no progress at all. On that instant, Hobday of the Forty-first Corps on the right telephoned. The failure of the Forty-fourth Corps to push forward their right wing–Green's division, in other words–had left their flank exposed. Curzon spoke to Green personally on the telephone. His division must be roused up and sent forward again. The positions in front of it must be stormed at all costs. At all costs, said Curzon with emphasis. No officer could plead ignorance of what that implied, or find excuses for disobedience. Curzon called for Deane, commanding his artillery, and ordered further artillery support for Green. Deane tended to demur; he pleaded the rigours of a set timetable and the disorder which would follow counter-order, but Curzon overrode him.

Sixth Army were on the telephone, demanding amplification of the meagre report Frobisher was doling out to them. Curzon dealt with them. He could not amplify the news yet. He was sending stringent orders to his divisional commanders for more details. But what was coming through was positive enough. As he rang off a glance at the clock surprised him. Time was racing by. According to plan his advance should be a mile deep in the German line by now, yet half of his forces had not advanced at all and the other half were fighting desperately to retain meagre gains. Halleck and the reserve division should be on the move now to reinforce the advance. That must be countermanded, and Halleck thrown in to complete Green's work for him and clear Hobday's flank. Curzon saw confusion ahead; he telephoned for Halleck to come over in person and have his orders explained to him, it would take hours to switch the division across and mount a new attack. Spiller would have to improvise a route with the help of the I.G.C.

Curzon could hardly believe that things could have gone so wrong. He got through to Sixth Army again for more news. The Tenth Corps and the Third Corps had failed worse than his. Only towards the Somme was definite progress being made. For a moment Curzon felt comforted, because other Lieutenant-Generals were worse off than he. But that feeling vanished at once. The failure of the attack meant the failure of the method of colossal bombardment, and Curzon could see no alternative to that method. Stalemate lay ahead–a hideous, unthinkable prospect. In savage desperation he sent the harshest orders he could devise to Terry and to Franklin to attack once more, and to snatch success where failure threatened. He knew he would be obeyed.

In the first few hours on the Somme the British Army lost three times as many men as the Boer War, with all its resounding defeats, had cost altogether. Little by little, as confirmation trickled in throughout the day, Curzon came to realize the truth. The result of the day, despite the capture of Mametz and Montauban and the advance of the French on the right, had been a decided set-back to British arms. The afternoon brought gloom; the night while the fighting still continued, black depression. It was not because of the losses. They could be borne and made up again. It was because the method of breaking through the trench line had failed–a method devised according to the very soundest military idea. Napoleon had said that artillery preparation was necessary for attack–they had employed an artillery preparation greater than the world had ever seen. Careful planning beforehand was desirable–the plans had worked perfectly, without a hitch, up to the moment of proof. Ample reserves–there had been ample reserves in hand. It would have only needed for Curzon that night to have discussed the tactical problems with some hard-bitten subaltern for him to have become convinced that the invention of machine-guns and barbed wire, which Napoleon had never heard of, called for a departure from Napoleon's tactical methods, and if Curzon had once been convinced it would have been hard to unconvince him.

But comfort came in the end, and from higher authority than an infantry subaltern. Hudson, the Sixth Army Chief of Staff, came down in person to explain to Curzon. The examination of prisoners which had been hastily proceeding through the night and revealed the fact that the German losses during the attack and the bombardment had been heavy. Several German units had been ruined. After their Verdun losses the Germans would not be able to stand a prolonged draining of their strength. If the pressure should be kept up long enough the German Army would break completely. Systematic bombardment and attack, relentlessly maintained, would wear them down.

'Their losses are bigger than ours,' said Hudson. 'And if they're only equal to ours we're bound to win in the end.

Hudson paused to sip at the drink at his side, before he brought in carelessly the blessed word which had occurred to someone at G.H.Q. with a more than military vocabulary.

'They key-note of the next series of operations,' said Hudson, 'is attrition.'

'Attrition,' said Curzon thoughtfully, and then he brightened as he realized the implications of the word. There would be no need for an unmilitary abandonment of the offensive; more than that, there would be a plan and a scheme to work to, and a future to look forward to. A General without these was a most unhappy creature, as Curzon's sleepless night had demonstrated to him.

'Yes,' said Curzon. 'I see what you mean, of course.'

'It's like this—' said Hudson, going on to expand his original thesis.

There was excuse to be found for them, and for G.H.Q. too. Anyone could realize the terrifying effects of a bombardment, but no one who had not lurked in a dug-out through one, emerging alive at the end–shaken, frightened, exhausted, perhaps, but alive and still capable of pressing the double button of a machine-gun–could appreciate the possibility of survival.

Two-thirds of yesterday's attack had failed, but there were considerable lengths of the German front line in British hands, where the Forty-fourth Corps and the Seventeenth and the Third had won footholds. From these points the pressure was to be maintained, bombardment and advance alternating. The Germans would go on losing men, and the advance would slowly progress. Something would give way in the end. The German strength would dwindle, their morale would break down under the ceaseless strain of the defensive, and, as a further possibility, the advance would in the end climb up to the top of the rolling crest ahead, and something would simply have to happen then.

Hudson's estimate of the enemy's losses was fantastic–he had selected the highest estimate put forward by the intelligence section, simply because anything less seemed fantastic to him. A month or two of losses on that scale would reduce the German Army to a wreck. There would be corresponding losses on the British side, but the British Army could bear them as long as the leaders kept their nerve–and that was the point which Hudson specially wanted to make with Curzon. Not all corps commanders could be trusted as Curzon could be, to push attacks home relentlessly, applying ceaseless pressure to divisional generals.

So that Curzon was to be maintained in charge of his present sector of the front. He would be supplied with new divisions as fast as they could be brought up to replace his exhausted ones, and he must see to it that the attacks were maintained with all the intensity the situation demanded. It was a high compliment which was being paid to Curzon (or at least both Hudson and Curzon saw it as one). He flushed with pleasure and with renewed hope; he had work to do, a plan to carry out, a goal in front of him, and he was one of the five lieutenant-generals who were charged with the execution of the offensive on which England was pinning her whole trust.

After Hudson's departure Curzon called his staff together. He outlined the work before them, and he quoted the figures of the German losses which Hudson had given him. He looked round at them. Miller, dark, sombre, and reliable, nodded approval; the others, even if they did not approve, had learned by now to keep their faces expressionless in the face of schemes they could not oppose.

'Our old Ninety-first Division is coming up to our sector,' concluded Curzon. 'We know what they can do. What do you suggest, Miller? Hadn't they—'

In this fashion began the orgy of bloodshed which is now looked upon as the second phase of the Battle of Somme, three agonizing months during which divisions, 'fattened up' in back areas on quiet sectors, were brought up into the line to dissipate in one wild day the strength built up during the previous months. They went into action ten thousand infantry strong; they won a few yards of shell-torn ground, a few trees of a shattered wood, or the cellars of a few houses, and they came out four thousand strong, to be filled up with recruits and made ready for the next ordeal. Kitchener's Army found its grave on the Somme just as the old Regular Army had done at Ypres.

Curzon worked with grim determination during those three months. There was always pressure to be applied to someone–transport officers who said that a thing could not be done, major-generals who flinched from exposing their divisions to some fresh ordeal, artillery colonels who pleaded that their men were on the point of exhaustion. He did his duty with all his nerve and all his strength, as was his way, while the higher command looked on him with growing approval; he was a man after their own heart, who allowed no consideration to impede him in the execution of his orders.

21

One morning there was a private letter (it was marked 'Private' on the envelope) for Curzon, and the sight of it gave Curzon an unpleasant sensation of disquietude. It was addressed to 'General Herbert Curzon', care of the regimental depot of the Twenty-second Lancers, and has been sent on to him via the War Office–and it was from Aunt Kate. He hesitated before he opened it; he did not want to open it; it was only by an effort of will he forced himself to open it and read it.

> Dear Bertie,
>
> Just a line to wish you all success and to ask you if you will do a favour for your aunt, because I have not asked you ever for one before. Our Dick had got to go out to the Front again. He was wounded and came back to the hospital, but now he is better and he is going back next week. Bertie, he does not want to go. He does not say so, but I know. He has done his bit because he has been wounded and has got the Military Medal. I showed him something about you that I saw in the paper, and he said joking that he wished you would give him a job. He said he would

rather clean out your stables than go over the top at Ginchy again. He said it as if he didn't mean it, but I know. Bertie, would you do that for me. You have only got to ask for him. Corporal R. Cole, 4/29 London Regiment, Duke of Connaught's Own. I swear that he won't say he is your cousin to your friends. Because he is your cousin, Bertie. He is my only son and I want him to come back to me safe. Please, Bertie, do this for me because I am only an old woman now. He doesn't know I am writing to you. It doesn't matter to you who cleans out your stables. Your Uncle Stanley and Maud send their love. Maud had a fine big baby boy now. We call him Bertie and he is ever such a tartar. Please do that for me.

Your loving
Aunt Kate

Curzon sat and fingered the letter. Aunt Kate was quite right when she said it did not matter to him who cleaned out his stables. Curzon really had not troubled his mind with regard to the dispensing of patronage at his headquarters. He had no knowledge of how the grooms and clerks and servants there had been appointed to their soft jobs–nor would he trouble as long as they were efficient. A single telephone message would suffice to give him Corporal Richard Cole's services–the 4/29 London was in Terry's division and coming back to the line soon.

But Curzon had no intention of sending for him; he formed the resolution after only brief reflection. Cole had his duty to do like everyone else, and there was no reason why he should be selected rather any other for a safe billet. Curzon had always frowned on favouritism–he reminded himself how he had sent back Horatio Winter-Willoughby to regimental duty. He was not going to deprive the fighting forces of the services of a valuable trained N.C.O. He tore the letter up slowly. He was glad that he had reached that decision, because otherwise a request by a Lieutenant-General for the services of a corporal would have been sure to excite comment, and Cole would be sure to talk about the relationship, and Greven would hear, and from Greven the news would reach the Duchess, and from the Duchess it would go on to Emily. He did not want Emily to know he had a Cockney cousin–to shake that thought from him he plunged back furiously into his work.

In fact he was able to forget all about his cousin again in the stress and strain of the last weeks of the Battle of the Somme, and the excitement of the first entry into action of the tanks, and the need to combat the growing paralysis caused by the October rains and the exhaustion of his units. Only was he reminded of the affair when yet another letter, addressed in the same way, was put into his hands. There was a telegraph form inside addressed to Shoesmith Road, Brixton–'Regret to inform you Corporal R. Cole killed in action Nov. 1st.' There was only one word on the sheet of notepaper enclosing the telegraph form, and that was printed large–MURDERER.

His hands shook a little as he tore the papers into fragments, and his face lost a little of its healthy colour. He had never been called that before. It was a hideous and unjust accusation, and it made him furiously angry; he was angrier still–although he did not know it–because he was subconsciously aware that there were plenty of people who would most unreasonably have agreed with Aunt Kate. He did not like to be thought a murderer even by fools with no knowledge of duty and honour.

The memory of the incident poisoned his thoughts for a long time afterwards. When he went on leave–his first leave for eleven months–he was almost moved to confide in Emily about it. He knew she would appreciate and approve of his motives, and he was in need of approval, but he put the insidious temptation aside. His common sense told him that a moment's sympathy would not be worth the humiliation of confessing the deceit he had practised for two years; and yet it was his need of sympathy which made him put his arms round Emily and kiss her with an urgency which brought colour to her cheeks and expectancy into her eyes.

After the stress and turmoil and overwork of active service it seemed like Paradise to be back in the quiet West Country, to ride a horse through the deep Somerset lanes with Emily beside him and not a soldier in sight. The freakishness of Fate had placed him in a position wherein he was compelled to work with his brain and his nerves. He had been gifted with a temperament ideal for a soldier in the presence of the enemy, knowing no fear and careless of danger, and yet his duty now consisted in never encountering danger, in forcing responsibility on others, in desk work and paper work and telephone work which drained his vitality and sapped his health.

Emily was worried about him. Despite the healthy red-brown of his cheeks (nothing whatever would attenuate that) she fretted over the lines in his forehead and the increasing whiteness of his hair, even though she tried to look upon these changes in him as her sacrifice for King and Country. There was anxiety in her eyes when she looked at him while they were in the train returning to London–the Duke had expressed a wish to have a long talk with Curzon before he went back to France, and, as he could not leave his official duties, Curzon was spending a day and night of his leave in London although Emily had met him at Folkestone and carried him straight off to her beloved Somerset.

The Duke was worried about the progress and conduct of the war. While talking with Curzon he seemed incapable of coming out with a downright statement or question or accusation. He listened to Curzon's bluff phrases, and said 'H'm', and stroked his chin, but an instant later he harked back again, seeking reassurance. Curzon found it difficult to understand his drift. Curzon was quite ready to admit that the offensive on the Somme had been quenched in the mud without decisive results, but he was insistent that it had done much towards bringing victory within reach. The German Army was shattered, bled white; and if it had not rained so continuously in October, just when the offensive had reached Sailly-Saillisel and Bouchavesnes on the crest of the ridge, the decisive victory might have taken place then and there.

'H'm,' said the Duke, and after a pause he harked back once more to the aspect of the question which was specially worrying to him. 'The casualties are heavy.'

The Duke felt that that was a very mild way of putting it, considering the terrible length of the daily lists–Englishmen were dying far faster than in the Great Plague.

'Yes,' said Curzon. 'But they're nothing to what the German casualties are like. Intelligence says—'

The conclusions that the General Staff Intelligence drew from the material collected by their agents and routine workers were naturally as optimistic as they could be. The material was in general correct, but necessarily vague. Exact figures could not be expected, and the data accumulated only permitted of guesses. Pessimists would have guessed much lower. Equally naturally to Curzon and his fellows approved of the conclusions reached by Intelligence. If this plan of attrition failed, there was no plan left to them, only the unthinkable alternative of stagnation in the trenches. With just that unmilitary confession of helplessness before them they would need a great deal of convincing that their only plan was unsuccessful.

'You're sure about this?' asked the Duke. He wanted to be convinced too. The task of finding someone to win the war was a heavy one for the Cabinet.

'Quite sure,' said Curzon, and he went on to say that as soon as fine weather permitted a resumption of the offensive a breakdown of the German defence could be looked for quite early. Tanks? Yes, he imagined that tanks might be a useful tactical accessory; they had not yet fought on his front at all, so that he could not speak from experience. It would take a great number of tanks, all the same, to kill the number of Germans necessary for victory. Only infantry, of course, can really win battles–the Duke was so eager to learn that Curzon could restate this axiom of military science without impatience. Keep the infantry up to strength, build up new divisions if possible, keep the ammunition dumps full, and victory must come inevitably.

'I'm glad,' said the Duke, 'that I've had this chance of talking to you. We've been a bit–despondent, lately, here in London.'

'There's nothing to be despondent about,' said Curzon. A despondent soldier means a bad soldier; Curzon would be as ashamed of being despondent as of being afraid–he would see little difference between the two conditions, in fact.

It may have been this conversation between the Duke and Curzon which turned the scale of history. Perhaps because of it the Cabinet allowed the Expeditionary Force to spend that winter preparing once more for an offensive on the present lines, and were only confirmed in their decision by the bloody failure of the great French attack launched by Nivelle with his new unlimited ideas. Curzon was at Arras when Nivelle failed, waiting to engage in his eternal task of sending divisions through the Moloch-fires of assaults on the German lines. So serious was the news that a general assembly of British generals was called to discuss it–Curzon was there, and half a dozen other Corps commanders, and Hudson and his chief, and Wayland-Leigh from the Sixth Army with Norton. When Curzon climbed out of his car with Miller behind him and saw the array of cars already arrived, and the different pennons drooping over the radiators, he guessed that something serious was in the wind. Wayland-Leigh's car stopped immediately after his, and Curzon waited to greet his old commander before going in. The Buffalo was lame with sciatica, and he took Curzon's arm as they went up the steps.

'Christ knows,' said Wayland-Leigh, hobbling along, 'what this new how d'ye do's about. Ouch! I bet the French have got 'emsleves into trouble again.'

Wayland-Leigh's shrewd guess was correct. When everyone was seated on the gilt chairs in the big dining-room of the château an officer on the General Staff at G.H.Q. rose to address the meeting. It was Hammond, very tall, very thin, with no chin and a lisp, but with a reputation which belied his appearance.

'Gentlemen,' said Hammond. 'The news I have to tell you is such that we have not dared to allow it to reach you by the ordinary channels. It must not be written about, or telephoned about, or even spoken about outside this room.'

He paused and looked round him as he said this, and one general looked at another all round the room, before Hammond went on.

'The French Army has mutinied.'

That made everyone stir in their seats. Half a dozen generals cleared their throats nervously. There were alarmists among them who had sometimes thought of mutiny.

'As you all know, gentlemen, the great French offensive on the Chemin-des-Dames has failed with very heavy losses, just as you all predicted. General Nivelle promised a great deal more than he could perform.'

Wayland-Leigh and Norton grinned at the mention of Nivelle's name, and others followed their example. Nivelle, with his gift of the gab and his vaulting ambitions, was an object of amusement to the British staff. They smiled when he was spoken about, like a music-hall audience when a comedian refers to Wigan or to kippers. But Hammond was deadly serious.

'The point is,' he went on, 'eight French divisions have refused to obey orders. It is not as serious as it might be, gentlemen. There has been no Socialist movement.' The word 'Bolshevik' had not yet crept into the English language, or Hammond would have used it. 'There are no political feelings at all in these divisions. They only objected to what they call unnecessary waste of life. It is a case of—'

'Cold feet,' interjected Wayland-Leigh, and got a laugh.

'Objection to a continuance of the offensive,' said Hammond. 'Nivelle has resigned and Pétain has taken his place. He is rounding up the mutineers with loyal troops. I don't know what measures Pétain will take–I suppose we all know what we should recommend to him. But the fact remains, gentlemen, that for this summer the duty of maintaining pressure upon the enemy will fall on us alone. We must attack, and attack again, and go on attacking. Otherwise the enemy will undoubtedly take the opportunity of falling on our gallant allies.'

There was a sneer in Hammond's tone at these last two words–for some time there had been a tendency in the British Army to say those words with just that same intonation; for a year no English staff officer had spoken of *les braves Belges* and meant it.

'So, gentlemen, the battle at present in progress at Arras will continue. The Second Army will deliver the attack at Messines which they have had ready for some time, while plans will be perfected for a transference of pressure to the northern face of the Ypres salient and drive to clear the Belgian coast. In this fashion, gentlemen—'

Hammond turned to the big map on the wall behind him, and introduced his hearers to the Third Battle of Ypres. It was not the Third Battle of Ypres as the long-suffering infantry were to know it. Polygon Wood and Paschendaele were mentioned, but only in passing. The concentrated efforts of the British Army for a whole summer would carry them far beyond these early objectives.

Hammond indicated the vital railway junctions far to the rear which must eventually fall to them; and he lingered for a moment over the relief it would afford the Navy in the struggle against submarines if the whole Belgian coast should be cleared.

Hammond's optimism was infectious, and his lisping eloquence was subtle. Curzon's mood changed, like that of the others, from one of do-or-die to one of hope and expectancy. There were seventy divisions, and tanks for those who believed in them, guns in thousands, shells in tens of millions. Surely nothing could stop them this time, no ill fortune, no bad weather, certainly not machine-guns nor barbed wire. The enemy *must* give way this time. All a successful attack demanded was material and determination. They had the first in plenty, and they would not be found lacking in the second. Curzon felt resolution surging up within him. His hands clenched as they lay in his lap.

The mood endured as his car bore him back to his own headquarters, and when he called his staff about him his enthusiasm gave wings to his words as he sketched out the approaching duties of the Forty-fourth Corps. Runcorn and Deane and Frobisher caught the infection. They began eagerly to outline the plans of attack which Army Headquarters demanded; they were deeply at work upon them while the divisions under their direction were expending themselves in the last long-drawn agony of Arras.

22

Curzon wrote to Emily that there was no chance at all of his taking leave this summer. He realized with a little regret that an officer at the head of an Army Corps would be far less easily spared for a few days than any regimental officer or divisional general. The troops of the line had their periods of rest, but he had none. His responsibility was always at full tension. He was signing plans for the future at the same time as he was executing those of the present. He was responsible for the discipline and movement and maintenance and activity of a force which sometimes exceeded a hundred thousand men.

And he was lonely in his responsibility too, although loneliness meant little to him. Save for Emily he had gone friendless through the world among his innumerable acquaintances. He would sometimes, during that summer of 1917, have been desperately unhappy if he had stopped to think about happiness. But according to his simple code a man who had attained the rank of Lieutenant-General, was the son-in-law of a duke, and had a loving wife, could not possibly be unhappy. There could be no reason for it. Unreasonable unhappiness was the weakness of poets and others with long hair, not of soldiers, and so he believed himself to be happy as the British Army plunged forward into the slaughter of Paschendaele.

For fifteen days–half as long again as at the Somme–twice the number of guns as at the Somme had pounded the German lines. Curzon's staff, Hobday's staff on his right, the staffs of six other army corps and of three

Armies had elaborated the most careful orders governing the targets to be searched for, the barrages to be laid, the tactics to be employed. The Tank Corps had early pointed out that this sort of bombardment would make the ground impassable for tanks, but after the success at Messines Curzon and all the other generals had decided that the tank was a weapon whose importance had been overrated, and it stood to reason that fortifications should not be attacked without preliminary bombardment.

Once more the reports came in describing the opening of the battle–large sections of the German line overrun, the advance once more held up, the usual heavy fighting in the German second line. Once more the weather broke, and the country, its drainage system battered to pieces, reverted under the unceasing rain to the condition of primeval swamp from which diligent Flemish peasants had reclaimed it in preceding centuries. Already intelligent privates in the ranks were discussing whether the Germans had a secret method of bringing rain whenever they wanted it for tactical purposes.

Curzon in his headquarters, as the days went on and the rain roared on the roof, began almost to feel a sinking of heart. The toll of casualties was mounting, and, significantly, the number of the sick, while progress was inordinately slow. Those optimistic early plans had envisaged an advance a mile deep, and here they were creeping forward only a hundred yards at a time. Tanks had proved utterly useless in the swamp. The Germans with their usual ingenuity and foresight had studded the country with concrete fortresses to hold the line where trenches were impossible to dig, and attacks were horribly costly. There were moments when Curzon hesitated before forcing hinself to read the casualty figures of the divisions he had sent into action.

His determination was maintained by the information which Army Headquarters supplied to him. The German losses were heavier than the British; the German morale was on the point of giving way; any moment might see a general collapse of the enemy's army. When Curzon rode out to inspect his long-suffering divisions in their rest billets he could see for himself that they were as reliable as ever, and that if they were not as high-spirited and hopeful as the early divisions of Kitchener's Army they were still ready, as he knew British soldiers always would be, to pour out their blood at the command of their leaders–and three years of eliminating had given the British Army leaders like Curzon, who could not be turned back by any difficulties, nor frightened by any responsibilities.

Cheered on by the encouragement of the highest command, Curzon threw himself into the work of maintaining the pressure upon the Germans, flinging his divisions, each time they had been filled up with drafts, once more in assaults upon the enemy's line battering away with the fiercest determination to win through in the end. Under his directions and those of his colleagues the British Army used up its strength in wild struggles like those of a buffalo caught in a net, or a madman in a straitjacket, rather than submit to what seemed the sole alternative, which was to do nothing.

A week or two more–no longer than that–of these nightmare losses and thwarted attacks would see the end of the war, a complete disintegration of the whole German front in the north-east; that was what the Army command deduced from their Intelligence reports. Victory was in sight. Then suddenly

Hudson, the Army Chief of Staff, dropped in with a bombshell. The Civilian Government at home had grown frightened at the casualty lists, and were losing their nerve, as might be expected of civilians. There was a suggestion that the Government–the 'frocks' as one famous staff officer significantly and humorously called them–were actually proposing to interfere with the military conduct of the war and to force some scheme of their own upon the command.

No self-respecting general could put up with that, of course. There would be wholesale resignations, and, if the Government persisted and could withstand the effect of these resignations upon public opinion, there would be more than resignations. There would be dismissals, until the Army was under the command of the pliant and subservient boot-licking type of general who always wins promotion under civilian command. It was not idle talk, but an imminent, urgent possibility; in fact, to such lengths were the civilians going that the politicians were actually coming out to France to see for themselves, not on the customary sight-seeing trip, but because they were pleased to doubt the word of the soldiers as to the present state of affairs. Something must be done to impress them immediately.

Curzon was in the heartiest agreement. He was genuinely horrified by what Hudson told him. Civilian interference in military affairs spelt ruin–all his teaching and experience told him that. If the present order of generals was swept away and their places taken by others (Bewly was an example of the type Curzon had in mind) there could be nothing but shame and disaster awaiting the British Army. Curzon did not tell himself that the present state of affairs must be the best possible because it was the present state of affairs, but that was a pointer to his line of thought. Innovations and charlatanry were indissolubly linked in his mind. He called upon his staff to make haste with their plans for the renewed attack upon Paschendaele. The surest reply to these busy-bodies would be a resounding success and thousands of prisoners.

Curzon was shaving early one morning, before the night's reports could arrive, on the third day of that last tragic offensive, when young Follett came into his room.

'G.H.Q. on the telephone, sir,' he said–and the tone of his voice indicated the momentous nature of the occasion. 'They want to speak to you personally.'

Curzon hurried out with the lather drying on his cheeks. In the inmost room of his headquarters Miller was at the telephone, and handed the receiver over to him.

'Curzon speaking,' he said.

'Right. You know who this is?' said the receiver.

'Yes,' said Curzon.

'Is anyone else present in the room in which you are?'

'My B.G.G.S.'

'Send him out.'

Curzon dismissed Miller with a gesture, and, when the door had closed he addressed himself again to the telephone.

'I'm alone now, sir,' he said.

'Then listen, Curzon. You know about the visitors we're entertaining at present?'

'Yes, sir.'

'They're coming to poke their noses about in your sector this morning.'

'Yes, sir.'

'They think we're asking too much of the troops by continuing the attack at Paschendaele. They as good as told me to my face last night that I was lying.'

'Good God!'

'You've got to show 'em they're wrong. What do you think of your corps at the present?'

Curzon reflected for a moment. All his divisions had been through the mill lately except for the good old Ninety-first under Challis.

'I've got nothing that would impress politicians, I'm afraid, at the moment,' said Curzon despondently.

'Well, you must. I don't care what you do. Who's that young A.D.C. that you've got? Greven, isn't it? He ought to be some use in this comic-opera business. Call him in and talk it over with him, and for God's sake remember that something's got to be done.'

Something was done and, as G.H.Q. advised, it was the result of Greven's inspiration.

There is no need to describe the telephone calls and the hurried motor-car journeys which were made in preparation for the politicians' visit. Preparations were hardly completed and Curzon had hardly strolled into the headquarters when an awed young staff officer looked up from his telephone and said: 'They're coming!'

In ten minutes a little fleet of motor cars came rolling up and stopped outside the house. From the radiators flew the pennons of G.H.Q. A motley crowd climbed out of the cars–the khaki and red of the General Staff, and new horizon blue of the French Army, officers in the 'maternity jackets' of the Royal Flying Corps; and among the crowd of uniforms were half a dozen figures in ludicrous civilian clothes. Curzon noted their long hair and shapeless garments with contempt. They gawked about them like yokels at a fair. They were stoop-shouldered and slack. He came forward reluctantly to be introduced.

'This is Lieutenant-General Curzon, sir, commanding the Forty-fourth Corps,' said the senior staff officer present. At the moment of making the introduction the staff officer, his face turned from the civilian, raised his eyebrows in inquiry, and Curzon nodded in return.

'We want to show these gentlemen, General,' said the staff officer, 'something of the troops that have been engaged at Paschendaele. Have you got any specimens on view?'

'Why, yes,' replied Curzon. 'There's the Ninety-first Division coming out of the line now. If we drive over to the cross-roads we ought to meet them.'

'They've had a pretty bad time,' put in Greven, with all the deference expected of a junior staff officer venturing to demur from a suggestion of his chief.

'That's just what we want to see,' put in the leader of the visitors. Yet the stilted artificiality of the conversation could hardly have escaped his attention–his mind was one of the keenest in Europe–had not the circumstances been so entirely natural.

The fleet of motor cars, augmented now by those of the Corps, continued their dreary way through the rain over the jolting *pavé*. Curzon found himself beside a sharp-featured little man whose manner reminded him of Sir Henry's on the first occasion on which he dined at the Duchess's. Curzon was plied with questions throughout the short journey, but none of the answers he gave was particularly revealing. For one thing Curzon had partly acquired the art by now of being uncommunicative without being rude; and for another he was so excited about the outcome of this very doubtful affair that he had hardly any words to spare for a civilian in a suit whose trousers bagged at the knees.

Suddenly the whole *cortège* slowed down and drew up at the side of the road. Everybody got out and splashed about in the slush.

'Here comes the Ninety-first,' said Miller, pointing. Greven pushed himself forward. 'Their numbers seem a little low,' he said, 'but that's only to be expected when they've had ten days in the line.'

The staff officers from G.H.Q. played up nobly. They shielded Curzon, who was the least accomplished actor of them all, by grouping themselves round him and surrounding him with a protective barrage of professsional explanation.

The Ninety-first came trailing down the long, straight road. They had believed that the War held no new surprise for them until today. They had been turned out of their comfortable rest billets at a moment's notice, formed up into column without explanation and sent marching post haste up the road towards the front. Everybody had naturally assumed that they were being sent in to make a new attack or to fill up some gap caused by a German counter-attack, and everybody's spirits had fallen accordingly. Then suddenly at a cross-roads their march had been diverted and they were being marched back post haste away from the line again. The explanation of the manoeuvre entirely escaped them, even when they saw the string of motor cars with fluttering pennons and the group of visitors watching them march by. They had had a fortnight's rest and they were extraordinarily cheered by their reprieve from front-line duty. Naturally they were wet and muddy and weary with their long march through the mud, but their spirits were high. They marched with all the spring and swing of men ready for anything–and this was carefully pointed out to the politicians by the staff officers from G.H.Q. Their mudiness and their wetness were nothing compared with the condition of the troops marching from the line at Paschendaele. Troops after that ordeal hardly had anything human about them; they were generally so sheeted in mud that only the whites of their eyes showed up uncannily out of uniform greyish-brown masks.

'There doesn't seem to be much the matter with these men,' said the sharp-nosed little politician who sat beside Curzon. He sounded disappointed as he said it.

'Of course not,' said Miller breezily.

Reeves, commanding the Rifle Battalion in the division's second brigade, had his men most in hand and was the officer upon whose historic ability Curzon's staff had placed most reliance. The Rifles were marching past the group just when Miller had made his last remark and at a signal from Reeves they broke into a wild burst of cheering. They did not know whom they were cheering nor why, but a British battalion after a fortnight's rest can generally be relied upon to cheer lustily as the call of a popular commanding officer.

'There,' said Miller. 'You'd never hear broken-spirited men cheering like that.'

And soon after that the drenched politicians and staff officers climbed back into their motor cars and returned to G.H.Q. Curzon had done his best for the Army. It would not be his fault if he and his brother soldiers were held back at the moment of victory.

But the rain which had poured down upon prisoners and politicians alike extinguished the last chance of victory. Paschendaele was taken–a statistician might have calculated that the miserable village cost, in the shells hurled against it and in pensions paid to the dependants of the dead, about three hundred times as much as a similar area in the most valuable part of New York covered with intact skyscrapers. The ridge was crowned, but the higher command had decided that there was nothing to be gained by trying to push on. The high hopes of capturing Bruges and Zeebrugge had vanished; even if further efforts could be asked of the troops (as Curzon maintained) there was no chance of keeping the troops in the front line supplied well enough to maintain an offensive across the three miles of shell-torn swamp which they had conquered.

Curzon was informed of this decision in the course of a visit to Sixth Army Headquarters; he was closeted alone with Hudson for a long time. Yet during that interview Hudson was disinclined to discuss the future of the War. His own efforts had ended in failure, and now the Third Army was planning a tank offensive in the Cambrai sector regarding which his opinion was not even being asked. Hudson skirted round controversial subjects with a good deal of tact. He was full of appreciation for Curzon's recent work, and as well as Curzon's relentlessness in command he was pleased to approve of Curzon's handling of the matter of the troops back from the front.

'That was first rate,' said Hudson, grinning. 'It was absolutely convincing–took 'em in completely. Serve 'em right.'

Curzon grinned back. There was joy in the thought that soldiers could outwit politicians in other things as well as military affairs.

'Oh, yes, by the way,' said Hudson. 'You'd better take your leave now while things are quiet.'

'Thank you very much,' said Curzon. 'I was intending to ask you.'

'There'll be a special reason for it though,' said Hudson.

'Indeed?'

'Yes.' Hudson's expression was one of ungainly whimsicality. He fumbled with the papers on his desk to prolong the dramatic moment. 'You will have to be present at an investiture.'

Curzon's heart leapt; he guessed now what Hudson was going to say–he had been modestly hoping for this ever since the Somme.

'The future Sir Herbert Curzon, K.C.M.G.,' said Hudson. 'Greven gets the D.S.O., of course. Yes, I'm glad I'm the first to congratulate you. The very strongest recommendations have gone through both from here and from G.H.Q., and I'm glad that someone in London's got sense enough to act on them. You'd better take your leave from the day after tomorrow.'

Curzon was genuinely delighted with the news. He was glad to be a knight. Socially it was a distinction, and professionally too–only a minority of corps commanders received knighthood. There would be a ribbon and star to wear with full-dress uniform, and it would be pleasant to be addressed by servants as 'Sir Herbert'. Incidentally he had never really liked being announced with his wife as 'General and Lady Emily Curzon.' 'Sir Herbert and Lady Emily Curzon', on the other hand, sounded much better.

When he reached England, Emily was inclined to agree; she was glad for Curzon's sake even though she herself was sorry because the investiture would take him from her side for a day and would compel them to stay in war-time November London, where the Duchess insisted on claiming (or, rather, assumed as a natural right) too much of his attention. The Duchess was full of gossip as usual–the Duke told Curzon that it beat him where she got it from–and although the Navy in its life-and-death struggle with German submarines was occupying more of her attention than the Army nowadays, she found time to try and pump Curzon about the new offensive, regarding which she had heard rumours.

Curzon was relieved to find that it was only rumours which she had heard–many of the leaks of information must have been stopped–and that the main reason for her curiosity was this very vagueness. Offensives of the ordinary sort had no more charm of novelty for London society by now than they had for the men in the trenches, but there was a quality about the new rumours which stimulated her interest. Curzon was tactfully reticent. He knew little enough about this Cambrai stunt as it was, and neither he nor his corps was to be employed. Moreover, it was to be a tank affair, and, frankly, he was not interested in tanks after they had disappointed him at Arras and Paschendaele. His unconcern actually deluded the Duchess into believing that the rumours had been exaggerated, and she went back to her new interest of trying to find out the latest about the new American Expeditionary Force.

However, she called upon Curzon and Emily at their hotel on the evening of the investiture–naturally she wanted to hear about that. So it came about that she was present when a servant came in with the information that the Duke of Bude would like to speak to Sir Herbert Curzon on the telephone.

'I wonder what your father wants, dear,' said the Duchess to Emily during Curzon's absence.

'I can't imagine, mother,' said Emily.

Meanwhile Curzon was standing in the little glass box (which was the home of the telephone at even luxurious hotels in 1917) listening in amazement to the Duke's voice and to the news it was conveying to him with excited volubility.

'There's good news, Curzon,' said the Duke. 'Best since the war began. There's no harm in my telling you–it's being made public as quickly as possible. We've won a big victory.'

'Where?'

'On the Western front, of course. Cambrai.'

'My God!'

'There's no doubt about it. Five miles advance up to now. Five thousand prisoners. Two hundred guns. The cavalry are being brought into action. The war's as good as won. It's the tanks that have done it.'

'God bless my soul.'

Three months of agony at Third Ypres had won no greater result.

'I'll come in later, if you're going to be in, and discuss it with you.'

'Very good.'

Emily and the Duchess thought that Curzon's expression on his return portended bad news; they were relieved when in reply to their startled 'Whatever's the matter?' Curzon told them that England had won a victory. It was irritating in the extreme to Curzon to have to recount that in his absence from France a battle had been won in which his corps had played no part, and that the principal instrument of victory had been a weapon he despised–he remembered his cutting rudeness to his Tank staff officer when the latter had ventured to make suggestions. He could have swallowed the affront of the success of the tank if he and his men had shared in it. As it was he was exceedingly angry; apprehensive, as well, because the Duke's preposterous optimism over the telephone had almost infected him with doubt lest the war should be won before his leave expired. He would be a fool in his own eyes then.

He was hardly as angry as the Duchess, all the same.

'I'll never forgive you, Bertie,' she said bitterly. 'And as for young Gordon, he's finished as far as I'm concerned. Here have I been going round, and whenever anyone's said that there was going to be a big push soon I've said: "Oh, no, I'm quite sure you're wrong. There's not going to be anything of the kind. I know for certain." I shan't be able to hold up my head again.'

Fortunately the Duke on his arrival was able to suggest a very satisfactory way out of the difficulty, presumably by the aid of his political experience.

'Don't worry, my dear,' he said. 'You'll be able to say that you knew about it all the time, but denied the rumours so that the Germans would be lulled into insecurity. You can say that you were acting in obedience to a Royal command, because it was well known that whatever you said was given great attention in Berlin.'

The Duchess thought that a brilliant suggestion.

23

In the morning the newspapers proclaimed England's victory in flaming headlines. There could be no doubt about it. Curzon's appetite for his war-time breakfast (not nearly as appetizing as the ones served him at his headquarters in France) quite failed him as he read. Envy and apprehension between them stirred up strange passions within him, to such an extent that after breakfast he made an excuse to Emily and slipped away to telephone to General Mackenzie at the War Office. He did not dare tell Emily that he was going to suggest that he sacrifice the remainder of his leave in order to make sure of missing no more of the glory which was to be found in France.

But Mackenzie seemed to be in an odd mood.

'I shouldn't worry, if I were you, Curzon,' he said.

'But I don't want to miss anything,' persisted Curzon.

'Well–no, look here, Curzon, take my advice and don't worry.'

'I don't understand I'm afraid.'

'Don't you? Perhaps that's my fault. But on the other hand perhaps it isn't. Now ring off, because I'm busy.'

There was a small grain of comfort in the conversation, Curzon supposed, but it was woefully small. Out in the streets as he went for his walk with Emily, the church bells were ringing a peal of victory, such as London had not heard for three dark years. Emily's happy chatter at his side received small attention from him. He brought tears into her eyes by declining flatly to go to Somerset for the rest of his leave–he felt that he did not dare to quit the centre of affairs and put himself six hours farther away from France. He could picture in his mind's eye the rolling downland on which the victory had been won, and his mind dwelt on the armies pouring forward to victory at that very moment while he was left behind here in England and ignominy

The evening papers told the same tale of a continued advance and of further captures. The whole Press was jubilant, and Curzon remembered bitterly the cautious half-praise which had been grudgingly dealt out to him in the Press (not by name, of course, but by implication) for his greatest efforts at Third Ypres. He began to lose confidence in himself, and when a soldier of Curzon's type loses confidence in himself there is little else for him to lose. He told himself repeatedly, and with truth, that he was not jealous of the success of others. It was not that which was troubling him, but the thought that there was still six days of his leave left.

Then in the morning there was a change. Curzon was no literary critic, but he sensed, even although he would not have been able to label it, the note of caution on the newspaper comments on the progress of the Battle of Cambrai. There was a decided tendency to warn the public not to expect too much. Curzon could imagine the sort of reports which would be coming in to Corps Commanders from Divisional Headquarters–he had received them often enough. Reports of a stiffening resistance, of the arrival of new German divisions at the front, of the establishment of a fresh defensive line which only prolonged bombardment could reduce. He could read the symptoms with certainty, and he knew now that General Mackenzie had been right when he told him not to worry–enough details must already have trickled through to the Imperial General Staff at that early stage of the battle for Mackenzie to have formed his judgment.

So Curzon was fully reconciled to spending the rest of his leave in England, and he brought a new pleasure into Emily's heart by consenting to go down into Somersetshire with her for his last four days. Emily was more anxious and worried about him than she had previously been. Perhaps the revelation of Curzon's attitude during the Battle of Cambrai had shown her an aspect of his character with which she had not been previously familiar, or perhaps with her woman's intuition she could guess at the changing state of affairs on the Western Front more accurately than Curzon could. In either case she had a premonition of danger. She clung to Bertie during those four idyllic days in Somerset.

There was just enough petrol in the Duke's reserves to supply the motor car which bore them across the loveliest and most typical stretches of the English countryside–lovely even in a war-time December–from Somerset to Folkestone at the end of Curzon's leave. Emily found it hard to keep her lips steady as she said good-bye to her husband at Folkestone Harbour, where the stream of khaki flowed steadily by on its way to the ships and to France; and Emily's cheeks were unashamedly wet with tears. Curzon actually had to swallow hard as he kissed her good-bye; he was moved inexpressibly by the renewal of the discovery that there was actually a woman on earth who could weep for him. His voice was gruff, and he patted her brusquely on the back before he turned away, spurs clinking, past the barriers where the red-hatted military police sprang to stiff attention, to where the steamer waited against the jetty, crammed nearly solid with pack-laden soldiers.

At the headquarters of the Forty-fourth Corps Curzon found a new atmosphere. The revelation of the efficacy of tanks to break the trench line had some too late. The alterations of plan forced on the Tank Corps Staff by G.H.Q. had reduced material results to a minimum, and occasioned such losses in tanks that it would be some time before a tank force sufficient to launch a new offensive could be accumulated. Meanwhile the collapse of Russia meant that Germany could transfer a million troops from East to West. Miller had ready for Curzon a long list of new German divisions already identified, and more were to be added to it every day. Where for three years three Allied soldiers confronted two Germans, there was now an equality, and there seemed to be every prospect that before long the balance would alter further yet until the Germans would possess a numerical superiority, which they had not been able to boast since First Ypres. The staff maps which showed the order of battle of the contending armies indicated an ominous clustering of the black squares of German divisions in front of the British line.

Curzon pored over them for long, scratching his cropped head, and turning repeatedly to the detailed trench maps as he forced himself to concentrate on this unusual problem of defence, with the help of the appreciations to which Miller and Frobisher devoted long hours in drawing up. He presided at long weary conferences with his divisional generals and their staffs, when defensive tactics were discussed. Universally the schemes laid before him took it for granted that ground would be lost in the first stages of the battle should the enemy attack, and he was puzzled at this. He tugged at his whitened moustache as he listened or read. This almost voluntary cession of soil was quite opposed to the traditions inherited from Wayland-Leigh, and the prospect irked him sorely. There had been a few occasions when the Forty-fourth Corps had yielded up blood-soaked fragments of trench in the height of a battle, but they had been very few. He would have preferred to have issued a few stringent orders to hold on to the front line to the last gasp, and threatening with a court-martial any officer who retreated. That was the kind of order which he understood and would have been ready to execute.

But Miller was able to back up his suggestions with a huge mass of orders from Sixth Army, bearing Hudson's signature, in which the greatest urgency was laid upon the need for the economy of life. Two-thirds of a million casualties, incurred at Arras and Paschendaele, had forced the British Army, for the first time in two years, to worry about losses. Curzon found the restriction irksome and unnatural. He had grown used to handling unlimited supplies of men and material, and in the Forty-fourth Corps a convention had grown up under which the prowess of a division was measured by the number of its men who were killed.

'Confound it, Miller,' he said angrily. 'You're surely not proposing that we should give up Saint-Victor like this?'

A hundred thousand men had died so that the ruins of Saint-Victor should be included in the British line.

'I think we'd better, sir,' said Miller. 'You see, it's like this. There's a weak flank *here*. We can't be sure of holding the sector along here to here. That'll mean a salient if we hang on to Saint-Victor. It would be all right if we could afford the men, but—'

'Oh, all right, have it your own way,' said Curzon testily. He could not withstand arguments about possible losses.

Into this atmosphere of nervous preparation there came a fresh bombshell from Sixth Army headquarters. The Forty-fourth Corps were being taken out of the line they were preparing to hold and transferred to take over a sector held up to that time by the French.

'Yes, I'm sorry about it,' said Hudson, when Curzon hotly denounced the scheme over the telephone to him. 'You don't think I want it, do you? My own idea is that G.H.Q. have been weak. We oughtn't to stretch our line any farther. But we've got to, old man, and there's an end of it. You'll find your new sector a bit weak. Buckle too, old man, and get it strengthened while you've got time.'

Weak it certainly was. Divisional generals and brigadiers, when the transfer was effected, inundated Corps headquarters with complaints regarding the inadequacy of the wiring, the absence of support trenches, and so on. Curzon passed on the complaints to Hudson.

'What do you expect from the French?' said Hudson. 'They can't fight and they can't work, and they expect us to do both for them. I can't help it. We've picked the Forty-fourth Corps for this sector for that special reason. If anyone can hold it, you can, Curzon, old chap. We're relying on you.'

Under this stimulus Curzon threw himself into the work of strengthening his line, while Miller and Frobisher and the others slaved at drawing up new orders to cover the changed conditions. Gone were the days when the front of the Forty-fourth Corps was marked out from all others by nightly fireworks and exceptional activity. Curzon's major-general had no desire to attract hostile attention to themselves. The waste of a night of labour in consequence of a barrage put down by the enemy was a disaster. They sought to extract as much labour from their men as they could–as much as the sacrifices of Paschendaele had left spirit in the men to give.

Curzon studied the new orders which Miller drew up. There were three divisions in front line and one in support–the attenuated divisions which the recent reduction in establishments had left to him. It was a woefully weak force, and as far as he could gather from a study of Sixth Army orders, and those issued by Fifth and Second Armies, there was precious little reinforcement to expect. At first sight the prospect was gloomy. There could be no doubting the menace of the accumulation of German forces in front of him, and the reports which Intelligence kept sending in of the piling up of German artillery and transport. Curzon actually experienced a quailing in his stomach as he envisaged a future of ruin and defeat. The inconceivable was at hand.

Largely because it was inconceivable to him Curzon later took heart. He forced himself to remember the offensives he himself had commanded and directed. Once he had looked upon them as tremendous victories, but, now, in a fresh light, he did not value them so highly. After all, what had they brought? A few square miles of ground, a few tens of thousands of casualties, and then stagnation. Why should he fear that the Germans would achieve more? They had no tanks worth mentioning with which to bring off a surprise like Cambrai. They had no new weapon, and would be compelled to fight with the old ones. When their bombardment commenced there would be ample time to move fresh divisions up to meet the assault–he remembered the number of times when he had imagined himself to be on the verge of victory, and had been held back by the arrival of German reserves; he remembered his exasperation on hearing of the identification of new divisions in his front. He forced himself to realize that he had launched attacks with a fourfold, fivefold superiority of numbers, and that not upon a settled piece of front, but on one hastily built up in the midst of a bombardment, and he had never broken through yet. He could rely upon his men to oppose a sturdier resistance than the Germans, and upon his own will to hold them together during the crisis–he set his mouth hard when he thought of that.

Moreover, the tactical arrangements of which he was approving would cost the Germans dear. There were a whole series of strong points against which the German waves would break in red ruin–how often had he not flung whole divisions unavailingly upon strong points in the enemy's line? He felt that he could await the attack with confidence, whatever might be the boastings of Ludendorff and his men.

'Intelligence,' said Miller, shuffling through a sheaf of reports, 'keep on insisting that the push is coming on March 21st. They say they've confirmed it a dozen different ways. Cavendish would bet his life on it. Sixth Army says so, too.'

'They may be right,' said Curzon. 'It doesn't matter to a day or two, except that the later they leave it the stronger we can make our line. I should have liked another week or two, myself. But beggars can't be choosers–I mean when you're on the defensive you can't expect to choose the day to be attacked on.'

24

Curzon presided at the dinner of the staff of the Forty-fourth Corps on the night of March 20th. He remembered how Wayland-Leigh had provided champagne on the eve of other battles, and he sent Greven all the way back to Amiens by car in order to obtain a full supply of the Clicquot 1900 which Curzon specially favoured. Conditions were a little different from those other evenings, for Terry and Whiteman, commanding two of the divisions in the line, had been compelled to refuse Curzon's invitation on the ground that they dared not leave their headquarters for so long. But Franklin was there, red-faced and be-ribboned, and Challis–for the glorious old Ninety-first Division had come back under Curzon's orders. Challis sat silently as usual, handling his knife and fork so as not to draw attention to his maimed hand, about which he was morbidly sensitive.

The dinner was dull enough at first, because everyone present was overtired, and the smooth flow of conversation was continually being checked by interruptions as messages came in which could only be dealt with by particular individuals. The wine only loosened tongues gradually, but by degrees a buzz of talk grew up round the table. Stanwell told his celebrated story of how once when he had a bad cold he had been deputed to show a sight-seeing party of important civilians round the front. They had arrived in the dark, and his sore throat had compelled him to whisper as he guided them to where they were spending the night–'Step wide here, please,' 'Stoop under this wire, please.'

At last one of the civilians whispered back to him: 'How far off are the Germans?'

'Oh, about ten miles.'

'Then what the hell are we whispering like this for?'

'I don't know why *you* are, but I've got a cold.'

Everyone laughed at that, even those who had heard it before; it was always good to hear of civilians and politicians making fools of themselves. Milward, the gas officer, down at the foot of the table (the Irregulars were dining with the Regulars on this special occasion) was tempted to tell how he had pleaded for a year with Curzon to experiment with dichlorethyl sulphide–mustard gas–and had been put off because he could not guarantee many deaths, but only thousands of disablements.

'We want something that will kill,' Curzon had said, and the British Army postponed the use of mustard gas until the Germans had proved its efficiency.

Milward almost began to tell this story, but he caught Curzon's eye along the length of the table and forebore. Curzon noticed his change of expression, and with unusual sensitiveness felt Milward's slight hostility. As host it was his duty to keep the party running smoothly; as commanding officer it was his duty too. He remembered Wayland-Leigh on the night before Loos quoting Shakespeare as he toasted the advance to the Rhine. He fingered his glass. There was no imminent advance before them, only a desperate defensive. Into his mind drifted a fragment which he remembered of one of Lewis Waller's speeches in the old days when he was playing Henry V.

'Come the four corners of the world in arms and we shall shock them,' said Curzon, turning to Challis on his right.

'Er–yes. Yes. Quite,' said Challis taken by surprise.

The presence of so many senior officers and the small number of young subalterns present prevented the evening developing into the sort of wild entertainment which Curzon had so often experienced in cavalry messes. The junior ranks were unusually quiet, too. Several of them withdrew early on the truthful plea that they had work to do, and Franklin, who was a determined bridge player, quietly collected a four and settled down, rather rudely and unsociably, Curzon thought.

He went out and stared through the darkness towards the line. The night was absolutely still. There was an aeroplane or two droning in the distance, but the sound of their passage was louder than any noise of guns from the front. The bobbing points of light which marked the line of trenches on the horizon were far fewer than he had ever noticed before. There was no breath of wind; the stars were just visible in a misty sky. Curzon went to bed. If Intelligence's forecast was correct he would need all his energies for the morrow. He told Mason to call him at five o'clock.

Curzon was soundly asleep when Mason came in–he had the trick of sleeping sound until the exact moment when he had planned to wake. Mason had to touch his shoulder to rouse him.

'Is it five o'clock?' said Curzon, moving his head on the pillow, with his moustache lopsided.

'It's four-thirty, sir,' said Mason. 'Here's Mr Greven wants to speak to you, sir.'

Curzon sat up.

'Bombardment's started, sir,' said Greven. 'Been going five minutes now.'

The house was trembling to the sound. A thousand German batteries–more guns than the whole world put together had possessed before the war–were firing at once.

'Mason, fill my bath,' said Curzon, leaping from the bed in his blue and white pyjamas.

'I've done it, sir,' said Mason.

'Any reports?' asked Curzon, flinging off his pyjamas.

'Not yet, sir,' said Greven.

'No, of course there wouldn't be,' said Curzon. Not for two days did he expect any vital report–the Germans would be fools of they attacked after a briefer bombardment than that.

Curzon had his bath, and shaved, and dressed, and walked into his headquarters office to hear the latest news before he had his breakfast.

'Bombardment's heavy, sir,' said Miller, sitting at a telephone. 'Gas, mostly. Queer that they're using gas at this stage of the preparation. And there's thick fog all along the line. I've warned everyone to expect local raids.'

'Quite right,' said Curzon, and went off to eat porridge and bacon and eggs.

When he had eaten his breakfast he came back again. Miller seemed unusually worried.

'Something very queer's going on, sir,' he said. 'Back areas are coming in for as much as the front line. They're flooding places with gas.'

He proffered half a dozen reports for inspection.

'And the cross-roads behind the line are catching it as well. *We've* never spread a bombardment out like this.'

'I expect they think they know better than us,' said Curzon lightly.

'Terry's reporting that all communication with his front line units has been broken already, but that's only to be expected, of course,' said Miller.

'Yes. Any raids?'

'Nothing yet, sir.'

Curzon found his stolidity a little shaken by Miller's alarmist attitude. There must be a long bombardment before the attack; in theory there would be no need to do anything for days, and yet–Curzon could not bring himself to order his horse and take his customary morning's exercise. He paced restlessly about headquarters instead. The thick ground mist showed no sign of lifting; the roar of the bombardment seemed to have increased in intensity.

When he came back Frobisher was speaking excitedly into a telephone.

'Yes,' he was saying. 'Yes,' and then he broke off. 'Hallo! Hallo! Oh, hell,' and he put the receiver back with a gesture of annoyance.

'Wire's gone, I suppose. That was General Whiteman, sir. Attack's begun. That's all I could hear.'

An orderly came running in with a message brought by a carrier pigeon and Frobisher snatched if from him. The attack had undoubtedly begun, and confusion descended upon headquarters.

Incredibly, it seemed, the line was crumbling along the whole corps front, and along the fronts of the corps on either flank as well. Curzon could hardly believe the reports which were coming in. One of the chief duties of a general is to sort out the true from the false, but here it was impossible to believe anything. One or two strong points in the front line whose communications had survived reported that they were holding out without difficulty; the entire absence of news from others might merely mean a rupture of communication. And yet from here and there in the second line came reports of the German advance–so far back in some places that Curzon felt inclined to dismiss them as the result of over-imagination on the part of the officers responsible. The mist and the gas were causing confusion; and the German bombardment had been cunningly directed so as to cause as much havoc as possible in the means of communication. Curzon found himself talking to an artillery colonel who was reporting by telephone that the Germans were assaulting his battery positions.

'Are you sure?' asked Curzon.

'Sure? We're firing over open sights with fuses set at zero,' blazed the colonel at the other end. 'God damn it, sir, d'you think I'm mad?'

Through all the weak places in the British line–and they were many–the German attack was pouring forward like a tide through a faulty dyke. The strong points were being steadily cut off and surrounded–there was no heroic expenditure of German life to storm them by main force. Little handfuls of machine gunners, assiduously trained, were creeping forward here and there, aided by the fog, taking up tactical positions which destroyed all possibility of unity in the defence.

Holnon and Dallon were lost. As the afternoon came Curzon sent orders to Challis and the Ninety-first Division to move up into the line and stop the advance. His old Ninety-first could be relied upon to do all their duty. Guns, ammunition dumps, bridges, all were falling intact into the hands of the enemy. At nightfall the British Army seemed to be on the verge of the greatest disaster it had ever experienced, and Curzon's frantic appeals to Army Headquarters were meeting with no response.

'We've got no reserves to give you at all,' said Hudson. 'You'll have to do the best you can with the Ninety-first. It'll be four days at least before we can give you any help. You've just got to hold on, Curzon. We know you'll do it.'

All through the night the bombardment raved along the line. Challis was reporting difficulties in executing his orders. Roads were under fire, other roads were blocked with retreating transport. He could get no useful information from his fellow divisional generals. But he was not despairing. He was deploying his division where it stood, to cover what he guessed to be the largest gap opening in the British line. Curzon clung to that hope. Surely the Ninety-first would stop the Huns.

At dawn Franklin reported that he was shifting his headquarters–the German advance had reached that far. There was no news from Terry at all. He must have been surrounded, or his headquarters hit by a shell–four motor cyclists had been sent to find him, and none had returned. The coloured pins on Miller's map indicated incredible bulgings of the line.

'Message from Whiteman, sir,' said Frobisher, white-cheeked. 'He's lost all his guns. Doesn't know where Thomas's brigade is. And he says Stanton's is legging it back as fast as it can, what there is left of it.'

That meant danger to the right flank of the Ninety-first. Before Curzon could reply Miller called to him.

'Challis on the telephone, sir. He says both flanks are turned. There are Huns in Saint-Félice, and nothing can get through Boncourt 'cause of mustard gas. Shall he hold on?'

Should he hold on? If he did the Ninety-first would be destroyed. If he did not there would be no solid point in the whole line, and in the absence of reserves there was no knowing how wide the gap would open. Could he trust the Ninety-first to hold together under the disintegrating stress of a retreat in the presence of the enemy; He went over to the telephone.

'Hallo, Challis.'

'Yes, sir.'

'What are your men like?'

'All right, sir. They'll do anything you ask of them–in reason.'

'Well—'

Frobisher came running over to him at that moment with a scrap of paper which an orderly had brought in–a message dropped from an aeroplane. It bore only three important words, and they were 'Enemy in Félcourt'. At that rate the Germans were far behind Challis's right flank, and on the point of intercepting his retreat. There could be no extricating the Ninety-first now.

'I can't order you to retreat, Challis,' said Curzon. 'The Huns are in Félcourt.'

'Christ!'

'There's nothing for it but for you to hold on while you can. You must maintain your present position to the last man, Challis.'

'Very good, sir. Good-bye.'

Those few words had condemned ten thousand men to death or mutilation.

'If the Huns are in Félcourt, sir,' said Miller, 'it's time we got out of here.'

Half a dozen eager pairs of eyes looked up at Curzon when Miller said that. He was voicing the general opinion.

'Yes,' said Curzon. What Miller said was only common sense. But Curzon suddenly felt very dispirited, almost apathetic. What was the use of withdrawing all this elaborate machinery of the Corps command when there was no Corps left? Three divisions were in ruins, and a fourth would be overwhelmed by converging attacks in the next two hours. And there was nothing to fill the gap. The Germans had achieved the break-through which the English had sought in vain for three years, and a break-through meant defeat and ruin. England had suffered a decisive defeat at a vital point. Curzon went back in his mind through a list of victories which had settled the fate of Europe–Sedan, Sadowa, Waterloo. Now England was among the conquered. He tried to find a precedent in English military history, and he went further and further back in his mind through the centuries. Not until he reached Hastings could he find a parallel. Hastings had laid England at the feet of the Normans, and this defeat would lay England at the feet of the Germans.

'We'll move in the usual two echelons,' Miller was saying. 'Frobisher, you'll go with the first.'

What was the use of it all? A vivid flash of imagination, like lightning at night, revealed the future to Curzon. He would return to England a defeated general, one of the men who had let England down. There would be public reproaches. Court-martial, perhaps. Emily would stand by him, but he did not want her to have to do so. In an excruciating moment he realized that even with Emily at his side he could not face a future of professional failure. Emily whom he loved would make it all the worse. He would rather die, the way the old Ninety-first was dying.

He swung round upon Greven, who was standing helpless, as was only to be expected, amid the bustle of preparation for the transfer.

'Send for my horse,' he said.

Those who heard him gaped.

'The motor cars are just coming round, sir,' said Miller respectfully.

'I shan't want mine,' replied Curzon. Even at that moment he sought to avoid the melodramatic by the use of curt military phrasing. 'I'm going up the line. I shall leave you in charge, Miller.'

'Up the line,' someone whispered, echoing his words. They knew now what he intended.

'I'll send for my horse too, sir,' said Follett. As A.D.C. it was his duty to stay by his general's side, even when the general was riding to his death. One or two people looked instinctively at Greven.

'And me too, of course,' said Greven slowly.

'Right,' said Curzon harshly. 'Miller, it'll be your duty to reorganize what's left of the Corps. We can still go down fighting.'

'Yes, sir.'

'Two minutes, Follett,' said Curzon, and under the gaze of every eye he strode across the room and through the green baize doors into his quarters.

Mason was running round like a squirrel in a cage, packing his officer's things.

'Get my sword,' snapped Curzon.

'Your sword, sir?'

'Yes, you fool.'

While Mason plunged in search of the sword into the rolled valise, Curzon wrenched open the silver photograph frame upon the wall. He stuffed Emily's photograph into the breast of his tunic.

'Here it is, sir,' said Mason.

Curzon slipped the sword into the frog of his Sam Browne. There was still a queer military pleasure to be found in the tap of the sheath against his left boot. Mason was talking some foolishness or other, but Curzon did not stop to listen. He walked out to the front of the house, where among the motor vehicles Greven and Follett were on horseback and a groom was holding his own horse. Curzon swung himself up into his saddle. The horse was full of oats and insufficiently exercised lately, besides being infected by the excitement and bustle. He plunged madly as Curzon's right foot found the stirrup. Curzon brought the brute back to the level with the cruel use of the curb, and swung his head round towards the gate. Then he dashed out to the road, with Greven and Follett clattering wildly behind him.

The road was crowded with evidence of a defeat. Transport of all sorts, ambulances, walking wounded, were all pouring down it with the one intention of escaping capture. Puzzled soldiers stared at the three red-tabbed officers, magnificently mounted, who were galloping so madly over the clattering *pavé* towards the enemy. Far ahead Curzon could hear the roar of the guns as the Ninety-first fought its last battle. His throat was dry although he swallowed repeatedly. There was no thought in his head as he abandoned himself to the smooth rhythm of his galloping horse. Suddenly a flash of colour penetrated into his consciousness. There was a group of unwounded soldiers on the road, and the little squares on their sleeves showed that they belonged to the Ninety-first. He pulled up his horse and turned upon them.

'What the hell are you doing here?' he demanded.

'We ain't got no officer, sir,' said one.

They were stragglers escaped by a miracle from the shattered left wing of their division.

'D'you need an officer to show you how to do your duty? Turn back at once. Follett, bring them on with you. I expect you'll find others up the road.'

Curzon wheeled his lathered horse round again and dashed on, only Greven followed him now. They approached the cross-roads where a red-capped military policeman was still directing traffic. An officer there was trying to sort out the able-bodied from the others.

'Ah!' said Curzon.

At that very moment a German battery four miles away opened fire. They were shooting by the map, and they made extraordinarily good practice as they sought for the vital spots in the enemy's rear. Shells came shrieking down out of the blue and burst full upon the cross-roads, and Curzon was hit both by a flying fragment of red-hot steel and by a jagged lump of *pavé*. His right leg was shattered, and his horse was killed.

Greven saved Curzon's life–or at least always thought he did, although the credit ought really to be given to the two lightly wounded R.A.M.C. men who came to the rescue, and put on bandages and tourniquets, and stopped a passing lorry by the authority of Greven's red tabs, and hoisted Curzon in.

Pain came almost at once. No torment the Inquisition devised could equal the agony Curzon knew as the lorry heaved and pitched over the uneven road, jolting his mangled leg so that the fragments of bone grated together. Soon he was groaning, with the sweat running over his chalk-white face, and when they reached the hospital he was crying out loud, a mere shattered fragment of a man despite his crossed swords and baton and crown, and his red tabs and his silly sword.

They had drugged him and they operated upon him, and they operated again and again, so that he lay for months in a muddle of pain and drugs while England fought with her back to the wall and closed by a miracle the gap which had been torn in her line at Saint-Quentin.

While he lay bathed in waves of agony, or inert under the drugs, he was sometimes conscious of Emily's presence beside him, and sometimes Emily was crying quietly, just as she had done at that revue he took her to on the last night of his last leave after Paschendaele and someone sang 'Roses of Picardy'. It was a long time before he was sure enough of this solid world again to put out his hand to her.

And now Lieutenant-General Sir Herbert Curzon and his wife, Lady Emily, are frequently to be seen on the promenade at Bournemouth, he in his bathchair with a plaid rug, she in tweed striding behind. He smiles his old-maidish smile at his friends, and his friends are pleased with that distinction, although he plays such bad bridge and is a little inclined to irascibility when the east wind blows.

The Captain from Connecticut

C. S. Forester

I

Although it was mid-afternoon it was nearly as dark as a summer night. The ship swayed uneasily at her anchor as the wind howled round her, the rigging giving out musical tones, from the deep bass of the shrouds to the high treble of the running rigging. Already the snow was thick enough on her to blur the outlines of the objects on the deck. On its forward side the square base of the binnacle was now a rounded mound; the flemished coils of the falls were now merely white cylinders. The officer of the watch stood shivering in the little shelter offered by the mizzen mast bitts, and forward across the snow-covered deck a few unhappy hands crouched vainly seeking shelter under the high bulwarks.

The two officers who emerged upon the quarterdeck held their hats on to their heads against the shrieking wind. The shorter, slighter one turned up the collar of his heavy coat, and attempted instinctively to pull the front of it tighter across his chest to keep out the penetrating air. As he spoke in the grey darkness he had to raise his voice to make himself heard, despite the confidential nature of what he was saying.

'It's your best chance, Peabody.'

The other turned about, and stood to windward with the snow driving into his face before he answered with a single word.

'Aye,' he said.

'The glass is still dropping. But it can't go much lower,' went on the other. It seemed as if he were talking for the purpose of encouraging himself, not the man he was speaking to. 'The west wind'll veer nor'-easterly to-morrow, but by that time you'll have weathered Montauk, please God.'

'Please God,' echoed Peabody–but it was more like a prayer, in the tone he employed, than the other man's speech.

'Well, good-bye, then. The best of good fortune, Captain Peabody.'

The two men shook hands in their heavy furred gloves. Peabody raised his voice against the storm–it was a penetrant voice, nasal yet with a tenor musical tone which somehow made it more readily audible against the wind.

'Call the Commodore's gig. Pipe the side for the Commodore,' he said.

'Compliments in this weather?' asked the Commodore, a little surprised, but Peabody gave him no explanation. He was not going to allow a blizzard to interfere with the decent and proper routine of his ship.

The figures huddling for shelter under the bulwark came to life and scuttled across the deck and down into the gig. Other figures, black against the snowy deck, came swarming up from below. It was strange and unnatural that their feet made no sound on the deck. They were like ghosts in their noiselessness, treading the thick carpet of snow. Not even the marines, in their heavy shoes, made any sound. Feebly the pipes of the boatswain's mates twittered in the shrieking wind as the Commodore went over the side down into his waiting gig. Peabody watched him down into the boat, saw the bowman cast off the painter, and then turned back to face the wind again.

'Man the capstan, there!' he shouted. 'Mr Hubbard, fore and main topmast staysails. Three reefs in the tops'ls, ready to sheet home.'

He stood with his hands behind him, facing into the bitter wind, and making no attempt whatever to shelter from it. Forward he could just hear the voice of the boatswain as he gave the word to the men at the capstan bars. Then he heard the clank-clank of the capstan; it was turning slowly–very slowly. It was hard work to drag the big frigate up to the anchor against that wind. There were men aloft, too; their movements disturbed the snow banked against the rigging, and it was drifting astern in big puffs visible through the snow. Another unexpected noise puzzled Peabody for a moment–it was the crackling of the frozen canvas as it was unrolled. And the frozen ropes crackled, too, like a whole succession of pistol shots, as they ran through the sheaves. Little lumps of ice stripped from them came raining down about him, whirled aft by the wind.

Peabody looked over the starboard quarter. Somewhere in that murk and darkness was the Long Island shore, and Willet's Point, too near to be pleasant, he knew, although invisible. On the larboard bow, equally invisible, lay Throg's Neck. It was only the protection of the guns of Fort Totten and Fort Schuyler on these two points which had enabled him to bring his ship thus far in peace. Beyond them the British Navy cruised unchallenged over the length and breadth of Long Island Sound, yet the watch over the Narrows was stricter still, so strict that in his considered judgement it had been better to make the attempt to reach the open sea by this back door to New York. Were it not for the land batteries the Hudson and Hell Gate would be at the mercy of the British squadrons, just as Long Island Sound was. Hardy–the captain who had kissed the dying Nelson in the cockpit of the *Victory* at Trafalgar–lorded it off New London in the *Ramillies,* burning fishing boats and capturing coasters, and keeping Decatur and Jones blockaded in the port. Peabody thought of the starving seamen and dockyard hands who begged their bread on the waterfronts of New York and Baltimore, of the ruined businesses and the disrupted national economy. Hardy and his brother captains were strangling the Union slowly but certainly. Whether the *Delaware* would help to break their stranglehold in the slightest was more than he could say. He could only carry out his orders, interpreting them as best he could towards that end. If necessary, he could die.

The gale bore back the boatswain's hail from forward.

'Straight up and down, sir!'

'Heave away!' shouted Peabody. 'Sheet home, Mr Hubbard.'

There were two quartermasters at the wheel beside him; the spokes turned in their hands as the *Delaware* gathered sternway. The canvas slatted wildly as the yards were braced round.

'Hard a-starboard,' said Peabody.

The *Delaware* hesitated and trembled. Her sails filled with a loud report, and Peabody felt the movement of the deck under his feet as the *Delaware* lost her sternway and began to move forward. She was heeling now as the treble-reefed topsails caught the wind. So thickly was the snow driving that it was impossible to see what was happening. Peabody had to rely on his other senses, on the feel of the ship, on his long-trained instincts, to draw his conclusions about what she was doing.

'Keep her to the wind,' he said to the quartermasters. They, too, would have only their long experience to help them in their task. Only by the feel of the wind in their faces, and by the sound of the sails if they steered too close to the wind, could they tell whether they were obeying their orders or not.

Under the pressure of the wind upon her scanty canvas the *Delaware* was moving forward precipitately through the water. The surface was rough enough to give her a distinct motion, and the sound of her bows crashing through the waves was audible through the noise of the wind. She was lying far over with the pressure of the wind, despite the fact that her top-gallant masts had been sent down; she was behaving like a blood horse in the hands of incompetent stable boys. No one save a madman or a blockaded captain would dream of taking a ship to sea in conditions like this, with a treacherous shore under her lee and snow so thick that it was hard to see a dozen fathoms away. But it was only in conditions like this that the *Delaware* stood any chance of evading the attention of Hardy and his watchdogs. She might as well, reflected Peabody bitterly, be piled up on the Long Island shore as lying rotting at Brooklyn.

He bent over the lighted binnacle, and studied the compass, and then turned his face back towards the snow while he made his calculations. His mind worked slowly but with infinite tenacity, and he had no need of paper and pencil as he moved mentally from point to point of the course he had in mind. They would weather Elm Point comfortably, he decided.

'Heave the log every glass, Mr Hubbard,' he ordered.

'Aye aye, sir,' said Hubbard. Hubbard's breast and front of his thighs were white with snow as he turned to acknowledge the order; glancing down, Peabody saw that his own clothes were similarly coated. A master's mate and a hand came aft, trudging through the snow on deck, their foothold precarious on that giddy slope. The hand would wet himself thoroughly with the dripping long line as he hauled it in again, and the water would freeze in that biting wind. It would be an uncomfortable night for him, thought Peabody, but discomfort was part of a sailor's life when necessary. The safety of the ship depended on the accurate estimate of her speed and distance travelled. He turned to the quartermasters.

'Are you cold?' he asked.

'A little, sir,' said one of them.

From those tough seamen the two words were the equivalent of a long wail of misery from a landsman. Peabody knew they would be numb and stupid before long.

'Mr Hubbard!' he said. 'Relieve these men at the wheel every half-hour.'

'Aye aye, sir,' said Hubbard.

Hubbard was marking on the traverse board the speed and course.

'What's the speed?'

'Five knots and a bit more, sir.' Even when Hubbard was shouting into a gale his voice bore the faint echo of the South Carolina which had given him birth.

The *Delaware* was showing her good points, doing five knots close-hauled under staysails and close-reefed topsails alone–the Baltimore shipwrights who built her way back in 1800 had left their impress on the shape of her hull, despite the specifications of the Navy Department. Five knots, and it would be more when they had weathered Elm Point and brought the wind abeam. High water at Montauk Point was at two a.m. Peabody stood with the wind whistling round him and the snow banking against his chest while he continued his calculations. In a blizzard like this he could be fairly certain that the British squadron would be blown out to sea; if not, it was so dark that he could hope to get through unobserved. In these conditions his ship was in a hundred times greater danger from the navigational difficulties than from the enemy, and it was only then, as he bitterly realised, that he stood any chance of getting to sea at all.

The relieved quartermasters were stumbling forward now, bent against the wind. He could tell from their gait how numb and stiff they were–they had been standing with their arms extended, holding the wheel, in an attitude which fairly invited the wind to pierce them to the heart. He would be feeling cold himself if he allowed himself to do so, but he would not. He went on facing stubbornly into the wind. They must be abreast of Elm Point by now.

'Nor'-east by east,' he said to the men at the wheel.

'Nor'-east by east, sir,' they echoed.

'Hands to the braces, Mr Hubbard.'

'Aye aye, sir.'

The *Delaware* steadied herself on her new course, heeling to the wind, rolling rather more now, and pitching far less. Peabody had never know the Sound to be as rough as this–it was the clearest proof of the violence of the blizzard.

'Seven and a half knots, sir,' said Hubbard, marking up the new course and speed.

That was what he had expected. Now they would weather Montauk comfortably before dawn. For a few hours he could relax a little–relax as far as an American captain could possibly relax when sailing in the heart of his own country's waters in the midst of enemies.

The wind that was blowing about him from the Connecticut shore must now–he worked out a neat trigonometrical problem in his head–have passed just over the farm where he was born and spent his childhood. The memory made him shiver a little, although the blizzard did not. It was not often that those memories came back to him, except in nightmares. Against his will they forced themselves into his mind as he stood staring into the darkness. It was not the poverty, or the hunger, or the winter cold, which he hated to remember, although they had been poignant enough at the time. The bare bones of that farm had stuck through the skin and the soil, and no one could have hoped to gain more than the barest living from it. There was nothing hateful now about the memory of poverty. But the other memories made him shudder again. That tall, gaunt father of his, with the yellow beard and the blazing blue eyes–he winced a little in the darkness at the vivid mental picture.

The bottle beside him and the Bible in front of him, and the furious texts foaming out of his mouth, drunk with rum and the Old Testament–that was one way in which he could remember his father. And then another memory, insidiously creeping into his mind, of his father lurching across the room, still mouthing texts, and unbuckling the heavy belt from his waist; lurching across the room to where a terrified little boy stood cornered, reaching for him with a huge calloused hand, dragging him away from the sheltering walls. How that little boy had screamed under that searing belt! That little boy was now Captain Josiah Peabody, of the frigate *Delaware*.

Those memories had him on their treadmill now, there was no escape from them. There was his mother, dark and beautiful–he had thought her beautiful–who used to take him into her arms and rock with him and pet him; as a big baby, before he became a little boy, he could remember the bliss of those embraces. Then after that he knew that her step was uncertain, that her laugh was too loud and misplaced. He knew the reason for her red cheeks and staring, foolish gaze. After that he shrank from his mother's drunken caresses just as he shrank from his father's clutches–they sickened him equally as much. He remembered the nausea which overtook him when he smelt her breath as her soft arms closed about him.

Then Uncle Josiah, for whom he was named, had come to the farm, very extraordinary in his appearance to the little boy, with his hair tied into a neat queue, and a laced neckcloth and gloves and riding boots. Uncle Josiah had taken him away–Uncle Josiah was an elegant gentleman, strangely enough; his nephew could guess that queer things had happened to Uncle Josiah during the past few years. Uncle Josiah had a lace handkerchief which wafted the perfumes of Paradise about the room when he applied it delicately to his nose; apparently he was a wealthy man, and the source of his wealth, unbelievable as it might be, was somehow connected with a war which had begun the other side of the ocean.

He was engaged in the most multifarious businesses, obviously, seeing that he received as many as six letters a day at one of the taverns when they stopped on their way to New York. He had friends, too. A mere word from him to one of those friends made young Josiah a boy in the Coastguard Service, where the beatings were not nearly as severe and where the nightmares of a loving mother gradually ceased in intensity. There was the fresh, clean wind of the sea to blow about him, and the boys who berthed with him were not weakly malicious, as had been his younger brothers and sisters. And the cities he visited were vast and intoxicating, from Portsmouth down to Charleston; and somehow the lessons which the master-commandant of the cutter taught him had a peculiar, delicious charm–algebra, when he was introduced to it, gave him pleasure as great as maple syrup or honey had done.

And then, when his voice had broken and his beard had begun to grow, there had come a call for officers in the new Federal Navy. Uncle Josiah said another word for him to another friend, a word which made his nephew a lieutenant at the age of sixteen. It was the last service Uncle Josiah was to do for him, for Uncle Josiah, two months later, paid the penalty of having become a gentleman, and died in Baltimore twelve paces from the pistol of another gentleman who had been his friend until the sudden disclosure of a queer scandal regarding the outfitting of privateers for the war against France.

Josiah knew nothing of his death for some months, for he was at sea in the *Constellation* with Truxtun. Josiah could remember with peculiar vividness those early battles, with the *Insurgente* and the *Vengeance*. He could remember as well the colour and the heat and the rain of the West India islands, where Truxtun had displayed the Stars and Stripes–the memories were a little overlayed by others, of Tripoli and Algiers and Malta, but they were still keen enough. He found himself wondering whether he would see those islands again, and then checked himself with a hard smile, for he was under orders to proceed there at present. The immediate problem of weathering Montauk Point and breaking the British blockade had for the moment driven the equally difficult problems of the future clean out of his head. But it was as well that he could smile–most of the times when his weakness had lured him into going back over old memories he could not smile at all.

He shook himself, now that the spell was broken, back into his proper state of mind. He lifted the traverse board into the dim light of the binnacle–he realised that he must have been standing on deck motionless during two or three hours. The *Delaware* had held her course steadily during those hours, and must be well out into the Sound now. New Haven must be on their larboard beam. He could feel his way about Long Island Sound as surely as he could about his own cabin, thanks to his years in the Coastguard Service and to further years commanding one of the gunboats on which Mr Jefferson had lavished so much of the national income in an attempt to buy security cheap.

The sea had been a second mother to him, and a kinder one than the traditional stepmother had ever been, he reflected, in an unusually analytical mood. The Navy had been his father. Then to continue the analogy the *Delaware* must be his wife, to whom he devoted all his kindly care, and all his waking thoughts. He was more fortunate in his family than most men were. He struggled again against this dangerous bit of brooding. He knew that with advancing age came a tendency to dwell upon the past. Perhaps now that he was thirty-two–close on thirty-three–he was beginning to show signs of it. Realistically he remembered how, as a lieutenant of sixteen, he had looked upon men of twice his age as old; and captains especially so. Truxtun, in the *Constellation*, had seemed almost senile, but then Truxtun must have been in his fifties or so. On the other hand, Decatur was the same age as himself, practically, and Decatur still seemed young to him. Perhaps, after all, he was not so very old at thirty-two. It was a satisfactory conclusion to reach, especially while he was the most junior captain in the list, and while his country's freedom had still to be defended–and while this very night he had to break a blockade enforced by a squadron of ships of the line.

Enough of this nonsense. He turned to face the snow-covered deck, and was surprised to find that he could hardly move; the bitter cold of the blizzard had stiffened him to such an extent that, now that his attention was called to it, he walked with difficulty. As the *Delaware* heeled before the shrieking wind his feet slipped in the treacherous snow, and he slid away to leeward and cannoned into the bulwarks, his feet struggling to find a foothold in the scuppers. That was the penalty for dreaming, he told himself grimly, as he rubbed his bruises. Uncontrollable shudders shook his body, and his teeth were chattering. It was ridiculous that he should have allowed himself to grow so cold. He struggled up the deck again to the weather side and under the slight shelter of the bulwark, where he flogged himself with his arms, beating off the thick layer of snow which had accumulated on the breast of his pea-jacket. He trudged forward along the spar deck to get his circulation going again; the foremast shrouds on the weather side here were coated completely with ice–the frozen spray taken in over the weather bow–so that shrouds and ratlines were like the frames of windows of ice, hard to see in this shrieking darkness, but plain enough to the touch. A fresh shower of spray blew into his face as he felt about him; there must be a good deal of ice accumulating on the running rigging. Certainly, the anchor at the cathead was welded to the ship's side by a solid block of ice.

He made his way aft again.

'Mr Murray!'

'Sir!' said the officer of the watch.

'Set the watch to work clearing away the ice. I want twenty hands clearing the running rigging.'

'Aye aye, sir.'

Even with the gale blowing he could hear a few yelps of dismay among the crew as Murray gave his orders. To lay aloft in the blizzard was to face a torture as exquisite as anything the Indians had ever devised, and there would be frostbite among the crew after this, even if no one broke his neck struggling along the frozen footropes with a precarious hold on the ice-coated yards. Yet it had to be done. The whole safety of the ship depended upon his ability to handle her promptly and to let go the anchor, if necessary. His calculations of her course and run might be faulty. He might find Orient Point close under his lee, when he really intended to give it a wide berth, and the knowledge that he might not be completely infallible gnawed at his conscience. Because of that, he stayed out on the exposed deck, where the blizzard could work its will on him. If the men had to suffer because he could not be sure of his position to within a quarter of a mile he was going to suffer with them; Peabody was not aware of how deeply ingrained into him was the Old Testament teaching of the father whom he had grown to despise.

Something white over the starboard quarter caught his eye–a fleck too big to be a mere breaking wave. He rushed across the deck to look more closely. There it was again–something white in the hurtling grey of the snow. He sprang up into the mizzen rigging, with the wind shrieking round his ears, and the sea hissing beneath his feet. That white fleck was the spray about the bows of a ship. As he leaped back again to the deck he found Murray there–Murray had seen it, too. Murray stabbed at the darkness with a gloved hand, and shouted in his ear, even grabbing his shoulder in the excitement of the moment, for Murray was of an excitable temperament. It was a ship, close hauled under storm canvas on the opposite tack to the *Delaware*. She was close abreast of them. She would cross their stern within a yard of them, Peabody decided; near enough. The bowspirit and martingale which circled in the air under their noses were coated with ice, he noted. Through the snow he could see the curve of her bow with two broad stripes of paint and a double line of checkers–a two decker, then, Hardy's *Ramillies* or Cochrane's *Superb*.

'A Britisher!' shrieked Murray, quite unnecessarily. There were no United States ships of the line. Murray turned away towards the helmsman, and then back to his captain for orders, quite unduly excited. There was nothing to be done. The ships were passing rapidly, and Peabody could be certain that the British guns, like his own, were secured by double breachings. By the time a gun could be loaded and run out the ships would be invisible to each other again; but Murray did not possess the imperturbability of his captain nor his fatalist ability to accept the inevitable.

Already the two decker was passing rapidly–a well-thrown stone would have landed on her deck. The glimmering snow with which she was coated showed up faintly in the darkness; against the whitened decks Peabody thought he could see the dark forms of her officers and crew. The poor devils were having as miserable a time of it as were his own men; worse, probably. Beating about Long Island Sound in a New England blizzard was no child's play, especially in a clumsy, pig-headed ship of the line–Peabody remembered how bluff and inelegant had been the bows she had presented to him when he first caught sight of her.

Now she was gone, engulfed in the darkness. She might put about in pursuit, but it did not matter. At a hundred yards the ships were as invisible to each other as at a hundred miles, and by the time the two decker could go about and settle on her new course she would be a couple of miles at least astern. It was even likely that she had not recognised the *Delaware* as American–there were few enough American frigates, and those all strictly blockaded. It was one of the ironies of history that the last vessel one would expect to see in Long Island Sound was an American frigate.

But on the other hand, the fact that he had been seen at all decided him to take one more risk on his passage to the open sea. It would be high water in Plum Gut in two hours from now, four and a half fathoms at least, and with this wind blowing probably rather more. He would head the *Delaware* through there, and chance all the dangers of Orient Point. Peabody did not think that any British battleship would have the nerve to follow him through.

Peabody studied the compass in the binnacle, and occupied his mind with the fresh problem in mental trigonometry as he worked out the conditions arising from the changed situation.

'Bring her two points farther off the wind,' he said.

'Two points farther off the wind, sir.'

Peabody looked aft into the darkness. The night had most certainly swallowed up the British two decker. He wondered whether there were any parallel mental processes going on in the British captain's mind. Whether there were or were not he could not tell, and certainly he was not going to stop to see. Daylight might perhaps show, and he was quite capable of waiting till daylight.

2

Lieutenant George Hubbard was officer of the morning watch. The glass had just been turned for the last time, and seven bells had been duly struck, and Hubbard was beginning to look forward to his relief and to wonder whether he would find any time for sleep during the day, when his captain loomed up beside him. With the cessation of the snow there was enough light now for details to be clearly distinguished.

'You can wear ship now, Mr Hubbard,' said Peabody. 'Course sou'-west by south.'

'Sou'-west by south, sir,' echoed Hubbard.

'And take those men out of the chains. We won't need the lead again.'

'Aye aye, sir.'

'See that they have something hot to drink.'

'Aye aye, sir.'

The wind had moderated as it veered, but now that they were in the open sea they were encountering the full force of the waves. Close hauled, the *Delaware* had been climbing wave after wave, heeling over to them, soaring upward with her bowsprit pointing at the sky, and then, as she reached the crest, rolling into the wind with her stern heaving upwards in a mad corkscrew roll with the spray bursting over her deck. Now she came round before the wind, and her motion changed. There was not so much feeling of battling with gigantic forces; much more was there an uneasy sensation of yielding to them. The following sea threw her about as if she had no will of her own. Standing by the wheel, Hubbard was conscious of a feeling of relief from the penetrating torture of the wind–so, undoubtedly, were the men at the wheel–but the feeling was counteracted by a sensation of uneasiness as the *Delaware* lurched along before the big grey-bearded waves which came sweeping after her. There was an even chance of her being pooped–Hubbard could tell, by the feel of the deck under his feet, how each of those grey mountains in its turn blanketed the close-reefed topsails, and robbed the ship of a trifle of her way. He could tell it, too, by the way the quartermasters had to saw back and forth at the wheel to meet the *Delaware*'s unhappy falling off as each wave passed under her counter. If she once broached-to, then good-bye to the *Delaware*.

'Steer small,' he growled at the quartermasters.

It was unsafe to run before this wind and sea. A cautious captain would have kept the *Delaware* upon the wind for a while longer, or would even heave-to until the sea moderated–provided, that is to say, that a cautious captain would have left port at all on such a night, which was quite inconceivable. As first lieutenant of the ship, and responsible to his captain for her material welfare, Hubbard could never quite reconcile in his mind the jarring claims of military necessity and common sense. He looked with something like dismay about the ship in the growing daylight, at the snow which covered her deck, and the ice which glittered on her standing rigging. The quarter-deck carronades beside him were mere rounded heaps of snow on their forward sides. When the forenoon watch was called he would have to set the hands at work shovelling the stuff away–queer work for a sailorman. The tradition of centuries was that the first work in the morning was washing down decks, not shovelling snow off them.

The captain was still prowling about the deck; Hubbard heard him lift up his voice in a hail.

'Masthead, there! Keep your wits about you.'

'Aye aye, sir.'

The poor devil of a lookout up there was the most uncomfortable man in the whole ship, Hubbard supposed, without much sympathy for him. It was interesting to note that the captain was apparently a little uneasy still about the possible appearance of British ships. Peabody had brilliantly brought the *Delaware* out to sea–the first United States ship to run the blockade for six months–as Hubbard grudgingly admitted to himself, yet with the open Atlantic about him he was still nervous. Hubbard shrugged his shoulders. He was glad that it was not his responsibility.

Here came that pesky young brother of the captain's. During the four weeks that the *Delaware* had lain at Brooklyn, Hubbard had come most heartily to dislike the boy. Captain's clerk, indeed, and he was hardly able to read or write! It was a pity that the *Delaware*'s midshipmen were all young boys. Jonathan Peabody was by several years the oldest of the gunroom mess, and in physique he was as tough as his elder brother, so that there was small chance of his being taught much sense there. He was sly, too; otherwise, as Hubbard was well aware, he would never have contrived for four weeks to avoid trouble in a ship whose First Lieutenant was anxious to make trouble for him.

'Take off your hat to the quarterdeck, you young cub,' snapped Hubbard.

'Aye aye, sir,' said Jonathan Peabody, and obeyed instantly. Yet there was a touch of elaboration about his gesture which conveyed exactly enough contempt both for the ceremony and for the First Lieutenant to annoy the latter intensely, and yet too little to make him liable to punishment under the Naval Regulations issued by command of the President of the United States of America–not even under that all-embracing regulation which decided that 'all other faults disorders and misdemeanours not herein mentioned shall be punished according to the laws and customs in such cases at sea.' The young cub flaunted his excellent clothes with a swagger which smacked of insolence, clothes which, as Hubbard knew, his captain had brought for him only four weeks ago. Until then Jonathan Peabody had been a barefooted follower of the plough, and presumably the furtive Lothario of some Connecticut village. Hubbard disliked him quite as much as he admired his grim elder brother; possibly the dislike and the admiration had some bearing on each other.

There came a yell from the maintopmast crosstrees.

'Sail, ho! Sail to wind'ard, sir.'

The captain appeared from nowhere upon the quarterdeck, leaping on the weather rail, and staring over the heaving sea into the wind over the quarter. Apparently he could see nothing from there, for he hailed the masthead again.

'What d'ye make of her?'

'She's a ship, sir, under tops'ls. Same course as us, sir, or pretty nigh.'

The captain took Hubbard's glass and swung himself into the mizzen rigging, running up the ratlines with the quite surprising agility of a big man. He was back again on deck shortly after, sliding down the backstay despite the handicap of his heavy clothing. Hubbard was not used to captains as athletic as that. The captain's hard face was set like a stone mask.

'That's the two decker we passed last night, Mr Hubbard,' he said. 'Turn up the hands. I'll have a reef out of those tops'ls, if you please. Set the jib and mizzen stays'l, too.'

'Aye aye, sir.'

All hands came pouring on deck as Hubbard shouted his orders, while Peabody walked aft to the taffrail and stared astern. The fresh canvas as it was spread crackled loudly behind him, and the *Delaware* plunged madly under the increased pressure. Peabody swung round to watch his ship's behaviour. In a full gale like this he was exposing more canvas than he should do in prudence. There was a risk that something might give way, that some portion of the rigging might part–leaving out of all account the possibility that he might run the *Delaware* bodily under. But if he did not take that risk the British ship would overhaul him. It was only under present conditions that a British ship of the line stood any chance in a race with an American frigate. The bigger ship, with her immensely strong gear, could make more sail than he dared, and her bluff bows and lofty freeboard which made her so clumsy on a wind were a huge advantage when running before a gale on a rough sea. By ensuring her appearance nearly dead to windward Providence had secured all these advantages for the British ship. But then, on the other hand, if she had appeared to leeward, although the *Delaware* could escape from her easily enough close-hauled, close-hauled she would be headed back for Montauk Point, back to the confinement of blockade–possibly straight into the waiting arms of the blockading squadron. What Providence took away in one fashion she restored in another, keeping an even balance so that a man's success or failure depended entirely on himself, as it should be.

Hubbard was looking up at the straining topmasts. There was a distinct sign of a whip there–they were bending, very slightly, but perceptibly to the naked eye. What the strain was upon the backstays and preventer braces could only be imagined; the tautness of the rigging had driven the perennial Aeolian harping of the wind quite a semitone up the scale. Hubbard turned to meet his captain's eye, and went as far in protest as to open his mouth, and then thought better of it, and shut his mouth and resumed his pacing of the deck, where the hands were at work shovelling away the snow. Peabody watched the antics of his ship for a moment longer, noting how low she lay in the water when the pressure of the wind forced her downwards in certain combinations of waves, noticing how the water boiled away from her bows, and then turned back to stare over the taffrail again. The *Delaware* rose upon a wave, heaving up her stern above the mad flurry of grey water, climbing higher and higher as she pitched, and in the very instant of her stern's highest ascent Peabody saw, far astern, on the very limit of the grey horizon, a tiny square of white. It was gone in a flash as the *Delaware* plunged down the farther slope, but Peabody knew it for what it was–the foretopsail of the British ship hoisted above the horizon for a moment. He had seen that foretopsail for a moment the night before; he had stared at it through his glass for two full minutes this morning, and he would recognise it again at any time in any part of the world. The sight of it from the deck meant that it was nearer, that his pursuer was over-hauling him.

'Set the mizzen tops'l, Mr Hubbard, with two reefs.'

'Aye aye, sir.'

'Have the relieving tackles manned, if you please.'

'Aye aye, sir.'

'Mr Crane, take charge of them.'

'Aye aye, sir.'

Peabody had noticed the difficulty the quartermasters had in holding the *Delaware* on her course with the following sea–it was partly to help them that he had had the jib set. Now the pressure of the big mizzen topsail would add to their difficulties, countering the steadying effect of the headsails. Six men below at the relieving tackles, applied direct to the tiller ropes, would not only be of assistance in turning the rudder, but would also damp down the rudder's sudden movements. And Mr Crane, the sailing master, with his lifetime of experience–he had commanded in twenty voyages to the Levant out of Boston–would be the best man for the difficult task of correlating the work of wheel and relieving tackles; standing on the grating with his eyes on wheel and sails and sea, he would shout his warnings down to the tiller ropes.

Peabody watched warily as the mizzen topsail was sheeted home. The *Delaware* reacted to the added pressure instantly. There was nothing light or graceful about her movements now. She was crashing from wave to wave like a rock down a hillside. Even with the wind well abaft the beam as it was she was leaning over to it, the white foam creaming along her lee side to join her boiling wake.

'Mr Murray, go aloft, and keep your eye on the strange sail.'

'Aye aye, sir.'

Peabody looked aft again, and at one of the *Delaware*'s extravagant plunges he once more caught that fleeting glimpse of the British topsail above the horizon. He did not need Murray's hail from above.

'Deck, there! If you please, sir, I think she's nearer.'

Peabody's expression did not change. The *Delaware* was showing all the canvas she could possibly carry, and he had done all he could for the moment. If the wind would only drop a little, or the sea moderate, she would walk away from that tub or two decker. If not, it would only be by the aid of special measures that she would be able to escape, and those measures, which involved considerable sacrifice, he would not take until the necessity was proved.

'Why don't we fight her, Jos?' asked Jonathan–when the crew were at quarters his station was on the quarterdeck at the captain's orders, so that he was in his right place, but Josiah wondered sadly how long it would take the boy to learn the other details of naval life.

'You must take your hat off when you speak to me, Jonathan,' he said, 'and you call me "sir," and you take your hand out of your pocket, too,' he repeated patiently–he had said it all before.

'Sorry, Jos–I mean sir,' said Jonathan, lifting his hat with the hand from his pocket. 'But why don't we fight her?'

He jerked his thumb over the taffrail to indicate the pursuing enemy.

'Because she's twice as strong as we are,' said Josiah. 'And with this sea running she's three times as strong–we could never open our maindeck ports. And besides—'

Josiah checked himself. Anxious though he was for Jonathan to learn, this was not the time for a long disquisition on tactics and strategy. The two decker had twice the guns the *Delaware* had, and some of them heavier than the *Delaware*'s heaviest. She had scantlings twice as thick, too–half the *Delaware*'s shot would never pierce her sides. However heavy a sea was running she would always be able to work her upper-deck guns as well as her quarterdeck and forecastle carronades, and her clumsy bulk made her a far steadier gun platform, too. From a tactical point of view it would be madness to fight her; and from a strategical point of view it would be worse than that. Here he was on the point of escaping into the open sea. Once let him get free, and he would exhaust England's strength far more effectively than by any battle with a ship of the line. He could harass her fleet of merchantmen so that twenty frigates each as big as the *Delaware* would be engaged in convoy duty. He could be here to-day and there to-morrow, threatening a dozen places at once. The brigs and the sloops with which England guarded her convoys from the privateers would be useless against a powerful frigate. If anything could force England into peace it would be the sort of pressure the *Delaware* could apply. There was nothing whatever to be gained by an immediate encounter with a superior force–such an encounter could only end in his having to put back for repairs and submitting once more to blockade.

Josiah felt all this strongly. To think strategically was as much part of his ordinary processes as breathing was; but he was not a man of words–it was not easy for him to put these ideas into phrases which could be readily understood, and he knew it, although he was not conscious of the other disadvantage under which he laboured; that of being a man of wildcat fighting blood forced to play a cautious part. But at the same time some explanation must be made to Jonathan, so that the boy would appreciate what was going on. He fell back on a more homely argument.

'That fellow there,' he said, with his thumb repeating Jonathan's gesture, 'wants us to fight him. Nothing would please him better than to see us heave to an wait for him to come up. Look how he's cracking on to overtake us. D'ye see any sense in doing what your enemy wants you to do?'

'P'raps not,' said Jonathan.

Josiah was glad to get even this grudging agreement, for Jonathan's good opinion meant much to him. He had grown fond of the youngest brother of his, whom he had never known before. His first action on his promotion to captain and appointment to the *Delaware* had been to use his one bit of patronage in the boy's favour, and nominate him as his clerk; to his mind it was a way of repaying Providence for Uncle Josiah's kindnesses to himself, and buying clothes for the boy and introducing him to naval life had somehow endeared the boy to him.

The *Delaware* was leaping and lurching under his feet, and he could hear Crane beside the wheel shouting instructions through the grating to the men at the relieving tackles. He looked up at the straining rigging but the Navy Yard at Brooklyn had done its work well. He looked aft. It was not on rare occasions now, but every time that the *Delaware* heaved her stern over a wave, that he could see that ominous little square of white on the horizon. The two decker was still overtaking them, despite the aid of the mizzen topsail and the shaken out reefs. He could set no more canvas–the *Delaware* would not bear another stitch without driving bodily under. He thought about knocking out the wedges in the steps of the masts to give the masts more play; sluggish sailors often benefited by that, but the *Delaware* would not. During the four weeks she was lying in the East River he had seen to it personally that everything had been done to give her every inch of speed. She was trimmed exactly right, he knew.

But she was low in the water. He had crammed her with all the stores she would hold before setting out in his determination to make her as independent as possible. There were six months stores on board. There were fifty tons of shot, and twenty of powder. There were fifteen tons of water–he could relieve the *Delaware* of that fifteen tons in a few minutes by merely starting the hogsheads and setting the hands to work at the pumps. On the spar deck there were eighteen carronades weighing a ton and a half each, and it would not be difficult with tackles to heave them over the side. But powder and shot, guns and drinking water were what gave the *Delaware* her usefulness in war. Without them he would be forced into port as surely as if he had been crippled in action.

'Mr Hubbard!'

'Sir!'

'Rig the tackles. I want the longboat and cutter hove overside.'

'Aye aye, sir.'

Longboat and cutter were on chocks amidships. Whips had to be rove at the fore and main yardarms at either side, and Peabody watched four hands running out along the yards to do so, bending to their work perched fifty feet up above the tormented sea. If any man of them lost his hold, that man was dead as surely as if he had been shot–the *Delaware* would not stop to pick him up even if he survived the fall into the icy sea. But the lines were passed without accident, and fifty men tailed on to them under the direction of Mr Rodgers, the boatswain. Tackles and boats were his particular province; even when the boats were being thrown away it was his duty to attend to the matter at the First Lieutenant's orders. At the last moment there was a hitch–young Midshipman Wallingford came running aft to his captain.

'What about the hogs, sir?' he asked breathlessly. 'And the chickens? Are they to go overside, too?'

'I'll give Mr Rodgers one minute to get them out,' said Peabody hastily.

Hogs and chickens lived in the longboat and cutter; they were the only source of fresh meat on board, and important in consequence. Peabody was annoyed with himself for having forgotten about them, with having let his head get full of advanced warlike ideas to the exclusion of matters like hogs and chickens. He watched the livestock being herded aft to where a temporary pen was hurriedly designed among the spare spars. The longboat rose, cradled in its sling, and hung half a dozen feet above the deck. Then the men began to heave in on the leeside tackles, and let go on the weather side, and the longboat slowly swung towards the leeside bulwarks. The *Delaware* felt the very considerable transference of weight, listing in a manner which was a trifle dangerous in that gale. But the business was ticklish enough, for she still rolled and plunged, and the vast deadweight of the longboat swung about madly as far as the four suspensory ropes allowed. Peabody walked slowly forward; he had no intention of interfering with Rodgers's execution of his task–Rodgers's technical knowledge probably matched his own–but instinct drew him there.

Rodgers looked warily to windward, and studied the send of the sea, watching for his moment.

'Heave!' he shouted to the leeside men.

The longboat went out with a run, hanging from the lee yardarms exclusively while the *Delaware* listed more sharply still.

'Let go,' shouted Rodgers to the men at the lee main yardarm tackles. When they were let go the boat would hang vertically down in the slings until she slid down out of them, and the men obeyed promptly enough. But the line ran only for a second in the sheaves and then jammed. The longboat hung at too small an angle to slide out of the slings, and remained dangling from the yardarms, imperilling the very life of the ship.

'God damn the thing to hell,' said Rodgers.

A couple of hands sprang into the rigging with the idea of getting out to the block and clearing it.

'Let go, there, you men!' roared Peabody suddenly at the men holding the lee fore yardarm line. With a start of surprise they did so. The other end of the boat fell; she tipped up more and more, and then fell from the slings into the sea while the *Delaware* righted herself. Rodgers had been caught off his guard by the jammed line. He had been intending all along to drop the longboat stern first, and did not possess the flexibility of mind to reverse his plans instantly when the hitch came.

'Let's see that line!' he said irritably. 'Who made this long splice? God damn it, any soldier could make a better long splice than this. I'll find out if it takes me a month o' Sundays.'

'Get the cutter overside, Mr Rodgers,' interrupted Peabody.

He walked aft again; the incident had made little impression on him save to confirm to him his already formed estimate of Rodgers's capacity. The gig which had been nested in the cutter was swayed out and deposited on the chocks of the longboat, and the cutter next rose in its slings from the *Delaware*'s deck, traversed slowly across to leeward, and then fell into the sea. Peabody watched it as it went astern, broken backed and full of water, white among the grey of the waves, a depressing sight, and he turned back again to study the *Delaware*'s behaviour now that she was relieved of six tons of deadweight. Peabody was not of the type to feel easy optimism. He approached the problem ready to see no appreciable difference, and yet, despite this discounting, he was forced to admit that the *Delaware* was moving a tiny bit more easily–the tiniest, tiniest bit. In that rough water it would give the *Delaware* no added speed, but it was the most he could do to ease her in her labours and still retain her efficiency. The deadweight had been taken from the point where it had most effect on the ship's behaviour–from the upper deck and forward. He glanced astern, and saw the fateful topsail on the horizon again.

The wind was still howling round his ears–it certainly ought to moderate soon, now that the glass had begun to move upward. But there was no sign of it at present. On the contrary–or he was mistaken–those topmasts were whipping badly. He was conscious as he stood that the wind had increased, and he felt in his bones that it was going to increase further. It was natural in a storm like this–he had seen the phenomenon a hundred times. The dying flurries of a storm were often more intense than anything that had preceded it. He felt a sudden wave of bitterness surge up within him. If he had to shorten sail the two decker would come romping up to him, and the voyage of the *Delaware* would come to an end. This was his first command, and he had been at sea less than twenty-four hours. The flurry of the gale might last no more than half an hour, and the wind might die away to a gentle breeze, but that half hour would be enough to do his business for him. God–he was on the point of stupid blasphemy when he mastered himself sternly.

A big grey wave hit the *Delaware* a shuddering blow, and she lurched uncertainly as the water creamed over the spar deck. The high-pitched note of the wind in the rigging screamed a warning to him, and Hubbard was looking round at him anxiously for orders.

'Get the mizzen tops'l in, Mr Hubbard,' said Peabody. 'And the jib.'

A dismasted ship would be of less use than a ship still under control, even if a two decker were overhauling her. The hands raced aloft, shuffling along the footropes of the mizzen topsail yard, and bending forward over the yard to wrestle with the obstinate canvas. The wind shrieked down at them all the harder–it was in the very nick of time that they had shortened sail, and there was a grim satisfaction in that. The men poured down the shrouds again, and one of them after he had leaped to the deck paused for a moment to examine his right forefinger. The nail had been torn almost completely off, and was hanging by a shred from the bloody fingertip–some sudden jerk of the mad canvas aloft had done that for him. He took the dangling nail between his teeth and jerked it off, spat out the nail and shook the blood from his hand and then ran forward after his fellows without a tremor. The crew was tough enough, thought Peabody grimly.

Murray was beside him, descended from his chilly post aloft.

'She's coming down on us fast, sir,' he said. He had a notable tendency to gesticulate with his hands when he spoke.

Hubbard was at his captain's other shoulder now, tall and saturnine, a master of his profession, and yet in this unhappy moment feeling the need for company and conversation.

'Those damned two deckers,' he said. 'They need a gale of wind to move 'em, and that one has it. Standing rigging like chain cable, sir, and canvas as thick as this pea-jacket of mine.'

The two of them looked sidelong at their captain, in need of reassurance. Hubbard was older than Peabody, Murray hardly younger, and yet he felt paternal towards them.

'D'you think he went through Plum Gut, sir?' asked Murray.

'No doubt about it,' said Hubbard, but Murray still looked to his captain for confirmation.

'Yes,' said Peabody.

The implications were manifold. A captain who had the nerve to take a two decker through Plum Gut had nerve enough for anything else whatever, and he had brains as well, and the ability to use them.

'They've had two years to learn in,' said Hubbard, his thin lips twisted into a bitter smile. For two years British ships had been studying American waters at first hand.

The wind shrieked down upon them with renewed force. The *Delaware* was labouring frightfully in the waves; even on deck, and despite the noise of the wind, they could hear the groans of the woodwork as she writhed in their grip.

'If you were down below, sir,' said Murray, 'and *he* wasn't behind us, I'd send down to you for permission to heave-to, sir.'

'And I'd give it,' said Peabody. He could smile at that, just as he could always smile in the midst of a struggle.

'Can we lighten the ship any more, sir?' asked Hubbard, with the extreme deference necessary at a moment when he might be suspected of offering advice to his captain.

'No,' said Peabody. Pitching the spar-deck carronades overside might ease her a little, but would give her no increase in speed in this rough water–only in smooth water with a faint wind would decrease in draft benefit them there, and he had already flung overboard the only weights which were not essential to the *Delaware*'s efficiency as a fighting force. The nod which Hubbard gave indicated his agreement with Peabody's unvoiced argument, and as if with one mind they turned to look back at the two decker. Something more than her topsails were in sight now–as the *Delaware* rose on a wave they could catch a glimpse of her black hull lifting menacingly above the horizon.

'She'll be within gunshot soon,' said Murray with despair in his voice, and Peabody looked at him searchingly. He wanted no cowards in his ship, nor men who would not fight a losing battle to the end. Yet Murray had come to him with the Commodore's enthusiastic recommendation, as the man who, in command of a gunboat flotilla in the Rappahannock had beaten off the boats of the British fleet in the Chesapeake.

'Yes,' said Peabody. 'And I want these two twelve pounders cleared for action. Rig double tackles on them, Mr Murray, if you please, so that they won't come adrift.'

'Aye aye, sir,' said Murray. Peabody could see the change in him now that he had something to do–so that was the kind of man he was. Peabody had no definite labels for human beings, and no vocabulary with which to express his thoughts about them, but he could estimate a character pretty closely.

The *Delaware*'s spar deck carried eighteen thirty-two pounder carronades, nine a side, but forward and aft at the end of each row was mounted a long twelve pounder. The Commodore at the Navy Yard had argued with Peabody about those long guns, pointing out how carronades instead would give the ship an additional forty pounds of broadside, but Peabody had been sure of what he wanted. On this raiding voyage he would either be running away or pursuing, and he wanted long guns on her upper deck to aid him in either of those tasks. He had even had the aftermost and foremost ports enlarged so as to allow these long guns to be trained fully round.

'By George, sir!' said Hubbard suddenly, as he watched the work. 'Do you remember what the Commodore said about these guns? You were right, sir. You were right.'

Peabody did not need Hubbard's approval; he needed no approval save his own.

Murray knew his business. He brought up a double crew–fourteen men–to each of the stern chasers. Cautious, they slacked away the breachings until the gun muzzles were free from the lintels of the ports, and even so, with the mad leaping of the *Delaware*, they careered up and down in the inch or two of slack in the breachings in a fashion which boded ill if they should take charge. Ten men tailed on to the tackles as the breachings were slacked away, keeping the guns steady against the breachings. As the ports were opened showers of spray came in through them, washing over the deck ankle deep. The gun captains took out the tompions, and tested with the rammers to see that the guns were loaded. One of them watched the spray bursting over the gun and shook his head. Despite its tarpaulin cover, the flintlock mechanism could not be expected to work in those conditions, at least, not until the gun was thoroughly hot with use. The powder boys sped forward and came running aft again each with a long coil of slow match in a tub, the ends smouldering and spluttering.

'Run 'em up, boys!' said Murray, and the men threw their weight on the tackles and ran the guns out.

'Ready to open fire, sir!' said Murray, lifting his hat to his captain.

'She's beyond cannon shot yet,' replied Peabody, looking over the grey-flecked sea, with the wind howling round his ears. The two decker was clearly in sight now, all the same, leaping and plunging over the mad sea. 'Mr Hubbard, hoist the colours, if you please.'

The flag went up to the peak and streamed forward in the wind, its eighteen stripes rippling wildly. There had been a discussion about that, too, with the Commodore; and Act of Congress had given the flag fifteen stars and stripes, and yet–as Peabody had seen with his own eyes–the flag that flew over the Hall of Congress bore no more than thirteen, while the Commodore had maintained that there should be a star and a stripe for every state in the union, as Congress had also laid down. It was the Commodore who had decided upon eighteen stripes and stars in the end–Peabody would have preferred the fifteen under which he had sailed into Tripoli harbour. He wondered if the two decker would ever be able to get near enough to count them for herself.

'You can try a shot now, Mr Murray,' said Peabody.

The gun captains already had their guns elevated to the last degree. Each snatched a priming quill from a powder boy, and thrust it in the vent of his gun. They took their matches in their hands, and peered once more along the sights. Then they stood back, watching the ship's motion, and each chose the same moment for firing. They waved their hands at the men at the train tackles to release their grip, and plunged the lighted matches into the quills. One gun hung fire for a moment, the quill sizzling and spluttering, and only exploded after the other gun had boomed out and recoiled to the limit of the breachings. The wind whirled the smoke forward in a flash, and that was all. There was nothing else to be seen; the sea was far too rough for the splash of a twelve-pounder ball to be seen at extreme range. The two decker came plunging along after them unhurt, as far as could be told, the spray still flying from her bluff bows. The hands had crept aft to see the sport, and a sort of groan of disappointment went up from them, even though they were all experienced men who ought to have known better than to expect anything.

'Try again, Mr Murray,' said Peabody–the guns were already being wiped and the powder charge rammed in.

He climbed up on the bulwark close behind the starboard, balancing with his hand on the mizzen rigging. The gun went off with a bang, while Peabody's keen eyes searched the line of flight. There it was! Like a momentary pencil mark–come and gone in a flash–upon the seascape, he could see the ball rise to the top of its trajectory, and drop again to the sea, where a minute white spot marked its fall.

'Half a mile short,' called Peabody. 'But the aim was good. Try again.'

The captain of the other gun had badly misjudged the roll of the ship–his shot plunged into the side of a wave not two cables' lengths away, in plain sight of everyone. Impatiently Murray thrust him on one side, and bent over the breach of the gun himself. Peabody watched the firing from his point of vantage; he was able to mark the fall of about half the shot fired, and nothing went nearer than a hundred yards from the target, as far as he could see, and he expected little else on that heaving sea, and with that gale blowing. But the firing was warming up the guns, so that they would soon be shooting with more powder and so that the lock mechanisms would soon begin to function–no one could be expected to judge the roll of the ship accurately when firing with a match, so that at least two seconds elapsed between the intention to fire and the explosion.

The range was down to a mile–to less than that. Peabody suddenly saw the two decker's maintopsail emerge beside her foretopsail, and the mizzen beside that. Her bluff bows lengthened and her bowsprit showed in profile as she turned. She was yawing to present her broadside to the *Delaware*–Peabody could see her yellow streak and her checkered side as she rolled madly in the trough of the sea. Next came a brief wave of smoke, blown instantly to nothing by the gale, and next came–nothing at all. A hoot of derision went up from the watching sailors at Peabody's back.

'Missed! Clean missed!' said somebody, dancing with joy. 'A whole broadside, and we didn't see where a single shot fell!'

Probably the two decker had fired the long guns on her upper deck–sixteen or seventeen, if she were the seventy-four Peabody estimated her to be. To him there was nothing surprising about the broadside missing, considering the difficulties under which it was discharged. The *Delaware* had fired a dozen shots so far, under better conditions, and not one had gone near the target–the men did not stop to think about that.

The two decker had come before the wind again, and was plunging after them, her bowsprit pointed straight at the *Delaware*. But she had lost a good half mile by yawing to fire her broadside; Peabody doubted if her captain would waste valuable distance again in that fashion. Most probably he would reserve his fire until the two ships were yardarm to yardarm, and when that moment would come depended on the wind. He turned his attention once more to scanning first the sky and then the *Delaware*'s behaviour under her storm canvas. He wanted most desperately for the wind to moderate, or to back, or to veer, for it to do anything rather than blow as it was doing, straight from the two decker to him. Perhaps his life, certainly the success of his voyage; possibly the good opinion of his brother captains, and certainly the good opinion of the American public, depended on that wind. The *Columbian Centinel* would have some scathing remarks in its column if the *Delaware* were captured, even by a ship of the line–not that he cared, save for the depressing effect on the people. His whole power to do anything at all in this war depended on the wind; it was the wind which would settle whether he was to range the Atlantic a free man or rot as a prisoner, and the wind was still blowing its hardest. Peabody had the feeling that it was as well that it was the wind upon which all this depended. If it were some human agency he might be declined to fret and chafe, possibly even to swear and blaspheme, but as it was he could await the decision of Providence calmly.

For some time he had been subconsciously noting the fall of the shot as the stern chasers banged away, and now suddenly his attention was called to the business with a jerk. The brief vision of the flying ball coincided with the two decker a mile astern, and terminated there.

'Good shot, Mr Murray!' he called. 'You hit her fair!'

Murray turned a smiling face back to him, unconscious that the fumes from the vent of the gun had stained his face as black as a negro's. One of the hands was leaping about on the quarterdeck shaking his fists above his head. Peabody's hope that the hit might goad the two decker into yawing again to use her broadside proved ill-founded; the two decker held on her course inexorably, driven by the gale. In half an hour she had gained a quarter of a mile, and in an hour she was no more than half a mile astern. Peabody sent the crew by watches to have their dinners–he did not want the men to have empty stomachs while they fought, although he himself felt not the slightest need for food. He walked round the spar deck to see that every carronade was properly manned. With no chance of employing the main-deck guns he could have fifteen men at every carronade, quite enough to ensure that no carronade would get loose during the battle. And at every carronade there was a good gunlayer–most of them had learned their duty in the British fleet–and still Hubbard had a hundred men under his orders to attend to the working of the ship.

It was a comforting sensation to have an ample crew, with every man an able seaman, and even the ship's boys seventeen years old and upward; there had been no difficulty whatever in enlisting a crew in New York when the *Delaware* commissioned. And yet the captain of the two decker, if he knew his business, would be able to nullify all these arrangements at his will. He could lie three cables' lengths from the *Delaware*, beyond the effective range of her carronades, and pound her to pieces with the long guns on his upper deck. Probably that English captain knew his business, too–he had proved it by bringing his big ship through Plum Gut in the night and guessing the *Delaware*'s future course. Peabody allowed the hatred he felt for his implacable foe to well up freely within him.

He went back to where the stern chasers were still banging away. 'We've hit her eight times, sir,' said Murray, in a sort of ecstasy. Powder smoke and the din of the guns were like drink to him.

'Aim high and try to wing him,' said Peabody.

'Aye, aye, sir,' said Murray, and then, respectfully, 'I've been trying to, sir.' He bent to squint along the gun again, gave a couple of twirls to the elevating screw, and then stood aside and jerked the lanyard. The gun roared out and recoiled; it was so hot now that it leaped in its carriage at the discharge.

'That went close,' said Peabody. 'Try again.'

The sponge on its flexible handle was thrust up the gun, and the water with which it was soaked hissed against the hot metal. Someone whipped a paper cartridge of powder from out of the bucket which guarded it from spray, ripped it open and pushed it into the muzzle. The rammer thrust it further in, and then the big felt wad was thrust in in its turn, the rammer packing the charge hard up into the breach; slovenly packing might diminish the power of the shot down on top of the charge, and another wad was rammed down upon it to hold everything secure. Murray stood aside with the lanyard in his hand, watching the motion of the ship. Suddenly he jerked the lanyard and the gun came leaping back upon its breachings while the wind whisked the smoke round the gun-crew's faces for a second before heaving it forward.

Peabody looked for the flight of the ball, but this time he missed it. And then, as he stared, he saw the two decker's foretopsail suddenly shut down upon itself. From a clear cut oblong it changed into a vague strip cock-eyed across the foremast and shaking in the wind. Someone started to cheer, and the cheering spread along the deck, but it had not reached its full volume before the two decker, deprived of the balancing pressure of her foretopsail, came round abruptly into the wind.

'That's her foretopsail tie gone, sir,' said Hubbard, standing at his side. His lean face with its high arched nose showed more animation than usual.

'More likely the slings,' said Peabody. He had whipped his glass to his eye, and through it he saw the fore rigging of the two decker black with men struggling with the wreckage. 'That was a good shot, Mr Murray.'

But Murray did not hear; he was already sighting his gun again, absorbed in the business of doing as much damage as possible. As Peabody put his glass to his eye again he saw the two decker's broadside momentarily shrouded in smoke, and directly afterwards he was conscious of a tremendous crash beside him. A shot from the two decker had smashed a hole in the bulwark and ploughed its way along the quarterdeck; splinters hummed round him and two men serving the other stern chaser lay mangled in pools of blood. There were other men staring stupidly at wounds inflicted by the splinters, and when he looked forward he saw other men lying dead on the deck, while two severed mainmast shrouds on the starboard side showed where the ball had found its way out of the ship again.

'Get those shrouds spliced and set up again, Mr Hubbard,' said Peabody.

Crippled the two decker might be, but she was determined on inflicting the utmost possible damage before her antagonist escaped out of range. The two stern chasers roared out their defiance; the surgeon's crew were already carrying the wounded below in their canvas chairs and dragging the dead out of the way. Again the two decker was wreathed in smoke, and Peabody found no time to feel a momentary misgiving lest this broadside should do more damage than merely parting a couple of shrouds. But even as the thought came into his head he saw two jets of water rise from a wave top a cable's length astern–the danger was past, and although two guns had been well pointed they had not been given sufficient elevation.

'She's out of range, sir,' said Murray, turning back to him from his gun.

'Yes, Mr Murray, thanks to you,' said Peabody.

Murray showed a gleam of white teeth in his smoke-blackened face.

'Thank you, sir,' he said.

Peabody remembered Stephen Decatur's words of thanks to him when they met, sword in hand, on the deck of the captured *Khaid-ed-Din* in Tripoli harbour, and how he himself had stood flushed and tongue-tied and unable to reply.

'I'll remember this in my report to the Commodore,' said Peabody. 'Now get those guns secured.'

He realised now that he and everyone else on the quarterdeck were soaked to the skin by the spray which had come in through the gunports, and he was shuddering with cold and lack of exercise. His heavy pea-jacket was wet as a soaked sponge and hung like lead from his shoulders. Looking through his glass he could see men still hard at work on the two decker's foretopsail yard; they looked like ants on a twig. It would be fully ten minutes before the two decker got before the wind again; in ten minutes they would be a mile farther away; to regain that mile would take the two decker at least two hours, if not more; and in less than four hours it would be dark. They were almost safe–as safe as any United States ship could be on a sea whose length and breadth was searched and scanned by the British fleet.

Hubbard had the hands at the braces trimming the sails, and Peabody looked sharply up at the commission pennant fluttering from the maintopmast. The wind had backed noticeably, and, just as important, it was moderating.

'Set the mizzen tops'l and jib again, Mr Hubbard,' said Peabody.

'Aye aye, sir.'

Hubbard stood beside his captain with his eyes on the men casting off the gaskets and a wry smile on his long face.

'We can just walk away from that old tub now, sir,' he said. 'It would ha' saved us a bit of trouble if the wind had made up its mind sooner.'

Peabody stared at him. The dead men were lying by the spars, forward; their lives would have been saved, undoubtedly, but apart from that–Providence helps those who help themselves. Peabody's philosophy was such–illogical though he would have admitted it to be if he had happened to analyse his feelings–that to him it was the most natural thing in the world for the wind to shift and moderate after his own efforts had made the change almost unnecessary. To grumble at the whims of uncontrolled natural forces–at the dictates of Providence–was a little absurd to him, like a heathen beating his god for not responding to prayer. He was growing a little set in his ways of thought.

3

The *Delaware* had crossed the blue water of the Gulf Stream. She had caught the north-east trades by now, and was thrashing along with the wind over her port quarter and with all sail set, driving so hard that Mr Hubbard was keeping an eye on the studding sails lest there should be a trifle too much strain on the booms. The blue water–so blue that it might have been a painted surface–turned to a dazzling white as the *Delaware* broke through it, and in the waves thrown off from her sharp bow a dozen dolphins tumbled and somersaulted.

The lookouts were at their dizzy posts at the fore and main topgallant mastheads, swinging in vast circles against the blue sky as the *Delaware* soared superbly over the waves. They were on duty; so were Mr Hubbard and Midshipman Quincy, walking the deck with their telescopes under their arms, and so were the men at the wheel. So were the two carpenter's mates at work on the deck planking aft by the taffrail–there was a bloodstain there which no amount of scrubbing during the past few days had been able to remove, and by Mr Hubbard's orders a section of planking was being replaced. Mr Hubbard would not on any account have bloodstains marring the spotless white of his decks.

Otherwise, in this dog watch, the ship's company was free. Forward the deck was covered with little groups of men, chattering, sewing their clothes, or merely lounging in idleness; aft the ship's officers were taking air and exercise, lieutenants, the master, the surgeon and his mate, walking solemnly up and down their little bits of deck, and turning inwards towards each other at each end of their beats without a break in their conversation, while up in the mizzen rigging half a dozen midshipman were valorously emulating the athletic feats of young master's mate Hayward who was leading a game of follow-my-leader.

On a day like this all troubles could be forgotten. The memory of the bitter cold of the blizzard in which they had started had vanished as completely as the ice which had festooned the ship, and already the memory of the dead whom they had left behind them was beginning to fade along with it. The sun was warm and not too warm; the ship had her studding sails set slow and aloft; there were sparkling rainbows in the spray tossed from the bows, and sail drill and gun drill had ceased for the day. There was nothing more that a sailor's heart could desire.

Peabody came on deck, a cigar all ready for smoking between his teeth, and the officers herded away respectfully from his side of the deck. He lit his cigar from the smouldering bit of punk which during the dog watches was left in a tub aft for the convenience of the officers, and inhaled deeply as he glanced round the ship as every captain since the world began has done on his arrival on deck. All sail set and drawing well–the cut of that main course was a perfect masterpiece. She must be going all of the eleven knots which he had noted on the traverse board on his way on deck. And tobacco was good on a sunny evening like this–he drew again deeply on his cigar. It was several hours since he last smoked, for Peabody had a strict rule against smoking below deck, and he had been confined below for several hours dealing with the ship's papers. Most of what he had been doing was the clerk's work, but Peabody was fully conscious of his own competence to deal with it, and guiltily conscious of the clerk's inability. And he had not wanted to bother the boy; he looked sharply across the deck and saw him leaning, gloomy and solitary, against the taffrail with his back to all the merriment and lightheartedness of the ship.

That was a pity. Peabody would have preferred to see Jonathan skylarking up in the rigging along with the midshipmen, and he sighed a little. The boy was a little too old to adapt himself readily to a life at sea. Peabody blamed himself for not having obtained his captaincy earlier so that he could have rescued the boy from the plough–from his mother and father–a little younger, before he got so set in his gloomy habits, when it would have been easy to initiate him into the pleasant delights of algebra and spherical trigonometry and gradually make him into a midshipman, a lieutenant, and in the end a captain. He himself was profoundly grateful to Providence for what he had received. He was captain of this superb ship. He had work to do which he felt competent to perform–that was a most gratifying feeling. And he was already wealthy. As captain he was paid the enormous salary of one hundred dollars a month–a stupendous amount. The Connecticut farm did not produce one hundred dollars a year in real money; the terrible father who had beaten him as a child had never in his whole life held in his hands the sum which his son received monthly. There was a grim, unpleasing pleasure in the thought.

But he should have reached this eminence five years ago, for Jonathan's sake, saving him five years of frightening tyranny, five years of a maudlin mother's insane antics. There was every excuse in the world for the boy; but tobacco did not taste so good now. He walked across the deck to pitch his half-smoked cigar overboard to leeward, and Hubbard took off his hat to his captain with the formal courtesy which characterised him–the formality of the Navy combined with the graces of the South.

Here came the marine band, all six of them marching stiffly behind their sergeant, two side drums and four fifes, the sergeant saluting captain and quarterdeck with a single gesture. He swung his brass-mounted cane, and the drums gave their triple roll before beginning their exhilarating rhythm while the fifes squeaked bravely away at 'Yankee Doodle.' Up and down, up and down, marched the marines; the fifers in their tall stocks were purple in the face with the effort of blowing. It was all very gay and lighthearted; even Peabody caught the infection. To be at sea again, to have broken the close blockade, was stimulating and exhilarating. The prospect of action cheered everyone on board. The sail drill and the gun drill during those tedious weeks in the East River had been dull and pointless, but now there was a chance of putting them to use. And every man on board, except for Jonathan Peabody and some of the midshipmen, was an experienced sailor, with the sea in his blood. The joys of home, of life in port, were not exaggerated, but were liable to cause surfeit, and some of the men on board had not been to sea for two years now. They felt as if they were free of chains.

On the starboard beam the sun was setting in a glory of red. Three bars of cloud, as straight as if drawn by parallel rulers, hung over the western horizon above the dying sun; typical trade wind clouds bearing the promise of unchanged weather, thought Peabody, noting them. He watched the red disk sink slowly into the sea while the light faded from the sky–in the east it was already dark. The young moon was just in sight in the western sky now that its light was not submerged in that of the sun.

'Deck there!' from the maintopgallant masthead. A pause.

'What is it?' hailed Hubbard.

'I thought I saw a sail. Yes, there she is, on the starboard bow, sir! Right to leeward, sir!'

All Peabody's instincts exploded into action. He did not stop to calculate that with night coming down so fast every second was of value, and he did not consciously allow for the waste of time if a junior had to report to him; his reactions were quicker than his thoughts. He snatched the glass and threw himself into the main rigging. Up the ratlines he went, up the futtock shrouds back downwards without pausing for breath, up to the maintopmast crosstrees, hand over hand to topgallant masthead. He was hard and lean despite his heavy shoulders, and his pumping heart and quickened respiration did nothing to unsteady him.

Up at this height there was perceptibly more light than on deck. Eastward all was black, with a star or two beginning to show, but to the westward the sky still showed a gleam of red. The awed lookout on his narrow perch pointed over the starboard bow, momentarily too impressed by the sudden appearance of his captain to speak. Peabody saw what he was pointing to. At the very edge of the colour in the sky, silhouetted sharply in black against the red, were two minute geometrical shapes close together. Peabody fixed them in his glass, swinging the instrument in accordance with the roll of the ship, but in that light the glass was not of any help to his own keen eyesight. The upper sails of a brig, royals and topgallants, decided Peabody, standing to the north close hauled on the opposite tack to the *Delaware*.

'Has she changed course since you saw her?' he demanded of the lookout.

'No, sir, not as far as I can tell.'

Peabody glanced back over his shoulder again; the eastward sky was quite black. The *Delaware*'s upper sails, viewed from the brig, would not stand out in the fashion hers did, and there was not enough light from the westward to illuminate them, either. The chances were that the brig had not seen her, and moreover if she had she would probably have put up her helm and hurried over the horizon as a precautionary measure. His eyes sought her again unavailingly, for the red patch had dwindled almost to nothing and the brig had disappeared into the darkness.

'Mr Hubbard!' he bellowed down to the deck.

'Sir!'

'Put the helm up. Bring her round on the other tack.'

'Aye aye, sir.'

Far below him he could hear the orders called, and he could just hear the bustle of the men hurrying to the braces. The *Delaware* rose momentarily to an even keel beneath him, and then heeled again. The darkness round him was filled with the creaking of ropes as the yards came round. As he looked forward he saw the starboard foretopmast studding sail blot out the last of the red patch of sky. The foretopsail followed round.

'Keep her at that!' he roared.

'Aye aye, sir!'

Now the *Delaware* had the wind nearly abeam, while the brig to leeward had been close hauled. The courses of the two ships were sharply convergent. Two hours, two hours and a half, perhaps, before they met–always provided, that is, that the brig did not alter course. But although Peabody strained his eyes peering into the night he could see nothing of her at all. He was about to descend, when he remembered the good services of the lookout.

'A tot of rum for you to-morrow,' he said.

'Thank'ee, sir. Please, sir—'

'Well?'

'Beg your pardon, sir, but could you make it 'baccy? A plug o' chawing, sir—'

'Yes. What's your name?'

'Gaines, sir.'

A seaman who preferred tobacco to rum was quite a rarity. Perhaps he had been through the same desperate struggle that Peabody had, when every nerve in his body shrieked for the drink he denied it. Peabody had won his victory over the monster as a lieutenant of twenty, after he realised that in the wardroom mess his behaviour, which he had thought so clever, was like that of his mother when she was wearing her stupid grin. There had been three months of torment, three years of temptation. Now even the temptation was gone, and Peabody could trust himself to have one drink, two drinks, when the occasion demanded, but perhaps this man Gaines was still in the period of temptation. He looked over the starboard sky, somehow oddly moved, and then he realised that he was in danger of having a favourite on board, which would not do at all. He grunted something inarticulate, swung himself into the rigging, and began his slow descent. Murray was officer of the watch now, but Hubbard was still on deck with him awaiting his captain.

'Send the hands to quarters, Mr Murray, and clear for action.'

The drums which had beaten so merry a tune an hour ago now went roaring through the ship calling the men to quarters. The *Delaware* was filled with the clatter and bustle of it all as the men rushed to begin their allotted tasks, and the weeks of drill during those grim days in the East River were justified now as even in the darkness the men did their work without confusion. The marines climbed to the tops with elephantine clumsiness; the powder boys came running to the guns with their buckets of cartridges. Down below the bulkheads were coming down, the guns were being cast loose, the sand was being scattered over the deck. Rodgers the boatswain formed up his two fire-fighting parties with the head pumps fore and aft and the canvas hoses coiled in the scuppers. Two boys hurried along the deck with their arms full of lanterns, hanging them on the gant lines which Rodgers had set up.

'I don't want a light in the ship until I give the word.'

'Very good, sir.'

The main-deck guns were being run out with a threatening rumble–the distant thunder of the approaching storm–while on the spar deck the crews of the carronades adjusted their pieces for elevation and primed the vents. The *Delaware* was singing through the sea; running thus, two points free, was perhaps her best point of sailing, and there was most decidedly a chance that she would pass ahead of the quarry.

'Get the stuns'l in, Mr Hubbard.'

'Aye aye, sir.'

There was not much chance of danger. A brig-rigged vessel even if she were a man-of-war, was bound to be smaller than a big frigate like the *Delaware*; if she were part of a convoy the escort would have been to windward of her and in plain sight. She must be sailing alone, and in that case she might be perhaps an American privateer or one of those footy little British Post Office packets. Peabody called up before his mind's eye the memory of those topsails silhouetted against the sky. Yes. The chances were that she was a Post Office packet, and in that case she must be overwhelmed before she could throw her mail bags overside. Yet at the same time he must be quite certain that she was not an American privateer; it would be disastrous if she were and he fired into her.

Peabody remembered the British naval officers whom he had encountered often enough in the cafés of Valetta. Many of them spoke in a curious throaty manner which he had been given to understand was looked upon nowadays as the newest fashion in England, with the vowels broadened and the consonants disregarded. He thought for a moment of Hubbard, but Hubbard's South Carolinian speech had nothing British about it. He turned upon Jonathan.

'Go and find O'Brien for me. Master's mate–he'll be at the headsail sheets.'

It was five long minutes before O'Brien came looming up on the quarterdeck; it was a pity that Jonathan had not yet familiarised himself with every part of the ship and every man on board.

'O'Brien, sir. Come to report.'

O'Brien's voice had not lost the Irish in it, even though it was twenty years since he had sailed from Cork.

'Stay by me. I want you to hail for me when the time comes.'

The night was clear although dark; the crescent moon, right down on the horizon, contributed almost no light, but the stars were bright. A ship could be seen at a couple of miles, certainly.

'Cover that binnacle light,' said Peabody.

The *Delaware* surged along through the darkness; it was fortunate that he had been able to spare the studding sails, because the reduction in speed would make a considerable difference to the visibility of her bow wave. There came a low hail from the foretop–the sergeant of marine there must be an intelligent man as well as having keen eyes.

'Deck, there! She's in sight, sir. On the larboard bow.'

Peabody put down his night glass–the thing was not of much use. There she was, most certainly, a black outline faintly showing against the slightly lighter surface of the sea, holding the same course as when he had seen her last, and the two vessels were closing fast. In five minutes–but she was wearing round on the instant.

'Loose the stuns'ls, Mr Hubbard, if you please. Put your helm up a point, quartermaster.'

Peabody had caught sight of the first movement of the brig's sails as she wore. The fact that her foretopsail came round before the mainsails proved that she had a small crew and was no man-of-war, and it also gave the *Delaware* two full minutes in which to cut the corner. She was tearing down upon the brig now.

'Pass the word to the starboard guns to stand by.'

A faint hail came from the brig.

'Ship ahoy! What ship's that?'

Peabody nudged O'Brien, but there was no need. The Irishman's tongue was ready enough.

'His Britannic Majesty's frigate *Calypso*. Heave to!'

There was a moment delay, while the *Delaware* still fore reached upon the brig. If the chase were American, she would open fire.

'Heave to, and wait for my boat!' hailed O'Brien.

These seconds were precious. There was no chance of escape for the brig now; in a few more seconds they could overwhelm her perhaps without firing a shot. The brig had not opened fire, and it was clear she was not American. Peabody was certain, as it was, that she was a Post Office packet; he recognised the cut of those sails. But at any second she could recognise in her turn the *Delaware* for what she was, by her clipper bows and raking masts and spar deck. There were no other ships at sea like the big American frigates. Peabody nudged O'Brien again.

'Heave to, damn your eyes!' yelled O'Brien into the speaking trumpet.

Five more seconds elapsed before the answer came–four bright orange flashes from the brig's side. A ball sang over Peabody's head, and at the same time there was a crash below as another struck home.

'Mr Murray!' shouted Peabody, and the words had hardly left his lips before the *Delaware*'s broadside replied–a little ragged, but just passable. The enormous orange flames from the quarterdeck carronades left Peabody momentarily blinded. All was dark around him and he could see nothing. But overside he could hear the results of what he had done–a clatter of falling blocks and a man shrieking in agony. He had not wanted to do this; he wanted to overwhelm the brig without effusion of blood, but once he had opened fire it was necessary to crush her before the mails could be thrown overboard.

He blinked his eyes until he could see again. The brig had come up into the wind a helpless wreck, braces and halliards shot away; the smashing broadside had almost torn her to pieces. He heard the *Delaware*'s guns rumble loudly as they were run out again.

'Back the mizzen tops'l, Mr Hubbard, if you please. Brig ahoy! Have you struck?'

'Yes, God rot you,' said a voice in the darkness.

'Take the quarterboat and take possession, O'Brien. Send the captain over to me.'

'Aye aye, sir.'

The wounded man on board the brig had stopped screaming as the quarterboat dropped into the water. Peabody took a restless turn or two about the deck–the two vessels were close enough together by now for him to hear voices on board the brig, and the sound of the oars being laid down in the boat as she went alongside.

'Mr Hubbard, take charge. I want a boatswain's chair to hoist the brig's captain in.'

Lights gleamed at the entry port, the sound of oars proclaimed the return of the quarterboat, and the tackles squealed as the brig's captain was hoisted on board. Someone led him aft to where Peabody stood in the faint light of the uncovered binnacle; he was short and square and stocky, with a stiff rheumatic gait. Peabody took off his hat. 'Your servant, sir.'

Truxtun in the *Constellation* had drilled his young officers in the manners expected of them, and Peabody's graces dated from that time. The British captain touched his hat in the new manner of the British service.

'Perhaps you would be so good as to come below with me, sir?' asked Peabody.

Down below they were just replacing the bulkheads of the main cabin; they had a glimpse of the long gun deck where, in the dim light of the lanterns, the men were securing their guns again. Washington, the negro servant, was trying to set the cabin to rights, bustling about with chairs, lighting the big cabin lamp, putting cushions on the lockers. He was flustered by the fact that his master was receiving company in a cabin which had been cleared for action. The British captain sat down in the chair which Washington dragged forward for him, while Peabody took his seat on the starboard side locker.

'What was your ship, sir?' asked Peabody. He knew how bitter the use of that word 'was' would be for his prisoner but there was no way round the difficulty.

'Brig *Princess Augusta*, seven days out from Kingston. My name's Stanton.'

'Post Office packet, Captain Stanton?'

'Yes.'

'Whither bound?'

'Halifax.'

Letters for the British troops in Canada, then. The capture was doubly important.

'And what ship is this?' asked the British captain in his turn.

'United States ship *Delaware*.'

There was no need to say whence or whither—this prisoner might be recaptured.

'I didn't guess you were a Yankee until it was too late,' said the British captain bitterly. 'There aren't so many Yankee frigates at sea nowadays.'

The *Delaware* was the only one, as far as Peabody knew, unless Decatur had managed to escape from New London.

'I hope my broadside did not do too much damage,' said Peabody.

'Four killed and seven wounded–two of 'em mortal, I think.'

Washington came back into the cabin and spread a cloth on the table. He had brought an appetising-looking tray, but the British captain waved away the food which Peabody offered.

'No thank you,' he said. 'I've no appetite for food.'

'I shall send my surgeon on board the *Princess Augusta*,' said Peabody. 'I hope he will be able to relieve the wounded.'

'Thank you, sir,' said the captain.

There came a knock at the cabin door, and Washington opened it.

'It's Mistah O'Brien, sir.'

'Tell him to come in.'

O'Brien was carrying two small but heavy leather bags, on the fastenings of which dangled leaded seals.

'I brought these over myself, sir. I didn't want to trust 'em to anyone else.'

The bags as he set them on the deck gave out the clink of gold; Peabody glanced at the British captain and saw the look of mortification which passed over his face. But now that the discovery had been made the captain took it with the best grace he could.

'Two thousand guineas,' he said. 'I was hoping you wouldn't find it before we were retaken.'

'That's pay for the British army in Canada,' said Peabody. 'You were quite right to bring it to me, O'Brien. Are the mail bags still on board?'

'Yes, sir.'

Stanton's hint about the chance of the *Princess Augusta* being retaken no more than echoed what was already in Peabody's mind. It was hard for the United States Navy to take prizes, but it was harder still to profit by them. The rigid blockade off every American port made it extraordinarily difficult to send in captured ships. Peabody's instructions from the Secretary of the Navy, locked in the desk at his elbow, expressly authorised him to destroy prizes–even neutral vessels with contraband–at his discretion. The gold would be far safer on board the *Delaware* than in charge of a prize crew. But the mails were a different matter. At Washington they might be able to extract valuable information from them. It was worth while trying to send the brig in with the mail bags, even though it meant exposing a prize crew to the risk of capture. He sent O'Brien away with instructions before he turned back to Captain Stanton.

'If you will give me your parole on behalf of yourself and your crew,' he said, 'not to attempt escape before you reach an American port, it will make your voyage far more comfortable.'

Stanton shook his head.

'You know as well as I do that I can't do that, sir,' he said.

'More's the pity,' said Peabody. Stanton and his men would be left battened down below, at that rate, until the *Princess Augusta* reached Charleston. 'You are sure you will have no refreshment before you leave, sir?'

'You're very kind, sir. Perhaps I will–only a small one, sir. Just four fingers. Thank'ee, sir.'

Stanton looked at Peabody over the top of his glass; he forbore to comment–wisely enough, perhaps, seeing that he was only a prisoner–on the smallness of his host's drink.

'Confusion to the French,' he said.

Peabody was a little startled. The French were at war with England; America was at war with England, but France and America were not allies. He wondered if he could drink such a toast, all the same, even in the privacy of his cabin. Stanton's homely wrinkled face broke into a smile at his confusion.

'Let's say "a speedy peace," then,' said Stanton.

'A speedy peace,' said Peabody, solemnly.

Stanton took a pull at his glass before speaking again.

'You've heard the latest from the Continent, sir?'

'What is it?' asked Peabody, with native caution.

'The news came in the day before we cleared from Kingston. Wellington's over the Pyrenees. The Russians are over the Rhine, and Boney's licked. Licked as sure as a gun.'

Peabody stared at him, but there was no doubt the man was speaking the truth. In Peabody's throat the weak rum that he had sipped burned with the fierce pleasure which he had always to disregard, and for a moment it distracted him from making any deductions from what he was being told.

'Come midsummer,' said Stanton, 'and France'll be neutral. Aye, or before that.'

Then the British Navy would be free to turn its whole strength against the American coast, the British Army would be free to strike at exposed points, and what hope would there be then of an honourable peace?

'And then we'll have nothing to fight over,' went on Stanton. 'We won't want to press your men, and we won't care how much wheat you sell to the French. I'm no naval officer, sir. England was at war when I took my first command to sea in '94, and we're still at war twenty years after. I'd like to make a voyage–just one voyage–without wondering whether I'd be in prison before I reached the end of it.'

He drank off his glass without winking an eyelid, and stood up, submissive to any orders which Peabody might give him. On deck in the darkness he shook hands with his captor before hobbling stiffly off to the ship's side. Peabody lingered on deck; Mason, his youngest lieutenant, had fifty men and all the skilled hands of the *Delaware* repairing the tattered rigging of the *Princess Augusta*, and when the work was finished Mason would retain six of them and make an attempt to reach Charleston–or Georgetown or Wilmington, or any other port where he could slip past the British cruisers.

Peabody suddenly became aware of Jonathan at his side, whispering urgently in the darkness.

'Jos,' he was saying,' Jos, is it true that ship's going back to America?'

'Yes, I'm sending the brig in with a prize crew.'

'Jos, send me back in it, too.'

'What's that?' said Peabody, quite unable to believe his ears.

'Send me back in that ship–brig, I mean. Please, Jos. Let me.'

'What in God's name are you saying?'

'I want to go back on that ship. I want to get out of here. I hate all this. I know they're going to the South, but I'll be able to get back to Connecticut somehow, Jos.'

'Call me "sir",' snapped Peabody. He was still too astonished to attempt to deal with the matter of what Jonathan was saying, and temporised by finding fault with the manner.

'"Sir", then. Won't you let me go?'

The boy was frantic now, plucking at his captain's sleeve. He had at least the grace to whisper his ridiculous request, but that was little enough in his favour–on the contrary, rather, for it showed he knew he ought to be ashamed of it.

'No, I will not,' said Peabody, coming to a decision. 'Get below, and don't let me see you again to-night. Get below, I said.'

The boy went off into the darkness with something like a sob, leaving Peabody tapping angrily with his foot on the deck as he debated this extraordinary happening. There must be something seriously the matter with Jonathan if he wanted to exchange this ideal life on board ship again for the hardships of home, the orderly discipline for the madness of his parents. Peabody went back in his mind to his first days at sea. Yes, he had been homesick, too, homesick for the green valleys and the rocky hills, even homesick for his chaff mattress in the corner of the room. But he had been only twelve, and Jonathan was twenty. Now he came to think of it, it was strange that Jonathan had endured the Connecticut farm up to that age; he could have escaped from it long ago into the West, into Ohio, where the farming was so good, or even into the Federal army during the past two years.

Peabody was conscious of a feeling of disillusionment, or of disappointment–in either case, it was something which he was always prepared for.

4

Peabody wiped his mouth with his napkin and looked down the table, the largest that could be rigged in the mess cabin. The afternoon sunlight was streaming in through the skylight, and the cabin was sweltering hot–there were trickles of sweat down his lean cheeks, while fat little Purser Styles beside him was mopping his face unashamedly.

'Damme, sir,' said Styles, 'but those beans were good. The weevils haven't got at 'em yet. Here, Washington, I'll have another cut o' that pork.'

Only skeletons remained of the four scrawny hens which had been sacrificed for dinner, but there was plenty of fat meat left on the two legs of fresh pork which had been served. Everyone had eaten well, and before Washington brought in the dessert it was time for a toast. Peabody was uneasily conscious that it was time for a speech, too, but that he would not be able to give. The toast would have to suffice–he could remember by heart well enough the formula he had heard repeated in past years. He got to his feet, glass in hand, and conversation died away as all eyes turned to him.

'To the memory of the immortal man whose birthday we are celebrating to-day,' he said. 'To the memory of George Washington.'

Everyone rose with inarticulate murmurs while the toast was drunk, and sat down again a trifle self-consciously.

Purser Styles, with his red face, took it for granted now that he could unbuckle the stock which was putting him in danger of apoplexy. Lieutenant Murray took wine across the table with his *vis-à-vis*, Acting Lieutenant Howard, Mr Crane, the master, beamed quite genially at the three lads at the end of the table–Midshipman Wallingford, Midshipman Shepherd, and Acting Midshipman Peabody.

The captain, at the head of the table, experienced a feeling of relief; he had proposed the toast without stumbling, and this formal dinner party was bidding fair to be a success–Peabody always felt qualms of doubt when responsible for a social occasion. He frowned a little as he noticed Jonathan refilling his glass. The boy was a little flushed as it was–although that might merely be the heat–and he did not like to see it. Jonathan had so obviously benefited by this appointment as acting midshipman. It really had been fortunate that they had captured the *Princess Augusta*, and that Mason had gone off in her as prize master; the acting promotion of Howard had left a vacancy which Peabody was entitled to fill. Now Jonathan was acting midshipman, and his foot on the ladder leading to executive rank, and with the discipline of Hubbard and Murray and Crane to drive out from his mind the fantastic troubles which had been worrying him. Peabody was well content, or would have been if Jonathan were not quite so flushed.

A knocking at the cabin door heralded the admission of Quincy, out of breath with hurrying.

'A message from Mr Hubbard, sir,' he panted. 'Cutter in sight, and bearing up for us.'

'My compliments to Mr Hubbard, and I'll come on deck.'

Peabody turned to his guests.

'I beg your pardon, gentlemen. I hope you will excuse me for a moment.'

They rose in reply–it was a continual mild surprise to Peabody that the conventional manners which he found it so hard to employ always worked so well.

Peabody ran up on deck; Hubbard was looking through his glass at the jaunty cutter which was running towards them–a typical island boat with patched brown sails.

'Heave to, Mr Hubbard, if you please.'

The cutter was bowling along quickly under a light air which had hardly been moving the *Delaware*, but then the latter had had no more than topsails set. The cutter, as Peabody saw through the glass, had a coloured hand in the bows and two more in the waist; aft, at the tiller, there sat a man in dazzling white clothes. He put up his tiller, and the cutter came neatly into the wind and took in her head sail; a moment later, the dinghy, which had been towing astern, came sculling briskly across the glittering water with the white-clad man in the stern sheets, and a half-naked negro at the sculls. Peabody met the visitor as he came dexterously up the side.

'Mr Hunningford?'

'Captain Hunningford, sir. And I have the honour to address—?'

'Josiah Peabody.'

'Of the United States frigate *Delaware*,' supplemented Hunningford, looking round the ship with a keen professional eye.

'I have been beating about waiting for you for the last week,' said Peabody irritably.

'And I, sir,' said Hunningford, with sublime insouciance, 'have been waiting for you for two months.'

He was a man as tall as Peabody, and even thinner, and without Peabody's heavy shoulders. He had a lean, mobile face and a twinkle in his eye–it was the face of a young man in strange contrast with his snow-white hair.

'What news have you for me?' demanded Peabody.

Hunningford looked round the deck.

'I would prefer,' he said gently, 'to tell you that in conditions a little more private.'

'Come below,' said Peabody curtly.

He led the visitor down the companion, pausing outside the door of the main cabin he heard Styles's voice lifted in song, and directly afterwards the rest of the company joined in the chorus.

'This way,' said Peabody, opening the door of the sleeping cabin.

Hunningford sat down on the locker and left the cot to Peabody.

'You are comfortable enough here,' he said, glancing about him. 'But I would prefer to have that skylight closed.'

Peabody followed his gaze, and reopened the door to give the order to the sentry outside. Then they waited in silence until the skylight closed over their heads.

'Well?' said Peabody.

'The Jamaica convoy sails in nine days' time,' said Hunningford. 'The escort will be the *Calypso*, 36, corvette *Racer*, 20, if she's back in time, which I expect, and the brig *Bulldog*, 14. They will sail by the Windward Passage, and will rendezvous with the Leeward Islands convoy in Latitude 25 North, Longitude 65 West.'

This was precise enough information, if it were correct.

'How do you know this?' asked Peabody.

Hunningford shrugged his shoulders.

'I am paid no commission for revealing that,' he said. 'But if you imagine that a convoy of a hundred sail can be assembled without certain facts leaking out you have a higher opinion of human nature than I have. My commercial connections give me certain opportunities and privileges.'

Peabody felt a certain surly hostility towards this elegant spy, partly because of his elaborate manner, and partly because of the way he lived, associating with honest merchants, and selling them to their enemies.

'Are you sure of what you say?' he asked.

'My dear sir,' said Hunningford, crossing his knees, 'you are treating me with a suspicion which is quite unwarranted. If I wished to betray you, you can be quite sure that it would not be my cutter which kept our appointment, but a squadron of British frigates.'

That was perfectly true, and it ought to have lessened Peabody's instinctive dislike for the man, but it did not. But he did not allow his dislike to interfere with his questioning.

'What news of the privateers?' he asked.

'Ah!' replied Hunningford archly. 'Now we approach the crux of the matter. I am in touch with the schooners *Emulation*, Captain Daniel Gooding, and *Oliver*, Captain James Curtis, both out of Baltimore. I have already passed on to them some valuable pieces of information, but the Jamaica convoy is rather more important, as both you and they agree. They are anxious to receive instructions from you. With your assistance, Captain, they hope to make themselves both wealthy for life. To me, it is more important that my commission on their captures will make me wealthier still.'

'I'll give you a letter to them.'

Hunningford put his fingers to his lean throat, and made a realistic choking noise.

'You must dislike me very much, Captain, if you are so anxious to see me cut off in my respected old age. I will carry any verbal message you like, but nothing in writing.'

Peabody looked his puzzlement, and Hunningford condescended to further explanation.

'I come and I go,' he said. 'My manifold business interests take me from island to island. As far as I know, no suspicion attaches to me. No one, save my negroes, knows that to-day I encounter you just out of sight of land, and to-morrow Captain Gooding. I could be arrested and examined at any moment, and I should welcome the examination, which could only clear my fair name. But if I carried a letter from a United States captain—'

He repeated his former gesture, putting his head on one side, and rolling up his eyes with hideous added realism.

'What do you want done, then?'

'You must tell me your plans, Captain, and I'll pass them on.'

Peabody rubbed his chin, and stared at Hunningford; the latter's malicious grey eyes met his own hard blue ones without flinching.

'What's the force of these two schooners?' he demanded.

'They're both big enough to take care of themselves. The *Emulation*'s two hundred and fifty tons, the *Oliver*'s over two hundred. *Oliver* has four long nine and ten twelve-pounder carronades. *Emulation* threw half her guns overboard last December, when the *Fox* chased her in a calm, but she's rearmed herself from prizes–sixes, nines, and a couple of twelves.'

Peabody's mind began to analyse the tactical problem presented.

'Neither Gooding nor Curtis,' said Hunningford, 'will fight a King's ship if they can help it.'

Peabody knew that; no privateer captain who knew his trade would risk his ship and face certain crippling damage in action with a man o' war. If he were to lock yardarms with the *Calypso* there was still the rest of the escort to consider–the *Bulldog* alone could probably beat off the privateers, and the *Racer*, if she were present, could outfight them both. But the disparity of force was not so great as to be insuperable; the West Indian convoy was a prize, indeed, and any serious loss to it would raise a storm among the merchants of London. It was most unlikely that, for some time to come, there would be any equally attractive objective for an attack at smaller risk.

'Tell them,' said Peabody, 'to meet me behind Tortuga on the second of next month.'

Hunningford nodded.

'They wouldn't come,' he said, 'unless I told them that there was a capable captain in command. I'll tell them that, too.'

Peabody shot a surprised glance at him, but Hunningford reverted instantly to his former tone of light cynicism as he rose to his feet.

'This has been a stimulating interview, Captain,' he said. 'I'm glad to see a ship of force in these island again. And I expect the prizes taken will return me a very handsome commission.'

Peabody watched the cutter go racing off again, wing-and-wing, to the southward. He wondered, as he saw her sink over the horizon, whether her captain was a mere venal person who took tainted money, or a very brave man who was cheerfully risking the gallows in his country's cause. He strongly suspected Hunningford to be the latter. When he reached his cabin again he found that his dinner party had progressed perfectly satisfactorily in his absence.

5

Captain Gooding was bluff and hospitable, but Captain Curtis was young and eager–quite half a dozen years Peabody's junior. They were both waiting at the side when Peabody came on board the *Emulation* to return their call, both in their best clothes, with swords at their sides and cocked hats on their heads. The *Emulation* copied man o' war's ways; the boatswain's mates twittered on their pipes, and there were side boys in white gloves ready to assist him, and twenty landsmen–the privateer's equivalent of marines–in green coats making a workmanlike job of presenting arms as Peabody stepped on the deck. The hands were uniformly dressed in red check shirts and white trousers, and the deck was as white as Captain Gooding's cravat.

'Honoured to receive you, sir,' said Gooding. 'Please be so good as to step this way. The coaming's high–*Emulation*'s a wet ship on a bowline–and the cabin's not as lofty as you've been accustomed to, I'm afraid. Mr Merton! Take Captain Peabody's hat and sword. Sit here, sir. I've a nice drop of Jamaica, sir, which I took out of the *Blandford*. No? There's some Madeira and a fair Marsala. Merton! The Madeira for Captain Peabody. Please take your ease, sir. There's no reason for worry as long as the wind's nor'-easterly. Merton! How's the wind?'

'Nor'-east by east, sir,' said Merton, in a tone of infinite patience.

He was tall, spare negro, who got his information, after a glance at the tell-tale compass over Gooding's head, by craning his neck up to the chink in the cabin skylight and looking up at the pennant at the maintopmast truck.

'Serve the dinner, then, you black pole mast.'

The ludicrous simile made Peabody grin; there was a strange likeness between the lean negro and a skysail mast without the skysail set.

'I would be glad to hear your suggestions again for the attack, sir,' said Curtis, the moment the flow of Gooding's talk was checked.

'Anyone would think Curtis and I hadn't spent the last two hours discussing 'em,' said Gooding promptly. 'This is dinner-time. How's the wind, Merton?'

'Nor'-east by east, sir.'

'The British don't know your ship's in these waters?' persisted Curtis.

'They can't know yet,' said Peabody, 'not unless Hunningford has told them.'

'Hunningford wouldn't say a word,' said Gooding. 'He has too keen an eye for business.'

The three captains exchanged glances, Peabody keenly observing the other two.

'Three fat commissions has he screwed out of me,' admitted Curtis.

Peabody had a flash of insight. The fact that these hard-headed Baltimore captains had to pay Hunningford good hard cash for his information made them far more ready to respect his suggestions. His heart warmed to the memory of the man.

'Try some of this alligator pear, sir,' said Gooding. 'I can't ever stomach it myself, but the natives of these parts don't think they've dined unless alligator pear has been served. Take plenty of the pepper sauce, sir. That'll help it down. How's the wind, Merton?'

'Nor'-east by east, sir. Mebbe east nor'-east.'

'Veering southerly a bit. The British know we're here, at least. That convoy'll sail in order of battle, just as it always does.'

'I followed the last convoy eleven days,' said Curtis, 'and ne'er a straggler was I able to pick up.'

'So you told us before, my lad. But I don't think your owners have much to complain about, so far,' said Gooding. 'May I carve you some of this cold brisket, sir? You're making a poor dinner. And look at your glass! Drink fair, sir.'

'*Calypso* has twelve pounders on her main deck,' said Curtis, thoughtfully.

'Yes,' said Peabody. He thought of his own long eighteens, and the good use he could put them to if he dared risk crippling the *Delaware*.

''Scuse me, sir,' said Merton, 'but the wind's east by south now, and still veering.'

'That interrupts our dinner,' said Gooding. 'If you're wrong, you black fathom o' pump water, I'll go a thousand miles out o' my course to sell you at Charleston under the hammer.'

'Yes, sir,' said Merton, quite unmoved. He craned his neck up to the skylight opening again and announced: 'Mr Crase says east by south. I should say east sou'-east, sir.'

'Would you, by God!' said Gooding.

They were all of them on their feet now, and Merton produced, as though it were a conjuring trick, Peabody's cocked hat and sword from nowhere.

'The black heathen'll be telling me what sail to set next,' protested Gooding, while Merton buckled the belt round Peabody's waist. 'Have you called Captain Peabody's gig?'

'Yes, sir,' said Merton.

Before Peabody went down the side Gooding held out his hand.

'When we meet again we'll be half a million dollars richer,' he said.

'Good luck, sir,' said Curtis, with a young man's enthusiasm in his eyes.

The gig took Peabody rapidly across the dancing water to where the *Delaware* lay hove-to, a beautiful sight. As she swung towards him he could see her lovely bows and round, sweet run. The rake of the bowsprit and of the masts was as beautiful as a quadratic equation–masts and bowsprit exactly complementary. The proportion between topsails and courses was ideal, and the painted gunports threw in the right note of menace, so that she was not merely a beautiful thing, but a beautiful fighting thing. He looked back at the schooners, with their heavy spars and long sharp bows. They were like birds of prey, ready for a sudden swoop upon the defenceless, but incapable of the smashing blow which the *Delaware* could deal. And yet it was only by schooners like these–save for his own ship–that the American flag was displayed anywhere through the wide Atlantic.

If only they had decided ten years ago in Washington to build a dozen seventy-fours! Gouverneur Morris had advocated it a score of times, but Mr Jefferson had decided against it. In this world only a display of force could exact respect. A battle fleet would have prevented the coming of this war, and would have saved the people of the United States a thousand times its cost. In normal times a hundred ships a day cleared from American ports, and a hundred entered them, but now two thousand American ships rotted at their moorings–flour in Boston was just twice the price it was at Baltimore, while Baltimore had to pay three times as much for sugar as the price demanded on the quay at New Orleans. The United States were dying of a slow gangrene. Unemployed sailors crowded the waterfronts of every seaport; for every hand in a privateer there were a hundred looking for work, and all because Mr Jefferson had not thought himself justified in spending money, and was obsessed with the quaint fear that a powerful navy would make an autocracy out of America.

And Mr Madison had proposed to establish a neutral zone in the Atlantic, as far as the Gulf Stream, and to bar foreign ships of war from it; Peabody had helped Commodore Rodgers to write a professional opinion of this proposal only a year before British ships of war dropped anchor at Sandy Hook and slammed the door of New York in Mr Madison's face. It was because of this kind of muddled logic that the *Delaware* was faced with a task for which a dozen ships of the line would not have been too powerful, and that he himself was prowling furtively like a jackal instead of challenging battle like a man.

The bowman hooked on to the chains as the gig came alongside, and Peabody climbed to the deck and raised his hat in acknowledgement of the salutes paid him. The schooners were still nodding and dipping across the water, awaiting the time when he would move; southward the mountains of Haiti rose from the horizon, and northward lay the rounded outline of Tortuga. The wind was veering more and more southerly, and close hauled the Jamaica convoy would be able to make the Windward Passage.

'Dip the colours and fire a gun to leeward as soon as the gig is hoisted in, Mr Hubbard,' said Peabody.

A flight of pelicans was flapping solemnly over the water, dark against the bright western sky, keeping their steady line ahead as they passed close to the *Delaware*'s side. The sudden bang of the gun and the jet of smoke threw them all aback in confusion, and they turned and flapped away in a disorderly line abreast.

'Square away, Mr Hubbard. Come west by south.'

'West by south, sir.'

Under easy sail the *Delaware* crept slowly along westward, with the mountains of Haiti towering up in the south, the white cliffs just visible at their foot. The two privateers were five miles off to windward, blotted out every now and then by the sudden rainstorms which passed over them on their way down to the *Delaware*. The storms were heavy while they lasted, and they kept busy Mr Hollins, the cooper, and his mates and working party. Hollins had a sail stretched aft from the knightheads to catch the rain water, the aftermost edge pulled down to form a lip from which, when it rained, the water poured in a cataract into the hogsheads which Hollins had his men trundle beneath it. Peabody watched the operation with a grin of satisfaction; as long as his water butts were full he was independent of the shore for three months at least–if the *Delaware*'s career should last so long.

Cape St Nicolas was close under their larboard bow, and night was coming down fast.

'Heave to, Mr Hubbard, if you please. And I'll have two lights hoisted at the peak.'

The Windward Passage was under the direct observation of his ship now, there was a beautiful three-quarter moon, and no convoy of a hundred sail could get by without his knowledge. He turned and went below to his cabin, where Washington was making up his cot.

'I 'spect your coat's wet, sir,' said Washington.

It was, of course–Peabody had stood out through half a dozen tropical showers–and so were his breeches.

'Now here's your nightshirt, and you get right into it, sir,' said Washington, fussing round the cabin.

Peabody had not been able to grow accustomed to having a body servant. Washington had thrown himself into his duties when he was first engaged with all the abandon of his race; perhaps with generations of dependence preceding him he was merely seeking to make himself quite indispensable as quickly as possible. Peabody had thrown cold water on some of his enthusiasms; Washington no longer crouched to him, holding out his breeches for him to step into, as he got out of bed, but Peabody had not yet been able to break him of his habit of touching him to see if he were wet, and of trying to dictate to him what he should wear and when he should sleep. Peabody could recognise each of his shirts individually, and during his years as a poor lieutenant had devised a satisfactory system of rotation of duties for them, and he still bore unconsciously some slight resentment against Washington for breaking into his orderly habits.

'I don't want my nightshirt,' he said curtly. 'Get me out a dry shirt–one of the plain ones, and take it from the top of the pile–and a pair of the white ducks. Hang my coat on the hook there where I can find it.'

'You ain't goin' to turn in all standing, sir,' said Washington resentfully.

'I am,' snapped Peabody.

He threw off his wet gala clothes–there was a queer uncontrollable uneasiness at being naked when he was not alone, but he fought against that because he felt it was not quite justifiable–and pulled on the shirt which Washington handed him. He put his feet into his trousers, balancing against the roll of the ship first on one leg and then on the other with a habitual facility of which he was unconscious, and stood tucking in his shirt.

'Put my shoes against the bulkhead and take that lamp away,' he ordered.

'Yes, sir. Good night, sir,' said Washington.

Alone in the darkness Peabody lay down on his cot, 'all standing'–with his clothes on–as Washington had protestingly said. He could lay his hands instantly on his shoes and coat, and could be on deck within forty seconds of an alarm; Peabody had no self-consciousness about appearing on deck with his nightshirt-tails flapping round him, but the picure did not coincide with his idea of a well-ordered ship. He bent his long length and turned on to his side, his hands clasped before his chest in the attitude of sleep he had habitually employed from babyhood, and he closed his eyes. There was a momentary temptation to lie awake and brood over the dangers before him, but he put it aside like the temptation to drink. There was a time for everything, and this was the time to sleep.

At midnight he was awake again; twenty years of watch-and-watch–four hours waking and four hours sleep–had formed a habit even he could not control. He went on deck and prowled round, although he had complete confidence in his officers' ability to carry out routine orders. The lights burned brightly at the peak, and the moon shone clearly from beyond the Windward Passage, while the *Delaware* rose and fell rhythmically over the long swell as she lay hove-to before the gentle wind. The atmosphere was warm and sticky, and on the side on which he had been lying his clothes were wet with sweat which hardly evaporated in the hot night. There was nothing to do except sleep, and he went below again to his stuffy cabin, lay down on his other side, emptied his mind of all thought for the second time, and went to sleep in the accustomed stuffiness, lulled by the *Delaware*'s easy motion over the waves.

Dawn brought him on deck again, and there was still no sign of the convoy, although the wind had stayed to the south of east all night. Five miles away to windward the schooners lay hove-to under their mainsails alone, and there was no need to signal to them, for privateer captains had as much need for patience as for dash in their work. All day long the *Delaware* lay-to off Cape St Nicolas–an easy day in the hot tropical sunshine, while the rainstorms came up to windward and burst over the ship and passed away to leeward in rainbows. The decks were washed down; the forenoon watch was spent in drill–gun drill, boarding drill, sail drill, and when the men's dinner-time arrived there was still no sign of the convoy. Last night had been the earliest possible moment it could appear, but Peabody was wise to the ways of convoys and knew quite well that he might have to wait a week.

In the afternoon Hubbard found work for the crew. He had the anchors and the ironwork tarred, while Rodgers, the boatswain, kept a select party doing neat work on the rigging–knots and flemish-eyes and pointings. The ship's boys were making sinnet, and the sailmaker had a party at work with needle and palm on a new foretopsail, while the spun yarn winch buzzed cheerfully away spinning yarns with which a few fortunate men–for some odd reason it was the most popular work in the ship–walked solemnly forward and aft. The rain squalls came up; sails and yarns were bundled under cover, and the helmsman had a moment's activity keeping the ship from being taken aback. Then in an instant, as it were, the rain was past, the deck steamed in the hot sun, and the wind began its cheerful note again.

The first watch was called, and work on the ship suspended. Peabody gave permission for clothes to be washed, taking advantage of all the unwanted fresh water on board, and soon the lines which had been rigged were gay with all the red and white shirts and white trousers of four hundred men. The sun was dipping to the west. Two bells were struck, and then three, and then came the hail which Peabody had been waiting for.

'Deck there! Sail to leeward! Two sails, sir! A whole fleet, sir!'

'Clear for action, Mr Hubbard, if you please. Hoist the colours, and dip them twice.'

The drums went roaring through the ship. Like magic the lines and the clothes vanished from forward. Boys went racing along the deck strewing sand. Groups of men came running to every gun, casting off the breachings, taking out the tompions, pulling rammers and sponges from their racks. The marines came pouring up into the quarterdeck, falling into stiff military line in their blue and white uniforms and jaunty shakoes, while the sergeants inspected them before taking their parties up into the tops.

'The schooners have hoisted their colours and dipped them twice, sir,' said Midshipman Wallingford.

'Yes,' said Peabody.

That was the acknowledgement of his prearranged signal for the convoy in sight to leeward–if the convoy had by some chance appeared to windward the colours would have been dipped once. Peabody took his glass and ran up the mizzen rigging. Halfway to the top was as far as he needed to go; with his feet astride and his back leaning against the shrouds he could see the convoy coming down upon him, close hauled on the starboard tack. There was only one ship-rigged vessel in sight although there were two barquentines and four brigs. None of the brigs was a man o' war, for he could recognise their familiar outlines as typical West India traders. But the ship–he looked at her more closely. She was flush-decked, and she showed a line of gun ports, checkered black against yellow. Fore and main topmasts were about equal, and her canvas was faintly grey instead of a lively white. She was a British ship-of-war, then, and presumably the twenty-gun corvette *Racer* whose presence Hunningford had been doubtful about.

'Ship cleared for action, sir,' hailed Hubbard from the quarterdeck.

There were more sails crowding up over the horizon now, and as Peabody turned his glass upon them he checked himself in instant certainty. There was no mistaking those topsails, that silhouette–a British frigate, or he had never seen one before in his life. He scanned the other sails closely, and then traversed his glass back again over the fleet. No, there was no sign whatever so far of the brig *Bulldog* which Hunningford had mentioned, and Peabody would have been surprised if there had been, yet. The senior officer of the British squadron, if he knew his business, would have the corvette to windward of the van–as she was, the frigate to windward of the main body where she could most easily cope with trouble–and she was there; and the brig in rear to keep her eye on the stragglers, where presumably she was. He closed his glass and descended to the deck.

Murray was positively dancing with excitement and anxiety, and even

Hubbard was walking up and down the quarterdeck with quick, rapid strides.

'Set all plain sail to the royal, Mr Hubbard, if you please, and put her before the wind.'

'Aye aye, sir. Before the wind, sir.'

'Mr Murray!'

'Sir!'

'I want the round shot drawn from the guns. Load with two rounds of dismantling shot.'

'Aye aye, air. And I'll point the guns high, sir.'

Murray was quick to grasp a plan. The *Delaware* had three ships-of-war to deal with, and must put all three out of action so as to leave a free hand for the privateers. Peabody watched the men at work on the quarterdeck carronades. With corkscrew rammers they drew the wads from their pieces. They twisted the elevating screws, forcing in the wedges under the breeches, until the carronades were pointing sharply downwards. With the roll of the ship the round shot came tumbling from the muzzles, falling with a thump on the deck, to be snatched up and replaced in the garlands against the bulwark. Next the dismantling shot was rammed in–cylindrical canvas bags, which concealed the missiles within. For these thirty-two pounders each bag contained a dozen six-foot lengths of iron chain, each joined to a single ring in the centre. On discharge they would fly like a hurtling star, effective to a range of five hundred feet, cutting ropes and tearing canvas to shreds. Sawyer, of the Boston Navy Yard, had long advocated the use of dismantling shot, but Peabody had yet to see it employed in action. Peabody was aware that the British thought its use unfair, but for the life of him he could not see why; he supposed it was because they had not thought of it for themselves.

Peabody looked ahead. The frigate had tacked about, and was heading towards the *Delaware*, to inspect this strange ship-of-war which had so suddenly appeared. The corvette had backed her mizzen topsail, and was allowing the convoy to catch up with her while she took the frigate's place; the British had been guarding convoys for twenty years continuously now, and understood their business. There was a string of flags rising to the frigate's main yardarm.

'M W P,' read off Wallingford. 'It doesn't make sense, sir.'

The private recognition signal, of course. There would be a code reply of which he was ignorant, but there was a reply he could make which would be quite sufficient.

'Bring her to the wind on the port tack, Mr Hubbard.'

As the ship came round the ensign at the peak became visible to the British frigate. Peabody smiled grimly as he saw the effect it produced–more signals soared up the frigate's halliards, and a white puff of smoke from her bows showed that she was firing a gun to demand the instant attention of her consorts and the convoy. This was the moment of surprise. No King's ship in the West Indies could know until that moment that a big American frigate was loose on the high seas. He watched his enemies warily to see what they would do.

The frigate was holding her course, parallel to the *Delaware*'s, both of them lying close hauled. Now the corvette was coming round, too; Peabody could only see her topsails, and she was six miles farther to leeward of the frigate. And dead to leeward of the frigate, and far beyond her, Peabody saw another pair of topsails on the horizon wink as they came round, differentiating themselves sharply from the others beyond. That was the brig, then. They were all three heading towards him, as he had hoped; the privateers, far astern of him and on a course diametrically opposite, were out of their sight and would soon have a free hand with the convoy.

Vigilant, he watched his enemies. If they were wise, they would close up together to meet his attack. The *Calypso* by herself was of slightly inferior force to the *Delaware*, and in a ship to ship duel he would fight with confidence in victory, even with his knowledge of the chanciness of war at sea. But the *Calypso* and the *Racer* together would be grave odds against him, and even the *Bulldog* could cause him serious annoyance if the *Delaware* were involved in a hot action. By bringing his ship to the wind he had made a pretence of refusing battle–they might chase him in heedless pursuit, as they were doing at this moment, widening their distance from the convoy, confident that there could not possibly be two United States ships at sea simultaneously and forgetting the lurking privateers.

It was a complex series of factors, and Peabody turned his attention to another complication–the setting of the sun. Red and angry it was setting, beyond the convoy. There was not much more than an hour's daylight left, and he needed daylight to do his work well. He glanced to windward; there was the familiar black cloud coming down with the wind, as might have been expected, for it was two hours at least since the last rainstorm. He held doggedly on his course, aware that Hubbard was looking at him with faint surprise and that even the men at the guns were glancing over their shoulders, wondering why their captain was running like this from the enemy. The enemy to leeward, the squall to windward; Peabody transferred his attention first to the one and then to the other. Now the squall was close upon them. There was a warning flap from the sails and Peabody heard Crane cautioning the men at the wheel. Now it was here, heavy fluky gusts of wind and torrential warm rain, heavy as if from a shower-bath, drumming on the decks and streaming like a cataract in the scuppers.

'Wear ship, Mr Hubbard, if you please. I'll have her before the wind again.'

Round she came, the heavy gusts of the squall thrusting her forward perceptibly. She was in the heart of the little storm, travelling down wind with it for several minutes before it drew ahead of her. As Peabody turned his head a little cascade of water poured out of the brim of his cocked hat, but the rain was already lessening. Even when it had ceased entirely, and the decks were beginning to steam in the hot evening, it was still ahead of blotting the *Calypso* from Peabody's sight, and presumably concealing the *Delaware* from the *Calypso*.

'Stand by your guns, men!' called Peabody. He was glad to see Murray attending to the distribution of lighted slowmatch round the ship–he wanted nothing to go wrong with that first broadside.

Only a scant mile ahead of the *Delaware* a grey shape emerged from the rainstorm–grey one moment, sharply defined the next; the *Calypso* still holding her course and beyond the immediate help of her consorts. Certainly there was no time now for the British ships to close together, not with the

Delaware rusing down upon them at eight knots. There was a chance of raking the *Calypso*, of crossing her bows and sweeping her from end to end, but her captain was too wary. As the two ships closed he put up his helm–Peabody saw her broadside lengthen and her masts separate.

'Larboard a point,' snapped Peabody to the helmsman. He wanted that broadside delivered at the closest possible range.

The *Calypso* was just steadying on her new course as the *Delaware* forged up alongside her. The forecastle twelve pounder went off with a bang; Peabody took note of that, for the captain of that gun must be punished for opening fire without orders. Peabody could see the white deck and gleaming hammocks of the British frigate, the gold lace of the officers, and the bright red coats of the marines on the quarterdeck. Where he stood by the mizzen rigging he was just opposite the frigate's taffrail; it was almost time for the broadside–it was interesting to see how Murray down on the main deck came through this test of nerves. At last it came–a crashing simultaneous roar from the main-deck guns, followed instantly by the spar-deck carronades. The *Delaware* heaved to the recoil of the guns, and the smoke poured upwards in a cloud, enshrouding Peabody so thickly that for a moment the *Calypso* was blotted from his sight. Something struck the bulwark beside him a tremendous blow which shook him as he stood. There was a gaping hole there; something else struck the mizzen-mast bitts and sprayed all the deck around with fragments. Peabody watched death flitting past him; and in the sublime knowledge that he had done all his duty he felt neither awe nor fear.

The carronades beside him, speedily reloaded, roared out again. The ship trembled to the recoil of the guns, while Peabody could feel, through the deck beneath his feet, the heavy blows which the *Calypso*'s guns were dealing in return. The British frigate was firing fast, accurately, and low; the earlier defeats of British single ships had shaken up the service into renewed attention to gunnery, as the action between the *Shannon* and the *Chesapeake* showed. Peabody peered through the smoke to see what damage was being done to the enemy, but with the wind directly abaft it was hard to see anything. There was the *Calypso*'s main mast standing out through the smoke, mistily visible from the main yard upward. Yet everything there was in such confusion that Peabody actually found it hard to recognise what he saw. The maintopsail was in ribbons, with strips of canvas blowing out from thc yard, which was cantcd wildly sideways and precariously supported the topgallant yard, which, slings, ties, and braces all shot away, was lying balanced upon it in a wild tangle of canvas and rigging. As Peabody watched, half the main shrouds parted as though a gigantic knife had been drawn across them, the mast lurched, and the whole mass of stuff came tumbling down into the smoke.

The *Delaware* was drawing ahead fast; the chance of crossing the *Calypso*'s bows and raking her was obvious. Peabody leaned forward to the man at the wheel.

'Larboard your helm,' he said.

Hubbard had seen the chance too, had heard his words, and was bellowing his orders into the smoke. Over went the helm, round came the yards, and Peabody turned back to watch the *Calypso*. But she was coming round too–the distance between her vague main mast and mizzen mast was slowly widening.

Peabody saw a red-coated marine come running out towards him along the *Calypso*'s mizzen topsail yard, musket in hand; the man must have been mad with the lust of battle to have attempted such a feat. He reached the yardarm, but as he was bringing his weapon to his shoulder something invisible struck him and he was tossed off the yard.

With the wind abeam they were passing out of the smoke, and the *Calypso*'s outlines became more distinct. From the deck upward she was more of a wreck than Peabody would ever have thought possible, her canvas in shreds and her running and standing rigging cut to pieces. Her headsails were trailing under her forefoot; her spanker gaff hung drunkenly with the upper half of the spanker blowing out from it like a sheet on a clothesline, and although the maintopgallant was the only yard which had fallen all her spars sagged and drooped as if a breath would bring them down. There could be no doubt whatever as to the efficacy of dismantling shot, Peabody decided.

Midshipman Shepherd was beside him. His cheek had been laid open over the bone, so that half his face was masked in blood which dripped down on to his torn coat.

'Number seven gun has burst, sir,' said Shepherd. His chest was heaving with his exertions as he tried to hold himself steady. 'Mr Atwell sent me to report. The ship caught fire on the main deck, but the fire's out now, sir.'

'Thank you, Mr Shepherd. Get that cut bandaged before you return to duty.'

Peabody made his reply steadily enough, but he had felt a wave of bitterness at the news. These cursed iron guns! The *Belvidera* had escaped from Rodgers in the *President* because of just such an accident. The Pennsylvania foundries had not learned yet to cast iron without flaws. Shepherd's report explained the slackening of the main-deck fire which Peabody had detected just before. Another shot hit the deck beside him at that instant, sending a ringbolt flying through the air with a menacing whirr–the *Calypso* was still firing rapidly and well; a wreck from the deck upwards, her gun power was not in the least impaired. Through the roar of the carronades beside him he could hear the smashing blows which the *Calypso*'s guns were still dealing out, but the main-deck guns were firing back again as fast as ever now. The *Calypso*'s tottering foretopmast came down, falling nearly vertically–she was dropping astern fast again. Peabody wanted to hurl his ship close along side of her, to pound her in a mad flurry of mutual destruction, to sink her, to burn her, to cover her deck with corpses. Mad lust for battle wrapped his mind like a cloak.

'Shall I back the mizzen topsail, sir?' asked Hubbard, crossing the deck towards him.

'No,' said Peabody.

Battle-madness passed and common sense returned at Hubbard's question. The level-headed Yankee temperament took charge when Peabody saw the swarthy Carolinian's blazing eyes. There was the *Racer* to think of, and the brig, and the convoy, and the approach of night. He looked away to leeward, and there was the *Racer* clawing gallantly up to windward to join in the fight. Aft, and there was the brig doing the same, while against the red western sunset were silhouetted the countless sails of the convoy. Another broadside from the *Calypso* crashed into the *Delaware* and shook him as he stood talking to Hubbard.

'Up helm, if you please, Mr Hubbard. We'll go down to the corvette.'

The *Delaware*'s sails filled as she bore away, and the infernal din of the battle died away magically. Borne on the wind came a wild cheer from the British ship–the fools thought they had made the *Delaware* seek safety in flight. There was a moment's temptation to tack about and show them that they were wrong, but Peabody put it aside.

Peabody looked round the ship. On the larboard side–the disengaged side–a carronade slide had been smashed and the carronade's crew was at work securing the clumsy lump of metal which lay on the deck. There were big holes in the bulwark and the deck was torn up in several places. Aloft someone was reeving fresh maintopsail halliards, and there were a few big holes in the sails. There were dead men here and there, but the *Delaware* was still an efficient fighting unit. Someone came running up to him–a carpenter's mate whose name Peabody could not instantly remember, Smith or Jones, perhaps.

'Mr MacKenzie sent me, sir. We've been holed twice below the bends, sir, on the starboard side for'rard. We've plugged one hole, but the other's beside the beef an' we've got to move the hogsheads, sir. But there's only a foot of water in the well and Mr MacKenzie's gotten the pumps to work.'

'Right. Get below again.'

They were coming down fast on the *Racer*; Peabody waved the man away as he peered keenly forward to watch her movements. A glance astern assured him again that the *Calypso* was out of action for good–she was wallowing quite helpless in the trough of the sea. But the *Racer* was not going to falter, all the same. She was holding her course steadily, the white ensign flying bravely from her peak. It was her duty to protect the convoy, even at the cost of her own destruction. Peabody swung round upon Shepherd.

'Go find Mr Murray,' he snapped. 'Tell him to load with dismantling shot again.'

The sun was completely below the horizon; there was not much daylight left and the moon would not be of much help for accurate gunfire. Peabody saw the *Racer*'s maintopsail swing round until it reflected the pink of the sunset in sharp contrast with the dark silhouettes of the other sails. She was laying it to the mast, heaving to for a steadier shot at the big frigate plunging down upon her. Her best chance of saving the convoy was to cripple the enemy while she still had the opportunity. Peabody felt a grim approval of the British captain's tactics as he waited for the broadside to come.

A neat row of white puffs of smoke appeared along the corvette's side, and Peabody's mathematical mind leaped into a calculation.

'One, two, three, four—' he counted.

The air was full of the sound of the balls overhead. A fresh hole appeared in the foretopsail, and the maintopsail halliards, just replaced, parted again, the loose ends tumbling to the deck. The *Delaware* was going six knots; there would be two more broadsides–three, if the corvette's guns were specially well served–before she was at close quarters. Peabody wondered what was the maximum damage the corvette's long nine pounders could inflict. He might actually lose a mast, although the chances were that he would not lose even a spar. The ship was deadly quiet now. There was only the clanking of the pumps forward to be heard beside the eternal note of the wind in the rigging and the sound of the sea under the bows. The men were standing quietly to their guns awaiting their orders; the rush and bustle of the powder boys had ceased now that each gun had its reserve cartridge beside it.

Again the puffs of smoke from the corvette's side.

'One, two, three—'

Elevation was bad this time, or the corvette's gunnery officer had mistimed the roll of his ship. One ball tore through the air close to Peabody's side, the wind of it making him stagger, but the others struck the *Delaware*'s hull, to judge from the splintering crash forward. The sound reminded Peabody suddenly of something he was astonished at having forgotten. The two guns of Jonathan's section were numbers seven and eight, main-deck starboard side–and number seven had burst. Jonathan might be dead; probably was. Peabody forced his mind to leave off thinking about Jonathan. The corvette was within easy cannon shot now–the shots came as soon as he saw the smoke.

There was a crash overhead; the spanker gaff was smashed, close to the vangs. The foretopsail lee braces were gone–no other damage; and the corvette's maintopsail was coming round again as she got under way ready to manoeuvre.

'Starboard a point,' snapped Peabody to the helmsman. There was a chance of crossing the corvette's bow, but she was well handled and parried the thrust.

'Let her have it, boys!' shouted Peabody as the ships came together, and the two broadsides roared out together.

Through the smoke Peabody saw a chance of crossing the corvette's stern, but she hove in stays and went about like clockwork, baulking him. The corvette was a handy craft, quicker in stays than the big frigate. Peabody followed her round, bellowing his orders to the helmsman through the maddening din of the guns; it was dark enough now for the big flames to be visible shooting from the muzzles of the guns. Peabody could see the corvette's rigging melting away under the hail of dismantling shot, although the corvette was hitting back as hard as she could with her nine pounders against the *Delaware*'s eighteens, contending fiercely against odds of five to one. The *Racer*'s main topmast fell suddenly, and along with it the mizzen topmast, just at the moment when the air round Peabody was filled with flying splinters from a shot which struck close by. As he rallied himself he found the *Delaware* flying round into the wind. There was a thunderous flap from the sails as she was taken all aback, and the guns fell abruptly silent as they ceased to bear. Peabody swung round upon the clumsy helmsman, and then shut his mouth with a snap upon the angry words he was intending to use. For the helmsman was dead, and so was the second helmsman, and so was Mr Crane the master, and where the wheel and binnacle had once stood was now a mere splintered mass of wreckage in the darkness.

'Man the relieving tackles, Mr Hubbard. Jib sheet, there! Haul out to starboard.'

The *Delaware* was rapidly gathering sternway; Peabody could hear the bubble of water under the counter in the eerie silence which had settled on the ship. It seemed to take a strangely long time to work the ship's head round and get her under control again.

'Jib sheets, there! Are you asleep?'

'Tiller rope's jammed with the helm a bit to starboard, sir,' reported Hubbard.

'Clear it, then. Jib sheets! Haul out to port!'

That was better; the *Delaware* was coming round again into control, but she was circling away from the *Racer*, which was barely visible as a dark mass a full half mile away. It would take some time to work to windward and close with her again.

'Tiller rope's cleared, sir.'

Keep her on the wind on this tack, then.'

The *Racer* was a disabled wreck, as helpless as the *Calypso*. She would be able to do nothing to-night to protect the convoy. Peabody searched the darkness to leeward. There was the brig! She had given up the attempt to join the battle, and was heading away with the wind on her quarter to evade the *Delaware* and rejoin the convoy. He might have guessed that she would.

There was not time to destroy the *Racer* and still be able to head off the *Bulldog*; he put the *Delaware* before the wind again and went charging down upon the brig in the darkness. The stars were already out, gleaming over the dark sea, and the moon was lighting a wide path over the waves, and two battered wrecks were being left far behind. Five minutes later Peabody saw the brig abruptly alter course to avoid being intercepted, and he brought the *Delaware* round in pursuit, staring after her amid the clatter and racket of the working party who were busy rigging a jury wheel. An hour later there came a hail from aloft.

'Deck there! There's a light way off on the starboard beam. Might be a burning ship, sir.'

It must have been a burning ship–two minutes after the hail the light was visible from the deck, reflected in a yellow glow from the clouds in the sky, lighting a quarter of the heavens. Evidently Gooding and Curtis were in among the convoy–that blaze meant that they were destroying a worthless capture. So the brig could go on holding that course until she ran aground in Cuba, if she wanted to. The *Delaware* had achieved what she had set out to do. All that remained to be done was to lay on such a course as would be likely to keep the escort ships from rejoining the convoy, and give a chance of picking up stragglers. Then to go round the ship and give what orders were necessary to make her as efficient a fighting unit as possible, and after that there would be a chance of finding out what had happened to Jonathan.

6

Captain Peabody looked over the side of the *Delaware* as she crawled along in the hot sunshine with bare steerage-way.

'Mr Atwell,' he said, harshly.

The young third lieutenant came running across to him.

'You're not attending to your duty, Mr Atwell. What is *that* floating there?'

Atwell followed with his gaze Peabody's gnarled forefinger.

'An orange, sir,' he said, haltingly. The orange rose on a little wave against the ship's quarter and drifted astern.

'Did you see anything about that orange which interested you?' asked Peabody.

'N-no, sir,' said Atwell.

'Then either your eyesight or your wits aren't as good as they should be,' said Peabody. 'That orange had a piece bitten out of it. And its sides were hollow instead of rounded. What does that tell you?'

'Someone has been sucking it, sir,' said Atwell, a little bewildered at all this fuss over a mere orange already a hundred yards back in the ship's wake.

'Yes,' said Peabody, and he was about to continue with his Socratic questioning when his expression changed and he pointed again to something floating past the ship.

'And what's *that*?' he snapped.

'Coco-nut shell, sir,' said Atwell, and a light dawned upon him. 'Some ship's emptied her slush bucket overside.'

'And not merely that, Mr Atwell. Oranges and coco-nuts–where does that ship hail from?'

'The West Indies, sir!' said Atwell.

'Yes,' said Peabody. 'That means we're in the track of some part of the convoy. Now do you understand why you should have seen it?'

'Yes, sir.'

'Don't neglect your duty again, Mr Atwell,' said Peabody, turning away.

Atwell was a 'good officer,' thought Peabody. There was never any slackness about the men when he had charge of the deck, and the sails were always properly set, and the helmsman was always on his course. But there was another side of the picture. Officers of that sort were so engrossed in the details of their routine duties that they had no thought to spare for anything else. And not merely that; years of routine duties had a stunting effect upon their imaginations and logical faculties. Atwell ought to have made deductions from the sight of that floating rubbish instantly. Peabody was afraid that Atwell would never develop into a great commander, into a Truxtun or a Decatur.

But the sight of that rubbish confirmed Peabody in his conclusions as to the movements of the convoy. He had acted correctly in taking the *Delaware* through the Caicos Passage. The convoy, scattering like sheep before the wolves of privateers, must have headed for the Atlantic by the first route open to them. A dozen rich prizes probably lay only just over the horizon ahead. He looked keenly aloft to make sure that the *Delaware* was getting every possible yard out of the feeble three-knot breeze which was wafting her lazily along. He would maintain the pursuit for even days–or until he had taken ten prizes–before he put his ship about again to see what further trouble he could make in the West Indies. He and the *Delaware* were like a farmer and his money on market day. He had to find the best value he could for her, lay her out to the best advantage in the sure and certain knowledge that sooner or later she would be expended. Lawrence in the *Chesapeake* had chosen badly; even if he had captured the *Shannon* a captured British frigate would have been a poor exchange for the cutting up and crippling of an American one. Porter had the better notion when he headed for the Pacific instead of making a dash for home–Peabody wondered how the cruise of the *Essex* in the Pacific was succeeding.

A sorry procession was coming on deck. The wounded and sick were returning from their morning visit to the surgeon. Jonathan was leading them, his left arm in a sling–a flying fragment of iron from the burst cannon had gone through the muscles above the elbow–and behind him followed men with bandaged heads, with bandaged legs, and after them came the sick-bay attendants carrying in canvas slings the men who were too injured to walk. Downing, the Surgeon, and Hoyle, the Surgeon's mate, followed, and supervised the laying of the wounded against the spars in the shadow of the mainsail. They were a couple of surgeons from New York, obsessed with fantastic ideas; they had the notion that sick men should not be kept in a comfortably dark 'tween decks. They were perfectly convinced that sunshine did sick men good, and they even declared that there was no danger for them in night air at sea. Downing was most emphatic on the point that air once breathed had a deleterious effect upon the system, in defiance of the common knowledge that air thoroughly warmed and humanised was far better than raw fresh stuff. Peabody himself could not sleep if there was a suspicion of a draught in his cabin, and as a New Englander born he was innately suspicious of Yorkers, but he had not been able to enforce his ideas upon the two mad doctors. By virtue of their warrants from the Secretary of the Navy they were independent of him in the matter of the sick, and they traded upon the fact quite shamelessly, littering the neat deck with sick men, and always willing to argue with their captain.

Peabody strolled forward.

'Good morning, Jonathan.'

'Good morning,' and then after an interval, 'sir.'

Jonathan was sick with his wound; otherwise he would not have spoken in such a surly fashion.

'How's the arm to-day?'

'Hurting like hell,' said Jonathan.

Peabody turned to the others.

'Doing well, sir,' said one of them.

'Stump's as clean as a whistle, sir,' said the one whose leg had been shattered below the knee. He was grey with loss of blood and weakness, but he made himself smile as he lay there.

'Cross and Huntley died during the night, sir,' said Downing, in a quiet aside to Peabody. 'I'm sorrry about Huntley–I thought he'd pull through. But I never had any hope for Cross.'

'So I remember,' said Peabody.

This would be the third successive day in which they had buried dead men overside, and he contemplated the approaching ceremony with distaste. Murray had come up, and was talking earnestly to Jonathan, and trying to catch his captain's eye at the same moment.

'Damn it, man,' Murray was saying, 'you *must* remember something about it.'

'I don't,' said Jonathan, doggedly.

'I was asking about that burst gun, sir,' explained Murray to Peabody. 'I was thinking, it might have been double-loaded, and it was in Mr Peabody's charge.'

'What makes you think it was double-loaded?'

'I'd just given the order for round shot, because the range was drawing out. If the gun was already loaded with dismantling shot the men might be excited and put in another charge and a round shot on top. That'd burst any gun.'

'So it would,' agreed Peabody, and he looked at his brother.

'He's trying to blame something on me, the same as always,' said Jonathan.

'It's important, sir,' explained Murray. 'If the men don't trust the guns they're serving—'

He left the sentence unfinished but adequate to the occasion.

'You're quite right, Mr Murray,' said Peabody, looking at his brother again; but Jonathan only shook his head.

'I don't know anything about any double-loading. Mr Murray wants me to say that's how it happened, of course–anybody can see why. And then he'd have me in trouble, which is what he wants just as much, too.'

'Don't speak so insolently,' snapped Murray.

'Mr Peabody cannot be asked questions which might incriminate him,' said Peabody, gently.

If it could be proved that Jonathan had allowed a gun under his immediate charge to be double-loaded, Murray might easily charge him with inattention to duty, and Jonathan was clearly aware of the danger, so that he was justified in being cautious in his replies, although not in his manner of making them–only the pain of his wound could excuse that. Murray must have seen all this, for he opened his mouth, shut it again, and turned away after raising his hat to his captain.

'You must be more respectful another time,' said Peabody, a little testily. He was annoyed that his capable second lieutenant should be annoyed.

'All right, all right,' said Jonathan.

Peabody left him to doze in the sun, and walked aft again to see that Atwell got every inch of speed out of the *Delaware*. The word had got round the crew that there were prizes ahead, and everyone was keyed up in anticipation. The hands worked with a will as the sails were trimmed to the fitful wind, and half the watch below spent their time aloft eagerly scanning the horizon for sails. When the wind backed northerly there were more frequent calls for the watch, because Peabody would not allow the *Delaware* to tack far off the direct course which he had mentally allotted to the flying convoy, but drove her along in a succession of short boards, tacking every half hour. But nobody minded the extra work; everyone realised that a weatherly ship like the *Delaware* had her best chance of overtaking dull-sailing merchant ships with a foul wind.

The first sail they sighted proved a disappointment. She showed up to windward on the opposite tack to the *Delaware*, and the latter intercepted her with ease because she made no attempt to escape. Midshipman Howard's sharp eyes first detected the fact that she was flying two flags, and a moment later a score of telescopes identified them as the Stars and Stripes flying above the Red Ensign. When they closed within hailing distance she announced herself for what she was–the ship *Dalbousie*, Kingston to London, prize to the *Emulation*, Daniel Stevens, prizemaster, heading for Charleston with prisoners.

'We've gotten together two hundred of 'em under hatches, sir,' yelled Stevens. 'Rum, sugar, an' coffee.'

She would be a nice prize if she could be taken through the British blockade into an American port; the prisoners themselves represented a fortune, with the Federal Government paying a hundred dollars a head for British seamen placed in the hands of a United States sheriff. Gooding had destroyed some of his smaller prizes, after stripping them of everything valuable, and had sent the *Dalbousie* in, with the hope that she might make an American port. She had nothing better than an even chance, Peabody decided, watching her sail over the horizon.

Six hours later the lookouts reported more sails, dead to windward, close hauled on the port tack.

'Two brigs an' two barquentines, sir,' reported master's mate O'Brien, all breathless, having run to the masthead with his glass and descended, all within two minutes. 'Merchantmen for sure, sir, an' sailing in company.'

That meant without a doubt that they were part of the disrupted convoy. There was small chance for them, with the *Delaware* to leeward of them, so that it was impossible for them to scatter far. The barquentines held on their course, and the brigs went about on the other tack, as soon as the *Delaware*'s dread topsails had climbed up over the horizon sufficiently far to be clearly identified.

'Keep her steady as she goes, Mr Hubbard,' said Peabody. 'We'll have the barquentine first.'

The *Delaware* could lie nearly a point closer to the wind than the clumsy merchant ships, and could sail almost two feet to their one–she was like a pike among minnows. Remorselessly she ran them down, Peabody watching grimly as the distance shortened.

'Try a shot from one of the bow guns, Mr Murray, if you please.'

The shot crashed out, and Peabody saw a black speck rise to the peak of the nearer barquentine, flutter a moment, and then descend. Apparently all on board were careless of what should happen to their ship now she was taken. She was allowed to fly up into the wind, and lay there all aback in a flurry of disordered canvas.

'Back the mizzen topsail, Mr Hubbard. Mr Sampson! Take the quarterboat and take possession. Mr Kidd! Take six men and go with Mr Sampson. Pull to the other barquentine and take possession as soon as she strikes. Square away, if you please, Mr Hubbard. Mr Murray, put a shot across that other barquentine's bows.'

The flag of the leading barquentine rose and fell again, and she hove-to. Peabody watched for a moment until he saw the *Delaware*'s boat pulling towards her.

'Tack after the brigs, please, Mr Hubbard.'

The brigs had won for themselves no more than an extra two hours of freedom; the *Delaware* caught up to them hot-foot. It was a little painful to see their flags come fluttering down–Peabody felt an odd twinge as he stood in the hot sunlight and watched his prizes come clustering together, obedient to his orders. He listened a little gloomily to the reports sent over by his prizemasters–Barquentine *Richmond*, three hundred and twenty tons, Kingston to London, cargo of sugar, twenty-nine of a crew; Barquentine *Faithful Wife*, three hundred and forty tons, Kingston to Liverpool, and so on. They were all bulk cargoes–no valuable specie for him to take under his special charge. Murray and Hubbard were eagerly turning over the pages of the prizes' logs, in search of possible hints as to the whereabouts of any other survivors of the convoy.

'Twenty-five sail took the Caicos Passage, sir,' announced Murray. 'The others must still be ahead.'

A laughing working party were swaying up a miscellaneous collection of livestock from the longboat of one of the barquentines, chickens and pigs and a score of big turtles; the city of London aldermen would go short of their favourite dish this coming winter, and the crew of the *Delaware* would have a brief taste of fresh food again. The four captured captains stood in a sullen group on the other side of the deck, saying nothing to each other, and trying to display no emotion while their captor decided on their fate; they might as well have been Mohegans awaiting the stake.

'Mr Hubbard!'

'Sir!'

'I'll have those two longboats on board. They'll serve instead of the boats we lost.'

'Aye aye, sir.'

'Which of you gentlemen is the captain of the *Laura Troughton*?'

'I am.'

The captain of the smaller of the two brigs came with a rolling gait across to Peabody, to listen sullenly to what Peabody had to say.

'I'm setting your brig free after my prize crew has thrown those guns of yours overboard. You will take on board the officers and crew of the other three vessels.'

'But Holy Peter! That'll make a hundred souls on board or more.'

'Yes.'

'The water won't last, sir. I've only ten tons on board.'

'You've a fair wind for the Cuban coast. Four days and you'll be in Havana.' Peabody turned to the other three captains. 'I'll give you twenty minutes to get your property transferred to the *Laura Troughton*. At four bells I shall set fire to your ship.'

It was the best thing to do. Releasing the prisoners meant a loss of ten thousand dollars in prize money; burning the ships meant a loss of ten times as much, but the *Delaware* had few men to spare for prize crews, and they must be reserved to take in really valuable captures–if there was any chance of evading the blockade. And sending the *Laura Troughton* in to Havana–the water shortage would ensure that she went nowhere else–would deprive England of her services and those of her crew for some time to come.

Peabody looked aft as the *Delaware* bore up to the northward again. The *Laura Troughton* was heading south with all the sail she could set, and the hot sun glared down on the other three vessels drifting aimlessly on the blue water.

Each of the three was enshrouded in a faint mist, rendering their outlines vague and shimmering. As he watched, he saw the sails of the *Richmond* suddenly whisk away into nothing as the flames, invisible in the bright sun, ran up her masts. The *Faithful Wife*'s main mast suddenly lurched drunkenly to one side, and a dense volume of black smoke poured out from her gaping decks, drifting to leeward in an ugly cloud. Sugar and rum made a fine blaze. A sudden hard explosion from the *Richmond* told how the flames had reached her small powder store–only a hundredweight or two, but enough to send a column of smoke shooting upwards. He could see that the whole of her stern had been blown away, and as the misshapen wreck drifted on the surface the billows of smoke told how the invading sea was battling with the roaring flames. The *Faithful Wife*'s masts had fallen now, and so had the brig's, and the two blazing hulks had drifted together and were wrapped, side by side, in the clouds of murky smoke. It was a horrible sight, and Peabody could hardly bear to look at it. But he made himself do so, for a strange mixture of reasons which he himself made no attempt to analyse. Under the influence of the New England conscience he was mortifying himself, making himself pay in person for his country's weakness, rubbing his own nose in the dirty fact that he was here as a skulking commerce destroyer and not as the fighting man which all his instincts guided him to be.

7

By the time that Peabody decided to turn back from the pursuit of the convoy the *Delaware* had overtaken and destroyed fourteen sail of merchant shipping. Another small brig had been released laden with the crews, and the ship *Three Sisters* had been despatched with a prize crew in the attempt to run the blockade into an American port. The *Three Sisters*' cargo of mahogany and log wood was not specially valuable, but she was armed with no less than twelve beautiful long brass nine pounders, and it was for this reason that Peabody had sent her in. There was a terrible shortage of cannons in the United States, as he well knew; there were privateers waiting in harbour fully equipped save for their guns. America was still laughing over the story of the privateer captain–a Connecticut man at that–who sold one of his prizes, as she lay at the quay, for a greatly enhanced price because she carried guns, and it was only later that the purchaser discovered that the guns for which he had paid so dearly were merely wooden 'Quaker' guns. It was an amusing story–especially amusing in the Wooden Nutmeg State–but it abundantly illustrated the shortage of weapons which was hampering the United States. Those twelve guns would serve to arm another *Emulation* or *Oliver*, while if the British retook them before they reached American shores it would be small gain to Britain, glutted as she was with the guns taken from a hundred thousand prizes.

Three of the ships overhauled were Spaniards, and Peabody had to let them go. Spain was an ally of England against France, and those cargoes, consigned to Passages, were almost certainly destined for the use of Wellington's army, but still, the United States were neither at war with Spain nor in alliance with France. Peabody's instructions were explicit–he read them through carefully again–and he had to let them go, sadly realising, for by no means the first time, that Mr Madison had not the least idea of how to fight a war. There was the comforting thought that perhaps, now that he had crippled the convoy escort, some French privateer or other might snap those Spaniards up when they reached European waters. It was a ridiculous political situation; Mr Madison's polished hair splitting might make it sound logical, but Peabody, the man who had to implement the policy at the risk of his life and liberty, was acutely aware of its practical fallacies.

And now he knew the convoy was scattered over the breadth of the Atlantic, with each ship laying its own course for home–what ships were left of it–and it would be an unprofitable use of the *Delaware* to proceed farther into that waste of waters in the hope of further captures. It was at focal points that he wished to strike; he thought for the moment of crossing the ocean and appearing in the mouth of the Channel, but decided against it. Those waters would be thick with British ships of war, and the arguments which had in the first place directed the *Delaware* to the West Indies still held good. The day they let the last of the Spaniards go Peabody gave the order which turned the *Delaware*'s bow to the southward again. Presumably the *Emulation* and the *Oliver* had taken every prize they could find a crew for, and had headed for Savannah days ago, so that there would be need of the *Delaware*'s presence.

It was comforting to think of the outcry which would arise in London when the news arrived there that two privateers and a frigate had got in among the West Indian convoy. There were Lloyd's underwriters who would drive home in their coaches broken men; there were shipowners who would lapse into bankruptcy. Perhaps it was only a pin prick in an elephant's hide, but it was Peabody's duty to go on pricking, until either his career should end in an ocean grave–or in Dartmoor prison–or until the enemy was pestered into asking for peace. It was not a very dignified part to play in a world convulsed in the titanic struggle which was going on at present, but it was the part which Providence had allotted him, along with other seemingly trivial and yet solidly satisfactory duties like keeping track of the consumption of ship's stores.

Peabody was at work on this very matter when the next break in his routine duties came. He was sitting at his desk with a plan of the *Delware*'s hull in front of him. Every week his crew consumed a ton of salt meat, and a ton of hard bread and other stores. Since they left Long Island Sound they had fired away nine tons of shot and six tons of powder, and the bursting of the long eighteen pounder on the main deck had relieved her of a further two tons of metal. He shaded in upon the outline the parts of the ship which had been relieved of weight, the tiers where only empty beef barrels stood and the bilges which had been emptied of shot. He sat back and looked at the result, and then narrowed his eyes as he visualised the *Delaware* afloat. She would be down by the stern a little–but then on the other hand he had the feeling that she would be a trifle handier and faster if she were. He was willing to give it a trial, even with the knowledge that the continued success of his voyage might depend at any moment on his being able to get every foot of speed out of his ship. He made a mental note to tell Fry, the gunner, to draw ammunition until further orders from the after magazine.

He had become aware a second or two before of a bustle on the deck above his head, of a hoarse voice hailing from the masthead, and he was not surprised when Midshipman Kidd came into his cabin after knocking at the door.

'Mr Murray's respects, sir. There's a sail in sight to the east'ard, sir.'

Peabody's eyes went up to the tell-tale compass over his head as Kidd went on speaking.

'She's on nearly the same course as us, sir, and she looks like a sloop of war.'

'Thank you,' said Peabody. 'My compliments to Mr Murray, and ask him to send the hands to quarters.'

He put his papers neatly away into the three upper right-hand pigeon-holes of his desk, each paper into its appropriate place, and he shut and locked the desk with unhurried movements. The roar of the drums sending the crew to quarters was already echoing through the ship, and when he stepped out of his cabin the main deck was swarming with men running madly to their posts, with petty officers snapping out sharp orders at the laggards. He put on his hat and moved towards the companion; the after guard came pouring past him and threw themselves into their task of pulling down the cabin bulkheads. He had been intending to put the crew through this exercise to-morrow, but it was better as it was. Even with a first-class crew drill was more effective when there was a definite goal in sight. On deck Hubbard and Murray uncovered to him; Hubbard had his watch in hand and was noting how long it took to clear for action.

'I'll give the order for the guns to be run out myself, Mr Murray.'

'Aye aye, sir.'

Hubbard pointed to windward to where a tiny triangle of white showed over the horizon.

'She looks like a man o' war, sir, but I can't make her out fully.'

'Bear up for her, if you please, Mr Hubbard.'

On converging courses the two ships neared rapidly.

'Masthead, there!' yelled Hubbard. 'Is there any other sail in sight?'

'No, sir. Ne'er a thing, sir.'

The strange sail was a ship of war without a doubt.

There was a man o' war pennant at her masthead, and a row of gun ports along her side, but she came sailing securely along as though with a perfectly clear conscience, strange for a ship of war in sight of another much larger. But there could hardly be any sort of ambush planned with nothing else in sight from the masthead.

'I reckon she's French, sir, to judge by the cut o' that foresail,' said Hubbard, squinting through his glass. 'A Frenchie'd run from us until he knew who we were.'

'Hoist the colours, Mr Hubbard, if you please,' said Peabody, looking at her through his own glass.

The odds were at least ten to one that any ship of war at sea was British–this might be a British prize, which would account for her French appearance, and if she were thinking the *Delaware* were British a careless captain might perhaps come down as confidently as that. But if she were a British ship her doom was sealed by now, for she would never be able to escape to windward from the *Delaware*. A victory over her, petty though it would be, would be a stimulus for the American people. It was over a year since the last King's ship had struck her flag to the Stars and Stripes.

The colours were at the peak now, and Peabody saw a dull ball run up to the sloop's peak in reply, and break into a flutter of white. The white ensign? Peabody looked through his glass again. No. It was a plain white flag, unrelieved by any red cross or Union in the hoist.

'What in hell—' said Hubbard beside him, peering at the flag. 'Maybe she's a cartel, sir.'

Hubbard meant that the white flag was a flag of truce, and that the ship was on her way to exchange prisoners or to deliver a message. But a cartel would fly the national colours above the white flag, and Peabody would hardly believe that any naval officer could be ignorant of that convention.

'Fire a gun to leeward,' he said.

That was the politest way of stressing his demand for further information. The sloop's course and position were sufficient proof that she was not bound for anywhere in the United States. If as a cartel she were a British vessel negotiating with France he would not recognise the white flag, he decided. France was no ally of America, and any temporary suspension of hostilities between France and England meant nothing to his country.

The gun went off, and every eye on deck watched the strange sloop. She did nothing whatever except to hold steadily on her course with the white flag at her peak, blandly ignoring the *Delaware* altogether.

'God-damned impertinence!' said Hubbard.

''Bout ship, Mr Hubbard. Mr Murray! Run out the guns and put a shot across her bows!'

Amid the bustle and hurry of going about came the dull thunder of the wooden gun trucks rumbling across the deck seams as the *Delaware* showed her teeth. As she steadied on her new course the other bow-chaser went off with a crash. Peabody saw the sloop's starboard jib-guy part like a cracked whip–Murray had put a liberal interpretation upon his orders. Immediately afterwards the sloop showed signs of life. She threw her topsails abruptly aback, and came up into the wind like a horse reined up from full gallop, her canvas slatting violently. Apparently the shot and the threatened broadside had had their effect.

The *Delaware* forged up alongside her, the gun captains looking along their sights, not a sound in the ship save for her sharp bows cleaving the water.

'Heave-to, if you please, Mr Hubbard,' said Peabody, taking up his speaking-trumpet.

'Sloop ahoy! What sloop's that?'

A high-pitched voice sent a reply back to him down wind, but the words were unintelligible.

'French, maybe. Or Eyetalian,' said Hubbard.

'What sloop's that?' asked Peabody again, irascibly.

There was a second's pause before the reply came, in English this time, with a marked foreign accent.

'Say it again!' roared Peabody.

One of the gold-laced officers on the sloop's quarterdeck raised his speaking-trumpet again. When he spoke his intonation betrayed quite as much exasperation as did Peabody's.

'His Most Christian Majesty's Ship—'

What the name was they could not be sure.

'Sounded like "negress," sir,' said Hubbard. 'Queer name for a ship. But she's a Dago, or mebbe a Portugee.'

'Neither of those,' said Peabody.

The King of Spain was His Most Catholic Majesty, and the King of Portugal was His Most Faithful Majesty–he had heard the pompous expressions used time and again when he was with Preble in the Mediterranean. He had never heard of His Most Christian Majesty.

'I'll send a boat,' he roared into the wind, and instantly decided that this was a business which he himself had better attend to; if an international incident were to grow out of this he wanted full responsibility.

'Pass the word for my servant to bring my sword,' he said. 'I'll go in the quarterboat, Mr Hubbard–and pass the word for Mr Peabody to come with me.'

Washington came running with sword and belt and boat cloak; Jonathan came up from his post below. There was a fair sea running, but they made a neat job of dropping the quarterboat into the lee which the ship afforded, with Jonathan sitting nursing his wounded arm in the stern sheets. Peabody swung himself down the fall, timed the rise of the boat as a wave lifted her, and dropped in a moment before she fell away again. With the spray that was flying he was glad of his boat cloak to preserve his uniform from salt.

'Give way,' he said to the boat's crew, and they thrust against the *Delaware*'s side and took up the stroke, the boat bobbing up and down over the big Atlantic waves.

'She's surely French enough in looks,' he said, examining the smart little ship towards which they were heading.

'Is she?' said Jonathan.

'Oars?' said Peabody to the crew, and the slow rhythmic pulling stopped while the boat ran alongside the sloop. The bowman got to his feet with a boat-hook. A boatswain's chair came dangling down to them, and Peabody threw off his cloak and swung himself on to it.

'Follow me,' he called to Jonathan, as the swell took the boat from under him.

A dozen curious faces looked up at him as he swung over the rail and dropped to the deck; he stepped down, removed his hat, and eyed the waiting group. With a little surprise he noticed two women standing aft by the taffrail, but he did not have time for more than a brief glance. A stout officer with massive epaulettes stepped forward.

'Captain Nicolas Dupont,' he said–his English was stilted and he pronounced the French names in French fashion, unintelligibly to Peabody, 'of His Most Christian Majesty's sloop *Tigresse*.'

'Captain Josiah Peabody, United States Ship *Delaware*,' said Peabody.

Malta had accustomed him to encounters with officers of foreign services, but there was for him still a vague sort of unreality about stiff formality.

'You wore your–your coat in the boat, Captain,' said Dupont. 'We could not see your rank. Please pardon me for not receiving you with the appropriate compliments.'

'Of course,' said Peabody.

All this was the preliminary salute before crossing swords, he felt. He and Dupont eyed each other so keenly that neither paid any attention to Jonathan swaying down in the boatswain's chair behind Peabody.

'And now, sir,' said Dupont. 'Would you have the goodness to explain why your ship fired upon me?'

'Why didn't you show your colours?' riposted Peabody. He was in no mood for a passive defensive.

Dupont's bushy brows came together angrily.

'We showed them, sir. We still show them.'

He gesticulated towards the peak, where the white flag fluttered. Peabody noticed for the first time a gleam of gold on the white, and felt a moment's misgiving which he was determined not to show.

'Where are your national colours?' he asked.

'Those are they. The flag of His Most Christian Majesty.'

'His Most Christian Majesty?'

'His Most Christian Majesty Louis, by the grace of God King of France and Navarre.'

Dupont's rage was joined to genuine and obvious distress, like a man facing approaching humiliation.

'King of France!' said Peabody.

'King of France and Navarre,' insisted Dupont.

Peabody began to see the light, and at the same time worse misgivings than ever began to assail him.

'Napoleon has fallen?' he said.

'The usurper Bonaparte has fallen,' said Dupont solemnly. 'Louis Eighteen sits on his rightful throne.' It was the most tremendous news for twenty years. The shadow which had lain across the whole world for twenty years had lifted. They were emerging into the sunshine of a new era.

Dupont's distress was evaporating as he guessed at Peabody's astonishment, and Peabody began to feel sympathy for Dupont in the quandary in which he had found himself. A simple hoisting of the tricolour flag which the world knew so well would have saved all this misunderstanding, but Dupont had not been able to bring himself to hoist it–it would have been a horrible humiliation to have received protection from the colours of the Revolution against which he had struggled for a lifetime. It must have been a humiliation, too, to discover that the world had forgotten that title of Most Christian Majesty which had at one time overawed Europe. And he knew immediate qualms at the thought that he had fired upon the flag of what was presumably a neutral country now. He saw the need for prompt apology, unreserved apology.

Mr Madison would be furiously angry if he heard of the incident, but that was not the point. The United States could not afford to antagonise anyone else, not while she was locked in a death struggle with the greatest antagonist of all. He had thought for the moment of laughing at the whole affair, turning to his heel and quitting the *Tigresse*, leaving the politicians to disentangle the business as best they could, but he put aside the insidious temptation to reckless arrogance. It was his duty to humble himself. He swallowed twice as he collected the words together in his mind.

'Sir,' he said slowly, 'I hope you will allow me to apologise, to apologise for this–this unfortunate thing that has happened. I am very sorry, sir.'

It was not the words of the apology which mollified Dupont as much as the tremendous reluctance with which the words came. A lion could hardly have given back a lamb to its mother more unreadily. An apology from a man so totally unaccustomed to apologising was doubly sweet to the fat little captain, and his face cleared.

'Let us say no more about it, sir,' said Dupont. He creased himself across his fat middle in a profound bow which Peabody tried to imitate, and then they looked at each other, Peabody at a loss as to what to say next. Polite small talk, always difficult to him, was more difficult than ever after the strain of the last few minutes, but Dupont was equal to the occasion. He glanced across at Jonathan.

'And this gentleman is—' he asked.

'My brother, Midshipman Peabody,' said Peabody gratefully.

'Your servant, sir,' said Dupont. He turned to the group of officers behind him, and the two brothers were engulfed in a wave of introductions. Everyone was bowing and scraping and making legs in the instant, and there was an immense amount of broken English being spoken. Peabody had yet to meet the naval officer of any nation who did not possess at least a few words of English, but these officers all had more than that, even though their syntax was doubtful and their accents marked. As the flurry died down Dupont said:

'Would you please come and be presented to my passengers?'

The whole business of bowings and scrapings began again the moment Dupont began to lead them away; it left Peabody a trifle dazed–as a young man he had always been a little amused during Captain Truxtun's careful lessons in the deportment of a gentleman and a naval officer, finding it hard to believe that grown men really did these things.

Across the deck, beside the taffrail, stood a little group of three people, including the two women whom Peabody had noticed some time back. The third member of the group was a man.

'Your Excellency,' said Dupont. 'May I present Captain Josiah Peabody of the United States Navy?–His Excellency the Marquis de St Amant de Boixe, Governor of His Most Christian Majesty's possessions in the Lesser Antilles.'

Peabody put his hand with his hat on his heart and moved his feet into the first position, but his bow was cut short by the Marquis stepping forward and offering his hand. His grip was hearty and firm. Peabody, a little more dazed still, had the impression of a strong face, extraordinarily handsome, with piercing blue eyes. The Marquis was a man in his early forties, with his hair clubbed at the back in a fashion a trifle old-fashioned; across his gold-laced blue coat he wore the broad ribbon of some order of nobility, of a vivid blue which complemented the blue of his eyes.

'It is a pleasure to meet you, Captain,' he said, without a trace of accent, 'and you, too, Mr Peabody. It would be a further pleasure to present you to my sister,

Madame la Comtesse d'Ernée, and my daughter, Mademoiselle de Breuil.'

Everything contributed to Peabody's bedazement; perhaps the fact that he had just shaken hands when he was preparing to bow had thrown him off his balance at the start. The two women had put back their veils, and revealed faces which strongly resembled the Marquis's. The sister was the older, and there was a line or two on her face and something in the set of her features which made for hardness and supplemented the widow's black which she wore. But the daughter–Peabody's wits drowned in those blue eyes. He had already bowed to the Countess and was preparing to bow again when he met their glance, but the bow was cut short while he stared. He was conscious of no other details about her; the Countess was speaking to him, but Peabody's ears registered the words as a flat series of meaningless sounds. She was going down in a curtsey to him, her eyes still on him, and it was only with an effort that he managed to push his foot forward and complete his bow. He tore his glance away to make himself listen to the Countess.

'Confess, Captain,' she was saying, 'you did not recognise our flag when you saw it.'

Peabody, until he could find words, looked up to where the golden lilies–visible enough from here–flapped on the white flag at the peak.

'I have been at sea twenty years, ma'am,' he said, 'but this is the first time I have seen it.'

'Fie,' said the Countess. 'The flag of Lafayette, of de Grasse, which freed you from King George, and yet you fire on it!'

'Louise,' said the Marquis. 'The captain did no such thing. I have Captain Dupont's word for it that not a shot has been fired this morning.'

Peabody looked at him gratefully, and caught at his cue.

'No indeed, sir,' he said, and then tried to correct himself: 'Your Excellency.'

These cursed titles of honour! He looked away and met those blue eyes again. There was a friendly twinkle in them which made his heart miss a beat. He wanted to wipe his face with his handkerchief, but he knew that would be inelegant. He was hot under the skin, and the burning sun was calling forth the sweat on his forehead. It may have been on account of his embarrassment that the Marquis brought the conversation round to business, so as to give him a chance to recover.

'The incident is forgotten,' he said. 'It is my intention, as soon as I reach Martinique, to maintain the strictest neutrality.'

'It will be a strange experience,' said the Countess, 'for French people to be neutral while there is a war on.'

'Yes,' said Peabody. His mind was already at work upon the problems set him by the defeat of France. 'Martinique is to be French again?'

'Martinique, Guadeloupe, and their dependencies.'

This was of lively interest. Up to this moment the British had conquered and ruled all the West Indies save for Haiti and the Spanish possessions; the former was not strong enough to defend her neutrality, and Spain, as an ally of Great Britain, although not at war with the United States, would hardly be likely to afford a safe refuge in her colonies to the *Delaware* should she need it. Until now there had been no neutrals worth mentioning in this war which had involved the whole world, and he was already wondering how he could put the new situation to use. A fresh consideration struck him, and he turned to include Dupont as well as the Marquis in his inquiry.

'You won't inform the British of my position of course, sir?' he said.

'That would be un-neutral,' said the Marquis, quickly, before the captain could reply.

'Thank you,' said Peabody, and then, remembering again: 'Your Excellency.'

Once again there was that twinkle in the girl's blue eyes.

'I hope you are planning to visit us at Fort de France, Captain Peabody,' she said.

'Anne!' exclaimed the Countess, a little scandalised.

'My daughter has said exactly what was in my mind,' interposed the Marquis. 'It would give me the greatest pleasure to be able to return some of the hospitality which my daughter and I owe to America.'

Peabody looked his inquiries.

'I was born in your country, Captain Peabody,' said the girl–Anne was her name, apparently.

'How's that again?' asked Peabody.

'Anne was born in Philadelphia,' explained the Marquis, and then, after a moment's hesitation, 'my wife is buried there. We were in America during the Terror. Anne was born the day they guillotined Robespierre.'

'We all thought then,' said the Countess, sadly, 'when the news came, that the world would soon be at peace again. And that is twenty years ago, and some of us are still at war.'

'But you haven't been living in America for the last twenty years?' said Peabody to Anne. As far as he was concerned there was practically no one else on deck.

Anne shook her head and twinkled again.

'I left when I was four,' she said. 'I have no memory of it, and I am sure that is a pity.'

'I acted as envoy from my King to your President,' explained the Marquis. 'After four years I was transferred to Europe. For the last five we have been living in London.'

Conversation died away at that. Peabody had too much to think about to be able to say anything while he digested the two remarkable facts that Napoleon had fallen and that Anne was American born. He shook himself back into politeness.

'This has been a delightful visit,' he said, racking his mind for the right words. 'I must thank you very much.'

The ladies went down in curtseys as he bowed; the Marquis shook hands, and Dupont prepared to accompany him to the ship's side.

'Don't forget you've promised to visit us!' said the Countess.

This time there were formalities, pipes twittering, and marines presenting arms as his boatswain's chair swung him off the deck, and then the boat danced back to the *Delaware*.

'A couple of peaches, they were,' said Jonathan.

'Good God!' said Peabody, turning on him.

He was simply amazed that anyone could possibly think of Anne as a peach; the two notions were so far removed from each other.

'The old 'un's getting long in the tooth,' said Jonathan, 'but I reckon she could still give a bit of sport. And the young 'un—'

'Shut your mouth!' snapped Peabody.

They ran under the *Delaware*'s counter and grabbed the falls; Peabody swung himself up, hat, sword, and all, on to the quarterdeck, hand over hand, where Hubbard called all hands to attention. Peabody blinked about him at the familiar surroundings. It was odd to be among these familiar things and yet to feel so strange, to have commonplace details to attend to during this moment of unusual exaltation.

'Mr Murray!' he yelled. 'A salute of nineteen guns, if you please! Mr Hubbard, dip the colours at the salute. Dismiss the watch below, and square away.'

The ensign ran slowly down and up again as the saluting gun barked out. The yards came round, and the *Delaware*'s idle pitching over the waves changed to a more purposeful rise and swoop. The sloop's sails were filling, too, and repeated puffs of smoke broke from her bows as she answered the *Delaware*'s salute. Peabody stood staring back at her while the two ships diverged; there was–he was almost sure–a speck of white waving from her quarterdeck, and he snatched off his hat and stood bareheaded.

8

Peabody sat pen in hand bending over the ship's log. 'Encountered French Government sloop *Tigresse* Captain Dupon, having on board—'

This was hard work. The name *Tigresse* came easily, because Peabody had read it cut into the ship's bell. He was fairly sure about the 'Dupon,' too, having heard the captain enunciate it clearly enough although with his French accent. But it was not so easy to describe the *Tigresse*. He was not at all anxious to write 'His Most Christian Majesty's,' or 'The French King's,' because he was by no means sure whether the American Government had recognised that potentate, and it had called for a little thought to devise a way round the difficulty. And now that he had come to the point of saying who else was on board he was quite at a loss. There was a Marquis, he knew–he had caught the word during the introductions–but what he was Marquis of Peabody had not the least recollection, even if he had ever really heard the cumbrous title. Somehow he had formed an accurate idea as to what were to be the Marquis's official duties, but the actual words used by Dupont in his presentation quite escaped him. Peabody scratched his nose with the end of the quill, pondered, and went on writing–'Having on board the new Governor of Martinique and his family.'

That solved the difficulty. She had blue eyes (Peabody's thoughts went off at an abrupt tangent) and very black hair whose curls were in the most vivid contrast with her white forehead. Her given name was Anne, but what the rest of it was he could not tell, not for the life of him. Anne de Something-or-other. That did not describe her in the least–she was somebody much more definite than that. Into those blue eyes there sometimes came a twinkle which was one of the most exciting things he had ever seen. But for the rest of her— Peabody tried methodically to piece his memories of her together. Tall? Short? Peabody forced himself, with rigid self-control, to remember what he had noticed about her before he had met her eyes; he tried to call up before his mental vision his glimpse of her on the quarterdeck when his only reaction to the sight of her had been surprise at the presence of females. The carronade beside her had been a twelve pounder, and that came up as far as–yes, of course, she was short. The Marquis was not a tall man, and she had appeared small beside him. She had been wearing some sort of veil which she had put back to twinkle at him. What else she was wearing he could not remember at all, not at all. But the black curls and the blue eyes and the pink-and-white skin he could remember more vividly than he had ever remembered anything. Jonathan had called her 'the young 'un,' and spoke of her as a peach. Jonathan was a young fool who was not fit to approach any young woman.

Peabody put the log on one side, rose from his desk, and walked up on deck; before his eyes, in the dark alleyway, there floated the vision of Anne, which only faded–just as a ghost would–as he entered the strong sunshine of the deck. Atwell uncovered to him, and he paced rapidly up and down the quarterdeck for a few turns while he looked over the ship. Everything there was just as it should be; the sails were drawing well, the ship was exactly on her course, the watch was at work in a quiet and orderly fashion. Peabody contrasted his own happy lot with that of the British captains. The maintenance of American ships of war–what few of them there were–was a mere flea-bite compared with the enormous resources available; there had been no need for niggardliness in any respect whatever, while the British, maintaining the largest fleet possible, during twenty continuous years of war, were compelled to skimp and scrape to make the supplies go round. When he had commissioned the *Delaware* he had been able to pick his crew from a number of applicants three times as great as he needed–every man on board was a seasoned seaman, every specialist had spent a lifetime in his trade, while the British officers had to man their ships by force and train their crews while actually on service. He was a fortunate man.

His eye caught sight of a midshipman forward in charge of a party setting up the lee foremast shrouds. He was lounging against a gun in a manner which no young officer should use when supervising hard work done by older men. It was Jonathan.

'Mr Peabody!' roared Peabody.

A little stir ran round the ship, unnoticed by him alone; Jonathan looked up.

'Mr Peabody!' roared Peabody again,

Jonathan came walking aft, a faint look of surprise on his face.

'Move quicker than that when I call you!' snapped Peabody. 'Pull yourself up straight and stand at attention!'

The look of faint surprise on Jonathan's face changed to one of deep, pained surprise.

'Take that look off your face!' said Peabody, but the surprise merely became genuine.

'I don't like to see you squatting about, Mr Peabody, when your division is at work.'

'But my arm—' said Jonathan.

'Damn your arm!' said Peabody; not so much because Downing had declared Jonathan fit for duty yesterday as because he was irritated that a member of his ship's company should plead bodily weakness when there was work to be done.

'I'm not feeling good,' said Jonathan, 'and you wouldn't either.'

It may have been surprise which had deprived Jonathan of his usual tact; he ought to have guessed that his brother was in an unusual mood, and he ought to have modelled his bearing for the moment on the slavish deference of the other officers which so excited his derision. Peabody for a couple of seconds could only gobble at him before he was able to find words for his indignation.

'Call me "sir"!' he roared. 'I don't like your damned impertinence, Mr Peabody.'

Jonathan, still amazingly obtuse, pushed out his lower lip, hunched his shoulders, and sulked.

'Fore top-gallant masthead! Wait there for further orders,' snapped Peabody. 'Run, you–you whipper-snapper.'

He was in a towering passion, and Jonathan, looking at him for the first time with seeing eyes, suddenly realised it and was afraid. He turned and ran, with every eye in the ship following him. Halfway up the foremast shrouds he paused for a moment and looked down, saw Peabody take an impatient step, and pelted up again. Peabody watched him to the masthead, and turned abruptly to continue pacing the deck while his fury subsided. He was actually trembling a little with emotion. He had been over-indulgent to the boy, and he knew it now. The realisation that he had actually had a favourite on board since the voyage began was a shock to him.

He was by no means self-analytical enough to know that he had been indulgent to Jonathan merely because he had already been indulgent to him–that he felt the natural fondness for him which was only to be expected after his kindness to him. And fortunately for the sake of his own peace of mind, he most certainly was unaware of the reason for his new perspicacity, which was Jonathan's ill-advised remark about the two women on board the *Tigresse*. He was angry with himself, not with Jonathan, although no one save himself knew it. Atwell turned and looked away to leeward, over the blue water, so as to hide a smile; the hands at work on deck were grinning secretly to each other; below deck already the excited whisper was going round that the captain had parted brass rags with that cub of a young brother of his. And at the fore top-gallant masthead, on his uncomfortable perch, with his arm linked through the fore royal halliards, Jonathan sat and shed tears as he bemoaned the fate which had dragged him into this unsympathetic service with its unyielding discipline and soulless self-centredness, which denied to his personality any play at all. Jonathan did not accept gladly the function of being a cog in a machine. He did not even bother to look up when the lookout began bellowing 'land-ho!'

In his present mood he cared for no land that was not his native Connecticut, where he could find sport in dodging the ire of his terrible father, who was at least a known hazard with human foibles as compared with this hard unknown brother of his. The romantic blue outline, dark against the bright sky and the silvered surface of the distant sea, had no appeal at all for him.

Down on deck Hubbard, whom the cry of land had brought up from below, was exhibiting the modest complacency natural after an exact landfall following thirty days at sea.

'Antigua, sir,' he said to his captain, fingering his telescope.

'Yes,' said Peabody, without much expression.

Now they were putting their heads into the lion's mouth. The chain of islands was one of the richest possessions of England–in sterling value hardly smaller than the whole extent of India. It was the most sensitive of all the spots in which he could deliver a pin prick. From the Virgins down to Trinidad wealth came seeping towards London. A myriad small island boats crept from island to island with the products that made England rich, accumulating them in the major ports until the time should come for a convoy to start for Europe. For several years the British had been undisputed masters here, conquering island after island–the Danish Virgins, the Dutch St Martin, the French Martinique–in their determination to allow no enemy to imperil their possessions.

The American privateers had effected little enough in this region; the small island vessels were not tempting as prizes, for they called for a disproportionate number of men as prize crews in relation to their size, while the distances between protected harbours were so short as to give them a fair chance of evading capture. Privateers fought for money; there were shareholders in Baltimore who demanded dividends, and mere destruction–especially when that destruction was bound, sooner or later, to call down upon them the undesirable attention of British ships of war–made no appeal to them. Peabody could foresee a rich harvest awaiting the *Delaware*'s reaping for a while, and perhaps ruin and perhaps death at the end of it. No one was expecting him here, for he had last been reported in the Windward Passage six hundred miles away. It was his business to wring every drop of advantage out of the surprise of his arrival, to ravage and destroy to the utmost before counter-measures could be taken against him. He looked through his glass at the steep outline of Antigua. His thin mobile lips were compressed, and the two lines which ran from the sides of his nose to the corners of his mouth showed deep in his face.

9

The cutter was only a small vessel–the mulatto captain had only two coloured hands to help him handle her–but she was all he owned. He squatted on the deck of the *Delaware* with his face in his hands, sobbing, while she burned; and Peabody and the other officers whose business brought them past him cast sympathetic glances at his unconscious back. They liked this callous destruction no better than he did, and she was the thirtieth vessel which had burned since the *Delaware* had come bursting into the Lesser Antilles. Sloops and cutters, and the little island schooners; the *Delaware* had interrupted and burned every one she had been able to catch from Antigua to Santa Cruz. The Leeward Islands must be in an uproar of consternation. Peabody walked the deck as the *Delaware* bore away from the scene; in these narrow waters where instant decision had to be taken he did not care to be even a few seconds removed from the position of control.

To windward lay St Kitts, green and lovely, towering out of the sea with its jagged outline climbing up to the summit of Mount Misery, and on the port bow lay Nevis, sharply triangular, the narrow channel between its base and St Kitts not yet opened up by the *Delaware*'s progress along the land. Over there in Basse-Terre people must be wringing their hands and shaking their fists in helpless anger at the sight of the American frigate sailing insolently past, Stars and Stripes flying. The soldiers in the batteries there must be impotently looking along their guns, measuring the impossible range, and praying without hope for some chance which might bring the enemy within range. There were strange feelings in Peabody's heart as he gazed. It was here, in this identical bit of sea, that the *Constellation* had fought the *Vengeance*. Peabody had been a lieutenant then, in charge of eight spar-deck guns. He remembered the battle in the wild sea, then destruction and ruin, and Truxtun on the quarterdeck with his long hair blowing.

Out here to-day in the lee of St Kitts the wind was uncertain and fluky. Every now and again the sails would flap thunderously as a puff came from an unexpected quarter, for it was at this time of day that the sea breeze might be counted upon to spring up and over-master the perpetual breath of the trades.

'There's shipping there, sir,' said Hubbard, stabbing the air with a long forefinger. Against the white of the surf could be seen three or four small cutters creeping along on the opposite course to the *Delaware*'s, hoping to reach the shelter of the batteries of Basse-Terre.

'I see them,' said Peabody.

'They'll catch the sea breeze before we do out here, sir,' went on Hubbard warningly.

'That's likely,' said Peabody. He swept his glass in a minute search of the shore line beyond Basse-Terre; there was no recent information at his disposal regarding the coastal defence of these islands, and he had no wish to incur a bloody repulse. But the most painstaking examination failed to reveal any battery hidden among the lush green of the island's steep sides.

'I'll have the boats ready to put over the side, Mr Hubbard, if you please,' said Peabody with the glass still at his side. 'Arm the boats' crews.'

'Aye aye, sir.'

The orders were briefly given, and the boats' crews bustled into their stations, excitedly buckling cutlasses about them and thrusting pistols into their belts.

'Uncock that pistol, damn you,' bawled Hubbard suddenly.

In the privateer in which Hubbard had served before joining the *Delaware* a landsman had once let off a pistol by accident, and the bullet, flying into the arms chest, had discharged a loaded musket which in turn had set off every weapon in the chest and caused a dozen casualties.

'Starboard a little,' said Peabody to the helmsman. 'Keep her at that!'

'Keep her at that, sir,' echoed the helmsman.

The *Delaware* edged in towards the shore, skirting the extreme range of the Basse-Terre batteries, so as to give the boats the shortest pull necessary. The tiny airs of wind sent her through the water with hardly a ripple. She crept along over the matt blue amid a breathless silence.

'Boats away, Mr Hubbard, if you please.'

'Boats away! Boats away-ay!'

Hubbard began to shout the order as soon as the first two words had left Peabody's lips; the polite remaining five were drowned in his yell. A hundred hands who had been awaiting the order went away on the run with the hoists. The two big boats rose and fell simultaneously into the water and their crews tumbled down into them, Murray commanding one and Atwell the other. They thrust clear and then flung their weight upon the oars, making the stout ash bend as they drove the big craft through the water, dashing for the shore.

'We might be a whaler, sir,' grinned Hubbard to Peabody, as he watched their progress.

The cutters saw their doom hurtling at them. The leading one manned four sweeps in a desperate effort to gain the shelter of the batteries; Peabody saw the long black blades begin their slow pulling, but the other three incontinently went about and headed for the shore. Atwell's longboat altered course for the cutter under sweeps, Peabody following her with his glass. A white pillar of water emerged suddenly from the surface of the blue sea a cable's length ahead of the longboat; the big guns at Basse-Terre were chancing their aim. But a minute later Atwell was alongside, and not long after that he was pulling away again. A crowded dinghy was taking the cutter's crew to the land, and a black cloud of smoke was slowly rising from the cutter and spreading over the surface of the sea.

Peabody swung his glass towards the other vessels. They had reached the shore, and their crews tumbled out into the surf in a wild rush for safety. Peabody watched Murray steady his boat on the edge of the surf for a moment and then dash in after them; it was interesting to see if Murray kept his head during his tenure of independent command. A little group of white-shirted men ran up the narrow beach as a guard against surprise, and another group moved along to the beached boats, while the longboats waited in the surf with oars out ready for instant departure. Murray was acting with perfect correctness, decided Peabody. His glass caught a glint of steel in the sunshine–someone was wielding an axe to stove in the cutters. Directly afterwards came the smoke as first one boat and then another was set afire; by the time Atwell's boat reached the scene all the cutters were on fire and blazing fiercely.

Something impelled Peabody to traverse his glass along the shore towards Basse-Terre. He saw a big red dot, the twinkle of steel–a detachment of the garrison was pelting hot foot along the coastal path to try to save the boats. But Murray still had ten minutes in hand, and he coolly made the most of them. Probably all three of the cutters had stove their bottoms running ashore, and certainly ten minutes' axe work upon them damaged them beyond repair, while the fire had time to take a good hold and sweep the upper works. The infantry detachment was a quarter of a mile away when Murray recalled his picket, and by the time the sweating soldiers had reached the scene of action the longboat had shoved off and was just out of musket range beside Atwell. It was a neat piece of work, as Peabody ungrudgingly told Murray when he reached the ship again.

'Thank'ee, sir,' said Murray. His eyes were still bright with excitement and his chest was still heaving in sympathy with his quickened pulse. 'Those sogers were black. Their facings were blue an' they had a white officer. West India Regiment, I reckon, sir.'

Another good mark for Murray, seeing that during the excitement of the retreat he had kept his head clear enough to identify his pursuers. The information was of trifling importance, but all information was of some potential value. Murray looked back at the beach, where the red-coated soldiers and white-clad inhabitants were trying to salve something of the wrecks.

'We didn't leave much for 'em, sir,' said Murray, grinning, but Peabody was no longer paying him attention. He was a-looking at Nevis, which was slowly growing more defined as the *Delaware* made her leisurely way along the coast. Already the two-mile-wide channel between Nevis and St Kitts was fully opened up from where he stood.

'Bring in the captain of the cutter we've got on board,' he said.

They brought him the mulatto, who stood sullenly in front of him in his ragged shirt and trousers. His bare feet were seemingly too hard to feel the hot planking under them.

'John O'Hara,' said Peabody, and the mulatto nodded. 'Your boat was registered at Charlestown, Nevis.'

Another nod.

'What soldiers are there?'

O'Hara said nothing.

'Did you hear me speak to you?'

'Yessir. I don't know nothin', sir.'

The mulatto's speech was accented like no other on earth. It was only with difficulty that Peabody could understand him.

'You know the answer to that question,' said Peabody.

'No, sir.'

Even if patriotism did not motivate him, O'Hara owed a grudge against this captain who had just destroyed his all. Peabody looked at the sullen face, and then away, at the blue sky and the blue sea, and the steep green slopes of Nevis. War was a merciless business.

'Listen to me, O'Hara,' he said. 'Tell me what I want to know, and I'll set you free. I'll give you fifty golden guineas as well.' He kept his hard blue eyes on O'Hara's face, but he could detect no sign of weakening at the offer of the reward. So it was time for threats.

'If you don't tell me, I'll sell you at New Orleans. I promise you that, and you know what it means.'

Peabody saw the expression of the mulatto's face change, he saw the melancholy black eyes with the yellow whites wander round the horizon, just as his own had done a moment before. The wretched man was thinking of his present life, free, in this blue and green paradise, and comparing it with the prospect offered him–the canebrake and the cotton field and the taskmaster's lash.

'I'll get eight hundred dollars for you,' said Peabody. 'Somebody'll get eight hundred dollars' worth out of you, and a profit beside.'

The mulatto shuddered as he emerged from his bad dream.

'I'll tell you,' he said.

Bit by bit Peabody drew the facts from him, halting every now and then to make sure he understood O'Hara's patois. No, there were no red-coated soldiers in Nevis, although there were plenty in St Kitts. There was a white militia, perhaps a thousand in the whole island, perhaps two hundred in Charlestown itself. They drilled once a month on Sunday afternoons. The coloured people, even the free ones, were not allowed arms except for the men enlisted in the West India Regiment. Yes, there were some guns mounted in Charlestown–two big ones, in a battery at the north end of the bay. There were two old white soldiers who looked after them all the time, and some of the white militia were supposed to be trained by them. Yes, that was the battery, there. Yes, those warehouses round the jetty were full. Sugar and molasses and coffee.

'Right,' said Peabody. 'If this is the truth, I'll set you free to-night. Take him away, and bring me the other two.'

The two negroes who had constituted the crew of the burned cutter were more easily frightened, though their speech was even more unintelligible than their captain's. Peabody did not have to use threats towards them; it sufficed for him merely to repeat his question once, with his eyes narrowed, for them to pour out their answers in their gobbling speech. They were silly with fright, and they knew little enough, but all they said went to confirm the information wrung from O'Hara. It was worth while to take the risk.

'I shall want the two quarterboats manned as well as the longboats,' said Peabody to his officers, and they stood in a semicircle before him as he gave them his orders.

They looked at each other as they listened, exchanging glances, and then looked back at him. His hard blue eyes had a light in them, and the firm compression of his lips seemed to make his thin nose more pronounced than ever in the frame of the deep lines beside it.

Two leadsmen in the chains chanted the depth as the *Delaware* glided round; steep-to as these West India islands all were there were soundings and a dangerous shoal in the shallow channel between these two island. Peabody looked over at Nevis, at the white houses of Charlestown broadcast over the green slopes like cubes of sugar, at the shallow crescent of the bay with its gleaming beach, and then back at St Kitts. The guns rumbled out as the ports were opened, and with a scampering of feet the men at the weatherbraces backed the maintopsail.

'You can go now, Mr Hubbard,' said Peabody.

There was a cheer from the crew as the four boats dropped into the sea, and the men at the oars needed no urging as they drove the blades foaming through the water. This was an expedition whose daring was obvious to everyone, and which appealed to everyone. It was paying back in her own coin the thousand mortifying insults which Britain had dealt out to American shores. British squadrons might lord it in the Chesapeake and in Long Island Sound, but they could not guard the West Indies against reprisals. Peabody walked slowly back and forth across the quarterdeck, keeping wary watch upon all the three points of stress, on Nevis and on the battery and upon the mole at Charlestown. Murray was leading the two fast gigs against the battery, the most vital point; Atwell with the two longboats was heading straight for the mole. There were a hundred and fifty men in those boats, every single one which the *Delaware* could spare and still remain a fighting entity; Peabody watched their progress with an anxiety which he found it hard to conceal.

A movement over on the St Kitts shore caught his attention.

'Mr Shepherd,' he said to the midshipman commanding the port-side quarterdeck guns. 'Try a shot with that twelve pounder at those boats.'

The gun roared out and a spout of water in the smooth shallow sea showed where it had pitched; the row boats which had crept out from shore manned by redcoated West Indians promptly turned back. There was no hope of crossing in row boats two miles of open water swept by the guns of the *Delaware*. The garrison of St Kitts would have to stand by impotently and watch the attack upon Nevis. Over in the battery appeared first one jet of smoke and then another; it was not until a quarter of a minute later that the sound of the shots, flat in the heated air, reached Peabody's ears. Peabody could see no sign of the fall of the shot; perhaps the gunners were using grape–at twice the effective range of grape shot–or perhaps they had utterly misjudged the range, or perhaps they had forgotten to put in any shot at all. Militia gunners were capable of anything, especially when taken by surprise, and there could hardly be a greater surprise for them than the arrival of a powerful enemy in the same week that everyone was drawing a long breath at the conclusion of a war twenty years old.

Murray's men were running up the beach; at three miles the flash of the sun on the cutlass blades was still reflected clearly back. There was no need to worry then any more, and Peabody turned his attention to the mole. He could see the longboats coming alongside, but he had to guess at the sequence of events–the blue marines marching methodically forward while the white-clad sailors set about the work of destruction. Even through his glass the drowsy town still seemed eminently peaceful.

A sudden tremendous roar startled him a little. It came from the battery, which was concealed in a cloud of smoke. Murray must have blown it up, battery, magazine, guns and all. Peabody hoped that none of the *Delaware*'s men had been hurt, for blowing up magazines was a tricky, chancy business. But there were the gigs pushing off from the beach, so that presumably all was well. They were heading along the arc of the bay towards the mole to act as a reserve to Atwell if necessary. Over in St Kitts row boats were making their appearance again, far away on the further side of the channel.

'Shall I try another shot at 'em, sir?' asked Shepherd, looking round at him.

'They're out of range,' said Peabody, shaking his head. The St Kitts' garrison was welcome to try and interfere as long as they circled round beyond the range of the *Delaware*'s guns–their course would land them on the far side of Nevis. After a four-mile row and a four-mile march they could do what they liked in Charlestown, seeing that the raid would be over long before their arrival.

Shepherd's wound had robbed him of his good looks; his scarred left cheek gave to his sunburned face a lopsided appearance which was utterly sinister, as he stood there beside his guns. Peabody looked back at Charlestown. There was still no sign of war in the drowsy town; the only things moving were Murray's gigs, creeping beetle-like over the blue water towards the mole, and he took the glass from his aching eye and walked slowly back and forth across the quarterdeck. Providence had decreed that he should be subjected to these long and dreary waits; it was that which robbed them of their sting. There was no break until the sound of another loud report came from the town, sending his glass to his eye again on the instant. It was a cannon shot without doubt, but search as he would with his glass he could see nothing whatever of the source of the sound. Murray had reached the mole and was landing his men. There were fifty marines and a hundred seamen there now, and Murray ought to be safe enough.

Yes, that was what he had been looking for. A wisp of black smoke was drifting slowly over the town, coming from the general direction of the warehouses grouped round the mole. It thickened even as he watched. There would be a maximum of twenty minutes or thereabouts to wait, and he resumed his pacing. The *Delaware* with her maintopsail aback, swung idly round in response to a fortuitous puff of wind–apparently the sea breeze was beginning to win its daily victory over the Trades. The black smoke was growing all the time in volume and intensity, and the sea breeze was spreading it like a fog over the slopes of Charlestown. Once those warehouses with their inflammable contents were well alight, no effort whatever on the part of the British could extinguish them.

Here came a little block of white down the mole to the boats, the first party of retiring seamen. First one longboat and then the other detached itself from the mole and began to crawl out into the bay, and then the swifter gigs followed.

'Square away, Mr Hubbard, if you please. We'll run down to the boats.'

On the quarterdeck Murray made his second report of the day.

'We blew the battery up, sir. Dismounted the guns and sent the whole place to glory. They only had time to fire two rounds at us–I guess you saw that, sir. There weren't more than twenty men serving the guns, an' they ran when we arrived. I had two men hurt, sir–Able Seaman Clarke and Seaman Hayes, both badly. They were hit by rocks when the magazine went up.'

Atwell took up the tale, with a side glance to where the wounded were being swayed up to the deck.

'I had two men killed, sir–Robinson and Krauss. Some of their Militia got an old gun–a six pounder, sir–hidden in a lane an' fired it slap into my picket. Herbert lost his leg. But we burned everything there–boats, warehouses, everything.'

Atwell looked back again to Peabody, and his expression hardened.

'And I have two men under arrest, sir–those two.'

He pointed to a couple of helpless figures, one of them a marine, hanging in the slings before they reached the deck. Atwell swallowed for a moment; what he was about to say was going to put those two men in peril of their lives, and he went on with the grimmest formality.

'They are charged with looting and being drunk on duty, sir. They swilled neat rum from the casks we were setting on fire.'

The two accused men were dumped roughly on the deck, and Peabody looked down on them. The marine was conscious enough to wave his arms slowly across his face while gurgling some drunken nonsense; the seaman was as motionless and helpless as if he had been stunned with a club, and pale under the mahogany skin. He must have filled his stomach with neat rum at a single draft. Peabody knew that passionate yearning for liquor, that wild desire for oblivion.

'Put them in irons in the peak,' he said harshly. 'I'll deal with them to-morrow. Ask the surgeon to look after this man after he has attended to the wounded.'

He turned away; the setting sun was gleaming across the bay at Charlestown, but it could not penetrate the vast cloud of smoke which engulfed the town, where a million dollars' worth of property was burning.

10

A court-martial had not been possible. Not until her voyage was completed–not until the war should be over–could the *Delaware* hope to be in a place where it would be possible to assemble the imposing array of officers who could try such an offence. But three lieutenants were able to compose a Court of Inquiry who could listen to Lieutenant Atwell's evidence and make recommendations to the Captain. Seaman and marine had no defence to offer, and could only throw themselves on the Captain's mercy. They stood white-faced while they listened to Lieutenant Hubbard's formal report to the Captain, studying the lean features and hard eyes of the man who could send them to their deaths in the next five minutes. Punishment in this little speck of a ship, encompassed by enemies and friendless through the oceans of the world, could be terrible and must be swift. Death, or such less penalty—

It was torment for Peabody. Far within him the devil was tempting him. He had two drunkards in his power, and he could repay on their persons the misery he had endured from a drunken father, the agonising distress caused him by a drunken mother, the torture he himself had gone through in his battle with the enemy. Deep down inside him a little well of blood-thirsty lust brought up into his mind the prospect of repayment. He submerged the hideous temptation and turned an expressionless face to the two wretched men.

This was a happy ship which he commanded; there had been punishments when she was lying at Brooklyn, but not a single one since she had escaped to sea. He felt a dull resentment towards these two who had imperilled the frail structure of happiness. If he should pardon them, he would be running the risk of unsettling the crew; there were some members–he knew it so well!–who would resent the pardoning of a crime which they had been tempted to commit. Yet punishment would not reform drunkards, would not make better men of them. But they had disobeyed orders, that was their worst crime. On this desperate venture every man on board must be shown that disobedience was instantly visited with punishment, and for men steeped in the tradition of the sea there was only one form of punishment besides death. Peabody passed sentence with a face set like stone.

The marine was bovine, phlegmatic, and suffered his flogging in stolid silence, but the seaman screamed under the lash. It was a horrible sound, which rent the fair beauty of the multi-coloured morning.

Montserrat lay in the distance, its jagged peaks purple and green against the sky; from the Soufrière at its southern end a cloud of white steam merged with the clouds which hung over it. In the opposite direction the low sun had waked a rainbow from the rainstorm which had just driven by. Its brilliant arch dipped to the sea at either end, and above it the reverse rainbow was visible, not as brilliant, but still beautiful. The sea was of such a vivid blue that it was hard to think of it as a lively liquid; with that deep colour it was more logical to think of it as of a creamy consistency through which the *Delaware* was cutting her way, leaving behind her a white wake lovely on the blue. It was Peabody's plan to spread desolation and misery and lamentation throughout this peaceful scene, to burn and harry and destroy, to sweep through the Lesser Antilles like a hurricane of destruction from end to end.

Here lay Montserrat; beyond lay Guadeloupe, French again now, but worth investigation on the chance of finding British shipping; beyond that Dominica, and then, after the French Martinique, a whole series of British possession, St Vincent, Barbados, Grenada, Trinidad, Guiana, stretching nearly to the Line. There might be convoys with which he would be unable to interfere, ships of war from which he might have to run, but there would be plenty of weak points–joints in the British armour–at which he could thrust. The *Delaware* was capable of keeping the sea for three months more at least–much longer if he could find the opportunity to reprovision from his prizes–and during that time he would do damage costing a hundred, a thousand, times as much as the Federal Government had expended on the ship. He refused to let his mind dwell again on what might have been the result if only Mr Jefferson had decided to build a squadron of ships of the line. With his glass levelled at Montserrat he gave the orders which set the *Delaware* to work again on the task she had begun.

The days that followed were monotonous only in their sameness–ships destroyed and anchorages raided, West India planters ruined, and West Indian merchants bankrupted. The smoke of the fires which the *Delaware* lighted drifted over the blue sea and up the green hillsides, while Peabody could only guess at the terror and the uncertainty he was spreading, at the paralysing of commerce and at the shocked outcry in London. And through it all there was the constant dribble-dribble of casualties; two men killed by a round shot from the battery at Plymouth, three wounded by the single desperate broadside fired by the trading brig intercepted off Basse-Terre, one drowned when the *Delaware* was caught under full canvas by a sudden squall near the Saintes. It was not want of food and water which was likely to put a period to the *Delaware*'s career, not even shortage of powder and shot, but the loss of mortal men. Of every six men who had come aboard in the East River one man was now dead or useless. When the hands were at divisions, Peabody used to find himself looking along the lines of sunburned faces and wondering who would be the next to go. British ships of war could find recruits whenever they met a British merchant ship, but the *Delaware* was alone.

If was off Roseau that they saw the big schooner. Hubbard himself announced the sighting of her to Peabody.

'Right to windward, sir, but she's bearing down on us fast.'

So fast, indeed, that when Peabody came on deck she was already nearly hull-up. The enormous extent of her fore and aft sails, the pronounced rake of her masts, her beautifully cut square topsails, were obvious at a glance, and as she came nearer Peabody could see the sharp lines of her bows and the beauty of her hull. Peabody took the glass from his eye and looked at Hubbard.

'Baltimore privateer,' said Hubbard, and then, slowly: 'Well, I don't know.'

Peabody had the same doubts. At first glance those bows and that canvas seemed eloquent of Baltimore, and yet at second glance they seemed nothing of the kind. If ever a ship had a foreign appearance it was this one.

'What d'you make of her, Mr Murray?'

'Baltimore schooner, re-rigged in some foreign port, I reckon, sir.'

Murray's home was in Baltimore; his earliest recollection were of the white wings of the schooners on the Patapsco; his judgment ought to be correct if any was.

'Privateer dismasted in action and refitted at Port-au-Prince, most likely,' said Hubbard.

That was by far the most probable explanation.

'She's carrying heavy metal, sir,' commented Murray.

So much the better. Peabody had been hoping that chance would bring him in contact with a privateer; not only did he need news and information, but he wanted to concoct fresh plans of attack. There ought to be a convoy due soon from Port of Spain, and Peabody would be glad to deal with the escort if only there was a privateer at hand to snap up prizes.

'Hoist the colours, Mr Hubbard.'

'She's rounding-to,' exclaimed Murray.

Much more than that. She had spun round on her heel, hauled in her sheets, and was beating her way back to windward as hard as she could go.

'Thought we were a merchantman until she saw our teeth,' chuckled Murray. 'Now she's having the fright of her life. I guess she'll be glad to see the Stars and Stripes.'

If the sight of the American flag brought any comfort to the schooner, she showed no sign of it, for she went on clawing up to windward in a desperate hurry.

'Fire a gun to leeward,' said Peabody testily.

But the gun brought no reply from the schooner.

'Nobody'd think we're trying to make the damned fools' fortune for 'em,' grumbled Hubbard, watching her go.

'Stand by to go about,' snapped Peabody. 'We'll look into this.'

The *Delaware* went on the other tack, and, hauled as close as she would lie, started in pursuit. The schooner was right to windward, two gun shots away, and heading for the open Atlantic with Dominica on her larboard beam. Far away to starboard the stark bald peak of Mont Pele showed above the horizon.

'Queer,' said Hubbard.

The schooner was heading neither for the active assistance of the British Dominica, nor for the neutral protection of French Martinque.

'If she was British you'd expect her to run for Roseau,' said Murray.

'And if she were anything else she wouldn't run at all,' said Hubbard.

'Maybe she's a Yankee with a British licence,' suggested Murray sagely.

The same thought had already passed through Peabody's mind. The New England merchants had not taken very seriously this war which Mr Madison had decided upon, and they had certainly resented the loss of their profitable trade with Britain. Massachusetts had come within an ace of declaring herself neutral, and a good many Yankee ships had continued in British service, supplying the British forces, under licence issued by British admirals. If this schooner were one of those, Peabody had every intention of making her a prize of war, and the schooner probably knew it.

Peabody looked up aloft. Every stitch that the *Delaware* could carry was set, and every sail was drawing its best. He looked through his telescope at the schooner.

'She's fore-reaching on us, damn her,' said Hubbard.

'I guess she's weathering on us, too,' supplemented Murray.

The schooner was going through the water a trifle faster than the *Delaware*; she was lying a trifle–half a point, perhaps–nearer the wind; and, as Murray had suggested, she probably was not sagging off bodily to leeward quite as much as the *Delaware*, although Heaven knew that the *Delaware* on a bowline was better than most.

'Call all hands,' said Peabody. 'Put the watch below in the weather shrouds. And I'll have the watch on deck carry the shot up to windward. Keep her up, quartermaster!'

'Keep her up, sir!'

Two hundred men in the weather shrouds, thicker than apples in a tree, meant over ten tons of human ballast, and the mere area of their bodies, exposed to the wind on the weather side, was a help to the *Delaware* in keeping closer to the wind. The rapid transference of shot from the garlands and lockers on the leeside to the weather side helped to stiffen her as well. The weather braces were hauled in taut, and every sail was as flat as a board and drawing to the utmost; the cast log gave them nearly eight knots.

'Eight knots!' said Murray surprised.

'She's still fore-reaching on us, all the same,' said Hubbard bitterly.

'Get those men out of the foremost shrouds,' said Peabody. 'Bring 'em aft. Run out the larboard side guns, and then bring the watch on deck aft as well.'

Running out the guns on the weather side would stiffen her enormously. Bringing the men aft would set her a little by the stern, and Peabody, his mind conjuring up diagrams of the *Delaware*'s underwater form, thought it just possible that she might give a few more yards of speed in that case–possible, but not probable. The guns rumbled out; the foremast men came running aft and scrambled up the mizzen rigging, packing themselves in among the men already there. The watch on deck came and clustered aft in an eager crowd, herded by the sharp orders of the petty officers.

'Heave the log again!' said Peabody to O'Brien.

O'Brien performed the duty with the utmost care. The seaman with him forced the peg into the log-ship and stood holding the reel of line above his head. O'Brien made a level base on the slide of the after carronade for the sand-glass. He did not intend to trust to the transmission of orders; he took the log himself and cast it, and as the fluttering marker of bunting passed his left hand, with his right he neatly inverted the glass. The spool rattled as the line ran out, so that the sailors' uplifted hands shook as if with the wind. O'Brien kept his eye on the glass during the twenty-eight seconds it took the sand to run out, and as the last grain fell he nipped the line.

'How much?' said Peabody.

'Seven, sir, an' a half. Nearer eight than seven, sir.'

No better than before, then, and perhaps a little worse; the wind had kept steady during those twenty-eight seconds. The tension on the seaman's hands ended as the peg was jerked out, and the log towed unresistingly. He began to reel the line.

'She's still fore-reaching on us, sir,' said Murray gently.

Even a glance showed that; the distance between the schooner and the *Delaware* had grown perceptibly.

'We'll keep after her, though,' said Peabody. 'She may carry something away.'

That was always the last hope, pursuing or pursued, that the other ship would damage herself in some fashion. It was not a very dignified thing to hope for, and in this case the hope was to bear no fruit. The strange schooner steadily increased her distance. By noon she was hull down before the first dog watch was called; Peabody gave the order to wear ship, and laid a course for St Lucia.

'But all the same, I'd like to know who the devil she is,' said Hubbard with a jerk of his head back to the vanishing topsails of the schooner.

For Peabody it was sufficient to be aware that there was a fast schooner in the vicinity which was not anxious for inspection; after that there was no use in regretting the hours wasted in pursuit of her. The next job to be done was to continue to exploit the surprise of the *Delaware*'s arrival among the Lesser Antilles, to continue to burn and destroy, even though his heart sickened of the wasteful business. Even though the towering peaks of Martinique looked down upon his exploits, so that Anne on some country picnic may have seen the sails of the *Delaware* as she passed her career of destruction. Peabody looked over at the mountains of Martinique; he was not proud at the thought that Anne might be watching him carefully striking down those powerless to strike back at him. And Martinique was now at peace; in that island the open wounds of war were beginning now to close. As a sensible man, Peabody was fully aware of the blessings of peace; the task which lay to his hand made him more aware still. They were very mixed feelings with which he looked over at Martinique.

II

During the hot night Peabody awoke to a knocking on his cabin door; and he had called 'Come in' before he was fully conscious. He sat up in his cot as someone came stumbling into the stuffy darkness. It was Midshipman Kidd, and he had hardly entered before Washington appeared with a candle lantern, his shirt outside his trousers, but ready for duty. Peabody suspected him of sleeping on the locker of the main cabin.

'Mr Atwell sent me, sir,' said Kidd. 'There's a strange sail to leeward he'd be glad to have you see, sir.'

'I'll come,' said Peabody, and swung his legs off his cot. In that instant of time Washington had snatched up his trousers and was crouching for Peabody to put his legs in them–Washington was always alert for opportunities to perform the most menial duties. He continued on his knees while Peabody buttoned his flaps, holding the shoes ready for his master's feet.

On deck the brilliant tropic moon illuminated everything, showing up the familiar shipboard objects in a strange new light, and illuminating a broad path all the way down to the western horizon. It was down this path that Atwell pointed, after lifting his hat to his captain.

'There she is, sir,' he said.

Certainly there was something there, an outline brighter than the sky behind it, darker than the sea below it. Peabody's eyes accustomed themselves to the light, and he could see more clearly. There were the upper sails of a ship, from the royals down the mainyard, reaching with the wind abeam on the opposite course to the *Delaware*'s. Peabody looked again, struck by the memory of something hauntingly familiar about the ship. He took the proffered night-glass and focused on the vessel, took the glass from his eye again, having once more convinced himself that at night his eyes saw no better with artificial assistance, and looked again with narrowed eyes. The distance between those fore- and maintopmasts, and the odd proportion between them, meant something to him, without his figuring it out, as he might remember an acquaintance's face without thinking whether one eye was bigger than the other or the nose a little out of the straight.

'I know her,' he said decisively.

'I thought you would, sir,' said Atwell.

'She's the *Racer*,' said Peabody. 'The corvette we dismantled in the Wind'ard Passage.'

'Yes, sir,' said Atwell.

'Turn up the hands, Mr Atwell. I want the ship cleared for action without noise.'

'Aye aye, sir.'

'No lights are to be shown without my orders.'

'No, sir.'

'Put up the helm and go down to her.'

'Aye aye, sir.'

On that still night, with a favouring wind and over such a kindly medium as water, the sound of the drums calling the men to quarters might easily reach acute ears on board the corvette, and there was always the possibility of surprise–faint, but in war no possible chance must ever be neglected. In all the bustle of clearing for action Peabody stood looking over the dark sea at the *Racer*. As the *Delaware* wore he watched closely. For several minutes she showed no sign of having seen her, and then suddenly her masts blended into one. She had turned tail, and Peabody nodded to himself as he did at the solution of a mathematical problem. It would have been suspicious if she had not acted in that way–he could not imagine a King's ship not sighting an enemy at that distance, not recognising her at once.

His mind attacked the problem of explaining the *Racer*'s presence here in the eastern Caribbean after he had last seen her six hundred miles away. It was necessary to be wary, to consider every step, in these conditions when any step might lead to destruction.

Murray was at his elbow, seeking his attention.

'Shall I load with round shot or dismantling, sir?'

'Canister in the carronades. Round shot in the long guns,' said Peabody, 'if you please, Mr Murray.'

Each of the eighteen carronades which the *Delaware* carried fired a thirty-two-pound missile, and a thirty-two-pound round of canister contained five hundred musket bullets. He would close with the *Racer*, sweep her deck with canister, and board her in the smoke. That would be the cheapest way of overpowering her, he decided and would give her least chance of disabling the *Delaware*; not that such a lightly armed ship had much chance of permanently disabling the *Delaware*, and slight damage aloft would be unimportant in the present situation, where, unlike during the attack on the convoy, seconds would not be vital.

The chances were that her presence in these waters was a mere matter of routine–Peabody knew how easy it was to suspect an enemy of some deep design when all he was doing was merely something for his own comfort. There had been a notable instance just before the attack on Tripoli. But on the other hand, he must be cautious. He must not run the *Delaware* into a trap. He had spent nearly every waking moment since he left New York on the watch for traps, and his alertness had not diminished with time.

'Deck there!' came the cry from the masthead. 'Please, sir, there's another sail to leeward!'

Atwell caught a nod from Peabody, and rushed aloft with his night glass.

'Yes, sir,' he hailed. 'I can see his royals sure enough, sir.'

'What is she?'

'Can't tell you yet, sir. But the chase seems to be making for her, sir.'

If the *Racer* was employed in guarding some small convoy, the last thing she would do would be to draw pursuit towards the ships she was escorting. It was unlikely that the new sail was a merchantman, then, unless she were a chance comer.

'I can see her better now, sir,' came Atwell's voice. 'She's ship rigged, and heading close hauled to cross our course. And–and–she's a British ship of war, sir.'

'Mr Hubbard! Put her on the starboard tack, if you please.'

The barest hint that there were British reinforcements awaiting the *Racer* over the horizon was enough to make Peabody alter his course. This might be the trap he had expected; certainly he was not going to plunge blindly into unknown dangers during the hours of darkness. By laying the *Delaware* on the starboard tack he was keeping well to windward of the enemy, so that when daylight should clear the situation he would be in a position to be able to offer or refuse battle at his own choice. As Hubbard roared 'Belay!' to the hands at the braces, Atwell appeared on the quarterdeck.

'I'm not sure about that second ship, sir,' he said, 'but–but she might be *Calypso*, sir.'

A ship whose masts and sails had been so thoroughly torn to pieces as had the *Calypso*'s, might well not be recognisable the next time she was seen. New masts and sails would disguise her as much as beard would disguise a man.

'It seems likely to me,' said Peabody steadily. 'Perhaps the brig's over there, too.'

'I don't think she was in sight, sir. Shall I go aloft again and see?'

'If you please, Mr Atwell. Mr Hubbard! The watch below can sleep at the guns.'

If there were to be a battle to-morrow, Peabody had no intention of fighting it with a crew weary after a sleepless night. He would need all his strength if he were to fight the *Calypso* and the *Racer* together; in fact he knew already that he would only engage if he could make, or if chance presented him with, a favourable opportunity. And after their experience in the Windward Passage he could be sure that these two ships would do their best to offer him no opportunity; he could be surer of it with them than with any other two ships out of the whole British Navy.

Meanwhile, he must consider his own position. On this tack he would weather Martinique not long after dawn to-morrow; if he were to fight the British it would be somewhere between Martinique and Dominica. If he did not, then the Atlantic would be open to him. If he wanted to escape he could do so; the *Delaware* could work to windward, out to sea, far faster than the British could–she would have as much advantage over them as that mysterious schooner had displayed over the *Delaware* herself. He could run the British ships out of sight, and free himself for his next move. Having drawn them to this end of the West Indian chain, logically his best course of action would be to run down to leeward, take the Mona Passage, say, and make a fresh drive at the Jamaica trade, unless he crossed the Atlantic–as he had considered doing once already–and tried to make havoc in the Channel. As long as the British were reduced merely to parrying his thrusts he was doing his duty. Two years of anxiety in America had already taught Peabody the disadvantages of the defensive.

'If you please, sir,' hailed Atwell. 'The brig's in sight. Right ahead, sir, and on the same tack as us.'

'Thank you, Mr Atwell.'

That was decisive, then. He would not fight if he could avoid it, or unless the British acted far more foolishly than he hoped for. Out of three ships, in a close fight, one would be able to cross his bows or his stern and rake him while he was engaged with one of the others. Even the little *Bulldog* in such a position would do the *Delaware* enormous damage. He could not fight three ships at once. The *Calypso* and the *Racer* were well out of range to leeward, silently, paralleling his course; he thought for a moment of bearing down to interpose between them and the *Bulldog*, and put the thought aside–the interposition would not save his having to fight all three simultaneously. He decided to maintain this course; the British ships on the larboard bow could come no closer to him and by his superior speed he would gradually head-reach on them, and possibly he might overtake the *Bulldog* and force a fight on better terms than might be the case. He would chase her until dawn and reach his own decision then.

Peacefully through the night the four ships held their steady course; on board the *Delaware* there was only the low music of the rigging and the creaking of the woodwork as seas came rolling up to her weather bow. The watch on deck talked only in whispers, while the watch below snatched an uneasy sleep on the hard planking between the guns. Peabody stood tireless by the rail, listening to the whisper of the seas going by, watching the faint shadows of the British ships to leeward, and the dim outline of the mountains of Martinique on the horizon to windward.

At eight bells the relieved watch quietly took their turn to try to sleep; there was no bustle and small excitement. This crew was a seasoned one; there were men on board who had fought, sixteen years ago, all through the night under Nelson at the Nile, and others who remembered the long chill night watch waiting to attack at Copenhagen. There were a couple of Dutchmen who had watched the British line come bearing down on them at Camperdown, and even if those men who had fought under other flags in fleet actions were only few, the majority had fought pirates off Penang, or had stood to their guns against privateers on the African coast. Heterogeneous the crew may have been once, but their recent career of success had given them a common enthusiasm, and they were bound together by a common chain of discipline, whose master link was the silent figure who stood with his hand on the quarterdeck rail.

To the eastward the sky grew pink. All of a sudden the mountains of Martinique changed from vague shadowy slopes to sharp hard outlines which might have been cut from black paper and laid against the brightness. Round the sides of the outline the light came seeping like flood water round an obstruction. To the westward the sky was still dark, the British ships were still vague, and then suddenly the light reached up into the sky above them and revealed them, all sail set, in line ahead, *Calypso* leading, *Racer* astern, the *Bulldog* four miles ahead and to windward of them.

As the seconds went by, the mountains of Martinique took on a new solidity. The bald crown of Mont Pele caught the sunlight and reflected it, while the hues of the sunrise faded, pink and lavender and green sinking into the blue. Still the sun was behind the mountains, which cast their long black shadow far out to sea, until with a kind of wink the edge of the yellow sun looked over the saddle between the mountains to the north and those to the south, and instantly it was full day. The mountain-sides were green now, and broad on the starboard beam opened the bay of Fort de France, with the steep pyramid of the Diamond Rock on the starboard quarter. Behind it, through Peabody's glass, showed the coloured sails of the fishing boats making for the town with their night's catch, and, beyond the white roofs and walls of Fort de France itself. The dwellers in the town would have a fine view of the battle, if one were to be fought soon. Perhaps the Marquis and his womenfolk were already being roused with the news that a battle was possible.

Peabody swung his glass back to the British squadron. They were holding their course steadily; during the night the *Delaware* had fore-reached upon them only a trifle, although she had perceptibly cut down upon the *Bulldog*. He had only to give the word for the wheel to be put to starboard and in twenty minutes he would be upon them, amid the roar of the guns and the clatter of battle. The temptation was grave, like that of a bottle two-thirds full. There was an analogy between the two prospects, too. In either case there would be an hour's mad satisfaction, and then, at the end, oblivion. Peabody knew the full force of that temptation, but he put it aside. He must play the game out to the bitter end, preserve the *Delaware* so that she could continue her career of destruction.

Beyond Mont Pele lay Cape St Martin; he could weather it easily on his present course, and, once through the straits, he could go about and vanish into the Atlantic distance. Shaking off pursuit, he would be free once more. Port of Spain or Port Royal or Bantry Bay; the British would not know where to seek him until he should announce his presence by further sinkings and burnings.

The shadow of the mizzen shrouds moved a little across his face, and in a vertical sense, too, not in the circular way which was the continual result of the pitch and roll of the ship. Her course was altering a little; if that were due to the quartermaster's negligence the shadow would move back in the next second, but it did not. In that one second Peabody's subconscious mind, trained in twenty years at sea, had made the whole deduction. His glance swept the pennant at the masthead, the spread of the maintopsail, the man at the wheel. The helmsman had not been negligent; the wind had backed northerly a trifle, and he had had to change course a trifle to keep the ship on the wind. Hubbard was already beside the wheel, along with Poynter, the acting master.

A faint uncertainty came into Peabody's mind, and he could see from

Hubbard's attitude as he talked with Poynter that his first lieutenant felt the same. With the rising of the sun it was not unnatural that the wind should grow fluky. Another puff breathed on his cheek and the *Delaware*'s bow came farther round still as the helmsman yielded to it. On this course it was by no means a certainty that the *Delaware* would be able to weather Cape St Martin, and with every point the wind veered by that much was he deprived of the advantage of the weather gauge. Until now the British ships had been powerless to get within range of him without his co-operation, and he could choose his own moment for battle. Now the freakishness of the West Indian wind was depriving him of the advantages which his forethought had won for him.

It was a random puff of wind which had been responsible for the *Constellation*'s overtaking the *Insurgente* when he was a lieutenant under Truxtun. Thirty years ago at the Battle of the Saintes a flaw in the wind had been responsible for the breaking of the French line and for Rodney's victory–which, if it had happened six years earlier, might well have postponed indefinitely the independence of the United States. Tremendous events sometimes resulted from the unpredictable vagaries of the wind. At this very moment the fate of the *Delaware*, his own life, depended on them. But as the vagaries were unpredictable, as they were dictated by a quite inscrutable Providence, there was no reason to allow them to anger him; it would be childish as well as irreverent to break into recriminations over them, the way Hubbard over there was doing. Hubbard was looking at the trend of the land, and then out to sea at the British squadron, and up at the pennant which told the direction of the wind, and the long black curses were pouring from his lips. Hubbard found it hard to bear the tension when it was obvious that if the wind veered another single point the *Delaware*'s escape round Cape St Martin would be impossible.

'Mr Hubbard! Hoist the colours, if you please.'

Peabody still stood by the rail, his lean face and his hard eyes expressionless as he awaited his fate, and within them he was just as unmoved, thanks to his self-mastery.

The British ships had hauled to the wind as it veered, keeping parallel with the *Delaware*'s course. Across four miles of blue water the *Calypso* and the *Racer* maintained their rigid line ahead, all sail set and drawing; as the Stars and Stripes went up to the *Delaware*'s peak the White Ensign rose to theirs, fluttering jauntily, and at that very moment Peabody felt the shadows move across his face again. The wind had veered one more point–two more points.

Now the *Delaware*'s bow was pointed straight for the foot of Mont Pele. The *Calypso* and the *Racer* must be exultant to see her cut off from the open sea. There were signal flags going up to the *Calypso*'s weather yardarm, and the *Bulldog* was answering them. Next moment she hove in stays and went about. On the opposite tack she was heading just for the spot where the *Delaware* would have to change her course is she were not to go aground–just for the spot where the *Calypso* and *Racer* would intercept her so that all the four ships would come together at once. Peabody studied the blank sky, the expressionless sea. He was trying to guess what the unpredictable wind would do next. If it were to back, he still would have a chance to reach the open sea, and to pound the *Bulldog* into the bargain while the other ships looked on helplessly. The wind was as likely to back as it was to veer; more likely, perhaps, as it had veered so far. Peabody held his course and issued no orders. He caught his fingers in the act of nervously drumming on the rail before him, and he peremptorily stilled them.

Five minutes went by. Ten minutes went by, and at the end of ten minutes the wind had veered half a point more. Peabody broke into action again. He made his body stand stiff and immovable, and he kept his voice at a conversational pitch, not for the sake of the example it gave, but because these servants of his mind must act without weakness.

'Mr Hubbard! Tack, if you please.'

Even a losing battle must be fought out to the end; if Providence had declared against him he must fight Providence to the last, for that was the only way to earn the approval of Providence. By tacking he would delay the encounter with the British squadron and have a chance of fighting at a better advantage than if he fought at present. Something might always happen. Providence might relent, the British might blunder, the wind might change or might drop altogether. Tacking would prolong the chase and give Providence a chance. The canvas slatted and the blocks rattled as the *Delaware* came up into the wind, and stilled again as she caught the wind on the other side. Now her bow was pointed straight towards the Bay of Fort de France with its rocky islets and its white cubes of houses; that was the corner into which he was being driven.

The *Calypso* had tacked the moment the *Delaware* did, and the *Racer* tacked in succession behind her, neatly backing her topsails for a second to maintain her interval–the British could handle ships, without a doubt. Astern came the *Bulldog*, revelling in the safety which the veering of the wind had given her. It was she who was to windward now, who held the weather gauge, who could select her moment for battle. Peabody could not turn and tack up to her without having the other ships upon him before he reached her. In the Windward Passage he had had all the advantages, the advantage of the weather gauge, the advantage of surprise, the advantage of the fact that the British ships were separated to guard a convoy, the advantage that the power of his ship was unknown–all of these advantages which he had won by his own foresight, but which had given him the opportunity to defeat his enemies in detail.

In the present encounter the wind had been unkind, and the British had learned caution. They were keeping their squadrom massed while he was being driven upon a lee shore where he could not refuse battle to their united forces. But the game was not lost yet; he still had some miles of sea room in which to prolong the chase. Standing out towards the Diamond Rock ahead was a white sail. Peabody whipped his glass to his eye; it was neither a friend nor another enemy–it was the *Tigresse*. Coming to see the sport, he supposed, a little bitterly. It would be an unusual experience for the French in these war-torn islands to witness a battle which did not affect them. Well, he could imagine the way boats would have poured out through the Narrows filled with sightseers three years ago if the rumour had gone round New York of an approaching battle between English and French off Sandy Hook.

He could claim the protection of French neutrality if he wanted to–run for

Fort de France and shelter under the guns and laugh at the British. He was sure that the Marquis would do his best to protect him, because he remembered what the Marquis had said about maintaining strict neutrality. Since he had given the order to tack, the idea had come into his mind more than once, and he had put it on one side, guiltily. It was what he ought to do, logically. If it were best to keep the *Delaware* afloat and as a fighting unit, it would be better for her to be blockaded in Fort de France than sunk or captured. But he would not do it, not even though it were his duty. He would rather fight–or to word it better, he was set on fighting in preference to accepting French protection, and he felt guilty about it because he fancied that an honourable defeat was the wrong choice from the naval point of view. On this vital matter, for the first time for twenty years, he was going to allow his personal predilections to outweigh his sense of duty. He was tired of running away.

He looked over at Fort de France and at the approching *Tigresse*. Time was growing short, and if he were going to fight it would be best to do it now while there was still a little room to manoeuvre, although God knew that once he was locked in battle with three British ships there would be small opportunity for a manoeuvre.

'Mr Hubbard,' he said, and in his determination to allow himself no emotion, the New England drawl which his Navy service had done much to eradicate was more pronounced than ever. 'Clew up the topgallants and royals, and then heave to, if you please. We'll wait for them to come up.'

Hubbard's dark-complexioned face showed his sardonic smile as the meaning of the words penetrated his understanding; he turned and bawled his orders, and the hands came running to the braces. The *Delaware*'s way diminished as the yards came round, and she lay there in the blinding sunlight, submitting to the waves instead of riding purposefully over them. Peabody turned to watch the British ships swooping down on him, and as he did so he heard a sound on the deck behind him. Somebody was cheering, and the cheering spread, echoing from the maindeck under his feet, taken up by the fighting parties in the tops. The whole crew was cheering and leaping about at the prospect of instant battle, and Peabody smiled as he looked over his shoulder at them. They were a fine lot of men.

But this was no time for sentiment. Peabody turned back again to his duty of observing the approaching attack; when the time should come he must have the *Delaware* under way again, handy and under control for the fight. The *Calypso* and the *Racer* were already shortening sail for action, while the *Bulldog*, still under all canvas, was moving so as to take station astern of them. Their plan would be to try to engage the *Delaware* all on the same side; he must do his best to prevent it. He eyed the narrowing stretch of blue water across which his fate was approaching.

He was surprised by the sudden appearance of the *Tigresse* close under the *Delaware*'s stern–she came by under all sail, tearing through the water only at pistol-shot distance away; in fact what first distracted Peabody's attention to her was the sound of her bows cleaving the waves as she approached. Startled, he looked down at the smart little sloop. She was cleared for action, her guns' crews standing ready round the dozen pop-guns which stood on her deck, and aft there was a glittering party in blue and gold. Standing out among them was the Marquis, conspicuous with his blue ribbon over his shoulder and the orders hung on his coat. He held a speaking-trumpet in his hand, and as the *Tigresse* slid by he raised it to his lips.

'Stay where you are!' he shouted. 'I'll come back to you!'

That was damned insolence, if ever there was such. Peabody's mouth opened a trifle in his astonishment, and he stared after the impertinent little vessel as she sailed by, heading straight for the British squadron with the white flag with the golden lilies fluttering at her peak. Peabody watched her round-to to square in the *Calypso*'s path, and he saw the white puff of smoke as she fired a signal gun, and directly afterwards the *Calypso* had to throw her sails aback to avoid an actual collision. The British squadron bunched and lost its rigid line as the three vessels clustered together.

'What's on his mind, sir?' asked Hubbard, as much in the dark as Peabody.

'Square away, Mr Hubbard. We'll go down and see.'

Possibly this might be a chance of catching the British off their guard. If the *Tigresse* got hurt in the mêlée it would only be her own fault. But the yards had hardly been braced round before a smart little gig dropped from the *Tigresse*'s side and began to pull towards the *Delaware*, the white flag at her bows. Dupont was in the stern, standing up signalling with his hand for attention. Peabody looked over at the halted British squadron, at the *Tigresse* between him and them.

'Oh, back the mizzen tops'l again, Mr Hubbard,' he said. His exasperation showed itself in the omission of the formal 'if you please.'

They dropped a rope ladder for Captain Dupont–in a ship cleared for action there was no way of offering him a more dignified entrance–and the fat little man came strutting aft to where Peabody had come halfway to meet him. At six paces he took off his hat and bowed; Peabody merely uncovered. To make a leg and double himself in the middle did not seem to be a natural thing to do on the deck of his own ship.

'His Excellency sends you his compliments,' said Dupont.

'Yes?'

'And His Excellency would consider it a favour if Monsieur le Capitaine Peabody would be kind enough to visit him aboard the *Tigresse*.'

'Oh, he would?' said Peabody. There were all sorts of replies possible, every one crushing, every one well designed to convey to the Marquis exactly what Peabody thought of this gratuitous interference. Peabody was making his selection when Dupont neatly spiked his guns.

'The British Commodore is there already,' he said, pointing over the blue water. Alongside the *Tigresse* bobbed a smart red gig, the straw-hatted crew fending her off. The sight left Peabody wordless.

'It would give me great pleasure,' said Dupont, 'if M. le Capitaine would make use of my boat, which is ready.'

'I'll come,' said Peabody. It was a mad world, and something madder than usual may have happened.

He slid down into Dupont's gig and took his seat beside the French captain, and the swarthy French sailors bent to their oars. On board the *Tigresse* every preparation had been made for the reception of officers of high rank, and beside the guard of honour stood the Marquis, bareheaded.

'Good morning, Captain,' said the Marquis. 'I trust you are enjoying the best of health?'

What Peabody wanted to say was 'Damn my health,' but he forced himself to mutter some form of politeness.

'I must present you to my other guest,' said the Marquis. His handsome mouth wore a smile, his bearing was one of perfect deference, but somehow there was the hint of the mailed fist within the velvet glove. 'Captain Josiah Peabody, United States' Ship *Delaware*–Captain the Honourable Sir Hubert Davenant, His Britannic Majesty's Ship *Calypso*, Senior Officer of the British Squadron.'

Davenant was a man in his early fifties, grey-haired, with a hard straight mouth like Peabody's and plainly in a very bad temper indeed.

'Morning,' said Davenant. 'The Frogs want to stop us fighting.'

He talked English with the gobbled 'o's and the hot-potato accent which Peabody had last heard used by certain exquisites at Valetta.

'His Most Christian Majesty's Government,' said the Marquis, politely, 'is determined to maintain its neutrality.'

Peabody looked from one to the other, and the Marquis took up the tale. He pointed across the water to the Point des Negres on one side of the ship, and to Cape Solomon on the other.

'You are within French territorial waters,' he said. 'I can permit no fighting here between any belligerents whatever.'

'But damn it, sir—' said Davenant.

'I shall fire,' went on the Marquis 'into any ship disobeying my instructions while within my jurisdiction.'

Davenant snorted and Peabody grinned. There was not any particular menace about the *Tigresse*'s pop-guns, but the Marquis was quite unmoved and continued placidly.

'I left orders on shore,' he said 'that the guns of Fort Bourbon and those of Trois-Islets were to follow my example. There are twenty thirty-two pounders trained on us at the present moment, I have no doubt.'

That was a very different story indeed. No frigate in the world could stand being knocked about by thirty-two pounders. The chances were that every ship in the bay, British and American, would be dismasted in a few minutes' firing. The Marquis still smiled, his manner was perfectly polite, but the mailed fist was quite obvious. He had every intention in the world of carrying out his threat.

'God rot all Frenchmen!' said Davenant, petulantly. His gold epaulettes flashed in the sun as he swung back and forth looking at the batteries. Then he rounded on Peabody. 'You came in here because you knew this would happen, damn you!'

'I did not, damn *you*, sir!' snapped Peabody.

'Then come out of the bay and fight me, then.'

'I was going to say the same thing,' blazed Peabody, shaking with wrath. 'Come on!'

'Gentlemen!' said the Marquis. There was an edge to his voice.

'Mind your own business!' said Peabody.

'Gentlemen!' said the Marquis again. 'Don't forget the twenty-four-hour rule.'

That halted them in their stride. A vague recollection of his reading of the almost forgotten laws of neutrality came into Peabody's mind.

'When the ships of two belligerents enter a neutral harbour,' said the Marquis, 'an interval of twenty-four hours must elapse between their respective departures. I cannot stop you leaving, but I can, and I will, stop your leaving together. I have to consider His Most Christian Majesty's dignity.'

It was perfectly true. In a world which had known no neutrals whatever for years the rule had been forgotten, and furthermore during earlier years Britain's overpowering naval might and the desperate exigencies of her position had forced her officers to ignore neutral susceptibilities–as Peabody well remembered. But here was a neutral with both the will and the power to enforce her neutrality, with a couple of batteries armed with thirty-two pounders loaded and pointed and ready. He caught Davenant's eye, and the British captain was so obviously crest-fallen that he could not help smiling. And with his smile his hot-headed passion evaporated, and his native shrewdness returned along with his clear common sense.

'Please do not consider it presumption on my part, gentlemen,' went on the Marquis. 'I must apologise in advance for any appearance of trying to advise you. But may I remind you that I do not expect either of your Governments would be too pleased if any offence were offered to that of His Most Christian Majesty?'

'Damn His Most—' began Davenant, and then he bit the words off short. The ways of statesmen were strange and inscrutable. There was a peace congress being summoned at Vienna, and a lively incident between the British and the new French Government might perhaps wreck some of the politicians' dealings. And in that case God help the career of the officer responsible! Peabody could see the struggle in Davenant's face as he tried to control his peppery temper and be tactful. The Marquis ignored the unfinished sentence, as a gentleman should ignore all unfinished sentences, while Davenant began to reframe his plans in accordance with this totally new situation. An idea clearly struck him, and he turned to Peabody.

'You can't go out first,' he said. 'There's nothing you'd like better than a twenty-four-hour start.'

Peabody was in agreement. Two hours start would be enough, for that matter. Once the *Delaware* was over the horizon the business of catching her would be far more complicated for the British. To the American Government a frigate loose on the high seas was worth two–was worth two dozen–in harbour or with their whereabouts known. But he kept his face expressionless; he was not going to yield any points in this argument if he could help it.

'I'll have to go out first,' said Davenant, thoughtfully. 'I'll wait for you to-morrow.'

Peabody was quite taken aback by this calm assumption. He felt he had never heard anything quite so British before in his life.

'*You'll* go out first?' he said. 'Why shouldn't *I* go out first? I came in first.'

'That's nothing to do with it,' replied Davenant tartly.

'I'll make it have something to do with it,' said Peabody.

'You will, will you?'

Davenant braced himself stiffly, his chin protruding as he put his head back to meet the taller man's eyes.

'That's what I said,' answered Peabody.

Then at that moment the ludicrous nature of the argument and of their attitudes suddenly struck him. He was reminded of the preliminaries to his first fight at sea, when he and Grant–the Grant who subsequently was killed at Tripoli–were squaring up to each other at the age of twelve on the foredeck of the coastguard cutter, *Beagle*. Peabody laughed, uncontrollably, and Davenant began to dance with rage. Only for a second, for his own sense of humour came to the rescue of his dignity and he laughed as well. The first round closed with the two of them grinning at each other. Davenant was the first to regain his composure.

'Seriously, sir,' he said, 'I don't know what the Admiralty would say if they heard I let you out of here after chasing you in. I'd be court-martialled–I'd be broke–I'd be on the beach for the rest of my life if they didn't shoot me.'

'And what about me?' said Peabody, this presentation of the case revealing a new light to him. 'What would they say about me in Washington? What would the Navy Department say if I let you go out of here on better terms than you came in? We have court-martials in our service, too, sir.'

'Yes, I suppose you have,' said Davenant thoughtfully. 'Damn all admiralties.'

Peabody had the feeling that each of them was sparring for an opening in this second round, after the heated exchanges of the first.

'Gentlemen,' said the Marquis. 'May I make a suggestion?'

They both turned and looked at him, suddenly reminded of his presence after some minutes of oblivion.

'Yes, sir,' said Davenant. Peabody noticed the hauteur of his manner–the irritating manner of one who represented the most powerful navy in the world.

'Can a question of this importance be decided in five minutes' conversation?' asked the Marquis. 'I must confess that I myself can see no way out of this impasse at the moment. And I might remind you that our five valuable ships are all of them hove-to on a lee shore. Why not drop anchor in Fort de France for to-night at least? You gentlemen may not be specially busy, but as Governor of this island I have other things to do besides listening to your arguments, educational though they are.'

Davenant looked back at Peabody, and Peabody looked at Davenant.

'How's your water?' asked Davenant.

'I've enough,' said Peabody cautiously.

'So've I. But I'd like some fresh. And I could do with some fresh vegetables after chasing you round the islands for five weeks. Is there any sign of scurvy among your men?'

'They'd be all the better for a run ashore,' admitted Peabody.

'I don't let my men ashore in a neutral port,' said Davenant. 'At least, only the few I can trust not to desert.'

He checked himself on the tempting edge of the abyss of professional conversation.

'I'm delighted to see you in agreement, gentlemen,' said the Marquis.

At first that seemed to be taking a good deal for granted, but the more the two captains considered the statement, the truer it appeared to be. To each of them the moment appeared to offer a golden opportunity to give his men a rest while at the same time conferring no advantage on his opponent.

12

'A letter for you, sir,' said the midshipman on duty, after knocking at Peabody's cabin door.

The seal on the back was elaborate–a coat of arms of many quarterings. Peabody broke it with care, and unfolded the paper.

The Governor's House,
Port de France
May 30, 1814

His Excellency the Governor and the Countess d'Ernée request the pleasure of the company of Captain Josiah Peabody and of his Lieutenants tonight at the Governor's House at 8 p.m.
Dancing.

Peabody scratched his big nose as he read this invitation. Certainly his instructions from the Secretary of the Navy enjoined the strictest regard for the susceptibilities of neutrals.

'Shore boat's waiting for an answer, sir,' said the midshipman.

There was no reason in the world why he should not accept, and every reason why he should. Peabody sat down at his desk and painstakingly repointed his quill before writing.

U.S.S. *Delaware*
May 30, 1814

Captain Josiah Peabody, Lieutenants Hubbard, Murray, and Atwell, and Acting Lieutenant Howard, have much pleasure in accepting the kind invitation of His Excellency the Governor and the Countess d'Ernée.

'Washington! Bring me a candle.'

It would be far more convenient, and, in a wooden ship a good deal more safe, to use a wafer to seal the letter, but there was the dignity of the United States to consider. Peabody melted the wax and impressed the ship's seal upon it with the thoughtless dexterity of his long bony fingers, and yet with the utmost deliberation. He was slow in handing the thing to the midshipman, slow in dismissing him. It was only when the door had closed, when the fussy Washington had tidied the desk and gone out, that he reached the moment which he had deliberately postponed while waiting for it impatiently, and abandoned himself to his thoughts.

He knew who would be there, whom he would see, to whom he would undoubtedly talk. He knew now that she had not been out of his thoughts since he had seen her. He had struggled honestly against those thoughts. They not only might have interfered with his duty, but they were sinful–twenty years at sea had not eradicated from his mind the idea of sin implanted in him during twelve years of childhood in New England. And now it was no use struggling against them any longer. He gave way to them. He would see those black curls and those blue eyes. He would feel her palm against his–there was sinful pleasure in that thought. The cabin suddenly became too cramped for him, too stuffy, and he went out with long hurried strides, up to where everything was illuminated by the rosy sunset.

On deck he addressed his four lieutenants, gravely, and yet with the lopsided smile which he always employed; Peabody had never seen any particular advantage to be gained from impressing it upon his subordinates that his requests were orders to disobey which involved a maximum penalty of death. Gravely they listened to him, just as they had done when he had been giving orders for the raiding of Nevis.

'You will all, of course, wear full dress,' said Peabody, after telling them of the invitation he had accepted on their behalf. 'Epaulettes, silk stockings, swords. Have you a silk cravat, Mr Howard?'

Howard had been only a midshipman when the *Delaware* commissioned, and Peabody knew by experience that midshipmen often sailed with inadequate outfits.

'Well, sir—'

'I'll see that Mr Howard has everything, sir,' interposed Hubbard.

The dandy from Charleston might be expected to have at least two of everything, even though when the voyage started the odds had been ten to one that defeat and death lay at the end of it.

'Very well,' said Peabody. He was racking his brains to remember what Truxtun had said in similar circumstances, when he was a young lieutenant. Truxtun had taken his young officers ashore to receptions, too, had worked conscientiously to educate them in the niceties of a society of which perforce they saw little enough, and of the necessity for which Peabody was still only convinced against his will.

'You will dance with every lady who needs a partner,' he said. 'I don't have to remind you of that. And there'll be plenty of wine–you'll be careful how you drink.'

'Aye aye, sir.'

'And–oh, that'll do. Dismiss.'

There were bright lights over at the quay when Peabody took his place at the tiller of his gig that evening among his officers, and as the boat made its way over the quiet water the lights gradually resolved themselves into flaming torches held by coloured servants in blue and white livery. A footman stooped to help the officers from their boat, and they climbed out. The solid stone of the jetty felt strange under their feet, for it was eighteen weeks since they had last trodden earth; they all stamped a little curiously as if to reassure themselves. The coloured footman welcomed them with a few words which none of them understood, and under the guidance of two torch-bearers they began their walk up into the town. On the far side of the jetty there were other torch-bearers, another boat coming in, and Peabody, glancing across, saw the red light of the torches reflected from gold epaulettes and buttons. Apparently the British officers were also attending the Marquis's reception; the Americans passed within a couple of yards of the waiting group, and on both sides a sudden silence fell over everyone, conversation dying away guiltily. No one knew whether or not to say 'good evening' to his enemies, and the situation was complicated by the fact that only Peabody and Davenant had been presented to each other. In the end the British officers looked out across the dark harbour while the Americans hurried by awkwardly.

There were lights at every window of the Governor's house, and long before they reached it they could hear music; at the open door stood a dozen coloured footmen, appearing strange to Peabody's eyes in their kneebreeches, their smart livery, and their white hair-powder. The Americans handed over their boat-cloaks and stood eyeing each other in the dazzling light as they adjusted cravats and ruffles; Peabody was conscious of a dryness of the throat and a queer feeling, comparable a little with hunger, in the pit of his stomach. Howard was as nervous as he was, he was glad to note–the boy's hands were not quite steady as he tried to shoot his cuffs. The calmest one among them was Atwell, who looked about him quite unabashed.

'I've a wife in New London,' said Atwell, with a grin on his homely face, 'who'll never forgive me if I can't tell her all about this evening. Please God I can remember what the women are wearing.'

At the head of the stairs stood three figures, the Marquis with a torrent of lace running from his chin to his waist, his blue ribbon crossing his breast, an order dangling from his neck and a star over his heart, as handsome a picture as one could see anywhere. Lace and ribbons and stars; Peabody thought of them all with instinctive suspicion, but when the Marquis wore them they had not that meretricious appearance which he expected. On the Marquis's right was the Countess d'Ernée in her black, her white shoulders a little solid, the smile with which she greeted the guests a little forced–so Peabody thought. And on the Marquis's left was Anne.

When Peabody looked at her all the rest of the glittering scene faded out; it was as if her face alone was standing out against a grey and misty background, like some miniature portrait. All Peabody's vagueness as to her appearance vanished with startling abruptness. Of course, he knew, he had always known, exactly what she looked like. He had been so sure of it that the minutest change would have been instantly apparent to him. He found himself smiling as their eyes met, the whole of his body singing with happiness, which, he told himself, was due to the extraordinary identity between her present appearance and what he remembered of her. There was something hugely satisfactory about that, like the solution of some involved mathematical problem, or like picking up moorings in a crowded harbour with a gale blowing.

Something that Atwell had said echoed in his mind, and he tried to force himself to take note of what she was wearing. But it was difficult; it was hard to focus his gaze upon her, just as it had been hard in the old days to focus upon the candle-flames of the mess table when he had been drinking. There was a white throat and white shoulders; Peabody's head swam as his gaze went lower down and he saw that Anne's gown did not begin until there was more than a hint of her bosom revealed. He expected a sudden consciousness of sin at the revelation and was a little taken aback when it did not come, as when an aching tooth suddenly ceases to hurt. There was something black and something red about her gown; he was sure of that. And there were pearls in the picture, too, which were just as mathematically satisfactory, but whether because of the pink-and-white skin or because of the contrast with the black curls, he could not decide.

He came to himself with the realisation that there were other guests on the stairway and he must lead his party to the ball-room; Captain Dupont was there to do the honours. Presumably it was his meeting with Anne which had made him hypersensitive, but Peabody felt himself suddenly in sympathy with the people in the room, telepathically aware of the sensation their entrance caused. The five officers, with their rolling gaits and their mahogany complexions, close-cropped hair and plain dress–despite their epaulettes and gold–were like a breath of sea air entering a hot-house. Round the room were many languid exquisites, many lovely and fragile women, and the men looked at the Americans with vague contempt, the women with awakening interest. Peabody was suddenly glad that his neckcloth was of plain pleatless silk, and that his sword-hilt was mere cut steel, unjewelled and ungilded.

At one end of the long room there were wide-open double doors through which could be seen a supper-room glittering with silver; at the other end was a low dais on which a negro orchestra was waiting. Captain Dupont had hardly begun to make presentations when the orchestra broke into a swinging, lively tune, and Peabody gaped a little as the dancers came on the floor. Each man took a woman in his arms, and each woman clasped her partner, perfectly shamelessly. The couples circled round the floor, each with a sort of wheel-like motion which reminded Peabody of the movement of the tiny water animalcules which he had observed as a boy in the stagnant water of summer pools; but it was not the motion which appeared so strange, as the cold-blooded way in which the embraces were publicly performed, the women looking up into the men's faces and talking as collectedly, as if they had no sense of shame whatever, regardless of clasped hands, of arms round waists, of hands on shoulders, of bosom against breast, or very nearly.

'That's the waltz,' said Hubbard between his teeth to Peabody. 'I heard it was all the rage in Europe.'

A languorous beauty in her late thirties to whom Peabody was being presented, overheard the remark.

'Indeed it is,' she said. 'All the world dances it. All the world has met together in Paris now, I hear. Excepting for us poor souls, doomed to an eternity of boredom on this little island. Tell me, Captain, do you intend to give your young officers a day ashore? It will be a pleasure to me to do what I can to make their visit enjoyable. I can send horses for them down to the port–my estate is St Barbara, six miles away from town.'

She flashed dark eyes from behind her fan at the circle of officers.

'That is extremely kind of you, ma'am,' said Peabody. 'Unfortunately I have no knowledge—'

There was so much bustle in the hall at this moment that he was compelled to break off his speech and look round. The English officers were entering the hall, Davenant in the lead, the naval officers in smart uniforms with the new white facings which Peabody had heard about and never seen before, the two marine officers in red coats and high polished boots.

'You mean,' said the languorous beauty, 'that you do not know when you are going to fight those gentlemen there. Well, it's in poor taste, now that the rest of the world is at peace. You should be ashamed to deprive us of the society of your charming Americans–it is years since we set eyes on one. We are accustomed to Englishmen, after the long English rule here. The sight of a red coat no longer rouses a thrill in our blasé hearts, Captain. But you Americans—'

'Yes, of course, ma'am,' said Peabody, as she obviously awaited some kind of answer, but there must have been a fount of hidden humour in the trite words, for the lady said 'La!' and flashed her fan again.

Peabody's eyes met Davenant's across the room. There was a moment's hesitation on the part of both parties of officers, and then they bowed to each other formally, the juniors copying the example of the seniors, and Peabody was glad to see that the gesture was performed just as badly by the English lieutenants as by his own, and that their gait was just as rolling and unfitted for a ball-room. Even Davenant, with his high fashionable neckcloth, and his red ribbon, and his star, was obviously someone straight off a quarterdeck.

Here came Dupont, very preoccupied.

'Captain Peabody, your commission as captain is a recent one, I fancy?'

'I have two years' seniority, sir.'

'Captain Davenant is the senior, then, his commission dating back eighteen years. Then he will dance the cotillion with Mme d'Ernée, and you, sir, will stand up with Mlle de Breuil.'

'Mamzelle d—?' asked Peabody, and was promptly annoyed with himself. Even if he could not pronounce Anne's name he ought to have recognised it instantly. To cover his confusion he fell back on formality. 'Of course I shall be delighted, sir.'

This was a serious moment. Not more than six times in his life had Peabody attended a ball, although in view of the occasional professional necessity of doing so, he had studied the conventions of dancing seriously enough, resolutely putting aside the nagging of his conscience on the matter. But this was something he had to go through, something unavoidable and inevitable; it was, therefore, no moment for doubt. The Marquis and Anne and the Countess were already entering the room, and Peabody braced himself, made a final adjustment of his cuffs, and strode over. He managed his bow, but try as he would, to his great surprise the formal request for the pleasure of the cotillion was a mere mumbled jumble of words. Anne smiled and curtseyed.

'I shall be delighted, Captain Peabody.'

In something like a dream he offered his arm, and she rested her hand on it. Walking in that fashion was a new experience. There was no sensation of weight; in fact it was quite the reverse. His arm felt all the lighter for the touch, as though a Montgolfier balloon were tied to it. She glided along beside him as weightless as a feather. Peabody had a feeling which reminded him of those few occasions when drink had exhilarated him without stupefying. In front of him Davenant was speaking to the Countess.

'I fear I don't know the drill, ma'am,' he was saying. 'As a matter of fact I'm damned awkward in a ball-room.'

'Never mind about that,' said the Countess. 'Charles will lead. All we have to do is to follow.'

That was doubly comforting, both to know that Davenant was nervous and that the Marquis would carry the responsibility; the Marquis was already leading out the languorous beauty of St Barbara, and the lines were falling in behind them. Peabody had recovered sufficiently to dart a quick glance round and to see that each of his officers was leading a lady into the dance. The band played a warning chord, and he turned to his partner and took her hand in his.

For Peabody that was his last clear recollection. The rest of the dance was just a divine madness. He was drunk with music and with the proximity of Anne. Awkwardness and the restraints of conscience vanished simultaneously. He bowed and scraped, he capered when the necessity arose, he strode with dignity, while sheer instinct–it could have been nothing else–saved him from allowing his sword to trip his partner or himself. The Marquis and his lady certainly knew how to lead a cotillion, and the orchestra did its part to perfection. A perfect wave of light-heartedness flooded the ball-room, everyone presumably infected by the gaiety of the Marquis. Everyone was smiling and laughing, even the elderly chaperones against the wall.

Peabody's mind was a whirl of tumultuous impressions, of pearls, and black curls, of white teeth between red lips when Anne smiled, of blue eyes and black lashes. When the dance ended he had an impression of awakening from some innocent and delightful dream, dreamed in a feather bed of unbelievable comfort. Yet his head was singularly clear.

'May I offer you some refreshment, ma'am?' he said, remembering his manners.

'The most grateful refreshment would be fresh air, don't you think, Captain?' said Anne.

She turned toward that side of the room which had no wall, opening on to a side porch, where the last breaths of the sea breeze were entering; her hand was on his arm again, and she glided along beside him across the ball-room. Out on the porch, with the light streaming behind her, she rested her hands on the rail and looked out across the town to the sea. The moon illuminated the bay, and the ships riding there at anchor, while from the garden before them arose a dozen strains of music–an orchestra which rivalled that of the ball-room–as frogs and crickets and a drowsy bird or two all chirped and croaked in unison.

'You dance very well indeed, Captain,' said Anne.

That singular clearness of head which had come over him saved him from imperilling the good impression with a mock modest reply.

'No one could dance otherwise with you, ma'am,' he said.

'And you pay a pretty compliment, too,' said Anne; there was more music in her chuckle, and Peabody was drunk with music.

'I speak the truth,' said Peabody, with a sincerity which was a greater compliment still.

'You must save those pretty speeches for Madame Clair,' said Anne.

'And who is she?'

'How hurt she would be to hear that, after ogling you from behind her fan for five minutes! She is the lady who danced with my father.'

'I remember her now.'

'She is looking for her fourth husband.'

'Where is he?'

'On earth somewhere, I have no doubt. But I do not know who he is, nor does Mme Clair, yet. Nevertheless, she will meet him soon enough. Perhaps she met him this evening.'

'God forbid!' said Peabody, fervently at the prospect of becoming Mme Clair's fourth husband.

'She waltzes beautifully. You should ask her for the pleasure of a dance.'

'I can't waltz.'

'Now that is serious, Captain Peabody. Naval officers should never visit neutral harbours without knowing the waltz. As ambassadors of good will–as diplomats on occasion–the knowledge would be of the highest advantage.'

Mlle de Breuil's expression was demure, but somewhere there was a hint of a twinkle, and Peabody could not tell whether he was being teased or not.

'I shall take lessons at once,' said Peabody.

As he spoke, there came low music from the violins in the ball-room.

'At once?' asked Anne.

It was a waltz which the violins were playing; Anne cast a hesitant glance behind her, for etiquette demanded that she should return to the ball-room the moment the next dance following the cotillion began. And yet–and yet—

'I am ready to learn,' said Peabody.

This extraordinary clarity of mind was quite amazing; it was intoxicating enough almost to defeat its own purpose.

'*One* two three *four* five six,' said Anne. She held up her arms as if she were in a partner's hold and danced by herself to the music. 'You slide the feet. You make the turn smooth as you can.'

She stopped, facing him, her hands still raised, and Peabody automatically held her.

'*One* two three *four* five six,' said Anne. 'Turn smoothly. Oh, that's better.'

If walking with Anne on his arm had been an amazing sensation, dancing with her in his arms was more amazing still. Peabody had not only been honest, he had been right when he said no one could help dancing well with Anne. She was like an armful of thistledown. The mere touch of her took off the weight from one's feet in a mysterious way; perhaps she was subtly guiding him so that he did not bump into the furniture on the porch, but if so she did it without his knowing, perhaps without her knowing. They slid smoothly over the mahogany floor, the violins inside wailing their hearts out under the bows of the negro musicians. Anne ceased to count aloud; her expression as Peabody looked down at her was a trifle distracted, as if she were seeing visions. The sight of her face, the round, firm chin and the soft mouth, the strange inspired calm of her expression, gave new lightness to Peabody's feet. He was a man inspired.

The music came to a heart-broken end.

'Oh!' said Anne, standing still in his arms, looking up into his face.

Next moment Peabody kissed her, quited unaware, until lip met lip, that he was doing so. She kissed him in return, her hands on his shoulders; for

Peabody everything had the awesome clarity of a dream; the touch of her, the scent of her, had an excruciating pleasure for him such as he had never known or dreamed of before. He looked down at her bewildered; he had never thought of a love affair being as simple as this, as free from the implications of sin, as inevitable and as natural as this.

'Oh!' said Anne again, but this time there was no disappointment in the voice, only wonder.

'I–I kissed you,' said Peabody. He was surprised at himself for being able to use such a word to a woman; it was like those dreams where one found oneself naked and unashamed amid a crowd of people.

'Yes,' said Anne, 'and I kissed you.'

They were still in each other's arms, the one looking up, the other down; with her left hand still on his shoulder she began to rearrange his neckcloth with her right.

'Shall I tell you?' she went on, her eyes no longer looking into his, but instead intent on the neckcloth.

'Shall you tell me what?' asked Peabody.

'That other time when I saw you–on board the *Tigresse*–when you looked at me–I said to myself: "that is the man that I would like to kiss." And then I said to myself that I was foolish, because–I had kissed no one except my father, and how should I know? But you see, I did know.'

She looked up again at him, a little fearful as to the effect of this confession, and Peabody's senses deserted him. All that boasted clarity of mind, all that extreme consciousness, vanished utterly. It was like a wave closing over his head, as he kissed her again. He found himself trembling as the wave subsided; he was a little frightened as he suddenly realised, for the first time, the depths of passion that there were within him. With a hint of panic he released her, and stood staring at her in the faint light. He was so intent on his own problems that he paid no attention to the footsteps that he heard approaching, and that was as well, because it saved him from betraying himself with a guilty start when one of the new-comers began to speak.

'Anne!' said Mme d'Ernée; she began to speak in French, but corrected herself and went on in English. 'I did not know you were here. Mme Clair will look after you while I am not in the ball-room.'

Peabody blinked at her, recovering his wits. The Countess was not angry. It even seemed incomprehensibly as if she were a little embarrassed, and then Peabody saw clearly again and realised that she actually was. Standing behind her was Davenant, and Davenant was a little awkward and self-conscious, too. He twitched at his neckcloth and shot his cuffs. It certainly was not to look for Anne that the Countess and Davenant had come out on to the porch.

'Yes, Aunt,' said Anne, perfectly steadily, albeit a little subdued. 'Shall we go in again, Captain Peabody?'

She put her hand on his arm, and they began to walk back. Davenant made way for them with a bow not quite of the perfect polish he had usually displayed.

13

Captain Dupont was arranging the guests for what he announced as a 'contre-danse.'

'It's nothing more than a Virginia reel, sir,' said Hubbard, sidelong to his captain whom he found at his side; Hubbard's wary glances were darting up and down the line and observing everything, quick to make deductions. Hubbard had no intention whatever of being betrayed into any uncouthness or of displaying provincial ignorance.

Peabody really did not know how he had come to be in that file of dancers, nor how he had come to be opposite the pretty girl who was his partner. Anne was farther down the line with a glow on her cheeks and a sparkle in her eyes. Craning his neck, Peabody could see that she was opposite the red-coated British marine officer, and as to how that had come about he was just as ignorant. All about him there was a babble of chatter, French and English intermixed, and some of the English he heard was strange enough. Not only was there the London accent of the naval officers, but there was the West Indian accent of the residents which was far more difficult; and Peabody guessed that the Martinique French which was being spoken around him was just as marked a dialect as West Indian English. Captain Dupont was performing prodigies, calling the figures first in French and then in English.

Peabody recaptured all the light-heartedness of the earlier part of the evening as the dance progressed. He felt no twinge of jealousy when he saw Anne's hand in the marine's; everything was extraordinarily natural as well as being merry. Once or twice she caught his eye–she was smiling already, but that did not detract from the smile she had for him; and when in the chain her hand touched his he was conscious of a message whose good fellowship surprised him. He had always thought that a love affair would contain a certain bitterness, or a certain remorse, which was certainly not the case at present.

The dance ended, and Peabody found himself in the supper-room with his new partner. The latter fell upon the food provided with a healthy appetite–over and over again Peabody had to intercept one of the numerous footmen who were circulating through the crowd and relieve his tray of something which had caught his partner's eye. Peabody himself found the food not so interesting. There were only made dishes to be had, things so fluffed up and maltreated as to be unrecognisable. There were little pies whose crusts were so fragile as to be unsatisfactorily ephemeral, and which contained a couple of mouthfuls of some meat or other, as minced and muddled as to be completely distasteful. There were stews of one sort or another, and Peabody took one look at them and decided not to venture farther–just anything could be concealed in them, and Peabody would rather have tried a stew produced in a ship six months out, which at its worst could hold nothing more than the rats and cockroaches to which he was accustomed. There were piles of fruit; his partner, dismayed at his lack of appetite, tried to press some on him, and secured for him a dish of some dismal pulp extracted from something like a vast orange–a 'shaddock,' his partner called it, otherwise known as the 'grape fruit,' rather inconsequentially. She even went on to explain that learned men had come to the conclusion that this thing was the veritable forbidden fruit which Eve had given to Adam, and yet Peabody did not find it attractive. Despite the damp heat he was hungry, but there was nothing to take his fancy, no honest roasts or grills, not even a dish of beans.

Corks were popping incessantly, and the footmen bore trays loaded with wide glasses filled with a golden wine; the bottles were cooled by being wrapped in wet cloths and hung in the draught, so the girl explained, her eyes looking at him over the rim of her glass. There was something enchanting about that wine, as Peabody admitted on tasting it. It was bubbling merrily as he drank, just like the sparkling water which Dr Townsend Speakman had for sale in Chestnut Street, Philadelphia. The light-heartedness of that wine re-echoed his own–the lamentable supper had done nothing to damp his spirits.

Davenant entered the supper-room at that moment, his eyes meeting Peabody's as though the pair of them were crossing swords. Each of the two instantly decided to look away again and not risk a further interchange of glances. Peabody's eyes travelled round the room; wherever he looked he could see the blue and gold and white of the British Navy, as well as the red coat of the Marine officer who was offering refreshments to Anne. Evidently the British Navy followed the same practice as the American, of leaving the watch in harbour in the charge of the master and the master's mates, so as to free the lieutenants; most of the lieutenants, at least, who could be serving in the three British ships must be present.

It was when he had formed that conclusion that Peabody decided on a new plan. It was so simple that he wondered why he had not thought of it before–except that all simple plans are exceedingly hard to think of. At one moment his mind had been void of ideas; at the next he had the whole scheme ready in his mind, its advantages and disadvantages balanced against each other, and his decision was taken for action. Quite without thinking he rose to his feet, rather to his partner's surprise, so that he sat down again. The essence of the plan lay in his not calling attention to himself, in his awaiting his opportunity to act unnoticed. He looked across at Hubbard, conversing in a lively group of mature females with all his Southern courtesy, and at Howard who was blushingly supping with Mme Clair. Murray was just in sight at the far end of the room, but Atwell was nowhere to be seen; Peabody wondered with extraordinary tolerance whether he was forgetting, somewhere out on one of the wide porches, the existence of that wife of his in New London. The four of them would be surprised when they knew what he had done.

'I don't think you heard what I said, Captain,' said his partner, a little tartly, breaking into his thoughts.

'I beg your pardon, ma'am,' said Peabody hastily. 'I can't think what came over me.'

'I can guess the cause of your distraction,' she said. 'It was either war or a woman.'

'Maybe so,' smiled Peabody.

He did his best to be conversational and natural, but the spell was broken, and his attention was not on the present. His partner was a trifle mortified, for here she had secured what was perhaps the greatest prize of the evening, in supping with the American captain, only to find she had no chance whatever of conquest. It occurred to her that it was still not too late to try again and see whether any of the lieutenants were not more susceptible, on the principle of a lieutenant in the hand being better then a captain in the bush.

'I think, Captain,' she said, 'that I had better be going back to mother.'

Peabody did his best to express regret, though only half convincingly. He escorted her out of the room and to her mother's side, and he forced himself to make the conventional remark and to bow leisurely when he left them–anything, rather than allow anyone to guess that he was in a hurry. He did not look back over his shoulder as he left the ball-room, for he knew that would be the surest way of calling attention to himself. He walked slowly down the deserted staircase, and slowly out to the main door. The coloured footman there addressed some remark to him in island French which he did not understand.

'Oh, yes,' he replied with a drawl. 'I guess so.'

He was through the main door now; the fact that his cloak was still in the house ought to persuade the footman that he was only intending to be absent a short time. He would have to abandon the cloak, just as he was abandoning his four lieutenants. A miracle might bring them back to him, but otherwise he would have to get along without them as best he could. There were some other capable midshipmen who might make useful acting lieutenants, and his master's mates were all of them experienced seamen. The *Delaware* might not be so efficient, but at least she would be free–if he got her out of the harbour to-night the British ships would be compelled to stay for another twenty-four hours, and he would have a whole day to forestall pursuit. There would be an outcry among the British, he could guess. They would condemn his action as a slick Yankee trick, without a doubt. Let them. He had made no promises, he had passed no parole, nor had he made any appearance of doing so. This was war; Davenant would be court-martialled and broke when it came out that he was at a ball when his enemy gave him the slip–that was hard luck on Davenant, but war always meant hard luck for somebody.

By now he had passed the sentry at the gate, had picked his way across the dark square, and was on his way down the steep street to the waterfront. Another thought made him hesitate in his stride, not because he had any idea of returning, but because it knocked him off his balance. Anne! He had forgotten all about Anne! He had had her soft lips against his hard ones. He had kissed her. Not only had he kissed a woman, but the woman he kissed was Anne. He was not the same man as had walked up that evening from the boat. There was a tremendous upheaval within him, even though he still hurried down the dark street.

It was perfectly likely that he would never see her again. Even if death did not come to him, the exigencies of the service and the chances of war would more likely than not keep him from her. An infinite sadness overcame him at the prospect. He had not even said good-bye to her–he knew that why such a notion had not occurred to him was because he never would have imperilled the success of his plan by doing anything of the sort. Peabody felt pain like a cancer in his breast as he thought of leaving Anne. Life had been gay and hopeful a few minutes ago, and now it was depressing and cruel. He was leaving Anne; he was sneaking away in the darkness, like a thief, to resume a hunted life, to go on ruining small traders and harmless fishermen, to be disquieted by every sail that showed on the horizon, slinking round the Caribbean like a wolf in the forest, and with destruction awaiting him at the end, and he would never see Anne again. In the darkness the hard lines deepened beside his mouth as he hurried on, stumbling over the inequalities of the street. The puff of warm wind that came down with him told him that the land breeze had just begun to blow–the land breeze which he had counted on to take him out past the Diamond Rock to freedom, to destruction.

At the waterfront the moon revealed his gig still waiting for him against the quay; most of the men were dozing uneasily, wrapped in their cloaks and doubled against the thwarts; three of them, including his coxswain, were standing on the quay chatting with a group of dusky women whose peals of laughter, he knew, must have been tempting to men who had been at sea for so long. But he knew there had been no desertion; he had selected his gig crew himself. As he approached, and the men recognised his tall figure looming in the darkness, they broke off their conversation abruptly and a little guiltily, although the women, unabashed, went on laughing and talking in their queer island French. Muggridge, the coxswain, sprang down into the gig to assist his captain, and the boat pushed off.

'Don't say I'm in the boat when they hail,' said Peabody quietly.

'Aye aye, sir.'

The boat glided over the moonlit water towards the phantom shape of the *Delaware*; on the other side of the bay the three British ships rode at their anchors. A little to seaward the remembered silhouette of a French coastguard cutter showed that the French Preventive Service was still awake, but it could not legally interfere with what he had in mind.

'Boat ahoy!' from the *Delaware*.

'No, no,' hailed Muggridge back.

That indicated there were no officers on board, just as 'aye aye' would have been warning of the presence of officers, or the answer '*Delaware*' would have announced the coming of the captain himself. Muggridge, like a sensible man, directed the course of the gig to the *Delaware*'s larboard side–only officers could use the starboard side. The boat hooked on, and Peabody went up the side in two sharp efforts. O'Brien was in the waist and peered through the puzzling light at the apparition of his captain arriving unannounced on the port side.

'What the hell—?' he began.

'Quietly!' whispered Peabody. 'I don't want a sound. Turn up all hands–quietly, remember. Ask Mr Poynter to come to the quarterdeck.'

'Aye aye, sir.'

His period of duty in a raiding frigate had already accustomed O'Brien to the strangest orders and occurrences. He turned to do his captain's bidding, while Peabody made his way to the quarterdeck. The drowsy hands stationed there started in surprise when he appeared; Peabody was aware that none of the men had had a proper night's sleep the night before–at best an hour or two snatched by the guns–but he clean forgot that he himself had not closed his eyes since he had been awakened twenty-four hours ago. Poynter loomed up before him; there was only the smallest noise as the hands came trooping to their stations from their broken sleep.

'I want all sail loosed to the royals, Mr Poynter,' said Peabody to the acting-master. 'Every stitch ready to set when I give the word. Have the cable buoyed and ready to slip. Mind you, Mr Poynter, I don't want a sound–not a sound, Mr Poynter.'

'Aye aye, sir.'

'The four lieutenants will not be returning on board,' went on Peabody. 'See that the warrant officers are warned. You will take over Mr Hubbard's duties.'

'Aye aye, sir.' Poynter waited in the darkness for any further surprising orders, and when none came he volunteered something on his own account. 'A letter came for you from the shore an hour or two back, sir.'

'Thank you,' said Peabody. He held the note in his hand while he hurried to the rail to stare through the darkness at the British squadron. He could see nothing and hear nothing suspicious, but this was a nervous moment. If the *Delaware* should get clear away it would be a resounding triumph for the United States Navy, and the British would be a laughing stock from the Caribbean to Whitehall. With a flash of insight Peabody realised that probably the most potent action he could take with the small means at his disposal, was to set the world laughing at the British. The land breeze was blowing well–the *Delaware* would be able to make a straight dash out of the bay.

'Cable's ready to slip, sir,' reported Poynter. Sail's all ready to set.'

'Thank you, Mr Poynter. Slip the cable.'

'Aye aye, sir.'

Poynter was of a plethoric type; Peabody could hear his laboured breathing, and could guess at the strain Poynter was undergoing at having to give in a whisper orders which he was accustomed to bawling at the top of his voice. Men were scurrying up the rigging in the darkness like rats in a barn, while Poynter vanished forward again, and Peabody remembered his letter. He opened it in the shielded light of the binnacle.

Bureau du Port,
Fort de France,
Martinique

The captains and masters of ships of belligerent powers in the ports of His Most Christian Majesty are informed that to avoid incidents of an international nature no movements of such ships will be permitted between sunset and sunrise. Ships violating this ordinance will be fired on.

Godron,
Capitaine du Port

Contresigne

Son Excellence le Gouverneur-Général, le Marquis Charles Armand de St Amant de Boixe.

So that was that. He felt he should have foreseen this, but it would not have been easy to have guessed at the promptness of the decision which the French authorities had taken. They were quite within their rights to take any measures they chose within reason for the proper control of their port and without a doubt the guns of the batteries were trained to sweep the sea on the exit to the bay. The avenue of escape which he saw before him was blocked. That cursed preventive cutter was probably waiting with rockets to signal any movement.

'Snub that cable!' he roared forward at the top of his voice, the sound breaking through a mystical stillness; he had to repeat himself before they heard or understood him. And there could only have been a fathom or two of cable left by the time the purport of the order penetrated their minds.

'Mr Poynter,' yelled Peabody, and Poynter came puffing aft; the spell of previous manoeuvres still bound him so closely that although Peabody spoke loudly, Poynter tried to puff quietly.

'Make all secure again, Mr Poynter, if you please,' said Peabody coldly, 'and then send the hands below.'

'Aye aye, sir,' said Mr Poynter. Discipline fought a losing battle with curiosity in Mr Poynter's breast, as could be guessed from the intonation of the monosyllables, but Peabody was not in a mood to gratify it.

'That will be all, Mr Poynter,' he said. Then Poynter turned away completely mystified. Peabody could accept the inevitable. He was not going to explain it to Poynter.

A moment later, a gig under oars went tearing by. Peabody saw in the stern sheets gold glittering in the moonlight, and he heard Davenant's voice.

'Pull, you bastards! Pull, you sons of bitches!'

Davenant's voice was cracking with anxiety–Peabody saw him leaning forward beating the air with his fists as he exhorted his men; Davenant must have had a tremendous fright at the prospect of the *Delaware* getting to sea without his knowledge. Peabody grinned to himself while the hands were shortening cable, and two minutes later another boat shot out of the darkness and came alongside, spewing on to the *Delaware*'s deck a quartette of excited officers in full dress.

'Were you going without us, sir?' asked Hubbard.

'That was in my mind,' snapped Peabody. He found himself on the verge of venting his ill-temper on innocent victims; he had done that once or twice in his career, and had found it an evilly attractive habit, like indulgence in strong drink. His iron self-restraint came down on him again and then allowed free play to his natural kindliness.

'Get below, the four of you, and get some sleep.'

14

After the moon had set there was half an hour or so of utter darkness. Peabody was still on the quarterdeck with his hand on the rail, ignorant of his fatigue and want of sleep. In this dark interval there might be a chance of escape, but Peabody hardly dallied with the idea for a moment. The French harbour guard was by now thoroughly aroused, and so, presumably, were the British. He had no doubt whatever that the big guns in the batteries were loaded and trained to converge on the exit, and that accursed cutter would send up her rockets. The *Delaware* would be badly knocked about; furthermore, if she violated harbour rules, the British might attack her at once and plead that in justification. It would not do.

But on the other hand the port captain's regulation distinctly laid it down that movement was permitted between sunrise and sunset–indeed, the French authorities could hardly say otherwise. That started an interesting train of possibilities. And the land breeze blew strongest at dawn. Peabody turned to the midshipman of the anchor watch with a series of orders, at the same time as he settled himself into a delightful calculation of what was the exact moment of sunrise on the morning of May 31st in Latitude 14° 20′ North. At three bells his orders began to bear fruit. The hands came up from below, while the dark sky above began to take on the faintest tinge of lilac, and the mountains of the island began to assume a sharper definition against it. The crew kept out of sight below the bulwark as they moved to their places under the direction of the petty officers; they were like the starters before a race–as indeed they were. Hubbard came up on deck and stood beside his captain. His eyes were a little red with fatigue, although he had had a full four hours' sleep in the last forty-eight.

'D'you think we'll do it, sir?' he asked.

'We'll know in ten minutes,' said Peabody.

There was enough light now for the British ships to be visible, and Peabody and Hubbard turned with one accord to look at them. They showed no sign of any activity–but then, neither did the *Delaware*. Peabody looked at his watch, put it back into his fob, and buttoned the flap with his usual care.

'Very good, Mr Hubbard,' he said.

The last syllable had not left his lips before Hubbard was pealing on his whistle and the ship broke into life. The cable roared out, the jibs shot up, the ship shied away from the wind. A second later courses and topsails and topgallants and royals were spread, and the *Delaware* jerked herself forward as the land breeze swelled the canvas. It was only a matter of moments before she was tearing through the blue water, under the brightening sky, at a full nine knots.

'Hurry up with those stu'ns'ls, there!' roared Hubbard. 'Are you asleep?'

On both sides, from royals to main and foreyard, the studding sails were being set, almost doubling the canvas which the *Delaware* had spread. The resultant increase in speed was perceptible–the *Delaware* leaped to the additional impulse.

'Look there, sir!' said Hubbard suddenly, but Peabody had seen some time ago what Hubbard was pointing to.

The three British ships had all sail set as well, had slipped their cables, and were racing for the open sea, on courses which would converge upon the *Delaware*'s. If even one of them crossed the line limiting territorial waters before the *Delaware* should, Peabody would have to turn back and stay twenty-four hours, while they could cruise outside and wait for him at their leisure.

'Clear for action and run out the guns, Mr Hubbard, if you please,' said Peabody.

With courses converging in this fashion, it would not be at all surprising if guns went off without orders, and if they should, Peabody had no intention of being caught napping. Should the British violate French neutrality he would give as good as he got. Ahead of them lay the *Tigresse*, periodically spilling the wind from her mainsail as she awaited their coming–she must have got under way long before dawn. And that accursed cutter was out, too, to see the sport. The *Calypso*, her bows foaming white against the blue of the water, was drawing closer and closer. She, too, had her guns run out and her men at quarters; Peabody could see the red coats of the marines drawn up on the poop. Her bows were a trifle ahead of the *Delaware*'s but the *Delaware* was gaining on her perceptibly. Peabody recognised Davenant; he had leaped upon a carronade slide and was bellowing through his speaking-trumpet at the *Delaware*.

'I lead!' he yelled. 'Peabody, you'll have to go back.'

Peabody snatched his own speaking-trumpet.

'You be damned!' he shouted. 'We're overtaking you.'

They were closing on the *Tigresse* now. She, too, had her pop-guns run out as she lay right across the bows of the charging frigates, and there were present all the ingredients for a violent explosion. There was a puff of smoke as she fired a gun.

'That was across our bows, sir,' said Hubbard.

'Across *his* bows, too,' said Peabody, with a jerk of his thumb at the *Calypso*. She showed no sign of heaving-to in obedience to the command, and Peabody would not give way before she did. He could see Davenant looking forward at the *Tigresse* with something of anxiety in his attitude. Something rumbled through the air over their heads and raised a fountain of water a cable's length from their port bow; they swung round in time to see a white puff of smoke from Fort Bourbon. It was an argument nothing could gainsay.

'Bring her to the wind, Mr Hubbard,' said Peabody.

As the *Delaware* came round, he saw the *Calypso*'s yards swing too. It might have been a well-executed drill, the way the two ships rounded-to exactly simultaneously. A moment later the *Bulldog* and the *Racer* did the same, and all four ships lay motionless in the bay while the *Tigresse* bore up for them.

They saw a boat drop from her side as she hove-to, and pull towards the *Delaware*, and directly afterwards Captain Dupont was being piped on board by the hurriedly assembled boatswain's mates.

'His Excellency,' said Dupont to Peabody, after the formal greetings had been exchanged, 'would esteem it an honour if you would visit him in the *Tigresse*.'

'His Excellency?' said Peabody.

The last time he had seen the Marquis was at the ball the night before. It seemed probable that no one had had much sleep last night.

'It would be a favour as well as an honour,' said Dupont gravely, creasing his rounded belly in another bow.

'Oh, I'll come,' said Peabody.

It was just the same as yesterday; it seemed as if nothing had happened during the last twenty-four hours as Peabody took off his hat once more to the Marquis on the deck of the *Tigresse*, and then bowed to Davenant. The Marquis was elegantly dressed in a buff-coloured coat with a pink and blue fancy waistcoat beneath it, and showed no sign of a disturbed night; Peabody, conscious of the disordered full dress which he still wore, and of his unshaven face, was glad to see that Davenant, too, was red-eyed and untidy, the grey sprouts of his beard showing on his cheeks.

'It is most pleasant,' said the Marquis, 'to have the honour of repeated visits from you two gentlemen like this.'

'You don't find it pleasant at all,' said Peabody. He was in no mood for airy and long-winded nothings.

'Hospitality would forbid my saying that even if it were true,' answered the Marquis. 'But your suggestion naturally encourages me to speak more freely. I must confess that I did not succeed in getting a wink of sleep last night owing to my anxiety lest the guests of France, for whose reception I am responsible to His Most Christian Majesty, should unconsciously violate any of the accepted conventions.'

'Look here, Your Excellency,' said Davenant, 'what we both want to know is why you stopped us this morning. We weren't breaking any of your rules.'

'I had reason to fear that one or other of you might do so shortly,' answered the Marquis. 'It was a very close race which you were sailing.'

'Well, what of it? There's nothing wrong in that. One or other of us, as you say, would have got out first.'

'And would the other one have stopped then?' The Marquis's expression was severe as he looked at them. 'You would have crossed the line almost together, and in five seconds you would have been fighting. How would the neutrality of France have appeared then, to have allowed such a thing to happen? It is my duty, gentlemen, to use every means in my power to prevent such an occurrence.'

There was much solid truth and common sense in what the Marquis was saying; Peabody stole a glance at Davenant and saw that the British captain was impressed by the argument–naturally the fact that the argument was backed up by twenty-four pounders gave it increased cogency.

'I must give you notice that whenever I see there is any possibility,' went on the Marquis, 'of your two ships leaving the bay together, I shall stop you, without hesitation.'

Davenant rubbed his bristling chin.

'I'm damned if I can see,' he said, 'why we ever gave Martinique back to you at all.'

The Marquis ignored the implied rudeness, which he could well do in his present position of authority.

'It has caused us all the loss of a night's sleep,' he said.

Meanwhile Peabody had been digesting the facts of the situation with results which were surprising him.

'But how are we ever going to get out of here?' he asked.

'That's what I want to know, by jingo,' said Davenant.

The glance which Davenant and Peabody exchanged showed that both of them saw the difficulties of the position. British and Americans would watch each other like hawks, and at the first sign of one making ready to leave the other would rush to forestall him. During daylight, at least, neither side would have a moment's leisure or relief from tension.

'I cannot see any answer to that question myself,' said the Marquis. 'I must apologise for it.'

'But dammit, sir,' said Davenant, 'you can't keep us here indefinitely.'

'I appreciate the pleasure of your company, Sir Hubert,' said the Marquis, 'but I assure you that I am making no effort to detain you. Please do not think me inhospitable when I point out that your presence here occasions me a considerable personal inconvenience. I should, of course, be delighted to oblige you two gentlemen in any way possible, if I might act as intermediary in any arguments you might care to enter into.'

Once more Peabody and Davenant exchanged glances.

'You might perhaps spin a coin for it,' suggested the Marquis.

The struggle apparent on the faces of both the captains at the suggestion made first the Marquis and then themselves, smile. It was tempting at first–an even chance of success or failure. But Davenant thought of the damage the *Delaware* might do if the spin of the coin were unlucky for him, and Peabody thought of the fact that the *Delaware* was the only United States ship of war not closely blockaded in an American port.

'I'm damned if I do,' said Davenant.

'I wouldn't have agreed if you'd wanted to,' said Peabody.

The Marquis sighed, as a very gentle reminder that his patience was being tried.

'You gentlemen can't agree upon anything?' he said.

'Why the hell should we?' said Davenant.

'Then I shall have to keep the *Tigresse* out here all day long and every day, and the battery guns manned and pointed,' said the Marquis. 'Really, gentlemen, you have very little consideration for your host.'

'That's nothing compared with what we'll be going through,' said Davenant irritably.

'Well, perhaps,' said the Marquis, tentatively, 'there is another course possible.'

'And what is that, sir?' asked Peabody, his curiosity roused.

'I was going to suggest, gentlemen, that perhaps you might agree on a short armistice. You might, for instance, give each other your promise not to make any attempt to leave Fort de France for some definite period–a week, might I say? That would give you an opportunity to water your ships and rest your men, and give me a chance to get some sleep. You would benefit and I would benefit and Martinique would benefit.'

'By Jove!' said Davenant. To him it was obviously a new idea, and Peabody, watching him closely, saw that he was tempted. He was tempted himself. There was a good deal of the *Delaware*'s standing rigging which needed resetting-up, and he might perhaps heave her over and do a good job of work on the troublesome shot-hole, forward. But then Davenant shook his head.

'But what would happen at the end of the week?' he asked.

'At the end of the week you would be no worse off than now,' said the Marquis. 'You might even be better off. You might even have received orders from your Admiral which would take some of the responsibility off your shoulders.'

That made the suggestion far more tempting still to Davenant.

'There's something in what you say, Excellency,' he said. In the tone of his voice, Peabody could hear the grudging underlying admission–unconvinced, of course–that for a Frenchman the Marquis was showing extraordinary intelligence.

'I'll promise if you will,' said Peabody, cutting the Gordian knot. He was weary of fencing, and his matter-of-fact mind saw the essentials clearly enough despite the unusualness of it all.

'But any moment I might get other orders,' said Davenant in a sudden wave of caution.

'That can be allowed for,' said the Marquis. 'An armistice can always be denounced on giving notice.'

'That's so,' admitted Davenant.

'Then, perhaps you two gentlemen will promise that for a week neither of you will make any attempt to leave the harbour. This promise will be subject to the condition that it can be terminated on–shall we say twelve hours' notice on either side?'

The two captains nodded.

'Then let me hear your promise,' said the Marquis.

Davenant's expression revealed a fresh struggle within him as he looked at Peabody. Davenant knew the worth of his own promise, he knew he would never do anything that would bring dishonour on the British Navy, but for a moment he knew doubt as to Peabody's promise. He found it hard to believe that a new nation and an upstart navy could be trusted. It was quite a plunge that he was taking, but at length he took it.

'I promise,' he said.

'So do I,' said Peabody.

'That's good,' said the Marquis, and then, abruptly changing the distasteful subject, 'I hope we shall be seeing a good deal of you two gentlemen at my house during the coming week–I am speaking not only on my own account, but for my sister and daughter.'

15

Captain Josiah Peabody was conversant with the usages of good society; at Malta, during the Mediterranean campaign he had served a hard apprenticeship, and it was then, when national rivalries culminated in a series of duels between American and British officers, that he had learned that the stricter the regard for the conventions the easier it was to avoid trouble. Those weeks at Malta had actually rubbed the lesson in more effectively than years of living in cramped and crowded quarters on board a ship.

So that in the afternoon, when he had set one watch to work upon the ship, and made arrangements for shore leave for the other watch, he had Washington get out his second best uniform coat, and he ordered his gig and went ashore to pay his digestion call upon the Governor, as good manners dictated. Always as soon as possible after a dinner party or a ball, one paid a personal call or at least left cards upon one's host, and in view of the fact that he would be representing all the five officers of his ship, he decided it would be more fitting to call in person. That was what he himself honestly believed; it did not cross his conscious mind that he might be at all influenced by the desire to see Mademoiselle Anne de Breuil again.

It might be pleaded for him that his usual keenness of mind was blunted by the fact that he had had no sleep for two nights, that he had gone through a good deal of emotional strain during the past forty-eight hours. It was only yesterday morning that he had turned with the intention of fighting his last fight against the British squadron; it was only last night that he had kissed Anne, and since then there had been the two attempts to break out of the harbour. Adventures had come in a flood, as they always did at sea. And the heat of the bay was sticky and stupefying, and the light was blinding in its intensity; Peabody, as he was rowed ashore, knew that he felt dazed and not as clear-headed as usual.

He landed at the quay and walked up into the town; the two hundred liberty men of the *Delaware* seemed to fill every corner of the place. They were to be seen at all of the out-of-doors drinking places, sitting at the little tables roaring remarks to each other, pawing the coloured girls who waited on them. Half of them would be quietly drunk and some of them–who would be un ortunate–would be noisily drunk when they came on board again. Shore leave to them meant rum and women and subsequent punishment one way or another. Sailors were like that; Peabody knew it and made allowances for them. He had conquered drink himself and had never allowed lust to overmaster him, but he knew that others had not been as fortunate as himself. The only lack of sympathy he displayed was with regard to their drinking publicly at tables on the street–he simply could not understand that. To him it appeared axiomatic that drinking should be done privately, and as little public attention as possible called to it. He knew that if ever he started drinking again–although he never would–it would be secretly, with hurried intoxicating nips out of a private bottle which no one would ever know about.

The sentry outside the Governor's house saluted him smartly as he passed, and he raised his hat in acknowledgement. At the front door the coloured butler recognised him and smiled. What the butler said in reply to his inquiry if the Governor were at home, he did not understand in the least. He was aware that the butler changed from Martinique French to Martinique English, but it did not make the butler more intelligible. But the butler was certainly ushering him inside, and he followed. The transition from the dazzling sunlight outside to the cool darkness within, quite blinded him. He stumbled over something in his path, trod on a mat which slipped treacherously under his foot on the polished floor, retained his balance with difficulty, and heard, as if in a dream, Anne's voice saying: 'Good afternoon, Captain Peabody.'

His eyes grew accustomed to the darkness, and the sudden mist which befogged them cleared away. There was Anne, in cool white, sitting gracefully in an armchair. He bowed and he mumbled; certainly his wits were not as clear as they should be. Something in Anne's attitude called his attention to another part of the room, and there was Davenant, newly risen from another armchair, and standing stiffly with his hat under his arm, and–possibly–feeling a little awkward, although there was no certainty about it. This meeting of one's country's enemies on neutral ground was embarrassing. But the suspicion that Davenant was not quite at ease was reassuring. Peabody was able to smile politely and bow formally in consequence.

'Very warm for this time of year,' said Peabody, utterly determined not to be discountenanced.

'Yes,' said Davenant. The way he pronounced it was more like 'yas.'

'But not as warm as it was last week,' said Anne.

'No,' said Peabody.

'No,' said Davenant, and conversation wilted. Peabody was momentarily distracted by the queer thought that if he met Davenant anywhere except on neutral soil it would be his duty to pull out his sword and fall upon him; that he would be liable to court-martial and to the severest penalties if he did not do his best to kill him as speedily as possible. He forced himself to abandon that line of thought.

'I have called to thank His Excellency on behalf of my officers and myself for the extremely pleasant evening we enjoyed yesterday,' he said.

'I'm glad to hear you enjoyed it,' said Anne, composedly, but as she said it her eyes met Peabody's and the next moment there was red colour flooding her cheeks and neck.

'Nice evenin',' said Davenant. 'There were some pretty women, by George. None of 'em a patch on you and Madame your aunt, though.'

'You are very kind, Sir Hubert.'

As if the mention of her had brought her in, the Countess entered on the words.

'Good afternoon, Sir Hubert. Good afternoon, Captain Peabody. I hope my niece has been entertaining you.'

'Delightfully, I assure you, ma'am,' said Davenant.

'His Excellency is still engaged with the Council,' went on the Countess. 'I was wondering if this would be a good opportunity while it isn't raining, to show you my orchids which I was telling you about last night, Sir Hubert.'

'Oh, yes, of course,' said Davenant.

'Sir Hubert is interested in orchids, you see, Captain Peabody,' explained the Countess, 'and His Excellency's predecessor in office, General Brown, made a most interesting collection. The British occupation of the island had its brighter side, we must admit.'

'Surely,' said Peabody.

'Anne,' said the Countess, 'will you offer Captain Peabody some tea?'

'Yes, Aunt Sophie.'

'Until we meet again, then, Captain,' said the Countess.

Next moment she was gone, through the glass door which Davenant opened for her and through which he followed her. The room was suddenly quiet, except for the faint whine of the fan in the ceiling–an ingenious arrangement by which a cord was taken over a pulley through a hole in the wall, so that a negro child outside the room could keep the air in motion without intruding on the privacy within. Peabody admired the contrivance for some seconds as if it were as fascinating as a snake. As the Countess and Davenant were leaving the room he had suddenly felt that he could not, for some unexplained reason, meet Anne's eyes. He remained on his feet, his left hand on his sword hilt, sliding the blade half an inch in and out.

'You went away!' said Anne suddenly, in the silence of the room.

He looked down at her, and she was looking up at him reproachfully.

'Anne!' he said, and he melted. There was never anything like this, like this unrestrainable surge of emotion. His head swam, and he came down on his knees at her side–he had never knelt to any woman before, but it was the most natural thing he had ever done in his life. She put her two hands into his, and they kissed; and when they drew back from each other he went on looking into her eyes.

'Anne!' was all he could say. He did not know what a volume of meaning he put into that monosyllable.

'I didn't mean what I said,' explained Anne.

'I had to go,' said Peabody. 'I had to try to go. I didn't want to.'

'I know, my dear,' said Anne.

She kissed him again, and then her lips left his and strayed over his mahogany cheek, fluttering as she murmured something to herself, some endearment or other.

'What am I going to do with you?' said Anne. 'This–this–I can't bear to have you out of my sight.'

She took one of her hands from him and put it on her breast where the emotion surged. Peabody knew just how she felt. He sawed at his stock with his free hand in a struggle against the passion which threatened to choke him. It seemed to be the last straw that she should so frankly admit to her emotion.

'Darling!' he said.

Her lips were the lips of innocence, of a sweetness and a simplicity which left him breathless in the delight which they conferred. There had never been anything like this in all his experience. Within him subconsciously stirred a twenty-year forgotten memory of his mother's tainted caresses, and he clung to Anne's hands and put his face to hers in the violence of the reaction.

'I couldn't bear it,' said Anne. 'You were gone. I thought I might never see you again.'

He looked into her eyes, and he remembered that death was awaiting him outside the bay, just beyond the Diamond Rock. The realisation shook him, and he tore himself from her and got to his feet.

'I'm a fool,' he said. 'I shouldn't ever have done this.'

It was a second or two before Anne answered, the fear that she felt revealing itself in her face and in her voice.

'Why not?' she whispered.

'Because—' said Peabody, 'because–oh—'

It was hard to put it all into words, the *Delaware*'s homelessness, the peril in which he stood, the losing fight which he was going to wage against the mightiest sea power the world had ever seen. Ironically, the love he bore for Anne crystallised his determination not to survive the eventual inevitable destruction of the *Delaware*; he did not say so to Anne, but it showed through the halting sentences with which he tried to explain his situation.

'I understand,' said Anne, nodding her head. It was odd, and yet it tore at Peabody's heart-strings, to see this very young woman contemplating problems of life and death, of war and peace.

'There is only this one week,' said Peabody.

'One week,' said Anne.

The little round chin under the soft mouth was firm for all its allure. Peabody had a moment's piercing insight; this was the sort of woman who would load her husband's long rifle while savages howled outside the log cabin, no more than twenty years old and yet willing to face anything beside the man she loved. He shook off the mental picture from before his eyes.

'That's all,' he said simply. 'I'm sorry.'

But all Anne's twenty years of life had been spent in a world in a turmoil of war. She had learned to think clearly through it.

'My dear,' she said, and her eyes met Peabody's unflinching. 'If we are lucky enough to have a week granted us, why should we waste it?'

Peabody's jaw dropped at that, and he looked at her with surprise. It was a view of the case which his far-seeing New England mind had not seen at all; he had paid so much attention to next week that to-morrow had escaped his notice.

'What do you mean?' his voice choking a little as the explication flooded in upon him.

Anne did not have the chance to explain, because the Marquis came in at that moment.

Peabody did not start at the sudden noise of the latch–his nerves were steady enough despite this present ordeal–and Anne retained her seat in the armchair with composure, but it would have been asking too much of them that their attitudes should not have revealed something of their preoccupation. The Marquis looked keenly from one to the other, and like a man of breeding he was prepared to pay no attention to the fact that his entrance had been at a difficult moment, but Peabody gave him no chance. He swung round on the Marquis, his brain labouring hard under the handicaps of strong emotion and recent sleeplessness.

'Good afternoon, Captain Peabody,' said the Marquis.

'I want to marry your daughter,' said Peabody, and even the Marquis's breeding was not proof against the surprise the statement occasioned. It was the sight of his discomposure which most helped Peabody to collect himself. The Marquis looked at them both again, as if during the last two seconds their appearance had undergone some radical change, and he waited some time before he spoke; even if Peabody's abrupt statement had taken him sufficiently off his guard to make him change countenance, years of training had taught him not to make an unguarded reply, and in theory, if not in practice, to count ten before he said anything decisive.

'The fact that you want to marry Mlle de Breuil,' he said, fencing for time, 'is a recommendation of your good taste, if not of your knowledge of the world.'

'Surely,' said Peabody. Now that he was in this affair he was not going to flinch, not for all the Marquises and Excellencies in His Most Christian Majesty's dominions.

'I know very little about you, Captain,' said the Marquis. 'Please forgive me–I intend no rudeness–but the name of Peabody does not enter into my genealogical knowledge. Can you tell me something about your family?'

'My father was a Connecticut farmer,' said Peabody sturdily, 'and so was his father, although he came from Massachusetts. And I don't know who *his* father was.'

'I see,' said the Marquis. 'You are not a man of great fortune, Captain?'

The question very nearly nonplussed Peabody. He was almost at the head of his profession, and he enjoyed a salary of one hundred dollars a month in hard money–a salary quite large enough to maintain a wife with dignity in New York or Philadelphia. But it was only now that his attention was called to the fact that this income–imposing enough to him–was insignificant compared with European fortunes, and it called for an effort on his part not to allow the realisation to unsettle him.

'I have my pay,' he said with dignity.

'I see,' said the Marquis again. 'Mlle de Breuil is a lady of fortune. She will have a very considerable *dot*–dowry, I think you call it. Did that influence you in reaching this rather surprising decision?'

'Good God!' said Peabody, completely thrown out of his stride this time. The idea had never occurred to him for a moment, and his face showed it. His astonishment was so genuine that it could hardly fail to make a favourable impression upon the Marquis–the latter's experiences might have accustomed him to American unconventionality, but they had not been able to eradicate the Frenchman's natural tendency to look upon matrimony as an occasion for financial bargaining.

'It is usual,' said the Marquis, 'when a marriage is being arranged, for the prospective bridegroom to match, franc for franc, his bride's fortune in the matter of settlements. You apparently had no intention of doing that?'

'No,' said Peabody. 'I didn't know that Mlle de Breuil had any money. I never thought about it, and I don't want it.'

He was conscious that he had made a frightful hash of the pronunciation of Anne's name, and it did not improve his temper, which was steadily rising.

'Josiah,' said Anne quietly. As far as Peabody knew, that was the first time Anne had ever spoken his name. It quieted him a good deal, and he made himself speak reasonably.

'All Anne and I want to do,' he said, 'is to get married. In my country we do not think about money in that connection. And one free man is as good as another.'

The Marquis suddenly became confidential.

'Do you know,' he said, 'it is my impression that just as many unsuccessful marriages result from the one system as from the other.'

Peabody grinned.

'You don't think our marriage is going to be unsuccessful, Father?' asked Anne.

'How long have you known each other?' continued the Marquis. 'You've seen each other twice—

'Three times, then—' said the Marquis, but he had been just sufficiently checked in the full flow of his argument to cause him to stumble, and his final words were a little lame. 'It's just madness, madness.'

The glass door opened to admit the Countess with Davenant, and the Marquis swung round on his sister.

'These two ridiculous people want to get married, Sophie,' he said.

'We are going to get married to-morrow, Aunt Sophie,' said Anne.

The Countess expressed her surprise in French; Davenant's face bore such a comic expression, of mixed astonishment and envy at this American who had carried off a prize in this fashion that Peabody was immensely comforted. He even began to enjoy himself. But Davenant was of stern stuff, and not for long would he ever allow himself to be discountenanced. If the right thing was there to be said, he was going to say it.

'I wish you joy, Mamzelle,' he said. 'Sir, my heartiest good wishes and congratulations.'

'Thank you, sir,' said Peabody.

'But—' began the Marquis.

'You are very kind, Sir Hubert,' said Anne, neatly interrupting him, and then she turned to her aunt with a torrent of French. The Countess's face softened, and she came towards her niece–Peabody had a clairvoyant moment, when telepathically he was aware of the sentimental appeal an imminent marriage has for any woman. Probably aunt and niece were closer together spiritually than ever before.

'But—' said the Marquis again.

'Father,' said Anne, turning from her aunt for a moment, 'I'm sure the gentlemen are thirsty. Won't you pull the bell?'

Not even his disapproval of his daughter's marriage could weigh in the scale against a lifetime of training in hospitality, and the Marquis broke off his speech to walk across to the bell-pull.

'Now listen to me—' he began as he returned.

'The white gown will do if we use a veil,' Anne was saying to her aunt, and

Peabody was careful to pay the strictest attention to her, so that the Marquis had only Davenant to whom he could address his remarks, which naturally died away undignified.

'Anne!' exclaimed the Marquis exasperated, 'don't—'

The entrance of the butler was the culminating interruption. The Marquis swung round upon him, and was immediately engulfed in orders to him. He actually never succeeded in giving any voice to his objections to the marriage.

16

Peabody came back on board the *Delaware* just at sunset. He looked round the familiar decks, and at the familiar faces, out at the red sun sinking in the blue Caribbean, and aloft to where the men were just finishing their work for the day. It was all so real, so ordinary, that for a moment he felt that the situation he had left behind at the Governor's house was an unreal one. It called for all his common sense to act normally in a world where at one moment he could have Anne's soft lips against his own, and at the next he could be putting the *Delaware* into shape for her last fight.

'Mr Hubbard,' he said, as his first lieutenant lifted his hat, 'we'll heave her over to-morrow. Run the even numbered starboard side guns over to larboard–that ought to be enough. You'll double-breech the others, of course. That'll bring her over by a couple of strokes and you can get at those shot-holes.'

'Aye aye, sir,' said Hubbard.

'I am going to get married to-morrow, Mr Hubbard,' went on Peabody.

'I didn't understand you, sir?'

Peabody repeated his words, but even so they did not convince Hubbard for a minute or two.

'Who is the lady, sir?' asked Hubbard, swallowing, and eyeing Peabody with some anxiety.

'Mamzelle Anne de Breuil,' said Peabody, and then he grinned, 'and the sooner she's Mrs Peabody, so that we don't have to try to say that name any more, the better.'

Hubbard's swarthy saturnine face grinned in response as the little human touch about the joke thawed him completely.

'She's a lovely lady, sir,' he said. 'I wish you joy, sir, and happiness, and prosperity.'

'Thank you, Mr Hubbard. Now what about that second best suit of sails? What did the committee of inquiry decide about them?'

There was a great deal to be done–there never was any ship yet in which a great deal did not have to be done, even when there was not the additional prospect of having to fight for her life within the week. Peabody went round the ship with his heads of department, his first lieutenant and his carpenter, his boatswain and his cooper and his purser and his gunner. The ship was noisy with the return at sunset of the tipsy liberty men whose last stragglers had been swept up by Atwell and a small party from the grogshops and the brothels, but Peabody like a sensible man, turned a blind eye and a deaf ear to the strange sights and sounds around him. His petty officers were the pick of all America, who could be relied upon not to incite trouble and to suppress it as soon as it showed–he paid no attention to the drunken figures which were being lashed into their hammocks like giant cocoons that could hurt neither themselves nor anyone else.

Washington was far more trouble than any drunken sailor; Peabody snapped the news at him as sternly and as unemotionally as he knew how, but that did not prevent the talkative negro from indulging in a long orgy of sentiment. That post of old family retainer was maddening to Peabody; so long had he been solitary, so long dependent on his own sole exertions that he resented bitterly Washington's continual attempt to establish himself in his intimacy; equally irritating was Washington's bland self-deception as he deliberately tried to make a god out of his master. Washington was uncomfortable without someone to worship, and paid small attention to Peabody's discomfort at being worshipped.

'Shut your mouth, you fool, and let's see those shirts,' growled Peabody.

'Yessir, yessir, immediately, sir,' protested Washington. 'Pity we haven't got a shirt of Chinee silk for the wedding, sir. And I haven't never seen the lady yet, sir, and—'

'Shut your mouth, I said!'

A little more of it and Washington would completely unsettle him–already Peabody was holding on to his self-control with a drowning man's grip. He had been two nights without sleep, and a third would leave him fit for nothing to-morrow, he told himself as he lay down on his cot in the sweltering night. He called up all his self-control, all his seaman's habits, to try to make certain of sleeping as soon as his head touched the pillow, grimly emptying his mind of all thoughts in the manner which up till now had proved infallible. Yet to-night sleep did not come at once. He turned over, once, twice, in his bath of sweat, fighting down the images which awaited their chance to flood into his mind like hungry wolves. He heard six bells strike, and seven, and it was nature which decided the struggle in the end. At eight bells she asserted herself, struck him unconscious as though with a club, as she demanded her rights, her usurious repayment for the demands Peabody had made on her during the last forty-eight hours–forty-eight hours without sleep, of ceaseless activity, of continual mental strain of every possible kind. Once he was asleep his seaman's habits reasserted themselves to the extent of giving him every ounce of benefit from the six hours granted him.

So his hand was steady when he shaved next morning, and his eyes had not fulfilled their threat of being bloodshot, and he could listen without attention to Washington's ecstatic maunderings. He was as unobtrusively well-clad a figure as heart could desire as he went down the ship's side and took his seat in the stern of the gig along with Jonathan and Murray, and Providence was kind, for the prodigious midsummer rain of Martinique held off during the short passage to the quay, although they were hardly inside the carriage which awaited them there when it roared down upon the roof thunderously enough to drown speech.

It was a pretty compliment which his men were paying him. The watch which had come on shore a few minutes earlier had resisted the temptation of drink and women–after eighteen weeks at sea!–and were waiting for him. They ran shouting and yelling beside the clattering carriage, whooping and capering in the rain, scaring the coloured girls who put their heads out of the windows. Cheering, they thronged the carriage when it halted, so that Peabody, smiling, had to push his way through them. Their cheerful antics directed the vast crowd of Martinique, of all ages, colours, and attire who had come hurrying at the amazing news of the immediate marriage of the Governor-General's daughter. They crowded the vast audience hall, and their cheerful babble rose to a deafening height, to die away magically when everyone peered on tiptoe to catch a glimpse of Anne in white when she entered. The Marquis asked Peabody and Anne grave questions, first in French and then in English as, in his capacity as magistrate, he carried through the civil ceremony.

Things grew vaguer and vaguer in Peabody's mind–he was only conscious of the warmth and perfume of Anne beside him, and then, with a slight shock of surprise, that Anne's brows were straight and level black above the blue. It puzzled him that he had not realised before how straight they were.

There were more ceremonies; there was the signing of documents, there was a half-formal procession into the big room which he had last seen cleared for dancing. There were toasts and then there was laughter. There were endless presentations. There was a brief moment when he saw Jonathan across the room, wine-glass in hand, laughing boisterously with Mme Clair.

It all passed, and he was back in the carriage with the rain thundering on the roof again, but this time Anne was beside him, and he was more delirious with happiness than ever before, even at his most drunken moments. There was a small house–what house it was he had no idea–where there were eager coloured servants who giggled excitedly when Anne spoke to them in their queer tongue. There was a bedroom with a mosquito-net hung over the bed in the vastest dome Peabody could ever remember seeing, and Washington was there, unpacking things and chattering feverishly about a variety of subjects, from his master's future happiness to the surprising differences between coloured girls in New York and in Martinique–an endless flow of babble which only ceased when Peabody turned on him and hurled him from the room like Adam from Eden.

Anne came to him, and came to his arms like a child. Time was brief; life was short, and happiness was there to be grasped, as elusive as an eel and as hard to retain once caught. The little French words which Anne used were elusive too, and no drink he had ever drunk was as madly intoxicating. An hour before dawn he had, he knew, to start his preparations for leaving Anne for the day. He wanted to be on the deck of the *Delaware* at the first peep of daylight to attend to the work of the ship.

17

Lieutenant Hubbard clearly had something unpleasant to report, after he had given an account of how the work of the ship progressed. He held his lanky figure rigid as he stood in the stuffy cabin, and he looked over the top of Peabody's head as he said the words.

'Midshipman Jonathan Peabody, sir. Absent without leave.'

'He didn't come back last night?'

'No, sir.'

Hubbard was saying no more than the formalities demanded.

'He was with Mr Atwell. What has Atwell to say about it?'

'Shall I pass the word for Mr Atwell to report so that you can ask him, sir?'

'Yes.'

Atwell's ugly face showed all the signs of anxiety.

'After the–the wedding, sir—'

'Yes, go on.'

'We was all invited to another house. Madame Clair's, sir–I don't mean that sort of house, sir.'

'I know Madame Clair. Go on.'

'I didn't see much of Mr Peabody while we was there. To tell the truth, sir, there was drinking going on and skylarking.'

'Yes.'

'But at seven bells I thought I'd leave, sir, and I looked for Mr Peabody and I had to look a long time. And when I found him—'

'Where was he?'

'He was with Madame Clair. She was very merry, sir. To tell the truth, she had her arms round him.'

'Go on.'

'I said it was time to go back to the ship. And he said—'

'Go on.'

'He said he'd be eternally damned if he'd ever go back to the damned ship again. He said I could go back to hell on water if I wanted to, but he wasn't such a damned fool as me.'

'What did you say to that?'

'I said I'd forget his insolence if he'd only come back with me. I'd let bygones be bygones. I could see he'd been drinking, sir.'

'And he refused to come?'

'Yes, sir. I tried to make him, sir, but—'

'But what?'

'To tell the truth, sir, Madame Clair called the servants and–and I had to go without him.'

'Very good, Mr Atwell. No blame attaches to you. Thank you, Mr Hubbard.'

This was added bitterness in his strangely mixed cup. Jonathan had deserted in the presence of the enemy, and if Jonathan had his deserts he would be dangling at the yardarm if he could once lay his hands upon him. If Jonathan came back voluntarily he would spare his life after the severest punishment he could devise–but he knew Jonathan had no intention whatever of coming back. Nor, in a neutral port, could any attempt be made to recapture him, for Jonathan could stand on the quay and merely laugh at them. Probably that was what he would do. Peabody reached for the log-book and wrote in it. 'Midshipman Jonathan Peabody deserted.' Peabody's expression as he wrote reflected his mood; it was that same mood in which Cato put his sword point to his breast. He did not spare himself any of the agony.

The pain was still there at the end of the day, when his gig carried him over the reddened, sunset-lit water to the quay where the carriage with its ridiculous little horses stood waiting in the shade of a warehouse. His shoulders were a little bowed with it as he set foot on shore, and the hard lines from nose to mouth were deeper than ever. Washington–trust that fool to be there!–was standing by the carriage door and pulled it open the instant Peabody appeared. There was a flutter of bright colours, a whirl of petticoats, as Anne sprang down and ran to him. He made no move to take her in his arms, but she put up her hands to his lapels and drew him to her as close as his rigidity would allow, smiling up at him, and she made herself smile despite the unrelenting hardness of his face. Whether he would have kissed her in the full light of day and in sight of all Fort de France, if he had not been oppressed with the thought of Jonathan, was not to be guessed–public kissing was sinful.

'Where does Madame Clair live?' were his first words.

'Over towards Ducos. Five miles away. Six, perhaps, dear.'

'Can we go there?'

'Of course, dear. Dinner can wait.'

Peabody was not experienced enough fully to appreciate the transcendent loyalty of that speech.

'Let us go there, then,' he said.

Washington elaborately guarded Anne's skirts from the wheel; Anne gave her orders to the coachman in a steady voice which forbade any comment even from Washington who thirsted to make some. The carriage lurched over the cobbles.

'I know about Jonathan, dear,' said Anne and there was sympathy in her voice. Atwell and Hubbard had not offered sympathy, had perhaps been repelled from offering it; nor, in his drab existence, had Peabody been aware until that moment that he would be grateful for sympathy. And in his mind Peabody had drawn a sharp dividing line between the familiar realities of his professional life and the delirious unrealities of his dream life. It was the first indication that the line could be crossed, that Anne–a woman, and French, and the leading figure of the dream life should be able to know instantly what it meant to a United States captain that his brother should be a deserter.

'I don't know whether you've heard everything, dear,' went on Anne, gently. 'The island's full of the news.'

'What news?'

'They were married to-day. Jonathan and Madame Clair.'

'No,' said Peabody. 'I hadn't heard that.'

It did not seem likely in that case that a personal appeal would have any effect in persuading Jonathan to return to duty, then. Jonathan must have found a new career for himself.

'She's the richest landowner in the whole island,' said Anne. 'There's another estate on the windward side, near Vauclin, which came to her from her second husband. Jonathan will be a rich man–there are four hundred slaves.'

It was quite certain that Jonathan would not return to duty. Peabody was suddenly left without a doubt about it; he was able now to see his brother's character perfectly clearly. He could understand his passionate resentment against any kind of discipline, and the slyness which had enabled him to evade it. But that a Peabody should have deserted, that his own brother should have disgraced him like this, was almost more than he could bear. He did not know how he could face the world. He was tempted to turn and go back again, but it was not in him to give up any enterprise, however hopeless, once he had begun upon it. The stuffy interior of the carriage, the stifling heat, and the irregularity of the motion as the carriage rolled unsteadily over the inequalities of the surface, were all depressing. Then the rain came to make matters worse, and the little horses laboured in the mud of the road, and more than once they had to be checked as the wheels verged upon the ditch in the darkness.

And the meeting with Jonathan was a shameful thing–Jonathan red-faced with wine, his arm round his new wife on whose cheeks the rouge was smeared and striped with sweat, the two of them laughing and jeering at him like obscene animals at the entrance to their inaccessible cave. Peabody was conscious of the sword at his side and was tempted to slash and carve at this loathsome brother of his, but the coloured servants closed round him and he was forced to break off the hideous interview.

It was still raining when they reached the carriage door.

'We'll go straight home, Washington,' said Peabody.

'Yessir, cert'nly sir, whatever you—'

'Shut your mouth and get on the box.'

The carriage lurched and squelched back through the mud. In the darkness Anne spoke. There was the faint French flavour in her accent combined with the London accent which Peabody found so irritating in every voice except Anne's.

'I hate him,' said Anne. 'He's your brother and I hate him.'

'So do I,' said Peabody bitterly.

'Dearest,' said Anne, 'what can I say? What can I do? It breaks my heart that you are unhappy.' There was a catch in her throat as she spoke and Peabody knew she was crying in the darkness, and it was more than he could bear.

'Don't–don't,' he said.

'I hate him more than anyone on earth,' said Anne. 'But–but I love you more, ever so much more. I couldn't hate as much as I love you.'

Her soft hand touched his horny one, and that changed the mood of both of them.

Peabody in the darkness knew that all this was madness. To snatch at a moment's happiness like this, when all the world was against him, was as foolish as to heave a sigh of relief during the ten seconds' calm in the centre of a hurricane. It was not merely foolish, but it savoured of the sinful. And yet–and yet–there was no help for it. He could not control himself, and the minority party in his mind was vociferously informing him that the very briefness of his happiness was a further argument in favour of snatching at it. There was an additional fearful pleasure in comparing his own actions with those of the sinful man who said, 'Eat, drink and be merry, for to-morrow we die.' Logic on the one hand and unwonted recklessness on the other combined with his own wild passion to force him into forgetting for a space the *Delaware* and the *Calypso*, his brother's defection and his own approaching end, even the history of the world in which he was playing a major part and even the peril of his own country. Anne's lips were sweet.

The torch which lit them from the carriage to the little house was hardly as bright as the white fireflies which winked on and off in hundreds all about them; the whine of the fan in the ceiling did nothing to mask the song of the frogs and the crickets in the wet undergrowth outside the dark windows. Across the table Anne's sweet face swam in a mist; the glass of wine which stood before him stood untouched and unthought of. It might be madness; it might even be sin, but it was happiness, and the first he had ever known.

The coloured maid who was wise only in the ways of Martinique brought him rum to drink in the dark morning of thunderous rain, and her white teeth accented her amused surprise when it was refused. The dawn which burst upon him as he rowed out to the *Delaware* was the dividing line between the two worlds–their world where happiness was so acute as to be distrusted, and the other world where there were hard facts to be clung to, comforting as soon as the mind had grown accustomed to them again like eyes to light.

18

The gig which rowed over from the *Calypso* was a smart little craft, with the White Ensign fluttering above the head of the supercilious midshipman in the stern who answered Hubbard's hail.

'Message for Captain er–Peabody,' said the midshipman, and his manner implied that the name in his mouth was as distasteful as medicine.

The gig hooked on to the chains, the British sailors looked up curiously at the American ones hard at work about the ship while the midshipman scrambled to the deck. He touched his hat to the quarterdeck in the new off-hand British fashion that compared so unfavourably with the American rule of uncovering, and handed over the note.

H.M.S. *Calypso*
Fort de France

Captain the Hon. Sir Hubert Davenant, K.B., presents his respects to Captain Josiah Peabody, U.S.S. *Delaware*. He would esteem it a favour if Captain Peabody

> could find it convenient to meet him as soon as his duties permit. Captain Davenant ventures to suggest that Captain Peabody should visit him aboard *Calypso*, and wishes to indicate that he is aware of the honour Captain Peabody would confer upon *Calypso* in that event. However, should Captain Peabody decide that he cannot do so, Captain Davenant would be delighted to wait upon Captain Peabody at any point on neutral territory that Captain Peabody may be pleased to indicate. But the matter is urgent.

Peabody read this missive in the privacy of the cabin.

'You say the midshipman's waiting for an answer?'

'Yes, sir.'

'Tell him he'll have it soon.'

'Aye aye, sir.'

Peabody's matter-of-fact mind dissected the clumsy wording. In the first place, it did not need the final sentence to impress upon him how urgent the matter was–if Davenant should eat humble pie to the extent of making the first advance that was proof enough in itself. In the second place, the note did not ask him to commit himself to anything. It did not ask him to make any promises; he was at liberty to get any advantage out of the invitation which was open to him and to make no return. There was a chance of gaining something–he knew not what–and no chance of losing anything. Clearly the thing to do was to accept, and Peabody cut himself a fresh pen and addressed himself to the task.

It was not so easy as that. Peabody found himself making innumerable erasures as he floundered in the pitfalls of the third person singular; he made a fair copy, and then had to do it all over again when carelessly he allowed sweat to smudge the completed note–it was just as well, he discovered, on recopying, because he had forgotten to put in the 'K.B.' after Davenant's name, and he was certainly not going to allow a United States captain to be outdone in the game of formal politeness by a British one.

> U.S.S. *Delaware*,
> Fort de France
>
> Captain Josiah Peabody presents his respects to Captain the Hon. Sir Hubert Davenant, K.B. He will be honoured to wait upon Captain Davenant at three p.m. this afternoon, if that will be convenient to him.

Washington brought a candle and he sealed the note and sent it on deck.

'Get me out one of my best shirts, Washington.'

'Best shirt, sir? Yes, indeed, sir.'

These last few days had been a perfect orgy for Washington. It irked him inexpressibly that his master should ever wear the second best of anything, however neatly patched and darned, and now for days Peabody had been wearing a succession of the precious best shirts which had rested unworn in the locker since leaving Brooklyn. On deck Peabody was aware that Hubbard's keen observation had detected that he was wearing his best clothes.

'I'm going on board the British frigate, Mr Hubbard. Call my gig's crew, if you please. I shall inspect them before I start.'

'Aye aye, sir.'

Hubbard passed on the order and turned back anxiously to his captain.

'Did you say you were going on board the British frigate, sir?'

'I did.'

Hubbard realised at the same moment as his captain that there was nothing more to say. The British might be domineering, ruthless, inconsiderate, but neither Peabody nor Hubbard could for a moment imagine them capable of false dealing. If at their invitation Peabody visited them, he could be perfectly certain of being offered no hindrance when he wanted to leave again.

Muggridge formed up the gig's crew abaft the mainmast, and Peabody walked forward and looked them over.

'Can't have that patched shirt,' he said. 'Go change it. Those trousers aren't the right colour. Well, go draw another pair from the purser. You, Harvey, straighten that hair of yours.'

No lover preparing to visit his mistress ever paid so strict an attention to his appearance as did Peabody to that of his gig's crew at the prospect of having them looked over by a rival service. He even looked sharply over the gig itself, at the spotless white canvas fendoffs and the geometrically exactly arranged oars and boat-hook, even though he knew Muggridge to be too conscientious a sailor altogether to allow the slightest fault to be found with his charge. At precisely four minutes before six bells he stepped into the stern sheets; on board the *Calypso* the striking of six bells accompanied the hail of 'boat ahoy!' from the officer of the watch.

'*Delaware*!' hailed Muggridge in return.

There was the most formal reception on the deck. The red-coated marines presented arms like a score of mechanical wooden soldiers; their pipe-clayed cross-belts and bright badges echoed the gleam of the spotless decks and metal work. The officer of the watch held his hand rigidly to his hat brim while the boatswain's mates twittered wildly on their pipes; the side boys had the freshest imaginable white gloves and their infant faces had been scrubbed into preternatural cleanliness. Peabody took off his own hat in salute, and kept it off as Davenant advanced to meet him.

'Good afternoon, sir. This is a great honour. Would you be kind enough to accompany me below?'

The great cabin of the *Calypso* was smaller than that of the *Delaware*, as was only to be expected, and its permanent fittings were if anything even more spartan. Peabody had an impression of a multiplicity of ornaments–objects collected by Davenant during thirty years of commissioned service–but he had no attention to spare for them because his attention was held by the persons in the room. There were two other British naval officers there, on their feet to welcome him–he recognised them as having been present at the ball–and looking over the shoulder of one of them was, of all people in the world, Hunningford the spy, Hunningford whom he had last seen sailing away from the secret rendezvous after giving him the information regarding the Jamaica convoy. As their eyes met Hunningford's left eyelid flickered momentarily; but Peabody's wits were about him and he kept his face expressionless and with no sign of recognition.

'Allow me to present,' said Davenant, 'Captain Fane, His Majesty's corvette *Racer*, Commander Maitland, His Majesty's armed brig *Bulldog*, and Mr Charles Hunningford, one of our most respected Kingston merchants–

Captain Josiah Peabody.'

Everybody bowed.

'There's a mixture of rum and lime which is popular on this island and which ought to be better known,' said Davenant. 'The secret lies in a grating of nutmeg, I fancy. Will you sit here, Captain Peabody? Maitland–Fane–Mr Hunningford.'

Peabody realised in an amused moment that Davenant was actually shy, oppressed by the strange circumstance of entertaining a hostile captain, and endeavouring to carry it off with bluff and bustle.

'Your health, gentlemen,' said Davenant, raising his glass, and everyone sipped solemnly, and then looked at everyone else, the ice still not broken.

'Haven't had the chance to congratulate you on your marriage, sir,' said Fane, stepping into the breach. 'Devilish lovely wife you've got.'

'Thank you, sir.'

'Here's to the bride,' said Maitland, and everyone sipped again, and then sat silent. Peabody was enjoying himself. He felt he had a position well up to windward, and had no intention of running down to meet the others. Let them beat up to him. Davenant cleared his throat.

'The fact is, Captain Peabody,' he began, 'we are all wondering how long this damned ridiculous situation is going to last.'

'Yes?' said Peabody. He could not have said less without being rude.

'Our armistice–if that is what you are pleased to call it–comes to an end shortly. And then what happens?'

'We each have ideas on that point,' said Peabody.

'You get up sail. I get up sail, just as we did before. We start out of the bay together, and that Jack in office of a French Governor–I beg your pardon, sir. I was forgetting he was your father-in-law, but all the same he threatens to turn the guns on us. Back we go and try again. You see what I mean?'

'Yes,' said Peabody. He had followed the same line of thought himself–so, for that matter had everyone in Martinique with any ideas in his head at all.

'So we sit and look at each other until we all go aground on our own damned beefbones?'

'My men like pork better,' said Peabody drily.

Something was coming of this interview, and he was prepared to wait indefinitely for it. His frivolous reply drew a gesture of impatience from Davenant.

'I might have guessed what your attitude would be, sir,' he said.

Peabody nearly said: 'Then why did you ask me to come?' but he kept his mouth shut and preserved his tactical advantage. He looked round at the three sullen British faces and the enigmatical expression of Hunningford, and it was the last named who broke the silence.

'Perhaps,' he began deferentially, with a glance at Davenant, 'if I told Captain Peabody my news it might influence him?'

'I want you to tell him,' said Davenant, and Hunningford addressed himself directly to Peabody.

'There are pirates at work in the Caribbean,' he said.

'Indeed?' said Peabody politely. 'I've never known the time when there weren't.'

That was true; minor piracy had flourished in the Caribbean from the days of Drake.

'Yes,' said Hunningford, 'but never on the scale of to-day. Now that peace has come half the privateersmen in the world are out of employment. Spaniards–negroes from Haiti–Frenchmen—'

'I can understand that,' said Peabody.

'Losses are heavy already and will be heavier still. The Cartagena packet was taken last week.'

'Oh, tell him what happened to you, Hunningford,' said Davenant impatiently.

'Yesterday my cutter was chased by a pirate schooner. It was only by the mercy of Providence that I got into St Pierre.'

'I'm glad you escaped,' said Peabody politely.

'I've been chased by pirates before. Big row boats putting out from San Domingo, and guarda-costa luggers whose crews have been starved into piracy by the Spanish Government. One expects that. But when it comes to a big schooner, ten guns on a side, and heavy metal at that—'

'I know the schooner you mean,' said Peabody, surprised into his first helpful remark.

'You've seen her?'

'Yes. I chased her off Dominica. She looked Baltimore built to me, and French rigged. I thought she was an American privateer.'

'Baltimore built and French rigged is nearly right. She was the *Susanna* of Baltimore, dismasted in a hurricane two years back and put into Port au Prince. A French syndicate bought her there. They put Lerouge in command–he's a Haitian negro who served in Boney's navy–and manned her with blacks.'

'What else do you expect of Frogs?' interposed Davenant bitterly.

'They'll never see a penny of their money, if that's any satisfaction,' said Hunningford. 'Lerouge has been nothing more than a pirate for months back. And now with all the Americas on the move against Spain he'll have plenty of plunder and plenty of chance to dispose of it, which is just as important to him. God knows how much he took out of the Cartagena packet. But there were three women on board–two of 'em young.'

'He'd look well at a yardarm,' said Davenant.

'But what has all this to do with me?' asked Peabody.

'How can I catch him and hang him when I'm tied up here in Fort de France with all these French neutrality laws and harbour rules and God-knows-what?' asked Davenant in reply. 'Let me get my ships out and he'll hang in a week.'

'D'ye think you'd catch him?' said Peabody.

'Catch him? Catch him? Why–why–what do you mean, sir?'

'The *Susanna* was one of the fastest schooners which ever left Baltimore, sir,' said Hunningford.

'She got to windward of the *Delaware* and was hull down in half a day,' said Peabody.

'The *Delaware*! He'd never get away from *Calypso* on a bowline,' said Davenant, but even as he said it the lofty confidence in his tone ebbed away.

He had not commanded British frigates for eighteen years without learning something of the deficiencies of the vessels, and he was quite enough of a realist to be able to allow for them. It was a wrench to have to admit their existence to an American captain and a civilian, all the same.

'I take it, then,' said Peabody, keeping the argument on a practical plane, 'that what you want me to do is to give you a free passage out of the bay to deal with this pirate?'

'That is correct, sir,' said Davenant. He had known beforehand that his plea would not have one chance in a hundred of being granted, which was probably why he had deferred stating it in plain words.

Peabody thought for a full minute, twisting his glass in his fingers and paying careful attention to the powdered nutmeg afloat on the surface.

'I think it is quite impossible,' he said slowly. 'I will give you my definite decision later.'

'But see here, sir,' expostulated Davenant, and then he changed his tone. 'It's what I might have expected of a Yankee skipper. You fellows can't see farther than your noses. Here's all America in a flame, as Hunningford has said. That fellow Bolivar's on the rampage through Venezuela–he licked the Dagoes at Carabobo last spring. These waters will be swarming with letters of marque and privateers with commissions from Bolivar and Morelos, flying the flags of Venezuela and New Granada and Mexico and God knows what next. Pirates? How long will it take a Venezuelan privateer to become a pirate? Give 'em a lesson now and it'll save two dozen next year.'

'Your country's trade with these islands is nearly as big as ours,' said Fane.

'Yes,' said Peabody, rising to his feet. He was not going to be rushed into a hasty decision by an eloquent Englishman. 'I'll think about it.'

He turned to Davenant and repeated the formula he had heard Preble use after an official reception at Valletta.

'I must thank you, sir, for a delightful entertainment.'

As he turned to bow to the others Hunningford was catching Davenant's eye.

'Take Mr Hunningford with you, sir,' pleaded Davenant. 'His business connections with the United States should enable him to put the case clearer than I have done, perhaps. You will be able to question him freely in private.'

Peabody made himself hesitate while he counted ten inside himself before he spoke.

'I really don't see the use of it,' he said. 'But if Mr–er–Hunningford would accompany me in my gig—?'

'I'll come gladly,' said Hunningford.

Down in the gig Hunningford looked up at the sun.

'Devilish hot even for this time of year,' he said.

'So I thought,' said Peabody politely.

It was not until they were safely in Peabody's cabin and the skylight was shut that Hunningford allowed himself to relax. He ran his finger round inside his collar.

'That feels better,' he said. 'Whenever I am on board a King's ship I feel a peculiar sense of constriction in the neighbourhood of my larynx.'

'What the devil were you doing there?' demanded Peabody.

'It is part of my duty to be where there's trouble,' said Hunningford. 'Naturally I paid my respects to the British Commodore in the hope of acquiring information which might be useful to the United States Navy in the person of yourself. But I must admit I did not anticipate all the subsequent developments.'

'Is it true about the pirate?'

'Yes, curiously enough it is. I made my little adventure with the *Susanna* the pretext for my visit to the *Calypso*. I was naturally going to wait for a dark night on shore before I saw you next. I had not made sufficient allowance for the excitement a mention of piracy rouses in the British Navy. I wish I could take all the credit for this present admirable arrangement, but, much to my regret, I cannot. My native honesty forbids.'

'And now you're here, what's the news?'

'Plenty. And some of it's bad. Decatur's gone.'

'Decatur? Is he–dead?'

Hunningford shook his head.

'No, he tried to escape from New York in the *President*. They caught him off Sandy Hook and he had to haul down his colours.'

'Good God!' Peabody thought of Decatur eating his heart out in Dartmoor Prison. It was a horrible mental picture. 'What else?'

'The *Argus* is lost, too. I don't know how, yet, except that she was taken in British waters.'

With the *President* and the *Argus* gone the same way as the *Chesapeake*, the United States Navy was diminishing to minute proportions. There were only the *Essex*, somewhere in the Pacific, and the *Delaware* left to display the Stars and Stripes at sea.

'What else?'

'A British force took Washington. The militia ran, and the Capitol's been burned, and the last I heard they were moving on Baltimore.'

Peabody had nothing to say now. He had no words left at all.

'But there's good news as well. You knew of Perry's victory on Lake Ontario? Yes. That was before you sailed. Now Macdonough's won a battle on Lake Champlain. The Canadian frontier's safe.'

Tom Macdonough was Peabody's immediate junior on the captain's list–Peabody remembered him at Tripoli under Decatur's command. Peabody called up before his mind's eye the map of the Canadian frontier. With the American flag triumphant on Champlain and Ontario there was nothing more to be feared from the north, as Hunningford had remarked. Perry and Macdonough could both of them be relied upon not to allow the local command they had attained to slip through their fingers again, and the strongest sea power in the world would for once be baulked on water.

'That puts a different complexion on it,' he said.

The long Atlantic seaboard was exposed to British attack, it was true, but it was hardly possible that the British should attempt serious conquest. The raid on Washington assumed smaller proportions immediately.

'And one more thing,' said Hunningford. 'Mr Madison has sent to Europe to discuss peace.' Hunningford's voice as well as his face were quite expressionless as he said this.

'Well?' said Peabody drily. 'That makes no difference to my position here.'

He was right. If he did his best to fight a war he would be doing his best to influence an advantageous peace, and if the peace discussions proved inconclusive he would not be found to have wasted any opportunity.

'It is my business to tell you all there is to know,' said Hunningford. 'Thank God I don't have to instruct you on how to act on the information as well. To say nothing of the fact that you'd see me damned before you allowed me to.'

Peabody grinned his agreement.

'I'd see you worse than that,' he said.

'What are you going to do about this proposal of Davenant's?'

'Nothing, I fancy,' said Peabody. 'I'm not going to let him out of here because of a pirate on better terms than I'd give him at any other time.'

'You're right,' said Hunningford. 'Not that you mind what I think, of course. But it's irksome, all the same, to think of that black devil, Lerouge, raising hell in the Caribbean.'

'I have the United States to think of first,' said Peabody.

'When honest men fall out,' said Hunningford, 'rogues come by other people's property. The world is at peace except for us. The Americas are open for trade for the first time since the world began. Every merchant in the world wants to start business again–I hope, Captain, that you will not take too violent objection if I inject a little treason into what I say. There's no reason on earth left why we should go on fighting. Trade with Europe is open again–or would be if the British Navy was not in the way. They don't want to press our men any more. They don't want to search our ships. And yet you and Davenant sit in Martinique watching each other like dogs across a bone. What is more, you allow gentlemen like Lerouge to run off with the bone while you watch each other. And I, who flatter myself that I might be a useful member of society, spend my days with a rope round my neck facing the imminent possibility that at any moment it may grow much tighter than is convenient. Please don't for a moment think I am complaining, Captain. I am merely commenting at large upon the inconsistencies of the situation. From my reading of history I would rather continue to court the end I have just mentioned than the usually much more unpleasant one of the man who sets out to put the world to rights.'

19

Mrs Josiah Peabody was at work with her needle in the candle-lit drawing room of the little house on the hill. Beside her stood her empty coffee cup, and opposite sat her husband. For once in a way his usually clear-thinking mind was in an extraordinary muddle. He had thought about the string of events which had helped to change the unpronounceable Mlle Anne de Breuil into Mrs Josiah Peabody. He had thought about the coincidence that those same events enabled him to sit here watching her, under the monotonous swaying of the fan, secure in the knowledge that the British squadron, restrained by its senior officer's pledged word, would make no attempt to steal a march on him for two more days. Naturally he had thought about the *Delaware*, for he was never awake five minutes consecutively without thinking about her. She was fully stored with provisions and water again, her crew rested, her rigging newly set-up, ready for a six months' campaign. The gold which he had taken from the *Princess Augusta* had paid for everything–the fresh provisions, the fruit which had got his men back into health, the shore leave which had utterly reconciled them to a fresh voyage. He was a lucky man, and what he could see of Anne's cheek and neck as she bent over her needlework was lovelier than the set of the *Delaware*'s foretopsail. And Lerouge was hanging about off Cape St Martin, paralysing shipping, and which his duty really was regarding him—

Anne looked up as Peabody stirred in his chair.

'Father told me about the pirate,' she said. Already it had ceased to be a surprise to Peabody when Anne's remarks exactly chimed in with his own thoughts.

'Yes, dear,' he said. There was still a pleasant novelty about using the endearment.

'And Aunt Sophie told me about what Captain Davenant wants to do,' went on Anne.

'Oh, did she?' said Peabody.

He felt a slight shrinking of the flesh at the words. This was a hint of something he had feared, deep down within him. Women were interfering in man's business, and that meant trouble. The phrase 'petticoat government' drifted into his mind; much as he loved his wife he would never give her the smallest opportunity of discussing–which meant diverting him from–his duty.

'Captain Davenant and Aunt Sophie are growing very friendly,' went on Anne.

And Davenant is trying to get the women to do his dirty work for him, thought Peabody, but aloud he only said: 'I suspected as much myself.'

'He's quite furious about the pirate. And the people here are distressed as well. I suppose you've seen the ships in the bay which daren't go out. They're the first ships to leave Martinique for France for eleven years, and it's going to cause a lot of trouble to everyone. Monsieur Godron was telling me that he's afraid he'll lose the market in France and it'll ruin him.'

'Wars often ruin people,' said Peabody unhelpfully. He felt all the irritation of a fighting man, whose life is in peril from day to day, against the man of peace whose worries about his money merely complicate the issue.

'But I can't help feeling sorry for Monsieur Godron all the same,' said Anne.

'Now look here,' said Peabody. 'I can't do anything about it, dear. That's as precise as I can make it. I've got to—'

He restrained himself. He had almost allowed himself to tell his wife of his intention to hang on in Fort de France, watching for an opportunity to escape, keeping the British squadron eating their heads off there, and hoping for some shift in the circumstances of which he could take advantage. But he shut his mouth tight; he was not going to allow even a hint of his military intentions to escape him. He had not told Hubbard, and he would not tell Anne.

'It's very difficult for you, dear, and I know it,' said Anne.

Peabody saw the softness in her eyes. He had the sudden fresh realisation that his problems were as important to her as to him; that the peril in which he stood was far more of a strain upon her than upon him. The knowledge was liable to lose its reality with the passage of time. He spent necessarily so many hours thinking about the inevitable eventual end to the adventures of the *Delaware*; he had to calculate upon the destruction of the *Delaware*, upon the extreme likelihood of his own death, upon the probable termination of his own professional career. Long thinking about his approaching ruin and death made them loom even larger in his emotion than they deserved, and made it hard to realise–what was undoubtedly true–that they meant to Anne as much as or more than they meant to him. And it was hard when he allowed childish resentment against Providence to master him, not to be resentful at the same time against Anne who had only to sit back and have no worries about the proper employment of the *Delaware*, no insidious inward thoughts about the round shot which would one day dash him in red ruin on his own quarterdeck–smash him into pulp as he remembered Crane the master smashed into pulp beside the wheel.

But Peabody knew again now that thoughts like that were not nearly as painful to him as Anne's thoughts were to her, and that she shut her mouth as firmly over them as he did over his military plans. He bent forward towards her and touched the hand with the long slender fingers.

'I love you so much, dear,' said Anne.

Peabody did not say 'I love you,' in return, as he well might have done. He gave instead the most positive proof of it, by allowing the inertia of his previous train of thought to carry him on into a technical discussion with a mere woman whose knowledge of ships was of course negligible.

'Davenant couldn't do anything even if I let him go,' he said. 'That schooner of Lerouge's is Baltimore built and as fast as anything that sails. He'd never catch her with that tub of a *Calypso*–not even the *Racer* would do it. I chased the *Susanna* myself, a week back–By God!'

He had broken off what he was saying and was staring at her. It was odd that even at this moment when a fresh plan was forming in his mind, with a rapidity and a completeness which startled him, that he should still be able to note simultaneously with a thrill of pleasure how straight her brows were and how steady were the blue eyes below them. They smiled at him now.

'You've thought of something interesting,' said Anne.

'Yes,' said Peabody.

He got to his feet and walked back and forward across the room. Davenant would agree, he was sure. Peabody's logical and essentially matter-of-fact mind brushed aside the fact that the plan he had in mind was probably unprecedented. That was no argument against it. On the surface the plan was ludicrous, too–and that was an argument in favour of it. And–there were new aspects, new developments, revealing themselves as he thought about it. He smacked his right fist into his left hand to clinch the argument with himself, and stopped short in his pacing of the room to look down at Anne who was looking up at him.

'I beg your pardon, dear,' he said.

'I like it,' said Anne, simply.

Peabody caught her up to him and kissed her, and she kissed him back, her lips moving against his. This was stranger and more delightful than ever. It had never occurred to Peabody that plans for war and passion for his wife could coexist. He would have said earlier that it was as impossible that two masses should occupy the same space at the same time. The one thing was perfectly possible, as the present moment proved, and everything was so delirious that he would not be surprised if the other were possible despite what Euclid might say to the contrary. The excitement of caution gave an edge to his passion. Because he had thought of a method of dealing with Lerouge he could kiss Anne with added fervour; conceivably the prospect of immediate action in place of possible weeks of inactivity played its part as well. Anne saw the light dancing in his eyes and was glad. To Peabody it was all mad–mad–mad. It was mad that he should have thought of his plan while Anne's hand was actually in his. It was mad that at the same moment that his brain was seething with suggestions for the destruction of Lerouge it should be seething with warm images of Anne. It was mad that he could kiss thus, and that he should have his passions sweep him away and yet that he should feel no sense of sin. The white throat on which he set his lips was sweeter than the sweetest honey he had known in his hard childhood. The soft sleep which came at last in Anne's scented arms was something life had never given him before. The drugged, swinish oblivion that drink had given him in his youth, and which had sometimes seemed so alluring, was not to be compared with this sleep, hopeful and yet with desire all burned away. And the oblivion of death of which he had sometimes allowed himself to think longingly, blank and loveless like his life until now, could no longer be thought of. Anne, in the darkness, his face against her breast, knew that he smiled in his sleep. She loved him enough to be happy on that account, whether he was smiling because he was in her arms or because in his sleep his mind was still at work upon the details of plans to deal with Lerouge the pirate.

20

Captain Sir Hubert Davenant had said it was most irregular. He had gobbled like a turkey cock about it when it had been first suggested to him, mouthing his words in his queer London accent, and yet it had only taken a few minutes to convince him both of the essential reasonableness of the scheme and also of its likelihood of success.

'Fox and geese, eh?' he said, with the chart spread before him. 'We'll chase Mr Fox Lerouge into a tighter trap than he knows of.'

The Marquis had given the scheme his unqualified assent when he was consulted about it. He had offered the services of the *Tigresse* to stop the least obvious of the bolt-holes through the Saintes' Passage, and he had looked upon his son-in-law with something more than approval when the scheme was made clear to him. The military details–the need for complete secrecy to ensure surprise–he accepted as a matter of course, even though Davenant and Peabody, glancing at each other across the council table, expressed secretly to each other by their look their certainty that the *Tigresse* with her French crew would be horribly mauled if ever she found herself broadside to broadside with the *Susanna*. The Marquis had pledged his word to the execution of his part of the scheme–the issuing of sealed orders to Dupont in the *Tigresse* and the sudden reversal of orders at sunset to the captain of the port and the officers commanding in the batteries.

Night was coming on apace when Peabody in the *Delaware* began to make the first of his preparations for sea. Eight p.m., well after dark, was the time appointed for the start.

'We don't want to spoil the ship for a ha'porth o' tar,' said Davenant when the time was being discussed–in other words, they did not want to risk disclosing their plans to any possible informers in Martinique for the sake of gaining an extra half hour perhaps of darkness; besides, by that time the first puffs of the land breeze would help to get them clear of the harbour.

'Mr Hubbard,' said Peabody. 'We are leaving Fort de France to-night.'

'Aye aye, sir,' said Hubbard, and then, 'pardon me, sir, but have you squared the port captain?'

'No,' said Peabody. 'But we'll be allowed to leave. The British squadron will be leaving at the same time. So will the *Tigresse*.'

'Geewhillikins, sir,' said Hubbard; the dark mobile face lengthened in surprise, and Peabody relented. There was no sense or purpose in keeping his first lieutenant in the dark.

'The unofficial armistice is still going on,' he said. 'All we're going to do is to catch this Haitian pirate, Lerouge. After that we meet again in Fort de France and start again on the same terms as before. I've given my parole to that effect.'

'I see, sir,' said Hubbard. He digested the astonishing information slowly. 'It won't do the men any harm to get them to sea again for a time.'

Curiosity struggled with discipline, and curiosity won in the end.

'Pardon me, sir,' said Hubbard again. 'But was this your idea?'

'Yes.'

'It's a damned clever idea, too, sir, if you'll allow me to say so.'

'I'll allow you to.'

'The French'll be as pleased as Punch if we get this Lerouge out of the way. I suppose they've said so, sir?'

'They have.'

'And we keep the ball rolling that much longer without risk to ourselves. Oh, that's great, sir.'

'I'm glad you think so, Mr Hubbard. We'll get under way at four bells in the second dog watch.'

'Aye aye, sir.'

The land breeze was breathing very faintly when the *Delaware* got under sail in the darkness–she crept over the black water with hardly a sound of water rippling under her sharp bows.

'There's the *Tigresse*, sir,' said Hubbard to Peabody, pointing through the darkness to where a faint nucleus of greater darkness was just visible.

'Yes,' said Peabody, and he pointed in return over the quarter. 'And here come the British.'

The *Calypso* in the van could be almost recognised; the *Bulldog* in the rear was hardly visible at all, but enough could be seen to make plain how well handled were the three ships in their line ahead. Peabody felt a queer feeling of comfort. For months he had been at sea in continuous imminent danger, with every man's hand against him and not a friend within call. Even though he knew this present interlude to be a brief one, there was something pleasant about having even temporary friends. The thought of friends carried his mind inevitably to his wife. By now she would have received his note–'Dearest, I shall not be coming home to-night, as I have duties to perform in the ship. Please keep the servants thinking that you still expect me, as it is important that the news that I am not returning be delayed as long as possible. And will you please forgive me for leaving you like this, dear? It is my duty that takes me from you. Your father will explain why to-morrow. I shall see you again in a week.'

That note had been hard to write–Peabody had written nothing except formal letters all his life. It had been the first time he had written the word 'dearest,' and the first time he had ever written 'dear' in the middle of a letter, but it had not been that which had made the writing hard. It had been hard to face the fact that he had not admitted his wife into his confidence, that in the deep secrecy in which the move had been planned he had not made an exception of Anne. But that was where his duty lay. Military secrets must be told to no one unnecessarily, and he had told no one. Anne, waiting for him, would be hurt and disappointed–that was what made it hard. Later she might be hurt again when she realised that he had not trusted her, and that would be harder still. Peabody drummed on the rail with his fingers, and then suddenly he knew that Anne would understand.

'Course South by East, Mr Hubbard,' he said.

'South by East, sir.'

They would weather Cape Solomon now. In three hours–less if the breeze freshened as it should–they would be rounding Cabrit. It would be a long reach back to the Caravelle, but they should be there well before dawn, and the British, weathering Cape St Martin in the opposite direction, would drive Lerouge straight into his grasp. And in any event it was a joy to feel the lift and surge of the *Delaware* again beneath his feet, to hear the wind in the rigging and the music of the sea under her forefoot. Peabody recalled himself guiltily at the thought that at this very moment he might instead have been in Anne's arms–a wife certainly deprived life of its primitive simplicity in exchange for enriching it. It was an effort to dismiss the thought from his mind. A wife was a wife and his duty was his duty. He bellowed a sharp reprimand at the captain of the foretop, and had the weather foretopgallant studdingsail taken in and reset, and, having relieved himself of some of this unaccustomed internal stress, he made himself go below to rest for a few hours before dawn. He was a little afraid as he composed himself to sleep, lest married life was softening him.

'Eight bells, sir,' said Washington, allowing the cabin door to slam as a gust of the fresh Trades came into the stuffy cabin. 'A clear night, sir. Ship's on the starboard tack, sir. What shirt, sir?'

'The one I've got on,' said Peabody, swinging himself out of his cot. 'Bring me a cup of coffee on the quarterdeck.'

Murray was officer of the watch; he came up in the darkness while Peabody sipped his coffee and studied the traverse board and the scrawled writing on the slate which constituted the deck log.

'We're nearly up to the Caravelle, sir. You can hear the surf on the cays.'

'It's a nasty coast,' said Peabody.

With all these Lesser Antilles, practically without exception, the Atlantic side, to windward, was without real harbours, and dangerous with reefs and cays. The main life of the islands was carried on on the leeward Caribbean side, where were to be found the anchorages and the large towns. The rule held true from Antigua down to Trinidad.

'Lay the ship on the other tack, Mr Murray, if you please. I want to be five miles farther to windward by dawn.'

Lerouge would certainly be taken by surprise. He would be aware of the dead end which had been reached in Fort de France by the *Delaware* and the British squadron, and he would be counting on a free hand until the matter had been decided and an action had been eventually fought and repairs effected; and he probably had sources of information in Martinique on which he would rely for ample warning. The sudden appearance at dawn of the British squadron would surprise him, but would hardly imperil him; he would set all sail and leave them easily behind. But it would be a very different story when the *Delaware*, fast and handy, appeared right across his course, with the British spread wide in pursuit behind him. The moon was behind clouds and setting fast.

'Mr Murray! I want the best men you've got at the mastheads at the next relief.'

'Aye aye, sir.'

The *Delaware* was beating to windward close-hauled; it would be safe to leave an even greater distance between her and the island. With the wind abaft the beam, Peabody fancied that she would be faster than the *Susanna*, and the courses would converge if Lerouge did not want to pile his schooner on the coast–although that might be the way to prolong his life to the maximum. The tops of the waves going by were already growing a little more visible; there was enough light from the eastern sky to show up their ghostly white. This trade wind air, clean and fresh after its journey across three thousand miles of sea, was delicious after the stuffiness of Fort de France. Along the eastern horizon now there was a decidedly noticeable line of brighter colour, almost green by comparison with the deep blue of the area above it. It was widening, too, and changing in colour; the green was shifting into yellow, and now the yellow was changing into orange and from orange to red. Miraculously the sky was brightening. During the last few minutes everything on deck had become visible. Then the *Delaware* rose on a wave, and as she rose a little fleck of bright gold was visible peeping over the horizon to the east. It disappeared as she sank again, but at the next wave it was there, larger and plainer, and at the following wave it was clear broad day, with the sun fully over the horizon.

'Now,' said Peabody to himself. 'Where's our friend, Lerouge?'

It would be a disappointment if he had doubled back on his track to run into the *Tigresse* in the Saintes' Passage; it would be a far worse disappointment if he had got clear away from the British altogether. But he had done all he could do, and he had nothing for which to blame himself in that event. He looked up at the masthead to make sure that the lookouts were attending to their duty; the *Delaware* was as close to the wind as she would lie, thrashing away with the big Atlantic rollers bursting under her bows and bright rainbows playing on either side of her. Far back on the lee quarter lay the mountains of Martinique, a pale purple against the blue sky. On the far side of them Anne was waking alone in the big bed with the vast dome of mosquito netting over it. Between the ship and the island were the innumerable cays and reefs of the windward shore, revealed mainly by the white surf which burst continually against them–the long peninsula of the Caravelle showed itself as a green chalk mark along the dazzling white.

'Sail on the weather beam!' came a hail from the masthead. Hubbard raced with half a dozen midshipmen up to various points of vantage aloft.

'She's that schooner, sir. And heading straight for us.'

'Clear for action, Mr Murray, if you please. Quartermaster! Keep her on the wind.'

'Schooner's hauling up, sir,' reported Murray.

'Will we weather her?'

'Yes, sir. Easily.'

So that was all right. If the *Delaware* had cut off her escape to windward, and Martinique lay to leeward, and astern of her lay the British squadron, the *Susanna*'s fate was sealed. It only remained to see which ship would take her–whether she would go about and face the British, or hold her course and fight the *Delaware*. The guns were being cast off and run out, the decks were being sanded, and from below came the clatter of the bulkheads being taken down. Peabody turned his glance to search the horizon on the larboard beam for any sign of the schooner, but the two ships were not near enough yet to be within sight of each other from the deck.

'If you please, sir,' hailed Hubbard, 'the schooner's put up her helm. She's come before the wind.'

''Bout ship, Mr Murray.'

The hands sprang from the guns to help at the sheets and braces, and the *Delaware* came round like a top. As she steadied on her new course Peabody caught his first glimpse of the schooner, the rectangles of her big topsails against the sky.

'Starboard a point,' he said to the helmsman, and then, hailing the masthead, 'you can come down now, Mr Hubbard.'

He had the schooner under his own personal observation now, and he could lay his own course. He would intercept her before either she could pile herself up on the cays or–as was probably Lerouge's hope–escape into dangerous waters where no ship would dare follow her.

'I thought I could see the *Racer*'s royals just before I came down, sir,' said Hubbard. 'I wasn't sure enough to report it.'

'I expect you were right,' said Peabody.

'Hope we get her before she comes up, sir,' said Hubbard.

'We will if she holds that course much longer.'

On their converging courses the schooner and the *Delaware* were nearing each other fast. Peabody could already see the gaffs of her big fore and mainsails. She was going through the water very fast, but no faster than the *Delaware* with all sail set and the trade wind blowing hard over her quarter.

'She's a lovely little ship,' said Hubbard. 'Pity she fell into the wrong hands.'

'She'll be in the right ones again soon enough,' said Peabody. 'Mr Murray! Load with canister. I want this done quick and clean. One broadside as we come alongside and then we'll board her in the smoke.'

'Aye aye, sir.'

But Lerouge had no intention of submitting to a close-range action without an attempt to dodge past the frigate which lay between him and life. Peabody saw the big fore and aft sails flap, saw the schooner spin on her heel as she wore round, and at the first sign of the manoeuvre he was already bawling the order which brought the *Delaware* to the wind, close hauled on the same track. Peabody knew that the schooner would not hold this course for long, heading as she was back towards the British squadron and narrowing her already small free area of sea. He saw the schooner's sails shiver again as though she were preparing to tack. No, she would not do that–it would bring her too close to the *Delaware*. It must be a feint to induce him to put the *Delaware* about so that while the big frigate was engaged in the manoeuvre Lerouge would dodge back again. He smiled to himself in the exciting pleasure of quick thinking and shouted further orders. The *Delaware* came up a little closer to the wind; the headsail sheets were brought across, and the *Delaware*'s sails flapped thunderously. That was convincing enough. Lerouge was expecting the *Delaware* to tack, and now that she showed all the signs of it he put his helm up again and spun the schooner round in his desperate effort to drive past the *Delaware*. But the moment Peabody saw his masts separate he was ready with his orders. Over went the helm, back came the headsail sheets, and he had beaten Lerouge in the race. Already the two ships were near.

'We've got her now!' yelled Murray at the top of his voice, apparently without knowing he was speaking.

Peabody could make out the individuals on the schooner's deck. Aft there was a red spot–that was Lerouge; perhaps to play on his name he wore habitually a red coat looted from the baggage of some British officer. He could see the bustle on the schooner's deck–could see the guns' crews bending to their work. Next moment the schooner was wreathed in smoke and the air was full of the sound of round shot. The maintopmast stay parted with a loud snap, but that was all the damage done, and the two vessels were still nearing each other. Once more Lerouge feinted, turning the schooner to port, towards the *Delaware*, and then spinning suddenly back to starboard, but Peabody was not to be deceived by the feint. He held his course for a few more seconds and then ported his helm–all the extra manoeuvrability of the schooner availed nothing when her captain was being outguessed by a shrewd opponent.

He was on the schooner's quarter now, and the vessels were not a cable's length apart. Another broadside–a crash below and a hole in the forecourse. The schooner would have to dodge again at once, or submit meekly to having the *Delaware* run alongside her. Here it came! Peabody had foreseen it and was ready.

'Hard a starboard!' he ordered to the quartermaster, and then lifting his voice, 'starboard guns!'

The neat turn brought the ships close together, heading in the same direction.

'Hard a port now,' said Peabody, and as the *Delaware*'s broadside crashed out, frigate and schooner came together in the smoke.

Peabody's fighting blood was racing through his veins. He had drawn his sword and swung himself into the mizzen rigging.

'Boarders!' he yelled.

There was no need for self-control now, no need for clear thinking. He could fling himself into the fight, abandoning himself to the mad impulse of it all, and recompense himself for months of rigid caution. He scrambled down into the mizzen chains and dropped on to the schooner's deck, sword in hand. Behind him the *Delaware* swung round pushing the schooner before her, widening the gap between the vessels' sterns and closing it at their bows, while the boarders jostled each other at the main-deck ports, and he was left all alone–and unconscious of it–abaft the wheel on the schooner's deck.

The hurricane of canister had swept the schooner like a broom. There were dead men everywhere, and only a few half-naked black figures were grabbing weapons to meet the attack. But not five yards from Peabody was Lerouge in his red coat with the gold lace flashing in the sun, eyes and teeth gleaming in his black face, and Peabody leaped forward to cut him down. His sword clashed on Lerouge's guard; Peabody cut again, the cut was warded off, and then he thrust and thrust again at the bosom of the red coat. He might as well have been thrusting at a stone wall.

It dawned upon him that Lerouge was a swordsman who must have picked up the art of fencing during his service in the French Navy. He feinted and lunged; the lunge was parried, and he lunged again desperately to anticipate the riposte. That riposte would come soon, he knew already. Only while he could maintain this fierce attack was his life safe–the moment it slackened Lerouge's blade would dart forward and kill him, he knew. He beat against Lerouge's blade, thrusting first over and then under, his iron strength and long reach only a poor compensation for his lack of skill, trying to remember his early lessons in swordsmanship, and the course of a dozen hours in fencing he had received twelve years ago from the Maltese fencing master in Valetta. The blades rasped harshly together, jarring his fingers as they gripped his sword-hilt, and only in the nick of time did he beat aside the first thrust which Lerouge had made. This was death, death in the hot sun; the loud noises of battle which he heard about him reached his consciousness as faintly as the squeaking of mice.

Lerouge's mirthless grin, as his thick lips parted snarling, seemed to grow wider and wider until Peabody seemed to see nothing else. The sword-blades slipped apart, and Peabody made a wild blind effort to cover himself. There was a sudden burning pain in his right forearm, and his sword-hilt escaped from his paralysed fingers. Desperately he leaped forward; chance–or his own rapid instinctive reactions–put Lerouge's sword-blade into his left hand, low down by the guard, and he tore the weapon out of his path as he closed with his powerful antagonist. His right arm was paralysed no longer as he flung it round Lerouge. His left hand battled against Lerouge's right for control of the sword, his right behind Lerouge's back seized the golden epaulette on Lerouge's right shoulder, and his right foot was behind Lerouge's heel. He put out all his strength for the fall, was baulked, swayed to his left, and heaved again on one last insane effort. Lerouge's feet left the deck, and he fell with a crash, Peabody staggering above him with the sword in his left hand and the golden threads of the torn-off epaulette in his right.

The deck was thronged by now with American sailors cheering and shouting, and the din they were raising reached Peabody's ears now in its natural volume. Someone came rushing forward with a pike to pin Lerouge to the deck as he rolled over on his face, but Peabody kicked the weapon up in the nick of time.

'Tie him up, Harvey,' he said, recognising the man, and a dozen willing hands grabbed lengths of rope and bound Lerouge until he was helpless.

The schooner was captured–here came O'Brien running breathlessly aft with an American flag to hoist at her peak while the *Calypso* came tearing up with all sail set too late to show in the honour of the capture, and here came Captain Davenant, as fast as he could heave his ship to, and as fast as his gig could whisk him across the big Atlantic rollers.

'Congratulations, Peabody,' he said.

'Thank you, sir,' said Peabody.

It was pleasant to have made a clean job of the business before the British arrived.

'You are wounded, sir!' said Davenant.

Peabody looked down; blood was dripping slowly, in heavy blobs, down his right hand and falling on the deck. His right sleeve was heavy with blood as he moved his arm. And his left hand hurt him too–as he looked at it he saw that the horny palm had several haggled cuts across it where the nearly blunt part of Lerouge's blade had scored it.

'It's nothing,' said Peabody.

'Wounds in this climate are always important, sir,' said Davenant. 'Have you a capable surgeon? Hamilton, go back and fetch Doctor Clarke.'

The midshipman touched his cap and dashed off.

'My doctors are quite capable, thank you, sir,' said Peabody. He was conscious of a lassitude which was unusual to him and he did not want to argue about anything–the sun seemed too hot.

'They will probably be glad of Clarke's opinion all the same,' said Davenant, and then, looking round the schooner, 'and I suppose this is Lerouge?'

The burly negro in his red coat snarled again in his bonds as attention was drawn to him–Peabody remembered that snarl vividly.

'A nasty-looking customer,' said Davenant. 'Any other survivors?'

There were six of them, grouped round the mainmast, all bound. Two of them were squatting on the deck weeping aloud. Lerouge looked at the two captains and saw his death in their faces.

'St Amant'll hang 'em if we take 'em back to Fort de France,' said Davenant. 'It'll mean a trial and evidence and depositions, though. He's a whale for the letter of the law–we both know that.'

'We've taken 'em red-handed,' said Peabody. He knew the law of the sea and the instant fate which awaited pirates. His head was beginning to swim in the heat, and there was a hint of sickness in his stomach, although Lerouge deserved nothing better than was going to happen to him–something worse, if anything. Pirates captured at sea by the officers of a navy were hanged on the spot. Hubbard had turned up from somewhere, and his dark saturnine face wore a message of doom for the pirates, too; Peabody saw the two deep grooves between the bushy black eyebrows. Those grooves seemed to fill the whole seascape at that moment.

'Hang them,' said Peabody. He hardly recognized his own voice as he spoke.

His head was swimming worse than ever, and his impressions of the rest of the business were confused. He would never forget the wild struggles of the bound Lerouge as the hands dragged him away down the heaving deck, nor the screams of one of the other negroes and the ugly sound with which they ended. But blended with those memories were others of the doctors grouped round him, of cool bandages applied to his burning arm.

'Bind it up in the blood and leave the bandage unopened for a week, that's my practice,' said the pontifical Doctor Clarke to Doctor Downing across Peabody's recumbent body–this Clarke wore hairpowder which soiled the shoulders of his coat, Peabody saw. He did not know how he had got back to his cabin, but there he was, undoubtedly; and overhead was the clatter and rumble of the guns being secured again.

'I make it a rule never to have a rule,' said Downing. 'Open your hand, sir, if you please. Ah, no more than a few fibres severed, I fancy.'

21

'Turn to the other side, sir, please,' said Washington. He was shaving his captain with all the gusto Peabody expected of him. Washington had been perfectly delighted to find Peabody crippled in both arms–it gave him enormous pleasure to wait upon him hand and foot, to pass his shirt over his head and part his hair, and Peabody hated it. He had forbidden Washington to chatter while attending on him–curious how the act of shaving someone else seemed to loosen a man's tongue–but Washington side-stepped the order by asking Peabody to move his head as the operation demanded. Washington might well have suffered some internal injury as a result of accumulated pressure had he not done so, in fact–for the chance to say those few words he was willing even to forgo the pleasure of tweaking his captain's nose and turning his chin from side to side.

It was hateful to have Washington attend to him, and yet it was delicious to have Anne do so. There was enchantment in the touch of her slender fingers, always cool somehow in the sweltering heat of the West Indian autumn. There was a queer pleasure in being dependent upon Anne, for him who had made it a rule all his life to be dependent upon nobody. There was a mad shock of joy when he discovered for certain that there was pleasure for her in looking after him. She would stoop and slip the pumps from off his feet, the stockings from his legs, and she could smile while she did it. And when she took his head on her shoulder and put her lips against his forehead, troubles and anxieties and responsibilities lost their weight. Memories of a red-coated figure writhing in bonds were not nearly so acute then; even the memories were dulled of fighting a losing fight on the deck of the *Susanna*, of the imminent approach of sudden death.

That crossing of swords with Lerouge had had a profound effect upon Peabody, which even he realised. He was not the same man as had laid his ship so deftly alongside the *Susanna*, perhaps because of the unexpected nature of the danger he had encountered. He had thought of death from disease, of death among the waves of the sea, of unseen death from a flying cannon shot, but the death he had seen face to face had been at the hands of a negro pirate, and as a direct result of his own shortcomings in the mere matter of handling a sword. It had had an effect upon him similar to the spiritual upheaval of a religious experience, making him take fresh stock of himself, unsettling him; to feel his face against Anne's smooth throat, to know himself to be loved dearly–these were matters of desperate importance now in the impermanence of life. Yet even so Washington had to shave him.

The wounds healed quickly enough. Downing grudgingly admitted that in this particular case Dr Clarke's method of binding up clean cuts in the blood and leaving them was justifiable. Downing had a theory that the inconsequential behaviour of wounds was not as inconsequential as people thought, and that whether they turned gangrenous or not depended to a certain extent on whether some foreign agency were introduced into them. He was a little nervous about this theory, because he had seen wounds heal even with a lump of lead inside them, and wounds go gangrenous and refuse to close when there was simply nothing foreign to be seen about them, so that he laughed a little deprecatingly when he hinted that the sword-blade which had transfixed Peabody's forearm and cut his hand must have been quite clean, and he saw to it that the wounds were exposed as little as possible to the tropical air.

In these conditions they healed quickly–within three days he was allowed to take his right arm out of its sling, and his ability to use the fingers of his right hand relieved him of his hated dependence upon Washington, and as soon as the cuts on his palm had closed over Downing encouraged him to use his left hand, as well. Otherwise, as Downing said, there was a danger lest the scars should prevent his being able to extend his hand fully. There only remained a soreness deep down inside his right forearm, and an angry red blotch to show where Lerouge's sword had entered. That was all–save for a mental soreness, that continual feeling of humiliation at the memory of his helplessness before Lerouge. Peabody was wrongheaded about it; he had not felt fear at the time, and yet he suspected himself of it in the light of his present reactions. It made Anne's kisses all the sweeter, and yet their added sweetness did not mask the bitterness of the distorted memory. Anne, under the vast dome of the mosquito-net, with her husband at her side, was aware–as of course she would be–of the tangled unhappiness of the man.

The convalescent captain came on board his ship to the usual compliments. She was ready for sea again, complete in every particular; it was good to look round her and lay new plans for the future. But Hubbard, who came up to greet him was worried about something–Peabody could see it in his long face.

'We've got a couple of deserters on board, sir,' he said.

'Deserters from where?'

Hubbard jerked his head towards the British squadron which lay on the other side of the bay.

'They're off the *Calypso*, sir,' he said. 'They had a flogging coming to them and they didn't stay for it.'

'How did they get on board?'

'They swam here, sir, and climbed up through the hawsehole during the middle watch. The anchor watch ought to have seen 'em, sir. I've punished 'em already.'

'And the deserters are still here?'

'Yes, sir. Would you like to speak to 'em, sir?'

The two men were a fair sample of the sailors the British Navy had been forced to use in their desperate struggle against the whole world. Larsen was elderly, a Swede, slow spoken, and still unfamiliar with English. Williams was a Cockney, hardly more than twenty, pert and sly and with a desperate squint, a warehouse boy in a London draper's before a boating frolic on the Thames had brought him within the clutches of the press.

'What in hell did you come to my ship for?' demanded Peabody.

Williams jerked his thumb across the bay and winked with the eye which was under his control.

'They row guard every night between the ships and the quay, sir,' he said. 'I seen too many o' the boys try it, an' I seen wot 'appened to 'em arterward. We couldn't come nowhere but 'ere, sir.'

'But what did you want to desert for?'

'Me, sir? Captain's coxs'n, 'e copped me prigging from the cabin stores, sir. It'd ha' been five dozen for me this morning, sir. An' Larsen, 'ere. Well, sir, you can see 'ow slow 'e is, sir. Boatswain's mate 'ad a down on 'im, sir. Always in 'ot water, 'e was, sir.'

'Dat is zo,' said Larsen.

Peabody looked the two over again. He knew well enough what life on the lower deck of British ships of war was like–the fierce discipline necessary both to restrain the motley crews and to inculcate the unquestioning obedience which had carried the Navy through such sore trials; the bad food and worse conditions which were all that a bankrupt Admiralty could afford for its slaves; the feeling of a lifetime's condemnation as the war dragged on and on and the desperate straits of the British Government gave no chance of leave or release. And some petty tyrant had been abusing his power and making Larsen's life hell for him. He was sorry for the Swede, although he could feel no sympathy for the squinting Cockney who had deserted his colours.

'Do you want to take service with me?' he asked.

'Yessir,' said Williams eagerly.

He was one of that kind, who to save his skin would even fight against his own country. Peabody dallied with the idea of returning them both, with his compliments, to the *Calypso*. For the first attempt at desertion in the British Navy the punishment was a thousand lashes. For the second attempt, a milder punishment–death, after the worse had been tried and had failed. Williams read the thought in his face.

'You ain't goio'!uo!seoe us back, sir?'

'I'll think about it,' said Peabody. 'Take 'em for'rard.'

He could not send them back, of course. He could not give back two trained seamen to his country's enemies. He could not (as he would have liked to do) return Williams and keep Larsen. He disliked deserters, and he could sympathise very strongly with what would of course be Davenant's rections when he should hear that his men had taken refuge on board the *Delaware*, but he could not, just on that account, hand them back again. From the point of view of the politicians at Washington he was achieving something worth while in weakening the British forces–that was an aspect of the case which only crossed his mind later in the day when he was making ready for the reception on shore which was being given by 'Captain Henri-Francçois Dupont and the officers of His Most Christian Majesty's Navy.'

It was a function to which Anne had been looking forward with eagerness.

'Now the world will be able to see how well you can waltz, dear,' she said in the darkness of the carriage as they drove to the reception, and the recollection that the words called up, and the pretty trick of speech, set him smiling despite his preoccupation. It was a surprise to him to find that he, too, was looking forward to the party, to encountering the world with a wife he was proud of on his arm. He had never believed that he would ever know a pleasurable sensation while on his way to a social function.

Captain Dupont was a courteous host, when he received them in the drawing-room of his house above the quay. He asked politely about Peabody's wounds and he turned a pretty compliment about Anne's appearance. It was only when he had finished speaking to her and had turned back to her husband that he saw Peabody standing rigid, staring across the room with the hard lines carved deep in his face. He followed his gaze; there was Jonathan Peabody laughing and joking with half a dozen pretty women, his new wife watchful at his side.

'It is unfortunate, sir,' said Dupont. 'I am ready enough to admit that. But His Most Christian Majesty's Government can, of course, take no official cognition of the fact that young Mr Peabody is a deserter. We only know him as the husband of one of the richest and most influential landowners in the island.'

'I understand,' said Peabody, and the tone he used made it clear enough that while he understood he did not excuse. He turned away; there was no pleasure in the party for him now. He nodded to Hubbard and the others, who were entering the room eagerly, with all the freshness of their white gloves and glittering lace. Behind them came the British officers, Davenant and Fane side by side and their juniors following them. Peabody bowed to them as good manners dictated–just the slightest unbending towards an enemy on neutral soil. The Marquis was entering now, the Countess beside him, and the whole room rose to its feet in deference to the embodied presence of the direct representative of His Most Christian Majesty.

A few minutes later Peabody found himself alone–the Countess had taken Anne from him and had carried her off to where she was now the centre of an eager group of chattering women. Peabody wondered what on earth they found to talk about, seeing that most of that group saw each other every day, but he tried to smile tolerantly while he wandered through the rooms. At the far end of the suite was a room where a few elderly people were sitting round card tables, and Davenant and Fane were just emerging. Peabody stood politely aside to make way for them, but Davenant halted and addressed him.

'Good evening, Captain,' he said. 'I trust you are going to return those two deserters of mine?'

The words which ended in 'g' nearly had no 'g' at all, the way Davenant pronounced them.

'I don't intend to, sir,' said Peabody. He was a little nettled at Davenant's calm assumption of certainty.

'You don't intend to?'

Davenant's face exhibited a surprise which was not in the least rhetorical. With the capture of the *Susanna*, Davenant had come unconsciously to look upon the *Delaware* as a ship of war which could work with his own in matters not connected with the war between their countries, and Davenant, after forty years at sea, had grown to believe that naval discipline was the most vital and important factor in the civilised world. Peabody's refusal to return deserters would unsettle the crews of all the British ships. If Peabody had announced a determined belief in the community of property or of the necessity for every man to have nine wives, he could not have been more shocked.

'I don't intend to, sir,' repeated Peabody firmly.

'But, man, you don't understand what this means. D'you think I'm goin' to let a couple of deserters flaunt themselves within a cable's length of my own ship?'

That 'g' quite disappeared as Davenant grew more heated.

'They will flaunt themselves, sir, as you say, if the discipline of my ship permits.'

'Good God!'

The exclamation, as Davenant made it, was extraordinarily like the gobbling of a turkey, and Davenant's cheeks were deepening in colour like the wattles of a turkey. Peabody made no reply, and stood waiting to pass.

'Haven't you any sense of decency, man?' exploded Davenant.

Long years as captain of a ship had made it an unusual experience for Davenant to be crossed in his will, and for as many years he had never made any attempt to control his fiery temper. He did not stop to think what he would have said in reply to a request for the return, say, of a couple of American deserters.

'As much as other people have,' said Peabody, 'or more.'

Hubbard had miraculously appeared from nowhere, and was standing at his shoulder; Peabody was aware of the hush which had fallen about them as people listened to their words, but he did not take his eyes from Davenant's. There were strange feelings within him. He knew just whither this argument was leading, and he was strangely glad. Somewhere in the back of his mind was the memory of his fight with Lerouge, and his grim New England conscience was accusing him of fear during the crossing of swords. He must prove to himself that he had not been afraid. And life had been too good. Anne's kisses had been too sweet. With a desperate contrariness he felt he must imperil all his unaccustomed happiness to deserve it.

Fane had put his hand on Davenant's shoulder and was trying to lead him away, while Davenant's fierce temper refused to be mollified.

'It's what one might expect of Yankee trickiness,' he said. 'It's in keeping with the way they use dismantling shot.'

That made Peabody smile despite himself, and the smile set the coping stone on Davenant's rage. He searched through his mind for the most wounding, the cruellest thing he could say to this upstart American who had dared to oppose him.

'Of course,' he said loudly. 'In the American service they marry their deserters to rich widows. Especially when they happen to be the captain's brothers.'

Peabody stepped back from the impact of the insult as if it had been a physical blow. His lean brown cheeks were white under their sunburn. When he spoke it was with an interval between the words as he exerted his will to keep himself from bursting out with undignified anger.

'Who is your friend, sir?' he asked.

Davenant's shoulders lifted a trifle as he suddenly realised into what fresh trouble his hot temper had led him. But there was no going back now; the next development was as inevitable as a rainstorm.

'Captain Fane will act for me, I am sure,' he said, and turned away, in obedience to the etiquette of the duel which demanded that he should not see his enemy again until they met upon the ground.

'Captain Fane,' said Peabody. 'May I have the pleasure of presenting Lieutenant Hubbard, first lieutenant of the United States ship *Delaware*?' Then he, too, turned away. Dupont was hurrying up, wringing his hands over this deplorable incident at his party, but Peabody brushed past him. All eyes in the room were upon him, but he only saw Anne, just as he had seen her once before, with her face outlined like a miniature against a background of mist. His acute tension relaxed as he met her eyes beneath their level brows, but the exhilaration of excitement still remained.

'Anne,' he said, coming to her, 'we shall have to go home.'

As she looked up to him she had nothing to say to this husband of hers, who in the mad manner of men had imperilled everything she loved in the world for a few words. There was nothing she could say, nothing she could do; these affairs of honour between men were something whose course no woman could divert in the slightest. Her eyes were moist.

'I'm sorry to have spoilt your party, dear,' said Peabody, smiling down upon her. He was still too stupidly excited to appreciate how much she was hurt. Her lips trembled before she spoke.

'Let us go,' she said.

When Peabody was getting his cloak Hubbard appeared, with his usual air of quiet efficiency. He was accustomed to handling–or participating in–affairs of honour.

'Dawn to-morrow,' he said. 'On the edge of the canebrake across the stream from your house. I know the place–it's barely half a mile from there. Pistols at twelve paces. We'll use mine–they're London made and reliable. I have to go back to the ship for them, and to tell Downing and Murray–we'll need another second. May I spend the night at your house–I've still got some details to settle when I get back?'

'I'll give orders to that effect,' said Peabody.

Back in the room where the mosquito-net reared its vast dome over the big bed, Peabody put his arms out to Anne. He saw that she was weeping now, and for the first time misgivings asserted themselves, though unavailingly in the face of his other emotions. That Old Testament conscience of his was grimly satisfied that he should have put this undeserved happiness of his at the disposition of Providence, and he knew now that he was no coward.

'Darling!' he said–the endearments which he had never used before came more readily now.

Anne looked at him, and both her eyebrows and her shoulders went up a little. There was no predicting what this husband of hers would do next, nor how he would feel about it. In seven short hours his life would be in terrible danger–danger that made her feel sick when she thought about it, and yet here he was unmoved. She fought back her tears; as she knew, she would not be able to divert him a hair's breadth from the course mapped out for him at dawn next day. If she were weak now she would do no good and just possibly might do harm. She must be strong, and she took a grip on herself and was strong–Peabody in his blindness knew nothing of it at the time.

As they kissed, a knock on the door made them draw apart. It was Anne's coloured maid still displaying evident signs of excitement over the affair about which the news had spread like wildfire round the island.

'Ma'ame d'Ernée,' she said.

'Madame d'Ernée? To see me?' asked Anne.

'Yes, ma'amselle.'

'I'll come,' said Anne.

Peabody was philosophic about it. He sat down in the bedroom and ran over in his mind the arrangements necessitated by to-morrow's affair. His will–he had made that, and had it witnessed, directly after his marriage. He had given orders about Hubbard, and a bedroom on the ground floor was being prepared for him. He had a black stock and cravat to wear to-morrow so that he would show no linen, and he would fight in his second-best coat without the epaulettes. Anne's aunt had probably come to see if with Anne she could not devise some means of stopping the affair–she ought to have more sense, but she was interested in Davenant, of course. Anne would not presume to meddle, naturally.

Anne came in again. There was a queer twist to her smile and an inscrutable lift to one eyebrow. But her expression softened as her eyes met his, and she melted towards him. She came warmly into his arms, and Peabody quite forgot to ask her what on earth Madame d'Ernée had wanted. He did not want to know anything, not with Anne's lips against his and this sweet passion and purity of conscience consuming him.

Later he slept heavily enough not to feel her slip away from his side and under the mosquito netting; he turned once and found she was gone, smiled in his half awakeness without any suspicion at all. He did not wake far enough to think about the morrow, and when, an hour before dawn, the maid came in to waken them, she was back at his side.

22

Hubbard was positively masterful.

'Don't walk too fast, sir,' he said, and the 'sir' was a most perfunctory addition. 'We can't have you arriving out of breath.'

He looked at his watch, and up at the brightening sky from which the rain still dripped monotonously.

'Just right,' he said. 'We don't want to wait when we get there. And no gentleman would keep the other side waiting, although I've known it done.'

They passed a small gang of negroes on their way to work in the fields, and the dark faces all turned to see this odd spectacle of two white men on foot in the rain before dawn. A babble of talk burst from the group–every member of it had heard the gossip about the quarrel between the English captain and the American captain, and what was to happen this morning.

'It's round this corner, sir,' said Hubbard. 'You can walk a bit slower–if you please, sir. Damn this rain.'

Round the corner Murray was waiting, and Downing with a big case of instruments resting on the ground at his feet. Their faces were pale in the brightening dawn. And here came Fane, with Doctor Clarke beside him, and in the background Peabody caught a glimpse of Davenant and Maitland.

'You're sure those gloves are comfortable, sir?' said Hubbard. 'Better to show white than have an awkward grip on the trigger.'

'They're all right,' said Peabody, passing the forefinger of his left hand between the fingers of his right. They were a pair of dark doeskin gloves lent by Hubbard; only his face would catch the light now that he had on his black stock and cravat and blue trousers. Fane was approaching, and Hubbard went to meet him, uncovering and bowing with the utmost formality. Downing and Clarke went off with their instruments into a nook in the canebrake out of the line of fire, leaving Murray alone. He caught Peabody's eye and smiled a sickly smile, so sickly that it made Peabody grin–the Baltimore lad was so acutely nervous, and this period of waiting was trying him hard, and his clothes were soaked.

Hubbard took the case of pistols from under his arm and opened it before Fane. He slid a ramrod down each barrel; each pistol was charged.

'I loaded 'em last night in case of rain this morning, sir,' he said. 'I'll draw the charges if you like—'

'Please do not trouble, sir,' said Fane.

'Would you please be so kind as to keep off the rain while I prime, sir?' said Hubbard.

Fane opened his cloak and held out the breast of it horizontally, and

Hubbard held each weapon in turn under this exiguous shelter, close against Fane's bosom, while he filled each priming pan with fine powder from the small canister he produced from his pocket.

'Have you seen the new percussion caps they are making in London, sir?' asked Fane, his polite small talk tinged with professional interest.

'Too damned new-fangled for my liking, sir,' said Hubbard. 'There, sir. Is that to your satisfaction? Then please take your choice, sir.'

With the weapons under their cloaks to screen them from the rain they looked up at the sky.

'The light's fair in any direction with these clouds,' said Fane. 'Better station them with the wind abeam.'

'I agree,' said Hubbard.

They stepped out twelve paces apart and looked round at their principals who came up and were posted on the exact spots indicated. Peabody saw Davenant's face for the first time since yesterday. It was composed, stolid, philosophic. Peabody knew himself to be calm and his hand was steady, so that his heart was joyful.

'Sir,' said Hubbard, 'I must ask you if it is not possible, at this last moment, to compose your differences with Captain Davenant and prevent the effusion of blood?'

'Not a chance,' said Peabody.

Fane had posed the same question to Davenant.

'Never,' said Davenant steadily.

'Then you will please turn your backs,' said Hubbard. He raised his voice. 'I will call "one–two–three–fire!" You will remain still until the word "fire," when you will turn and fire at your leisure.

'Captain Fane, did your principal hear what I said, or shall I repeat?'

'My principal heard,' said Fane.

Hubbard took the pistol from under his coat and put it into Peabody's hand; the butt felt reassuringly solid through the doeskin glove. Peabody made sure of his grip, made sure his finger was securely against the trigger, raised the pistol so that his eye was along the barrel, made sure that there was no chance of his feet slipping. He tensed himself ready to wheel round while Hubbard's footsteps died away.

'One!' came Hubbard's voice. 'Two–three–fire!'

Peabody swung round, careful to point his right shoulder to his enemy so as to reduce the surface presented to the shot. Davenant's face showed clear at the end of the pistol-barrel, and he began a steady squeeze on the trigger. At that moment came a bang and a puff of smoke. Davenant had fired–presumably he had fired as he wheeled. The aim must have been poor, for Peabody did not even feel the wind of the bullet. Davenant was at his mercy now, and he could take his own time over his shot. Not that there was any need, for Davenant's face, seen clearly through the rain, was there along his pistol-barrel. As surely as anything in this life he could place a bullet right between his eyes and kill him. Davenant's eyes looked back at him without a sign of faltering.

Peabody's first instinct was one of mercy. He did not want Davenant's life. He did not want to kill anyone except to the benefit of the United States of America. It raced through his mind that Hunningford had told him of the imminent possibility of peace–the peace of the years to come would not be helped by a memory of a captain slain in a duel. He just had time to point the pistol vertically into the air before it went off.

The four seconds came pressing forward.

'My principal has stood your principal's fire,' said Hubbard, and Peabody noticed that Hubbard's voice sounded strained. All that careful unconcern had been merely a pose, and he was off his guard now and showed it. 'He has deliberately missed. Honour is completely satisfied, and both parties will leave the ground.'

'No second shot?' asked Maitland, and Hubbard turned upon him with an icy politeness barely concealing his poor opinion of a man who could display such ignorance of the code of honour.

'Your principal had his shot and it was not returned,' he said. 'You cannot expect him to be accorded further opportunities.'

That was perfectly true–it had been at the back of Peabody's mind when he missed. A duellist whose life had been spared must remain satisfied with that.

'Mr Hubbard is quite right,' said Fane. 'Both parties must leave the ground. But I must remind everyone that this is a most suitable opportunity, now that honour is satisfied, to make whatever concessions are compatible with honour and gentlemanly conduct. Mr Hubbard, would you perhaps be good enough to approach your principal again?'

Hubbard strode over to Peabody and spoke in a low voice.

'You could accept an apology, sir,' he said. 'You could do a good deal more than that, even, seeing that you've stood his fire.'

'What happens if I don't?' asked Peabody. He was vague on the point–he was familiar with the code of honour, but had never come across the practical application of this particular item.

'Nothing,' said Hubbard. 'You can never admit his existence, sir, that's all, and the same with him. You never see each other when you meet. It's awkward when you're in the same ship–I saw it with Clough and Brown in the old *Constitution*–but as things are it'll hardly affect you.'

'I see,' said Peabody. It probably would not affect him much, not even though Davenant was on a familiar footing with his wife's aunt. He would probably never again have dealings with Davenant now that the affair of the *Susanna* was settled. And then at that very moment the germ of an idea came into his mind, engendered by this thought. He might be able to wring very considerable advantages for the Service if he could keep in touch with Davenant.

'Fane and I will be speaking together,' explained Hubbard further. 'Fane might be able to make a lot of concessions, seeing that the world will not know who made the first advance, so to speak.'

'I'll accept anything in reason,' said Peabody. 'I can leave it all to you, I know, Hubbard. But I don't want to be put out of touch with Davenant if it can possibly be helped. Remember that.'

'I will, sir,' said Hubbard, and turned back. Fane left Davenant a moment later and joined him, as the two talked together in low voices. Davenant and Peabody stood and fidgeted in the drenching rain–their eyes met once and Peabody had difficulty, in his present excitement over his new plan, in keeping his features in their proper expression of stony indifference. Hubbard came back.

'He's ready,' he said, 'to express through Fane profound regret that the incident ever happened. That's not a full apology, sir. It's only a half measure, and if shots hadn't been exchanged I should strongly advise against acceptance. But as things are, and remembering what you told me about wanting to remain in touch, I've taken it upon myself to accept.'

'Good,' said Peabody. 'What do I do now?'

'Merely acknowledge him, sir, before we leave the ground.'

All very well, thought Peabody, to say that so airily, but actually it was a difficult moment. Peabody felt positively awkward as he came up to Davenant. He made his stiff spine bend in the middle.

'Your servant, sir,' he said.

Davenant bowed with an equal lack of grace.

'Your servant, sir,' and then constraint suddenly vanishing: 'Dammit, man, I'm glad I missed you.'

Walking home, Hubbard and Murray and Downing were in the highest spirits despite their wet clothes.

'By God, sir,' said Hubbard, 'this'll look well in the newspapers at home. You spared his life, sir. I could see that. I could see how you had him along your pistol.'

'Davenant's a dead shot,' said Downing.

'Yes, sir,' said Murray. 'They say he can hit a pigeon on the wing.'

'I didn't tell you that, sir, before you met him,' said Hubbard, with a laugh.

No damn you, thought Peabody, a little embittered at the thought, and he said nothing.

'He's lost some of his reputation now, anyway,' said Downing.

'I can't think how he came to miss,' said Murray.

'He shot from the waist without sighting,' said Hubbard. 'That takes practice.'

'But it looked to me,' said Murray, 'as if he couldn't miss.'

'So it did to me, by God,' said Hubbard. 'Did you hear the bullet, sir?'

'No,' said Peabody.

It was a most unpleasant conversation in his opinion, although he could not have said why, seeing that the affair was over. There was Anne standing at the door of the house, and she ran down the path through the rain when she saw them. She threw herself into Peabody's arms without shame, and he kissed her without shame in the presence of his subordinates. He had purged himself of his inward doubts, he had put this happiness of his at the disposition of Providence and Providence had returned it to him, so that shame had disappeared. There was coffee waiting for them, and the usual glass of rum which they all refused to touch.

'I can drink this coffee now,' said Murray, smacking his lips. 'I couldn't swallow a mouthful in the ship before I came up this morning. I hadn't the heart for anything.'

'The captain drank his,' said Hubbard. 'I watched him. Not a sign–he might have been getting ready to come on deck at anchor in the Chesapeake.'

'The captain's an interesting physiological subject,' said Downing, and then, suddenly: 'Gentlemen, although this is only coffee, can't we drink his health?'

'The captain,' said Hubbard, raising his glass.

'The captain!' echoed the others–Anne among them–and they drank to him as he grinned awkwardly at the compliment.

'The ship's waiting for us,' he said, to change the subject. 'I'll see you on board after I've changed my clothes.'

The bedroom with its dome of mosquito netting had been put to rights while he was gone; he got himself out dry clothes from the inlaid tallboy–married life played the devil with systematic rotation of his wardrobe when he had to keep half his clothes on land. He laid out a fresh white neckcloth on the dressing table among Anne's tortoise-shell toilet things, shoving aside her reticule to do so. The thing fell with a thump on the floor, and he stooped to pick it up. Two things had rolled out of its open mouth across the polished floor, and he pursued them. Marbles?

Beads? He picked them up. They were unexpectedly heavy, of a dull metallic hue. Pistol bullets! He stood looking at the half-inch spheres of lead on his palm, lost in thought.

'Anne!' he called. 'Anne!'

She came running–he heard her light step on the stairs–and as she entered the room she saw what he held in his hand and stopped short. The smile that was on her lips remained there, rigid, in shocking contrast with the terror in her eyes. If it had not been for that she might have been able to disarm his suspicions, so utterly incredible had they seemed to him.

'What are these doing here?' he asked, even now more bewildered than stern.

'You–you know,' she said. She was sick with fright at the knowledge that her terrible husband had caught her interfering with his precious masculine foolishness–imperilling his precious honour.

'I *don't* know,' he said. 'Tell me.'

'I took them out,' she whispered, faltering. 'Aunt Sophie and I.'

'But how in the name of–of anything at all—?'

'I went into Mr Hubbard's room,' she said. 'Aunt Sophie was here. You were asleep, and I crept out. I went into Mr Hubbard's room when he was asleep. Aunt Sophie waited by the door–I went in my bare feet, and I took the–the pistols. We dug out the–the wads with my stiletto and shook the bullets out.'

'But the pistols were loaded–I saw Hubbard test with the ramrod.'

'We thought he would. So we had to put in something hard which wouldn't hurt anybody. It was all we could do.'

'But what was it you did?'

'It took us a long time to think of something. In the end I got two bits of bread and baked them as hard as I could. I thought they'd fly to powder when the pistols went off and not do any damage.'

'You were right,' said Peabody grimly. 'And then?'

'That's all. We put the bits of toast into the pistols and stuck the wads in again on top, and I went back into Mr Hubbard's room and put them back in the case. Mr Hubbard snored and I nearly dropped them.'

'I wish you had,' he said bitterly. Her lips had lost their rigidity now and were trembling as he stared at her, the pistol bullets still in his hand. He suddenly remembered their existence and hurled them with a crash across the room.

'I was going to tell you about it,' she said, 'not to-day. Not to-morrow. But sometime I was going to tell you.'

'Much good that would do,' he sneered.

And then his saving common sense came to their rescue. After all, he had gone through the affair in good faith. He had stood Davenant's fire and he had not trembled. He had spared Davenant's life in the same good faith as Davenant had tried to take his. And the thought of Davenant, the man who could hit a pigeon on the wing, trying to bring down an American captain with a piece of toast, was marvellously funny. A laugh rose suddenly within him quite irrepressibly. And what made the joke more perfect was that the new plan he had in mind–a plan of whose success he was quite certain–would never have stood any chance of success if it had not been for the duel. Davenant would never have listened to his new suggestion for a moment if it were not for the mortification of knowing that all the world had heard that his life had been spared. If he had killed Davenant–and most assuredly if Davenant had killed him–the new plan would have had no chance. That was amusing as well. The laugh that was welling up inside him burst out to the surface beyond his control. He laughed and he laughed. He thought of Hubbard's grave dignity, of Murray's scared apprehension, while all the time two fragments of toast lay hidden in the barrels of the pistols, and that made him laugh the harder.

He turned grave again when another thought struck him.

'What about your aunt?' he asked. 'Can she keep the secret?'

'Yes,' said Anne, after a moment's serious reflection. 'Yes. She would always keep a secret for me. And this time it concerns Captain Davenant. She wouldn't want the world to know about this.'

'I suppose not,' said Peabody.

Mischief danced in his eyes which were so often cold and hard. Anne's steady gaze met his and she could not help smiling back at him. She smiled and she laughed, and Peabody laughed back at her.

23

Peabody's carefully worded letter had suggested neutral ground for the interview with Davenant, and Davenant's cautious reply had accepted the suggestion, and in the end Peabody had had to make use of 'petticoat influence' in violation of his prejudices, although by now not of his judgement. A word to Anne about his difficulty had been passed on to Aunt Sophie, and Aunt Sophie had responded with an invitation to Captain Peabody to drink a dish of tea with her at the Governor's house–a much more private and comfortable place in which to talk to Davenant than any café in

Fort de France or any hill-side in Martinique. Women were of some use even in men's affairs, decided Peabody, as he walked past the well-remembered sentry outside the gate and followed the butler into the Countess's drawing-room.

Naturally there was some constraint perceptible at the beginning of the meeting. Aunt Sophie was all charm, and she poured the tea with admirable grace, the rings on her fingers flashing back the light which leaked in past the shaded windows, but Davenant was ill at ease, displaying a British surliness vastly emphasised by a not unnatural antipathy towards the man who had condescended to spare his life. Peabody on his side was cautious and uncommunicative, a little afraid of showing his hand prematurely, so that all Aunt Sophie's conversational efforts met with a poor reception–especially as both her guests detested tea and were too polite to say so. But Peabody, noting the Englishman's ill temper, and clairvoyantly realising the reasons for it, was glad. It might be easier to induce him to agree to making a step which could only be thought of as rash–to goad the bull, so to speak, into making a charge which would lay him open to a sword-thrust.

Aunt Sophie replaced her cup in her saucer.

'Tea, Captain Peabody? Tea, Sir Hubert? No? Then if you will forgive me, I will leave you alone for a few minutes. There are some domestic trifles I must attend to.'

Davenant hurried across the room to open the door for her, and she sailed out with all her stately grace, turning before she left them with a few final words.

'I shall see personally that no one listens at this door,' she said. 'There is a sentry at the garden door who speaks no English.'

'Thank you, ma'am,' said Davenant, bowing her out and shutting the door before turning back to Peabody. 'A fine woman that. You have married into an admirable family, Peabody.'

'I thought so myself,' said Peabody, sitting down with all the coolness he could display. 'But it is most kind of you to say so, sir.'

Davenant sat himself opposite him. He, too, was doing his best to display cool indifference, crossing his right ankle over his left knee, and leaning back relaxed in his chair. But beneath his lowered lids he was watching Peabody closely, and he was drumming with his fingers on the arm of the chair.

'Well, what is it, sir?' he said at length.

'A challenge, sir' said Peabody. 'Another one.'

Those last two words were the darts to infuriate the bull, as he could remember seeing them employed in the bullfight at Algeciras. Davenant flushed a little, but he kept his reply down to one word.

'Yes?' he said.

'I'm tired of watching you across the bay,' said Peabody, 'and I guess you're tired of watching me.'

'I'm tired of all this tomfoolery,' said Davenant.

'I'm not surprised,' agreed Peabody. 'The whole island, of course, is amused at you.'

'At me?' said Davenant, on a rising note.

'Yes,' said Peabody. 'Of course, they do not understand the whole circumstances of the case. They can only see that you have twice my force and are having to wait here just because I do.'

'They think that, do they?'

'I'm afraid so, sir. You and I know it's not true, but you can hardly blame them for judging by appearances. The mob thinks much the same all the world over.'

'Damn the mob,' said Davenant. But another shaft had gone home. He was thinking of the British mob, of the English newspapers, and the rash conclusions they might draw regarding his conduct. 'Come out and fight me, Peabody.'

'I want to,' said Peabody, with an edge to his voice. 'I said I had a challenge for you. Come out in the *Calypso* and fight me ship to ship.'

'I'd like to, by God,' said Davenant, and then, trying to keep his head: 'What about these damned neutrality laws?'

'We'll have to obey the twenty-four hour rule,' said Peabody. 'But if I go out first I'll give you my parole to wait for the *Calypso* outside territorial waters. I'd be glad to let the *Calypso* go out first on the same understanding–it does not matter either way.'

'You mean me to leave *Racer* and *Bulldog* out of the action?'

As a sailor Davenant was trying to remain clear headed even while as a man his fierce instincts were overmastering him.

'Yes.'

'Thirty-eight guns to thirty-six, and a hundred and fifty tons advantage to you.'

'I know that, sir. But it's the nearest match we can arrange. You can draw extra hands from your other two ships which will help redress the balance. As many as you care to have.'

'So I can.'

'I'll be glad to do it. My officers have been discontented ever since our last meeting because they were sure I ought to have closed and captured the *Calypso*.'

'Closed and–by God, sir, what do you mean by that? I still had every gun in service. If you had closed instead of cutting my rigging to pieces–by God, sir, you'd have learned a lesson you sadly need.'

The bull had charged.

'I'll close with you this time, I promise you, sir,' said Peabody. 'I won't have a convoy to destroy as I had before.'

The mention of the convoy brought Davenant out of his chair. Its destruction must have called down upon his head an official reprimand whose memory still galled him. He gobbled at Peabody, his cheeks flushed, as Peabody effected his last prod.

'Let's hope conditions will be fair,' said Peabody. 'When we took the *Guerriere* and the *Java* and the *Peacock* we heard afterwards that the wind or the sea favoured the British. We must see that neither of us has that kind of excuse to offer this time.'

'You're insolent, sir!' raved Davenant. 'Meet me how and when you like, if you dare!'

'I have already said I would,' said Peabody. 'We have only the details to settle. Which of us will go out first, *Calypso* or *Delaware*?'

'Have it your own way.'

'As you will, sir.'

'I'll take *Calypso* out at noon to-morrow, then you can leave next day, and I'll be waiting for you ten miles west of Diamond Rock.'

'I think that will suit admirably, sir,' said Peabody, rising to his feet.

He was hard put to it to maintain his expression of cool indifference and to conceal his elation, and he did not want to run even the slight risk of Davenant's reconsidering his decision.

'Ten miles west of Diamond Rock the day after to-morrow,' he said. 'Until then, sir, I must hope that you enjoy the best of health. Would you be kind enough to convey to the Countess my thanks for her hospitality and kindness?'

'I will, sir,' said Davenant, with his stiff bow.

Outside, in the muggy heat of Fort de France on his way to the quay, Peabody walked as if on air. The plan had succeeded. He had got the best of the bargain. His presence in Fort de France had retained twice the force to watch him–but when England had a navy a hundred times as strong as the American what did that count? An American ship loose at sea, free to ravage and destroy, forcing the British to impose all the hampering restrictions of convoy on their trade, was worth a hundred American frigates in harbour.

He knew he could defeat the *Calypso* if the latter were unsupported by the *Racer* and *Bulldog*. It would be a hard fight, but he would win it, and there would be enough left of the *Delaware* to patch up and conduct on a fresh voyage of destruction–a weakened crew–Peabody made himself contemplate calmly a total of a hundred and fifty casualties–and patched sails and jury rigging, but she would still be strong enough and fast enough to play Old Harry with merchant ships. And the *Racer* and *Bulldog* had depleted crews already, if he knew anything about King's ships; Davenant would deplete them still further to give *Calypso* a full complement for what he must know would be the fight of his life. They would not be in a position to hamper his activity very much–they would be an easy prey for him if they dared to cross his path after he had finished with the *Calypso*.

Delegates were discussing terms of peace in Europe. What the basis of peace might be he had no idea, but of one thing he was sure, and that was that it would do his country no harm during the discussions if it were known that an American frigate was at large again in the West Indies. Perhaps in the United States they were tired of the war, disheartened, despondent. The loss of the *Essex* and of the *President* would not have helped to cheer them up either; the news of the capture of the *Calypso* would act as a tonic to them–if the peace negotiations broke down and further sacrifices were required of them this victory would give them the necessary tonic. The White House–or what was left of it, if Hunningford's account of the raid on Washington were correct–would be all the better for the stimulus of a little victory, too. Mr Madison might be an admirable President–as to that Peabody knew little and cared less–but as a war minister he had been a woeful failure.

By the time Peabody reached the quay his step was light and he was breathing the muggy air of Fort de France as if it were the keen winter air of Connecticut. Out in the bay the pelicans flapped in their rigid formations;

egrets and herons, white in the bright sun, haunted the waters of the edge of the bay, and overhead flew the manifold gulls with their haunting cries. Soon he would be as free as they. It crossed his mind that in the history books of the future he would be noted as the man who captured the *Calypso*, but the thought only crossed his mind and did not linger in it. He simply did not care whether the history books mentioned his name or not, as long as what he had done met with his own grudging approval. He knew himself to have done a good day's work for his country, and he was pleased.

It only remained–Peabody was being rowed across the bay in his gig by this time–to put the *Delaware* into as perfect shape as possible for the forthcoming struggle. He would have an hour's exercise at the guns this afternoon, before nightfall. To-morrow morning Hubbard could put the crew through sail drill while he and Murray went through the watch bill to make certain that every man was posted where he could do most good–those forward carronades, starboard side, would not be under good supervision if Corling became a casualty and they had the poorest gun captains–and in the afternoon there would be a chance for a final polish on the gun drill.

He would come out of the bay with all top hamper sent down, every stick of it, and fight the *Calypso* under topsails alone. A fallen mast then would do least damage, with the courses furled and wetted as a precaution against fire. He would not need speed, because Davenant would try to close with him as rapidly as possible, and under topsails he could still outmanoeuvre him until the ships came broadside to broadside. Then they would fight it out at pistol shot. It would be better not to board, for *Calypso* would be full of men and his gunners were the more efficient. Pistol-shot distance, with grape from the carronades and round shot from the long guns. By closing his eyes Peabody could call up the whole scene before him, the deafening roar of the guns and the choking fog of smoke, the splintering of woodwork and the cheers and the screams. *Calypso* would have to be beaten into a wreck, half her crew dead and the other half dropping with exhaustion, before Davenant would surrender. Davenant would probably be dead, too. And he himself? He might be dead. There was at least an even chance of it. But he knew that what he had done was the best he could do for his country.

As Peabody came on deck he blinked, blindly, as though he had just emerged from his dark cabin instead of having been for the last half hour in the blinding light of the sun. In a clairvoyant moment he had been seeing the deck littered with wreckage and corpses, guns dismounted and bulwarks smashed. So vivid had the vision been that he was taken a little aback by the sight of the gleaming white decks and the orderly crew and the guns all snugly secured. It was a couple of seconds before he recovered and began, coldly, to give those orders to Hubbard which were to make his vision into a reality.

24

Eight bells in the forenoon watch, and the hands just dismissed for dinner.

'*Calypso*'s making sail, sir,' reported Kidd.

'Thank you,' said Peabody.

Since yesterday the British frigate had been under the closest observation. They had watched her top hamper being sent down; they had counted every man who had been rowed across to her from the *Racer* and *Bulldog*. Twenty marines, conspicuous in their red coats, had been sent by the *Racer*, every marine she had, probably. That meant possibly that Davenant had it in his mind to board, but the seamen who had also been ferried over were probably quarter gunners and gun captains who might improve *Calypso*'s gunnery. Peabody's guess was that *Calypso* had now at least a full complement, a most unusual thing for a British ship of war. He himself had suggested to Davenant this supplementing of *Calypso*'s crew, but his conscience was clear, for Davenant would have thought of it himself before the time came for sailing.

Calypso was getting under way in the fashion to be expected of a King's ship, the anchor hove short, every sail set exactly simultaneously, anchor up, and the ship on the move instantly. She made a brave sight, even with her topgallants sent down, as she beat against the sea breeze over the enamelled green water of the bay. Her first tack was bringing her over towards the *Delaware*, whose crew was lining the hammock nettings to watch her. There was a little murmur forward, swelling instantly into a deep-chested roar. The crew of the *Delaware* was cheering their opponent as she passed, cheering wildly. From the deck of the *Calypso* came one single stern cheer in reply; Davenant was visible on his quarterdeck, conspicuous with his red ribbon and his epaulettes, and he raised his cocked hat in acknowledgement of the compliment. Then the noise from the *Calypso* ceased abruptly as discipline took hold again and the crew stood by for their ship to go about.

Peabody found himself swallowing, and the iron depths of him were even a trifle shaken, for he was luring those brave men over there to their deaths, and to-morrow the brave men here under his command would be dying at his word. His thin, mobile lips were even thinner during the brief space that he allowed himself to think about it. There was no written word between himself and Davenant either, no public parole. He realised with a start that it had not occurred to him to doubt the other's good faith for a single moment, nor had it occurred to Davenant to doubt his. A single sentence had sufficed to settle the details of the combat, and to come to an agreement far more binding than any treaty between statesmen. He bore no rancour against Davenant, and he knew–allowances being made for Davenant's fiery temper–that Davenant bore none against him. He remembered something of the 'treason' which

Hunningford had talked at their last interview, and he felt a twinge of regret that fine men and fine ships should be doomed to destruction on the morrow. In a sudden panic he shook the thoughts from him, consumed with misgivings as to whither they were leading him.

'Well, Mr Styles?' he said to the purser more sternly then usual.

Mr Styles produced his lists to prove that the *Delaware*'s stores were complete in every detail, that every water butt was full, that every brine cask was charged with meat–bought with the *Princess Augusta*'s gold from Martinique butchers at prices which made Mr Styles groan–and every bread bag full of biscuit. Wood for fuel, rum, tobacco, clothing; the *Delaware* was as fully supplied as the day she left Brooklyn. After the *Calypso* should be dealt with she would be free to continue her operations for months without being dependent on the shore for anything.

The *Calypso* was rounding Cape Solomon now, hull down at the mouth of the bay as she headed for her rendezvous ten miles west of the Diamond Rock. Peabody took one last look at her before he went down to the maindeck. Wooden slats had been nailed to the planking there beside the guns, to serve as pointers for concentrated broadsides, at such angles as to ensure that if the guns were laid along them their fire would all be aimed at a point fifty yards on the beam. He called for his big protractor and went along carefully checking the angles. Broke in the *Shannon* had made use of the method when he fought the *Chesapeake*, as Peabody had read in a copy of the *Jamaica Gazette* he had picked up in Fort de France; the same method might be invaluable if there were not enough wind to blow away the smoke and he laid the *Delaware* athwartships to the *Calypso*. There was no harm in learning from the enemy.

He was busy enough, and therefore one might almost say happy enough, until nightfall, by which time he had tired out his crew. He wanted them to sleep soundly that night, ready for the next day, and they perhaps would not do so in their present state of excitement without a good deal of exercise first. So he kept them hauling at the gun tackles in the sweltering heat, and he devised imaginary emergencies for them to deal with, until it was too dark to see. Then he dismissed them to rest. He looked out once more over the dark water, wondering what was happening aboard the *Calypso*, hove-to under shortened canvas out there at her rendezvous in the Caribbean, before he nerved himself to call for his gig.

He did not want to go ashore; he did not want to see Anne again. He doubted so much his ability to bear what he foresaw would be an agonising strain. The premonition of approaching death was strong upon him. This love of his, these few days of happiness, had been a tiny interlude of joy during his joyless life. Perhaps no bitterness, no disappointment, no privation, could ever be too much for his iron temperament, but he was afraid of happiness. He was afraid of himself, afraid lest he might weaken, lest this last glimpse of the happiness he was losing should break him down and betray him into some demonstration of weakness which would be sinful if anything was, which he would be ashamed of when he remembered it broadside to broadside with the *Calypso*, and which Anne would remember of him when–if ever–she thought of him in after years.

But he had to go through with it. That was all. It was something that he had to do, and so there was no use in grimacing as he swallowed his medicine.

'Good night, sir,' said Hubbard, hat in hand.

'Good night, Mr Hubbard,' said Peabody as he went over the side in the darkness.

There was the little carriage, which had been waiting at the quay ever since sunset, and there was Anne, faintly illumined in the light of the lantern which the coachman held. She held up her mouth to be kissed, and he kissed her, and he knew then, at the touch of her lips, that all his fears regarding his weakness were nonsensical. It was a moment of fresh recognition, like the time when he had seen her again at the Marquis's house–he had forgotten what she was like until he saw her again. Anne could never be a cause of weakness; she could never be a drain on any man's strength. Rather was she a fortifiant, strengthening him and revivifying him. Peabody remembered the *Pilgrim's Progress*, and how Christian's burden dropped from him when he reached the Cross. His own burden dropped from him as he felt Anne's slim shoulders under his hands and her lips against his, and there was nothing impious about the comparison, not even to his morbid conscience.

Later that night he tried to tell her about it. He even mentioned Christian and the Cross a little shamefacedly, for he was quite unliterary and high-flown similes did not come easily to him, and he felt her lie suddenly still in his arms. It was a second or so before she replied, in that London accent with its French quality that he loved so dearly, and she stroked his cheek as she spoke.

'Dear,' she said, 'darling. When I'm an old woman I'll remember what you've just said and I'll still be proud of it. But you've got it all wrong, dear. It isn't me. It's *you*. To you I'm what you think I am, of course–oh, how can I explain it? You're so good yourself, you're so honest and you think no evil. It's because you're like what you are that you think other people are the same. And my dear, it's because you think that that we try to be. Oh, what a muddle I'm saying, and yet to me it's as clear as clear. Sweetheart–darling—'

The night was passing and the dawn was approaching; the maid's knock on the door awoke them as they slept still in each other's arms. When Peabody was dressed the carriage was waiting to take him down to the quay, and Peabody stood to bid his wife good-bye. Their eyes met as he stretched out his hands and she put hers into them.

'Good-bye, dear,' he said.

'Good-bye, dear,' she answered, looking at him with level gaze, unflinching. 'You'll come back to me soon?'

'As soon as ever I can,' he said; the premonition of death had not left him.

He bent his head to kiss her hands, and he felt their impassioned clasp as he did so, but her eyes were still dry when he looked up again, and her voice was steady. It was not until he had gone that she wept, bitterly, heartbroken, alone in her room.

On board the *Delaware* the early morning routine was under way, just as ever. Rank by rank, their trousers rolled above the knee, the hands were washing the deck, polishing metal work, scrubbing canvas.

'Good morning, Mr Hubbard.'

'Good morning, sir.'

'It looks as if we're going to have a fine day.'

'The glass rose during the night, sir.'

The tropical sun was already glaring down at them over the hills, and one or two belated fishing boats were still returning to the bay with the night's catch. The little revenue cutter was standing out from the quay and hove-to close under the *Delaware*'s quarter. Dupont was on board, in full uniform, and he hailed the American ship.

'You will be allowed to sail at fifteen minutes past noon,' he shouted, bringing out his watch from his fob. 'I keep the time, and it is now six-thirty.'

Peabody looked at his own watch. He had forgotten to wind it the night before, and even on his wedding night he had remembered it. But he managed to keep his expression nonchalant as he synchronised his watch with Dupont's, and he called no attention to his actions when he next slipped the key over the winding post and gave it a few casual turns.

'Very good, Captain,' he hailed back.

'Isn't it sickening the way these Frogs can order us about, sir?' said Hubbard.

'It's for the last time,' said Peabody. 'Mr Hubbard, I've left duplicate orders for you should I be killed this afternoon.'

'Yes, sir,' said Hubbard, steadily. He did not cheapen himself with any conventional 'I hope not.' He was like Anne in that respect.

'One set is in my desk,' went on Peabody. 'The other is in a sealed envelope which the gunner has in the magazine in case our upper works are wrecked. However hard hit the ship may be, you are to repair her at sea.'

'Yes, sir.'

'The British have some sort of expedition fitting out at Jamaica,' went on Peabody. 'It may have sailed by now, but you are to track it down. My own guess is that they'll send it against New Orleans.'

'Yes, sir.'

'Hang on to it and do it all the damage you can. If you catch it at sea you may be able to snap up a transport or two–a couple of thousand redcoats for prisoners wouldn't do us any harm.'

'I guess not, sir.'

'But remember this, Mr Hubbard. You are not to fight any British ship of war if you can help it.'

'I understand, sir.'

'I hope you do.'

'I'm fighting *Calypso* this afternoon because it's the only way to get out of this damned harbour.'

'And you've been damned clever to arrange it, sir.'

'That will be all, Mr Hubbard. See that the men get their dinners at six bells.'

'Aye aye, sir.'

Peabody was aware that to an outsider the worst of having made all his preparations in plenty of time would be that now there was nothing to do except wait–Peabody remembered how careful Hubbard had been, the morning before the duel, that there should be no waiting on either side. And yet this morning waiting was a pleasure; it gave him time to enjoy his present tranquillity of mind and soul. He felt at his best; he could look up at the green slopes of Martinique and across the blue waters of the Caribbean and take pleasure in them. There was something purifying in his certainty that he was to die that afternoon. He had done everything he could, and he had left nothing undone, nor, looking back over the voyage, had he done anything he ought not to have done. America would register him among her heroes. And he would live in Anne's memory, which was the immortality he desired. He felt no shame in remembering her sweetness and the dear delights he had shared with her. That was strange, that he should feel this purity, as of a mediaeval knight watching over his arms, having known her ardent passion. It was the crowning of his present happiness.

An hour before noon the pipes of the boatswain's mates began to twitter as the men were called to their dinners. The sea breeze had begun to blow, and would reach appreciable strength when the time came to sail, Peabody decided. He looked up at the pennant at the masthead; if the wind did not shift they would be able to weather Cape Solomon in a single board. Close-hauled, they would very nearly make the rendezvous–it would depend on how soon they would pick up the trade wind out in the Caribbean. He looked out again over his projected course and started with surprise. There was a ship under full sail just coming into sight round Cape Solomon. She had every sail set, studdingsails as far as the royals on both sides, and was heading for the bay with the wind well abaft the beam at a speed so great that even at that distance he could see the white water under her bows. She was the *Calypso*, or so his eyes told him. His brain refused to believe any such thing. There was no possible reason for her to be returning.

'*Calypso* coming into the bay, sir!' yelled the lookout, but there was that in his voice which told that the lookout did not believe his eyes either.

Atwell across the deck had his telescope to his eye.

'Well, I'll be God-damned,' he said, turning to his captain, and then hastily added–'Sir.'

The officers were hurrying up from below, cluttering the quarterdeck and staring at the beautiful vision as the sea breeze brought her in fast.

'Davenant must have remembered something,' said Hubbard, and one or two of those who heard him laughed.

'Sprung a leak, perhaps?' suggested Atwell, seriously. 'On fire down below? Yellow Jack among the crew?'

All the suggestions were plausible, and the laughter stilled as every eye strained to see if there was anything to be seen which might confirm one of them. She was well into the bay now, and her studdingsails came in altogether.

'They've an anchor ready to let go, sir,' said Hubbard, without taking the glass from his eye.

'Heave our anchor short, Mr Hubbard,' said Peabody.

It might be a nice legal point, as to whether the return of the *Calypso* nullified the application of the twenty-four hour rule. It still wanted twenty-five minutes before noon, but he wished to be ready to dash out of the harbour the moment the *Calypso* anchored, before *Racer* or *Bulldog* could take a hand in the game. To escape into the Caribbean without a battle was better than any hard-won victory. He was prepared to go and leave the diplomats to argue the case subsequently. The loud clanking of the capstan served as a monotonous accompaniment to the excited comments on the quarterdeck.

'Turn up all hands, Mr Hubbard, if you please. I want all sail ready to set.'

Calypso was heading straight for the *Delaware*; at no more than a cable's length's distance she rounded to. Every sail was taken in simultaneously, and the roar of the cable through the hawsehole was plainly audible from the *Delaware*.

'Nothing wrong with the way she's handled,' commented Hubbard, grudgingly. The sudden bang of a gun made them all start, and then they all felt a trifle sheepish at the realization that *Calypso* was only firing off her salute to the forts.

'Anchor's aweigh, sir!' came the yell from forward.

'Set sail, Mr Hubbard.'

Courses and topsails were spread on the instant, as the headsails brought her round.

'*Calypso*'s launched a boat, sir,' said Kidd.

So she had; a gig had dropped from her quarter and was pulling madly across to intercept the *Delaware* as she gathered way.

'Keep her close-hauled on this tack, if you please, Mr Hubbard,' said Peabody. He could think of no message whatever which would keep him in Fort de France if once he had the chance to escape.

The gig's crew were bending frantically to their oars, making the little craft fly over the surface. Peabody could see the officer in the stern gesticulating wildly as he urged the men to greater efforts. Then as they came close the men lay on their oars and the officer jumped to his feet in the stern sheets, his hands as a speaking-trumpet to his mouth; it was the same supercilious midshipman who had once before brought a letter from the *Calypso*.

'Message from Captain Davenant,' yelled the midshipman as the gig was at the level of the *Delaware*'s mainmast. Peabody paid no attention. If he had the chance of getting to sea he was going to take it.

'Message for Captain Peabody,' yelled the midshipman as the mizzen mast went by.

The gig bobbed suddenly as the wave thrown off by the *Delaware*'s bows reached her, but the midshipman retained his balance with the practice of years. He put his hands to his mouth in one last desperate yell as the gig passed under the *Delaware*'s quarter.

'It's peace!' he yelled. 'Peace!'

'Bring her to the wind, Mr Hubbard,' said Peabody. After all, that was the one message which would keep him in harbour; and he had not thought about it before.

The gig overtook the *Delaware* as she lay hove to.

'Captain Peabody?' hailed the midshipman.

'I am Captain Peabody.'

'Sir Hubert's respects, sir, and would it be convenient for him to visit your ship?'

'My respects to Sir Hubert, and it will be convenient whenever he wishes.'

The gig turned about and rowed back, while Peabody gave his orders.

'Anchor the ship again, Mr Hubbard, if you please. Be ready to compliment Captain Davenant when he comes on board.'

Peabody dashed below, where the gun deck was cleared of all bulkheads and obstructions ready for action. There was only an exiguous canvas curtain hung to preserve for the ship's captain a shred of privacy up to the moment of action commencing.

'Washington! My best coat! White breeches. Silk stockings. Hurry, d'you hear me?'

'Lord ha' mercy, sir. What are you wanting those for?'

'Jump to it, damn you, and shut your mouth.'

Washington could not obey the last order, could not have done so to save his life, but he muffled his remarks in the sea chest into which he had to bend his head as he sought for the clothes, in the highly inconvenient corner of the cabin where the chest had been thrust while clearing for action. Peabody had thrown off coat and trousers and was standing in his shirt before Washington had found the other clothes; as Washington got to his feet the jarring rumble of the cable shook the ship.

'Lordy!' said Washington, and shut his mouth with a snap as Peabody turned a terrible eye on him. He could only roll his eyes when the tramp of the marines' heavy shoes sounded on the deck overhead as they poured up to the entry port.

'Tell the captain of the afterguard to set my cabin to rights directly,' said Peabody, buckling on his sword. As he set his foot on the companion he heard Hubbard's warning yell, and he reached the deck just as the boatswain's mates' pipes pealed and the marines presented arms.

'Ah, Peabody,' said Davenant, coming toward him with outstretched hand. He was smiling in kindly fashion, the wrinkles showing round his eyes.

'I am glad to see you, sir,' said Peabody, a little stiffly.

Davenant was struggling with the overwhelming curiosity which consumes a captain of a ship of war when by some chance he finds himself on the deck of a rival ship. Even at that moment it was hard to keep his eyes from straying.

'Here,' he said, opening the paper which he held in his left hand and passing it over to Peabody. 'The damned despatch boat from Port of Spain sighted me this morning and gave me this. It's conclusive as far as I'm concerned.'

Peabody read the despatch; the seal was official enough and it was addressed from the Admiralty at Whitehall—

> 'I am directed by my Lords Commissioners of the Admiralty to inform all captains of His Britannic Majesty's Ships that in consequence of peace having been concluded at Ghent between His Majesty and the United States of America hostilities will cease forthwith and to request and require all such captains to refrain from any hostile action whatsoever immediately upon receipt of this order.
> E. Nepean, Secretary to the Board.'

'I suppose it needn't bind you,' said Davenant. 'You can wait until you receive your orders from Washington.'

'It binds me too, of course,' said Peabody. If he went out to sea in the face of that evidence and began a career of destruction he would be in bad odour, to say the least of it, with the Secretary of the Navy.

'It's a damned shame,' said Davenant. 'No, damn it, I can't say that. I don't know whether to be pleased or sorry, damn it. We'd have had as neat a single ship action as there's been these twenty years.'

Peabody was not ready with a reply. He was looking forward into a new future, one which he had never allowed himself to think about until now. A future of a world at peace, a world of thriving commerce. His own life would be dull and without incident, and anyone who did not know him would say that the most interesting chapter of his career had finished. But Peabody–such was the nature of the man–thought that the most interesting chapter had now begun. He took control of his thoughts just as they were drifting towards Anne and brought them back to less romantic matters. There were three dozen scrawny Martinique hens in coops on the spardeck, and, boiled, a couple of them would be just edible.

'Can I have the pleasure of your company to dinner, sir?' he said.

'That's very kind of you,' said Davenant, looking at him keenly. 'But I suspect that you would rather go and tell this good news to that pretty wife of yours.'

Peabody hesitated, torn between love of truth and ordinary politeness.

'Don't mind my feelings, sir,' went on Davenant, and he laughed apologetically. 'To tell the truth, I have business of the same sort on shore myself. I suppose there's no harm in my telling you that I have the prospect–the imminent prospect, now–of marrying into the same family as you have done. We shall be relations in law, Peabody.'

Davenant looked oddly sheepish as he said this.

'I wish you joy, sir,' said Peabody, restraining a smile. 'Long life and happiness to you and to the future Lady Davenant.'

'But let's count this invitation as only postponed,' said Davenant. 'We'll celebrate the peace together.'

'Yes, uncle,' said Peabody.

THE AFRICAN QUEEN

C. S. FORESTER

I

Although she herself was ill enough to justify being in bed had she been a person weak-minded enough to give up, Rose Sayer could see that her brother, the Reverend Samuel Sayer, was far more ill. He was very, very weak indeed, and when he knelt to offer up the evening prayer the movement was more like an involuntary collapse than a purposed gesture, and the hands which he raised trembled violently. Rose could see, in the moment before she devoutly closed her eyes, how thin and transparent those hands were, and how the bones of the wrists could be seen with almost the definition of a skeleton's.

The damp heat of the African forest seemed to be intensified with the coming of the night, which closed in upon them while they prayed. The hands which Rose clasped together were wet as though dipped in water, and she could feel the streams of sweat running down beneath her clothes as she knelt, and forming two little pools at the backs of her bent knees. It was this sensation which helped most to reconcile Rose's conscience to the absence, in this her approaching middle age, of her corset–a garment without which, so she had always been taught, no woman of the age of fourteen and upwards ever appeared in public. A corset, in fact, was quite an impossibility in Central Africa, although Rose had resolutely put aside, as promptings of the evil one, all the thoughts she had occasionally found forming in her mind of wearing no underclothing at all beneath her white drill frock.

Under the stress of this wet heat that notion even returned at this solemn moment of prayer, but Rose spurned it away and bent her mind once more with anguished intensity to the prayer which Samuel was offering in his feeble voice and with his halting utterance. Samuel prayed for heavenly guidance in the ordering of their lives, and for the forgiveness of their sins. Then as he began to utter his customary petition for the blessing of God upon the mission, his voice faltered more and more. The mission, to which they had given their lives, could hardly be said to exist, now that von Hanneken and his troops had descended upon the place and had swept off the entire village, converts and heathen alike, to be soldiers or bearers in the Army of German Central Africa, which he was assembling. Livestock and poultry, pots and pans and foodstuffs, all had been taken, even the portable chapel, leaving only the mission bungalow standing on the edge of the deserted clearing. So the weakness vanished from Samuel's voice as he went on to pray that the awful calamity of war which had descended upon the world would soon pass away, that the slaughter and destruction would cease, and that when they had regained their sanity men would turn from war to universal peace. And with the utterance of the last of his petition Samuel's voice grew stronger yet, as he prayed that the Almighty would bless the arms of England and carry her safely through this the severest of all her trials, and would crown her efforts with victory over the godless militarists who had brought about this disaster. There was a ring of fighting spirit in Samuel's voice as he said this, and an Old Testament flavour in his speech, as another Samuel had once prayed for victory over the Amalekites.

'Amen! Amen! Amen!' sobbed Rose with her head bowed over her clasped hands.

They knelt in silence for a few seconds when the prayer was finished, and then they rose to their feet. There was still just light enough for Rose to see Samuel's white-clad figure and his white face as he stood there swaying. She made no move to light the lamp. Now that German Central Africa was in arms against England no one could tell when next they would be able to obtain oil, or matches. They were cut off from all communication with the world save through hostile territory.

'I think, sister,' said Samuel, faintly, 'that I shall retire now.'

Rose did not help him to undress–they were brother and sister and strictly brought up and it would have been impossible to her unless he had been quite incapable of helping himself–but she crept in in the dark after he was in bed to see that his mosquito curtains were properly closed round him.

'Good night, sister,' said Samuel. Even in that sweltering heat his teeth were chattering.

She herself went back to her own room and lay on her string bed in a torment of heat, although she wore only her thin nightdress. Outside she could hear the noise of the African night, the howling of the monkeys, the shriek of some beast of prey and the bellow of crocodiles down by the river, with, as an accompaniment to it all–so familiar that she did not notice it–the continuous high-pitched whine of the cloud of mosquitoes outside her curtains.

It may have been midnight before she fell asleep, moving uneasily in the heat, but it was almost dawn when she awoke. Samuel must have been calling to her. Barefooted, she hurried out of her bedroom and across the living-room into Samuel's room. But if Samuel had been sufficiently conscious to call to her he was not so now. Most of what he was saying seemed unintelligible. For a moment it appeared as if he was explaining the failure of his life to the tribunal before which he was so soon to appear.

'The poor Mission,' he said, and–'It was the Germans, the Germans.'

He died very soon after that, while Rose wept at his bedside. When her paroxysm of grief passed away she slowly got to her feet. The morning sun was pouring down upon the forest and lighting the deserted clearing, and she was all alone.

The fear which followed her grief did not last long. Rose Sayer had not lived to the age of thirty-three, had not spent ten years in the Central African forest, without acquiring a capable self-reliance to add to the simple faith of her religion. It was not long before a wild resentment against Germany and the Germans began to inflame her as she stood in the quiet bungalow with the dead man. She told herself that Samuel would not have died if his heart had not been broken by the catastrophe of von Hanneken's requisitions. It was that which had killed Samuel, the sight of the labours of ten years being swept away in an hour.

Rose told herself that the Germans had worse than Samuel's death upon their souls. They had injured the work of God; Rose had no illusion how much Christianity would be left to the converts after a campaign in the forest in the ranks of a native army of which ninety-nine men out of a hundred would be rank heathen.

Rose knew the forest. In a vague way she could picture a war fought over a hundred thousand square miles of it. Even if any of the mission converts were to survive they would never make their way back to the mission–and even if they should, Samuel was dead.

Rose tried to persuade herself that this damage done to the holy cause was a worse sin than being instrumental in Samuel's death, but she could not succeed in doing so. From childhood she had been taught to love and admire her brother. When she was only a girl he had attained the wonderful, almost mystic distinction of the ministry, and was invested in her eyes with all the superiority which that implied. Her very father and mother, hard devout Christians that they were, who had never spared the rod in the upbringing of their children, deferred to him then, and heard his words with respect. It was solely due to him that she had risen in the social scale over the immeasurable gap between being a small tradesman's daughter and a minister's sister. She had been his housekeeper and the most devoted of his admirers, his most faithful disciple and his most trusted helper for a dozen years. There is small wonder at her feeling an un-Christian rancour against the nation who had caused his death.

And naturally she could not see the other side of the question. Von Hanneken, with no more than five hundred white men in a colony peopled by a million Negroes of whom not more than a few thousand even knew they were subjects of the German flag, had to face the task of defending German Central Africa against the attacks of the overwhelming forces which would instantly be directed upon him. It was his duty to fight to the bitter end, to keep occupied as many of the enemy as possible for as long as possible, and to die in the last ditch if necessary while the real decision was being fought out in France. Thanks to the British command of the sea he could expect no help whatever from outside; he must depend on his own resources entirely, while there was no limit to the reinforcements which might reach the enemy. It was only natural, then, that with German military thoroughness he should have called up every man and woman and child within reach, as bearers or soldiers, and that he should have swept away every atom of food or material he could lay his hands on.

Rose saw no excuse for him at all. She remembered she had always disliked the Germans. She remembered how on her first arrival in the colony with her brother German officialdom had plagued them with inquisitions and restrictions, had treated them with scorn and contempt, and with the suspicion which German officials would naturally evince at the intrusion of a British missionary in a German colony. She found she hated their manners, their morals, their laws, and their ideals–in fact Rose was carried away in the wave of international hatred which engulfed the rest of the world in August 1914.

Had not her martyred brother prayed for the success of British arms and the defeat of the Germans? She looked down at the dead man, and into her mind there flowed a river of jagged Old Testament texts which he might have employed to suit the occasion. She yearned to strike a blow for England, to smite the Amalekites, the Philistines, the Midianites. Yet even as the hot wave of fervour swept over her she pulled herself up with scorn of herself for day-dreaming. Here she was alone in the Central African forest, alone with a dead man. There was no possible chance of her achieving anything.

It was at this very moment that Rose looked out across the veranda of the bungalow and saw Opportunity peering cautiously at her from the edge of the clearing. She did not recognize it as Opportunity; she had no idea that the man who had appeared there would be the instrument she would employ to strike her blow for England. All she recognized at the moment was that it was Allnutt, the Cockney engineer employed by the Belgian gold-mining company two hundred miles up the river–a man her brother had been inclined to set his face sternly against as an un-Christian example.

But it was an English face, and a friendly one, and the sight of it made her more appreciative of the horrors of solitude in the forest. She hurried on to the veranda and waved a welcome to Allnutt.

2

Allnutt was still apprehensive. He looked round him cautiously as he picked his way through the native gardens towards her.

'Where's everybody, miss?' he asked as he came up to her.

'They've all gone,' said Rose.

'Where's the Reverend–your brother?'

'He's in there–He's dead,' said Rose.

Her lips began to tremble a little as they stood there in the blazing sunlight, but she would not allow herself to show weakness. She shut her mouth like a trap into its usual hard line.

'Dead, is 'e? That's bad, miss,' said Allnutt–but it was clear that for the moment his sympathy was purely perfunctory. Allnutt's apprehension was such that he could only think about one subject at a time. He had to go on asking questions.

''Ave the Germans been 'ere, miss?' he asked.

'Yes,' said Rose. 'Look.'

The wave of her hand indicated the bare central circle of the village. Had it not been for von Hanneken this would have been thronged with a native market, full of chattering, smiling Negroes with chickens and eggs and a hundred other things for barter, and there would have been naked pot-bellied children running about, and a few cows in sight, and women working in the gardens, and perhaps a group of men coming up from the direction of the river laden with fish. As it was there was nothing, only the bare earth and the ring of deserted huts, and the silent forest hemming them in.

'It's like 'ell, isn't it, miss?' said Allnutt. 'Up at the mine I found it just the sime when I got back from Limbasi. Clean sweep of everything. What they've done with the Belgians God only knows. And God 'elp 'em, too. I wouldn't like to be a prisoner in the forest of that long chap with the glass eye–'Anneken's 'is nime, isn't it, miss? Not a thing stirring at the mine until a nigger who'd esciped showed up. My niggers just bolted for the woods when they 'eard the news. Don't know if they were afride of me or the Germans. Just skipped in the night and left me with the launch.'

'The launch?' said Rose, sharply.

'Yerss, miss. The *African Queen*. I'd been up the river to Limbasi with the launch for stores. Up there they'd 'eard about this war, but they didn't think von 'Anneken would fight. Just 'anded the stuff over to me and let me go agine. I fort all the time it wouldn't be as easy as they said. Bet they're sorry now. Bet von 'Anneken done the sime to them as 'e done at the mine. But 'e 'asn't got the launch, nor yet what's in 'er, which 'e'd be glad to 'ave, I dare say.'

'And what's that?' demanded Rose.

'Blasting gelatine, miss. Eight boxes of it. An' tinned grub. An' cylinders of oxygen and hydrogen for that weldin' job on the crusher. 'Eaps of things. Old von 'Anneken'd find a use for it all. Trust 'im for that.'

They were inside the bungalow now, and Allnutt took off his battered sun-hat as he realized he was in the presence of death. He bowed his head and lapsed into unintelligibility. Garrulous as he might be when talking of war or of his own experiences, he was a poor hand at formal condolences. But there was one obvious thing to say.

''Scuse me, miss, but 'ow long 'as 'e been dead?'

'He died this morning,' said Rose. The same thought came into her mind as was already in Allnutt's. In the tropics a dead man must be buried within six hours, and Allnutt was further obsessed with his desire to get away quickly, to retire again to his sanctuary in the river backwaters far from German observation.

'I'll bury 'im, miss,' said Allnutt. 'Don't you worry yourself, miss. I'll do it all right. I know some of the service. I've 'eard it often enough.'

'I have my prayer book here. I can read the service,' she said, keeping her voice from trembling.

Allnutt came out on the veranda again. His shifty gaze swept the edge of the forest for Germans, before it was directed upon the clearing to find a site for a grave.

'Just there'd be the best place,' he said. 'The ground'll be light there and 'e'd like to be in the shide, I expect. Where can I find a spide, miss?'

The pressing importance of outside affairs was of such magnitude in Allnutt's mind that he could not help but say, in the midst of the grisly business—

'We'd better be quick, miss, in case the Germans come back agine.'

And when it was all over and Rose stood in sorrow beside the grave with its makeshift cross. Allnutt moved restlessly beside her.

'Come on darn to the river, miss,' he urged. 'Let's get awye from 'ere.'

Down through the forest towards the river ran a steep path; where it reached the marshy flats it degenerated into something worse than a track. Sometimes they were up to their knees in mud. They slipped and staggered, sweating under the scanty load of Rose's possessions. Sometimes tree-roots gave them momentary foothold. At every step the rank marigold smell of the river grew stronger in their nostrils. Then they emerged from the dense vegetation into blinding sunlight again. The launch swung at anchor, bow upstream, close to the water's edge. The rushing brown water made a noisy ripple round anchor chain and bows.

'Careful now, miss,' said Allnutt. 'Put your foot on that stump. That's right.'

Rose sat in the launch which was to be so terribly important to her and looked about her. The launch hardly seemed worthy of her grandiloquent name of *African Queen*. She was squat, flat-bottomed, and thirty feet long. Her paint was peeling off her, and she reeked of decay. A tattered awning roofed in six feet of the stern; amidships stood the engine and boiler, with the stumpy funnel reaching up just higher than the awning. Rose could feel the heat from the thing where she sat, as an addition to the heat of the sun.

'Excuse me, miss,' said Allnutt. He knelt in the bottom of the boat and addressed himself to the engine. He hauled out a panful of hot ashes and dumped them over-side with a sizzle and a splutter. He filled the furnace with fresh wood from the pile beside him, and soon smoke appeared from the funnel and Rose could hear the roar of the draught. The engine began to sigh and splutter–Rose was later to come to know the sequence of sounds so well–and then began to leak grey pencils of steam. In fact the most noticeable point about the appearance of the engine was the presence of those leaks of steam, which poured out here, there, and everywhere from it. Allnutt peered at his gauges, thrust some more wood into the furnace, and then leaped forward round the engine. With grunts and heaves at the small windlass he proceeded to haul in the anchor, the sweat pouring from him in rivers. As the anchor came clear and the rushing current began to sweep the boat in to the bank he came dashing aft again to the engine. There was a clanking noise, and Rose felt the propeller begin to vibrate beneath her. Allnutt thrust mightily at the muddy bank with a long pole, snatched the latter on board again, and then came rushing aft to the tiller.

'Excuse me, miss,' said Allnutt again. He swept her aside unceremoniously as he put the tiller over just in time to save the boat from running into the bank. They headed, grinding and clattering, out into the racing brown water.

'I fort, miss,' said Allnutt, ''ow we might find somewhere quiet be'ind a island where we couldn't be seen. Then we could talk about what we could do.'

'I should think that would be best,' said Rose.

The river Ulanga at this point of its course has a rather indefinite channel. It loops and it winds, and its banks are marshy, and it is studded with islands–so frequent indeed are the islands that in some reaches the river appears to be more like a score of different channels winding their way tortuously through clumps of vegetation. The *African Queen* churned her slow way against the current, quartering across the broad arm in which they had started. Half a mile up on the other bank half a dozen channels offered themselves, and Allnutt swung the boat's nose towards the midmost of them.

'Would you mind 'olding this tiller, miss, just as it is now?' asked Allnutt.

Rose silently took hold of the iron rod; it was so hot that it seemed to burn her hand. She held it resolutely, with almost a thrill at feeling the *African*

Queen waver obediently in her course as she shifted the tiller ever so little. Allnutt was violently active once more. He had pulled open the furnace door and thrust in a few more sticks of fuel, and then he scrambled up into the bows and stood balanced on the cargo, peering up the channel for snags and shoals.

'Port a little, miss,' he called. 'Pull it over this side, I mean. That's it! Steady!'

The boat crawled up into a narrow tunnel formed by the meeting of the foliage overhead. Allnutt came leaping back over the cargo, and shut off the engine so that the propeller ceased to vibrate. Then he dashed into the bows once more, and just as the trees at Rose's side began apparently to move forward again as the current overcame the boat's way, he let go the anchor with a crash and rattle, and almost without a jerk the *African Queen* came to a standstill in the green-lighted channel. As the noise of the anchor chain died away a great silence seemed to close in upon them, the silence of a tropical river at noon. There was only to be heard the rush and gurgle of the water, and the sighing and spluttering of the engine. The green coolness might almost have been paradise. And then with a rush came the insects from the island thickets. They came in clouds, stinging mercilessly.

Allnutt came back into the sternsheets. A cigarette hung from his upper lip; Rose had not the faintest idea when he had lighted it, but that dangling cigarette was the finishing touch to Allnutt's portrait. Without it he looked incomplete. In later years Rose could never picture Allnutt to herself without a cigarette–generally allowed to go out–stuck to his upper lip half-way between the centre and the left corner of his mouth. A thin straggling beard, only a few score black hairs in all, was beginning to sprout on his lean cheeks. He still seemed restless and unnerved, as he battled with the flies, but now that they were away from the dangerous mainland he was better able to master his jumpiness, or at least to attempt to conceal it under an appearance of jocularity.

'Well, 'ere we are, miss,' he said. 'Safe. *And* sound, as you might say. The question is, wot next?'

Rose was slow of speech and of decision. She remained silent while Allnutt's nervousness betrayed itself in further volubility.

'We've got 'eaps of grub 'ere, miss, so we're all right as far as that goes. Two thousand fags. Two cases of gin. We can stay 'ere for months, if we want to. Question is, do we? 'Ow long d'you fink this war'll last, miss?'

Rose could only look at him in silence. The implication of his speech was obvious–he was suggesting that they should remain here in this marshy backwater until the war should be over and they could emerge in safety. And it was equally obvious that he thought it easily the best thing to do, provided that their stores were sufficient. He had not the remotest idea of striking a blow for England. Rose's astonishment kept her from replying, and allowed free rein to Allnutt's garrulity.

'Trouble is,' said Allnutt, 'we don't know which way 'elp'll come. I s'pose they're going to fight. Old von 'Anneken doesn't seem to be in two minds about it, does 'e? If our lot comes from the sea they'd fight their way up the railway to Limbasi, I s'pose. But that wouldn't be much 'elp, when all is said an' done. If they was to, though, we could stay 'ere an' just go up to Limbasi when the time came. I don't know that wouldn't be best, after all. Course, they might come down from British East. They'd stand a better chance of catching von 'Anneken that way, although 'unting for 'im in the forest won't be no child's play. But if they do that, we'll 'ave 'im between us an' them all the time. Same if they come from Rhodesia or Portuguese East. We're in a bit of a fix whichever way you look at it, miss.'

Allnutt's native Cockney wit combined with his knowledge of the country enabled him to expatiate with fluency on the strategical situation. At that very moment sweating generals were racking their brains over appreciations very similar–although differently worded–drawn up for them by their staffs. An invasion of German Central Africa in the face of a well-led enemy was an operation not lightly to be contemplated.

'One thing's sure, anyway, miss. They won't come up from the Congo side. Not even if the Belgians want to. There's only one way to come that way, and that's across the Lake. And nothing won't cross the Lake while the *Louisa*'s there.

'That's true enough,' agreed Rose.

The *Königin Luise*, whose name Allnutt characteristically anglicized to *Louisa*, was the police steamer which the German government maintained on the Lake. Rose remembered when she had been brought up from the coast, overland, in sections, eight years before. The country had been swept for bearers and workmen then as now, for there had been roads to hack through the forest, and enormous burdens to be carried. The *Königin Luise*'s boiler needed to be transported in one piece, and every furlong of its transport had cost the life of a man in the forest. Once she had been assembled and launched, however, she had swept the lake free immediately from the canoe pirates who had infested its waters from time immemorial. With her ten-knot speed she could run down any canoe fleet, and with her six-pounder gun she could shell any pirate village into submission, so that commerce had begun to develop on the Lake, and agriculture had begun to spread along such of its shores as were not marshy, and the *Königin Luise*, turning for the moment her sword into a ploughshare, had carried on such an efficient mail and passenger service across the Lake that the greater part of German Central Africa was now more accessible from the Atlantic coast across the whole width of the Belgian Congo than from the Indian Ocean.

Yet it was a very significant lesson in sea power that the bare mention of the name of the *Königin Luise* was sufficient to convince two people with a wide experience of the country, like Rose and Allnutt, of the impregnability of German Central Africa on the side of the Congo. No invasion whatever could be pushed across the Lake in the face of a hundred-ton steamer with a six-pounder popgun. Germany ruled the waters of the Lake as indisputably as England ruled those of the Straits of Dover, and the advantage to Germany which could be derived from this localized sea power was instantly obvious to the two in the launch.

'If it wasn't for the *Louisa*,' said Allnutt, 'there wouldn't be no trouble here. Old von 'Anneken couldn't last a month if they could get at 'im across the Lake. But as it is—'

Allnutt's gesture indicated that, screened on the other three sides by the forest, von Hanneken might prolong his resistance indefinitely. Allnutt tapped his cigarette with his finger so that the ash fell down on his dirty white coat. That saved the trouble of detaching the cigarette from his lip.

'But all this doesn't get us any nearer 'ome, does it, miss? But b–bless me if I can fink what we can do.'

'We must do something for England,' said Rose, instantly. She would have said, 'We must do our bit,' if she had been acquainted with the wartime slang which was at that moment beginning to circulate in England. But what she said meant the same thing, and it did not sound too melodramatic in the African forest.

'Coo!' said Allnutt.

His notion had been to put the maximum possible distance between himself and the struggle; he had taken it for granted that this war, like other wars, should be fought by the people paid and trained for the purpose. Out of touch with the patriotic fervour of the Press, nothing had been further from his thoughts than that he should interfere. Even his travels, which had necessarily been extensive, had not increased his patriotism beyond the point to which it had been brought by the waving of a penny Union Jack on Empire Day at his board school; perhaps they had even diminished it–it would be tactless to ask by what road and for what reason an Englishman came to be acting as a mechanic-of-all-work on a Belgian concession in a German colony; it was not the sort of question anyone asked, not even missionaries or their sisters.

'Coo!' said Allnutt again. There was something infectious, something inspiring, about the notion of 'doing something for England'.

But after a moment's excitement Allnutt put the alluring vision aside. He was a man of machinery, a man of facts, not of fancies. It was the sort of thing a kid might think of, and when you came to look into it there was nothing really there. Yet, having regard to the light which shone in Rose's face it might be as well to temporize, just to humour her.

'Yerss, miss,' he said, 'if there was anyfink we *could* do I'd be the first to say we ought ter. What's your notion, specially?'

He dropped the question carelessly enough, secure in his certainty that there was nothing she could suggest–nothing, anyway, which could stand against argument. And it seemed as if he were right. Rose put her big chin into her hand and pulled at it. Two vertical lines showed between her thick eyebrows as she tried to think. It seemed absurd that there was nothing two people with a boat full of high explosive could do to an enemy in whose midst they found themselves, and yet so it appeared. Rose sought in her mind for what little she knew about war.

Of the Russo-Japanese War all she could remember was that the Japanese were very brave men with a habit of shouting 'Banzai!' The Boer War had been different–she was twenty then, just when Samuel had entered the ministry, and she could remember that khaki had been a fashionable colour, and that people wore buttons bearing generals' portraits, and that the Queen had sent packets of chocolate to the men at the Front. She had read the newspapers occasionally at that time–it was excusable for a girl of twenty to do that in a national crisis.

Then after the Black Week, and after Roberts had gained the inevitable victories, and entered Pretoria, and come home in triumph, there had still been years of fighting. Someone called de Wet had been 'elusive'–no one had ever mentioned him without using that adjective. He used to charge down on the railways and blow them up.

Rose sat up with a jerk, thinking at first that the inspiration had come. But next moment the hope faded. There was a railway, it was true, but it ran from a sea which was dominated by England to the head of navigation on the Ulanga at Limbasi. It would be of small use to the Germans now, and to reach any bridge along it she and Allnutt would have to go upstream to Limbasi, which might still be in German hands, and then strike out overland carrying their explosives with them, with the probability of capture at any moment. Rose had made enough forest journeys to realize the impossibility of the task, and her economical soul was pained at the thought of running a risk of that sort for a highly problematical advantage. Allnutt saw the struggle on her face.

'It's a bit of a teaser, isn't it, miss?' he said.

It was then that Rose saw the light.

'Allnutt,' she said, 'this river, the Ulanga, runs into the Lake, doesn't it?'

The question was a disquieting one.

'Well, miss, it does. But if you was thinking of going to the Lake in this launch–well, you needn't think about it any more. We can't, and that's certain.'

'Why not?'

'Rapids, miss. Rocks an' cataracts an' gorges. You 'aven't been there, miss. I 'ave. There's a nundred miles of rapids down there. Why, the river's got a different nime where it comes out in the Lake to what it's called up 'ere. It's the Bora down there. That just shows you. No one knew they was the same river until that chap Spengler—'

'He got down it. I remember.'

'Yerss, miss. In a dugout canoe. 'E 'ad half a dozen Swahili paddlers. Map making, 'e was. There's places where this 'ole river isn't more than twenty yards wide, an' the water goes shooting down there like–like out of a tap, miss. Canoe might be all right there, but we couldn't never get this ole launch through.'

'Then how did the launch get here, in the first place?'

'By rile, miss, I suppose, like all the other 'eavy stuff. 'Spect they sent 'er up to Limbasi from the coast in sections, and put 'er together on the bank. Why, they *carried* the *Louisa* to the Lake, by 'and, miss.'

'Yes, I remember.'

Samuel had nearly got himself expelled from the colony because of the vehement protests he had made on behalf of the natives on that occasion. Now her brother was dead, and he had been the best man on earth.

Rose had been accustomed all her life to follow the guidance of another–her father, her mother, or her brother. She had stood stoutly by her brother's side during his endless bickerings with the German authorities. She had been his appreciative if uncomprehending audience when he had seen fit to discuss doctrine with her. For his sake she had slaved–rather ineffectively–to learn Swahili, and German, and the other languages, thereby suffering her share of the punishment which mankind had to bear (so Samuel assured her) for the sin committed at Babel. She would have been horrified if anyone had told her that if her brother had elected to be a Papist or an infidel she would have been the same, but it was perfectly true. Rose came of a stratum of society and of history in which woman adhered to her menfolk's opinions. She was thinking for herself now for the first time in her life, if exception be made of housekeeping problems.

It was not easy, this forming of her own judgements; especially when it involved making an estimate of a man's character and veracity. She stared fixedly at Allnutt's face, through the cloud of flies that hovered round it, and Allnutt, conscious of her scrutiny, fidgeted uncomfortably. Resolve was hardening in Rose's heart.

Ten years ago she had come out here, sailing with her brother in the cheap and nasty Italian cargo boat in which the Argyll Society had secured passages for them. The first officer of that ship had been an ingratiating Italian, and not even Rose's frozen spinsterhood had sufficed to keep him away. Her figure at twenty-three had displayed the promise which now at thirty-three it had fulfilled. The first officer had been unable to keep his eyes from its solid curves, and she was the only woman on board–in fact, for long intervals she was the only woman within a hundred miles–and he could no more stop himself from wooing her than he could stop breathing. He was the sort of man who would make love to a brass idol if nothing better presented itself.

It was a queer wooing, and one which had never progressed even as far as a hand-clasp–Rose had not even known that she was being made up to. But one of the manoeuvres which the Italian had adopted with which to ingratiate himself had been ingenious. At Gibraltar, at Malta, at Alexandria, at Port Said, he had spoken eloquently, in his fascinating broken English, about the far-flung British Empire, and he had called her attention to the big ships, grimly beautiful, and the White Ensign fluttering at the stern, and he had spoken of it as the flag upon which the sun never sets. It had been a subtle method of flattery, and one deserving of more success than the unfortunate Italian actually achieved.

It had caught Rose's imagination for the moment, the sight of the rigid line of the Mediterranean squadron battling its way into Valetta harbour through the high steep seas of a Levanter with the red-crossed Admiral's flag in the van, and the thought of the wide Empire that squadron guarded, and all the glamour and romance of Imperial dominion.

For ten years those thoughts had been suppressed out of loyalty to her brother, who was a man of peace, and saw no beauty in Empire, nor object in spending money on battleships while there remained poor to be fed and heathen to be converted. Now, with her brother dead, the thoughts surged up once more. The war he had said would never come had come at last, and had killed him with its coming. The Empire was in danger. As Rose sat sweating in the sternsheets of the *African Queen* she felt within her a boiling flood of patriotism. Her hands clasped and unclasped; there was a flush of pink showing through the sallow sunburn of her cheeks.

Restlessly, she rose from her seat and went forward, sidling past the engine, to where the stores were heaped up gunwale-high in the bows–all the miscellany of stuff comprised in the regular fortnight's consignment to the half a dozen white men at the Belgian mine. She looked at it for inspiration, just as she had looked at the contents of the larder for inspiration when confronted with a housekeeping problem. Allnutt came and stood beside her.

'What are those boxes with the red lines on them?' she demanded.

'That's the blasting gelatine I told you about, miss.'

'Isn't it dangerous?'

'Coo, bless you, miss, no.' Allnutt was glad of the opportunity of displaying his indifference in the presence of this woman who was growing peremptory and uppish. 'This is safety stuff, this is. It's quite 'appy in its cases 'ere. You can let it get wet an' it doesn't do no 'arm. If you set fire to it it just burns. You can 'it it wiv a 'ammer an' it won't go off–at least, I don't fink it will. What you mustn't do is to bang off detonators, gunpowder, like, or cartridges, into it. But we won't be doing that, miss. I'll put it over the side if it worries you, though.'

'No!' said Rose, sharply. 'We may want it.'

Even if there were no bridges to blow up, there ought to be a satisfactory employment to be found in wartime for a couple of hundredweight of explosive–and lingering in Rose's mind there were still the beginnings of a plan, even though it was a vague plan, and despite Allnutt's decisive statement that the descent of the river was impossible.

In the very bottom of the boat, half covered with boxes, lay two large iron tubes, rounded at one end, conical at the other, and in the conical ends were brass fittings–taps and pressure gauges.

'What are those?' asked Rose.

'They're the cylinders of oxygen and hydrogen. We couldn't find no use for *them*, miss, not anyhow. First time we shift cargo I'll drop 'em over.'

'No, I shouldn't do that,' said Rose. All sorts of incredibly vague memories were stirring in her mind. She looked at the long black cylinders again.

'They look like–like torpedoes,' she said at length, musingly, and with the words her plan began to develop apace. She turned upon the Cockney mechanic.

'Allnutt,' she demanded. 'Could you make a torpedo?'

Allnutt smiled pityingly at that.

'Could I mike a torpedo?' he said. 'Could I mike—? Arst me to build you a dreadnought and do the thing in style. You don't really know what you're saying, miss. It's this way, you see, miss. A torpedo—'

Allnutt's little lecture on the nature of torpedoes was in the main correct, and his estimate of his incapacity to make one was absolutely correct. Torpedoes are representative of the last refinements of human ingenuity. They cost at least a thousand pounds apiece. The inventive power of a large body of men, picked under a rigorous system of selection, has been devoted for thirty years to perfecting this method of destroying what thousands of other inventors have helped to construct. To make a torpedo capable of running true, in a straight line and at a uniform depth, as Allnutt pointed out, would call for a workshop full of skilled mechanics, supplied with accurate tools, and working under the direction of a specialist on the subject. No one could expect Allnutt working by himself in the heart of the African forest with only the *African Queen*'s repair outfit to achieve even the veriest botch of an attempt at it. Allnutt fairly let himself go on the allied subjects of gyroscopes, and compressed air chambers, and vertical rudders, and horizontal rudders, and compensating weights. He fairly spouted technicalities. Not even the Cockney spirit of enterprise with its willingness to try anything once, which was still alive somewhere deep in Allnutt's interior, could induce him to make the slightest effort at constructing a locomotive torpedo.

Most of the technicalities fell upon deaf ears. Rose heard them without hearing. Inspiration was in full flood.

'But all these things,' she said, when at last Allnutt's dissertation on torpedoes came to an end. 'All these gyroscopes and things, they're only to make the thing *go*, aren't they?'

'M'm. I suppose so.'

'Well,' said Rose with decision, at the topmost pinnacle of her inventive phase. 'We've got the *African Queen*. If we put this–this blasting gelatine in the front of the boat, with a–what did you say–a detonator there, that would be a torpedo, wouldn't it? Those cylinders. They could stick out over the end, with the gunpowder stuff in them, and the detonators in the tips, where those taps are. Then if we ran the boat against the side of a ship, they'd go off, just like a torpedo.'

There was almost admiration mingled with the tolerant pity with which Allnutt regarded Rose now. He had a respect for original ideas, and as far as Allnutt knew this was an original idea. He did not know that the earliest form of torpedo ever used had embodied this invention fifty years ago, although the early users of it took the precaution of attaching the explosive to a spar rigged out ahead of the launch in fashion minimizing the danger of the crew's being hoist with its own petard. Allnutt, in fact, made this objection while developing the others which were to come.

'Yerss,' he said, 'and supposing we did that. Supposing we found something we wanted to torpedo–an' what that would be I dunno, 'cos this is the only boat on this river–and supposing we did torpedo it, what would happen to *us*? It would blow this ole launch and us and everything else all to Kingdom Come. You think again, miss.'

Rose thought, with an unwonted rapidity and lucidity. She was sizing up Allnutt's mental attitude to a nicety. She knew perfectly well what it was she wanted to torpedo. As for going to Kingdom Come, as Allnutt put it with some hint of profanity, she had no objection at all. Rose sincerely believed that if she were to go to heaven she would spend eternity wearing a golden crown and singing perpetual hosannas to a harp accompaniment, and–although this appeared a little strange to her–enjoying herself immensely. And when the question was put to her point-blank by circumstances, she had to admit to herself that it appeared on the face of it that she was more likely to go to heaven than elsewhere. She had followed devoutly her brother's teachings; she had tried to lead a Christian life; and, above all, if that life were to end as a result of an effort to help the Empire, the crown and harp would be hers for sure.

But at the same time she knew that no certainty of a crown and harp would induce Allnutt to risk his life, even if there was the faintest possibility of his end counterbalancing his earlier sins–a matter on which Rose felt uncertainty. To obtain his necessary co-operation she would have to employ guile. She employed it as if she had done nothing else all her life.

'I wasn't thinking,' she said, 'that we should be in the launch. Couldn't we get everything ready, and have a–what do you call it?–a good head of steam up, and then just point the launch towards the ship and send her off. Wouldn't that do?'

Allnutt tried to keep his amusement out of sight. He felt it would be useless to point out to this woman all the flaws in the scheme, the fact that the *African Queen*'s boiler was long past the days when it could take a 'good head of steam', and that her propeller, like all single propellers, had a tendency to drive the boat round in a curve so that taking aim would be a matter of chance, and that the *African Queen*'s four knots would be quite insufficient to allow her approach to take any ship by surprise. There wasn't anything to torpedo, anyway, so nothing could come of this woman's hare-brained suggestions. He might as well try to humour her.

'That might work,' he said, gravely.

'And these cylinders would do all right for torpedoes?'

'I think so, miss. They're good an' thick to stand pressure. I could let the gas out of 'em, an' fill 'em up with the gelignite. I could fix up a detonator all right. Revolver cartridge would do.'

Allnutt warmed to his subject, his imagination expanding as he let himself go.

'We could cut 'oles in the bows of the launch, and 'ave the cyclinders sticking out through them so as to get the explosion as near the water as possible. Fix 'em down tight wiv battens. It might do the trick, miss.'

'All right,' said Rose. 'We'll go down to the Lake and torpedo the *Louisa*.'

'Don't talk silly, miss. You can't do that. Honest you can't. I told you before. We can't get down the river.'

'Spengler did.'

'In a canoe, miss, wiv—'

'That just shows we can, too.'

Allnutt sighed ostentatiously. He knew perfectly well that there was no possible chance of inducing the *African Queen* to make the descent of the rapids of the Ulanga. He appreciated, in a way Rose could not, the difference between a handy canoe with half a dozen skilled paddlers and a clumsy launch like the *African Queen*. He knew, even if Rose did not, the terrific strength and terrifying appearance of water running at high speed.

Yet on the other hand Rose represented–constituted, in fact–public opinion. Allnutt might be ready to admit to himself that he was a coward, that he would not lift a hand for England, but he was not ready to tell the world so. Also, although Allnutt had played lone hands occasionally in his life, they were not to his liking. Sooner than plan or work for himself he preferred to be guided–or driven. He was not avid for responsibility. He was glad to hand over leadership to those who desired it, even to the ugly sister of a deceased despised missionary. He had arrived in Central Africa as a result of his habit of drifting, when all was said and done.

That was one side of the picture. On the other, Rose's scheme appeared to him to be a lunatic's dream. He had not the least belief in their ability to descend the Ulanga, and no greater belief in the possibility of torpedoing the *Königin Luise*. The one part of the scheme which appeared to him to rest on the slightest foundation of reality was that concerned with the making of the torpedoes. He could rely on himself to make detonators capable of going off, and he was quite sure that a couple of gas cylinders full of high explosive would do all the damage one could desire; but as there did not appear the remotest chance of using them he did not allow his thoughts to dwell long on the subject.

What he expected was that after one or two experiences of minor rapids, the sight of a major one might bring the woman to her senses so that they could settle down in comfortable quiescence and wait–as he wished–for something else to turn up. Failing that, he hoped for an unspectacular and safe shipwreck which would solve the problem for them. Or the extremely unreliable machinery of the *African Queen* might give way irreparably or even–happy thought–might be induced to do so. And anyway, there were two hundred miles of comfortable river ahead before the rapids began, and Allnutt's temperament was such that anything a week off was hardly worth worrying about.

''Ave it yer own wye, then, miss,' he said resignedly. 'Only don't blame me. That's all.'

He threw his extinct cigarette into the rapid brown water over-side and proceeded to take another out of the tin of fifty in the side pocket of his greyish-white jacket. He sat down leisurely beside the engine, cocked his feet up on a pile of wood, and lit the fresh cigarette. He drew in a deep lungful of smoke and expelled it again with satisfaction. Then he allowed the fire in the end to die down towards extinction. The cigarette drooped from his upper lip. His eyelid drooped in sympathy. His wandering gaze strayed to Rose's feet, and from her feet up her white drill frock. He became aware that Rose was still standing opposite him, as if expecting something of him. Startled, he raised his eyes to her face.

'Come on,' said Rose. 'Aren't we going to start?'

'Wot, *now*, miss?'

'Yes, now. Come along.'

Allnutt was up against hard facts again. It was enough in his opinion to have agreed with the lady, to have admitted her to be right as a gentleman should. Allnutt's impression was that they might start tomorrow if the gods were unkind; next week if they were favourable. To set off like this, at half an hour's notice, to torpedo the German navy seemed to him unseemly, or at least unnatural.

'There isn't two hours of daylight left, miss,' he said, looking down the backwater to the light on the river.

'We can go a long way in two hours,' said Rose, shutting her mouth tight. In much the same way her mother had been accustomed to saying 'a penny saved is a penny earned', in the days of the little general shop in the small north country manufacturing town.

'I'll 'ave to get the ole kettle to boil agine,' said Allnutt. Yet he got down from his seat and took up his habitual attitude beside the engine.

There were embers still glowing in the furnace; it was only a few minutes after filling it with wood and slamming the door that it began its cheerful roar, and soon after that the engine began to sigh and splutter and leak steam. Allnutt commenced the activities which had been forced upon him by the desertion of his two Negro hands–winding in the anchor, shoving off from the bank, and starting the propeller turning, all as nearly simultaneously as might be. In that atmosphere, where the slightest exertion brought out a sweat, these activities caused it to run in streams; his dirty jacket was soaked between his shoulder-blades. And, once under way, constant attention to the furnace and the engine gave him no chance to cool down.

Rose watched his movements. She was anxious to learn all about this boat. She took the tiller and set herself to learn to steer. During the first few minutes of the lesson she thought to herself that it was a typical man-made arrangement that the tiller had to be put to the right to turn the boat to the left, but that feeling vanished very quickly; in fact, under Allnutt's coaching, it was not very long before she even began to see sense in a convention which spoke of 'port' and 'starboard'–Rose had always previously had a suspicion that that particular convention had its roots in man's queer taste for ceremonial and fuss.

The voyage began with a bit of navigation which was exciting and interesting, as they threaded their way through backwaters among the islands. There were snags about, and floating vegetation, nearly submerged, which might entangle the screw, and there were shoals and mudbanks to be avoided. It was not until some minutes had elapsed, and they were already a mile or two on their way, that a stretch of easy water gave Rose leisure to think, and she realized with a shock that she had left behind the mission station where she had laboured for ten years, her brother's grave, her home, everything there was in her world, in fact, and all without a thought.

That was the moment when a little wave of emotion almost overcame her. Her eyes were moist and she sniffed a little. She reproached herself with not having been more sentimental about it. Yet immediately after a new surge of feeling overcame the weakness. She thought of the *Königin Luise* flaunting her iron-cross flag on the Lake where never a White Ensign could come to challenge her, and of the Empire needing help, and of her brother's death to avenge. And, womanlike, she remembered the rudenesses and insults to which Samuel had patiently submitted from the officialdom of the colony; they had to be avenged, too. And–although Rose never suspected it–there was within her a lust for adventure, patiently suppressed during her brother's life, and during the monotonous years at the mission. Rose did not realize that she was gratified by the freedom which her brother's death had brought her. She would have been all contrition if she had realized it, but she never did.

As it was, the moment of weakness passed, and she took a firmer grip of the tiller, and peered forward with narrowed eyelids over the glaring surface of the river. Allnutt was being fantastically active with the engine. All those grey pencils of steam oozing from it were indicative of the age of that piece of machinery and the neglect from which it had suffered. For years the muddy river water had been pumped direct into the boiler, with the result that the water tubes were rotten with rust where they were not plugged with scale.

The water-feed pump, naturally, had a habit of choking, and always at important moments, demanding instant attention lest the whole boiler should go to perdition–Allnutt had to work it frantically by hand occasionally, and there were indications that in the past he or his Negro assistants had neglected this precaution, disregarding the doubtful indication of the water gauge, with the result that every water-tube joint leaked. Practically every one had been mended at some time or other, in the botched and unsatisfactory manner with which the African climate leads man to be content at unimportant moments; some had been brazed in, but more had been patched with nothing more solid than sheet iron, red lead, and wire.

As a result, a careful watch had to be maintained on the pressure gauge. In the incredibly distant past, when that engine had been new, a boiler pressure of eighty pounds to the square inch could be maintained, giving the launch a speed of twelve knots. Nowadays if the pressure mounted above fifteen the engine showed unmistakable signs of dissolution, and no speed greater than four knots could be reached. So that Allnutt had the delicate task of keeping the pressure just there, and no higher and no lower, which called for a continuous light diet for the furnace and a familiarity with the eccentricities of the pressure gauge which could only be acquired by long and continuous study. Nor was this attention to the furnace made any easier by the tendency of the wood fuel to choke the draught with ash–Allnutt, when stoking, had to plan his campaign like a chess player, looking six moves ahead at least, bearing in mind the effect on the draught of emptying the ash pan, the relative inflammability of any one of the half a dozen different kinds of wood, the quite noticeable influence of direct sunlight on the boiler, the chances of the safety valve sticking (someone had once dropped something heavy on this, and no amount of subsequent work on it could make it quite reliable again) and the likelihood of his attention being shortly called away to deal with some other crisis.

For the lubrication was in no way automatic nowadays; oil had to be stuffed down the oil-cups on the tops of the cylinders, and there were never less than two bearings calling for instant cooling and lubrication, so that Allnutt when the *African Queen* was under way was as active as a squirrel in a cage. It was quite remarkable that he had been able to bring the launch down single-handed from the mine to the mission station after the desertion of his crew, for then he had to steer the boat as well, and keep the necessary lookout for snags and shoals.

'Wood's running short,' said Allnutt, looking up from his labours, his face grey with grime, and streaked with sweat. 'We'll have to anchor soon.'

Rose looked round at where the sun had sunk to the tree-tops on the distant bank.

'All right,' she said, grudgingly. 'We'll find somewhere to spend the night.'

They went on, with the engine clanking lugubriously, to where the river broke up again into a fresh batch of distributaries. Allnutt cast a last lingering glance over his engine, and scuttled up into the bows.

'Round 'ere, miss,' he called, with a wave of his arm.

Rose put the tiller over and they surged into a narrow channel.

'Round 'ere again,' said Allnutt. 'Steady! There's a channel 'ere. Bring 'er up into it. Steady! Keep 'er at that!'

They were heading upstream now, in a narrow passage roofed over by trees, whose roots, washed bare by the rushing brown water, and tangled together almost as thick as basketwork, constituted the surface of the banks. Against the sweeping current the *African Queen* made bare headway. Allnutt let go the anchor, and, running back, shut off steam. The launch swung stationary to her mooring with hardly a jerk.

For once in a way Rose had been interested in the manoeuvres, and she filled with pride at the thought that she had understood them–she never usually troubled; when travelling by train she never tried to understand railway signals, and even the Italian first officer had never been able to rouse her interest in ships' work. But today she had understood the significance of it all, of the necessity to moor bows upstream in that narrow fast channel, in consequence of the anchor being in the bows. Rose could not quite imagine what that fast current would do to a boat if it caught it while jammed broadside on across a narrow waterway, but she could hazard a guess that it would be a damaging business. Allnutt stood watching attentively for a moment to make certain that the anchor was not dragging, and then sat down with a sigh in the sternsheets.

'Coo,' he said, 'it's 'ot work, ain't it, miss? I could do with a drink.'

From the locker beside her he produced a dirty enamel mug, and then a second one.

'Going to 'ave one, miss?' Allnutt asked.

'No,' said Rose, shortly. She knew instinctively that she was about to come into opposition with what Samuel always called Rum. She watched fascinated. From under the bench on which he sat Allnutt dragged out a wooden case, and from out of the case he brought a bottle, full of some clear liquid like water. He proceeded to pour a liberal portion into the tin mug.

'What is that?' asked Rose.

'Gin, miss,' said Allnutt. 'An' there's only river water to drink it with.'

Rose's knowledge of strong drink was quite hazy. The first time she had ever sat at a table where it was served had been in the Italian steamer; she remembered the polite amusement of the officers when she and her brother had stiffly refused to drink the purple-red wine which appeared at every meal. During her brother's ministry in England she had heard drink and its evil effects discussed; there were even bad characters in the congregation who were addicted to it, and with whom she had sometimes tried to reason. At the mission Samuel had striven ineffectively for ten years to persuade his coloured flock to abandon the use of the beer they had been accustomed to brew from time immemorial–Rose knew how very ineffective his arguments had been. And there were festivals when everybody brewed and drank stronger liquors still, and got raging drunk, and made fearful noises, and all had sore heads the next morning, and not even the sore heads had reconciled Samuel to the backsliding of his congregation the night before.

And the few white men all drank, too–although up to this minute Rose, influenced by Samuel's metaphorical description, had been under the impression that their tipple was a fearsome stuff called Rum, and not this innocent-appearing gin. Rum, and the formation of unhallowed unions with native women, and the brutal conscription of native labour, had been the triple-headed enemy Samuel was always in arms against. Now Rose found herself face to face with the first of these sins. Drink made men madmen. Drink rotted their bodies and corrupted their souls. Drink brought ruin in this world and damnation in the next.

Allnutt had filled the other mug over-side, and was now decanting water into the gin, trying carefully but not very effectively, to prevent too much river alluvium from entering his drink. Rose watched with increasing fascination. She wanted to protest, to appeal to Allnutt's better feelings, even to snatch the terrible thing from him, and yet she stayed inert, unmoving. Possibly it was that common sense of hers which kept her quiescent. Allnutt drank the frightful stuff and smacked his lips.

'That's better,' he said.

He put the mug down. He did not start being maniacal, nor to sing songs, nor to reel about the boat. Instead, with his sinfulness still wet on his lips he swung open the gates of Paradise for Rose.

'Now I can think about supper,' he said. 'What about a cup o' tea, miss?'

Tea! Heat and thirst and fatigue and excitement had done their worst for Rose. She was limp and weary and her throat ached. The imminent prospects of a cup of tea roused her to trembling excitement. Twelve cups of tea each Samuel and she had drunk daily for years. Today she had had none–she had eaten no food either, but at the moment that meant nothing to her. Tea! A cup of tea! Two cups of tea! Half a dozen great mugs of tea, strong, delicious, revivifying! Her mind was suffused with rosy pictures of an evening's tea drinking, a debauch compared with which the spring sowing festivities at the village by the mission station were only a pale shade.

'I'd like a cup of tea,' she said.

'Water's still boiling in the engine,' said Allnutt, heaving himself to his feet. 'Won't take a minute.'

The tinned meat that they ate was, as a result of the heat, reduced to a greasy semi-liquid mass. The native bread was dark and unpalatable. But the tea was marvellous. Rose was forced to use sweetened condensed milk in it, which she hated–at the mission they had cows until von Hanneken commandeered them–but not even that spoilt her enjoyment of the tea. She drank it strong, mug after mug of it, as she had promised herself, with never a thought of what it was doing inside her to the lining of her stomach; probably it was making as pretty a picture of that as ever she had seen at a Band of Hope lantern lecture where they exhibited enlarged photographs of a drunkard's liver. She gulped down mug after mug. For a moment her body temperature shot up to fever heat, but presently there came a blissful perspiration–not the sticky, prickly sweat in which she moved all day long, but a beneficent and cooling fluid, bringing with it a feeling of ease and well-being.

'Those Belgians up at the mine wouldn't never drink tea,' said Allnutt, tilting the condensed milk tin over his mug of black liquid. 'They didn't know what was good.'

'Yes,' said Rose. She felt positive friendship for Allnutt welling up within her. She slapped at the mosquitoes without irritation.

When the scanty crockery had been washed and put away Allnutt stood up and looked about him; the light was just failing.

'Ain't seen no crocodiles in this arm, miss, 'ave you?' he asked.

'No,' said Rose.

'No shallows for 'em 'ere,' said Allnutt. 'And current's too fast.'

He coughed a little self-consciously.

'I want to 'ave a bath before bedtime,' he said.

'So do I.'

'I'll go up in the bows an' 'ave mine 'olding on to the anchor chain,' said Allnutt. 'You stay down 'ere and do what you like, miss. Then if we don't look it won't matter.'

Rose found herself stripping herself naked right out in the open, with only a dozen feet away a man doing the same, and only a slender funnel six inches thick between them. Somehow it did not matter. Rose was conscious that out of the tail of her eye she could see a greyish white shape lower itself over the launch's bows, and she could hear prodigious kickings and splashings as Allnutt took his bath. She sat naked on the low gunwale in the stern and lowered her legs into the water. The fast current boiled round them, deliciously cool, tugging at her ankles, insidiously luring her farther. She slipped over completely, holding on to the boat, trailing her length on the surface of the water. It was like Paradise–ever so much better than her evening bath at the mission, in a shallow tin trough of lukewarm water, and obsessed with the continual worry lest the unceasing curiosity of the natives should cause prying eyes to be peering at her through some chink or crevice in the walls.

Then she began to pull herself out. It was not easy, what with the pull of the current and the height of the gunwale, but a final effort of her powerful arms drew her up far enough to wriggle at last over the edge. Only then did she realize that she had been quite calmly contemplating calling to Allnutt for assistance, and she felt that she ought to be disgusted with herself, but she could not manage it. She fished a towel out of her tin box of clothes and dried herself, and dressed again. It was almost dark by now, dark enough, anyway, for a firefly on the bank to be visible, and for the noises of the forest to have stilled so much that the sound of the river boiling along the banks seemed to have grown much louder.

'Are you ready, miss?' called Allnutt, starting to come aft.

'Yes,' said Rose.

'You better sleep 'ere in the stern,' said Allnutt, 'case it rains. I got a couple of rugs 'ere. There ain't no fleas in 'em.'

'Where are you going to sleep?'

'For'rard, miss. I can make a sort of bed out o' them cases.'

'What, on the–the explosives?'

'Yerss, miss. Won't do it no 'arm.'

That was not what had called for the question. To Rose there seemed something against nature in the idea of actually sleeping on a couple of hundredweights of explosive, enough to lay a city in ruins–or to blow in the side of a ship. But she thrust the strangeness of the thought out of her mind; everything was strange now.

'All right,' she said, briefly.

'You cover up well,' said Allnutt, warningly. 'It gets nearly cold on the river towards morning–look at the mist now.'

A low white haze was already drifting over the surface of the river.

'All right,' said Rose again.

Allnutt retraced his steps into the bows, and Rose made her brief preparations for the night. She did not allow herself to think about the skins–black or white, clean or dirty–which had already been in contact with those rugs. She laid herself on the hard floor-boards with the rugs about her and her head on a pillow of her spare clothing. Her mind was like a whirlpool in which circled a mad inconsequence of thoughts. Her brother had died only that morning and it seemed at least a month ago. The memory of his white face was vague although urgent. With her eyes closed her retinas were haunted with persistent after-images of running water–water foaming round snags and rippling over shallows, and all agleam with sunshine where the wind played upon it. She thought of the *Königin Luise* queening it on the Lake. She thought of Allnutt, only a yard or two from her virgin bed, and of his naked body vanishing over the side of the launch. She thought again of the dead Samuel. The instant resolution which followed to avenge his death caught her on the point of going to sleep. She turned over restlessly. The flies were biting like fiends. She thought of Allnutt's drooping cigarette, and of how she had cheated him into accompanying her. She thought of the play of the light and shade on the water when they had first anchored. And with that shifting pattern in her mind's eye she fell asleep for good, utterly worn out.

3

Rose actually contrived to sleep most of the night. It was the rain which woke her up, the rain and the thunder and lightning. It took her a little while to think where she was, lying there in the dark on those terribly hard floor-boards. All round her was an inferno of noise. The rain was pouring down as it only can in Central Africa. It was drumming on the awning over her, and streaming in miniature waterfalls from the trees above into the river. The lightning was lighting up brilliantly even this dark backwater, and the thunder roared almost without intermission. A warm wind came sweeping along the backwater, blowing the launch upstream a little so that whenever it dropped for a moment the pull of the current brought her back with a jerk against her moorings like a small earthquake. Almost at once Rose felt the warm rain on her face, blown in by the wind under the awning, and then the awning began to leak, discharging little cataracts of water on to the floor-boards round her.

It all seemed to happen at once–one moment she was asleep, and the next she was wet and uncomfortable and the launch was tugging at her anchor chain. Something moved in the waist of the launch, and the lightning revealed Allnutt crawling towards her, very wet and miserable, dragging his bedding with him. He came pattering up beside her, whimpering for all the world like a little dog. The leaky awning shot a cataract of water down his neck.

'Coo!' he said, and shifted his position abruptly.

By some kind chance Rose's position was such that none of these direct streams descended upon her; she was only incommoded by the rain in the wind and the splashes from the floor-boards. But that was the only space under the awning as well protected. Allnutt spent much time moving abruptly here and there, with the pitiless streams searching him out every time. Rose heard his teeth chattering as he came near her, and was for a moment minded to put out her arm and draw him to her like a child; she blushed secretly at discovering such a plan in her mind, for Allnutt was no more a child than she was.

Instead she sat up and asked—

'What can we do?'

'N-nothing, miss,' said Allnutt miserably and definitely.

'Can't you shelter anywhere?'

'No, miss. But this won't last long.'

Allnutt spoke with the spiritless patience bred by a lifetime's bad luck. He moved out of one stream of water into another. Samuel in the same conditions would have displayed a trace of bad temper–Rose had to measure men by Samuel's standard, because she knew no other man so well.

'You poor man!' said Rose.

'You poor chap' or 'You poor old thing' might have sounded more comradely or sympathetic, but Rose had never yet spoken of men as 'chaps' or 'old things'.

'I'm so sorry,' said Rose, but Allnutt only shifted uncomfortably again.

Then the storm passed as quickly as it came. In a country where it rains an inch in an hour an annual rainfall of two hundred inches means only two hundred hours' rain a year. For a little while the trees above still tossed and roared in the wind and then the wind died away, and there was a little light in the backwater, and with the stillness of dawn the sound of the river coursing through the tree-roots overshadowed every other noise. The day came with a rush, and for once the sun and the heat were beneficent and life-giving, instead of being malignant tyrants. Rose and Allnutt roused themselves; the whole backwater steamed like a laundry.

'What's to be done before we move on?' asked Rose. It did not occur to her that there was anything they might do instead of moving on. Allnutt scratched at his sprouting beard.

'Got no wood,' he said. ''Ave to fill up with thet. Plenty of dead stuff 'ere, I should fink. An' we'll 'ave to pump out. The ole boat leaks anyways, an' wiv all this rine—'

'Show me how to do that.'

So Rose was introduced to the hand pump, which was as old and as inefficient as everything else on board. In theory one stuck the foot of it down between the skin and the floor-boards, and then worked a handle up and down, whereupon the water beneath the boards was sucked up and discharged through a spout over-side; by inclining the boat over to the side where the pump was the boat could be got reasonably dry. But that pump made a hard job of it. It choked and refused duty and squeaked and jammed, and pinched the hands that worked it, all with an ingenuity which seemed quite diabolical. Rose came in the end to hate that pump more bitterly than anything she had ever hated before. Allnutt showed her how to begin the job.

'You go and get the wood,' said Rose, settling the pump into the scuppers and preparing to work the handle. 'I'll do this by myself.'

Allnutt produced an axe which was just as rusty and woebegone as everything else in the boat, hooked the bank with the boat-hook, and swung himself ashore with the stern painter in his hand. He vanished into the undergrowth, looking cautiously round at every step for fear of snakes, while Rose toiled away at the pump. There was nothing on earth so ingeniously designed to abolish the feeling of morning freshness. Rose's face empurpled, and the sweat poured down as she toiled away with the cranky thing. At intervals Allnutt appeared on the bank, dumping down fresh discoveries of dead wood to add to the growing pile at the landing place, and then, pulling in on the stern painter, he began the ticklish job of loading the fuel on board, standing swaying periously on the slippery uneven foothold.

Rose quitted her work at the pump to help him–there was by now only a very little water slopping below the floor-boards–and when the wood was all on board, the waist piled high with it, they stopped for breath and looked at each other.

'We had better start now,' said Rose.

'Breakfast?' said Allnutt, and then, playing his trump card, 'Tea?'

'We'll have that going along,' said Rose. 'Let's get started now.'

Perhaps Rose had all her life been a woman of action and decision, but she had spent all her adult life under the influence of her brother. Samuel had been not merely a man but a minister, and therefore had a twofold–perhaps fourfold–right to order the doings of his womenfolk. Rose had always been content to follow his advice and abide by his judgement.

But now that she was alone the reaction was violent. She was carrying out a plan of her own devising, and she would allow nothing to stop her, nothing to delay her. She was consumed by a fever for action. That is not to belittle the patriotic fervour which actuated her as well. She was most bitterly determined upon doing something for England; she was so set and rigid in this determination that she never had to think about it, any more than she had to think about breathing or the beating of her pulse. She was more conscious of the motive of avenging her brother's death; but perhaps the motive of which she was most conscious was her desire to wipe out the ten years of insults from German officialdom to which the meek Samuel had so mildly submitted. It was the thought of those slights and insults which brought a flush to her cheek and a firmer grip to her hand, and spurred her on to fresh haste.

Allnutt philosophically shrugged his shoulders, much as he had seen his Belgian employers do up at the mine. The woman was a bit mad, but it would be more trouble to argue with her than to obey her, at present; Allnutt was not sufficiently self-analytical to appreciate that most of the troubles of his life resulted from attempts to avoid trouble. He addressed himself, in his usual attitude of prayer, to the task of getting the engine fire going again, and while the boiler was heating he continued the endless task of lubrication. When the boiler began to sigh and gurgle he looked inquiringly at Rose, and received a nod from her. Rose was interested to see how Allnutt proposed to extricate the launch from the narrow channel in which she was moored.

It was a process which called for much activity on Allnutt's part. First he strained at the anchor winch, ineffectively, because the current which was running was too strong to allow him to wind the heavy boat up to the anchor.

So he started the screw turning until the *African Queen* was just making headway against the current, and then, rushing forward, he got the anchor clear and wound in. But he did not proceed up the backwater–there was no means of knowing if the way was clear all the way up to the main-stream, and some of these backwaters were half a dozen miles long. Instead, he hurried back to the engine and throttled down until the launch was just being carried down by the current although the engine was still going ahead.

This gave her a queer contrariwise steerage way in which one thought in terms of the stern instead of the bow. Allnutt left the engine to look after itself and hastened back to take the tiller from Rose's hand; he could not trust her with it. He eased the *African Queen* gently down until they reached the junction with the broad channel of the main backwater. Then he scuttled forward and jerked the engine over into reverse, and then, scuttling back to the tiller, he swept the stern round upstream, keeping a wary eye on the bow meanwhile lest the current should push it into the bank, and then, the moment the bow was clear, while catastrophe threatened astern, he dashed forward again, started the screw in the opposite direction, and came leaping back once more to the tiller to hold the boat steady while she gathered way downstream. It was a neat bit of boatmanship; Rose, even with her limited experience, could appreciate it even though some of the implications were lost upon her–the careful balance of eddy against current at the bend, for instance, and the subtle employment of the set of the screw to help in the turn. She nodded and smiled her approval, but Allnutt could not stay for applause. Already there were danger signals from the engine, and Allnutt had to hand over the tiller and resume his work over it.

The *African Queen* resumed her solemn career down the river, with Rose happily directing her. This was the main backwater of the section, a stream a hundred yards wide, so there was no reason to apprehend serious navigational difficulties. Rose had already learned to recognize the ugly V-shaped ripple on the surface caused by a snag just below, and the choppy appearance which indicated shallows, and she understood now the useful point that the *African Queen*'s draught was such that if an under-water danger was so deep as to make no alteration in the appearance of the surface she could be relied upon to go over it without damage. The main possible source of trouble was in the wind; a brisk breeze whipped the surface of the river into choppy wavelets which obscured the warning signs.

At present today there was no wind blowing. Everything was well. In this backwater, running between marshy uninhabited islands, there was no fear of observation from the shore, the navigation was easy, and the *African Queen*'s engines were in a specially helpful mood so that she squattered along without any particular crisis arising. Allnutt was even able to snatch half a dozen separate minutes away from them in which to prepare breakfast. He brought Rose's share to her, and she did not even notice the filthy oiliness of his hands. She ate and drank as she held the tiller and was almost happy.

With a four-knot current to help her the launch slid along between the banks at a flattering speed, and slithered round the bends most fascinatingly. Quite subconsciously Rose was learning things about water in motion, about eddies and swirls, which would be very valuable to her later on.

The heat increased, and as the sun rose higher Rose was no longer able to keep the launch in the shade of the huge trees on the banks. The direct sunlight hit them like a club when they emerged into it, and even back in the sternsheets Rose could feel the devastating heat of the fire and boiler.

She felt sorry for Allnutt, and could sympathize with him over his unhygienic habit of drinking unfiltered river water. At the mission she had seen to it that every drop of water she and Samuel drank was first filtered and then boiled for fear of hookworm and typhoid and all the other plagues which water can carry. It did not seem to matter now. Under the worn awning she had at least a little shade. Allnutt was labouring in the blazing sun.

Allnutt, as a matter of fact, was one of those men who have become inured to work in impossible temperatures. He had worked as a greaser in merchant ships passing down the Red Sea, in engine rooms at a temperature of a hundred and forty degrees; to him the free air of the Ulanga river was far less stifling, even in the direct sun, than many atmospheres with which he was acquainted. It did not occur to him to complain about this part of his life; there was even an aesthetic pleasure to be found in inducing that rotten old engine to keep on moving.

Later the backwater came to an end, merging with the main river again. The banks fell away as they came out on to the broad stately stream, a full half-mile wide, brilliantly blue in prospect under the cloudless sky, although it still appeared its turbid brown when looked into over the side. Allnutt did not like these open reaches. Von Hanneken and his army were somewhere on the banks of the river; perhaps he had outposts watching everywhere. It was only when she was threading her way between islands that the *African Queen* could escape observation. He stood up on the gunwale anxiously, peering at the banks for a sign of a break in them.

Rose was aware of his anxiety and its cause, but she did not share his feelings. She was completely reckless. She did not think it even remotely possible that anything could impede her in the mission she had undertaken. As for being taken prisoners by von Hanneken, she could not believe such a thing could happen–and naturally she had none of the misgivings which worried Allnutt as to what von Hanneken would do to them if he caught them obviously planning mischief in the *African Queen*. But she indulged Allnutt in his odd fancy; she swung the *African Queen* round so that she headed across to the far side of the bend, where at the foot of the forest-clad bluffs the head of a long narrow island was to be seen–Rose already knew enough about the river to know that the backwater behind the island was almost for certain the entrance to a fresh chain of minor channels winding between tangled islands and not rejoining the main river for perhaps as much as ten miles.

The *African Queen* clanked solemnly across the river. Her propeller shaft was a trifle out of truth, and numerous contacts with submerged obstructions had bent her propeller blades a little, so that her progress was noisy and the whole boat shook to the thrust of the screw, but by now Rose was used to the noise and the vibration. It passed unnoticed. Rose stood up and looked forward keenly as they neared the mouth of the backwater. She was quite unconscious of the dramatic picture she presented, sunburned, with set jaw and narrowed eyes, standing at the tiller of the battered old launch in the blinding sunlight. All she was doing was looking out for snags and obstructions.

They glided out of the sunlight into the blessed shade of the narrow channel. The wash of the launch began to break close behind them in greyish-brown waves against the bank; the water plants close to the side began to bow in solemn succession as the boat approached them, lifting their heads again when they were exactly opposite, and then being immediately buried in the dirty foam of the wash. The channel along which they were passing broke into three, and Rose had to exercise quick decision in selecting the one which appeared the most navigable. Then there were periods of anxiety when the channel narrowed and the current quickened, and it seemed possible that they might not get through after all, and the anxiety would only end when the channel suddenly joined a new channel whose breadth and placidity promised freedom from worry for a space.

Those island backwaters were silent places. Even the birds and the insects seemed to be silent in that steaming heat. There were only the tall trees, and the tangled undergrowth, and the aspiring creeper, and the naked tree-roots along the banks. It seemed as if the *African Queen*'s clanking progress was the first sound ever to be heard there, and when that sound was stilled, when they anchored to collect more fuel, Rose found herself speaking in whispers until she shook off the crushing influence of the silence.

That first day was typical of all the days they spent descending the river before they reached the rapids. There were incidents, of course. There were times when the backwater they were navigating proved to be jammed by a tangle of tree-trunks, and they had to go back cautiously in reverse until they found another channel. There was one occasion when their channel broadened out into a wide, almost stagnant lake surrounded by marshy islands, and full of lilies and weeds that twined themselves round the propeller and actually brought the boat to a standstill, so that Allnutt had to strip himself half-naked and lower himself into the water and hack the screw clear with a knife, and then pole the launch out again. Every push of the pole against the loose mud of the bottom brought forth volleys of bubbles from the rotting vegetation, so that the place stank in the sunlight.

It might have been that incident which caused the subsequent trouble with the propeller thrust block, which held them up for half a day while Allnutt laboured over it.

There were times now and then during the day when the heavens opened and cataracts of rain poured down–rain so heavy as to set the floor-boards awash and to cause Rose to toil long and painfully with that malignant bit of apparatus, the hand pump. They had to expect rain now, for it was the time of the autumn rains. Rose was only thankful that it was not springtime, for during the spring rains the storms were much longer and heavier than those they had to endure now. These little daily thunderstorms were a mere nothing.

Rose was really alive for the first time in her life. She was not aware of it in her mind, although her body told her so when she stopped to listen. She had passed ten years in Central Africa, but she had not lived during those ten years. That mission station had been a dreary place. Rose had not read books of adventure which might have told her what an adventurous place tropical Africa was. Samuel was not an adventurous person–he had not even taken a missionary's interest in botany or philology or entomology. He had tried drearily yet persistently to convert the heathen without enough success to maintain dinner-table conversation over so long a time as ten years. It had been his one interest in life (small wonder that von Hanneken's sweeping requisitions had broken his heart) and it had therefore been Rose's one interest–and a woefully small one at that.

Housekeeping in a Central African village was a far duller business than housekeeping in a busy provincial town, and German Central Africa was the dullest colony of all Africa. There was only a tiny sprinkling of white men, and the Kaiser's imperial mandate ran only in the fringes of the country, in patches along the coast, and along the border of the Lake, and about the head-waters of the Ulanga where the gold mine was, and along the railway from the Swahili coast. Save for a very few officials, who conducted themselves towards the missionaries as soldiers and officials might be expected to act towards mere civilians of no standing and aliens to boot, Rose had seen no white men besides Allnutt–he, by arrangement with the Belgian company, used to bring down their monthly consignments of stores and mail from Limbasi–and his visits were conditional upon the *African Queen* being fit to travel and upon there being no work upon the mining machinery demanding his immediate attention.

And Samuel had not allowed Rose even to be interested in Allnutt's visits. The letters that had come had all been for him, always, and Allnutt was a sinner who lived in unhallowed union with a Negress up at the mine. They had to give him food and hospitality when he came, and to bring into the family prayers a mention of their wish for his redemption, but that was all. Those ten years had been a period of heat-ridden monotony.

It was different enough now. There was the broad scheme of proceeding to the Lake and freeing it from the mastery of the Germans; that in itself was enough to keep anyone happy. And for detail to fill in the day there was the river, wide, mutable, always different. There could be no monotony on a river with its snags and mudbars, its bends and its backwaters, its eddies and its swirls. Perhaps those few days of active happiness were sufficient recompense to Rose for thirty-three years of passive misery.

4

There came an evening when Allnutt was silent and moody, as though labouring under some secret grievance. Rose noticed his mood, and looked sharply at him once or twice. There was no feeling of companionship this evening as they drank their tea. And when the tea was drunk Allnutt actually got out the gin bottle and poured himself a drink, the second that day, and drank, and filled his cup again, still silent and sulky. He drank again, and the drink seemed to increase his moodiness. Rose watched these proceedings, disconcerted. She realized by instinct that she must do something to maintain the morale of her crew. There was trouble in the wind, and this gloomy silent drinking would only increase it.

'What's the matter, Allnutt?' she asked, gently. She was genuinely concerned about the unhappiness of the little Cockney, quite apart from any thought of what bearing it might have upon the success of her enterprise.

Allnutt only drank again, and looked sullenly down at the ragged canvas shoes on his feet. Rose came over nearer to him.

'Tell me,' she said, gently, again, and then Allnutt answered.

'We ain't goin' no farther down the river,' he said. 'We gone far enough. All this rot about goin' to the Lake.'

Allnutt did not use the word 'rot', but although the word he used was quite unfamiliar to Rose she guessed that it meant something like that. Rose was shocked–not at the language, but at the sentiment. She had been ready, she thought, for any surprising declaration by Allnutt, but it had not occurred to her that there was anything like this in his mind.

'No going any farther?' she said. 'Allnutt! Of course we must!'

'No bloody "of course" about it,' said Allnutt.

'I can't think what's the matter,' said Rose, with perfect truth.

'The river's the matter, that's what. And Shona.'

'Shona!' repeated Rose. At last she had an inkling of what was worrying Allnutt.

'If we go on tomorrer,' said Allnutt, 'we'll be in the rapids tomorrer night. An' before we get to the rapids we'll 'ave to go past Shona. I'd forgotten about Shona until last night.'

'But nothing's going to happen to us at Shona.'

'Ain't it? Ain't it? 'Ow do you know? If there's anywheres on this river the Germans are watching it'll be Shona. That's where the road from the south crosses the river. There was a nigger ferry there before the Germans ever came 'ere. They'll 'ave a gang watching there. Strike-me-dead-certain. An' there ain't no sneaking past Shona. I been there, in this old *African Queen*. I knows what the river's like. It's just one big bend. There ain't no backwaters there, nor nothing. You can see clear across from one side to the other, an' Shona's on a 'ill on the bank.'

'But they won't be able to stop us.'

'Won't be able—! Don't talk silly, miss. They'll 'ave rifles. Some of them machine-guns, p'raps. Cannons, p'raps. The river ain't more than 'alf a mile wide.'

'Let's go past at night, then.'

'That won't do, neither. 'Cause the rapids start just below Shona. That 'ill Shona stands on is the beginning of the cliffs the river runs between. If we was to go past Shona in the dark we'd 'ave to go on darn the rapids in the dark. An' I ain't goin' darn no rapids in the dark, neither. An' I ain't goin' darn no rapids at all, neither, neither. We didn't ought to 'ave come darn as far as this. It's all damn-bloody barmy. They might find us '*ere* if they was to come out in a canoe from Shona. I'm goin' back tomorrer up to that other backwater we was in yesterdye. That's the sifest plice for us.'

Allnutt had shaken off all shame and false modesty. He preferred appearing a coward in Rose's eyes to risking going under fire at Shona or to attempting the impossible descent of the gorges of the Ulanga. There was not going to be any more hanky-panky about it. He drank neat gin to set the seal on his resolution.

Rose was white with angry disappointment. She tried to keep her temper, to plead, to cajole, but Allnutt was in no mood for argument. For a while he was silent now, and made no attempt to combat Rose's urgings, merely opposing to them a stolid inertia. Only when, in the growing darkness, Rose called him a liar and a coward–and Rose in her sedate upbringing had never used those words to anyone before–did he reply.

'Coward, yourself,' he said. 'You ain't no lady. No, miss. That's what my poor ole mother would 'ave said to *you*. If my mother was to 'ear you—'

When a man who is drinking neat gin starts talking about his mother he is past all argument, as Rose began to suspect. She drew herself stiffly together in the sternsheets while Allnutt's small orgy continued. She was alone in a small boat with a drunken man–a most dreadful situation. She sat tense in the darkness, ready to battle for her life or her virtue, and quite certain that one or the other would be imperilled before morning. Every one of Allnutt's blundering movements in the darkness put her on the *qui vive*. When Allnutt knocked over his mug or poured himself out another drink she sat with clenched fists, convinced that he was preparing for an assault. There was a frightful period of time while Allnutt was in muddled fashion reaching beneath the bench for the case of gin to find another bottle, during which she thought he was crawling towards her.

But Allnutt was neither amorous nor violent in his cups. His mention of his mother brought tears into his eyes. He wept at his mother's memory, and then he wept over the fate of Carrie, which was his name for the brawny Swahili-speaking Negress who had been his mistress at the mine and who was now Heaven knew where in the train of von Hanneken's army. Then he mourned over his own expatriation, and he sobbed through his hiccups at the thought of his boyhood's friends in London. He began to sing, with a tunelessness which was almost unbelievable, a song which suited his mood–

'Gimmy regards ter Leicester Square
Sweet Piccadilly an' Myefair
Remember me to the folks darn ther
They'll understa-and.'

He dragged out the last note to such a length that he forgot what he was singing, and he made two or three unavailing attempts to recapture the first fine careless rapture before he ceased from song. Then in his mutterings he began to discuss the question of sleep, and, sure enough, the sound of his snores came before long through the darkness to Rose's straining ears. She had almost relaxed when a thump and a clatter from Allnutt's direction brought her up to full tension again. But his peevish exclamations told her that he had only fallen from the seat to the floor-boards, mugs, bottle and all, and in two minutes he was happily snoring again, while Rose sat stiff and still, and chewed the cud of her resentment against him, and the reek of the spilt gin filled the night air.

Despair and hatred kept her from sleep. At that moment she had no hope left on earth. Her knowledge of men–which meant her knowledge of Samuel and of her father–told her that when a man said a thing he meant it and nothing on earth would budge him from that decision. She could not believe that Allnutt would ever be induced, or persuaded, or bullied, into attempting to pass Shona, and she hated him for it. It was the first time she had ever really set her heart on anything, and Allnutt stood in her way immovable. Rose wasted no idle dreams on quixotic plans of getting rid of Allnutt and conducting the *African Queen* single-handed; she was level-headed enough and sufficiently aware of her own limitations not to think of that for a second.

At the same time she seethed with revolt and resentment, even against the god-like male. Although for thirty years she had submitted quite naturally to the arbitrary decisions of the superior sex, this occasion was different. She wanted most passionately to go on, she knew she ought to; conscience and inclination combined to make her resent Allnutt's change of front. There was nothing left to live for if she could not get the *African Queen* down to the Lake to strike her blow for England; and such was the obvious sanctity of such a mission that she stood convicted in her own mind of mortal sin if she did not achieve it. Her bitterness against Allnutt increased.

She resolved, as the night wore on, to make Allnutt pay for his arbitrariness. She set her teeth, she chewed at her nails–and Rose's mother's slipper had cured her of nail-biting at the age of twelve–as she swore to herself to make Allnutt's life Hell for him. Rose had never tried to raise Hell in her life, but in her passion of resentment she felt inspired to it. In the darkness her jaw came forward and her lips compressed until her mouth was no more than a thin line and there were deep parentheses from her nostrils to the corners of her mouth. Anyone who could have seen Rose at that moment would have taken her for a shrew, a woman with a temper of a fiend. Now that Samuel was dead Rose had no use for patience or resignation or charity or forgiveness or any of the passive Christian virtues.

Nor was her temper improved by a night of discomfort. Cramps and aches made her change her position, but she could not, even if she would, lie down in the sternsheets where Allnutt was all asprawl across the boat, and she would not make her way forward to take up Allnutt's usual nest among the explosives. She sat and suffered on the ribbed bench, on which she had sat all day, and even her shapely and well-covered hind-quarters protested. She slept, towards morning, by fits and starts, but that amount of sleep did nothing towards mollifying her cold rage.

Dawn revealed to her Allnutt lying like a corpse on the floor-boards. His face, hardly veiled by the sprouting beard, was a dirty grey, and from his open mouth came soft but unpleasing sounds. There was no pleasure in the sight of him. Rose got to her feet and stepped over him; she would have spurned him with her foot save that she did not want to rouse him to violent opposition to what she was going to do. She dragged out the case of gin, took out a bottle and stripped the lead foil from the end. The cork was of the convenient kind which needs no corkscrew. She poured the stuff over-side, dropped the bottle in after it, and began on another.

When for the third time the glug-glug-glug of poured liquid reached Allnutt's ears he muttered something, opened his eyes, and tried to sit up.

'Jesus!' he said.

It was not the sight of what Rose was doing which called forth the exclamation, for he still did not know the reason for the noise which had roused him. Allnutt's head was like a lump of red-hot pain. And it felt as if his head, besides, were nailed to the floor-boards, so that any attempt at raising it caused him agony. And his eyes could not stand the light; opening them intensified the pain. He shut his eyes and moaned; his mouth was parched and his throat ached, too.

Allnutt was not a natural-born drinker; his wretched frame could not tolerate alcohol. It is possible that his small capacity for liquor played a part in the unknown explanation of his presence in German Central Africa. And one single night's drinking always reduced him to this pitiful state, sick and white and trembling, and ready to swear never to drink again–quite content, in fact, not to drink for a month at least.

Rose paid no attention to his moaning and whimpering. She flung one look of scorn at him, and then poured the last bottle of the case over-side. She went forward and dragged the second case of gin out from among the boxes of stores. She took Allnutt's favourite screwdriver and began to prise the case open, with vicious wrenches of her powerful wrist. As the deal came away from the nails with a splintering crash Allnutt rolled over to look at her again. With infinite trouble he got himself into a sitting position, with his hands at his temples, which felt as if they were being battered with white-hot hammers. He looked at her quite uncomprehending with his aching eyes.

'Coo Jesus!' he said, pitifully.

Rose wasted neither time nor sympathy on him; she went calmly on pouring gin over-side. Allnutt got to his knees with his arms on the bench. At the second attempt he got his knees up on the bench, with his body hanging over-side. Rose thought he would fall in, but she did not care. He leaned over the gurgling brown water and drank feverishly. Then he slumped back on the bench and promptly brought up all the water he had drunk, but he felt better, all the same. The light did not hurt his eyes now.

Rose dropped the last bottle into the river, and made certain there was no other in the case. She returned to the sternsheets, passing him close enough to touch him, but apparently without noticing his presence. She took her toilet things from her tin box, picked up a rug, and went back again into the bows. By the time Allnutt was able to turn his head in that direction the rug was pinned from the funnel stay to the funnel, screening her from view. When she took down the rug again her toilet was obviously finished; she folded the rug, still without paying him the least attention, and began to prepare her breakfast, and then to eat it with perfect composure. Breakfast completed, she cleared all away, and came back into the stern, but she still gave him neither look nor word. With an appearance of complete abstraction she picked out the dirty clothes from her tin box and began to wash them over-side, pinning each garment out to dry to the awning overhead. And when she had finished the washing she sat down and did nothing; she did not even look at Allnutt. This was, in fact, the beginning of the Great Silence.

Rose had been able to think of no better way of making Allnutt's life a hell–she did not realize that it was the most effective way possible. Rose had remembered occasions when Samuel had seen fit to be annoyed with her, and had in consequence withdrawn from her the light of his notice and the charm of his conversation, sometimes for as much as twenty-four hours together. Rose remembered what a dreadful place the bungalow had become then, and how Samuel's silence had wrought upon her nerves, until the blessed moment of forgiveness. She could not hope to equal Samuel's icily impersonal quality, but she would do her best, especially as she could not, anyway, bring herself to speak to the hateful Allnutt. She had no reliance in her ability to nag, and nagging was the only other practicable method of making Allnutt's life hell for him.

During the morning Allnutt did not take very special notice of his isolation. His wretched mind and body were too much occupied in getting over the effects of drinking a bottle and a half of overproof spirit in a tropical climate. But as the hours passed, and draught after draught of river water had done much towards restoring their proper rhythm to his physiological processes, he grew restless. He felt that by now he had earned forgiveness for his late carouse; and it irked him unbearably not to be able to talk as much as he was accustomed. He thought Rose was angry at him for his drunkenness; he attached little importance, in his present state, to the matter of his refusal to go on past Shona and down the rapids.

'Coo, ain't it 'ot?' he said. Rose paid him no attention.

'We could do wiv anuvver storm,' said Allnutt. 'Does get yer cool fer a minute, even if these little b–beggars bite 'arder than ever after it.'

Rose remembered a couple of buttons that had to be sewn on. She got out the garment and her housewife, and calmly set about the business. At her first movement Allnutt had thought some notice of his existence was about to be taken, and he felt disappointed when the purpose of the movement became apparent.

'Puttin' yer things to rights prop'ly, ain't yer, miss?' he said.

A woman sewing has a powerful weapon at her disposition when engaged in a duel with a man. Her bent head enables her to conceal her expression without apparently trying; it is the easiest matter in the world for her to simulate complete absorption in the work in hand when actually she is listening attentively; and if even then she feels disconcerted or needs a moment to think she can always play for time by reaching for her scissors. And some men–Allnutt was an example–are irritated effectively by the attention paid to trifles of sewing instead of to their fascinating selves.

It took only a few minutes for Allnutt to acknowledge the loss of the first round of the contest.

'Ain't yer goin' to answer me, miss?' he said, and then, still eliciting no notice, he went on–'I'm sorry for what I done last night. There! I don't mind sayin' it, miss. What wiv the gin bein' there to my 'and, like, an' the 'eat, an' what not, I couldn't 'elp 'avin' a drop more than I should 'ave. You've pied me back proper already, pourin' all the rest of it awye, now 'aven't you, miss? Fair's fair.'

Rose made no sign of having heard, although a better psychologist than Allnutt might have made deductions from the manner of twirling the thread round the shank and the decisive way in which she oversewed to end off. Allnutt lost his temper.

''Ave it yer own wye, then, yer psalm-singing ole bitch,' he said, and pitched his cigarette-end over-side with disgust and lurched up into the bows–Rose's heart came up into her mouth at his first movement, for she thought he was about to proceed to physical violence. His true purpose fortunately became apparent before she had time to obey her first impulse and put down her sewing to defend herself. She converted her slight start into a test of the ability of the button to pass through the hole.

From his earliest days, from his slum-bred father and mother, Allnutt had heard, and believed, that the ideal life was one with nothing to do, nothing whatever, and plenty to eat. Yet up to today he had never experienced that ideal combination. He had never been put to the necessity of amusing himself; he had always had companions in his leisure periods. Solitude was as distressing to him as responsibility, which was why, when his Negro crew had deserted him at the mine, he had involved himself in considerable personal exertion to come down to the mission station and find Rose and Samuel. And to be cooped, compulsorily, in a thirty-foot boat was harassing to the nerves, especially nerves as jangled as Allnutt's. Allnutt fidgeted about in the bows until he got on Rose's nerves as well; but Rose kept herself under control.

It was not long before Allnutt, moving restlessly about the boat, began to occupy himself with overhauling the engine. For a long time that engine had not had so much attention as Allnutt lavished on it today. It was greased and cleaned and nurse-maided, and a couple of the botched joints were botched a little more effectively. Then Allnutt found he was thoroughly dirty, and he washed himself with care, and in the middle of the washing he thought of something else, and he went to his locker and got out his razor and cleaned it of the thick grease which kept it from rusting and set himself to shave. It was only sheer laziness which had caused him to cease to shave when war broke out, and which accounted for that melodramatic beard. Shaving a beard like that was painful, but Allnutt went through with it, and when it was over he stroked his baby-smooth cheeks with satisfaction. He put cylinder oil on his tousled hair and worked at it until he had achieved the ideal coiffure with an artistic quiff along his forehead. He replaced his things in his locker with elaborate care and sat down to recover. Five minutes later he was on his feet again, moving about the cramped space wondering what he could do now. And all round him was the silence of the river; that in itself was sufficient to get on his nerves.

5

A man of stronger will than Allnutt, or a more intelligent one, might have won that duel with Rose. But Allnutt was far too handicapped. He could not do chess problems in his head, or devote his thoughts to wondering what was the military situation in Europe, or debate with himself the pros and cons of Imperial Preference, or piece together all the fragments of Shakespeare he could remember. He knew no fragments of Shakespeare at all, and his mind had never been accustomed to doing any continuous thinking, so that in a situation in which there was nothing to do but think he was helpless. In the end it was the noise of the river eternally gurgling round the tree-roots which broke down his last obstinacy.

Allnutt had made several attempts to get back on a conversational footing with Rose, and only once had he managed to induce her to say anything.

'I hate you,' she had said then. 'You're a coward and you tell lies, and I won't speak to you ever.'

And she had shaken herself free. The very first advance Allnutt had made had surprised her. All she had hoped to achieve was revenge, to make Allnutt suffer for the failure of her scheme. She had not believed it possible that she might reduce him to obedience by this means. She had no idea of the power at her disposal, and she had never had to do with a weak-willed man before. Her brother and her father were men with streaks of flint-like obstinacy within their pulpy exteriors. It was only when Allnutt began to ask for mercy that it dawned upon her that she might be able to coerce him into obeying her. By that time, too, she had a better appreciation of the monotony of the river, and its possible effect on Allnutt.

Her one fear was lest Allnutt should become violent. She had steeled herself to hear unmoved anything he might say to her, or any indelicate expressions he might employ, but the thought of physical force undoubtedly gave her a qualm. But she was a well-set-up woman, and she put unobtrusively into her waist-belt the stiletto from her work-bag. If he should try to rape her (Rose did not use the word 'rape' to herself; she thought of his trying to 'do that to her') she would dig at him with it; its point was sharp.

She need not have worried. Physical violence, even towards a woman, was a long way from Allnutt's thoughts. It might have been different if there had been any gin left to give him the necessary stimulus, but providentially all the gin was in the river.

Just as Rose had underestimated her power, so had Allnutt underestimated his offence. At first he had taken it for granted that Rose was angry with him because he had got drunk. Her scheme for going on down the river was so ludicrously wild that he hardly thought about it when the silence began; it was only by degrees that he came to realize that Rose was in earnest about it, and that she would give him no word and no look until he had agreed to it. It was this realization which stiffened up his obstinacy after his preliminary apologies and strengthened him to endure another twenty-four hours of torture.

For it was torture, of a refinement only to be imagined by people of Allnutt's temperament who have undergone something like his experiences. There was nothing to do at all except to listen to the gurgle of the river among the tree-roots and to endure the attack of insects in the crushing heat. Allnutt could not even walk about in the cumbered little launch. Silence was one of the things he could not endure; his childhood in shrieking streets and his subsequent life in machine shops and engine-rooms had given him no taste for it. But the silence was only a minor part of the torture; what Allnutt felt more keenly still was Rose's presence, and her manner of ignoring him. That riled him inexpressibly. It was possible that he could have borne the silence of the river if it had not been for the continuous irksomeness of Rose's silent presence. That hurt him in a sensitive spot, his vanity, in a manner of speaking, or his self-consciousness.

In the end it even interfered with Allnutt's sleep, which was the surest sign of its effectiveness. Insomnia was a quite new phenomenon to Allnutt, and worried him enormously. Days without exercise for either body or mind, a slightly disordered digestion, and highly irritable nerves combined to deprive Allnutt of sleep for one entire night. He shifted and twisted and turned on his uncomfortable bed on the explosives; he sat up and smoked cigarettes; he fidgeted and he tried again unavailingly. He really thought there was something seriously wrong with him. Then in the morning, faced with yet another appalling blank day, he gave in.

'Let's 'ear wotcha wanter do, miss,' he said. 'Tell us, and we'll do it. There, miss.'

'I want to go down the river,' said Rose.

Once more appalling visions swept across Allnutt's imagination, of machine-guns and rocks and whirlpools, of death by drowning, of capture by the Germans and death in the forest of disease and exhaustion. He was frightened, and yet he felt he could not stay a minute longer in this backwater. He was panicky with the desire to get away, and in his panic he plunged.

'All right, miss,' he said. 'Carm on.'

Some time later the *African Queen* steamed out of the backwater into the main river. It was a broad, imposing piece of water here. There was more wind blowing than there had been for some time, and up the length of the river ran long easy waves, two feet high, on which the *African Queen* pitched in realistic fashion, with splashes of spray from the bows which sizzled occasionally on the boiler.

Rose sat at the tiller in a fever of content. They were on their way to help England once more. The monotony of inaction was at an end. The wind and the waves suited her mood. It is even possible that the thought that they were about to run into danger added to her ecstasy.

'That's the 'ill Shona stands on,' Allnutt yelled to Rose, gesticulating. Rose only nodded, and Allnutt bent over the fire again cursing under his breath. Even when they had started Allnutt had still hoped. He had not been quite sure how far down Shona was. Something might easily happen to postpone the issue before they reached there. He really meant to burn out a water tube at the right moment, so that they would have to lie up again for repairs before making the attempt. But now they were in sight of Shona unexpectedly; if the engine were disabled the current would bring them right down to the place, and there was no shelter on either bank. They would be prisoners instantly, and, appalling though the choice was, Allnut would rather risk his life than be taken prisoner. He began feverishly to nurse the engine into giving its best possible running.

The waist of the launch was heaped with the wood collected that morning; Allnutt crouched behind the pile and hoped it could stop a bullet. He saw that ready to his hand were the chunks of rotten wood which would give an instant blaze and a quick head of extra steam when the moment came. He peered at the gauges. The *African Queen* came clattering majestically down the river, a feather of smoke from her funnel, spray flying from her bows, a white wake behind her.

The Askaris on the hills saw her coming, and ran to fetch the white commandant of the place. He came hurriedly to the mud walls (Shona is a walled village) and mounted the parapet, staring at the approaching launch through his field-glasses. He took them from his eyes with a grunt of satisfaction; he recognized her as the *African Queen*, the only launch on the Ulanga, for which he had received special orders from von Hanneken to keep a sharp look-out. She had been lost to sight–skulking in backwaters, presumably–for some time, and her capture was desirable. The German captain of reserve was glad to see her coming in like this. Presumably the English missionaries and the mechanic had tired of hiding, or had run short of food, and were coming in to surrender.

There could be no doubt that that was what they intended, for a mile below Shona, just beyond the next bend, in fact, the navigation of the river ceased where it plunged into the gorges. She would be a useful addition to his establishment; he would be able to get about in her far more comfortably than by the forest paths. And if ever the English, coming up by the old caravan route, reached the opposite side of the river, the launch would be of great assistance in the defence of the crossing. The mere mention of her capture would be a welcome change in the eternal dull reports he had to send by runner to von Hanneken.

He was glad she was coming in. He stood and watched her, a white speck on the broad river. Clearly the people in her did not know where the best landing-place was. They were keeping to the outside of the bend in the fast current, on the opposite side to the town. They must be intending to come in below the place, where there was a belt of marshy undergrowth–it was silly of them. When they came in he would send a message to them to come back up the river to the canoe-landing place, where he could come and inspect them without getting himself filthy and without having to climb the cliff.

He walked over to the adjacent face of the town to observe her further progress round the bend. The fools were still keeping to the outside of the bend. They showed no signs of coming in at all. He put his hands to his helmet brim, for they were moving now between him and the sun, and the glare was dazzling. They weren't coming in to surrender after all. God knew what they intended, but whatever it was, they must be stopped. He lifted up his voice in a bellow, and his dozen Askaris came trotting up, their cartridge belts over their naked chests, their Martini rifles in their hands. He gave them their orders, and they grinned happily, for they enjoyed firing off cartridges, and it was a pleasure which the stern German discipline denied them for most of their time. They slipped cartridges into the breeches, and snapped up the levers. Some of them lay down to take aim. Some of them kept their feet, and aimed standing up, as their instincts taught them. The sergeant chanted the mystic words, which he did not understand, telling them first to aim and then to fire. It was a ragged enough volley when it came.

The captain of reserve looked through his glasses; the launch showed no signs of wavering from her course, and kept steadily on, although the fools in her must have heard the volley, and some at least of the bullets must have gone somewhere near.

'Again,' he growled, and a second volley rang out, and still there was no alteration of course towards the town on the part of the launch. This was growing serious. They were almost below the town now, and approaching the farther bend. He snatched a rifle from one of the Askaris and threw himself on his stomach on the ramparts. Someone gave him a handful of cartridges, and he loaded and took aim. They were right in the eye of the sun now, and the glare off the water made the foresight indistinct. It was very easy to lose sight of the white awning of the boat as he aimed.

A thousand metres was a long range for a Martini rifle with worn rifling. He fired, reloaded, fired again, and again, and again. Still the launch kept steadily on. As he pointed the rifle once more at her something came between him and the launch; it was the trees on the farther point. They were round the corner. With a curse he jumped to his feet, and, rifle in hand, he ran lumbering along the ramparts with his Askaris behind him. Sweating, he galloped down across the village clearing and up the steep path through the forest the other side. Climbing until he thought his heart would burst he broke through the undergrowth at last at the top of the cliff where he could look down the last reach of the river before the cataract. They had almost reached the farther end; the launch was just swinging round to take the turn. The captain of reserve put his rifle to his shoulder and fired hurriedly, twice, although, panting as he was, there was no chance of hitting. Then they vanished down the gorge, and there was nothing more he could do.

Yet he stood staring down between the cliffs for a long minute. Von Hanneken would be furious at the news of the loss of the launch, but what more could he have done? He could not justly be expected to have foreseen this. No one in their senses would have taken a steam launch into the cataract, and a reserve officer's training does not teach a man to guard against cases of insanity. The poor devils were probably dead already, dashed to pieces against the rocks; and the launch was gone for good and all. He could not even take steps to recover fragments, for the tall cliffs between which the river ran were overhanging and unscalable, and not five kilometres from Shona the country became so broken and dense that the course of the Lower Ulanga was the least known, least explored part of German Central Africa. Only Spengler–another born fool–had got through it.

The captain of the reserve was not going to try; he formed that resolve as he turned away from the cliff-top. And as he walked back to Shona, bathed in sweat, he was still undecided whether he should make any mention of this incident in his report to von Hanneken. It would only mean trouble if he did; von Hanneken would be certain it was all his fault, and von Hanneken was a tyrant. It might be better to keep quiet about it. The launch was gone and the poor devils in it were dead. That little worm of a missionary and his horse-faced wife–or was it his sister? Sister, of course. And the English mechanic who worked on the Belgian mine. He had a face like a rat. The world would not miss them much. But he was sorry for the poor devils, all the same.

When he came up through the gate again into Shona he was still not sure whether or not he would inform von Hanneken of the incident. The Askaris would gossip, of course, but it would be a long time before the gossip reached von Hanneken's ears.

6

The rivers of Africa are nearly all rendered unnavigable along some part of their course by waterfalls and cataracts. The rivers on their way to the sea fall from the central tableland into the coastal plain, but the Ulanga is not one of this category. Its course is inland, towards the Great Lakes, and its cataracts mark the edge of the Great Rift Valley. For in the centre of Africa an enormous tract of territory, longer than it is wide, has sunk bodily far below the level of the tableland, forming a deep trough, of a total area approaching that of Europe, in which are found the Great Lakes with their own river system, and, ultimately, the source of the Nile.

Along much of their length the sides of this trough are quite steep, but the Ulanga, as befits the noble river it is, has scoured out its bed and cut back along it so that nowhere in its course is there an actual waterfall; its cataracts indicate the situation of strata of harder rock which have not been cut away as efficiently as have the softer beds. The natural result is that in its course from the tableland to the valley the Ulanga flows frequently through deep sunless gorges between high cliffs; overhead is rough steep country untravelled and unmapped in which the presence of a river could hardly be suspected.

At Shona the river begins its descent; because that is the last point at which the river may be crossed by raft or canoe, the old slave caravan route along the edge of the rift passes the Ulanga here, and Shona grew up as the market at the point of intersection of caravan route and river route. The choice of site at the top of the cliff overlooking the river, where the gorge has actually begun, was of course due to the need of protection from slave-raiders who, being quite willing to sell their own fathers if they saw a profit in it, were never averse to snapping up business acquaintances should they be so careless as not to take proper precautions.

It was down the outside of the great bend on which Shona stands that Rose steered the *African Queen*. It was convenient that on this course they not merely kept in the fastest current but also were as far away as possible from the village. She looked up the steep bank, across the wide expanse of water. The forest came to an end half-way up the slope; near the crest she could see high red walls, and above them the thatched roofs of the huts on the very top of the hill. It was too far to see details. She could see no sign of their coming being noticed. There was no sign of life on the banks; and as they went on down the river the banks grew rapidly higher and steeper into nearly vertical walls of rock, fringed at the foot with a precarious growth of vegetation.

She looked at the red walls on the top of the cliff; she thought she could see a movement there, but it was half a mile off and she could not be sure. Perhaps von Hanneken had swept off the inhabitants here as he had done along the rest of the river, to leave a desert in the possible path of the approach of the English. They were practically opposite the town now, and nothing had happened. A glance at the near bank showed her the speed at which they were moving; the river was already running much faster in its approach to the cataracts.

Suddenly there was a peculiar multiple noise in the air, like bees in a violent hurry accompanied by the sound of tearing paper. Rose's mind had just time to take note of the sound when she heard the straggling reports of the rifles which had caused it. The volley echoed back from cliff to cliff, growing flatter the longer the sound lasted.

'They've got us!' said Allnutt, leaping up in the waist. His face was lop-sided with excitement. Rose could pay no attention to him. She was looking keenly ahead at the swirls on the surface. She was keeping the *African Queen* in the fastest water along the very edge of the back eddy off the bank.

There came another volley which still left them untouched. Rose edged the tiller over so as to get more in mid-stream, in order to take the reverse bend which was rapidly approaching. Allnutt remained standing in the waist; he had forgotten all about taking shelter behind the woodpile. Rose swung the tiller over for the bend; so absorbed was she in her steering that she did not notice the bullet which whipped close by her as she did so. A moment later the whole boat suddenly rang like a harp and Allnutt turned with a jump. The wire funnelstay on the starboard side had parted close above the gunwale; the long end hung down by the funnel. Even as Allnutt noticed it there was a metallic smack and two holes showed high up in the funnel. Rose had brought the tiller over again, straightening the launch on her course after taking the bend. Next moment Shona vanished behind the point, and Allnutt stood shaking his fists in derision at the invisible enemy and shouting at the top of his voice.

'Look after the engine!' screamed Rose.

They were flying along now, for the river was narrowing and its current increasing with every yard. The wind could not reach the surface here, between the cliffs. Most of the surface was smooth and sleek like greased metal, but here and there were ominous furrows and ripples betraying the hidden inequalities of its bed. Rose steered carefully through the smooth water. She found she had to make ample allowance for leeway now; so fast was the current that the boat went flying down broadside on towards these obstructions in the course of the turn. There was another bend close ahead, a very sharp one from all appearance. She dragged the tiller across; she found she was not satisfied with her field of view ahead, and leaped up on to the bench, holding the tiller down by her right knee. With her left hand she reached up and tore the rotten canvas awning from its stanchions. They neither of them noticed the last two shots which the German captain of reserve fired at them at this moment.

The *African Queen* slithered round the corner, and lurched and rolled and heaved as she encountered the swirls which awaited her there. But the steady thrust of her screw carried her through them; that was Allnutt's job, to see that the launch had steerage way to take her through the eddies and to enable Rose to steer some sort of course with the following current.

There were rocks in the channel now, with white water boiling round them, and Rose saw them coming up towards her with terrifying rapidity. There was need for instant decision in picking the right course, and yet Rose could not help noticing, even in that wild moment, that the water had lost its brown colour and was now a clear glassy green. She pulled the tiller over and the rocks flashed by. Lower down, the channel was almost obstructed by rocks. She saw a passage wide enough for the boat and swung the bows into it. Stretching down before her there was a long green slope of racing water. And even as the *African Queen* heaved up her stern to plunge down it she saw at the lower end of the fairway a wicked black rock just protruded above the surface–it would rip the whole bottom out of the boat if they touched it. She had to keep the boat steady on her course for a fraction of a second until the channel widened a trifle, and then fling herself on the tiller to swing her over. The boat swayed and rocked, and wriggled like a live thing as she brought the tiller back again to straighten her out. For a dreadful second it seemed as if the eddy would defeat her efforts, but the engine stuck to its work and the kick of the propeller forced the boat through the water. They shaved through the gap with inches to spare, and the bows lurched as Rose fought with the tiller and they swung into the racing eddies at the tail of the rapid. Next moment they had reached the comparative quiet of the deep fast reach below, and Rose had time to sweep the streaming sweat from her face with the back of her left forearm.

All the air was full of spray and of the roar of rushing water, whose din was magnified by the cliffs close at either side. The sound was terrifying to Allnutt, and so were the lurches and lunges of the boat, but he had no time to look about him. He was far too busy keeping the engine running. He knew, even better than did Rose, that their lives depended on the propeller giving them steerage way. He had to keep the steam pressure well up and yet well below danger point; he had to work the feed pump; he had to keep the engine lubricated. He knew that they would be lost if he had to stop the engine, even for a second. So he bent to his work with panic in his soul while the boat beneath his feet leaped and bucked and lurched worse than any restive horse, and while out of the tail of his eye he could glimpse rocks flashing past with a speed which told him how great was their own velocity.

'Our Father which art in Heaven–' said Allnutt to himself, slamming shut the furnace door. He had not prayed since he left his Board School.

It was only a few seconds before they reached the next rapid, like the last a stretch of ugly rocks and boiling eddies and green inclined slopes of hurtling water, where the eye had to be quick and the brain quicker still, where the hand had to be steady and strong and subtle and the will resolute. Half-way down the rapid there was a wild confusion of tossing water in which the eye was necessarily slower in catching sight of those rocks just awash whose touch meant death. Rose rode the mad whirlwind like a Valkyrie. She was conscious of an elation and an excitement such as only the best of her brother's sermons had ever aroused. Her mind was working like a machine with delirious rapidity. She forced the *African Queen* to obey her will and weave a safe course through the clustering dangers. The spray flew in sheets where the currents conflicted.

Lower down still the river tore with incredible speed and without obstruction along a narrow gorge walled in with vertical faces of rock. To Rose, with a moment to think during this comparative inaction, it seemed as if this must be almost as fine as travelling in a motor-car–an experience she had never enjoyed but had often longed for.

It was only for a moment that she could relax, however, for close ahead the gorge turned a corner, so sharply that it looked as if the river plunged into the rock face, and Rose had to make ready for the turn and brace herself to face whatever imminent dangers lay beyond out of sight. She kept her eye on the rock at the water's edge on the inside of the bend, and steered to pass it close. So the *African Queen* was beginning to turn just before she reached the bend, and it was as well that it was so.

The sweep of the current took her over to the opposite bank as if she were no more than a chip of wood, while Rose tugged at the tiller with all her strength. The bows came round, but it looked for a space as if her stern would be flung against the rocks. The propeller battled against the current; the boat just held her own, and then as they drifted down the backwash caught her and flung her out again into mid-stream so that Rose had to force the tiller across like lightning, and hardly were they straight than she had instantly to pick out a fresh course through the rocks that studded the surface in flurries of white foam.

Later she saw that Allnutt was trying to attract her attention. In the roar of the rapids he could not make his voice reach her. He stood up with one anxious eye still on his gauges, and he held up a billet of wood, tapped it, and waved a hand to the shore. It was a warning that fuel was running short, and fuel they must have. She nodded, although the next moment she had to look away and peer ahead at the rocks. They shot another series of rapids, and down another gorge, where, the half-mile river compressed into fifty yards, they seemed to be travelling at the speed of a train. It was becoming vitally urgent that they should find somewhere to stop, but nowhere in that lightning six miles was there a chance of mooring. Allnutt was standing up brandishing his billet of wood again. Rose waved him impatiently aside. She was as much aware of the urgency of the situation as he was; there was no need for these continued demonstrations. They ran on, with Rose doggedly at the tiller.

Then she saw what she wanted. Ahead a ridge of rocks ran almost across the stream, only broken in the centre, where the water piled up and burst through the gap in a vast green hump. Below the wings of this natural dam there was clear water–an absence of obvious rocks, at least; each corner was a circling foam-striped eddy. She put the *African Queen* at the gap. She reared up as she hit the piled-up water, put down her nose and heaved up her stern, and shot down the slope. At the foot were high green waves, each one quite stationary, and each one hard and unyielding. The launch hit them with a crash. Green water came boiling over the short deck forward and into the boat. Anyone with less faith than Rose would have thought that the *African Queen* was doomed to put her nose deeper and deeper while the torrent thrust against the up-heaved stern until she was overwhelmed. But at the last possible moment she lurched and wallowed and shook herself loose like some fat pig climbing out of a muddy pond. And even as she came clear Rose was throwing her weight on the tiller, her mind a lightning calculating machine juggling with currents and eddies. The launch came round, hung steady as the tiller went back, shot forward in one eddy, nosed her way into another.

'Stop!' shrieked Rose. Her voice cut like a knife through the din of the fall, and Allnutt, dazed, obeyed.

It was nicely calculated. The launch's residual way carried her through the edge of the eddy into the tiny strip of quite slack water under the lip of the dam. She came up against this natural pier with hardly a bump, and instantly a shaking Allnutt was fastening painters to rocks, half a dozen of them, to make quite sure, while the *African Queen* lay placid in the one bit of still water. Close under her stern the furious Ulanga boiled over the ridge; downstream it broke in clamour round a new series of rocks. Above the dam it chafed at its banks and roared against the rocks which Rose had just avoided. All about them was frantic noise; the air was filled with spray, but they were at peace.

'Coo!' said Allnutt, looking about them. Even he did not hear the word as he said it.

And Rose found herself weak at the knees, and with an odd empty feeling in her stomach, and with such an aching, overwhelming need to relieve herself that she did not care if Allnutt saw her doing so or not.

One reaction followed another rapidly in their minds, but despite their weariness and hunger they were both of them conscious of a wild exhilaration. No one could spend half a day shooting rapids without exhilaration. There was a sense of achievement which affected even Allnutt. He was garrulous with excitement. He chattered volubly to Rose, although she could not hear a word he said, and he smiled and nodded and gesticulated, filled with a most unusual sense of well-being. This deep gorge was cool and pleasant. Up above, trees grew to the very edge of the cliffs, so that the light which came down to them was largely filtered through their leaves and was green and restful. For once they were out of the sweltering heat and glare of Africa. There were no insects. There was no fear of discovery by the Germans.

With a shock Allnutt suddenly realized that only that morning they had been under fire; it seemed like weeks ago. He had to look round at the dangling funnel stay to confirm his memory, and automatically he went over to it and set himself to splice the broken wire. With that, the work of the boat got under way once more. Rose set up that wicked old hand pump and began to free the boat of the water which had come in; it slopped over the floor-boards as they moved. But pumping in that restful coolness was not nearly as irksome as pumping on the glaring upper river. Even the pump, which one might have thought to be beyond reformation, was better behaved.

Allnutt climbed out of the boat in search of fuel, and any doubts as to the possibility of finding wood in the gorge were soon dispelled. There was driftwood in plenty. On shelves in the steep cliff past floods had left wood in heaps, much of it the dry friable kind which best suited the *African Queen*'s delicate digestion. Allnutt brought loads of it down to the boat, and to eke out its supply the slack water above the shore end of the dam was thick with sticks and logs brought down from above and caught up here. Allnutt fished out a great mass of it and left it to drain on the steep rocky side; by next morning it would be ready for use in the furnace if helped out with plenty of the dry stuff.

Rose had in fact been really fortunate in finding the *African Queen* ready to her hand. The steam launch with all its defects possessed a self-contained mobility denied to any other method of transport. No gang of carriers in the forest could compare with her. Had she been fitted with an internal combustion engine she could not have carried sufficient liquid fuel for two days' running. As it was, taking her water supply from over-side and sure of finding sufficient combustibles on shore she was free of the two overwhelming difficulties which at that very moment were hampering the *Emden* in the Indian Ocean and were holding the *Königsberg* useless and quiescent in the Rufiji delta. Regarded as the captain of a raiding cruiser Rose was happily situated. She had overcome her difficulties with her crew, and the stock of provisions heaped up in the bows showed as yet hardly a sign of diminution. She had only navigational difficulties to contend with; difficulties represented by the rocks and the rapids of the Lower Ulanga.

For the present neither Rose nor Allnutt cared about navigational difficulties in the future. They were content with what they had done that day. Nor did they moralize about the *African Queen*'s peculiar advantages. The everlasting roar of water in their ears was unfavourable to continuous thought and rendered conversation quite impossible. They could only grin at each other to indicate their satisfaction, and eat enormously, and swill tea in vast mugs with lots of condensed milk and sugar–Rose found herself craving for sugar after the excitement of the day, and, significantly enough, made no effort to combat the craving. She had forgotten at the moment that any desire of the body should be suspect and treated as an instigation of the devil.

Freedom and responsibility and an open-air life and a foretaste of success were working wonders on her. She had spent ten years in Africa, but those ten years, immured in a dark bungalow, with hardly anyone save Samuel to talk to, had no more forwarded her development than ten years in a nunnery would have done. She had lived in subjection all her life, and subjection offers small scope to personality. And no woman with Rose's upbringing could live for ten days in a small boat with a man–even a man like Allnutt–without broadening her ideas and smoothing away the jagged corners and making of her something more like a human being. These last ten days had brought her into flower.

Those big breasts of hers, which had begun to sag when she had begun to lapse into spinsterhood, were firm and upstanding now again, and she could look down on them swelling out the bosom of her white drill frock without misgiving. Even in these ten days her body had done much towards replacing fat where fat should be and eliminating it from those areas where it should not.

Her face had filled out, and though there were puckers round her eyes caused by the sun they went well with her healthy tan and lent piquancy to the ripe femininity of her body. She drank her tea with her mouth full in a way which would have horrified her a month back.

When their stomachs were full the excitement and fatigue of the day began to take effect. Their eyelids began to droop and their heads began to nod even as they sat with their dishes on their knees. The delicious coolness of the gorge played its part. Down between those lofty cliffs darkness came imperceptibly; they were once more in a land where there was twilight. Rose actually found herself nodding off fast asleep while Allnutt was putting the dishes away. The tremendous din of the water all round her was hardly noticed by her weary ears. For three nights now she had slept very badly in consequence of worrying about Allnutt. She felt now that she had nothing more to worry about; although the fire of her mission still burned true and strong she was supremely content. She smiled as she composed herself to sleep, and she smiled as she slept, to the blaring song of the Ulanga.

And Allnutt snuggled down on the boxes of explosives in a similar condition of beautiful haziness. What with fatigue and natural disability and the roar of the river he was in no condition for continuous thought, and the night before had been sleepless because of Rose's treatment of him. It was astonishing that it should only be the night before. It seemed more like a childish memory. After that had been settled they had come down past Shona. Coo, they had sucked the old Germans in proper. The poor beggars hadn't thought of shooting at them until they were past the town. Bet they were surprised to see the old *African Queen* come kiting past. They hadn't believed anyone would try to get down those gorges. Didn't believe nobody could. Well, this'd show 'em. Allnutt smiled too, in company with Rose, as he slid off into sleep to the music of the Ulanga.

It is a pretty problem of psychology to decide why Allnutt should have found a little manhood–not much, but a little–in Rose's society, among the broad reaches of the Ulanga, and in the roaring gorges, and under the fire of the German Askaris, when it had been so long denied him in the slums of his youth, and the stokeholds and the engine-rooms and brothels, and the easy-going condescension of the white men's mess of the Ulanga Goldfields. The explanation may lie in the fact that Allnutt in this voyage so far had just sufficient experience of danger to give him a taste for it so that he liked it while he hated it, paradoxically. Surfeit was yet to come.

7

It almost seemed, next morning, as if surfeit had come already. To look back on dangers past is a very different thing from looking forward to dangers close at hand and still to come. Allnutt looked at the roaring water of the fall, and at the rocky cataract which they would have to negotiate next, and he was frightened. There was an empty sick feeling in his stomach and a curious feeling of pins and needles down the backs of his legs and in the soles of his feet. The next fifty yards, even, might find the boat caught on those rocks and battered to pieces, while he and Rose were beaten down by the racing current, crushed and drowned. He almost felt the strangling water at his nostrils as he thought about it. He had no appetite at all for breakfast.

But there was a vague comfort in the knowledge that there was nothing for them to do save go on. If they stayed where they were they would starve when their provisions came to an end. The only possible route to anywhere lay down the gorge. And the din of the water made it hard to think clearly. Allnutt got up steam in the boiler, and heaped the boat with fuel, and untied the painters, with a feeling of unreality, as if all this was not really happening to him, although it was unpleasant.

Rose got up on to her seat and took the tiller. She studied the eddies of the pool in which they lay; she looked down the cataract which awaited them. There was no fear in her at all. The flutter of her bosom was caused by elation and excitement–the mere act of taking hold of the tiller started her heart beating faster. She gave directions to Allnutt by means of signs; a wave of her hand over-side and Allnutt pushed off cautiously with the boat-hook; she beckoned him to her and he put the engine into reverse for a revolution or two, just enough to get the bows clear. She watched the swirls and the slow motion of the launch backward towards the fall. Then she waved with a forward motion, and Allnutt started the propeller turning. The *African Queen* gathered slow headway, while the shaft vibrated underfoot. Rose brought the tiller over; the launch circled in the eddy, lurched into the main stream, the next moment was flying down with the current, and the madness of the day had begun.

That ability to think like lightning descended upon Rose's mind as they reached the main stream. She threaded her way through the rocks of the cataract as if it were child's play. It had become child's play to watch the banked-up white water round the rocks, to calculate the speed of the current and the boat's speed through the water, when to start the turn and what allowance to make for the rebound of the water from the rock they were passing in planning their approach to the next. The big stationary wave which marked an under-water rock was noted subconsciously. Mechanically she decided how close to it she could go and what the effect of the eddy would be.

Later, when the descent of the river was completed, Rose found she could not remember the details of that second day among the rapids with half the clearness of the first day. Those first rapids were impressed upon her memory with perfect faithfulness; she could remember every bend, every rock, every eddy; she could visualize them just by closing her eyes. But the memories of the second day were far more jumbled and vague. Rose only remembered clearly that first cataract. The subsequent ones remained in her mind only as long sequences of roaring white water. There was spray which wetted her face, and there were some nasty corners–how many she could not tell. Her mind had grown accustomed to it all.

Yet the elation remained. There was sheer joy in crashing through those waves. Rose, with never a thought that the frail fabric of the *African Queen* might be severely tried by some of those jolts and jars, found it exhilarating to head the launch into the stiff rigid waves which marked the junction of two currents, and to feel her buck and lurch under her, and to see the spray come flying back from the bows. The finest sensation of all now was the heave upwards of the stern as the *African Queen* reached the summit of one of those long deep descents of green water and went racing down it with death on either hand and destruction seemingly awaiting them below.

Towards afternoon there was a cessation of cataracts. The river widened a trifle, but the walls of the gorge, although not quite so high, remained nearly vertical still. Between these walls the river raced with terrific velocity, but without impediment. There was time now to think and to enjoy oneself, to revel in the thrill of sending the *African Queen* skating round the corners, pushed far out by the current until the outside bank was perilously close to one's elbow. Even Allnutt, noticing the sudden smoothness of the passage, suspended his rigid concentration over the engines and raised his head. He watched in amazement the precipices flashing by at either hand, and he marvelled at the dizzy way they slithered round the bends. There was something agonizingly pleasant about it. The feeling of constriction about the breast which he felt as he watched gave him an odd sense of satisfaction. He was full of the pride of achievement.

The mooring place which they desired presented itself along this cataract-free portion of the river. A tributary to the Ulanga came in here–not in any conventional way, but by two bold leaps down the precipice, to plunge bodily into the water after a forty-foot drop. Rose just had time to notice it, to steer clear and be drenched by the spray, when she saw that a sudden little widening of the channel just below, where the current had eaten away the rocky bank at a spot where the rock was presumably softer, offered them the assistance of a back eddy in mooring. She called to attract Allnutt's attention, signalled for half-speed and then for reverse. Allnutt's boat-hook helped in the manoeuvre, and the *African Queen* came gently to a stop under the steep bank. Allnutt made fast the boat while Rose looked about her.

'How lovely!' said Rose, involuntarily.

She had not noticed the loveliness before; all that had caught her attention had been the back eddy. They had moored in what must have been one of the loveliest corners of Africa. The high banks here were not quite precipices, and there were numerous shelves in the rock bearing blue and purple flowering plants, which trailed shimmering wreaths down the steep faces. From the crest down to flood level the rock face was covered with the mystic blue of them. Higher upstream was the spot where the little tributary came foaming down the cliff face. A beam of sunlight reached down over the edge of the gorge and turned its spray into a dancing rainbow. The noise of its fall was not deafening; to ears grown used to the roar of the Ulanga cataracts it was just a pleasant musical accompaniment to the joyful singing of the calm rapid river here. Under the rocky bank it was cool and delicious with the clear green river coursing alongside. The rocks were reds and browns and greys where they could be seen through the flowers, and had a smooth well-washed appearance. There was no dust; there were no flies. It was no hotter than a summer noon in England.

Rose had never before found pleasure in scenery, just as scenery. Samuel never had. If as a girl some bluebell wood in England (perhaps Rose had never seen a bluebell wood; it is possible) had brought a thrill into her bosom and a catch into her throat she would have viewed such symptoms with suspicion, as betokening a frivolity of mind verging upon wantonness. Samuel was narrow and practical about these things.

But Rose was free now from Samuel and his joyless, bilious outlook; it was a freedom all the more insidious because she was not conscious of it. She stood in the stern and drank in the sweet beauty of it all, smiling at the play of colour in the rainbow at the waterfall. Her mind played with memories, of the broad sun-soaked reaches of the Upper Ulanga, of the cataracts and dangers they had just passed.

There was further happiness in that. There was a thrill of achievement. Rose knew that in bringing the *African Queen* down those rapids she had really accomplished something, something which in her present mood she ranked far above any successful baking of bread, or even (it is to be feared) any winning of infidel souls to righteousness. For once in her joyless life she could feel pleased with herself, and it was a sensation intoxicating in its novelty. Her body seethed with life.

Allnutt came climbing back into the boat from the shore. He was limping a little.

'D'you mind 'aving a look at my foot, miss?' he said. 'Got a splinter in it up on the bank an' I dunno if it's all out.'

'Of course,' said Rose.

He sat up on the bench in the stern, and made to take off his canvas shoe, but Rose was beforehand with him. On her knees she slipped the shoe off and took his slender, rather appealing foot into her hands. She found the place of entry of the splinter, and pressed it with her finger-tip while Allnutt twitched with ridiculous ticklishness. She watched the blood come back again.

'No, there's nothing there now,' she said, and let his foot go. It was the first time she had touched him since they had left the mission.

'Thank you, miss,' said Allnutt.

He lingered on the bench gazing up at the flowers, while Rose lingered on her knees at his feet.

'Coo, ain't it pretty,' said Allnutt. There was a little awe in his tone, and his voice was hardly raised loud enough to be heard above the sound of the river.

The long twenty-four hours spent in the echoing turmoil of the cataracts seemed to have muddled their thoughts. Neither of them was thinking clearly. Both of them felt oddly happy and companionable, and yet at the same time they were conscious that something was missing, although they felt it close at hand. Rose watched Allnutt's face as he looked wondering round him. There was something appealing, almost childlike, about the little man with his dazed smile. She wanted to pet him, and then, noticing this desire in herself, she put it aside as not expressing exactly what it was she wanted, although she could find no better words for it. Both of them were breathing harder than usual, as though undergoing some strain.

'That waterfall there,' said Allnutt, hesitatingly, 'reminds me—'

He never said of what it reminded him. He looked down at Rose beside him, her sweet bosom close to him. He, too, was glowing with life and inspired by the awesome beauty of the place. He did not know what he was doing when he put out his hand to her throat, sunburned and cool. Rose caught at his hands, to hold them, not to put them away, and he came down to his knees and their bodies came together.

Rose was conscious of kisses, of her racing pulse and her swimming head. She was conscious of hands which pulled at her clothing and which she could not deny if she would. She was conscious of pain which made her put up her arms round Allnutt's slight body and press him to her, holding him to her breasts while he did his will–her will–upon her.

8

Probably it had all been inevitable. They had been urged into it by all their circumstances–their solitude, their close proximity, the dangers they had encountered, their healthy life. Even their quarrels had helped. Rose's ingrained prudery had been drastically eradicated during these days of living in close contact with a man, and it was that prudery which had constituted the main barrier between them. There is no room for false modesty or physical shame in a small boat.

Rose was made for love; she had been ashamed of it, frightened of it, once upon a time, and had averted her eyes from the truth, but she could not maintain that suppression amid the wild beauty of the Ulanga. And once one started making allowances for Allnutt he became a likeable little figure. He was no more responsible for his deficiencies than a child would be. His very frailties had their appeal for Rose. It must have been that little gesture of his in coming to her with a splinter in his foot which broke down the last barrier of Rose's reserve. And she wanted to give, and to give again, and to go on giving; it was her nature.

There was not even the difficulty of differences of social rank interposed between them. Clergyman's sister notwithstanding, there was no denying that Rose was a small tradesman's daughter. Allnutt's Cockney accent was different from her own provincial twang, but it did not grate on her nerves. She had been accustomed for much of her life to meet upon terms of social equality people with just as much accent. If Allnutt and Rose had met in England and decided to marry, Rose's circle might not have thought she was doing well for herself, but they would not have looked upon her as descending more than a single step of the social ladder at most.

Most important factor of all, perhaps, was the influence of the doctrine of the imperfection of man (as opposed to woman) which Rose had imbibed all through her girlhood. Her mother, her aunts, all the married women she knew, had a supreme contempt for men regarded in the light of house-inhabiting creatures. They were careless, and clumsy, and untidy. They were incapable of dusting a room or cooking a joint. They were subject to fits of tantrums. Women had to devote themselves to clearing their path for them and smoothing their way. Yet at the same time it was a point of faith that these incomprehensible creatures were the lords of creation for whom nothing could be too good. For them the largest portion of the supper haddock must always be reserved. For them on Sunday afternoons one must step quietly lest their nap be disturbed. Their trivial illnesses must be coddled, their peevish complaints heard with patience, their bad tempers condoned. In fact–perhaps it is the explanation of this state of affairs–men were, in their inscrutable oddity, and in the unquestioned deference accorded them, just like miniatures of the exacting and all-powerful God whom the women worshipped.

So Rose did not look for perfection in the man she loved. She took it for granted that she would not respect him. He would not be so dear to her if she did. If, as to her certain knowledge he did, he got drunk and was not enamoured of a prospect of personal danger, that was only on a par with her father's dyspeptic malignity, or Uncle Albert's habit of betting, or Samuel's fits of cold ill temper. It was not a question of knowing all and forgiving all, but of knowing all except that she was entitled to forgive. And these very frailties of his made an insidious appeal to the maternal part of her, and so did his corporal frailty, and the hard luck he had always experienced. She yearned for him in a way which differed from and reinforced the clamourings of her emancipated body. As the flame of passion died down in him, and, with his lips to her rich throat, he murmured a few odd sleepy words to her, she was very happy, and cradled him in her strong arms.

Allnutt was very happy too. Whatever he might do in the heat of passion, his need was just as much for a mother as for a mistress. To him there was a comfort in Rose's arms he had never known before. He felt he could trust her and depend on her as he had never trusted nor depended upon a woman in his life. All the misery and tension of his life dropped away from him as he pillowed his head on her firm bosom.

Sanity did not come to them until morning, and not until late morning at that, and when it came it was only a partial sort of sanity. There was a moment in the early morning light when Rose found herself blushing at the memory of last night's immodesties, and filled with disquiet at the thought of her unmarried condition, but Allnutt's lips were close to hers, and her arms were about his slender body, and there was red blood in her veins, and memories and disquietude alike vanished as she caught him to her. There was a blushing interval when she had to own that she did not know his name, and, when he told her, shyly, she savoured the name 'Charlie' over to herself like a schoolgirl, and she thought it a very nice name, too.

When the yearning for the morning cup of tea became quite uncontrollable–and after a night of love Rose found herself aching for tea just as much as after a day's cataract-running–it was she who insisted on rising and preparing breakfast. That 'better portion of the haddock' convention worked strongly on her. She had not minded in the least having meals prepared by Allnutt her assistant, but it seemed wrong to her that Charlie (whom already she called 'husband' to herself, being quite ignorant of the word 'lover') should be bothered with domestic details. She felt supremely pleased and flattered when he insisted on helping her; she positively fluttered. And she laughed outright when he cracked a couple of jokes.

All the same, and in a fashion completely devoid of casuistry, Rose was appreciative of the difference between business and pleasure. When breakfast was finished she took control of the expedition again without a second thought. She took it for granted that they were going on, and that in the end they were going to torpedo the *Königin Luise*, and it did not occur to Allnutt that now that he occupied a privileged position he might take advantage of it to protest. He was a man simply made to be henpecked. What with the success they had met with under Rose's command up to now, and with the events of the night, Rose's ascendancy over him was complete. He was quite happy to cast all the responsibility on to her shoulders and to await philosophically whatever destiny might send. He gathered fuel and he got up steam with the indifference engendered by routine.

Only when they were on the point of departure did either of them waver. Rose found him close beside her murmuring in a broken voice—

'Give us another kiss, old girl.'

And Rose put her arms round him and kissed him, and whispered–'Charlie, Charlie, dear Charlie.' She patted his shoulder, and she looked round at the beauty all about them, where she had given him her virginity, and her eyes were wet. Then they cast off, and Allnutt pushed off with the boat-hook, and a second later they were in the mad riot of the Ulanga once more, coursing down between the precipices.

In some moment of sensible conversation that morning Allnutt had advanced the suggestion that the last cataract had been left behind and this portion of the river was merely the approach to the flat land round the Lake. He proved to be wrong. After ten wild minutes of smooth water the familiar din of an approaching cataract reached Rose's ears. There was need to brace herself once more, to hold the tiller steady, and to stare forward to pick out the continuous line of clear water, a winding one to avoid the rocks, and yet with no turn in it too sharp, which it was necessary to select in the few fleeting seconds between the sighting of the cataract and the moment when the *African Queen* began to heave among the first waves of the race.

So they went on down the wild river, deafened and drenched. Amazingly they survived each successive peril, although it was too much to hope that their luck would hold. They came to a place where the channel was too narrow and obstructed to offer in its whole width a single inch of clear water. Rose could only pick the point where the wild smoother foam was lowest, and try to judge from the portions of the rocks exposed what course was taken by the water that boiled between them. The *African Queen* reared up and crashed into the tangle of meeting waves. She shook with the impact; water flew back high over the top of the funnel. Rose saw clear water ahead, and then as the launch surged through there was a crash beneath her, followed by a horrid vibration which seemed as if it would rattle the boat into pieces. With the instinct of the engineer Allnutt shut off steam.

'Keep her *going*, Charlie!' screamed Rose.

Allnutt opened the throttle a trifle. The devastating vibration began again, but apparently the propeller still revolved. The *African Queen* retained a little steerage way, while Allnutt prayed that the bottom would not be wrenched out of the boat. Rose, looking over the side, saw that they were progressing slowly through the water, while the current hurried them on at its usual breakneck speed. She could tell that it was vitally urgent that they should stop as soon as may be, but they were faced with the eternal problem of finding a mooring place in the narrow gorge with its tearing current. Certainly they must find one before the next cataract. With that small speed through the water she would never be able to steer the *African Queen* down a cataract; moreover, swinging the tiller experimentally, she found that something was seriously wrong with the steering. The propeller had a tendency now to swing the boat round crabwise, and it called for a good deal of rudder to counteract it. The cliffs streamed by on either side, while the clattering vibration beneath her seemed to grow worse, and she fought to keep the boat in mid-current. A long way ahead she could see the familiar dark rocks rearing out of the river, ringed at the base with foam. They *must* moor. Down on the left a big rock jutting out into the river offered them a tiny bit of shelter in the angle below it.

'Charlie!' she screamed above the roar of the river.

He heard her and understood her gesticulations. The operation had to be timed to perfection. If they turned too soon they would be dashed on to the rock; if they turned too late they would miss the opportunity and would be swept, stern first and helpless, down the cataract. Rose had to make allowance for the changed speed of the boat, for this new twisting effect of the screw, for the acceleration of the current as it neared the cataract. With her lips compressed she put the tiller across and watched the bows anxiously as the boat came round.

It was too much to hope that the manoeuvre would be completely successful. The bow came up behind the rock true enough, but the turn was not complete. The launch still lay partly across the river as her bow grounded in the angle. Instantly she heeled and rolled. A mass of water came boiling in over the gunwale. The boiler fire was extinguished in a wild flurry of steam whose crackling was heard above the confusion of other sounds.

Allnutt it was who saved the situation. Grabbing the painter he leaped like an athlete, in a split second of time, nearly waistdeep in a swirling eddy, and he got his shoulder under the bows and heaved like a Hercules. The bows slid off and the boat righted herself, wallowing three-quarters full of water; the tug of the current instantly began to take her downstream. Allnutt leaped up the face of the rock, still clutching the painter. He braced himself against the strain. His shoulder joints cracked as the rope tightened. His feet slipped, but he recovered himself. With another Herculean effort he made time for himself to get a purchase with the rope round an angle of the rock, and braced himself again. Slowly the boat swung in to shore, and the strain eased as the eddy began to balance the current. Five seconds later she was safe, just fitting into the little eddy behind the rock, as full of water as she could be without sinking, while Allnutt made painter after painter fast to the shore, and Rose still stood on the bench in the stern, the water slopping about below her feet. She managed to smile at him; she was feeling a little sick and faint now that it was over. The memory of that green wave coming in over the gunwale still troubled her. Allnutt sat down on a rock and grinned back at her.

'We nearly done it that time,' he said; she could not catch the words because of the noise of the river, but clearly he was not discomposed.

Allnutt was acquiring a taste for riverine dangers–rapid-running can become as insidious a habit as morphine-taking–apart from his new happiness in Rose's society. Rose sat on the gunwale and kept her feet out of the water. She would not let her weakness be seen; she forced herself to be matter of fact. Allnutt swung himself on board.

'Coo, what a mess!' he said. 'Wonder 'ow much we've lost.'

'Let's get this water out and see,' said Rose.

Allnutt splashed down into the waist and fished about for the bailer. He found it under the bench and handed it to Rose. He took the big basin out of the locker for himself. Before Rose got down to start bailing she tucked her skirt up into her underclothes as though she were a little girl at the seaside–the sensation of intimacy with Charlie, combating piquantly with her modesty, was extraordinarily pleasant.

The basin and the bailer between them soon lowered the level of the water in the boat; it was not long before Rose was getting out the wicked old hand pump so as to pump out what remained under the floor-boards.

''Ere, I'll do that, Rosie,' said Allnutt.

'No, you sit down and rest yourself,' said Rose. 'And mind you don't catch cold.'

Pumping out the boat was about the nearest approach to dusting a room which could be found in their domestic life. Naturally it was not a man's work.

'First question is,' said Allnutt, as the pumping drew to a close, ''ow much does she leak?'

They pumped until the pump brought up no more water while Allnutt addressed himself to getting up a couple of floor-boards in the waist. A wait of half an hour revealed no measurable increase in the bilge.

'Coo blimey,' said Allnutt. 'That's better than we could 'ave 'oped for. We 'aven't lorst nothing as far as I can see, an' we 'aven't damaged 'er skin worth mentioning. I should 'ave fort there'd 'a been a 'ole in 'er somewheres after what she's been through.'

'What was all that clattering just before we stopped?' asked Rose.

'We still got to find that out, old girl,' said Allnutt.

There was a cautious sympathy in his voice. He feared the very worst, and he knew what it would mean in disappointment to Rose. He had already looked up the side of the ravine, and found a small comfort in the fact that it was just accessible. If the *African Queen* was as much disabled as he feared they would have to climb up there and wander in the forest until the Germans found them–or until they starved to death. It said much for his new-found manliness that he kept out of his voice the doubts that he felt.

'How are you going to do that, dear?' asked Rose.

Allnutt looked at the steep bank against which they were lying, and at the gentle eddy alongside.

'I'll 'ave to go underneath an' look,' said he. 'There ain't no other wye, not 'ere.'

The bank was steep-to. There was four feet of water on the shore side of the boat, six feet on the river side, as Allnutt measured it with the boat-hook.

''Ere goes,' said Allnutt, pulling off his singlet and his trousers. They were wet through already, but it runs counter to a man's instincts to immerse himself in water with his clothes on.

'You stay 'andy wiv that rope, case there's a funny current darn at the bottom.'

Rose, looking anxiously over the side, saw his naked body disappear under the bottom of the boat. His feet stayed in view and kicked reassuringly. Then they grew more agitated as Allnutt thrust himself out from under again. He stood on the rocky bottom beside the boat, the water streaming from his hair.

'Did you see anything, dear?' asked Rose, hovering anxiously over him.

'Yerss,' answered Allnutt. He said no more until he had climbed back into the boat; he wanted time to compose himself. Rose sat beside him and waited. She put out her dry hand and clasped his wet one.

'Shaft's bent to blazes. Like a corkscrew,' said Allnutt, dully. 'An' there's a blade gone off the prop.'

Rose could only guess at the magnitude of the disaster from the tone he used, and she underestimated it.

'We'll have to mend it then,' she said.

'Mend it?' said Allnutt. He laughed bitterly. Already in imagination he and Rose were wandering through the forest, sick and starving. Rose was silent before the savage despondency of his tone.

'Must 'a' just 'it a rock with the tip of the prop,' went on Allnutt, more to himself than her. 'There ain't nothink to notice on the deadwood. Christ only knows 'ow the shaft 'eld on while we was getting in 'ere. Like a bloody corkscrew.'

'Never mind, dear,' said Rose. The use of the words 'Christ' and 'bloody' seemed so oddly natural here, up against primitive facts, that she hardly noticed them, any more than she noticed Charlie's nakedness. 'Let's get everything dry, and have some dinner, and then we can talk about it.'

She could not have given better advice. The simple acts of hanging things to dry, and getting out greasy tins from the boxes of stores, went far to soothe Allnutt's jangled nerves. Later, with a meal inside him, and strong tea making a hideous mixture in his stomach with bully beef, he felt better still. Rose returned then to the vital issue.

'What shall we have to do before we go on?' she asked.

'I'll tell you what we could do,' said Allnutt, 'if we 'ad a workshop, an' a landin' slip, an' if the parcel post was to call 'ere. We could pull this old tub out on the slip and take the shaft down. Then we might be able to forge it straight agine. I dunno if we could, though, 'cause I ain't no blacksmith. Then we could write to the makers an' get a new prop. They might 'ave one in stock, 'cause this boat ain't over twenty years old. While we was waitin' we might clean 'er bottom 'an paint 'er. Then we could put in the shaft an' the new prop, an' launch 'er an' go on as if nothink 'ad 'appened. But we 'aven't got nothink at all, an' so we can't.'

Thoughts of the forest were still thronging in Allnutt's mind.

It was Rose's complete ignorance of all things mechanical which kept them from lapsing into despair. Despite Allnutt's depression, she was filled with a sublime confidence in his ability; after all, she had never yet found him wanting in his trade. In her mind the problem of getting a disabled steamboat to go again was quite parallel with, say, the difficulties she would meet if she were suddenly called upon to run a strange household whose womenfolk were down with sickness. She would have to get to know where things were, and deal with strange tradesmen, and accustom herself to new likes and dislikes on the part of the men. But she would tackle the job in complete confidence, just as she would any other household problem that might present itself. She might have to employ makeshifts which she hated; so might Allnutt. In her own limited sphere she did not know the word 'impossible'. She could not conceive of a man finding anything impossible in his, as long as he was not bothered, and given plenty to eat.

'Can't you get the shaft off without pulling the boat on shore?' she asked.

'M'm. I dunno. I might,' said Allnutt. 'Means goin' under water an' gettin' the prop off. *Could* do it, p'raps.'

'Well, if you had the shaft up on shore you could straighten it.'

'You got a hope,' said Allnutt. 'Ain't got no hearth, ain't got no anvil, ain't got no coal, ain't got nothink, an' I ain't no blacksmith, like I said.'

Rose raked back in her memory for what she had seen of blacksmiths' work in Africa.

'I saw a Masai native working once. He used charcoal. On a big hollow stone. He had a boy to fan the charcoal.'

'Yerss, I seen that, too, but I'd use bellers myself,' said Allnutt. 'Make 'em easy enough.'

'Well, if you think that would be better–' said Rose.

''Ow d'you mike charcoal?' asked Allnutt. For the life of him, he could not help entering into this discussion, although it still seemed to him to be purely academic–'all moonshine', as he phrased it to himself.

'Charcoal?' said Rose vaguely. 'You set fire to great beehives of stuff–wood, of course, how silly I am–and after it's burnt there's charcoal inside. I've seen them do it somewhere.'

'We might try it,' said Allnutt. 'There's 'eaps an' 'eaps of driftwood upon the bank.'

'Well, then—' said Rose, plunging more eagerly into the discussion.

It was not easy to convince Allnutt. All his shop training had given him a profound prejudice against inexact work, experimental work, hit-or-miss work. He had been spoiled by an education with exact tools and adequate appliances; in the days of his apprenticeship mechanical engineering had progressed far from the time when Stephenson thought it a matter of self-congratulation that the *Rocket*'s pistons fitted her cylinder with only half an inch to spare.

Yet all the same, flattered by Rose's sublime confidence in him, and moved by the urgency of the situation, he gradually came round until he was half disposed to try his hand on the shaft. Then suddenly he shied away from the idea again. Like a fool, he had been forgetting the difficulty which made the whole scheme pointless.

'No,' he said. 'It ain't no go, Rosie, old girl. I was forgetting that prop. It ain't no go wiv a blade gone.'

'It got us along a bit just now,' said Rose.

'Yerss,' said Allnutt, 'but—'

He sighed with the difficulty of talking mechanics to an unmechanical person.

'There's a torque,' he said. 'It ain't balanced—'

Any mechanic would have understood his drift at once. If a three-bladed propeller loses a blade, there are two blades left on one-third of its circumference, and nothing on the other two-thirds. All the resistance to its rotation under water is consequently concentrated upon one small section of the shaft, and a smooth revolution would be rendered impossible. It would be bad enough for the engine, and what the effect would be on a shaft fresh from the hands of an amateur blacksmith could be better imagined than described. If it did not break it would soon be like the corkscrew again of Allnutt's vivid simile. He did his best to explain this to Rose.

'Well, you'll have to make another blade,' said Rose. 'There's lots of iron and stuff you can use.'

'An' tie it on, I serpose?' said Allnutt. He could not help smiling when his irony missed its mark altogether.

'Yes,' said Rose. 'If you think that will do. But couldn't you stick it on, somehow? *Weld* it. That's the right word, isn't it? Weld it on.'

'Coo lumme,' said Allnutt. 'You are a one, Rosie. Reely you are.'

Allnutt's imagination trifled with the idea of forging a propeller blade out of scrap iron, and hand-welding it into position, and affixing this botched propeller to a botched shaft, and then expecting the old *African Queen* to go. He laughed at the idea, laughed and laughed, so that Rose had to laugh with him. Allnutt found it so amusing that for the moment he forgot the seriousness of their position. Directly afterwards they found themselves in each other's arms–how, neither of them could remember–and they kissed as two people might be expected to kiss on the second day of their honeymoon. They loved each other dearly, and cares dropped away from them for a space. Yet all the same, while Rose held Allnutt in her arms, she reverted to the old subject.

'Why did you laugh like that when I spoke about welding?' she asked in all seriousness. 'Wasn't it the right word after all? You know what I mean, dear, even if it's not, don't you?'

'Crikey,' said Allnutt. 'Well, look here—'

There was no denying Rose; and Allnutt especially was not of the type to deny her. Moreover, Allnutt's mercurial spirits could hardly help rising under the influence of Rose's persistent optimism. The disaster they had experienced would have cast him into unfathomable despair if she had not been with him–despair, perhaps, which might have resulted in his not raising a finger to help himself. As it was, the discussion ended eventually, as was quite inevitable, in Allnutt's saying that 'he would see what he could do,' just as some other uxorious husband in civilization might see what could be done about buying a new drawing-room suite. And from that first yielding grew the hard week's work into which they plunged.

The first ray of hope came at the very beginning, when Allnutt, after much toil under water, with bursting lungs, managed to get the propeller off and out of the water. The missing blade had not broken off quite short. It had left a very considerable stump, two inches or so. In consequence it appeared more possible to bolt or fasten on a new blade–the propeller, of course, was of bronze, and as the new blade would have to be of iron, there could be no question of welding or brazing. Allnutt put the propeller aside and devoted himself next to getting the shaft free; if he could not repair that it was useless to work on the propeller.

It was extraordinary what a prolonged business it was to free the shaft. Partly this was because it called for two pairs of hands, one pair inside the boat and one pair underneath the boat, and Rose had to be instructed in the use of spanners, and a very comprehensive code of signals had to be arranged so that Allnutt, crouching in the water underneath the boat, could communicate his wishes to her.

The need for all these signals was only discovered by trial and error, and there were maddening moments before they were fully workable.

That shaft was kinked in two places, close above and close below the bracket which held it steady, two feet from where it emerged from the glands, just above the propeller. There was no sliding it out through these bearings in either direction, as Allnutt discovered after a couple of trials. In consequence Allnutt had to work with spanner and screw-driver under water, taking the whole bracket to pieces, and, seeing that he had never set eyes on it in his life, and had to find out all about it by touch, it was not surprising that it took a long time. He would stand in the water beside the boat, his screw-driver in his hand and his spanner in his belt, taking deep breaths, and then he would plunge under, feel hastily for the bracket, and work on it for a few fleeting seconds before his breath gave out and he had to come out again.

The *African Queen* was moored in moderately still water in the eddy below the rock, but only a yard or two away there was a racing seven-knot current tearing downstream, and occasionally some whim of the water expressed itself in a fierce under-water swirl, which swung the launch about and usually turned Allnutt upside down, holding on like grim death in case the eddy should take him out into the main current from which there would be no escape alive. It was in one of those swirls that Allnutt dropped a screw, which was naturally irreplaceable and must be recovered–it took a good deal of groping among the rocks beneath the boat before he found it again.

Before he had finished Allnutt developed a surprising capacity for holding his breath, and as a result of his prolonged immersions and exposures, his skin peeled off in flakes all over him. It was an important moment for Rose when at last, bending over the shaft in the bottom of the boat, she saw it at last slide out through the glands, and Allnutt emerged wet and dripping beside the boat with it in his hands.

Allnutt shook his head over the kinks and bends now revealed in the light of day–the terminal one was nearly half a right angle–but the two of them set themselves doggedly to the business of forging the thing straight again.

The sight of those kinks brought relief to Allnutt's mind in one respect. The fact that the metal had bent instead of breaking revealed that its temper was such that it might not suffer much from his amateur blacksmith's work–Allnutt was very well aware that what he knew about tempering was extraordinarily little. He comforted himself philosophically by telling himself that after all he was not dealing with a tool steel, and that obviously the shaft had a good deal of reserve strength and that if he did not use extravagantly high temperatures and if he annealed the thing cautiously he might not do too much harm.

There was not the slightest chance of their using very high temperatures, as they quickly discovered.

Their attempts at making charcoal were complete and utter failures. When trying to reconstruct from memory what they had seen done they soon discovered that they had seen with eyes unseeing. All they had to show in return for several piles of wood were heaps of white ashes and a few bits of what only a kindly person could possibly have called charcoal. In desperation Allnutt resolved to try if he could not obtain a great enough heat with a wood fire and bellows. He made the bellows neatly enough with a couple of slabs of wood and inch or two of piping and a pair of black elbow-length gloves which Rose had carried in her tin box for ten years of Central Africa without wearing. When they found at last a good shape for their hearth of piled rocks Allnutt was relieved to discover that by energetic working of the bellows they could heat up that unwieldy shaft until he could actually alter its shape with his light hand hammer. They scorched themselves pretty well all over while using the flaring inconsistent fuel, but all the same, the metal became soft enough to work in a manner of speaking, and Allnutt was becoming reconciled to makeshifts by now.

All the same, under the urging of the bellows, at which Rose worked feverishly on her knees with scorched face, the open hearth consumed wood at an incredible rate. It was not long before they had gathered in every scrap of driftwood accessible in the ravine, and the work was as yet hardly begun. They had to climb the steep face of the ravine into the forest, and gather wood there. The heat was sweltering, they were bitten by insects of all sorts, they wore themselves out and their clothes into rags hacking paths through the undergrowth. No one on earth could have climbed down that cliff face with a load of wood; they had to drag the bundles to the verge and push them over the edge, and some fell direct into the river, and one or two caught on inaccessible ledges and were lost just as thoroughly although they were in sight, but they managed to profit by about half the wood they collected in the forest.

Curiously enough, they were as happy as children during these days of hectic work. Hard regular labour suited both of them, and as soon as Allnutt had become infected by Rose's passion to complete the job they had a common interest all day long. And every day there was the blessed satisfaction of knocking off work in the late afternoon and revelling in the feeling of comradely friendliness which drew them close together until passion was aroused and hand went out to hand and lip met lip. Rose had never known such happiness before nor perhaps had Allnutt either. They could laugh and joke together; Rose had never laughed nor joked like that in the whole thirty-three years of her existence. Her father had taken shopkeeping as seriously as he (and her brother) had taken religion. She had never realized before that friendliness and merriment could exist along with a serious purpose in life any more than she had realized that there was pleasure in the intercourse of the sexes. There was something intensely satisfying in their companionship.

Little by little that propeller shaft was straightened. Patient heating and patient hammering did their work. The major bends disappeared and Allnutt turned his attention to the minor ones. He had to use a taut string now to judge of the straightness of the shaft and he had to make himself a gauge of wire for testing the diameter, so nearly true was it, and there came a blessed morning when even his exacting mind was satisfied, and he pronounced the shaft to be as good as he could make it. He could lay it aside now, and turn his attention to the far more difficult matter of the propeller blade.

In the end Allnutt made that new blade out of half a spare boiler tube. The operations on the shaft had taught him a good deal of the practical side of smith's work, and his experience with the propeller blade practically completed his education. Under the urging of necessity, and with the stimulus given him by Rose's confiding faith in his ability, Allnutt devised all sorts of ways of dealing with that boiler tube; it might almost he said that he re-invented some of his processes. He welded one end into a solid plate, and he worked upon it and beat it and shaped it until it gradually began to assume an appearance reminiscent of the other two blades which were his models.

The ravine rang with the sound of his hammer. Rose was his diligent assistant. She tended the fire, and worked the bellows, and, her hands shielded with rags, held the nominally cool end of the tube under Allnutt's instructions. Her nostrils were filled with the smell of scorching cloth, and she burned her fingers over and over again and nearly every single garment she and Allnutt possessed between them was burned and torn until they gave up the hopeless pursuit after decency, and she somehow enjoyed every minute of it.

There was intense interest in watching how the new blade took shape; there were exciting discussions as to how this difficulty or that was to be evaded. Allnutt found it all to his taste; there was gratification in the primitive pleasure of making things with his own hands.

'If my old dad,' said Allnutt once, 'had put me to blacksmithing when I was a kid, I don't think I should never have come to Africa. Coo! I might still—'

Allnutt lost himself in a pictured fantasy of a London working-class shopping district on a Saturday night, redolent with fried-fish shops, garish with lights, and all a-bustle with people. He experienced a little qualm of homesickness before he came back to real life again, to the ravine with its pale red rocks, and the singing river, and the dazzling light, and the *African Queen* rocking in the eddy down below, and Rose beside him.

'But then I shouldn't never have met you, Rosie, old girl,' he went on. He fingered the embryo propeller blade. 'Nor done all this. It's worth it. Every time it is, honest.'

Allnutt would not have exchanged Rose for all the fried-fish shops in the world.

Later the propeller blade began to demand accurate measurement, so like had it grown to its fellows. Allnutt had to invent gauges of intricate shape to make sure that the curvature and contour of the old blades were accurately reproduced, and before this part of the work was quite completed he turned his attention to the other end and set to work to forge a socket to fit over the broken stump, and to drilling holes by which it might be made comparatively safe. The moment actually came at last when the completed blade was slipped on over the stump, and Rose was given a practical demonstration of riveting–Allnutt made the rivets out of stumps of nails, and Rose had a trying time as 'holder-on'; neither spanner nor pincers were really effective tongs.

The new blade was in position now, an exact match of its fellows, and to a casual inspection seemingly secure, but Allnutt was not yet satisfied. He could appreciate the leverage exerted upon a propeller blade in swift rotation, and the strain that would come upon the base–upon his makeshift joint. At the risk of slightly reducing the propeller's efficiency he joined all three blades together with a series of triangles of wire strained taut. That would help to distribute the strain round the whole propeller.

'That ought to do now,' said Allnutt. 'Let's 'ope it does.'

Putting the propeller shaft back into position, and settling it into its bracket, and putting on the propeller again, called for a fresh spell of subaqueous activity on the part of Allnutt.

'Coo blimey,' said Allnutt, emerging dripping at the side of the *African Queen*. 'I oughter been a diver, not a blinkin' blacksmith. Let's 'ave that other spanner, Rosie, an' I'll 'ave another go.'

Allnutt was very dear to her now, and she thought his remarks extraordinarily witty.

When shaft and propeller were in position, there was very little chance of testing the work. Once they left the bank they would have to go on down the next cataract, willynilly. Allnutt got up steam in the boiler, and sent the propeller ahead for a few revolutions, until the mooring ropes strained taut, and then he went astern for a few revolutions more. It was a good enough proof that shaft and propeller would turn, but it proved nothing else. It did not prove that the propeller would stand up to a full strain, nor that the shaft would not buckle under the impulse of a head of steam. They would have to find that out amid the rapids and cataracts, with death as their portion if Allnutt's work should fail them.

The night before they had both of them visualized this situation, and they had neither of them ventured to discuss it. They had lain in each other's arms. Rose's eyes had been wet, and Allnutt's embrace had been urgent and possessive, each of them consumed with fear of losing the other. And this morning they tacitly acknowledged their danger, still without mentioning it. Steam was up, a full cargo of wood was on board, they were all ready for departure. Allnutt looked about him for the last time, at their rock-built hearth, and his rock-built anvil, and the heap of ashes that marked the site of one of their charcoal-burning experiments. He turned to Rose, who was standing stiff and dry-eyed beside the tiller. She could not speak; she could only nod to him. Without a word he cast off the moorings, and held the *African Queen* steady in the eddy with the boat-hook, while Rose scanned the surface of the river.

'Right!' said Rose, and her voice cracked as she said it. The sound of it hardly reached Allnutt's ears above the noise of the river and the hiss of steam. Allnutt pushed with the boat-hook, and as the bows came out into the current he gingerly opened the throttle.

'Good-bye, darling,' said Allnutt, bent over the engine.

'Good-bye, darling,' said Rose at the tiller.

Neither of them heard the other, and neither was meant to: there was a high courage in them both.

The *African Queen* surged out into the stream. For a moment they both of them felt as if something was wrong, because the shaft clanked no longer–it was straighter than it had been before the accident. Shaft and propeller held firm, all the same. The launch spun round as her bows met the current and Rose put the tiller across. Next moment they were flying downstream once more, with Allnutt attentive to the engines and Rose at the tiller, staring rigidly forward to pick her course through the weltering foam of the cataract ahead.

9

Somewhere along their route that day they passed the spot where the Ulanga river changes its name and becomes the Bora. The spot is marked in no map, for the sufficient reason that no map of the country has ever been made, except for the hazy sketches which Spengler drew the year before. Until Spengler and his Swahili boatmen managed to make the descent of the river by canoe no one had known, even if they had suspected it, that the big rapid river which looped its way across the upland plateau and vanished into the gorges at Shona was the same as the stream which appeared in the tangled jungle of the Rift Valley a hundred miles from Shona and promptly lost itself again in the vast delta which it had built up for itself on the shore of the Lake.

The native population before the arrival of the Germans had never troubled their heads about it. The delta of the Bora was a pestilential fever swamp; the rapids of the Ulanga were as Rose and Allnutt found them. No one in their senses would waste a minute's thought about one or the other, and since there was no practicable connection between the upper river and the lower it was of no importance whatever that they should happen to have different names.

When all was said and done, the difference in their names was justified by the difference in appearance. The change from the steep slope of the side of the Rift Valley to its flat bottom was most noticeable. The speed of the river diminished abruptly, and the character of the banks changed as well.

For the Ulanga, travelling at its usual breakneck speed, is charged with all sorts of detritus, and rolls much of its bed with it. No sooner does it reach the flat land than all this matter in suspension is dropped in the form of mud and gravel; the river spreads out, chokes itself with islands, finds new sluggish routes for itself. It is to be supposed that when the Lake was first formed it lapped nearly up to the edge of the Rift Valley in which it lay, but for untold centuries the Ulanga–the Bora, as it must now be called–has deposited its masses of soil on the edge of its waters until a huge delta, as much as thirty miles along each of its three sides, has been formed, encroaching upon the Lake, a dreary, marshy, amphibious country, half black mud and half water, steaming in a tropical heat, overgrown with dense vegetation, the home of very little animal life, and pestilent with insects.

Rose and Allnutt quite soon noted indications that the transition was at hand. For some time the current was as fast as ever, and the stream irregular, but the cliffs which walled it in diminished steadily in height and in steepness, until at last they were in no more than a shallow valley, with a vast creeper entangled forest close at hand, and when they emerged from the shade the sun blazed down upon them with a crushing violence they had not known in the sunless gorges of the upper river. The heat was colossal. Despite their motion through the stifling air they were instantly bathed in a sweat which refused to evaporate, and streamed down their bodies and formed puddles wherever its channel was impeded, and dripped into their eyes, and stung them and blinded them.

Rose was sweeping it from her face as she steered the *African Queen* down the last flurry of rapids–not the roaring cataracts she had once known, but a wider, shallower channel down which the water poured with a velocity deceptively great, and where tree-trunks and shallows took the place of the foaming rocks of the upper river. There was still need for quick thinking and careful steering, because shallows grew up in the middle of the river, and the deep channels divided and redivided, coursing ever faster over the bottom, and growing ever shallower until at last the rocky ledge underneath was passed and the water slid over a steep sharp edge into water comparatively deep and comparatively slow.

Then there would be a respite for a time until a fresh change of colour in the water, and fresh danger signals ahead in the form of glittering patches of ripples, told of a new series of shallows approaching, and Rose had to plan a course for half a mile ahead, picking out some continuous deep channel, like a route through a maze, as far as the distant line of the steep edge. She knew enough about boats by now to guess that were she to choose a channel which died away into mere rushing shallows they would be hurried along until they bumped against the bottom, propeller and shaft damaged again, and probably, seeing how fast the river was running, the boat would be swung round, buried under the water piling against it, rolled over and torn to pieces while she and Charlie–she would not allow her mind to dwell on that, but bent her attention, with knitted brows, to seeing that the channels she chose did not come to that sort of end.

The weather changed with all the suddenness associated with the Rift Valley. Huge black clouds came rushing up the sky, intensifying the dampness of the heat until it could hardly be borne. Directly after came the lightning and the thunder, and the rain came pouring down, blotting out the landscape as effectively as a fog would do. At the first sight of the approaching storm Rose had begun to edge the *African Queen* in towards the shore, and the rain was just beginning when Allnutt got his boat-hook into the stump of a huge tree which, still half alive, grew precariously on the edge of the water with half its roots exposed. The river had eaten away the bank all round it so that it formed a little island surrounded by dark rushing water, and, swinging by their painter to this mooring, they sat uncomfortably through the storm.

The light was wan and menacing, the thunder rolled without ceasing to the accompaniment of a constant flicker of lightning. Yet the roar of the rain upon the boat and the river was as loud as the roar of the thunder. It beat upon them pitilessly, stupefying them. There was not even an awning now to offer them its flimsy shelter. All they could do was to sit and endure it, as if they were under the very heaviest type of lukewarm shower bath, hardly able to open their eyes.

The warm wind which came with the rain set the *African Queen* jerking at her painter despite the constant tug of the current, and before the storm had passed the wind blew from two-thirds of the points of the compass, veering jerkily until at last Allnutt, blinded and stupefied though he was, had to get out the boat-hook and hold the boat out from the shore lest the wind should blow her aground and imperil the shaft and propeller. Then at last the storm passed as quickly as it had come, the wind died away, and the afternoon sun came out to scorch them, setting the whole surface of the river steaming, and they could get out the pump and labour to empty the boat of the water which had filled it to the level of the floor-boards.

With the cessation of the rain came the insects, clouds of them, hungry for blood, filling the air with their whining. Not even Rose's and Allnutt's experience of insects on the upper plateau had prepared them for an attack by these insects of the lower valley. They were ten times, twenty times, as bad as they had known them on the Ulanga; and moreover their comparative freedom in deep gorges had rendered them less accustomed and more susceptible still. Down here there was a type of fly new to them, a small black kind, which bit like a red-hot needle and left a drop of blood at every bite, and this type was as numerous as any of the dozen species of fly and mosquito which sang around them, flying into their eyes and their nostrils and their mouths, biting mercilessly at every exposed bit of skin. It was torment to be alive.

The coming of the evening and the sudden descent of night did nothing towards enfeebling their attacks. It seemed impossible to hope for sleep in that inferno of sticky heat under the constant torture of those winged fiends. The memory of yesterday's fairly cool, insect-free bed, when they had lain side by side in happy intimacy, seemed like the vague recollection of a dream. Tonight they shrank from contact with each other, writhing on their uncomfortable bed as if on the rack. Sleep seemed unattainable and yet they were both of them worn out with the excitement of the day.

Some time in the night Allnutt rose and fumbled about in the darkness.

''Ere,' he said. 'Let's try this, old girl. It can't be no worse.'

He had found the old canvas awning, and he spread it over the two of them, although it seemed as if they would die under any sort of covering. They drew the canvas about their faces and ears, streaming with sweat in the stifling heat. Yet the heat was more endurable than the insects. They slept in the end, half-boiled, half-suffocated; and they awoke in the morning with their heads swimming with pain, their joints aching, their throats constricted so that they could hardly swallow. And the insects still attacked them.

They had to wallow ashore through stinking mud to find wood although it seemed agony to move; it took half a dozen journeys before the *African Queen* was fully charged with fuel again, sufficient to get them through the day. Already the sun was so hot that the floor-boards seemed to burn their feet, and it was only Allnutt's calloused hands which could bear the touch of metal work. How he could bear the heat of the fire and the boiler was inconceivable to Rose; the heat which was wafted back to her in the stern was sufficient for her.

Yet being under way at least brought relief from insects. The speed of the

African Queen was sufficient to leave that plague behind, and out in the middle of the river, half a mile broad here, there were no new ones to be found. It was worth enduring the sledge-hammer heat of the sun for that.

The character of the river and the landscape was changing rapidly. Overside the water, which had regained its familiar brown tint of the upper reaches, was growing darker and darker until it was almost black. The current was noticeably less, and quite early in the day they ran the last of the rapids of the type they had encountered so frequently yesterday. That indicated the last rocky ledge extending across the bed of the river; they were definitely down the slope and in the bottom of the Rift Valley now. There were no snags now; the river was far too deep. With its half-mile of width and sixty feet of depth the current slackened until it was almost unnoticeable, although a river engineer could have calculated that the volume of water passing a given point in a given time was equal to that higher up where the constricted shallow channel had raced between its precipices.

On either bank now appeared broad fringes of reeds–papyrus and ambash–and beyond them belts of cane indicated the marshy banks, and beyond the cane could be seen the forest, dark and impenetrable. Out in the centre of the river there was silence save for the clatter of the engine and the breaking of the wash; the *African Queen* clove her way through the black water under the burning sun. In that vast extent of water they seemed to be going at a snail's pace; there were loops and bends in the river's course which they took a full two hours to get round–motiveless bends, to all appearance, for there was no alteration in the flat monotony of the banks.

Although there was no need now to keep watch against snags or rapids, there was still need for some degree of vigilance on Rose's part. Much of the surface of the river was cumbered with floating rubbish, tangles of weed and cane, branches and logs of wood which might imperil the propeller; the current was too slow here to force this flotsam out to the banks and strand it there. It was a relief from the monotony of steering to keep a look-out for the dangerous type of log floating almost entirely submerged; and soon Rose began to lay a course which took her close to each successive floating mass, and she and Allnutt were able to select and pull in those bits of wood of a size suitable for use in the fire. It comforted Rose's economical soul in some inexpressible way to render the *African Queen* by this means still more independent of the shore, and in point of fact, as Rose observed to herself, it was quite as well to maintain the supply of fuel as fully as possible, having regard to the marshiness and inaccessibility of the banks. The fuel they gathered in this way was sufficient to help considerably towards maintaining their stock in hand, even though it did not compensate for their whole consumption.

That day of monotonous sun and monotonous river wore slowly towards its close. Allnutt came aft with a surprising suggestion.

'We needn't tie up to the bank tonight, old girl,' he said. 'It's a muddy bottom, and we can use the anchor agine. I vote we anchor out 'ere. Mosquitoes won't find us 'ere. We don't want another night like last night if we can 'elp it.'

'Anchor here?' said Rose. The possibility had not occurred to her. Five yards had been the farthest from land they had ever lain at night, and that was in the backwaters of the upper river–months ago, she felt. It seemed queer to stop in that tiny boat a quarter of a mile from land, and yet obviously there was no reason against it.

'All right,' she said, at length.

'I won't stoke no more then, and where we stops we—'

'Anchors' was the word Allnutt was going to use, but he did not have time to say it, some minor crisis in the engine summoning him forward on the jump. He turned and grinned reassurance to Rose after he had put matters right.

Gradually the beat of the engine grew slower, and the *African Queen*'s progress through the water died away until it was almost imperceptible. Allnutt went forward and let go the anchor, which took out its chain with a mighty rattle that echoed across the river and brought flights of birds out from the forest.

'Not sure that it's touching bottom,' said Allnutt philosophically. 'But it doesn't matter. If we start driftin' near trouble, that ole anchor'll stop us before the trouble gets too near. There ain't nothing that can 'urt us in sixty foot o' water. Now for Christ's sake let's rig up somethink to give us a bit o' shade. I seen enough o' that sun to last me a lifetime.'

The sun was still blazing malignantly down on them although the day was so far advanced, but Allnutt stretched the remains of the awning overhead and a rug along the awning stanchions, and there was a blessed patch of shade in the sternsheets in which they could recline with their eyes shielded from the persistent glare. As Allnutt had predicted, they were nearly free from the mosquito curse here; the few insects that came to bite were almost unnoticeable to people who had endured the assault of millions yesterday.

Rose and Allnutt could even endure contact with each other again now; they could kiss and be friendly. Rose could draw Allnutt's head down to her breast, and clasp him to her in a new access of emotion. Later on when peace had descended upon them they could talk together, in quiet voices to suit the immense silence of the river.

'Well,' said Allnutt. 'We done it, old girl. We got down the Ulanga all right. I didn't think it could be done. It was you who said we could. If it 'adn't been for you, sweet'eart, we shouldn't be 'ere now. Don't yer feel prard o' yerself, dear?'

'No,' said Rose, indignantly. 'Of course not. It was you who did it. Look at the way you've made the engine go. Look how you mended the propeller. It wasn't me at all.'

Rose really meant what she said. She was actually beginning to forget the time when she had had to coerce him by silence into continuing the voyage. In some ways this was excusable, for so much had happened since then; if Rose had not known that it was only four weeks since the voyage had started she would have guessed it to be at least three months. But her forgetfulness was due to another cause as well; she was forgetting because she wanted to forget. Now that she had a man of her own again it seemed unnatural to her that she should have forgotten her femininity so far as to have made plans, and coerced Allnutt, and so on. It was Charlie who ought to have the credit.

'I don't think,' she said, very definitely indeed, 'there's another man alive who could have done it.'

'Don't think anyone's likely to try,' said Allnutt, which was a very witty remark and made Rose smile.

'We'll have a good supper tonight,' said Rose, jumping up. 'No, don't you move, dear. You just sit still and smoke your old cigarette.'

They had their good supper, all of the special delicacies which the Belgian manager of the mine received in his fortnightly consignment–tinned tomato soup, and tinned lobster and a tin of asparagus, and a tin of apricots with condensed milk, and a tin of biscuits. They experimented with a tin of *pâté de foie gras*, but they neither of them liked it, and by mutual consent they put it over-side half finished. And, swilling tea afterwards, they were both of them firmly convinced that they had dined well. They were of the generation and class which had been educated to think that all good food came out of tins, and their years in Africa had not undeceived them.

The night came down and the river stretched on either side immeasurable and vast in the starlight. The water was like black glass, unruffled by any wind, and deep within it the reflection of the stars glowed like real things. They fell into a dream-like state of mind in which it was easy to believe that they were suspended high above the earth, with stars above and stars below; the gentle motion of the boat as they moved helped in the illusion.

'Coo!' said Allnutt, his head on Rose's shoulder. 'Ain't it lovely?' Rose agreed.

Yet for all this hypnotic peace, for all the love they bore each other, in the hearts of both was the determination of war. Rose's high resolve to clear the Lake of England's enemies burned as high as ever, unexpressed though it might be. Von Hanneken would not continue long to flaunt the iron-cross flag unchallenged on Lake Wittelsbach if she could prevent it. Every little while she thought of those gas cylinders and boxes of explosive up in the bow with a quiet confidence, in the same way as she might in other circumstances think of a store-cupboard shelf full of soap laid up ready for spring-cleaning. There was no flaunting ambition about it, no desire to rival the fame of Florence Nightingale or Grace Darling or Joan of Arc. It was a duty to be done, comparable with washing dishes. Rose asked nothing more of life than something to do.

For details, Charlie would have to attend to those–fuses and explosives were more in a man's line. Charlie would see to it all right. It was a perfectly natural gesture that at the thought of Charlie making an efficient torpedo she should clasp his arm more tightly to her, evoking in response a grunt of peaceful satisfaction.

That uxorious individual had no will of his own left now. What little there was had evaporated by the second day of shooting the rapids, the day when Rose had miraculously admitted him to her arms. He was content to have someone to admire and to follow. Even though Rose had no thought of rivalling Joan of Arc she resembled her in this power she exerted over her staff. The last few days had been one long miracle in Allnutt's eyes. Her complete fearlessness in the wild rapids which had turned his bowels to water affected him indescribably.

There was constantly present in his mind's eye the remembered picture, a composite formed during hundreds of anxious glances over his shoulder, of

Rose erect at the tiller, vigilant and unafraid amidst the frantic turmoil of the cataracts–it was the lack of fear, not the vigilance, which impressed him so profoundly. She had not been cast down when the propeller broke. Her confidence had been unimpaired. She had been quite sure he could mend it, although he had been quite sure he could not, and behold, she was right. Allnutt was by now quite sure that she would be right again in the matter of torpedoing the *Königin Luise*, and he was ready to follow her into any mad adventure to achieve it.

The very intimacy to which she admitted him, her tenderness for him, confirmed him in this state of mind. No other women had been tender to Charlie Allnutt, not his drunken mother, nor the drabs of the East End, nor the enslaved prostitutes of Port Said, nor Carrie his mistress at the mine, whom he had always suspected of betraying him with the filthy native labourers. Rose was sweet and tender and maternal, and in all this she was different from everyone else. He could abandon all thought of himself and his troubles while he was with her. It did not matter if he was a hopeless failure as long as she forbore to tell him so.

When she pressed his arm he held her more closely to reassure himself once more, and her kiss brought him peace and comfort.

10

To the tranquillity of the night succeeded the fever of the day. No sooner had the sun climbed up out of the forest than it began to pour its heat with insane violence upon the little boat exposed upon the broad face of the river. It demanded attention in a manner that would take no denial. The discomfort of immobility in the sun was such that the instinctive reaction was to make instant preparations to move somewhere else, even though bitter experience taught that there was no relief in movement–even the reverse in fact, in consequence of the need for firing up the boiler.

They headed on down the wide black river. Everything was still; the surface was glassy as they approached it. Behind them the ripples of their course and their spreading wake left behind a wedge-shaped area of disturbed water, expanding farther and farther until a long way astern, almost as far as the eye could see, it reached the reedy banks. They went on through the breathless heat, winding eternally round the vast motiveless bends of the river. There was just enough mist prevailing to make the distance unreal and indistinct.

Rose brought the *African Queen* slowly round one more bend. The mist was thicker here. She could not determine the future course of the river, whether at the bend of this reach it turned to the left or to the right. It did not matter here, where the river was so wide and so deep. Tranquilly she held on down the middle of the channel, a quarter of a mile from either shore. She could be sure of seeing the direction of the next bend when it came nearer.

Only slowly did it dawn upon her that the river had widened. In that misty heat the banks looked much the same at half a mile as at a quarter of a mile. Undoubtedly they were farther from both banks now. It did not matter. She kept the *African Queen* to her old course, heading for the mist-enshrouded forest right ahead. She was sure that sooner or later they would open up the next reach.

Somehow even half an hour's steaming did not reveal the channel. They were nearing the dark green of the forest and the brighter green strip of the reeds now. Rose could see a vast length of it with some precision, but there was no break. She came to the conclusion that the river must have doubled nearly back upon itself, and she put the tiller over to starboard to approach the left-hand bank again. There was no satisfaction to be found here. There was only the unbroken bank of reeds and the eternal forest, and moreover, something in the contour of that skyline seemed to tell her that it was not in this direction that the river found an exit.

For a moment she dallied with the idea that perhaps the river ended altogether somewhere in this neighbourhood, but she immediately put the notion aside as ridiculous. Rivers only end thus abruptly in deserts, not in rain-beaten forests of this sort. This was German Central Africa, not the Sahara. She looked back whence they had come, but the last stretch of comparatively narrow river was at least three miles back by now, low down on the horizon and shrouded with mist and out of sight.

There was only one course to adopt which promised definite results. She put the tiller over again and began to steer the *African Queen* steadily along the edge of the fringe of weeds. Whatever happened to the river, she was bound to find out if she kept along its bank for long enough.

'D'you think this is the delta, dearie?' called Allnutt from the bows. He was standing on the gunwale looking over the wide expanse of water.

'I don't know,' said Rose, and added, doggedly: 'I'll tell you soon.'

Her notion of a delta was a lot of channels and islands, not a lake five miles wide with no apparent outlet.

They steamed along the fringe of reeds. A change in the character of the water became noticeable to Rose's eye, practised through many long days in watching the surface. It was black water here, and although it had been black enough a little higher up, there was something different about it. It was lifeless, lack-lustre water here. There were long curling streaks upon it indicative of some infinitely slow eddy circling in its depths. There was far more trash and rubbish afloat on the surface than usual. In fact there seemed every indication that here they had reached, in defiance of all laws of nature, an ultimate dead end to the river.

'Beats me to guess where we've come to,' said Allnutt. 'Anywye, there's a nell of a lot of wood 'ere. Let's stop and fill up while we can.'

It was not at all difficult to collect a full charge of fuel of all the sorts Allnutt liked, from the long dead stuff which would give a quick blaze to solid boughs which could be relied upon to burn for a considerable time. Allnutt fished the wood out of the water. Even here, a mile from solid land, there was insect life to be found. He shook all sorts of semi-aquatic little creatures off it as he lifted it in. With his axe he cut it into handy lengths, as well as he could in the boat, and spread it out to dry over the floor-boards. Only an hour or two in that blazing sun was necessary to bring even waterlogged wood into such a condition that it would burn.

'I should fink we got enough now, Rosie,' said Allnutt at last.

They continued their journey along the reeds. Rose was conscious that she was steadily bringing the tiller over to port. They must be making a wide curve round the edge of this lake; a glance at the sun told her that they were heading in a direction nearly opposite to the one in which they had entered. On their left hand the bank of reeds grew wider and wider, so wide in fact that it was hard to see any details of the forest beyond it. Yet as a half-mile river must make an exit somewhere along here, Rose remained confident, despite her wavering doubts, that sooner or later they would come to a break. Strangely, there was no break to be seen as the afternoon wore on. Here and there were vague indications of tiny channels through the reeds, but they were very indefinite indeed. Certainly they were not passages clear of reeds; it was only that the reeds were sparser, as though there were a deeper bit of water up to the shore in which only the tallest reeds could hope to reach the surface. The forest was too distant and dense for any indication to show there.

The only break in the monotony came when they scared a herd of hippopotami, twenty or so of the beasts, in a wild panic through water, reeds, and mud, until they all with one accord took cover beneath the surface and vanished as mysteriously as they had appeared. Rose had hardly a thought or a look for the hippopotami. She was thinking too hard about this extraordinary behaviour of the river. She was still using port helm to keep them at a constant distance from the bank. As far as she could judge by the sun they were now nearly on the same course as they had been when she first noticed the widening of the river. They must in consequence have come round almost in a full circle.

To confirm this opinion she looked over to starboard at the opposite bank which had been barely in sight a quarter of an hour ago. It was nearer now, far nearer. At the end of another ten minutes the horrid suspicion was confirmed. They were back again at the mouth of the river, at the point of its emergence into the Lake. She only had to starboard the helm to head the *African Queen* upstream, towards the rapids whence they had come. It was a shock to her. A week or two ago she might have wept with humiliation and disappointment, but she was of sterner stuff now; and after her recent experiences there was hardly anything an African river could do which would surprise her.

As a matter of fact, her mistake was perfectly excusable, as the behaviour of the Bora and one or two other rivers which flow into Lake Wittelsbach is very unusual, and is the result of the prolific character of the aquatic vegetation of tropical Africa. The channels of the delta of the Bora are narrow, floored with rich silt, and with hardly any current to scour them–ideal conditions in that climate for the growth of water weed. As a result the channels are nearly choked with weeds and reeds, the flow through them grows less and less, and the river finds itself dammed back at its outlet.

As a result it banks up into a lagoon behind its delta. The slight increase in pressure which follows does, in the end, force some of the water out through creeks and channels winding a precarious way through the delta, but the lagoon itself increases in size with the steady inflow from the river until in the end it turns the flank of the delta on one side or the other, and bursts its way through into the Lake by a new mouth. Then the level of the lagoon drops sharply, the current through this new channel diminishes in proportion, and the whole process is resumed, so that in the progress of centuries the delta extends itself steadily from side to side.

In 1914, when Rose and Allnutt came down the river, it was fifteen years since the last time the Bora had made a new mouth for itself, the lagoon was nearly at its maximum size, and the few channels which remained unchoked were so overgrown and winding that there was really nothing surprising at Rose's missing them. She was not the fool she felt herself to be in that bitter moment.

She was soothed to some extent by the stupidity of Allnutt. He, engrossed in the supervision of the engines, had paid only small attention to their course. When Rose called to him to stop he was surprised. Looking about him at the wide river he quite failed to recognize it. He thought Rose had found the outlet to the lake which they had entered at a different point. It was only when Rose made him drop the anchor and showed him that the slight, hardly perceptible current was running in the opposite direction to the one he wished to take that he admitted his mistake.

'These blinking banks look all one to me,' he said.

'They do to me, too,' said Rose, bitterly, but Allnutt remained cheerfully optimistic.

'Anywye,' he said. ''Ere we are. We got a good mooring agine for tonight, old girl. No mosquitoes. We might just as well be comfy and forget abart things for a bit.'

'All right,' said Rose.

Yet she went on standing on the gunwale, one hand on the awning stanchion and the other shading her eyes, staring across the lagoon at the distant opposite shore, veiled in its greyish-purple mist.

'That's where the way out must be,' she decided. 'A lot of little channels. I noticed quite a lot through the reeds and wouldn't take them. Where we saw those hippos. We'll pick the best one tomorrow, and get through somehow. It can't be very far to the Lake.'

If English explorers had turned back at the sight of apparent impossibilities the British Empire would not be nearly its present size.

The night was not of the tranquillity which had characterized the preceding one. Rose was discontented with the day's progress, and filled with a vague disquiet about her capacity as a pilot. She was not used to failure, and was annoyed with herself. Even at the end of two hours' peace in the shade of the awning and screen which Allnutt rigged, she had not regained her optimism. Instead she was merely filled with a bitter determination to fight her way through that delta cost what it might, or to die in the attempt–a resolution which hardened the set of her mouth and made her conversation with Allnutt a little abstracted, and made sleep slow in coming.

And just as distracting was the sound of the frogs in the reeds. Hereabouts there must have been a colony of thousands, millions, of the little brutes, to whom presumably the attraction of the place lay in the suitability of the still water for spawning. They croaked in unison; Rose could distinguish two distinct kinds of croak, a deep-voiced kind whose volume never altered, and a higher-pitched kind which waxed and waned with monotonous regularity. Despite the distance of the boat from the reeds the din of that croaking came over the water to them as loud as the noise of a heavy surf on a reef, and with much the same variations of loudness and pitch. It was an infuriating noise, and it went on all night.

It did not disturb Allnutt, for no accountable noise could do that, and Allnutt's peaceful sleeping was nearly as annoying as the croaking of the frogs to Rose in her wakefulness. She lay and sweated in the breathless night, disturbed, uncomfortable, irritated. If Rose had ever indulged in scolding or shrewishness she would have been an evil companion the next morning, but a rigid upbringing had had sufficient effect on her to prevent her from indulging in such a wanton abuse of power. She did not yet know she could scold; she had never tasted the sweet delights of giving rein to ill temper.

Instead, she was only curt and impatient, and Allnutt, after a sidelong glance at her in response to some brief reply of hers to his loquaciousness, had the sense to hold his tongue. He wagged his head to himself and felt immensely wise, as he pondered over the inscrutable ways of womanhood, and he saw to it that steam was raised and the boat made ready for departure with the smallest possible delay.

Rose steered the *African Queen* straight out across the lagoon towards the place where she had decided she would find the best way through the delta. The low band of trees across the horizon grew more and more distinct. Soon they could distinguish the rich lush green of the reeds.

'Go slower now!' called Rose to Allnutt, and the beat of the engine slackened as Allnutt closed the throttle.

She took a course as close along the margin of the reeds as she dared. She did not like the appearance of them at all, pretty though they were. They grew in tough-looking, solid clumps, each stalk expanding at the top into a rather charming flower-head, and, apart from a few bold outliers, the clumps grew close together, while farther in towards the shore they were crowded in a manner which would make progress through them practically impossible. She did not know that probably this very species had provided the 'bulrushes' which composed the ark in which Moses had been set afloat on the Nile, nor that the learning of the world was most deeply indebted to it for the paper it had provided all through antiquity; and if she had known she would not have cared. All she sought was a way through.

Twice she hesitated as they neared points where the reeds did not grow quite so thickly, but each time she held on past them; there was the channel beyond through the forest of the delta to be considered as well. Such trivial indications of a waterway meant that its continuation through the delta might be impassable. Then they reached a broader, better defined passage. Rose raked back through her memory and decided this was at least as good as any she had noticed yesterday. She put the tiller over and turned the nose of the boat into the opening.

Nervously, Allnutt closed the throttle until the propeller was hardly revolving, and the *African Queen* glided among the reeds at a snail's pace; Rose nodded approval, for they did not want to run any risks with that patched propeller. The channel remained fairly clear of reeds as it wound this way and that. Sometines a clump scraped along the side with a prodigious rustling; Allnutt was sounding over-side with the boat-hook. It seemed that providentially the reeds refused to grow in water a little deeper than the *African Queen*'s draught; a channel which was clear of them was just navigable for her.

There came the inevitable moment when the channel bifurcated and a choice had to be made. Rose stared out over the sea of reeds at the nearing trees and brought the boat round into the most promising channel. They glided on; at each side the growth of reeds became denser and denser. And then the *African Queen* seemed to hesitate in her progress; there was something different about the feel of her, and Allnutt reached hastily to the throttle and shut off steam.

'We're aground, dearie,' he said.

'I know that,' snapped Rose. 'But we've got to go on.'

Allnutt poked at the bottom with the boat-hook; it was deep semi-liquid mud. There was no hope in consequence of their getting out and towing her, which was the first idea which occurred to him. He displayed the dripping boat-hook to Rose. 'We must pull her along by the reeds,' she said, harshly. 'The keel will go through mud like that even though we can't use the propeller.'

They addressed themselves to the task, Rose reaching out with her hands to the clumps she could reach, and Allnutt with the boat-hook. Soon their technique improved with experiment and experience. The papyrus reed grows from a long solid root which extends a considerable distance horizontally in the mud before turning upwards to form the head. Perched up in the bows, Allnutt reached forward with the boat-hook, fumbled about until he found a good grip, and then tugged the boat forward for a couple of feet through the ooze. Then he had to abandon the root he had found and search for a new one to gain another couple of feet.

It was terribly hot work among the reeds, which were not high enough to give shade although they cut off what little wind there was, and the sun glared down upon them with its noonday intensity. And soon the insects found them; they came in clouds until the air was thick with them, mad with the thirst for blood. The work was heavy and tiring, too. Two hours of it left Allnutt gasping for breath, and whenever he gasped he spluttered, in consequence of the insects he had drawn into his mouth.

'Sorry, miss,' he said at last, apologetically. 'Can't keep on at this, not any'ow.'

The face he turned towards Rose was as wet with perspiration as if he had been under a shower bath; so were his rags of clothes. Neither he nor Rose noticed his use of 'miss'–it sounded perfectly natural from a beast of burden such as he had become.

'All right,' said Rose. 'Give me the boat-hook.'

'The work's a bit 'eavy,' said Allnutt, with a note of protest in his tone.

Rose took no notice, but climbed past him on to the little fore-deck, the boat-hook in her hand. Allnutt made as if to argue further, but did not. He was too exhausted even to argue. He could only sink down into the bottom of the boat and lie there with the sweat drip-drip-dripping about him. For Rose, he had, literally, worked until he dropped. Rose certainly found the work heavy. Reaching forward to get a grip with the boat-hook was a strain. To get the boat to move forward over the mud and the reed-roots called for the exertion of every particle of strength she possessed–convulsive effort, to be followed immediately by the need for another, and another after that, interminably.

It did not take very long to exhaust her completely. In the end she put down the boat-hook with a clatter and reeled down the boat into the waist, her clothes hanging about her in wet wisps. The flies followed her, in myriads.

'We'll go on again tomorrow,' she gasped to Allnutt, who opened his eyes at her as he slowly came back to normality.

The reeds were higher about them now, for in their progress under this new method of traction they had practically left the papyrus behind and were come into the territory of another genus, and the sun was lower. They were in the shade at last; the boat, which had seemed as hot as a gridiron to the touch, became almost bearable, and the flies bit worse than ever. In time Rose recovered sufficiently to try to find out how close they were to the shore. She climbed on the gunwale, but the giant reeds stretched up over her head, and she could see nothing but reeds and sky. How far they had come, how far they were from the forest, she could not guess. She certainly had not anticipated taking a whole day to get through a belt of reeds a mile wide, but here was the first day ended and as far as she could tell they were only half-way in, and there was nothing to indicate that they would ever get through at all. No matter. They would go on trying tomorrow.

Anyone less stout-hearted than Rose might have begun to wonder what would happen to them if their forward progress became impossible. There was no chance at all of their pulling the boat back stern first the way they had come. They would be held there until they starved like trapped animals, or until they drowned themselves in the mud and slime beneath the reeds, trying to make their way ashore on foot. Rose did not allow that sort of notion to trouble her. Her resolution was such that no mere possibility could alarm her. She was like Napoleon's ideal general, in that she did not make pictures of might be–just as, all through this voyage, she had acted on Nelson's dictum, 'Lose not an hour'. If following, however unconsciously, the advice of the greatest soldier and the greatest sailor the world has ever seen would bring success to this land-and-water campaign, success would be theirs. And if they failed it would not be through lack of trying–that was what Rose was vowing to herself as she fought the flies.

II

There had been no need to moor the boat that night. No ordinary manifestation of Nature could have stirred her far from where she lay among those tall reeds. The wind that came with the thunder-storm that night was hardly felt by them at all–it bowed the reeds right across the boat, but sitting beneath the arch they formed they did not notice the wind. They had to endure all the discomforts of the rain as it poured down upon them in the dark, but even in those miserable conditions the ruling passion of that quaint pair displayed itself again.

'One thing abart this rine,' said Allnutt during a lull. 'It may deepen the water in this 'ere channel–if you can call it a channel. This afternoon we wasn't drorin' much more than there was 'ere. 'Alf a inch would mike a 'ell of a big difference. It can't rine too much for me, it can't.'

Then later that night, when the rain had long ceased, and Allnutt had somehow got to sleep despite the mosquitoes, Rose was suddenly aware of a noise. It was only the tiniest, smallest possible murmur, and only the ear of faith could have heard it through the whining of the mosquitoes. It was the noise of running water. From all around there came this gentle sound, slighter than the quietest breathing–water seeping and dribbling through the reeds as the level rose in the lagoon, helped on by the gathered rain which the Bora was bringing down. Rose almost woke up Allnutt, to listen to it, but refrained, and contented herself with vowing to make an early start in the morning so as to take full advantage of any rise before it could leak away through the delta–although seeing that they always started at the first possible moment it is hard to understand what Rose meant by an 'early start'.

There was this much variation, all the same, in their routine on rising that morning, in that they did not have to spend time in firing up the boiler and getting up steam. The sun was still below the tall reeds when they were ready to start, and already before Allnutt had come up into the bows to resume his yesterday's toil Rose was standing there, gazing into the reeds, trying to make out what she could about their course.

There really was no denying that they were still in some sort of waterway leading through the weeds. It was ill-defined; all there was to be seen was a winding line along which the reeds grew less densely, but it surely must lead somewhere.

'I fink she's afloat,' said Allnutt with satisfaction, taking the boat-hook.

He reached out, found a hold, and pulled. There seemed to be a freer movement then yesterday.

'No doubt about it,' reported Allnutt. 'We got all the water we want. If it wasn't for these blasted reeds—'

The channel was narrower here than when they had entered it, and the reeds caught against the sides as they moved along. Some had to be crushed under the boat, with the result that as each pull progressed the boat met with an increasing resistance; sometimes, maddeningly, she even went back an inch or two as Allnutt sought for a fresh grip. The resistance of the reeds, all the same, was far less unrelenting than the resistance of yesterday's mud, and Rose was able to be of some help by hastening about the boat freeing the sides from the reeds which impeded them.

They crawled on, slowly but hopefully. From what they could see of the sun there was no doubt that they were preserving a certain general direction towards the delta. Suddenly there came a squeal of joy from Allnutt.

'There's another channel 'ere!' he said, and Rose scrambled up into the bows to see.

It was perfectly true. The channel they were in joined at an acute angle a similar vague passage-way through the reeds, and the combined channel was broader, better defined, freer from reeds. As they looked at its dark water they could see that the fragments afloat on it were in motion–as slow as a slow tortoise, but in motion nevertheless.

'Coo!' said Allnutt. 'Look at the current! Better look out, Rosie, old girl. It'll be rapids next.'

They could still laugh.

Allnutt drew the *African Queen* into the channel. It was delightful to feel the boat floating free again, even though she could not swing more than an inch to either side. He hooked a root and gave a hearty pull; the boat made a good four feet through the water, and, what was more, retained her way, creeping along steadily while Allnutt sought for a new purchase.

'Blimey,' said Allnutt. 'We're going at a rate of knots now.'

A little later, as they came round a bend in the channel, Rose caught sight of the trees of the delta. They were instantly obscured again by the reeds, but the next bend brought them in sight again, not more than two hundred yards off, and right ahead. She watched them coming nearer. Almost without warning the passage through the weeds widened. Then, abruptly, the reeds ceased, and the *African Queen* drifted sluggishly forward for a yard or two and then stopped. They were in a wide pool, bordered on the farther side by dark trees, and the surface of the pool was covered with water-lilies, pink and white, growing so closely that it seemed as if the whole pool was a mass of vegetation.

The sunlight was dazzling after the green shade of the reeds; it took a little while for their eyes to grow accustomed to the new conditions.

'That's the delta all right,' said Allnutt, sniffing.

A dank smell of rotting vegetation came to them across the water; the farther bank was a wild tangle of trees of nightmare shape wreathed with creepers.

'We won't 'alf 'ave a gime getting this old tub through that lot,' said Allnutt.

'There's a channel over that way,' said Rose, pointing, 'Look!'

There certainly was some sort of opening into the forest there; they could see white water-lilies blooming in the entrance.

'I 'spect you're right,' said Allnutt. 'All we got to do now, in a manner of speaking, is to get there.'

He remembered the last water-lily pool they had encountered, high up on the Ulanga. There all they had to do was to get out again, having once entered. Here there was a hundred yards of weed-grown water to traverse.

'Let's try it,' said Rose.

'Course we're going to try it,' answered Allnutt, a little hurt.

It was not easy–nothing about that voyage to the Lake was easy. Those water-lily plants seemed to yield at a touch of the boat-hook, and afforded no purchase at all by which they could draw themselves along. Yet at the same time they clung so thick about the boat as to limit its progress as much as the reeds had done. Allnutt darkly suspected from the behaviour of the boat that they were being caught upon the screw–that precious screw with the weak blade–and rudder. The bottom was of such liquidity that it offered practically no resistance to the thrust of the boat-hook when used as a punt-pole, and in drawing the pole out again Allnutt found that he pulled the boat back almost as much as he had previously shoved it forward. Volleys of gas bubbles rose whenever the boat-hook touched the bottom; the stink was atrocious.

'Can't we try rowing?' asked Rose. Time was passing with the rapidity they always noticed when progress was slow, and they had hardly left the edge of the pool.

'We might,' said Allnutt.

One item in the gear of the *African Queen* was a canoe paddle. Allnutt went forward and found it and gave it to Rose. He brought back a billet of firewood for his own use.

Paddling the boat along made their progress a little quicker. There could be nothing slapdash nor carefree about wielding a paddle in those weeds. It had to be dipped carefully and vertically, reaching well forward, and it had to be drawn back with equal care, without twisting, lest at the moment of withdrawal it should be found so entangled as to call for the use of a knife to free it.

It was not a rapid method of transport. Rose would note some cluster of blooms up by the bows, and it would be at least a minute's toilsome work before it was back alongside her. Nor was the *African Queen* adapted for paddling. She had to sit on the bench in the sternsheets twisted uncomfortably sideways; a few minutes' paddling set up a piercing ache under her shoulder-blade like the worst kind of indigestion. She and Allnutt had continually to change sides for relief.

So slowly did they move that when they came completely to a standstill they neither of them realized it at once, and went on paddling while the suspicion grew until they looked round at each other through the streaming sweat and found each had been thinking the same thing.

'We're caught up on something,' said Allnutt.

'Yes.'

'It's that ole prop. Can't wonder at it in this mess.'

They stood together at the side of the boat, but of course there was no judging the state of affairs from there.

'Only one thing for it,' said Allnutt. He took out his knife, opened it, and looked at its edge.

'A spot of diving is the next item on the programme, lidies and gents,' he said. He tried to grin as he said it.

Rose wanted to expostulate; there was danger in that massed weed, but

Allnutt must chance the danger if the voyage was to go on.

'We'll have to be careful,' was all she could say.

'Yerss.'

Allnutt fetched a length of rope.

'We'll tie that round my waist,' he said, as he stripped off his clothes. 'You count firty from the time I go under, an' if I ain't coming up by then, you pull at that rope, an' pull, an' pull, an' go on pulling.'

'All right,' said Rose.

Allnutt sat naked on the gunwale and swung his legs over.

'Good crocodile country this,' he said, and then, seeing the look on Rose's face, he went on hastily: 'Nao it ain't. There ain't no croc on earth could get through these weeds.'

Allnutt was not too sure about it himself. He was rising to an unbelievable height of heroism in what he was doing. Not even Rose could guess at the sick fear within him, but in reaction from his cowardice he was growing foolhardy. He took his knife in his hand and dropped into the water. Holding on to the gunwale, he breathed deeply half a dozen times, and then ducked his head under the boat. His legs vanished under the carpet of weed, while Rose began to count with trembling lips. At 'thirty' she began to pull on the rope, and she sighed with relief as Allnutt emerged, all tangled with weed. He had to put up a weed-clustered hand to pull a mask of the stuff from his face before he could breathe or see.

'There's a lump like a beehive round that prop,' he said as he gasped for breath. 'An' 'alf the weeds in the lake are anchored on to it.'

'Is it any use trying to clear it?'

'Ooh yerss. Stuff cuts easy enough. I'd done a good bit already when I 'ad to come up. Well, 'ere goes agine.'

At the fourth ascent Allnutt grinned with pleasure.

'All clear,' he said. ''Old the knife, will you, old girl? I'm comin' in.'

He pulled himself up over the gunwale with Rose's assistance. The water streamed off him and from the masses of weed which clung to his body. Rose fussed over him, helping to pick him clean. Suddenly she gave a little cry, which was instantly echoed by Allnutt.

'Just look at the little beggars!' said Allnutt–the swear words he still refrained from using were those which, never having come Rose's way, she did not know to be swear words.

On Allnutt's body and arms and legs were leeches, a score or more of them, clinging to his skin. They were swelling with his blood as Rose looked at them. They were disgusting things. Allnutt was moved at the sight of them to more panic than he had felt about crocodiles.

'Can't you pull 'em off?' he said, his voice cracking. 'Arhh! The beasts.'

Rose remembered that if a leech is pulled off before he is gorged he is liable to leave his jaws in the wound, and blood-poisoning may ensue.

'Salt gets them off,' she said, and sprang to fetch the tin in which the salt was kept.

Damp salt dabbed on the leeches' bodies worked like magic. Each one contorted himself for a moment, elongated himself and thickened himself, and then fell messily to the floor-boards. Allnutt stamped on the first one in his panic, and blood–his own blood–and other liquid spurted from under his foot. Rose scooped the remains and the other leeches up with the paddle and flung them into the water. Blood still ran freely from the triangular bites, drying in brown smears on Allnutt's body under the blazing sun; it was some time before they could induce it to clot at the wounds, and even when it was all over Allnutt was still shuddering with distaste. He hated leeches worse than anything else on earth.

'Let's get awye from 'ere,' was all the reply he could make to Rose's anxious questionings.

They paddled on across the lily-pool. With the coming of the afternoon some of the pink blooms began to close. Other buds opened, ivory-coloured buds with the faintest tinge of blue at the petal tips. That carpet of lilies was a lovely sight, but neither of them had any eyes for its beauty. They sank into a condition of dull stupidity, their minds deadened by the sun; they said nothing to each other even when they exchanged places. Their course across the pool was as slow as a slug's in a garden. They dipped and pulled on their paddles like mechanical contrivances, save when their rhythm was broken by the clutch of the maddening weeds upon the paddles.

The sun was lower by now; there was a band of shade on the rim of the pool which they were approaching. With infinite slowness the *African Queen*'s nose gained the shade. Allnutt nerved himself for a few more strokes, and then, as the shade slid up to the stern and reached them, he let fall his billet of wood.

'I can't do no more,' he said, and he laid his head down upon the bench.

He was nearly weeping with exhaustion, and he turned his face away from Rose so that she would not see. Yet later on, when he had eaten and drunk, his Cockney resilience of spirits showed itself despite the misery the mosquitoes were causing.

'What we want 'ere,' he said, 'is a good big cataract. You know, like the first one below Shona. We'd 'ave got 'ere from the other side of the reeds in about a minute an' a 'alf, I should say, 'stead of a couple of dyes an' not there yet.'

Later in the evening he was facetious again.

'We've come along under steam, an' we've paddled, an' we've pushed, an' we've pulled the ole boat along wiv the 'ook. What we 'aven't done yet is get out an' carry 'er along. I s'pose that'll come next.'

Rose remembered those words, later in the following day, and thought they had tempted Providence.

12

In the morning there was only a narrow strip of water-lily lake to cross under the urgings of the early sun. They fought their way across it with renewed hope, for they could see the very definite spot where the lilies ceased to grow, and the beginning of a channel through the delta, and they felt that no obstacle to navigation could be as infuriating and exhausting as those lilies.

The delta of the Bora is a mangrove swamp, for the water of Lake Wittelsbach, although drinkable, is very slightly brackish, sufficiently so for some species of mangrove to grow, and where mangroves can grow there is no chance of survival for other trees. Where the mangroves began, too, the water-lilies ended, abruptly, for they could not endure life in the deep shade which the mangroves cast.

They reached the mouth of the channel and peered down it. It was like a deep tunnel; only very rare shafts of light from the blazing sky above penetrated its gloomy depths. The stench as of decaying marigolds filled their nostrils. The walls and roof of the tunnel were composed of mangrove roots, and branches, tangled into a fantastic conglomeration of shapes as wild as any nightmare could conceive.

Nevertheless, the repellent ugliness of the place meant no more to them than had the beauty of the water-lilies. These days of travel had obsessed them with the desire to go on. They were so set upon bringing their voyage to its consummation that no place could be beautiful that presented navigational difficulties, and they were ready to find no place ugly if the water route through it were easy. When they crawled out from the last clinging embrace of the water-lilies they both with one accord ceased paddling to look into the water, each to his separate side.

'Coo,' said Allnutt, in tones of deep disgust. 'It's grass now.'

The weed which grew here from the bottom of the water was like some rank meadow grass. The water was nearly solid with it. The only encouraging feature it displayed was that the long strands which lay along the surface all pointed in the direction in which they were headed–a sure sign that there was some faint current down the channel, and where the current went was where they wanted to go too.

'No going under steam 'ere,' said Allnutt. 'Never get the prop to go round in that muck.'

Rose looked down the bank of mangroves, along the edge of the lily pool. They might try to seek some other way through the delta, but it seemed likely that any other channel would be as choked with weed, while any attempts to find another channel would involve more slow paddling through water-lilies. She formed her decision with little enough delay.

'Come on,' was all she said. She had never heard Lord Fisher's advice, 'Never explain,' but she acted upon it by instinct.

They leant forward to their work again and the *African Queen* entered into the mangrove swamp with the slowness to be expected of a steam launch moved by one canoe paddle and one bit of wood shaped rather like a paddle.

It was a region in which water put up a good fight against the land which was slowly invading it. Through the mangrove roots which closed round them they could see black pools of water reaching far inwards; the mud in which the trees grew was half water, as black and nearly as liquid. The very air was dripping with moisture. Everything was wet and yet among the trees it was as hot as in an oven. It made breathing oppressive.

'Shall I try 'ooking 'er along, now, Rosie?' said Allnutt. He was refusing to allow the horror of the place to oppress his spirits. 'We get along a bit better that wye.'

'We could both of us use hooks here,' said Rose. 'Can you make a hook?'

'Easy,' said Allnutt. Rose was fortunate in having an assistant like him.

He produced a four-foot boat-hook quickly enough, beating the metal hook out of an angle iron from an awning stanchion, binding it tightly to the shaft with wire.

With both of them using hooks their progress grew more rapid. They stood side by side in the bows, and almost always there was a root or branch of the mangroves within reach on one side or the other, or up above, so that they could creep along the channel, zigzagging from either side. Reckoning the mangrove swamp as ten miles across, and allowing fifty per cent extra for bends in the channel, and calling their speed half a mile an hour–it was something like that–thirty hours of this sort of effort ought to have seen them through. It took much longer than that, all the same.

First of all, there were the obstructions in the channel. They encountered one almost as soon as they entered among the mangroves, and after that they recurred every few hundred yards. The *African Queen* came to a standstill with a bump and a jar which they came to know only too well–some log was hidden in the black depths or the water, stretching unseen across the channel. They had to sound along its length. Sometimes when they were fortunate there was sufficient depth of water over it at some point or other to float the boat across, but if there was not they had to devise some other means of getting forward. The funnel early came down; Allnutt dismantled that and the awning stanchions quite soon in consequence of the need for creeping under overhanging branches.

Generally if the channel were blocked they could find some passage round the obstruction through the pools of water which constituted a sort of side channel here and there, but to work the *African Queen* through them called for convulsive efforts, which usually involved Allnutt's disembarking and floundering in the mud and warping the launch round the corners. It was as the *African Queen* was slithering and grating over the mud and the tree-roots that Allnutt's ill-omened words about getting out and carrying the boat recurred to Rose's mind.

If there were no way over or round they had to shift the obstruction in the channel somehow, ascertaining its shape and weight and attachments by probings with the boat-hooks, heaving it in the end, with efforts which in that Turkish-bath atmosphere made them feel as if their hearts would burst, the necessary few inches this way or that. They grew ingenious at devising methods of rigging tackle to branches above, and fixing ropes to the obstructions beneath, so as to sway the things out of their way. And Allnutt, perforce, overcame his shuddering hatred of leeches–on one occasion they squatted in mud and water for a couple of hours while with knives they made two cuts in a submerged root which barred the only possible bit of water through which they could float the *African Queen*.

It was a nightmare time of filth and sludge and stench. Be as careful as they would, the all-pervading mud spread by degrees over everything in and upon the boat, upon themselves, everywhere, and with it came its sickening stink. It was a place of twilight, where everything had to be looked at twice to make sure what it was, so that, as every step might disturb a snake whose bite would be death, their flounderings in the mud were of necessity cautious.

Worse than anything else it was a place of malaria. The infection had probably gained their blood anew in the lower reaches of the Bora before they reached the delta, but it was in the delta that they were first incapacitated. Every morning they were prostrated by it, almost simultaneously. Their heads ached, and they felt a dull coldness creeping over them, and their teeth began to chatter, until they were helpless in the paroxysm, their faces drawn and lined and their finger-nails blue with cold. They lay side by side in the bottom of the boat, with the silent mangrove forest round them, clutching their filthy rags despite the sweltering steamy heat which they could not feel. Then at last the cold would pass and the fever would take its place, a nightmare fever of delirium and thirst and racking pain, until when it seemed they could bear no more the blessed sweat would appear, and the fever die away, so that they slept for an hour or two, to wake in the end capable once more of moving about–capable of continuing the task of getting the *African Queen* through the Bora delta.

Rose dosed herself and Allnutt regularly with quinine from the portable medicine chest in her tin trunk; had it not been for that they would probably have died and their bones would have mouldered in the rotting hull of the *African Queen* among the mangroves.

They never saw the sun while they were in that twilight nightmare land, and the channel twisted and turned so that they lost all sense of direction and had no idea at all to which point of the compass they were heading. When the channel they were following joined another one, they had to look to see which way the water was flowing to decide in which direction to turn, and where it was so dark that even the water grass would not grow, as happened here and there, they had to note the direction of drift of bits of wood placed on the surface–an almost imperceptible drift, not more than a few yards an hour.

It was worse on the two occasions when they lost the channel altogether as a result of forced detours through pools round obstacles. That was easy enough to do, where every tangle of aerial roots looked like every other tangle, where the light was poor and there was nothing to help fix one's direction, and where to step from the islands of ankle-deep slime meant sinking waist-deep in mud in which the hidden roots tore the skin. When they were lost like this they could only struggle on from pool to pool, if necessary cutting a path for the boat with the axe by infinite toil, until at last it was like Paradise to rejoin a murky, root-encumbered channel on which they might progress as much as fifty yards at a time without being held up by some obstacle or other.

They lost all count of time in that swamp. Days came and went, each with its bout of chill and fever; it was day when there was light enough to see, and night when the twilight had encroached so much that they could do no more, and how many days they passed thus they never knew. They ate little, and what they ate stank of the marshes before they got it to their mouths. It was a worse life than any animal's, for no animal was ever set the task of coaxing the *African Queen* through those mangroves–with never a moment's carelessness, lest that precious propeller should be damaged.

No matter how slippery the foothold, nor how awkward the angle of the tow-rope, nor how imminent an attack of malaria, the launch had always to be eased round the corner inch by inch, without a jerk, in case during her lateral progress the propeller should be swung sideways against some hidden root. There was never the satisfaction of a vicious tug at the rope or a whole-hearted shove with the pole.

They did not notice the first hopeful signs of their progress. The channel they were in was like any other channel, and when it joined another channel it was only what had happened a hundred times before; they presumed that there would be a bifurcation farther on. But when yet another large channel came in they began to fill with hope. The boughs were thinning overhead so that it grew steadily lighter; the channel was deep and wide, and although it was choked with water grass that was only a mere trifle to them now after some of the obstacles they had been through, and they had developed extraordinary dexterity at hooking the *African Queen* along by the branches. They did not dare to speak to each other as the channel wound about, a full ten feet from side to side.

And then the channel broadened so that real sunlight reached them, and Allnutt could wait no longer before speaking about it, even if it should be unlucky.

'Rosie,' he said. 'D'you fink we got through, Rosie?'

Rose hesitated before she spoke. It seemed far too good to be true. She got a good hold on an aerial root and gave a brisk pull which helped the *African Queen* bravely on her way before she dared to reply.

'Yes,' she said at length. 'I think we have.'

They managed to smile at each other across the boat. They were horrible to look at, although they had grown used to each other. They were filthy with mud–Rose's long chestnut hair, and Allnutt's hair, and the beard which had grown again since they had entered into the delta were all matted into lumps with it. Their sojourn in the semi-darkness had changed their deep sunburn into an unhealthy yellow colour which was accentuated by their malaria. Their cheeks were hollow and their eyes sunken, and through the holes in their filthy rags could be seen their yellow skins, with the bones almost protruding through them. The boat and all its contents were covered with mud, brought in by hurried boardings after negotiating difficult turns. They looked more like diseased savages of the Stone Age than such products of civilization as a missionary's sister and a skilled mechanic. They still smiled at each other, all the same.

Then the channel took another turn, and before them there lay a vista in which mangroves played hardly any part.

'Reeds!' whispered Allnutt, as though he hardly dared to say it. 'Reeds!'

He had experienced reeds before, and much preferred them to mangroves. Rose was on tiptoe on the bench by now, looking over the reeds as far as she could.

'The Lake's just the other side,' she said.

Instantly Rose's mind began to deal with ways and means, as if she had just heard that an unexpected guest was about to arrive to dinner.

'How much wood have we got?' she asked.

'Good deal,' said Allnutt, running a calculating eye over the piles in the waist. ''Bout enough for half a dye.'

'We ought to have more than that,' said Rose, decisively.

Out on the Lake there would not be the ready means of replenishment which they had found up to now. The *African Queen* might soon be contending with difficulties of refuelling beside which those of Muller and von Spee would seem child's play. There was only one effort to be asked of the *African Queen*, but she must be equipped as completely as they could manage it for that effort.

'Let's stop here and get some,' she decided.

To Allnutt, most decidedly, and to herself in some degree, the decision was painful. Both of them, now that they had seen a blue sky and a wide horizon, were filled with a wild unreasoning panic. They were madly anxious to get clear away from those hated mangroves without a second's delay. The thought of an extra hour among them caused them distress; certainly, if Allnutt had been by himself he would have dashed off and left the question of fuel supply to solve itself. But as it was he bowed to Rose's authority, and when he demurred it was for the general good, not to suit his own predilections.

'Green wood's not much good under our boiler, you know,' he said.

'It's better than nothing,' replied Rose. 'And I expect it'll have a day or two to dry off before we want it.'

They exchanged a glance when she said that. All the voyage so far had been designed for one end, The torpedoing of the *Königin Luise*. That end, which had seemed so utterly fantastic to Allnutt once upon a time, was at hand now; he had not thought about it very definitely for weeks, but the time was close upon him when he would have to give it consideration. Yet even now he could not think about it in an independent fashion; he could only tell himself that quite soon he would form some resolve upon the matter. For the present he had not a thought in his head. He moored the *African Queen* up against the mangroves and took his axe and cut at the soft pulpy wood until there was a great heap piled in the waist. And then at last they could leave the mangroves for the happy sanctuary of the reeds.

13

It was a very definite mouth of the Bora by which they had emerged. There was a fairly wide channel through the reeds, and they had no sooner entered it and turned one single corner than the limitless prospect of the Lake opened before them–golden water as far as the eye could see ahead, broken by only one or two tree-grown islands. On either side of the channel were shoals, marked by continuous reeds, extending far out into the Lake, but those they could ignore. There was clear water, forty miles broad and eighty long, in front of them, not a rock, nor a shoal, nor a water-lily, nor a reed, nor a mangrove to impede them–unless they should go out of their way to seek for them. The sensation of freedom and relief was absolutely delicious. They were like animals escaped from a cage. Moored among the reeds, with the *African Queen* actually rocking a little to a minute swell coming in from the Lake, they slept more peacefully, plagued though they were with frogs and flies, then they had done for days.

And in the morning there was still no discussion of the torpedoing of the *Königin Luise*. To Rose with her methodical mind it was necessary to complete one step before thinking about the next.

'Let's get the boat cleaned out,' she said. 'I can't bear all this.'

Indeed, in the glaring sunlight the filth and mess in the boat were perfectly horrible. Rose literally could not think or plan surrounded by such conditions. They jangled her nerves unbearably. No matter if the *African Queen* were shortly to be blown to pieces when she should immolate herself against the *Königin Luise*'s side, Rose could not bear the thought of passing even two or three days unnecessarily in that dirt.

The water over-side was clear and clean. By degrees they washed the whole boat, although it involved moving everything from place to place while they washed. Allnutt got the floor-boards up and cleaned out the reeking bilge, while Rose knelt up in the sternsheets and gradually worked clean the rugs and the clothing and the articles of domestic utility. It was a splendid day, and in that sunshine even a thick rug dried almost while you looked at it. Such a domestic interlude was the best sort of holiday Rose could have had; perhaps it was not only coincidence that they both of them missed their attacks of malaria that morning.

Rose got herself clean, too, for the first time since their entry into the mangroves, and felt once more the thrill of putting on a fresh clean frock on a fresh clean body. That was literally the case, because Rose had taken the step which she had tried to put aside in the old days of the mission station–she was wearing no underclothes. Most of them had been consumed in the service of the boat–as hand shields when the propeller shaft was straightened and so on–and the rest was dedicated to Allnutt's use. His own clothing had disintegrated, and now he moved chastely about the boat in Rose's chemise and drawers; the modest trimming round the neck and the infinite number of tucks about his thighs were in comical contrast with his lean unfeminine form.

Perhaps it was as a result of these civilized preoccupations that Rose that night thought of something which had slipped from her memory utterly and completely from the moment she had left the mission station. She herself, later, believed on occasions that it was God Himself who came and roused her from her sleep, her breast throbbing and the blood pulsing warm under her skin, although when she was in a more modest mood she attributed it to her 'better self' or her conscience.

She had not said her prayers since she joined the *African Queen*; she had not even thought about God. She woke with a start as this realization came upon her, and she lay with wave after wave of remorse–and fear, too–sweeping over her. She could not understand how it was that the God she worshipped had not sent the lightning, which had so frequently torn the sky about her, to destroy her. She was in an agony lest He should do so now before she could appease Him. She scrambled up to her knees and clasped her hands and bowed her head and prayed in a passion of remorse.

Allnutt, waking in the night, saw the profile of her bowed figure in the starlight, and saw her lift her face to Heaven with her cheeks wet with tears and her lips moving. He was awed by the sight. He did not pray himself, and never had done so. The fact that Rose was able to pray in tears and agony showed him the superiority of her clay over his. But it was a superiority of which he had long been aware. He was content to leave the appeal for Heavenly guidance to Rose just as he had left to her the negotiation of the rapids of the Ulanga. It took a very great deal to deprive Allnutt of his sleep. His eyes closed and he drifted off again, leaving Rose to bear her agony alone.

In that awful moment Rose would have found no comfort in Allnutt anyway. It was a matter only for her and God. There was no trace of the iron-nerved woman, who had brought the *African Queen* down the Ulanga, in the weeping figure who besought God for forgiveness of her neglect. She could make no attempt to compound with God, to offer future good behaviour in exchange for forgiveness of the past, because her training did not permit it. She could only plead utter abject penitence, and beg for forgiveness as an arbitrary favour from the stern God about whom her brother had taught her. She was torn with misery. She could not tell if she were forgiven or not. She did not know how much of hellfire she would have to endure on account of these days of forgetfulness.

Worse still, she could not tell whether or not her angry God might not see fit to punish her additionally by blasting her present expedition with failure. It would be an apt punishment, seeing that the expedition was the cause of her neglect. There was a Biblical flavour about it which tore her with apprehension. In redoubled agony she begged and prayed to God to look with favour on this voyage of the *African Queen*, to grant them an opportunity of finding the *Königin Luise* and of sinking her, so that the hated iron-cross flag would disappear from the waters of Lake Wittelsbach and the Allies might pour across to the conquest of German Central Africa. She was quite frantic with doubts and fear; the joints of her fingers cracked with the violence with which she clasped them.

It was only then that she remembered another sin–a worse one, the worst sin of all in the bleak minds of those who had taught her, a sin whose name she had only used when reading aloud from the Bible. She had lain with a man in unlicensed lust. For a moment she remembered with shocked horror the things she had done with that man, her wanton immodesty. It made matters worse still that she had actually *enjoyed* it, as no woman should ever dream of doing.

She looked down at the vague white figure of Allnutt asleep in the bottom of the boat, and with that came reaction. She could not, she absolutely could not, feel a conviction of sin with regard to him. He was as much a husband to Rose as any married woman's husband was to her, whatever the formalities with which she and Charlie had dispensed. She took courage from the notion, although she did not rise (or sink) to the level of actually wording to herself her opinion of the marriage sacrament as a formality. She lapsed insensibly into the heresy of believing that it might be possible that natural forces could be too strong for her, and that if they were she was not to blame.

Much of her remorse and terror departed from her in that moment, and she calmed perceptibly. The last of her prayers were delivered with reason as well as feeling, and she asked favours now as one friend might ask of another. The sincerity of her conviction that what she meditated doing on England's behalf must be right came to her rescue, so that hope and confidence came flooding back again despite the weakness which the first agony had brought to her sick body. There descended upon her at last a certainty of righteousness as immovable and as unreasoning as her previous conviction of sin.

In the end she lay down again to sleep with her serenity quite restored, completely fanatical again about the justice and the certainty of success of the blow she was going to strike for England. The only perceptible difference the whole harrowing experience made to her conduct was that next morning when she rose she prayed again for a moment, on her knees with her head bowed, while Allnutt fidgeted shyly in the bows. She was her old self again, with level brows and composed features, when she rose from her knees to look round the horizon.

There was something in sight out there, something besides water and reeds and sky and islands. It was not a cloud; it was a smudge of black smoke, and beneath it a white dot. Rose's heart leaped violently in her breast, but she forced composure on herself.

'Charlie,' she called, quietly enough. 'Come up here. What's *that*?'

One glance was sufficient for Allnutt, as it had been for Rose.

'That's the *Louisa*.'

Partisanship affected Allnutt much as it affects the Association football crowds which are constituted of thousands of people just like Allnutt. No words could be bad enough for the other side, just because it happened to be the other side. Although Allnutt had not had a chance to be infected by the propaganda which seethed at that moment in the British Press, he became at sight of the *Königin Luise* as rabidly an anti-German as any plump city clerk over military age.

'Yerss,' he said, standing up on the gunwale. 'That's the *Louisa* all right. Ther beasts! Ther swine!'

He shook his fist at the white speck.

'Which way are they going?' asked Rose, cutting through his objurgations. Allnutt peered over the water, but before he could announce his decision Rose announced it for him.

'They're coming this way!' she said, and then she forced herself again to stay calm.

'They mustn't see us here,' she went on, in a natural tone. 'Can we get far enough among the reeds for them not to see us?'

Allnutt was already leaping about the boat, picking things up and putting them down again. It was more of an effort for him to speak calmly.

'They'll see the funnel and the awning,' he said, in a lucid interval. Putting up the funnel and the awning stanchions had been part of the spring-cleaning of yesterday.

For answer Rose tore the ragged awning down again from its supports.

'You've got plenty of time to get the funnel down,' she said. 'They won't be able to see it yet, and the reeds are between them and us. I'll see about the stanchions. Give me a screwdriver.'

Rose had the sense and presence of mind to realize that if a ship the size of the *Königin Luise* was only a dot to them, they must be less than a dot to it.

With the top hamper stowed away the *African Queen* had a freeboard of hardly three feet; they would be quite safe among the reeds unless they were looked for specially–and Rose knew that the Germans would have no idea that the *African Queen* was on the Lake. She looked up and watched the *Königin Luise* carefully. She was nearer, coasting steadily southward along the margin of the Lake. From one dot she had grown into two–her white hull being visible under her high bridge. It would be fully an hour before she opened up the mouth of the river and could see the *African Queen* against the reeds.

'Let's get the boat in now,' she said.

They swung her round so that her bows pointed into the reeds. Pulling and tugging with the boat-hooks against the reed-roots they got her half-way in, but all her stern still projected out into the channel.

'You'll have to cut some of those reeds down. How deep is the mud?' said Rose.

Allnutt probed the mud about the *African Queen*'s bows and dubiously contemplated the result.

'Hurry up,' snapped Rose, testily, and Allnutt took his knife and went in over the bows among the reeds. He sank in the mud until the surface water was up to his armpits. Floundering about, he cut every reed within reach as low as he could manage it. Then, holding the bow painter, with Rose's help he was able to pull himself out of the clinging mud, and lay across the fore-deck while Rose worked the *African Queen* up into the space he had cleared.

'There's still a bit sticking out,' said Rose. 'Once more will do it.'

Allnutt splashed back among the reeds and went on cutting. When he had finished and climbed on board again, between the two of them they hauled the boat up into the cleared space. The reeds which the bows had thrust aside when they entered began to close again round the stern.

'It would be better if we were a bit farther in still,' said Rose, and without a word Allnutt went in among the reeds once more.

This time the gain was sufficient. The *African Queen* lay in thick reeds; about her stern was a thin but satisfactory screen of the reeds at the edge, which, coming back to the vertical, made her safe against anything but close observation even if–as was obviously unlikely–the *Königin Luise* should see fit to come up the reed-bordered channel to the delta.

Standing on the gunwale, Rose and Allnutt could just see over the reeds. The *Königin Luise* was holding steadily on her course, a full mile from the treacherous shoals of the shore. She was nearly opposite the mouth of the channel now, and she showed no signs of turning. They watched her for five minutes. She looked beautiful in her glittering white paint against the vivid blue of the water. A long pennant streamed from the brief pole-mast beside her funnel; at her stern there floated the flag of the Imperial German Navy with its black cross. On her deck in the bows they could just discern the six-pounder gun which gave the Germans the command of Lake Wittelsbach. No Arab dhow, no canoe, could show her nose outside the creeks and inlets of the Lake unless the *Königin Luise* gave permission.

She was past the channel now, still keeping rigidly to the south. There was clearly no danger of discovery; she was on a cruise of inspection round the Lake, just making certain that there was no furtive flouting of authority. Rose watched her go, and then got down heavily into the sternsheets.

'My malaria's started again,' she said, wearily.

Her face was drawn and apprehensive as a result of the ache she had been enduring in her joints, and her teeth were already chattering. Allnutt wrapped her in the rugs and made what preparations he could for the fever which would follow.

'Mine's begun too,' he said then. Soon both of them were helpless and shivering, and moaning a little, under the blazing sun.

14

When the attack was over in the late afternoon Rose got uncertainly to her feet again. Allnutt was only now coming out of the deep reviving sleep which follows the fever of malaria in fortunate persons. The first thing Rose did was what everyone living in a boat comes to do after an unguarded interval. She stood up and looked about her, craning her neck over the reeds so as to sweep the horizon.

Down in the south she saw it again, that smudge of smoke and that white speck. She formed and then discarded the idea that the *Königin Luise* was still holding her old course. The gunboat was returning; she must have cruised down out of sight to the south and then begun to retrace her course. Allnutt came and stood beside her, and without a word they watched the *Königin Luise* gradually grow larger and more distinct as she came back along the coast. It was Allnutt who broke the silence.

'D'you fink she's looking for us?' he asked, hoarsely.

'No,' said Rose, with instant decision. 'Not at all. She's only keeping guard on the coast.'

Rose was influenced more by faith than by judgement. Her mission would be too difficult to succeed if the Germans were on the look-out for them, and therefore it could not be so.

'Hope you're right,' said Allnutt. 'Matter of fact, I fink you are myself.'

'She's going a different way now!' said Rose, suddenly.

The *Königin Luise* had altered course a trifle, and was standing out from the shore.

'She's not looking for us, then,' said Allnutt.

They watched her as she steamed across the Lake, keeping just above their horizon, heading for the islands which they could see straight opposite them.

'Wonder what she's goin' to do?' said Allnutt, but all the same it was he who first noticed that she had come to a stop.

'She's anchoring there for the night,' said Allnutt. 'Look!'

The flag at the stern disappeared, as is laid down as a rule to be followed at sunset in the Imperial Instructions for Captains of Ships of the Imperial German Marine.

'Did you 'ear anything then?' asked Allnutt.

'No.'

'I fought I 'eard a bugle.' Allnutt could not possibly have heard a bugle over four miles of water, not even in the stillness which prevailed, but undoubtedly there were bugles blowing in the *Königin Luise* at approximately that time. Even though the crew of the *Königin Luise* consisted only of six white officers and twenty-five coloured ratings everything was done on board as befitted the exacting standards of the navy of which the ship was a part.

'Well, there they are,' said Allnutt. 'And there they'll stop. That's a good anchorage out there among the islands. We'll see 'em go in the morning.'

He got down from the gunwale while Rose yet lingered. The sun had set in a sudden blaze of colour, and it was already almost too dark to see the distant white speck. She could not accept as philosophically as Allnutt the inevitability of their present inaction. They were on the threshold of events. They must make ready, and plan, and strike their blow for England, even though any scheme seemed more fantastic now than when viewed from the misty distance of the Upper Ulanga.

'We ought to have been ready for them today,' said Rose, turning bitterly to Allnutt, the glow of whose cigarette she could just see in the dark.

Allnutt puffed at his cigarette, and then brought out a surprisingly helpful suggestion.

'Coo,' he said, 'don't you worry. I been thinking. They'll come 'ere agine, you just see if they don't. You know what these Germans are. They lays down systems and they sticks to 'em. Mondays they're at one plice, Tuesdays they're somewhere else, Wednesdays p'raps they're 'ere–I dunno what dye it is todye. Saturday nights I expect they goes into Port Livingstone an' lay up over Sunday. Then they start agine on Monday, same ole round. *You* know.'

Allnutt was without doubt the psychologist of the two. What he said was so much in agreement with what Rose had seen of official German methods that she could not but think there must be truth in it. He went on to press home his point by example.

'Up at the mine,' he said. 'Old Kauffmann, the inspector, 'oo' ad the job of seeing that the mine was being run right–an' a fat lot o' good all those rules of theirs was, too–'e used to turn up once a week regular as clockwork. Always knew when 'e was coming, the Belgians did, an' they'd 'ave everything ready for 'im. 'E'd come in an' look round, and 'ave a drink, an' then off 'e'd go agine wiv 'is Askaris an' 'is bearers. Used to mike me laugh even then.'

'Yes, I remember,' said Rose, absently. She could remember how Samuel had sometimes chafed against the woodenness of German rules and routine. There could be no doubt that if the *Königin Luise* had once moored among those islands she would do so again. Then–her plan was already formed.

'Charlie,' she said, and her voice was gentle.

'Yerss, old girl?'

'You must start getting those torpedoes ready. Tomorrow morning, as soon as it's light. How long will it take?'

'I can get the stuff into the tubes in no time, as you might say. Dunno about the detonators. Got to mike 'em, you see. Might take a coupler dyes easy. Matter of fact, I 'aven't thought about 'em prop'ly. Then we got to cut those 'oles in the bows–that won't tike long. Might 'ave it all done in a coupler dyes. Everything. If we don't 'ave malaria too bad. Depends on them detonators.'

'All right.' There was something unnatural about Rose's voice.

'Rosie, old girl,' said Allnutt. 'Rosie.'

'Yes, dear?'

'I know what you're thinkin' about doing. You needn't try to 'ide it from me.'

Had it not been for the discordant Cockney accent Allnutt's voice in its gentleness might have been that of some actor in a sentimental moment on the stage. He took her hand in the darkness and pressed it, unresponsive as it was.

'Not now, you needn't 'ide it, darling,' he said. Even at that moment his Cockney self-consciousness came to embarrass him and he tried to keep the emotion out of his voice. For them there was neither the unrestraint of primitive people nor the acquired self-control of other classes of society.

'You want to tike the *African Queen* out at night next time the *Louisa*'s 'ere, don't yer, old girl?' said Allnutt.

'Yes.'

'I fink it's the best chance we got of all,' said Allnutt. 'We oughter manage it.'

Allnutt was silent for a second or two, making ready for his next argument. Then he spoke.

'You needn't come, old girl. There ain't no need for us both to–to do it. I can manage it meself, easy.'

'Of course not,' said Rose. 'That wouldn't be fair. It's you who ought to stay behind. I can manage the launch on my own as far as those islands. That's what I was meaning to do.'

'I know,' said Allnutt, surprisingly. 'But it's me that ought to do it. Besides, with them beggars—'

It was an odd argument that developed. Allnutt was perfectly prepared by now to throw away the life that had seemed so precious to him. This plan of Rose's which had already materialized so far and so surprisingly had become like a living thing to him–like a piece of machinery would perhaps be a better analogy in Allnutt's case. There would be something wrong about leaving it incomplete. And somehow the sight of the *Königin Luise* cruising about the Lake 'as bold as brass' had irritated Allnutt. He was aflame with partisanship. He was ready for any mad sacrifice which would upset those beggars' apple-cart–presumably Allnutt's contact with the German nation had been unfortunate; the Germans were a race it was easy to hate if hatred came easily, as it did in those days. There was a fierce recklessness about him, in odd contrast with his earlier cowardice.

Perhaps no one can really understand the state of mind of a man who volunteers in war for a duty that may lead to death, but that such volunteers are always forthcoming has been proved by too many pitiful events in history.

Allnutt tried to reason with Rose. Although they had both of them tacitly dropped their earlier plan of sending the *African Queen* out on her last voyage with no crew on board–Rose knew too much about the launch's little ways by now–Allnutt tried to argue that for him there would be no serious risk. He could dive off the stern of the boat a second before the crash, as soon as he was sure she would attain the target. Even if he were at the tiller (as privately he meant to be, to make certain), the explosion right up in the bows might not hurt him–Allnutt had the nerve to suggest that, even when he had a very sound knowledge of the power of explosives and could guess fairly accurately what two hundredweight of high explosive would do if it went off all at once. In fact, Allnutt was on the point of arguing that blowing up the *Königin Luise* would be a perfectly safe proceeding for anybody, until he saw what loophole that would leave for Rose's argument.

It all ended, as was inevitable, in their agreeing in the end that they would both go. There was no denying that their best chance of success lay in having one person to steer and one to tend the engine. It was further agreed between them that when they were fifty yards from the *Königin Luise* one of them would jump overboard with the lifebuoy; but Allnutt thought that it was settled that Rose should do the jumping, and Rose thought that it would be Allnutt.

'Not more'n a week from now,' said Allnutt, meditatively.

They had a feeling of anticipation which if not exactly pleasurable was not really unpleasant. They had been working like slaves for weeks now at imminent risk of their lives to this one end, and they had grown so obsessed with the idea that they could not willingly contemplate any action which might imperil its consummation. And in Rose there burned the flame of fanatical patriotism as well. She was so convinced of the rightness of the action she contemplated, and of the necessity for it, that other considerations–even Charlie's safety–weighed with her hardly at all. She could reconcile herself to Charlie's peril as she might have reconciled herself if he were seriously ill, as something quite necessary and unavoidable. The conquest of German Central Africa was vastly, immeasurably more important that their own welfare–so immeasurably more important that it never occurred to her to weigh the one against the other. She glowed, she actually felt a hot flush, when she thought of the triumph of England.

She rose in the darkness, with Allnutt beside her, and looked over the vague reeds across the Lake. There were stars overhead, and stars faintly reflected in the water. The moon had not yet risen. But right over there was a bundle of faint lights which were neither stars nor their reflections. She clasped Allnutt's arm.

'That's them, all right,' said Allnutt.

Rose only realized then what a practical sailor would have thought of long before, that if the Germans took the precaution of hiding all lights when they were anchored the task of finding them on a dark night might well be impossible. Yet as they were in the only ship on the Lake, and forty miles from their nearest earth-bound enemy, there was obviously no need for precaution.

The sight of those lights made their success absolutely certain, at the moment when Rose first realized that it might not have been quite so certain. She felt a warm gratitude towards the fate which had been so kind. It was in wild exaltation that she clasped Allnutt's arm. In all the uncertainty of future peril and all the certainty of future triumph she clung to him in overwhelming passion. Her love for him and her passion for her country were blended inextricably, strangely. She kissed him in the starlight as Joan of Arc might have kissed a holy relic.

15

In the morning they saw the *Königin Luise* get under way and steam off to the northward again on her interminable patrolling of the Lake.

'We'll be ready for her when she comes back,' said Rose, tensely.

'Yerss,' said Allnutt.

With Rose's help he extricated the two heavy gas cylinders from the bottom of the boat and slid them back handily to the waist. They were foul with rust, but so thick was the steel that they could have borne months more of such exposure without weakening. Allnutt turned on the taps, and all the air was filled with an explosive hissing, as the gas poured out and the pressure-gauge needles moved slowly back to zero. When the hissing had subsided Allnutt got to work with his tools and extracted the whole nose-fitting from each cylinder. There was left a round blank hole in each, opening into the empty dark within.

Very carefully they prised open the boxes of explosive. They were packed with what looked like fat candles of pale yellow wax, each wrapped in oiled paper. Allnutt began methodically and cautiously to pack the cylinders with them, putting his arm far down into the interior.

'M'm,' said Allnutt. 'It'd be better if they weren't loose like this.'

He looked round the boat for packing material, and was momentarily at a loss. His ingenuity had been sharpened by all the recent necessity to employ makeshifts.

'Mud's the stuff,' he announced.

He went up into the bows, and, leaning over the side, he began to scoop up handfuls of the black mud from the bottom, and slapped them down upon the fore-deck to become nearly dry in the sun.

'I'll do that,' said Rose, as soon as she realized what he intended.

She squeezed the water from the stinking black mud, and then spread the handfuls on the hot deck, and worked upon them until they were nearly hard. Then she carried the sticky mass back to Allnutt and set herself to preparing more.

Bit by bit Allnutt filled the cylinders, cementing each layer of explosive hard and firm with mud. When each was full right up to the neck he stood up to ease his aching back. 'That's done prop'ly,' he said with pride, looking down at the results of his morning's work, and Rose nodded approval, contemplating the deadly things lying on the floor-boards. They neither of them saw anything in the least fantastic in the situation.

'We got to make them detonators now,' he said. 'I got an idea. Thought of it last night.'

From the locker in which his toilet things were stored he brought out a revolver, heavily greased to preserve it from the air. Rose stared at the thing in amazement; it was the first she knew of the presence of such a weapon in the boat.

'I'ad to 'ave this,' explained Allnutt. 'I used to 'ave a 'ole lot o' gold on board 'ere goin' up to Limbasi sometimes. A hundred ounces an' more some weeks. I never 'ad to shoot nobody, though.'

'I'm glad you didn't,' said Rose. To shoot a thief in time of peace seemed a much more unpleasant thing than to blow up a whole ship in time of war.

Allnutt broke open the revolver and took the cartridges into his hand, replacing the empty revolver in the locker.

'Now let me see,' he said, musingly.

Rose watched the idea gradually taking shape under his hands; the things took time to construct–what with meals, and sleep, and malaria it was all of the two days of Allnutt's previous rough estimate before they were ready.

First, he had, very laboriously, to shape with his knife two round discs of hard wood which would screw tightly into the noses of the cylinders. Then in each disc he pierced three holes of such a size that he could just force the cartridges into them. When the discs were in position in the nozzles the bullets and the ends of the brass cartridge cases would now rest in among the explosive.

The rest of the work was far more niggling and delicate, and Allnutt discarded several pieces before he was satisfied. He cut two more discs of wood of the same size as the previous two, and he was meticulous about what sort of wood he used. He wanted it neither hard nor rotten, something through which a nail could be driven as easily as possible and yet which would hold the nail firmly without allowing it to wobble. He made several experiments in driving nails into the various kinds of wood at his disposal before he eventually decided to use a piece of one of the floor-boards.

Rose quite failed to guess at the motive of these experiments, but she was content to sit and watch, and hand things to him, as he worked away in the flaming sunlight with the masses of mosquitoes always about him.

When the new discs were cut Allnutt carefully laid them on the others and noted exactly where the bases of the cartridges would rest against them. At these points he made ready to drive nails through the new discs, and, as a final meticulous precaution, he filed the points of the nails to the maximum of sharpness. He drove the nails gingerly through the discs at the points which he had marked, and on the other side he pared away small circles of wood into which the bases of the cartridges would fit exactly, so when that was done the points of the nails were just showing as gleaming traces of metal exactly in the middle of each shallow depression, while on the other side the heads of the nails protruded for a full inch.

Finally, he screwed his pairs of discs together.

'That's all right now,' said Allnutt.

Each pair of discs was now one disc. On one side of the disc showed the nail-heads, whose points rested against the percussion caps in the bases of the cartridges, the bullets of which showed on the opposite side. It was easy to see now that when the disc was in its place in the cylinder nose, and the cylinder pointing out beyond the bows of the *African Queen*, the boat would be herself a locomotive torpedo. When she was driven at full speed against the side of a ship the nails would be struck sharply against the cartridges. They would explode into the high explosive packed tight in the cylinders.

'I don't think I could do it any better,' said Allnutt, half apologetically. 'They ought to work all right.'

There were three cartridges to each cylinder; one at least ought to explode; there were two cylinders, each containing nearly a hundredweight of explosive–one cylinder, let alone two, ought to settle a little ship like the *Königin Luise.*

'Yes,' said Rose, with all the gravity the situation demanded. 'They ought to work all right.'

They had all the seriousness of children discussing the construction of a sand castle.

'Can't put 'em into the cylinders yet,' explained Allnutt. 'They're a bit tricky. We better get the cylinders into position now an' leave the detonators till last. We can put 'em in when we're all ready to start. After we got out of these reeds.'

'Yes,' said Rose. 'It'll be dark, then, of course. Will you be able to do it in the dark?'

'It's a case of 'ave to,' said Allnutt. 'Yerss, I can do it all right.'

Rose formed a mental picture of their starting out; it certainly would be risky to try to push the *African Queen* out from the reeds in the darkness with two torpedoes which would explode at a touch protruding from the bow.

Allnutt put the detonators away in the locker with the utmost care and turned to think out the remainder of the preparations necessary.

'We want to 'ave the explosion right down low,' he said. 'Can't ave it too low. Fink it's best to make those 'oles for the cylinders.'

It was a toilsome, back-breaking job, although it called for no particular skill, to cut two holes, one each side of the stem, in the *African Queen*'s bows, just above the water-line. When they were finished, Rose and Allnutt dragged and pushed the cylinders forward until their noses were well out through the holes, a good foot in front of any of the boat. Allnutt stuffed the ragged edges with chips of wood and rags.

'Doesn't matter if it leaks a little,' he said. 'It's only splashes which'll be coming in, 'cause the bow rides up when we're goin' along. All we got to do now is to fix them cylinders down tight.'

He nailed them solidly into position with battens split from the cases of provisions, adding batten to batten and piling all the available loose gear on top to make quite sure. The more those cylinders were confined the more effective would be their explosion against the side of the *Königin Luise.* When the last thing was added Allnutt sat down.

'Well, old girl,' he said, 'we done it all now. Everything. We're all ready.'

It was a solemn moment. The consummation of all their efforts, their descent of the rapids of the Ulanga, their running the gauntlet at Shona, the mending of the propeller, their toil in the water-lily pool and their agony in the delta, was at hand.

'Coo,' said Allnutt, reminiscently, ''aven't we just 'ad a time! Been a regular bank 'oliday.'

Rose forgave him his irreverence.

As a result of having completed the work so speedily they now had to endure the strain of waiting. They were idle now for the first time since the dreadful occasion–which they were both so anxious to forget–when Rose had refused to speak to Allnutt. From that time they had been ceaselessly busy; they had an odd empty feeling when they contemplated the blank days ahead of them, even though they were to be their last days on earth.

Those last days were rather terrible. There was one frightening interval when Allnutt felt his resolution waver. He felt like a man in a condemned cell waiting for the last few days before his execution to expire. As a young man in England he had often read about that, in the ghoulish Sunday newspaper which had constituted his only reading. Somehow it was his memory of what he had read which frightened him, not the thought of the imminent explosion–it deprived him of his new-won manhood and took him back into his pulpy youth, so that he clung to Rose with a new urgency, and she, marvellously, understood, and soothed him and comforted him.

The sun glared down upon them pitilessly; they were without even the shelter of the awning, which might betray them if it showed above the reeds. Every hour was pregnant with monotony and weariness; there was always the lurking danger that they might come to hate each other, crouching there among the reeds as in a grave. They felt that danger, and they fought against it.

Even the thunderstorms were a relief; they came with black clouds, and a mighty breath of wind which whipped the lake into fury so that they could hear breakers roar upon the shoals, and the whole lake was covered with tossing white horses, until even in their reedy sanctuary the violence of the water reached them so that the *African Queen* heaved uneasily and sluggishly under them.

To pass away the time they overhauled the engine thoroughly, so as to make quite certain that it would function properly on its last run. Allnutt wallowed in the mud beneath the boat and ascertained by touch that the propeller and shaft were as sound as they could be hoped to be. Every few minutes throughout every day one or the other of them climbed on the gunwale and looked out over the reeds across the Lake, scanning the horizon for sight of the *Königin Luise*. They saw a couple of dhows–or it may have been the same one twice–sailing down what was evidently the main passage through the islands, but that was all the sign of life thay saw for some days. They even came to doubt whether the *Königin Luise* would ever appear again in her previous anchorage. They had grown unaccustomed to counting the passage of time, and they actually were not sure how many days had lapsed since they saw her last. Even after the most careful counting back they could not come to an agreement on the point, and they had begun to eye each other regretfully and wonder whether they had not better issue forth from their hiding place and coast along the edge of the Lake in search of their victim. In black moments they began to doubt whether they would ever achieve their object.

Until one morning they looked out over the reeds and saw her just as before, a smudge of smoke and a white dot, coming down from the north. Just as before she steamed steadily to the south and vanished below their low horizon, and the hours crawled by painfully until the afternoon revealed her smoke again returning, and they were sure she would anchor again among the islands. Allnutt had been nearly right in his guess about the methodical habits of the Germans. In their careful patrolling of the Lake they never omitted a periodical cruise into this, the most desolate corner of the Wittelsbach Nyanza, just to see that all was well, even though the forbidding marshes of the Bora delta and the wild forests beyond made it unlikely that any menace to the German command of the Lake could develop here.

Allnutt and Rose watched the *Königin Luise* come back from her excursion to the south, and they saw her head over towards the islands, and, as the day was waning, they saw her come to a stop at the point where she had anchored before. Both their hearts were beating faster. It was then that the question they had debated in academic fashion a week earlier without reaching a satisfactory conclusion solved itself. They had just turned away from looking at the *Königin Luise*, about to make their preparations to start, when they found themselves holding each other's hands and looking into each other's eyes. Each of them knew what was in the other's mind.

'Rosie, old girl,' said Allnutt, hoarsely. 'We're going out *together*, aren't we?'

Rose nodded.

'Yes, dear,' she said. 'I should like it that way.'

Confronted with the sternest need for a decision they had reached it without difficulty. They would share all the danger, and stand the same chance, side by side, when the *African Queen* drove her torpedoes smashing against the side of the *Königin Luise*. They could not endure the thought of being parted, now. They could even smile at the prospect of going into eternity together.

It was almost dark by now. The young moon was low in the sky; soon there would only be the stars to give them light.

'It's safe for us to get ready now,' said Rose. 'Good-bye, dear.'

'Good-bye, darling, sweet'eart,' said Allnutt.

Their preparations took much time, as they had anticipated. They had all night before them, and they knew that as it was a question of surprise the best time they could reach the *Königin Luise* would be in the early hours of the morning. Allnutt had to go down into the mud and water and cut away the reeds about the *African Queen*'s stern before they could slide her out into the channel again–the reeds which had parted before her bows resisted obstinately the passage of her stern and propeller.

When they were in the river, moored lightly to a great bundle of reeds, Allnutt quietly took the detonators from the locker and went into the water again over the bows. He was a long time there, standing in mud and deep water while he screwed the detonators home into the noses of the cylinders. The rough-and-ready screw-threads he had scratched in the edges of his discs did not enter kindly into their functions. Allnutt had to use force, and it was a slow process to use force in the dark on a detonator in contact with a hundredweight of high explosive. Rose stood in the bows to help him at need as he worked patiently at the task. If his hand should slip against those nail-heads they would be blown into fragments, and the *Königin Luise* would still rule the waves of the Lake.

Nor did the fact the *African Queen* was pitching a little in a slight swell coming in from the Lake help Allnutt at all in his task, but he finished it in the end. In the almost pitch-dark, Rose saw him back away from the torpedoes and come round at a safe distance to the side of the boat. His hands reached up and he swung himself on board dripping.

'Done it,' he whispered–they could not help whispering in that darkness with the obsession of their future errand upon them.

Allnutt groped about the boat putting up the funnel again. He made a faint noise with his spanner as he tightened up the nuts on the funnel-stay bolts. It all took time.

The furnace was already charged with fuel–that much, at any rate, they had been able to make ready days ago–and the tin canister of matches was in its right place, and he could light the dry friable stuff and close down to force the draughts. He knew just where abouts to lay his hands on the various sorts of wood he might need before they reached the *Königin Luise*.

There was a wind blowing now, and the *African Queen* was very definitely pitching to the motion of the water. The noise of the draught seemed loud to their anxious ears, and when Allnutt recharged the furnace a volley of sparks shot from the funnel and was swept away overhead. Rose had never seen sparks issue from that funnel before–she had only been in the *African Queen* under way in daylight–and she realized the danger that the sparks might reveal their approach. She spoke quietly to Allnutt about it.

'Can't 'elp it, miss, sometimes,' he whispered back. 'I'll see it don't 'appen when we're getting close to 'em.'

The engine was sighing and slobbering now; if it had been daylight they would have seen the steam oozing out of the leaky joints.

'S'ss, s'ss,' whistled Allnutt, between his teeth.

'All right,' said Rose.

Allnutt unfastened the side painter and took the boat-hook. A good thrust against a clump of reeds sent the boat out into the fairway; he laid the boat-hook down and felt for the throttle valve and opened it. The propeller began its beat and the engine its muffled clanking. Rose stood at the tiller and steered out down the dark river mouth. They were off now, to strike their blow for the land of hope and glory of which Rose had sung as a child at concerts in Sunday school choirs. They were going to set wider those bounds and make the mighty country mightier yet.

The *African Queen* issued forth upon the Lake to gain which they had run such dangers and undergone such toil. Out through her bows pointed the torpedoes, two hundredweight of explosive which a touch could set off. Down by the engine crouched Allnutt, his whole attention concentrated on ascertaining by ear what he had been accustomed to judge by sight–steam pressure and water level and lubrication. Rose stood in the tossing stern, and her straining eyes could just see the tiny light which marked the presence of the *Königin Luise*; there were no stars overhead.

If it had been daylight they would have marked the banking-up of the clouds overhead, the tense stickiness of the electricity-charged atmosphere. If they had been experienced in Lake conditions they would have known what that ominous wind foretold; they had no knowledge of the incredible speed with which the wind whipping down from the mountains of the north roused the shallow waters of the Lake to maniacal fury.

Rose had had her training in rivers; it did not occur to her to look for danger where there were no rocks, nor weeds, nor rapids. When in the darkness the *African Queen* began to pitch and wallow in rough water she cared nothing for it. She felt no appreciation of the fact that the shallow draught launch was not constructed to encounter rough water, and that she was out of reach of land now in a boat whose wall sides and flat bottom made her the least seaworthy vessel it is possible to imagine. She found it difficult to keep her feet as the *African Queen* swayed and staggered about in haphazard fashion. In the darkness there was no way of anticipating her extravagant rolling. Waves were crashing against the flat sides; the tops of them were coming in over the edge, but that sort of thing was in Rose's mind only to be expected in open water. She had no fear at all.

The wind seemed to have dropped for a moment, but the water was still rough. Then suddenly the darkness was torn away for a second by a dazzling flash of lightning which revealed the wild water round them and the thunder followed with a single loud bang like a thousand cannons fired at once. Then came the rain, pouring down through the blackness in solid rivers, numbing and stupefying, and with the rain came the wind, suddenly, from a fresh quarter, laying its grip on the torn surface of the Lake and heaving it up into mountains, while the lightning still flashed and the thunder bellowed in madness. With the shift of the wind the *African Queen* began to pound, Heaving her bows out of the water and bringing them down again with a shattering crash. It was as well that Allnutt had selected the type of fuse he had employed; any other might have been touched off by the pounding waves, but the water which could toss about a two-ton boat like a toy could not drive nails.

It was all dark; Rose had no way of knowing if the stupefying water which was deluging her was rain or spray or waves. In that chaos all she could do was to keep her hand on the tiller and try to keep her footing. There was no possible chance of seeing the lights of the *Königin Luise*.

Allnutt was at her side. He was putting her arm through the huge lumbering life-buoy which had always seemed to bulk so unnecessarily large in the boat's equipment. Then as they tottered and swayed in the drenching dark he was taken from her. She tried to call to him unavailingly. She felt a surge of solid water round her waist. A wave smacked her in the face; she was strangling with the water in her nostrils.

The *African Queen* had sunk, and with her ended the gallant attempt to torpedo the *Königin Luise* for England's sake. And as though the storm had been raised just for Germany's benefit it died away with the sinking of the *African Queen*, and the wayward water fell smooth again, just as it had done once long ago on another inland sea, that of Galilee.

16

The President of the Court looked with curiosity at the prisoner. He tried conscientiously not to see him as he was now, but as he might have looked in civilized array. He tried to discount the mop of long tangled hair, and the sprouting beard, and he told himself that it was an ordinary face, one that might pass quite unnoticed on the Kurfurstendamm any day of the week. The prisoner was a sick man. That was obvious additionally to his weary and disheartened manner, and his feebleness was due to illness as well as to fatigue. The President of the Court told himself that if ever he had seen the characteristic features of malaria he saw them now in the prisoner.

The rags he was dressed in added to the drama of his appearance–and here the President suddenly leaned forward (the shoulders of his tunic had stuck to the back of his chair with sweat) and he looked with greater attention. The ragged singlet the man was wearing had some kind of tattered frilling at the throat. His breeches had frills and tucks, ragged but recognizable. The President sat back in his chair again; the man was wearing a woman's underclothing. That made the case more interesting; he might be mad, or–whatever it was, it was not the simple case of spying he had anticipated. There might be something in his defence.

The prosecuting officer stated the case against the prisoner; there must be due regard to formalities, even though it involved telling the Court facts which were perfectly well known to it. The prisoner had been seen on the island of Prinze Eitel at dawn, and, having been promptly hunted down and arrested, could give no account of himself. The Court was aware of this, seeing that it had been the President of the Court who had observed him from the deck of the *Königin Luise*, and the other members of the Court who had questioned him.

The prosecuting officer pointed out that on the island were kept reserve stores of fuel for the *Königin Luise*, which an evilly disposed person might easily destroy; this was additional to the fact that the island offered unrivalled opportunities for spying upon the movements of the *Königin Luise*. And it was hardly necessary to press these points, because the prisoner was obviously an alien, and he had been found in an area prohibited to all but members of the forces of His Imperial Majesty the Kaiser and King, by a proclamation of His Excellency General Baron von Hanneken, and so he was liable to the death penalty. The prosecuting officer made the quite unnecessary addition that a court of two officers, such as the one he was addressing, was perfectly competent to award a penalty of death for espionage in a field court martial.

This peroration annoyed the President; it was almost impertinence on the part of a mere lieutenant to tell a commander what was the extent of his powers. He knew them already; it was by his orders that the Court had constituted itself. The man would be giving him the information that he was the captain of the *Königin Luise* next, and similar irrelevancies. The President turned to the officer charged with the defence.

But Lieutenant Schumann was rather at a loss. He was not a very intelligent officer, but he was the only one available. Of the *Königin Luise*'s six officers, one was watch-keeping on deck, and one in the engine-room, two constituted the Court, one was prosecuting, and only old Schumann was left for the defence. He uttered a few halting words, and stopped, tongue-tied. He was shy when it came to public speaking. The President of the Court looked inquiringly at the prisoner.

Allnutt was too dazed and weary and ill to take much note of his surroundings. He was aware in a way that he was being subjected to some sort of trial–the attitude of the two officers in their white suits with the gold braid and buttons told him that–but he was not specifically aware of the charges against him, nor of the penalty which might be inflicted. He would not have cared very much anyway. Nothing mattered much now, that he had lost Rosie and the old *African Queen* was sunk and the great endeavour was at an end. He was ill, and he almost wished he was dead.

He looked up at the President of the Court, and his eyes drifted round to the prosecuting officer and the defending officer. Clearly they were expecting him to say something. It was too much trouble, and they could not understand him, anyway. He looked down at the floor again, and swayed a little on his feet.

The President of the Court knew that it was his duty, failing anyone else, to ascertain anything in the accused's favour. He leant forward and tapped the table sharply with his pencil.

'What is your nationality?' he asked in German.

Allnutt looked at him stupidly.

'Belgian?' asked the President. 'English?'

At the word 'English' Allnutt nodded.

'English,' he said. 'British.'

'Your name?' asked the President in German, and then, doing his best to remember his English, he repeated the question.

'Charles Allnutt.'

It took a long time to get that down correctly, translating the English names of the letters into German ones.

'What–did–you–on–ve–ve–Insel?' asked the President. He could not be surprised when the prisoner did not understand him. By a sudden stroke of genius he realized that the man might speak Swahili, the universal lingua franca of East and Central Africa, half Bantu, half Arabic, the same language as he used to his native sailors. He asked the questions again in Swahili, and he saw a gleam of understanding in the prisoner's face. Then instantly he assumed a mask of sullen stupidity again. The President of the Court asked again in Swahili what the prisoner was doing on the island.

'Nothing,' said Allnutt sullenly. He was not going to own up to the affair of the *African Queen*; he thought, anyway, that it was wiser not to do so.

'Nothing,' he said again in reply to a fresh question.

The President of the Court sighed a little. He would have to pass sentence of death, he could see. He had already done so once since the outbreak of hostilities, and the wretched Arab half-caste had at his orders swung on a gallows at the lake-side as a deterrent to other spies–but bodies did not last long in this climate.

At that moment there was a bustle outside the tiny crowded cabin. The door opened and a coloured petty officer came in, dragging with him a fresh prisoner. At sight of her the President rose to his feet, stooping under the low deck, for the prisoner was a woman, and obviously a white woman despite her deep tan. There was a tangled mass of chestnut hair about her face, and she wore only a single garment, which torn open at the bosom, revealed breasts which made the President feel uneasy.

The petty officer explained that they had found the woman on another of the islands, and, with her, something else. He swung into view a life-buoy, and on the life-buoy they could see the name *African Queen*.

'*African Queen*?' said the President, to himself, raking back in his memory for something half-forgotten.

He opened the drawer in his table, and searched through a mass of papers until he found what he sought. It was a duplicate of the notice sent by von Hanneken to the captain of reserve. Until that moment the news of a missing steam launch on the Upper Ulanga had had no interest at all for the captain of the *Königin Luise*, but now it was different. He looked at the female prisoner, and his awkwardness about that exposed body returned. She, too, was trying to hold the rags about her. The captain gave a short order to the prosecuting officer, who rose and opened a locker–the cabin in which they were was wardroom and cabin for three officers together–and produced a white uniform jacket, into which he proceeded to help Rose. The making of the gesture produced a reflex of courtesy and deference in the men; with just the same gesture they had helped women into their opera cloaks.

'A chair,' said the Captain, and the defending officer hastened to proffer his.

'Get out,' said the Captain to the coloured ratings, and they withdrew, making a good deal more room in the stifling cabin.

'And now, gracious lady,' said the Captain to Rose. Already he had guessed much. These two people must be the mechanic and the missionary's sister; presumably they had abandoned their launch on the Upper Ulanga and had come down in a canoe, and had been wrecked in last night's storm when trying to cross the Lake to the Belgian Congo. He began to question Rose in Swahili; it was an enormous relief to find, from her use of the German variants of that language, that she actually knew a little German–those weary days spent with grammar-book and vocabulary under Samuel's sarcastic tutorship were bearing fruit at last.

It was far more of a surprise when it came out that Allnutt and Rose had brought the *African Queen* down the rapids of the Ulanga and through the Bora delta.

'But, gracious lady—' protested the Captain.

There could be no doubting her statement, all the same. The Captain looked at Rose and marvelled. He had heard from Spengler's own lips an account of the rapids and the delta.

'It was very dangerous,' said the Captain.

Rose shrugged her shoulders. It did not matter. Nothing mattered now. Although she had been glad to see him in the cabin, even her love for Allnutt seemed to be dead, now that the *African Queen* was lost and the *Königin Luise* still ruled the Lake.

The Captain had heard about the stoicism and ability of Englishwomen; here was a clear proof.

Anyway, there could be no question now of espionage and the death penalty. He could not hang the one person without the other, and he never thought for a moment of hanging Rose. He would not have done so even if he thought her guilty; white women were so rare in Central Africa that he would have thought it monstrous. Beyond all else, she had brought a steam launch from the Upper Ulanga to the Lake, and that was a feat for which he could feel professional admiration. He gazed at her and marvelled.

'But why,' he asked, 'did not your friend here tell us?'

Rose looked round at Allnutt, and became conscious of his sick weariness as he still stood, swaying. All her instincts were aroused now. She got up from her chair and went to him protectively.

'He is ill and tired,' she said, and then, with indignation, 'He ought to be in bed.'

Allnutt drooped against her, while she struggled to say in German and Swahili just what she thought of men who could treat a poor creature thus. She stroked his bristly face and murmured endearments to him. In the white uniform jacket and tattered dress she made a fine figure, despite the ravages of malaria.

'But you, madam,' said the Captain. 'You are ill, too.'

Rose did not bother to answer him.

The Captain looked round the cabin.

'The Court is dismissed,' he snapped.

His colleague, and the prosecuting officer and the defending officer leaped up to their feet and saluted. They filed out of the cabin while the Captain tapped on the table meditatively with his pencil and decided on his future action. These two ought of course to be interned; that was what von Hanneken would do if he took them into the mainland. But they were ill, and they might die in imprisonment. It was not right that two people who had achieved so much should die in an enemy's hands. All the laws of chivalry dictated that he should do more than that for them. In German Central Africa there would be small comfort for captured enemy civilians. And what difference would one sick man and one sick woman make to the balance of a war between two nations?

Von Hanneken would curse when he knew, but after all the Captain of the *Königin Luise* was his own master on the Lake and could do what he liked in his own ship. The Captain formed his resolve almost before the blundering Schumann had closed the cabin door.

17

The post of Senior Naval Officer, Port Albert, Belgian Congo, was of very new creation. It was only the night before that it had come into being. It was a chance of war that the senior naval officer in a Belgian port should be an English lieutenant-commander. He was standing pacing along the jetty inspecting the preparation for sea of the squadron under his command. Seeing that it comprised only two small motor-boats, it seemed a dignified name for it. But those motor-boats had cost in blood and sweat and treasure more than destroyers might have done, for they had been sent out from England, and had been brought with incredible effort overland through jungles, by rail and by river, to the harbour in which they lay.

They were thirty-knot boats, and in their bows each would have–when the mounting was completed–an automatic three-pounder gun. Thirty knots and those guns would make short work of the *Königin Luise* with her maximum of nine knots and her old-fashioned six-pounder. The lieutenant-commander paced the jetty impatiently; he was anxious to get to work now that the weary task of transport was completed. It was irksome that there should remain a scrap of water on which the White Ensign did not reign supreme. The sooner they came out on the hunt for the *Königin Luise* the better. He gazed out over the Lake and stopped suddenly. There was smoke on the horizon, and below it a white dot. As he looked, a lieutenant came running along the jetty to him; he had binoculars in his hand.

'That's the *Königin Luise* in sight, sir,' he said breathlessly, and offered the glasses.

The lieutenant-commander stared through them at the approaching vessel.

'She's nearly hull up from the artillery observing station, sir,'

'M'm,' said the lieutenant-commander, and looked again.

'She looks as if she's expecting action from the number of flags she's got flying,' he said. 'M'm–half a minute. That's not a German ens'n on the foremast. It's–what do you make of it?'

The lieutenant looked though the glasses in his turn.

'I think—' he said, and looked again.

'It's a white flag,' he said at last.

'I think so too,' said the lieutenant-commander, and the two officers looked at each other.

They had both of them heard stories–which in later years they would be sorry that they had believed–about the misuse of the white flag by the Germans.

'Wonder what they're after,' mused the lieutenant-commander. 'Perhaps—'

There was no need for him to explain, even if there were time. If the

Germans had heard of the arrival of the motor-boats on the lake shore they had one last chance to maintain their command of the Lake waters. A bold attack–for which a white flag might afford admirable cover–a couple of well-placed shells, and the *Königin Luise* could resume her unchallenged patrol of the Lake. The lieutenant-commander ran as fast as his legs would carry him along the jetty and up the slope to the artillery observing station. The Belgian artillery captain was there with his field-glasses; below him in concealed emplacements were the two mountain guns which guarded the port.

'If they're up to any monkey tricks,' said the lieutenant-commander, 'they'll catch it hot. I can lay one of those mountain guns even if these Belgians can't.'

But the Germans had apparently no monkey tricks in mind. The lieutenant-commander had hardly finished speaking before the *Königin Luise* rounded to, broadside on to the shore, far out of range of her six-pounder. The officers in the observing station saw a puff of white smoke from her bow, and the report of a gun came slowly over to them. They saw the white flag at the foremast come down half-way, and then mount again to the masthead.

'That means they want a parley,' said the lieutenant-commander; he had never used the word 'parley' before in his life, but it was the only one which suited the occasion.

'I'll go,' decided the lieutenant-commander. It was not his way to send others on dangerous duties, and there might be danger here, white flag or no white flag.

'You stay here,' went on the lieutenant-commander to the lieutenant. 'You're in command while I'm out there. If you see any need to fire, fire like blazes–don't mind about me. Understand?'

The lieutenant nodded.

'I'll have to go in one of those dhows,' decided the lieutenant-commander, indicating the little cluster of native boats at the far end of the jetty, where they had lain for months for fear of the *Königin Luise*, and where they now screened the activity round the motor-boats. He stopped to sort his French sentences out.

'Mon capitaine,' he began, addressing the Belgian captain. 'Voulez-vous—'

There is no need to describe the lieutenant-commander's linguistic achievements.

The lieutenant watched through his glasses as the dhow headed out from shore with a native crew. The lieutenant-commander in the stern had taken the precaution of changing his jacket for one of plain white drill. The lieutenant watched him steer towards the gunboat, far out on the Lake, and in appearance just like a white-painted Thames tug. Soon the yellow sail was all he could see of the dhow; he saw it reach the gunboat, and vanish as it was furled when the dhow ran alongside. There was an anxious delay. Then at last the dhow's sail reappeared; she was coming back. There came another puff of smoke as the *Königin Luise* fired a parting salute, and then she turned away and headed back again towards the invisible German shore. The whole scene had a touch of the formal chivalry of the Napoleonic Wars.

When the *Königin Luise* was hull down over the horizon and the dhow was close in-shore the lieutenant left his post and went down to the jetty to meet his senior officer. The dhow ran briskly in, and the native crew furled the sail as she slid alongside the jetty. The lieutenant-commander was there in the sternsheets. Lying in the bottom of the boat were two new passengers, at whom the lieutenant stared in surprise. One was a woman; she was dressed in a skirt of gay canvas–once part of an awning of the *Königin Luise*–and a white linen jacket whose gold buttons and braid showed that it had once belonged to a German naval officer. The other, at whom the lieutenant hardly looked, so astonished was he at the sight of a woman, was dressed in a singlet and shorts of the kind worn by German native ratings.

'Get a carrying party,' said the lieutenant-commander, proffering no further explanation. 'They're pretty far gone.'

They were both of them in the feverish stage of malaria, hardly conscious. The lieutenant had them carried up on shore, each in the bight of a blanket, and looked round helplessly to see what he could do with them. In the end he had to lay them in one of the tents allotted to the English sailors, for Port Albert is only a collection of filthy native huts.

'They'll be all right in an hour or two,' said the surgeon lieutenant after examining them.

'Christ knows what I'm going to do with 'em,' said the lieutenant-commander bitterly. 'This isn't the place for sick women.'

'Who the devil is she?' asked the lieutenant.

'Some missionary woman or other. The *Königin Luise* found her cast away somewhere on the Lake trying to escape over here.'

'Pretty decent of the Huns to bring 'em over.'

'Yes,' said the lieutenant-commander shortly. It was all very well for a junior officer to say that; he was not harassed as was the lieutenant-commander by constant problems of housing and rations and medical supplies–by all the knotty points in fact which beset a man in command of a force whose lines of communication are a thousand miles long.

'They may be able to give us a bit of useful information about the Huns,' said the lieutenant.

'Can we ask them?' interposed the surgeon. 'Flag of truce and all that. I don't know the etiquette of these things.'

'Oh, you can ask them, all right,' said the lieutenant-commander. 'There's nothing against it. But you won't get any good out of 'em. I've never met a female devil-dodger yet who was any more use than a sick headache.'

And when the officers came to question Rose and Allnutt about the German military arrangements they found, indeed, that they had very little to tell them. Von Hanneken had ringed himself about the desert, and had mobilized every man and woman so as to be ready to strike back at any force which came to molest him, but that the English knew already. The surgeon asked with professional interest about the extent of sleeping sickness among the German forces, but they could tell him nothing about that. The lieutenant wanted to know details of the *Königin Luise*'s crew and equipment; neither Allnutt nor Rose could tell him more than he knew already, more than the Admiralty and the Belgian government had told him.

The lieutenant-commander looked for a moment beyond the battle which would decide the mastery of the Lake, to the future when a fleet of dhows escorted by the motor-boats would take over an invading army which would settle von Hanneken for good and all. He asked if the Germans had made any active preparations to resist a landing on their shore of the Lake.

'Didn't see nothing,' said Allnutt.

Rose understood the drift of the question better.

'You couldn't land anyone were we came from,' she said. 'It's just a delta–all mud and weed and malaria. It doesn't lead to anywhere.'

'No,' agreed the lieutenant-commander, who, like an intelligent officer, had studied the technique of combined operations. 'I don't think I could, if it's like that. How did you get down to the Lake, then?'

The question was only one of politeness.

'We came down the Ulanga river,' said Rose.

'Really?' It was not a matter of great interest to the lieutenant-commander. 'I didn't know it was navigable.'

'It ain't. Corblimey, it ain't,' said Allnutt.

He would not be more explicit about it; the wells of his loquacity were dried up by these glittering officers in their white uniforms with their gentlemen's voices and la-di-da manners. Rose was awkward too. She did not feel at ease with these real gentlemen either, and she was sullenly angry with herself because of the absurd anticlimax in which all her high hopes and high endeavour had ended. Naturally she did not know who the officers were who were questioning her, nor what weapons they were making ready to wield. Naval officers on the eve of an important enterprise would not explain themselves to casual strangers.

'That's interesting,' said the lieutenant-commander, in tones which were not in agreement with his words. 'You must let me hear about it later on.'

He was to be excused for his lack of interest in the petty adventures of these two excessively ordinary people who had made fools of themselves by losing their boat. Tomorrow he had to lead a fleet into action, achieving at this early age the ambition of every naval officer, and he had much to think about.

'They may be all right,' said he when they came away. 'They look like it. But on the other hand they may not. All this may be just a stunt of old von Hanneken's to get a couple of his friends over here. I wouldn't put it past him. They're not coming out of their tents until the *Königin Luise* is sunk. They don't seem to be married, but although they're lived together all those weeks it wouldn't be decent if the Royal Navy stuck them in a tent together. I can't really spare another tent. I won't have the camp arrangements jiggered up any more than they are. As it is I've got to take a man off the work to act sentry over them. Can't trust these Belgian natives. Not a ha'p'orth. You see to it, Bones, old man, will you? I've got to go and have a look at *Matilda*'s gun mounting.'

18

The next day the *Königin Luise* as she steamed in solemn dignity over the Lake she had ruled so long saw two long grey shapes come hurtling over the water towards her, half-screened in a smother of spray. The commander who had been President of the court martial of two days before looked at them through his glasses as they tore along straight towards him. Beyond the high-tossed bow waves he could see two fluttering squares of white. He saw red crosses and a flash of gay colour in the upper corners. They were White Ensigns, flying where no White Ensign had ever been seen before.

'Action stations!' he snapped. 'Get that gun firing!'

The prosecuting officer ran madly to the gun; the defending officer sprang to the wheel to oversee the coloured quartermaster and to make sure the commander's orders were promptly obeyed. Round came the *Königin Luise* to face her enemies. Her feeble gun spoke once, twice, with pitiful slowness. H.M.S. *Matilda* and H.M.S. *Amelia* swerved to one side. At thirty knots they came tearing round in a wide sweep, just outside the longest range of that old six-pounder. The *Königin Luise* was slow on her helm and with a vast turning circle. She could not wheel quick enough to keep her bows towards those flying grey shapes which swept round her in a decreasing spiral. Their engines roared to full throttle as they heeled over on the turn. They had four times the speed and ten times the handiness of the old gunboat. The prosecuting officer looking over his sights could see only their boiling wake now. He could train the gun no farther round, and the gunboat could turn no faster.

The lieutenant-commander stood amidships in the *Matilda*. A thirty-knot gale howled past his ears. The engine bellowed fit to deafen him, but he eyed coolly the lessening range between him and the *Königin Luise*, and the curving course which was bringing his ship fast towards the enemy's stern where there was no gun to bear. It was his duty not merely to win the easy victory, but to see that victory was won at the smallest cost. He looked back to see that the *Amelia* was in her proper station, looked at the range again, shouted an order into the ear of the man at the wheel, and then waved his hand to the sub-lieutenant in the bows by the gun. The three-pounder broke into staccato firing, report following report so that the ear could hardly distinguish one sound from the next. It was a vicious, spiteful sound, implying untold menace and danger.

The three-pounder shells began to burst about the *Königin Luise*'s stern. At first they merely blew holes in the thin plating, and then soon there was no plating left to explode them, and they flew on into the bowels of the ship spreading destruction and fire everywhere, each of them two pounds of flying metal and a pound of high explosive. The steering gear was smashed to fragments, and the *Königin Luise* swerved back suddenly from her circling course and headed on in a wavering straight line. The lieutenant-commander in the *Matilda* gave a new order to the man at the wheel, and kept his boats dead astern, and from that safe position sent the deadly little shells raking through and through the ship from stern to bow.

The *Königin Luise* had not really been designed as a fighting ship; her engines and boilers were above water line instead of being far below under a protective deck. Soon one of those little shells came flying through the bulkhead, followed by another and another. There was a deep sullen roar as the boiler was hit, and the *Königin Luise* was wreathed in a cloud of steam. The engine-room staff were boiled alive in that moment.

The lieutenant-commander in the *Matilda* had been expecting that moment; his cool brain had thought of everything. When he saw the steam gush out he gave a quick order, and the roar of the *Matilda*'s engine was stilled as the throttle closed and the engine put out of gear. When the steam cleared away the *Königin Luise* was lying a helpless hulk on the water, drifting very slowly with the remnants of her way, and the motor-boats were lying silent, still safely astern. He looked for a sign of surrender, but he could see none; the black cross was still flying, challenging the red. Something hit the water beside the *Matilda* with a plop and a jet of water; he could hear a faint crackling from the *Königin Luise*. Some heroic souls there were firing at them with rifles, and even at a mile and a half a Mauser bullet can kill, and on the great lakes of Africa where white men are numbered only in tens and every white man can lead a hundred black men to battle white men's lives are precious. He must not expose his sailors to this danger longer than he need.

'Hell,' said the lieutenant-commander. He did not want to kill the wretched Germans, who were achieving nothing in prolonging their defence. 'God damn it; all right, then.'

He shouted an order to the gun's crew in the bows, and the fire recommenced, elevated a little so as to sweep the deck. One shell killed three coloured ratings who were lying on the deck firing with their rifles; the prosecuting officer never knew how he escaped. Another shell burst on the tall bridge, and killed Lieutenant Schumann, but it did not harm the commander, who had gone down below a minute before, venturing with his coat over his face into the scalding steam of the engine-room to do his last duty.

'Perhaps that'll settle 'em,' said the lieutenant-commander, signalling for fire to cease. Even three-pounder shells are troublesome to replace over lines of communication a thousand miles long. He looked at the *Königin Luise* again. She lay motionless, hazed around with smoke and steam. There was no firing now, but the black-cross flag was still flying, drooping in the still air.

Then the lieutenant-commander saw that she was lower in the water, and as he noticed it the *Königin Luise* very suddenly fell over to one side. The commander had done his duty; he had groped his way through the wrecked engines to the sea cocks and had opened them.

'Hope we can save the poor beggars,' said the lieutenant-commander, calling for full speed.

The *Matilda* and the *Amelia* came rushing up just as the German ensign, the last thing to disappear, dipped below the surface. They were in time to save all the living except the hopelessly wounded.

19

There is an elation in victory, even when wounded men have to be borne very carefully along the jetty to the hospital tent; even when a telegraphic report has to be composed and sent to the Lords Commissioners of the Admiralty; even when a lieutenant-commander of no linguistic ability has to put together another report in French for the Belgian governor. He could at least congratulate himself on having won a naval victory as decisive as the Falklands or Tsu-Shima, and he could look forward to receiving the D.S.O. and the Belgian Order of the Crown and a step in promotion which would help to make him an Admiral some day.

His mind was already hard at work on his new plans, busily anticipating the time soon to come when he would escort the invading army across the Lake. 'Strike quickly, strike hard, and keep on striking'; the sooner the invaders were on their way the less time would von Hanneken have to recover from this totally unexpected blow and make arrangements to oppose a landing. The lieutenant-commander was urgent in his representations to the senior Belgian officer on the spot, to the Belgian headquarters, to the British headquarters in East Africa.

Yet meanwhile he could not be free from the worry of all commanders-in-chief. That long line of communications was a dreadful nuisance, and he had fifty bluejackets who expected English rations in Central Africa, and now he had some captured German wounded–coloured men mostly, it is true, but a drain on his resources all the same–on his hands as well as some unwounded prisoners. He had to act promptly in the matter. He sent for Rose and Allnutt.

'There's a Belgian escort going down to the coast with prisoners,' he said, shortly. 'I'm going to send you with them. That will be all right for you, I suppose.'

'I suppose so,' said Allnutt. Until this moment they had been people without a future. Even the destruction of the *Königin Luise* had increased that feeling of nothingness ahead.

'You'll be going to join up, I suppose,' said the lieutenant-commander. 'I can't enlist you here, of course. I can't do anything about it. But down on the coast you'll find a British consul, at Matadi, I think, or somewhere there. The Belgians'll put you on the right track, anyway. Any British consul will do your business for you. As soon as you are over your malaria, of course. They'll send you round to join one of the South African units, I expect. So you'll be all right.'

'Yessir,' said Allnutt.

'And you, Mrs–er–Miss Sayer, isn't it?' went on the lieutenant-commander. 'I think the West Coast's the best solution of the problem for you, too, don't you? You can get back to England from there. A British consul—'

'Yes,' said Rose.

'That's all right then,' said the lieutenant-commander with relief. 'You'll be starting in two or three hours.'

It was hard to expect a young officer planning the conquest of a country half the size of Europe to devote more attention to two civilian castaways. It was that 'Mrs–er–Miss' of the lieutenant-commander's which really settled Rose's future–or unsettled it, if that view be taken. When they came out of the lieutenant-commander's presence Rose was seething with shame. Until then she had been a woman without a future and in consequence without any real care. It was different now. The lieutenant-commander had mentioned the possibility of a return to England; to Rose that meant a picture of poor streets and censorious people and prying aunts–that aunts should be prying was in Rose's experience an essential characteristic of aunts. And it was terribly painful to contemplate a separation from Allnutt; he had been so much to her; she had hardly been out of his sight for weeks now; to lose him now would be like losing a limb, even if her feelings towards him had changed; she could not contemplate this unforeseen future of hers without Allnutt.

'Charlie,' she said, urgently. 'We've got to get married.'

'Coo,' said Allnutt. This was an aspect of the situation he actually had not thought of.

'We must do it as quickly as we can,' said Rose. 'A consul can marry people. That officer in there spoke about a consul. As soon as we get to the coast—'

Allnutt was a little dazed and stupid. This unlooked-for transfer to the West Coast of Africa, this taken-for-granted enlistment in the South African Forces, and now this new proposal left him with hardly a word to say. He thought of Rose's moderate superiority in social status. He thought about money; presumably he would receive pay in the South African army. He thought about the girl he had married twelve years ago when he was eighteen. She had probably been through half a dozen men's hands now, but there had never been a divorce and presumably he was still married to her. Oh well, South Africa and England were a long way apart, and she couldn't trouble him much.

'Righto, Rosie,' he said. 'Let's.'

So they left the Lake and began the long journey to Matadi and marriage. As to whether or not they lived happily ever after is not easily decided.

STER C. S. FORESTE
C. S. FORESTER C. S
ORESTER C. S. FORE
ER C. S. FORESTER C
S. FORESTER C. S. FO
STER C. S. FORESTE
C. S. FORESTER C. S
ORESTER C. S. FORE
ER C. S. FORESTER C
S. FORESTER C. S. FO
STER C. S. FORESTE
C. S. FORESTER C. S
ORESTER C. S. FORE
ER C. S. FORESTER C
S. FORESTER C. S. FO
STER C. S. FORESTE
C. S. FORESTER C. S
ORESTER C. S. FORE